Apotheosis

Act III

of

The
Forward
To
GLORY
Quartet

by

Brian Paul Bach

Fiction

The FORWARD TO GLORY Quartet
VAMPIRE OF THE YEAR
MYSTERIOUS AGENCY
NOX NOVA LUNÆ: CONFESSIONS IN THE GLOW OF A NEW MOON
LURID *or* HOWRAH BRIDGE
CARSTAIRS *or* FINITE AGONY
THE ADVENTURES OF LORD WILLOWBY
COULDN'T RESIST

Non-Fiction

The BPB'S ARTPOURING Series
BUSTED BOOM: THE BUMMER OF BEING A BOOMER
IF THIS IS THE FUTURE, THEN I DON'T WANNA…
CALCUTTA'S EDIFICE: THE BUILDINGS OF A GREAT CITY
THE GRAND TRUNK ROAD FROM THE FRONT SEAT
(2 editions)
A GRAND TRUNK ROAD GUIDE AND GAZETTEER
WHEELS OF LIFE

Short Stories

THE ELECTRIC PUNKAH

Plays & Screenplays

A REPRESENTATIVE OF THE OUTSIDE WORLD
WHEN THE LAST LAMP IS SHATTERED
THE KDIM PAPERS
MISH-MASH
DEATH DESERT

Poetry

THE GOTHIC GLARE

A Carnival D'Bloat Presentation

Forward
To
GLORY

A Quartet In Four Acts

III.

Apotheosis

Brian Paul Bach

A Goth House *of* Howrah Book

London | New York

2018

Goth House

(conceived in Howrah, Bengal)

<<Publishers to Oddballs>>

Howrah ~ Seebpore ~ Chowringhee ~ The Burg ~ London ~ Rangoon ~ Pipewell

Snappertuna ~ Chefoo ~ Peshawar ~ Ghubbah ~ Dresden ~ Wei Hai Wei

Calcutta

a division of

BPB's ArtPouring, Ltd.

http://forwardtogloryquartet.wordpress.com

forwardtogloryquartet@gmail.com

Illustrations and Cover Art by Brian Paul Bach

Cover Layout by Samit Roychoudhury

http://samit.org

Published by Clink Street Publishing 2018

978-1-912262-97-7 paperback
978-1-912262-98-4 ebook

'Forward... *to glory!*'

– Julian 'Gramps' Northrup, as played by Lionel Barrymore in Paul Osborn's

'On Borrowed Time' (MGM, 1939)

This is a work of fiction. It couldn't be anything else. 'Nothing like it has ever happened, *nor will it.* I just don't think such things are *possible.*'

– so said Somebody…

To

Samuel Bronston

(1908–1994)

Independent producer par excellence,
creator of epic worlds never to be forgotten, or surpassed

The Forward To Glory Quartet

Act III:

Apotheosis

Repetitious But Necessary Notes

When referencing films throughout the **Forward To Glory** quartet, I have included the name of the studio or distributor responsible for a given picture. The year of release is added when citing films of the past. As an avid reader of the showbiz periodical 'Variety' in the 1970s, such assignations, especially within Hollywood's greatest era, were always sure to indicate certain styles and personnel, as well as preferences in production and presentation. To we students of the Seventh Art, important stuff indeed.

A complete list of studios, a glossary, a comprehensive filmography of 1001 films, and a farewell essay: Notes on Sources, are all located at the end of the quartet's concluding volume, **Beyond *Fin***.

Although the quartet is a novel in the *epic-noir-satire* style, matters of a 'footnote' nature occasionally appear. In order that their somewhat recondite contents will not overly distract the Reader, I have placed them within [brackets], and in smaller type.

Showbiz is a *name-oriented* enterprise, and so is **Forward To Glory**. Therefore, studious readers may want to consider having easy access to handy resources like Wikipedia and the Internet Movie Database close at hand. Just in case any probings into the universe of Entertainment's players and supporters are desired. The expanse of casts and crews may be vast, but the findings are most rewarding – not to mention fascinating. Those names in the quartet's four volumes which do *not* appear in these or any other sources – and they are legion – are either not deemed worthy, or else they are Author-invented.

However, the entire quartet may be absorbed without reference works of any kind, as its prime directive is one of entertainment rather than study. At least that is the dearest wish of its Author.

Disclaimer: Any references to actual persons within the pages of the **Forward To Glory** quartet, whether living or dead, are made for fictional purposes only. They are exclusively the inventions of the Author, and the Author alone. Whatever real names are cited, any resemblance to the actual personage is purely coincidental (and generally complimentary).

No animals were harmed in the making of this production. Indeed, they were only loved.

And now...

Dear Reader: *Quiet On The Set!*

Three times have we been in this place! Three times the director has called for quiet, so that *action* may proceed! Three times it has been our honor to say: for your total convenience, the heralding blurb that once conventionally appeared in the flyleaf or on the back cover of books (in traditions long past) is here placed, complete and unabridged, for any of your 'warm-up' needs, should you require them, just below:

Act I: Tempering – Effort and Obscurity

Act II: Exposition – Attainment and Achievement

Act III: Apotheosis – Triumph and Transcendence

Act IV: Beyond *Fin* – Legacy and Summation

Advertisement

III. Apotheosis

Butterbugs is *somebody* now. He has arrived – at the top. In fact, he's higher, much higher than that. He has arrived at unprecedented stardom – *ultra*stardom, they call it. He is the world's first *ultra*star (and first trillionaire, too), though these things have nothing to do with him as an actor. They merely reflect his astounding singularity. He is still compelled to act for its own sake, and to thrive from wonders encountered in the process – of which there are many. Taking the lead in the most ambitious film ever to be made, he will need all the gathered resources within him for the staggering job ahead.

Way below his stratospheric plane though, threatening undercurrents coil in unholy pools, similar to many found in his finest roles before the camera. His own deep dimensions of character and the diversity of creatures around him make for a formidable force that extends far past mere entertainment as a strolling player. In fact, Butterbugs has become a phenomenon for billions. However, that does not mean that every last person on Earth is in his thrall.

The canvas, or to put it in cinematic terms, the screen, upon which *APOTHEOSIS* is projected is properly gigantic, and while such a prospect may be off-putting, the story downright commands it. Remember, *FORWARD TO GLORY* is nothing less than an epic noir satire – or a satirical noir epic, or a – Whatever the label, all those elements are here, and in every combination. The momentum built by *TEMPERING* and *EXPOSITION* does not let up for a second. By its very name, *APOTHEOSIS* is required to propel the reader toward a merciless climax, the only possible way it can end.

Fortunately, after so long on the deficient side, Butterbugs is blessed with the very best of friends and associates who surround him in his triumphs: Saskia and Justy – closer than ever, though mostly with each other; Sonny Projector – his agenting only rises higher and higher, along with his client; Edna Tzu – a favorite director and facilitator of the ultrastar's curative powers; Hyman Goth – ruthless studio mogul with a dreaded knowledge; Mayella – his stabilizing Israeli/Palestinian/ Polish lover; Egaz D'Varzim – transcendent director, who uncannily matches his actor's talents; Keenah LaVine – the mate Butterbugs has waited for… possibly; The Seven Muses of The Lazaretto – each of whom excels at their job: to inspire and strengthen the ultrastar in his most challenging role yet; Marshall Vogg – the disabled vet who, influenced by Butterbugs, virtually changes the course of the nation; and Heatherette – always a force for good, always reappearing at the perfect time.

Everything seems to be good, thus, his going forward, *FORWARD TO…*

Critical Mass:
Scattered Shot

When a patiently-waiting firearm is aimed right at your face, you can get all sorts of cinematic images blasting into your mind. That is, if you're blessed with a few seconds to consider them. Well, maybe you're a hostage or something, so you might be staring at one all day.

Bor-ring!

There's always the obvious: when you're in the audience, looking down the barrel of the suicide scene in Hitchcock's 'Spellbound' (Selznick, 1945), with its gunmetal b&w transformation into bloody color when the trigger's pulled. Pretty easy to imagine what happened.

However, depending on the nomenclature of the gun, quite a few non-weapon thoughts can also occur. A train tunnel surrounded by a fine metallic gateway. An electrical conduit awaiting wire. A telescope with the glass busted out. A dark jewel in a navel. A skull's sightless eye socket. A mouse-hole, even. Holes can draw you in, but it's more likely that something is going to come crawling, or hastening, or spewing out. Mice, spiders, dust… sewage… or even more dangerous objects.

But when the firearm is one of those blunderbuss/matchlock/flintlock jobs, the associations can turn tuneful. A trombone's bell, like in a Glenn Miller musical, but without a mute. Or a Rudy Vallee megaphone. Or blaring brass in a film biography of John Phillip Sousa. Or any one of seventy-six euphoniums. In any case, there should be music to accompany the image.

But there was no music now. Not with the type of trombone aimed at Butterbugs' face at this moment in time. Of course, the instrument in play wasn't musical at all, but a real instrument of death. Indeed, it was one of those blunderbuss-type things, polished, cleaned, primed, loaded, ready to broadcast shot as surely as an old Victrola's limited-spectrum sound waves could.

Only it wasn't just this deadly museum piece with which he was now having such an intimate relationship. Another kind of inanimate object usually focused on him, also known to shoot things – through a lens rather than through a barrel.

To be brutally frank, it was a kind of 'Fuck it; fuck it *all*' moment that had come squarely face to face with Butterbugs, the world's one true ultrastar. *Ultra*star meant above and beyond anyone else on Earth. Nevertheless, right now, it was all… just… too… much.

Things, that is.

To Butterbugs, suicide had always been a tangible concept. Reasonable, sensible, realistic. And specifically scripted, documented, written down or spoken or

1

transcribed somehow. If a given role required it, he would indeed write something actual down while the cameras rolled, as every self-respecting suicide pens a farewell note before the self-slaying begins. It's all part of the great tradition of the human need for communication.

Of course, with Century 21's new standards, the courtesy of note-leaving has been largely replaced with mainstream media coverage, social media momentum, and pretty much live documentation by the end-it-all ones themselves. Indeed, showbiz temptations have swept the intimacy of shuffling off the coil aside, to be replaced by global online stardom, just because of an exit with a bang. Mass murder suicides are of course the most heinous division of chosen death, especially those who do not do the right thing by committing the suicide portion first.

At any rate, how many times, and in how many fine scripts, had Butterbugs been required to enact the 'offing one's self' commitment in his career? That's why suicide was such a 'safe' notion to him. Always somebody else, never him, even though he had, like 98% of humanity, indeed contemplated it. Like that time when he almost...

Nevertheless, exercising distance was one of the easiest parts of doing acting for a living.

But whoa – there wasn't any scripted safety net under him right now. Some genuine reasons had piled up, reasons to say 'fuck it *all*'. For starters, the film he was starring in, the biggest ever attempted in the known universe, was in severe jeopardy. Long story that cannot be made short. And then, get this: he was on the run from his home country, and maybe even from the President and Administration of that country. First-hand attempts had just been made on his life by intelligence agency forces, in which his assaulter had been reduced to a bloody pulp (some of which still remained on his person). And another agent, too late a friend, had been murdered before his very eyes, as a result of his own brain-dead conduct. To top it off, his lover, the woman he cared about more than anything else in the world – never mind that he'd achieved unprecedented *ultra*star status and was one of the richest individuals who had ever strode the globe – had left him for another.

That was the big stuff, and there was plenty of small stuff too, to link everything together, like shrouds of suffocating cobwebs.

Preposterous and inexcusable, but true. He had fucked up. Fucked it *all* up.

Funny, some people have done themselves in over losing five bucks in a poker game, or having failed to deliver a packet of meth-making supplies by going to a trap house instead of a safe house. So he figured his own woeful lineup rated consideration for taking a fast escape route out of such a collective mess.

For an actor so well schooled in many a classic monologue that featured end-it-all language of much stateliness, he was coming up embarrassingly dry as far as farewell addresses were concerned. Not even the epic simplicity (or simplemindedness) of Gary Gilmore's 'Let's Do It' crossed the blank cue-card panels of his mind. Granted, his present situation was no great example to project upon his public, from either an æsthetic aspect or even a scripted one (made out of whole cloth). This was

probably because he knew how ignoble his position was, not to mention indefensi-
ble. Especially when everything was added up. In other words, there wasn't one of
his problems that couldn't be successfully resolved in itself, but when taken collec-
tively, the sum total was a little – overwhelming, even for a very human ultrastar.
Thus, with no defense possible, no other action was probable.

It was a cultural fact: when things get overwhelming, bail. Don't answer the
phone. Ignore emails, texts, tweets, sprinkles. Remain silent in discussions. Declare bankruptcy. Etc. Accountability was for losers, weaklings and perverts.

It's not as if he were actually suicidal, or even depressed. As a professional
picture show actor, his primary job in life was to respond to the dual commands of
'action' and 'cut'. Never mind the 'creativity' that may lie between. The simplicity
of this imperative is certainly a reduction that makes the lowest military person's
operatives look complex. But the problem was, Butterbugs' psyche, mind and
character were as big as all outdoors, so no one, least of all the man himself, could
get off the hook by relying on a few banal-isms like 'stress' or 'sleep deprivation'
or 'cuckoldry' or 'career disaster' or 'politically subversive target', or 'violence
trauma' to define his desperation at this one gun-barrel-staring point in time.

It was just that a whole lot of shit had added up for this ultrastar dude, and in
ways that went beyond the capabilities of a 'two-command' kind of guy. For once
it was a relief to fall back on the notion that all actors are mere dumbos who do
just that: e.g. follow dog commands with all the fidelity of an earnest puppy. Thus,
in such a process, in the name of the Industry that spawned him and the Bottom
Line that propelled him, he was ready to finally screw the 'Method over-intellec-
tualizing of every syllable' crap.

That, of course, is actor-speak for 'take the money and run', versus 'take the
role and be true to it'. Butterbugs, who had always been basically unclassifiable
in every way, was of course way beyond this debate. Yet the compound impacts
coming at him at this juncture made him scoot back to a few time-honored (and
out-of-date) arguments for just *cooling*-it. Like when things were so much simpler
and resolves more possible after everybody simmered down with a few beverages
and remembered the pleasures of humbleness. For it was genuine, heartfelt humbleness that usually cured most of an actor's ills.

He did chuckle for a second though, as he thought of a pleasant and dog-ori-
ented eatery called Fred's on Broadway in NYC. Their advertising gimmick was
'Come. Sit. Stay.'

If only he *could!*

There were many times in the past when he'd show up at old Fred's, often accompanied by his amiable and intellectual dogs Hugo and Hudson, in town from
their Lazarushian wilderland bliss, in order to catch a few shows. Usually acting
as his best friends' Obedient One, the human liked to kick things off before grub
by prefacing his conversations with, 'We dogs...' And he'd always manage to pull
off a delightful conference with many engaging persons, aided by his chick-mag-
net pups of course.

'We dogs… have our gravy rights, you know!' declared man, fondly watching his masters yick their trays, shake rangy brush-mouths, realign big jazzy lips, then cuzzle their haunches before two or three circlings, and elegant flumps on the ground, capped by satisfied exhaling in harmony.

Afterwards, a couple of Shakespeares (in the Park), new Yampsterdam perambulations, over to Henery Hudson, chats with the Roerich Museum gals, Gothic moments below Riverside's high gargoyles, replaying the tape of MLK's electrifying 'A Time To Break Silence' speech, Columbian symposia with the Ms. Alma Mater statue, McKim, Mead & White contemplations, progressive sermons at divine St. John, mouth harp lessons with TABP's dad under the Cotton Club, and late soul fude at Grabby's above the Golden Goon in Harlem.

What fond memory *didn't* he have of those halcyon New York City days, in which he rediscovered his urban imperatives and spread his purposeful endowment amongst so many who needed it?

It was just after the world premiere of his monster hit, Bob Wise's big Ottoman picture, 'Mehmed The Sixth' (Columbia) at the new Loew's Arbutus on W. 42nd St., and simultaneously, at the newer Loew's Amabilis on W. 43rd, combined with the smash run of his leading role in LaGozz Pate-Chimp's legit drama, 'The Life and Times of Sir Charles Montgomery Rivaz, Lt.-Governor of the Punjab', majestically played out on the great stage at Radio City, that Butterbugs chose to hide out for a time in his favorite Wall St. tree-house. Specifically, the upper reaches of the 1931-vintage former City Bank-Farmer's Trust Building, rechristened High Gotham Hall after he'd purchased it outright from the creditors of an aged, destitute The Donald (Drumpf).

One day, following that particular foreclosure, having heard of the artless deals that were dividing the spoils of his erstwhile 'empire', the now rag-clad 'emperor' happened to spy out the Broadway star on his way to that very Hall, and attempted to claw at him with his tiny fingers.

At this juncture, Butterbugs had been hoping to bag some zees aloft after his popular Afternoon Showtime Favorite matinee (always free admission for orphans, widows, retired seamen, sappers and miners), so he was in no mood for feigned beggary.

'Away, churl!'

Pawing and clawing.

'Leave me be, you crude oaf!'

The intruder's clumsy efforts rendered him so puffed that he let out a bark-like cough, spraying greyish-green sputum before him. Horrifyingly, if the chancre and gumma on his pursed lips were any indication (and the occult, indolent bubo lurking further down), it was probably laced with syphilitic contamination. Happily, it and any related dejecta were taken up in a fortuitously-placed sanitary pedestal, hard by.

'Hold your distance in disgrace, vulgarian!'

The vulgarian's thrashings, grunts and farts faded, only to be replaced by a withering whine.

'Insufferable mooncalf! Begone, lest I toot my crime-whistle and beadle's wrath ensue!'

The star was still immersed in his Victorian Raj-Era character, having contemplated his lines all the long way from the stage door canteen.

A chiaroscuro of obvious wetness fanned out from the crotch of the mooncalf's desiccated trousers.

'Why you – *dotard!*'

'You fucking *FAKE!*' the dotard rasped.

At this Butterbugs snapped back into his mod self and realized who it was: one who once famously mocked poverty now lived its tedious privation out of spite rather than humility.

'Oh. It's *you.* What then, do you want of me, 'The'?'

The Donald groveled, lower, still lower. His beat-up trucker's hat, once bright red, sported a psychedelic-green pot-leaf patch, taped-on instead of sewn-on. Only the first and last words of a slogan it covered remained on show: MAKE and AGAIN – whatever *that* meant.

'Lemme have one more trip to the top, Little Buttermilk! You *owe* me!'

'And let you fling yourself off in glory, with the world watching, cursing my very name – all on account of your own catastrophic choices in this world? Not on your sweet life.'

'Gimme a chance to *win* again, you... stupid... little... *schruzz*... So's I can *win big!* Again! And again-again-again! And *then* some!'

'The deal is *closed.*'

'Hey, you – you – *bub!*' wheezed the washed-up shill. 'Sour Little Buttermilk! Just a Sour Little Buttermilk. You better believe me! All the good people, the best people, believe me. Always have. Everybody does... Everybody does...'

Manhattan's onetime good-time (and most-hated) doyen squinted sullenly at the actor from a visage of atrabilious complexion, ruined from the excessive application of processed snack food dust: 'To keep me young!' The fœtid hogo of poorly-applied Preparation X that so polluted his presence reminded Butterbugs just how comprehensively disgusting this Drumpf thingie always was – and *still* was.

The Ancient Orange! Big, proud, bawling baby! Perpetually bullshitting! As if some kind of hot *deal* surely awaited, made possible by cheap charm, shallow emceeing, poncing nerve, cowardly meanness, and old-fashioned guile.

For a second, Butterbugs experienced a déjà vu, starring that unsavory Moby Kenderson, of Moby's Corner pop shoppe fame, whom he'd encountered on his way to Hollywood back in those unknown days, and later ran across once stardom had been visited upon him. Its significance: the delusions of those who believe they have power over another, despite their own inarguable powerlessness and decay. Resolved: these were they whose self-loathing was too monumental to ever instill anything like pity, let alone sympathy, for any thinking person to consider.

'The matter is completely and utterly concluded. And if you choose not to believe *me,* it's your call. Now if you'll excuse me, I'm off.'

This actor was certainly a humanitarian, though a just one.

'You *klinkabell*... Well, *OK* then! *Be* that way. So *what.'* Then, his tone became dismissive, almost wistful. 'Just... well... use that building... *my* building... wiser than *I* ever did... I guess...'

A brief flicker of uncharacteristic humbleness?

'Undoubtedly faked,' the humanitarian thought to himself.

'That is, until I sue – *then buy your cheapie ass out!'*

Humanitarianism requires realism in its makeup, just as much as idealism.

To think that this dude with the stumblebum look was nothing but a preening popinjay all through those disco years, when the bigness of the apple was rotting, while he was plastering enough gold-tinted foil in his dreary apartments to cover seven old Moulmein pagodas!

> East trash, west trash
> All around the alley.
> Tripping over the gutters
> Of the sidewalks of New York...

Defeated yet again, the old cat-anus blabbermouth attempted to comb over the few remaining strands of his erstwhile specially-made hair, once spun in Filipino sweatshops, before shuffling back to where he felt most at home. His haven for brooding on the past was more bizarre than wretched: the steam vents in the service crawlspace aft the rump of the unremarkable Boompah Building, way, way behind old Canal St.

Actors appearing in photoplays do not necessarily think in cinematic terms, but Butterbugs did, always. Even though he should've proceeded in haste to his sanctum high above these storied streets, the scene before him, in the naked city light, compelled him to linger until the anticipated fadeout. It was a melancholic ending, but a finely composed shot, certain to be memorable. Only the dialogue, echoing unto the fire escapes above, smacked of rinkydinkery, as the performing egomaniac toddled down the alley, ruining his own exit.

His voice rose into a cracked cry. 'I coulda been *President* of all this... Doesn't anybody *care?* About my *glory*...? About my *power*...?'

Just another pavement nut, hardly worth hauling in anymore, whether committing nuisance behind a dumpster, or just bitch-bitch-bitching to anyone who (wouldn't) listen.

'I can do *anything.* I'm the *best* pussy-grabber. I cherish women! With both hands, too. And they're very big hands. *Good* hands. Everybody says so. Everyone knows. Good people. The best people. They said I wasn't, but I *was*... Is... Whatever...'

He'd fiddled with an old Kloonk-Klonk breath mint container in his grimy pocket for decades, only now its fatigued plastic was about to break up in little pieces.

'And I have a very stable and better temperament than anybody. Like nobody's ever seen. You are going to *love* my temperament. You can think what you want, but... And I'm not a racist. The best not-a-racist ever. Take my word for it. Tremendous... Believe me... GENIUS!!' (Etc.)

Upon hearing these stagey mutterings, Butterbugs thought, 'He's never acknowledged, never accepted, or even comprehended that everyone's ceased to listen to him, ceased to put up with him... Pathetic. Sickmaking. Dismal.' Then, in a brilliantly-delivered whisper, 'Kaput. *Finished.*'

Resuming his robust pace via a shortcut through Klerker's Passage, the working actor couldn't help but self-declare, 'That is a man I will never grace by enacting his life story within any screen biography, no matter how 'kitsch' or 'box office' or horrorshow his dubious deeds may have been.'

Still, the drama! The larger-than-lifeness! Or was it, in actuality, something more vacuous, bordering on lesser-than-lifelessness? To square such a debate, the ever-progressive actor recalled the sagacious words of his good friend and intellectual guru Robert Hughes:

Where were the kind of structures that had stirred its social heart and bolstered its civic confidence from the 1880s to the 1930s – the symbols of promethean America...? Nowhere – only a succession of ticky-tacky post-modernist confections by Philip Johnson and his favored younger architects, the pediment-quoting Ralph Laurens of their profession: formica-thin memorials to the vanity of this or that corporate raider, gilded (Drumpfery), visual propaganda for the empire of Donald Duck. ('Culture of Complaint: The Fraying of America' New York & Oxford: Oxford University Press)

'Thank you, Bob!'

Then there was always that matchless Drumpf-documentor (and mentor-friend) Pot Carvus to turn to for guidance:

(Drumpf) taught the nation the anti-art of Continuous Partial Attention, in an unwitting but hugely successful war on critical thinking. ('My Scrawlings' Herbertpur: Parl, Purd & Jaykax)

Well then, a high concept for a biopic, consisting of nothing more than stale flatus; its subject an indwelling bore, bloated by clubbed publicity for the sole purpose of mass production of between-the-ads filler.

No, high standards must not only be kept, they must be *lived.*

Finally, before calling it a day as far as this odious and intrusive subject was concerned (e.g. The Drumpf), the only thing left to acknowledge was the standard time-tested epithet, achieved through much analysis and deliberation, based on proven theories of empirical and chronicled fact, universally employed by the many, both high and low: *'FUCKING MORON...!'*

And Butterbugs, actor, ultrastar, reformer, philanthropist, visionary... and humanitarian, et al, had done so – in scotching any and all Drumpf biopic entreaties and electing to run that particular bozo's properties infinitely better – to the very best of his integrity.

In fact, his heroics in Lower Manhattan were exemplary. With the collapse of such corrupt Wall St. firms as GoldbarryMuldman Saxs; Smith, Wong & Ghjugzhcucx; Tiggs & Kraupper; Associates & Maurie Pitzup, Inc., and so many others, he had helped transform the whole neighborhood into a Bohemian fertility ground, a hip/cool/happenin' workplace, and a showbiz Valhalla for the retireds. This kind of thing was one of his favorite hobbies: 'inmates taking over an asylum', and what he'd managed to achieve down there was nothing but success after success, to savor and keep savoring.

Therefore, he was nothing if not serene when he chose to take his straw-beverage up to the roof terrace for a bit of late afternoon/early sunset relaxation. He had recently overseen the removal of the monstrous steel framework that had blighted the crown of the building for these many years. It had been evacuated by a chopper borrowed from the Queens studios of Blackhawk Films, and the process had been a huge media event. The liftoff had gone smoothly, but unfortunately, en route to its disassembly point on Cuptip Island down in the Lower Harbor, the cable snapped and the whole assembly plummeted nine hundred feet onto Battery Park. No one was injured or killed, but 'The Sphere' by Fritzi Koenig, surviving relic of the twin towers' collapse, was smashed beyond recognition.

'I am extremely sorry', the ultrastar publicly declared, paying for its careful restoration to post-9/11-damaged status out of his own bottomless pocket.

As one of the Great Iconic Three of Lower Manhattan, and the centerpiece between the sharp-spired duo of the Cities Service Building and the Bank of Manhattan Co. (another ex-Drumpf) building, architects Cross & Cross had elected to make the 59-story City/Farmer's a flat top, its white slimness more feminine than phallic, despite its shaft's aggressive verticality.

[Shaft, upthrust, tower, erection; skyscraperism wasn't *completely* concerned with the biggest dick in town. After all, Butterbugs was an expert on the inverted (and admittedly non-masculine) culture of the crustscraper, e.g. the Isaac Davis Building disaster. Ever since that Biblical event, the fashion of ramming high-rises into the ground had all but died. But none of this had anything to do with the elegance at hand in Lower Manhattan, *in the least...*]

With its sets of three great arched windows near the top on all four sides, High Gotham Hall exuded a campanile-like quality that always bespoke that a bell would surely toll for those who practiced capitalistic corruptness within its earshot. Thanks to Butterbugs' reforms, actual hardware did not have to sound for the uncleanness to be banished, in toto.

In any event, the shaft's noble, even haunting, profile exemplified the sheer *drop* that resulted from its smart Deco profile. Butterbugs, from his suite in one of those huge belfry windows, loved the thrill of looking straight down. Down, onto what would surely be splat-pavement in front of Delmonico's, with any atomized flesh surely spreading as far as the tankard-strewn doors of the Fraunces Tavern, a block away. But due to the powerful drafts that surged from below, the actor always felt uplifted by this experience, and never drawn downward. Indeed, it was his commonest wakeful dream that he actually, maybe, might, just *might*, pull off being able to flap his arms and fly. If he'd only catch the right surge, at the right moment... and *believed*.

That's what he'd done with his career, wasn't it? *Believed?*

Well, on that particular big city night, there was no need for high-flying fantasies. With a masterpiece motion picture before the public, and a terrific new five-acter set to run for years after his launching of it, high life resulted in high achievement. Plus, high enjoyment in high places. The plan was, he'd play the lead in 'Rivaz' for a month at the restored Ziegfeld Theatre, then turn the role over to the eminently-qualified Yinker Brapp-Pile. Yink was currently his favorite protégé. Why, if he had to, he'd will his whole career to the guy without blinking. Of an up-and-comer like Yink, it was typical of Butterbugs to declare, 'I wish that *I too* had been born in an abandoned gravel chute in Adi Ugri, Eritrea!'

He'd certainly meant it. Such secure sincerity made him glow with more than just his usual internal incandescence.

Butterbugs and architecture!

If buildings might be called frozen music, Butterbugs, as an actor fully appreciative of the built worlds surrounding him, whether a set on stage or an existing location, might himself be classified as a mobile construction, for he identified with certain structures' conventional realities more than most. Kate Hepburn always told him she'd love to come back to Earth in another life as an oak tree. This clicked with him because he'd always thought he might return himself as an apartment building or something similar, with life coursing through his rooms as surely as instincts like thinking or lovemaking. Passionate or even lustful in its given vibes, a sexy building could give him a hard-on as surely as both Mindy DeVerandy and Miriam Lane (his current co-stars in 'Rivaz') did with every performance.

As with his Æyrie, The Lazaretto, and Vinejuice pads in LA, or his Bramham Gardens pied-à-terre in London, his secret bungalow in Seebpore, or his Bakelite capsule in Tokyo's Shinjuku-ku, this limestone-sheathed high-rise, with its carved-coin entrance, zig-zagged lobby, and helmeted guard-goyles way up there (that made damn sure no one tried to pull any shit when approaching), got his appropriate juices going every time he entered its exalted, rigid frame.

9

What better than to steal away on a solo afternoon in early spring – sunny, but with remote warmth seen on the sun setting beyond Liberty's tireless torch way off there, with only the wind sound in the rigging and some curls rising from a genteel joint puffed exactly twice (all he ever needed, really) behind the immense plate glass of his VistaVisionary window on the world to the southwest?

And after the sun was low and the lights came on in the gloaming, the solemnity of the heights became all sophisticated and Hefneresque, and the wit of the city below would bespeak low-cut little black dresses, dark swoops of hair, and tilted champagne glasses that reflected the subtle colors from way outside the window. Cool nightlife that warms one's cockles, and related parts, through a Gjon Mili or Stan Malinowski lens… (Cheryl Lampley was here once, sipping LeVeon Supérbus 1958 with finesse).

One time, in such a mood, he put on his LP of Gordon Jenkins' 'Manhattan Tower' and ran through the whole cinematic wonderment of its tonal poetics, which he was content to enjoy as a private show in his mind rather than via some over-produced package for those who couldn't actually be here, couldn't actually ascend to this level, couldn't actually experience an experience that had to be experienced in a certain way, one way only. No, even the cinema can't be allowed in on some avenues of storytelling, for the considerable powers of film could not, cannot, never will be able to capture the solid elusives he felt at moments like these. So he left well enough alone, and let the architecture that surrounded him have the first and final say. He loved to shed a few tears of music-inspired joy at times like these, but didn't want anybody to know, perhaps on the childish assumption they might think he was intrinsically sad or that he was putting on some pretentious show. But no, no *way* was he acting. He had no choice but to *re*act to lyricism with emotion, and without script, without direction.

How strange, for an artist to respond to… art.

That was the thing with Butterbugs and his many NYC pause-spots: they played themselves, not necessarily in any form that was overt, mainly because of characteristics built-in, often deep within, and way beyond the organic.

On up by Grand Central a ways, there's the Lincoln Building, on a truly crushing scale… Its Venetian Gothic capping, persistently providing the rest of Midtown's high-rises with some sense of chosen historicity, generated one of his first amazement statements the day he hit town: 'Well, I'll be daahned…'. Naturally, it captured the ultrastar's awe so that he had to have it, and so he got it, and when he was inside it, he thought only of the image it was projecting outside, so that he wished he could crawl along its horror-inducing heights and discern the power of its imagery on those who might meet its mass every day from opera-box windows adjacent. Without a doubt, the Lincoln and its kind was a drama card that Butterbugs sought out in megalopoli anywhere in the world.

To him, the buildings of a city like New York qualified as *actors* so much more than mere transitory humans had a right to claim. As far as the Lincoln's mediæval-Adriatic topside was concerned, he'd even entered into talks with Old Atrocity and John Box about constructing a raked stage, to be cantilevered from the face of the building, five hundred feet above 42nd, on which to perform 'Othello', with the striking polychrome arches as a backdrop with more power than the Hall of Supreme Harmony in Beijing's Forbidden City when used for a production of 'Turandot'. What's more, the performances, whether on stormy nights or humid mornings, or even in the snow on this railing-less platform, would be filmed in six-camera technique from adjacent buildings, to create what Butterbugs knew would be a ' – stunning, and unprecedented, too!' production.

[So far, the plan was stalled, due to sour grape juice from both the Port Authority and the Triborough Bridge Authority, who somehow had joint jurisdiction over air space 499ft and higher, above sidewalks and streets. But they had not yet encountered the *will* of Sonny Projector the ultra-agent, or the passion personally produced by Porter Pud Parker, who were said to be 'very much on top' of the idea. Parker suggested that the level of the stage be lowered to a mere 495ft, and a heartbroken Butterbugs was forced to accede.]

'Why, these are the *great stages* that we are fortunate to live amongst, to witness, to touch, to feel! And they, for their part, feel our touch too, and witness our presence and all that we do, as surely and as silently (but as mightily) as the bottomless ravines of dim Tine Gair or the shining crags of fabled Yosemite! Oh yes, these – these streets, these bricks, these posts and lintels, pilasters and stanchions, these piers and spandrels, these, *these* are the great stages for performance... and I'm not excluding my beloved Radio City in this, my gentle thesis, my friends... Indeed, that which has been built around us serves as one great set of boards upon which we, as strolling players of aspirational attitudes, might plead our case, as we need, first and foremost, somewhere to *stand*, if not to *make* a stand, somewhere to pose, to perch, to strut: indeed, to *stroll*, if we are to ply our trade before a rightfully demanding public!'

Butterbugs and holism!

Well, thus spake the ultrastar one crazy, crazy night at The Bitter End down in the Village, sharing the humble stage with Mpasa Huorgi, Bob Dylan, Dr. Dre, L. Gaga, TABP, B.B. King, Richard & Teddy Thompson, Dua Lipa, Mr. T, Viscardo Bloop, Edna Tzu, Luis Miguel, Glen Greenwald, Joni Mitchell, Amy MacDonald, Lee Fang, David Miranda, Juan Gonzalez, Ahamafule J. Oluo, Sarah Heath (ex-Palin), Udo Kier, Paul Moravec, Carroll Baker, Martin Clunes, Farooq Sheik, Brooke Baldwin, Mike Burke, Suzanne Vega, Tarana Burke, John McLaughlin, Amy Goodman, Esa-Pekka Salonen, Ed Snowden, Alicia Garza, Debasree Roy, Nellie McKay, Slavoj Žižek, Lou Jacobi, Monti Ling, Nancy Wilson, Laura Poitras (who was filming), Helena Guàrez, George Monbiot, Györgi Ligeti, Jack Germond, Andrew Sarris, Chelsea Manning, Victoria Bond, Mickey Rooney, Jules Feiffer, Shirley Chisholm, Woodys Harrelson and Allen, Gwen Ifill, Ari Herstand, Milton Gla-

ser, Jeremy Scahill, Chris Hedges, Freddy The Beetle Barnes, Abby Martin, Laura Ingraham, Savario Ghoom, Julian Assange, Kellyanne Conway, Jack Garfein,
Seymour Chwast, Ting Vhommalungtikkakorn, Cornel West, Jon Korkes, Harris
Faulkner, George Harris, and Rebecca Correia, in order to quell a drunken riot that
had started between Ed Koch, Festel McMoorarty, Bill de Blasio, Mikey & Ivanka
Bloomberg and Charlie Sheen over 'Uptown' and 'Downtown' musicianship (e.g.
which one was better).

Realizing that refereeing such a tussle between titans was pointless, Butterbugs
decided to lower the tension by employing reason, rather than rules. He aligned
their (rather stupid) argument with the seminal, subtle backdrop of architecture as
a rhetorical raison d'être – shelter itself – so as to make the performance of music,
any music, eastside, westside, all around the town, possible at all, under any condition, as his premise.

He had to raise his voice a little.

'Because, like Brahmā, who is the Earth itself, and upon whom we stand with
outrageous entitlement, the fabric of shelter hereabouts enables all and sundry to
freely express whatever we need to... well... express. Super-banal, is this not? –
but super-true, doncha know! And I never heard Bob Moses, dictator-general as
far as what he thought was good for NYC, say anything like that!'

Fantastic cheers welled up from the boisterous celebrants.

Robert A. Caro, distinguished biographer of the very same Moses, who happened
to be a member of an audience that suspended its brawling upon the ultrastar's first be-
seechment, was scrunched against the brick wall near the stage by a merrily hopped-
up Rev. Al Sharpton, but was able to howl out his approval with a resounding 'Yoe!'

'Peace now, New Yorkers!' The ultrastar's entreaty was bright and bountiful.
'And Peace again, for we have *new creation* in the works this night! We are surrounded by its wonders as it is, and it can only grow and grow!'

The audience wasn't exactly sure what Butterbugs was referring to, but after the
resultant cheers died down, the melee turned, all by itself, into an architectural seminar co-chaired by Ada Louise Huxtable and Robert A.M. Stern, who'd just dropped
by. You know: the values of a built environment, how to interact with it, etc.

Tension banished, the ultrastar and Rev. Al backslapped and gabbed for a spell.
Then, with greater ease than at any Cannes shindig, Butterbugs huddled with writer Caro.

With the cool jazz of Vijay Iyer & Co. providing atmospheric assistance in the
background, Butterbugs skillfully blended bluntness with sincerity.

'Because, why don't we just *do* 'The Power Broker', Mr. Caro? I mean, let's
just *make* it!'

There followed a mere thirty-five seconds, in which the two were able to firm
up an irresistible proposal: talented player to star and erudite expert to script what
would turn out to be the ultimate Bob Moses biopic.

'Yeah,' was all that was necessary for the Pulitzer-winner to clinch the deal, in
reply.

And so it came to be. Sidney Lumet, summoned from a booth back by the Green Room, couldn't wait to direct. It could only be a Foonman Stvdio release. (Foonman *always* granted Butterbugs more carte blanche quicker than any other moviemaking outfit.)

So simply, then, are great pictures ignited, for 'Power Broker' was destined to be one of the greats – instantly. No futzing in the name of fixing necessary. Cinema has long operated on such winning formulæ, but the so-called 'Butterbugs Effect' always ensured the swiftest of fast tracks into production.

Well, that was NYC for you – a successful deal could always be factored pronto, usually out of some initial challenge, or even conflict, such as on this memorable night. Enthusiasm seeped from the pavements hereabouts.

Catching wind of this impromptu and effortlessly-brokered movie pact, Gwen Ifill, always keen on a story, zeroed in on Caro after Butterbugs eased away. Tonight she'd come with Dr. Cornel West, Mr. T, and Rep. Shirley Chisholm as a foursome, and being a Caro fan, she was already formulating questions regarding what promised to be a momentous production.

Mr. T beat her to the punch.

'Hey man – Mr. Robert A. *Caro* – what's all this guff I hear about Bob Moses building only ONE playground in Harlem when he ruled this here city, and 254 playgrounds in other neighborhoods? Huh??'

'Sad but true, Mr. *T.*' The writer was always gratified when anyone quoted his book accurately. 'Indeed, Robert Moses built only one. Robert Moses wasn't interested in building any more than that in Harlem. Robert Moses built only *one* playground in Bedford-Stuyvesant. And Robert Moses built *none* in South Jamaica.'

The Hon. Ms. Chisholm knew the whole story.

'Yup. That's about it, T,' she said. 'Bigotry… abidingly institutionalized.'

'Robert Moses was indeed an unabashed bigot,' added the biographer. 'And even though Robert Moses is no longer with us, plenty of Robert Moses remains. Some good Robert Moses. Some not so good Robert Moses. That is, Robert Moses in *effect,* more than Robert Moses in *name.* Robert Moses is actually pretty easy to reduce to such terms. Robert Moses always thought the public was ungrateful. Robert Moses may have 'gotten things done', but in the process, at the end of a long, long day, Robert Moses hadn't a clue about the public. Reassuringly, the Moses *they* knew wasn't some damn power broker, but the Moses of the Pentateuch.'

'And the Moses of… Charlton Heston!' Gwen chimed in, with a touch of wryness.

'Hey! Remember 'Black Moses'?' interjected T, with excited respect. 'Double album, by my man, Mr. Isaac Hayes!'

'And remember *Charlottesville,* Brother T. Not an album, or the place, but the *event.* Among others…' Dr. West certainly felt a responsibility to propriety, but of course, he dug Hayes, too.

'We all remember, all the time, Brother West,' replied the Hon. Ms. Chisholm calmly. 'Rev. Dr. King said we've a ways to go, and I always got my best walkin' shoes on!'

Sobriety over Robert Moses (and much worse things) segued into a sort of same-page geniality.

Mr. Caro turned to the Congresswoman. 'By the way, we need you as POTUS more than ever, Shirl.'

'Most kind of you, Robert A. I'll do my best.'

[The Hon. Ms. Chisholm may not have achieved the White House, but she did secure the governor's mansion in Albany, and after that, the senior senate seat for NY.]

Dr. West then drew nigh.

'Brother Caro, your work is unimpeachable in its factual reality and integrity. I salute you as a co-laborer. We must bestir that which should be known.'

'I am honored, sir, and I fully agree.'

'That being the happy case, one question, Brother Caro.'

'Shoot!'

'If I may ask, with informality, why do you so respectfully style this broker of past power *Robert* Moses, all the while? Why not... just... 'Brother Bob'?'

Mr. Caro smiled puckishly.

'Dr. West, why do you refer to everyone as 'Brother' – or 'Sister', if I may ask?'

'Why Brother Caro, you know that all men are brothers. All women sisters. Thus, the family of man – whoops – *hu*-man-*ity*. New coinage of terms needed!'

Mr. Caro was amiable but firm. 'Robert Moses is no family of mine. Thus, the formality.'

Brother West's gap-toothed smile widened, and its accompanying guffaw was similarly-sized and wholly appreciative.

'Brother Caro – (somewhat conservative brother) – I read you loud and clear! But my goodness, yes indeed, sometimes that very family's what we now call *dys-funk-tion-al!* Just plain *funky*, too!'

The two embraced in mutual harmony – and hilarity.

Gwen was mentally formatting this encounter for a 'News Hour' (PBS) segment. Tomorrow's show had a seven minute gap awaiting content.

Mr. T approved, wordlessly.

The Hon. Ms. Chisholm smiled.

'That's a rather elegant explanation, you two!'

Elegance was then superseded by a load of the Bitter's high-volume (though civilized and sophisticated) bedlam. Brothers West and Caro made their way to the placid sub-Green Room in the very back, there to hobnob further.

Butterbugs discreetly followed, and peered in for a few moments, unbeknownst to the two passionate thinkers.

'Tonight – the exchanges... they spark me into a notion,' said Brother Caro.

'I like that terminology, Brother C!'

'It's just that, I'd dearly like to interest Butterbugs in playing the lead when it comes time to film my multi-volume biography of Lyndon Baines Johnson.'

'LBJ... *Brother* LBJ, huh?' Brother West was surprised but intrigued. 'Great Society brother and poverty's enemy, or militarist co-operator and order-giver to bump JFK off?'

'Are you adhering to that particularly American (and annoying) trend of considering most issues, persons, and events in terms of extremes?'

'Nope. The whole story, end to end. Lotsa grey betwixt.'

'Brother West? You are a seeker of truth!'

'God loves ya, and I am duly touched. Truth is bigger than all of us. And I engage with the justice therein, whether it goes for me, or against me. You seek the truth through writin' and research. I seek through faith and follow-up. Now Brother Butterbugs? He seeks through right action, dramatic example, and story-actin'. Powerful. Just plain powerful. That's the needful, right there!'

'That's why I so want him for... *Brother*... Lyndon. After the... *Bob* Moses picture, that is...'

Brother West smiled warmly.

'I'm glad you're lettin' 'em into the family circle – if only a little. All sisters and brothers need help – and that means love... all the time.'

At his doorjamb observation post, Butterbugs teared up. Then he stole away before he was discovered, returning to the twangy action, as zither-Theremin-ocarina-meistersinger Brerrold Lumslutcher had wrapped, and the Muckluck Jones Trio's set was just taking off.

Meanwhile, fraternal affairs of a different kind were being thrashed out. Mayor Koch was pretty enthusiastic all right, and he wasn't done fighting. He picked up a ball of yarn from his mom's knitting bag and was about to fling it at Mayor Bloomberg, when –

'Ed – no! Ed!' shouted Mayor Sheen, as the two ex-hizzoners snorted and puffed in their mutually impotent raging.

'Those boys!' Butterbugs mused, '*Alvez mit der jokes!*'

The evening ended around 3:00AM, when Bob DeNiro, who was getting mighty sick of what he was hearing from a Sheen who'd gotten into a fourth-wind rowdiness, decided to slug Charlie right in the gut, despite Snoop Dogg's attempts to restrain him. The raging bull's tactic worked: it basically re-set that poor mixed-up boy's aggression dial, so that by the time he was heading out the door, he was quoting Swami Vivekananda to uncertain souls all along the way, and deep into the sleet-spackled night. Charlie's subsequent retirement into private life as an Abbé at the Belur Math in Howrah generated great international praise.

'DeNiro's violence may have pushed me into peace,' the ex-bad boy stated later. 'But it was *Butterbugs* who made it all possible.'

15

All Dave Letterman, who had emceed since 5:15 the previous afternoon, could say as a wrap-up to a legendary night was, 'Awfully darn glad to have been here...'

That was Butterbugs' *theme statement*, wasn't it? That's all he needed, wasn't it? To get him through *anything*, right? To *be here*, the here and now, and to be awfully darn glad about it, too.

So then, up on his High Gotham terrace, he was indeed glad to be there, at that right moment, as so many moments in his life now *were* right. It was something never to feel guilty about, for he had served long in the *not*-so-right-moment world. Why waste irreplaceable time reviewing extinct issues?

'Right on!'

He breathed in the heady bouquet from his Chibbs Cup – that combo of Lemburg herb liqueur, Famous Sovetsk Tinctures and Gandolph sprouts, concocted by Allthimblesfingers the MixMeister, fifty-nine floors below, while the fly-birds just above were shooting higher, always higher, expertly riding the updrafts that the asphalt and manholes, in desperate need of cooling, helped propel from below.

Mellow was his countenance through and through as he sank in slow motion into a barrel-chair to continue his savorment. Each second brought with it pleasure akin to discovering a duckling-shaped bar of soap on his pillow, or a text by Goethe for the first time.

Then, a few sipperkins later, from just around the corner, a voice, spoken in normal tones, though neither censored nor aided by the great upper outdoors surrounding them, began to engage in English-language conversation. This terrace, like the entire building beneath it, being a wholly-owned freehold by Butterbugs, was nevertheless completely accessible to all residents. Many were the pleasantry-laden chats he'd had way up here with virtually all the intriguing and gifted occupants of this, his rent-controlled alternative for those who might have been turned out of fringe rooms in the Chelsea Hotel. It was sheer Providence for they who lacked even the scrap-change to afford a broken window ledge in Beekman Alley. Of course, the mix entailed the top-hatted and opera-jeweled as well, but all were primarily people in the brave, the bold, and the beautiful molds – a most enthralling combo. Such relish, scooped out in such big-city helpings! Because, when all was said and done, Butterbugs was essentially interested in *people*.

'Be that a lone voice I hear? Come, sit. Talk of your findings, Stranger, for none who come up this far under my ægis shall long remain strange to we High Gotham denizens! Indeed, to cushion any possible discomfort, first, would you take tea? No? Would you take *wine?* You have only to take of the soft fruitage, mighty nuts, patchleaf seltzer, and nourishing root-meats – an Eden of all plenteousness – from yon vending machine; the override key to which I shall cheerfully give you custody, be it only for the hour!' was what he'd *prepared* himself to say (not surprisingly, in the showy manner of his period role in 'Rivaz'), but when he chanced to hear the voice from just around the corner's next sentence, his own was instantly stilled before any such casual delivery.

'Why'd you think I came up here, anyway? To blow my nose on all the jizz-mis-takes below? Yeah, right! Now you tell *me* why I'm up here, why don't you, and don't take that long to say it, cuz you can't stall me. There's *no way* you can get here in time…'

'Oh dear,' thought Butterbugs, 'Trouble!'

He was about to venture round the corner and present himself to this voice of such potential conflict, then thought better of it and applied restraint. Ultrastar or no, what right did he have to barge into some citizen's private affairs? He'd made enough picture shows by this point and had enough life experience – well, *perhaps* – to give pause. Besides, had he actually scooted round the bend, his forbidding appearance, seen in such weeping twilight as now descended upon the metropolis, could possibly alarm the poor person into rashness or some worse action (e.g. fleeing in terror and accidentally falling over the parapet, or crashing into the vending machine, etc.), especially as he still wore his Sir Charles Mont-gomery Rivaz costume and makeup, a practice he often engaged in when B'way stage acting, and indeed, often *had* to do, lest his true identity cause distress for everyday folk who, perchance exhausted from a livelong day's work, just want to get home in one piece, free of celebration burdens when encountering unexpected noteworthies. To be sure, the vision of a subtropical-Victorian-clad gentleman with a huge mustache and spear grass-proof boots on, emerging from the stream-lined shadows on this lofty plane, just might cause a medical distress – or even undue expiration of an innocent.

So he remained seated, though with ear cupped so as to get an ear trumpet-full of data so as to make his next move – if any.

'So that's what you think, huh?' the voice resumed after a timespan that couldn't allow any stalling strategy from the other end to survive. 'Well, you're part right, but you don't know the half of it – or even the seven-eighths of it…'

Butterbugs thought that he (for it was clearly a man attached to the voice) was now the one doing the stalling. Such verbosity of dialogue! But then, why was he on the phone up here in the first place? He must have something important to announce – or maybe a secret or even a surprise to divulge! Maybe he wasn't supposed to find out about his birthday party, or something.

'I tell you, I'm *sick of it!* The sick society! And me, part of it! I mean, how do you like being *part* of something like that? Well, I just can't stand it anymore. And now… and now, you're… you're gonna have to call me… *Jumper* – ever after! That's right lady, Jumper!'

'Oh… Hmm…,' thought Butterbugs, never thinking that that name had any-thing to do with how far above sea level they were at this very moment (over seven hundred feet, in point of fact).

And then, when the sunset was reaching its sweetest time and an afterglow of much promise was spreading its goodness over the terrace, the voice, remaining in the realm of gathering duskiness, undertook a narration of real depth…

However, Butterbugs, still with superficial and carefree intentions, and so as not to butt in on someone's private business, stole away from his chair momentarily to make a call from the alcoved pay-phone down the terrace a piece.

The pay-phone had FinalityGloo-clogged coin slots.

'Those darn *kids!*'

So, he whipped out his mobile and peeped it. Sonny had always warned him that capturement of his cell phone chats was always probable, and that a call from what pay relics remained in the world couldn't end up as fodder for Twitterheads, TMZombies, Smirking Gun clubbers, or even as audio smug-lumps for NPR pinwheels to annoyingly rotate over, but he took this brief chance.

'Taffy? Taffy! Oh, Taffy-lovey, come and jiggle thy booty! Got a new playsuit, do ya? Super! Top 'o the Gotham. 'Bout eightish? Seeee yah!'

When he discreetly returned to his chair, the ultrastar fully expected this 'Jumper' voice to be successfully recovered from its societal sickness, and, introductions properly made, ready to join him in the nipperkin of his choice.

But –

'Oh girl, if you'd just listen for a few minutes, you'd know what a *remnant* I am – of anything decent. You *will* listen? That's novel – I mean, I'd hoped so. I *do* love – But no, there are things you'll never know, cuz revealing them to you wouldn't be as bad as revealing them to myself. But… Hey, time is short. I wanna get this off my chest before… Well, before night *falls*. I've got about five minutes. OK. I just came from Cambian Heights. My ex's brownstone? Know what? She just threw my three kids off the roof. Uh-huh. That's four stories. They landed in a dumpster full of busted glass – just like she planned. To get back at me for her discovery of *us*. She didn't get mad, she got even, by way of her slaughter of the innocents. That's right. My three wonders, all still under ten – dead! Oh, unutterable calumny! You might say I was responsible for them – never mind that you *know* I tried for the past three years to get custody. But yeah, I'm to blame, aren't I, for not getting them away from a certifiable psychopath in time. That's my first and most primal sin. No, I'm past shock. I'm very calm, very sane. How else could I tell you what I just told you? You know me well enough to understand such… such, a… thing…

'Do you know that, before this… unspeakable tragedy, I was already set in my downward course. But – and this makes me laugh (probably for the last ti –), I actually thought that I might reinvent myself, perhaps as a lush or a feeble-minded foon, or as a street hustler, even! I stood for over seven hours on Broadway, directly across from the Standard Oil Building, holding a sign that said, TOO UGLY FOR PROSTITUTION. All my effort yielded a buck. That's right, one. In note form, too.

'But boy, how my – (wry) – humor quietens your voice! All right then, that's enough of *that*. After I quickly cast away that sign and its accompanying dollar, more excrement hit the ventilation system. Too much to tell, and I ain't in the mood to write it all down, you know? Even today, believe it or not, I was still trying to intellectualize my failed life, still thinking that paths of change might be attempted. I climbed every step to where I stand now (and there were many, I can tell you that right now), to see if my misfortune might wear off the higher I got. But *no...*'

And the voice went on. And on. And... And in the most measured tones too, so that the listeners, the one at the other end of his Ding!Gull/Barry *fernsprecher*, and the one transfixed in the barrel-chair knew – they just *knew* – that he was probably understating things at the very least. Surely the mention of his babes' demise had taken the initial sarcasm out of his voice, so that now there was nothing left in the poor man's truths but naked facts. In short, everything bad that could happen to an individual had apparently happened. About ninety-nine times *worse* than bad. Job had it made, compared with this hapless one. Like the late Emperor Franz-Joseph, he might well have said, 'I have been spared *nothing*.' Yet, there was no whining, no request for the pathos of solo violins, no self-pity, so that amongst the egregious tragedies, the boils, the tears, the locusts, and the tornadoes, a kind of grace emerged, but it was a grace that plainly had an expiration date of *minutes*, not days.

This résumé was so relentlessly meticulous, yet so concise, that it was delivered within the span of an average between-the-ads segment of a national newscast. Nevertheless, despite this inherent digestibility, Butterbugs, detail-oriented student to a host of directors and scriptors that he was, began to flag after Jumper's rundown of his legal woes reached its first intermission.

'You won't *believe* what came next,' Jumper said as a kind of segue to regions even more forbidding. 'Because, dear lady, I know we haven't talked in a month, but it was a month as perfectly enacted as in one of Butterbugs' finest Greek tragedies...'

Butterbugs naturally took note of this, and because of the heavy cheer of Jumper's reportage, the name-drop of his own self was an ego-free relief. That is, if Jumper were cogent enough to mention a mere actor's name in the midst of his horror, it meant that perhaps he still had some zest for life, some taste for the drama, the kind limited to auditoria and not transferable to life itself, except as an edification or an entertainment. Many a fan had told him, often in a tear-streaked face-to-face, that for them, without the dramatic joys and theatrical gifts that he, Butterbugs, had endowed upon the Earth's peoples, life was not at all worth living.

He wondered though, was Jumper referring to his Broadway performance as Jason in the utterly crushing 'Medea' (Euripides, additional dialogue by Hy Averback and Everett Greenbaum, directed by Alan Rafkin) last year at the Ethel Barrymore, or was it his devastating Agamemnonian triumph at Ticker's TimeStage behind the Apollo in Harlem last month (seating capacity, 17!)? He certainly hoped his thespian activities didn't contribute to or even *cause* this hellish month in question. (An actor's vanity can often eclipse an actor's charity...)

'But you know, somebody like *Butterbugs*, well, he's always been on the royal path of life, hasn't he? I mean, everything always goes his way, doesn't it? While

I, obviously cursed, must tread a trail of genuine grimness, and one not limited to the safety of stage and screen…'

Butterbugs nearly leapt into the breech with a 'Now you looka here'-type energy, but again he thought this man's private agony did not merit such a cheap intervention. Every last audience member is entitled to their personal opinions and interpretations.

Sometimes in this life, the quest for justice must be… abandoned…

And then came, in mind-destroying detail, Jumper's actual description of his Greek-tragic month just past. Butterbugs was fully reduced to a puddle of helpless tears by this incredible 'non-fiction' performance, wrung from the depths of this non-actor's very soul.

Notwithstanding this, the ultrastar could not help but think: 'Whatever then, is this poor fellow *doing* up here, aloft and far away from she who obviously still cares for him, still loves him, still listens to him, even now?' The dimness of this question was certainly understandable, given the impact of the soliloquy he was hearing.

A minute or so passed… hard to tell how long. Butterbugs' sobs became downright projective. Certainly he who caused them could hear such an audience reaction.

'He now knows of my presence, and that I share his grief. Its effects! Its consequences! Its total tragedy! We who are not made of stone must respond in some civilized way! Perhaps so moved, I can help, perchance to change his mind,' thought Butterbugs, knowing that, as an actor of pathos, empathy from all those wonderful people out there in the dark gives strength to a performer and a conviction to *go on*, regardless of the challenge. Simultaneously, he gathered an inkling of the larger context, because he was putting it all together at last. The self-assigned name of 'Jumper' meant only one thing. It meant that he was going to –

'He's going to do it!' Butterbugs whispered. Then, out loud, 'I tell you, he's *going to do it!*'

It was getting late, but not yet *too* late.

He rose quickly and boldly went round the bend.

The terrace, which circled the rooftop crown of the building, was wide open and without population now. Where was Jumper? The ultrastar rounded one of the chamfered corners and there, ahead, outlined against the blazing sunset, was Jumper, his integrity intact, *up on top of the parapet.*

Yet now, a cinematic interlude entered itself upon Butterbugs' consciousness. How many times had *he*, as actor, been up on a such a ledge somewhere, enacting what Script wanted, what Director ordered, and what Producer was paying for? In how many rushes, test previews and premieres had he seen himself up there on the screen, pretending to be in some situation like this Jumper fellow was now, for real?

As Martha said in 'Who's Afraid of Virginia Woolf?' (WB, 1966), 'Truth and illusion, George. You don't know the difference.'

'Yes I do,' the actor stage-whispered. 'Oh, but yes I *do*. Maybe more than anyone else.'

This poor, mad – perhaps even holy – fool on the edge! His appearance betokened an impulsive disposition and a restless energy. His active and somewhat attenuated frame seemed a prison-house which had been gradually worn away by the fluttering of the eager soul within.

And of himself, Butterbugs thought in contrast, 'The fire within me does not kindle so readily, and when excited, burns slower...'

In other words, one has the guts to get up there and do what he thinks needful, while the other only has the skills to *pretend* such a thing.

The interlude passed.

'Oh! No! You don't wanna do *that!*' Butterbugs called out, loudly but weakly.

Yes, but he knew full well: the man *did* wanna do that, and nothing he could have said would have made any difference whatsoever. Therefore, the gesture made, Butterbugs advanced to the edge of the parapet, to at least make sure that Jumper got all the way down safely.

He did not.

Though his last declaration before he stepped into the void was a good one: 'I take off now – to see my babes – *in bliss!*', and though he was true to his 'name', perhaps Jumper hadn't researched the drop-off factor of this particular skyscraper's upper reaches. Granted, seen from directly below, High Gotham looked like an extremely principled shaft, a straight up-and-down affair, lacking way station or climber's rest – with the sole exception of an ornamental recitation balcony. However, as was the style in those legendary days before the crash of '29, when reaching for a moon was so suddenly denied because of the Great Depression, the upper reaches of these super-tall ones were usually tapered in many decorative ways, so that anyone peering from your average Observation Deck would have at least one setback placed directly below them. This buffer zone served to calm nervous Nellies & Nelsons, and with a very high success rate. But after the fashionable high-mortality jump-off ledge of the old Singer Building became unavailable, such crafty/subversive designs involving setback 'safety' ledges, put into responsible practice in the world's supreme high-rise environment, would surely and soundly defeat would-be suicides once and for all. Thus, potential Jumpers would hopefully turn about and reform somewhere along the transcontinental journey to the only acceptable alternative: the Golden Gate Bridge. Who knew how many lives this brick and mortar psychology had saved through the ages? Indeed, the upper levels of the Empire State Building appear almost as casually-placed condominiums in Acapulco, and any high-diving candidate would have to have access to the several lower planes, from which to take the big cannonball run *all* the way down. The point was for visitors at this height to look *out* at what the far horizon offered, and not directly, truly, unavoidably, along any plumb-lines *down*.

Jumper had indeed gone over the edge.

However, outside the arcade that enclosed the rooftop terrace, a significant setback happened to form itself, and he duly ended up on its own individual parapet, safe but for the fact that he landed horribly wrong, so wrong that his left leg snapped into a sort of terrible compound fracture, red tibia wobbling, itself a victim of total confusion upon greeting the high-altitude air outside its protective tissue so suddenly, so rudely.

His mind, so beaten, so bowed, produced no reactionary shriek. Nor was there – when Jumper's head jerked back and noticed Butterbugs looking down – any entreaty or change of plan. Indeed, thinking that some mustachioed, Knickerbockerian detective (that looked remarkably like Butterbugs, the well-known actor) was about to throw a safety net over him, he figured that any subsequent legal action would merely prolong his intolerable torment. So, best to decamp with all possible dispatch. Jumper did his namesake act again, this time so as to do it up fit and proper, and with perfect freedom.

At that very second though, from the stack of one of the nearby ventilation shafts connected to the Brooklyn–Battery Tunnel, came a tremendous blast of hot air, shooting skyward as no common updraft ever could. Whether it was some underground disaster or a particularly robust purge of monoxide-laden tunnel air did not matter at the moment.

[Media would later reveal it was the latter, though it was truthfully the former (news to be repressed), as it would reflect badly on the Triborough authority that ran the facility. In fact, it was a case of a disgruntled worker who had tossed a cigar end into an open drum of boilage solvent, stored in a service anteroom midway on the Manhattan-bound side. The ensuing draft-expulsion was turbo-powered and deadly. 42 people were killed, 326 were injured, and the tunnel was closed for a week until wreckage was cleared. The resulting scandal, which dragged on for months, was more explosive than the original impact, and its positive momentum led to great advances in de-corrupting such offices. (An *oblique* 'Butterbugs Effect'?)]

What did matter was that it changed Jumper's downward course, and quite radically, too.

Astonished at this phenomenon, Butterbugs' breath was momentarily taken away.

'Oh, now *fly*, stolid Jumper!' Butterbugs declared tearily after him. 'Fly with angelic skill, for it might yet save ye!'

For the duration of who knows how many milliseconds, Butterbugs experienced a tremendous rush, way beyond any tinker-toy bungee jumper's, because the variation of Jumper's intentions, combined with this 'schedule change', made for the sort of amazement that the average audience member feels when, say, first beholding the wonders of Cinerama. It's called being thunderstruck.

'He's *flying!* I knew it was possible. From this magic perch! I knew it the first moment I stood here. He surely knew it, too!'

Astounded, he watched the graceful flight of Jumper, experiencing the one true freedom: a tour of these high-topped towers without wires, bungees, spongy-cords, powered backpacks or safety nets.

A freedom such as an ultrastar always coveted?

'Now is *my* chance!' he exclaimed, waving his hand out into the realm of pure architecture, and most importantly, architecture's pure empty spaces.

He actually got up on the parapet, and, totally mindful of the pesky setback just below, and seeing the strange success of one who intended on dying instead of flying and riding the wave of possibility, thought he might just emulate the pioneer who had gone before. And the guy was even a cripple, too.

Despite such a majestic hope, any possible poetics to be gleaned from this latent tragedy were indeed spoiled by that disturbing busted leg. While the achievements of any disabled person may be impressive, often the æsthetics that come along with them are, quite frankly, a stumbling block.

'That is just so – *ugly*,' thought Butterbugs, used to critiquing a flaw in a take that could be redone simply and ingeniously, especially with an Old Atrocity or other problem-solver wizard on the set. Any director worth their salt would call out, hopefully in not too great a rage, 'Who stuck the raw meat on my diver? Property? Lose it, NOW. Camera? Get ready for Take 14!'

In fact, battered and busted though he was, with suicide as his mission, Jumper got to see what it was like to fly, really *fly*. This air blast, totally artificial in nature, propelled its passenger via its expanding billows, so that he didn't even have to flap any of his three good limbs to keep up the momentum, and the blast was so strong that even his wrecked leg, as it flopped around, did not influence his route as any sort of spastic rudder.

Indeed, he was heading downward, but at a trapezoidal angle. If there had been no architectural obstacles between High Gotham and the Hudson yonder, Jumper would have been allowed a clean and graceful sweep, perchance to make an aquatic landing that would have been more thrilling than deadly – though that lower leg would have been steak tartare for any shark venturing this far upstream.

Alas, a significant structure *was* in his path: Ralph Walker's dazzling Irving Trust Company Building, its Deco shaft a fitting (albeit slightly lower in elevation) limestone companion to Butterbugs' own High Gotham Hall.

No magnificent man *sans* flying machine, Jumper was not even allowed the dignity of a fast-track splat to conclude his nightmare life. No, he was catapulted into the arcane glass of the Irving's sepulchral Board Room window, that intentionally high-up-and-far-away badge that was to remind neck-craners of the Olympian solemnity and exclusivity of its all-powerful occupants. Now was its sacrosanct party crashed, and not by firebomb-hurling anarchist nor bewigged terrorist cell, but by this flying rebel who merely longed for the relief of release – which was *yet to be denied him*. Alas, it took six horrific hours for rescue teams to extract his still-conscious remains from the Perribaux chandelier in mid-chamber. When he finally did expire, it was just before an ER worker was about to inject him with a massive pain-killer, and Jumper, who in past real life had been no stranger to such Board Rooms, thought, in his chaotic delusion, that the ER worker was none other than 'Dr. Death' – Dr. Jack Kevorkian himself, providentially-arrived to issue the healing shot.

'A syringe! A syringe! I'm *saved!*'

And he fell back and spoke no more.

'Truly, the slaughter of an innocent...,' Butterbugs said in a stunned whisper, gesturing wanly at the Irving Trust window across the deep way, now buzzing with reactive personnel. 'He – over there, me – up here.' He gazed, through tear-blurs, up into the full-color sky and wondered how such hellacious acts, not scripted for motion picture entertainments, might be allowed to occur before such glorious backdrops. But they do, as he knew perfectly well, and this one did, only to destroy his day of high-up splendor.

'What *are* we, anyway?'

He placed his right hand on his breast in Balzac-like pose, and then held it out entreatingly to the Irving.

'Two mere specks of nothin'! Oh, the complete and utter evanescence of life, the incandescence of which burns off... into the æther!'

It was a spiritual devastation that not even the good godhead-consciousness of his Gothpore ashram could assuage. As with his best Broadway performances in O'Neill's 'Long Day's Journey Into Night' or T'milledniff's 'The Gong Cracked And Fell Across The Universe', this great and powerful actor was reduced to the detritus of an emotional boneyard.

Then, guilt.

Butterbugs and architecture again: if only... if he'd just... Well, he couldn't help but think that, if these high-rises, these audacious up-thrusts *were not here*, if they *did not exist*, the poor man's life might yet have been saved! Had this tower's terrace been off limits, limits that he, Butterbugs, had shorn of restrictions and thrown open for the joy of all, the man might have reconsidered, rejoined his lover, and built his life back up from the ruins! These buildings! Certainly complicit in the blame! And was he himself not a signal accomplice?

In his next powerful insight, he couldn't help but paraphrase Byron:

> The half-barbaric Gotham's minarets
> Gleam in the sun, but 'tis a sun that *sets!*
> New York! thou limit of his long career!
> For which ruined Jumper shed his frozen tear.

Sickened by an irony that then weaseled into his mind, he actually waxed narcissistic.

'And *my* career, *my* tear? I wonder if things would ever progress so that *I* would do what he did. I know I've had similar moments, but to *actually do* the deed –

now that would be a state to see myself in! Oh, but I'd be too self-aware, too self-conscious.'

Or would it just be self-loathing? The self must hate the self very much for the self to wish self-extinguishment.

'Naw, not me!'

Narcissism can be a self-preservation instinct that rivals even the most determined sperm facing tied tubes up ahead. As the actor stood at the edge, it served up its restorative elixir faster than the speedball punch of a laudanum injection directly into his brainpan. Suddenly life was so overwhelmingly precious that he cursed his folly – that of being seduced by suicidal thrills – and wavered on the ledge. He knew that if he fell he would be saved by the setback below, but what if some further air blast carried him out over that nether parapet, and he was compelled to follow the Resolved One? No doubt his flight plan would be ne'er so grand. An inglorious streaking, at stern Gravity's insistence, with some back alley's basement waste vent waiting to harbor his shattered remains...

So no, no, no, not this way! Not down, down! Only back, back!

In his frenzy, he spun about, and there was Taffy, oh Taffy, all chic and glowing, new playsuit shed and tossed on the tiles, ready with any number of witty comments on the day's experiences to whisper in his pillowed ear after they'd made love. And after that monstrous monoxide balloon from below, which plainly made his mind so temporarily diseased, had dissipated, he might even detect his cock scent on her lips and her pussy scent on his cock and he'd know that the earth was still the place to be, because it produced such good reliable musks, and the comfort would be complete as they'd roll back in both bodily and atmospheric afterglow and wonder how many stars might be visible from down here in perma-lit Manhattan. But being a bit higher than the street, perhaps if they were lucky, they might spot one of Orion's belt buckles. They had certainly pulled it off that last time, in central Central Park.

Because it came down to this: Butterbugs would rather fuck than fucking fly.

'Wow!' Taffy was incredulous, but totally used to show people pulling stunts. '*You're* adventurous tonight! What are you intending to do, start *flying lessons* or something?'

She raised her arms over her head and lavished her big raven tresses. There was enough flight power generated by her stripped poise to carry them both over the rainbow, so he very sensibly got right down off Foolish Edge, approached her with theatrical ecstasy, dropped his period costume (and mustache) and flew into a luscious contact kiss with her big lips, which were primed for well-grounded earthiness and terrific, firm lovemaking that can only be labeled cathartic.

Oh, but out of respect for both the tragedy of departure and the life instinct of coitus, perhaps it's best to tilt up from the loving couple and glide, ever so grandly, to the edge of the terrace, to the limits of the parapet, and take one last look at the Manhattan sunset as it transitions to ConEd-punctuated twilight.

To a talented director of cinema shows, it would be poor form, at least within any respected canon of cinematic technique, to dissolve from glamorous sky-scrapers (as seen from another skyscraper), into looking down the barrel of a cannon-like gun. To make this come off as a credible transition... well... it would be too pretentious, and to an audience, it couldn't be anything other than hokey. Similarly, from a reassured Butterbugs saying *'Naw, not me'*, to a shocking new Butterbugs thinking, *'Now, it's me'*, such a jagged jump would be compatible with the rebellion of Jean-Luc Godard instead of the establishment of George Stevens. That is, in terms applicable to the screen, it's a jump to the uncomfort-able avant-garde from the comforts of polished storytelling. A disassociated *cut* instead of a contemplative *dissolve*.

(When one works in film, so long as assembled pictures are created for people to see, film theory is never not applicable, whatever the situation.)

But there he was in the here and now – Butterbugs – in an utterly differ-ent environment, a different time, facing a gun, for God's sake, of his own arrangement, facing a moment of Jumper-like truth, Jumper-like awareness, Jumper-like consciousness – and Jumper-like loathing – though in circumstanc-es other than those that are self-generated. To be sure, he still believed in him-self, but now there were just too many things, too many movements, too many judgments, against him.

This wasn't the top o' Gotham now. Not NYC. And Taffy was nowhere to be found.

Like Jumper's had been, his own phone was nearby, available for use, to call anyone in the world he desired. Heaven knows, they'd all be thrilled to hear from him. But unlike Jumper, he couldn't think of anyone to ring. At least Jumper had had an anchor to talk to before he took his final kamikaze flight.

Butterbugs? *No one.*

The phone was right there, mobile, cellular, and willing.

'Naw, not me!' kept him from picking it up.

Jumper!

Or whatever his name really was... He-who-jumped-that-time, or whatever.

Butterbugs went over it yet again. How could a person *do* something like that? Something to *think* of, yes. But *do?* Well, if things were bad enough, he supposed so. Well, *maybe*... The thing was, when you're not *there*, when you're not in the moment, it's just so much sitting-in-the-audience voyeurism. Sure, empathy helps, and sympathy is a whole lot safer than that, but nothing can replace the urgency of being cornered by real or imagined enemies, while the tide rises, or the spiked walls advance inward, or the hopelessness and despair become codified into an irreversible reality.

But there was another thing. Jumper had meant to make a clean break with life. Granted, a long haul down to streets and bricks is a much bigger production that pointblank destruction by an armament, but it leaves open the probability of a whole shitload of 'the unexpected' to be delivered on site, as was certainly witnessed that time in New York.

In the here and now, Butterbugs, staring at a simpler way to go, was determined there would be no misfires, such as those in Jumper's final agony. In fact, there *better not* be any misfires at *his* moment of no-return truth. Not being half the man Jumper was, he wouldn't be able to bear it.

'Now, it's *me...*'

Oh hell, there was only one thing left to do: wrap this mess up by pulling the trigger. Get *on* with it. Ready, steady, FIRE.

But this takes place later on – Other things happen first...

Prelude:

Intermission

I, your host, Jonny Cide Hamete Benengeli, welcome you to this, the second of two intermissions. Let's get to know each other yet more! Really! Even you folks out there, way up in the *second balcony upper lobby.* I know you can hear me while you get your beverages and other refreshments, cuz my voice is piped right on through, to where it counts!

Hey! How do you like the picture, huh?

[Major, energetic applause]

Oh my lord, you're deafening me! Help! No, really, it's terrific, huh? Boy, *I'll* say! I have to tell ya, I ain't never seen so many human beings in one building at once. Look at those aisles! Everybody's filling all the spare space. We might have to set up the folding chairs and put 'em on scaffolding in all this empty space between the balconies and me! Just kidding. But, uh...

Our fine Intermission Music will play, regardless of what *I* do or say. Is it not a splendid sound? Uno Spaccalavacci – now at the keyboards, Ladies and Gentlemen! Wait! What do they say about Uno?

'He played and played and played and played and played...!'

[Pleasing applause and laughter]

And now: Intermission the Second!

[Standardized intermission behavior: stretching, yakking, refreshmenting, and pit stops, for some seventeen minutes; then:]

I, uh... I...If I could corral your attention for several secs, while you're getting your kits together for the duration, I... Well, I'll let y'all get, uh... settled, and...

[Several more minutes of standardized intermission behavior, before the host again appears in front of the massive curtain, and the Super Trouper spot from way up high again fades in on him; then:]

As Carson would say, 'We are back!'

28

[Applause from those paying attention]

I have a few short remarks I'd like to make though, regarding our Industry, and what has happened to it. And more importantly, what has happened to YOU, the audience, the paying audience.

[Cheerful applause]

I'd uh, I'd just like to say – hey! There's Joe Bubb over there! Hiding in the third row left, huh Joey? Great camerawork on 'The Meredith Bentley Story' (MGM), baby! And Mike Brad! Great production of 'And He's A Nut' (Your Basic), sweetheart! Sorry, but I have to drink a toast – *to all my friends!!*

Well by golly, thanks for the applause. All the warmth from all that applause. I tell ya… I could keep going, moving from seat to seat, row to row, as I see *such* a stellar gathering tonight. All my friends! You know? I could get a little choked up. All the terrific talent here. And let's not forget those who *aren't* here. Oh, hell, I'm gonna cry!

[More generous and loving applause; audience fully engaged now]

Thank you, thank you, folks. Now listen, let me, uh, let me get back to what I wanted to say. I'd uh, I'd just like to say – a few things about – the abatement of viewer apathy. Huh? I like the sound of that. I mean, don't you? Because, heck, anything that makes me look good, hey, I'm interested in it! Really! But let me tell you. It's a funny thing, when a whole *audience* changes – not just the pictures they watch. Maybe, could this be *because of* the pictures they watch? I gotta say, this is so.

Get into my rhythm here, Laties and Chentlemen, Poys and Kirls.

Listen to this! It's because of New Ideas, New Ways, New Faces. I suppose that, in the supersized scheme of things, something had to *give*. Nothing's new under the sun, and yet, each second is something unprecedented for each and every one of us. Notice how I include everybody, now! Of course, there have always been new faces in town. And boy, are we all glad of *that!*

This… apathy thing. Mostly most of any of you who work in the Industry, and I know not all of our fabulous audience tonight actually does, but all of you, and all those wonderful people out in every dark house in front of the sheen of a motion picture screen tonight, should know what I mean when I say, we all *love pictures*. Don't we?

[Total-agreement applause and hoots]

But, for the longest time, those audiences, why, they were going wobbly. With apathy, man! I mean it! Where you *been?* We all knew it. And on the production side, it was happening all over the place. And it was bad.

But then, things changed. It took a few pictures to show it, but those New Ideas, New Ways, and New Faces had caused some kind of change to come about. We all knew it in our guts, but come on, none of us knew what the hell we would *say* about it, or even how to approach talking about it. But at last, we *did* learn how to talk about it. In the simplest ways, really. Single words, mostly. Like 'swell', and 'different', and 'afoot'. Remember those? All around the motion picture community, there was a certain kind of talk. Not your usual 'I want him EXECUTED' banter, but something more. Some folks might call it extraordinary. Extraordinary! I tell you, I love the sound of the word, even better than 'abatement' or 'viewer' or 'apathy'. Yeah! A single word to describe it, this change: 'extraordinary'...

[Pleasing applause]

Thank you. Thanks. I, uh, I have to mention names now. Or rather, *name*. One name. Singular. I said, New Face*s*. Notice the plural. I really should have said 'Face'. Because, all of you out there might know of whom I speak.

[Some audience disquiet]

No?

No one can handle such a new face without, to paraphrase Clifford Bax, 'incredulity and a sense of outrage'. But in this case, this specific face, which, by the way, we see at the beginning of every 20th Century-Fox picture – Thanks, Darryl. Are you out there? I think you are! Darryl of the Blessed Aisles? There he is! Ladies and Gentlemen: may I present Darryl Francis Zanuck!

[Stormy applause]

Nice shades, Darryl! Hope you take 'em off during the picture! But, uh... Thank you. So, like I was saying, see? That face – up on our gigantic screen tonight – which we've seen now on so many screens, is different. It does not incite jealousy, or envy, or really anything negative. In fact, I'd like a show of hands now – is there anybody out there who finds the face that I'm talking about to be something of contempt, of negativity – of apathy, even?

[Total silence in the auditorium; no coughing, tittering, or fidgeting; even the background accompaniment of the organ leaves off]

'Who the hell are you talking about, Jonny??'

John! John Huston! I see you brought your handy, portable Bakelite megaphone with you! Ready to direct me at any moment, huh? Get to the point, huh? Well listen, I suppose I really *should* name names at this point. Or do I actually have to?

[The audience erupts with 'No! No!' chanting, that eventually segues into a growing chorus of – 'Butterbugs! Butterbugs!', which the returning organ converts into a tuneful cantata for some minutes, before fading down to:]

My goodness, my goodness, my goodness. We are all of the same mind tonight, are we not. Are we *not??*

[Cheers]

Well now. Well, well, well now. That's just fine. Butterbugs it *is*. I tell you, how was our town, our people, our very Industry so fortunate so as to have been blessed with this thing they call Butterbugs? What gave us the right? How was it possible for him to come out of nowhere to change us all, as he has done? How did we become so worthy? Why did he emerge at this time, in this place? Who could have dreamt of the gifts that he would bring? We have seen him now, in a whole host of pictures, and who can say that he has *not* transformed us? Who among you? By his very being, by the transmission of his ignited soul, by the simple delivery of his inner offerings, he brings us something of value. It is subtle at first, but when we see him, in anything he is in, we know – we just know – that he is approaching us in the way he knows best: his real, natural way. It is an approach via a trail, a byway, a lane, an alley, a road, a thoroughfare, an arterial, a superhighway, a – cosmic path to a galaxy (!), here clearly drawn, that we can all tread! He brings us forward, and there is no one too high up, or anyone too near the ground, that he has not noticed, or spoken to, or spoken for, and the goodness therein makes us all happy equals in his presence. How, I ask you, can anyone not understand? Well, I am no agent for this fellow, only an observer. And how we observe! Who amongst you would not be able to say the same things that I have, were you up upon this glossy stage? It is that truth, that essential center of one's existence, not only in the here and now, but in the past-and-future spectrum of the whole, cozy universe, that is distilled and made real, and into something that you can hold in your hand, and stretch out to offer to the person next to you, in back of you, and in front of you, that Butterbugs makes plain, if we choose to take it! And we *do!*

[Emotional applause, with sounds of weeping, both joyful and poignant, plainly heard]

But, you *know all of this.*
Oh, audience! You're wonderful. You *get* it! If that isn't an abatement – no – not good enough – if that ain't an *annihilation* of viewer apathy, I just don't know what the fuck *would* be!!

[Really big applause, not only for the words spoken, but for each audience member, from each audience member, to another, for they all get it]

31

Me? Like I told you, a couple of times now already, I tend to like all kinds of pictures, but they better be pretty challenging. I can get mighty sick of a whole bunch of scenes comin' at me like Pamplona's – what're they – elephants? Too easy. Triumphalism can be overwhelming. But let's see what we've got coming up. It can't be all good... Hah! Oh, well...

[The crowd simmers, a little disoriented by the host's latter lines, but having gotten the larger message, settles into readiness for the last act of tonight's Roadshow Presentation; the houselights slowly dim, the Wurlitzerian intermezzo swells into a fugal climax as the voice fades, the houselights are doused, and the curtains part, and the screen becomes incandescent with blank film glow...]

That said, Great Group, remember one thing: there's something in motion picture entertainment for every single one of you! Terrific! Dig it! You're beautiful. Love it, baby! We will help you. We will entertain you.

[Coming to the multi-faceted climax of Intermission:]

And at last, to paraphrase my good buddy, Al Jolson: Wait a minute! Wait a minute! You *ain't seen <u>nothin'</u> yet!*

Vale.

1.

Hollywood In The Epoch Of Butterbugs

Hollywood!

It was still there. More 'there' than ever, actually. Big things were rolling, and in all directions, whether they were cameras or dollies or script conferences or production schedules.

Not since the apex year of 1939 had the motion picture capital been so in-ter-sewn with so much activity on a scale of such high quality. Everybody worked. The studios were running three shifts. Old-timers preferred graveyard, where they could get away with employing techniques from the halcyon days, some of which were responsible for the new renaissance, such as literate writing, emphasis on character development, full-bodied scoring, a banishment of white lettering on black background for opening/closing titles (except for Woody Allen and Stanley Kubrick productions) and a return to proper title presentation, a rebirth of the over-ture quality to the Main Title music, a cessation of the 'opening jab' soundtrack over said white-on-black titles, the elimination of faux-Orff choral treatments in scores (that had been plaguing the Industry for decades), and on and on and on.

It wasn't just old guys and gals that were exercising winning ways. The Indus-try was reforming itself from the ground up. It was almost an organic process, like the development of carbon-based life forms. Except that Hollywood, always turbo-impatient, ratcheted up the evolution, not just by the reinvestment of ul-tra-B.O. dollars, but by strategic positioning of talent and management.

This phenomenon, and it was nothing short of a phenomenon, is not the sub-ject of the present report, but if it were to be distilled even more essentially than a Reader's Digest Condensing, the progression was this: Corporate control was OUT, baby, OUT. The inmates had truly taken over the asylum again. This was thanks to a new wave of handpicked immigrants from Central and Eastern Europe, Gabon, Bihar, Tenasserim, Venezuela, and Oregon. People like Yobadiah Gezelzner, D'lugna M'amjaimbo, Yuther Gold, Nurburia Trane, NorMann Telp, Seeta Varmah, Muazzam von Gwadar, Polycarp Davis (Isaac's other, enlight-ened brother) Horemheb Jigbash, and SantaRosita Bellah!

These moguls proved they really knew how to make pictures, to slam them out with vim, and not only that, to create new classics of quality and worthiness. And their track record rendered the aging bean-counters irrelevant. And as the prestige and the power grew, a whole complex of wedded finance and production was constructed, built by Industry people in the Industry town. Its people, from the executive branches down to the paper cup picker-uppers: they made their own way, and soon it outclassed what Wall St. could give (or mostly take). So the silly Suits were bought out and relegated to historical dustbin-dom. It was certainly a matter of money, but those who led the Industry now knew there had to be a reformed mode of progress if they as a group were ever to be free of the exploitive yoke of the retrograde bottom-liners. The transition to Hollywood-centered control took place, amazingly, within the space of one bare year.

A fair amount of giganticism was afoot. This being Hollywood, and LA in general, it was essentially a good development. No one does gigantic better than Hollywood. In the vast scheme of things, it was not only systems, services and production that were being constructed. There was the exhibition side, too. Mammoth new picture palaces were making Hollywood more of a destination site than ever. The latest kick was to actually see a picture – to experience it – *in* Hollywood! Such an event became the goal, or regular goal, of millions per year, and so new venues for unique motion picture experiences had to be designed and built at a furious and demanding pace.

Sid Grauman, not surprisingly, was the most innovative. It was a time to pull all stops out, and to do it right. Grauman's Tirukkalikundram was the grandest effort Sid had yet made in this universe. A multi-acre movie complex based on the layout of one of Tamilnadu's best temple towns. And its mighty gopurams rose into the air above what was once the dullest stretch of the Hollywood Blvd straightaway. At 10,001 seats, it pushed the Metropolitan into second place in west coast seating rankings, though that particular house, newly restored to original luster, remained his flagship.

Aside from the Tirukkalikundram's massive auditorium, which was based, not on a temple's more intimate inner sanctum, but on the secular inner vastness of the Tirumalai Nayak palace in Madurai, with its titanic *chunam* pillars and lofty scalloped arches composed of materials from far-off Tamilnadu itself, there was a Thousand Pillared Hall, two 'sacred' tanks, a refreshment kiosk in the center of the complex, with a golden dome that rivaled anything to be seen at Tirumala, and while there was a certain air of propriety about the place, no effect was spared in Sid's insistence on catering to the picture that was playing at the moment.

With seven gopurams populated with every member of the Hindu canon, painted in cheerful day-glo and hailed by Hindu and non-Hindu alike, the opening of Sid's ambitious addition to the LA showplace lineup proved to be *the* event of a brilliant season.

The opener was the latest Butterbugs epic: 'Shree Jambukeshwar, Meenakshi – and Shunya' (Mega|Goth), a lavish mythological, with Hema Malini, Dimple, Shabana Azmi, Shilpa Shetty, Sweetie Surapalayam, Rogi Kutterbutty, and Aishwarya Rai. They all attended, surrounding the star himself in a protective escort.

'They are my *gopis*,' Butterbugs joked.

If this was not an age of gold, or even silver, then it was platinum, or perhaps even vanadium.

Most importantly, production was absolutely flourishing. Not overheated, but the friction from rolling cameras must have upped the ambient temperature of LA at least six degrees, so surging was the wave of creativity and hustling effort that the film community was generating these days.

As far as the physical studios themselves, their plants were expanding.

Vitagraph was big again, releasing sixteen features in the past year, half of them blockbusters.

Biograph, another illustrious name, wasn't far behind.

Oddball David Lynch's fittingly esoteric studio had five pictures slated, which was ambitious, to say the least. The world always anxiously awaited the latest weird wonder to emerge from that quinoa–fired hothouse of a film factory, which was truly unencumbered by convention.

Dino De Laurentiis and his outfit might be more prosaic, but the Maestro and his brood were as adventurous as ever, with twenty-seven pix on the docket.

And that was just a tiny sampling from the 'growers' (as these 'boutique' studios came to be known in 'Variety' lingo), who were surprising everyone with their product.

Groaning from overwork, the Majors encouraged more studio construction and investment. Now that Wall St. was out of the picture (and largely out of pictures, thank heavens), there was much more freedom for Industry-supervised development and experimentation. Mini-studios (aside from the Growers), nurtured by the Majors, sprang up all over the Great Plains of the Grid.

Looking down from his Æyrie, Butterbugs could see them rising where once had been urban detritus. Off to the southwest, Sid's Tirukkalikundram made its memorable profile remain long in the memory with each sunset, and on up the boulevards, many welcome structures with studio associations sprouted, with benefit of conscientious and imaginative architecture. Thus, a true Hollywood style evolved: part Deco, part Mission, part Streamline Moderne, part National Romantic. The results were enchanting, compelling, powerful. At last, a true *gesamtkunstwerk* of the cinema city was being *borned* (another word term variation for creative innovation realized).

As far as these developing studio facilities were concerned, that was where a lot of state of the art cinema was happening. Many a significant scene were shot at places like former Deco petrol stations in Culver City, or once-abandoned warehouses downtown. There was even talk of developing the late Isaac Davis Disaster Site into a multi-level location facility (*no* underground arrangements allowed; all of the site would be open to the sky). Toxicity abatement was still in progress though, and it would be months before studies could be properly made.

Nevertheless, that was about the only example of any roadblock standing in the way of the Industry's thrust-forth activities these days. Power brokers such as Shonnaleen Gubbins, Sonny Projector, Mike Prike ('The First Mike of Showbiz'), Charlie Feldman, Sherry Lansing, TABP, Bobbo D-Vult, and others knew how to throw the levers and engage the clutches and baby the accelerator pedals of the

Industry, and their talents went ahead, as they were key players in the nouveau re-naissance which beneficently showered over every and all players and crew now engaged.

Audiences were *back*, big time. Devices were utterly interlinked, but had now found their proper, less dominant places. Tots were willing to listen and not mock, young people were focused, burghers and dullards were agreeable in venturing to these new picture pagodas, middle agers were not so taciturn and withdrawn, and seniors were energized as never before. And the new management in Hollywood recognized these advantages and did not play down to them. Instead, they who ran the big show had the big wisdom to raise them up.

All across the vast canvas of the gigantic matrix of the Hollywood map, the life-cycle of the photoplay breathed mightily in layer upon layer: creation, nego-tiation, preparation, rehearsal, construction, enactment, shooting, re-takes, SFX, post-production, publicity, premiere, exhibition, circulation, preservation...

It was a time of vitality, of importance, of exhilaration, of achievement, and of greatness.

And who set all of this rolling? Who could really be credited? Who instilled the creation of reinvention where it was most needed – where it was most effective?

Everyone knew who.

2.

The Big Time

The Roxy!

Servandoni could have envisioned it! Garnier could have realized it! Khufu would have built it! The dream was vast, the intention was one of service, and its siting would have to be of milestone quality to the world, for the whole world would inevitably come to see it. It was left to Ahlschlager, with his nerdish mustache and hotel-designing background, upon whom the heavy task rested to erect this, the Cathedral of the Motion Picture! The greatest house in the East, venerated, along with its stylistically foreign mate, Radio City, as the Big Apple's premiere showroom, the very presence of which always left audiences gasping from its sheer grandeur. Under Roxy himself was it built, and in his spirit did it stand and provide performance.

Thus, the Roxy took its place as one of the great public buildings of the modern world.

New York, 6:30PM.

The great city in retreat, or rather, shifting its duties, from the mundaneness of day to the magic of the night, when the sealed-beam of the automotive headlamp, the lanterns of hospitality, and the neon of sensation begin to outweigh the consequences of purply skies, leafy park walks and hydrant-spray parties in this Atlantean conurbation's four-season mix.

The entire intersection of Seventh & 50th was almost gridlocked, not with vehicles, but with people. Ballyhoo was out in full force. Klieg-lights of particularly wide coverage sought out inhabitants far above, even beyond the top pediment of the Voiraquellen & Bombo Building, who might be viewing the gala from seats in highest heaven.

It was an occasion of full significance. Persons of consequence were here, as well as the everyday all-around-the-town New Yorker, out for a sighting of – persons of prominence. No Hollywood premiere, this. No premiere at all. Just an ultra-special event.

A fleet of black limousines, retrofitted with flexion-powered plants, purred along 50th in orderly fashion, their way kept clear by Roxy-provided rope railings and standards. There were so many of these newly-efficient land barges that the street looked, from above, as if populated by creeping patent leather shoes, some with fins, some with bubble tops, and others with mafia-type funereal bunker-domes. All were in transit, in the same direction, with one destination: the curb outside the Roxy.

Butterbugs rode with Saskia and Justy in his favorite NY-based '57 Imperial Ghia limo, which matched his favorite LA-based mate, both of which naturally co-starred with Butterbugs in his beloved comedy, 'The Solid Platinum '57 Imperial LeBaron' (Columbia). It was his home away from home. He knew every ash receiver, every fold of the mouse-haired ceiling, every honest shift of the TorqueFlite transmission, and so he was at ease, despite the import of the eve.

On the other hand, his accompanying couple, firmly part of his most inner of circles, were at the moment, in awe.

'The Roxy!' exclaimed Justy in an honorific whisper as they each peered up at the mighty Spanish Renaissance window ensemble, way up on the façade.

'Butterbugs – this means you have *arrived!*'

'So have *you!*' he replied cheerily. 'And the front door is nigh!'

They were able to accomplish a quick frolic before disembarkation, for the two lovers were all over Butterbugs in a matter of seconds.

'Not that this situation is an aphrodisiac or anything…,' he quipped.

As their rig finally pulled up to the quay under the great oval 'Roxy' trademark on the marquee, the crowd, which was extremely well mannered, went wild. Not physically though, save some ecstatic jumping in place and arm waving. No puppetry was in evidence, just honest but sensibly contained energy. It was their voices that rose, in an ascending cheer, each voice expressing its owner's healthy enthusiasm without any cult of personality baggage. But this was another example of Butterbugs' influential consciousness. He had successfully inculcated the masses to take up the path toward continual civilization again.

'Take it up' was the rallying cry, based on Butterbugs' famous line, 'Come, take it up!' in 'The Prize of the Ages' (Oddball), David Lynch's practically indescribable masterpiece of clarity, vision and hope, which dealt with the subject 'Are we going to do this 'civilization' thing or not?' In that one remarkable picture, Butterbugs' performance quotient had expanded multifold.

The moment was at hand to present himself to the people.

The klieg-lights shone into the darkening sky, some of their white beams catching the specially fabricated, bevel-edged letters on the marquee, for which the Roxy was famous.

BUTTERBUGS

…was all that was spelled out, for this was no premiere, no regular presentation. No picture per se would even grind this night. It was all *his* night – devoted to *him*. A celebration more than an honoring. A momentous occurrence rather than a retrospective. This was because Butterbugs needed no review or explanation. There wasn't one soul there who did not already know about this fellow, and each carried his or her own thoughts and memories of his contributions to their lives, thus far.

That understood, it was a *darshan*, a witnessing, a sharing of the same air, that would ensue. And, remarkably, it was all to be done under the premise that Butterbugs occupied no pedestal, nor was he deified by any agency. He was as he was: a fellow humanoid who offered what he offered, and that was good enough for all.

Though he was and always would be a man of the people – for it was a given that he was admired for every conceivable reason, though he was impossible to admire for admiration's sake alone – there was nevertheless a tone of exaltation during his progression unto the Cathedral of the Motion Picture. There he went, up-the-Pikk of the Roxy-logo'd TyLaMats. Through the Box Office 'starting gates', up the introductory passage to the Grand Foyer. A special pilgrimage to the Drowsy Ladies, statues that guarded the passages to the Upper Balcony Loges. He laid commemorative chiltberry wreathes at their feet. Then, a circular expedition round the undulating entwinement fringe of the Great Carpet, pausing to acknowledge and greet every New York light who could be crammed under the enormous Greater Chandelier. Thus, into the cavernous auditorium, but via the furthest doorway to the right, so as to fully appreciate the aspect of the stage at its most compelling. But also, as was Butterbugs' wont. He felt compelled to make a heartfelt gesture of modesty, in keeping with his heritage of having entered the motion picture world from a route of comparative obscurity and humbleness.

And there were none at hand who thought for a second that this unconventionality was any sort of stunt or an attempt at indirect pomposity. They did not want a king's entrance down any central avenue, nor some ruler, either already wearing a crown or expecting a coronation. For it always had to be kept in mind that the public *got* Butterbugs, so to speak. They understood. His clarity was not to be misinterpreted or taken advantage of. It was exploited, of course, but in a very special way. Never was exploitation so non-exploitive. Such a singular set of characteristics he had, of bringing out the best in people, and setting that quality as a cycle to be repeated, from person to person, shoulder to shoulder, mind to mind, heart to heart. And this was accomplished not by a spiritual or religious belief, or via any sort of dogma or creed, but by the power of the Drama, through an Industry that created and exhibited picture shows, with strolling players, for folks to see and hear.

Butterbugs noted there were two camera crew units filming the proceedings. Both were tracking on opposite sides of the passage, and he worried there might be a possibility their coverages might conflict. But he relaxed when he saw that Ping Wang was directing one unit, and Howard Hawks the other.

Then came the majestic descent into the three acres of seats. At one particular row, BB, near the second seat in from the aisle, here on the periphery, next the bulwark of the wall, the mayor of New York, Hyman Hoggston Blutz, awaited.

'Butterbugs!' he announced, 'Welcome to the Roxy. And, I might add, welcome to our out-of-the-ordinary metropolis! I will be your usher this night.'

And he conducted him the three feet or so to his place in BB-46, then handed him the lavishly illustrated 612-page programme (one of 7012 copies printed and presented to patrons tonight, personally initialed by Butterbugs, by way of autograph), and then withdrew to his usher's station after seating a street person from Hackensack and a peasant from Henan Province (two of hundreds specially invited to the occasion, by virtue of chance) on either side of him.

The street person offered the star a swig from his half-empty/half-full bottle of Tokay, and the peasant made an offering from her bag of sauerkraut candy. In return, Butterbugs could only offer whispered thanks.

How much could a person take, of tones of antique gold everywhere? Well, all in the audience here tonight discovered their capacity was infinite, for having entered the portals of this august establishment, no appetite was too restrained *not* to be enabled in absorbing all that it contained. It was because Butterbugs himself was here.

The houselights dimmed. The entire theatre crackled with expectant magic. The symphony struck up, led by Ray Heindorf, who had arranged 'A Butterbugs Overture', consisting of themes both major and minor from many of his pictures.

Suddenly flooded with emotion, Butterbugs' easy tears made his cheeks striped with phosphorescent trails. The peasant next door's compassion, ignited by her sighting of his passion, gave her cause to search her tucker-bag with concern, and when she proffered a burlap kerchief to staunch his tears, he was almost as overcome again – with appreciation this time – as he was at hearing the dear and familiar music.

Here, next to him, was a person of devotion, he knew, who had no doubt seen his pictures, if not in subtitled form, then surely dubbed, perhaps on a screen no more grand than a suspended sheet, hung in a familiar courtyard, with a single 16mm projector, powered by a crank generator, which made his visage flicker, nickelodeon-style, for those who crouched on the good earth, looking up in wonder at the player who spoke to them in ways they immediately grasped.

[Butterbugs did all his own dubbing for foreign versions, advised by the best vernacular coaches; that is, if he did not happen to know the language in question.]

As a measure of comfort for her not to worry too much, he placed his grateful hand on her shoulder, and knew she knew that her own tears were in the right place and for the right reasons.

Butterbugs pulled minds together, not apart.

The overture rose to a glorious climax, and then the houselights went out completely. So did every other lamp in the house, even the aisle lights and the exit signs.

Then, in the stunned silence that followed, a faint light, as in a dream barely perceived, began to form on the wall near the Stage Right organ grille. And as its spotted light began to grow, a Gothic pulpit way up there further was gradually revealed. A robed and hooded figure, more Gurnemanz than Mosaic, but with the same gravity, ascended the stairs to the announcement position, and spake:

40

'Lo! Those out there, who come to this place in witness, if only to see for yourselves, in person, that which you have seen elsewhere, in a different form, in a different way, in another time, perhaps in a world apart, have sought the right path. Because tonight, the goal has been reached. We all breathe the same air, and here, in this chamber, is an enrichment of which we formerly could not conceive...'

'Hey,' thought Butterbugs, 'that's Chuck Heston!'

The monk/prophet continued.

'Who among you has not heard of he whom we present tonight? If there be one amongst you who has not, let them come forth so as to tell their tale of deprivation! No one comes? I knew it. I sensed it. If that is the case, then, my task is complete, for I came to this setting on high at this time for one purpose: to proclaim the awareness, and because that imperative has been met, my one remaining action...' He stretched out his palm toward the curtained stage. '...is to now present, with the loftiest of pleasures – BUTTERBUGS!'

The spot was extinguished, the orchestra crashed into a specially composed fanfare and tone poem by Leonard Bernstein, and the curtains slowly parted. There followed a two hour retrospective of Butterbugs clips, both famous and obscure, compiled by Chuck Workman, with original scoring by Elmer Bernstein, and with interview segments directed by Warren Beatty, Michael Moore, Sergio Leone, Alexandra Pelosi, Barbara Walters, Eugene Jarecki, and Ferdooz. No mere documentary, this work was the first genuinely cinematic attempt to delve into how the extraordinariness of Butterbugs actually worked. While it failed in that mission, valuable questions were raised, as monk/prophet Heston intimated, that awareness was the most important thing at this point. Butterbugs, witnessing it from his seat, was non-analytical, though his immediate neighbors had some interesting insights from their obvious vantage points, which they were keen to share. At the very least, it charted the actor's very extraordinariness, his most elusive factor. To be aware, though not necessarily with scientific methodology, but with the magic of drama, not necessarily with fluorescent-lit clinical inspection, of the phenomena of the unifying wonder this particular actor brought to the viewers of the world.

Ending on a major chord, the film had the entire audience on their feet for the longest time. And from the bronze dome far above, a follow-spot's white light selected Butterbugs himself, who had no objection to the singled-out treatment, but he happened to have his hands full at the moment, as Davy the street person (to his left) had unfortunately vomited, and Butterbugs and Liao Shur the peasant woman were in the process of cleaning up the effluvia.

As Butterbugs had been sharing Davy's paper-bagged swill, he could not find any evidence that the Tokay was in any way tainted, until in the spew-up, he discovered undigested bits of chicken beaks and feet, plus obviously rotted pine nuts and vermin-infested asparagus tips that the disenfranchised fellow had been

41

reduced to assemble as a poor-fare meal from the gourmet alley dumpsters of Mid-Town's China Blue Restaurant.

Liao Shur and Mayor Blutz did yeoman duty in scraping the emetic rime that had projected onto the star's person, and just in time for him to stand up, take a bow, then exit into the adjacent aisle.

Then Sonny and TABP came out of nowhere and flanked Butterbugs.

'Ascend now,' Sonny's voice struggled to overcome the huge applause and cheering. 'Your place on stage! Your presence is requested!'

'Look at them!' said TABP. 'Listen! I never heard such cheering!'

'Oh, but yes you have!' smiled Butterbugs. 'Your concert at the Morumbi in São Paulo, remember?'

'Yeah, I guess so,' he agreed. 'But now's your time, baby. Now's your big step. To what we laughingly refer as 'the upper echelon'.'

'I'm glad I can sense quotation marks around that, TABP.'

'Yeah, well, I knew you'd discern what the program really is, and dig it.'

'I dig. It's for us not only to enjoy, but to share.'

'You *do* dig. I have to say, I knew it the first time I beheld your mug, baby. That we'd be here, some day. But shit, I didn't exactly know what that would really mean. What kind of energy would be found, and such.'

'You speak the truth as usual, TABP. The world is full of marvels.'

Sonny went into producer mode.

'Sir Butterbugs, we could easily set up lawn chairs here with appropriate beverages and bask in the clap-glow until the cows come home – They'd do it, you know; such is their devotion. – But you owe it to them to take the stage in short order, as you must now deliver.'

'To give back some of what they have taken. From the screen, I mean,' said Butterbugs.

'I know what you're driving at, pal. Now get your sacred ass the hell up unto glory before I hogtie and haul ye!'

'I *will*, sir!' the star laughed.

Thus escorted by Sonny (known to only so many millions), and then yet further by TABP (known by so many more), to where the proscenium's foundations were rooted and sprang upwards, the audience went even more wild as Butterbugs came fully into view by all.

'It's yours now,' TABP said in epic tones as a sendoff. 'As you step up into the big time, know of your mortality, but also know of the possibilities and the truths way beyond!'

Butterbugs gave him such a look of comprehension, intelligence and joy, that his face, seen by these fortunate masses, and further afield, on the media murals of the world, instantly became an icon of transcendent sureness and magnificence.

In the pit, Ray pulled off a fine musical ad-lib. The music that accompanied Butterbugs' lengthy trek to center stage was Korngold's 'The Sea Hawk' (WB, 1940) Main Title, and its heights competed well with the applause that was wearing out determined palms, and cheers and hoots that were enhoarsening vocal cords. But New York is a spirited city, and where else could Honored Ones be elevated so far?

So Butterbugs proceeded up the heavily carpeted steps to the Roxyian altar. It was true: he had never heard such cheering. His form was highlighted by the spot's pale tincture of 'lux sit', while behind him, the stage was matte-black-dark.

Then, where starring credit names usually appear on screen, nicely centered letters spelling 'BUTTERBUGS' faded in, to a bright handwriting-on-the-wall radiance, clearly delineated in a razor-cut, industrially bold font. (Behind a solid scrim, there was in fact active pyrotechnical activity employed for this effect: miniature but huge-scale-quality fireworks were activated inside contained boxes located in back of each stencil-cut letter composing Butterbugs' name; it was a beautiful effect, later much copied, both on stage and screen.)

As the Korngold masterpiece concluded, Butterbugs reached his position. The crowd quietened in pukka Butterbugsian fashion (e.g. orderly, without ego, desirous of receivership of what they came for, etc.)

No microphone awaited him. As if he needed one. It was not only the Roxy's bell-clear acoustics that enabled him to be heard to the topmost urns, it was his inherent ability to communicate, his projection, with not only refined diaphragmatic technique, but a sort of astral grace, in which the listener was effortlessly engaged without being roped-in or finagled. Naturalness was here in an order, ever so – natural.

And, as befitted any big production, there comes that moment of truth, when the power of the Drama will out, and the task becomes clear. The audience must and shall be galvanized.

Recent movie trends had sought to accomplish this via aggressive plot twists, loud noises, and other SFX surprises. Tonight, there were no such mechanisms in play, nor were any even accessible. Hell, the stage crew (under Old Atrocity) were busy enough with the pyro demands, backstage.

It was all boiled down to Butterbugs himself, the man, the entity, the actor, the star, alone on stage, in front of his audience.

For a time he said nothing. He just stood there, regarding the moment. All those in the SRO hall returned the compliment. The exit signs were back on, but you could hear a soft contact lens drop in the sacred silence.

BUTTERBUGS: *Know*, that, by my coming here, to this place, on this transfigured night, I fulfill a sort of quest. And a desire, as well. To see a house like this, in full spate, at high tide. Or perhaps I just mean maximum capacity. Except that, in a world where 'normal' is only to be found on a washing machine's dial, here, in this environment, 'normal' is always high tide, full spate, maximum capacity.

If I, and I speak in the singular – yet in the plural of all who practice what I pretend to practice – have been contributory to the condition of which I speak, then truly, my heart is full. If my name be on this stage and also the marquee without, it is not solely my own. Countless others are contained therein. It is as if, when a nation's single name is considered, the understanding that that lone word brings with it the names, lives, and significances of each and every citizen and their guests who embody its very substance. So, the aspects of community are as a given. If my name be used, it can only be under that canopy.

I gaze out into your faces, and so many are familiar. Those that I know well and have worked with, and also, those I have never beheld before. They are all known to me. How can this be? How can one, as a cinema player, feel one's audience within so detached an apparatus? I have to tell you that, as I act in front of the cameras, I can feel your presence. You, out there in the audience. Yes, this is true, because it is possible. I knew it the first time I saw you. You knew it, too.

My person was meant to dwell in mystery. It is not for me to discern why I feel what I do. Those of you who choose to form a construct or a method in ascertaining this system are welcome to do so, but I shall not join you in the process. I am not superstitious, and I am completely and utterly open to all realms of thought, but I am bound to my task: to enact and communicate the assigned role I have undertaken at any given moment, for the ultimate purpose of your – the audience's – requirements. I can only serve that goal.

Thus, mine is not to reason why.

Off the hook I am. Is this, then, a moment to give thanks? Is this the requisite expectation of all you who now behold my solo existence at this juncture in time? I could say, 'Hell, no! I climbed to this level of my own free will and by mine own gumption and cussedness!' If I did say this, would you forgive me? Would you then turn away from my pictures and abandon them (in the name of my haughtiness) to obscurity and neglect? Or, if this great dome, which hovers above us right now, suddenly was rent asunder and a shaft of heaven-sent light descended unto me and caused me to fall to my knees, so as to invoke the godhead, possibly truantly, in an act of desperate appeasement due to all the sinful acts I have committed... would that impress you? Would that make me whole again in your eyes?

Alas and alack, I have no such luxuries, no such gimmicks. If gratefulness be a tool for self worth or aggrandizement, I have none to offer. But if it be a built-in component of living and breathing, then I offer up not only my body to you in thanks, but my soul as well.

The thing is this: I don't know who all to thank. There are the clearly obvious ones, to be sure, and I do, and I have all along, thanked them. Most of your names are writ large on motion picture screens or cheques of considerable sums. But there are so many, so many more whom I am at a tragic loss to recount. Ever since I came out of the wastes to the east of the Hollywood mass, there have been beings of aid to my cause. I have not always known that fact, but I know it now, and treasure it always. However, it is my everlasting failure that I have no record or recall of so many who mattered, and matter still.

Up in the mezzanine sat Shawna Lee, the former stripper who had taken off to Vegas after some days of absorbing (the ante-Hollywood) Butterbugs' sincere but ultimately unpromising puppy love. Her honey-blonde hair, still fabulous, hung in an aggressive peek-a-boo bang, which concealed a savage scar on her forehead, installed there by a drunken strip-lurker who had stabbed her in a DT fever, thinking that she was a grizzly bear cub. She had returned to her Jersey hometown, and now worked in a second-string bead shop. Her eyes overflowed. She would not trouble him this night – or ever. It was sufficient to see him way down there on the huge stage, speaking from his heart, which was full, directly to *her* heart, which had been empty for so long. But now, at this instant, expanded so swiftly, with love. It was her 'Stella Dallas' (Goldwyn, 1937) moment, and she'd waited a lifetime for it. Yes, she'd left him that day, but if she hadn't, he would have tagged along to Vegas, and surely, no stardom would have resulted. In fact, it probably would have been he who received the knife blow, and not her. Yet, from this time onward, she was at peace, and simply happy to be here.

'I love you,' she whispered. 'I *love* you...'

And way up the balcony, off to the left side, sat none other than Sanchez the scaffold worker, fresh in from his co-workers' clubbed-together airfare flight, that had propelled him into this *darshan* occasion. Though the frame gang had worked with Butterbugs in that dusty lot on Pico, it was a distant recollection to most, but for Sanchez, Butterbugs had made a remarkable impression. Never had he seen an outsider who was so willing to drop pretensions and just be himself. He was hurt when Butterbugs, who had committed to coming to his fiesta, never showed. His high hopes were shattered, as were his attitudes concerning El Gringo. In fact, part of the reason for his trek to this affair was to try and confront the actor in person, in search of an explanation for being stood up. But after he heard and saw tonight's presentation, pride pushed away resentment, into a corner. He thought, 'I am one of those whom Butterbugs thanks personally tonight!' After all, if he *had* shown up for the Sanchez fiesta, there is no doubt that Butterbugs would have bonded with his family, their hospitality, and their food, which would have helped settle him into the scaffolders' world, thus removing his incentive to struggle onward as a strolling player. Like a proud papa, he gazed at his protégé, way down there on the stage, and whispered 'Bravo! Viva El Butterbugs!' before blowing his nose and wiping his eyes.

There were others in the audience who had similar heritage contacts with Butterbugs in their various forms from the past. So many, from so many associations, many non-professional, and most by chance. But the star's humility became theirs as well. Each had his or her reasoning behind their presence in the great Roxy, but each one, as they came to truly understand Butterbugs, was in agreement as to the significance of tonight's event. It was a time to simply *be*, to pause and recognize unique greatness, and to let it live, and let it grow, and let it be.

The star's words continued for another 110 minutes or so. And in that time, his character was solidified yet more. Concreted, in fact. His soliloquy was not so much a manifesto as it was a commitment to flexibility. Expansion, he noted, was what the actor's prime directive should be. Truth was contained within it, as were all the other imperatives for leading a progressive and consistently rewarding life – not just for an actor, but for all audiences.

Just in case this testimony might be considered pretentious in its gravitas, Butterbugs chose to wrap up his perf with a couple of vaudeville touches. First off, he attempted to juggle several bubble-wrapped china vases, with Maestro Heindorf supplying the appropriate showbizzy accompaniment. He ended up busting one vase outright, dropping another (its bubbles failed), but succeeded in keeping three of them in the air all the way to the end of one of Stephen Foster's tunes.

Then, to ring down the curtain, and out of respect for all the now-forgotten hoofers who had come before him – many on this very stage, he delivered a pretty decent tap-cum-soft shoe patter of the Red Roberts variety, which somehow percolated to his consciousness by way of vicarious knowledge of the Goth Theatre's past acts, way back in Carstairs.

There. Tributes delivered.

Applause now, applause for the dance, for the whole memorable evening, and for a monumental career thus far.

By the time he sank into Justy's and Saskia's arms back in the limo, after a full regime of re-greeting known faces and old faces not recently seen, hanging out with Sanchez at the crush bar and burying the hatchet ('Can you forgive me, Sanchez?' 'Nothing to forgive, Señor.' 'Am I still welcome in your home?' 'Any time, Butterbugs.' 'We'll get together soon.' And they did.), finally finding Liao Shur in the Grand Centralness of the Grand Foyer and insisting she be his escort for the duration of the eve, doing a quick radio show and interview in the Roxy's Hello Everybody Studio upstairs, posing with the lovely Roxyettes on the

Great Stage, goofing off with the crew behind the scenes, sharing Old Atrocity anecdotes in front of OA himself, getting a ride up the 'counterweight elevator', taking a tour of the entire premises, which culminated in inspecting Gloria Swanson's love letter to Roxy, inscribed in the plaster way up in the Great Dome, some late partying with all types back in the Grand Foyer, and then, with the house cleared out, a solo stroll once more across the great stage, the best place to watch the lights go out, group by group – all except the exit signs, so that after all this, well, he was pretty conked.

As he snuggled into Justy's bosom, she asked softly:

'Was it all that you thought it would be?'

He smooched her bared breast.

'What I thought it would be? It's funny... I didn't think about it at all...'

'You didn't have to, baby...' Saskia moved in to negotiate his fly's zipper. 'It's not a question of thinking. It's all about acting.'

Butterbugs smiled.

'I'm glad I don't have to think. I only have to act...'

Postscript

Headline in 'The Hackensack Daily Grinder' (a P. Parwell Mindy Conservative Society publication):

THIS IS WHAT HAPPENS WHEN A VERY VERY IMPORTANT PERSON SITS AMONGST "THE PEOPLE"

(with a wire photo and caption:)

'New York's mayor daubs a guttersnite's [sic] bilious wine gravy from Butterbugs' velveteen tux, as a frowning old Chinawoman bosses our Blutz around, making for a tawdry scene at humungous Roxy faun-gala last night'.

The flash bulb caught Liao Shur at a moment when she actually prevented some of the scrubbed vomit rubbish from unceremoniously hitting the Mayor, whom she was warning, in fine Hakka diction. Her facial expression was as intense and purposeful as one of Longmen Cave's finest stone warrior's.

Long story short: at this point, any anti-Butterbugsian sentiment in the media could be written off – and generally *was* by the public – as the purest of sour grapes. And because of this particularly offensive reference to his newfound friends, Butterbugs successfully sued for a retraction.

In after days, through the star's efforts, Liao Shur attained a Lecturer on Peasant Culture position at Shijiazhuang University, and he quickly got Davy into rehab, eventually setting him up in a job at Mega|Goth Studios after discovering that he had an as yet unrealized penchant for historical interpretation and scholarship. Any appearance of Davy Drummond's name in the credits of a period picture ensured enhanced box office receipts.

Butterbugs was fast learning all about the divers fringe benefits of the Big Time that now framed him so favorably.

3.

A Questionnaire Recalled

After the Roxological exam of Butterbugs' career to date, a fair number of attendant 'fame devices' were trolleyed to and fro along the avenues of easygoing entertainment, mostly for fun's sake. Oh, how the public loved 'em. They loved 'em all. The lighter side of high-octane stardom brought with it a whole further world of magic, cheeriness, and good, old-fashioned hilarity.

Butterbugsian goof-arounds were all over the media, TV and vaudeville.

Once, while perambulating through the Musée Carnavalet in Paris on holiday, the star became somewhat tuckered, as a result of relentless tourist-taking of the city's lightness and brightness. Faun, his lovely resident escort, was absent on this go-round, so he had to content himself with a cheap incognito-causing beret and peasant smock to sustain his anonymity.

Alone he came, and alone he succumbed to worn-downness and dehydration. Nothing serious, but for a star on his own in the midst of many Parisian prowls, it was something of a return to obscure behaviors of the past.

Way out in the far reaches of the museum's probings into Parisienne sweet nothings, he found himself needful of a prone plane upon which to rest his weary frame, if only for a few minutes of recharge time. After all, he'd been going, going, going-gone for more than a fortnight now, what with filming and Fauning and holiday-making and partying and dining throughout most of the capital's best crème-pourings.

Settees there were none. Creaky parquet floors, imported from all sorts of chateaux, were well polished and historic, but hard and unyielding as Genet's disquieting bunk in Fontevrault prison. A ledge outside the Louvre in chill wee hours would be more hospitable!

He dared not ask for succor, lest a tsunami of ill-timed attention engulf his enfeebled bod. The capital, along with the nation in general, was pretty Butterbugs-oriented right now, mainly because his classic 'Toilers of the Sea' (20th-Fox) was being re-released, with a French Liner full of extras, interviews, seminars and documentaries, running at different cinema houses throughout the city. His favorite cinematic bolt-hole, the Studio Galande, was running all this stuff 24/7, booked for two months, to sold-out houses!

So no, let beret & blouse shield him from intensity. He even managed to sketch curling mustachios on his upper lip, with a Gauloises butt he found in an ash receiver next the loo.

Plus, the 'Toilers' trip was even more boosted, by a hit parody, 'Boilers of the

Planet C', exhibited locally as 'Chaudières de la planète « C »' (ImagesLumenoniY-eux), a wacky jape about a space bubble that gets caught in a wormhole. Starring Le Gang Fou as 'Mutterbugs', 'Shutterbugs', 'Cutterbugs', 'Putterbugs', 'Utterbugs', and 'Blubberbugs', with Yvette Mimieux as 'La Belle Clutterbugs', and special guest star, Jerry Lewis, as 'Stutterbugs'. Les Hees Hee!

Meanwhile, back in the Musée, the unidentified star now entered a narrow conduit leading from the Hunchbackian findings of pre-Haussmann Paris to more nouveau trails of discovery. Just before the threat of fainting away brought him down, he spied an actual metal-framed bed, scarcely meritorious of museum quality, but spread with a silken duvet of royal blue. A cozy companion's chair was hard by, with comfy bedside table and lamp in between. Watching over the group was a folding chinoiserie screen.

'Plainly a rest stop for the enwearied', as his uncharacteristically-wobbled logic encouraged him. 'A safe harbor, ponderously located in this maison's attic of a collection, but a most Gallic of homey courtesies!'

It seemed to have his weary hulk's name written all over it. So he flopped down on its feathery sinkhole, and awaited the assured recharge. Slumbering now, dreams instantly accessed, suspended in bliss, and infinitely enjoyable.

Out of nowhere, an agreeable voice asked him some questions in the local tongue. Easy to understand, and easier to answer. And answer he did, in his best reciprocal French (here translated):

What is your idea of perfect happiness?

Slurping a barrel of gumball stew, ladled out by an old hag I could call my own. Or maybe, now that I think of it, reposing here, on this spot, at this time.

What is your greatest fear?

Not remembering the greasiest line of dialogue that Prassy Jeighms has just carefully written out for me.

Which historical figure do you most identify with?

DogBoy of the Upper Lakotan tribes. Sai Baba's coolie. The head of the Camera Dept. at 20th Century-Fox Studios.

Which living person do you most admire?

I cannot honestly say that it is Butterbugs, who I believe actually exists, but failing such speculation, Wungus Phrérule, my part-time plant waterer, wins hands down.

What is the trait you most deplore in yourself?

The tendency to be distracted by the availability of potted bloater paste, and also by the shrieking call of online sex, which in actuality is at least enjoyable as a brief diversion.

What is the trait you most deplore in others?

Narcissistic preoccupations, now institutionalized as legitimate.

What is your greatest extravagance?

The sincere admiration of Raquel Welch's torso.

What is your favorite journey?

Across the Hooghly River from Howrah (and back), in order to get a kati-roll from Chikkervurity's Super-Best Roll Palace in Jupper Lane, Calcutta.

What do you consider the most overrated virtue?

Feigned interest when curiosity and genuineness would be far more effective.

On what occasion do you lie?

When I detect feigned interest and narcissism as the standard bearers for normal human interaction.

What do you dislike most about your appearance?

That my private parts cannot be publicly displayed for the public's enjoyment.

Which living person do you most despise?

The cretin who runs a little bubble gum shoppe in Grubbidgetown, Kentucky, and won't let little kids leaf through his collection of 'Humpty Dumpty' magazines that he has tantalizingly displayed well within their reach. Bastard-fuck!

Which words or phrases do you most overuse?

'I want some cooperation here!', 'I *FEEL!*', 'I swear, the tide is rising!'

What is your greatest regret?

To not have been believably bold when people needed me.

What or who is the greatest love of your life?

That's an easy one. I don't rightly know, yet.

When and where were you happiest?

Couple of months ago, at Dr. Kamales Kapat's Sweet Shop, Nellie Sengupta Sarani, Lindsay Street, Calcutta. *That I know*, for sure!

Which talent would you most like to have?

Symphonic composer, with advantageous contractual options for playing my works in the orchestra pit of a small vaudeville thiertre in the provinces. Oh, yeah!

What is your current state of mind?

Asleep in the fields of St. Geneviève, patron saint of Paris, while she is watching over the city, as depicted by Pierre Puvis de Chavannes. That *is* Paris down there, isn't it?

If you could change one thing about yourself, what would it be?

That I would actually have an *identity* of note.

If you could change one thing about your family, what would it be?

Why, whatever are you talking about? *What* family?

What do you consider your greatest achievement?

To have honored a person I mistakenly led into perdition.

If you were to die and could choose a person or thing to come back as, what would it be?

Grauman's Metropolitan Thiertre. Sid would really like that.

What is your most treasured possession?

The key to Grauman's Metropolitan Thiertre. Sid himself entrusted me with it.

What do you regard as the lowest depth of misery?

Losing the key to Grauman's Metropolitan Thiertre. Sid told me never to let that happen.

Where would you like to live?

On Mars!

What is your favorite occupation?

Probably running a little newsstand and candy counter in the lobby of a seedy, threadbare hotel in a faded, anonymous city.

What is your most marked characteristic?

A passionate, compassionate drift.

What is the quality you most like in a man?

To wage peace instead of war all the time.

What is the quality you most like in a woman?

To be confident in her wonderfulness.

What do you most value in your friends?

A little bit o' lovin'.

Who are your favorite writers?

Saskia Pingles, Sawl Cane, Norton Juster, Rowland Emett, Shawn Levy, Tennyson, Robt. Hughes, John Murray, Karl Baedeker, Byron, Scott, Scott Eyman, Mundella Sicoarg, Anne Terry White, Bango Yywutite, Chig Fang, a whole bunch of others, too.

Who is your most favorite hero of fiction?

Harry The Goth in D. Keith Mano's 'The Death and Life of Harry Goth', Blixie Bimber in Carl Sandburg's 'Rootabaga Stories', Odysseus, the three Mulla Mulgars, Romola in Mary Ann Evans' eponymous novel, the dog in Kipling's 'Bubbling Well Road', Saladin in Sir Walter Scott's 'The Betrothed' – or was it 'The Talisman'? Pearl Chavez. Others...

Who are your heroes in real life?

Let's see, TABP, Saskia Pingles, Justina Mwam-Projector, Sonny – of course. Uh, Yevo Yevtushenko. Oh, there's Shonnie and Cody, Alfred and Leon. Dear Mitya – Shostakov… you know the rest… Uzaka Goro, Amava Bhattacharyah – who always has such nice sarees. Dr. Ambedkar, of course. Bunch of others. And the dreamlike girl who lives in a big mansion on Yniguez Terrace – can't remember her name right now…

What are your favorite names?

Tucker Tidswhildth, Churchy, Mendel, Teezy, Minda, Lockhorrenhoft, Dizzy, Preeti, Mbabane. Oh, and Larry.

What is it that you most dislike?

Everything! Everybody! And all things in between! Heh!

How would you like to die?

With an expiration date that finds me full of gravy, full of cheer, and full as an egg.

What is your motto?

'People who think deeply and constructively don't rattle'. Frances Partridge told me that, during a card game. Really, she did.

Then, a rudeness occurred.

'Monsieur, s'il vous plaît désabonnez-vous de cette relique sacrée immédiatement! La Société Proust vous poursuivre pour des dommages si ils trouvent que je l'ai pas dans ma tutelle! Maintenant, RETIREZ-VOUS, citoyen!'

['Monsieur, please remove yourself from this sacred relic immediately! The Proust Society will sue you for damages if they find I have failed in my guardianship! Now REMOVE YOURSELF, citizen!' (translation courtesy of 'The Everything That Ever Happened To Butterbugs Compendium & One-Stop Shopping Centre For All Things Butterbugsian', Kansas Otulu & Jim Dim, eds. (Middlesbrough: Keeperfry & Elmoth)]

About six minutes after he'd drifted off, he awoke as a result of being roused by a museum guard for violating one of the exhibits. There wasn't one thing that Butterbugs could remember from the things just past. Or dreamt.

The voices that came screaming over the phone to Sonny, from the 3rd Arrondissement's Mairie, were hopping mad. The only thing the groggy derelict-peasant had uttered to the arresting gendarmes was Sonny's phone number, as if recited from a dog tag. In his hyper-fluent French, Sonny ironed out the controversy in about two seconds.

The very next day, Mayor Sanscoulotte declared 'Le jour Butterbugs d'appréciation'. The star was appreciated, all right. And fêted as a cause célèbre all over again.

At a huge banquet at the Hôtel de Ville, Fernandel toasted the star with a fitting capstone:

'Je suis ravi que Butterbugs a quelque peu indirectement nous a rappelé à rattraper notre Proust... Rappelez-vous que!' ['I'm delighted that Butterbugs has somewhat indirectly reminded us to catch up on our Proust...Remember that!]

Snagging him via transcontinental long-distance, Sonny glanced at the wirephoto of the disguised star before his arrest for trespassing, plastered all over 'Le Cyber-Journal-Revue de Rue Perrée Soir-Telegraph', and commented tamely, 'Nice costume, Butterbugs. A little hokey...'

'I'm so sorry I shamed Paris and the Parisians through my petty exhaustion...'

'And you don't remember anything about your time there? You know, lying on that bed?'

'Not a thing!'

Ever after, the Carnavalet Commune, in creative association with the Proust Society, installed a sign, penned by Simone de Beauvoir, and specially executed by Banksy, who was guest-graffitiing in the city, that read: 'BUTTERBUGS FOIS DORMI ICI, RÊVER PEUT-ÊTRE', ['Butterbugs once slept here, perchance to dream'], placed on the wall above the bed. Never had the Musée seen such enthusiastic crowds, or the Society such a resurgence of remembrance.

A remarkable bit of lovable, loving mockery was particularly beloved by the star. It occupied a special hall at Dismaland (the cherished bemusement park, featuring 'art, amusements, and entry-level anarchism') at Weston-Ultra-Mare, in old Somerset, UK. Simply titled 'Bitterbugs', the interactive exhibits took on 'everything withered, wonky, and wanky' about the actor-star. All throughout his vomiting during that happy horrorshow, Butterbugs couldn't stop laughing.

There were plenty of Butterbugsian celebratory notions stateside, too. Some were pretty elaborate and involved motion picture production. Thus, a decent cargo of Butterbugsian parodies appeared.

Aside from 'Boilers', a dumpster full of fun awaited tipping over. 'A Dirty Bubble' (Oddball), 'The Kid From The Wastes' (Columbia), 'He Thought He Was Going To Be A Star' (RKO), 'Kid Impossible? I'm Gonna GIT You!' (Chunkwood/Dr. Zempf Pictureshows), and other treacly trifles rattled off the waggish assembly line.

Once such, 'Extreme Desire: The Budderbuggs Story' (Strapidzneah), easily the best of the bunch, had Butterbugs rolling on the floor in jollity. On a lark, he even appeared in a cameo. He was also amazed by its attention to detail, and the unexpected mix (daring litigation) of real and invented characters. The press kit told all in proper Industry form:

STRAPIDZNEAH INTERNATIONAL

in association with Logan Gold, John Smith,

Meena Merry, Harry Silverfisch, Milt Delp,

Sawlohmunn Rabinowicz Cane,

Larry Schimmelklutcher, John Steves, Steav Tiggs,

Irving Fendleman, Irving Chiggs,

Irv 'Czech' Jones, Cartright Jones, CobyJones,

and especially WARREN SARJENT

Present

A Sidney Steveston Schmutz Film

From **THE STRAPIDZNEAH STvDIO**

Hollywood's Most Important Picture To Date!

In WarnerSuperScope 70mm / In WarnerColor! /In UltraSound!

THE STORY THAT *DEEPLY SHOCKED*

THE NATION!!!!!!!!!!!!!!!!!!

EXTREME DESIRE

THE BUDDERBUGGS STORY

HOW ONE TOUGH KID FOUGHT TOOTH 'N' NAIL
TO HAVE HIS DREAMS PROSECUTED WITH EXTREME PREJUDICE,
AND HOW HE TROD THE RUGGED PATH ALONG THE WAY!

YES, HE WAS A FIGHTER,
BORN INTO A HELL'S KITCHEN OF ROLLICKING, ROMPING,
JUST-PLAIN-SUPER ACTIVITIES!

THRILL to Action-Pack'd scenes of how he clumb [sic] his way up to the pinnacle of LIFE and how his name was graven into the Publicly-Recognized Temple of FAME!

Soon All Peoples in All Lands were saying:
'Budderbuggs, Butterbuggs, Butterbuggs, BUDDERbuggs!!'
And Budderbuggs replied:
'YEAH!!!!'

Laughter! Tears! Equivocation! Goofball Stuff! Fun!
Incredibly Detailed Interactions With Post-Marxian Dialectics!
Business School Tips!
Danish Cuisine Experiences!
The Cell Phone Dialogues!
How It All Began!

*YOU JUST CAN'T LOSE BY CHECKING OUT THIS INCREDIBLE PICTURE!
IT SETS A NEW BENCHMARK IN MOTION PICTURE HIGH FIDELITY –
THE BEST SINCE '59!*

*Hop into the family transport wagon and head on down to the picture show to see this pretty darn special production!
Something for the whole darn tribe!!*

Hey Wait Just A Minute

THE REVIEWS ARE COMING IN!!!:

'A mammoth, utterly Gothic piece of cinema, which tells a story so big, so crushingly wonderful, that I am still wailing, "Oh, OH! What a beautiful show!" to every ruffian I encountered within six minutes of being privileged to witness this landmark of motion picture fashionable art!'
– *Mike Douglas, on 'The Mike Douglas Show' reruns*

'I laughed to the bottom of my soul at the funny bits, then was transported beyond the Milky Way during the lengthy inspirational sequences! O Butterbugs, why do you *do* these things to us? Do them some more, will ya?' – *Kywooza Bo-Mo-Ko, 'Comedy Sub-Basement & Profound Penthouse'*

'I can't wait to see the ten hour Director's Cut version in a DVD Tri-Pak kit! I find myself panting with existential excitement whenever I steer my Attention Deficit Disorder-oriented mind towards 'EXTREME DESIRE: The Budderbuggs Story'. Why can't I have such an experience every day, every minute?!' – *Ursula Harmonikah, 'ADD Today!'*

'Thank you, thank you, THANK YOU, The Strapidzneah International team, for bringing this joltingly fabulous story to the screen!' – *Relishman Goth on 'The Relishman Goth Show'*

The Picture Features:

Wrich Little, Schecky Green, Wrip Taylor, Dohn Rickle, Whit Bis'l, Frank Gorschen,
Patt Boone, Gharry Crosby, Mimsy Pharmer, Dickie Smuthers, Jill SinJohn, Anji Dickinson, Baub Ivers, Willy Keth, Butterbugs, Jœy Heathertone
with Barbie Bentohn as 'The Girl' and Gaston LeBru
as 'The Old Man'

and DANA ANDREWS

Special Guest Stars: Monty Hall, Bob Barker, Al Nitz, Dohn Martin *(in his first picture show)* MICHAEL DEAVER
and

JERRY SPRINGER

Scripted by James Lee Fink and Hukkah Washington Spizzitsky
based on the Ultra-Best Selling Novel
by President Richard M. Nixon and Harold Crud
Music presented by Wishram Hogjowl; score by Blue Oyster Cult and the East Cincinnati Philharmonic Orchestra, featuring the
St. Louis Aquarium Choir, entirely
Conducted and Controlled by Yogi Brinkley,

showcasing the Voice of

AL JOLSON

Consultant: Wawrd (representing Wawrd Pictures)
Produced by Waddington Ching

Running time: 292 minutes, not counting two Intermissions

Photoplayed in
THE STRAPIDZNEAH STvDIO
thru
STRAPIDZNEAH INTERNATIONAL PICTURES

EMERGENCY NOTE:
BOOK NOW
OR
FOREVER HOLD YOUR PIECE!

Fans glommed onto these pictures like you wouldn't believe. Popcorn Tours were organized, rolling with much merriment through the midnight LA streets, from theatre to thiertre where the pictures that fit into this terrific new sub-genre played and played and played. Butterbugs himself tagged along, and had big fun with the rollicking gang, quoting lines, oddballing around, and engaging in bozo antics on the open-topped bus which shuttled them around under the buttery streetlights, forming sweet times and comfortable ties.

When the distinguished producer Edwin Knopf rang up Butterbugs and complained about the childish fonts used in the posters for these parodies, the star replied, 'Oh Edwin, the children enjoy them so!'

Serious and dedicated picture show player that he was, Butterbugs never shirked from humor, be it highbrow or browless. That's what both vaudeville and Shakespeare can do for an actor.

4.

On Up Yellowjacket Creek A Ways

Idyll.

Mark Twain could have written it without disguise! Neil Young could have balladized it! Vonnegut could have wrung it through a wringer! The trees, the breeze, the altitude, the silence, the afternoon meadows, the winged vermin, the safety, the retreat, the sanity…

It was time for escape, for its own sake, to pause and refresh, to reconnoiter, to take leave of Big Time life, here amongst the purple dusk of the American outback, without seeking its portfolio or its exploitive characteristics.

There would be no searching for evanescent lodges or their appealing inhabitants this time. Besides, wrong region. Anyway, Butterbugs was past all that now. What he wanted was a little down-time up there in the Oregon Territory.

It was a back-ended bit of obscure genuineness that was found, via a rutted lane of pillowy dust, stirred up by a borrowed VW Westphalia, all beat-up cosmetically, but with air purring coolly over the cylinder heads, like normal. A lazy harmonica day, in deep salubrity, with Butterbugs at the wheel, encountering no human in the region surrounding, but accompanied by a happy band within. Saskia and Justy, of course, but with Ave Imperatrix, the rising Broadway director, riding shotgun. Vet lenser Joe MacDonald was also in the party, but he'd elected to stay back at Ronaldshay Hut, free to lounge with his watery starfruit drinks, and gawp at the passing broads through his CinemaScope viewfinder.

As the day was exceedingly fair, and certain clouds of hame-flies had taken off for parts unknown, the four easily elected to become nudists on an attractive mead next to the burbulating Yellowjacket, the creek o' this gentle canyon, where they might gambol, recline, eat figs, and toast the sun with mildly-chilled white zinfandel and mellow weed products.

The mone-bark, the pines, and the cacklewood that overarched them became as a seraglio dome, where pleasure might be dispensed without hesitance. Simple pleasures, those of escape and natural appreciation easily transpired, tumbling effortlessly, one after another. It seemed as if the local 'Life Is Good Department' was managing these people with tremendous success.

Nude each one was born, and nude they now lay, in sculpture-park poses, enhancing the landscape with beauty, truth, and no Hollywood enhancements. Breasts were real, genitalia were respectably organized, and flesh was flesh, but of extraordinarily high quality.

No orgy, this. Nor was one attempted

Before she stripped, Justy set up a shamiana so as to house her Saskia in quarters that would keep her Olympia (by Manet) complexion intact, while she herself preferred the Renoiresque dappling nearby, but adopted her treasured odalisque-watcher position, as immortalized by Benouville.

Ave, rugged as Victor Mature, as urbane as Jeremy Irons, as wise as Woody Harrelson, nevertheless did not gaze on the loveliness of the women with dick-thought and other lusts, nor could he deny the Louvre-like standards of womankind before him. However, he was surprisingly neutral and restrained for being in such sensual circles. The fact was, he was profoundly in love, with MarLane Sugerterry, his leading lady in the political hit 'After Downing Street'. She was all he could think of, all he saw, and relieved he was that no one here would lay a seduction trip either for or against him.

The others knew of his distraction, but weren't the types to heckle or even humor for its own sake. They were all way beyond either stuffy protocol or superficial funning. This was a group in harmony with itself, where philosophical tenets of open liberality and mutual respect were a given, and successful careers did not impinge on any achievement of true leisure and true carefree moments.

There was mutual approval amongst them all, but that did not run the show of the moment. Those were the precepts of this occasion, and no one was going to muck it up with ding-dong needs or offerings.

As the wine bar opened and stayed open, warmed by both sun and the fun above and around it, the gang moved into golden time. Simple being in this world at this time brought ecstasy. Wonders were everywhere. The guys looked on, in genuine awe at the systematic love of Justy and Saskia, and how the two worked out the minor logistics of their relaxation headquarters. Saskia obviously enjoyed being treasured and Justy would be nothing but the treasurer. They were mild and sensible with each other, and it was obvious that everything fit together between them in all the right ways.

'You love your assets so, Justy,' Ave observed.

'Does it show, babe?' she replied.

'I'll bet you two have fantastic sex!'

The other three all laughed, especially Butterbugs.

'I can vouch for that,' the actor said, with some authority.

Amidst her plumped pillows, Saskia appeared as a pale Pre-Raphaelite damsel, but with enough Erda earthiness in her to instill a measured power and respect, as well as self-evident admiration.

And just at hand, Justy stood in all her sculptural curves and strengths, Modernist, but linked to her lover's era, a carbon fiber erection of womanliness, arms with akimbo'd strength, set against the eastern blue atmosphere, unaffected by stage lighting or its cheap attempts at mood.

'You stand there, Justy, like a colossus of consequence!' Ave announced.

Butterbugs liked that statement. He was in bliss.

Justy herself noticed the contrast.

'We are beyond yin and yang,' she said with a broad smile on her face. 'We are simply beauty itself!'

'We are?' asked Saskia joyfully. 'Oh, Justy!'

'Oh yes, you are!' said Ave.

'Indeed, you are,' added Butterbugs, stating a simple fact.

'Saskia is my daystar. And me? I am the universe itself – the background, black! – (you notice yet, babe?) – or so it appears, which everyone sees but does not perceive. I am content in my role, and to let the daystar shine, but I remind you, without the background, the stars would be as nothing.'

'You are the cyclorama!' marveled Ave.

'The glamé!' Saskia enthused.

'That is both glitter and ground,' replied Ave, legitimate stage man.

'Now you're catching on!' cooed Saskia.

'You see?' added Justy, 'The stars would *be*... as nothing...'

'Are you, uh, making an indirect comment about me?' laughed Butterbugs. 'I already thanked all the peoples, big and small, at the Roxy, last!'

Justy was genuinely nonplused.

'Oh, baby! I didn't mean you or your kind! I was talking about race, lover. I thought you'd get it.'

'Race? What's that?' asked the actor who'd played every race imaginable at least thrice by now, and with minimal makeup, too.

'Your cue, actor,' Justy gestured toward him.

'Is it not a sub-division, a Linnæan classification? Or further, a non-scientific name, for difference, gauged by type?' Butterbugs spoke in the lyrical light. 'The great races! The color dial... One of the fundamentals of our existence, particularly in the crock-pot aspect ratio, which is our heritage and our duty to examine. Why does it bring out so much surliness, or crankiness, or coterie gripes? The anxiety to identify, to contain, to rest assured that judgment has been passed so that nightly sleep might be intact. For is that not the spirit of peace? That is, to have all conflict and the threat of conflict nicely placed under powerlessness' confines?

'What then, is so established a threat as those carrying *difference* with their appearance and their guise? Documented through the ages, I cannot possibly add to the mix. But I cast my gaze across the rustic yard of this here encampment, and see nothing but love. In the color sense, variation detected. Opposites, in fact. The basic starting point. But there it is. I love, despite opposite dynamics. I take no science as my guide; only feeling, which transcends classification. Here, at this emotional stoop, I disappoint both tractist and reactionary. Race dissolves. Personage becomes emboldened. I am in the luxurious position to call the populace before me in *real* rather than packaged terms. I luxuriate in that elitism. Would that it spread!'

Butterbugs indeed cut a stunning profile, like a statue on a Finnish bridge. He confronted what he deemed the truth, with all honesty and steadfastness. If others did not entirely buy his spiel, he at least came across with sincerity.

'Your thoughts, sir,' Justy conceded, though without approbation.

'You have identified your vantage point,' said Ave. 'And you have spoken it. I applaud.'

Justy, hardly in a willing position to debunk her co-lover's naïve but whole-some tenet at this point, gazed at his pose, and her eyes moistened, so she gave a golf-tournament-type of applause for his performance: polite clapping, made trite by outdoor video sound-capture. Still, if a ball was headed in the right direction, hope shall be noted. The world might well be capable of a New Good, even yet.

Saskia was careful in her referencing a thinker who was germane to the subject of the individual's projected consciousness.

'Fasco Tarpé, whom I have been reading of late, says we must be as demanding on ourselves as we possibly can, but without giving anything away.'

'"The Classification of the Awarenesses', right?' Ave swiftly responded.

'As a matter of fact, yes. DeLuxe edition.'

'That's a coincidence. I've been reading it as well. For different reasons.'

'What do you mean, different?'

'Personal reasons. To assuage something inner –'

Justy wanted to say something.

'But Tarpé talks about race as the hidden imperative in each person's ruling consciousness. It is the definer, rooted in surface dimensions, yet most noticeable and, thus, most commanding. I don't necessarily live that truth, but I can acknowl-edge it. Without contempt, actually. You have to *live* the layers to know them. Majorities tend not to venture there so much.'

'No doubt, black woman. 'Tis lovely that you are.' Ave smiled.

Justy approached him and kissed him on the right knee.

'Grape beverage?' she addressed all.

'Mmmm!' murmured Saskia.

She genuflected to all.

'I will!' said Butterbugs.

'Aye, aye, and I!' Ave followed through.

'You know,' Justy waxed reflective on filling the boys' vessels, 'I think that it all blends together once it gets flowing. Problem is, it has *trouble* getting going. Flowing.'

'The 'it' of which you speak –,' Saskia started to say.

'Silence, Writer!'

Justy held out her hand with understanding. She wanted to hear it from some-one else.

Butterbugs duly took it up.

'The 'it'. (We use 'it' rather a lot, don't we?) This, this 'it'… It flows. It – goes. It… knows. What it is, is… Well, I find it hard to say, because I live 'it'. At least I think I do.'

'I know you do, Butterbugs,' said Saskia.

'You're talking about a melding, right?' Butterbugs was thinking well out of the script-box now. 'A melding, where you don't have to differentiate.'

'Starting to take form,' mused Justy.

'But I know,' said Butterbugs.

'Of course you do,' agreed Saskia. 'You're with us. But what about –'

'Others?' Ave filled in. 'As in, race as role determiner.'

'I see why you're a director,' said Justy. 'Intuition.'

'Yeah, well, I'd be cooked if I couldn't recognize motivation as a definer of character, or a factor in plot development.'

'Well, of course. Certainly. And you have some great shows already, Ave.'

Justy was sincere in every way. She and Sonny had seen several of Ave's stagings of everyone from O'Neill to Tiggs.

'Thanks, Justy.'

'So, is it us, all four of us, who understand what the surface forces are?' continued Justy. 'And so can we move up, a further step, in a progression forward, without prejudice, but with the memory of that prejudice, like the lamp at the stern of the ship, so we know where we've been… Right?'

Butterbugs leaned back, feeling the same sun that had shone on Odysseus, because at that moment he felt such ancient energy, despite Justy's train of thought.

'Oh, I think that…' He stretched his knuckles ionosphere-ward. 'That, um, the chambers we inhabit, the windows therein, and the arterials in and out of them, are, uh, barely known. Can we know them? Will we know them? If we can. If we must. We must. We can. We do.'

Justy, more interested now in a massage than a pursuit of the inexhaustible argument, looked lovingly at Butterbugs, then crossed the open ground to his perch and kissed him fully and lovingly. Pulling back, she gazed into his eyes.

'An unfinished statement,' she said. 'You are unfinished. But more finished than the rest of us.'

Then they all laughed and kissed and cuzzled and sipped and were glad that each had the power to feel others, whether it was skin, sweat, bone or hair. Or lips or toes or the dirt, grass, trickly creek, or pine needles, as support between.

Then Butterbugs set about creating a set for an imminent performance. He gathered many a branch, preferably of dark tint, and fashioned a sort of Gothic spire. Its raggedy façade rose up, black and impressive against the dun and sage-green landscape, and once the stage was set, curtains could part, as great as all outdoors. If they were now in LA, who knows, Butterbugs might have gone to great pains in restoring weedy patches near stacked concrete conduits next outbuildings, just to give this scene needed credibility. After all, that was what the Tailgate Performances were all about.

At any rate, this matinee's theme: color prejudice averted, though the setting was deep in adverse territory.

'I have another gripe,' Justy declared.

'Let's hear it!' Ave hooted.

'I'd like you to know!' Saskia chimed in.

'As you like,' added Butterbugs.

'It's just that,' Justy sat back and squeezed some vintner's cheap white zin, that was the order of the day, past her glorious lips, 'I cannot get past the complexities of complexion.'

'Oh, J-J, enough!' Saskia complained. 'Let's all not be Colour peoples, let's be Drama peoples!'

'Hey babe, you've told me that you, as super-white girl, have experienced prejudicial behavior from your own (privileged) kind.'

'Like, I'm too extreme.'

'They named the whole *race* after you, babe!'

'Everybody needs milk, but licorice is an acquired taste,' joked Ave.

'Oh man,' Justy laughed, 'you should come to sub-Saharan Africa and say that!'

'That's why we fit so well, my girl,' said Saskia ardently. 'We've had similar experiences in that respect.'

'In that particular respect, yes babe. But in your Home Counties, or even in Italy, you're an angel.'

'To be sure, Justified-Love, but color isn't the only factor. Personality and behavior, not to mention culture, traditions, beliefs, practices, all form the mindset, too.'

Justy obviously agreed with these basics, so she shot Saskia a look of love, not argumentative defense. But by that look, she requested (and got) a tad bit more indulgence from her lover, so as to announce the following:

'I, I feel a need to say, that, you know, because of my background, which youze here have to take my word for, that, uh, I am usually offended at the prejudicial attitudes displayed against my race in most Western urban environments!'

This line landed flat with her audience, which she duly noted: BORING!

'Except!' she quickly added, 'In Edinburgh, capital of Scotland, OK?'

The listeners, well-traveled and exposed to the world's variable tones on most subjects, prepared to groan, or question, or at least register some kind of hesitation...

Justy did not wait for war to develop in the camp.

'Because, when you look around that city, the complexion of some chief players in its architecture has come under a scrutiny of value.'

The others smiled, then relaxed. Justy's leadership was always the best option for one to take when she was present. She had no desire to eclipse Butterbugs, but her animation was building, and foundations were being laid in preparation of his desired entrance onstage.

'And nothing illustrates this more than the Scott Monument!'

Justy stood up and gave a Butterbugsian reach up unto the sky. The kineticism she generated caused the cheat grass pods to project off her breasts and hips in sunlight-highlighted slow motion.

'For there it stands!' she continued. 'As a black-coated spire, in the midst of a nation that has scrubbed its facades down to a lighter shade of pale! Because, if they indeed scrubbed Sir Walter's spire, if they returned it to its lassie-like face of original stone, all character acquired these long years would be reduced to Mother's Pride white bread! But note! They have not! And that is credit to my face!'

'Or, your *race!*' the actor corrected.

'Race, face, same thing,' Justy proclaimed with a mischievous smile. 'Ass, too!' She didn't even need to do a turnabout. Her buns were well known to prove any point they took on.

Saskia bounded up and drew a hickey on her girl's righthand booty with white lipstick.

In the beauty of the moment, Butterbugs grasped a further cue: a tale from the realm of free associations. (Told in light of his semi-recent role as the author of 'Waverley' himself, in the biopic, 'Late Afternoon at Dryburgh Abbey' (Biograph).)

'So what the hell!' the actor exclaimed. 'Testimonials in stone, supposedly lasting, fall in the line of intervention every day, and that's a fine state of affairs, all right! Let me tell you that right now!

'On the other hand, I'm all worked up now! Perfect timing to make a perfect-moment response to one of the cheerier subjects that has been brought up of late: Sir Walt's mega-memorial in Old Edinburgh, Schkottland! Have you looked at that glorious monstrosity? Well, have you?

'When I climbed it, alone, the only other humanoid around was the deaf ticket-fellow. Here, in the solo atmosphere, swirling with literary Wizardry of the North, few of us, in all probability, could properly contemplate the most obvious subject at hand!'

Having taken wine, the actor's performance grew steadily affected, but that was quite all right. It was the first time he had ever willingly performed under the influence of intoxicants. It was also the last time, so the audience knew they were witnessing an historical occasion, which only added to their delight.

'Up, up, relentlessly up, into the brazen but driven world of historicity that Sir Walt loved, full of winding staircases and niches, begrimed with Gothic black – wholly black; darker than any documented complexion – Grime! Yet, freshly adventurous in lifting me up, up, relentlessly up, above the Prince's pavements and the Jenner's shops and oh, how far over the longing puppy poses of Walter's beloved hound Maida, perpetually placed so that onlookers can remind themselves of their Waverley heritage (railway station adjacent, indeed styled 'Waverley'!) and what that means in their daily lives…! So that the soul of Scotlund can soar, not only with Sir Woultre and his bardish hymns, but with each person's heart, as part of the whole scheme.

'As I clumb, I felt dependent on the strong and skillfully-laid stone for my preservation. How high we – uh, me – rose! How sexy the sensation! Gothicism upon Gothicism raised meself to almost breathtaking heights. And the clean wind, certainly the same that Quentin, or James Fitz-James, or your average black dwarf breathed, how it smote my up-climbing form and threatened to fling me from this great height and lay me humbly next to the Abbotsfordian's humble fireside statue with brush-mouthed Maida (sigh!)!

'But nay, laddie and lassies! I fought to cling to Monument's burly side, and good stout Scottie construction, sensible and strong, came to mine rescue and saw me to the very tip top, in all its 1840s weirdlaw-ness.

'The Summit! At Last! And I thought, this pile should stand out on the plains of the Punjab, or right at the entrance to this here canyon, or the vale thereabouts, to shock first, but then inspire!

'For it is inspiration of quality that our everyday folk need, when they look up from the curb and gutter of the street just passed...!'

Butterbugs then gave on to a certain, obvious rest, indicating that he had reached the end of his soliloquizing sequence of improv. The others applauded, as the actor stood there in noble Greek Revival nudity, arm outstretched in classic Butterbugs fashion.

'I tell you, sir, you shall star in one of my Broadway productions!' enthused Ave. 'Can't you see it, girls? There's talk of a revival of 'Let My People Come'.'

'Sounds like fun,' said Saskia. 'Should you require any additional dialogue...'

'I don't know if I want to share him like that,' Justy pouted.

'It has to be *sans togs*, dear,' Ave made clear.

'In our profession, J-J, it is possible to share what we treasure, without the treasury being plundered,' said Saskia.

'All based on the honor system,' replied Justy.

'Why J-J, I do believe you're possessive-jealous!'

'True!' she answered, 'Below the basement of race, you will find jealousy and envy filling a few cubic meters!'

At least she could smile while she said it.

'Let's all take wine now, and talk of no more business like show business, my friends and associates!' Butterbugs joyfully announced.

Long indeed was the long, golden afternoon. These four deserved it, and knowing this, the Earthen globe's managerial mind that controls rotation therefore elongated its privilege to such appreciators, so as to expand their attitudes in all things real and all things under-appreciated. For the listening Earth, it was good to hear such talk amongst humans.

After they awoke from their nap, Butterbugs asked Ave,

'Where's your TarlMate, Ave? You could be talking with MarLane right now!'

'I tell you, I forgot it. Willingly!'

'On-purpose negligence? Why ever did you?'

'Because I wanted to think of her without guile, without misinterpretation, without distraction.'

'So, I take it you haven't been distracted for one second with thoughts of that fair lassie, then?' Butterbugs asked, in the thickest Borders brogue he could manufacture.

'Nay, Sir Walt. My whole *being* is a distraction! As we speak, everything is MarLane.'

'Akin to Sri Aurobindo's 'Everything-is-Krishna'.'

'Precisely. Except, instead of a blue god, I see MarLane's tanned ass and rosy bubs.'

'As it should be, my dear fellow! In such things is divinity native!'

'We heard that!' Justy sounded off.

'Good!' returned the star. 'I learned it all from you, anyway.'

Justy waxed feisty. 'Damn right, SweetLoops! Ave, give that Sugerterry a ring and get her tanned ass out here. I want to size her up. See if she's good enough for me – er – you.'

'Justina!' Saskia mock-hissed. 'Beware of *my* jealousy!'

'Don't give me what I want, dear!' Justy padded into Catwoman mode. 'Deny me! Continue to deny me!'

The two gals and Butterbugs exploded with laughter. Mockery of non-existent emotions was always a welcome game.

But Ave did not laugh. Instead, he started to weep.

'I can't tell you how remote I feel,' he said. 'She acts so distant from me. I direct her on stage left, and on stage right. I give her *center* stage at every opportunity, and it's as if she were as far away then as we are right now, even though we occupy the same stretch of boards on the same stage. I am crushed. I don't know if she'll ever accept me, beyond me being her director. Even if the show runs a year, with MarLane, I face a finiteness that I cannot bear! I'm so in love, and the love is an ache that persists beyond all my consciences. She has taken me, taken me away, but she does not realize she has done it, so she does not know where she has put me! Oh, friends! I don't know what to do...'

Saskia roused herself once more from her plush cushion and dashed, naiad-like, over to Ave, quickly followed by Justy, who held a wispy kerchief over her to protect against the late afternoon sun.

As Ave's tears dropped into the weedy dust, Saskia stroked his Sicilian-style hair, got her hands greasy, then laved his dick in the lubricant, and assisted in its hardening.

'Let me make you forget, if but for a moment, baby,' Saskia whispered caringly.

She positioned herself in doggie style and aimed her soft butt facing the saddened director's face. Justy made sure that additional wetness was added to the mix, and as her tongue ceremoniously retreated, she herself tenderly guided the sorrowful one's lonely member to surrogate lips. They may have been attached to a bottom whiter than he'd like, but with similar long waves of back-cloaking hair, to remind him of she who really mattered. And Justy, now standing protectively over the couple, let the kerchief's fabric out in the gentle zephyr, so that its un-furled flag flapped faintly above them. Firmly was she anchored as the statuesque goddess of virtue and ultimate courtesy, who silently approved, with all the so-lemnity necessary for summer memories to be realized.

Such a compassionate act of distraction qualified as a sacred trust.

Butterbugs, respectable star of stage and screen, was nevertheless made some-what goony by white zinfandel in the blanch-sky'd sun. He noted the compas-sionate sex scene with interest from some distance away and became fittingly stimulated on account of its breathtaking open-heartedness. Respect was the only proper response, so he vetoed any interruption of its poetics. Thus, feeling capable as a result of some recent advanced yoga classes, he clumsily attempted auto-fel-latio amongst the cheat-grass. His failure was a bit comic, but certainly not slap-stick. So, he continued to satisfy himself, like the others were doing, yonder. For the freedom to follow pleasure in this world was palpable all around them. There was nothing for it but to proceed in all honesty.

Such was the true nature, found in all here, revealed.

Final Check of their campsite followed in the morn, when everyone was a tad rough-around-the-edges. The impromptu Scott Monument would stay, as its æs-thetics would soon rate it a Protected Monument of the Forests. Only the standard rubbish and occupation remains were left to be cleared.

'Let us cleanse the wilderness, my friends,' Ave chirped, 'and leave no trace!'

Perhaps because of the previous orgy, and how it went, Butterbugs was feeling a bit grungy, and so waxed wry.

'No trace? Why, I was practicing 'leave no trace' way before there was even any 'trace' to 'leave'!'

Idyll.

'We are pleasantly dating now, Butterbugs,' Ave said a couple weeks later over the phone. 'It's great to be back, back, BAAACK on Broadway! I cannot tell you how helpful Saskia and Justy were in breaking the obsession that was destroying me. Did you know that was the sole reason MarLane was distant from me? She could sense it, and she was... Well, quite frankly, she was *afraid* of me. Not just the big, bossy director, but the big, bossy, *obsessed* director! Who could possibly blame her? I ask you! I can't believe how stupid I was. Or selfish! But once the spell was broken, we could court each other. And it was in the old-fashioned style! Turns out she was longing to all the time, but my craziness, which she picked up on, had freaked her out. You know what I mean? You know what that's *like?* When I got back, I just – I just told her *everything*, and she was ecstatic. I even told her just *how* the spell was broken, and how your ménage pulled it off. You know what she said about the 'intimate' part? She thought it was *beautiful!* Really, and her tears were joyful ones! How lucky are we, anyway?? Hey, the three gals – Sasky, Justy, 'n' MarLaney – are even planning a long weekend in Marigot, in the

Caribbean! Unbelievable, but true! True friend Butterbugs, we're so happy with each other! I'm so, so grateful. I just called S and J, and you know what they said? 'We're glad you went along with us, and didn't fight it.' Really! That's what they said! And you! The Facilitator! Other guys would have strung me up in the toolies for bear meat, but you knew – you *knew* what they were doing! You are the Caliph of Cool! And you know what? We think the 'Downing Street' show's going to be a flop, and we're actually thrilled. It's bringing us even closer together. I love her more than ever, and she loves me! And we love you guys – just as much! Thanks, buddy! Thanks for everything!!'

Though he subsequently acquired a passing fair ranch with manor house and romantic outbuildings with verandahs and fine prospects below the mouth of the Yellowjacket canyon, and many called upon him to set up a country studio by which alternative and truthful Butterbugs vehicles might be launched under their own auspices, the actor did not elect to erect any sort of duplicate Scott Monument anywhere in those wild marches. His point was already proven: to persist in living the language that others only intimated. To venture past the verbally safe, predictable and banal. To continue, and to maintain. His monuments were composed of celluloid, not stone.

The Earth and its occupants would pass, but thought was eternal.

5.

Butterbugs On The Gantry

Butterbugs reined in his mule.

A distant trumpet sounded (fanfare by Dimitri Tiomkin). The sullen forces of holy war were gathering on the battle plain. A strange phosphorescence was in the sky. Desolate day. A low-level, tense rumbling, as a storm gathering. Electrifying environment. Deep, deep portending.

Action was called. In character now, Butterbugs, as Severe Revenger Teijuk, moved into the range of the WarnerSuperScope lens.

TEIJUK: How my heart pants for the battlefield!

MUNDGRUP: They are on the horizon, my overlord. They come!

KHRADRAP: My chief! I am afraid!

TEIJUK: I tell you, don't buy into it!

KHRADRAP: I *will* not!

ZIDDHOARVALLOCKX: With you as our leader, fearsome Teijuk, cowardice is an impossibility.

OKOLLAVADSHATT: That we know! That we live! That we *kill* for!

JHARNKLAKX: We are wild! *Wild*, I tell you!

BHOGBRAKK: My overlord and my underparts, drink with me this one last time!

VHAAD-KEN-DHURRUCK: Never the last! If here, so be it, but forever more in Dhlogvhast!

KUZZ-ZADD: We drink, my warrior-hogs!

BAUDVAUDEZLIZ: To the Shun-lords!

ZIDDGHARKAKK: To the Unnamables!

RIÓUSLIEUMAI: Like, *Hatred*, my honeys! Ooooh! Woo-woo!

SCHADDBLOKK: I can only kill! *Then* swill!

IXT-ZHOX-MUZ: Always in Dhlogvast!

VUZZUZZAH: Quick-dipped in enemy blood!

UDDGHLUDD: In watermelon sugar!

KAXSCHRINKOX: In bakes of stone and iron!

ISCHBAUG: Wyarzim! *(battle-cry)*

SHIDZHTROKK: The curséd liquor of Ziyxunn!

WAMMHRAGG: It will boil our blud!

THODD-PWIZZ: It will make us laugh!

JEXXTANK: It will make us strong!

THARK-KWANK: It will make us fully capable of rape, later on!

RIÓUSLIEUMAI: Ready on my end, girls!

DHRUZZSHAPP: It will make us *kill!*

DAZZFKUKK: Dark revenge is all I care to hit, on the anvil's head.

TEIJAK: Your entire tribe shall be avenged this gothic day!

VIME-GHASCHT: War!! I want war! NOW!!!

TEIJAK: Drink now, my pustules! My killer-bugs! We destroy ALL!

ALL: Wy-aaaaaar-zimmmmm!!!!!

    Suddenly a cry pierced the air.

    'Cut! I tell you, cut!' Director Æneas Pigboy-Schadrach was ecstatic. 'All the right faces! All the right expressions! The music will sound like The Last

Trumpet! Shamroy, line up shot 465 B! Yak, get the second unit over beyond the ridge! PLACES!'

Assistant Director Wingate Smith shouted out:

'Cue War Horns! Cue War Drums – all seven tiers!'

Butterbugs was tremendously excited. This picture was going to be earth-shaking. It was his first role as an unremittingly savage villain. His character, utterly evil and without quarter, absolutely triumphs beyond his dreams, opening up a new Permanent Era of Total Repression and Unpleasantness.

Gwyneth Paltrow's daughter, Apple Martin, was in for a cameo appearance. She was bawling up a storm, which was perfect for her role as a peasant tot who vehemently opposes the Vuggoth Invasions.

'That little smallie is one heck of an actress!' Butterbugs exclaimed. 'She just might steal all our scenes!'

With Gunther Ngummah as Chuchkuk the Blaster, Peter O'Toole as Vuhfaasch the Order-Giver, Ving Rhames as Dhugjhugg the Hacker, Julie Cox as Stastadna the Necromancette, Yaphet Kotto as Yimjheb the Curser, Covity Shirity Kabadi as Condellina the War Princesse, and Liv Tyler as Gondra, the Wandering Princessina! With Robert Hardy, Richard Briers, Richard Wilson, Derek Jacobi, Adam Faith, Ian MacShane, Ian Holm, Ian Richardson and Ian McKellen as the Nine Parths (Judge-Philosophers).

In between shots, Butterbugs applied more bear grease to his shaven dome, while Makeup dribbled cow saliva onto his Vuggoth-style beard, which protruded from his right-hand cheek and down to his leaden armor.

Lessingham Westmore, the Makeup Buddy, muttered, 'We're gonna git yiew nice and raunchy fer the battle scenes!'

'Raunch me out!' crowed Butterbugs, who then adjusted his purple prosthetic teeth. He wore contacts that made his eyes look like corroded ball bearings, a suggestion from Ray Milland, who played Old King Shetzchrag. No one even thought of Randi Chuzzlewit and his infamous ferric glare.

All preps accomplished, Butterbugs sat in his saddle and pondered life.

'This picture!'

He reveled in the power of the role. It had planted a seed, which grew into a single fiber, then advanced up his spine. The prospects of the future were vast, indescribably wonderful... stupefying, even. But his hand was steady on the pommel, and all contemplation was in proper places of accessibility and purposefulness.

It was suddenly quiet enough for him to hear himself think. This was what he wanted to do: to participate in this cherished picture at all cost and to the fullest of life's capacities. A simple concept. It was just that there was so much of the unknown to portray on the screen – yet. Coverage of ground had become increasingly important to him. Aside from the plains to be ridden over, there were other planes that beckoned seductively and sensibly.

The very air was different out here. Bouquets of Silk Road implications, not silken in reality, but gruff, gritty, yet filled with honesty and unburdened hope.

Openness implied possibilities, and Butterbugs was elated that they were filming on the actual historic stretches that could be assigned to this epic tale.

Atop his steed, he was aware of its needs, but they were not pressing, so he cast his eye around the vast space awaiting cinematic battle circuses. Off to the south, an ancient Tartar tower, dolled up to dress the far background. A vital scenic ingredient that Tiomkin's music would make even more distant, yet exalted. In the basin to the west, an entire army of Khoraghichtic extras awaited the signal. To the north, the camera crew of three units, spread out in Napoleonic configurations. They were ready to catch the angled light and all the action from the most imaginative and artistic angles. The inspired Pigboy-Schadrach, having planned every detail throughout all those bitter months of uncertain illness and anticipation, now turned to realizing them with robust ecstasy.

The grandeur of the imminent situation struck Butterbugs as worthy of documentation on its own, a motion picture capturement of all that he now beheld. But the more he thought of it, the more he was pushed away. What robbery it was, to show the moment and the method of what a picture's participants beheld, at the expense of the final picture, which becomes minimized by description, instead of standing on its own merits. Therefore, he would remember these moments as jewels attached in sequence to a caparison, which was itself a-building, as his career allowed.

So, for a picture of war, he was at peace.

The offensive nature of his kit and its outrageous sensual assets began to take his attention away from purely observant thoughts as to the significance of his position in the center of this enterprise. That was good. Reduced to a grotty reality as far as hygiene and potential were concerned, Butterbugs became surly with reaction to the stale hogo-broadcasts of bear effluvia and other sour makeup applications, be they ever so genuine. The putridity of yesterday's soup was everywhere. Perfect! And in the order of things, pure Method rammed its message home. These obnoxious ointments and salves, *they* are what made these warriors ill-tempered, aggressive and bellicose in their beings and in their purposes. Not a bad argument, considering the modern person's aversion to things *not* reeking of safe pleasure and packaged intentions.

Not that Butterbugs wholly fitted into such a handy category. He fit in now, though. He *was* Severe Revenger Teijuk, ready to mete out awful justice for his own concerns.

The hordes were assembled and awaited their opening commands. The sky was increasingly dark overhead, but ringed with bronzed and oblique sidelight, as if some menacing, extinguishing element was biding time before finalizing its power by crashing in. Or else its threat was deceptive. Perhaps it was a force of theatrical effect. Benign, yet carrying mass misinterpretation of the feelings it instilled in human souls. Could be that it came with cooperation and care, maintaining its appropriate ambience as a courtesy, to be sustained while this difficult sequence was filmed. In any case, the weather was proving ideal.

The production team, the artists and the artisans (including Frank Frazetta), were all riveted with anxiety that the mood would not hold, as it was cinematic perfection itself.

Thus, it was now or never.

Again, the horns of Dimitri's next and infinitely more anticipatory fanfare blared across the field as a prelude for moody action. The savagery of its tones put every mind on the plain in the most fitting of states.

Several constructed parallels held multiple camera setups, so that every angle was covered, but the most important was the portable unit atop a seven-story gantry on the main runway into the battlefield's heart. That is, at Butterbugs' starting point.

The interval after the fanfare sounded was rather longer than might be considered usual. However, cover shots were accomplished. Then a lull set in. No one seemed to really know why, but due to this style of location filming (grandly-enhanced reality, in all ways), lulls were to be expected, even under transcendent conditions, such as this day's.

The quietude became disarming. Many a steed stood and pranced in anticipation, jingling and snorting. The atmospheric pressure was terrible. Heat was not an issue, but cold sweat was, enough to precipitate migrainey filaments of worry and distraction before one's eyes.

From the control centers about the battlefield, no word came, nor did any emit from the HQ where director Pigboy-Schadrach supposedly hovered in front of schematic tables, communication hardwares, monitors and viewfinder.

2nd, 3rd and 4th units (helmed by Yakima Canutt, Andrew Marton, and José López Rodero, respectively) stood by. And by. Nervous, restless, but attentive.

And near to Butterbugs, the shockingly-high gantry stood ready, with the master shot camera atop it, linked with the Shelenkov-Bondarchuk boom that would 'inherit' the camera for the desired sweep-in effect, tackled within the same take. No cuts or fakery were to be tolerated.

The gantry was committed to a certain track route that would naturally have to be followed by Butterbugs and his brigade, and what rehearsals were possible proved that the trickiness of the setup would require great skill and intuition.

Butterbugs loved this aspect of picture making. He embraced the challenge with incredible relish and insisted on doing his own stunts, as usual. This made his presence amongst the masses of stunt persons with whom he would be riding – the actors themselves sat this one out – all the more heroic. Besides, the camera would be pulling into a full close-up of the Severe Revenger on his ride, after it descended from the gantry via the boom, gathering speed, dollying closer to Butterbugs while he was in faster and faster transit, then angling around into a splendid, straight-on CU of the fearsome leader.

That was the plan.

The delay continued. So did the magnificently atmospheric and natural lighting conditions all around them. All was on hold. Now more than ever, it was now or never.

Because the army of unit assistant directors had no commands – yet – Butterbugs did his own reccy of the scene. All his men were in their places, and associated actors were all as they should be.

Even baby Apple was ready to start bawling on cue (she had been in rehearsal for some time, as most of the hordes were painfully aware). There she was, in swaddling rags, upon the pagan stone Altar of All the Sacrifices that stood atop the seminal Well of the Sorrows, right in the middle of things. The battle was due to rage around it. Eerily, the Well and Altar were benefitting from one of the most phenomenal features of the current natural lighting. As if from the eye of a pantheonic dome, fresh overhead beams were cast down upon the well, making its stage all set in harmonious terms that even the scriptwriting team of Zephaniah Lazarus, Saskia Pingles, and Philip Dunne could not have conceived.

In the midst of his awaiting destruction, the Chaos Lord would find himself, in this planned take, making an astounding rescue: Apple's character, Baby Sheeboilb. In his stony heart, a child's cry would serve as jackhammer. It would be his defining, Ashokan moment, when the course of history would be changed, due to shrieking, wordless vocal cords.

Thus, the signal importance of this whole, lengthy one-take sequence was self-evident, and its complexity was the most notable since the Battle of Borodino in 'War and Peace' (Mosfilm/Continental, 1968).

His vision rendered into rough charcoal sketches of reality due to his ball bearing contact lenses, Butterbugs nevertheless enjoyed a particular clarity of perception. To him, all was in high contrast, and because of the uncertain subtleties in play all throughout this environment, it was as if he possessed a grasp on logistics the director himself should have (but couldn't), despite his tech-heavy HQ control.

Glancing up at the summit of the gantry tower, from where the sequence, upon notification, would ignite, Butterbugs noticed that the camera operator, Vance Van Vund, seemed less than committed to his normal eagle-eye focus on task. His head bobbed, as if he were inebriated – or ill.

All other crew were singularly occupied at their own posts, whether to activate pulleys or pull ropes or guide animals or assure safety for both their own or for many an extra's welfare. Tedium was apparent though, and stamina was being tried on all fronts.

Because he was the only one of the talent who was not in shot until his dramatic highpoint entrance from stage right, once the mechanism of this sequence was well underway, and after action was rolling inexorably forward, Butterbugs had the luxury of doing what he now did.

Sensing conflict due to Vance's conspicuous wavering, the star made his move. Dismounting from his thoroughly-trained steed Mhlagaz-cherg, who kept a sidelong glance attached to his master, the Severe Revenger, in full costume and character (essentially), hopped onto the vast gantry assembly and made his way toward the upward-slanting stairs.

Just at that point, the air was ripped with a general announcement.

'Places!'

'Oh, *scheisse!*' hissed Butterbugs.

Because the gantry was basically a movable tower assigned to a pre-determined route of track, and the lowest level consisted of a flat 'lobby' floored with plate metal set in ballroom style to cover the basement substructure, which provided a plain of passage for those who would dare ascend and its ballast properties kept the upper realms in balance, the actual steadfastness of the whole assembly was dubious at best.

As he ascended the first flight, further PA proclamations were heard. The motors to power the gantry's progress, one per wheel, were idling and awaiting remote control commands, so the actor had to strain his ears to hear the announcements over the heavy-duty humming.

'Your director is speaking now. Warning! This is the most complex take of all our careers! Thus, the regretted delay. Take care. You all know your instructions, and your procedures. This is a big deal. Conditions are optimum. The world is watching. So are the ages! When I call 'Action', the great mechanism we have designed and constructed will go forward, and none of us can stop it. Nor would we, even if we could! Let all our hearts be filled with joy, and may all our motions in this great duty be successful beyond our highest expectations!'

'Oh, *scheiser!*' spat Butterbugs.

The bear grease was liquefying due to the sweat produced by his strenuous upward mobility. He knew that any second now, the tipping point would be reached, and all could be lost – or gained.

At the fourth level, the luxury of the stairs ended and mere ladders were required, as the gantry tower's profile narrowed as surely as the gopurams of Grauman's Tirukkalikundram Thiertre, so far away at this moment, which the star knew so well.

The ladders were nominally anchored, but because of Butterbugs' weighty kit and leaden armor, which he was obliged to keep wearing on his haul upward, the tie-down strips were sorely taken to task, and with each level gained, at the next level, the anchorage was distressingly dislodged.

Higher and higher, as if in some soon-to-be demolished high-rise apartment block, where airiness is all that is left, the insecurity of the heights linked with the actor's latent fantasy of flying. It intermixed with a dreamlike falling, falling, to fight the pressing duty of yet more ascension in the midst of the prime conflict while facing this irrefutable crisis.

Crisis it was, because the inexorable process was now in play, and ears pricked, the dreaded shoe was about to drop.

It occurred on the sixth level, just when he was moving up the rickety final ladder.

'Peoples of the plain!' Pigboy-Schadrach's voice bellowed triumphantly over the region, 'It is *now* that we select to move! Think of it! You are at the nexus! Participate presently, in this, the full-bore complexity of orchestrated elements of the Seventh Art! Now! It is upon us! I call, and in the most commanding but solemn and respectable tone possible, the high motion of: **ACTION!!**'

That was it. Design was everything. And because of that, all that followed was based on the fact that the gantry, which Butterbugs now nearly stood atop, had to commence its course in order to accommodate all associated and subsequent actions of the interrelated and retroactive extras and main players that were now required to realize this most elaborate of any live cinematic progression yet undertaken in known cinematic history.

Across the plain, at his HQ, the master director could not watch. Once his mechanism had been set upon its course, he retired to his tented chambers and gazed at his self-portrait in a mirror. (He would later be heavily criticized for this.)

'Have I attempted too much?' he queried his shadowy side. 'Were we too complicated? Have I the right to request such planning in such a chaotic world? Is this my way of making sense of it all…?'

Nevertheless, as the designer questions his wisdom, the scheme moves into enactment. At least there was a conscience in the arena, signifying a soul somewhere hereabouts…

Reaching the point in the gantry tower by which man's erection met the sky, its fecund possibilities of art and science could be found at last. Where, on this roof of the world, naked truth was the only point on which to light, Butterbugs beheld the key element in the acute imperative now laid down upon the world. It consisted of all it took to capture what followed successfully on motion picture film.

Due to the action call, the gantry had now been set trundling on its hard rubber mega-casters. Butterbugs could feel it far below. And on this bare rooftop, all the personnel required to make magic happen under the tremendous duress had… fallen! The medic squad, the backup crew, the support grips, all were prone and without power.

'Anticipation-stroke!' whispered Butterbugs, immediately recognizing the baleful force that had laid these outstanding professionals low.

Hastily, he looked toward the massive camera, mounted like an antiaircraft cannon, and at its eyepiece, gallant operator Vance Van Vund, unhappily collapsed in involuntary surrender, but still in his chair, brought low by the stress of an impossible schedule, and also, unknown sodium deficiencies.

Without wasting a microsecond, Butterbugs made his way up to the mounted instrument of capture and saw to the noble operator's needs. Escorting his weepingly weak form to prone safety near his mates, he attained the seat in front of the trigger of the 70mm monster, and without even glancing through the non-reflex system to check for parallax, and knowing that Vance had set it up in splendid style, Butterbugs let 'er roll, then set the lock on.

In one of the most poignant acts in the history of the cinema, Đặng Từk Nn, the clapper fellow, roused himself from his confounding malaise and was able to raise his instrument for a few seconds in order to identify this, the take of the ages, before succumbing to his overriding ailment, and turning over the destiny at hand to he who came to complete what he and these others could not.

'Butterbugs!' gasped the ecstatic Nn. 'You, of all, have come! Take this, our composite creation! Make it real for us! Oh, Butterbugs, do not fall down, as we have!'

And the gesture of his hand, out beyond his duties of the matte box, stretched across the plain below. It was the most epic and sincere statement that Butterbugs had yet beheld in all his cinematic encounters. And as the clapper sank, Butterbugs rose to the occasion.

They were rolling, and the gantry was in motion, and Butterbugs could see the extras in alignment, properly framed in the camera's coverage, and the progression was suddenly almost of an automated nature. Such were the calculations of the creators and the technicians, who had sweated blood to not only work out these logistics, but to ensure that all enactment was foolproof on their part. So that the director, working with live actors, would not be encumbered with non-drama-oriented issues. In short, it was up to the actors now to prosecute this sequence in the most efficacious manner possible, as all the technical aspects had been solved and planned upon.

Knowing this inherently, and sensing some potential animation in the person of Vance the operator, Butterbugs kept at the eyepiece, making small adjustments to keep the gathering momentum of the surging hordes – his very men – within the generous frame of the photographing device he now captained.

Speed was increasing, both in the gantry's route, and the army's advance. Soon a cruise was reached. They were rumbling along. A nice movement was felt at this tip-top of the gantry, which Butterbugs reckoned would provide a nice sense of exalted importance in the rhythm of this scene so far, especially to the rising triads of Tiomkin's anticipated score. The composer himself was occupied in his own observation tower, sketching steadily, with an adjacent toy piano to test any questionable fifths.

And sure enough, because the mechanics were proceeding so smoothly, there appeared, off to the right, the approaching high-rise entity of the Shelenkov-Bondarchuk boom, leading into the gantry's route, in the mission of taking up the camera for greater distributary coverage of this mass movement.

Knowing its linking to be synchronized on the highest levels of sophistication, Butterbugs expected harmony in the passing of the baton, as it were. The boom was indeed manned, by Sherry Nederland, a rookie operator. She waved enthusiastically, in anticipation of a happy mating with the solemn switchover of the immense camera, from fixed mount to floating boom. If the handover was not accomplished without a hitch, many would die. Numerous souls were linked to this machinery, and they were so vulnerable in its operation, that flawless progression was the only acceptable program.

Sherry duly rose while advancing, and nearing Butterbugs, despite the surprise of seeing the star as her co-techie, she was able to give him a quick primer on his newfound tasks in de-securing the camera and sliding it into its adoptive seating in the boom. Her instructive dialogue was steady and well-delivered, step-by-step, so that Butterbugs, the consummate actor, and now the rising apprentice, was able to pull off the all-new requirements in making sure this thing was able to continue without the disaster and humiliation of interruption.

At such a height, with only the uncertainty of the holding sky above, and the threats of perdition below, Butterbugs and Sherry achieved the near-impossible. Sliding over the unencumbered rolling-film machine into its new berth, the team knew they'd nailed it, with only a slight jar that aficionados would appreciate, as charming.

[As with the rise of Hal Rosson's crane over Munchkinland in 'The Wizard of Oz' (MGM, 1939), or in the big pull-back, executed by Ray June, in 'Born to Dance' (MGM, 1936); MGM being famous for their 'the audience will never notice' wobbles in their pull-backs, which are, to most fans' thinking, one of the most endearing things about the studios' attempts at making big, big, big statements.]

The slot-locks did what they were supposed to, in securing the great camera, and now it was all Sherry's ride, all the way down to the Well of Sorrow and Sheeboilb's heartfelt bawling, a long, long way from here.

The handover sealed, Butterbugs knew he must surrender the glorious post of operator's advantage and get back down to the plain of action, where it was vital that he appear at the assigned second, so that the mathematics of this whole sequence could proceed in peace, and so that the sensational effect could be had – decisively.

'Gawrsch!' Butterbugs ejaculated, upon seeing Sherry descend somewhat rapidly, now that the hand-over had been pulled off successfully. 'How, then, shall I reach my mount in time?'

It was perhaps the most pressing question of the hour. Way, way up here above the artfully-blighted plain, the view was fantastic, but for the leading player, stage-death!

Conventional descent was utterly out of the question. Urgency began to grip him, and cobalt-tinted sweat condensation rimmed his eyes with a terrifying effect (which Makeup would certainly appreciate as a dramatic enhancement).

'What then – what – am I going to do??'

There was no time even to panic, but if he had had the opportunity, that emotion would have uncharacteristically crippled him if he had not made his leap of faith at that very second.

It was because the Shelenkov-Bondarchuk boom, which was based in principle on Eiffel's drawbridge over the Cisse, at that precise moment had its counterweight positioned in scissors-type articulation aft from the camera mount. Butterbugs saw an opening. The ingenious engineering enabled both ends to rise and lower in opposite directions. Therefore this special scissors-suspension allowed for great flexibility, a centrally-located drive train and grip stations, and its zeppelin-light girders of titanium could carry the heaviest cinematographic hardware with all the nimbleness of flouncing girls in a *midsommar* pageant parade.

So, as the camera descended, the bulk of the counterweight ascended. But as the tracks of the gantry tower and those of the boom had reached a Y so that the gantry would be well out of the picture when the camera panned to take in the spectacular mass of extras, divergence between the two was immediate, though their speeds of progression were approximately the same.

For Butterbugs, no thought was necessary, no debate, no dithering over what to do any longer. If this were to be his end, his final gesture as a working actor, then at least it would be within the sphere of nobility which, by virtue of his creative associations with filmmakers, actors, and other artistes, he had fashioned himself by doing what he was meant to do. And if his final stroll as a player was an attempt to save the day in an impossible situation, then those who came after him would have to assess and judge it as worthwhile. Or not. The picture was nearly finished, and it could still be a success without him.

That was why all fear vanished, and he jumped.

If he had waited three more seconds, he would have plummeted the full fathom down to a destiny of dust instead of colliding, metal-to-metal, with the counterweight housing one story below, rather than six more.

His lead armor gave him a horrible jar when it thudded against the far lighter element that now saved him. His torso reverberated violently within this carapace, but aside from that, he clung like grim death to the sleek surface, which was made slick by his coating of bear grease.

The gantry, relieved of the non-calculated weight of Butterbugs and his costume tonnage, veered off to the left on its pre-arranged tracking, but all seven stories nearly toppled over as a result. It and the lives at the top were saved by the quick-witted instincts of Beaky Brennion, the grip running the remote control. Easing back the trainset-style controls at just the right rate, he lowered the gantry's speed to a crawl, so that it could round its exit-corner without catastrophe, and just in time to get out of the shot, too.

Back on the boom, in mid-shot, the first thing Butterbugs thought was not 'Are my bones intact?' but 'Did I ruin the shot?'

Surely his landing on the counterweight carriage caused the camera to lurch, but no, the flexion capacity of the superstructure had been hyper-engineered to accommodate blows far greater than any Butterbugs might deliver. After all, the mechanism was several steps past Stedicam technology and an intricate system of gimbals and gyros ensured that the frame of coverage had been rock-steady all along. If this knowledge was unknown to the actor as of now, nothing more could be done about it. So he set to in tackling the next step. How to get from this rising mechanism down to his loyal steed, which he could see in the distance, already on the move, herded by hostlers (in war costume) to its appointed place of rendezvous?

By now the boom had picked up speed, and, under director's orders, it was necessary for it to surpass the raging mounted warriors behind the vanguard, who were already moving along at full tilt.

Constantly in danger of falling off because of his blucky makeup, Butterbugs placed all his immediate talent on the project of negotiating this slippery slope without making the camera waver or dodge or hunt (though he needn't have worried). In the process, the job of working his way down to a pausing point was one of the most difficult things he had ever attempted in life. But achieve it he did.

Observation platform as base, he was able to pause for a moment and appreciate the threatening majesty of the spectacle before him, all noise and fury, orchestrated and timed, and dependent on every participant to make it work.

Again, had he the opportunity to analyze the import of all within the mega-wide scope of things at some leisure, surely he would be overcome with enough rushing thought to send him into a dive and end up as ground-down road-kill beneath the stout onslaught of cheval, mule and tapir now raging beside him.

'I will not fail,' he thought, obtaining a moment of inner sanctum quietude amidst the absolute tension and tamasha that his gantry acts had let loose.

While prepping the grand pan in mid-rush that would usher Butterbugs' entrance into the shot, Sherry, up on the operator's deck, caught sight of him and gasped.

'What the hell are you doing *here?*' she mouthed.

'Shere-dear,' he mouthed back, 'we're going to have to be a bit fancy with this maneuver. No deviations from basic plan, but you're going to have to slow down your pan when it comes time for me to jump ship and take up my mount. Can you work something out?'

Sherry grinned the grin of one who is exalted by such challenges.

'I shall execute the task without trickery,' she hooted. 'Just you wait and see!'

Her confidence was unabashed because, unbeknownst to Butterbugs and even most of her crew, this particular Shelenkov-Bondarchuk boom was the latest model, equipped with operator-located control pedals and throttle, and, wonder of wonders, Sherry had been futzing and training on it for the past two and a half weeks. Needless to say, as an operator for every great, from Zsigmund to Harlan to Nykvist to Willis to Renoir (Claude-type) to Shamroy (her boss today), she mastered the machine in a few hours, and the rest of the time had been spent perfecting her art. There was no one on earth more competent at the controls. That fact Butterbugs knew, so now, his own confidence entirely restored and the situation manageable, he returned to his essential duties: to define and project character for the motion picture screen, no matter how complex the context was, or how austere.

There entered his mind a certain serenity, not brought on by detachment or ego, but by concentration on the holistic fabric of the moment, in which both future and past were appreciated and duly filed. But they did not stand in the way of the imperative of dramatic creation, when the spark of guidance flares, and the trail ahead is lighted by a pyrotechnical display which is discriminate in its coverage, but concise in its essence.

Thus, the rest of the sequence was realized with almost a mechanical progression. But because competence was not in question, artistic interpretation could flower, and many memorable insights and innuendoes were brought forth in Butterbugs' performance, despite the premise of this scene being a vast and war-like sequence of bluntness and anti-subtleties.

The crew was right on it. Sherry buzzed some grips, who picked up on Butterbugs' dilemma, and dispatched a Tackerball Flying Doodlebug motorcycle, the largest in existence, over to the boom to allow him to hop on and joyride over to his oncoming charger.

The driver, Encrescenden Dundan, who happened to be Associate Executive Producer on the picture, but preferred risky grip work, pulled up to the boom and instructed Butterbugs to hop on, then smuggled him over to his galloping steed through the streaky hoof-charged dust, all the while keeping close watch on Sherry's adjusted pan of the huge scope camera, working completely in concert with it, so that the lead actor could be installed in the saddle just in time for the Big Close Up.

Securely in saddle seconds before the invasion of Sherry's camera in capturing the wind-blown savagery of this next leg of the sequence, Butterbugs was able to get out:

'Bravo Encrescenden! You and so many others have this day entered the pantheon of cinema's selfless endeavorers, in order to make this picture what it shall be: a striking gesture of personal and public statements regarding the concept of warfare. And now, I ride into the deceptive concept of desired cataclysm!'

The Big Close Up, in all its grotesque glory, was beautiful beyond words.

And the subsequent eighteen minutes of the continuous sequence, ending with a screen-filling Turbo-Close Up of Apple's tonsils, yowling out her non-verbal commentary on the senselessness of aggression, communicating its message to the Severe Revenger with earthquaking effect, went without a hitch. Indeed, every aspect of the shot was heightened and made splendid by all involved.

'**CUT!!!!**' shrieked Director Pigboy-Schadrach. 'I am complete. I am fulfilled. Bow down, everyone on this field, for you shall all be knighted this day!'

He was beyond ecstatic.

The first thing Butterbugs did the second 'cut' was called, he commandeered Encrescenden and the Tackerball Flying Doodlebug and plowed over to where the gantry was parked.

'Medic!' he bellowed, while shedding his war-costume into the dust.

'Here, star, here!' Milt the Medic called out, already on the seventh level. 'I am here, and we have revivers!'

'Just plain *good!*' exclaimed Butterbugs as he ascended by ramp, stair, and unanchored ladder.

All the crew, still prone but pillowed and blanketed, were accounted for and alive.

'Đặng Tửk Nn! You live yet!'

Butterbugs cradled him in his arms, and wept.

'Oh, dear Butterbugs,' breathed Nn with relief, 'We all shared a cask of Schragg-water for refreshment, and it turned out that the enhancement-pump on it was out of date, so we got infusions of lerna-gas into our beverages! Nothing worse than that, but at such a time!'

'And I thought you dead! All! All of you fine ones up here!' He gestured to each crew-member with love.

'Nay, Butterbugs. We live yet! But... But the shot! We failed it. By our failure, the film fails.'

'Speak not that way, Nn! For the shot is safe – in the can, and is perfection!'

Then did Nn and the others regard Butterbugs with hopeful disbelief.

'Truly? Oh, but how could such a wonderful dream be true, and in the light of our failures here?'

'Technician! You must *believe!*'

'Help us to believe, Butterbugs! Help us to *behave!*'

'All of you! You already have, my friends! If you can't believe my tidings, I shall depart, and you shall learn the facts that *are*, in your own time. But if your trust is intact, rely upon my convenience, for I recite *truth*, not *script!*'

'Oh Butterbugs, what you say restores us. If I was indeed lying on my death-bed, I should release in bliss, just now...'

'If that were the case! But 'tis hardly. So, rise when you all can. Lerna's effects are mild. Join me at table for pork-and-gravy when the dinner gong roils!'

'We will, Butterbugs, we will! Our humblest of thanks.'

'Knowing this, seeing you here, breathing, alive, restored... Why, it makes my day! A day previously incomplete, now wholly fulfilled!'

When it was released, the audiences of 'Out Of The Advancing Fiery Curtain' (WB) were absolutely bowled over by this new aspect of Butterbugs, the star. It was as if they were in shock for a time, but actually wanted to dwell in that state for a while, to be suspended in the compelling and at times harrowing process of witnessing his character's sway over the earth's governance.

If Butterbugs was famous for leading his audiences to not only water, but to sustenance for the heart and for the soul, he now led them to an acid bath. But in it they discovered, even there, the same nourishment awaited them. Its form was foreign, but through absorption came interpretation, and not one viewer fell through the cracks.

All drank of its offerings.

6.

Wunndie Yingland, Cool Party Grrrrl!

Old Atrocity was having a party.

Just a few friends, from all corners of the Industry. Butterbugs wasn't there (couldn't make it – on location in Moldova for 'Ish-Pish' (UA)), but to make up for it, the Industry's Most Amazing Grip put on his dancing shoes and let 'er rip with his latest monologue.

'It started with this,' OA stated, by way of introduction. 'And let me tell you, we were in high geniality. Butterbugs 'n' me, that is. We got into our usual generational latitudes.

'I said, 'Our generation learned how to mock, but not necessarily create. I know, mocking's a little worse than just making fun. But we had to do *something* that passed as 'important'. As we grew up, here we were, bursting with energy, minds going a million miles an hour. What do we *do*, anyway? So yeah, we learned how to mock. To mock what we couldn't create. To mock because we couldn't be part of what we *wanted* to create. To mock because, what came before us was better than 'most anything we were capable of. And we knew it, so we mocked it. Because, we probably couldn't sustain the creation of anything better, anyway. We mocked because we were… weak. We mocked because we were lazy. We mocked because we were lackadaisical. We mocked because there were so many riches for us to consume, we never developed our own talents. Finally, we mocked because we were a failed generation. (I did a big fat pause here.) No, *more* finally, we mocked because it was the easiest thing to do.'

'So Butterbugs, he said, 'There you go again! Always with the generation gap!'

'I said, 'If you had come before me, Butterbugs, I would probably now be mocking *you* and all you have done, no matter how good everything was.'

'He said, 'But – but *whie??*' (He always does that 'but *whie??*' thing whenever we get into it.)

'I said, 'Cuz, man, because you're so fuckin' *good*, and there's no way I can compete with you.' Not that I ever *could* compete, or anything. With our generation, it's the *idea* that counts, not the action itself. A pail of bullshit, I know, but that's just 'how we are', ya know?

'He said, 'But I have come *after* you. Will you now mock me, or will there be praise?'

'He got me there! I could not mock him, nor could I praise him highly enough. Nor could I say to his face at that hour what I really thought of him. That he was the most extraordinary person I had ever known, and what he was doing for our Industry was essentially beyond the realms of my being a rather articulate grip! So I just stood there with my best Michael J. Pollard grin. He understood.

'We tend to have a lot of fun like that. But let me tell you, he can be intense. Really, super-intense. So, I might add, can I, on occasion. One of those occasions is now! You know, we all go way back, don't we? You all realize that I could have been a triple threat in this town. Orson hounded me about it. He said, 'Get off the earth closet, OA, and teach RKO a lesson!' Well, I didn't wanna write, direct and/ or produce! Nothing makes me happier than gripping for the stars or the Whits. But the thing is, with Butterbugs in the game, I started to have ideas.

'If you'll allow me, I'd, uh, like to do a little 'free association'. I'm not gonna translate it all for yas, cuz y'all can figure it out, but lemme let you in on a yak-fest B-bugs 'n' I had not too long ago. We were terrorizing each other about a 'project'.

'Keep in mind, it was a period piece, so don't worry about the minutiæ of our lingo. You'll figure it out as we go. Remember though, I'm *letting you IN*. It's a sanctum, but not very 'inner'. You don't have to figure it all out, but see if you can. So roll with it, babies! Let's see, I think I can replicate it...:

'Now looka here, try not to be too hard on li'l Wunndie – she just might be a key player in Administration Destruction! That scrappy little brat might be bigger than mega-Monica, more profound than 'Deep Throat' (Aquarius, 1972) – er, I didn't mean the picture – and throw a mightier kick-box to Warren G. Harding's crotch than Teapot Dome ever did! I just heard most of the Sec'y of Defense Show on the wireless. Wow, I was impressed at the 'responsible' behavior of the questioners (even Liddy Pineapple!), who essentially lined our Sec'y up in front of a firing squad. True, it was pretty much water balloons instead of bullets, but the thing's rolling now, and that's all that matters. The Sec'y, in lots of moments when that particularly reedy quality of his voice was made apparent, admitted it 'wasn't a pretty picture'. And when he got pissed off 'n' feisty, no one seemed to be too intimidated, which is unusual. He tried being aw-shucks 'n' remorseful at the beginning, but quickly trashed that bozo act in order to return to his hell-bent-for-leather, circle-the-wagons Li'l Tuff-Huff-Puff Guy stance. (Boy, I'd love to see him come up against tuff, barking li'l Wunndie!) Connie the Prez's gonna have to let him go. That pathetic Cryers fellow (Chare, Joynt Cheaphs), who would seem to be a nice old fellow, is nothing more than a whipping poodle in this whole affaire. C'est merde, man! There are many more pix and wideos (more Wunndie!! Please??) awaiting, and now said Sec'y's seen 'em. Tricky Dick was brought down on much less. The question of the moment is, will it go past SecDef, or will the scandal fade? *CAN* it fade? I think there is Mayday(!) in the W. Haus right now. This Nouveau Worst Nightmare makes R. 'Dick' Clarke et al look quaint.

'So I said all *that*, but what I said wasn't that big a deal, so in response, out of the blue, Butterbugs waxed poetic, as is his wont:

'**W**unndie! Alas, Alas For Wunndie!

Oh Wunndie!
Perverted Punky Brewster!
Storm chaser!
Tough little onion
From the farm of bitterness!
Now – hear –
Eleven years!
In deepest stir!
At least that is the threat —
Because of a wink, a cig, a thumbs up!
Oh! Oh! Oh! Oh! Oh!
Why didst thou go with Prong the Seducer,
Unto unholy works
In Papa's Park of the Damned?
Was it your Oxygen-deprived silence?
Or your will to follow,
Not reading in any way
The signs towards your misfortune?

But, thy infant child!
Thy one bare hope!
Seed of trailer trash
Bound for grimness,
Nevertheless, could well rise
From the fumes of failure.
In the years ahead, of future dynastic tyranny,
Towards triumph,
When he testifies in front of Congress all,
To reveal the truth about his unhappy mother:
That The Sec'y himself,
Knowing the Private's cell phone number,
Made, with approbation from assistant The Putz,
Who, comb in mouth,
Hovering over his boss's wrestler's shoulder
In timid but commanding form,
Chuckled, as The Sec'y
Gave direct writ to sullied Wunndie,
To go, make merry with Eye-Racky flesh;
Pose, in trophy hunt form,
Have big fun, and go in saturnalian joy.

But do not ask – yea – and do not tell,
Of these arcane orders – evermore.
Under a threat that cannot be named.

And Wunndie, tough punky pipsqueak,
Kept silent, as was her old way, those long years,
Bitter, but resolved, to retain her merit as loyal
To they who commanded her,
Be it unto the grave.

Yet, in son's noble quest for justice,
They who made their princely plots from afar
Will still come unto judgment,
Ultimately in a court far higher
Than any now known.

Oh Wunndie, *young* Wunndie!
– If 20s be still young –
How could you have known,
In your trailerian days in old W. Virginny,
That you could have made
Pentagonian trusses tremble,
And the inhabitants therein cry
Unto heaven for mercy?

As you sit out your youth
In the not unpleasant cooler
In an as yet undetermined military facility,
But without a Freedom nor Liberty
Of which the Leader hath benevolently
And magnanimously brought
To they whom you posed with,
Know this: ye can still shake ye foundations
Via a bestseller, so that The Sec'ys and The Putzes
And all they who are of them,
Have ye to fear!
Suckle thy gaol-child
To thy breast, Punky!
Milkflow matters –
Sour power does not.'

'And when Butterbugs finished his tale, he brooded for a time, then uttered, in cryptic tones, 'How d'ya like *them* apples?'

"Maybe so, maybe so,' I replied. 'But 'The Daily Wrestling' offers a fascinating twist. Do they mean that the Sec'y himself might've employed this diversion tactic, or was it anti-Sec'y elements? After all, many in the P'gon hated him from the start, for his 'transformation' plans for the military. If they could 'bump him off' so to speak, many would be glad. Homely Putzi waits in the wings, but he's so controversial and polluted that I don't see how any confirmation committee could approve his taking up the mantle of Essential War Emperor. Maybe Bowell Powel could do 'double duty' until he too falls under the stack of '2001' monolith-shaped dominoes.'

'Butterbugs looked kinda impassive, so I continued to act like we were in a fucking story conference: 'Yesterday, I rang up the DeaSea offices of our two titanic CA senators' offices to politely request that Sec'y plus Putzi's heads jointly appear on a burlap pillow for Ye Publick to… react to, and when I asked if they wanted my name, they said, 'No, that's OK, we're just keeping a tally'! So, many a call must be coming in. (Incidentally, Senate offices are pretty good: you always talk to a real person!)

'Well, gang, you know what? Our actor was silent. He looked down. A sure sign that fair-minded Thought was in process. I was thinking satirically, while he… He was much more serious, more intense.

'Primed, I continued to spout. 'Have you actually *seen* that Wunndie twerp from the W. Virginia trailer park (no kidding) who's in those Eye-Rack prison porno pix? What a punk twerp show-off!'

'He said, 'I'm sure there's a serious aspect to the story, OA, and that it's not really the kind of thing to mock until it's told in full.'

'Shit, I couldn't argue with that. He's so damn *fair-minded!* Still, I took a sort of adversarial route, to perk him a bit. I thought, isn't this what they do when they brainstorm in story conferences? Isn't this what I have to do to make the leap into director/writer/doer-hood? You know, *creating* whole fucking movies 'n' stuff?

'So I continued, with: 'She cracks me up. And that bum with the glasses, that doofus who knocked her up? Reminds me of the entire fringe used car scene I used to witness so regularly, and the 'folks' therein. Remember the stark horrah of seeing my old felon pal Carled Kooke at that last-stop-before-the-Saturday-night-gun-shop on Southsarcoma Way? Still dinkin' around with junky cars to sell to unsuspecting working poors? That's Wunndie's world, all right!

'All he said was, 'Oh. Yeah? Oh, I suppose so…'

'He'd really been *thinking*. Even at this late stage, I puffed up, in response to his previous Byronic canto, with a pretty clever exercise in techie's impatience: a thoughtful haiku:

> 'Prong drips
> With putridity.
> When will those
> Who matter
> Wise-up and
> Reject?

'All Butterbugs said was, 'I think hers is a consummately sad story…'

'I could add nothing more. Our – or, my – satire deflated in the face of Abu Ghraib's true horrors…'

OA's party froze in silence. The rest was awkwardness.

'The show is concluded, folks,' an exhausted Old Atrocity announced to his fireside audience. 'Now, I retire unto my repose.'

'Hey OA,' said Kenna Bamuku, Best Girl of OA's 'A' team, as all were leaving. 'It's OK. You tried.'

'See what I mean?' OA replied, almost in a whine. 'Our generation is pretty shitty at creating stuff. Here I was, trying to make a satire out of events from our epoch, and Butterbugs rises above and makes fucking *poetry* out of it!'

'Isn't that in itself really cool?' she asked.

'Kenny, you don't know how happy it makes me. I don't *have* to compete. I don't *have* to create. I add on to *his* stuff. I help *him*. That's my job. That's what I do. And that's good enough for me. I've found my place, and I love it there. See ya on set tomorrow, 5:00AM on the dot, OK?'

The participants went home, the fires went out, and night-tide Hollywood underwent a midnight rain.

Goldwyn Studios. Day. Interior.

Butterbugs set down his morning mega-jumbo-sized can of double-caliber Jellidon's Non-Esspressoh Corfee-Flavoured Water and gazed at the latest 'Daily Variety'.

Old Atrocity, just opposite, and with the selfsame edition, snorted and said:

'Listen to this. Headline on page three. 'Warren Sarjent slated to woo Butterbugs and ProwlerCat to team in hot version of 'The Wunndie Yingland Story'. Watch out man, Warren's on the warpath!'

Now it was Butterbugs' turn to snort.

'Yup, that's how I thought you'd react.'

'First I've heard of it. Sonny'll put the k'bosch on it, pronto.'

Butterbugs went silent. He located the article and read it.

Old Atrocity gave Butterbugs a particularly grizzled look.

'You, uh, ain't thinkin' of makin' such a career move, are yas?'

Butterbugs was silent.

Old Atrocity stared at him with penetrating insight.

'Oh, I get it. You wanna do it! And you knew about it! Hell, boy, d'you know this here would be the *fourth* version of that there raunchy saga?'

'But with Jack Garfein at the helm…'

'Ollie Stone wants it.'

'And so does Henry Koster.'

'Hell, he'll massacre Stone.'

'I want Garfein. Jack Garfein.'

'What's that, boy? He hasn't made a picture since '61!'

"Something Wild' (UA, 1961)'.

'Wasn't he –'

'Auschwitz, et al survivor.'

'Uh-oh...'

'No, he'd be perfect. Confused girl passing as self-assured tomboy gets snagged into shocking situations. I can coax him out of retirement.'

'Dammit boy, you're determined!'

Butterbugs had the gravitas.

Old Atrocity grew respectful. 'A new re-telling?'

'I think so. I know so.'

'And the lead – ProwlerCat. Are you sure?'

'Actually, no. I think it's best for young wisp Plurr Plurree.'

'My stars, Butterbugs, you beat us all to the essentials. You couldn't be more on target.'

'It's just that, if I am to play the awful dragger of that poor girl into error, dynamics can already be set by the dramatic capabilities of Plurr, whom I have acted with of late, in the photoplay, 'In Neek Akavaranzah' (De Laurentiis).'

'I immediately agree.'

'So do I. Oh, *so do I*.'

Their debate continued, outside of any fireside or studio venue. In fact, Old Atrocity actually agreed to a rap session about this picture with Butterbugs at The Æyrie.

'Butterbugs, Ollie Stone wants to direct you in the Miss Wunndie story. You know that. Battles with Henry Koster ('The Robe' (20th-Fox, 1953) and 'The Singing Nun' (MGM, 1968)) over the chores have been intense, as you – er – know. Butterbugs, you'd give your left pinkie toe to play Prong the badass. Relax! I hear on good authority that you will, I tell you, you will!'

Butterbugs was silent, but wholly connected.

Old Atrocity continued, as if he were producing.

'In the plot, Miss Wunndie runs to Prong to escape the clutches of the possessive Gen'l Worris Gappannsky, who, after a brief affair, decides she wants Wunndie full time, as she can't live without her. Wunndie escapes to the brutal side of the prison and gets involved with that bum with the 1980s glasses (Prong). Woody Harrelson's slated for the Slimik role. Sally Benson's in, as scriptor. That's a step in the right direction.'

Old Atrocity, who knew and loved his place in life and in the Industry, couldn't quite let go of another try at doing a creative deal with the world's hottest star.

'OK, OK, let's look at the premise. Let's put ourselves back in the date and time. That... that... Punky Brewster gone wild, that feisty product of mo-byle home kul-chah, that wisecracking tomboy whose favorite film is 'Twister' (WB, 1996), is *ALL OVER* the media now! Aside the sacred icon of saintly Pvt. 1st Class, Jennarefer Lunch is now placed an unbelievable portrait of this sneaky little demon gal, Miss

Wunndie, to show the good/bad, either/or, with me/against me polarization package this here homeland believes in so fervently. Even the Euro press has not mentioned (quite yet) that, just being in the lower echelons of our nation's military has the same effect of corruption as our nation's prison culture has, even on such tough li'l fighters as Miss Wunndie. There are so many scrap people in the army, that fact alone explains Miss Wunndie's stumble into bad company. Just consider my felon pal's creep brother, Pvt. Corrul Kooke, as one mega-minor example! (Mediocre kid gone more mediocre...) If she is successful in completing her mission in bringing down the Dude Who Knew in the POTUS' administration (for starters), I'm going to do everything in my power to ensure that she receives the coveted (and covert) Distinguished Star for Doing Stuff That Most Of America Thinks Is Bad But Is Really Pretty Good Award.'

Butterbugs continued to let Old Atrocity brainstorm. He was a tad sleepy, but it was good to keep up a pacific front.

'Let me put myself in the period. Like I said. That'll bring this thing *alive* more. Consider the cumulative effects. For adjustment! The Capitol Hill sequences now. In an abrupt policy change, the opposition in Congress is now in *FAVOR* of retaining Lord Sec'y in the P-gon. But, but *WHIE?* So that the Sec'y can continue to squint his way through controversy after controversy, and thus become more of a liability than he already is. On the other side of the aisle, the current mascot for Ultimate Change in the White House is, not surprisingly, Miss Wunndie, who could bring them all down. They're putting their chips on the 'trickle up' effect, in which the higher-ups pay more dearly than the bozos who actually did the torture. They *DO* hope they throw a very large book at that psycho dude with the 1980s glasses who knocked up Miss Wunndie, that sick-making Prong dude. (Er – *YOU*.) Speaking of the little muskrat, she is now at Fort Braggadocio in precious N'Cahlynah, doing 'odd jobs' like warshing walls! It's amazing how the Net is *PACKED* with Miss W. talk, song lyrics, advocates, enemies, and chatter. Resources aplenty! Essays are being written that she is the nation's dominatrix, or the end result of feminism, as well as setting fashion trends! Oh, that hog-person you thought was her mom is actually the mom of the guy who blew the whistle on the whole thing, a hog-person with a conscience. The Carraghpur fellow. They aren't talking about him very much. Yet. He may be eligible for People's Herodom, that is, if Administrations come crashing down. Can you believe what trailer trash is doing to the supposedly invincible, nuclear-armed cadre of Lord Sec'y & Co.?! It's phenomenal. Only in 'Murica! Forget 'Gays in the Military'! Now it's '*Scrap* in the Military' that will come to the fore. The whole white trash thing has presented itself as a rather unpleasantly-burst pustule on the nation's face. What the hell do you *DO* with these people if you can't vacuum them into the military dumpster?

'I confess to having kind of a soft spot for Miss Wunndie though. She may be a rat, a brat, a naughty, snotty imp of perversity, but I truly think she got mixed up with those fringe psychos runnin' wild in old Awbou 'Grave'. I think she got used by them as much as they were using the prisoners. That mop-top kid was too stupid to realize what they were doing to her. As a result, the nuclear lords of the Pentagon tremble in their shoes!'

'The majestic extravaganza continues,' said Butterbugs, rousing himself.

'Easy, Butterbugs, easy. Yes, that was my euphemism for this girl, this Wunndie Yingland (wow, what a name!). This twerp, this little wisp of a thing who, in tomboy haughtiness, is seen posing with these humiliated Iraqi prisoners, and appearing to be having a good time. I was being a bit sarcastic in referring to her as Punky-like. In her first interview Wunndie says she was ordered to pose in those pix, as it is particularly shameful for a woman to be intimidating a male in Iraqi society. Her higher-ups knew this would be an effective tool in getting prisoners to 'talk'. I think she's probably telling the truth. I also think that all of them willingly participated in the non-supervised party scene in that lurid prison. Thus, Wunndie takes on the role of porno actress: bossed around to do stuff that she wouldn't normally do, yet not objecting too much, either. And we mustn't forget about how the whole martial culture works, i.e. following orders, the clannishness, the hierarchy, etc. Also, there is another thing that isn't talked about very much. And that's the issue of scum in the military. Yeah, I'll say it again. We're getting all this propaganda about how glorious our troops are, and what perfect, selfless people they are. It is also a fact that more than a few of them are little better than criminals. Scum, scrap people who joined the military for any number of sleazy reasons. The media doesn't want you to know about them, but they come in mighty handy when you want dirty work done. As for Miss Wunndie, whom I've actually become a bit sympathetic with, as I said, I think she got mixed up with some badass types who used her like they were using the prisoners: for their own agenda. Kind of like our Sec'y of Def & Co., who use the USA in general for their own dark purposes. That's why I'm rooting for Wunndie (at least for now). She is not above reproach (she did other naughty things that have yet to come out), but if she can be instrumental in bringing Lord Sec'y and even the Murn Administration *DOWN* (it could really happen – I tell you, it *COULD!*), then she gets a gold star from me. She is actually quite a tragic figure, and when you have a war situation, you have exponential tragedy. The horror that many innocent Iraqis face every day will continue to come out in stark relief.'

Butterbugs was impressed.

'You are in the middle of it, Old Atrocity. It's obvious.'

OA, still in half-hearted aspiring-producer mold, carried on the premise a little further. He recited a few lines of dialogue he had scrawled the night before.

'So *YES*, I wanted to see this scandal go all the way to the top, so we could get on with repairing the hideous damage we have done in the world. Does this all make sense? The horrah of caurrent ivents must have rendered you speechless. It's been months since you've sent a cable. I have to admit, I was shocked myself, at the apparent 'normality' – if I can use that word – of Missy Wunndie in her first of countless interviews. Sounding like the archetypal army brat (rattling off such army-oid phrases as 'persons in my chain of command'), she sent a thinly veiled message to Lord Sec'y of Def: 'I'm gonna git yieu!'

'Hell, the Lord Sec'y got so shaken that he had to leave the country, feeling safer with his foxhole buddies in lurid Papa's Park than within the increasingly transparent walls of Fort P'gon.

'So, with all this firestorm going on, you must've retreated to the mild and soothing ocean of forgetfulness which can only be found in the Bubble Room of Your Choice. Heck! I don't blame you one bit! But let me tell you: let me know when you are ready to face the ongoing trials and tribulations, storm and schtryph, and, above all, the equivocations of our daily life and our daily bread.

'Poor Wunndie, she got screwed, not the least because, uh, you know, she grew up in, uh, a trailer, and you know the rest. That psycho bum with the glasses who knocked her up, Prong: it doesn't take too much to figure out what kind of gentle-man *HE* is.'

OA paused, almost breathless.

'Well, movie star, whadaya think??'

Butterbugs' response was polite.

'Uh-huh. OK.'

Needless to say, the picture, under Butterbugs' sponsorship, proceeded to pro-duction, post-production, and big box office and acclaim.

To shut Old Atrocity up, if nothing else.

OA declined screen story credit. Producing was way too complicated. As he had known all along in his heart, he vastly preferred nailing a temp set together. It was easily torn down and the lumber re-utilized for the next set. Tangible prob-lem-solving was for him. Something he could do with his hands…

7.

Things Get Going

In this politically-aware time zone, Butterbugs scanned not only the trades but the DC wonkette rags, too. What he found was enlightening, only because he was startled at the elaborate parallels betwixt marble capitol and tinsel capital, and it set his mind to pondering.

Where then, does power find a firm enough foundation for its interested parties to build upon and make their way upwards, toward the envy-inducing stratosphere of power-achieved, as opposed to mere power-dreamt?

He rang up a bald and overweight pandit he knew and got a kick out of, Everembulum Kasks, late of Riga's trenchant lineup of politico commentators-general of international acclaim.

'Everembulum, what is the secret of... power?'

'Ah, Butterbugs! I knew you would ask me that question sooner or later! Consider this: you have, in your ever-expanding repertoire of cinema roles, portrayed a variety of, oh, how shall I put it, 'exercisers of power', have you not?'

'I have!'

'Well then, in your – Method, or whatever the hell you'd call it these days, what with you tearing up all precedents and Greek-style labels for pigeon-holing comfort zones for all who might question your offering rather than blindly consuming them (no offense!) – well, I must say, let's take a look at the current situation at the Pentagon.'

'What situation at the Pentagon?'

'Well, I'll tell you. From that great five-sided imprint upon the New Land, nouveau aspirations rise, and rise and rise, into the mote-filled air well above commonwealth and district. Level upon level it rises. 99 further levels upward, with a pyramid effect! It shall be the highest and most armed-to-the-teeth structure in the world, not only with nukulur devices, but with crossbows, slingshots and hot tar. Molten metal, too. At the top will be a pedestal for a Guest Statue Program, whereby monumental and heroic likenesses of notable milli-terry persons will be loaded/unloaded by Black Hawk Down heelicopters and bolted into place. Current shortlist: President of the United States of America George Wokkerbush (in toga, with erection), V.I. Lenin (surplus from Communist Russia), Dr. Josep Stalin (not the Soviet dictator Iosef Vissarionovich Djugashvili, but an obscure, pipe-smoking country doctor with a bushy mustache, who traveled from gulag to gulag, performing helpful experiments on the traitors to the strong central government, in heavy, heavy Red Army overcoat and captain's hat), Pall D. Woofowitz (shriveled nude), Dohn Rumnsfield (life-size, in Botany 500), the Busch Twins (in Party-Girl Mode, doing the twist), Fat Fruddie Kaganagain (the Hero of the Surge), Kritchurd Puerile (in whimsical Darth Vader costume), and, of course, Bobbura Busch (in Sears catalogue attire). That's just the beginning. Coll Rohv will be nowhere, as he did not ever serve in the milli-terry.'

'Such, it seems, is a nation in imperial phase.'

'Aye,' Everembulum replied grimly. 'In aspic, for all to see.'

'But we look elsewhere.'

'Toward you, on the screen!'

'A worthy enterprise?'

'In comparison, most assuredly. Even without connecting the two, your efforts win by far!'

'Win! What is to be won if statues stand high, with only spare space between them and the sun?'

'They are too high up and far away.'

'Perhaps...'

Butterbugs indeed wondered if the permanence of stone and bronze was maybe more significant than persistence of vision flashings on a silver panel in a darkened room. The former were prone to environmental erosion, but the latter were subject to oblivion, if the Attention Deficit (+Hyperactive) Disorder tendencies of an intellectually challenged public were any criterion. (Butterbugs still didn't think of himself as any kind of profound influence on society – which he in fact was, inarguably.)

It was just that, after playing many roles involving characters of grandeur, he couldn't help but feel, especially knowing the grandiosity of the powers now in play back East, what was it *like?* How did it *feel?* To be one of them, that is.

Subjects for further thought. In the course of character development, of course.

Despite images of inanimate matter being raised to pinnacles of power, was it not possible to perchance raise a hollowing nation to a higher pilaster through example, via art?

In the meantime, each moment of his consciousness was summarily devoted to motion picture contemplation and execution. Butterbugs was the ideal student, absorbing as much as he secreted, the symbiotic action resembling one hand washing the other, with mutual service and advancement of cause.

In a way, it was almost as if one hand were clapping, while the other was cupping an ear to hear it.

To be sure, there were leisure hours to be had, but most were dedicated to cinematic experience and expansion. The Æyrie was the ideal hermitage for concentration, for in the Populuxe lines of its uncluttered confines, with expansion out onto the LA matrix from this height, the freedom to learn and the desire to engulf – in cinema – held elaborate and total sway. Those were privileged hours, alone up there. Many a Main Title and Entr'acte could be heard emanating from the Projector Screening Hall (named in Sonny's honor) on the Second Cantilever Level, aft the Butterfly Room wing.

Sex partners were generally absent from these premises. No distractions, please! And all who were involved and cared about the star's needs naturally abided by these liberal rules. Those who mattered kept to the peripheries, prepping beverages and snacks, but were always ready for a review when the actor emerged from his chosen session.

'Butterbugs, you have *seen God!*' proclaimed his dear lover-friend Kang Kevereschu after they both crawled out of the Projector after a viewing of 'Bad Day At Black Rock' (MGM, 1955).

'Nay!' he told her, 'I have seen Spence Tracy!'

The next week, after he'd spent the evening on 'Hot Summer Night' (MGM, 1957), Kang was tempted to parrot her own remark of before, so as to make a happy tradition out of his revelatory movie-going. She needn't have said anything.

'I have seen Edward Andrews!' was all he said, and all he needed to say.

In spite of the technical perfection of BKV's alternative capture-stock, Zuk-Plate, with its better-than-real presentation of motion pictures of every kind, and in every width and format, Butterbugs often preferred battered prints from the Golden and Silver Ages (as opposed to the Butterbugs-led Vanadium Age, as aficionados labeled the contemporary production scene).

After viewing a lined, faded, and aperture-wandering print of 'Dragon Seed' (MGM, 1944), he came out into the electric-blue sunset from his privacy in the Projector room, solo, weeping almost uncontrollably. And he was indescribably happy.

With another viewing of the same Jack Conway/Harold S. Bucquet production, via the latest ZukPlate edition, all the picture's sentiments were intact, and in some ways enhanced. Sid Wagner's cinematography, for one, was stunning. But the resulting emotions were more out of respect and observance of technique, as if Butterbugs were in the picture himself, and so had the contextual view. It was akin to the empathy he well knew with the cast and crew, rather than with the characters and the audience's consumption of them. The experience was thus not quite perfect. The charm was diminished. In this and like instances, the old and hackneyed comparison of 'cold' CD sound, as opposed to 'warm' vinyl sound, despite pings and pops, still stubbornly lingered.

Therefore, on some of his subsequent pictures, Butterbugs and his production team custom-made certain effects of wear and tear, but only if the tenor of the film required it.

Audience response was generally enthusiastic, largely based on lobby overhearings, such as:

'That picture really looked beat-up. Ripped into me. A rough ride. But, it made me feel like I was actually part of it…' etc.

Porter Parker was most cooperative and intrigued with these techniques of subliminal filmmaking, which he dubbed 'Butterbugs' Dragon Seeding'.

Well, in any case, Butterbugs studied and studied many a picture show on a permanent ongoing basis. It was a question of personal preference, and he made the most of it, confining his study sessions to what he knew and what he liked, and the proper way to do it was, to him, in the darkened room.

8.

The Very Thrill Of It All

The next week, Butterbugs had to depart for Socotra, to enact the lead role in 'Blaze of the Summer Islands' (Selznick) a huge pirate picture set in the Indian Ocean of the early 1800s.

It was an ecstatic proposition, a dizzying prospect, a rapturous project.

'We will set sail,' he proclaimed to those who loved him, upon departing his vine-clad canyon. 'Until the sky grows dark in the east, and all we can expect is for the west to carry us through the long night!'

Justy looked at Saskia.

'He is in need of an epic.'

'And I have done so. I have given him his 'Blaze',' Saskia said in matching epic tones.

'To work, whereby to live.'

'Oh yes, but in need of *living* it, not just posing within it.'

'You speak the truth. I hope he can find it, anon.'

'I will write now, lover.'

'For him?'

'Always. For him.'

'Our love.'

'Our inclusive love, yes.'

'Saskia, do you think, those who see his pictures –'

'Everyone?'

'Everyone, yes. Do you think, that they know of *our* love. We three?'

Saskia watched Butterbugs' motorcar convey him into the gathering dusk and wondered the same thing herself.

'If they do, it is because he is true to us. In his craft, in my words, in your anchoring support, the thing intangible becomes what it needs to be in every viewer's heart. In that way, the word spreads, and the truth is known.'

Both also wondered though, every time they saw him off, if each time might be the time when he wasn't coming back. So perfect was the triangulation of their love, that any built-in anxieties were routinely given their token air-time as a courtesy, then wisely abandoned in the name of common sense, not to mention the privilege of joy.

In the dissolve of time and distance, Butterbugs stepped into action on that far island place and in out-of-sequence understanding, built his character from a growing need to transcend even further than what he had achieved so far. Pushing the limits of his finite turf of familiarity and capability, he adopted an almost greedy ethic in gaining more territory from which to work, as the work-space for the acting of leadership required certain vastness, by which freedom of expression might be drawn in terms large enough – or small enough – to accomplish the task.

His very ethnicity in the role was a challenge: part Bulgarian, part Rohingya, part Omani. Therefore, the actor had to master each corresponding language in order to facilitate the patois concocted by Saskia and her associate, the esteemed polymath, Aman Mascera.

'Truly, one of my most *international* pictures,' the star enthused to the press.

And truly, one of his most *problem-prone* pictures.

Drave Appleyard was the line producer. He had a reputation for iron-handed control, but here on Socotra, his stamina was breaking down. It happened at a point when the cameras hadn't even started to roll yet.

The heavy Technirama units were on a barge off the boiling isle of Perim, bound for customs in Aden, which would take a minimum of two weeks.

The star's death scene, where he is nailed to a Dragon's Blood tree, would have to be shot quickly (only one week was skedded), as the actual close-ups showing the nails entering the tree (after passing through Butterbugs' hands) could only be secured in one take, period. This was because the ichor of the tree flowed out in the most luridly splendid display of bright, red, bulging, pulsing ooze. It was an opportunity not to be missed.

The director was Stigh Chuk, the brilliant auteur from Kyzl, Tannu Tuva, who, born in a Stalinist gulag, had swept streets in the deadly-dull district town of Svyettchetsniahkash in the Lena River basin of forgotten Siberia. Harsh instruc-tion in the Vidmukh Better School. Long winters in Boshmush. Temporary jobs as an itinerant 9.5mm film developer, with his lab in a covered ox wagon. This orientation led to producer Sidney Balderdasch picking him above such action stalwarts as Henry Hathaway, Tim Burton, Joel Schumacher (gawd, he would have been an *awful* choice!), and Drina Comm-Post.

The final chase sequence, a fugal masterpiece that was projected to run 75 minutes, would be scored by the incomparable Dimitri Tiomkin.

'Dear Timmy,' Balderdasch wrote to Tiomkin, 'Please make this score pretty interesting.'

As far as lensing was concerned, there was talk that the huge Super Technirama 70 cameras might be a little heavy on this shoot, but Chuk was determined. Bob Surtees, thankfully lensing, could only sigh:

'Whatever the kid wants.'

Conditions on the island could be rather nightmarish. The pre-production crew were already in situ and suffering accordingly. Huge, sticky, yellow webs spun by hog-spiders would be found covering the sets and equipment every morning. The waste from the Ning beetle was everywhere, even in the freezer units. Temperatures rose to 51°C by 10:00AM, and humidity exhaustion, prickly heat, damp-staining, and even a couple of cases of cholera were reported, though thankfully made non-fatal due to prompt evacuation to the eminent curative facility at Conjeeveram.

Strangeness was everywhere, from the balaustine pollen of the pomegranate trees to the antics of the upward-tending sewerage worm, a colony of which spread out in the canteen like jars of smashed sweet-pickle relish. At the maximum heat-hour (generally 2:09 to 3:17PM), the boles of the cucumber tree tended to explode from built-up boilage pressure. After a couple of incidents, in which viscous gwamm-juice from within splattered all over the Super-T camera and bathed several extras, shooting was strategically planned away from these stands and groves, especially at that specific hour. The splatter was basically harmless, but thick and oily and quite warm to the touch. A significant glob landed on Butterbugs' nose.

'Hey! Tastes like broasted pumpkin!' he cackled. 'Cookie? Git yer kettles and ladles and gravy-boats! We'll dine on hot tree sap this night!' Then he burst into the old song: 'Oh-del Ladle! OOOOOH'd'l-Ladle!!'

The many who came here were busy viewing these and other spectacles with minds blown. Or else they were locked into a sort of rhapsody, Butterbugs-guided. Because they were in this place at this time, and what an exception it was to the lives they'd always led.

A kind of enchantment, really.

The old British haven of Port Gribbsy was headquarters for much of the Socotra shoot. Just down the coast from Cape Sombre, and in from the Secluded Bight, it was a virtual Yorkshirish scene, here on the torrid rocks of the northwest coast. As if the Brits of the 1820s had intended to create a virtual Whitby, but after about 1/64th of the project was built, the absurdity and the heat took over. Nevertheless, there were proper moles and a pukka lighthouse. Opium godowns stood (empty) next to ornamental ghats, and a heat-damaged, Doric-columned Customs House, where every room had a coal-grated fireplace, under a roof rated to withstand five feet of snow. These were still the centerpieces of the tiny Harbour. There were even old abbey ruins up on a bluff. In their haunted shadows lurked many a degraded grave of those who had no choice but to stay on. Among the living were a handful of stubborn expats from the pre-1967 colonial era, colorful, but a bit loony.

Production designer Wilfred Shingleton and his crew got right to work on the woebegone locale, which had only one operating emporium, and a lone beadle. Plus, the dusty remains of a hand-cranked picture show. But after the privations of Ghubbah and Howlef up the coast, 'Old Gribbs', as it was affectionately called, seemed like Bombay or Karachi in comparison.

'As picturesque as a faded aquatint by Edward Lear, I should think,' observed Butterbugs to Leo McKern, who was playing Kid Brogoworth, an extortionist merchant in the port.

'A vase of dry faded stock, plonked with ullage, on a wan window ledge, high up the wall in a shut-up house,' Leo mused.

'Quite a contrast to this sun-blasted cove, away from the world.'

'Nevertheless, that's what it reminds me of, my boy.'

'It's quite remarkable, Leo. A place like this, way out here! It was either a noble attempt at reproducing familiarity for the benefit of a foreign race, or a scheme of mad hats and sugar-mice!' He scanned the scorched remnants with a glass.

Leo knew of Lear the painter of course, but thought the scene needed a bit of... drollery.

'Lear, you say! How about this:

> There was an old tar from Socotra
> Who hopped from boat-tra to boat-tra.
> Quaffing dragon-tree blood by day,
> And cucumber-tree porridge at night,
> What a wasted old burnout from Socotra!'

'Hey, that's pretty good!' Butterbugs exclaimed. 'Did Lear *really* write that?' Leo winked his glass eye.

The consumption of beer was staggering. Busted brew bottles littered the jetties and bunds. Producer Appleyard had to send for mega-shipments from Zanzibar. When those were exhausted, a relief ship arrived from far-off Moçambique, bearing a product of strange Portuguese-ish hop-fluid that gave everyone midnight hallucinations.

'Oh, but isn't it glorious?' howled Butterbugs, boiled out of his mind on Nova Mambone slime-suds, as he appeared out of the darkness of a side-alley.

And those who were uncertain about their own current boil-outs were suddenly transformed into thinking:

'This is frightful, awful, and dubiously threatening, but – could it not *also be* glorious?'

'It could!' came the usual reply.

'It *is!*' came the usual conclusion.

When the cast and the rest of the crew arrived in Qadub, the pathetic but pictorially perfect location for certain scenes on shore, after a sizzling sea journey down the Red Sea from Suez, they felt they were landing on another planet.

An angry, red planet.

'Reminds me of the plains on the southern hemisphere of Mercury,' quipped Sir Ernesto Rollicksworth, the stalwart West Ender, who was to play a corrupt port official. 'The Searing Coast nearby does a tremendous summer season, with excellent dance bands...'

His rival at the National Theatre, Sir Mucius Snade-Grain, arrived a day later, in a brown study, and without any wit at all. He was there to get his role over with as soon as possible, but his scenes required him to stay for the duration. He was playing a sort of Prester John character – a mad vicar actually, who tries to keep the local dried-up church alive, with its sparse graveyard of past parishioners (the blank plots become obsessions to him). His big moment comes with a chaotic fight in the church's belfry (which was a-building in Old Gribbs, by coolies brought from Zanzibar). He plummets to his doom, naturally.

The same sort of trepidation-cum-emphaticness went for Mimsy Farmer, Emmanuel Lewis, Reynolds Kenwick, and old pal Art Linkletter (now quite frail, but cheerful), who were to play key roles in this ultra-important picture.

For a time, the set in Old Gribbs became a sort of chic port of call for the beautiful people – a dangerous holiday or long weekend – in which to make the scene. Lord Carl-Pepperbibs Mathews was there with the Duke and Duchess of Kent, among scads of others.

Even the Queen stopped by, as this was a former British possession. A perfect pro in remote ex-Empire exploration, her digs were a tree house in the vermin-free Kwuk-stalk, slightly cooled by the old Hindoo tank hard by. Tea was rushed in from Aden, and all was well. Even Boofy and Gregarowink, two of her Corgi patrol, had the time of their lives.

Then the Italians came, with their designer X-ray specs, and the Côte de Azur set, and it all became rather a circus of the pretty and the prissy, the macho and the mean.

Norman Mailer, upon landing at Meean Meer jetty, shook his two sticks and squawked:

'What the hell is this, Ibiza?' before settling into the wild scene at the Crisparkle Hotel (under Armenian management), the headquarters of the literary crowd.

It was a shuttered-window/lazy-punkah/G+T sort of place, while across the road was Tinker's, the happenin' disco scene, where Young People and New People hung out till the rancid dawn, when crippled pie-dogs with mushroom-mange reclaimed the blighted streets as their own.

Mailer slugged Brando (in for his cameo as Governor Catbrain-Quarrey) smack-dab in the gut after their rather animated discussion about Tahitian broads ended up in a fistfight. Brando was on the ground, muttering something about 'the horrah', but they soon made up and were seen hanging out at the bar at Tibbs Point (named for an obscure British collector who plunged off the nearby Snake Fang Parapet in 1842), talking about old times. They even managed to cajole director Chuk into bringing Norman into the picture. Brando mumbled his way through his antagonistic Governor bit, and Mailer played Collector Tibbs himself, who pens a woeful final soliloquy on the way to the waves below. Everyone who saw the rushes knew in their hearts that it was one of Brando's finest performances, and Mailer's best dialogue since 'Of A Fire On The Moon'.

And what, oh what, of Butterbugs?

This particular picture was a mighty revelation to him, not only because of the tale's epicness, its pages and pages of complex text to memorize, the hazardous swashbuckling, and the dizzying publicity playing the very lead, but because of a hidden mandate.

Early on, Drave Appleyard had collapsed from the stress, the beverage intake, and the hashish usage. He implored Butterbugs to take over chores as producer. Butterbugs accepted the challenge, on the condition that it be kept as secret as possible, and that Appleyard would still get sole producer credit. Three times did Butterbugs refuse any sort of screen credit for the elephantine tasks he took on, and at last Appleyard had to give up imploring. He was rendered speechless for a whole day (an utterly unheard-of occurrence), because of the majesty and nobility of the young, bright-shining star.

By the time the picture pulled up stakes and moved on to locations in the Nicobar Islands and the Mergui Archipelago off Burmah, the circus came to a halt, the sets came down, and Socotra's brief starring moment had passed.

Butterbugs was oddly abbreviated after it was all over. His sole comment: 'A tough shoot!'

9.

What The Lights of LA Spell

It all started with Bea Lillie.

She said to Chaplin, one summer's night when silence was golden, above the fray, way up in the H'wood Hills, with the jacaranda blooming, while it was lilac time way back in Missouri:

'Charlie,' she said softly, 'If the lights down there could spell out names, they'd read... 'Douglas Fairbanks'.'

There is no record as to how far the Little Tramp's crest fell. The artists were supposed to be united in their cause.

However, such were the days of united artistic egos, however justified.

But in the Hollywood of Century 21, there was little of the innocence of scented romance left.

Instead, a message had to be sent from the plains, some sort of sign. It was because, for some time now, a longing had been building in the minds of photo-play audiences everywhere. Not just in the Id of LA, but everywhere.

It was an excitement, really. The sort of anxiousness that something especially good was surely impending, only no one seemed to know what the dynamics or the proportions of this amorphous something might be.

Not surprisingly, this visceral, cinematic mood concerned Butterbugs. Or rather, he was uncertain how he should be received, now that –

Now that – what?

There is nothing *official* about being a star. Where was it written that any sort of 'Rule of Law' applied? Nevertheless, a public wants its stars as people you can rely on. 'Official' meant governmental or institutional. A better adjective for stars might be 'consummate', or 'fixed', as in the heavens (or 'falling' – long a gloater's fave). In any case, there was always a public demand for sureness, and closure was desirable, in order to set that sureness in concrete, as it were.

Not only Sid Grauman and those kids in Reepsville required it, every mov-ie-going person from Hollywood to Curitiba to Taze (Burma) to Cape Agulhas to Hermannstadt and back to Hollywood required it. It was as if a communal child was asking the providing powers above:

'Are you my mama? Or not?'

So, approaching the inevitable question, straight on:

Was Butterbugs an *ultrastar* now?

Some discussion is perhaps necessary here and now, for the benefit of towns-men, householders, and other assorted burghers who perhaps do not place the Seventh Art in so august a position in their lives (unlike 98% of the world's consta-burgeoning populations), in order to expound on the ultrastar theme a bit.

In Linnæan taxonomy, everything, assuredly, has its place. In Maslow's hier-archy, ditto, though in a more subjective, even existential context. In the Industry, informality is intrinsic to its comfort zone, but box office simplicity has cre-ated its own mandate, going back to the Nickelodeon Era. That is, B.O. rules. Whatever entity that brings coin into B.O. gets to wear the Emperor's clothes for at least a day, so as to appear, at the very least, to rule. If identifiable names are responsible for B.O.-filling, all the better. Wasn't it a desperate PR department at General Motors (and not a Hollywood studio) who came up with the brilliant catchphrase, 'Stick With The Names You *Know*'?

Thus, the pertinent corollary: actor, nobody, wannabe, starlet, starling, co-star, star, superstar, megastar… and… *ultra*star.

Well, maybe. Nobody had ever been an ultrastar before.

Nobody, not no how.

The thing was, Butterbugs assuredly merited big B.O. But that was only the starting point. Nothing so banal could define him. As everyone knew, he was much more than that. For some time now, in the urge to classify him, all manner of methods had been applied, in the hopes of explaining the eponymous Phenomenon. Cult of personality, sex appeal, talent, photogenics, vibes, roles, likability, worshipfulness, contributing talent behind the camera, agent connec-tions, and on and on. There had to be a *reason*.

However, each one of these prosaic threads led into a box canyon – not office – when some assemblage of a skein was attempted. That is, the Industry wanted a formula. Like an $E=mc^2$ (that highest of high concepts), so it could be replicated, adapted, cloned, exploited, and distributed to potential properties, like groundnut pretzels or lover mints.

No one in Hollywood ever gambled on a one-of-a-kind property for long. Unless it was, well, a property worthy of – ultrastardom. Whatever that was. This happened to be ultra-undiscovered country. Too impossible, too Utopian, too deistic, too good to be true. Unless – unless one person was achieving it, even as they quaffed their designer drinks at Mlellen's or Ma Maison.

Mega-agent (or would he be considered an *ultra*-agent now?) Sonny Projector would always protect his client from these sort of cheap and greedy notions, but the fact remained, because every indication and truth pointed toward a universal acknowledgment of Butterbugs' extraordinariness, why not, with characteristic showbiz aplomb, just get on with it and give him the popular label? It was just what the public wanted, and what the public should get, closure in the declaration of a fact. Butterbugs was an ultrastar now, dammit.

Butterbugs *is* an ultrastar.

Transition labels like 'superstar' and 'megastar' were never really brought to bear in this case, as if the public knew their validity simply wouldn't apply for very long.

Ultrastardom was... forever...

So was it written. So was it done.

Life goes on.

It didn't even particularly matter that no one, really, knew exactly what an ultrastar *was*, but as the term continued to evolve into its own, perhaps the following minor example could give an indication of its just intentions.

Ultrastardom might have come under controversy regarding its definitions, its responsibilities, its seriousness.

Maybe, but efforts were afoot by those who were in the front lines of longing for an outcome. During the season in LA before Hiatus (when film production cools it for a spell), citizens and city and utility workers drew together into one vast community of service, the result being a spectacular, unprecedented feat.

It was a brilliant idea for a brilliant season. It wasn't that another mere monarch of Hollywood would be crowned. It was rather more like a new galaxy, or something even bigger, had been discovered. But it wasn't one positioned 73 grillion inconvenient light years away. It was here, now, and as close as your nearest picture show, to explore.

So, the idea having been born in the miraculous mind of Old Atrocity, and casually spread to his Chief Electrician pals, who broached it with their City Light and Greater LA County Utilities pole gangs and switch-throwers, a cogent team of pros set to work.

They were able to rig up a grid of organized chiaroscuro, in which civic and commercial interests were joined, whose purposes were to provide public and private lighting, whether for street or sign or kitchen, that every day spent the power produced at the Southland's diverse plants or propellers.

There was only one way to describe it: on terra firma, from the Observatory terrace in Griffith Park, or any residence, from The Æyrie to Jimmy Cagney's hunting lodge near the Hollywoodland sign, public and private lighting within a specific configuration was rigged so that for a single sixty minutes, it spelt BUTTERBUGS.

From the high balcony of Mulholland's palazzi, or a hot balloon basket, or passing zeppelin's window, there were the letters, in elementary progression, perfect for a first-grader learning to spell. Failing those sites, this major event could actually be discerned from Tranquility Base. If Richard Nixon's signature, plastered on a plaque commemorating the touchdown in '69, cannot be easily detected from our native planet, then, well, any 'naut standing at said plaque on the moon at this prime moment could actually, without the aid of optic enhancement, make out UTTRUGS – no, wait a minute, BUTTERBUGS – the strolling player! As surely as a 'Toilet Occupied' sign can be seen from the rear seat in a jetliner!

The procedure to pull off this up-in-lights gambit was extremely involved, and could only be accomplished not only by a team of massed computers, but through skillful manipulation of century-old Cutler-Hammer fuse blocks of hard rubber and copper.

So it glowed, filling in the space 'twixt mountains and seaboard, for one grand hour. And in the shadows beyond the borders of that illuminated Roman script, all dubious activity ceased, as if any crime or illegal gesture was at once un-empowered. As if they in those zones knew, in their anonymity, that they were, for one mere hour, part of something exceptional. As if they were tied, by the narrowest of capillaries, to the magic of Butterbugsian energies, of Butterbugsian roles, of Butterbugsian integrity, to the Butterbugs Phenomenon itself, which seemed to give pause for a revaluation of all values.

Butterbugs himself, with characteristic modesty, was out on location, this time in the central Irtysh River basin, shooting 'Siberian Song of the Forests' for 20th-Fox, to be followed by 'Evenings on a Farm Near Dikanka' (also 20th-Fox).

He saw it all on the tube via satellite, and was strangely and silently gratified, though he did murmur 'Well I'll be daahned', in the manner of Elia Kazan, or even John Randolph in 'Little Murders' (20th-Fox, 1971).

But then it was back to work. Way back in his mind, though, a bulb went on…

Resolved: an ultrastar is something more than a megastar, which is something more than a superstar, which is something more than a star, which is something more than a co-star, which is something more than a starlet, which is something more than a wannabe, which is something more than a nobody from out of town who lived an inordinately long time in a DeSoto wagon while becoming increasingly alienated from the realities of the world, be they ever so harsh and heartless.

But this is showbiz.

Can you tap dance?

10.

Of Pomp And Higher Pomp

Wieriold-Tim Macanda, eminent helmer of erudite, dignified, elegant and tasteful spectacles, not to mention chamber pieces and historical dramas of all sizes, directed Butterbugs in 'Known Knowns And Known Unknowns' (RKO).

It was a full-blown tragic story which charted the scandals, corruption and fall of the power cabal that surrounded and included a US president, and solidly based on fact. But what was most important was that it was a darn good story. Every detail had to be attended-to if this thing was going to fly high above the darling-of-the-critics curse, Butterbugs-as-star or no Butterbugs-as-star.

Naturally, Butterbugs had the plum role as Sec'y of Defense, but it was one of his most challenging parts, ever. He couldn't quite get past the fact that he was playing in an aggressively-true drama of recent vintage, still throbbing with controversy. Its real-life players were still excruciatingly active in suits both civil and criminal, and there was no getting around the fact that, because it was recent-recent history, the burden of authenticity was naturally... pronounced.

Here was melodrama on such a scale as to propose satire. Woven with blatant banality in its real life characters, and a high-toned building of climaxes that involved forced resignations resulting in murder-suicide pacts, stoning by mobs, humiliation brought by an avenging public, and the crowning ugh-drama of the leading character taking a swan dive from the upper gallery of the US Capitol, every instinct was against this picture coming off as the tart, articulate and profound drama that it became.

But Macanda! The actor's dream! He had led Butterbugs around the brick-pits of temptation, avoiding any documentary or mockumentary tendencies that a less than idyllic script (by Norman Corwin, Zoë Akins, Frances Marion and Ben Hecht, no less!) carried within it. But because of Bbs' perf, all bathos was avoided and a dimensional, original interpretation of his role had emerged, due to the brain-numbing interplay between star and director, that led toward this monumental work.

Ultra-high suspense.

The director, an orthodox Jew, was himself *beyond* dramatic. Every one of his gestures was larger than life, yet he was completely credible and respected. Not a caricature, but some of his behavioral aspects might easily be parodied.

'I am an original,' was all Wieriold-Tim Macanda could say to his critics.

Butterbugs was in on the scoring, because Macanda wanted him to give the composer, Ilya Vuzzhukhevkhovskiy, freshly arrived from Russia, his input. Butterbugs spent several sessions with him, just talking about his role. It was remarkable chemistry, and Ilya Ilyich emerged inspired, and wrote the score in a white heat.

There was no mention of the star's associations with Ovchinnikov, Tiomkin, Yevtushenko, or Shostakovich. No need to cloud this sensitive composer's receptors. As a result, Butterbugs was sure that his rapport made the score clear of influence, which is what the director wanted. Despite his own thoughts on Russian film composers and poets, there was nothing more important than complying with whatever the director of the moment desired.

Today, all were in the preview room to look at the finale sequence, just scored. It was lengthy, but all were riveted, and it was a full house, as the director wanted everyone there, so to be in on the actual making of the sequence. The experience was so powerful that the director, who had not seen it before in this form, and who had crafted the film itself, was writhing on the floor.

Horrified, Butterbugs thought he had collapsed in a falling-sickness attack. He approached his respected director.

'I am here, chief!'

'Leave me be!'

Butterbugs took up the burden. Anything to save him from disaster, or the gurney.

'Wieriold-Tim, I can alter my performance –'

'Leave me be, I tell you! I – I am in – ecstasy!'

Fortunately, Ilya Ilyich's Exit Music had been wisely attached to the work print by Don the Miracle Projectionist, so the director's pronouncements were, as Butterbugs regarded him on the floor, perfectly and powerfully scored. The effect certainly worked on the actor.

The houselights came up. All were stunned. And when the arc light unit in the projector was turned off (its faint familiar buzzing was beloved by veterans of the long dark hours in this chamber by the gang who made movies on this lot), there was nothing left but a blank screen and complete stillness and silence all around.

Then, on the side aisle, a hand rose from the floor, and grasped at the armrest. There was a slight communal rustle, and just a bit of excruciating leather jacket scrape-creaking, as everyone turned towards this Lazarushian gesture.

Macanda rose up, as if from pre-death, shaking, gasping, pushing, as he advanced upward, against the wall, so that the heavy acoustic drape encased him in a robe-like configuration, which, with the exposed fireproof mesh behind, gave an interesting textured background to this instantly iconic image, though his orthodox kit was understated.

He stared at the ceiling, still gasping, as if searching at noon for a lantern to light.

'Where is Ilya?' he managed to call out.

'Ilya Ilyich is over here!' the composer sounded off. Cossack-Blurryap that he

110

was, fearless, brilliant, and always willing to be poignant, despite the turbo-diesel passion of his score.

'Come to me! Orpheus of the Orthochromes! Minstrel above Meistersingers! My mate in creation!'

Ilya approached the icon.

'Respected Jew!' Ilya started. 'Or, let me rephrase that: Respected fellow Abrahamic follower of similar but different ways! Tell me!'

'Associate! Though my forebears were from beyond the Pale, like you, there is nothing else to say...'

Macanda went flat. It was as if it was all over for him.

Butterbugs felt helpless, though he noted the thick curtain, drawn about his face in Tiepolo-approved under-lit chiaroscuro, made even the director's Woody Allen glasses resemble what the Doge was probably wearing this season. Everything added up to an especially arresting visual ensemble. Total cinema, to be lived as well as worked.

And so was the dialogue, despite the fact that it was a little corny. Wieriold-Tim was a better director than he was an actor. By a long shot.

Yet, while it might have been because the audience of professional picture people were still being transfixed by the sequence they had just seen on the preview screen, and credit must be given them for knowing that Butterbugs himself was in the room (and thus, some of his incandescence might shower down as an influence on the creative persons thereabouts), Macanda nevertheless made a deep impact on them. Because, each one asked themselves, what was the significance of all this?

Suddenly a Macanda cry shattered the dense air.

'Ilya!'

'My God, he's dying!' whispered an associate art director to a Foley technician.

More silence, with a better build-up than Garbo got in her 'Camille' (MGM, 1936) death scene.

'Ilya!' came the cry again.

Pause, to much effect.

Then:

'Your score! PERFECTION!!'

And with the unbearable tension now relieved, the entire company let out a joined exhaust-sigh, immediately followed by deafening cheers.

Then Macanda, effortlessly risen, dragged the composer to the front of the house, and waxed Charles Foster Kane-ish under the direct overhead lighting, with a big hand extended toward his musician.

'I just can't imagine...' The roar died down. 'You know, *imagine* – a better score!!'

The roar returned, solid confirmation that the concept this important director had for his picture had been borne out.

'This – this – this – *Russian*, this Cossack from the steppes! He has done it!

He has, with the audial method, drawn out the soul of my picture into an emblem as golden as my mother's first wedding ring! As wonderstruck as a canter's first cry of Kaddish! I weep! Weep for the glory! And I hired him! I can't – I just can't tell of the joy, right now!'

Then he really started bawling, and didn't let up.

To Butterbugs, this 'show' was entirely justified, be it an artistic license concoction, or a mere act of blow-off-steam thiertre. He felt, for more than just a moment, that he had been part of an incredible achievement, that this picture was part of the wider purpose for which not only he, but multitudes of others exercising their talent and their wit, their sweat and their sincerity, had been placed upon this earth to do. He could not quite fully appreciate though, how gratified he felt in being reduced to a 'mere' associate, or rather, a participant, in this whole production. That others could be elevated to the rarified platform upon which the lime-most of lights shone was nothing short of a deeply-defined comfort to him. It was one reason why he held Macanda so highly. Plus, he was a mucking fine director, who, Christ-like (despite his religious convictions), bore all the sins and conventions of his troupe, and with good cheer.

The assembled cheers and huzzahs were so reverberative from the enthusiastic audience that those who passed in the busy thoroughfares just outside were given pause to startle and then share in the wonder at what must be taking place inside. The general sense indicated something wonderful had indeed transpired. Those who ascribed this phenomenon to the fact that they indeed knew Butterbugs was on the lot this day were in for a treat. There were undoubtedly other exceptional incandescents who strode this earth and contributed their efforts to that which they themselves aspired to. But here was one they knew to be bona fide and present. Truly, a marvelous realization. Perhaps one was spreading the light to others, and in turn, they to yet others.

The audience filed out. For ultimo exit music, Don the Miracle Projectionist put on something entirely different: 'Spring Morning' by Frederick Delius, a tone poem of poignant hope, and by the time they reached the soundstage alley outside, most of them were sniffling and daubing the corners of their eyes.

Leo Tover, co-lenser, cleared his throat as he watched his fellow audience members react to their memories of the picture just ended. He leaned toward Malcolm Bert, who'd designed the production.

'L.B. Mayer told me once that a picture that makes people bawl is head and shoulders ahead in any horserace it's running in.'

Mal didn't need to do his own reccy for a second longer.

'Proof positive today, old fellow. Photo finish not needed. The proof is in the tears!'

He then reached for an already damp tissue, to absorb his own renewed flow.

'Do you see a messiah on the horizon, ever?' asked Butterbugs when both he and Macanda were enjoying a kosher ruby wine, several days later.

Macanda was calm, circumspect.

'Listen! I used to think it was *me*. Really, I did. What, I ask you, would you think of it, if you had such a burden cast upon you?'

'What sort of burden?' Butterbugs expected to hear about some kind of occult tragic condition as a lead-in to –.

'To get to the mailbox and back in one piece!' Wieriold-Tim spread his palms out wide. 'Life, baby, *life!* God's curse on those he supposedly chose – er – loves.'

Butterbugs suppressed a chuckle.

'Now, my fine acting – I mean – actor friend, after these long triumphs in Hollywood, I think I shall dare to take a thought from my dear associates, the Sufis. Could it be that, such a being, a *messiah*, as it were – you know, the one we're always promised – is closer to us, right now, than the vein in our neck? (God, I hate blood and thinking about arteries!) But I don't know anymore. If it's not particularly *that* close, it could still be in the general neighborhood. But I swear, the tide is rising.'

11.

I, Butterbugs, Ultrastar

The Proclamation had been made across the face of the world: Butterbugs was now an ultrastar.

You mean you hadn't heard? Where you *been?*

Some elements of the public still had to be educated. Not in Bangladesh, or Japan, or most of the world, in fact, as culture and education provided the bulwark of background for the ability to recognize human remarkableness without too much explanation. But there were blocks in the US union (even though that particular entity must and shall be preserved), that failed to really grasp the common sense of the Butterbugs Phenomenon. It is unnecessary to declare the geographic locations of these blocks, but suffice it to say, they were chronically known to be deficient in the judgment of progressive movements everywhere. No slam, just fact.

So, once more: in the hierarchy of stardom, which was nowhere inscribed but everywhere understood, one could ascend from anonymity to starletdom, thence to stardom, perhaps to superstardom, but rarely to megastardom. Of course this staircase applied only to true stars, and not Whits, who had their own path upwards – a servant's staircase, as it were. The Whit of Whits, Bissell himself, occupied, as all knew, his own special niche. So did Benin's own galaxy of stars for that matter, and those in the Bollywood universe as well, naturally. Amitabh? Well, let's just call him a *magna*star. His own category. Namaste, Amitabh.

But *ultra*stardom? They say that Gable could have achieved it, or Elvis, or Liz. Or Piaf. Johnny Hallyday? Maybe. Dimple? Could be. James Wainwright thought he might get there. To many, Toshiro Mifune achieved something even higher. Rosemary Forsyth aspired to it, as did countless others, including Samm-Art Williams. But *ultra*stardom?

Watch Butterbugs. His pictures, that is. End of questioning.

The message eventually got through, and because of that, cultural progress was made in these previously 'unaware' blocks of territory.

There came a time when the formalization of fame came calling, in the guise of a cute dress-for-success redhead named Jilleeun Gold-Coast. A quick-read hardback-straight-to-paperback biography (or as Orson Welles called it, 'bee-ography') was now required for the public's comfort-food consumption. Jilleeun was

114

'Now', and 'A-Go-Go', and pretty cool. Her style was tart, a tad sassy, and she would happily border on the hagiographic, if necessary.

To Gellenstart/Pworer, the corporation that owned massive Jimmy House Publishers, it was necessary. Jilleeun's brother, Brunyun McPheeters, was studio head of Oxidized/Onion Pictures (bankrolled by G/P Inc.), and he, linking with white-water rafting partner Sonny Projector, got his sis the bee-ography gig.

Could Oxidized/Onion have a biopic property in mind? Assuredly.

Sonny P. had allowed Oxidized/Onion exclusive motion picture rights to the life of his client. Mega|Goth and 20th – the only other contenders – were squeezed out, sans even a bidding war. The matter was not open to negotiation. DFZ and Hyman Goth were *NOT PLEASED*.

O/O was a comparatively new kid in town, started by they who came out of the Irving Thalberg Building one summer night in great tribulation, similar to the UA exodus to the promised but finite land of Orion Pictures.

The only other contractual requirement for a Butterbugs biopic was that it be shot in Ultra Panavision 70, the ultrastar's favorite widescreen process, which the term 'ultra' had nothing to do with. And that meant one thing: Bob Surtees, the Dean of Ultra-P-vision 70, would be the lenser. Fine, fine. Few but Butterbugs and the high-echelon production team cared, anyway. But the thing was, all the viewing public *would* care if things weren't done 'just so', and Bob was one of the many who knew how to pull that shit off.

But first, the bee-ography. Upon instructions from Sonny, Butterbugs agreed to take three weeks off during summer Hiatus to be interviewed by Jilleeun. The actor was amenable to the project, as long as it remained truthful and that every page was not devoted to him. He wanted to concentrate more on the issues that interested him, and the passion he had for just causes.

'Oh, you can be coy,' he teased her. 'Just make it worth laughing about.'

Jilleeun laughed herself, in reply.

They met in the sleek and somewhat neutral security of Butterbugs' agency pent-bungalow, up amongst the sheltering palms, bamboo, and mushweed.

Jilleeun liked her herbal liqueurs, so a wet bar was provided, and while she got pleasantly tipsy (but no more), Butterbugs enjoyed a gentle cascade of pure rain water and cranberry juice.

'Now then Butterbugs, you 'saxy dreamer', what about all the flood of admirers?'

He gave her his best charm smile.

'It's MORE than a flood! It's a deluge.'

And it went from there...

Jilleeun left in fulsome smugness, stilettos having strengthened the ankles inside them enough to not slip-slide to the deck, but without enough gumption to pull the micro-mini down to conceal garter clips, well up toned thighs.

'Hey, Red!' Butterbugs playfully called after her.

'My name's Jill-ee-*un!*' she returned, not bothering to look about. Those thighs were now completely bumpled with goose bumps.

'You forgot your iPoddyRikkorduk. Want me to keep it till our next session?'

She had no idea he was this risqué. She turned round, and with a snare-drum strut, hiked up her mini to reveal whatever he chose to notice. She knew she could have him, but would she be up to an ultrastar's standards? Gawd, was she glad she was sprightfully-spiffed, otherwise the exalted nature of her interviewee would become too crushing, too –

Wait, all this thought was a dumpster of bullshit. He wasn't like that at all. He was nice, and low key, and kind, and un-starry, without guile or conceit. And so sexy that her peddied toenails could easily curl into blast-off mode.

'I think I'd better take it...' She tried to sound over-confident. Not to play a game, but just in case he thought she was a pushover. 'I like to do my pieces in stages, and not all at once.'

'Of course. Very sensible.'

'I try to be sensible. All the time.'

She didn't realize that her nipples were in high relief and her *crème fraîche* left butt cheek was delightfully visible above its crease, both being known to Butterbugs, as she stood in semi-cautious profile.

'Good plan. I knew it. I sensed it. That's why my personal limo awaits you.'

'It does?'

Thus was her hometown girlness revealed.

Butterbugs, from a hometown smaller than hers, had no choice but to be down-right neighborly.

'Yes, ma'am.'

'You're a find – a real griggly-mirrpurr *find!* Oh! *Erp* – perhaps I shouldn't have said that.'

'Oh, but yes, you should have. That's all right. I think you're super, too.'

'Butterbugs!'

She grew dreamy, almost woozy.

'But look,' the actor replied, without acting, 'Let's wrap 'er up now. If we're going to do this thing, let's do it without ribbons attached, be they ever so appealing.'

He scanned her body, somewhat boldly, as if grabbing all he could while the chance was prime, fantasy ammo for a later firing.

'Really? You're so smart, Butterbugs! That's so right-on. I love – I mean, I respect you – er – that.'

'And after you're done with this thing, would you care to join me on a cruise around Sint Maarten on my waiting sailboat?'

'That is a noble goal, Butterbugs! It will help me in my application to this... undertaking. I now bid you good eve.'

'I'm crazy about your bangs, Jilleeun!'

In about one month's time, the thing was done, the bee-ography, It was a big success, and the two went on the cruise and had a super time. It was hot, heavy (but pleasantly low-cal), and Jilleeun was added to his roster of regular callers. Chronicler of contemporary history that she was, she never lost the mentality that reminded her she was part of something great, something of consequence, and thus, she learned humility in the process. The quality and depth of her writing vastly improved, and it was she who, down the road, was to produce the definitive biography, a grander set of volumes, which came to be compared to Ellman, Mrs. Gaskell, Vuppramana, Zweig, Troyat, and Caro.

And better, too.

Charlie Rose, a tol'ble interviewer for gen'l purposes, if not understanding and depth, after his national confession in which he pled guilty to having not enough understanding and depth, was out of town/in possible holiday rehab, but sent a big Charlie 'WELCOME' to Butterbugs via an mp23 ZapperZone moment nevertheless. In his absence, the avenue was open for an important interview on the Peter Bradley Show (on the Jiggs Network), with guest host Larry Pine.

Based on his latest picture, 'Beggars of Life' (Paramount), Larry asked Butterbugs about his Carstairs life.

LP: You apparently came from a family of sluggards and dullards.

Bb: You know, Larry, that's not half-wrong.

LP: Butterbugs, why are you in so many bee-ographical pictures? Your Sri Sankara picture, 'I Am The Seer' (Grandad Ted) is just out.

Bb: Well Larry, as Meyton Pharps, my favorite historian, said, 'Bee-ography is Story'. Where else can we in the picture business get terrific stories than from bee-ography, current or otherwise? I ask you.

LP: Dahn good pernt, Butterbugs. I like how Pharps, who was on the show last week in fact, got her start as a greeter at Goob-Mart in the year before that concern's complete and utter collapse in on itself. And she saw every kind of creature God ever made, and she had to respond to those she 'greeted', and to usher them onward. And she found she didn't believe any more in what she was ushering them towards. So, one by one, she started to introduce doubt into the minds of those who came into contact with –'

Bb: Excuse me for interrupting, but I think it was a healthy skepticism rather than doubt. At least that's what she told me.

LP: You're right! I tell you, you're right! I respect your up-front clarity. So characteristic! At any rate, our Meyton found she was already transcending her environment, and so decided to be a prominent historian.

Bb: She was also prescient. Collapse from corruption was imminent for such an entity, as said Mart was so deliberately built on the sands of greed. What she told those consumers was *right on*, baby!

LP: Isn't that great?

Bb: I think valuable perspectives like that are good for all of us, Larry.

LP: Agreed. Now then, Butterbugs, you're taking some time out to do some touring.

Bb: Yep. I'm gooning around. Stopping by some places of the past.

LP: Sounds like a *picture* in the making!

Bb: That's what I laughingly refer to as 'Sonny Talk'.

LP: In other words, 'Ask my agent, not me', right?

Bb: Yep!

And it came to pass that, driving a three-wheeled Tempo ('for fun'), Butterbugs made a much publicized return to Pepito de Tacos-Queveres Memorial Avenue, in order to kick ass and to teach that wheelchair guy and those hooligan kids from the P.U. (Pre-Ultrastar) Era a lesson.

While much of the metropolis had been purged of the human crustbucket slime that throve on the cult of crack-cocaine-'n'-meth, Pepito de Tacos-Queveres Memorial Avenue remained hardass in its stubborn allegiance to this longtime industry.

Butterbugs, out of the generosity of his heart, offered to make the scene as a gesture of solidarity to Mayor Rico-Rico, who would also be there, serving punch and cookies to the kids and outraged parents who wanted their Memorial Avenue back. Even Pepito de Tacos-Queveres himself and his wife Mixi would be there, as well as Arnie (Schvartzn'gar), and Gouvernail Gubbub, Governor-Elect.

[The 'Memorial' appellation stemmed from the fact that after de Tacos-Queveres, a onetime gang-lord, was finally busted, he made a deal to rat on all his rivals. His sentence was drastically reduced, and the DA fixed it so that 'Daughters of the American Revolution – Los Angeles Branch – Avenue' was duly renamed 'Pepito de Tacos-Queveres Memorial Avenue'. Because the term 'Memorial' appeared in this honorarium, his potential enemies thought he was dead. So after de Tacos-Queveres did his time and fully reformed, he achieved enough security to become a cheerful 'Roach Coach' proprietor and pillar of society.]

Well, despite the big build-up and the VIPs present, things didn't go very well that day.

The event was designed to make a major impact on the Recall crowd, but when Butterbugs tooled down the Avenue in his wheezy Tempo, to the prescribed place, there wasn't one sign of any event to be found. Indeed, all he saw were the familiar sights known to him as on that terrible day, the day of his first introduction to LA, which had driven him out to the further fields of the Southland, and a time of exile.

From the safety of his shaky rig he observed the same types of louts, layabouts, ruffians and other human rubbish, going about their daily druggie dances, throwing punches, arguing, betraying, stabbing and kicking. Wheelchair guy was nowhere to be seen, though. So Butterbugs himself became nowhere to be seen, as he wised up to the racket in play.

'Still a tad bit of work to do on this thing yet,' was his gentle Butterbugsian commentary.

It reached the media, and within days, hellcats in the Justice Dept. were clearing out the corrupt ones, and soon the sun of promise began to shine over poor, blighted Pepito de Tacos-Queveres Memorial Avenue for the first time ever. And for *sure*, this time.

Butterbugs' Fulltime Fanclub (BbFtFc), arguably *the* premiere effort in ultrastar admiration, came into being, almost overnight. Their aim was to document every ultrastarry moment, to be presented not only in web form, but in formal bound volumes. Documentation would be comprehensive, both currently and retrospectively – the most complete coverage of a human being's life ever attempted.

Funded by public subscription, the BbFtFc completed their purpose-built headquarters just opposite Swennoweth Park in record time. Housing an Institute, Library, Viewing Salons, Gallery, and Mvsevm, it was quickly established as *the* starting point for all studies of things Butterbugsian. The difference was that it was no ditzy fan site. Bubblegum was politely left at the door. The accent was on scholarship and respectful probing.

Not surprisingly, film viewing facilities were state of the art. Not meant to compete with commercial venues, the three auditoria therein were meant for retrospective, repertory, and instructional exhibition. Uniquely, each hall was devoted to certain gauges of film, each bigger than the last. The 8mm/9.5mm/16mm Salon was intimate and home-like. The 35mm Salon was conventionally-sized, and the 70mm Grand Salle was appropriately amphitheatrical. Each was lavishly appointed and ornately decorated.

The building itself was a domed and encolumned exercise in the National Romantic style, with an astonishing array of craftsmanship in its every aspect, from hugely cinematic murals in the Rotunda, to each and every hand-beaten door hinge and light switch plate. It precipitated a whole nouveau movement in Arts &

Crafts architecture. The architect was Årwyn Karolsellius, who, at Butterbugs' request, usually did the production design for the ultrastar's Scan-oriented pictures. Despite his name, he was one of the Sami peoples, and he always found a way to integrate their traditional elements into his own creative schemes.

'I love it, Årw, but *whie* did they choose this particular school of architecture for this clubhouse?' Butterbugs innocently asked, after a wide-eyed tour. 'Your design is stunning, but its pronounced Nordic features, combined with all those palms out front, remind me of the Collectorate Club in old Nagpur, Maharashtra!'

'Why? Well, no matter what picture you are in Butterbugs, these fans of yours, the ones who raised this 'living memorial' (heh-heh!) to you – I think, to them, you're somebody who just strode out of Asgard, probably to set the world straight or something! Whereas, you and I can just sit back and say, agornybornygornyborn!'

Their booming laughter echoed throughout the stately halls.

In spite of the giganticism of this and many other ongoing honorings, the ultrastar was adjusted not a bit. Hardwired with humbleness, he approached the BbFtFc and their activities with good cheer.

'If it makes them happy…,' he said, though certain aspects of discretion were to be expected.

His everyday trips to the loo, 'private' matters, (e.g. his dirty bits and naughty bits), not to mention other activities that might lead to prurient interpretation, were handled judiciously by the BbFtFc's very wise editors. An Esoteric Branch handled these 'tricky-cum-dicey' items of interest, but with impartiality and class. That was why Butterbugs decided to go along with this particular project.

[In the days and months to come, as his cinema roles intensified, Butterbugs was to become more… evasive… Or else he delivered info to the BbFtFc in more guarded or 'managed' ways. After the actor-ultrastar finally admitted he could no longer put quill to paper in order to answer all sincere fan mail, Nayland Gribgrib took over nearly all tasks related to fan management.]

One of the BbFtFc's Mvsevm's most prized possessions was one of its most ephemeral. Somehow, someone had found the Free Photo and Fun Book that Butterbugs had acquired at Mr. Sy's Casino of Fun in Vegas, during his sequence of pre-stardom surreality. When shown this relic by Kester Kearsarge, Curator of the Mvsevm, Butterbugs uttered nary a word. Yet all who saw him ever after, knew that indeed, it was he in the cheap head & shoulders mug shot (possibly the ultrastar's first 'photoshoot'), so deep was his range of world experience and world thought.

No explanation was necessary.

Actually, Butterbugs was most excited about the Mvsevm's first big exhibition, 'The Hirschfeld Version: One Hundred And One Depictions of One Hundred And One Butterbugs Roles'. The inimitable Maestro Al would be at the opening himself, with Mrs. H. (Louise), and beloved daughter Nina, whose name was naturally hidden in at least half the drawings.

Having been so thoroughly and masterfully Hirschfeldized, even modest Butterbugs had to admit he had *arrived.*

'I, Butterbugs, have...'

But he couldn't finish the sentence.

The Kid from Carstairs!

And what of... Carstairs itself?

It was being transformed, certainly. The sites of the man's nativity and youth were being discovered, developed and exploited faster than an arsonist's fung-grass fire in August, one of which had burnt the Shack that Butterbugs had assembled as a kid, way out on Old Dad's outermost acres.

Lost in the illegal flames were Butterbugs' stash of Playboys. Hef was person-ally impressed that an intact Dec. '68 issue was found amidst the ruins, and told Butterbugs so.

'I don't know where *that* came from,' said the ultrastar in a broadcast multi-fo-rum, with Hef himself, Larry Flynt, Bob Guccione, Woody Harrelson, some Henry Miller footage, John Cusack and Kate Walsh, on 'The View'...

Also, there were several tins of Peper's Pouch and a couple of Van Roy pipes, signs that perhaps his puberty was rather more normal than his most ardent wor-shipers might have wished. Had they known about such caches, they might have raided their fastness and hoarded any relics in their shrines, while repressing even the slightest reference to their existence.

The ultrastar seemed to be everywhere, involved in all the situations of the day.

He was in the fields of Darfur, shooting the message pic, 'Prince Moombah' (Oxidized/Onion), the entire profits of which (€1.2 billion) went to the protected fledgling nation, providing a hopeful base of operations for the first time ever in the region.

He was up at Great Bear Lake, on location near Port Radium, dealing with the crisis of the Northwest Territories becoming known as 'Bob'.

He was lower down, in Alberta, helping the tar sands horror to be healed after it was fully decommissioned and shut down forever.

He was concerned about the de-naturalization of South Georgia, and made a special trek there to communicate that fact to the inhabitants thereof.

And so many others...

Simultaneous with Butterbugs' rise as a phenomenon, in ruralia, a humble schoolteacher (one Chandrakins Digelius) was achieving the same kind of effect with her kids as the ultrastar had with his audiences. No one knew it quite yet, but these were the ultrapeople, who would 'save' Urth in the long run. That much was sure.

Butterbugs' work was showing up in diverse mega-ways, via pop culture. Chandrakins' efforts, allied in every way, would be as of the earth. A geological process: slow, steady, and inexorable. Supremely subtle, as well.

After the huge success of the Butterbugs Parody Pictures (a website and Institute of that name plied a brisk business in its Studies and Store divisions), there emerged a wannabe rival, Chet Plang, who for a few days copped some attention as an aspiring challenger to the ultrastar's status. Serious challenger that he was, he attempted to float a picture concept called 'Butterjugs', and pitched it to every studio in town. Unfortunately, most thought it was a parody, and green-lighted it in that context. Plang, however, thought he was a great artiste and nixed every opportunity provided to at least get his foot in the door. He thought he should be allowed to start at the top and ascend effortlessly and infinitely upward. Butterbugs attempted parley with him, but the fellow was haughty, uncommunicative, impossible. Thus, withering faster than a mosquito wing held over an oil refinery's burn-off stack, one week after his much-vaunted assault on the thing that was Butterbugs, he was heard of in Hollywood and the Industry no more. Not even the term 'planging' (e.g. doing the impossible, but with pluck) lasted out that laughable week.

Finally, it was a time when Butterbugs could indulge some of his most cherished pursuits. Not particularly in the realms of hollow pleasure (though pleasure flourished without hollowness), but in beneficence.

Finally, he was able to formalize one of many charitable ventures: the Russel Arms Foundation. Its Statement of Purpose was spread throughout the realms of all media: 'To aid those who, even in the midst of mainstream prosperity, are lacking the necessities of civilization, by which they are kept shunted into the rear, away from the best which life has to give.'

There was no doubt this was high-flying language, but to Butterbugs, it was a mere formality. Not only did the new organization delve into the reality of what might be called the 'Russel Arms Mentality', but it was a movement that spread far and wide in the world.

No coercion or even persuasion were used. Those who wished to stay in the regressive lifestyle were respected (there was a very effective 'happiness' test which everyone concerned cheerfully undertook), but offers were tendered towards betterment, and the percentage of those in need of embracing them was overwhelming. No free lunches, but an opening of doors. That was what this thing was all about.

Intentions were philanthropic, and due to the genius of the minds put forward in prosecuting actions needed, results were not only encouraging, they were downright trendsetting. Russel Arms was a signal influence in turning around the low expectations in life, levied on persons of obscurity, at all levels in contemporary life. No one could deny that Progress had been attempted, and due to such efforts, it had been achieved to certain degrees.

As for Butterbugs, who got things rolling in the first place, he was in awe.

'I never imagined that suggestions could turn into answers,' he confessed in interviews.

He was being unusually modest. There was evidence of major ethical change, of Wilberforce, of Dickens, of Miss Cardwell, of M.K. Gandhi, of MLK, of Tutu, of Francis (both saint and pope-saint). It was the next step towards Decency.

In private, Butterbugs waxed circumspect at times. Receiving the Foundation's quarterly reports between takes on the set of Bergman's 'Thunder Emanating From The Seats of Highest Heaven' (Svensk Filmindustri), he could only gape in wonderment at the verified facts of achievement.

'I don't recall much from those (Russel Arms) days, but I cannot forget them...'

His confession was strictly private.

Of Marshall, the heavily damaged human remains whom he had held, lifted, and set upon their course, all trace had vanished. It was Marshall, Marshall above all, who had served as the lasting inspiration for the Foundation and all it meant. There wasn't one day, one week, when Butterbugs did not recall his essence. It did not haunt, but it did inspire.

And there were others, many others, founded and sustained by Butterbugs, to bring about exerted good in the world. What else was there to do? Having swept aside the trends of decline that had so gripped the American world from the 1980s to the early new millennium, new zephyrs were beginning to take hold in their activity of blowing against the collective cheek of those with comfort, power and money in the world, the world over.

This was no naïve Ruskinian self-improvement notion, produced out of guilt or feel-good response. It was a tone change. And in this tired old world, when air circulates in refreshed jets, adherence to new ways and new ideas is as natural as breathing itself.

12.

Ring of Rings

With the splendor of 'The Lord of the Rings' (New Line, 2001–03) and 'The Hobbit' (New Line/MGM, 2012–14) now safely consigned to filmic lore, it was officially and ethically permissible to shoot its companion piece in tone and import that until now had been confined to the world's greatest stages, but confined nevertheless. And what's more, to shoot it in definitive terms.

When Butterbugs was formally and repeatedly asked, by Kathi Wagner, over a schnapps lunch in Weimar, after a stroll along the Ilm, during lollies in the Park, and a polite snog in Goethe's Garten Haus, if he would ever consider playing the role of Siegfried in the full-length fully-cinematic filmization of her ancestor Richard Wagner's 'Der Ring des Nibelungen', there was nothing to say but:

'*Ja*'.

'*Ja*', he said, to the heirs of the Meister's legacy.

Butterbugs certainly qualified as a heldentenor, and after several weeks of training in Bayreuth, he was ready for his first Siegmund scenes.

Filming was naturally arduous, but after it was all in the can the ultrastar was overheard as saying that he rather liked singing opera, and might have considered switching over to it entire, as an alternative acting career, if he weren't so busy these days.

Some personnel notes follow. Because to those in the know, *who* all were working on a picture series of this importance naturally indicated the degree of quality to come. The very best were working with the very best.

Consultant: The Angry Black Priest

Butterbugs: 'I want you on the set all the time I'm there, TABP!'

TABP also delivered a sizzling performance as Fafnir, as both giant and dragon.

Musical Director: Alfred Newman; associate: Ken Darby. With this successful package, Newman and his team became associated with the Wagner operas in the same way they had with Rodgers & Hammerstein. Berlin, Vienna, NY, LA and Prome duly contributed their philharmonics.

'A terrifying prospect,' Alfred had said at the outset, then found he rather fancied the whole affair and its accompanying status.

Art Direction: Årwyn Karolsellius, Albert Nozaki, Hoah Fendsman and a team of hundreds.

Camera: Vittorio Storaro and Sven Nykvist, and other masters, painting with light.

The cumulative production was helmed by Yakki Dzuzdkgyg, Werner Herzog, Henry King and David Lynch.

The plan, which Butterbugs himself suggested, entailed that each director took a single Act (or in the case of 'Rheingold', a scene) that alternated throughout the cycle, unto the grand finale, which was harmoniously directed by all four. On further thought, everyone decided to shoot three versions: 1) One director per opera; 2) One director per Act/scene; 3) One director per *leitmotif.*

'That oughta do it,' Butterbugs commented drily upon the plan's acceptance. 'Let's git 'er done!'

The end results were some of the strangest, most perfect amalgamations of cinematic art, or art in general, that the world had yet beheld.

Der Meister would have flipped right out of his Bayreuth burial vault, free from madness.

Stylistically, this daring interweaving of directorial diversity was perfect for tackling Wagner's grand concept, which, in actuality, is a saga of intimacy, of one-on-one conversations, rather than epic battle scenes and a cast of millions. But the scope is indeed vast, and via the freedom of cinema leaving the walls of the *opern haus* behind, the four directors were able to build their own grand designs.

King, who handled the opening scene at the bottom of the Rhine (with effective location work), brought the traditions of straightforward storytelling within established frameworks of clarity and realistic composition. Thus, the approach of the whole tetrology was set and adhered to.

Dzuzdkgyg, with her characteristic youthfulness and vivacity, expanded the drama with huge close-ups and lavished in the characters' attractiveness (svelteness was preferred over hoggishness), be it poignant or grotesque.

Herzog was, well, Herzogian, and while he did not particularly exploit the Germanic inevitability of the saga, he injected the proper Wagnerian imperatives without cliché or parody, and resisted all temptations of excess.

Lynch of course expounded on the saga's generously wide avenues of bizarreness, but never had his touch been lighter, or his nuances more skillful. His sensitive portrayal of the Fafnir (as dragon) sequence was sheer genius, and it was a natural maturation of a creative evolution that stretched all the way back to The Baby (e.g. 'They're not even sure if it *is* a baby!') of 'Eraserhead' (Libra, 1977).

As musical leitmotifs ruled the score, each director created his or her own *cinematic* motifs, which were honored and utilized by the others. And in the other versions, which were released according to a sophisticated meister plan of ingenious exhibition, the masala in the Norn-stirred kettle turned out to be even more compelling. In each version, all the threads meshed and held throughout the colossal running time of nearly nineteen hours (not counting intermissions, naturally). Even with this fascination, and even with the presence of Butterbugs, it was Wagner's show all the way.

Publicity was especially heavy in Mitteleuropa, what with its big metro centers, and their foundations and endowments, and in certain opera-loving Texas towns.

'Great news for Wagner fans', ran many a tagline. 'Butterbugs will be playing the roles of Siegmund and Siegfried (and Donner in 'Rheingold' – an unusual departure) in the complete 'Ring', after all!'

In the planning stages, after extensive negotiations with the Wagner family, whose Peyton Place wrangles provided regular news not only for the opera world, but the Deutsche Presse in general, a deal was made.

Word has leaked out that certain members of the family wanted a Brazilian Indian to take the demanding central role, but apparently Butterbugs' technically accurate and easily-manufactured heroic looks, self-manufactured for the occasion, won out. Plus his superstar name was not a liability. There was even a big campaign (in light of the Meister's dictum: '*alles neues, Kinder*') that Butterbugs should perform the role in blackface (which Butterbugs himself and his people balked at, despite the intriguing and controversial avant-garde premise), but the family relented in favor of a hyper-realistic cinematic presentation.

[As any sensible and terrified opera company usually did, after the universal condemnation of the Carvlovian National Opera's 1999 staging of the 'Ring', entirely in the clean-out trap of an abattoir's cistern.]

Adherence to the New Realism would also ensure maximum box office. Indeed, the four-picture cycle stood a good chance to be a hit in Reepsville.

Filming in Norway, Iceland, Svalbard, the Rhine canyon, the Black Forest and Switzerland took all summer and autumn. Real storms had to be generated in the usually calm fjords, and, despite tempting the condemnation of the New Realism Patrol, planes seeded the clouds for days.

The staging of the Ride of the Valkyries on top of, aside, and below Pulpit Rock in Norge's Lysefjorden was as hair-raising a shoot as any the ultrastar had participated in. There were no casualties, except for quite a bit of acrophobic vomiting, including the usually impervious Butterbugs (he played Waltraute, in well-disguised drag). It was an unconscious act of solidarity on his part for his horned-helmeted sisters, for once they saw his emetic discharge join theirs, which rained into the purifying waters hundreds of meters below, they took heart and sang to the stormy heavens above, in voices that were beyond extraordinary, the sour upchuck having cauterized or embronzed their vocal cords, somehow.

There were many such transcendent acts from the heldenstern all throughout this magnificent four-part shoot.

There was already talk among some producers at Cannes to plan filming 'Die Feen', 'Rienzi', and even a cycle of Siegfried Wagner's operas.

'And what about 'Parsifal'?' everybody asked.

'We shall see, meine Kinder,' the star replied.

Business was huge worldwide, especially in the usual operatic hangouts: Japan, Indonesia – and Brazil, despite the disappointment over an Amazonian being turned down for the lead. (Wulutan Memeo, a Xhootha tribe member, did get the role of Wotan though, and went on to a huge operatic career, at Butterbugs' urging.) The cycle ran continuously at the Manaus Opera House for six months before moving to Fitzcarraldo's Picture Palace.

Produced by Jerry Wald, Zev Duckman, Waltraute Kemmoo and Heinrich Vult, American, Hungarian Jew, Ghanian and Cherman hands were joined in a pact that *worked*. Because of Butterbugs.

The cycle had healing qualities. Read anew, but with its essence intact, 'Ring' was SRO in Tel Aviv, as it was in Dinkelsbuhl.

Also, seeing their ancestor's magnum opus so definitively filmed, the Family Wagner declared universal peace with itself at last. For the first time, truly, the family seat of Wahnfried was free of madness.

The play was the thing.

Once more, as the Meister himself uttered, '*Alles neues, Kinder!*'

Emerging from an all-day marathon of the whole tetrology in Newark, a kid was heard to ask: 'Are they gonna make a sequel?'

13.

And In The Open Air

Butterbugs fell five miles.

He did not pass out. He had time to think, to observe, to review. He experienced the full horrah, the expansive majesty, and finally, the serenity of certain death.

It was a true story they were filming, but the falling-out-of-it part wasn't true. Because both the Sikh stowaways who glommed onto a 747's landing gear for a flight from Umritsar to Manchester made it without falling. One of them froze to death though, while the other was arrested upon touchdown, only to be deported.

'If My Pilot Be Of Khalsa' (UA) was their story, and because Butterbugs dearly wanted to tell it, he had to produce it himself, in creative association with Porter Pud Parker. That being the case, having total control over the production, and filming in international airspaces, he was under no obligation *not* to do his own stunt work.

When Porter balked, Butterbugs looked at him with an expression that almost made the portly producer pass out, so profound were its intentions.

'How can I face my audience if it is not me who, like the real life characters, placed themselves in such peril, and whether 'twas foolish or no, made their way of transport into a message for all?'

'I concede. But you are not required to carry their mission on your shoulders.'

Butterbugs turned away and thought:

'He has a point. I don't entirely know why I said that...'

But if there was face to be lost, this was no time to indulge it. Not with the plane climbing to 30,000 and the courageous crew waiting down amongst the apparatus for the call to action. (The very plane was the same that had seen the actual events.)

'I go down now,' was all he said to his producer, before squeezing through the bilge-box shaft into the underbelly of the craft.

'Sorry Yak, you're out,' Butterbugs announced to the vet stunter Canutt, who'd suited up in identical pugree and no-hair-clipped visage.

Yakima didn't particularly like his producer's mandate behavior, but at this stage, it couldn't be helped.

He took it well.

'Only thing is, Butterbugs, they sprayed the surface metal with a no-stick agent to make it two million miles younger. Mind what ya do.'

'Check. Let's have a curry later.'

'Places!' called out the director, action ace J. Lee Thompson, via public address. He was in a cruiser cab behind the camera, manned personally by vet Ernie Laszlo.

Art Malik was in place, playing Shoga Singh, who was supposed to be slowly freezing to expiration levels in this scene, and Butterbugs' character attempts to move him to a less vulnerable position. But he would have to move him across the valley of the ship's belly, to where hot water lines provided just enough heat to grasp, and possibly save their lives.

Gurupaonta Singh, whom Butterbugs was playing, was illiterate but extremely intelligent. However, he was unable to read the severe and boldly-printed warning signs that covered the panels over which he now advanced.

Granted, a jetliner's hatches are always battened when underway, but on this particular model of this airline's 747 series, a breakaway flexibility panel could be activated to expel any rubbish or object that had gathered on the landing gear's tires. The design provided for any offending item, whether inanimate or offendingly animate, to be dislodged due to normal vibration and standard auto-cleaning procedures enacted after every takeoff, and ejection would happen quickly and safely by way of this 'flappable' belly panel.

'Action!' J. Lee sounded off above the constant din of the general landing gear chamber in high transit.

Butterbugs advanced, with difficulty, across the concave sacrum of the plane.

Two cameras were covering the scene, one in master shot and the other in tight CU of the actor's face, to register the extreme anxiety in play, mixed with the character's obvious courage and heroism – not to mention the actor's own virtues. He proceeded, with all the integrity of portraying the rural Punjabi, trying to make sense of his high-risk environs. But, a moment of involuntary instinct intervened.

His gaze was fixed on the route ahead, but as his actor's eyes beheld the EXTREME AND ABSOLUTELY FINAL WARNING! OPENABLE PANEL – DO *NOT* STAND OR PUSH WHILE INFLIGHT! sign, they moved from left to right: text read as normal.

Violation!

Gurupaonta Singh could not read, a fact made very clear in the script. The close-up shot was therein betrayed.

'Sorry J. Lee! I blew it. I read the sign. I blew the shot.'

'Cut!' came the director's order. 'Again, please!'

Musing on his malfunction, Butterbugs read the sign again, as if to process its message, *so as to purge it*. All assumption was that, while the sign was authentic, any sort of flappable panel had been duly secured in the name of credible but safe filmmaking. He advanced toward it, in order to take a second to confer with Malik, who was practicing Method and remaining in frozen and non-verbal mode, preparing for his death scene, which would follow this shot. Thus would his partner's daring heroism in a lost cause be made more powerful and poignant.

'That's a remarkable sign,' Butterbugs sounded off to no one in particular. 'It's good that we don't really have to be warned!'

'Oh gad! Yes you do!' propmeister Ed Willis yelled.

Butterbugs had insisted that the plane not be altered in any way, so that complete and utter authenticity could be respected at all times. Producer as god. And aloft over who knows where, no California safety laws need apply, except in principle and as a courtesy.

'You mean —'

Butterbugs' hand, made slick by the coating Yak had warned about, slipped off the support pole he'd been gripping, and the curve of the belly floor caused him to lose traction, slide down – as in a half-pipe – so as to be completely and efficiently ejected from the craft, by means of the flappable panel, like so much sick-bag discharge, to be dissolved in the rare elements this far above the globe.

The real Gurupaonta Singh had not fallen. He had been lucky, because, in similar circumstances, he had grabbed onto a landing gear strut just above, in the right place and at the right time. Butterbugs was different. He was only an actor. He fell through the flappable panel, as surely as gathered storm waste on the landing tires is regularly expunged, for dissipation at high altitudes.

'Man overboard,' radioed J. Lee, too shocked to add an exclamation point.

'Should we do a pickup?' queried Bogdanoff Rend, the studio's stunt pilot extraordinaire, who at this time was 20,000 feet below, goofing off over the Tien Shan Mountains, with nothing much to do.

'Over.'

'I think you'd better, Bog.' replied Tin Sheh, the pilot. 'Over.'

'Roger. Will eyeball it. Shouldn't have to use instruments. Clear day. Over.'

'Yeah, it is up here, too. Over.'

'So where's his parachute? Can't spot it. Over.'

'Doesn't have one. Over.'

'He didn't go with a 'chute? Over.'

'No, he didn't. Not on his costume manifest. Over.'

'Roger. He'll be hard to spot. Over.'

'He's got a bubblegum-pink turban on, though.'

'That'll help.'

'Do your best. Over and out.'

Five minutes passed.

'We got 'im,' Bogdanoff blandly rattled off. 'Over.'

'Is he OK?' queried J. Lee. 'Over.'

'He's, uh…'

'Is he – is he *saved*, then? Over!!'

'He's on board. Over.'

'I tell you, *IS HE OK?* Over.'

'He's fine, Pops. A little weather-beaten. Over.'

'Jesu cryptos! How?? What th – Over.'

'Well, he unwrapped that turban. Kinda made a 'chute of sorts. Pretty smart. Slowed him down a tad. Helped to spot him, too. Uh… over.'

'For heaven sakes, let me talk with him. Over.'

'Is that you, chief?'

'Butterbugs! Over.'

'Yeah. Over.'

'And?? Over.'

'Let's do another take. Now I know where to grab.'

As Butterbugs' strong stomach acid had recently made many a stout Valkyrie's heart yet stouter in the face of yawning voids below, now had its residual power come forward to make his own gravitational trial seem as nothing.

And in the open air, way up high, he'd found a kind of home.

14.

Trames Bucolicus

There was once again – yet, oh-so-yet again – a producer named Parker in the picture. And it wasn't just a couple of meetings and a brief bit of timidity, as in the case of 'If My Pilot...' (UA).

No, it was time for Porter's prime project 'to see air', as he would say. It was time for the 'Bucolic Byways', as Sonny often put it, somewhat mockingly, to go into production.

'The public clamors!' ranted Porter.

'It's all Butterbugs' effort. What's left? Your ego,' quipped Sonny.

'Oh, but you don't know!' portly Porter sounded off. 'I have delivered! Here we have an ultrastar, and I'm *in* with him! Now how about *that?*'

'You are *old*, Father William...'

'You! Doggone you! I –'

'Listen, Parker, let's get beyond the childish rancor. You're producing. You're up to it. Now shut the fuck up and produce your dream-cycle.'

'OK. I will. I'm on board, Sonny.'

'Right. Bank on Butterbugs' new status. These are 'humble' roles. Let's build his benevolence. As if we needed help! But Porter, baby, these are going to be heartbreaker pictures! Future classics, I know. Don't think it doesn't make me drool. Guys and gals will both be filled with the longing of the ages. Because, these are great stories, but it will make the viewer think he or she has stakes in the outcome. Can we expect nothing less?'

'Exactly what I've been thinking these long months, Sonny! I was like, well, how can we bring the audience in to think that, 'would it were *me* that had these challenges'. That is, that which they see on screen –'

'I read you, baby. Audience totally identifies with character.'

Sonny couldn't help but interject an opportunity for cream-puff snideness... Why did these junior producers not give credit for life experience on their seniors' parts? And not very much more senior, either.

'You mean you *know* what I mean?' continued Porter. 'Really? Anyway, I want these pictures to touch the heart and soul of whomever they encounter, for was it not the unremarkable Drew Carey who –'

'Can it, not-ready for big, ultrastar-vehicle pictures-type producer –'

'I am *so!* I have produced, and I will continue to! Butterbugs and I are *close!*'

'Yeah, yeah. Swell, yeah. Now listen, let's really fucking *produce* these pictures. Butterbugs needs solidarity in the massed consciousness of the steady, in-the-daily-grind audience. He stands out as an exceptional type, but as far as humdrum character roles, he could use some empire-building.'

'I hear you, Sonny. Your trumpet-like truths cause me to recognize a nouveau sunrise: that I am the one to uplift and carry on the mission you charge me with. I salute you! And I will carry it through!'

And he charged out of Sonny's office with all the sincerity of a reformed and experienced member of Boy's Town, who only needed to know what happened to the Peewee of the Moment to catch on, to know what must be done. It was the harrowing of Porter's maturity, acted out in Sonny's own office, as he knew it might be, some day.

The door closed, and Sonny sat back, confident that he, super– or mega-agent, had facilitated the maturing of a producer who was really, genuinely, *finally* coming into his own. So the tedium of the long hours of expectant patience and indulgence had been worth it, no? There was no doubt about it in his mind: Porter was *in*, and the Bucolics would, quite possibly, be his high-water mark.

Porter Pud Parker may have been a flippery boor oftentimes, but he definitely did not have a 'tin eye' for things artistic, like many producers he knew.

'I've put a lot of effort into that fat boy. A *helluva* lot of effort...,' Sonny mused.

No such expectations though, dared be made as far as Butterbugs was concerned. Producers had to claim their niches, but it was indeterminate what ultrastars had to do to maintain their status. So they all strove under that umbrella, to achieve an excellence worthy of the sheltering dome above them.

In the case of Porter Parker, excellence followed upon excellence.

Pleasingly, he engaged Saskia to take on the scripting chores for the cycle, as chief and supervising writer. It was an inspired choice, but not really an obvious one, as the Butterbugs/Saskia/Justy lifestyle was one of Hollywood's most respected bits of earth-knowledge.

'I wonder if she scripts all their love-lives...,' he muttered.

Saskia's scenarios were impeccably fine, but they needed a bit of prepping and polishing. She was currently booked into location scripting on a Mads Mikkelsen vehicle in Spøttrup Slott out Jutland way. No onlining right now. She needed the solitude. Anyway, her co-scriptors were no longer under contract, so Porter would probably have to call in Ben Hecht to save the day, if the day needed saving. Ben was always willing to drop everything and apply first aid to anything Butterbugsian. Sonya Levien and Jesse Lasky Jr. always came through, too.

But this time, it was not only Porter Parker who was involved, but such a cultured gentleman as Jonnathun Kendramin Cottsbower. He was a brilliant choice on Porter's part to bring in as Associate Producer. A former editor at Borzoi, literati connector, friend of Hemingway, Vonnegut, Tidd and Grace White (very handy for this production lineup), he would ensure that his own particular kind of erudition be exercised. That was saying something, considering the rural tone of these properties. Highest of qualities was ensured. Locked-in, even.

Aside from that, none, absolutely none, of the sleaze surrounding the last attempt to realize the Bucolics polluted this go-around. All of Porter's shenanigans over contracts and dicking around with the pre-star Butterbugs were… forgiven. Had been for some time. This whole picture biz was about progression.

Progress.

'I'm only as good as my last picture.'

Or as DeMille would say:

'My next picture is always my best picture.'

The casting and crewing were not at all the same as envisioned by Porter those long months before (except for Olivier and Whit, that is).

But oh, the tones to create! Additive, to what already lay planned from before.

'Harold of the Country' remained the ultimate. Here would be the fleeting autumn of wistfulness, spiked with elements of everyday tragedy and comedy, with characters of fullness and longing (rather like Jilleeun and Butterbugs these days). The lives of the people in the landscape: up at the crossroads, down at St. Eustace's Tower, at the edge of the plain, to the side, in the morning, at the harvest, in the store, down Chinaberry Lane! Life itself!

Charlize Theron as Cherry! Paris Hilton as Missy! Winona Ryder as Sassy! Connie Nielsen as Lukettah! Dennis Hopper as Homer! Whit Bissell would play the country parson – perfect! Theo Marcuse as Archway, the greedy grain merchant! Oprah Winfrey as the grandmother! Larry Olivier and Ian MacShane as the strolling players! Marinette Jeck as the traveling clip-joint proprietor! Also: Jack Nance, Jack Soo, Victor Sen Yung, Little Milton, John W. McNiven, Lynn Redgrave and Warner St. Waller. With Art Fleming. And Freida Pinto (as Heelie!) made it in the door just before it closed. It was an unbelievable cast. Sometimes dreams come true. Porter Parker would see to that.

And above it all was the *Country* itself! The soul of the land – it had to be found. Whole teams of art directors were dispatched to the most mint-condition 19th-century-appearing landscapes in over ten temperate zone countries, to fully capture the tone of Tidd's esteemed Peking Prize novel. Aside from Saskia's overseeing, Norman Corwin, Francis Marion, Isobel Lennart, Florence Ryerson and Edgar Allan Woolf scripted, with Ben Hecht, who got screen credit for once.

In a gesture as potent as Newman and Herrmann's teaming on scoring 'The Egyptian' (20th-Fox, 1954), or Miklós Rózsa and Alex North for 'Candles In The Sun' (Selznick), Parker secured Franz Waxman and Jerry Goldsmith to collaborate on the score. In the Newman/Herrmann case it was an arrangement of necessity, on account of crunch-time scheduling. In the case of 'Candles', the teaming was a contractual blunder that ended happily. With the 'Harold' picture, it was a deliberate choice on Porter Parker's part. (Though some townsfolk insisted it was Fred Kohlmar's idea and his alone; a seasoned concept, coming from one hell of a seasoned producer). Nevertheless, it was Parker who green-lighted it, and the two composers were thrilled. In the great tradition of non-rivalry established by the previous example in '54, they would alternate cues, and thus separate development would be applied to the two great themes: one system of leitmotifs for Harold and another for Homer.

Pre-production was moving right along.

And YES: another dream prosecuted: Jack Nicholson was IN. Big role in 'Harold'. Porter could die happy (decades and decades from now, of course). It was a coup, though his part had to be whittled down a tad, as he was skedded to light up a Tchervis Lendrill picture in West Virginia after ten days on set.

Because 'Tess of the Storm Country' ran like clockwork, and 'True Heart Susie' was only two days behind schedule, and 'Harold of the Country' was ready to plow into location shooting at the very hour pre-determined, Porter won over Mega|Goth to green-light 'Born On Bread Tray Mountain' and a remake of 'Tol'ble David', just like he'd talked so loosely about with his new star, that time. It was his resolute and dedicated focus on essentials and goals that allowed Porter to enter into Upper Echelon Producer status, which 'Variety' and 'The Hollywood Reporter' subsequently acknowledged.

'You're cranking these Bucolics out, in quick succession, with closely-following release dates,' Butterbugs confided in his producer over cold green Jell-O at a location Mom's Café somewhere in the Shenandoah hills.

'You mean an O.D. is in the making?'

'Yoe.'

'I'm a traveler on less-traveled paths,' he told Butterbugs. 'But I want the many to come along with me. It's an invitation, and it's quite a route I'm leading them on. They will follow.'

To Butterbugs this was not preposterous. He never would have thought such a thing of the formerly feckless Parker. But now, given the opportunity to bloom, just like he said he would, there were tangible results of conspicuous quality, and there was someone there to admire.

15.

Sinatra,
A Script Conference,
And Mashed Yeast Drinks

It just didn't occur to Butterbugs that he would have any impact at all on the Chairman of the Board.

Because, the coolness never waned in the ageless Ol' Blue Eyes. Who *wouldn't* be in awe?

But for Butterbugs, he had long looked forward to working with the Oscar-winner.

Frank had done it ALL, and he was still doing it.

'And I'm still *DOIN*' it,' was his rejoinder.

Everybody was still scared shitless of him. Leave us not forget, the orange sweater, the thin, thin 16mm ties, the Dual Ghia (still bashed from that episode of bossing his way out of Charlie Feldman's to escape a party he didn't like), and, yes, the associations with the Boys still resonated with high octane fire, not only in Vegas and Palm Springs, but all around Hollywood, too.

Not for the last time did Don Rickles lay his life on the line with, 'Come on in, Frank. Hit somebody!'

And Sinatra hit back.

'Rickle – I'm not callin' you in the plural 'cause there better be just *one* of you…'

And the insult banter would rumble on, till the wee hours, ending with smile-weary laffs and goodnight kisses full of scotch & rye.

'You Jews kiss awful wet' was Frank's final zing for the night.

And Rickles was speechless amidst his tears of delight.

Sonny was beside himself with joy.

'Know what you're having today?' He rubbed his hands. 'Script Conference 'n' Sinatra!'

He had come through. Negotiations had been in the works for about a month. 'Dice Roll Roll Dice' (WB) was set to be the ultimate Vegas tribute/exposé, and what could it possibly be but a brutal parody without the screen presence of he who did things His Way?

The confab was at Warners.

Jack L. was at the track, so his associate was subbing. Thing was, it warn't going so good. Maybe it was the tension of the VIPs in camera (as opposed to a much less stressful *in-front-of*-camera). The expectation was that egos would collide. The picture biz was fun, and for some (like Butterbugs) it was a blast, while for others (like the exec in charge today), it was just 'Suffer, Suffer'.

All of a sudden, Jack L.'s associate collapsed. Carroll W. Beggarplastic was coughing up blood.

Sinatra shook his head.

'That's what happens when you've got blood in your alcohol system.'

Butterbugs stared in horror at the poor Temp Head of Production.

'Same thing happened to Buddy Adler over at 20th,' the Chairman of the Board added.

Butterbugs saw the exec slump to the floor. Before he could even lurch up to help or save, a couple of Yes Men rushed to assist him.

'We all gotta go sometime,' observed Ol' Blue Eyes.

Tiny, the saloon singer's favorite 350 lb. Samoan bodyguard, plucked up the fallen one and packed him over his shoulder.

'He's losin' it', Francis Albert commented as his lit a cig.

After studio medics evacuated Beggarplastic, the script conference resumed.

'Too bad about –,' began Butterbugs.

'Yeah, Beggplazz... Sweet guy...,' Frank cut in.

'He must've been –'

'Listen, baby, Joe E. Lewis always used to tell me that after he had his throat cut out, he made a VOW, baby, a vow, never to spit up anything red again. He kept that vow, I wanna tell you that right now.'

Sinatra was serious.

'He sure was –'

'But naah, in this business, ya gotta be tough.'

'Like that –'

'Take it from me, baby, I been around.'

'You –'

'Yeah, I been around. *WAY* around, man. *SOME KIND* of around! Studio to studio. Band to band. Club to club. Gutter to gutter. Bedroom to bedroom.'

'Sa –'

'You know somethin'? Ava and I never even jumped into the sack before she'd lasso'd me into tyin' the knot. Creep!'

'T –'

'But well, what the hell. She's still a helluva dame. Listen baby, I'm outa here. Later.'

The Chairman got up, threw his orange sweater over his shoulder, donned his sport hat, lit another cig, and Lippy the Doorman had to scramble in order to have the Boardroom door open in time. He pulled it off. Everyone at the table knew that it was Frank's world. They only rented space in it.

Butterbugs looked over at Israel Gold, the Associate Head of Production, who in turn glanced at Tony Morettavicci, Mr. Sinatra's right-hand gentleman in cine-matic affairs.

Tony milked the moment, then spake.

'Frank likes the project.'

That was it. Ashtrays smoldered like incense braziers. Glasses clanked down on the great plains of the table. Lots of departure sounds, chairs shuffling, coats rustling, crumpling of dry-fry paper trays, hawking, biting of c-gar ends, throat-clearing, hawking, and mumbling.

Sinatra's sommelier packed up the wines and trolleyed them back to the star's bungalow.

So Butterbugs would be playing The Kid. Sinatra as the Owner of Vegas, or 'The Owner', or just 'O.V.'.

TABP had a huge role as a rival club operator. 'Sammy he ain't', Frank quipped admiringly, after the two played their first scene together. 'Therefore, I am justly appointing you the Pack's Chief Operating Officer, Tappin' Tab.'

Sinatra was the only person TABP would ever allow to address him so.

TABP: 'You gonna polish my tap shoes, or bust 'em?'

Sinatra: 'Yeah, I know you ain't no tap-dancer, Tab. No hunter, neither…' was just one example from their genial hassle-banter.

At the insistence of cast, crew, and studio, there was only one dude who could produce this kind of picture. None other than Sonny Projector. He acceded to the drafting gladly, making a rare screen appearance as Doagie, the dice-cleaner.

With Joey Bishop, Angie Dickinson, Jill St. John, Henry Silva, Rocky Don Brewer, Johnny Seven, Samm-Art Williams, Baby Laine, Phil Harris and Alice Faye, Paris Hilton, Angelina Jolie, Gugg the Great, Penelope Cruz, Herbie Faye, Jessica Pastor, Richard B. Shull, Shug Fisher, Jesslyn Fax and EDWARD AN-DREWS.

Butterbugs was thrilled. At last, he would get to do a scene, one-on-one, with Edward Andrews!

Butterbugs was in 'this-is-going-to-be-*fun*' mode, respective of his hobby as an ongoing student of film. He couldn't help but gush to a phone-blabber, Ted-Mike Mawn, friend and supporting roll player in the hit cable series, 'The Jack Soo and Myoshi Umeki Show' (The Birney Stratton Cable TV Networks – TBSCTVN).

'This amazing Ed discovery, Ted-Mike! You know, Edward Andrews! Coupled with Tony Randall's recent knighting, reminds me of the picture in which they BOTH appeared, the picture that I consider one of the crown jewels of comedy, 'Send Me No Flowers' (Universal, 1964)! Ed as the casual doctor who mixes up Rock's X-rays. It just doesn't get any better. I'm also reminded of one of Mr. Andrews' most memorable TV appearances, in 'The 'Wild Wild West' (CBS, 1965–69), where he plays a villain confined to a STEAM POWERED bathchair! I'll never forget those close-ups of him with the smokestack of his bathchair be-hind him. Priceless! Confronting Ed in his evil cave headquarters, James T. West outsmarts him by creating a diversion, so that Ed's bathchair, coming straight for him at top speed, and with a deadly spike protruding, goes off a cliff and into a bottomless pit! One of the most sensational things I've ever witnessed on the screen!'

Carroll W. Beggarplastic, Temp Head of Production, was resting quite comfortably in his office. He pressed the Bakelite button on his intercom.

'Marci, could you please bring in some Baby's Bum Wipes?'

As he gingerly crumpled a couple of spent ketchup packets and cleansed his hands of the overflow, he confided to his secretary.

'You know Marci, I love Frank and all, but those confabs really twist me into a pretzel. So I bail. Last time it was the old LSD-overdose trick, but I gotta keep coming up with something new. Besides, with Butterbugs there, I figured everything would be OK. Frank reveres him, you know. He's just got a funny way of showing it.'

16.

Cardinal Or Ordinal?

He just stood there, tryin' not to blaspheme, atop a blasted crag torn from the pages of Mrs. Radcliffe.

But it could only be a scene out of Sidney Wakhovich's script of Joris-Karl Huysmans' best seller, 'The Agonies of Cardinal Lemoine'. Current buzz indicated it was rapidly adding up as the season's most eagerly anticipated picture (Allied Artists).

The Cardinal, in eclipse, climbs amongst the wastes of the Accursed Lands, in search of transubstantiation. He wants to rail at the heavens, but it does not come.

Butterbugs just stood there, in firm and utter concentration, whispering his lines, becoming the character. A bit of improv, followed by some importation of words he thought the director (Ping Wang) might appreciate. There wasn't much room to move about on this dizzying æyrie. So he stood in ragged tarnishment, immersed in the intellectual development of his role. In addition, he wasn't the only one up there. His somber tableau was populated. Others were in their proper places. Extras occasionally shuffled on their blocking marks. Extras who were nothing remotely smacking of humankind. It was the tissue of vulture lungs that breathed the studio air hereabouts. Seven in number, of the kite variety, imported from Rajasthan. Totally professional, well-behaved, well-fed for the duration of their gig in Hollywood, and a dream to work with. And huge. Squeaky clean. Shiny feathers. They sat, nearly as tall as Butterbugs, and concentrating on their roles just as deeply.

From far below, on the mediævally-misty plains, came a chattering, which gave way to a clucking, which turned into a bickering.

'It looks like the Swedish flag – warped through PicturePlasticks!'

'You bitch! It's yellow dawn, with blue fringies.'

'André – don't be such a fool. Paint the whole cyclorama with fuchsia, all in little humps.'

'Yes, dear, just dainty references to Jennie Anus-ton's pert little ass, throughout the Last Sunset's sky. What the hell do you think this is? 'Along Came Plocowicz' (Union-Brandi)? Right-O!'

Nathalie van den Praze-an-Beeble, art director of the picture, actually laughed. 'Hmm! Cute!'

André Devizes, production designer of the picture, looked at her with an evil grin. 'You see, this ain't Västmanland, Bobby-Sox!'

'I hate it, André!'

'You can't read color. I know that now.'
She grabbed his peacock-tinted cravat.
'I'll show YOU who can't read color!'
He clutched her puce snood.
'Tie me up, baby!'
She pushed his wide-brimmed straw hat off his balding dome.
'Say it ain't so, love-muscle!'
He pulled down her stretch-elastic bronze-lamé pants.
'Ooo, you've got my favorite PeptoDismal pink panties on today!'
She flashed her bubs at him, then spun about and mooned him.
'The only flesh you've ever stripped are your bum-boys, buster!'
He put on his ultra-dim Russel Popecock shades and sniffed.
'You make me limp all over, sister!'
She shimmied back into presentability and spat.
'Fie upon YOU, monster-boy!'
He squealed like a brat whose double-scoop cone has dropped in the dirt.
'Fie back, you awful sis, you horrible-horrible!'
She regarded him with complete and utter disgust.
'You oily blot! Monochrome moron!'
He removed the shades, then added a low, droopy-drawers tone to his voice.
'So, I guess it's time to sic the Technicolor color director on you! Hmm?'
'Which one? It makes a lot of difference!'
'Jaffa!'
'Henri!'
'Padelford!'
'Morgan!'
'Mrs.!'
'Kalmus!'
'Leonard!'
'Doss!' she cackled, 'You're disqualified! He's DeLuxe!'
'Saucy thing!'
'Swishy swill!'
'Ya old *RAG!*'
'Fag!'
'Fag *hag!*'
'You are a dirty piece of slime!'
At this point, Butterbugs, up on the plastic landscape in fowl company (some of whom had commenced emitting showery streams of silvery vulture waste), roused himself from his structured reverie of mental exercise and took note of the sound of war in the camp.
In his best sympathetic voice delivery (rather along the vein of one of the Industry's most prominent Whits – not specifically Whit Bissell, who, in Butterbugs' respect-ful estimation, did not really have an outstanding voice, despite his unforgettable

141

performance abilities – but more along the lines of Harold J. Stone, rather than James Gregory, and, come to think of it, more in the style of Gene Lockhart than Harold J. Stone), and in the self-assigned role of a candy-ass peacemaker (as he was taking into account who he was dealing with: two 'sensitive' designers), he ventured forth with a question:

'May I speak?'

The question, projecting downwards in an acoustical cone so perfect in its dynamics as to make a THX nerd cream his bib overalls, descended upon the jabbering couple with mellifluous yet overriding authority. It cancelled out their petty little creative snit – instantly. Wowed beyond belief, the design team gazed up, never expecting to actually see the consummate ultrastar of their Industrial town so positioned. But there he was, with dress extras, already on set, research-ing their roles, days before their call.

Butterbugs' words would have been in Hebrew if he thought that would do the trick to bring peace in the valley. But there were no stern Mosaic words that would come down from the mountain today. Chuck wasn't up to those things anymore, and Butterbugs, respectful of DeMille and Bronston-era Heston, would not cross over Jordan to use that actor's masterly techniques of epic oratory, just now. No, on this occasion he would employ delivery out of some goddam Warner Bros., or even an RKO, groove-thang. And now that silence reigned on set, he graciously continued.

'May I suggest?'

'May we listen?' André answered, with a liverdumpling in his throat.

'It will be what you see, not what you hear.'

Without any further wasted words, Butterbugs' hand entered his jute tunic and brought out his wireless CobbyDeck VoonderPack ConnectToCut KeeBord. Tweaking the controls, he accessed, via the cloudy Net, the Stage 19 server, in which the cyclorama's lighting plot coordinates, gobo projections, and glass painting slide images were stored.

With arcane keystrokes, the ultrastar adjusted the entire light, tone and color of the grand and pricey 'cyc' here on the big Stage 87. It was a light show of great dimension, and it didn't stop until all the strata, all the nuances, and all the appro-priate drama-through-settings were achieved.

'Behold!' was all he uttered.

There, sweeping from a far peak in the west, was a sea of light, tinted with unexpected subtlety, yet sickly, inspirational of remorse, regret, and spiritual desiccation. And the crag, horror-lighted from below, was splendidly composed in an atmosphere reminiscent of over-stewed suet pudding.

Just what the script demanded.

'My God, André-kins, it is as we imagined things!'

'I don't *believe* it!

'As if from 'The East is Red' (August 1st Studios, 1965) – here in front of us now! Ping will be agog!'

'And the sky! Those tones! It's that watery look – that, that rice-water thing!'

'Andraay-yay! Yes! Like a bowl of second-hand Sino egg soup, with drippy mushrooms!'

'The perfect ickiness! Oh, yes, Natty! Oh, baby!'

'The yellowish scum on top!'

They embraced. Butterbugs smiled from on high.

Nathalie noticed the strands of vulture guano, now brought out into raised relief by the transformed backdrop and the key lighting.

'Nice touch! Nice highlight!'

André also stared in wonder.

'Very Bob Ross! Happy vultures, shitting in their own little world! O Natty, I could just *cry!*'

Actually, creative perfection such as this brought with it a plain sexual arousal to the two old vets – perhaps the beginning of something beautiful between them. They both praised Butterbugs for this gesture, which they ascribed to his wranglership of the set-friendly and artistically-sensitive vultures. Then, tear-stained kerchiefs tucked into places of fashionable display, hearts fulfilled, the two left the plain, arm-in-arm, hearts uplifted, and spirits rejoicing.

17.

The Uh... J, Uh... F, Uh... K, Uh... Papers. And, Uh...

Sonny Projector called.

'Butterbugs! This just might be the ultimate property for the ultimate JFK picture! Lemme put Blerrie on the phone to cue you in!'

'Hey B'bugs!' quoth the famed dealmaker Blerrie con Crebbah.

'My dear fellow,' answered the actor, just emerging from his wine vault below Vinejuice's mellow patio, with a bottle of grape-chip fluid from the terroirs of Ste. Vauz et Fontrevault.

'What do you have for me, today?'

'Taste this! You're gonna love it, baby! This being, uh, J, uh, F, and uh, K Week, I've been watching all the docus on the TV. Tonite UBC has a two-hour special at 9:00. GeeBS too, I think. Did you hear about that History Channel documentary that blames LBJ for the assassination? What the...? I don't know if the Perris Match Theory will surface or not. JFK himself would probably suppress it in this country. But the Britney Spears controversy continues to bloat.'

'Which one?' asked Butterbugs, almost innocently.

'Yeah! Right! So watch out. David Chetley said the same thing to the Yung Peiple of today, that JFK is no more than the subject for a quiz show question. Hopefully, by this time next term, Conny the Murn will be in the same category, if not worse.

'So listen. The following is TRUE. There is a very controversial article in Parris Match that claims some shocking things about the whole Kennedy assassination thang, these 50+++ years ago. Heelda Westerling was up here a few days ago, and I got her to translate enough of the article to put together the following tale. You're not gonna believe it, but here it is:

'Mac Wallace, Mike Wallace's (of '60 Minutes' (CBS) fame) brother and a failed insurance company executive bumped off JFK for big bucks. Yup! Cuban exiles were involved, as was financial trickster and cat fancier Billie Sol Estes (whose Texan antics helped put LBJ in the White House). And of course the Mafia were mixed up in it too, so the Ratty Pack MUST HAVE KNOWN. Lee Oswald, a Bolshie janitor, was blackmailed into taking the fall. He was supposed to make his escape back to Communist Russia with the cooperative aid of the CIA and the Mafia, in creative association with KGB. However, Jonny Mondell, an up and coming ganglord in Dallas, wanted a piece of the action, so he double-crossed everyone by ratting on

Oswald, and hired Jacky Ruby to finish off Lee so he wouldn't squawk, see? Jacky knew nothing about Jonny Mondell, so Mondell was safe.

'And here's the clincher, as reported by the 'Match': the guy who was actually assassinated by Mac Wallace WASN'T JFK! He was Patrick Cranepeist Ridgeway, an obscure but professional JFK impressionist, who played clubs in Kansas City, Tulsa, and Kimball for several months before being noticed by the President's agents. He was offered the gig of riding through Dallas with Jackie, as there was a rumor that someone might be up to some mischief that fateful 22 of November. Bobby (Kennedy) suggested that JFK remain seated in a shadowy bar across town while the procession played itself out. That way, they could have an alibi if they needed one.

'The premise would be that li'l Nikita (you know, Khrushchev) was on the line, and the President was rather busy with the call. Ridgeway was offered $10,000 and an option for a contract at one of Vegas' 'up and coming' showrooms (read 'second string' casinos in North Vegas, doncha know!). He was specifically *not given* a heads-up that his head might indeed be blown off. Eyewitnesses on the scene say that even Jackie was completely taken in by the hoax.

'Let's see, this is what the 'Match' article says:

"Le President Kennedy en cas subtle dans en pleine face morceau. De Mac Wallace chiffres fingerprint proves without la shadow de la doubt that Monsieur Wallace is ze guilty de la assassination pour le JFK.

Mon dieu! Eet ees, how you say, mon incredible zat zis ouass not mentioned et le time de la assassination. Le photo officielle de l'autopsie du JFK le possible how do you say, fraude. Ajourde Bobby les complisitor de la plot. Combein sur la Billie Sol Estes avec le chat! Et dupuis 'Monsieur Le Corruption' de tout! Tout le monde! Sacred bleu!'

'How do you say, I hope zees translation explain to you ze real truth par JFK et le plot. And pardon my French! Heh-heh-he-HAW!

'At least Ridgeway didn't even know what hit him. The rest is history. It is Patrick Donal Ridgeway who lies beneath the Eternal Flame up on the Arlington hill. Conclusive! Isn't that something?'

'I thought you said his middle name was Cranepeist,' interjected Butterbugs.

'Oh yeah. Cranepeist. And JFK? What happened to him, you ask? The Perris Matsch goes on to complete the tale. It is a story that, once the anti-French feeling ever settles down in the US (which probably won't be until after the post-Murn/Bush II/Cheney I-II/Bush III Dynasty is over, i.e. third term for Dubya, followed by two terms of Dick! Cheney, followed by two terms of Jebber, followed by a Special Guest Star Presidency of 1000 days only, featuring an aged but still feisty Barbara 'Bar' Bush), and once translators can be located and paid enough to render it into Good English, it will be a story that will deeply shock the Nation.

'But anyway, after JFK and Bobby were somewhat surprised that Pat Ridgeway met his end in the '63 Continental next Jackie, Bobby professionally advised the President to 'play possum' for the foreseeable future. JFK concurred, and the Perris Matsch says he concurred with RELISH! The Oval Office job was beginning to bore him anyway, as was Jackie, who was really getting in the way of his penchant for unrehearsed and spontaneous 'love trysts' with a growing number of applicants. So, with a false mustache and an attaché case, the now legally dead ex-Prez hopped into his '62 Plymouth Hertz rent-a-car and hightailed it to parts unknown. But he didn't go out of circulation. Not by a long shot. Urging everyone he met to please keep in mind that 'mum's the word' cuz he's an ex-Prez on the lam, he engaged in a career of 'professional intimacy' with a huge cast of characters.

'Since Marilyn's demise, Hollywood was never the same, so he hung in Vegas, Tahoe, and Sun Valley most of the time, and sported 'bachelor lodges' in all three places. Even before the Burton/Taylor thing had run its course, Jack was spending a LOT of time with Liz. Lincoln Shulman, Miss Taylor's former lawyer (who now works for Kim Novak) has revealed to the French press that Miss Taylor has written a controversial volume of confessions: 'Why I Will Never Talk About My Ongoing (and Still Going) Affair With The Late President John Fitzgerald Kennedy', soon to be published by La Canard.

'The years hardly slowed him down. He recently went through a 'young pop vocalist' phase, which will surprise many of today's Young People. There is a substantiated rumor that Britney Spears has written a memoir, now locked away in a Swiss bank, called 'How JFK Made Me Into A Lipstick Lesbian'. This shocker is mute evidence of the way JFK left a trail of carnage behind him as far as his relationships were concerned.

'Today, in his 100s, JFK, though occasionally confined to a bathchair as a result of Darel's disease (not to be confused with Darrell's disease; a priapic-oriented disorder affecting nether region specifics), is still engaged in a social whirl, in his huge unfinished and already decaying pleasure palace by the sea, in some unspecified locality. He occasionally does covert PT boat duty for some of his old Signal Corps pals, even unto the shores of the Strait of Hormuz, where he recently earned a decoration for Classified Bravery. Maybe we could get him to swing a cameo. I know some of those old generals!

'It's all such a beautiful story – an American Epic of Our Times! So whatta ya think, B'bugs?'

'Thanks, Blerrie. Good stuff! Can I talk to Sonny for a second?'

'Sure, kid! See you on the set! Sonny, the kid wants ya…'

'So what's shakin', Butterbugs?'

'Sonny, I uh, and uh, I think I'll pass on the J, uh, FK Papers option. I know it sounds goofy, but I don't want Frank mad at me.'

'You think Sinatra's gonna take it out on you? This is history – Bub!'

'Funny, I thought you were going to say 'Mumpkin Boy'…'

'Easy, Butterbugs, easy. Uh. You've got a point. I don't want Frank mad at me, either. I guess.'

'We don't want Frank mad at either of us, Sonny.'

'No, of course not. But this is gonna be so damn BIG, man!'

'Are we not big *enough*, Sonny?'

Big pause.

'Uh… yeah.'

'Plus, Frank isn't mad. At either of us.'

'He has no reason to be!'

'I want Frank on *our* side.'

'Oh yeah! Yeah! That's *so* right! So do I, Butterbugs. *So do I!*'

'That's right, Sonny.'

'I… I hear you.'

'Later, Sonny.'

'…*Later*…' (sniff)

18.

People's Blood-Red Sunrise...
Over The East...
Which Happens To Be...
Red

SHANGHAI

Butterbugs was strolling along the Bund.

He gazed out onto the busy Whangpoo and over at the titanic architectural forest of Poodong. He liked it over here on the Bund side, preferring the grey Deco glory of the Peace Hotel to the chromium heights that proliferated across the river.

Barely audible, from hailers mounted beneath the lotus lamps all along the way, 'The East is Red' played and played and played. Cheerfully did he whistle that catchy tune as he rotated the key in the mahogany door to his suite. The hard rubber phone on the teapoy was ringing. As he gazed out the window to the chuggers and junks on the latte-colored river of ancient legend far below, he heard Sonny's tinny voice.

'Butterbugs, I know you are on holiday in old Shanghai, but what would you think of appearing in a music and dance extravaganza?'

'I did the entire 'Ring' not too long ago, you know. The closest Wagner gets to dance is gesture, but boy, did I do a lot of gesturing!'

'Listen, sweetheart, Wagner may be the hottest thing in the Hohhot Opera House right now (due, incidentally, to the interminable but lovable cycle you just referred to; biz is great in outer Asia...). But this is a different package. It's within the limits of the old People's Entertainment thang. You know, heroic poses, in a vast orchestral something or other.'

'Wagneriana à la Cultural Revolution?'

'Oui, la critique mon cher! Or whatever. Listen, 'Cultural Revolution' is a dirty term, but I know what you're shakin' out. Propaganda, via good production values.'

'Is that what it seems?'

'Well, I'm receptive, mainly due to the historicity of the styles involved.'

'I concur. If that's the case, I'm in.'

'Just plain *good*.'

No specific films were mentioned, but that was how the Butterbugs/Sonny System of Ongoing Trust worked. No further explanation was needed, because no further explanation was possible. Never mind that he had already agreed to a deal, but via another, non-agented avenue.

He returned to his Bund stroll and gazed at the murals in the dome of the De-Corrupted Hongkong and Shanghai Banking Corporation's HQ. His eyes drifted to the 'Calcutta' mural and he was reminded of the Victoria Memorial and its lofty scenes of the Victorian life-saga. A wave of homesickness for Hooghlyside swept over him. How good it would be to see Swami Ghukandananda at Dakshineswar and Samaren Roy & greater family in Behala again! It had been too long.

'But no,' he whispered to himself. 'No, this is a purposeful China sequence now. My pictures here are key. As to *why*, it is a matter I have not yet... divined.'

Refreshed by a short-beer at the Bund Brewery, the spring in his step was restored. He was certainly recognized as a star here, but, unlike in India, Chinese practicality of restraint was in play. Faces smiled, but they did not go wild.

Up in his high suite in the Peace, he meditated on the role to come, as an express delivery of the script landed in his hands the moment he returned.

'Grave, dignified and loyal' were words that crossed his mind while reading.

'I will prepare myself by becoming grave, dignified, and loyal.'

Thus was his strategy set, and the next day he caught the People's Red Star Super Express for the capital.

BEIJING

One week later.

Broiler-house days, Canton-hot/wet, but Peiping-style. Fiery afternoons, baking the forbidden bricks of the Googong yet further. Yellow tile roofs like caps of gelatinous lava. Jewel-blue toppings at the Temple of Heaven, like slopes of butane flares, burning only in the daylight.

In the studios though, cameras ground on, twenty-four hours a day. 'Lucky was the graveyard shift in the namesake month', the saying went around this particular studio.

Chairman Shing adjusted his monocle and prepped his rice bowl of puppy meat. It was an auspicious occasion. For it was in fact August 1st, and it was here, at August 1st Studios, that one of the biggest events in the People's Republic was about to take place: principal photography was to commence on the remake of the People's Classic 'The East is Red'!

The Chairman wanted to see the inaugural takes for himself.

Who would have ever thought that Butterbugs, some months before, would have personally answered the phone call that came shrieking through the night, in Mandarin, with a passionate plea from Gong Li herself: to cross the seas and come to old China, to appear in 'The East is Red', and to share of the honors therein?

'We cannot pay you very much,' she had said. 'But we want you. Yes, we *want* you!'

149

'I tell you, I will do it!' exclaimed Butterbugs.

'Joy!'

'My agent Sonny will be intermixed with this commitment, in due course.'

'More joy!'

The young American ultrastar, feeling instantly relaxed with the young Chinese superstar, nevertheless overstepped his bounds a bit as far as etiquette was concerned. That it was a bit of Western brashness, combined with naïveté, there wasn't any doubt, but there was never any intention on his part to make anyone lose face.

He asked:

'Tell me, Li, just for curiosity, how did you get my number?'

She could only murmur, 'Your telephone number?'

'Yeah! I mean, cuz, it's amazing, you getting through to me, and all!'

Gong Li could hardly reveal the fact that this seemingly impossible feat was accomplished by means of very high-level, secure, governmental (People's Central Committee for Mega-High Security, International Affairs and Horticulture) action, via the complex of cadres and People's Committee avenues, through which such informations were procured. Assuredly, she was not keen on creating an international incident out of a bungled explanation, so all she could do was resort to a bit of levity, extracted from Arte Johnson on a recently-seen original version episode of 'Rowan and Martin's Laugh-In' (NBC, 1968–73): 'Ve haf veys uff knowing thees thinks!'

Butterbugs lost it. He couldn't stop laughing. At the other end, she knew it wasn't out of mockery, but relief at discovering the interlocking connectivity between them, made possible without words or misinterpretation of any kind. From then on he was fast friends with Gong Li.

So, months later, when Sonny made his cryptic pitch to Butterbugs while in Shanghai, the actor was already well ahead of his agent, and positioned for immediate uptake on this exciting picture show prospect.

The ultrastar spent whole days in the Temple of Agriculture, savoring the quietude, studying his role, and reading texts of Mencius, Mao, and Carl Ting.

He had made a picture on this spot earlier, 'The Temple of Agriculture' (Janus) was one of his most obscure pictures, but its cult status grew with every re-release. The business of that time and assignment had kept him from understanding the significance and the importance of this 'second string' site of the Capital Ancient.

In the evenings he would practice his choreography and Death Scimitar gestures with Dr. Xzu at the People's Activity Centre, located on Posthumously Rehabilitated President Liu Shaoqi Avenue.

After a steamboat meal and an urn of pejou, he would stroll the hutongs behind the little Colonel statue at Kentucky Fried Chicken and then retire to the rejuvenating obscurity of Jardine & Bong's Rest House.

The studio was absolutely abuzz. Jimmy 'Shanghai' Tang was the costume director. He turned out to be an inspired choice, as his shop had a tremendous supply of Cultural Revolution era threads. He accurately predicted that the Mao jacket would make a huge comeback, along with the ubiquitous green, blue and black Chairman caps. And filming hadn't even started yet. Until today.

And today, Butterbugs entered the largest soundstage in East Asia – bigger than Sir Run Run Shaw's Old Chen Memorial Soundstage at Junk Bay, Hong Kong. Under its overarching superstructure, a complete scale replica of the mammoth People's Main Auditorium in the Great Hall of the People had been commissioned and successfully built. Its 10,000 seats were already packed with extras, 70% of whom had appeared in the original picture in 1965, and all wore their People's Hero medals as a consequence.

Butterbugs, as the sole westerner in the place, could only stare in wonder at this giganticism in action, and the utter organization of it all. Above everything floated the huge red star in the ceiling, countless meters above.

Even the original hardware was being used: dollying along the central aisle was an aged crane, c.1939, and 'MGM' could still be seen on the side, in faded stenciled letters. It was all breathtaking, ingenious, and even a little scary. Mainly because every authenticity was being achieved right here, in a massive bubble, contained within the hyper-modern, state-of-the-art context of August 1st Studios at large. In contemporary fast lanes, it was one of the foremost engines within the complex that was the Chinese photoplay industry. Ever since the Old Days, facilities were split between Shanghai and Beijing, and the rivalry tended to be brisk, but friendly. Shollywood rarely conflicted with Jollywood. (The 'Jolly' was hip patois terminology extracted from the northern city's 'jing' so as not to usurp Bollywood from the jargon of the trades…) Besides, the People's Cinema was all for the common cause of the People.

Mun Kee, Butterbugs' personal assistant and calligraphic translator, approached. (The ultrastar was fluent in Mandarin, but many of the characters still threw him.)

'Nihau, Butterbugs! And, as your Charlie Rose would say, '*WELC*OME!' Are you ready?'

'Nihau, Mun Kee! I am! Oh, how I am! And tell me, how *is* Charlie?'

'We had a very fine interview, Butterbugs. Most of the show was dedicated to you and this production. Much stir here and in the States. It airs tonight.'

'Good. I'm keen to see it. But now, please advise, have I the right look for the Chairman in the Yunnan Days sequence?'

'You do. Taller, slimmer, more matinee… Sorry, not to joke…'

'Not at all!'

'You have played him before, I know.'

'I have. But that was a through-the-years biopic. Here we have iconography.'

'And not through rose glass, either.'

'But historical, objective lenses.'

'Correct. Your latter-day interpretation should be compelling. We shall see what others think.'

'Indeed!'

In between takes, Butterbugs could hear his surrounding cast and crew-mates saying, 'We serve only you, Chairman Shing!'

With long traditions of power management within the Chinese systems of the ages, Butterbugs knew that an etiquette was in play that transcended socio-political constructions. Nevertheless, he was here to appear in a commissioned role for a first class August 1st production. He posed, and awaited 'Action!'

Mun Kee again approached him on set, in full prep for the all-important solo slot that kicks off his aria.

'Butterbugs,' he whispered. 'Pardon, but a mandate has come down – not from heaven, but from our present power source. He wishes to see you for a few minutes.'

'But Mun Kee, we are about to do a take of the most signal and significant shot in the picture! Billions of waiting audience members want it done right! I am in the middle of it!'

'I hear you, Butterbugs. But the fact remains that the Chairman is the Chairman, and when the Chairman wants those below the Chairman to come for Chairman words and Chairman attentions, all heed the Chairman, because... the Chairman is the Chairman...'

The star almost burst out in broad laughter at the wit of his assistant, until the assistant shushed him, and pointed to the mike overhead.

Mun Kee continued, 'Would that I had the clout to inform him that, because of your ultrastar status, and your generous guest appearance in this great production, you are, in point of fact, *higher than he* – as far as power to and of the people is concerned. It is an easy-to-prove fact that...'

'Mun Kee, how dare you address me so, with me in full makeup, under full lighting, in front of cameras with full magazines! You are poised, by way of your craft, to stoke my ego, thus precipitating an event that might come off as political. I cannot consider your request in terms other than simply social, and –'

Mun Kee broke in: 'Butterbugs, once again, pardon, but you don't necessarily understand. Right here, right now, it is best if we adhere to the desires of he who is, essentially, the exec producer of this here shindig, to use Hollywood terminology.'

'Well then, why didn't you put it in those terms?'

'Because I thought that you, Butterbugs, were cool enough to read the general tenor of a given situation, and as ultrastar, you wouldn't get too hung up on protocol, given the politico-artistic situation at hand.'

Butterbugs reflected positively on Mun Kee's statement. He devoted an interim moment to reviewing a distinctly bigger-caliber political situation. It was loaded with the shocking weight of high corruptions and associated sociopathic behavior. Such elements were found in his role as Sec'y of Defense, in Macanda's rousing-ly-received 'Known Knowns and Known Unknowns' (RKO). So the present state of affairs concerning Chairman Shing seemed as nothing.

'Mun Kee, ye are a gift, whether from heaven's mandate or from the common, livelong day of the provinces! In your articulation, I find true comfort and sense, for you have chucked the 'ultrastar' bullshit and approached me as any other, which is naturally my preference. Why, TABP has been lecturing me about these potential moments for the longest time...'

'Thanks, Butterbugs. I appreciate your sensitivity. The fact is, will you speak to Chairman Shing *RIGHT NOW*, or have we an incident by which all of us, who are far below you stellar occupiers, must sift strength with sweat – and possibly blood?'

Butterbugs was as if thunderstruck.

'Mun Kee, you transform me, even as I spew my stupid words. I attach myself to your reason, and your easy understandings. Forgive me. I am of the mind that an actor, when hired, shows up to do his gig, then vanishes, as does the northwest wind from old Beijing, when the season is right.'

'Oh Butterbugs, your speech is touched with desirable Tang Dynasty aspects of poetry – late Tang – because, had it not been so, I would have had to conclude that you, like so many Westerner personalities, had no interest in approaching our collective mindset, not only here at August 1st Studios, but in the Middle King-dom as well, and there would have been no point in continuing any rapport with you except in the tiresome by-standard mode of patience by way of politeness, so that –'

'Mun Kee! While I appreciate your acute sensitivities regarding intercultural relationships between the Chairman and me, I must remind you of expediency, as it is, on a film set, preferred procedure. You have requested that I confer with the Chairman. Is that not an urgent enough request so that our debate might be continued at a later time, or is this an exercise in the batting about of absurdities?'

'It is not. You speak essential truth, Butterbugs.'

'Excellent! I shall be delighted to meet with Chairman Shing in the immediate sense!'

'Thank you, Butterbugs, for honoring Chinese and not necessarily Western rea-son. It is so rare to run into any who truly understand what we, in our own country, be it the Middle Kingdom or not, but –'

There were no more explanations derived from diplomacy or any other genteel source, to back up or commingle with the...

'Butterbugs! At last, a moment to commune with you!'

It was Chairman Shing, centerpiece of power in the Chinese world, who strode onto the stage, under the harsh People's Colour lights, surrounded by the artifice of cinema-making, with full crew, massive cast behind, massed chorus in tiers on either side of the proscenium, three CinemaScope cameras, ready to roll upon command from the elderly but super-esteemed Ping Wang (known as 'The Great Helmsperson' in Jollywood). All stood at riveted and expectant attention.

Because the scene had become impromptu in the very midst of what was probably the most controlled production in the history of the studio, Ping Wang sensed that she had better get her cameras rolling, because as the Chairman was making his way across the far-flung stage, not only a photo-op was shaping up, but the makings of a full-blown brigade painting were fast forming into a living mural of historical import. Transferred into posters, the scene would look stupendous in Tiananmen, along the General Promenade in Chungking, and of course on the Bund. The footage would also appear in newsreels, to assured acclaim.

'Action!' she said quietly, into the operator crew's mike.

'I receive you!' answered Butterbugs in his most impeccable Mandarin (though sharpened with a rakishly noticeable flash here and there of the classic Beijing 'Err' dialect. Full diplomatic convenience was employed.

'And what's more, I recognize your great appreciation for the Cinematic Sciences! Welcome! Oh, *welcome* to my guest appearance in this important picture! Heartiest of welcomes!'

Butterbugs well knew that the Chairman was keen on science or faux-science in the forefront of the nation's publicity, concerning the arts.

'I, I am of the arts!' the Chairman exclaimed.

Butterbugs, surprised by the leader's informality, registered delight.

'I am happy to hear that, Chairman Shing.'

'There is, in the world, now more than ever, a need for the arts – assisted realization for our People's fulfillment and enjoyment. Yet, how can it be that those who might know little or nothing of the important merits and harmonies of these arts plow ahead with a creative sense every day of their lives, though they carry great weights on their shoulders? Could you imagine your own nation proceeding with a shallow agenda which is related to all sorts of plundering? Ah, but these are modern economic challenges resulting from the fruits of those who create, often from nothing more than pure thought. As calligraphy is our ancient heritage, and painting an elucidating of our thoughts and best noticings about nature's beauties, we naturally embrace the cinema! The sciences of chemistry, optics, engineering and logistics are happily wedded to the arts of writing, acting, photography, music, design, and drama. These Four Sciences and these Six Arts form the Ten Factors of the Seventh Art. All these ingredients, as well as their end result, must be championed, as I have done and as I always *will* do.'

'It is heartwarming to know of your deep knowledge and profound devotion to these endeavors of goodness, Chairman Shing.'

'I am similarly honored, Butterbugs! It is exciting to be here on this ingenious set, under the direction of the awe-inspiring Ping Wang.' He gestured generously to the director, who rose from her chair with the help of her production assistants. 'And surrounded by these fine creators and performers! Look at the fine things they do! My people! *Our* people. Is that not so, Butterbugs?'

'Oh yes! Yes, Chairman Shing!'

Chairman and star then shook hands, and the entire throng burst into stormy applause, which went on for some minutes. By chance, the scene, which continued to be captured on film, perfectly resembled the actual scene that awaited shooting from the script, sans the proper music, naturally.

Then the Chairman graciously stepped aside, retired to his Exec Producer chair not far from Ping Wang, and the shooting got underway (with only 37 minutes of studio time lost).

Just then, Butterbugs thought of something and stole over to the Chairman's chair. As long as the leader was enacting his role as Exec Producer, the star grabbed the opportunity to ask about an important issue regarding the picture at hand.

'Producer Shing – might I inquire…'

'Please, Butterbugs, do take advantage of our newfound openness of conversation!'

The anticipation of utilizing his good listener skills excited him.

'I was hoping that – well, will the beautiful and moving prelude music from the original production be retained in this, the new version?'

It was a most appropriate question. The Chairman was equally passionate about the entire score. He gazed up at the Great Red Star in the ceiling's center of the auditorium far above and Butterbugs could see near tears well up between his eyelids. Somehow he found words by which to reply.

'Oh, Butterbugs – your question is of great value! Who else might think of such things! And you have stimulated me into remembering each and every detail! Yes, yes. I insist that all aspects of the score shall be retained, and with the same effects. Rather like the 'Warner Bros. sound', don't you think? That very *presence*, in which the orchestra is shown to greatest effect. We had that in the original version, and it shall be upheld! All integrities are to be preserved without hesitation, and not just because I say so. All our filmmakers here today agree.'

He gestured to Ping Wang in this regard, and the director enthusiastically concurred, and not just because it was coming from any old Chairman.

'Same orchestrations and arrangements,' she announced, acknowledging everyone in the orchestra pit. 'Same sound equipment as well, to reproduce the inimitable tones. And mostly the same persons, too! Look at them in their finery of poise and musical instruments, and also, listen!'

Now was Butterbugs' heart full. He hastened to his blocking mark, and greatness was at hand.

On cue, the full orchestra, conducted by the legendary Ding Shande, carried Butterbugs to the dizzying heights of the People's Pre-Cultural Revolution Song and Dance Epicness.

Though the previous Chairman (Mao) was now officially categorized as 5% correct and 95% incorrect in his governance of China, this performance, by a non-Chinese (though ultrastar), was immediately regarded as historic and admirable in every sense of the word. In this one cameo, the generosity and openness of the Chinese peoples toward other peoples of the world was made manifest: to allow a foreigner to appear in such a key role was the height of hospitality and artistic respect.

Butterbugs' aria, in which he greets the incoming People's Liberation Army, thus signaling the beginning of the end of the days of exile, came off as perfection in the very first take. Two further takes were made, but Chairman Shing and Ping Wang agreed with Butterbugs that the first was indeed the best.

Applause from the entire company, as well as the VIP observers, rocked the soundstage. After a respectable amount of time, in which Butterbugs bowed and blew kisses (which the audience especially appreciated), Chairman Shing rose and engaged in supportive presentation clapping in the actor's direction. He had a large parcel under his arm, and when he ascended the stage again and drew unto Butterbugs, the expectation of the adoring crowd reached yet higher planes. All three cameras still rolled, of course.

'Hail to Butterbugs!' he exhorted. 'He is in the upper echelon of achievement for our peoples! Praise him in all your councils! Encourage his spirit!'

A whole new range of applause now filled the air.

When it began to subside, the leader of China said:

'I am very impressed with your performance. And that being the case, I make the following request before you and the entire nation now! It is: would you be interested in playing the lead in a tremendous new biopic I have scripted myself? It's called 'Shing of Shings', and you, proven actor, would play 'Yours Truly' in what promises to be an absolutely terrific show! And before you answer, please, allow me to present the script to you for your perusal.'

He handed over a weighty tome, bound in brads, with the proper title of the work, its characters (both in Pinyin and Simplified Chinese) inscribed by hand on the exposed spine, just like they'd be at Republic or Mega|Goth Studios.

Chairman Shing was a professional.

Nearly overcome with emotion, Butterbugs accepted the script wholeheartedly, and proclaimed:

'Chairman Shing, I will appear in your picture, *script unread*. It is not necessary to read it at this time for approval. Privilege is the deciding factor. For you, I will do it without qualification. For you. And *our* people!'

The Chairman and the entire company could scarcely believe their ears. They naturally applauded to show their emotions.

The leader then said, 'Butterbugs, you are more than enough evidence that goodness returns to the world!'

'If you say that about me,' replied the actor, 'I can only say, it is because you have provided the avenue, cleared of doubt and inspired by example!'

And in the rain of rapture that emanated from all who were there, a glorious peace came down and stayed amongst the people. And in its midst, a deal had been made, for Butterbugs to not only do the lead in 'Shing of Shings', but to appear on a cameo basis in the subsequent series of magnificent pictures collected into a 'Rulers of China' series, including 'Ming of Mings' and 'Ching of Chings' (all August 1st).

[Some playful parodies resulted: 'Ning of Nings' and 'Ying of Yings' and one Peking Opera/hootenanny/KTV musical: 'Sung of Sungs' (or 'Song of Songs') set in the Sung (Song) dynasty. Series wrapped with 'Tang of Tangs' (produced by Mun Kee) devoted to the poets of the period, and not a historical epic.]

Then they drank a toast with Fifteen Thousand Year-Old Rice-Flavored Brandy, and the contract was set.

No wonder Chairman Shing was the most beloved leader in China's history. His approval rating passed even that of King Bhumibol in Thailand. He was justifiably famed for his benevolence, his wisdom, and his unprecedented capacity to steer the vast People's nation from strength to strength. For his own part, Butterbugs was monumentally gratified and humbled to be in his presence at all, let alone have him as a fan of his picture shows. China's enlightened leader was amazing the world. As was Butterbugs. It was in the order of things that they should link in accord, and produce one helluva picture together, which is exactly what 'The East Is Red' and then 'Shing Of Shings' turned out to be.

19.

The Three Lucky Gorges

Butterbugs stared at the solemn and vast Great Wall of Three Gorges Dam.

Next week he would start shooting 'The Gardens of Yin' (Tinker Pixint) at Old Shen (not to be confused with Old Chen) soundstage in the Hong Kong Special Administrative Area, so Mun Kee suggested they take a Yangtze cruise and a bit of holiday-making in the suburbs of Wuhan and other huge but obscure metropolises.

'Look, Mun Kee, that bright and shiny boat down there! Someone must have set out from Marina del Rey, crossed the Pacific and sailed on up the river! Hyman Goth has one just like it!'

'Come, Butterbugs, there is a small assembly gathering down at the People's Concrete Terrace for Best Viewing of the Far Eastern Powerhouse of the Great Barrier Across Chang Jiang to Prevent Flooding and Spread Electric Power to All Chinese Peoples. Let's see what's up.'

The white-gloved District Supervisor for People's Enrichment and Recognition of Local Enterprises In Order To Achieve Late Leader Deng Xiaopeng's Three Dictates On Getting Rich Is Glorious pulled out a booklet, waited for the enthused group to settle down, and spoke in a clear voice which rose above the very high voltage vibrations nearby:

'Now reading People's Poem Celebrating Opening of the Seven Jubilees Yacht Fabrication Works and Club, Fooching, Hubei Province.

> 'Great glory to the cadres
> Who caused the beautiful view
> Of Bayliner junks
> Bobbing on Crescent Moon Pool,
> Lotus showers falling
> From high up power pylon,
> Crackling with electric might.
> Major recognitions and applause
> To our hearty captain and sailors,
> Keeping the treasure boat
> From being sucked into
> Dangerous-turning turbine drain!
> Great glory to Chairman Shing
> Speaking to the Tenth Party Congress

Deep in the Auditorium
Of the Great Hall of the People,
In far-off capital city of old,
For allowing our local cadres
To give reason for progress here,
Making Bayliner and perhaps other reliable brands,
For sale to the non-Chinese peoples of the world
For a price both cheap and clever,
In order to undercut the
Running Capitalistic Hoodlums
And beat them at their own game.
Great glory to the peoples of the
Midday Luck Hull Processing and Protecting Unit
Who work on Bayliner and probably other fine brands,
And spread the Chairman's poetry
So that right here starts our
Great Domination of the World's Economy!
Long live all Chairmen who bring such glory!
Long live our expanding but not overheated economy!
Great success to all Bayliner-oriented workers!
Glory! Glory! Now!'

Butterbugs, who had been following along with the English translation, printed on a wispy tissue paper insert in the Programme, joined in the golf-clapping that was led by a brigade of People's Liberation Army teens. He adjusted his blue workers' cap and then he and Mun Kee enjoyed a cold noodle lunch on the Second Platform Linking Conduit Corridor #734 With Garden Of The Nine Crooked Imported Cherry Branches.

'Interesting, Mun, this heavy, industrial atmosphere. The austere, age-old cliffs of the gorge, and the arresting barrier of the dam!'

'Yeah, it's a real shock to the system all right. I have no idea where this will all go, or if it really *will* prevent flooding...'

Butterbugs picked up the tissue paper translation of the poem, and because the glory of the moment was so apparent, and the creative urge of expression so surging, rather like the whirlpools and eddies in the yellow Yangtze just below, the dun sky somewhat oppressive, yet highlighting the People's blue of the workers, the PLA green of the soldiers, and the limited numbers of black-clad cadres who formed the masses hereabouts, he then read the poem, in English, off the cuff. The crowd around him grew and grew, and so did the wonderment.

Fortunately, the famous film director Xi Czu was nearby, and happened to have a crew filming the tremendous features of the dam, in Cinerama. She hastily got the operator to dolly in on Butterbugs during his grand recitation, capturing the performance in its entirety, and in nine-track optical stereo.

Before he got off the boat at the landing ghat in Kowloon, Butterbugs was approached by the Mongkok cadre for the People's Special Administrative Area of Hong Kong and was presented with a special certificate: Recipient of Special Status Award for Permanent Welcome in the People's Republic of China.

20.

At Junk Bay

The headlines howled:

'Comin' At Ya: Butterbugs' Chop Socky Adventures??!!'
'From Canton to Can Do: Butterbugs Does HK Smash-and-Kick...!'
'Just You Wait – Butterbugs Knocks Over Kowloon!'
'Butterbugs Mashes Mongkok!'

All these appeared in the dignified 'South China Morning Post' alone.

Every expectation was that Butterbugs was in town to show the chop socky film industry a thing or two. But the Special Administrative Area's Privacy Providing Agency wouldn't let any scribes near him. His Red Flag limo passed into the Shaw Brothers' big black compound next the yellow waters of Junk Bay, without incident.

It was the kind of day that Thomas Mann would have identified as liable to plague. There wasn't any in the air, but SARS had only recently vanished from the scene, having taken 30% of the individual populations of Kwangsi, Kwangtung, Yoonan, and Hainan provinces into a cataclysm of sickroom hell. So there was a slightly jaundiced tinge to the edges of things.

After all that, the populace was in the mood to be entertained again.

Butterbugs, fresh from his triumph in the lavish but hardass polemics of 'The East is Red' and his 'Rulers of China' (all August 1st) series, was here to help. Shaw Brothers graciously allowed Tinker Pictures to lease their crown jewel Old Chen soundstage in between koong foo epics, only because Butterbugs was starring.

But it was a very odd picture in which he would appear. 'The Gardens of Yin', freely adapted from, or 'suggested by' – just like Rogg Corman used to do with the Ed Poe tales – the poem by H.P. Lovecraft, here told as a tale set in the China of 1832. It was something about a group of misfits and intellectuals not gaining access to the fabled gardens in the title. By means of chamber-piece dialogues, table talk, and itemized lists, they eventually enter the gardens, only to find a similar environment of nausea and wobbliness. It was sort of a parable on the notion of expectations rumored to be 'great'.

The Old Joss House was a set that took up a quiet corner of the cavernous space within the mega-soundstage, the rest of which was devoted to a wide range of environments, all with the same theme. And it was a truly sickly theme, mostly expressed through color. That sallow, droopy world of poorly-presented reds and yellows, blacks, whites, and the indescribable putridnesses in between. The whole unpalatable palette was here manufactured with stunning skill, in order to serve the picture. Plus, egg-roll tints, gizzard-y splotches on exposed but empty lunchmeat veins, and other second-hand tones reminiscent of dried nasal mucus. But it was a work of art. Sort of like a primitively-printed paper placemat in a tatty chowmeinery, stained with oil, coagulated food scum, and perhaps even some spit-up.

Filming was going well – if 'well' was an applicable term. The director, the 'brainiac' of it all, Vycod Raymundschneider, asked much of his cast and crew, and he got what he wanted.

'I want each of you to eat a bowl of cold 'n' stale seaweed and pork marrow in watery corn starch sauce – with used chopsticks!'

Then, to himself he added, 'The ambience of a public toilet in Tingking! That oughta do it!'

Some of the second-hand chopsticks had specially-placed bits of dried rice kernels and pot sticker detritus still on them. Each rice bowl was a horrorshow of pallid porcelain or cheap stamped pot-plastic, with cracks containing pre-digested bacteria remains, suspicious crazing, and even uncleanness. During the filming, everyone involved had a sort of low-level nausea because of the sickly vittles, colors, sets, and ambience of the whole thing.

It was true: the auteur's entire cast had the look of utter biliousness on their faces, with cold sweat, uneasy expressions, and the anxiety of imminent gastric illness on their faces. Jaundiced light the color of moribund mouse urine was cast onto the backdrop. In front of it, with the Old Joss House off to the side, the cast would perform their scene.

And it was with a wonderfully wambling belly that Butterbugs delivered his hopped-up soliloquy, in Mandarin for the first takes, then Cantonese in the next set, and in Yinglish (specially formulated for this picture) during the next. Yinglish wasn't entirely pidgin, but it was close:

'Now you taika walky-walky, wah!' substituted for 'We may now perambulate'.

A fourth version was also shot, in the Augustan English of Alexander Pope, in which 'We may now perambulate' substituted for 'Now you taika walky-walky, wah!'

The thing was, 'Yin' was a work of genius, and Butterbugs, initially reading only a single page of the script, knew it. He had been amazed at its powerful effect. Even when reviewing it in the mellowness of his comfy Shek-O balcony pad, after a beautiful five-spice tiffin, an ickiness had descended upon him. But it was a feeling of *purpose*. He instantly wanted to be a part of it.

And so it was through the wonder of Sonny Projector's ways and means that Butterbugs now found himself in the PortaLoo outside of Old Chen, evacuating the slop he had ingested in order to properly deliver his lines. For the past four weeks it had been so, and there were two more weeks of shooting to go. Such was the price for being part of a production that was already legendary in the Annals of Cinema.

He knew his condition was temporary. Yet, because the stimulation of the creative process was inherent, he literally couldn't wait to get sick every day. He'd had everything from boiled (to death) wolf's penis parts to whale fœtus blubber, each dish presented in the most sickly, liquidly, thin, and spittle-like manner as was possible.

Yet! It was no gross-out film. Nor violent, nor prurient. There was no trace of anything anti-Sinic, either. It was all in the power of its tone and of its look, and nobody had ever seen anything like it.

Some scenes were filmed in a lurid Canton studio. The metallic blue tint of the fluorescent tubes was unforgettable. People's Music, like 'Little Sisters of the Grasslands' and 'Song of Horseback Mountain' made the time noble.

With Richard Loo, Tiny Tim, Lucy Lum, Lucy Liu, Gim Ling, Gong Li, and Wellington Cheh as Chimm.

The price of the picture was high. Not in cost, but in lives. All who worked on the picture were subject to its rigors, and not just those who appeared on screen.

Producer Mun Kee, Butterbugs' right hand man, so loyal from the 'East' days, died of starvation due to his system's rejection of the horrific 'Yin' diet. Butterbugs was devastated, but he was comforted by the fact that he died for a great cause. A picture of substance was better to die for than, say, a war promulgated by sissyhawks.

There would be both a mighty monument at Junk Bay and a stele-surrounded plaque at August 1st Studios, dedicated to his memory. The grief-stricken ultrastar sponsored the casting of the Ming-style heroic statue of Mun that would forever gaze out over the junk-scattered waters.

Butterbugs weighed about 117 pounds by the time filming wrapped. The flight home was rough. His aircraft almost went down near Yokohama. He kept vomiting up the skewed airplane grub. Strangely, his belly pined for the Yin Gardens menus.

At LAX he was greeted like a hero. Long lines of fans stood for hours in the lowering smog to see what was left of the ultrastar, wheeled in a special bathchair to a waiting Packard sedambulance. Never had the player looked so wan, so bent, so... broken. He lifted one forearm, one hand, one *finger* to the crowds, as a gesture of still-breathing life. A collective gasp went up among them.

'At least he will expire on his home hemisphere...' one fan was heard to utter, before collapsing into a sobbing, fœtal-positioned mess.

The rescue rig sped, non-stop, to The Lazaretto, Butterbugs' recently-acquired zone of sequesterment, beyond the fringe of predictable Hollywood.

Once there, a strict regime of recovery was embarked upon by his personal surgeon, Dr. Cantrell. It was only hoped that within a certain amount of time, Butterbugs could be back in the pink, to be busier than his usual pup-in-a-room-full-of-rubber-balls status, puttin' on the pounds, playing shuttle-board, and indulging in fatty-sheened Sunday roasts.

Alas, maybe not...!

Did Butterbugs look upon his recent harrowing experience as indeed harrowing? Did he consider this picture an entirely stupid and unnecessary risk? No frikkin' way! He knew that he had been a part of something truly great. A whole room in The Lazaretto was devoted to 'Things Yin-ish'. He was astounded and fascinated by the whole phenomenon.

Dmitri Shostakovich once told him, 'I compose music to make people sick.' Well, that was a loaded statement, and not to be taken at face value, of course. It was an intellectual challenge, a conundrum of value to the soul, even if it is never resolved. Butterbugs now knew what the composer meant, though. That things are not what they seem when they seem to be something as simple as visceral. More dimensions are required for consideration, on multiple levels. They would have to be determined in each case, and the task would never let up.

'The Gardens of Yin' bombed at the box office. But it was there, in all its media forms, for the future to regard its nobility, profundity, and undoubted merit. The first societies devoted to its study happened to be in Canton and Kowloon.

Others would sprout and bloom.

21.

He Lives Yet,
Or,
The Lazaretto

Time had stopped.

His shaky, uncertain recovery from the purposeful horrors at Junk Bay allowed Butterbugs a furlough from the excitements of the fast track. His hulking frame, appallingly diminished by the ordeal, sallow in the tenuous morning light, resembled a bigger-boned version of a frail survivor of the Cultural Revolution's farm duties.

Early on, he was not ashamed to submit to some transport via bathchair. Like FDR, he agreed to have one in the house only if it was constructed on the spot, using a Populuxe kitchen chair, balloon bicycle tires found in the potting shed, and castors taken from a Coke machine-looking steam cleaner from the 1940s, discovered in some obscure outbuilding near the limits of the estate.

Old Atrocity, along with his apprentice, Randy, came over from the studio and accomplished the task of building this vehicle before lunch, on his second day home.

'Give me a trundle!' said Butterbugs feebly. 'I wish to see the world!'

If there was any homoeroticism in the process of tough old Old Atrocity's lifting the emaciated superstar's dhoti-clad body – a Mahatma Gandhi/Christ moment – from his circular rotating bed into the rickety but functional conveyance, it quickly melted into genuine but mellow emotion.

Two tears – but only two – welled up in each of Old Atrocity's eyes, but they did not fall on the khadi cloth below.

Instead, he steeled himself, swallowed, and in an unfortunately-wavering voice that betrayed his wobbly feelings, said:

'Mr. Butterbugs, this is the first part of the first step in the trip of your coming back to us...'

Apprentice Randy, who actually was gay but didn't know it quite yet, just stood there in his torn sleeveless sweatshirt, Brando muscles and other things bulging. He had to look away. This was not a turn-on situation for him. Instead, his mind concentrated on his second job. Tonight, after 10:00PM, he had to do a stud scene in one of the 'Meat Rack' (Hoo Hoo Hoo! Films) series. Two hundred bucks, firm. Could he perform on command...?

Nevertheless, Randy was indeed honored to assist in the ultrastar's needs, but privately thought, upon wiping Butterbugs' gravy-stained ass, that the great actor would not be seeing another New Year.

165

However, ever so slowly, it began to seem that Randy was likely to be wrong.

In the weeks that followed, Butterbugs glided through the days with reflective elegance. For the first time, he really had the leisure to appreciate The Lazaretto. He found he quite loved the place. The austere Italianate walls and roofs, with their deep eaves and tiled tops, filled him with gentle calm. The vine-clad Toretta di Segnalatore Acustico, a mini version of Santa Francesca Romano's campanile in Rome, guarded the Parte Posteriore Terrazzo, which in turn looked out over the pool and the rusticated garden, with its cypresses, grem-trees, pame-vines, and herbal bouquets of sage and rosemary, their entwinements wafting through the loggia's wispy curtains on sunny afternoons.

The estate was rich in memories and lore. Though built as recently as 1912–20, by the silent film superstar Marius Wumbo, who died only several months previously – shortly before Butterbugs acquired it, The Lazaretto had all the ambience of an Umbrian palazzo. As in: Chianti and olives waiting on the table under the arbor, and Pietro Mascagni's 'La Amico Fritz' or the 'Inno del Sole' from 'Iris' playing on a portable gramophone. In point of fact, the Maestro himself had taken a beer lunch on the premises in April of '21, hosted by Mr. & Mrs. Wumbo, who were prime opera patrons. Mascagni, on tour with his 'Il piccolo Marat', was enchanted. He declared though, that the ambience of the estate was infinitely more Tuscan than Umbrian. And sure enough, all the columns on the estate did have Tuscan capitals. Sid Grauman was present at the occasion, and sensibly brought his Concrétier with him. In a portable crate of wet, waiting mud, the composer performed the ritual of signature, a musical quotation and imprints, with Sid making sure that Mascagni's famous cranial fortress of hair was successfully immortalized in cement.

[It wasn't until much later that Sid had the brainstorm of thrusting John Barrymore's cheek, temple and chin into prepared batter at the Chinese, much to the Great Profile's chagrin.]

The cheerful composer of 'Parisina' was much amused with his shampoo, and requested that his autographed block remain under Wumbo stewardship, on these very grounds. Sid generously agreed, and to Butterbugs' delight, he found that the venerable souvenir still occupied its own special kiosk, designed by the eminent William Lee Woollett in his strange Antediluvian Style, which was not, oddly enough, incongruous within this classical landscape. It had always been one of The Lazaretto's favorite trysting spots.

In fact, 'Il Lazaretto d'ell Los Angeles' was a one-and-a-half-act opera Mascagni composed in memory of his visit. The original manuscript – the only copy known to exist – was recently discovered by Butterbugs in a tool drawer over in the estate's wood shops. Eventually premiered at the Goth Theatre in the ultrastar's home town of Carstairs (after it was finally restored to glory as a festival venue), it was an immediate hit and soon enjoyed as popular a spot in the international repertoire as 'Cavalleria Rusticana', with which it is often triple-billed with Leoncavallo's 'Pagliacci'. A serio-comedy, the opera concerns – surprise – a disparate group of actors who are 'quarantined' in a movie star's estate and, as a diversion, they stage an amateur opera. The opera-within-the-opera, with libretto by D'Annunzio, gloriously scored in ultra-romantic tones, concerns rival brothers in the 1820s. They struggle over ownership of The Lazaretto, which a dying padre has gifted them, now that the plagues are gone from old California. Fraternal relations erupt, with consequences: a duel over The Girl (La Ragazza) ends in an agreement for a ménage à trois, but a duel over The Lazaretto leads to mutual assured destruction – and two dead brothers, naturally. The 'buffa' epilogue has the actors pitching their opera project to a superstar impresario – Sid Grauman himself. A happy ending after all.

This important discovery – due to Butterbugs' innocent 'snooping around' – led to a welcome reappraisal of Mascagni as Maestro equal to Puccini.

Truly, this wondrous enclave was a verismo kind of place, with vivid stained glass illuminating the ominous interior of the Segnalatore tower, rough-hewn walls, dramatic pavilions, ancient lights, contemplative walks and nostalgic groves. Valentino, Mabel Normand, Nazimova, Gilbert, Bara, Negri, Ploaf-Pluff, and any Silent who was anybody, put in plenty of gamboling time hereabouts, in both pool and boudoir.

The 'bottomless' well in the southern courtyard was said to be a place where Caruso's ghost could be seen (and heard) on occasion. Indeed, the legendary tenor, who just missed linking with Mascagni by a couple days, showed up for a party in his honor, with Geraldine Farrar on his arm. DeMille, who happened to be there, gave a bit of impromptu coaching, and they sang duets from Charpentier's 'Julien'. The director pleaded with her to return to pictures, but the Met was her first love (along with Toscanini).

Weeks later, shortly before his final return to Naples, Caruso sang a spontaneous aria in the courtyard, 'The Burro-Minder's Serenade', from Spizzioni's 'Il Spaccelavacchi Padrone', using the well as a stage setting for the martyrdom sequence. The passion of his singing was enhanced by the well's depths, which made for astounding reverberations. It was said that burros from miles around were attracted to The Lazaretto's walls, but couldn't enter, and their distant braying provided an enchanting accompaniment.

Such music-making was on many of those star-spangled silent superstar nights, when all those present were far from silent, making festal sounds, and all was cast in tones of antique gold, and the constellations above were as coins tossed onto dark velvet.

Even after Old Atrocity's bathchair busted down from off-road usage in the upper heights of the estate, Butterbugs liked to sit in its remains, tilted on the courtyard gravel, clad in his recovery garments, dipping an orange wedge into his Ur-Sonoma red and noting how the dusky light was falling on the rubbly wall, from which the heat of the day still emanated.

Zemlinsky's 'A Florentine Tragedy' was airing over the wireless from a distant room, followed by some late choral work by Bax. The fingernail moon rose above the verticality of the cypresses, and lamps were lighted.

Staff were very respectful of Butterbugs' recovery, and most of the time he was left to himself, with careful periodic checks by the experts. All cinematic and tech items were put in the drawer for the time being, and communication with his professional interests was achieved through handwritten notes.

Discretion was the key; cartes de nom arrived on platters for the ultrastar to see, with the ever-so-briefest of jottings on their embossed surfaces.

'Kisses' – Cody

'We can't wait for your return' – Hy

'Every day you're stronger, and so am I!' – Sonny

'You are the ONE' – P. Pud P.

'Hey you: MEOW!' – ProwlerCat

'Mwah!' – Faun

'Your very coolness shall *cure*' – TABP

'You're the song in my heart!' – Parlor McK

'Get well. Then get hard…' – Jilleeun

'Mega-hugs – from afar – lest you be smother'd with love, babe! – Shonnaleen

That sort of thing.

It was with the utmost effort that Butterbugs was able to put a faint, penciled check mark on each one, and then call for new staffers such as Tuan Jim, or Ching, or Mbane to take the tray away.

'For them!' was all he could utter, and each servant knew that each item would be duly returned to he or she who had sent it, as signs of life at The Lazaretto.

One night, when Butterbugs was a tad stronger, and able to sit up in a trolley-chair on the Terrazzo, Sonny arranged a bit of entertainment for the puppy-like patient.

Shana and Utopia, two of the raunchiest, most spectacular strippers from Coquette's Off Los Feliz, showed up without notice. Their floorshow, which was more softcore for sophomores than the Accelerated Turbo-Urban Blandishments they were used to pulling off, rendered Butterbugs speechless with memories of horny joy. He got all choked up, and after the three cuddled together, he, not fully functional yet, was nevertheless able to rasp:

'Tell Sonny… Tell him, my new intimate friends, you shall be in my next picture where sex kittens are required. That I promise! I tell you now, be I ever so diminished in appearance and tenor!'

They wiggle-wagged their tails, mewed a bit, and went on purring all night.

The next day, Butterbugs awoke, refreshed. He even thought he could take a little soft-cooked 'oaf-meal' today.

There was Shana, butt-naked except for a choker and platforms, drawing aside the drapes. The mid-morning sun cast through her short blonde hair, while Utopia massaged his kneecaps with her Moorish lips, voluptuous breasts buttressing his scrawny thigh. A Saskia/Justy combo in tint and tone, though much more machined and urban.

Funny, his fellow ménage-ists S and J were currently on civic and artistic duty in the CentraAfriRepub, but sent their explicit blessings to this proxy enterprise, fully knowing their counterparts would be conspicuous players in healing their ultrastar.

'Oh, oh, oh, oh!' he moaned, the oral caresses feeding his shorted-out libido. 'If I could have a bit of beef tea... perhaps...'

'*Tea??*' exclaimed Shana, whose haughty accent revealed she was a runaway from one of Shropshire's more aristocratic tribes. 'The hell with *that*. You're going to have beef STEAK to break your fast! Steady, ready, get set for a Bobby Dazzler!'

Grabbing a tray, she approached Butterbugs, squatted, and raised the protective bells that covered The Big Breakfast underneath. Utopia sensually cut the meat, daubed it in lakes of alfredo, Pour-A-Plateful spicings, and caper-drippings, raised it to her mouth and sucked. Chewing slowly with her spotlight-bright teeth, she kissed him squarely on his vomit-stained lips. With her skillful tongue she propelled the masticated cutlet into his trembling yet eager mouth, mother bird-like. Breathlessly he processed what little chewing remained before its passage down his gullet.

'M-m-more... M-m-more...,' he snuffled.

When the puppy was ready to advance past basic nipple-nurture, he was able to lap spread bloater paste off Shana's sleek thighs. For her part, Utopia drippled fish oil onto the small of her back, which he nuzzled nutritiously.

Hopefully, profitable results would occur.

In this and other ingeniously loving ways, the kittens saved the superstar's life. Through meat and love and lust and nourishment. No drugs, no BlimpDiet, no gimmicks. Just the basics, though not by bread alone.

And the man grew stronger. In time, he bulked up, sat up, and soon the three were exploring The Lazaretto in detail. At first Butterbugs was so frail he rode between the two stalwarts, his arms around their shoulders, Mahatma Gandhi-style. Soon he was able to have his arms around their waists, far enough to tickle their belly buttons. Then they marched arm-in-arm, the gals clad in their racy Planet Zorkex outfits, and he in homespun khadi, still.

'Great fun!' the actor hooted.

There was scarcely nook or alcove or turret or attic or chamber or grotto or byway or lean-to in which they didn't get it on in some variation.

'Oh, my wonders,' he would say each time, 'I am back, and you have brought me!' Each time a little louder.

'Ours is a friendship not noted for its orthodoxy,' whirred Utopia quite matter-of-factly, while massaging his prostate with her toes.

'Orthodoxy, heterodoxy, homodoxy, bidoxy…! We make our *own* doxies, my love-entities,' added Shana, while massaging his dome with her bunnies.

'Resoundingly *therapeutic!*' was all he could say.

When Heatherette – yes – long-ago-seen Heatherette – making a rare venture out of her station, showed up on the front arcade and pulled the bell chain, on a mission to inquire how Butterbugs was doing, Tuan Jim, protective of his master's reasoned privacy at the moment, engraved his words in stone to her:

'He is healing.'

Heatherette was comforted. That was enough. No one knew her from Eve here-abouts anyway. Her Renaissance presence graced the arcade for some time before she finally left in the wistful haze of the season's mid-afternoon.

All would be well now.

22.

The Dreary Sweven

If, after tedious weeks of recovery in seclusion at The Lazaretto, during which he never was in the least dispirited or depressed or despairing (thanks to the bright luxury of his sexy therapy), Butterbugs could now cite one particularly unique thing about his career at this point. It was that his merest suggestion for the subject of a picture would be taken seriously by the multi-dimensional matrix of elements in the Industry, who vigorously undertook any enterprise with which he was associated.

For a player who strolled into town with such anti-grand aspirations, advantage achieved.

Thus, when he had a nighttime dream in the surreality of his early convalescence, of a gigantic Masonic temple collapsing, he happened to relate it via handwritten note to Sonny, as a mere conversation detail. Without delay, Sonny put the topflight team of Robert Benton, Jack Gariss, and Waddington Ching on it, and a scenario was born. The writers and Sonny wanted the credit to read: 'Based on a dream, one strange night, by Butterbugs'. But the star himself nixed it, on account of his fidelity to modesty.

Anyway, how could the ravings of a sick star be a credible source for such an important picture?

'Because,' Sonny argued, 'It's from your *mind*, and many will thus follow.'

It was an access to power that Butterbugs was intrigued by, yet wary of.

The actual fall of a Masonic temple came to appear in 'The Further Adventures of John Melmoth', sequel to the fabulously successful 'Melmoth the Wanderer' (both 20th-Fox). The writing team integrated the star's idea into the Melmoth saga, thus relieving Butterbugs of having to take up the burden of credit. Besides, his role in 'Wanderer' had been so intense that it had given him many dreams of much vision and vividness.

'I tell you, there was enough material in those dreams to create a whole Melmoth *Cycle*, Sonny.'

'Super! I'll get a crack secretarial pool in here to serve as your amanuensis!'

'That's a fancy word, Sonny.'

Sonny grinned widely, and did a Richard Crenna-style 'Well...', always his indication of modesty, a thin cover for what was essentially pride.

'No, Sonny. I couldn't speak it! Those incredible tales will never be told, but they remain up in the lower mid-levels of my brain-pan.'

171

Sonny knew better than to push Butterbugs any further. He fervently hoped that as time went on, his star would be compelled to release yet further potential volumes in this new Cycle, which promised to be more filthily lucrative than the old George Lucas stuff. Therefore, he retained a whole semi-covert Melmoth Unit, to keep the already-prepped elements of Melmothia well-lubed and ready to utilize.

The actual filming of this dream-induced extravaganza was led on and on by Butterbugs' supplemental dreams, which the star recited to the writing team while lying on a casting couch. Consequently, their own attitudes waxed feverish and *traum*ish, so intoxicated were they with this actor's vivid wonders, born in drowsy half-light…

1840. Day, interior to exterior.

Its collapse precipitated by the Oracle (filmy female character, played by La Penelope Cruz), the fall of the huge Mason-built temple, about a half-mile long, in the Groman style, would be captured by the camera on a track, with motorized trolley. Starting far inside, the collapse would begin with the camera backing out as the destruction came forward, in domino fashion.

Butterbugs wanted to ride with the camera, if only to provide the proper perspective for his reaction shots. It was a notion based on his success with the gantry-to-steed sequence in the Teijuk picture. That is, if he and the operator, Kep Wing, were up for it.

They were. Very dangerous, and very unnecessary, as they could just cut into a separate shot to get his reaction of the disaster from afar. But the actor wanted Authenticity. If the character was supposed to simply escape death by running from it, well then, so should the player playing him.

'Don't tell anyone, Kep,' the actor said mischievously. 'We can handle 'er.'

The Temple was compartmentalized by interior walls with heroic texts graven on them, about fifty meters high. As the collapse started, the remote-controlled trolley moved as it should. But as they got up to full speed, it became unsteady, way beyond the often attractive old 'MGM wobble'. If it hadn't been for Butterbugs constantly shifting his weight with total accuracy, due to instinct, plenty of muscle, and sheer brilliance of innate engineering skill, they would've gone off track and perished. Death would've been by crash impact, followed by falling girders, plaster, and Masonic masonry.

The whole sequence was therefore captured, and the lengthy passage away from the building ended in triumph. The continuous shot concluded with the camera at the terminus of its track, panning 180° and dollying into a MS of Butterbugs, in costume, as Melmoth, freshly escaped from the disaster. As the camera was panning, he hopped off the trolley and stood perfectly poised, huffing and puffing as if he'd just run the distance, regarding the spectacle with heavy cheer, all perfectly within frame.

'CUT!'

Old pro Joe MacDonald, Director of Photography, who also directed second unit today, was enraged. 'How the fuck did *that* happen?? It's not some god-dammed amusement park ride, ya know! You both could've wrapped!'

He moved for a lawsuit, but Butterbugs became transcendent, a state that was enhanced by his late indisposition. All who witnessed him now felt like dropping to their knees. He declared *pax*, and all obeyed.

'It was a tremendous shot, Joe. I know, I was there. I saw it. Lived it. But you would have prevented me from doing it, had you known I was on the trolley.'

'It's because you're such a big star, Butterbugs.'

'In your opinion,' he replied.

The old cameraman smiled.

'If I took a piss right now, over five billion humanoids would spill out. All of the same opinion. *My* opinion.'

23.

Wallace & Davis
Booked For Xmas Eve!

'**W**ell howdy-do, Perry! Better, thanks. Much better. Yes, it was an ordeal, but yes, it was worth it. Have you seen 'Gardens/Yin'? You haven't? Well, you should certainly give it a whirl, because – What is it, Perry? Whatever could be the matter in this brilliant season? Why, I saw your latest hit, 'Marion Begglurr In The Campagna' (Lopert) on my porta-widescreen, in proper aspect ratio, last eve, and I tell you, it was really jim-dand – You sound – Perry, what is it? I charge you, you have to tell me. Now tell.'

'Butterbugs. You're right. I have to tell you. *And I will.*'

'Proceed, fellow actor.'

'Couldst thou cometh to mine own estates, which now knoweth peril, as their master is fated by change… (?)'

'Good rendition of the famous line from 'Gunther', Perry. Although I get the feeling that you're not acting this time.'

'Couldst… thou… (?)…'

Perry's voice clicked off.

Butterbugs knew at that second he'd better kick into usual executable energy mode and locate the key-packet to Saskia's Quatroporto, the swiftest vehicle now stationed at The Lazaretto.

Tuan Jim rolled away the garage door. The growler burst out, then into the byway of Koth Lane, so as to take the shortcut over Dina Martina Bluff, and thus, down to the Drygardens. With the great sedan's magnificent handling abilities realized due to Butterbugs' driving craft, which was honed during the filming of 'Gunda's Very Grand Prix' (Oxidized/Onion), dealing with an endurance run in the Hindu Kush, the journey took only seven minutes.

The Drygardens had an august look and mood this time of day, a late afternoon that only Los Angeles can lend. Exquisitely peaceful and eminently respectable. Any of the California Impressionists might have captured it in oils!

After the V-18 was switched off, only a few tekkerbirds tekked from a bank of dustbranch shrubbery, to score the otherwise still and expectant air. The estate's trademark crunchy leopard-gravel led right up to the front portal, which was – ajar.

All of a sudden, it was as if Butterbugs cast aside his semi-droopy recuperative husk and became filled with the fluid of expectation, which glowed bright chartreuse, as a warning that the following sequence just might be composed of anxiety-inducing nutrients. An indicator that the old pleasurable days of many parties and long afternoons and sweet downtime with the freedom to wander within this generous parcel – might be over.

Resolved: they were over.

Butterbugs swept open the door, with its Norman Sicilian hardware yielding to his gentle forward motion. This, despite battering-ram protection capabilities for those who inhabited the spaces within. But those who did, or at any rate, *he* who did, forfeited that protection by such easy access. The visiting actor entered and beheld the actor of the house in clear, VistaVision-caliber definition.

Across the brightly-polished neem-wood floor, against the picture windows that looked down and around Spindrift Canyon, was the image of his friend, fellow player Perry Flask, in superb silhouette, standing upright. With an automatic firearm pointed toward his upper head. Like a gentleman, not in his mouth.

Besides, the choice of blowout-hole starter-locations indicated there was still something unsaid. If he talked, it would not be with his mouth full.

Thinking of his own earlier end-of-all-things flirtation dance on his terrace up at The Æyrie, surmising that a plunge might do the job of problem-solving better than sweat and tedium, Butterbugs came very near to saying, as if delivering a line late-in-a-day of filming, after one-hundred-and-one Wylerian takes:

'So Perry, you've come to this. What's it going to be then, eh?'

But he didn't. Instead it came out as:

'I come to you, friend, in your hour of... need.'

'Oh, I don't know,' replied Perry, in a voice elevated by the combine of intoxication and dread for the voyage into another being or a new nothingness, on which he might be about to embark, 'I'm in a position of choice, and not necessarily *need.*'

'And this is how you choose to announce it?'

'I don't know yet. As I said.'

'Perry, have you... *gone off,* or something?'

This questioning, not in the best taste, just leaked out. Ejaculations – and not very Butterbugsian ones, at that. If his erstwhile acting partner was going to engage in snottiness, and if this was all just an attention-getting show, then it deserved a bit of Randi Chuzzlewitting, perhaps as a prophylactic against more of the same.

'You know...,' Perry started to say.

Then his voice broke and he started to sag, slowly sinking behind the settee that barricaded him from all on-comers. Not once, though, did he relax the Beretta's hot Italian design from his slab-sided temple.

The compassion of Butterbugs could now take hold.

'Perry, whatever ye choose as your destiny, pray, let me enter and draw nigh, for what time remains.'

'Go ahead. I *trust* you, after all.'

His voice had now become as thin and un-poached as a runny sparrow's egg, smashed by a disinterested wolverine.

'Thank you, Perry.'

'It's why I called you, you know…'

'*Thank* you, Perry.'

Butterbugs was truly grateful. He perched on the edge of an ottoman, not three meters from Perry's barricade.

'We are both settled. And now, would you care to tell me what's… What's on your…heart?'

He already knew what was next the poor fellow's head.

Perry's voice came as from a land of regrets, though with a quality of wistfulness. As if, just earlier in the day, circumstances positively magical in comparison with those now commanding him, had been at hand, in which to luxuriate and qualify an easy statement, such as, 'Life is Good.'

'Oh, Butterbugs, yes, if only our lives did not give us the power to *choose*. If only we could be as brutish beasts, loyal solely to our own instincts or our own masters! Ah, but this is a Vale of Tears! If only… If only…'

His voice trailed off. Then, after some discreet digital beeping and peeping, another voice altogether, this one low, solid, but bland, even clinical, made the following statement:

'Hello. Police? There's been a murder.'

The proper street address was delivered, his own name stated, and he acknowledged that indeed, an investigation detail was on its way over. Before he rang off, he added, as if from the bottom-most of footnotes:

'And I did it.'

As an actor, Butterbugs had always regarded Perry not so much in a profound light, but certainly with an admiration for his inventiveness. A selection of multiple character voices indicated a diversity of creatures, of talents. Never had there been evidence of a schizoid personality. But now he wasn't so sure.

'Perry. Don't do it. Put the gun down. You have everything to live for. You cannot murder yourself. What would Darcie say and think? It would destroy her. And the babes!'

The ultrastar thought a heads-up announcement to the authorities of one's self-murder, thus sparing unpleasant discoveries by family and friends, a downright courtesy.

'Ah, Darcie!' Perry's voice had returned to the land of regrets.

'You have an unstained life as of now, Perry. You cannot murder yourself. Any reason is not satisfactory enough. What is amiss? Your career? I can and *will* work with all my associates, to resolve any conflict you may have. Is it financial? I have untold amounts. From those funds I might assist you. In perpetuity, if need be. And what about your little ones, Uncas and Thisbe? You wish to see them attend Wem Hall, do you not? No, Perry, thou canst not murder thyself!'

The two actors always relished a bit of the archaic form in their dialogues. That alone might restore the troubled one.

Perry had had enough. The cops were on the way, so time was short. His voice and delivery lost all traces of affectation, and became his own.

'Here's the deal, Butterbugs. Just listen, will you? You're the only one I could call. We have very little time. This isn't about me slaying myself. That's just a collateral effect. The *real* reason looms large, and it cannot go away. Upon me and me alone rests the responsibility for my stagemom's passing from this earth, not three bare hours ago. I did it. *I did it*, I tell you. I am a murderer. Of mine own kind.

'Never, never could such a deed have been a thought within me. Not until – well, the last phase, this long last phase. So I guess I had plenty of opportunity to contemplate the final outcome and its consequences, because the plans were set into motion some time ago.'

'Perry!' Butterbugs cut in, 'You can't have –'

Perry ignored the interjection, but its occurrence reminded him that he owed Butterbugs an explanation of another kind.

'Don't concern yourself as to the liabilities to which I expose you at this moment, my friend. You are not an accomplice, but are subject only to my preliminary confession. This scene is being taped from three security camera angles (in D-150), as well as being taped in PerspectaSound via yonder Nagra with Neumann mikes, with THX-Unkra enhancements. The evidence I thus provide is unimpeachable.'

Butterbugs always had a feeling that Perry's career, though it might tank in front of the camera, would probably find full-flower fulfillment behind it, so tech-savvy was he.

'As to the deed itself,' continued the confessor, 'Here is a concise version of what happened.

'First off, I am in my right mind. I will defend that statement no further. You remember my stagemom, of course. You know where she lived, and how. A mere squirrel cage in the Drylands, out back! Bizarre, to be sure. Even my stagemom admitted it, but to her it was home. She'd say, all tucked-up and curled-up in her cage, 'Aren't I just a princess? A little squirrel princess?''

He shook his head (while keeping the Beretta perfectly aligned), then righted himself.

'But anyway, even Darcie never knew about her. Nor the kids. Nobody was interested in the further Drylands, except you. That's one reason why I protect you with this testimony, lest your effects on that one brief evening cause you investigative attention.'

Perry drifted a bit. Then he stood and faced a direction in which he knew one of the cameras was placed, to capture the plain view of the scene. He went into performance mode, à la legitimate theatre:

'Witnesses and watchers! Know, that if this head that now articulates its pathetic tale to you by way of explanation is about to be transformed into sanguine pulp, the explosion of which will, if willed, certainly be shown across every medium, from YouTube to AlwaysWatch to kinescopes (for those digitally-lacking), you might think that such an act would be done out of pure vanity (as my greatest, if not most widely-seen performance!), instead of… uh, as an escape from my tragic and guilty situation. I can assure you, it is not out of vanity, for I would rather be regarded mistakenly as a conceited actor than as a sorry-ass egotist whose final exit would be regarded by gawping millions as an insipid failure. So no, no vanity here! Merely escape from the misery I hath made for myself.

'That established, I have to add another personal note. Viewers will notice that none other than Butterbugs, strolling player and now ultrastar, himself is here with me at this time. How many of you will ever be able to say such a thing throughout the course of your lives? If there is one success I have left to me, it is this, it is this, it is this: he is here, he is here, he is *here!*

'My… My *friend!*

'Because… (sniff)… we were cub stage-mates together, and his rise was loftier and much more spectacular than mine could ever be. Therefore, I honor him above all men. Thus do I wish to make it official that he had *nothing whatsoever* to do with any act of illegality I have committed, or ever will commit! You saw him try to save me, you heard his attempts to recapture my fainting soul. You saw him cast out the line of hope, which I elected not to take up!'

He stretched out his non-gun-toting hand toward Butterbugs, not as a defiant act against his last sentence, but to embolden the ultrastar's very presence.

'Behold, this man!' Perry exclaimed. 'My friend, my associate, my fellow seeker upon the path toward our strolling through whatever plays and photoplays came our way! I cannot tell you what Butterbugs has meant to me! All you doubters out there, who may regard this actor as merely an ultrastar, you do not know him! Please understand, he never meant me anything but good! And here, now, as witness to my brain's impending exposure to purer air than that which surrounds its housing now, as in a grievous fog, he displays nothing short of friendship in the highest order. I salute him, as all of us salute him!'

He allowed for anticipated applause, in the event that this sequence made it to a variety of commercial media formats, perchance to support Darcie in her grieving hermitage and into her dotage, and to keep the little ones in shoes. A disturbing thought crossed his mind though. What if a laugh track be inserted, for use in comedy and late-night talk, chat, and yak shows?

His Butterbugs tribute off his chest, Perry paused again, thinking that he'd be hearing sirens by now, with any pre-climax necessities handily out of the way, and only the final decision of when to pull the trigger (to the greatest advantage) yet awaiting.

That would be the last thing to do before this turkey was wrapped.

But none were heard.

'The interplay of traffic on the streets of the valley below, no doubt, is bad…'

He had half a mind to call 911 again, on the outside chance that his demi-celebrity identity was being utilized by another, crankier caller, thus causing confusion for an overworked Samaritan staff, seasoned in name-calling abuse. He decided to hold fast though, gun firmly in place, and develop his confession to his actor-friend a bit more.

'So Butterbugs, let me take this opportunity to expand on what the hell happened. She was indeed in the cage. The truth is stark. She starved to death. She was constantly sedated. I started it months ago, after she exhibited signs of – of *going off*, as you would put it. She was becoming impossible. Hurtful, hateful. I grew to genuinely abhor her. This was not the stagemom I once knew! I wanted to have nothing further to do with her. Also, I didn't want to have anything to do with this weird transformation into a squirrel that she was so interested in. Squirrels are cheerful little creatures, but she was turning into a wild beast. I had to do something, though I couldn't bear to share the burden.'

'No one else knew?'

'None! Er – no one! The tales of artifice and avoidance I had to enact this whole time would fill several large volumes.

'So, since she craved her cage, I decided that that was where she should stay. One night, when she slumbered after a particularly terrifying rampage against me, I embedded a hypo of Nyaprinansquaresin into her, subcutaneously, as with an actual squirrel. The effects seemed to be beneficial. She simmered, preferred to hibernate, and let me be. I never locked the cage. She could have crawled out at any time. But as things proceeded, her hibernation was, in fact, a torpor that led to her expiration! 'Twas not my intent, I swear. *I swear it to you, and the world, now!*

'I tell you, this sounds like a movie plot, and maybe it is; in fact, weren't we both in something like –'

Then, the distant trumpets of fate were heard. The anti-romance of LAPD sirens is always a bitter tonic of hopelessness and despair for those on their receiving end.

The two actors looked at each other, and knew civil structure within the Rule of Law was about to descend upon their exchange. As a canny result, their lines to each other began to be delivered at a crisper clip.

'I thought that the sedation would keep her under control, Butterbugs.'

'And you weren't working with qualified help.'

'Not at all. Securing the Nyaprinansquaresin and its simple paraphernalia from ruffians on the streets of the night was the only illegal activity I thought I was engaging in.'

'You should have done this, by...' Butterbugs cut himself off.

'Of course I should have! Of course I should have – a lot of things...'

'I am deeply and permanently sorry, Perry.'

'I... But I have to tell you –'

'Again, I am sorry, Perry, but I can't possibly take any more of your testimony. It will have to come out at trial.'

'How do you know there will *be* a trial?'

'Because, my dear fellow, you will face it. I will support you, as I *know* you. You are a *man*, and I am your *friend.*'

Perry lowered the Beretta he'd been aiming at his temple-cum-cheekbone the whole while.

'You will?'

'I tell you, I will. Why, of course. You know I speak the truth, as you have spoken it to me.'

Any deliberate addressing the three cameras or microphones directly in this chamber was unnecessary, and entirely un-Butterbugsian as well.

'Butterbugs, I can't tell you how that makes me feel.'

'Better, I hope?'

'Yes. Oh, Butterbugs, it's been so hard…'

'Darcie, is she…?'

'She will be with me. No matter what.'

'I knew it. So will we all. Now, you have moved past your end-it-all thoughts, have you not?'

'I – I have. Totally.'

Deftly, despite the pressure of the moment, Perry placed the trigger lock back in the firearm and then threw the keys into the Bruxelles firepot, which blazed incongruously near to him.

'There. I am past it. How did you know?'

'Because you are not a murderer. Of your stagemom, nor of yourself. Neither can I call you temporarily insane, though that's what you were. You were rendered thus by being cornered in an emergency. It is not my place right now to comment further. At trial, Perry, at trial.'

'You have given me my courage back again, Butterbugs. My zest, even! Ingmar Bergman was right: we are not Hollywood types, you and I. We are Jangtown Friends! Actors of a feather!'

'Well-spoken, sir.'

And when the authorities, who were nothing short of genteel when dealing with these two, hauled Perry out, leaving Butterbugs to do mop-up with the inspector team, not to mention Darcie and the kids, who had just driven up, Perry's proclamation could be heard:

'I was imprisoned by her power, Butterbugs! But you, a free man in so many ways, are always to be unchained!'

The trades were absolutely overrun with bits and pieces of the Perry Flask case, and most of them added up to a dubious standing. Heaven knew, Flickerville had had more of its share of scandals and other Babylonian activities, but the trades generally avoided rapacious comment. Butterbugs wasn't pleased, and after he wrote terse letters to Heino Gapp himself at the 'Hollywood Reporter', and Hime Silverman himself at 'Daily Variety', the madness passed.

Also sprach Butterbugs.

The mainstream media, however, were flooded with Hollywood Gothic coverage, which took the Flask name down, down, down to the realm of Cerberus, just short of a one-way ticket into the Underworld. Black balls loomed in the sky above the defendant's cubicle in bail-less incarceration. Once they were allowed to rain down, the effect would be more thorough and appalling than a point-blank pistol. One effect left far more humiliating remains than the other.

Perry, in his wretched confinement, got wind of these blasts, and the determination of self-execution returned. On suicide watch, even his wrists were restrained, as he'd tried to strangle himself with his own trembling hands.

When Butterbugs beheld his Jangtown friend's public excoriation on color television, generally delivered by many in broadcasting whom he knew personally, most of whom should've known better than to engage in this sort of tumbrel loading & rolling, he got on the blower. Not with the non-committal Sonny, but with Justy, just then in Cannes. At Festival. She easily set up a slot in golden palm time, with a full suite at the Carlton (with promenade view), in order to launch an effective response.

'We'll see how 'they' like it when a so-called ultrastar wields his ultrastar pecs and accomplishes ultrastar deeds!' exclaimed Justy.

The ultrastar himself laughed, somewhat weakly. He was already en route to the aerodrome.

'Oh Justy!' he was able to get out as he plowed into her loving breast region upon arriving, with a significant quantity of celluloid reels illustrating Perry Flask's career in tow, 'Your goodness is the most palpable thing on earth to me right now. Is there a chance that we can roll a Flask retrospective all week before the finals?'

'You star-power generator, you! You know you can. M. Voux and Mme. Fraisch await your command. Max von Sydow's chairing this year. Perry F's pix start grinding in twenty minutes over at La Madame President Salon Cinema Magnum. It's all set up. That is, if you'll release 'em from your hot little hands.'

The plastic keys to the reel chests he'd clutched the whole transcontinental and transatlantic voyages instantly fell from his iron grip and were immediately snatched up by the tech crew, who had those frames in front of arc-light so fast that Butterbugs didn't even have time to utter a single 'alles'.

Perhaps it was the legend '*BUTTERBUGS PRÉSENTE*' on the marquee that did it, or else the negative publicity – largely in the US – aimed at all things Flaskian, or the fact that the star of these pictures was currently in gaol, that packed 'em into SRO mode this balmy night on the Côte. But there was no doubt: Butterbugs' Perry Flask retro was a spellbinding success.

'I never knew these Flask pictures were so significant (as *films*, for God's sake!)' wrote Herman G. Weinberg in 'Coffee, Brandy and Cigars'. 'Everywhere in them is found the influence of Butterbugs. No wonder he fronted this retrospective. But Flask stands proudly on his own. Helluva actor. Have you noticed? We should all be ashamed of ourselves, whether it's pre-trial or not.'

In his first public appearance since his ghastly illness, Butterbugs himself showed up to do a multilingual intro and Q&A for one of the pictures in which they both starred. Which, as chance would have it, concerned a fellow with a problematic stagemom, who'd alienated herself to such an extent that there was nothing for it but to –

But it was just a movie, no? 'She Is No More' (Your Basic) was a 'small' film, with art house pretensions, but it was an excellent little thing, and it set those who read its subtitles and those who understood its stagy dialogue to ask certain questions concerning the fine line between fact and fiction.

Then, trial.

'Who among you,' asked Butterbugs, standing in front of the crushingly huge Poelaert-designed San Pino County Courthouse, 'Have not seen Perry Flask in 'She Is No More' (Your Basic)?'

'Aye, aye!' the hugely approving crowd replied. 'But we have seen YOU in it, as well!'

'We are after a cause here, masses, not glory!'

The masses exploded in cheers.

Up inside the pile, the prosecution looked down from their immense gallery windows and knew they were cooked.

O'Moore Parsons-Szaarck, the Imperial Prosecutor, mused:

'This day, I wish I were a janitor in the confines of Yucca Mountain. Only then would I experience the solitude that I so desire at this moment!'

'We're gonna get our noses buried in santorum!' said Jayjay J. Shagbag, his associate. 'I'm ready to bail right now. Who among you are with me?'

The entire team of twenty-six souls began to grumble.

'Do we want our careers destroyed – *by strolling players?*' P.J. Drunton, DA, asked no one in particular.

Associate Imperial Prosecutor Sterry Turm-Bwongo tossed down her attaché with its potentially damning indictments against Perry in the case of The State of California vs. Flask, and adjusted her designer specs, making sure her WonderBra was aimed correctly.

'Yes, but *what* strolling players they are! Or *he* is! It's Butterbugs, girls, and there he is in person, right below! Any of you wanna just *ditch* this melting glacier by leaping out and sacrificing ourselves on his hunky altar right now?'

Half the team was female, and all of them, even the six declared lesbians, wiggled into the windows' box seats, effectively displacing the good ol' boys, except the I.P.

Parsons-Szaarck was truly worried.

'Let's not lose our heads over a movie star, gals!'

He tried to be folksy, but was utterly ignored. He gazed down at the noble figure, who had the huge crowd completely mesmerized by his oratory.

'Butterbugs!' he thought to himself amidst the mixed ecstasy and panic displayed by his team. 'This is the first time I have seen him in the flesh. I, too, have to admit to his magnetism. He is a leader. We are as cat dirt. Soiled, no less. In comparison, we haven't even portfolios to speak of. He has The People. We only have The Law. He will triumph, every time.'

Then he turned to gather his things. He would not lead the way out of these courts, but he would follow along. Perhaps he would achieve his desire for custodianship of some remote and radioactive site, as this affair would certainly 86 his tenure as Imperial Prosecutor. An official announcement was quite in order, though.

'Ladies and Gentlemen,' Parsons-Szaarck cleared his throat and took courage. 'Due to the extraordinary circumstances which have, of a sudden, been delivered before the venue of this case this very day, and indeed, as I speak, and as a result of the mixed grill of feelings displayed by you, my Team Extraordinaire, I am compelled to honor your dearest wish. And that is, to scuttle this case here and now.'

'Right on, O'Moore!' crowed Assistant Prosecutorial Engineer Peal Bigdom. 'Cower in the face of challenge, and git ready for obscurity!'

'Maybe,' the I.P. replied, with growing indignant feelings. 'But how can we *do this* to Butterbugs? What gives us the *right?*'

The rest of the team became almost violent in their passionate agreement.

'Yes! Yes! Oyez! Oyez! Hark ye! Hear ye! An end now! An end to all!'

Even Bigdom came to say:

'I guess you're correct. What were we *thinking?*'

'I'm glad you concur, Peal,' said the I.P. 'We have a universal accord. Shall we adjourn?'

There was a good deal of hullaballoo in the chamber, as the ultrastar's speech had ended outside and everyone was in the process of chucking the case. They were already casting folio upon folio of germane papers into the now-glowing fireplace on the far wall.

Then I.P. Parsons-Szaarck ascended the ceremonial lecture lectern and announced:

'I do declare that this case, that of The State of California vs. Flask, is hereby and herein discarded from this chancery, under the provisions of Bylaw No. 7738-A, carrying the popular title, 'In the event of dark and unusual needs'.

'And now, a personal note, in form of commentary, which shall not be a part of the record of these here preparatory proceedings: I do not know what the future holds for us, but I hereby and herein request all of you to vacate this here chamber immediately at the sound of this descending gavel contacting its smash-pad.'

He raised the venerable hammer up, but before he could finalize his imperative with a BAM!, the great double doors to the chamber burst open.

'You CANNOT!' a voice sounded off. 'You cannot discard this here case! YOU CANNOT *DO THAT!* Equal justice, I say! Under *lawr!*'

It was Butterbugs, freshly arrived from the heady barricade lust of the pressing crowds below. A legal eagle had tipped him off as to the radical intentions of the prosecutorial team. He entered the room, as if on a chariot, and raised his arms in civic warning. He was accompanied by a host of bailiffs, attorneys, law enforcement officers, ATM agents, puisne judges, Whit Bissell, the Rev. Al Sharpton, Graydon Carter, Bianca Jagger, Dennis Weaver, Paris Hilton, Edward Andrews, Lily Tomlin, Norman Mailer, Deal Kailers, Dr. Dre, Ravana Mundrendrannacan, Kate Moss, James Wolcott, Joan Baez, Sheenah Creenah, Ranald MacDougall, Amy MacDonald, Dougal Haston, Neil Armstrong, Ray Teal, Maureen O'Hara, Cesar Chavez, and Bill Buckley, Jr.

'You can, will, and *must* proceed with this case, as ordered by the mandates of our statutes at large!'

Many in the throng, witnessing Butterbugs' power, had to bolster themselves so that they wouldn't pass out.

Remembering that he was indeed a lawyer, Parsons-Szaarck plucked up enough fortitude that remained in him.

'May I speak? But Butterbugs, sir, is this not what you desire? To wit, our withdrawal?'

'How dare you ask such a question of a feature picture player! Who am I to stop the grand wheels of organized judicature and the virtual pharaonic sway it has over The People, its combine of Solomonic wisdom, combined with the Ashokan Edicts, the Teachings of Dith, the writings of Wm. O. Douglas, and the mighty achievement of Roman jurisprudence, guiding us through the treacherous by-lanes and gullies of modern life and its effects? How came I to stand at this juncture, with power of life or death? Do not give me this authority, if it be only just a jiffy in the popular mind of followers! Are we so desirous of detaching ourselves from the already established terra firma of civilized order? Or, in our modern perception of standing at the peak of humanity's achievements thus far, have we concluded that it is all so corrupt, that the entire mass of our progress to this point has become so riddled with hypocrisy and purposelessness, that 'tis best to surrender the baton to lesser lights and decamp into a dropped-out state?

'I come not to lecture, but to charge; to charge that this trial must and shall proceed – with immediate dispatch! This day! Now! As *scheduled!!!*'

His voice echoed unto the Rubenesque frescoes above. The affirmative cheers that followed left the Imperial Prosecutor and his team absolutely no option but to gather their items and indeed decamp, not into any, as Butterbugs warned, drop-out plane, but into the ornate and cavernous High End Court, with its theatrical ambience (consulting architects: Rapp & Rapp; consulting producer: Sid Grauman), and its handy seating capacity of 2020 persons. Today, it was SRO.

The trial commenced, Judge Lakey Broath III presiding.

With all the precision of one of Sid's prologues, everyone found their proper places while a processional overture by Berlioz was played, which, by the way, all found very helpful in blocking and prepping for this ambitious and complex examination, so that one might live or die.

As Judge Broath ran a conservative courtroom – wigs, robes, women's doily cravats, and other de rigueur accessories, as in the style of silk – the gathered heat and stuffiness approached that of the Madras High Court. Which was where, incidentally, Butterbugs had made a courtroom drama once: 'They Came To Triplicane' (Ziggurat). Certain comfort items found in movie palaces, such as ice-cold A/C, were not embraced by sober judge and bland bureaucrat in this vast judicial palace.

Though personnel high and low were gussied and dolled-up in this operating theatre, Butterbugs, who was here to do star testimony, displayed the garb of a worker. In fact, he wore what he wore when he was a scaffold laborer. In this dress was he a glaring standout, and there were many who felt hypocritical for their blatantly contrasting garments. Yet, they did not feel humiliated by Butterbugs' guile-free and apolitical appearance, so much as instructed by it.

Then, as the oppressive sub-drama of legalia went about its mannered course, it came time for Butterbugs to mount the dock.

Judge Broath acknowledged the testifier with admiration and extra decorum. Butterbugs knew this, and so wished to use his influence, blatantly if necessary, to get Perry off this plainly bum rap.

But his was all a sincere and honest approach. Really, it was.

'Really, my friends.' Butterbugs began his testimony with these three words, which catapulted to legendary status almost instantly. And the implication was, listen, and understand a truth that may not yet be known.

Upon Judge Broath's invitation, Butterbugs undertook his speech, as the trial had reached a tipping point. If Perry had indeed allowed his stagemom to pass from among the living due to certain circumstances, were said circumstances due to negligence, or malicious mischief?

Butterbugs was to propose neither.

Confident, urbane, non-confrontational, he began to speak while standing between the wide tables of the opposing sides in the case. To his right, the Imperial Prosecutor, having rested his case, sat at the head of his formidable lineup of ten assistants, and the look he gave Butterbugs was not one of challenge, but an expression of hope. Deliverance, even.

To his left, Mr. Flask sat, his wrists free at last, calmly placed on the sage velvet of the defendant's well-worn seat, next his lone council, M. Prerrer Prêtre, late of the Naumburg Courts of Burgenlandkreis.

Behind him, Darcie and the kids sat anxiously, tears filling the little girl Thisbe's eyes, her pale face topped by a bluebird beanie, while Uncas sat in sailor-suit presentation; his gazing up and around the magnificent ceiling with wonder betrayed a mind yet too young to realize the gravity of the procedure now running in the room at large.

And Darcie, oh, Darcie was there in body and soul, as wife, mother, lover. A dream of a face, shining with elegance and belief. The more cares that were heaped upon her, the more like a serene saint she looked. No pretensions to saint-

hood though. Only a beautiful woman of great dimension, who loved her husband.

'How could I have not known of this?' Darcie thought. 'My lack of dimension
only increases dear Pair-Perr's sweetness in my eyes! My heavens above! Deliver
him from gruesomeness! Empower Butterbugs to achieve transcendent justice,
with Polyhymnian inspiration! Please spare delicate Thisbe and blameless Uncas
from ruin!'

So, in the name of they, Darcie and the kids, if no one else, did Butterbugs
anchor his words.

'Really, my friends, there will always be debate, on all levels of existence, and
in all moments of life, and between all who are wont to know, about what truth *is*.
Ever elusive in perception, but ever-present in fact, truth the subjective and truth
the imperishable are both our double-destinies in this experience of life. Aren't
they? Life! Truth! Yea, or nay! I cannot tell you my version of it, nor can you tell
me thine. For it is all a matter of opinion – at first.

'Far be it from me to state a truth and have it end up as chronicle. I come from
a world of construction, of realization, or specific intent. So does he who requires
defense, this day. For what is a moving picture but an assembly of manufactured
concretions, meant to come into an entity as surely undeniable, and indeed, as de-
finable as this cherished chamber itself, which currently surrounds us and protects
us from the elements, both natural and man-made, without?

'Therefore,' he continued, gaining in momentum and volume as he proceeded
at a stately pace, down the crimson-plush carpet toward the high Bench, all uphol-
stered in japanned teak and tarwood, 'do not take my utterances as anything other
than opinion. Because, as we all know, for every brain cell that has ever existed,
there is at least one opinion. And for every brain, there is one opinion for every
cell of its composition.

'However, I care not to entertain you with such obvious trifles. Essentials boil
quickly in murder trials. Evidence displayed, adds up.'

He spun about and pointed at the defendant.

'How dost thou plead, protagonist? Guilty! Aye, aye. 'Tis guilty that ye be. But
to what extent? Under your watch then, did said stagemom expire. Under your
protection. We know that much, and in the air of written legal language, you are
within the realm of *actus reus*. But, were it not true that the honeybee gives life
to the fig flower so that we may have figs, is it also not possible for one to allow
a death of an oppressor, not for the sake of that oppressor's death at all, but so
that the oppressed may be *free?* For was it not Ed Coke who said, '*actus non facit
reum nisi mens sit rea*'? Really, my friends, an act (in this case, the allowance of
a death), does not make one guilty, unless one's mind – our defendant's mind – is
also committed to that act.

'People,' he resumed his progression toward the Bench, 'I confess, and let me
tell you, a court such as this is a good place for an all-out confession, I will not
continue to wow you with legalistic gobbledygook. Truth does not seek obfusca-

tion, regardless of its seductive tendencies. Where else do we enjoy our private vices, our secret perversions, our wished-for aberrations, but in the privacy of veiled and heavy covertness?

'Day, our best hope in reconciling the terror of the night with our hopes for the future, casts its light on truths we can all understand. Therefore and thus, mystery, begone!

'See! See, how day's noontide wash streams through yon lofty windows! See where it casts its truth-seeking rays! There! There, onto that place in this court, where our defendant sits! Is it not striking? Does it not reveal a truth? Not an opinion, but a truth. But what *kind* of truth? Does it mean he is truthful in all ways, and this trial was just a pathway toward our obvious conclusion, that indeed, he was responsible for stagemom's death, but he remains a virtuous man, husband and father, nevertheless?

'Oh, light of the day's apogee, do not let us think that your canny timing in shedding your bounty on he who gives us reason to assemble here is a full explanation for an ecce homo epiphany. Rather, let it serve as an introduction to my tale.

'It is a tale that needs to be told by one who shares the profession of making mud pies for the public, except on a motion picture screen. And I speak proverbially, especially in this, the metropolis of invention. A moving mural of the moment perhaps, animated by drama, and made with care, though via artifice.

'Artifice! For purposes sometimes edifying and purposeful, or diversionary. And that's certainly purposeful in our activities today, as well. Consider all the joys that we in pictures have brought to audiences worldwide. So, do not necessarily dismiss our activities as puffy play-acting, or mental masturbation for distraction's sake. Although, I must say, I call 'guilty' to many in our Industry for doing just that, and to their numbers I sheepishly add my raised hand from time to time...'

The court chuckled politely.

'But, no!'

Butterbugs continued in a more forceful vein, having reached the heights of the terrace that served as a virtual stage in front of the judge's high console. The lighting was sophisticated. Lee Garmes could have plotted it! And the surroundings, Roland Anderson obviously had a hand in them!

Not since his appearance on the broad boards of Grauman's Metropolitan had Butterbugs a better stage from which to expound.

'Really, my friends, no, I make it plain. I work from scripts and take direction so as to conform to the needs of each specific picture. And so, as a strolling player, I wish to illustrate the following example, so that the court will come to better understand what the hell happened in the case of Perry Flask and his stagemom.

'At this important juncture, I mildly request – nay! I *demand*, like Hades itself, or even *him*self, that certain footage be mechanically projected here and now. Scenes conceived and put into motion by the man Flask himself! They show –

without trickery or pre-planned pontifications, without manipulative rhetoric or persuasive rubbish, or *anything* meant to deflect or decry evidence, as already presented in this exhausting case – THE TRUTH, with appropriate twists, regarding this 'bumping off of said stagemom' business. It shall serve as prelude to what I will then add as substantial testimony.

'For I was *there*, at the actual Flask residence, and I am a vital participant, not a mere strutting poseur in its drama, in which insight as to this defendant's real role shall stand revealed. Ye shall see the extreme circumstances of our moments together, in which we debate the gravity of existence itself!

'After this essential viewing, I invite you, Judge Broath, to terminate this mess of a trial with pace-express, for you will find no other consensus by which to do so *even possible.*'

'Please proceed, Butterbugs,' the Judge answered brightly.

'Thank you, your honor. And now, I present an approved motion picture presentation of the footage I referred to earlier. See it and duly ponder! Jimmy?! Ready!'

The huge glowing gondolas far above began to dim. Heavy drapes were silently drawn across the high windows. A drive-in-sized screen was lowered behind the Bench, while a special flat-panel rose in front of the Decider so that he did not have to turn about and strain to visually assemble the giant images to be projected for the courtesy of the people. Then, into the center aisle at the back of the audiotoriumite, a soundproofed 65mm projector was wheeled. Perry's footage had been blown up to BKV-enhanced size from high-res digital files. A Porta-Vox of the Thiertre sound system was hooked up and tested. Almost instantaneously, the rustling and murmuring subsided so that the much-anticipated scenes could now unspool.

All humans present were soon sitting on the edge of their seats.

Fully did it play, from a proem spoken by Flask to prepare the viewer for what was to come, his phone call to his trusted friend, a seven minute filler-medley of organ intermezzi, featuring afternoon showtime favorites from a cherished Ethel Smith album, followed by the Butterbugs scenes, intact and uncut.

The picture ended with the defendant, captured by the telephoto capabilities of an exterior camera's zoomar lens, calling out nobly, 'I was imprisoned by her power, Butterbugs! But you, a free man in so many ways, are always to be unchained!'

Slow fade to black, followed by a modest credit roll of a minute or so, judiciously lacking scoring of any kind. Butterbugs produced the venture, with generous gratis distribution by Kemmendine Pictures, who owed the ultrastar a remunerative or equivalent motion, due to a contractual settlement of some months before.

Thus did Butterbugs understand and utilize his Industry.

After the house was restored to In-Session settings, many in the audience were to be seen daubing an eye or two with kerchiefs, while others blew their noses so as to assuage the gathered mucus of stirred feelings.

So *many* feelings, keenly felt, in this courtroom today!

Butterbugs returned to center stage. In lieu of responding to any applause, which Judge Broath naturally forbade (even in cases involving Butterbugs), the testifier made simple obeisance to the Bench before continuing. The judge was absolutely awed by this gesture, though he did not betray it. His throat was crowded with the lump of favorable emotion, and were he to deliver any verbal proclamation or teaching at that moment, his voice would have been distorted by a liverdumpling timbre – an unsustainable condition for any judge.

'Really, my friends,' Butterbugs resumed with a debonair flourish, 'a while ago, at a rally outside this very mega-structure, this very day, I exhorted a gath-eréd crowd to be reminded of a certain picture I starred in – along with one Perry Flask. It is titled 'She Is No More'. It was released by Columbia Pictures... No, no, I believe it was Your Basic Pictures International. (See? I told you, opinion must by needs give way to shining truth!)

'In any case, it is a simple tale, scripted by Oscar Saul, Art Cohen, Dalton Trumbo, Daniel Taradash and Pearl Bailey. Its screen story and scenario are re-ferred to, as you might have noticed, in the form of an incomplete innuendo in the testimonial motion picture you have just seen. To describe it in brief, 'No More' tells of an honest fellow who is trying manfully to keep his family not only from the jaws of debtors' prison, but also from the associated impact of certain degra-dation from want. That is the premise from which we start to absorb this picture.

'So, the mise en scène is set. One day, a selfish and baleful relative in the form of an aged and sick aunt comes into the lives of our given family. A mother and a father and two kids. They are conventionally set up in life, living in modest cir-cumstances. Therefore, sincerity is their principal frame of reference. The inter-loper is demanding and shrill, with a ghoulish, even zombie-like appearance. (Su-perbly played by Kathleen Freeman.) She then restlessly desires certain courses of action to be taken. Her goal is to seek revenge for damage wrought in childhood, and she proceeds to take it out on the family unit, who are completely and utterly unassociated with that which deformed her mind. With a diseased and toxic soul, she actually inflicts her unhappiness upon they who have selflessly taken her in.

'It is a universal story, your honor! Perhaps more universal than any of us mak-ing it at the time ever contemplated. (Verily, each of us thought ourselves in the midst of *something great...*)

'The scale of the aunt's offenses reaches such a pitch that the dad, isolated in his dearest desire to make every facet of his gathered situations work out the best for all involved, perhaps with the exception of himself (regarded last, if at all), finally resolves to remove the offending cinder from the eye of the family unit, while that unit still holds together.

'With no murderous intent, and only desirous of recapturing the simpler and happier days of the past, the dad conspires to cause the aunt to be released from her earthly sufferings in as humane a way as possible.

'This is where, in this motion picture, the element of, to use a legal term, *tem-*

189

porary insanity comes into play. It is no condition of convenience! Rather, a torturous storm, to threaten a responsible citizen's sincerity! How it rages, over his
head. How it weighs him down! Oh, put yourself in *his* place...!'

Within the matrix of his actor's eye-contact strategy while in performance,
Butterbugs caught a glance at the significantly-affected expression that Judge
Broath wore on his learned face. His wig was sopped with sweat, his lips were
pursed with concentration, and he fiddled with his favorite calabash pipe, which
he elected not to puff on for once. In a micro-second of internal debate, the testifier wondered whether the expression was one of a rapt audience member, or a
preliminary legal-minded response leading to potential displeasure over his own
dramatization of a not-quite-germane sidetrack away from the destiny of Perry
Flask the man, rather than Perry Flask the actor. The ultrastar wisely decided to
simmer his performance a bit.

'But really, your honor. The universality of this scenario must be borne out,
and I shall do so without too much further exposition or equivocation. You see,
the similarities between the fictional drama, which I describe, and the nonfictional
drama that *you*, your honor, shall decide, becomes more acute, more remarkable,
and more *urgent* with every second that passes in this here court hall.

'The dad, so grievously affected and afraid for those he provides for and protects, employs pre-meditated craft, but without conscience, so preoccupied is he
with the vicissitudes of daily life. This mission of elimination is simply added to
his list of things needful for daily evolution.

'So he embarks on a program to phase the already verifiably sick aunt out of
their lives by means of meds sneaked into her daily routine. So that she may find
that life *fades* rather than ends. His intentions are solidly humanitarian, in spite of
the aunt's beastliness. He regales her with the gramophone ballads of her youth
and gives her wistful thoughts to consider within a glow of benign nostalgia.
While all this time, a fog about her grows as he proceeds with the plan to ensure
her exit from their lives, and her own.

'I must say, even at the point of this advanced state, in which there is no going
back, all the characters in this photoplay are unavoidably sympathetic. Really!
Particularly the dad. The scriptors have ingeniously introduced means by which
the dad converses with all family members, including the aunt. They wholeheartedly agree with him as far as his philosophy of life be concerned, and even encourage him to enact whatever means are necessary to open up all avenues of
potential happiness. *Including* the aunt. In the penultimate scene, the aunt virtually condones what her nephew is in fact doing to her, for she knows it is the only
possible route to be taken on this, the royal path of life.

'Think of it! A decent person fully embarked on a course by which certain
problems will engage with solutions, for they are best for everyone concerned,
including society at large. Except for the fact that they are slightly illegal when
viewed within the strict canon of law.

'Really, my friends, how can humanity be regulated by law which does not allow for poignancy? Have you ever thought about such things? Huh? I know that, were it not for my participation in this picture (as Parson Spuxlurr), and Perry Flask's role as the dad, and my visitation to Perry's Drylands tracts, as you saw for yourselves in the previously-projected picture, I would never have cause to contemplate these here issues. Even the presence of Jack Kevorkian, who did a non-MD cameo (he played a friendly neighborhood greengrocer, I believe) was no reason to suspect that the effects of this picture might influence any future acts or schemes by any of the cast therein, *including* Dr. Kevorkian.

'But I tell you, I think that this be the case. In fact, I know it. I know it to be the truth. 'She Is No More' *was* an influence to its star, albeit subjectively, but *not* subversively! Really, my friends, I know Perry Flask to be of impressionable and artistically-oriented mind. By his intense concentration on this role, seeds were planted, dormant perhaps, for a set amount of time. But once the circumstances of fertilization by chance occurred in the theatrics of his brainpan, a familiar, already-scripted scenario was at the ready, to which hands made desperate by offenses shown by an offending party, lay their claim. And without ceremony or conspiracy or even very much thought, a course of action was embarked upon, as surely as the subliminal power of a commercial for Frosty's Mix lays claim to the decision-making of millions. Because, when an ad for a new product in the Frosty's lineup hits the media outlets of print, stage, screen, and color television, as well as the information superhighways and byways, all who behold it shall be impressioned!

'Where then, does guilt lie? With the team that wrote this powerful picture? By he who directed it? Or photographed it (in Panavision)? Guilt lies, of course, with he or she who prosecutes a deed. Yet, by the influence of other forces shall that guilt be somewhat shared.

'And now, after a brief interval in which rest stops might be effected – (WC ushers await your needs, as the path to the loo is labyrinthine in this nonfiction-the-atrical venue) – I therefore charge the Court with a Special Evidential Viewing of said picture, 'She Is No More', if your judgeship is willing.'

'The Court and presiding judgeship are *willing*,' replied Judge Broath.

'Well, that's pretty good!' replied Butterbugs cheerily.

The interval passed in utterly orderly and solemn fashion. No one at all tried to be either comedian or critic to allay the gravity of the occasion. All were re-sponsible citizens, guided by the propriety that was its structure. The Press were particularly respectful, being fully occupied with gavel-to-gavel coverage.

'And now?' Butterbugs as Advocate stated, as the stragglers anxiously re-claimed their seats, 'Why! We shall view the Your Basic Films' presentation of the Terry Grubulon/Mingus Orb production, 'She Is No More'. A Blaby ParTu-rion picture. It will provide deep, deep background in the direction of this case's imperatives. The picture is in black and white, and in scope. There will be no intermission. Thank you for your attention.'

Then two 35mm projectors replaced the senior 65mm unit, just retired, and

'She Is No More' rolled. In each of its 142 minutes, those who saw it, if even for the fifth time, were nothing less than electrified.

After 'The End', once again the great lanterns were illuminated, and a later, wiser daylight was allowed back into the stunned vastness of the courtroom.

'A helluva picture, eh?' said its star, after the final fadeout and AMPA rating card.

The Court was too moved to respond, so, in church-like fashion, Butterbugs picked up the ball.

'To which I append, in this photoplay, as in the Flask case itself, guilt is shared not in the legal, but in the ethical sense. Such is the power of we who are part of picture shows, and it effectively demonstrates, without the specter of a doubt, the cinema's relations of validity with *life itself*.'

Butterbugs bowed to both jury and Bench, but not as an add-on. It was a posture he'd worked toward, so the impact of its humbleness was especially noteworthy to all essential observers.

'And then –'

Butterbugs was interrupted by an usher who approached him and pulled his workers' denim sleeve in order to deliver a note without interrupting his actual speech. Interrupt it he did, though.

Butterbugs deemed it mandatory to cease his oration to see what the message contained. He opened the envelope amidst some of the most intense anticipation he'd ever felt in any live forum or performance. There was muttering and whispering aplenty from all quarters of the courtroom.

'I would, uh, like to announce, as this is a matter of extreme importance, that uh, it says here, as this paper I hold contains the results of high-level laboratory functions, that, after triple-checking DNA hyper, hypo, and mean-range tests, it has been determined beyond the remotest shadow of the most overwhelming doubt, that Perry Flask is NOT, I repeat, NOT blood-related to the late corpse known as his stagemom.'

The court went absolutely wild with chatterment and marveldom. Judge Broath rained down his gavel, initially out of instinct over the Butterbugsian idyll being cut short, and then out of rage that his court was turning into a circus. But beyond his gavel's power in cutting down the mob's excesses was the voice of Butterbugs made more effective yet. If more words of import were to come, that was reason enough to return the court to sensible control.

'I, uh... I think it would be only fitting... if I now submitted this new and shocking evidence to the Bench, so that it may be perused by not only the supreme authority in this tabernacle of justice, but also by yonder jury, to whom I have not particularly catered, if only because I am not an advocate, but merely a testifier. I surrender my dominance now, so that verdict and sentencing may ensue without further equivocation, after wisdom has been meted out.'

Judge Broath struggled to contain how much he was hit with this whole thing by carefully doling out his thanks via looks more than words.

'The court is – well, beyond grateful, Butterbugs,' he nevertheless managed to say. 'Your multi-media testimony is not only of great value, it promises to affect the outcome of this case more than any attorneys' time-filling rhetoric.'

Then, he cleared his throat with lawful authority.

'Bailiff, I now submit this evidential report to the jury, so that it can proceed to its conclusion *without further equivocation*, hear?'

The use of Butterbugs' phrase did not go unnoticed by either of the actors in the room. The ultrastar noted it with satisfaction, as did the defendant.

The bailiff, weighted down by the bulky ceremonial robes he was obliged to wear, made to receive the slight text of the lab report from the judge. He was a husky, if not overweight, direct descendant of slaves, and his pride was such that he had bailiffed at most of the county's excelsior cases these many years now. However, the Tamil-heat and the heavy responsibility of this particular case had inflicted him with a breakdown that was not fatal, but it effectively ended his high privilege of serving his judge's wishes in this court hall today.

He faltered, and made to collapse, but Butterbugs reached him just in time and provided relief, accompanying him in his descent to the carpet in easy stages, and once there, delivered a few drops of liquid resuscitation in the form of sprinklings from the boda bag he pulled from his workers' kit. Also, he applied certain massages to the bailiff's dome, thus preventing an occult aneurism, if one threatened, and was in fact imminent, from reaching climax. Continuing the massage also ensured that unhappy condition's total banishment from his person, as pressure was brought to bear where none had ever been present before. Thus, the vessels in question were appeased. A simple solution to complex consequences.

'Butterbugs,' whispered the bailiff, while the court was anxiously suspended, 'You played a scene with Moses Gunn in his portrayal of one of my ancestors in your outstanding epoch-making picture, 'Before The Late Unpleasantness' (Selznick). I am eternally grateful for your humanitarian approach to that story. It is a gratitude upon which I might be, well, pleased enough to surrender my life... at this very moment.'

'Bailiff!' Butterbugs replied, 'You are not going to die at this time. You have too much to do yet. But you will heed not my warning, but your overwrought body's, and you will return to your duty here upon completing a TICE-like transformation of slimming, re-evaluation of your health pursuits, and then implement a remedial plan involving recovery. Medic?? Place this gentleman into your care!'

'Oh, Butterbugs! Thanks be to you!' the bailiff responded with joy in his heart.

While the medic detail tenderly hauled the bailiff off on a porta-gurney, Butterbugs cheerfully completed his interrupted assignment of delivering the lab report to the jury.

By the choreography of court procedure, provided by law, the grindings that often take eons were enabled to clock a natural time, which was, in this case, about an hour.

Judge Broath was fighting back tears. How could he throw the book at Perry Flask? How could he do such a thing to *Butterbugs?*

The gavel seemed to take four seasons to fall. When it finally did, sentence was pronounced.

'One year in a no-labor, academic research-allowing, child-playtime, no-security facility, with early release for good behavior fully anticipated and utterly expected.'

There. Butterbugs' Rule of Law had been duly observed, practiced, and carried out. Perry Flask served illustriously for 199 days, at the end of which he was once again a free man. Like Butterbugs.

'We must *party*, friend,' were Butterbugs' first words to his fellow actor, newly reformed.

To celebrate, Butterbugs took the whole legally-oriented and reunified gang to see a terrific new show at the Capitol in NYC: Wallace & Davis!

So numerous was the party that the star had to buy most of the orchestra seats. How else to celebrate such a huge triumph?

Wallace & Davis bounced in, and 'Playing Around' really got going. Music and lyrics by Irving Berlin. Book by Krasna, Panama & Frank.

Keen on the new show, Butterbugs took notes.

– What do you do with a general?
– When they stop wining and dining him...
– Two and three and four star generals... unemployed...
– In the immortal words of Bob Wallace: 'We open *Christmas Eve!*'
– Sounds very Vermonty.
– Boy, girl, boy, girl. The Sisters Act. The Haynes Sisters.
– Freckle-faced Haynes, the dog-faced boy!
– Boy, he sure was a good lookin' kid (cameo by Carl 'Alfalfa' Switzer).
– Betty! Judy!
– Snow! It won't be long!
– I dream about liverwurst.
– A tall cool blonde, a little on the scatback side, but SEXY, SEXY!
– Grab the cow.
– The kid played a percentage.
– They're doin' choreography.
– Chaps, who dig taps.
– Mr. Bones,
– Mr. Bones, how are ya doin', Mr. Bones?
– Rattlin'!
– Everybody's got an angle.
– That's a pretty cynical point of view.
– I'm sorry, it's the best I can do.
– Well, I guess there's a lot about show business I don't understand.
– You read it to me, son.

– What's it gonna do to his pride?

– A Vermont volleyball!

– Mutual, I'm sure.

– Give me a Joe who has winter and snow – in his heart.

– Love – you didn't do right by me.

– At the Carousel Club.

– Stuck with a Weirdsmobile for life.

– Get me Ed Harrison on the phone.

– Don't forget the key role: Susan Waverly.

– Christmas 1944.

– Irving gets top billing – that's in his contract!

– Der Bingle and the Gang.

– Not Mitzi, but Mitzi-ish: VeeraEllun: elfish & endless legs.

– With Tean Chagger and Percy 'Club Caah' Helton, and special guest star, JOHN-NY GRANT as ED HARRISON.

– Pine Tree.

– Coming in to Pine Tree.

– The curtain-pulling sequence.

– Mike 'Crazy Hungarian' Curtiz directed – just like the picture version, first ever in VistaVision, lensed by Loyal 'I'd work at any studio' Griggs! (Paramount, 1954). 120 min. Technicolor.

Despite that heritage, wasn't seeing a show with all that talent live on stage really something? Better than a courtroom drama, that was for sure.

After the final curtain, Perry and Butterbugs looked at each other, the silver-accented auditorium highlighting their thoughts.

'It's amazing,' reflected Butterbugs. 'Irving practically wrote our story. He *rules*, baby. He sent best wishes telegrams to both of us! Here's yours. I was waiting for the right moment. No squawks, no beefs. And no stagemoms, as far as the mind can reach. But hell, let's go backstage and meet Wallace and Davis. They make us look like goofballs in a gopher hole!'

'Butterbugs,' said Perry, 'You will have to get used to a life without thanks. We in your service have lost our ability to speak it…'

24.

Weirdsmobiles and Spirochetes

PADRÉ ESTEBAN: Abomination!

ERNESTO: Old man! Hide me in the bell tower!

PADRÉ: I *will* not!

ERNESTO: You get me a monk's robe. NOW!

PADRÉ: Get out! You – you apostate!

'CUT!' yelled the director, Edna Tzu.

'Butterbugs! Don't come on so strong! Your make-up tones will be tweaked into the most homely and lurid colors in final print. You are overdoing it.'

The company suddenly grew dead silent. A director, telling Butterbugs how to act?

Butterbugs approached the Kwangsi province native, who was a little over half as tall as the ultrastar.

'What did you just say to me?'

'Butterbugs, we are telling this story with *colors* as much as we are through dialogue. You know that.'

'I do. It was my idea, remember?'

'Yes, Butterbugs, but I am *implementing* your respectable idea.'

'So you are, Miss Edna.'

'That's better.'

'*Direct* me, Miss Edna.'

'Butterbugs, come with me for a moment. Krenston, tell the company to take fifteen.'

'Yes, Miss,' said the a.d., anticipating shrieks emanating from the rushes trailer.

Miss Edna led the Mexi-clad Butterbugs into the trailer.

'Sash, leave us.'

'Yes, Miss,' said the switcher.

'But before you do, wind back to take 31, and switch on the Goofballizer.'

'Yes, Miss.'

'Butterbugs, this is the medium CU of you threatening the terrified padré.'

'I know dat...' Butterbugs was trying not to be snotty.

'Now, let's go into CU #7. See your facial lines? See what we're doing?'

As the take rolled, she adjusted the Goofballizer so that Butterbugs' serape, mustache, makeup and mariachi sombrero were rendered in colors approximating a sickeningly blurry and tinted polychrome postcard of, say, a 1930s bungalow motel. As if certain foodie combos might have been plowed into his mouth, like peanut brittle with mayonnaise, or maraschino cherries in prune gravy with Demerara sugar sprinkled on top, Butterbugs felt bilious.

Then they went to the super CU that showed his putrid-looking eyes glaring directly at the camera. Not hallucinogenic, these images, but certainly nightmarish, rather like the bathos of a sour stomach hangover in a damp, distress-filled sleeping bag (for Butterbugs had vivid memories of such things).

'Turn it off!!!!' wailed Butterbugs, exactly like George C. Scott, when seeing his daughter in a peepshow porno pic in 'Hardcore' (Columbia, 1979).

'I like that, Butterbugs. We'll use it. Just like George C. Scott. You'll say it when you're strapped into the electric chair. Did they have electric chairs in 1906?'

'I now see what you're doing with the colors, Miss Edna. But is it cinema?'

'It's cinema, Butterbugs. And thiertre, too. Remember that. And don't forget about the art factor.'

'You're right. I tell you, you're right! Could I be *that* detached by my new dizzying stardom?'

'Perhaps. But I know what is on your heart. I know of your experience, and your multi-dimensional capacity for contextual interpretation through true empathetic exposition. How do you think you came out of those long times in the wilderlands, to lead us all with your inspiration, your talents, and your selfless contributions to those who adore you so? Who taught you to steer towards that destination of destiny, that has offered up so much via the cinema screen, except by your own heart? You have taught us not to live by popcorn alone! Can you not now understand that you must see yourself through, in order to complete your soul-searching, in order to deliver what you were really meant to do, and how to do it? How could you not feel these passions without the triple ribbons of art and drama and performance, weaving their tapestry of purpose around your aura? What do you think drove you out of obscurity, in order to bear such gifts to we who wait so needfully, and yes, so desperately, for them?'

Butterbugs was in tears. Oh, but he knew that Miss Edna was trying to help him *do* all those things!

'No. No, Butterbugs, you are not complete yet. And this is as it should be. There is no fear in this, nor dishonor.'

Butterbugs' tears made his hideous makeup even more outrageous.

'You... you...' He could hardly get out the words. 'You are so good, Miss Edna. And beautiful, too.'

'Oh, you Butterbugs.'

She reached up and pulled his face down to hers, and then she licked his cheek. She giggled.

'Chinese food coloring! Perfect for sick hues! I told Uncle Checkers to mix it in. All organic! Hypoallergenic! And edible! And I could eat you up!'

She let him straighten up and made sure that he could see how high the slit in her Madame Sin dress extended.

'You big bug!'

'Miss Edna!'

'Too bad fifteen minutes are up.'

'Oh yes, Miss Edna.'

'Back to set!'

'Back to... Yes, back to set!'

Even though the communication mike had been left on in the rushes trailer, and even though the entire cast and crew had listened (to *hell* with I.A.T.S.E. break rules!) spellbound, to their director and her star, the returning couple were greeted with nothing but reverence. Some were overwhelmed with sentiment.

For Butterbugs? Why, this was a turning point in his evolution. His acting had turned a corner. Now the artistry could flow without filter or barrage. Nor with flood, for it was in an advanced level of restraint – yes, restraint – that Butterbugs finished the picture. It was just such a surprise to audiences that 'We Ride, Muchachos!' (MGM) was such a profoundly moving, joyous, and devastating motion picture experience. And the fact that Butterbugs had outdone himself proved to all that this star was going to deliver an elemental display of performance drama that was nothing short of a revolution. And for every soul who saw him on the screen, every last one of them was, in their heart, a revolutionist who followed he who inspired them.

Another factor in this ascendancy toward new planes was an incident that occurred on the last day of filming. It was the kind of precision close-up shot that required a skeleton crew, best tackled after hours, without all the daily mix & match vibrations surrounding the sensibilities of cinematic artistes and their strivings.

After the shot was in the can, the crew went home, and the great soundstage door of Metro's Stage 27 was opened all the way, letting in the balmy pre-evening air of release and relief. Butterbugs and Edna tarried in their director chairs, enjoying cigars and grappa in this, the savory verandah hour.

Legs stretched out, Edna placed a pointy-toed boot on top of Butterbugs' FlopperHoof sandals and said:

'The calm before the wrap party and the peace before the separation anxiety, you know?'

'I've never felt that, Miss Edna.'

'Never? I always do. A part of me ends. You know the cliché.'

'I know it but I've never felt it. What's it like?'

'Sad. But there's an edge to it. A bend to be rounded, a gasp that's coming. Something not yet attempted. Something not yet contemplated.'

'Wistful?'

'Sometimes.'

The activity in the 'tween soundstage lanes was almost non-existent now, though the studio forge was alight across the way, ready to cast a temple altar lid, for use in Anthony Mann's latest, a production dealing with the Assyrian world.

'I think we have a good picture, Butterbugs. Remarkable, even.'

'I'm glad I didn't disappoint you.'

'How could you have? It is *me* who can only disappoint *you*.'

'I can never get over how it all happens. How it all comes together. From ideas do we build, and we move toward our goal, and we have purpose. And then we have an outcome.'

'My business is 'construction management'!' Edna joked.

'And mine? To swing the hammer. To tote that bale.'

'And get a little drunk and wind up in jail!'

Edna toasted him with the grape-y rocket fuel.

'Oh yes. All so remarkable. Isn't it?'

Edna smiled back. She wasn't thinking of pictures. She was thinking of Butterbugs. Energized suddenly, despite the long day full of directives. Her smile right then was because of acting, not directing. Her own acting.

Butterbugs, having just finished a picture with this insightful director, still enjoyed professional mind-meld with her, and the avenue of creative and sensational exchange between them remained open and operating. No secrets had any chance of surviving.

'Miss Edna, what did you mean by 'It is me who can only disappoint *you*.'?'

The director of course knew that it was a two-way avenue, so she got on with it.

'I got a doc report today, Butterbugs. I've got an STD. So now, do you.'

Butterbugs had only recently taken his controversial makeup off, but some elements of it were still to be seen as influences on his face, and when he looked over at Edna, it was neither his character nor his real self that was transported in visual communication.

Edna picked up on the understandably mutant development.

'They don't know what it is yet, jewel. It's an STD, but an unusual one.'

Butterbugs was almost casual.

'AIDS, I suppose? HIV?'

'I tell you, they don't know.'

Edna wasn't particularly worked up, either.

'Shall we go down the list? All the way down to the dreaded CNULTI-FLIX-990?'

Edna was turned on by this. She'd spent her creative effort in today's demanding wrap of this picture, an effort that could very well fly or very well flop, and here was Butterbugs, hers to boss about cinematically. And now, uttering these sexy unscripted lines – not as far as content was concerned, silly, but it was all in the tone. She was helpless with desire.

'Oh, Power-Lover! What a hit you are!'

She grew breathy and twisted her arms in his.

'High Loyal Art-Crafter!' he replied, with a shakiness that did not imply STD knowledge, but sheer libido unleashed, 'Kiss!'

She complied, splitting her Madam Sin dress to the hips as she hopped up and clamped her thighs around his pelvis.

'No worries at this moment, my star.'

'We are sharing. We have shared. We are immingled. Me inside you, and now, you inside me. Do you think we're doomed?'

'All I know is that we are *alive*. We are feeling good. Great, in fact. Wonderful, even. And we will feel yet better. *More* wonderful.'

'That is the same, but we are changed.'

'You want to hit me, Butterbugs?'

'I do not want to hit you.'

'Kill me, then?'

'I do not want to kill you.'

'There has to be something you'd like to do.'

'I don't wish to harm you in any way.'

'What, then? Go home?'

'I want to fuck you.'

'Ohhh? With what, then? And how? There is good fucking and bad fucking. And fucked-up fucking.'

'With joy.'

With this coitus, Butterbugs found the higher plane, never elusive when it came to Miss Edna. It was certainly elevated, because the Tantric achievement was undeniable. There was chemistry, unprecedented in his sexual experience, which was undeniably present. It could be defined no further, though. Not in the currents of passion, for love was not the question here. It was high-level, high-frequency lust that incited both of them. Chemistry, then, generated by intimate parts moving and sharing in a concert neither of them understood except within the realms of pure heat. Yet it was exactly that friction under these circumstances, combined with the shared STD particles that really got going into a Petri dish made possible by each side's collaboration. It was a culmination of the mixed elements of sex and death, fear and desire, anti-bodies and pro-bodies, viral commands and cellular stopping points. From this surging give/take, a crazy combine came to be: the life force itself. Not an embryo or a zygote, or any of that reproductive stuff. Here was no product but plain existence, not the creation *of* it, but its sustenance. It remained, it would continue.

In this *masala* then, apparently, a cure was born.

The next checkup, which both followed up the next day, returned no evidence of any malady within either one of their persons. None. And this, in light of the rock-solid sureness of the previous test, in which Edna was pronounced stricken beyond the most wobbly shade, standing in the way of doubt.

Two more sophisticated tests also came back negative.

They were cured, all right. And they had done it themselves. Science would not know why. But now a case study would ensue. It would have to arrive at the same conclusion on its own.

But here is what Butterbugs took away from the encounter. Joined with Edna in especially vivid congress, and with the knowledge implanted that malevolent items ranged in his systems, with the surety of terminal mischief, his whole world-view shifted. There was a decision to be made. If, as the threat promised, doom now stood at hand, and with less predictable abstractions than a little while before, then his acting would naturally be affected. For the time left to him, he was resolved to act in picture shows like there was no tomorrow. Granted, a banal and amusing notion, but he had been shown the grandeur of THE END, and there was nothing for it but to be transformed, if only till his health gave out. Besides, he had been exposed to all sorts of interior influences and suggestions, which darted and parried and flitted and barged through his mind at any given moment of creative processing. On set after set after set. Externally, contributions from directors and other actors had molded his performances all along. But these were internal impulses, bold and glowing and ingenious... Well, he usually avoided them, and was chary about accepting their instinctual power. Besides, doing so might be regarded as egotistical or 'over the top', as the overused expression goes. In his Inner Sanctum though, he knew these were forces for good, for enhancement, for elevation, and for fulfilling his role, whatever it was at the moment.

So now, with the hooded monk of mortality introduced to his mentality by means other than his own half-baked flirtations, timeliness was of the essence. Internal instructional instincts would be paid attention, accessed, utilized, but under proper standards of scrutiny, of course.

This freedom-promise led, not surprisingly, to elation. He bowed down to Miss Edna's body-temple, and in performing every kind of enjoyable sex act with her, proclaimed his gratitude for this gift. If nothing else, she had proclaimed her trust for him, a trust he wouldn't react negatively towards, even in light of a positive test.

The thing was, once Butterbugs had been declared free of all sexually transmitted threats, the mandate of timeliness, which included all liberation of internal creative possibilities, did not leave him. In fact, it grew more foundational, and provided a sure and immovable buttress below the sill of his starting point as an actor.

Dimensions of belief stretched ever deeper, as did credibility and credence. Audiences noticed the additions, and became even more moved. Persons who never turned on to Butterbugs before now, positively *latched* on, by whatever coincidences or synchronicity that led them thither. Exposure to his pictures might occur around any corner, or just plain up ahead. A unanimity of appreciation made the ultrastar's light shine, not necessarily brighter, but with ever-expanding depth, and sureness of purpose.

Plus, he was apparently a healer.

But if his powers could not be harnessed by the scientific community, they could be conveyed through the Drama, surely.

Who can measure such a phenomenon, and how could it ever be reduced to such a primitive mechanism as scientific method?

25.

Deil Busch For President!
– If Not Of The USA,
Then Of Halliburton!

In the first decades of the new millennium, which were actually pathetic, overrated times in terms of general civilization, there were some figures of note that popped up here and there, and they stuck out quite a ways.

The comfort of the maxim 'You are either for me or against me' had come to full fruition in the Land of the Brave. Many talked of polarization, but few rolled up their sleeves to grind into attendant problems, as the profits from said problems were really rather fucking spectacular, thank you very much.

Error was everywhere, but not everywhere within the Industry. Not any more. Butterbugs and his Effect had shaken things up, not seismically, but the trees were full of newly-exposed fruits, and there was new breath breathing in the exec suites of the studios, as well as every location set and exhibition house involving the Seventh Art.

It is not fair to entertain the idea, 'If it hadn't been Butterbugs who was responsible, it would've been someone else'. No, such an insipid observation was necessary, because no one now questioned what Butterbugs was or what he was about. In this way was the world of cinema way ahead of other systems of American administration and guidance, at this point in time.

In no other way but American politics was this divide so clearly demonstrated. New lows, even surpassing those of the first few years of the century, were reached and settled upon. For despite the growing influence of Butterbugs' life-affirmness, there seemed little hope, and the populace was stymied by fear and intimidation.

But here is where the Butterbugs Effect was really coming to the fore. Revaluation of all values was now a possibility, and it was phasing into the public's sensibilities via moving picture entertainment, rather than the more time-honored routes of civics and Congressional procedure.

If Barry Goldwater had referred to a pendulum swinging back and forth between the limits of both the house of government's rooms, in which each side gets its time in the sun, then the Effect of Butterbugs was breaking new ground.

Perhaps that pendulum was turning into a *tetherball*. Which, suspended from a central pole, it might be directed in one orbital direction or the other. But the ball always ends up at a centrally-located apex. Yet, despite the pole's 'middle of the aisle' stance in the physical sense, as things were going now, lateral progression wasn't possible. It was, however, a question of elevation. It was all about ascendancy, not a pit and a pendulum.

That tetherball had chances to fly high and wide in its orbit. It was up to those who chose to give it a shove. An actor could only suggest or imply.

Naturally, when applied to Butterbugs' Effect, this concept could open him up to all sorts of social and political accusations, from holier-than-thou-ism to turbo-socialism, and even Antichrist branding...

Talk about sounding like a movie!

Well, things weren't turning out to be like that at all. When it came to this ultrastar of the cinema, the media waxed refreshingly mature in its perceptions. Fortunately, even though he displayed characteristics that were archetypal, he was never portrayed as a Messiah figure, or a prophet, or even another Dalai Lama. No pope-ishness or wigged-out charismata-character, either. Not because those roles involved things spiritual, but any non-political leader who influenced peoples without portfolio tended to be religionized. In the case of Butterbugs, there was no reason for any such notions to crop up.

The strange thing – strange because it was so unexpected – was that the media was *getting it*, and so were the public.

Of course the starting point was that he was an actor. Then, artist, character-realizer, personality, celebrity, all-around neat guy, sex symbol, star-into-ultrastar and all that. But one who could *act*. And how he acted was compelling, attractive, inspirational.

So, in actuality, he really *did* project elements of spirituality after all, though not in any conventional sense. Mostly his Effect was transparent, as if of the æther. Subtle, mostly. But decisively influential. In that sense, he was more of a Swami Vivekananda figure. Illustrative, presentational, confident in ever-expanding ways of wisdom. And likable. They liked him in Winnipeg and Yemen to the same degree. Love was certainly right in there, too, but not in primitive versions.

Observers often referred to what Butterbugs was *not*. He was not a religious leader, nor a political one, nor was he conventional, etc. etc. This was because they did not yet know what he particularly *was*, except what they could see, hear and feel. So that's where things rested for the present.

Deil Busch, a lesser member of the Busch Cartel, was a key player in a new picture about the always-controversial Halliburton Corporation, 'I Thus And Only Serve' (Mega|Goth). Butterbugs was very enthusiastic about it. This ne'er-do-well, who'd never found success in his many ventures, was now trying... well, acting.

His connections were impressive enough to get him into a Butterbugs picture, mainly due to Hyman Goth's intimate relationship with the Cartel. Mega|Goth Studios was, in due course, 'encouraged' to give the kid a chance.

Butterbugs had a strange sense of pity for Deil, and sensed that being a movie player just might be his bag. He would play Tracy Sears, President of the corporation, who gets bumped off on a trip to Merraguay. Butterbugs would play a lowly chow server, contracted to Halliburton, who makes an exciting discovery.

Though they didn't share any scenes onscreen, Butterbugs nevertheless cultivated the peripheral embryo. It happened when he had a moment after makeup tests (he was to portray an Uzbek in the picture named 'Jess' Úknad).

'Why hi, Deil. Welcome aboard.'

'Hey, call me Peil! My brother made the name up. When I had a dog as a kid, it peed on the carpet! Funny!'

'OK, Peal – heh, I, uh, know a lawyer with that name.' Butterbugs stuck with the proper orthography.

'Ya do? Did he have a dog that peed on him, too? Bet he sued it!'

'Ha ha. Well, Peal, do you know your lines?'

'I'm excitin' my lines as I speak. I'll be cordial with 'em.'

'Perfect, Peal. Perfect.'

And the ultrastar moved on. It was an opportunity to meditate on the meaning of power in America.

Certainly then, it was a new life for Peil, and he had to admit, it had the promise of being a pretty exciting one. He was part of the exodus of former non-fiction personalities who were now devoting their careers to the art of the fictionalized Drama. No, these weren't people who were getting into literary gigs (some of them couldn't scrawl a pleading note to a Purgatory warden to save their souls!). They were getting involved in pictures. Mainly due to Hyman Goth's loyalist virtues, as was the case with Peil.

Ever since a recent 'Life' magazine cover story ('Discredited Politicians Blunder Into Pictures'), the rush was on. Toani Blare was in hit after hit on the West End stage, mostly in odious, over-plummy, and swishy roles. Wink Dinkerson had just inked him for his Broadway debut in 'Porno Shopping Center Confidential'. Kritchurd Puerile was doing very well as a Whit (at least in a couple of C-pictures at Mascot), and Georg Tennunt was dickering with Sonny Projector over a big new action pic, for a key role as head of an international intelligence organization, no less. (Negotiations fell off the edge of the Earth, though.) Duggi Fieth was a prof for a while, but now he couldn't find a job, even as a greeter at a Boal-Mart. Hy Goth's reach only extended so far. And Steve Camboned? What else but playing a comedy trombone in a Joby Baker picture! It was intoxicating and swingin', and the former DeaSea crowd turned out to make fairly decent B.O. for all concerned (albeit of the second-string variety).

Thus the crap shoot of Peil's big screen debut.

'Keep him away from Bangkok, and keep him away from hookers,' was Hy's warning to Eymun Memncamn, the producer. There was, in fact, a Bangkok sequence, but maybe LA's Chinatown could be substituted for the location.

Players on the non-cinema side, though, were not exactly amused. The entire structure of Halliburton positively seethed over the fact that 'I Thus And Only

Serve' was skedded and prepped for production. The trades were making a pretty big deal about it, too.

Halliburton's Chief Emperor Officer Davy Sleasor, from high atop his pyramidal penthouse in Dubai, was preparing the mother of all lawsuits, until his phalanx of law people, horrified, completely and finally censured him.

'In a Butterbugs case, we'd be made meatloaf in court, anywhere on the globe!' his Team Leader declared.

Filming went ahead, unencumbered. Peil Busch was a moderate hit, too.

26.

Shot At A Public Appearance

$\mathbf{N}$ow came a time of pictures that promised their own sets of controversies.

Here was a particularly controversial role for Butterbugs, in which he played a prominent Jew, Nahum Fermé. He is opposed to the concept of Greater Israel, a piece of agenda that floats around in private power circles, with members who fully intend on enacting it. Personally, Fermé supports the successful Permanent Settlement, already brokered by Zxu Yaxi of Chengdu and Darrold Demoines Drumbo of East Liverpool, Ohio. It is the instrument that drew the Israeli/Palestinian conflict to a close by the development of technology that created a duo-plane complex of overlapping realities, both accessible in non-sci-fi ways, so that every side could exist and enjoy the sacred ground simultaneously.

At the same time, Fermé discovers occult but authoritative scriptures that prove the transcendent holiness of a Lost Ground, way, way out in Siberia. That is, the Far Eastern Jewish Autonomous Republic of the old Soviet Union. Ironically, it had been originally sanctioned in the Stalinist Era. Because the Jewish people decamp for the new Promised Land in the film, the Mideast problem is solved. *SOLVED*, do you hear?

An avalanche of criticism followed, on the pretense that the evacuation of a people to a more worthy ground was a cheap-ass solution... But, you know, it really worked.

The picture, based on the bestseller by Yæl Tæzl, 'My Name Is Sholem Goldkorn' (Tinker) predictably caused conflict with the hardass crowd, but mostly because of mindlessly non-kosher refreshments offered on set. Surprisingly, no Jewish comedian emerged to levitate the absurdity. Not one would touch it. Even Henny Youngman was reticent: 'Take that joke – *please.*' Despite the prominent Jews who were responsible, producers Jeremiah Muschtabb, Ezekiel Schimmelklutscher, Shmuel Mestre and the Hummbelhertzl Brothers, the picture was condemned as Possibly Anti-Semitic. Director Edna Tzu was roundly pilloried for being a 'collaborator'. Even Ehel Fetzman, the prop supervisor (and Talmudic scholar), was scolded by noisy, ganged-up hardliners.

Properly recognized by Butterbugs, the non-kosher food problem was quickly tackled by an emergency delivery from Kanter's on Fairfax. After the pic's release, consequent reviews were surprisingly enthusiastic. Sir Nicholas Winton, as brilliant and spry as ever in his 100s, had an important cameo, and Norman Finkelstein sensitively co-scripted. B'nai B'rith endorsed the 159-minute film without reservation, as did Teddy Kolleck and Simon Wiesenthal. Legitimacy achieved.

In pursuit of stories germane to the nightmares of the present age, Butterbugs sought out an intelligent script regarding the Palestinian POV, and he found it in 'To Ramallah in Time' (UA), insightfully scripted by Leon Uris and Edward Said. The ultrastar played the role of a charismatic street person who essentially tells the Palestinians to 'cool it' and when they do, they have every success in settling the age-old agony with a new sense of serenity.

Well, pictures like these would, sooner or later, really piss people off. Not balanced people, or those familiar with Butterbugs' Effect. But every living/breathing person on the globe could never be expected to understand the actor's motives, especially if they were the type who only went to the picture show once per decade or less, or when the Industry condescended to tell a story that mattered to them.

One such, a certain Whimpei Groyle, of Pott's Gully, in northern southern Gee-ohh-jia, chanced to take in a showing of 'My Name Is Sholem Goldkorn' at the non-A/C Hootenanny Theatre, one torrid eve.

What he saw utterly transformed him. Granted, he hadn't seen a 'flick' since 'Porky's' (20th-Fox, 1982), which he thought was an exposé on trichinosis. The telltale words 'Sholem Goldkorn' in the title promised to put to bed his anxiety about 'Who ARE these Jews, anyway?' once and for all. To him, the Jews had killed his Lord without license. Why? From not knowing that Jesus had become a Christian, via his own transformation. That was why.

Of uncertain countenance, Groyle was nevertheless supremely confident that he was an intellectual. Therefore, he would go about this whole Jewish thing intelligently, and probably with a lot more smarts than anybody else. Indeed, he was offended by the message of the picture: that Jews might be revitalized-anew. And what's more, within a gifted context that all could be happy to embrace. Thus empowered out there in Siberia, they just might kill *another* messiah – and kill again!

His Rambler American had fold-down seats, so he had free lodging all the way out to the foreign marches of Hollywood. Because that's where this thing had to be addressed. He did not know anyone, so there was no one to see him off as he departed the (Erskine) Caldwellian dumbo country of the Peachy State. No one would know what he was about to do. Never mind that routine satellite coverage, showing his Rambler's blue streak of oil smoke, could easily trace his passage to the Coast...

There was only one imperative: to resolve this issue once and for all, and to teach those rascals who promulgated this sort of junk a lesson – once and for all.

Like the Ruffinites, sometimes showing up at the source was the only way to achieve final – even terminal – resolve. But Groyle was a lone wolf, and lone he would stay. Besides, why should he share his intellect with anyone else – or the glory that would result?

And so he came to the town of films. He and his Rambler were immediately pulled over on pollution charges, but his plates being Georgian, a stern warning was all that resulted. After a fortnight of determined wandering, he chanced upon Butterbugs himself, making a live appearance at a premiere. As luck would have it, it was for his very next picture, 'To Ramallah In Time' (UA).

When Whimpei Groyle saw 'Ramallah' up there on the marquee, it meant nothing to him. But when he saw 'Butterbugs' up there as well, the inner crucifixion he'd felt over 'Sholem Goldkorn' came back with full force, traumatizing his palms and feet, as if railroad spikes were piercing them.

'If… if The Cross awaits my body,' he wailed, 'then let it be *here!*'

The glitzy extravaganza was unwinding in front of both the Mayan and the nearby Belasco theatres, as crowds were so thick the venue had to be divvied up. Butterbugs intended to introduce the pic to both audiences individually, with unique care and content to each. Such was his style, to ever invent, ever to offer, to expand only, with no contraction.

But Whimpei Groyle, positioned behind an innocuous tank of cow's milk, ladled by the tin cup to those on the sidewalk, held a parlor pistol, with which to cut down this misguided sin-portrayer. That was how he would save the world from further global pollution. That was how he would ensure his own immortality – by knowing when to put on the brakes, where radical movements are concerned.

The events were simple. When Butterbugs raised his right hand to wave at the burgeoning crowds, Groyle perked up, aimed, and fired. Butterbugs stood there, but his arm collapsed. Without a struggle, Groyle was taken into custody. The crowds were orderly, and figured there was some kind of gag going on, possibly as publicity for Butterbugs' forthcoming detective pic, 'Worst Case Fantasy' (WB). So, they genially proceeded into the auditoria. Entertainers were meant to entertain, not to get everybody *worked up* about something…

The star had to specifically request that his assailant not be beaten. In fact, as he was lying on the pavement, the warm blood bathing him like oil, he made a special plea.

'When the pictures in this dual premiere have ground forward – though without my special introductions – and when I am fixed up in hospital, bring him to me. The shootist, that is. P'raps this minor insistence shall be my final request… ever…'

In due course, lying in hospital (in fact, a makeshift sick-bay for homeless street folk, the tents of which stood behind the Belasco), Butterbugs contemplated his assailant. The flesh-wound in his upper left forearm hurt a tad, but it was really quite all right. He'd hurt his palms much worse when nailed to the dragon's blood tree in 'Blaze Of The Summer Islands' (Selznick). Talk about a crucifixion!

'What would I do if I were impressionable as he?' the actor mused, as the shootist was brought forth.

Whimpei Groyle was presented at the entrance to the tented enclosure. Just the two of them, face to face. The whole periphery without was lined with armaments to eliminate this Groyle person, if need be. General John-Thomas 'J-T' Gather, specially imported from Ft. Zukor, was in command of the Authority Forces, which was good. He was no hothead, and a big fan of Butterbugs' performance in 'Sholem Goldkorn' and 'The Little White Kitten and His Pal Dog' (20th-Fox).

One of the reserve troops started bawling inconsolably. Gen. Gather approached him.

'Oh, terrible times! What… what if he dies? What if our own Butterbugs *dies?* What if he is taken from us? In his (sniff) *prime?* What would we do? How could we do *anything?* What a shocking eon we occupy! Oh, grief! Why have you visited me? That's *Butterbugs* in there!!'

'Courage, Troop!' Gen. Gather counseled quietly. 'If Butterbugs breathes his last in the moments to come, you shall join me in the front lines of wreaking comprehensive vengeance on the Hater and Murderer, which this marauder might turn out to be!'

'Thanks, Dad,' the rank-and-file youth replied, brightening.

The shootist, sans weapon, stood rooted at the threshold, his chains jingling.

'Come to me – I cannot see ye clearly in the failing light,' said Butterbugs, after Groyle was pushed into the tent.

The northerly southern Georgian was plainly in shock over what he had done. In fact, he was full of wonder at being in the presence of he whom he tried to erase from the face of the Earth, and for the sketchiest of reasons.

'Are you… a… Jew?' the assailant asked timidly.

'You know, I do not really know *what* I am. I play the parts in photoplays, Whimpei. For those who watch me, who love me, who like me, who think I'm just OK, and yes, for those who do not care very much for me, it calls for an open mind, and an appetite for adventure. Think of how many adventures it takes for one to play a part in a moving picture! I could be anything. I could be a bit of protoplasmic slime. But you would see me up on the screen, and in its sheen ye would, if I have done my job properly, *believe* in what I was – for all that it's worth – in the time I'm up there. For what reason is there, not to imagine the possibilities of other lives lived, other existences told? Well beyond our own limits, be they mud puddles or snow-capped peaks.'

Butterbugs wasn't entirely sure of the IQ of this fellow, nor the limits of his perceived softening of the brain. His 'hick-ccent' was not overly pronounced.

'I have always wanted to scale a snow-capped peak,' said Whimpei carefully, so as not to worsen the wounded one's condition further.

'You have?' Butterbugs thought immediately of Sri Aurobindo's 'Savitri', and reflected upon the fact that it might make a terrific picture.

'It is only an idea…,' said the violent one.

'I myself can be impressionable to suggestions. Your snow-capped peak is an inspirational one.'

'I wish I was on one right now, if you please.' Whimpei sank to his knees and clasped his hands.

'A motion picture can go there, and many other places besides.'

He sensed a dormant intellect in his would-be assassin's soul.

'I am a fool,' quoth Whimpei. 'I know that now.'

'Are you contrite, shootist?'

'I am. I am indeed contrite.' He spread out his arms and gazed to the heavens, but no light illuminated him. 'O! How could I have done this thing?'

Never had the actor seen a more effective plea-without-words for a come-to-Jesus talk!

'You were not aware of what I was about, nor were you privy to the saga of the Jews and their searches in this world.'

Whimpei wanted to learn. He lowered his eyes to the one he'd laid low.

'True! Now I am better equipped, and I can't wait to see 'To Ramallah In Time'. I only wish there was a picture that existed, a drama for all humanity, in which the reaches of power could be made plain to we who can only guess at them, and in the process of our ignorances, we make our foolish and disastrous choices.'

'Well by golly, Whimpei, I tell you, let us see the present picture as it unspools next door. Just now. Together!'

'But what about my impending incarceration, assured imprisonment, and possible execution for my crimes?'

'Oh, we'll deal with that later.'

'OK, but what about the effects of my toy pistol's cap-and-ball penetration of your person, which I feel wretched for having occasioned?'

'Your consideration and eloquence pleases me, Whimpei. Great! We can sneak in while the Overture plays, which I think I hear, faintly. I am all right now. I think you should see 'Ramallah', as it would correct your misunderstanding and enhance your understanding of these issues. Come, help me up.'

So the assaulter aided the assaulted, and on their way past the bricks of the Belasco's back alley stage door, Whimpei was able to confide:

'I tell you, Butterbugs, I meant not to extinguish your flame. Now I know how brilliantly it burns, for even doofusses like me to see. This morning I was a nothing and a nowhere. I think I must've wanted to *hurt* you, but not *kill* you. Either way, I would have become 'someone' in the process, perchance to become a footnote in your legend. You are generous indeed to allow me to see your picture before I am flung into prison, but know that I wish to learn, and that contrition is only a starting point from which to take your wisdom and make my life whole again.'

'Why Whimpei, you blow me away –'

They exploded in laughter.

'I mean, I mean, well, listen, let's just see the picture right now and thrash this out after,' exclaimed Butterbugs. 'Hark! The Overture is drawing to a climax. Let us unto the second balcony. Seats are being held for latecomers up there. Come! We can catch the Overture in full at the beginning of the second showing! Come *on!*'

During the Golan Heights build-up sequence, Butterbugs' character strides out to where the Heights are most visible from any challengers, whether Ottoman or Mesopotamian or Hadhrami. On the massive screen, he gestures grandly to the vast landscape before him.

'War – is *what we do!*' the character exclaims.

Then appears the following inscription, in Hebraic-style lettering across the screen: 'Some prefer war over all things'.

'I shall never touch firearms again, Butterbugs, whether pea-shooter or hulking railcar with mortar!' Whimpei whispered as David Amram's potent score filled the dramatic doughnut before the climactic scene to come.

'Good on you, Whimpei. A terrific reason why this picture should circulate widely. To save lives like mine.'

Whimpei clasped his hands. 'Yes! *Yes!* And it has saved mine!'

After the show, which they decided to sit through a second time in its entirety, Butterbugs and Whimpei were joined by Saskia, and the three of them adjourned to Vinejuice for drinks and late hors d'œuvres. They talked well into the night. Close to dawn, Whimpei had accepted a post in the Butterbugs organization, as a consultant in matters pertaining to what people in the world didn't know, as opposed to what they did; e.g. anti-knowledge, as opposed to knowledge. There was much to be learned.

Saskia and Whimpei helped change Butterbugs' dressing.

'Well, this isn't any *big deal*…,' Saskia commented.

'Naw,' agreed Whimpei.

As the ultrastar was showing Whimpei to one of the guest rooms (where Valentino and Rambova had once frolicked), he noticed something.

'Whimpei, pray, settle thyself before retiring. Hafta make a phone call. Be right back.'

'No problem!' Whimpei replied.

'Yes, uh, Gen. J-T Gather, please. Butterbugs calling. J-T? Butterbugs here. So sorry for the super-late hour. But say, do you happen to have the keys to Whimpei's chains…?'

Alone with his thoughts once more, Butterbugs pondered, 'So, a drama for all humanity… hmm?'

[In the credits for the subsequent production of 'Savitri' (Selznick), Whimpei Groyle was given a special title card, 'For Providing An Inkling of Approaching The Subject of the Present Photoplay'.]

27.

The Anodyne

'**I**'ve gotta be over at Grandad Ted Studios next Monday at noon. Lomo St. Blair and Hez Huntz will be there for legal council. Is there anything else I can do for you?'

'I've got another problem, Stu.'

Stuart Tibbs-Curtain, mega-lawyer that he was, personal consigliere to the Wassermans, the Zanucks, the Warners, the Loews, the Plablocks, the Gummindipundys, and practically anyone else worth anything in the Industry – virtual Viceroy of Hollywood where legal matters were concerned – and 28 years old next July, bent his ear into the receiver, expecting small talk to ensue.

('I'm the freakin' Irv Thalberg of Legalia in this Burg!' he was wont to crow, after ingesting SixMixDrinx, as he called them, at Jug Town every Friday.)

Stuart had to admit though, that he was a tad annoyed over the fact that Hy Goth had 'another problem'. But it was *the* Hy Goth on the line, and he would just have to behave himself, shut up, and listen. It was probably about a sex toy on the blink, or something.

'Yes, Hy,' he answered, with as much sickeningly-sweet, jellied-up fakery he could fabricate, 'Annnnd, what can we do for ya, today?'

'Listen, Curtain! If you're gonna be a slime-assed no-good wise guy punk with me, I'll see ya burn. I – will – *assassinate* – you.'

'Hyman, sorry, I was just –'

'You were JUST thinking about your 1959 DKW four door sedan with three-cylinder two-stroke engine, that's what you were thinking! You think I don't know?? Huh??'

In the apparently not-so-private chambers of his mind, Stu had to admit, uh, yes, that's what he was thinking. Some people had strap-on mistresses with whips, others had a golf fetish, an alkie buggy, or a Bella Darvi obsession. His happened to be obscure postwar German oddball cars, 'Goon Cars' as he called them. What was so wrong about that? After all, it wasn't a *drug addiction*, or anything...

'Stu, listen to me, you DKW doughboy! I'm addicted to crack cocaine.'

Hy's voice was as steady and withering as it had been all along in this conversation. As usual.

Well, speak of the devil.

'I'll be dahned,' thought Stu. Then he announced, with court-roomy clarity, 'Why Hy, I'm sorry to hear that. *Really.*'

'Listen, fuck,' Hy rasped, 'You're not only *not* sorry to hear it, you're thinking,

'Old Hy's cooked. I can cross him off my list, while cleaning him out at the same time.' Well, you're drastically wrong, I can tell you that right now. And you're the only one who's ever going to hear about my 'problem', as you'd view it. The *only one* in this town, in this whole gawdam'd universe, understand?'

'I understand perfectly, Hy.'

'Good. Not even Oriana knows. Not Gabby, or Prissy, neither.'

'I think that's wise, Hy.' Especially when it came to the Borzois.

'Yeah...' Hy was starting to sound circumspect.

'Let's get to work on a solution.'

'Yeah...'

'Hy?'

'Yeah...'

'Hy, are you OK?'

'Yeah...' The impatience returned. 'Stu, for Cryssakes, I was just getting my crack pipe out of the desk. Don't tell anyone.'

'I won't, Hy.'

'Gimme a second.'

Strong inhalation sounds were transmitted over the phone. Stu suddenly tapped on the digital recording cell (with minimally-detectable Q-ray 456-bit encryption standards).

Amidst the heavy imbibage process, Hy was able to croak:

'Stuart, don't be an ass. Shut off the damn tape recorder, or whatever the hell it is. I got DETECTION, baby!'

Stu obeyed, chastened.

Yowzah!, what a HASSLE some of these clients were! Why was it that the head of the largest studio in Hollywood, a man of intense personality and mighty achievement, was currently at the mercy of the neighborhood Candyman?

Or similarly, was Hyman Goth at the mercy, right now, at this very second, of Stuart Tibbs-Curtain, the neighborhood legal handyman? Hmm?

'Stuart?'

'Yes, Hyman.'

'You forgot to do something for me.'

'What's that, Hyman?'

'Delete it.'

'Delete what, Hyman?'

'Cut the crap, Baby Solon. You think I don't know?? Hit 'Delete' on that recording file you just created – of my Q-ray-detectable inhalation sounds. Erase. Or hit 'eject' on your little pocket k-set recorder, or whatever the fuck it is. Might not sound so good to the DA downtown. You're a potential untrustworthy complicit informer/traitor/bastard, baby.'

Once again, Stu obeyed, not only further chastened, but truly impressed.

'Now listen, Stu, you're going to do something else for me. You're just getting started. *We're* just getting started. You're not only gonna listen, you're gonna act. And you're gonna obey. Just like a good superstar loyyer.'

Stu deeply, deeply regretted his decision to have taken this one last Friday afternoon phone call before heading over in the '59 DKW for the annual Messerschmitt Goon Car convention at Searchlight, across the border in the Sovereign Nation of Nevada. He would've been safe there, beyond Hollywoodian extradition. For a guy so young and on top of the world, he suddenly felt the *weight* of that world. He could only emit a stunned whisper, akin to the pivotal scene in 'Midnight Cowboy' (UA, 1969), when Joe Buck asks the appalling question, put to that bathrobe-wearing fundamentalist fruitcake (played expertly by John 'Lord Beasley' McGiver), after he tells Joe to 'Get down on your knees'...!

'Whut...?'

Hyman Goth, mogul of infinite power, totally unmindful of such petty minutiæ, resumed.

'Stuart? Are you listening to me? You'd better. Your very soul's in danger, if you let any of this out of the cage we're both now in, pal. My, uh, *supplier* was bumped off a few hours back. Not here at my palace – but over in Alhambra somewheres. Pearl Chavez was the best in the biz, baby. But those bastards took her out. [Super-deep inhalation sounds.] So, what you're gonna do, is *this*. You're gonna be my new supplier. Oh, yeah. You maybe think not? I maybe think, *yeah*. With your connections, you shouldn't have any problem. You BETTER not have any problem!'

Hy cackled, high and happy now.

'You corrupt sonofabitch!'

Nonplused in the extreme, Stuart wasn't sure if he could even make a drooling sound.

Hy cough-laughed.

'Welly welly, well! Got your pot-metal tongue for the first time!'

Then the mirth switched to severity.

'Now looka here. Stuart? You're gonna *do* this. Oh, yes you are. Total commitment. And here's the threat. Ironclad. If you don't cooperate, I'll expose your role in the Einselgänger-Woody Woodbury case. You, uh, DO remember the fact that, uh, I know everything. EVERYTHING, pinwheel! Got it? There are penalties for slipping into disloyalty. Wanna hear 'em? I'll recite a couple, for your convenience. In case you need a little persuasion. Huh?? Your little empire will be incinerated in one brilliant move of mine. You will get the Triple-Death Penalty Without Hope of Mercy. All I have to do is hit 'Send' in my little email program. Backed up on twelve different servers, worldwide, my friend. The main one's in Püke, Albania, but out of modesty, I won't tell you the exact address. How about *that* for security?! Got a ticket? Can you git there in time to throw the thing out the window? OK then, you gotta make eleven more stops around the world, in, what, about eighty seconds, if you wanna get 'em all. As if you knew their exact and fucking secret locations! And if I'm not around to hit the right code every day at 3:00PM (which is when you will make your daily delivery to my Inner Sanctum, just to make sure you see I do it), I won't be able to personally cancel the HackFree AutoSend command that tells that ditzy li'l ol' email from hell to go dy-rectly to ZondaChannelMedia TwentyFourSeven News! Ha, ha, ha, HA!'

It was settled. Without debate, discussion, or disagreement. Stu was fried. Been-had. Screwed. Checkmated. *Fucked.* And he knew it.

Hy hadn't hard-scrabbled his way to the top just by producing marvelous pictures. Even the wild success of Butterbugs' influxes hadn't built the pyramid of power on whose apex he securely sat. The superstructure had been built over the years, the pipes laid, and the gas had flowed for the longest time now. Any Butterbugs grosses only secured the fastness.

Therefore the Irv Thalberg of Legalia could not muster up one single gesture of acknowledgment. Aghast with horror, he sat as if a fuse had blown. But it hadn't. He was 28, and in great physical shape.

'Stu-Stu-Stu. Here's the deal, dear ol' Stuey, and it'll blow the lid off your small-scale li'l ol' legal mind. The deal is, I don't wanna ever quit. Get it? I want my druggie-wugs, and I'm having a good time. In fact, I like to have a *super* time. Get it? I plan to use 'em till I wrap at the early age of 109 – maybe 110, to call it even – beating out George Abbott as the biggest fucking elder in the Industry. And if you let loose any therapy goons, or fuzz, or Uzbek mafia on me, that email gets sent pronto-express, baby. And with me always safe, secure, and higher than a non-doomed zeppelin, and *you* as my rock-of-ages Deliver-the-Candy Dude, so to speak, we'll have the solid structure of a beautiful friendship forevermore. Forevermore... And the neat thing is (for me, that is), you're already paid off. So I don't have to keep books on this deal. And you don't either. Talk about a carefree deal for both of us, huh? Nothin' in writing, nothin' to be traced. Fucking *genius!* It's all about you *owing me.* And that owing will continue, baby, from here on in. But – hell – remember, I've also got friends in high places. And low! Remember Manuel 'Pineapple-Face' Noriega? Huh? *Remember* that guy? You're no doubt too much of a young-fuck to even know what I'm talking about most of the time. But listen up anyway. Well, I gave ol' Pineapple-Face that beloved nickname, BTW. I was there. I saw it. So, sport, how's it all sound? What you say?'

Predictably (as of this afternoon, anyway), Stuart Curtain couldn't quite find the words. Not quite.

'And Stu? Say, there's also a tiny additional matter. Something else is riding with this monkey on my – and now your – back. A little picture called 'Unholy War Hymn', which, it is my understanding, you and your clients have considerable interests in. Well, I *want in*, and you're gonna open the door. Wide. Wider. All the way.'

How much injury added to insult could a young superstar lawyer take?

'Are the tears flowing yet, Stu? Tears are silent, but they say so much! Tears of hatred, I'll bet. You bet your boots! But you made your bed with this one, and I've kept your sorry ass nice 'n' perfumed. Nice 'n' *prim,* like the good little mogul I am. You OWE ME, Sunny Jim.'

Then he attempted a cheap imitation of the fake southern accent that Sinatra used in his legendary monologue that incredible night at the Sands in '66:

'Tell you what. You is mute, but you is not deaf. All you do raht now is tap that phone. Tap away, Green River guzzler! That weigh, I *knows* you agree!'

Stu tapped. He tapped as if his life depended on it. Which it did. As if his Goon Cars depended on it. Which they did. His accounts, slushy or otherwise. His wife, kids, three mistresses, and casa by the sea. Everything. It was that big.

Hy was back in character now.

'That's right, Stu, just make that tapping noise as a sign you agree. That's our 'gentleman's agreement'. Heh. Our contract. Heh-heh. And it's writ in blood, baby. Heh-heh-heh!'

There was nothing else to do but keep tapping.

'You start tomorrow. The Inner Sanctum. 3-in-the-P. *Be there.*'

CAH-LICK.

28.

The Oddballs

Then there was the incident when Butterbugs' private parts were discovered by virtually everyone in the world. It happened just outside The Lazaretto.

It was one of those situations that could not be captured properly, even in film noir, for the reality was far less stylish, and its monotone B&W-quality all more depressing. So it had little cinematic value when viewed in long shot. That's all the camera was able to capture.

With Tuan Jim on holiday, only Butterbugs himself knew where to water the four-o'clocks out by the gateway's pilasters. A great job to do in one's boxers, as carefree as a Tydee-Warsh commercial. Then, in the thoroughfare nearby, traffic confusion, and a screech of brake pads and rubber on sloopy tar. Butterbugs ran out to help a kid hit by a van. Squatting, helping the medics, his privates poured forth from boxer flimsiness.

It was a matter of ancient, arcane knowledge though, known from Hindoo backwaters to Haitian ceremonies outside Jéremie, that certain energies may be passed from human to human, with beneficial effects. Such transfers might occur via any body part *to* any body part. No mind meld, just a sharing of helpful vibes when and where they're needed most. No thinking involved.

Tragically, the kid's injuries were in the region of the groin.

Today, in this particular instance, when Butterbugs' sac, liberated from its modesty, inadvertently sagged and chastely contacted the kid's traumatized region, Shar-Pei folds blessing it, as it were, there was enough evidence to suggest a magic wand effect. Wherein certain powers of healing and/or aural effect were transferred from giver to receiver, and the receiver, empowered, was able to respond.

For the record, the kid did indeed recover completely, had four children with his high school sweetheart, and his life went on to be even-tempered and successful. His own modesty forbade him from attributing it all to his one unconscious encounter with the world's ultrastar. It was just a simple matter of one vibe-producer providing vibe services to another. No doubt the receiver would pass them on to someone else, in time.

Odd, but true!

These were the true circumstances surrounding Butterbugs' intimate exposure to the public. Incidentally, he was up to the task, as usual. There was no one who had cause for critical comment, and not even Mike Angelo's David or Carl

Milles' Uppsala Railway Station's Pan were ever mentioned as qualifiers when it came to the matter of someone so *above* common vicissitude.

And soon after came another remarkable incident, this one of much more tragic dimensions. It was the seventh time some wacko parked his SUV on the commuter tracks at the San Padré dos Retiros grade crossing. Again, there was derailment, destruction, and death. Butterbugs, who happened to be picking up some AA batteries at Pimbles' Peoples' hard by, bounded into the breach and saved dozens from a fiery end, or from impact with dangerous objects suddenly disassembled and projected. Spectators were in advanced awe.

'He's just like Mr. Charles Dickens at the Staplehurst railway disaster,' one Chicano shopping trolley attendant uttered to a prominent African-American college professor from USC, hard by.

'Aye, he is for a fact,' replied the professor, 'Come! Let we who are inspired by this leader of men hasten to his aid. We shall follow him in his methods of rescue!'

And many more responded to this call.

The ultrastar even apprehended the culprit, who, in the great tradition of San Padré dos Retiros grade-crossing tragedies, had gotten cold feet in intending to slay himself, evacuating his SUV in the key position 'twixt rail and rail. Making a limp attempt to escape the scene, Butterbugs merely stood in front of the dishonorable man. And then, this reprehensible excuse for a human being, seeing Butterbugs' power, passed out.

In the aftermath of the disaster, the very presence of Butterbugs on location enabled all mop-up operations to proceed in orderly fashion. There was no hysteria, either at his august status, or over the actuality of the terrible wreck that surrounded them, because the nobility and serenity with which he enacted his purposeful deeds spread to all involved.

After the many injured were gurney-d away to Seniors/Cyanide Hospital, and all the many dead were conveyed to New Dawn Funerary Emporia at various locations, Butterbugs brought peace and comfort to those who were left behind to mourn.

'He is not a Christ,' proclaimed a solemn pastor from a nearby chapel to the companions in his task force group. 'At least we do not *think* he could be... But he is someone to watch, and I do not mean up on the picture show screen alone. He may yet emerge as someone wholly Christ-*like*, and that bears watching.'

One padre's opinion...

Regardless, surely – *surely* this man was a force for good in the world.

'Talk to me. Sidney. Baby! Talk to me. Yeah, OK. That's right, baby. Now listen, let me tell you something. Where is it written that I do not ever come through with a helluva deal? Hunh? You're just not gonna believe this. Charlie Feldman should be so lucky. Fred Kohlmar, ditto! Am I making sense out there? Have I started yet? Lemme tell you something Sidney. Remember this. Back in

'39, I was the FIRST agent in New York to say over the phone that vaudeville was dead. I tell you, I was the first to do it. It was when that *kid* called and said he wanted to be the greatest tap artiste in the vaude world. Yeah, I know you were, Sidney. I know you were in the office and that you gave me credit in 'Variety'. Sime himself *knighted* me over it. So here's the deal. You can trust me. Can't you? What? Whadaya mean Baby Tucker just spit up his oat flakes across the table? You're taking breakfast with Baby Tucker? Where's the maid? Or, what-the-who, the nanny(goat), or whatevah... Oh, oh, oh. You've got the kid till 11:30. OK, baby. We'll take lunch at Chorl's at 1:15, then. Now listen, Sidney... What? He did it again? Sprayed 'em across the table at *you*, full in the face? I'm sawry to hear that, Sidney. Give the kid a bromo. You keep mopping it up, and lemme tell you. Now here's the deal. It's all in the property. I KNOW that's what Mike Todd said. I was there in the office when he said it! You weren't, baby. Remember that. Hey, did you hear that Mike's coming back? Yeah. Dig-it-tal Rest-tor-ay-shun, baby. I'm gonna have to corner Mike when he's back and lean on him about the money I put up for that stupid Mule Train number in Mike's BugEye Lens Follies ('The Big Show in Todd-AO'!). But let me tell you. This prop'ty is potentially hot. The one I'm trying to talk to you about. In the midst of your oat flakes storm. Hell yes! But I can't *wait* till 1:15. I'm so worked up, I gotta tell ya *now!* So I will. Just can it and listen. OK. It's an unpublished novel, see? It's by Sawlohmunn Cane, see? Yes, Sidney, I know you were his bar mitzvah coordinator. I *know* that, Sidney. And I always have. And I always will. *Maybe.* Yeah, Sidney. Now look. I know another Cane novel isn't the biggest news in the world to you, Sidney. I know he has written over 500 novels, Sidney. I know over 700 pictures have resulted, Sidney. Let's toss around numbers, Sidney. You wanna do the numbers? Hundreds and hundreds of numbers. Are you sick of it yet, Sidney? Hell, Stanley is over at Severe Jurist Pictures now, making a picture based on TWO LINES from an obscure poem Cane wrote when he was four years old, for God's sake! Listen Sidney. Shut up, Sidney. Sit up and shut down, Sidney. Look at that, you've got me so worked up now, Sidney, you're making me flub my lines. Send Tucker out of the kitchen, Sidney. Tucker. *Your* Tucker. I don't care if your burp-rag is full. Let him get another from the dirt bag. The kid's gotta pull for himself some day. You want him in the Industry, or not? OK then. I know, you want him to 'carry on'. Fine. A little quaint, maybe. But fine. Plan ahead and start now. Yes, Sidney, I know he can't even toddle yet, but the kid'll work it out. Instinct. C'mon, start him off early. Yes, Sidney, I can hear him in the background. No Sidney, I don't want you to flip on the camera option so's I can see how much upchuck is on the table right now. Yes, Sidney, I know you're suffering there. I want you to wear a clean FitzGlolldo at table in a few hours, Sidney. We'll do martinis today. OK. So Cane says to me, he says, 'Maury, I can't get behind this book as a picture right now. It's too timely. History in the making.' That's what he says to me, Sidney. Can you believe it? And then he goes, 'Maury, I want *you* to take the book and peddle it to a studio first, then we'll publish as the picture is being made. I'll script, of course. We'll get Waddington Ching to do another treatment, just for good measure. The timing will be close: one coming hot on the heels of the other.' Well, Sidney, I read the book. It's talking about events that took place just eight days ago, for crying out loud. Well, eighteen days. We gotta move fast. What's it about? Sidney, it's 1200 pages. I'm on page 20! But I know it's gonna be big. Sawl will script, and The Little Wadd'll brush it up. That's all I care about. I dunno, it's about some crazy mideast oil freak or something. Indiana? Missouri? Iowa, or somethin'. No, that's mid-west. What was I think-ing? I talkin' about where the oil is. I dunno, Sidney. I just don't know. Big story. Big characters. I wanna secure a deal before Mike Todd is restored to life – I can tell you that right now! Sidney, baby. That's why I'm calling you, sweetheart. I want you to get me in to Hy Goth. I know that's the stratosphere, baby. That's why I wanna go to the top. A brunch thingie. That's the best time of day for this operation. Sidney? You read me, or what? Get me a brunch with Sam Goldfish, too. I know he is, Sidney, but I want Hy to think that I'm hungry. Who do you think I am? I'm not Sonny Mucking-Projector! Sidney, I'm NOT using curse words! No I'm not. I know Baby Tucker is in the same room with you. He can't hear me, Sidney. I know you know he can't hear me but you don't want him in the same room with you when I am substituting fake curse words for real curse words in case the false vibes get to him, baby. Did you get him that bromo? Why not? Why are you treating me this way? What did I ever do to you? Why do you hurt me, Sidney? Uh-huh… Well, I think we can wangle some percentages out of this that will buy Baby Tucker into Princeton, for Pete's sake. Rutgers, maybe. OK, Brandeis – *Done,* already. Yeah. So can you do this for me today, Sidney? The Hy Goth brunch trick? Do I have to remind you? Do I remind you of all I've done for you? I need this today, Sidney. To-day. You *said* you would! You'll *try?* Try harder, Sidney. You'll try harder. You'll do this for me, Sidney. You're a good boy, Sidney. What? I don't wanna hear about it, Sidney. I told you that if you are having a baby in your seventies, Sidney, things are likely to involve spit-up and ca-ca. Sidney? Are you still there? Yes, I *know* you can still get it up, Sidney. Bezzie's a very attractive girl. The blonde you always wanted. Very æsthetic, too. She's a sweet girl. Everybody respects her, Sidney. I do, too. But you're old enough to be the kid's great-grandfather. Or something. I *know* he put VapoRub in your martini yesterday, Sidney. I'll make it up to you at lunch. But Hy is an oddball, Sidney. You know how to play him. You know his cracks and his venereal warts. That was not a curse word, Sidney. My middle daughter is an executive at Betty Ford, Sidney. She knows those words. She uses them on me. I'm not going to tell you the celebrities who have venereal warts, Sidney. No, it was not Taylor. It was not Björk. No, Sidney. Miley? No. I'm not going to tell you, Sidney. Did you get a chance to see if Hy still likes those 'piquant' capers that I ordered for him from Varna, Bulgaria? He does? I'll get him a *case*. My associate is leaving tonight for Varna, on a location reccy. That is not a problem. I'll email him. This is big, Sidney. See you at 1:30, baby. Verna sends her love.

My lovey-love to Thelma – oh sorry, I mean Bezzie. And to Baby Tucker. Kid's got a big future. Ciao.'

Click.

In times of reflective leisure, Butterbugs' disciplined mind could readily tilt into soulful pondering on the fate of humanity, and its strategic plans for future advantageous management. His priorities and directions were well-regulated and balanced, on a scale that would rival that of sagacious world leaders. The few of which existed.

It was this benevolent leaning that led him into the works of Cageworth Mumfa Blaintain, the beekeeper-philosopher. In the rarefied air of his mediations, Mumfa Blaintain addressed the issues of our times within a neutron-beam-steady state of grace, so to speak. And Butterbugs, in his advanced position of power, who could transform the attitude of onlookers by a mere glance at a bookcase lighted by early morning sunbeams, chose to turn his attention to an austere but entirely germane work of Mumfa Plantain's for consideration as a photoplay. It was her seminal text, 'Most Of The Universe Is Cold', and for a period of some months, Butterbugs entered into a sustained state of enhanced reality because of it.

He made a special trip to the great lady's estates at Tiddery-Twoo, deep in the somber vales of Humberside.

House by Ned Lutyens, garden by Gertrude Jekyll, and bee-metropolis by Dame Cageworth Mumfa Blaintain.

Still bee-ing every day in her late 90s, she and Butterbugs took tea in their favorite folly, also a Lutyens confection. Luxurious bee-perches abounded, populated by thousands of buzzers in all shapes and sizes. Under the tutelage of their patroness, they were extremely well-behaved and ornamental.

'So, Biggsy' (she called him Biggsy), 'you seek my approbation for capturing 'Most/Universe/Cold', do you?'

'I do, Cagey, with a humbleness that can only be described as –'

'As *unnecessary*,' she interjected.

'You mean –'

'I mean, make this picture one of your best ever, Biggsy. I expect it to play at the Old Conkwood Arms in the village before my next Pollination Festival in the coming season. Otherwise I shall have to unleash my Zipperstripe Marauders on you.'

'I'll be there, dear,' was his only reply. He knew she was serious.

Of course the project was green-lighted, and Sawl Cane embarked on the script, his most demanding ever.

'But,' Cane asked, 'will anyone *care* about such a picture? Will anyone come to the picture show to be enveloped in light?'

'They will. I tell you, they will!' uttered Butterbugs over a midnight nipperkin of Benedictus Quafficus at Sawl's place in Plaster City, during that extraordinary time.

'Sawl. Sawl! I have to tell you, look about us! Cast your sensors beyond the cinema circle we occupy. Look at the *people*. Behold their regard for the truths in life. Then, move past, to the edges. Consider which way the peoples are looking. Ever outwards! Those who occupy the marches on the borderland, they look askance at their immediacy, but concentrate their quiet but sure efforts *beyond* the horizon! It is there that Cageworth Mumfa Blaintain's concept of the here and now is held. And it will be held in this picture, as well. You will sustain it in words, as I will do so myself, on the very screen upon which it shall be projected!'

And Sawl Cane, great and hearty man of many letters that he was, witnessing Butterbugs' power, passed out.

It was not that Butterbugs held a charismatic or even messianic power over those who came into his sphere. Or those who even passed through it unawares. It was just that such a fine simplicity of truth hung about him. A truth that still mattered, after society had gone on for some decades after the death of religion, of psychology, of Elvis, of New Ageism, of Marxism (maybe), the miserable flop of the preposterous and vulgar 'Cellophane Prophesy', and even the wearying titan of Nouveau Colonialism. Plus, the New Selfishness.

As Sinatra said to a hostile Press, Down Under, 'You people are all dead.'

But the society and its world did indeed survive these losses.

There was something innocent again in the air, a new refurbishment of nothing that had come before. An oxymoron that made sense. How was one to sum it up, except to temporarily disengage from the Greco-Roman penchant for labeling everything that existed in the world, and accede to the nameless submission of pure acceptance without analysis?

Thus, 'Most Of The Universe Is Cold' shaped up as one of the most profound projects in which the erstwhile loner from Carstairs was ever involved.

True to his word, Butterbugs personally fostered the world premiere of 'Most/Universe/Cold' at the Conkwood Arms pub in Dame Mumfa Blaintain's home village of Kemberston Stixnox. It was a very intimate occasion. The Dame strolled the two miles from her estates, arriving just a few minutes before showtime. About twenty villagers attended, and Sir Peter Ustinov happened to drop by, in search of a jar of beer.

'Join us!' the star entreated.

'Perfect, dear boy,' Sir P replied. 'As chance would have it, I'm escaping for the full evening, after a tedious session of being interviewed by Jonathan Woss, over in York...'

'Poor fellow! Then we have a special limited treat tonight, Peterkins. A premiere, in fact.'

'Ah! Cagey!' Sir P exclaimed. 'Might I perch by you for the eve? Home movies, is it?'

'You are most perceptive, Yoostie!' the philosopher-beekeeper replied.

'Nothing buzzing in your pockets, I hope...?'

While everyone was getting settled, arranging the equipment took a bit of doing. Since it was only himself and some cans of film on the scene, Butterbugs did everything from start to finish, and it was his pleasure to do so. A crank-operated projector was located at the old abandoned cinema over in Bopworth, still well-oiled and ready to roll. A rape-oil lamp with reflector was rigged up as its light source. The screen was a sheet from the inn-beds upstairs.

With stocked pints and suitably moody weather outside, the cozy Conkwood Arms was a pleasing world premiere venue indeed.

Butterbugs himself hand-cranked the magic lantern-ish projector for the film's 127 minute duration. He played the soundtrack on a portable cassette deck, with the horn from the pub's very own Victrola serving as amplifier. Thanks to the star's own 'rhythm method', synchronization was surprisingly successful. When the cassette needed to be turned over, he simply stopped cranking. When the reel needed to be changed, he simply hit Pause.

'The Vitaphone *lives!*' Sir P whispered to the Dame.

When the cranking stopped, the cassette clicked off, and the gas-lamps came up, the pub witnessed its profoundest full-house silence ever.

No one could speak.

Finally, Dame Cageworth herself managed a minimal but consummate statement.

'This picture will pollinate goodness further and wider than any of my forces ever could...!'

But there was another profound project that awaited.

'Savitri'.

29.

Savitri

A particularly exciting project was handed to Sonny Projector one day.

It appeared on a jute tray, which perfectly matched the sophisticated greens framed by the sleek, brushed stainless steel window frames of his Pent-bungalow. Because the late afternoon light hit it askance, the jute provided a kind of tingling, rough-textured look that struck him as iconic.

Yana Jabberjee, one of Sonny P's assistants, held the tray. Her eyes flashed.

'Read this proposal,' she uttered, then set the tray down on the cool-grey ottoman (designed by IKEA graduate Jørn Okkakkstaad), and floated out.

There happened to be a butter lamp glowing across the room, which gave off an aura of mellow Tantric ecstasy. The proposal on the tray was hand-lettered in ochre ink, on saffron-tinted paper with wheaten flecks. The first thing Sonny saw, as far as written text was concerned, was the legend, 'Dhraja Chuckerverrity Presents' on the top of the page.

'Wow...' Sonny was in awe. 'Dhraja Chuckerverrity! Returning to producing! I don't believe it!'

This was big. It reminded him of Sam Bronston's happy return to production after years of wasted legal tangles. And he was further blown away by the picture's subject and personnel. A full-length cinematic realization of Sri Aurobindo's epic poem, 'Savitri'! Omigod. With Amitabh Bachchan. The tagline: 'The Universe is *formed*, rather than destroyed. Big stuff. It takes a lot of responsibility.'

It may have been a mere proposal, but Sonny already thought it a reality.

Script by the Aurobindo Ashram. Music: Karë Huuoöahuüah, the brilliant Finnish composer, rumored to be descended from the Sami people, whose score to 'Larry of the Churchyard' (Lomax) had the same strange wild hopes as in Bernardo Segall's music for 'Custer of the West' (Cinerama, 1969). Could they get him?

Locations: Calcutta's Tollywood sound stages, the dry jungle near Cooch Behar, and, specific settings way further east, near Mt. Kipling, in the most obscure expanses of the forbidden eastern Himalayas. Here the cosmic sequences would be shot, demanding tons of supplies and a whole supportive infrastructure where none at all currently existed. A narrow gauge steam railway would have to be constructed to access the area, and countless other logistic nightmares – strike that – challenges, would have to be negotiated.

To be directed by the darling of the Paraguayan cinema, none other than Javier-Gomez Prutmop.

225

It was all there. All the ingredients for transcendent greatness, but greatness without ego. Very Butterbugsian. The whole project, though, was contingent on one thing: Butterbugs must be one of the stars. Sonny couldn't wait to green-light it. But Butterbugs' schedule was always filling up for the foreseeable future. Still, he was determined not to let the august Sri Dhraja Chuckerverrity down. That would be unforgivable.

He picked up his Noki-Noki.

'Yana, we have to take a meeting with Butterbugs. How's lunch for tomorrow?'

'You forgot, Sonny. Butterbugs is currently on the shores of Lake Balkhash, on location for 'Nikolai the Cossack Chief' (WB), produced in cooperation with Yugg-Balk Tartar Pictures.'

'Sumbitsch! That's right, I *did* forget. I guess we'll have to go out there. This is too gaddam important. I'm gonna have to shuffle the deck. We'll see him out on location. We march tonight.'

Savitri! Bane of filmmakers! Its profundities, its difficulty of conceptualization, the very logistics of it meant that, in a way, the cosmic nirvana of Sri Aurobindo's majestic vision would have to be realized on Earth somehow. On an ordinary Earth. But maybe not. The far eastern Himalayas were so mysterious, and rumored to be of transcendental status, that there was nothing for it but to pack up and for everyone involved to see for themselves. The line-scriptor, Harold Washington Spizzitsky, had an extraordinarily inspired sense of vision, and upon him the burden of realization lay. (He would adopt the French term of 'Realiseur' for this production, out of devotion to the picture's inherent goodness, and out of humility to its purpose.)

Plus, the remarkable capabilities of Butterbugs would be called into play on such a level of reliance that no one knew if the demands would be too much for even the Great Player's reserves. Action on the set would certainly tell.

And Amitabh! What could even be said about him? This production would be blessed by semi-divine talent, and Sonny knew it.

Butterbugs would of course play Satyavan, with Amitabh as Yama, Lord of the Underworld.

'But whom', said Sonny to Yana, once their Airbus was on its way, 'shall we secure to play Savitri?'

Yana leaned back, and on this night of power, stood up and announced:

'You shall have *me*.'

And Sonny stared in wonder.

30.

The Great Question
Of Our Times

'**N**ow listen people, today I want your undivided (no, REALLY, *undivided!*) attention. I'm gonna tell ya a story.'

Some groans erupted from around the table. Stanley Wig-Gash was the kind of producer/exec that liked to be didactic in order to make a point. He had been a strolling monologist back in vaudeville, and he could really go *on*, sometimes. Plus, it was always interesting to find out what parts of the impending cavalcade of words didn't make sense. That was part of Stanley's charm – his business matters always had a high entertainment factor. However, his points were usually irrefutable.

'Now looka here, this is history, and let me tell you, it's BIG TIME history. It involves Butterbugs!'

Immediately the group quietened down.

'That's better. Now here goes, awright?:

'As you know, the thousand injuries inflicted on me by the Creative and Semi-Creative Artists Management Agency I had borne the best I could.

'Hollywood can be cruel. Cru-El. You know that. I know that. Therefore, it came as a super-surprise when Irving suggested I take Harry up on his offer of early-mid-morning cupcakes and a nipperkin of high-malt Scotch over at his office. As you know, his office is directly across from Selznick Studios, so every time I look out Harry's window, it's like that dandy beginning to any Selznick picture. Only thing missing is Alfred's fanfare, so I guess I'll have to smuggle in a little tape recorder or something next time, just so I can properly score the scene. It's like we used to do in silents: crank up the gramophone or get a violinist from Fanchon's to play an obscure, preferably Central European ballad full of sap while shooting a scene...

'So Harry and I sat down for a talk, see? It was a yellow afternoon outside, sort of like being in the United Artists motion picture cathedral down on Broadway for a matinee, and being surrounded with all that sub-creepy dark golden plaster and burgundian curtains, and, perchance wandering along the corridor under the mezzanine and encountering the great stained glass window on the west, and suddenly, flooded with all that amber light, one stands, transfixed in a forced reverie of sallow and somewhat sickly moods.

'Harry could see me spacing out with this hallucinogenic tone poem, so, like he usually does, he grabbed me by my thin tie and chicken-flicked my ear lobes. So then I was able to settle down to some jim-dandy cupcakes and high-spirited malt beverage.

'Harry obviously had something of great importance to tell me.

"Just a rumor. You know the scene, Manny and his wife Jerry were yakking up a storm at L.B.'s breakfast garden party last night. They was saying that Milt Yurkasinowicz Cane (author Sawl's brother), who is probably the biggest lit agent in the greater LA-San Pino area, was spilling his guts out over something really big. Big, baby. BIG.'

'Harry dawdled, savoring the suspense. So I sez to him I sez:

"Harry, where is it written that you should torture me so?'

'Harry fiddled with the buttons on his Corus Kester suit. One by one he plucked them off and left them in a haughty pile on the floor. I kid you not. Those of you who know Harry, and I think it's pretty much everybody in this here room, if not this here office block, if not this here whole frikkin' studio, *know* Harry, and know he'd do something like that. I just want all you to know that I'm not makin' this up, nor am I makin' *any* of this up.

'I knew he had a spare suit out in his Terraplane, and he could suit up again out there, if he had to. That Harry! Always mit th' jokes! Always trashing his haberdashery when trying to make a point! Well, we finished our lox and then downed an urn of Mogan David Fortified 20/20.

'By then, Harry was really ready to talk. But the shreds of his Kester were all on the floor of the booth we populated. So, unless he wanted to make an emergency run out to the car, he had to mutter-up. He decided he'd rather put on the new suit though. I was getting steamed, but he'd hooked me, so I had to toddle along behind him like a good little dope.

'Now you all know how vain Harry is. New suit on, he had to show it off. We motored over to Ma Maison.

' 'Aw-right, Harry, aw-right Harry,' I said each time he did a play-by-play on the way over. Finally we get a table. A helluva table. I suddenly realized, Harry always likes to spill big news in a public place. So everybody can see he's doing some spilling, and that's how he plants his seeds of power, to be carefully nurtured, I can tell you that right now. Yeah, I know. Bozo Village.

"OK, baby,' Harry finally says in a stunned stage-whisper, 'get ready for this…'

'I was panting with existential excitement *so much* that the wine-enriched drool that flowed out of my trembling mouth was adding up into a puce specimen-sized puddle on Ma M's table in front of me. Think of it! Orson Swelles often sits where I am right now! The mega-girth of his bodily frame had made a huge swale in the cushion below. There were still some of Orson's cigar ash burns on the table, which my drool now irrigated with blood-tinted waves. So comfortably and ecstatically positioned, I was now ready to receive the biggest news in Hollywood since the word that Maxie Steiner had been hired at Warners by Jack L.

"Somebody's made a *deal*,' was all he uttered.

'And then I knew. I knew all about it. And I knew what Harry was going to say.

"One of the biggies has been after the hottest property in Hollywood, as hot as in 1959, when Sawlohmunn Rabinowicz Cane's ultra-blockbuster novel 'Judah's Big Deal' hit the stands. Well, *now* – today, that is – Cane's got something bigger in the hopper. Bigger than 'Judah's Big'. Rumors are flying. Phones are ringing. But mostly in secret, boys and girls. Hands are grabbing. You know Cane properties; is there a gold in Fort Knox, maybe, for instance? This new opus: something about a High Mad Doctor. I know *I'm* gonna chase this one.' And Harry wasn't even drunk.

'Harry's next statement was searingly terse, and more powerful than when C.B. DeMille got semi-mad at me for asking who his barber was.

"They're going to make it a picture, from Sawl's novel. And I don't mean 'Judah's Big Deal' (which was optioned, but never made – yet).'

'Luckily, I was able to fumble in my duffle bag and found the Porta-Ox bottle. I inhaled so deeply that I hallucinated that we were on one of Neptune's more obscure moons for a few seconds. Such was my distant joy at being in this place, and at this time in the space-time continuum we call 'Home Sweet Home'.

'Harry sliced another cupcake in half – he always likes to brown bag-it at Ma M's – and inspected the goose-spine gelatin within.

"You know, Schtan,' he said, calmly now, 'I think we are entering a very, very, great epoch.'

'I agreed.

'Then he asked the question which was at the very nexus of the known universe:

"Who can we get to play the High Mad Doctor in whatever this picture turns out to be?'

'I thought, 'Such a role would be the greatest part in the history of post-vaudeville entertainment in this solar system. And Neptune's moons, too!' I was high, but I knew it, probably before anybody. NO – *definitely* before anybody.

'All I could say next was: "I know a kid. He can play the part. I tell you, he can play it."

Stanley fell silent, and so were all those who now sat in the boardroom, for their numbers had increased to SRO. He finished his beaker of high-malt in front of him.

'Well, that was some time ago, as you know. Since then, the Rise of Butterbugs has become the stuff of Always Living Legend. Now, I know all of you understand that Butterbugs *can* play the part, but listen, I ask you, will he *want* to play the part? That, I declare to you, is the great question of our careers.'

Shmuel Wolensak spake:

'Butterbugs just left for that big Hindoo picture, doncha know. Who the hell has any idea how long they'll be on location! Huh? It's slated for eleven weeks' location shooting. Prob'ly more. He's in gawdam Further Bengal or some gawf'saken place!'

Nootka Lannaberry of Standard Pictures raised his hand. He looked every one of the bigwigs in the eye, and his scan ended up with Hyman Goth, who was sitting in his special highchair, to accommodate the bib he always wore in preparation for board-room doughnuts.

'Thing is,' Nootka said, 'no deal has been struck yet, for this High Mad Doctor concept. Whatever the picture turns out to be, and I assume it's got commercial potential, and not just greatness up its sleeves? I suppose somebody's got it lassoed, but has it been pulled in yet? I prizzoom Projector's got this one in his cupboard, but nobody's talking. It's making me nervous, friends and neighbors, cuz –'

'Just a minute!'

Hy Goth was present, and he was in crisis, and not solely because he was worried shitless about securing Butterbugs for the role of his lifetime. That nagging addiction was upon him, even though he'd stoked up right before the confab. It was a sign of this particular deal's import that his body's anxiousness had used up the cokey rocket fuel before its usual time, so he stole away to the Exec Loo, flipped on the fart-fan, took advantage of a conveniently outrageous defecation, popped out his crack pipe and did some cargo.

During his absence, there wasn't one suited board member or guest exec who didn't start sweating razor blades over Butterbugs.

Stanley was almost gobbling.

'I mean, what if he's… he's…'

Jesus von Gold wasn't shy.

'I'll finish your sentence, Stanley. Get ready. What if he's *not coming back?* Right? Am I right? Is that what you were going to say?'

Sir St. Pancras Jubilee-Blubberminster was erudite.

'Gentlemen, after having served in His Imperial Majesty's forces in that part of India during the Raj, I have to tell you that life is a bit dicey in such a neighborhood. At the best of times.'

Hazel Snyder (*the* Hazel Snyder – of Hazel Snyder Presents) spoke in her hi-fi voice of sane authority.

'St. Pan, we were aware that this production of 'Savitri' was a risk, but you're saying it's really hazardous?'

'Quite, my dear,' replied St. Pan.

'Hazel, for a while there, everyone in Hollywood was trying to talk him out of it,' said Jesus. 'And nobody succeeded. You couldn't even get into the sub-corridor that led to Sonny's office. Nobody could do *nothing*.'

'It's a quandary, but we shouldn't be intimidated,' she replied.

'Intimidated by the, er, possibilities,' interjected super-producer Durmdrullt Hennipour.

'That's right, Durm. We're in a hazardous biz. Butterbugs is constantly in risk-fever.'

'That's a good way of putting it, Haze. I can't imagine the dimensions of his insurance package.'

'Or the liabilities clauses,' Jesus said, just to complicate things.

'Oh, let's not go there.' Hazel rubbed her temples through her red tresses. 'Such a subject just makes my producing talents go slack.'

'Sonny handles all of that rubbish, I should think,' offered St. Pan, concerned about his great dame Hazel, whom he'd been banging for over a year now. Her producing talents were very dear to him, as his bankrupted estates in Salop had little to offer him now.

'So what're we *gonna do?*' Stanley asked, almost whining and worried sick, all passion for monologuing spent.

Hy, higher than shit, entered grandly.

'We do nothing,' he announced. 'We wait. And in the meantime, deals on bigger pix than this mystery Megillah you're yammering on about have yet to be made! Don't get all steamed about High Mad Doctors. Never you mind. And if that's not enough, I got someone who can perform miracles, right here! May I present the little guy who's gonna make our lives easier from now on. Come on out, Gupta!'

From the shadows of the private passage that connected with his office suite, Hy almost dragged out a tall, distinctive gentleman of singular appearance.

'Gang, meet Swami Guptanally –'

'Oh no, Mistar Got-h, you see, I am Swami Guptanarabandananda!'

'Yeah. Whatever. We'll call you Swami Gupta!'

'That is fine with me,' smiled the Swami: salt and pepper-bearded, jolly cheeks, topknot, Vaishnavite markings, khadi garments, accoutrements, tray of sacred flame, etc.

'As long as Butterbugs is working on this East Indian picture –'

'I assume your goodself is very much referring to eastern Hindustan, instead of the eastern tribes of Red Indians, Mistar Got-h,' the Swami interjected, like the academic he was. That is, before he went sannyas.

'Whatever! You – Don't interrupt me again, or else – or, or take your magic else-where, holy man!'

The Swami smiled beatifically, while Hy continued.

'So listen, we can't lose now! We've got this here li'l Swami Gupta to back us up and guide us along.'

'It is a fact that I will offer you guidance!' the 6'5" Swami cheerfully declared, fingers arranged in a Ramakrishnaic pose in the cigarish air.

'So look!' Hy addressed his group of power. 'If we're gonna get through this thing, follow along with what Swami says and does. Swami Sez. Yeah, Swami Sez! Now, he's gonna be coming around to each of you, and I want you to pass your hand through that little fire he's got going there. OK Swami, get this package going.'

With the lights dimmed, the little oil flame, surrounded by dhoop plugs, circulated amongst the high and mighty with bouquets of patchleaf chewing gum and jasmine. And that was how the whole room engaged in the puja, without equivocation.

For this time, and not for the last time on this picture, there were none who could claim either a Christian or a Jewish background.

All was Brahma.

31.

Esteemed Immensity

Far, far, up the terai, still in the safe dryjungle in this, the extreme east of Arunachal Pradesh – barely Hindustan, but more Brahmanic than most of the world, and not just because of all the recent memories of steaming up the *Brahma*putra – they went inexorably onward. For some weeks after leaving that lonely ghat at river's edge, seen off by only a lone sadhoo with a feeble tray of sacred fire in a cloud of dusky dhoop smoke at sunset, their trek had been through a land of wonder.

The avian life was active, the villages were receptive, and even their interaction with the wandering Chimm tribe was cordial and mutually beneficial. In this remote tract, Hindoo began to meld with animism, and the peculiarity of the resulting aggregate found expression in odd little temples, pagodahs and shrines: Bengali-walled, Assam-roofed, with tribal symbology attached, in the form of spikes, spears, sickles, and other exterior designations of trans-Meghalayan/ cis-Burmese micro-cultures.

But soon the knots of pint-sized hut children and beggar brats thinned, the braided trails amongst the thickets became one, the bird life decreased, and the climatological limitations of the plains began to broaden.

The locals along the way tended to think this grand procession was a shikar party, bound for the distant legendary mountain terraces where the snow-rhinoceri surely dwelt, and whence said party would certainly never return. Thus their detachment from even the realization that a mega-star such as Amitabh was in their company. Also, due to the traveling video-wallahs, Butterbugs was not unknown to them, either.

All the Subcontinent, from Gwadar to Chittagong, from Dalhousie to Nagercoil, had loved his performance as the Raj Kapoor character in the remake of 'Gopichand Jasoos' (Sippy Pix, filmed a while ago in Bombay), but when they saw his benevolent face in this marching company, they were respectful, yet restrained. Bad luck to engage a doomed enterprise, however venerated its members. Nevertheless, the visitors were not at all rejected, and every hospitality was extended them, whether in procuring a sack of split pulse in a village gunge or securing a bit of ground upon which to rest their weary heads at night, guarded over (mainly from night animals) by their sepoy escort. There were reports of indeterminate panic down in Manipur, but up here, out back, with the wilderland all about them, things were downright hospitable.

And Amitabh was largely silent, attracting little or no attention at the communal water tap, waiting his turn behind the bheesti and drinking his share of tube-well refreshment, railway style: from the chained cup, a waterfall into his parched mouth. On this shoot he wasn't Big B so much as just another mortal. Yet inside his head, he was exalted by his upcoming role, as no other. He began to wear saffron, but instead of mantras, he uttered his lines in a whisper, which he'd already memorized from the dictionary-thick script, the library of which was toted and curated by a special script-wallah porter from Nepal, who had gone to the top of Kanchenjunga four times.

It was a case of insistent, communal propulsion, ever forward, but under the hybrid cover of slatted palmyra fronds and rotund sal leaves. Scored, as it were, by Franz Waxman in matinee mode. Far from the intermittent aisle lights in a thousand different mezzanines. Or the exposed-insulation interiors of a score of soundstages, more remote at the moment, than the Saturnian satellite system.

As the trek went on and on, certain alterations in mindsets began to occur without external impetus. It was true, the stimuli around them lessened and became more limited in look and feel. But it was the moods, attached to each marcher as surely as the rucksacks and porter mechanisms on their backs, that were the determining factors along the path they were now taking. Some could not sleep and knew not why. Grown men would wake up sobbing, for unknown reasons. It was not an anxiety nor even an anxiousness so much as an awareness, identifiable as something imminent, something coming.

One afternoon, after a highly-strung slog, the tension was becoming unbearable. Butterbugs found himself in a senseless argument with Ravana Pal, one of the production designers, and the horribleness he felt when Pal stomped off only added to the collective agony that plagued them all. Doubt, uncertainty, and a fear of loss of control were now endemic. This thing, it seemed, could just fly apart or collapse at any moment.

They proceeded eastward without even knowing why. No sound came from the environment surrounding them, so the aural generations they themselves made in their strained blundering along were strangely deafening in an alarming sort of way, akin to being in the dead zone of a live room, where sound bytes are born and die in illogical time spans.

It was Tegh Singh, a risaldar in Hodson's Horse, whose cry pierced the silent air: 'Dekho! Himayalastan, achcha!' ('Look! The Abode of the Snows! Certainly!').

He was the first to stumble through the final edge of the receding dryjungle to see, *to see*, in all their far-flung splendor, the Snowy Range of the greatest mountains in the Known Non-Oceanic World.

All of a sudden, every one of those who made up the company simultaneously experienced a total cessation of pressure. There was a moment when all experienced a complete absence of thought, or perception, or even existence. Some sort of tone-change occurred.

Short-out. Reset. Return.

Supporting players Rana and Sharli, without even knowing Sanskrit, erupted into Vedic hymns, and even Fat Chance Parker (Porter's younger brother, Line Producer on this one) joined in, effortlessly and naturally. Supporting superstars Rekha and Dimple wept tears of happiness and relief.

Look, look at it there! Just over there. The main mass rose, at an improbable angle, a range of high snows, impossible to take in except by extreme wide-angle panning of one's head. Which suggested to the director that this was perhaps the last best place to grab an establishing shot of the grand range, the temple of the ages, that would house their lofty story of 'Savitri'!

So much came with this moment of Return. To the geographers and scientists aboard, subjects like the appalling knowledge that the Salween River must be 'over there' somewhere arrested their thoughts and only heightened their sense of excitement. The porters were certainly joyous, now that they would be back in familiar environments once again.

Those who did the tech side of the film work were imbued with a glorious challenge. And those who would act out the great saga were simultaneously gratified and humbled.

Suddenly everything was possible again.

The Sherpa porters, who were becoming more refreshed by the slightly higher altitude than the previous period of trekking along the lower valleys, now rose to the task of lugging the immense Super Technirama 70 camera #1 onto the tripod, a task they would do countless times in the months ahead.

The whole company, all 1430 of them, then watched in complete silence as the camera captured the mountains' enormous dialogue on BKV celluloid, running sideways through the aperture, which was most appropriate for this astounding block of vertically-scored horizontalism. And that very night, when the starlight was almost as bright as the waxing moon, they watched again, as the camera, now on a quarter km-long railway, covered the same shot, except with shadowy verticals of palm and pine tracking in the foreground: a remarkable and awe-inspiring vision.

Butterbugs, immersed in the glory of the half-light behind the camera, gazed with the others in wonder. Amongst the quiet shuffling of the crew associated with the tracking shot, he found Chandra Lal, the company's spiritual guide, who stood in rapture. Knowing of Butterbugs' extraordinary transcendental powers – as yet unrealized – he opened his sensors and wordlessly invited the star to share his thoughts of the moment.

'Why, Chandra-baba, did we suffer so in these last days before we saw the mountains?'

'Because, my child, we were going through the Gate, in which conflicting forces are channeled and pushing, always pushing.'

'Shakti?'

'You are touching on the truth, my child.'

'Why did we have to feel those things, and why do we not feel them now?'

'I too felt them.'

'You?'

'Yes, certainly.'

'And now?'

'We are emerging on the other side.'

'The other side? Of what?'

'I cannot tell you with veracity right now, my chela. It is not possible.'

'I am content. I am at peace!'

Butterbugs drifted down into a shadowy grove. In the dimness there was a presence, but he could not identify it, and because of his elevated state of mind, there was no need. Unbeknownst to him, overarching above was the hood of a super-sized nag, one of Shiva's hamadryads. And the cobra watched over him protectively.

Enveloped in this remarkable æther, Butterbugs whispered in the dark.

'This, *this*, is what I became an ultrastar for.'

No more words were necessary. The magic night was soft and velvety, and all continued to exult in its aura.

Elation.

Joy.

Ecstasy.

Bliss.

32.

Ascent And Nirvana

Dawn, and all were ready to take the upward path.

No one quite knew what their destiny, either collective or individual, might be. But no one wished to turn back. All faces were aimed upwards and onwards. There was no alternative now.

It wasn't as if all had achieved an exalted state of being. No one could chart the exact location of each individual's station of soul. But one thing was clear: each knew a certain extraordinariness was present, even palpable, all around them. It was as if, that being the case, all trepidation and questioning had fallen away, so that any path, not just the one that led up into the mountains, might lie open to them now. The world of hindrances had passed away.

So they went on up.

Though they were a heavy cavalry in volume and appearance, the company left little mark upon the land. A lightness of foot and an easy flow of lung were both upon them, and they moved along, up into the mystic layers of mists, thick at first, but with each stratum past, clarity increased.

As they settled down into their ascent, groupings formed. Butterbugs, not in the vanguard, but still near the front, chanced to partner with Yana Jabberjee. It was her first stroll in the eastern Himalayas. This erstwhile assistant to Sonny was not yet 21, and she had never acted before in her life. Butterbugs knew this. Now she had a co-lead in an extremely important picture.

The terrain not quite requiring rest-step methods, and his diaphragmatic adjustments to the changing altitude working perfectly, the ultrastar was able to converse without any huffing and puffing.

'Yana, you climb well.'

'Thank you, Butterbugs. I am hale.'

'You inspire me.'

'Good. The mere fact that you say this very thing serves to calm my mind.'

'Why, Yana, you are a model of pacific bearing.'

'I am indeed at peace. Yet, on the plane of the world we left behind, I think I should collapse with stress.'

'Oh, but why, dear Yana?'

'What right did I have to magnify my ego to snowy heights and wrest this role from others, who are a thousand times worthier? Would ProwlerCat not have been a more natural choice? Or Koogah Mantell?'

'Perhaps, but we all know that your gesture of offering, which Sonny took up without question, was the only option. We do not know why, precisely, though.'

'Ours is not to reason why?'

'We all believe in you.'

'But, do I believe in myself now? I –'

Butterbugs smiled. Then he paused at a romantic crag and gestured grandly out at the vast vista below.

'Cwm Gothpore!' he declared. 'There's Gothpore town – far, far down the cirque-ish valley. I fancy I see the monorail tram depot. And a bit of smoke from the engine's stack, as it departs on its morning run. That ride up, all the way from Vishnoogunge, seems a million years past!'

'Can you really see that far, Butterbugs?'

'Well, no, not that far, in fact. Not without a platformate-powered glass, anyway.'

'Are you trying to keep my feet on the ground, then?'

She smiled warmly and knowingly.

'Oh, Yana, you're too smart for me!'

'You want me to keep in touch with our past world, don't you?'

'Well, not really. I don't wish you stress at all. Ever since we all entered this transcendent realm, we are no longer burdened with conventional life's complications. In a way, speaking for myself, I'm testing my sensibilities, to see what my limits are. I'm involving you at this moment, because we must be bonded – firmly bonded – in our leading roles in this picture. We must both know how far we can come and go within its realities.'

They resumed their upward progression.

'What about Amitabh?' Yana asked.

The superstar was a ways ahead of them, riding in a jinrickshaw, powered by stout bearers. The fairly steep grade was as nothing to them.

'He is in meditation,' replied Butterbugs. 'And being a tad bit older than we, he has a right to preserve some of his strength. The billions who admire him are all sending thoughts, vibrations, and prayers his way, at any given second. Think of it! He is as Brahma. But as the third great role in this supreme drama, he will meld with us without any preparation or treatment. He is already in an advanced state.'

'That, too, inspires me.'

'Good. The mere fact that you say this very thing serves to calm my mind.'

'That's what *I* said, just now.'

'I know! We are as talking mirrors. We are melding.'

'Butterbugs, I am settled into a proper excitement now. This is an elation!'

'I too feel it, Yana. Are we not honored?'

It became a jolly climb, with much geniality and responsible conduct, based on courtesy and caring. The two leads accomplished such deeds as helping porters with their tares when they clearly needed it, and attending to a cast of supporting players in their directives of ascent. They even toted loads for Sherpas full on when they were taking tiffin, and for substantial stretches, too. It was their high privilege to generally assist in every possible way they could find.

Merrily passing a pack of motion picture film stock to a porter, after giving him a break in its hauling, Yana called out:

'Oh, how this day is leading to the greatness of existence!'

Butterbugs, who was now far away, was glad she finished her statement, for he had a feeling that some sort of transformation was about to take place. Amitabh and Gooroo Chunder, as well as Chandra-baba, happened to be in her immediate vicinity, as well. They all took note of her rising cadence.

Suddenly Yana, even though she was relieved of her burden, began to teeter, then topple.

Though they were in the midst of an incline that was not harshly vertical, still, it rose many hundreds of meters in one grand sweep. Nevertheless, Yana was standing at a point which, if she lost her footing, would place her in an unstoppable pattern of descent such that even a rolling rock of the most obtuse shape, were it human, would not be able to avoid a brain-battering ride toward a grassy grave in the lines of whomp-weed that bordered the slopes of folded and rising rock. The distance to that place was indeed measurable, but unfathomable, unthinkable.

Chandra-baba's voice rang out in the poor conductivity of high altitude air.

'Attend! See! *See* how she enters samadhi!'

Gooroo Chunder's words followed.

'Her physical being is now placed in an attitude of interval!'

Amitabh, reminded of the life-threatening impact on his spleen while filming 'Coolie' (Aasia, 1983), shouted out, 'Yana-rani! It is the samadhi! It is upon you! Can you hear?? Oh, but how could you? We are coming!'

All three enlightened gentlemen were, unfortunately, too far removed from her person to be at her side within the few seconds she would be allowed before inevitably tilting toward the magnetic downside of the encouraging but merciless mountain.

'Butterbugs!' Amitabh sounded off. 'Can you, being within sprinting distance of our dear Yana, save her from certain doom?'

Butterbugs did not have to answer. He was already in transit, lunging toward the parapet she currently decorated, though not for long.

His was indeed a lunge, but it was not without footing, for he found he could providentially negotiate the coarse gravel of the landscape between he and her with startling facility.

Indeed, it was almost as if he were traversing a velveteen-draped bank next a river of universal nectar. Time was not a problem, because, as he advanced, Yana did not embark in any direction of tumble. Yet, there was an inarguable imperative, and because of the transcendence upon all of them, it was possible to accomplish. The ultrastar simply made his way to her side, and though no quality of slow or retarded motion was in play, he beheld her condition as a subject for severe and rapid descent, then measured the angle by which she might commence this action. When she actually did, he was ready to intervene.

'It is the moment!' Chandra-baba declared while he and the others closed in to provide any needed support.

'And so it is,' added Butterbugs, just as he spread his arms and leaned over, to retrieve the fallen human in supra-human trance.

He had indeed leaned over, toward the person he wished to save. It was too steep to jump down and place himself underneath, in order to catch her like a falling sack of spudatoes, so he chose, in his split-second but generously-timed decision-making, to act as crane, in order to pluck, rather than grab.

It was no slight on Butterbugs, but as the others approached and provided buttress and anchor to Butterbugs' engineering, it became a wholly group effort in sustaining her from any death-fall (if a person in samadhi can indeed die of a fall). They became a four-person unit of savement, an engine of multiple joints and movements, which nevertheless depended on one set of hands to do the lion's share of rescuing. Butterbugs possessed these, of course, and their grappling technique, tested in the context of that hideous crone's grip on his person that time in Paris, now came to him in clamping onto the gentle form of Yana's upper arm and lower thigh, both on her right side.

The squeeze on, Butterbugs knew he was inflicting bruises, but better that than the full pummeling of a brutal bomb-fall. In any case, the samadhi was protecting her from both destruction-fear and preservation-pain. He was in full possession, and she was a precious found object indeed.

The four had her, really had her, and they would not lose her now. Gooroo Chunder then provided the rotation capability that allowed the whole humanoid superstructure to sway onto safe ground, and the process of relief began, in which grips were fully loosened and the cargo was softly returned to firmness and levelness.

There she lay, head pillowed with homespun wool generously laid, body coverletted and comfy, as the four gazed upon her with poignancy and sheer joy. They allowed themselves a bit of pride, too, as they were still, even up here, part human.

In the beauty of the gravel, Yana lay in perfect harmony with herself. Large eyes peacefully closed most of the way, the lavish lashes revealed, only slightly, the advanced status of crossed eyes underneath. As if instructed by Sri Ramakrishna or another high-flyer in the fine lines of samadhi, Yana proved herself to be unimpeachable in her lofty repose, and they all knew what an exalted state she was in.

'It is in the order of things,' murmured Chandra-baba as they regarded her. 'Butterbugs, do you know her?'

The ultrastar nodded.

'*She is Savitri*,' he replied gravely.

'We are here, and she is Savitri!' said Amitabh.

Butterbugs leaned down tenderly in the same crane-like posture by which he and the others saved her from mahasamadhi. He drew her up into a position of transport, and the others attended.

And so he carried her in his arms, on up the mountain, without a thought, and without impairment. And the hours went by as the climb went on. Many hours, many meters.

Yana rode, in peaceful suspension.

And then there was a change. A natural occurrence. She emerged from samadhi as he carried her upward.

This near to him, she gazed with total conviction at his profile as it cut the rare air with tranquil but directed purpose.

Her voice did not surprise him. Rather, he expected it, and was ready to accommodate.

'Butterbugs, might I lie next to you these nights?'

His focus remaining fixed by necessity to the steepening lane ahead. The ultrastar was glad his co-star had returned to conventional consciousness.

'Indeed, come! Lie next to me either day or night, as it is a natural fit, and it is beyond meaningful. It is a love of bliss and a bliss of love. We must consummate it.'

'Butterbugs, what happened to me?'

'You went into samadhi. It's true, wonderfully true. Gooroo Chunder, Amitabh, and Chandra-baba attended me. We celebrate your ecstasy.'

'I know I cannot verbalize its reaches to you; my samadhi...'

'Not needed, Yana. You are becoming Savitri. You *are* Savitri!'

'Is that what the gooroos told you?'

'No. Not verbally. Well, yes, in effect. It is what they said, without saying it. I also knew it in my heart. That is why we can bond further, closer. To share your shakti.'

She was overjoyed at this.

They continued onward.

And when Yana was walking again, and her vim was equal to Butterbugs', the company paused at a wide ledge near the snow line for several days, and the first scenes were shot.

'Where, oh where, is our line producer, Butterbugs?' queried director Javier-Gomez Prutmop, an artiste in the highest sense.

'Well now,' replied Butterbugs, placing his script on a podium of blue ice. 'That is a very good question... But that's what people say today when they do not know a question's answer.'

Fat Chance had followed up the rear. He was indeed a bloated bub, and because he had not yet reached a certain elevation, the line producer felt something odd beginning to form in his consciousness. Things began to spin, but not because of any extreme or dangerous condition. Or even because of the elevation factor. Actually, the change that now came over him did nothing but provide engagement, and it finally took possession of him. Far it was from a hostile takeover. Conversely, it was all about truth, a condition he had never really known in toto before. He turned about and descended the trail, which was, at this point, only starting to become a challenge for anyone going up its course.

Several months later, with the lofty photoplay drama in the can, all who were in it and had made it, descended to the still-high base-camp of Gothpore, with its ragtag likability in Tuscan-columned dress, providing invitational comfort to a company still lost in the stars of true transcendental space and time.

One afternoon, Butterbugs was wandering idly amongst the chick-shaded loggias, hands behind khadi-clad back, pondering the busted chips of terracotta chai cups that peppered the gutter along here, chatting in Hindi and the local Baracala tongue with the shop-folk, townsmen, and idlers along the way, while all the time remaining on call, in case any retakes on the lower heights were needed.

He turned into a by-lane in this not-much-more-than-a-main-drag thana village, and noted the obscure attractions of the cubbyhole dwellings and storage facilities that made up the micro-urban composition in these parts.

Then two ornate pilasters gave way to a modest courtyard under a neem tree, and he found himself in an ashram of sorts. Though this was far from the plains, he had the feeling that he was in a neat little nook in, say, Betul District, which always provided fond memories for him.

He had to keep in mind he had virtually completed one of the most philosophically-advanced roles he had yet taken on in this maya existence, so a walk like this into such a cozy but unexceptional locale might have been construed by any onlooker as an act committed by a sadhoo with other, more remotely thoughtful things on his mind.

But Butterbugs, even with his native garments and his post-in-character mien, was known here. Because...

'Hey Butterbugs!' a familiar voice chimed.

The ultrastar looked over where the twanging sound came from – an earthen cubicle, old as time, beneath a monkey nest midway up the trunk of the spreading neem, the plain headquarters of any acolyte who professed dedication to this hidden but obviously worthwhile shrine.

There was the plump 'n' pale meat of a familiar personage, late of the 'Savitri' location unit; a person of erstwhile consequence.

'Fat Chance! I've found you at last!'

'Namaskar, Butterbugs! Välkommen, in fact!'

'You're here! You! *You!*'

'All success, above?'

He gestured toward the Himalayan mass, the tops of which peeped over the modest village skyline of sikharas and domelings.

'I think we have achieved something remarkable, yes. I say that on behalf of everyone, and with utmost humility.'

'Fantastic!'

'Now, Fat Chance, it's great to see you prospering. Tell of your new deal.'

'What did you think of me? These long months, that is.'

'Well, I did not think you dead. I thought, 'He has moved on, to a different plane', perhaps one not known by the likes of me. I sensed it. I *knew* it. Or at the very least, I can only hope I am worthy of knowing it.'

'So measured. So sane. So accurate!'

'Then – I am? Accurate?'

'Yea, Butterbugs. I have found my place.'

'Oh my, but it is fine. Very good. I'm glad you weren't disappointed.'

'Was I missed?'

'Of course. But when I knew in my heart that you were safe, we got on with things. Nobody was angry, or even irked. We just weren't *doing* that stuff. Bob Evans filled in, covering your duties. You'll still get partial screen credit.'

'Good old Bob.'

'Well, yes. Good old Fat Chance! Yes, yes. Achcha... Soon the monorail tram will bear us back, ultimately to old Hollywood.'

Adjusting his indigenous garb whilst sitting cross-legged, Fat Chance paused in his response to this important statement, as if the long afternoon, with its sunlit rays now planting their effects on a broken column adjacent to the box of the temple itself, instilled a nostalgic interruption that overrode all desires inherent in all humans present. The local colony of langur monkeys above were unaffected.

At length, Fat Chance elected to make his statement.

'I'm staying on, Butterbugs. You see, I'm – I'm... *staying on*. I have had a vision, and it has come to pass. I have been welcomed as a chela here. It's the chance of a lifetime, and I'm not going to turn it down. The District Collector has offered me instant citizenship, on account of my cheerful enthusiasm to join this estate and make it my own. Confirmation has just arrived from Delhi! I think I knew, when our ship left Suez, that I would never return. When I retreated from those mystic mists on the mountain slopes, I knew it was for a good reason. I knew it the first moment I turned back. I also knew you wouldn't be angry with me for not fulfilling my line producer duties, but that's all behind me now. Also, I am in pink health, and I am already slimming. Soon I shall be as classically shapely as a Calcutta beggar-trainer! I am living the days of the Beloved here.

'This is what I always wanted, Butterbugs. I am here and now. *In* the here and now, and it is better than I thought it would be – by far. I have already studied copious sacred texts, and I am learning Sanskrit. I can read you the palm frond of your choice! I trust you will give Big Brother Porter my best greetings and felicitations.'

'I will, with all my heart!' exclaimed Butterbugs.

'And Butterbugs?'

'Yes, my child?'
'One last thing. Please remit the remainder of my earnings to:

> 'The Baboo
> Carzon Hall
> The Mall
> Gothpore
> Arunachal Pradesh
> Hindustan'

'I will, with all my heart! In fact, I will personally supervise the dissolution of your estates, the liquidation of which shall be dispatched in full form and transferred into rupees, so that you may apply it to your nouveau charitable concerns in this here community,' added the ultrastar.

'Thank you, Butterbugs. I know that our town will now be a place of pilgrimage because of our production of 'Savitri', but I want it to happen in the right way.'

'It will. I tell you, it will! I and all the gooroos, sadhoos, sannyasis and swamis, from worldly to austere, will make this dream a reality.'

'Oh-so-good! The monorail tram will have to run more than once a day, I should think. Perhaps we can acquire another engine and bogies. Perhaps the Maharaja of Patiala can donate his spares. Please apply to the railway and locomotive works at Kharagpur. We have six bighas of pleasing land on the edge of town, donated by the Wala of Jumboolah, upon which to build a picturesque pilgrimage center. We will need a dharmsala, and a small talkies, with dual Philips 70mm capability, in which to screen 'Savitri' daily, and an expanded ashram and a rest house and a cookery and a cutchery and a sacred tank for ablutions with ghats, and a...'

They planned well into the night, and were joined the next morn by the essential team of designers and guiders who would make this tremendous enterprise real.

Saying their farewells, the two friends, actor and producer-turned-baba, tarried long on the platform, waiting for the monorail tram engine's toot from around the palmyra-ornamented bend.

'I so admire your new life,' Butterbugs remarked.

The other adjusted his dhoti and shifted his weight in his new plastic slippers.

'Not bad for a fat boy from west Texas, huh?'

The apparatus for Gothpore's new spiritual centers now completely set-up, safely and properly with his help, Butterbugs called upon dear friends in Cooch Behar, spending equal time in both palace and mulgie. He then made his way down to Dacca, where he lodged in the Ahsan Manzil for several days' stay, as a guest of the city. The wonderfully gloomy suites sported haircut-height punkahs, and he hosted several banquets, where many old acquaintances, from as far away as Chittagong, Cox's Bazar, and Sylhet, wined and dined with him until the dog wars in the by-lanes nearby faded away, and the creeping, sensual steam from the Burigunga, accompanied by the nightly boom from the Barisal guns – when lonely Bibi Mariam still calls for her lost mate Kale Jham Jham, from under the waters off the Buckland Bund – enveloped them in pleasance... All these and much more, made their days and nights complete.

'This is one of my *homes!*' the star proclaimed, with much sentiment.

One day, Butterbugs' pal Moonshee Kharak Tenh took him to a small ceremony at the Tara Masjid, where he was welcomed as an honorary Fellow.

All standing Fellows had assembled in the ravishing courtyard, and gazed at the pleasing structure, freshly dolled up, as it was, daily.

'One of the benefits of your status, Butterbugs Bahadur, is that now, as of this here moment, the central dome of this mosque shall be colloquially (but with dignity) called Butterbugs Gumbauz, as its stars shine in Allah's glory. But they might be a mild reminder of your own glory, as well. We say this now. Inshallah!' proclaimed the Moonshee.

All were in admiration.

'You will note that the central dome is a small one,' he added. 'Because we know of your perfect humility. Yet your signal importance is undeniable, as well!'

Butterbugs, with tears in his eyes, could only whisper, 'Inshallah!' in reply.

This visitation, in this always-loving environ, was particularly fulfilling to the ultrastar's soul.

Yana joined him at Judd Ghat, where they took ship for the west.

It was with the regret of many involved that the expansive saga of the filming of 'Savitri' (Selznick) could not be laid down on pages numbering less than four digits. The overarching majesty of that enterprise was as big as the Himalayas themselves. There nevertheless came into existence a super-limited-edition three-volume set, which documented the undertaking in stunning scope and detail, published by Benedikt Taschen and priced at US$12,000. Aside from hour-by-hour entries from a superb staff of historians, it featured essays by Khushwant Singh, Vikram Chandra, Swami Guptanarabandananda, Jean-Paul Sartre, Noam Chomsky, Vikram Seth, Nisith Ranjan Ray, Cardinal Vaughn, The Mother, P.T. Nair, Pat Buchanan, Stanley Crouch, Moti Charbi Bewkoof Baba (Fat Chance Parker), Pupul Jayakar, Samaren Roy, Jug Suraya, Bibhutibhushan Bandopadhyay, Cornel West, Jiggs Kohlra, and Sarah Chayes, with special guest, the Dalai Lama. The volumes appeared in mega-size format, with their own special container chests and trolleys. 95% of the profits were channeled to charitable organizations, including the Gothpore Leelasthana – the venue, for the divine sports of... (Butterbugs?)...

[A Cheap Edition (price: Rs 42 only) appeared after a respectable time in which the specific charities fully received their proceeds from the instant sellout of the limited edition.]

No hyperbole was to be found anywhere amongst the effects of the 'Savitri' production, whether in the picture itself, or in its associated literature, promotion or exhibition. It was simply fact. It existed. And wonder existed also.

In the world today, there are indeed heroes, and so it was that they who enacted and realized this picture, ostensibly for entertainment, ended up achieving so much more than that. Thus, the reader must be referred at this point to that far-off ideal, achieved through the cinema, as well as in these multiple volumes. A fourth volume was devoted exclusively to plates, and a fifth was a packet of DVDs, CD-ROMs, CDs, microfilm, microfiche, and digital files, which ever expanded on the entire phenomenon.

Not for the last time did Butterbugs contemplate a post-strolling player career as a sannyasi, doing daily puja amidst the serene and unfolding marvels of the Gothpore Leelasthana tank's languid and reverie-filled ghats, on a long and vintage afternoon...

33.

In Epoch Ultra

It was as if Butterbugs wanted to give it all up.
All.

Perhaps it was because of the letdown upon returning to the maya of Earthly existence, having experienced the nirvanic bliss of his late 'Savitri' voyage through transcendent layers and planets. Sri Aurobindo was not even the reason. As author of the
epic poem, it was as if he was the agent for freedom. So, no mundane personage had
a part in this interior dialogue. Essences themselves were of the essence.

Justy was doing some office time in the Central African Revised Republic,
where she was having great success being Prime Minister Without Portfolio,
while Saskia was in purposeful hermitage in Gränna, Sverige, hammering on a
script of unknown content. His lovers were well-provided-for to do their important work. He never had to worry about them. Was he in their thoughts, or did they
even have time?

So, was it a sadhoo's renouncement of the world, or a 'post-partum' depression
for the ultrastar?

Though J and S were never regarded in his mind as security blankets, the
conspicuous physical lack of one or both of them at this time, despite close techie
contact, reminded him of how, that's right – he – Butterbugs, was decisively a
single gentleman, without possession of a directly intimate relationship with the
girl of his dreams, or even musings.

The latest, Yana, was heavenly, the perfect cerebral mate for him, and physically, nirvanic, even. Love was easily optioned. But, she was still Savitri. She
was indeed, ever since that moment on the alm, when Butterbugs, Amitabh &
Co. had prevented her from The Drop-Out. She *was* Savitri.

(They who were her rescuers had all concurred later that Yana had, at that very
moment, experienced transcendent powers truly imbued in her person, which
never would have allowed for her to fall. She may even have been granted the
power of flight just then. No, they had been merely servants of courtesy, to ensure
her dignity and her quality of ascent...)

Yana was somewhat easy to categorize, only because she was so impossible
in her goals and her bearing. She had been set up via all the proper channels as
an entity of consequence in all Sri Aurobindo institutions in the Southland, and
she acquiesced to their entreaties toward enlightenment. Thus, to the ultrastar, no
opportunity for love, really.

He reviewed other perspectives in his private life, regarding – fulfillment. He didn't come up with much. Strange, how a star of ultra standing could be so – wanting.

Recent experiences of profundity having dominated his reason, his more banal sensitivities looked askance at historical subjects to scrutinize as food for thought – even though it be 'filler' thought. That being the case, the tone of the idyll surrounding Pepper Carlson and Prairie Browne kept him up nights. That was an idyll worth obsessing over, because it seemed so accessible, yet it was denied him. Distraction yes, but where was the resolve?

There was a certain incongruity over the juxtaposition of that dreamlike world with the uplifted particulate matter and fly-ash that sometimes settled like black snowflakes on his panoramic bedroom window, up there in The Æyrie.

After he'd talked with Leonard Bernstein late one night, and the great composer/conductor told him about his own world-weariness – all the cocktail parties and social requirements, the very burden of it all, the succession of it, and the cumulative effect it can have on one's soul... there was plenty of reason for the actor to think, 'Greater artistes than myself have suffered from the same malaise. But how did they survive it?'

'How did you survive it?' asked Butterbugs.

The composer/conductor did not hesitate.

'I took solace in the farewell nature of Mahler's 9th Symphony.'

'But you were lucky enough to conduct it,' said Butterbugs. 'You got to *experience* it!'

'And I was healed,' replied Lenny.

Some, like Lenny, were fortunate. They could live by music alone.

Then there were a few moments when the ultrastar felt a particular descent into the flames, as in Dave McCallum's slow-motion fall in that fantastically deserted set in 'The Greatest Story Ever Told' (UA, 1965). A slo-mo realization of resolve. Perhaps it could be accomplished here in Upper LA, from the ledge of The Æyrie's Populuxe-drawn thin line, between deck and sky.

Again?

(He never did have those railings installed...)

But there was an overriding factor that was very important, and just because it overrode his success did not mean it was recognized as being most important. It being: despair was not what he felt. Rather, he longed to return, to ascend, nay, *transcend* to some elevated vista plain, from which to spy out the land in purposeful survey. That way there could be navigable authority over his apparent destiny.

Should he repair to Gothpore, perchance to entertain options with the babas of the Leelasthana? Fat Chance – er – Moti Charbi Bewkoof Baba, wrote a kind and newsy ærogramme, in which he narrated how they'd just finished constructing an attractive ambulatory for reflection that encircled the old Perpendicular Gothic monument to Waycreft Goth (most appropriate). He had been the first Collector, for whom the station was named, serving way back in the good old days of John Company. The eroded crockets on its spire did no obtrusive harm to the devotees' daily regime. Here peace was not only achievable, it was non-intrusive. Butterbugs was welcome to come and bunk in the barracks, to stay for as long as he wished, if only he would let them know.

(For mature audiences only, as peace cannot be maintained by bozos.)

Oh, but that was not it. The source of his malaise was not to be found in any retrievable pocket, though he retained his Gothpore ticket packet until ten days past due. As a sort of security blanket, if nothing else.

What then, was happening to him?

Something was coming. That he knew. An amorphous mass. On the horizon.

'What, I ask you,' he asked himself, 'is it all about?'

You see, Butterbugs was, in point of fact, not all that hip a person, so he did not sardonically add the expected 'Alfie' at the ending of his query, as might be expected, even in an exchange from himself to himself.

(Not long ago, he had seen Lewis Gilbert's Mike Caine's 'Alfie' (Paramount, 1966) and liked it, though he had thought it would be a comedy).

Then, once he realized his Gothpore tickets had expired, he booked passage again.

A veil of tears! Did it drape itself about our planet in the here and now? Oftentimes now, it seemed so.

He was a man in need of security. A feeling that, past the pomp and the glory, something else awaited, and was accessible, if need be.

He was a typical American.

34.

Some Good Things

These were good times, hopeful times.

They were times when it was proven it was OK to be positive, and to be comfortable with it, too. To feel so without any agency telling you that's *how* you had to feel. Life was on the upswing. There were new ideas, new feelings, new plans all around. People called it the Butterbugs Effect.

For many, things were looking up. For others, at least the hope that things were looking up was a possibility. Someone always gets left behind in the scheme of things, but fewer happened to be in that category these days. Butterbugs' own Russel Arms Foundation, which had grown into an Oxfam-sized organization, was only one of the reasons why.

People were saying things like:

'My sister is no saint, but she's a helluva lot more saint-like than I am.'

Giving credit and benefit of the doubt were pushing hostility, suspicion, frustration, and cynicism right off the roster of public behavior.

The ultrastar had taken some interest in politics, naturally. Not as a player, though.

'Photoplays are the venue where I make my stand,' he told both friends and the media. 'Not from the tiers of any Congress' chambers, nor any Parliament's benches, nor from the ovoid center of any world-grasper or progressive's pinnacle of power. Not from within the humble interior of a council room in any village of dust, nor from the courthouse of Kidder County, Northakota either, for that matter. No, my statements of politico natures, if any, remain confined to the shows in which I appear. We all should have our say from where we belong. I will not retreat, however, from identifying myself with any worthy cause, be it vetted by myself or by people I trust.'

He certainly did not shirk. Butterbugs was involved in many charities, movements of global concern, as well as the Dryburgh Abbey Preservation Trust, which kept the moss off Sir Walter Scott's tomb.

As far as political interests in which to contribute, Sonny had suggestions as to where he should cast his gaze. None of them had Bolivian copper mine owners as members, or types like that. Yet some were fairly high in the corporate world, as Sonny made it clear that the Industry needed to watch out for its own interests.

'What do you mean by 'interests', Sonny?'

'Well, bub, that sounds odd coming from you at this latter-day juncture.

Concerns, outfits, and persons of consequence who are friendly to we who make picture shows.'

'The Motion Picture Relief Fund?'

'Why sure! 'Sright, son! And well, you know, investors and the like.'

'Corporate types?'

'Now don't go sayin' nothin' agin *them* again. You know we couldn't make your pictures without them.'

'I don't know about that...'

'You mean – you're referring to your own untold reserves?'

'I am. Why do we need such grubbers when I have a fulcrum by which to shift the line of control from they who celebrate B.O. receipts for a living back to where it has belonged all these lengthy decades: to we who, as you say, *make* the pictures?'

'Butterbugs, you know I have always admired your egalitarian principles. I have supported them whenever I could. Why, I was right behind you when you excoriated the Defense Policy Board in your and Bob Altman's outstanding Your Basic Pictures release, 'When I Get Up In Front Of Congress', but if it hadn't been for Mingus Orb, who made his platinum from beet farmer monopolies across the face of the temperate world, your cause-stricken speeches never would have reached audiences – to electrify them like you did.'

'Everybody lives with lies, Sonny. And it took a lot to bring Mingus around, if you remember. I even got him to sell his slaves on his private estates in Longon-golongongo.'

'So you did. At least it sounds like you're a realist when it comes to hypocrisy.'

'It's only because it bugs us, you and me, that we notice it so regularly. To them – those who live the hypocritical life – hypocrisy is not anything bad. Freeing one's mind from the burden of bad is exhilarating.'

'Is that what they taught you at 'Gothpore'??'

Sonny always got a bit playful when any reference to the Leelasthana was made. It had nothing to do with the coincidence of names (i.e. Gothpore – Mega|Goth Studios – Hyman Goth), and it was no cue for him to exercise his dubious feelings for Hy Goth, or anything gothic, for that matter. As a distraction, that faraway Indian magnet of spiritual attraction had the power to pull his ultrastar right out of active duty. So the playfulness was actually anxiousness.

Butterbugs looked at him with marked disappointment.

'Look, Butterbugs, I know that, as you have achieved ultrastardom, you feel as if you have taken on a greater responsibility as a humanoid on this here planet. Bravo! But sir, as Pappy Ford once told me, don't start inflating your head with hydrogen yet. You know what'll happen.'

'I will abide...' was all Butterbugs said.

A certain amount of shaking and rattling and rolling was nevertheless going on, with or without the world's only ultrastar's participation.

After serving as governor of Michigan, overseeing the final breakup of GM (a cherished dream), and ushering the implementation of Pyragon propulsion technology on through to the assembly line, Michael Moore ran for governor of California after Arnie's fall from grace in the DurjaTorque/DumBelle controversy. He won. After decades of making millions squirm, Mike was now respected in all quarters, but only because of his achievement of good things for all.

Water wars became settled, 79% (gigantic!) of movie folk were now employed, and while corporate domination of world operation was bigger than ever, there was a marked tone change in its approach to independent moral pathways. After all, everything was a matter of peaceful coexistence. At this point in the world's history, there actually *was* money enough for all. (Resources were another matter, though…)

It wasn't long before critics, seers, and trend-watchers like Eek Tchesteretsch, O'Farrell Milgers, and Charity Poptart – and even Mark Mutty Mullun, were giving credit for these and other things to the proverbial *Butterbugs Effect*.

That in itself was a phenomenon.

Sonny and others continued to point out his Effects' effects on humanity, hoping that the ultrastar would be jarred out of what they called 'The Gothpore Soul Suckers'. Not that they viewed the respected pilgrimage center as a cultish trap. They just wanted the ultrastarry universe to be without end.

They would have to keep him happier, somehow.

And, as agents are supposed to do, Sonny took Butterbugs by the shoulders and guided him into a chute of opportunity. He'd long ago given up trying to match him with starlets and turbo-gals he knew. After all, his own ex was Butterbugs' demi-life partner. Rather, his guidance came in the form of hot properties and the discussions therein. He was ever on the lookout for a picture that might satisfy the star's thirst for do-gooding. After the vastness of 'Savitri', the need was perhaps bigger than ever.

'Hell for Stout' (20th-Fox) was a complicated construction worker pic. The first part, set in NYC, becomes deeply involved with high-rises, and climaxes with the '39 World's Fair. After intermission (pic runs nearly five hours), the scene changes to LA. Butterbugs' character, a Promethean builder (no, it wasn't some sort of 'Fountainhead' (WB, 1949) remake…), now a big time visionary after laborious rising through experience, is charged with rebuilding all of LA after it is consummately devastated in the ultimate quake.

The thing was, despite all the improvements on many a front, the languor in Butterbugs' heart was there. It existed, and it could not be denied.

Something though, was coming. It was still an amorphous mass.

35.

I Cannot Choose Now

And now occurred a great unveiling.

For many months, the heaviest of draperies had hung round an entity that was known by a few, coveted by most of the few, and once it was secured by one, lorded over *all* of the few.

There was one thing Hyman Goth loved more than his crack cocaine, and that was to make the biggest splash in Hollywood. Over and over. All the time.

Butterbugs had just returned to town after filming a short, Wim Wenders' 'Rage Over A Lost Penny' (Continental). Vienna, 1800. Inspired by the Beethoven piano piece. It was destined to win an Oscar as Best Short Subject.

Having just finished a pimento sandwich and the last wedge of a schlagobers-slathered strudel he'd personally packed all the way from his favorite Kaffeklatsch-O-Matic, run by his pal Adi Berber just this side of the Ring, his most private telecommunication device rang.

When such a thing occurred, he always picked it up. Not surprisingly, it was Sonny.

'Butterbugs, I cannot speak long now...'

Sonny was absolutely solemn, almost whispering, as if calling from just out-side the door to an operating room where surgeons were fighting for the very life of the President of the United States – or someone even more important.

'Then how come, old Sonny, did you ring? I am in Wiener-mode now. Wanna hear my brief run-down? I got a virtual key to the Stadt! I guest-conducted Bruckner's Ninth at the Grosse Musikvereinsaal. Really! Herbert coached me. Just for fun I did a cameo in a reenactment of the coronation of Charles I at the Burg Thiertre. A bunch of us did nude body painting at MUMOK. Kinda squiggly. Then I got to take Archduke Frauncis Ferdinand's Gräf-und-Stift death-mobile for a spin around the Ring. I really 'opened her up' on the Hauptallee! Quite the honor! Spritzers with Mindikins and Sissi at the good old Gumpoldskirchnergarten. My *favorite*. And guess what? I even won a Franz-Joseph II lookalike contest! Oh, yeah. (Breena did makeup!) Naturally, I donated the 3000-florin prize to the Beggar's Guild. Just yesterday I did an ad for the Zentralfriedhof with Darcey Bussell – gratis. We were dancing up a storm around the mausolea! You really should've been there, Sonny. It's been a *blast!* Why, at the State Opera, I –'

'If you could report to the Negotiation Block over at Mega|Goth as soon as you possibly can, there is a one-on-one conference waiting to happen for you. In this short, urgent exchange, I cannot possibly convey the total importance of such an impending encounter. You are strenuously requested to attend at earliest.'

When Sonny said 'earliest', it meant, not an hour ago, or fifteen minutes ago, or any of those smartass wordplays, but just as soon as it was convenient, as if convenient meant 'the next thing you do'. This was decent code to the ultrastar. That was why the two associates had always remained close.

Soberly placing his strudel down on the counter, Butterbugs replied in carefully measured tones.

'I will, Sonny. Right now, and without equivocation or hesitation of any kind.'

Sonny hung up in his usual manner of not saying goodbye, and the thing was done. The Vienna to LAX flight was non-stop.

'This is going to be a very serious picture, Butterbugs. Probably your most profound.'

Arimanes J. Jugbash was one of the finest Assistant Associate Executive producers in the Industry. His wife, Astarte, was even more respected in pictures, mainly as a result of her work on the legendary 'Cheng' (Oddball).

Butterbugs politely scanned a pre-pre-production press kit, unreleased but for his eyes only.

'Aye, it looks it. But what a cast!'

'The whole range of show business is represented therein, son.'

'It's not going to be like 'Pepe' (Columbia, 1960), is it?'

'No. No, it is not.'

'How could it be anything but a very serious picture?'

'That's right.'

A.J.J. did not usually smile, and he did not now. His grave and stately mien was unfazed by the present human interaction. The thin, thin, 16mm tie, camel-hair jacket, lightly oiled hair and almost imperceptible (rumored to be smokeless) cigs, spoke of an exec whose careful planning was always trustworthy. But that wasn't the point here.

Butterbugs was silent.

A.J.J. knew the ultrastar did not indulge in any sort of petty games.

'Is Edward Andrews in?'

As an actor, Butterbugs had to get down to basics.

'From the start. Key role, as Grand Ward.'

'Hmm. Excellent. Sawl Cane's powerful roles!'

'And yours, Butterbugs.'

'I only know of the novel. It's new and busting blocks all over, and it is a big read.'

'You have not yet read it?'

Butterbugs' reply was awkward and poorly-toned:

'New...'

'It is tremendous power itself!'

'But this picture – of it – Cane's latest – wouldn't it be rather like my 'Holy Water Sprinkler War On The Volga Plains' (Bronston)? I thought that *that* was the very summit of my Modern Morality Melodramas, and should never be eclipsed. You were not there. Do you have any idea what we *did* with that picture?'

If A.J.J. betrayed a sort of worshipfulness towards Butterbugs, it practically sneaked out now, here, in this sedate and Scan-cool environment.

'One of your greatest pictures!'

If there was any way he thought he could've gotten away with truly speaking his mind on this one particular subject, as in 'If they had let *me* associate exec produce 'HWSWOTVP', then, truly, it would have indeed been your *greatest* picture!' Never mind the appendix that might follow: 'But now, with this as-of-now untitled Sawl Cane Project, here is my chance to be, if not the principal producer, then at least the Assistant Associate Executive Producer of this, the most outstanding picture to be made – ever.' Yet, he dared not speak these thoughts (even though Butterbugs, who respected him, would invariably be sympathetic).

A.J.J. remained low-key.

'But Butterbugs, this as-of-now untitled Sawl Cane Project is something entirely of the *beyond*. The beyond, I tell you.'

Was he too low key?

He was. Butterbugs held out empty hands, expecting nothing.

'Then here, take it,' said Arimanes.

The novel itself.

He continued, 'Take this latest deluxe edition, fresh off the New York press! Read it! Read it, and –'

'Weep?'

A curled Butterbugsian smile ensued.

'Sometimes –'

The producer didn't wish to get off into sitcom humor procedures in getting his point across. His resolve was to remain grave.

'It will impact your soul, Butterbugs. Weeping, wailing, amazement, and yes, some laughter, too, all will be yours. You will have everything.'

A.J.J. then placed, almost reverently, the massive 3099-page volume, bound in hog-skin – (while its satellite accouterments were rife with supplementary folios, broadsides, explanatory charts and engravings; the whole forming a kit of light steamer-trunk size) – onto the alpaca-lined daveno beside the star. It was a gesture of kings.

With all his vast experience, Butterbugs now drew back, remained suspended, and upheld his progress within this ashlar-lined chamber. It wasn't A.J.J. or his reserved but peerless bearing that was the problem.

'My mind is – attempting something. Something I do not readily know. I cannot speak it.'

'Speak, memory…'

That was exactly what Yevtushenko told him that night, way up in the vampiric high-rise in Moscow. The Nabokovian flashback method. Back when poets, artists, intellectuals, franklins, carters, ash-burners – the whole wide world – were trying to establish what the Butterbugs phenomenon actually *was*. And what it meant to them. If all in the outside world now knew, did the phenomenon himself, at this, the very latest moment, still know?

Butterbugs waxed urbane.

'In point of fact, I happen to be, A.J.J., if I can really tell you, a sort of prisoner of something unknowable right now.'

'Why, naturally, in your advanced state of achievement, you are perhaps worried lest –'

'No, A.J.J., it's nothing like a therapeutic or dysfunctional crisis. Far from it. It's just that, I don't really know what to do with the rest of my life.'

Even though this was not exactly true, Butterbugs decided to affect a construct of reasonable probability, so that the producer might not be too troubled by the star's own apparent flakiness, and thus, take it unto his breast as understood. There was a bridge of trust between the two, and its lanes and curbs were free of conflicting traffic. Most importantly, there was no one wanting to throw themselves off its heights in sight.

'Then, Butterbugs, I propose that this here picture, to be based on the great work now in your hands, might be just the elemental item to get you *back on track*, so to speak.'

Butterbugs abandoned his gentle fib.

'I'm sorry A.J.J. I… I cannot choose now.'

A.J.J. remained unruffled. Not only was he in the presence of Butterbugs, it was simply not his style to apply constriction to any troubled vein in his vicinity, however brightly red it leaked. With an entire back wall of books as a cyclorama, he poured them both a cascade of white grape juice, and placed a pale stalk of asparagus in each.

'Someone more erudite than I will then talk to you about it.'

'And try to change my mind.'

'Or at least try to convince you to 'hook on'. You are conclusive, then?'

'I tell you, Arimanes, I don't know! I just don't know.'

The rest of the time was a poor scene. Neither knew how to shed the rubbish that had been acquired in this session and speak the plain and simple truth.

And he took Sawl Cane's big new novel home with him that night, to The Lazaretto. Courtesy was a hallmark, based on gentlemanly treatment.

It was a fact that, while he was now much experienced with picture people on the management side, those who enabled and booked and opportunized the whole process, usually under the premise of profit, there were nevertheless some gleanings of wisdom to be found in their obvious manipulations.

Now A.J.J. was an honorable man, so Butterbugs trusted him, but it wasn't as if the powers of persuasion were to be found amidst his sophistication.

He hauled the tome home, manually, and after grunting it from the trunk of his Bristol coupe, he simply left it in the foyer. The kit sat under the gentle glow of the chain-held lantern overhead, alone and abandoned by the master of the house, so that the hour grew late, and staff went about securing the property for the night.

Tuan Jim knew everything about The Lazaretto, so he tended to notice any alteration his employer might make, whether it was a toothpaste repair to a stucco wall from a dart being misplaced in a basement back room, or a pair of ladies' gloves, forgotten by a visiting legendary cinema personality on a mail table in the anteroom connecting with a ninth-string bathroom out in the Guest Wing.

Tuan Jim noticed the volume kit where Butterbugs had left it. The trolley was hard to miss. It being the late hour, the last of the clocked day, Tuan Jim thought he might take a bit of relaxation and peruse this mass as left by his squire. His Malacca days had been filled with survey after survey of the world's great reads, so he was accustomed to pausing in any midstream he happened to paddle at the moment, and extract a textual tincture or two.

He knew Sawl Cane, probably as well as Butterbugs did, as the author had been a guest here many times. Consequently, the two had struck up an intellectual rapport of great value. But to Tuan Jim, this was the most ambitious work he had yet witnessed from the prolific Cane's pen.

He became so engrossed in the novel that he glanced up at the timepiece down the hall and noted that it was 3:30 in the AM. No matter. To continue...

By 10:00AM the next day, Tuan Jim had read steadily, non-stop, while holed up on one of those furnitures that no one ever sits on, except perhaps when a boggling message comes over the phone, and the receiving ears command their owner to tread a few steps, then collapse onto the nearest chair... And though the novel was indeed a page turner, it nevertheless was up to the task of gripping the turner's very soul, so as to emit a 'I have never read so deep a book' message that told one's body to forget any imperatives except those that would maintain the reader's stamina, until the full tale of said book's saga had been told.

Well, Tuan Jim wasn't that fast a reader, because come mid-morn, he was only less than one half through the bulk.

At that point though, he knew it was his urgent duty to notify his employer as to the magnitude of the book, as he, Tuan Jim, knew that it would make an irresistibly-great picture. A picture for the ages.

'Tuan Butterbugs! Might I intrude?'

Tuan Jim knew that he could intrude at any time, as he had the complete trust of Butterbugs, so he opened the louvered double doors and strode into the ultrastar's suite.

The ultrastar had slept alone this night, so all the better to approach him with bed tea and a buttery citrus beverage, as well as the Cane novel, in tow.

'Butterbugs?' The very high-pitched tone of Tuan Jim's voice, uncharacteristic though it was, caught Butterbugs' receptive attention.

'Speak, Tuan Jim.'

'This, this *novel*, by our erstwhile houseguest Cane. You must read it and embrace it. No other input to your life right now could be so acute.'

Still languid in his nightclothes, cozened in his cocoonment amidst the stagey sweep of his bed's breeze-opened curtains, but aware that a levee must be certain, Butterbugs took the signal.

'Cane's labor? You have it?'

'Right here, Butterbugs. A hefty piece.'

'I know. I lugged it last night, late, with more difficulty than the trolley system which you now use.'

'I have made it orderly and accessible. Here, it is. Commence it without delay. I will provide all needs, beverages, grub, and advisement, as well as secretarial blocking to any distractions that might impact you, *for the duration*.'

Butterbugs was pleased rather than amused.

'You insist, then?'

'I do. I tell you, I do. Cane's finest work! You cannot ignore it. It came up to you, and you cannot *not* react.'

'That's meaningful to me, Tuan Jim. So, bring it forward. While I'm in my morning loo, prep the text, if you please.'

'A distinct pleasure, Butterbugs!'

'I might add, I'm a slow reader.'

'Absorbent! Comprehensive! Have at it, person of importance!!'

Butterbugs read it, every word. Day after day in the Agfachrome noon, he sat by the pool, lunging after each page. Even the gamboling nudes just at hand did not sway him from his sole purpose on Earth right now. Not even Marranee Morgroath, whose pussy lips crawled relentlessly toward him after each fresh-squeezed orange juice breakfast upon levee. Now *that* was something.

'All right my friends,' he thought, facing an imagined audience of James Ensor masks (the actor's perfect test audience, with a convenient anonymity, but noted for their propensity to be nightmarishly demanding), 'I'm almost in, and...'

In?

Variety-ese for joining a picture, of course.

And days later – it was days, not weeks – as he put down the huge volume, with its India paper practically turned to meal, and its flyleaves scrawled with notes, and the overflow inserts protruding from the body like intermittent feathers, he leaned over on the leaden table at sunset, severely exhausted, but simultaneously proto-electrified, as if 880 volts of pure dynamo-flash power had replaced the bloody ichor of his veins, and because his brain, virtually a new control center, based on elusive yet forceful amperage, had replaced the wet chemicals of his birth, it became a crown of insight and enlightenment as far as the roles of the ages were concerned.

His voice, needing recovery from not speaking a single word all this time, was fully coated in liverdumpling extracts and built-up oils. Yet, called to service upon the book's final line and 'The End' below it, and performing to the new strong standards of what entailed some mighty thing so transcendent that it was equivalent to achieving an operational plane loftier than carbon-based life as we know it, he managed to utter, starting in basso profundo but soon liberated into a clear heldentenor of urgency:

'I tell you, I'm IN…! I'm in, and it is the truth! Yes. I know it now. I always knew it. I'm in. You'd better believe it: I'm… *in!*'

36.

Embarkation

After that – after the solemn decision had been taken, did Butterbugs fully come to terms with what he had taken on. With new strength, he instantly decided that he was up to the task. He took it in. On, then in.

Further matters had to be worked out yet. Naturally. Though he was ecstatic about the book, the official deed of joining up was still not finalized. Seduced he was, but pen had not yet scrawled onto legalized papers. He needed to be absolutely *sure*, and he wasn't quite there yet. He would need some bolstering.

Vanished, at least for the present, was the vacuum pocket in his soul that had caused so much consternation since the rarefied 'Savitri' days. Now loomed something that was perhaps far grander. Not that grandeur was his goal, but big things seemed to carry more meaning these days, and any ultrastar, if he or she was responsible enough, was required to pay attention to such things. And if this new production was indeed the actual, troubling mass of unknown-ness that he sensed was coming his way, it now had shape and form.

His passage to Gothpore moldered and grew quaint.

A whole wing – the Le Corbusier wing – of The Lazaretto had become a sort of museum. Here were arranged in dynamic but curatorial style, artifacts and exhibits germane to his huge new role, tastefully laid out by close friend Malcolm Bert and associates McClure Capps and Lyle Wheeler, with Rolf Gerard and Cedric Gibbons as consultants. The gallery lighting, from the translucent skylit ceiling, lent a calm, objective aspect to the diverse items. Everything had a matte finish; nothing was shiny. In this moderne setting, Butterbugs could indulge in the abstract thought needed to engineer the structure of his character, and the dimensions of its labyrinthine construction.

The mood? Elliot Carter could have scored it! Dani Karavan might have done the layout! Giacometti could have sculpted under the lighting plot! Chillida should have done the floors and the walls, rendering them unforgettable!

The physical, the three-dimensional – both were already seen-to. It was the back-up crap that awaited firming.

Before anything legal was agreed on, the ultrastar was allowed to receive injections of the scenario as it appeared from the adaptors' efforts. There was a lot of ground to cover.

Packets of script from the team arrived daily, sometimes twice a day. The impact of the material caused an ecstatic absorption that Tuan Jim, in his supporting position, could well appreciate. It was at times a frightfully challenging onslaught of dramatic implication, and with its charting, the opportunities for creative interpretation began to stand out in high relief.

How the actor studied! He even resorted to having a special pair of reading glasses assembled, so that when the warmth of the skylight faded into later hours, he could still read by the electric blue of the lens-lit specs, and his mood of imaging and imagining was only enhanced.

All in the household knew it was a foregone conclusion he would soon set up a single-occupant cot in the gallery, where he would surely dwell in high monastic fashion.

For quite some time now, Butterbugs had been nurturing a scene at The Lazaretto that allowed for a community of creative minds to gather in a convenient environment of fooding and lodging, in order to explore artistic pursuits. There were more than enough bungalows, picturesque shacks, and even lean-tos set amongst the mellow and quiet landscape to inspire cultures as diversely-oriented as Rad, Avant-garde, Modernistic, Neoclassical, and all the way up to Virgilian Pastoral, as far as output was concerned.

Most of the occupants were young or fairly young persons, of significant talent, which was only natural. Not one of them would have identified themselves as members of any 'clique', or in the case of female artistes, a 'harem'. They were there because they wanted to be. They were there because it was a privilege. They were there for reasons of friendship and love, and liking, too. No funkadelics, sleaze or mush-brained substance abuse, either. Indeed, beverage alcohol flowed in Omar Khayamian rills, and a Mosaic and Sephoraic-appearing hip-oid couple or two did a bit of witchweed and noxious cultivation of the sweetest kind, but the maturity level was high, and the appreciation of this kaleidoscopic idyll ran deep. Creative work was a mandate no one wasted time in questioning.

A fair bit of creative activity here was sexual, based on the tried and true principles of mutual consent. Because that was what much of this groove-thang was about. Creating pleasure, not just product. Pigeonholes such as 'libertine' had no meaning here, and 'free love' lacked the scene's sophistication. The joy of sex was really all there was to it, and it didn't take Alex Comfort to point it out (which he did on one of his visits, much to everyone's playful amusement).

Their ultrastar was known affectionately by many names, some of them randy and naughty, like Big Hunque and Little Protector, Wirehaired Pointing Griffon, and even, most coyly, Priapus Maximus.

To be sure, Butterbugs was no Hef (though Hef was himself impressed with the setup), and this was no Playboy Mansion, though sensuality seeped from every pore of the place, and *someone* had to lead the way and set the tone, to spread it around, then let it soak in.

Speaking of Griffons, there were plenty of other beings around, of the non-primate variety. Several of that actual breed of dog were in residence; Marengo,

Magenta, Pupp, Hudson, and Hugo being the most noteworthy. The latter two starred in Butterbugs' 'Hugo, Dog Of Peace' (20th-Fox) series. They sniffed and cuzzled, tracked and whizzled, plopped and sang in operatic bass commentary, and gave screen-door yawns, dealing dignity to strangers and loyalty to regulars.

Aside from the pluppies, there were glamorous and wise cats and kittens, like Prunella, Julian, Gupta, Gopi, Mutz Muttlington, Col. George, Lurr, and Condell who lounged on pillars, lolled like fat worms in contented dirt, and yowled in the pure joy of cat politics. Plus, fuzzy ponies like Twinkletoes and McMasters, and fuzzcuddle ducklings, and on and on. It was indeed a Merrie Menagerie.

No one would ever have cause to use the term 'artists' colony' when mentioning The Lazaretto. Art was always involved, though. Numerous practitioners of note – or of significantly obscure status – came and went at their leisure. Emil Kosa was always welcome, Davy Hockney guested when he was in town. As did Mark Tansey, Jane Orleman, Mars MacDonald, Becky Parnins, Jim Woodring, Dennis Hopper, Arno Rink, Rick Altergott, Cindy Sherman, Steven Appleby, Tony Millionaire, James Yamasaki, Hans Rickheit, Lee-Lenna, Rowland Emett, Komar & Melamid, Shag, Kaz, Michael Kuppermann, and Dong Kingman. Manish Shaw did pencil portraits of everyone. Noguchi showed up to do some 'girl watching'. Calatrava looked in about once a month in order to get back to his earth-control, whence he sprang in all directions. While in-house, Lord Norman Foster designed the Bangui Air Terminals (all seven of them) – at Justy's request, making it the most important hub on the African continent. Up in the Il Padrone Bungalow, which sported a large studio space, with expandable tables built by Eliel Saarinen, Ms. Sherman did photo shoots that were really adding up, as documentary evidence, that this whole thing at The Lazaretto was actually… *working out*. Everybody was a friend, everybody was cool, and harmony was entirely possible and probable.

Industry types were not ignored, either. Romantic comedy stars hung out with key grips. Too many personalities to list. Even Old Atrocity maintained rights to a getaway love-shack in the remote Upper Levels tract. Man, did he throw some far-out parties, at which Laurie Anderson, Trumper the Big, Betty Box, Lindsey Lohan, Bill Burroughs, and Crispin Glover usually showed.

Things could get name-droppy at times, but all pretension was left outside the dryvine-covered entrance archway.

Scandal was virtually impossible. Hard feelings or rivalries were unheard of, and unthought of. No Peyton Places could take seed at The Lazaretto. No cult-worship (only body-worship), no mind-robbing, no sleaze-bagging, no violence ('cept scene rehearsals), no creephood lurkings. They just didn't happen. It was the Butterbugs Effect in play, and everyone knew it, and was glad of it.

However, because of recent developments concerning Butterbugs' career moves, some of the girls resident at the estate, such as Brydie and Chandrakins, Turtle, Joni, Xi Ci-Ci, Srivannanavanna, Magenta, Cheenah, Maggie, Taffy (oh, Taffy, oh, Taffy!), Moorah, and MacKenna, and particularly the 'Seven Muses':

Mitzi, Rahvundrah, Terpsichore, Cydalise, Uriyurr, Darcie, and Jody, plainly suffered from hurt feelings.

[Darcie – the same Darcie Flask that served as such a faithful wife when her husband Perry had his ordeal, had spent quite a bit of chaste and contemplative time at The Lazaretto, while Perry had famously served his time. Now she enjoyed making cameo appearances when she wished for an especially cheerful retreat. Her specialty was pleasantative poetry. She was always an inspiration to all.]

A group of them gathered in the torch-lit vestibule not far from the Corbu gallery.
'I don't even get to show him my new playsuit,' mourned Brydie.
'And I dedicated my latest flower painting to him, but he's said nothing to me all day!' added Turtle. Her bobbed bangs, always sprightly, seemed so sad tonight.
'Come on, girls,' said Chandrakins. 'Grow up, and grow up *now*. This isn't some bratty boarding school. This is The Big One. And I'm not necessarily referring to you-know-what, in this instance. Not necessarily.'

[Chandrakins Digelius was a former humble schoolteacher who, after orienting many of her students toward the wonder of Butterbugs, chanced to make her way to his door, seeking to confirm her beliefs. Her total sincerity and earnestness was undeniable. She was not disappointed, and indeed, she was invited to come and go as she pleased. To teach, perchance to earn. After an afternoon of observation of the general scene, she thought what he had was a harem, and for a moment all faith vanished. Then she discovered the forum aspect of the group gathered here, and with it, a dignity and sincerity which she herself embodied. Thereafter, she embraced Butterbugs' community with easy enthusiasm. Her judicious term of trial was typical among her peers.]

'Oh Chandrakins, you are so cute, but so am I! Is he going to be this way from now on, or what?' Brydie replied.
Immanâla Nōōmanossi, who was lodging in The Monsoon Shack in preparation for her sequence in Butterbugs' new picture, spoke with arresting authority.
'I tell you, he is in the middle of it! It is all high up and fantastical. We should not question what he does. He needs us.'
Her exotic Munzan accent faded as she continued: 'I feel we are on the verge of a great truth, though I cannot speak it.'
The young women murmured amongst themselves for a short time, then disbanded. They went their separate ways, to the dipping pools or to their chambers, sobered, but with new hope in their hearts. If there was one thing that the ambience of Butterbugs brought with it, it was harmony.

One by one, the Muses made their contributions to his welfare. They took their responsibilities very seriously. At seven in number, they were two Muses short of really thorough coverage, so they had to hustle more.

'You go first, Mitzi!' hissed Rahvundrah, with a big Andhra smile on her face.

Mitzi tried not to let a giggle escape, as she was thrilled and a bit nervous at the same time.

'Catch him as he goes up to The Folly, to light the Gloaming Tripod up on Albert Moore Terrace!'

'But he'll see me approach!' whispered Mitzi.

'Good! Although I *doubt* it. He takes the ritual with a lot of solemnity. He's focused on the lighting procedure. Perfect romantic moment, Mitz-Mitz!'

Encouraged, Mitzi knew Rahvundrah was right.

'I'll tell him about the pickle jugs I threw over in our Pot City Studio, this afternoon!'

'Sex pots! Don't just tell! *Show!*' snickered the beauty from Hyderabad (Deccan).

A leather-hard pickle jug in each graceful but farm-girl-firm hand, noble-boned Mitzi glided across The Oval's terracotta gravel with scarcely a crunch. She had the sort of statuesque figure that was perfect for potters, with wide, pear-ish hips that anchored solidly before a wheel, but with breasts delicate enough not to collide with any clay thrown off the hump, and a curly raven mane that framed an elegantly narrow face, highlighted by Akhenaten lips.

Indeed, she spied the ultrastar up on The Terrace, wearing his familiar early evening toga.

Proceeding toward him, she downshifted her hips with the kind of heroic saunter that snagged appreciators high and low, most of whom would never admit that a badass ass and front-loaded thighs could be the prime directive in getting wood prepped and hauled to its proper loading dock.

'I, Mitzi, your Muse of Ceramix, approach, honey!'

'Why Mitzi, my dear. I didn't – well, I wasn't aware... of your oncoming tack.'

'If I did not approach, I could not draw near.'

'True... Too true!'

'And if I could not draw near, I could not show you these, the fruits of my creative womb. We women are creators, but in any number of ways, different ways, even amongst ourselves. Mine is the forming of the primæval clay, though not as preliminary Creators were wont to do. I treat the beginning clay with more patience. Vessels and conversation pieces do I fashion.'

'And what, if conversation enters into it, is the subject of your dialogue?'

He was beginning to respond to her moisture-oriented presence – moisture combined with supple graspability, in keeping with the sculptural structure of her oncoming form.

'A word with you, pray...'

She drew both the pickle jugs into the region of his cheeks so that he was compelled to regard one or the other. Instinctively he opened his mouth, just in time for the right jug to come into contact with it. His lips sensing that the material was easily masticated, he opened his jaw and gently chomped down on the still-pliable clay. It gave, and indeed, resembled a bar of Amul chocolate, with added grit factors.

'Mmmm', he moaned. 'The very suppleness of your... creation!'

It was the easiest thing for her to then usher him through the bolt hole that connected with The Throwery, the massive pottery studio that took up the lion's share of the halls beneath The Terrace.

They descended and ended up in a happy slump near the pug mills. The bouquet of earthy clay filled both their open-ended sensibilities.

She came to lick his nostrils, prepping them for clean clayey input, in which cloth imbued with ball clay was duly shed, and because kiln-wash had made the tablets of firing furniture dry and without biology, it was a fitting place for Butterbugs and Muse to roll their molds, rotating, drawing ever closer, until squirting-cementing-bonding caused engagement as a result of inevitable close contact. Fireworks spun out of their union like a pulsating pinwheel of gunpowder and light.

'I remember you now,' whispered the ultrastar, his balls barely glowing blue from their frictional work. 'You are as the Earth, in which sex becomes *defined!* You are at the beginning; clarity is at the beginning... Or *under* the beginning. Now is clarity clear to me.'

They both laughed out loud.

'Regardless,' he added, 'I love you.'

Mitzi smiled in eyes-shut post-coital bliss. She had done her bit for him, and for herself and her fellow Muses.

He was still grounded, via earthiness, on Earth.

Rahvundrah spied him, walking thoughtfully down The Stroll, that long and much-beloved arcade of metal arches, designed by Halsey Ricardo. Butterbugs particularly liked its name, as it reminded him of his profession. It was the scene of some of his best soliloquy rehearsals. At 300 meters long, it was a perfect place for chatting or reading or reflection, whether sitting on a bench or perambulating to and fro. It was also the perfect place for a dusk tryst. Traditionally unlighted by any sort of lamp, its rear wall set into the hillside and its one open side looking toward the west, it was famous for extolling afterglow moods. Or, in the moonlight, allowing for mysterious and pleasurable night acts.

At this moment though, it offered neither, as the afterglow was faded, adding to the contemplative mood in which Butterbugs was obviously immersed.

She decided to be stately, rather than pixyish.

As Muse of Creative Technical Writing, Rahvundrah had to maintain an overt mien of propriety. Besides, as a Chundrah dynasty member, there was a requirement in setting up dignified understandings, from imparter all the way to receiver.

She found his gentlemanly bearing consistently thrilling. No one was more honorable towards her. He understood all the myriad threads of her enculturation, and always let her lead. This trust was mutual, and led to his edification as far as her specialty was concerned. She was scholarly but not academic. Indeed, her current project here at The Lazaretto was to present a complete and re-invented documentation of all the technical aspects of the cinema, from its embryonic chemistry all the way to the color temperatures generated by the FlexLight system of optics. Early on, she had particularly endeared herself to the ultrastar by presenting him with a bound (and autographed) copy of her definitive examination of Ultra-Panavision 70, and the whole film community was abuzz over her forthcoming 'How The Industry Awoke From Its Cumulative Maya: The Complete and Utter Explanation of the BKV™ (B.K. Vendacardamom) Method of Motion Picture Film Stock Cosmology, Epistemology, Creation, Production, and Marketing'.

Now, on this less than perfect evening, he spied her several arches down, and as a courtesy, was the first to fold his hands into a namaste greeting.

She followed suit, and approached him. She never addressed him as anything other than 'Butterbugs'. That is, she did not preface or append his name with 'Shree' or 'Lord' or 'Babu' or 'Bahadur' or any other multi-cultural enhancement from her heritage's orientation. But tonight she didn't formally address him at all, which meant the coast was clear for probable intimacy, based on intellectual equality.

She being a child of Bharat, there was no question as to her Kama-sutric depth of knowledge. She was capable of generating her own unique kind of intimacy, as a link between intellectual, spiritual and temporal conjoinings.

'Technicalities,' she had always argued, 'also apply to the production of love, be it high art or entertaining kitsch!'

She repeated that statement now, in the hush of the hurrying dark.

'I like that inference,' said Butterbugs, under the arch they now shared. His heart fluttered.

He lay down in the Śavāsana position, as if to isolate himself yogically, in order to ponder this matter.

But this was not a time for purposeful isolation, she thought. Moreover, it was an opportunity to experience joint realization.

'Of what?' Butterbugs asked, her yogic powers of non-verbal broadcasting enabling him to pick up on her vibes.

'The layering of our imprints,' she replied out loud, then asked him to disrobe and lie on his stomach.

Jasmine oil was spread on her hands, and she proceeded to apply it spreadingly to his back in order to establish a fluid medium between their actual and individual physicalities. The massage was crude on the bodily level, but lofty on the spiritual. Beams of realization passed between them, informing Butterbugs as to the constant interplay of universe upon, and with, universe, a reality easily acknowledged and infinitely benevolent.

Their mutual orgasms, which followed after an indeterminate timespan-cum-spacespan, were of the most illuminating kind, as per his incandescent creativity and her explanatory presentation.

They both lay on the floor of the airy gallery, in opposite directions yet next to each other, he still on his verso and she on her recto. Then his hand and her hand found each other, linked, and by that connection was their intimacy on this occasion consummated and concluded.

'From now on, Rahvundrah, I shall know the power of your translation: of mere thought into the mechanics of perceived sensual joy and Tantric climax.'

'As from the thoughts, born in your mind, when you are taking on a role in front of the cameras, and their nuts-and-bolts transition, up onto the motion picture screen, thence into the minds of your audience,' she added.

'I am thus bolstered for the task ahead. (If indeed I am able to execute it.)'

'You are indeed able,' she murmured. 'I have felt so, just now.'

The peace they had created together was more beautiful than the evening shadows.

'He is content in this,' she thought, though she did not let him know it. No need, as their melding had occurred on a higher plane, which was, at this moment, the thing most needful.

Terpsichore! As chance would have it, her name and most of her persuasion lined up with her Classical forebear, except that this Terpsichore was Muse of the Ritual Burlesque Dance. At the Rivoli in Seattle did she learn her trade, and trade it she did. Regularly did she dare all onlookers to start out with doubting her art. Then she would extemporize the Dance's more esoteric opportunities for laying a story out via gesture, without wasting too much time and effort in unnecessary embellishment, except to convey her message.

Her walk carried with it the recollection of a drum set invariably beating out the renowned David Rose anthem, a cliché always regenerated by her re-inventive talents. Straw-blonde, organically-buxom, and high heel-wearing and strutting, despite the most arduous of conditions, wherever they might pop up. A Dutch confection complete, but without the Volendam hat and the titty windmills made immortal in Merv LeRoy's 'Gypsy' (WB, 1962). This muse was professional all the way, but simultaneously, a distributor of pure love.

She of course treasured the gotta-have gimmicks of the old burlie shows, and the hurly secrets and knacks of the Hovick school, but Terpsichore's particular tricks 'n' acts really got into one's soul. With guys' adoration and gals' respect, she'd revitalized the whole culture she practiced, and every Friday week head-lined two shows at the Wiltern, attended by such biggies as Governor Moore, QE2, a few Habsburgs, Crown Prince Naruhito, and Chief Lone Biceps of the Wolf and Bear Cub First Nation.

There was a little theatre at The Lazaretto, naturally, called the Pix. It was available mostly for picture show use, but there was a fully equipped stage, with basement dressing rooms down a genuine spiral staircase. It was a rattly old place, with grapelights in the wall sconces, wandering tracery tacked onto the walls that passed as 'respectable' décor, and a tawdry orchestra pit. Butterbugs was fond of it though, and didn't engage in any restorations, as it blended well with the informal, sleepy summeryness of the Further Acreages. The one-line marquee had the ultrastar's favorite white letters on black background, though not very well lighted. When there was a Terpsichore show on, just her name was up there, nothing else. Across the square from it, stood a feeble attempt at a civil fixture: one of those early digital readout clocks, this one surplused from Carlos Motors, a last-stop-before-the-junkyard car lot in east LA. Most of the bulbs were burned out, so no one ever knew what the real time 'n' temp were, and after a while, only a few remaining lights flashed at all.

Terpsichore loved doing shows there, even though five or six souls might show up. Never mind that they might be Sonny Projector or John Huston or Debbie Watson or Spike Lee or John Singleton – (directors tended to take in the shows for a little nostalgic relaxation) – or even Ruth Warrick or Queen Latifah on a Ladies' Night... If nothing else, her Pix shows allowed for handy practice or just honing her Hovicks, or even master classes and workshop programs. It was a sweet set-up, and all due to the Butterbugs Effect. Spawned, in this particular territory, by Butterbugs himself.

At any rate, this strippin' Muse had a mission. Right now she was in search of the man himself. She'd set out to nurture his apparent lack of simple 'good times' diversions. How else could the great impending decisions be negotiated? How else could the stress of distractions give way to relief at last? Plus, if a striptease couldn't get his attention, only a point blank-fired bullet could. There were times when she was compelled to tuck a derringer into her garter, just in case.

Armed with only those smooth implements attached to her svelte but hourglass figure, she stalked the ultrastar all throughout the estate and finally nailed him as he sauntered down a leafy lane. He was kitted out in boring JC Penney slacks and bland Sears sweatshirt, as well as featureless tennashoes purchased at Peoples'.

'Hey there, Mr. Average, Borax, and Deprived Citizen!' she called out from an ornamental garden aisle, 'You look like you could use some revision! Might I interest you in an interlude, of the ecdysiastical kind?'

He perked, and as a result, became less boring.

'Oh, Miss! I couldn't possibly think that you'd find the time to devote to me, a mere shuffler-along in these parts...'

Terpsichore was an authority on what she knew. It translated to her management skills, and for that, Butterbugs was grateful. He'd been privately yearning for some sort of bawdy entertainment in these mannered grounds for some time now.

'Come. With. *Me...!*'

'I follow! Lead on, stately babe!'

She was indeed impressive. There was mystery garb keeping her barely modest, but the lines and the curves and the folds and the features were more than hinted at. There was a terrific showgirl ambience about this marauder that he, in this sequence of purposeful but pressured isolation, found absolutely irresistible.

Now, he didn't know Terpsichore well, but he knew her to be a formidable institution, and therefore, he could well appreciate her demand in the entertainment world at large. Yet here she was, all to himself, with no denying her power was worth following. His muses were impeccably benevolent. But that didn't mean they were priggish. He emitted a few short pants in watching how she moved along in the Bois de Boulogne-ish gravel, in high heels, no less. That was enough to bring him about. That was it.

They came together up in the Oceanides Grotto, with its carnival of Pitti Palatial grotesques. One such, everyone's favorite, was a flabby nincompoop in sandstone. There was usually just a dribble from his pee-pee, but thanks to the stripper's friskiness, today it flowed like spray from a wasp-killer can. Poseidon, Triton and Nereid masks spewed greenwater from squidmouths, and high-foreheaded dolphins frolicked in the carved travertine foam, creating an ambience so convincing that visitors always swore they'd suddenly been transported into one of the more out of the way nooks at Caserta (rather than Florence), which undoubtedly served as this construction's inspiration.

'Terpsich, I get the feeling, I get it strong and clear, that a bit of a show might be about to unfold.'

'You could be right, Borax-one! But pay heed. You need to own up to your responsibilities. What better than sex-flashy female-flesh to bring you back to your responsible self? Don't you want someone to show some *interest* in you? A pretty girl, perhaps? Someone to make you an upstanding citizen again?'

'Mmm' was all he could say.

Switching on the weatherproof Voxes of the Amphithiertre sound system, she had no idea what was on the playlist. She could, however, work with most anything. There was a striptease to be found even in white noise.

'Sieg Howdy!' by Jello Biafra and The Melvins was just finishing up, cross-fading (by resident DJ, Pepp Credible) into Chunky Urine's stone-gashing 'Plie Plant Gondombo'. Surprisingly, the music came forth in such clean-limbed sound patterns that it complemented Terpsichore's oncoming routine. She found herself inventing as she went.

In a hard-pounding garden party then, did this very professional stripperkins make her mark on the landlord. Unlike the usual Pix show, today boobies were totally bared, and without pasties, too. Plus, wonder of wonders, the only mount of Venus in the Grotto, fresh and friendly, was yielded unto the viewer – just this once, and all.

The campanile clock chimed 11:00.

'How, then, do you like my truth?'

She proceeded to scale her fetlock gloves back on, and the pearl necklace, and the bustier and the garter belt (panties first!)…

'Wellllll... How can I, you know, deny it?'

'I'm not asking for philosophical certitude, Butterbugs. Was I hot or not?'

'You were – oh yes, you were – hot. Very... very hot.'

'Which technique or detail did you like the best?'

'Well... I liked it when you'd done all the obvious stuff, and then, when you'd blown your cover, you still had your pearls on, and you sort of shifted your hips, suddenly but smoothly, as if to say, 'Oh, well...''

'Funny fellow! You're so prosaic.'

'I am a *simple* fellow.'

'Just the way you should be!'

'And your pronouncement?'

'Butterbugs, you know I'm just a stripper with a heart of gold. I don't make pronouncements.'

'But have you... something to... say... ?'

'I've already said it, sport. I showed you my body. It's what I have. I have a great figure. I share it. I can only say, if one has great talent, one should share it.'

'I will soon have to tell them of my intent, then. About the looming picture.'

'I think so.'

And it came to pass that she tucked him up nice and comfy in his beddy-boo. No music now, just pillow time after a stripper's dignified union with her audience of one. It wasn't that a Muse's job was to *seduce* her victim, then prove her point via sex. Everyone here was too smart for that racket. It's just that the sex part was a nice gooey frosting on the cake of substance they had sought and found. What better than to decorate it with love? Loving sex worked better than anything to make mortals mild, and to introduce peace as the first choice for those who wished to achieve something in this mixed-message life. With so much unhappiness in the world, nirvana needs were acute. The spreading had to start somewhere.

The ultrastar, simple fellow that he was, then slept. She could yet get a bit of work in, tonight.

Up at Old Atrocity's, they were probably already falling-down drunk. Well, maybe not quite this early. She could certainly do a late show and expect a few coppers in her g-string. Then wrap things up with a cozy cuppa sufferin' sassafras tea, before curling her lusciousness up in her old fashioned brass bed, contentedly solo.

As Muse of Montage in the Cinema, Cydalise knew how to capture visuals, assign appropriate audios, and condense a scene down to essentials, often dispensing with dialogue altogether, preferring music to carry the other half of the experience.

This eve she wielded a windup Eyemo of WWII vintage – in fact it had been at Midway, cranked by Pappy Ford himself – and she caught some expository shots of Butterbugs from all angles, before concentrating on the art aspects.

She was spying on him, for tonight he was in a traveler-of-the-past mood, all decked out like a tropical timmy: wrinkled white linen suit and white shoes, poor-ly-done thin tie for contrast, walking stick and Panama hat. He was little unsteady, not because of oncoming yellow fever, but because he had overdressed a bit on this hot end-of-day, so he paused and daubed his forehead.

Nice effects in play, and she was all over the place as far as angles were con-cerned, stealthy, fast, and composed.

'You look like von Eschenbach on Prickly Pear Island, or something.'

Butterbugs was hardly taken aback. Cydalise was noted for getting 'good shots' around The Lazaretto.

His reply was full of propriety. 'Not in Venice, then?'

'Nah! No boys on the beach here! I already checked.'

He chuckled.

'Oh, Cyd, I overplayed tonight's costume.'

'Yes, well, it has a very nice feel. You're actually *glowing* against the dark shrubbery behind.'

'Every one of your waking hours is a film, no?'

'And my dreaming ones, too, cherie.'

'Have you a pint of refreshment to ease some of this tottering white man's burden?'

'Oh, sir, you have come in time. I was just preparing a pitcher of cool rum crunch.'

Fanning himself with his drippy Panama, Butterbugs approached with sweaty glee.

'Rum crunch at Cyd's Shack, run crunch at Cyd's!!'

'Hold it. Let me get that in medium shot. Do the fanning again. Action!'

He cheerfully redid the scene.

'Now, come into my Ramshackle. I'm calling it that now, instead of just The Shack.'

'I like it better, too. And this is one of my favorite places in The Lazaretto.'

Indeed, it was a fabulous pad. Not that the greater estate wasn't peppered with oddities of all kinds, none of which were pretentious in the least. Just like the squire who oversaw it all. And what he oversaw was no theme park, but an organ-ism of much curiosity and naturalness.

Ramshackle was a real old-time dwelling, with half-collapsed verandahs pop-ulated by weathered couches and teapoys, and a getaway interior that was funky without being mean. Cydalise had invaded everywhere, with her Moviola editing equipment and her reels and her film clips, which only added to the romance of these walls. They could have been in Sumatra or Suriname.

She took his damp hand and led him into her bedroom, which was a tad stuffy, so she switched on the electric punkah overhead.

'Before rum crunch, lie down on the bed. Fully clothed. Get all uncomfortable. Disarrayed. Leave the hat out. Good, your hair's all greasy. Sprawl. Let's try some low light shots. Effects…'

'Ready when you are, C…'

'Damn, out of film!'

She went over to a work desk and reloaded. He found her entrancing.

From old Cayenne in the French Guiana had she come, and even if no one knew it, her descent from the advantageous amalgamating of Liberian-freed slaves with members of the Nenka tribe, a Maroon Creole people from down along the Lawa in Papaïchton canton, made for the kind of exoticism everyone plumped for. Butterbugs himself, at that very location, had invited her to muse at The Lazaretto on the strength of her three-minute super-8mm gizmo film, 'Pop-Off!' (CydShow International). She'd run it for him between takes of his appearance in 'Gomez of the Guianas' (Ziggurat), David Lean's superb filmization of the classic 1850s saga.

To all who were lucky enough to come in contact with her, her sensibilities conveyed confidence and competence. She was heavenly to work with. She knew your questions before you had wit to ask, and before that, their answers. Cerebral, but wired to the ground. Physicality came with her. Similarly, her body brought along a bouquet of smoky ardor, a mien that was both striking and soft, a fantastic balloon of hair that floated in perfect balance about her dreamy face. And if those plump lips loved nothing more than to kiss, well, just everywhere, she had, not at all surprisingly, a worshipful effect on Butterbugs.

How important it was to have a Muse with specialties within the range of cinematic craftspersonship! He could always approach Cydalise, cuddle next to her soft belly, and relax while she made insightful small talk about the influence of Vorkapich on newsreels, or the success of the transition sequence she'd just finished for 'Savitri', or how she planned to do the dissolves in whatever picture it was that Butterbugs was now churning over, because she'd just signed up to do its montages this very morn. And thanks to Butterbugs, she'd worked with practically every editor of merit in the Industry to date.

She aimed the Eyemo at the ultrastar as he rolled on her mattress in his smudged trop suit, below the punkah's strobing whisperbreeze, and the frames chuttered away. Then she went into lithe-mode, covering him from all angles, sometimes just pinching the shutter a tad, to make fleeting images to serve as underlay ghostshots, for interweaving during the editing process.

When the space got a little tight between a hanging lattice and the wall, she peeled off her jeans and t-shirt so that the perspiration from her skin made a nice lubrication, and slipped into the confined space and got some great shots.

'Your nips are protruding through the lattice holes, Cyd.'

'Perfect. Adds to the way you're looking toward me, actor.'

The camera sounded like a sewing machine.

'Now look lower.'

'How do I get there?'

'Follow the line of hairs. The ones you love.'

'Oh! Those! From your roll, down to your Aphrodite.'

'That's right. Nice and slow now.'

'You are fucking gorgeous, girl.'

'They'll be able to read your lips on the screen.'

'Let them think I am a monomaniac, with Onanist tendencies!'

'They'll be able to read that, too.'

'My fantasy. My self-absorbed, narcissist, fucking fantasy.'

'Which goes nowhere.'

'Which goes nowhere – only nowhere…'

'To me, it's *somewhere*, cuz I got it on film.'

'Cyd, you should direct.'

'Think so, huh? Dressed like this?'

'Oh, yeah…!'

'Start… I don't know, *writhing* or something…'

Some inner talent allowed her to practically turn into aspic at moments like these. She was able to squilge down and flow out of the rat chase below the lattice and ooze onto the mattress, winding and filming at the same time. She was not a dancer but she had the special powers that only a Pilobolus troupe member could achieve, even in silhouette. This had nothing to do with the fact that she was a bit thick in places.

For once Butterbugs wished he'd be the one with camera, if only to capture her motions so that people would not always think he was straining the truth a little when he related her marvels to others.

She had emerged feet first, so that her heels had pressed into his already ring-around collar, and further smudging added to his suffering sweatbox role.

'Cyd, hand me the Eyemo and do that squiggle again. Can't I secure it on film this time?'

'No way. I'm on a roll. And this is B-roll. I need it. Keep thrashing. I like the dirt on your collar. My contribution.'

He complied. There wasn't much suffering on his part, though. By now she was a virtual bedmate, and her musky underarms and monkfish muff whetted his appetite, rum crunch or no rum crunch.

She was indeed shooting silent, so he talked freely, almost over-articulating in describing her charms, for all those lip-readers out there.

'Cyd, how do you do that stuff, that jelly-o-y stuff with your beautiful bod?'

'That's a good word for it, star-kid. But I can't tell you. It's tribal. It's secret. Comes in handy in the jungle.'

'The way you shape yourself! It's beyond poetry.'

'I like to think it influences my work.'

'You make me hard. This is a very, very sexy sequence. You're doing it to me. You're showing off, because you *can!*'

'Yeah, baby. Boy, do I love to show off for you!'

'May I have a rum crunch now? You've drained my tear ducts. I can't even weep for joy at your stunning self no more.'

'Not yet. Thirst on, baby. Keep gawping at me.'

She did some strategic wiggles to make this writhing sahib, marooned up-country, even more antagonized.

'If only we colonial hacks could be as you are! If only we had the guts to go native! But then we would be ostracized and shut out of our own kampongs, and you, on the noble savage side, would not accept us either, even though we expressed a sincere interest!'

'I'll let you aspire, but I'll never let you in! Keep doing that jerking-off thing. It implies frustration. Good touch.'

'Cyd, will you be my director?'

'Hold that expression.'

'Really, Cyd, will you make the leap to features? I'll spot you.'

'I have no desire, elf. I like what I'm doing. Directing is too fussy.'

'What are you doing now, then?'

'I'm making love to you, sweat-mop! Can't you tell, even now?'

She morphed into squatting position so that Butterbugs could see her fine classic rawness, sculptural and Vigeland-like.

'Oh, I know there's love coming through that lens, but I'd like some lip time, not just lip service.'

'My lips really are quite spectacular, aren't they?'

Butterbugs got immediately aroused whenever she complimented herself like that, always with his sloppy goading.

She decided to give in, saying, 'Damn! Out of film!' even when she had 55 feet left. The Eyemo was tossed to the side.

'Come here, you soggy sinner!'

She cozened up to him, the closeness of her sensuous sinewy-ness made him run out of perspiration, but not drool. She wiped his mouthful of it with her fingers then licked them, then stroked her clit, then gave them to him in his mouth. He was ready to be made comfortable now.

He lay there like a dubious baby as she stripped him and daubed his discharges, then sashayed over to the barie-poo and made them both cracking good rum crunches, Cayenne style, with three dashes of Dave's Insanity Sauce as relish.

They simmered. Then they got all mutually horny and did some really A-class lovemaking, heated, but in superb taste. Cydalise was a moaner, but Ramshackle was secluded enough for any hearer on the outside (and there were in fact, none) to mistake her orgasmic approach with, say, a Latvian cuckoo who happened to show up on this cooling eve.

They puffed on Cubans for a time, and the punkah kept them aired.

'You performed well in the impromptu today, Butterbugs.'

'Thanks rum-love. But yours was a silent. I am faced with a talkie. I'm not at all sure about the weighty drape of verbal augustness that will surely result from the rich text format of the lofty script before me.'

She planted her lips on his forehead for a time.

'Oh, Butterbugs, I have tasted your anxiety with my incredible tongue. As a concept, it tastes bitter. But you, as a filter, taste so sweet. How are you allowing these influences to infiltrate your waters? Why is it that you are even thinking such things? I would never have thought that you, who brought me to this place after so minimal a proving, should himself be brought low by doubt and distress!'

'I know, but I'm not as… agile, somehow.'

'You must be everywhere, Butterbugs. Do all things. Some people cannot, but you were made for it. How do you think you became an ultrastar?'

'That's what others call me.'

'That's what *all* others, not just *some* others, call you. Can *all* others be wrong?'

'What you propose is not unreasonable.'

'Of course it isn't. Think of my film montages, and how they will come together. I will craft something evanescent from the footage I took of you this night. It will be as a chameleon fish in a fluorescent sea, with the rays of the sun playing in the shallow blue, causing limits to be lifted and physics to be set free.'

'Cydalise, you are as the æther itself! Subtle, but in our midst. Never was transparency so bold!'

Her big lips met his, and their curative power was upon them.

Cydalise soon nodded and fell asleep in his arms, just after he fell asleep in hers. That was all she wanted to hear.

Uriyurr took Butterbugs by the hand and gently led him to the great hangar doors of her studio. Similar to Jess Lasky's 'Squaw Man' barn, this building had once stood on the old Dee Dub Griffith lot and had been imported here, stick by stick, when it was slated for razing. In it Richard Barthelmess had done his 'Broken Blossoms' (UA, 1919) scenes with Lillian Gish.

Uriyurr got to use the enormous Billy Bitzer Room because, as Muse of Brigade Painting, she usually needed the space for her Cinerama screen-sized works.

The two were close and potentially cuddlesome when she loosened the hasp and let go the perfectly balanced mechanism, which, as it opened, revealed a Jan Styka-sized mural. It was basically an allegorical scene, stretched out amidst a harsh landscape, with storm approaching. In a vaguely historic but steadfastly indeterminate setting, a group of characters were sited on heights, moodily key-lit in the manner of camera-maestro Bill Mellor, so that each figure attained a place of significance, posed amongst the tussocks in a severe environment, concerning some forgotten victory somewhere. The technique was of course superb, and the finished product worthy of the Versailles Battle Gallery, or somewhere similar.

As if three projectors were simultaneously contributing their 35mm territory to the collective mural, and the process was overwhelmingly eclipsed by the content, the piece indeed spoke for itself. There was a figure resembling Butterbugs, seemingly in command, whether before the ensuing decisive battle, or after its fortunes, that commanded the attention of any viewer. Certainly that was because of the sophisticated lighting plot that Uriyurr had skillfully fashioned (she was not for nothing a Muse), and within it, a focal point of éminence ingénieux had been created: the commanding figure of the painting, in whatever historical context it was, tended to dominate the scene. Not only because it was key-lit, but because it was nude.

Not charming in deepest summer was this scene. Indeed, uncertain and unsettled weather filled out the painting's ecology. A nude figure in such a context must by needs be placed there for symbolic reasons, either as an exposure to character, or an exposure to a role within a larger scene. In any event, a classically embellished nude garners attention, and the question is: why?

They both regarded the expansive painterly production in proper patron-cum-artist style. She, as artist, sure that what she'd done was right, if not pretty damn good. He, as patron, no matter how modest his mien, had to adjust to a particular artist's vision, and awaited explanation for aspects that – required explanation. Both were up to the task. And the task was, what they were doing here was worthy of reactive comment!

'Though I am usually the leader of a brigade, I did this one all by myself, Butterbugs, in the style of David. Do you fancy it?'

'Oh, Uriyurr! You know I do!'

She may have exhorted the name of Napoleon's best *pictor*, but, for heaven's sake, the style was entirely hers: lush, well-rounded, and passionate. Like architecture created at its most artistically personal, such as the Itmad-ud-Daulah in Agra, the Peacock House in Kensington, or the Stockholm Stadthuset, her paintings were total turn-ons, and just as three-dimensional in their impact.

After an almost cursory time-capsule period in which an artist could potentially revel in such praise, she drew closer to him and in a slow-pitch loop, swung her hand around until it cupped his crotch.

'Do you fancy *me?*'

'Oh, Uriyurr! You know I do!'

Actually he wasn't sure, because of his visceral distractions, the urgency of horniness had not visited him this day. So far.

She was certainly patient, and did not take anything personally.

With her other hand she gestured to the left of center, spot-lit figure of the ultrastar up there on the canvas, not in xenon-projected light, but in permanent pigments still drying under Damar protection.

'You see where you are in the scene, my lord and lover? Noble, I know. But there are a few things I don't quite like about it. Because this is a surprise painting, I only was able to paint you from (vivid!) memory. Would you now care to spare an hour or so, to pose in person, so that in my depiction, I might be anatomically correct in every sense of the word? If you don't wish to do it for me personally, do it for the public, because in the ages ahead, after the motion picture technology passes from the Earth, the people will still see you in ageless tableau here, and know, such was this ultrastar, this *man!'*

She wasn't serious about his motion pictures being so temporal, but she knew he always got a kick out of her attention-getting methods, not the least of which were her pulsating hands right now, one intimately-placed, the other expansively-placed.

Not subject to the potentially flattering reaction to seeing his nudeness up there (and thinking the likeness was finished enough for even the artist's satisfaction), he willingly and wordlessly acquiesced to her desires. She tugged the French farmer blouse he wore over his head and quickly rendered his culottes to the floor.

'My,' she said before she kissed his now imposing erection, 'That's just the revision I want to make!'

'You mean I'm no longer going to have the Louvre statue look?'

'Uh-uhh. Mmrph – er – nope. I want correctness. Boldness. No need for timidity.'

'Timidity adieu, I agree, but is it hubris you want?'

'I don't know what that is, l'amore, but I'll take your word for it. All I want is to show your dick like it is. Like it is at this moment. I am the artist! I have a license, you know!'

'Oh, Uriyurr, your Mediterranean passion almost borders on bawdiness!'

'In Naples we have a saying, baby: 'Gimme a light!' That's what the little kids crow to anybody, in order to get their cig lit. It also means, 'Wow me, huh?''

'Does that translation take in the Neapolitan dialect?'

'Hey, 'dammi una luce, si' means what it means: I'm paying you a rather nice compliment from down here on my knees.'

'You mean I'm wowing you?'

Cock-teasing with purpose, she backed off and simply said, 'Now hold that pose, dear.'

Shucking away her own artsy artist's model's robe, and clad only in Greek-style sandals laced up to her knees, her jaybird curves advanced toward the scaffold, so that she could arrive in front of the figure that needed repainting. Hair all the way up, so that it would stay away from the paint, except for two super-strands that flanked her soft face, so that she puckered her lips and blew 'em to the side when they tickled, her head looked proportionately small for her butt, but when her cheeks creased with normal propulsion, there was no other fitting description than to refer to her as a moving painting. Right now, the movies as medium seemed wholly archaic in light of this vision of naturalism, which he wished could only be captured on canvas.

She climbed up with effortless muscularity. She knew the way she moved made him – excited. Her own bod might have been brand-named Rubenesque, although it wasn't quite that generous. Really, it was more Bourguereau-like, while from some angles it even had a few Kustodiev qualities. Butterbugs had to conclude though, that right now, seeing her up there on the scaffold, holding that palette, with the dappled light coming in through the clerestory, she was nothing less than a lovely creation by Renoir.

She was doing all this for him. The least he could do was to give her what she wanted.

So he did.

Butterbugs needed more contemplation time. The script was jousting with him. Could he master its language? Would he be able to successfully memorize some of the pages-long speeches that he knew any director would want to tackle in one sustained take?

He thought, in order to maintain solitude so as to tussle mentally with these and other knotty problems, he would repair to the popular Fountain of the Dawn, which he knew would be deserted, as eventide was coming on.

But it wasn't. He nearly turned about and sought the Sylvan Hermitage, which was further out, but the vision in front of him was so beauteous that he simply had to stand there and luxuriate in it. He may have been a major actor who belonged to the world, but he was not averse to *consuming* a moment of æsthetic enjoyment instead of always *providing* it.

There was Darcie, pretty as a nymph, and dressed in the same Attic manner, as was her wont when on these grounds, reading an Insel Verlag book of verse. Her hair, usually up or woven in the public modes of a non-Classical world outside, here, in a Classical world achieved, cascaded down with full private glory, in a score of homemade-honey shades, a framework that kept her bare shoulders and pert breasts modestly presented.

As Guest Muse of Pleasantative Poesy, Darcie Flask was the one to turn to when appreciations of the outside world's sincerity were needed, especially in the light of that same world's nastiness.

How pleased he was then, to encounter her in this genteel manner.

They were deep friends. There was never, ever, any fooling around between them, though they freely touched and cuddled each other, in the Euro style of familiarity. Therein was their security with each other well-based.

Mmm, but was she yummy. Many were the times Butterbugs declared, to Perry directly, how lovely his wife was. And Perry, ever generous and sincere, always beamed with mega-pride. In the great tradition of trusting friends in other cultures who have similar assets, Perry graciously offered to open the doors of intimacy with his wife without reservation – not as a three-way, but as an exclusive encounter, pending her own approval, of course. Naturally, the ultrastar declined, but with compliments.

The three of them knew all these aspects, and celebrated their three-sided admiration in (nearly) all its combinations. Thus was their relationship unencumbered by tiresome jealousies or rancor.

Therefore, because it was hot out, Butterbugs shed his undistinguished garments down to his boxers, and invited Darcie to do the same.

'Here at The Lazaretto, we're into comfort,' he chirped. All this Muse-inspiration was making him downright bouncy. Besides, the light spray from the fountain, always infused with rose petals, lent a relaxing lilt to the hour.

Without missing a beat, she crossed her arms and raised the chaste nymphet frock over her head and stood there, still covered only with a black and tight tank top (with spaghetti straps!), and her pair of Victorian sharp-toed boots, which, to be blunt, defied any weather, because her feet ran cool.

(As anyone who acts in pictures knows, attention to costuming details becomes as an ongoing hobby; how will it look on the screen?; will it fit the character's personality?; does it make me look 'hot'?; etc.)

He drew close to her and they touched each other. Not near any naughty bits, but in regions of potential foreplay: her hands on his broad shoulders, his round her tiny middle.

There was much that could be said and done, but Darcie, looking into his eyes at these close quarters, and he into her powder blues, simply said:

'May I share, Butterbugs, a tiny example of one of my Modern Morality Melodramas?'

'Why of course, sweet Darcie!'

He could practically join his hands around her dance-snug-clad waist, everything was so firm and sleek. Then he let go and softly pushed her protruding belly button, as if to roll tape.

'But wait a minute, Darse, I thought all you did was *pleasantative* poesy?'

She smiled warmly and wagged her index finger fake-chidingly.

'It's a broader field than most people think, saxy dreamer. Pay heed now, and let's have some fun.'

Butterbugs just about busted his boxers with good feeling. In those first dark days of Perry's incarceration, with the kids at their grandsire's, Darcie had confided in him:

'Butterbugs,' she had said, 'I don't know if I want to go on living.'

And for the second Flask time, Butterbugs had brought one he loved back from the edge.

'I went to the abyss and looked in,' she'd told him upon her rebound. 'And I knew, because you showed me, that any abyss is really unnecessary, because there is no need for anything that adds up to nothing.'

A tear welled up in his eye as he thought of that time, but its characteristics turned from poignancy to zowie-grade, as this babe in front of him was as fine an enhancement to the scenery of The Lazaretto as had ever been witnessed.

She turned about and got her peachy buns up on top of a Corinthian capital, so placed as to be reminiscent of a ruined Theseum, and there she stood in booted glory, arms akimbo, so as to begin her recitation.

'And now,

'**P**rimrose M'Cullum'
   by – me!

Primrose M'Cullum,
Simmered as in stew,
Left the place of her nativity
And joined a strange crew.
She jostled and jollied
Her way half-roun' the earth,
And costled and collied
Into a marriage at Perth.
In wist Oz did she learn
That impossible 'Strine,
Quipped all and every
Quaffer of both Foster's and wine,
Then bandied about
Beyond her borders with him
Into the realms of the range
Of those who practice ghastly vim.
She'd fallen and she'd fared
As sailors do not,
In and out of bays both round and squared,
No pay, no mission,
Just a drifting gal,
No substantial commission.
On up Malay's dangling leg
She'd slept her way up it and down,
Ending up in Port Swettenham's bed.
'So if Primrose be at the bottom,' she thought,
'And this be the state of the wit,
To reconnoiter, to think it over, I ought
To really come clean on this bit,
And might as well make it mine.
If this is all there is – then this be *it*,
The will in the matter be *thine!*"

Not knowing the rubato-challenged ditty was concluded, Butterbugs remained in fully absorbed and appreciating mode, arms fully crossed, mouth slightly opened and slightly smiled, rather like his dog regarded him when in hopeful expectation, tongue not yet wagging.

She spread out her hands in vaude climax and then cocked her crotch so that her puffball was a few centimeters closer to him, as if to imply, 'That's all, folks! Really!'

'That's all?'

'That's it. Thank you, thank you, my attentive, but really quite dull, audience.'

She hopped down and draped the light nymphet dress elegantly round her slim hips, then sat on the Corinthian stage and waited to see if he would approach.

He did, eventually. Privately, he thought Darcie capable of more than this leaky trickle. Nevertheless, he came up to her, smiled, and kissed her hand.

'You're pissed, aren't you?' She was wildly attractive when she was somewhat imperious.

'No, dear. Not... pissed. Maybe...Just a little. I don't know, *let down*. Or something.'

'You were expecting Yemily Dickinson, or someone?'

He merely chuckled.

She encircled him with her boots as he stood there, and thus clamped, he paid her his undivided attention.

'Yeah...?' was all he could think of.

'I want to talk to you about *choice*, Butterbugs.'

She grew serious.

'Ur, hokay.'

'Choice of pathway. Right now, I see unavoidable disaster for you.'

He hooted out a brief stream-shriek of amazed laughter.

'No, really,' she continued.

'Really?'

'Undoubtedly. That is, if you persist in the course you are following.'

'I thought we had achieved a lot here at The Lazaretto.'

'I'm not talking about that. I'm saying that equivocation will be your downfall.'

It was the first time Butterbugs ever thought of himself as being in any sort of position that could possibly involve downward action. In his perception of things, he'd *already* been downfallen. A long time ago. That was where he'd sprung from.

Like Mervyn LeRoy always said, when accused of leading a charmed life, 'My family and I lost everything in the '06 San Fran earthquake. Everything since then has been gravy!'

But the ultrastar supposed that if one springs up from the depths, a certain elevation-change meant one could spring right back down again. Or fall.

'So Darcie, you think I'm in a tenuous spot?'

'Not at all. But your agonizing over this role has left you vulnerable.'

'Yes! To you Muses!'

'You got me there, Butterbugs.'

'So now...'

'If you can avoid the equivocation pickle, then you will be a man, my son!'

She loosened her grip, hopped down and stood in front of him, then kissed him tenderly.

They walked in quiet promenade and rounded a bend by the Spenserian Urn.

Whom should they encounter but none other than The Angry Black Priest, who sported a new battery-operated clerical collar with an ultraviolet glow that looked particularly harmonious with the painterly eve all about them.

'Hey, gentlefolk,' said TABP. 'Might I intrude?'

'Well, I don't know...,' Butterbugs drawled.

'I was fulfilling an appointment, that's all. I'm to escort this here foxy lady to the Coconut Grove for dinner and dancing. After which, P. Flask will join us for late table at Friend Fritz's. Will you not make our party a foursome?'

'Man, oh man, TABP, I can't. Big role coming up. You know.'

'Of course, baby. I'm *in*, y'know. Co-producing. Team shit, but I'm up for it. In fact, I'm fucking honored.'

'Just plain *good!*'

'Also, I'm in the music supervision team, too.'

'I didn't know, I didn't know,' Butterbugs replied, relief obviously relaxing his frame, made somewhat erect by his fancy escort.

'Go and prepare, B-bugs,' advised best friend TABP.

'I will. I tell you, I will! Now, Darse, I turn you over to overly capable hands.'

'Oh, thanks, pretty boys. But TABP, pray, shall I change?'

TABP adjusted the carbon fiber lenses of his shades and eyed the skimpy wrap about her midsection, the cool tank top, and the boots on the ground.

'I think I share the same tastes and appreciations as your hus-band, whom we are soon to rendezvous with. If I were he, I'd rather come up against the sight of this criterion of class who stands before us now, in those babe-alicious boots, than practically any other vision of loveliness in this here state. Except of course, for my closely-knit babe of my own, Keremeos, who happens to be on location in Ungava right now.'

TABP held out his elbow in escort style, Darcie went on over, and the trans-action was complete.

Oh, but was this parting melodious, for Butterbugs felt as if dipped in a vat of spun song, a TABP ballad, like 'Lady Turnaround', which was fully compatible with the rhyme and reason of 'Primrose M'Cullum'.

How he loved those whom he knew so well and trusted so far!

Love. Knowing. Trust. Made sense. It took a Muse to show him.

As Muse of Erotic Comedy and Eros-Imparted Wisdom, Jody, proud stunner that she was, felt empowered, and for once in her life, she was doing what she ought to do. After years of breathing rubbish to and from neighborhood boys and campus squirrels, she'd finally listened to her inner voice, wised up, packed her bags, hit the road, learned about life, and made her way back to LA, for to seek a venue by which to impart her happier and wiser wisdom, gleaned from her picaresque wanderings.

Jody, heartbreaker, with her bronzy/pop appearance, scrumpdiddlyump-tious in every way, nevertheless was not what might be called a... mainstream personality. She was much more dimensional than that. Not that she was born that way. Shallowness and haughty conceit had been her hallmarks, especially in her UCLA days, when she was just hanging out on campus, to get laid and/or flip shit to anyone and everyone who wasn't good enough for her hottie audiences.

When, by means too roundabout to be thoroughly sized up here, she found out she had actually encountered Butterbugs when he'd chanced to stumble into that campus' ditzy dorm world when he did, and she'd joined forces with her dingdong sorority mates and mercilessly mocked this uncertain but alternatively intriguing figure from beyond the pale of safe affluence, there was a crisis of consciousness that ensued. It was because she'd felt some sort of impact because of her deeds. Something different. Otherwise she probably would've retained her bubble-brained ways, and indeed, further capitalized on them.

But the recollection of the encounter haunted her, and finally came to alter her whole progression as a promising and sexy college babe for our times.

The only thing that saved her from self-mutilation as punishment was the fact that at that one specific crossroads moment in the distant past, as Butterbugs had been driven away by her and her mates' ridicule, she'd thought maybe he was a being of extraordinary caliber, in spite of superficial impressions.

'And then I came to myself!' she announced, having prefaced this statement by mentally informing him as to her history, but not out loud. He did not seem to respond to her vibes in this matter.

So now, with all this history built up, she had, as a Muse hereabouts, to consider just what such a crisis of conscience meant at this point. Absenting herself from a dreaded knowledge seemed the only way. So she took off into the wilds.

It was, after all the ultrastar's Muse-trysts of late, the only one that was a chance encounter. Jody hadn't been seeking him. If anything, the increasing oppression of the truth – the truth she'd mocked him with, and in effect, cursed him with, began to weigh on her. So she reckoned she should therefore banish herself and fall into a consumptive lifestyle of dissipation, by which to atone for her outrageous and thoughtless acts.

Head downcast, the girl who'd been so snottily sure of herself sought the little-known Late Postern by which to exit The Lazaretto's vast estate, in the most obscure way possible. Hard by the one-way gate was a sort of faux chapel, placed here years ago to provide a bit of picturesque distraction upon which to focus. That is, if any explorer stout enough ever happened to venture in this remote quarter. There was even an ersatz graveyard, with overgrown markers, most of which poetically leant in the Californian sun, or under the deep shade of an incongruous yew.

But this was the region of Hollywood where every and all environments were duplicated for the purposes of entertainments, from mainstream to obscure.

She paused beneath the shabby arch of the chapel's door, and eyed the overgrown postern, so little used that even in this climate, its gate, which hung ajar, was red with rust. Beyond it, she did not know if life would go on. She could not imagine it, even with her attained wisdom. With this helpless prospect, she shed tears of sorrow. For what might have been, and even more, for what *should* have been.

Meanwhile, down the lane…

His rucksack packed with good stürm fromage and quenching william-wine, Butterbugs was taking a mid-morning ramble, seeking the Upper Pastures as a getaway to formulate more advanced approaches amidst the gathering strength of his strategy in discerning his upcoming role's demands.

Clad as a Hardy-esque county lad – Wessex waistcoat, floppy straw hat of summer, billowy blouse and loose bow tie, to appear presentable to any land-owner class who might consider any less dress improper, he roamed these fur-ther reaches and found the lyrical natures therein enriching and intriguing. Now he knew where to come if atmospheric solitude of the gentlest kind needed accessing.

There – an ecclesiastical ruin of some sort, and before it, buried remains only, devoid of human life. But –

As if cued by the prelude to Act II of 'Parsifal', the definitive film version which Butterbugs had appeared in not long ago (Oceanus), he saw a figure bowed low. Framed by the pointed arch, it was preparing to steal away amidst the obfuscation of the graves, in some sort of gesture, he guessed, of escape. A wave of almost chill wind swept over the graveyard, rippling its rank grass and propelling the wayfarer up and through it, in mid-current, until he drew nigh to the cloaked and hooded figure that was making its way toward the postern.

Mysterious, moody, the figure struck him as certainly clandestine in its appar-ent mission. Then, he caught a sudden but fleeting glance of trim ankle, revealed by the cloak's failure to conceal.

'Jody!' Butterbugs called out. 'Oh! *Jody* is it?'

The figure came to a halt.

'*Quo vadis?*'

His question carried genuine incredulity. Did his guests ever try to escape from The Lazaretto? Was this one in progress? As host, what had he done to merit this?

The figure, Jody indeed, slowly lowered her hood, and turned about. The breeze cleared her face of errant locks, and, pulling in close, Butterbugs could see her eyes were full of mist.

'Jody. *Muse* Jody! You! What – what were you about?'

She maintained a close hold on the cloak's coverage, clasping it near her throat.

Here was he whom she was charged to inspire, in front of her now. Straight in front. She was compelled to be straight, in return.

'I was stealing away,' she decided to announce.

'Away? From we here at The Lazaretto? From *me*…?'

'I had to, loved one. I was becoming beside myself.'

'So much so, you have come to such an abandoned spot as this! So unlike frolicsome and frisky Jody! Ohhhh…. *Jody!*'

She smiled, and the joyous and randy memories were all still there. But a cloud surrounded them now.

'Butterbugs, I am not worthy.'

She turned and made ready to exit through the postern, knowing full well that once she crossed its border, there would be no turning back. Not ever.

'Wait, Muse! You are still one of their number, Jody. You cannot pull away with only that statement. Why-ever – Whatever were you thinking? *Worthy?* Our life here is not circumscribed by any bureaucracy, nor clerical mandate, nor cultish bizarreness. You know we live by our art here. Nay, *for* our art.'

Jody kept her head about her, and though she was sorely tempted to cry, more tears did not come.

'I have a confession.'

He spread his arms wide. Even in her diminished state, he found her to be so fetching in appeal and wonder, he could've easily embraced her without further ado, so as to reset their relationship. Any emotional complications would be left by the wayside. But the incredulity continued.

'Confession??'

'It was *me*,' she said in a low voice.

'That...?'

'You know it, Butterbugs. Do not feel you have to protect me any longer.'

'Jody, most kittenish of Muses, you are not known for your leading games.'

He was becoming more frustrated than anything now. The lyricism of the day, which was what he'd sought, was dissolving into a somber elegy in a country churchyard.

Her courage failed her. All she wished was for him to take up the burden of truth and chastise her for what she had done.

'I wanted to leave before you had to have me sent away.'

Again, she took steps toward the derelict pilasters on the estate's edge.

'Speak the truth now. As if I did not know it. Please. Here and now.'

His impatience meant one thing: it was a moment for truth. Once more she turned toward him, this time with a dramatic flair, for she flung open her cloak and her true identity was unmasked.

Then she cast the wrap into the waving grass, and stood without any instrument of deception, hands on hips, defiantly, boldly, unabashedly.

'There, Butterbugs! Behold, your mocker, in all her fancy foxiness!'

A stab from the past. From the little black choker down to the baby-chick-yellow halter top, full of orbéd contours. The red miniskirt that flared out like an upside-down tulip, the kind that willingly showed off what color panties were just underneath, by the tiniest of genuflections. Here was the same girl who'd been particularly coy – and then mean – to him that retarded day long ago at UCLA's Jugg Hall dormitory. It was only her so-fine pictoriality that even allowed for him to recall anything from that checked-out time. But there she was, better than ever, demonstrating history, instead of Erotic Comedy and Wisdom.

Yet it was certainly sheer eroticism she was conveying, and when she spun about and reminded him to 'Kiss my little round ass', comedy got tossed in as well. And then wisdom.

'I was one of them, Butterbugs. The central one. Miss Jubilee to my left, Jemymah to my right. Together we hassled you and made fun of you. At your expense.'

'You mean, *you* were one of those three?'

'I was. I'm telling you, I was. I stand before you in the light of truth, Butterbugs.'

Though he knew he had to observe the proper decorum when dealing with a Muse, he couldn't help but remember that day in the same light now, as then: she, so cute, but what a bitch! He nearly smiled.

Holy shit, but she looked so sexy here and in the present. And back then. Same outfit, too.

'I thought it only fitting that I depart your presence wearing what I wore when I assaulted you like that. (Still fits perfectly, too!) So as to complete the closure.'

She was truly contrite. But she had yet another confession.

'You have to believe me now, sir, when I say, I knew it then, that I *believed* in you!'

'Oh, but Jody, why did you deride me so?'

'Because, dear one, I was in a hateful air. I was surrounded by cattle. And then you were there, of a sudden. And none of us had ever seen such a being. We did not know what to do. So I defaulted into moronics.'

'You said those things –'

'Aye! I did. For which I am heartily sorry. Alas, we have never talked about this! I thought if I sought you out and made myself into something, I could make up for my offense, by serving you – though not in servile ways. Then my conscience began to overload me with so many distortions and oppressions. I thought I should retreat... to what or where, I could not imagine. Probably oblivion, out of shame. But I now know you forgave me the first moment you saw me again, just now. I knew it too. Besides, you knew me to have the surest, sweetest little body you'd seen in a long time, and you stripped me in your mind. And you have not been disappointed. And you knew me to generally think loftily, which I do every day. And not just about you! Attraction is always a starting-point, to be taken up by intellect and character. Which I have in abundance. As do you.'

He was impressed that she stood up for herself and did not devolve into defeatism or self-loathing. Needless to say, all was forgiven! A no-brainer, for sure.

'You know I wouldn't want to have anything just one way, Jody-sugar! Come back, with newness all around!'

'Kiss me, Butterbugs! I am your right hand.'

'Better than my right hand!' he said breathily, playfully.

'Card-boy! You know what I mean!'

'I know. You are my Athena.'

'That's better!' she replied, mock-snottily, then gave him the sexiest kiss of the day. Pallas was never so seductive.

Once they had savored the revived rural idyll, in which the old chapel and its accoutrements were fully noted and appreciated, and they'd lounged under the yew until the breeze's letting up reminded them that refreshment awaited back at The Lazaretto's familiar facilities, they wended their way homeward.

Further on, Butterbugs walked after her, admiring that coy behind that had once been used as a tool to deride him, and he thought, how sweet destiny can be. He reached out and patted her skirt in accordance with her rhythmic gait.

'Why girl, we forgot your cloak!'

'I didn't forget it. I left it. It's no longer something I care to have. It is my Error, and as a symbol, I have abandoned it.'

'Smart, sassy… and sensible, too!'

'Perhaps we'll use it as a picnic blanket sometime, and we'll make graveyard love on its weathered but comfy fabric.'

'Country lover!'

'That's right, sex object!'

'Say, Jody! Impart some of Eros' cheer as we near our humble quarters!'

'All right!' She turned about and kissed his caressing fingers. 'I love kissing you after you've touched me.'

'And before.'

'Of course. But, I've a joke from the hoary mediæval days, for your amusement. It may bomb, you know.'

'That's part of the fun, baby.'

'Well, there's this Germanic barbarian who's happened to have tagged along on one of the Crusades. The Third, I think. He doesn't believe in its mission or anything. He's just along for the pillaging, rape, etc. Anyway, he ends up with this Moorish Amazon who is a houri-type member of Saladin's harem. He's positively blown away by her, and she tames, even civilizes, him. They fall in lust, and then in love. They know, if they're caught, they'd be executed on the spot, perhaps *in flagrante delicto*. They're standing there in this secret hammam, nude, looking at each other. Perhaps for the last time. They realize their dilemma. They scan each other's bodies. He, her incredibly pendulous labiæ. She, his floppy sac and other droopy skins. 'If we hang,' she quips, 'I guess we hang together!' That's it. Well??'

'Hmm,' he snort-laughed. 'Lousy joke! Where's the hook?' He smiled slyly, 'But, uh, is that a hint?'

'That we do some 'hanging out'? It's your call. After all, I'm here to inspire, not necessarily instruct.'

'But was it a happy ending? Did they make a life for themselves?'

'Oh Butterbugs,' mock-moaned Jody, 'Would I be interested in tragedy?'

'Of course not, Muse of Erotic Comedy and Eros-Imparted Wisdom!'

She then instructively led him on through the loggia of the Herculaneum wing, dropping an article of clothing under each arch whilst reciting a line from one of Euschynæus' most erotic sonnets, and in the antique Greek tongue, no less.

She loved the way her ass drew him effortlessly onward, and at every pirouette with accompanying lyric, she exhibited the pleasantly-puffy bulbs on her chest in ever more unveiled states. UCLA attire, adieu.

Aside from her obvious T&A attributes, he had always been particularly fascinated (and turned on) by her magical and expressive eyebrows. They rose as he rose.

They spent the rest of the afternoon in the Nova Pompeii baths, taking, in turn, steam, tepidarium, and divan-sex under the skylights, 'neath mottled walls of blood red, gold lines, and black panels.

Jody was the embodiment of courage, truth, and revaluation of values. The simplicity of her recovery, and her redemption through love, were all that he needed to cap his analysis of The Self at this juncture. In this oneness was Butterbugs fully and finally restored, more whole than ever, more matured, ready, cemented into place, as it were.

'I am now prepared for this role,' he announced, coming up for air after advanced cunnilingus. Then he dove back in.

Jody had no end of thrills.

'Oh, Butterbugs! Oh, yes! Hail, transcendent hour! Ohhhh! Yesssss!'

The Seven Muses had done their work well.
Mitzi had inspired him to be grounded.
Rahvundrah had inspired him to be aware.
Terpsichore had inspired him to be accountable.
Cydalise had inspired him to be flexible.
Uriyurr had inspired him to be trustworthy.
Darcie had inspired him to be decisive.
Jody had inspired him to be magnanimous.
Ideal leadership qualities, all.

'Strength now', went their chant, 'Strength, *to Butterbugs!*'

37.

Foundational Basement Supersubstructure

Every Ultra-Panavision 70 camera in existence was being overhauled, upgraded and cleaned. Robert Surtees and Leon Shamroy had just been inked for the co-lenser chores. It was cemented into the contract that Butterbugs' most preferred screen process would be utilized in this upcoming and exceptional picture, for the contract was *duly signed* on this day.

There was a ceremony, appropriately, at Mega|Goth Stvdios, on Stage 19, the showiest on the lot. Everybody was there, and there was lots of glitz. Publicity was of course vital, though not much effort was needed, as this thing was going to play itself.

Sonny and Butterbugs intrinsically knew that Hy Goth was a person of dubious character, but as a mogul, few could top his top-flight tastes 'n' techniques.

'An unholy alliance?' quipped Old Atrocity to Porter Parker, while they watched the wet ink bleed on the parchment, as the ultrastar signed up amongst fellow eagles, on the banner-draped dais.

'We are witnesses to history, OA. But go ahead and be droll. You'll see. This picture has the capacity to change the world.'

'Into what?'

'Can it, OA, would you now? Wait for some scenes to unfold before you start nipping and needling. You're key-gripping on this one, aren't you?'

'Pretty much the whole way through, baby. You can't get more witnessy to history than that.'

'Consider yourself lucky, sir. The list of the blessed is legion, but limited. Hy's generously allowing the two Sams – Bronston (who headed the august list) and Goldwyn, DFZ, Sol Siegel, DeMille, Merv LeRoy, Dorean Dellavonda, Dino De L, Haze Snyder, Edmund Mark Mad, plus Yxlö and Britta Svenendensen to guest produce, with screen credit under 'Associate Producer'. Even Sonny's in. TABP will enjoy Associate Assistant Executive Producer billing. So will we all. How's that?'

'That's a step in the right direction. Producer P. Pud Parker!'

'They're all damn grateful, sport. So damn grateful, as am I, as Associate Executive Producer! (And I correct you.) Isn't that incredible?'

'Awfully-very incredible.'

'It's all happening so fast. So furiously fast! Are you *ready*, OA? Oh, *are you?*'

'I will be. Relatively immediately.'

'Oh, be a fussbudget then. This is going to be *fun!*'

Inside, away from producers, Old Atrocity was really quite exalted at being part of this production. And he didn't know it yet, but he would receive a unique screen credit, as Director of Systematic Realization, which was sure to (privately) thrill him to no end.

And now, **UNHOLY WAR HYMN.**

'UWH', the abbreviation| by which this picture became universally and instantly known, (thanks to the colloquialists at 'Variety'), was inspired by the saga of Ool-Akzad Nazah, Chief Martial Law Administrator of Khwhyreziumn. You know, that trans-Caspian-cum-cis-Oxus nation-oid 'twixt Aral and legitimacy that everyone was yakking about these days.

The work was written in blank verse, in eighteen cantos in the heroic style of John Milton, by that titan of contemporary literature and popular texts, Sawlohmunn Rabinowicz Cane. The High Mad Doctor (HMD, that is, the virtual 'Generalissimus' status to which the character ascends) was based on the actual Ool-Akzad-type person.

And the thing was, it was all so 'recent'. In point of fact, it was instant history, or one mind's interpretation of it, as it happened, as it just might happen. History was still unfolding even as the book was being released. Therefore, it would actually be up to the *film version* to tidy things up, to make them cogent, and to present a consummate ending, which would of course be amended in any future book edition. Indeed, both author and filmmakers were watching the headlines, constantly seeking plot twistables and turnables.

No docudrama this, but what were the headlines saying?

In the White House, the Murn Administration had taken a fanatical interest in this Nazah fellow, especially after he categorically declared 'war' on America some time ago, rather in the manner of that old saw, the 'Global War on Tare', that got international trade interests so hopped up on rage.

President Con Murn and his cabal were thus mad keen on making the most of the opportunity. What they thought of this film project, though, remained to be seen.

Here then, was a 'nation' that had been carved out of the detritus of the Regional Shakeup War that had resulted from the catastrophic antagonism instilled by an unhappy US invasion of Iraq. Culturally and ethnically, the nation of Khwhyreziumn was something out of the Prester John myth: something Circassian, something Uzbek, something Azerbaijanian, something Turkmenian, something just a little bit Kazakh... A hotchpotch really, and also with some generic Caucususian aspects thrown in (a new term actually sanctioned by the Oxford English Dictionary, as a lexicographic way of patching up an already dreadful nomenclature-situation). Khwhyreziumn was without intrinsic heritage, identity, or, for that matter, raison d'être. At least ostensibly.

Such a nation would normally be relegated to permanent reliance on greater powers for its crutches and training wheels, in order to keep its doors partially open for business. But there had been a recent discovery within its borders.

It happened on a night when a distant star, Arkabeetes, known since the ancient ages for its evil intent, was at its millennial brightest, as seen in skies within the temperate latitudes. That meant anyone looking up in DC could see it, and know in their hearts that somewhere, someone was up to something sneaky. But it wasn't as if what was recently discovered had been planned, or that a certain star was not complicit except for having reigned at such a nativity. For science has proven that stars are more concerned with their own fates than those of worthless humans on a mere ball of dust in a grade-Z neighborhood of the omniverse.

It was just the sort of discovery that came in the form of a gift, which turned out to be an ace in the hole. This discovery was, well, this: because the Aral Sea oil fields had played out, as had the Aral Sea itself, having reached a stage of enshrinkment so that it could now only be called the Aral Tank, most of Khwhyreziumn had become the world's most unwanted real estate. 'Polluted' was in no way an adequate enough term. However, the eminent Schottishe scientist-cum-explorer Sir Jon Duckling, whilst promenading these wasted tracts in search of amusement, embarked on a series of geo-soil experiments, just to see if anything jolly might turn up.

One escartulate examination preceded another, and the next thing Sir Jon knew, he had several score steamer trunks full of brave new evidence of unique and unnaturally-occurring chemical percolations and sediments that promised radical exploitation in multiple directions.

Why, it was a revelation! The precursor to a revolution! Here in this hideous rubbish-land were any number of synthetic fast tracks, having mutated into considerable mineral and ichor deposits, due wholly to the unspeakable environmental degradation that had been laid out hereabouts, these many decades.

Sir Jon knew those scientists who cooked up today's amazement-compounds that make life and industry so much more convenient and profitable would be spinning like tops when they found out that not only Contamulate-BX 362 'naturally' occurred in a particular swale, where signs of Svignanion 57-bologet were also noted, Etex 9000-Z was there, as well! Just this one simple, esoteric knowledge promised to bust the shoes of any research team stupid enough to approach it with the slightest cockiness. It would permanently blow away any operating officers of an enabling exploitive company who weren't capable of greatness, and the associated merchant network specializing in the threshold market of Famlap-based pharmaceuticals better be up for the humungous task of managing this entire world-shaking, world-grasping package.

Here, literally oozing from the ground, were bona fide organics, that tens of thousands of incomplete lab workings and strivings in a field that was at least a decade out from conclusive achievements hadn't come close to accomplishing yet, just begging to be slopped into buckets and capitalized with the highest of exploitations.

But that was only one of hundreds of startling offerings to be had from this putrid plain of chemical mush. The possibilities were mind-nova-ing.

Sir Jon, having assembled his necessary presentations for preliminary proposition in utter secrecy, quickly made plans to decamp, and soon was on his way via palkee-gharry, followed by camel caravan, hauling his steamer trunks with their priceless contents, ultimately bound for Victoria Station in London town.

One blustery afternoon near Vhop, a portmanteau that was poorly attached to the last camel-of-the-line's howdah chanced to break away, and when it hit the hardpan below, some papers let fly. They were chemical compound charts and advanced structural formulæ, personally penned and tinted by Sir Jon, of supreme importance to this entire scheme of discovery, development, and exploitation.

However, one Farmer Mkluq, who attempted hopeless tillage of the soil hard by, spied an especially significant chart amidst the stinging sands, plucked it up, failed to interpret the markings, and so assumed they were the devil's tool. Reporting to the nearby garrison village of Whup, F. Mkluq turned in the evidence to a certain Judge-Constable Slucpztc, who happened to be a brilliant non-amateur sleuth. He correctly inferred the chart was discharge from the foreigner-led caravan, which was at that very moment to be found making its way toward the exit post at the border to the southwest.

Consequently, the über-authorities in the semi-ruined capital of Atlasaxis were contacted, and appropriate forces were dispatched with alacrity. Just six furlongs before the border crossing, the caravan was tracked down by elite prætorian patrol in Citröen half-tracks, and the palkee-gharry was requested to pull over.

'Sir Jon!' declared Juncture-Sheriff Stissztapfcx of Contra-Aral District, who happened to be a Keele graduate, 'I arrest you on charges of ripping off the Chief Martial Law Administrator's personal 'n' private property.'

The knight had no defense.

For his efforts, Sir Jon, too valuable an instrument to be allowed escape unto the corporate hegemony in the West that surely awaited, was taken away and imprisoned in the castle fortress of Dhrapcx. There he was forced to cooperate with the Permanent Martial Law Authority in developing these resources, upon threat of having his eyelids sewn shut within the context of solitary confinement in a backroom basement cistern.

He and his mercenary teams set to work, and in less than a year had the entire resource area cataloged, assigned and controlled. Negotiations opened up with panting interests in the West, who were obliged to take things and make deals on Khwhyreziumnite terms. Canniness and craftiness, not previously endemic in this tawdry country, were now instantly acquired. Systems to empower the owner of powerful resources were locked and loaded.

To review, the vast Aral Tank zone's creativity spawned a new fulcrum in the world's balance of power. Not bad for a failed state. When certain chemical responses are unique in all the world, and toxicity has given way to advantageous opportunities, the dilemma of control inevitably results. Such was the case now.

Chemistry is power. All growing things in Khwhy (abbreviation unanimous-ly approved by the Intercontinental Labeling and Agreements Organize; ILAO) were now rapidly mutating into any number of The New Products. Everything from groundbreaking pharma to the basic composition chemicals that made up cinema's new physical medium – the BKV Method would be impossible with-out imports of one-of-a-kind KhwhyChems (also an OED-embraced term, out of sheer desperation, really). So the stakes were ionospheric, and the Industry was involved on the highest of levels.

Problem was, the Ruler. It's always the Ruler. He was *something else*. He wasn't exactly a kluck, either. He had stuff everybody wanted, and wanted badly. So he wrote his own ticket. Far simpler than oil or tin or even bauxite, the KhwhyChems factor immediately became the mandate inflicted on all dependent corporations, governments and consumers on the planet Earth. Inflicted because the Chief Mar-tial Law Administrator was not at all a pleasant dude. Having learned the lessons of Hitler, Stalin, Saddam, and Jumbo Tinks (whose gambit of creating an Afric superpower that, for a time, extended from the Ashanti savannahs down to Vic-toria Falls, almost came off, before it was scotched by Roberson Oils 'n' Mines), Ool-Akzad Nazah played his cards in the most sly sets, which of course infuriated the pale paternal penis people of Western boardrooms and ministerial sanctums. They wanted in. *Way* in, without hooks or strap-ons of any kind.

In fact, the late Isaac Davis had been *in* at the start of this business. 'Can we really work with this darn guy?' had been his most persistent question.

Well, the world *had* to, and they were getting sick of it. The tactics encountered were strict and ruthless, so tightly controlled that they made the late Richard X. Cheney look like a male slut – all talk, and a yard wide. Big biz concerns wanted their rights back. *Now*.

Pressure from their ranks was soon brought to bear on Nazah's rinkydink but growing-in-power regime. He plotted in his HQ, in forbidden Arkbash. Vibes rose into the world from that place. He didn't stay bought, and decided, if mafia tech-niques were to be used on him (crude attempts to bump him off were the West's innocent efforts to solve the situation), then by God, that's what he would deliver in return.

Speaking of God, the Deity had nothing whatsoever to do with any aspect of the mounting crisis. Though the region was historically Islamic in its cultural hearth, Nazah and his nation were not. Absolutely not. Back in the 1880s, certain proselytizers from the Utilitarian Chapel sect out of Sepeepsee, Oklahoma, had successfully converted fringe inhabitants of the area to their bleak and hopeless faith. Now, so long later, those very fringe-oids, corralled so unintelligibly and by mere chance from the war settlement acts, found themselves in power in this funky blip of a nation. Personally, Nazah had no spiritual development whatever. He wasn't even interested in stoking his cause with any gimmicks of the religious kind. He didn't have to. It all boiled down to one vacuous greedy businessman versus others. Thus, especially in this super-region, he was an oddball. No one really knew how to even start thinking about him, or how to approach him – or how to hogtie him. So he got more and more empowered, and richer, and richer yet. The Sultan of Brunei was knocked down a notch. He also enjoyed extreme approval from his populace. Even though he plowed absolutely none of his wealth toward the benefit of his citizens, they were truly 'his' people, and indigenousness prevailed. This reality was one of the true successes of the war settlement acts.

The stage was set, dressed, and ready for blocking. If not shooting.

Nazah thus demanded severe terms in dealing with those who required his goods. 80% commissions would be charged on all transactions, and the world at large found itself gummed up and hamstrung, instead of being the one to tie the ham and stuff it full of gum. They protested. Therefore, the Ruler had no choice but to declare war.

Sawl Cane was perceptive enough to seize this ultra-historical situation and define it in the poetics of his exceptional style. And because it was Cane, the world listened. Because it was *now*, the world grabbed it and ran. Because it was timely, Hy Goth nabbed it. Because it would only do as a mega-production, it would be mega-expensive. Because it was assumed that 'Unholy War Hymn' would publicize their cause beyond their craziest expectations, the corporations concerned (and many who weren't) backed Hy's project to the hilt. Because money was no object, all lights were green. And because Butterbugs was now on board, greatness was presumed, as was success in every way.

But here was Butterbugs, himself having tasted the corporate lifestyle from so bitter a goblet, signing on to the most corporate undertaking of his career. So far. What, then, did he think?

First of all, he had read Cane's work. All of it. Had anyone who wore a corporate suit? If any had, they would have found it to be as trenchant and devastating a critique of their own enterprises as it was of the Ruler's mad practice of power-political medicine. Apparently, due to the synopses' strengths alone, the suits took it on, thinking themselves above history, of course. But even more than that, the very tone of the cause alone would grant them special powers of public approval to proceed in any damn way they wanted. What better than a picture show – with Butterbugs – to romanticize it?

So Butterbugs was concerned, all right. It was in the term that followed his Equivocation (as his chroniclers now officially called it), cured by the Muses, that this new concern now came into its own. But he'd found the script to be totally loyal to Cane's vision.

So what was the problem?

Scripts, though, were pretty little things. Delicate, subject to change. Even a Cane/Butterbugs script. This being the titanic production it was, though, nothing had surfaced as of yet. Prepping, plus locations, could alter much. Plus, *the weather*, for crying out loud. This was, after all, the New Reality. No cheating.

In fact, Butterbugs now ensconced himself at the monasterial The Æyrie to learn his lines. His jaw dropped and kept dropping at the majesty, the magnificence. It was an ecstatic and elevating process, quite unlike any production prep he'd ever done before. Sure, he'd played leaders. Lenin, Mao, Brokk-brok, St. Stephen, James Abram Garfield, Panchard, Dr. Ambedkar, and Napoleon – in the incredible 'Fromage à Tilsit' (Warren Sarjent) – and none of them had been easy Easter pageants to pull off. Yet they and others were historical actualities, and usually well-documented through materials laid out for his easy reference. Cane's High Mad Doctor (HMD) was more a character consisting largely of a state of mind, with events attached. Or at least that's how it appeared. He and his director would see to it. It would be up to them to realize the role's cult of personality.

Oh, and Cane himself would undoubtedly have things to say. As would Old Atrocity. Inexorably, imminently.

OA remained one of Butterbugs' most high-level consiglieres. Never an actor to rely on committee, though, despite his innate egalitarianism, the character's light would emanate from within him. How, he did not yet know, nor did anyone else. That was the best thing about incandescence. It was its own creation. Witnesses appreciated its existence rather than probing its origins. Wonder spoke for itself, and needed no explanation or investigation.

Indeed, the ultrastar felt in complete control of his powers. The vast script would unleash them in the best unbridled manner. This was not to say his acting would lack discipline or focus. He just knew this was the Role of the Ages. Instinct would win out over intellectualizing, because it was all so right and all so natural.

'Sawl, I don't know why my character would mutter: 'In accounts kept, sugar adds up as sugar, and solstice ends solstice / Ambience jerks ambience even past the end of all things / Though we know it not, I say!' '

Cane's voice was singularly tinny at the other end of the line.

'You make a good point, Butterbugs. I'll confer with the script crew. The peerless Tulameen and Similkameen Spuzzum-Judgeship sisters are working on an adaptation. There's plenty of leeway. Your... suggestion?'

'I don't know yet. When it happens, I *will know*.'

'I trust you, naturally. We will leave it open. This and everything else.'

'It will not be an improv though, Sawl.'

'That I know. You don't know how to do that method, anyway.'

'You know, I guess you're right. It's just something I've never employed. I figure that when I know the script, the invention follows.'

'To be sure. That's obvious from all your roles. You will invent, and I will marvel, then inspect, then approve. But you will not improvise.'

'I guess I'm just not that kind of guy.'

'And that is all our fortune, Butterbugs.'

The script crew was formidable.

Justy rang him from her Mairie in the Central African Revised And Now Reformed Republic.

'Sweetiebugs, are you sure this is the right move for you? This particular picture? I miss you!'

'And I you, Queen of Justice, Maid of Bangui, she of whom the CARANRR will soon be renamed 'Justinia' aka 'République de la Justine l'Afrique'!'

'It is true that I have accomplished miracles here. And they are spreading from this here nexus-location.'

'Would that I could, here. Yes, with this particular picture. You are my model.'

'Could you, phone-sex lover? And how could you?'

She was not being coy. She was excited, in more ways than one.

'Well, for one, or should I say two, squeeze your breasts closer to the phone. By being, well, a bit subversive.'

'You like that? They're both in my hands as I whisper to you, tongue in phone, phone-tongue in your ear. I am wet, honey. Here, in a dry land! What a time not to have a Picturephone! You really can't do that, Butterbutter. You can't even fake 'subversive'! Neither can I!'

'I feel their warmth, baby. If only my tongue could transpose your own, and if only it could do more than talk, just now! Ahh! I think that if I craft my part in the sense that Sawl suggests – that all parties are culpable in today's world, then a message-mélange might get through.'

'Oh baby, closer! I hear you. I can just imagine what you're doing now – down below. Well, that sounds pretty basic, Buttery. You can come up with something more substantial than that. I myself certainly have to, when I've got the Purbah Rural District Water Board standing in front of me, still dripping with deserty dust, because no tube-well will yield any more. (We conquered that prob, too, w/o subversion of any kind!)'

'Quick question, Just.'

'Anytime, anyplace, Bee.'

'I was wondering, you are not a native Central African Republican. It's obviously not a problem, but I thought that...'

'Africans are tribalists, first and foremost?'

'Well, I...'

'A common mindset. Believe it or not, my non-tribal, non-border-dependent presence is actually an asset. There's a new awareness of pan-Afric sensibilities everywhere here. It's part of Ali Mazrui's thesis on Pax Africana, which new generations across the continent are embracing, and – But sweets, that isn't why you called... Is it...?'

'Not particularly. But I'm tickled with the newness!'

'Thanks, Baby B. Will keep you apprised. Meanwhile, back in the mind of an actor...'

'Oh Justica, you've got me so distracted! How can I fairly address you about strategy when we're in the midst of making love?'

'Yeah, further – further in! Oooh! You've got a point, heroic lover. But maybe that's just it: to make love. To do it. With love. You know, real *love* – love.'

'Not Maybe-love?'

For a moment a Vonda-lump formed in his voice. Justy could tell.

'That's right, savory-lips. *She'd* want it that way.'

'You think so?'

He was instantly comforted.

'I know so. Vonda was so into love, she never knew how far. She changed your life. And therefore she changed us all.'

'Oh Justy, and you have, too! And Sasky! Where is that Saskatoon now, anyway? Would that we were all in each other's arms and thighs right now!'

'Of course we have changed each other's lives! We all have. And we are together in spirit. Always are. On the surface, I miss both of you keenly, but I'm immersed in your love here, and you are there, and so is Saskykins, off in the Highlands somewhere.'

'So *that's* where she's been! Scripting for 'UWH' calls.'

'Yes, she is needed to help construct the frame upon which your performance must stand. She will help you, as no muse can!'

'That's a great comfort, baby.'

'That's my specialty, love-cup.'

'Why is love so simple, Justy-baba?'

'Because it speaks to us without having to have words. Like music. We can feel it with just the emotions that matter. We can have it anywhere, everywhere, without conditions, and for free!'

'I love you, Justy.'

'Yeah, baby, you're loved, as well.'

'Free! Love for free – not for sale!'

'You got it, love-love!'

'Can I tell that to my corporate chums? Can I get away with it? You must understand that, no matter what we creators have as treasury, and no matter our will to spread it unto the masses, the higher pomp of the company brass still determines how brilliant the season will be. So can I tell them? Indeed, *dare* I? Even *I?* I repeat, can I get away with it?'

'Oh, no, don't tell them. Here is where you can be subversive. Integrate it into the role. Steal it past them and give it to the audience. Your masses. Just like on the tailgate. It is for them only.'

'How, exactly?'

'You must find your own way, Butterbugs. I had to do it here, so you can do it there.'

He could tell she was smiling when she said this.

'I'll find a way!'

'How about a little improvisation?'

'I don't know… It's not my skill. I lack the confidence. Besides, I promised Sawl…'

'You?? You are a maharaja of improv! In bed, I've never felt a more inventive dude! Saskatoon'll back me up, because we've whispered the same thing to each other. We pillow-talk about you all the time.'

'Why didn't you whisper it to me?'

'Improvised invention don't need no praise. It just needs to be… enjoyed.'

'Justy… you've, you've got something there.'

'And I gotta-lotta lovin' to do with you.'

'You babe! You improvisational muse!'

'Just stay with love, Butterbugs. Do not get seduced by – anything – else. This is too high a plane from which to fall.'

'I have indeed fallen from a high plane, you know.'

'This is a great deal higher, my one.'

38.

The Type Of Business This Business Is

Production began to get underway.

Filming in Khwhyreziumn itself was utterly, totally, and completely out of the question.

No director was yet set, but cameras were actually rolling. Second unit directors were kicking things off, grabbing mood shots in the field, from Kurrachee to Kuzzah, Spiriol to Spubbah, Kyzl to Kashgar.

As word of the coming cinematic onslaught spread, the 'UWH' company was receiving tenders from every direction of the winds. All the 'Woods' perked up, from Hollywood to Shollywood to Tollywood to Gollywood (wherever *that* was…), including Nigeria's burgeoning Nollywood CinemaCities, a studio compound the size of Connecticut.

Hy Goth was a conservative, though. Not only politically, but in his cheapskate reasoning. The drugs usually worked in his favor, but not in every instance. Though he would never admit it to the actual filmmakers, as far as facilities and locations were concerned, he planned to readily accept whatever recommendations they would make. The stakes were too high on this one to get overly 'big dick' about things. He was certainly secure in his home base, and to him, that was all that mattered.

Location was everything.

A frontline unit was in Jash County, WesTex, scouting the blighted plaques of land that were consummately spoiled from all kinds of spoilage, but with cloud formations more true to Cain's specifications than the actual Aral-zone skies. The latter were currently going through an unfortunate smudge era, due to rising grease-spray from any number of pollutant appurtenances connected to systems and concerns in the region.

Problem was, this bit of attractive Jash County sky happened to be over one of the US nation's worstest splatter tracts, where nuclear-oriented items of all kinds had been carelessly stored, waiting for the Big Day of Finality, when all such material would be trundled to the Absolute and Conclusive Turbo-Vault and Terminally Somber Repository of Everlasting Stasis and Repose at Yucca Mount… in old Nevada. *Some* day, but not yet, as the Qwuckford Fields were still streaked with radioactive putridity, and freedom seemed so far off as to be some distant memory of the future.

But its skies! Claude (Lorraine) could have painted them! John Ford could have put them to good use! (and he might, if he would just quit scratching his balls and crawl out of bed to direct this one, as many had been clambering for him to do). The Montgolfiers would have looked apropos puffing through skies like this! Louis XIV would have ordered their appearance!

Kings' Weather skies!

Bill Skall, lenser on one of the units, reckoned that with a P-78 red filter, cumulus resolution would outdo anything ever seen in the cinema before. Perfect for the big B&W dream sequences.

'But Butterbugs, I have right here, the 'Report', submitted by the Senatorial Sectional Committee for the Study of Land Locations in West Texas and the Texican Sphere of Influence That Might Come Under Certain Scrutinies of Motion Picture Crews In Search of Evocative Locations in Lieu of Shooting At Actual Locations Due to Political Upheaval or Environmental Degradation, and they say in said 'Report', dated just six months previous to today, that:

'Jash County is especially particularly indeed damaged, probably beyond repair, but if location crews elected to dwell not more than 196 hours in that land for purposes of photoplay dramatics, no adverse reaction is probable and probably possible under those terms. However, if that sum of hours be exceeded, if only by just a jiffy, statistical probability increases immediately and exponentially in the likelihood of cases of carcinoma of the entire senior canal, as well as the lung and cartilage bits, and this includes heart cancer. Aside from that, Hollywood studios will recognize this area as a most attractive and valuable site in which to engage in 'quick shoot' sequences, particularly in picture shows where certain centralized Near Asian locales are to be replicated. In these cases, all personnel shall be required to wear 'beep buttons' that sound off when the resident body has reached near capacity of harm-waves. After the beep, said person has, at the very least, 6.5 hours to clear out of the contaminated area.'

There was a pause.

'So you see, Butterbugs, it seems to me that we'll all be OK and that everything will be all right.'

'Mayella! *Oh*, Mayella! You are fairly youthful and cheerful! You are near my age and mindset, yet –'

Mayella was ring-a-ding-ding, in the happy extreme, and she and Butterbugs were currently gettin' it on, but when it came to Production Management, she was nothing but business. So right now, she had an announcement to make to Butterbugs. For the good of the picture, she would use all her clout with Hy Goth to push for this location. Butterbugs would surely thank her in the end.

'And yet??' she asked, content for the moment, to delay her announcement.

Mayella may have been all business, but she still toggled into the heady reality that she was dating an ultrastar, which tended to preclude all career-based reason and logic.

Butterbugs did not yet finish his thought out loud.

Mayella set aside the hefty government 'Report' and took the periodical that Butterbugs now silently handed her. It was the latest issue of 'The Journal Of The Mega-Concerned Atomic Scientists'. She instinctively opened to the Contents page, and he placed his finger on a certain article title: 'West Tex Tamasha' by Bob Oppenheimer, Niels Bohr, Ravlev Muhkhukkjhukk, and Keinrich Suzooza-vluk, in creative association with the late Jack Wong. She quickly paged to the appropriate starting point and proceeded to read the text of the cautionary article:

'Apparently, as far as the Qwuckford Fields are concerned, we, the experienced authors, think because it's out of sight (confined to the awesome and shocking wastes of Horribilis Mountain – elevation about 20 meters (!) – and vicinity), it's certainly out of mind. There was a fire burning out there last week, and black smoke formed, not a mushroom cloud, but a vague skull formation in the sky. Probably a mere and routine accidental combustion of yet another rotting 55-gallon drum of C-65095-X compound, peppered with feisty plutonium and neptunium bits, which invariably creates a boring old lake of fire in which dozens, perhaps scores, of workers – just a bunch of illegal aliens, whose tongues have been cut out for security reasons – perish yet again in a lurid holocaust. It's no big deal, really. The things that bull-dozers have covered up out there are enough to loosen your remaining molars and disrupt your hair plugs: a complete train, a half mile long, diesel-electric locomo-tive included; hundreds of baby calves with unicorn horns and three sets of hips and various sphincters (average number: 26) on their right sides only; thousands of punctured astronaut suits, in which illegal alien day-laborers writhed in secret agony while unwanted penis-like protrusions bulleted out of their sacrums (no ben-nies, no extra cost, easily replaceable); and scads of monster fœtuses from the Grik Medical Center in nearby Leonardtown, monstrosities that look more like Hot Stuff the Li'l Devil and Casper the Friendly Ghost than bouncing standard-issue human-oids. Upcountry folk should be darn grateful to Zeus that He doth command ye wind to blow northwesterly to southeasterly, and that the great Nywarpsundun Range and further on, Jerry Peak, provide a happy earthen bulwark against the creeping veins of subterranean FC-7000.07 Master Mix leaks.

The general situation is, well, fucked.

Our clock is set to go. It's just ten seconds to midnight.

We say this *now*.'

'Butterbugs, are they *kidding* with this crap? And the *language!*'

Mayella then looked at him and became absolutely wordless, but not for long.

'You are familiar with the authors of that article?' she asked.

'Some personally, my wonder. Oppie and I have –'

'But Ultra-bugs, come on now. Whadaya think?'

'We shall not shoot our picture in that sector, my Mayella. Ever. I don't care if the cloud formations turn up wrong elsewhere.'

'But Butterbugs, dear Thing and Ultrastar of this picture, that would defy the Reepsville Accord! Not to mention Mega|Goth Stvdios and Feature Pictures, and the Producers' Team, with DFZ, et al.'

'Do you not think that that very issue hasn't been weighing on my complete person and its associated personality? Do you not know how I have brooded? Have you not noticed, Mayella, my agony over this here subject? Oh, the awesome *gravity* of it all! I tell you, I too have been tormented much, and more, about it. But we durst not risk precious cast 'n' crew lives on a mere picture. Besides, what if it's a flop?'

'I hadn't even thought of that,' answered Mayella, almost gasping.

'Thus, we shall not shoot in that land.'

'And the Producers' Team? I am their liaison.'

'Leave off them. They cannot refuse me.'

'And Reepsville?'

'The Accord shall not be violated. Light can be bent. It will bend, but it will not break.'

'Oh, dear Thing, your power almost makes me pass out!'

'Do not pass out, Mayella. What is power? It is invisible.'

'Can *it* be bent, like light?'

'Ah, yes, yes it can. My character, HMD, is adept at it, and I have learned from him. I am rising. Rising above the layers of control we exercise over each other. Straight routes to solutions are now needed, and I can enact them.'

'Spoken like a true ultrastar!' Mayella thought, but she dared not speak it. She could not imagine what the *anger* of an ultrastar would be like, in the case he misinterpreted her, so she did not take the risk.

For his own part, Butterbugs was lacking of speech, but full of thought, as well. *And* he was full of disgust.

'In America,' he thought, 'everyone thinks they're in such *control*. I love this country, that's why I critique it.'

Mayella undressed down to her choker, which pleased Butterbugs.

'And everyone also,' he appended to his thought before engaging in sexual refreshment, 'thinks they *know* everything. So they tell you all about it.'

It was a rare bit of sourness that pickled his observation, but he was right. He had never surrounded himself with sycophants; quite the contrary. But in doing so, he was exposed to the realization that everyone was an opinionist, everyone a critic.

He did it right now – criticism. That is, appreciative criticism. His eyes traveled down the sleek lines of Mayella's torso, to the impossibly slim waist (she could not even fake womanly lipids) back up to the dark thatch on top of her head, and zoomed out for a full view. Just then, if she'd asked him to commit to filming here, he would have acquiesced, and all would have risked radiation because of her glowing stature. She also had an unusually strong sensual magnetism, which made their lovemaking into such a heady and intoxicating whirl. Indeed, her power almost made *him* pass out, and she knew how much he loved it.

But she did not misuse her power, nor did she even attempt to curve it a tad.

The production was wrestling with certain fundamentals that kept turning things around. Sawl Cane and Butterbugs had regular revelations and regular phone calls. Both might last for hours. Shooting would be divided between Mega|Goth in Hollywood, various atmospheric locales, as well as a dummy for Khwhyreziumn itself.

'What is the real reason for this picture, Sawl?' queried Butterbugs, in one of his academic moods.

'In point of fact, Butterbugs, its contents dislodge a charge against the toleration of humanity.'

'You mean, what we all put up with?'

'Precisely. I'm glad you didn't get diverted into the wrong spur line of thought.'

'No, no, that's what I immediately thought. Your clarity is always apparent. Through the whole work. I ask the question simply as a participant. My character – his behavior – the world's response – the world's acceptance.'

'Advantageous acceptance.'

'Right. Advantageous to *some*.'

'Oh yes, and we know who they are. Those who benefit the most from it.'

'Toleration based on opportunism.'

'Opportunities to limitless wealth.'

'Aye! 'Tis grim. A grim reality.'

'And we will expose it.'

Butterbugs smiled craftily into his mobile.

'On all sides.'

'In all its permutations.'

'Yeah.'

'You see, Butterbugs, nefariousness in its mafia manifestations has come to dominate certain sovereign powers. Yet, it evolves into a sort of non-specific world. No places are recognizable, nor cultures. Only atmospheric names and the message remain. Such is the forward thrust-power of the work. Locations and environment are all-important, but tone and intent end up ruling, to a tremendously dominating and transitional extent.'

'So, Sawl, the tone of our 'UWH' epic is paratactic.'

'That's right, star, structures occur side by side in their progression.'

Meanwhile, in old Hollywood, news of the ultrastar's nixing of a perfect location had taken the Industry by storm. It was not a Butterbugsian edict, only a fact of reality. They would not film in that land, *because Butterbugs said so.* Acceptance ensued. Yet, the dedication to realism had to be revised, maintained. Otherwise audience rejection could kill pictures.

The lengths the filmmaker community went to were almost beyond absurd. But audiences would accept nothing else than problems of correct depiction solved. This of course was because of the audience's obsession with the need for Absolute Realism and Truth in the Cinema. A ReaLife Board (its name hijacked from the old widescreen film process) was instituted to inspect and approve of all filmed scenes (even screen tests) for proper realistic capturement. Not at all a censorship agency, ReaLife was entirely sympathetic to the Industry and worked in concert to solve any problem that might come up in a realistic way. If tests were passed, ReaLife awarded a certificate to the picture in question. There was too much money at stake for any other alternative to be considered.

But, in cinematic sub-plot style, an underground movement, supported by corrupt Government elements (no one knew how high-up) was working on a quasi-surreptitious technique to wholly create digital realities that made old existing methods look like dog waste, all as raw material, all on computer. Way beyond mere animation, the technology would be indistinguishable from in-the-here-and-now reality.

Oh, but all this stuff was absolutely worlds away from the immediacy of Butterbugs' current location on planet Earth.

'Sonny *Projector!*' exclaimed Mayella, with her characteristic emphasis on words that mattered, wiping away Butterbugs' seed from her bee-stung lips just in time.

'Where is the kid?' asked the mega-agent, who had taken off his Old Fitzgerald Bourbon shades just before entering the cheap motel room, unannounced.

Mayella hastened to finish tying her kimono string, though Sonny surely caught a gander of one boob and then a peek too-far-up one thigh.

The agent raised an eyebrow.

'Late morning recovery?'

'We – uh, he – was up till wee hours, deep in script study. Oh, so deep!'

Sonny smiled but did not smirk. He liked Mayella, but didn't think she was any more than a diversion for the ultrastar, in light of Saskia and Justy's busy and intense professional lives. However, he was no cop, and knew Butterbugs' maturity to be beyond his own ken. Besides, he knew she wasn't lying or even kidding. The ultrastar *would* stay up late to study his lines. At any rate, he could well understand a morning roll on the Motel .006 Magic Fingers slab. When a cast member wants to be present for second unit location shooting, and he isn't even in any scenes, time weighs in waiting.

'Might I inquire – May I have a yak with the man of the house?' he asked kindly.

'Why sure, Sonny. You want a cup of good-morning-America?'

'Real jitter juice?'

'You *know* it!'

'Don't mind if I do. But you don't have to go to no trouble...'

'No problem! None whatsoever! I'll just toddle down to the check-*in* and get the real thing. No doubt it's been stewing there, in the half-light before the yellow dawn.'

'But Mayella, you're not stepping out in that get-up, surely?'

She looked down at her scant covering; patterned, but filmy.

'You're right, Son.' She paused, finger to lower lip. 'I've got just the thing.'

She went into the bathroom and quickly emerged with a black garter belt, which she shimmied into, only fairly discreetly.

'Holy shit,' thought Sonny, who actually felt like pleasuring himself just then. Never mind the mammoth motion picture that needed guiding and prepping right now.

'You – uh, that's *it?*'

'Oh, I'll cover up good! See? After all, the management knows we're picture folk. Gotta put on a show!'

'You're doin' it, baby!'

She giggled, then called out, 'Bee-bugs! Oh, *BEE*-Bugs! Sonny the *Projector's* here, probably to chide you for coming in my mouth this morning!'

She sashayed out the door, dark curls & furls bobbing on her fake heaven-fur shoulders.

'She's *funny!*' mused Sonny, who was used to her on-the-job propriety. He caught a voyeur glimpse of her sensuous progression toward the office.

'Hoo, what a contraption!'

'Sonny?'

'Just here. Mayla's gone out for corfee. Might I intrude?'

'I am no longer nude, Sonny. Sex be my waiting room activity when the work of the day awaits.'

'I hear you. I'm not so equipped right now, because I'm waiting for stuff myself, but I'm not lying about.'

'Forgive me, Sonny.'

'Nothing to forgive, HMD. Now dig this.'

He ventured into the musky chamber and beheld a truly relaxed Butterbugs, in cheap terrycloth robe, who made no attempt to rearrange the sex-play plain upon which he lay.

Sonny approved. They were family, after all.

'Now looka here. 'UWH' has yet to get a signed director.'

'I know that fact.'

'Yoe.'

It's not that the producers were getting sick of this reccy in Peagle, TX. It was just that decisions had to be made, and selecting a director for the picture was an issue that had become quite acute.

'Whom, then, can we get to helm this venture?' asked its principal star.

'There is a short list.'

'Jack Ford?'

'He's certainly at the top, but Pappy's kind of lazy right now.'

'J. Lee Thompson?'

'Already booked elsewhere.'

'Hawks?'

'Ditto.'

'Why would Howard want to pass something like this up?'

'I don't know if I'd want to ask him that question.'

'Marvie Minnwinn?'

'She'd be perfecto, but she just birthed twins.'

'How about Joe Mankiewicz?'

'Nay. Tony Mann, neither.'

'Janey Nukumba?'

'Unfortunately, no, as well.'

'Lean?'

'Almost! But he's committed to his Glubb Pasha/Harry St. John Bridger Philby duo-biopic dream project now, out in the Trucial States. Prince Charlie's producing, too. Damn, but was he really lusting for our little old unholy war.'

'Henry King?'

'Now you're talkin'. He's agreed to fill-in direct until there's a full-timer. He'll be glad to take Assist Dir credit. Sweet guy.'

'Always gracious. Strong. Principled. Mentorian.'

'Check. One of nature's true noblemen. And never any trouble.'

'Well, that's a step in the right direction. I can rest easy now.'

'You already appeared to *be* in that particular state of mind. Or is 'satisfied' more accurate?'

'Rest! It is *rest* that I'll take, just at hand!'

'Not right now, sport. Get in the lav and snap out of love-mode. We're flying out tonight.'

'Er, hokay. Locations?'

'You got it.'

'You mean, you're not contesting my recommendation – nixing Texas?'

'Affirmative.'

'I am gratified, Sonny.'

'I thought you would be.'

'And, uh…,' the star asked, somewhat morosely, 'the skies?'

'Ah yes, the skies. They must match!'

'And does the mismatch do us in?'

'I could string you along with a mock entertainment pal, but we haven't time. A match was found. Perhaps better than over these sickening tracts right outside your very own door, here. Over in the East, on past Suez, in an unknown and forgotten land. Well sir, our location has been found!'

'Sonny! Exciting news! Transcendent!'

'Discovered by none other than Charlie Clarke and his wandering camera crew. He's already got one week of tests in the can.'

'Good old Charlie!'

'He gets a gold star.'

'To say the least. Knighthood, I'd say! Very well, time to pack now. Mayella, too?'

'Mayella, too. You'll need her.'

And the agent winked.

Bronze light, from the east, rose like a warning chorus, vocalizing so as to lift a curtain, revealing a spectacle of high altitude architecture, highest in the world. A rolled needle, its cylinders rising to nearly Frank Lloyd Wright's Mile-High Skyscraper elevation, stood in reflective and curved verticality before them. A constructed thorn, to prick the lofty air over an already over-skyscraped city. Air on a level never touched by human hands, nor their ground-based creations directly, was now accessible. Dreamlike flying, without encumbrance of fuely machine, was surely possible, even probable.

'*Anything* is possible in Burj Khalifa!'

Rare, rare was the atmosphere here. So much so, Butterbugs could only think of his death-defying dive from the belly of the jet, that time. And all for a picture show.

Today, he was on top of the man-made world, occupying the climactic Apex Suite of the Burj Khalifa itself. Where things were probable.

Baked was the dun air, as if in heated barns, with particulate metallic effect, causing extreme sun-drama, at both rise and set.

It wasn't exactly his turf.

'I am *certainly* a stranger here,' he mused as he walked the perimeter of floor-to-ceiling PerroPlastic windows that lined the entire circumference of this top-most-turret chamber of extreme luxury.

Philip Johnson might have designed it! A Pierre Koenig Case Study in the Arab/Gulfene sky! (his Æyrie associations did make him feel somewhat at home). Halliburton might have bankrolled it! After all, they were a neighbor around here somewhere. Dubai the Spectacular had more villains per square meter than France had ever harbored.

Ugh.

No, wait...

In fact, it was Skidmore, Owings & Merrill who were responsible for the pile. Barcelona chairs were at key positions, and Kimco+Kimcorp, a Korean consortium tied to Malagasy interests, actually forked over the lettuce-leaves to get this pad erected. Peace in the international valley, as it were.

'Let's not go into the '*why*' while we're here, Butterbugs.'

Mayella's entreaty made sense. Why shouldn't they marvel at their environs just a little bit?

'I agree,' replied Butterbugs.

It was just that he felt like he was in a *real* lazaretto of sorts, but one of sterile, elite, and remote character.

'This is a way station, Butterbugs. A rather significant one. But the moment is momentous. Tonight we get our ongoing instructions. Tonight we meet – our director.'

'True! This is as good a place as any. Might not be so bad after all. Good, fresh, contemporary design, too. Tonight... tonight...'

He gazed down at the mega-city-state coming to life in the already 130F-degree heat, and beheld a vast dust storm approaching from the west. In the Rub' al Khali was it born, and massive enough to stretch from Muscat all the way up to the Neutral Zones.

'Behold, the spreading sand of the numerous ages! See how it redistributes itself! It survives by expansion; a colonial effort, domineering and commanding, and we in its pathway, tremble.'

'This building is hell-for-stout, Butterbugs.'

'That was an interesting picture to make.'

"Hell For Stout' (20th-Fox) certainly was! There was no height you did not take on, no ledge too narrow, no perch shunned! You were heroic in your willingness to take chances, just so the shot would be perfect. Safety last! You are the Torch of the Industry – a light to be followed.'

'Only, this building...'

'You're uncertain? It is verily strong!'

'Like that of Isaac Davis?'

Mayella knew of his epic role in that tragedy.

'Oh, but we shall weather it! Together!'

She cuddled him as the Cinerama spectacle advanced to envelope their A/C-soothed vantage point. She presented a Voix de la Quexaire mimosa to him, followed by a finger-tray of Semmie's Buttered Tart Mints, fresh from the 121st Floor boutiques, and he was won over.

'It's going to be a great show!' he enthused, after they kissed romantically.

They lolled on fake cubskin rugs (the very best) and could not even hear the nuggets of æolian-projected desert pummel the ÆliusWax-protected sheath of the Burj, just decimeters away.

'It always *has* been!' she replied. '*You* are the great show! We are always in the midst of it.'

'You know, Maymyo, I do indeed appreciate the certain touches of quality that strolling playing has brought about. I do! I tell you, I do! Like this moment. Who would think that a humanoid could even endure the marvels of this very reality right here, right now, without a smidgeon of introspection as to the worthiness of its participants?'

The surge of specks was creating a baroque light show of multi-hued graininess without, like a huge presentation of scratchy sepia-toned leader film, but without numbers counting down.

Mayella, that rare combo of Israeli/Palestinian/Polish heritage, nevertheless found it normal to manage her tripartite Abrahamic background as an instrument of peace, especially whilst in the region. Personally, she could hardly wait until there were more such meldings of culture, for she knew countless others were in the making, even as she thought on the subject.

'Oh Butterbugs, no introspection is necessary. Nature and its – or her – perpetual motion is larger than the largest screen process. Bigger than the most comprehensive DeMille picture. Grander than even Sawl Cane's 'Unholy War Hymn'!'

'Girl, you liberate me,' Butterbugs said quietly, and they both kissed with their eyes open so that they wouldn't miss a second of the storm.

The intensity increased, and kept increasing. Butterbugs looked at the Wind Speed Readout at the Unit Control Centre in the Main Kitchen on the Suite's second floor.

'212 km/h!' he reported back to Mayella, who seemed thrilled.

'Zowie!' she hooted.

'I don't know, May-bee, I think there's a moment of truth ahead, because –'

Suddenly a synthesized blare pierced the air, and red neon strips in the coving all around the suite started flashing. Reader-bars, formerly invisible or camouflaged into the décor, proceeded to spell out: EXTREME WARNING: EVACUATE ENTIRE SUPERSTRUCTURE ABOVE GROUND AT ONCE. NO EXCEPTIONS. THIS IS NOT A DRILL. OBEY ATTENDER AND CONDUCTOR TEAMS, *NOW EN ROUTE* TO YOUR LOCATION. EXTREME WARNING! EVACUATION PROCEDURE NOW BEING ENACTED. EXTREME WARNING! in fourteen different languages, with companion narration (voiced by rotating celebrities; the Burj's management was set to approach Butterbugs for a contribution before his stay ended), broadcast between blares.

'Kind of like the 'Horror Horn' and the 'Fear Flasher' in Bill Castle's 'Chamber of Horrors' (WB, 1966), isn't it?' the well-schooled ultrastar commented, as his mate was frantically packing survival kits.

A crack team of Attenders and Conductors appeared with Staff to ensure the VIPs' safe evacuation from the Main and Highest Stem, the inhabitants of which enjoyed a straight-through shaft to the very bottom of the colossus, with instant access to the Redoubt Bunker, which spread subterraneously off into the body of the Arabian Peninsula, well past the complex's Fall Zone. Getting there was a piece of cake, with driverless express trains, designed to outrun the fastest-falling Burj, leaving every fifteen seconds.

Within five minutes, the ultrastar and party were in that very sanctuary, surrounded by as much luxury as at the Apex. Maybe more. Their privacy was intact.

'You thought of everything,' said Mayella to one of the Conductors as she settled into an Irv Lomoani love-seat.

'We aim to be *first* quality, ma'am,' he replied.

'Excuse me, boy, but where are you from?'

'Nairobi, ma'am. Isn't everybody?'

Butterbugs chuckled.

'Ah, the typical Nairobian greeting!'

'I am Conductor Ukaiji. I am a big fan of yours, Mr. Butterbugs.'

'Why thank you, Mr. Conductor. And thank you for saving our lives.'

'My turbo-pleasure, sir. I so enjoyed your portrayal of Kenyatta in the picture, 'Jomo' (MUZ Studios), in recent times.'

'Thanks! It was an inspiring role. We filmed all over Keenya that month. My favorite location was Nujumbah.'

'My hometown! My grandsire runs the Imperialists' Hotel there.'

'Where I stayed! Is he Kettikut Ukaiji?'

'The same, sir! He is the very man!'

'Excellent. His resources were invaluable. His name is in the credits, you know. One whole title card!'

'I did not know! I will seek it out in the credit crawl.'

'Would you join us for eine tasse iced coffee?' asked Mayella.

'I acknowledge your gracious invitation with thanks, ma'am, but I am on-shift and others need conducting and organizing.'

'Of course, please, don't let us keep you.'

'Jolly good, Conductor,' said Butterbugs. 'Here's my card. We can use you in the main production unit of 'UWH', if you can manage a leave of absence. Interested?'

'In *the* 'UWH'?'

Conductor Ukaiji was aghast, but with joy.

'The same. We're moving into it with vigah. Contact Mega|Goth, collect, with my compliments. I'll set it up.'

'I will, sir.'

'Good. We need *first quality* personnel.'

'In me you already have it, sir. A note before I depart. You will see the chartreuse RETURN notice flash in place of the EVACUATE warning, when the coast is clear. You may wait for our escort service or, because you are young fit folks who might not want to be fussed over, just through yon double door is a Staff's Own Shortcut back to the Third Orbit Access Hub, from which you may embark on any Electronic Express Rickshaw to take you on in. Simple. Safe. Fast.'

'Hail, Conductor Ukaiji, and thanks!'

The Kenyan saluted with civil obedience and went to help the Bathchair and Seniors Crew further on down the line.

Pressing a button on the VIP Lounge Entertainer remote, the couple witnessed the Burj's current ordeal as presented on a humungous flatscreen, photo-captured from the adjacent (and less storm-beaten) Burj Dirham. The mad fury of the sketchy sand in full storm still hogged the view, though after about twenty minutes, actual thinning could be detected.

'I wonder,' said Butterbugs gravely, 'if we shall see a ruin where once we kissed, far aloft?'

'No one can say,' replied Mayella anxiously. But, remembering the intimacy of the kiss, she smiled and winked.

Then, as more occlusions whirled around in the diminishing frenzy, the grandeur of terror was replaced by the grandeur of triumph. Thus stood the Burj, revealed. It was intact! Just then, a shaft of sunlight, free now to travel via a passage through the devilish dust, slanted onto the entire structure, proving its hyper-polished surface was indeed totally unscathed.

Pre-programmed into the emergency procedures coverage was a specially commissioned fanfare and triumphant tone poem by Jerry Goldsmith, which played as the Burj emerged. The effect was electrifying. All who saw it were properly in awe. And the sand continued to retreat, into amorphous defeat.

'Say, I'll have to give Jere a call,' Butterbugs said admiringly. 'That would be cool if he could use a few of those leitmotifs in a future score...'

'He never likes to repeat himself, ya know, Butter-guy,' replied Mayella.

'OK, OK, I know... Boy, the whole dust-mess looks like the locust plague in 'The Good Earth' (MGM, 1937), only in reverse.'

'But on a much bigger scale.'

'Now I don't know about *that*. You see, those clouds of locusts in Anhui Province can get so huge that –'

At that very second, the RETURN / HEARTIEST OF WELCOMES BACK TO THE BURJ'S WONDERS! notice started flashing everywhere, accompanied by audio confirmation, voiced by trusted Walter Cronkite and Norman Rose, live from New York, indicating the Burj was entirely safe for re-occupation. In addition, special Announcements of Reassurance proclaimed all personal goods were safe and intact. In this, its first real trial, the Auto UpLock System throughout the entire complex succeeded brilliantly in its executions, as it was always activated in the event of any Evacuation. If conditions required, the system could only be unlocked by each occupant giving Breath Recognition at the Welcome Centre at every entrance to each private residence or hotel suite. Happily, no such conditions today.

'Short cut?' Mayella proposed.

'Short cut!' replied the ultrastar.

It was with some regret that they decamped, as they had actually been quite happy in the Evacuata Zone. Plus, a bit of important business had been accomplished with the virtual recruitment of Conductor Ukaiji for 'UWH''s Elite Production Unit.

'I didn't want to freak him out by telling him how *totally elite* the Unit is. I think he could really humanize it, as that's what I have in mind for him.'

'I'm sure he will perform with aplomb,' Mayella said. She found him a most attractive fellow.

The 'short cut' was actually an immensely long corridor, probably a half-kilometer in toto, consisting of interlinked pre-cast concrete caissons, and lighted by sickly fluorescence, at surprisingly sparse frequencies. It was the only non-adorned environment in the entire complex, probably because it was brand new, and plans to make it barely palatable were still incomplete.

At any rate, they made their way along without any problem.

Three quarters of the way through, they were startled by the jarring, echoey noise of a double-access door opening, and a person entered, almost colliding with their brisk progression.

Mayella, who was in 'business' mode, and tended to be somewhat abrupt in her responses, could not but help blurting out:

'Why *you...!!*'

The door slammed shut. The echoes died and all was silence, except for the hum of the nickel-shiny tubelight's transformer, above. It seemed deafening, but then the face of the intruder, at once arresting, yet so serene as a South Indian sannyasi's, made the upheld interval transcendent somehow.

All three were in suspension.

'I saw you... once,' said the actor, almost absently.

'And I you,' the director – for he was indeed a director – replied.

Another pause of indeterminate length.

'Excuse us,' Mayella finally said. 'We must be bustling along. Forgive this intrusion to... or, on... your solitude.'

Butterbugs silently thought this an acceptable exit strategy. So without settling whether each of them actually had seen each other before, or even mentioning the late emergency, each party proceeded in detached manner, though headed in the same direction. Near the end of the corridor, Butterbugs looked back, and the other person, the director (unbeknownst to him) was far back, under a tubelight, advancing, but almost in slow motion. He wondered if the man was indeed capable of... samadhi...

Now, at sunset, the skies had cleared, absolutely cleared, so that the clean recessive rainbow of the entirely hopeful sunset made the resolve of the day conclusively glorious. The layers were like one of those showpiece chemical cocktails, where bars of color stay in place, based on weight, for us to marvel at, even though marveling (in an un-drugged stasis) was far out of style.

The couple had marveled several times how swiftly everything and every person in the Burj had returned to normal. For a mere five hours, all had been in flux. But now, in the evening hour, all was as if in the midst of the Venetian lagoon in the days of the Serenissima.

The door gong rang. Butterbugs, eschewing the live-in butler Billpopff, answered it himself, in person. There was Sonny, and with him, Associate Assistant Producer Kennedy Kitchen, awaiting entrance.

'Heard about your trek all the way down,' were Sonny's first words. 'We just got in. Circled over Bushire until the winds cleared. This burg's grown. This Burj, too. Heh-heh. No one hurt in the scramble, I trust?'

'No –'

'Kend Kitch's along on this one. With studio directness, concerning decisions. Key decisions. Nigh.'

'Welcome, Kennedy! It's been ten pictures or more, since. Glad you're in, K.K!'

'You know it! Say… This is an exalted place, Butterbugs!'

Kennedy was plainly excited to be here.

'Yes, I guess it's closer to heaven than most human-made platforms.'

'Drinks now, baby. For thirsty travelers!'

Sonny could be a bit pushy when stakes were obviously high, and not just in altitude. He could also be somewhat boorish, even rude, as far as social protocol was concerned.

Though the two entered the Apex Suite, a third person remained in the outer hallway, and he stood directly under the light-emitting diodes in the can overhead. He would have gone entirely unnoticed had Butterbugs not seen his plain, guest-like presence through the peephole as he closed the portal. After Sonny and Kennedy went gallivanting in to the bar, Butterbugs slowly re-opened the door, not sure if the hallway presence was in fact a servant in waiting, or just an aberration of evacuation-memory.

The flameproof door swung open, and there, now in the lesser light of the threshold, a vision presented itself to the actor, as connectable as any iconic face, based on previous viewings, no matter how brief. Mystic but not exotic, powerful but peaceful, unconventional but preferable, attractive but not cloying, a face from many different directions was there, framed by wavy oiled locks to the shoulder, eyes downcast in an obeisance of impending hospitality, hands joined in the western-prayer/eastern-namaste greeting, shirt untucked, feet bare, but integrity clearly purposeful. This person, this straggler, begged acceptance and access at this high elevation, based on those who had come and gone in before.

It was not that he could be anything but authorized to reach such a rarefied point, especially at this great height and this restricted an access. Yet, he was significantly unknown.

Deeper, there were recognized linkings. That time, just a while ago, downstairs, so far down, just under Earth's surface. And one thing more. That time, in the 'Long March' corridor, when he was covered with Teeny Topper's slobber, so long ago.

'You!' exclaimed Butterbugs. 'It is… *you!* I *thought* I had a feeling about you!'

'And I you,' the fellow humanoid said, in a line spoken with cinematic comprehension.

'Do come in. You are with Sonny and Kennedy?'

'I follow them, but I am not necessarily *of* them. Please consult them for my credentials.'

'I'd rather get them from you, yourself.'

Butterbugs heard the others greeting Mayella in the far background. They were loud, even boisterous.

'So, present your mission, if it please you.'

'Well, I'm being considered… to direct.'

'To direct. 'UWH'?'

No answer was immediately forthcoming. Instead:

'Perhaps you will find me discombobulating,' the third one said, 'For I am based on a tri-continental gathering of mutually interested parties. I am part Portuguese, part Moçambiquan, part Timorean, part Angolan, part Macauan, part Goan, part Damanian, and part Diuian – which makes the Indian influence the most prevalent in my DNA display gallery. That is why I greet you with Indic signs, as they are closest to my soul – which is a signal example of colonial unification, amidst perceived disarray. I am its living proof. You may ask me to leave at this instant, and I will not contest you.'

'Did you not hear?' asked Butterbugs in wonder, 'I had a *feeling* about you!'

'I link, because I know exactly of what you speak, Butterbugs. We go way back, I think.'

'I think so, too. And not just earlier today. Come in, connected one.'

'I am grateful. This is a swingin' pad!'

'You think so? I suppose it is. It's very high up.'

'The highest! Levels are transitory, but in the time and the place, they should be appreciated.'

'You know, I suppose you have a point there.'

'There are also different levels to the most level of planes.'

'I agree! Come in, come in and make yourself to home. Sonny and Kennedy brought you.'

'Indeed. I am no deceiver.'

'Then, what are you?'

'A candidate for directing 'UWH'. As I said.'

At that moment, Butterbugs almost hit the deck out of amazement. But he didn't.

'As... principal director?'

'Yes. To helm the whole shootin' match.'

'Well now, that's a tall order. I suppose you should be subject for review.'

'Thus, my humbleness.'

'That's appropriate, for such a Herculean task.'

'I endeavor.'

'Friend, enter, refresh yourself via any source of preference. Bars on all floors. You may bathe in facilities on floors Two and Four of this here five-story mega-suite.'

'You're obviously not showing off what you have here.'

'I'm not! I'm as much a guest here as you are. Perhaps more so.'

'I can see why. Amidst the wonders are always the letters that spell out 'WHY'. And a question mark, too.'

'You make a reasonable point, though there is no true existentialist twist at the bottom of my presentation to you as host. Rather, this is a mere way station between pictures.'

'I follow you. For me, I hope it is a launching pad.'

'It is certainly *high* enough!'

'But my question is, is it advantageously-placed?'

'As many questions as stories in this pile! Pray, friend, refresh yourself now, whilst I see to my other guests. Wander at will.'

'Many thanks, sir.'

'Call me Butterbugs.'

'Butterbugs!'

Sonny, Mayella, and Kennedy were whooping it up on the Apex Against The Sky Terrace, which, thrillingly, had access to the Uppermost Slopes of the Needle. There were plentiful oxygen masks for those who caught the dizzio, and all could enjoy the protection of a special air-vacuum return system that ensured safe delivery of inebriated persons who might teeter over the edge. Though the direct drop was only 279 meters, careless partyers would surely mend their ways after a lesson-learning, sobriety-inducing trip to the cubic meters just shy of splatterment. In no way was it an amusement ride.

Butterbugs made his way to the dimmer quarters of his five-story Eden container, to see where this director-apparent had wandered off.

'Perhaps he is suffering from intimidation,' Butterbugs thought, 'And indeed, lies despondent somewhere.'

He knew a first time director, given the promise of a weighty assignment, could easily go wobbly under the multifarious tonnage of both expectations and promissory bravado.

'May I call you – what?' Butterbugs asked with uncharacteristic bluntness.

He located the guest in a salon centered around an immense fish tank, stocked with mini-sharks and jullundur-tench. They glowed fluorescently as the sophisticate lamps of greater Dubai and the Emirates-at-large glowed out the vistarama windows,

'Egaz would be fine. For I am Egaz D'Varzim.'

Butterbugs expected to know the name and respond to it with formality, but he didn't recognize it.

'Very well, Egaz. Well, let's face it, we're all at a high level here.'

'Much at stake?'

'I suppose so, though I never think in those terms.'

'Producers' terms! Not those of performing artist and directing artist.'

'A cultural divide?'

'I don't think so, no. I don't mean to create any divides. I wish to bridge them.'

'No walls set up by terminology.'

'Not at all. I hate that sort of thing.'

'As do I.'

'I'm just struck at the encounters we've had.'

'Two of them, right?' Butterbugs had to think.

'Yes. Two. I'm sure that's all there were. And now, three.'

'Indeed. And in such obscure places, cloaked in anonymity.'

'Yet, amounting to something.'

'I hope so.'

'Take our environment here.'

'Yes, we could not have walked in from the street.'

'But I did!'

'With support.'

'That's true. An overview always brings with it advantage.'

'A necessity for directing a picture.'

'And necessary for showing others the way.'

'Like actors.'

'And tech side.' Egaz was showing a thoroughness.

'Why of course. How quickly we actors forget.'

'An overview, like, out there.'

'We have only to approach the window glass and gaze out in any direction, as if from the clouds.'

'It's a view from which a god could make decisions,' said Egaz. 'A fairly powerful god, too.'

'You know, I think you've just articulated what I myself was thinking the first moment I gazed down there. A position of power.'

'And judgment. Consequences result from an overview.'

'I agree.'

'The camera always lies.'

'How could it not, when what it captures is so crafted?'

'Lies are not the worst thing in the world.'

'Especially when they are devoted to dramatic purposes.'

'Artifice is real.'

'Always has been. Always must be.'

'Creation is artifice.'

'Entirely appropriate. Why do we not accept that fact?'

'Glad to meet you – finally, and properly – Butterbugs!'

'Oh yes! And I you, Egaz!'

After all the others had slithered off to their repose, Egaz and Butterbugs sat attentively in their Barcelona chairs next the big god-view below. They supped on marinated mullet plugs and jeremiah-weed punch, with a goat-brain powder dip from the Hejaz, as accent to the Arabia Felix olive cones that Staff proffered upon them.

'I have to tell you, Butterbugs, I've followed your career for some time.'

Butterbugs didn't mean to snort, but he did. He couldn't help himself, he really couldn't. But hell, much of the world had followed his career at this point.

Notwithstanding this, all he did was snort, which could be interpreted as a compliment for the Bedouin fare they were sampling, so Egaz did not get the wrong idea.

'Oh, yes? Have you now?'

'To be sure. For one thing, I knew that when I saw you at the Teeny Topper gig, which I worked as a techie, you were the one for my 'I Wanna Marry A Chimp Cage Cleaner' (20th-Fox).'

'But that was a Richard Fleischer production, with Elmo Williams, associate.'

'That's how it turned out, but 'Chimp Cage Cleaner' was my baby from the start. From my mind was it born, and in the process, because of my inexperience, I was sidelined, then ejected outright from any and all aspects of the picture. Contractually, I got screwed. I don't want to go into all that here with you, especially at this magnificent viewpoint, and with me on the rumored verge of directing 'UWH', and all. I just wanted you to know of my dedication to your acting persona, which dates from before the world discovered you.'

'Well I'll be dahned,' marveled Butterbugs. 'I had no idea of the ramifications.'

'How could you? But I, I never forgot. And so I persisted, prepping a high concept to 'UWH''s producers, and to Sonny.'

He paused.

'Sonny! Who really listened to me.'

Butterbugs wondered if there wasn't something extraordinary about this Indo-Afro-Sino-Malayo-Porto octoroon, something of the Invisible Universe, where energy fields and wavelengths streaked and did good work, all the livelong day, whilst we in this current dimension lived out our lives in muddy potholes.

'But tell me, Egaz, you mean, you are not signed on yet?'

'Absolutely not. I'm strictly on trial. A host of biggies could squash me like a rame-bug on a knife blade's edge.'

'Sounds messy.'

'That's why I use the analogy. If sliced in half, I'd spill everywhere.'

Butterbugs laughed. 'I tell you what. You say you've brought a short film with you. Might I see it now? In private?'

'Assuredly. Here is the disk. Please play it at your leisure whilst I meditate under the hornéd moon for twenty-three minutes.'

'The short's duration?'

'Yeah.'

'Sounds just plain *good*.'

So the young director retired to the Star Plane balcony whilst the young actor watched Egaz D'Varzim's short, 'Kay Kwuff Kwig Seffah' (Lemon International).

Six minutes into it, Butterbugs knew that Egaz was the one and only person, mind, and soul to direct 'UWH'. It was just that simple. He knew also that Sonny and Kennedy and all the other producers had already arrived at the same conclusion. That's why he was here, in tow, well behind Sonny and Kennedy, waiting in the hallway. It was all out of respect for Butterbugs, because others thought the ultrastar had to be approached on soft cat feet over this matter.

Call it shaky vibes, but in point of fact, it was Butterbugs himself who had always felt Egaz was the one, *though he knew it not*. Not until just now. Subliminal mind-texts pick up on connections, no matter how obscure, no matter how disjointed in time. Two brushes with Egaz in the past, in passing, had proved nothing but contact points. But they were points of ignition toward an encounter where sense and consciousness met, and as it happened, everything computed into the most cogent slots. All was understood now.

Butterbugs was fulfilled by these jujus, and put great credence in them.

'I'm glad you've signed, Egaz!' said the ultrastar, as the contract dried. 'The others will witness it in the morning. Besides, it's all been video'd.'

'I know. I directed it.'

They guffawed.

'That's a good day's work,' sighed Butterbugs.

'Indeed. May we kick back?'

'Be my guest, director.'

They enjoyed the sophisticated nighttime panorama.

'I also want to tell you something shocking, Butterbugs. And I hope it will not trash your thoughts of me.'

'Shoot.'

'As you know, I am of mixed race from several different networked colonial vestiges. That makes me rich in associations.'

'Agreed, agreed!'

Butterbugs was fascinated with Egaz's diversity, and wanted to hear more.

'I too, am a mutt, though not so determinate!'

'Well, one tack I've decided to take on this picture is, in my direction of it, to evince a certain limitation regarding English-language performance in my directorial – er – direction.'

'I'm not sure I follow you, old boy.'

'Uh, taking my cue from Mike Curtiz, and some of the other pantheon directors, I think that if I minimize my elucidation while directing and maximize my passion, or my instinct, I think I can get more out of my actors. In fact, I *know* I can.'

'So, what will you use, Butler English, or 'pidgin'?'

'Well, first off, I'm glad you understand. That is, you have offered up two options rather than razzing me over this idea.'

'Capt. Gill calls Pigeon English, 'A grotesque gibberish which would be laughable if it were not almost melancholy'. Is that the sort of thing you shall be engaging?'

'I just didn't want to shock you if, on set, I engaged in a sort of baby talk –'

'My dear fellow, I am at least experienced enough to know that lack of language can certainly be key in great direction. I worked for Tuzuzuki Michichizi in 'Urekii Fujujinku' (Toho) for the better part of a season, without one word of English or Japanese between us, and I think we achieved, well – something.'

'Urekii Fujujinku' is a masterwork, Butterbugs. I honor you and Michichizi like no others!'

'So, what have you in mind?'

'Well, I thought I would direct in *stunted* English, so that a certain edge of understanding might prove effective to my actors.'

'I think you're on to something, Egaz. I support you, and entirely in private.'

'Thankest thou, Butterbugs! Thanks for believing in me.'

'I won't tell a soul. I do hope, however, that the results will not be comical, except when it's needed.'

'Well, I'm not big in the standup department, but there will undoubtedly be some gaffes.'

'This is a great moment, Egaz.'

'That I know, Butterbugs.'

'Cheers, then. To this vast undertaking.'

'Cheers. May it not *take us under!*'

39.

Life In Jambutterbugsabad

'This is *it!*' enthused Butterbugs, once he was out of the way of the chopper.

The previous week had been full of 'This is not it!', 'This is NOT it!', 'This is not IT!' 'This is NOT IT!', and especially, 'THIS IS *NOT IT!!!*' and on and on. It was because, even though they were deep in the Makran, it wasn't until they got into the deep, *deep* Makran that the locations started to get promising. Then, up the Kurr Valley, just 60 km north of Butterbugs' old stomping ground of Gwadar, a whole succession of ideal setups presented themselves. Butterbugs, Sawl, Egaz, Bob (Surtees), and Mayella were ecstatic.

'Better than Khwhy itself!' whispered Sawl, stunned, as they strolled amongst the formidable rock formations under skies that could only be called Khan's Weather, for they outdid Jash County in WesTex by a country mile.

'If we had only known this before we blew all that money on Texas,' said Porter Parker, just arrived.

Egaz took Porter aside.

'Butterbugs knew – when all of us doubted.'

'But he didn't know *where,* specifically, ya know.'

'Not overtly, but below the surface, I know he knew. He revealed, on the chopper lift as we were coming here, that he'd had a dream of great clarity in the Burj Khalifa. He dreamt that remarkable things would happen *west of Las Bela*, in Baluchistan – Only, only in Baluchistan. Now, naturally I wondered about the veracity of such a statement, until I found that, despite his previous visits to the region for various photoplays, he did not in fact have any association with Las Bela District, or Bela town. In this visionary dream, he even pledged to make a respectful offering at Sandeman Sahib's tomb in the latter locale, perhaps during a hiatus in shooting. That was proof to me, there is some extraordinary connection Butterbugs has with the locations of this picture.'

'I honor your observations, D'V. My mind's wide open – especially when it comes to things Butterbugsian. An ultrastar apparently has powers of consciousness that we producers – and directors – do not possess or even comprehend.'

'The faith factor…'

'It's tempting to get all religious-y and apply messianic tackiness to our ultrastar, but I think I'll give that line of thought a miss, Mr. Director.'

'I was talking about faith in his instincts.'

'Yeah, well, I've got that kind of faith, for sure. With this mega-budget, I jolly well should have, pal. Super-secret powers beyond that, I ain't got.'

'Speak for yourself, Parker.'

'I just did.'

'Well, just before, you said 'we producers and directors'. My record stands clear. I have elucidated it through numerous personal entries. I have had feelings about Butterbugs for the longest time.'

'You mean, you're in *love* with him, or something?'

'Ha! Leave it to Hollywood minds on the surface, the prurient surface, who think only with their dicks! No, there is no association with sexuality in my regard for Butterbugs. I speak simply as an artist who connects with a fellow artist on a plane others do not comprehend. Closeness – intimacy – on such terms, are usually assumed to be on a perverse level. How come I have to explain this to you?'

'Actually, you don't,' replied Porter. 'You wouldn't believe how I have matured as a person – because of Butterbugs. I agree to all the metes and bounds when it comes to the ultrastar I serve. I hope others who serve him feel the same way, newcomer.'

'I'm glad you understand. It's just that, as his director on this picture, I must achieve an intimacy that *rivals* a sexual relationship. Ours must not be sexual, but sensual. For the Seventh Art is nothing but feeling.'

'As long as you maintain those standards, Egaz, I will produce what you do.'

'You are accepted into my intimate circle, friend and producer. I'm glad you're on the line with me. And with Butterbugs.'

'I hope it's not a firing line.'

Butterbugs went away from the chopper and the landing pad, and the present signs of humanity. He went out into the realm of ancient nature. Here was a land that was harsh with difficulty – an environment, even though it was largely unknown, that had minded its own business for these many millennia and had been of little consequence to the larger world.

Never mind that the bones of some Macedonians had mingled with the grains of the plains beneath the escarpments hereabouts. History, especially involving superstars such as Alex LeGrande, meant little in the here and now. The important thing was that the land endured, no matter the drama played upon its surface, no matter how rarely.

It was this respect that Egaz the director knew, and Butterbugs the actor discovered, once he'd wandered past the barriers of expectation.

'Look at him striding away, with such purpose,' Egaz commented to Porter. 'Look at him and see how natural it is for him to be noble!'

Butterbugs went far afield, so that the dialogue between he and the natural setting became valid. It wasn't as if he sought permission as much as acceptance. One land would have to substitute for another, and was that OK? Because, this other land, which the Makran would have to play a role as, was inferior as far as economic status was concerned. So, was it OK with the land itself that it enact a role of dubious associations?

The ultrastar stood on a low pillar of flaséd lodestar, facing the interior. Nullahs crept uphill amidst waste-stone and bare patches of cribweed. Ochery-orange landforms stood against a profoundly blue atmosphere. Here was clean desolation, beautiful and intact. His voice flowed out in caresses to his audience.

'May I ask you, land, Makran that you are, a bald prospect? Might I take advantage, in the artistic sense, of your uncanny resemblance to a distant tract that your visage provides, a tract we dearly want to emulate, for the sake of this brief (in geological time) picture show, to utilize your remarkable characteristics and topographic personality, so that we might achieve something akin to relevance in the capturement of scenes, so as to promote credibility, while we tread your marches?'

Actually, this particular spot bore little resemblance to the once virgin lands of Khwhy, but Butterbugs' entreaty was to the region as a whole, which provided a diversity of orographical variance, with plateau and coastal plain in equal doses. (The only terrain lacking was riverain, but there was always the mighty Indus to the east...)

And the land replied:

'Most certainly! Do what you need to do. You have all the trust you can use. You understand. You will not abuse the opportunity. You have – carte blanche.'

The Jam of Kelat, who was naturally invited to participate, was nothing if not sanguine. So, because of his regional knowledge and authority, he was credited as Unit Production Manager and Associate Producer, as were most of the members of his cabinet, the Dewan, and affiliated figures. It was because they were invaluable in negotiating the realities of this somewhat forbidding land.

An entire city was constructed that served as The Complete and Utter Base of Operations Concerning Location Sites for 'UWH' (aka: TCUBOCLS'UWH'), that soon was officially dubbed Jambutterbugsabad because it was easier for everyone, both locals and foreigners, to pronounce.

[Application of any 'wood' suffix (e.g. Bollywood, et al) was strictly avoided, mainly to avoid silliness creeping into the preferred gravitas, and to keep the moniker in a class by itself. Butterbugs & Co. were even able to convince the 'Variety' muggs to eschew compressions of convenience, such as 'Jambad', 'Butterbad', 'Bugsybad', and other dubious mutations. 'J-bad' or 'J'bad' was permissible though, to keep telegrams and Quiverings brief. 'Jambutterbugsabad' was coined by Associate Art Director Aldobrandino Camposanto, who had just signed onto the picture. The eminent designer also had a PhD in Linguistics, and was a colleague of Noam Chomsky at MIT.]

A frontier town! Sergio Leone might have ordered it built! Carlo Simi might have seen it through!

But no western set, this town, for it was styled not on whiskey or spaghetti or curry. Instead, the Jam's government authorities intended to make a Dinocittà or Churubusco out of it, a permanent cinema-gunge, devoted to picture show production, way out here on the Makrani hardpan, and they drew upon multiple sources and resources to make the baby grow. Mega|Goth was delighted to go along, as was the whole growing 'UWH' mechanism.

And in the way that frontier folk saw development as a boon and not a curse, it came to be. And quickly, too. Its pukka nature ensured that a complete cantonment and Mall were laid out, with a Dalhousie Institute, a Lady Dufferin Hospital, and a Quaid-i-Azam Centre, amongst other necessities in the establishment of a community of consequence.

'We are proud that 'UWH' is to be shot within our auspices,' said Ulama Yusuf Malik Khan, the newly appointed *jirga*-meister, who became alcalde of the new town.

'I'm glad you appreciate our opportunism here,' said Butterbugs in all frankness. He really did relish going amongst those thespians, crew, maintenancers, extras, sooners, boomers, and wildcatters in the new town.

'You think you're taking advantage of us for your photoplay, no?' asked the Khan.

'Well, aren't we?' answered Butterbugs, in precise but over-enunciated Baluch.

'To your point of view, certainly.'

'In the corporate sense…'

'Agreed. Your conundrum of guilt.'

'It's true.'

'But, I tell you, to we in need, and I speak of the collective 'we' for those hereabouts, the establishment of this entrepôt and railhead (with Karachi) is just the ticket in creating an outpost of destiny in this here tract of relatively virgin territory.'

Butterbugs could see the alcalde's realism and its instant link with pragmatism and his own sense of opportunism. When things were seen in their actual terms, down on this level, *fuck* the corporate influence, because in the long run, everybody here would be on their own, sink or swim, after the Ultra-Panavision 70 cameras were safely home.

'Obviously, a regional center, somewhat inland, is needed,' Butterbugs rationalized.

'Very well,' said the Khan. 'You're looking past your 'evanescent' movie.'

'Bravo!' replied the ultrastar. 'But I also let out a cry so that the nature of this region can retain its own unique personality.'

'Butterbugs, I have highest regard for you and yours, but please believe me, Bahadur Burra Sahib! If I thought that *not* to be the case, you and your entire company would have been reduced to 'strawberry jam', as they say. Because, violations of our code of the land are not to be tolerated, even from guests. And even – from ultrastars.'

Then was Butterbugs glad, because he knew he was dealing with the sincere minds of the real inhabitants, and their principled protocol would not be altered, but its practitioners would obviously stand firm in all circumstances.

Thus did Butterbugs do the job of producers and lay out the basement foundations for a major motion picture to be realized. No one got in his way, or had their shoes busted, because Butterbugs was achieving things no one else could do.

'Leave the lad alone,' was all Old Atrocity said when Mayella first beheld the ultrastar's technique in negotiating with Industrial bigwigs over Mega|Goth responsibilities for Jambutterbugsabad.

'But he doesn't have to worry about that stuff. It's the Producer Team's job!'

'What the Producer Team realizes is purely practical. They're getting a great deal for doing virtually nothing in these respects. They know *they* don't have to worry about this 'local' stuff. Butterbugs is in a unique position. Unprecedented, really.'

'What he wants, he gets?'

'That's not it at all. Haven't you figured this out yet, Ms?'

'No. No, I haven't.' Mayella put on a catty expression. 'I want to *mold* him.'

'You want to mold him, huh?'

'For his own good, Old A! He's so childlike. So vulnerable.'

'That's what I thought once. Not the child bit, but the vulnerability.'

'See? My instincts are right-on!'

'Not yet they aren't. Even though you two are swapping bodily fluids, you don't know him yet. Vulnerable he isn't. I'd use the word 'invincible', just between you and me.'

'Really?'

'You sound very naïve, my child.'

'Well, I'm not. You see, he never puts on acts.'

'Or airs. How's *that* for an ultrastar?'

Mayella grew serene. 'He is a star, all right. And he burns clean…'

As sets were built and tracks were laid and full-blown sound stages rose into the arid but clear air, the designed town known as Jambutterbugsabad came into existence with dispatch. Happily, the face of it was in a Victorian mold, as spares were culled from a multitude of Raj Era creations, such as Jacobabad, Quetta, Jamshedpur, Simla and Murree, as well as the Coronation Durbar site in Delhi. Under the brilliant eyes of designers like Colasanti & Moore, Camposanto, and Razah Ulamshah, a period coherence was achieved. And pretty cheaply, too. They came up with an astonishing supply of mint-condition articles, such as lampposts, gateways, Larymore boilers, pilasters, staircases, bandstands, fountains, barge-boards, building stone, bridges, furnitures, and even a complete, unbuilt railway station, with cast iron platform sheds, built to take a four-foot snow load, with unused electric punkahs. The whole station-kit had lain in a Karachi godown since 1906. Perfectly useful blueprints of essential buildings from the same period, tracked down in dusty archives from Dera Ghazi Khan to Dehra-on-Sone, could now be built and utilized with an attention to detail that would be lasting. This thematic approach also spoke of a seriousness of intent, to make this Makran ins-ta-town a worthwhile player in intercontinental motion picture production, while at the same time providing for an attractive and historically-familiar regional cen-ter and its amenities.

Taking up the most amount of space in the back lot north of town was the site for what would become the largest outdoor set in the world: the pleasure-dome high-rise of the High Mad Doctor. The priority was high, as it would have to be ready for when the climax sequence was to be filmed, still some time out, yet. It would take many suns to build, and would have to be more than worthy, which the designers, Richard Day and Sayvie Mooharram, pledged it would be.

On the eve of the first day of location shooting, Butterbugs strolled the streets of the new garden city with Yusuf Malik Khan.

'I especially like the finishing work on this approach to the choultry,' comment-ed Butterbugs.

'I, too, have noticed its quality. My team and I have noticed all details. I hope not obsessively. But if the finishing work is poor, so will the whole town be poor in body and spirit.'

'O great Khan, you have achieved much, and in such an abbreviated time. I will do everything I can to encourage and even commission cinematic creation and production in this place. It's a blessed spot! I must say, I am a bit wistful at seeing this town come out of the wilderness. You have not ruined anything. In-deed, I know the land itself, upon which it sits, is a willing host. I talk to this land, every day, and in Baluch as well as my native tongue. I am confident, that is why I endorse your enterprise, so closely coupled with my own.'

'We cannot thank you enough, Butterbugs. For all you have done.'

'I have done little,' replied the actor. 'Except to participate in a transient enter-prise. You have gleaned concretions from it, and they will live on in stone and iron and wood. My contribution is a mere will o' the wisp – gone with the wind. And I am not referring to Margaret Mitchell's tale of the Old South…'

40.

The Cast

'**E**veryone Who's Ever Been Anyone Is In It!' ran the tagline.

Saul and Elaine Bass were working feverishly on their most ingenious title sequence yet, as well as the extensive poster series and associated appearance themes. These and other identifying appliances would actually be released as short 'teaser' films in themselves. They would also be vital elements in the projected Director's Completely and Utterly Final Cut Package.

'UWH''s cast and crew were the most international ever to grace an international cinemashow production. Ever. Not in the 'global' sense, but rather with an 'All of humanity'-type inclusion, the kind FDR had spoken so passionately of at the opening of the 1939 World of Tomorrow Exposition in New York.

Hyman Goth inherently opposed this 'liberal' approach, but crack-coke-pleasure kept him singularly occupied just now, even though the greatest film of his studio was now in highest production.

Stuart Curtain chafed, but was chained to his role as Supplier to the ingenious mogul. He couldn't quite bring himself to ring up Butterbugs and confess, for whom else could he turn to? So he turned to no one.

But what a cast! And here they are, in order of appearance:

Richard Wilson was in it, as were Tufariu Tumatana Haamoeura, Richard Briers, Robert Hardy, Jesslyn Fax, Michael Dunn, Thelma Ritter, Yana Jabberjee, Drave Appleyard, Kathleen 'Mrs. Hardtack' Freeman, Jay-Z, Richard Widmark, Sir David 'Frostie' Frost, Greta Scacchi, Bobs Watson, I.S. Johar, Anna May Wong, Mantan Moreland, Gene Palma, Camilla Sparv, Murray Melvin, Burt Mustin, Beah Richards, Godfrey Quigley, Samm-Art Williams, Michael Douglas, Kirk Douglas, John Hoyt, Khigh Deigh, Hank Worden, Mickey Rooney, José Greco, Emmanuel Lewis, Sergei Bondarchuk, Moms Mabley, Mrs. Miller, William Hung, Julie Christie, Medwin Kennoway, Geraldine Chaplin, William Demarest, Harry Davenport, Norma West, Whit Bissell, Jennifer Jones, Ursel Mumoth, Jack Burns, Michael Kitchen, Ray Teal, Frances O'Connor, Hope Summers, Dabney Coleman, Moses Gunn, Jane Birkin, Dominique Sanda, Catherine Deneuve, Keenah LaVine, Elsa Martinelli, Philip Bruns, Michael Feast, Debbie Watson, Kirsty Mitchell, Emma Thompson, John C. Reilly, Leo McKern, John Mills, Martin Shaw, Uriyurr, Sir Jesus Smock-Carabinierei, Joe E. Lewis, Liv Tyler, Frank Sinatra, Ralph Williams, Whoopi Goldberg, Marlon Brando, Cal Worthington,

Powers Boothe, Jerry Lewis, Richard Crenna, Amitabh Bachchan, Waycroft
Pamiel, Kuksi Ix Freresco, Jon Korkes, Shirley Jones, Edu Dyetz, Ronald Squire,
Steve Reeves, Vincent Gardenia, Elizabeth Wilson, Lou Jacobi, John Randolph,
Hector W. Braneparth, Doris Roberts, Peg Leg Sam, Woody Harrelson, Percy
Helton, Lisa Chappell, Mickey Maga, Eugene Mazzola, Shabana Azmi, Leslie
Uggams, Art Linkletter, Sheryl Crow, Juliette Greco, Bella Darvi, Hal Holbrooke,
Dan Hedaya, Ricardo Montalban, Madge Blake, Patricia Routledge, Chris Rock,
Penny Edwards, Jack Elam, Kate Beckinsale, Eddie Quillam, Aubrey Mather,
Marcia Rodd, Dame Kreesta Lainwaith, Robert Morley, John McGiver, S.Z.
'Cuddles' Sakall, Andrew Buchan, Victor Buono, Vahina Giocante, Neville Brand,
Paul Lynde, Dave Willock, Michael Rennie, Philip Ahn, James Westerfield,
Yvonne Craig, Ron Feinberg, Morgan Freeman, Audrey Dalton, Woody Allen,
Romolo Valli, Washington Xisolo, Niall MacGinnis, John Fiedler, Shug Fisher,
Perdita Robinson, Don Sullivan, Sir Norcroft Pantiwaste-Semm, Jack Nance, Si-
mon Oakland, Casey Adams, Harry Hickox, John Goodman, Cairley Kreekoss,
Frank Welker, M. Emmett Walsh, Rena Riffel, Vittorio Gassman, Juliette Lewis,
Judy Davis, Raj Kapoor, Victor Bannerjee, Merrimint O'Columcraddie, Norman
Rodway, Art Malik, Nipsey Russell, Laela Knight, David Opatoshu, Utopia, Jody
Twen, Gianni Di Gregorio, Lennison Tinkchears, Paul Newman, Michael Culkin,
Samantha Harper, Larry Gates, Virginia Mayo, Butterbugs, Isabelle Adjani, Nas-
tassija Kinski, Dennis Waterman, Lerrie Pfumonah, Woodrow Parfry, Halle Berry,
Neil Hamilton, Sonny Basic, Steve Smith, Alan Mandell, Mark Gupta, Bill Dana,
Gary Crosby, Ronald Pickup, Viggo Mortensen, Barksdale Tidd, Shikshak Mun-
dra, Don Rickles, Farooq Sheik, Sue Lyon, Jeremy Irons, Matt Dillon, Johnny
Seven, Harry Swoger, James Fox, John Cusack, Cornel West, Abby Martin,
Prunejuice Lávah, Goozaard de Hogo, Diana Quick, Herbie Faye, Mucellus Plau-
rinka, Henry Daniel, George Macready, Cydalise, Patrick McKenna, Richard
Egan, Harold J. Stone, Willem Dafoe, Kate Winslett, Ringo Starr, Christopher
Walken, Anthony Perkins, Rebecca Romijn, Burl Ives, Edward Fox, Sarah Miles,
Sir Vyvyan Claudeburst, Manuel Padilla, Jr., Tim Piggott-Smith, Percy Rodri-
guez, Claire de Lorez, Wallace Shawn, Josh Mostel, Betty Blythe, James Best,
Tender Kerrison, Yesterday's Soup Bilbullen, Ken Berry, Ken Stott, James Wain-
wright, Juanita Hall, Edward Norton, John Kerr, Joan Baez, Jon Hall, Ed Reimers,
Dennis Haysbert, Huntz Hall, André Morrell, Walter Abel, Agnes Moorehead,
Gong Li, Aasif Mandvi, George Sanders, Rosanna Arquette, George Carlin, Linda
Fiorentino, Joe E. Brown, Rob Brydon, Arnold Stang, Dimple, Barrie Chase, Jon-
athan Winters, Robert Emhardt, Jessica Pastor, James Bolam, Huitzilopochtli
Wong, Robert Duvall, Ron Jeremy, Ian Holm, Brad Dourif, The Ronettes, The
Timbertones, The ShangriLas, Naomi Watts, Tim Dutton, Patricia Arquette, Chris
Cooper, Mercedes McCambridge, Harry Wilson, Hank Henry, Ray Charles, Rich-
ard Burton, Harry Andrews, B.B. King, Christopher Jones, Peter O'Toole, Joe
Flynn, Björk, Mazhaan Munir, Kansas DeForrest, Pixie Hopkin, Dennis Hopper,
John Savage, John Cazale, Fred Willard, Jack Soo, Malcolm McDowell, Michael

Gothard, Roscoe Karns, Wallison Bendz, Shahid Ahmed, Edward Andrews, Roger C. Carmel, Aishwarya Rai, Ian McShane, Walter Hampton, Joan Chen, Rupert Graves, Hugh Marlowe, Jay Robinson, Consuelo Gómez, Country Joe, Julie Cox, Frank Thring, Jack Palance, Kuumba, Roy Poole, Julie Newmar, Maureen Stapleton, Carroll Baker, Richard A. Dysart, Susan Lynch, Joanne Woodward, Roscoe Lee Browne, Richard Pasco, Vaughn Taylor, Frank Ferguson, Joey Bishop, Ray McAnally, James Earl Jones, Ron Perlman, Shirley Temple Black, John McIntire, Gore Vidal, Joey Heatherton, Rich Little, Charlie Callas, Steve Martin, David Nelson, Lyle Talbot, Eric Idle, Albert Hall, John Astin, Ted Danson, Milton Frome, Thayer David, Kasey Chambers, Ian Richardson, Christopher Lee, Miles Anderson, Jenny Funnell, Lucinda Williams, Laurence Fishburne, Philip Bretherton, Michael Palin, Howard Cosell, Jerry Colonna, Barbara Rush, Paul Chapman, Alfred Newman, Bradford Dillman, Ben Stiller, Saskia Reeves, Bob Dylan, The Churl, Martin Mull, Christopher Guest, William Charles Mitchell, Karen Black, Abraham Sofaer, Omar Sharif, Jürgen Strelnikov, Jayne Atkinson, Billy House, Michael Gambon, Samuel L. Jackson, Alan Howard, John Woodvine, Roger Rees, Kyle McLaughlin, Berry Pumpkin, Maria Bello, William H. Macy, Nick Nolte, Alec Baldwin, Will Ferrell, The Incredible Jimmy Smith, Avery Schreiber, Alfonso Bedoya, Jerry Van Dyke, Bob Balaban, George Maharis, Heinz Bennent, Katherine Hepburn, Al Thomas, Benecio del Toro, Sir Paul McCartney, Tim Blake Nelson, Louise Fletcher, Darcie Flask, Jennifer Anniston, Josh Brolin, Michael J. Pollard, Pepe Serna, Brittany Murphy, Terry Jones, Luis Guzmán, Valerie French, Norman Mailer, Rex Ingram, Samuel West, John Cleese, Miklós Rózsa, Arpita Chatterjee, Gerard Depardieu, Perrison Jheeblak, Bill Baldwin, Sr., Marisa Berenson, Alex Kingston, John Mills, Robin Williams, Kenneth Griffith, Jenda Larx, Slappy Elleth McGuire, Jeff Bridges, Kenneth Mars, Patrick Bergin, Juliette Binoche, John Smith, Poodles Hanneford, Luis Guzman, Elijah Wood, Catherine Spaak, Carla Gugino, Henry Jones, Adolfo Celi, Patrick Cargill, Bo Hopkins, Jay C. Flippen, Sheridan Morley, Paul Stevens, Æmelia Clohaskin, Robert Redford, Mary Morris, Viktor Stanitsyn, Milton Selzer, Carol Lloyd, Ned Glass, Annette Carell, Giuli Chokhonelidze, John Hurt, Dick Martin, Crispin Glover, Kiva, Al Checco, Jody, Dump Kroger, James Millhollin, Finlay Currie, Jean-Louis Trintignant, Cynthia Patrick, Richard Blupp, Jim Begg, Parker Fennelly, Mina Olivera, S.N.C.F. Smith, MarLane Sugerterry, Suzi Quatro, Corin Redgrave, Sir SanFrancisco Bone, DeForest Covan, Leo Genn, Richard Barthelmess, Peter Egan, John Carradine, Maria Newman, Elodie Bouchez, William F. Buckley, Viola Davis, John McLaughlin, Nichole Galicia, Jeanne Bates, Kent Smith, Gina McKee, Baby Gramps, Dahliah Lavi, Fabian Lavender, Kelly Brook, Paul Fix, Andrew Duggan, Jodi Kreakers, Paradise Likkerkins, Frank DeKova, Billy Barty, Chris 'Eric' Jury, Bobbywood Chuckerjee, Denis Lawson, Fiona Shaw, James Whitmore, Saffron Burrows, Martin Landau, Alexis Kanner, Terry Gilliam, Boris Zakhava, Jonathan Miller, Slim Summerville, Suze Rotolo, Octavian Jones, Slim Pickens, Henry Hull, Oskar Werner, Burgess Meredith, Arthur Hill, Jack Buetel, William Atherton, Angelo Muscat, Shana, Lelia Goldoni, Paul Stewart, Chance Telemachus, Maria Bonnevie, Cedric the Entertainer, Keir Dullea, Marilyn Chambers, Prasenjit Chatterjee, Nigel Havers, Mary Badham, Christopher Waltz, Bess Flowers, Kerry Armstrong, Jeff Donnell, Bobby Rydell, Steve Coogan, Barbara Nichols, John Dall, Mimsy Farmer, Angela Davis, Richard Arlen, Lillian Gish, Shawnee Smith, Paul Winfield, Parsons St. Squirrel, Damian Lewis, Yacanda DeeOldevvo, Charlie Rose, Cesare Danova, Saeed Jaffrey, Robin Weigert, William Eythe, Tun Tun, Alun Armstrong, Elliot Gould, Donald Sutherland, Dabbs Greer, Hannah Donaldson, Dub Taylor, Billie Piper, Marne Maitland, Michael Lerner, Michele Derriere, Patty McCormick, Edward Fox, Michael Hordern, Vyacheslav Tikhonov, Ralph Richardson, Emanuel Lewis, Cerise ConCubbah, Sylvester Stallone, Lady Jame, Michelle Rodriguez, Laurence Olivier, Lyudmila Savelyeva, John Gielgud, Edith Evans, Snoop Dogg, Patricia Neal, Patrick O'Neal, Melton Malton, Cora Bissett, Julie Delpy, Sir Neal Prinxchop, James Mason, Sasha Frost, Mitzi, Eddie Mayehoff, David Letterman, Jack Carson, Maureen O'Hara, Natalie Portman, Kevin Spacey, Warren Clarke, Sir Ernesto Rollicksworth, Stacy Keach, Sylvia Kristel, Kelly LeBrock, Stephen Fry, Stephen Tompkinson, Graham Chapman, Jonathan Moore, Banksy, Arthur Malet, John Wood, Martin Gabel, Bruce Dern, Johnny Knoxville, Koogah Mantell, Buck Henry, Anna Chancellor, Godfrey Cambridge, Eileen Atkins, Daniel Craig, Gabriella Licudi, Chutney Brassington, Bart., Richard Ayoade, Al Freeman, Jr., Julie Graham, Mel Brooks, Karin Dor, John Brotherton, Jr., NTR, Brock Peters, Marton Csokas, Kate Nelligan, Valery Gergiev, Dame Rondelle Pinnium, Dudley Sutton, Anna Lee, Edward Herrmann, Sam Waterston, Lena von Martens, Peter Bowles, Iain Glen, Lummox O'Charlie, Vaundelle de Uieune, Sorrell Brooke, Dolores Gray, Charitable Jones, Steeple Aston, Allen Joseph, Belinda Lang, Paul Sorvino, Nick Apollo Forte, ellboy.com, Derrun Kindlunn, Aidan McArdle, Phyllis Logan, Roy Scheider, Sofia Vergara, Jean Marsh, James Woods, Simon Callow, J. Scott Smart, Clinton Sundberg, Reggie Rymal, Nedrick Young, Robin Wright, Lucy Phelps, Chips Rafferty, Prissy Starspangled, Jack Pennick, Tilda Swinton, Porkfat Russell, Lucky Johnson, Sophie Marceau, MGR, Ian MacNeice, Eddie Murphy, James Karen, Philip Seymour Hoffman, Parley Baer, Marcello Mastroianni, Famke Janssen, Helmut Berger, Leon Askin, Marvin Kaplan, Ravundrah, Arnold Stang, Judith Anna Roberts, Randy Quaid, Albert Brooks, Katharine Isabelle, Zachary Scott, Frank Stallone, Irvin S. Cobb, Gheglux St. Jon-de-la-Primrose, Claudia Cardinale, Nigel Green, Salina Godden, Udo Kier, Tim McInnerny, Mary Beth Hurt, Keira Knightly, Susan Vidler, Mario Adorf, Dennison Lutz, Leslie Caron, Hag Haggadorn, Belle Bennett, Philip Stone, Bapi Green Taxi, Scarlett Johansson, Jason Welterswelter, Robert Rietty, James Robertson Justice, Fawndell Windwoods, Teretiaiti Teyahineheipua Maifano, Percy Herbert, Peter Bergman, Andreas Teuber, Richard Deacon, Martha Hyer, Leon Redbone, Paterson Joseph, Diane Baker, Terpsichore, William 'Pete' Fawcett, Wingo Kornbahl, Trixie Friganza, Peter Boyle, J. Pat O'Malley, Brooke Baldwin, Lillete Dubey, Pell James, Jimmy Boyd, Stephen

Moore, Richard Johnson, Charlize Theron, Sverre Anker Onsdal, Elizabeth Banks, Sydney Pollack, Amelia Warner, Phil Austin, Art Gilmore, David Ossman, Rebecca Ferguson, Norman Vellman, Kate Dickie, Kenny Baker, Bobby Clark, Patrick Malahide, Plurr Plurree, Philip Proctor, Tom Smothers, Jacques Aubuchon, Florence Pernel, Amanda Redman, Stellan Skarsgård, Egregia Mitten, ProwlerCat, Zoë Wanamaker, Meat Loaf, Jack Nicholson, Téa Leoni, Rand Brooks, Elana Eden, Ina Balin, Melvyn Van Peebles, Eleazeth Grose, Dietrich Bader, Julianne Phillips, Fred Ward, Fan Faehrt, Stella Stevens, Uma Thurman, Shashi Kapoor, May Britt, Britt Eklund, Turl Square, Tom Courtenay, Hope Lange, Laird Cregar, Kristanna Loken, Hurd Hatfield, Melvin Stewart, Amminadab Bogdrombash, Bill Nighy, Alex Désert, Nigel Stock, Turhan Bey, James Keach, Jim Belushi, James May, Kiki Relisch, Curd Jurgens, Maylie Menue, Beau Bridges, Ephreum Rhuel, Barrett Blensons, George Takei, Lupita Nyong'o, Heinz Bennent, Mahershala Ali, Viceroy Cribbs, Lockwood West, Brer Soul, House Jameson, Laura Dern, Robert X. Cringely, Irfan Khan, John Waters, Jessica Biel, G.D. Spradlin, Christopher Plummer, Andy Garcia, Nickolas Grace, Steven 'The Street' Mackintosh, Michael V. Gazzo, Smita Patil, Belinda Stewart-Wilson, Nicholas Selby, Frank McGrath, Adam Faith, Jessica Alba, Jeremy Clarke, Brian Dennehy, Mike Judge, Sylvester McCoy, Pads Tarcoil, Chief Dan George, Joan Greenwood, Suky Appleby, Sir Drawbridge Kame, Bekka Sar Anthonius, Tartina Gondell, Peter Plumpstead, Gugg the Great, Mindelwood Brepps, Jon Stewart, Mark Rylance, Rowena King, Stan Boreson, Mustache, Jeffrey Wright, Jeffrey Mishlove, Shelley Fabares, Roy Marsden, Mitzi McCall, Charlie Brill, Karin Krick, Christopher Eccleston, Susannah York, Jenny Agutter, Cameron Mitchell, Freddie Jones, Amanda Peet, Elth Kith, Issa Rae, Sven Norden, Barrie Ingham, Alberta Hunter, Wendis Way, Shannyn Sossamon, Stephen Root, Dick Smothers, Barrison Pekpup, Larry Storch, Al Lewis, Robert Joy, Eddie 'Rochester' Anderson, Daniel Stern, Dianne Wiest, Deepanjan Ghosh, Jennifer Connelly, Howard St. John, Keith David, Ahamafule J. Oluo, F. Murray Abraham, Lurchie Channunn, Teeny Topper, Ballard Berkeley, Per Christian Ellefsen, Craig Charles, Jason Mitchell, Fansell Kajurga, Jack Carter, Brennan Fig, Leonard Watkins, Mindy Merrills, Lothaire Bluteau, Winneslavw Kinneus Murkpeace, Gilbert & George, Parker Posey, Kamalahasan, Harry Shannon, Amy Adams, Lee Melons, Billy Bob Thornton, Helô Pinheiro, Harry Barris, Stephen Colbert, Mindy Mubba, Patricia Hodge, Hutton Cobb, Paradise McKenna, Per Oscarsson, Tuesday Weld, Victoria Catlin, Shawn Michael Howard, Maria Sansone, Prunella Ching, Mads Mikkelson, Janie Dee, Felicity Kendal, Jester Hairston, Village, Ajay Naidu, Jim Jarmusch, Meryl Streep, Churchman Kerrison-Muldball, Jeremy Kemp, Hugh Fraser, Chris Barrie, Henry Gibson, Amanda Donohoe, Sammi Davis, Leslie Parrish, Timothy Spall, Arthur Dignam, Slavoj Žižek, Paul Brooke, Mos Def, Suzy Parker, Anthony Sharp, Shelley Duvall, Kitty Aldridge, Sir Mucius Snade-Grane, Jesse White, Norman Lovett, Hershey Benson, Thandie Newton, Yinker Brapp-Pile, Sven Nordin, Linda Lou Allen, Bérénice Bejo, Ed Harris, Jeffrusun

329

Drum Cone, Djimon Hounsou, Frank and Agnes Flanagan, Linda Hutchings, Terry Crews, Carol Lynley, Anthony Hopkins, Brastis ConnaGremmenden, Shelley Winters, Ed Fury, Mitzi Gaynor, Italo Zingarelli, Immanâla Nōōmanossi, Sonny Chiba, Nimrat Kaur, Tim Edward Rhoze, Eva Green, Richard B. Shull, Raj Kapoor, John Oliver, Shashi Kapoor, McHenry Boatright, Peter Ronson, Dhurrumnudranath Bhadralok, Diane Fletcher, Patricia Owens, Hans Presston Bluck, Nancy Kwan, Robert Easton, Calvert DeForest, Karl Michael Vogler, Miriam Lane, Dan Vadis, Roshan Seth, Andie MacDowell, Mai Tai Sing, Sarah Silverman, Alexis Bledel, Stevenson Jacket, Waldo Bubble (making a rare screen appearance), Lola Albright, Melissa Gilbert, Apple Martin, Francis L. Sullivan, Ana Cabrera, Celia Imrie, Penelope Cruz, Anthony James, Joe Strnad, Perry Flask, Ser Woultre Scot, Eva Longoria, Helena Bonham Carter, Brambin Bon Bindinbomb, Rajnikanth, Michelle Ryan, Benson Fong, Lord Willyumn Cragmount Jasps, Jennifer Garner, Visbulite Lacplesis, Jack Weston, Marjorie Rambeau, Victor Sen Yung, Charles Lane, Miyoshi Umeki, Aislín McGuckin, Martin Clunes, Duckwallow Marsh, Sonny Bupp, Buddy Swan, James Shigeta, Barry Newman, Danny John-Jules, Maisie MacFarquhar, Miriam LaVelle, Harry Holcomb, Peapoh Dandello, Ty Ziegel, Rachel Ward, Rev. Wm Barber, Florinda Bolkan, Cal Worthington, Terry Farrell, James Anderson, John Westbrook, Carlos Zaza, Dr. Dre, Millis Kerritonay, Mindy DeVerandy, Pierre Segui, Julian Peedle-Calloo, Hattie Winston, Tuppence Middleton, Michelle Rodriguez, Dixie Dunbar, Sacha Baron Cohen, Adalyn Schloss, Harry Dean Stanton, Susannah Harker, Ta-Nehisi Coates, Neil Dudgeon, George Dzundza, Daphne Zukvuk, Erik Crary, Bob Hastings, Doutzen Kroes, Vincent Price, Jack Black, Cara Delevigne, Victoria Hamilton, Megan Fox, Sean Connery, Nuala McGovern, Teyonah Parris, Paul Onsongo, Jerry Maren, McParken Janeway, Robert DoQui, James Wilby, William Fichter, John Thomson and Cheeky Monkey, Franka Potente, Prunella Scales, Audrey Tautou, Meeonee Diaz-Durango, Kristen Wiig, Margot Robbie, Matthew McConaughey, Urk-Uh, Woona Greenslit, Lizzy Caplan, Nawazuddin Siddiqui, Amy Schumer, Sir Ling Wuzzeerovitch, Honeysuckle Weeks, Jim Carter, Saverio Guerra, Sally Hawkins, Peter Ustinov, Kindly Parrparrow, Johnny Grant, Marie-Josée Croze, Timothy Carey, Feather Saltchurch, Ziyi Zhang, Dorothy Malone, Nick Abbot, Damien Dar Degguns, Boyfriend Bamber, Blill Feeconk, Beyoncé Knowles, Sir Chips Trolleypinch, Helena Chase, Ken Murray, Anthony 'The Mooch' Scaramucci, Adi Berber, Tenzin Gyatso (the Dalai Lama), Eevy Sprarestnopp, Cate Blanchett, Phil Harris, Joan Tetzel, Madhur Jaffrey, Bongo Enumba, Walter Brooke, Johnny Sekka, Chuck Aspegren, George Clooney, Maribel Verdú, Neptoon Jones, Frederick Treves as Frank, Theo Marcuse, William Tracy, Saoirse Ronan, Elias Ringquist, Lata Mangeshkar, Juba Xudr, Richard Attenborough, Frank Ching, Georg Stanford Brown, Naura Hayden, Mollycoddle Muethington-Spares, Irving Perris-Skrennenniss-Sugarbaker, Little Chickens Muethington-Spares, Charlton Heston, Fabia Drake, Dorothy Dandridge, Marvel Mirkry, Shawna Lee LePraise, Sir Parabola Manewayster, Luetha Lome, Evangeline Lilly, Robert Middleton, Frank Craven, Edward Petherbridge. Narrated by Norman Rose, David Austin, Nancy Wilson, and Linda Hunt.

And many more.

Indeed, there were many names: many famous, many who were stars, many who were Whits, and many who were both obscure actors and obscurer extras, eligible for addition to this list. At this juncture, it was nothing if not preliminary. The final cast sheet would be issued after the studio's Accounts Payable Dept. did their numbers, and after final editing of the film itself had been completed to directorial satisfaction (for Egaz retained Final Cut rights, in creative association with Butterbugs). No doubt numerous others not on this list would pop up in the entire process of counting-and-making-and-editing, as having creatively participated in the picture, so much having transpired over such a grand, lengthy shoot.

For example, it was actually forgotten by persons of significance that Orson Welles had done part of the voiceover narration, a task shared by four others. A pretty damn substantial element, obviously. With such a vast production, slop would inevitably sneak in, sooner or later. One day, Orson rang up to request that his fee be advanced before the pre-arranged date, as he had some bills to pay at Ma Maison and at BKV Labs, for some film stock.

Orson's old ally, DFZ, growled, 'Pay him off!'

No one in the pebble-counting office could find any evidence of his voice work, until actual physical evidence was stumbled-upon by a conscientious janitor. Sweeping up in the Audio House, he'd spotted several important-appearing audio boxes in the rubbish, obviously dumped there by accident. Totally proficient with the tech hardware, he engaged the audio files within and cranked up the volume. Booming through was the Wellesian mellifluousness all right, safely stored on MegaPerspectaMagnaSound Fugue-File Audiella-Cones, neatly catalogued and awaiting sound marriage in the BKV Bootee-Mixee Method.

'Can't you people keep your achievements in order, if not in mind?' bellowed DFZ at his team, upon hearing of the temporary misplacement of his pal Orson's quite expensive and quite extensive contributions to the picture.

'Hell, he can now finish 'Don Quixote' (El Silencio Film) for what I paid him! Whomever blew that one gets his ass canned.'

'Sorry, chief,' plucked up Porter right away. He was hardly responsible for the actual oversight, though courage was one of his newfound virtues.

'No more bozo-behavior like that again, OK, Parker?'

'No, no. Certainly not. But it's fun to rediscover such a buried treasure. Plus, it's a terrific surprise.'

'Fun...,' brooded DFZ. 'Fun. Surprise...!'

He nearly grew mocking, then checked himself.

'Fun... Heh! You know... you're right, Parker. Fun. Making pictures is fun. It is fun. In fact, it's a fucking blast. OK then kid, you can stay on the picture.'

331

NB: The latest late addition to the list (to be placed at the end):

And the voice of Orson Welles.

[The janitor, Crurgan Mo'Betr T-shammah, was given screen credit as 'Associate Sound Steward' and instantly promoted to the Sound Department, as a genuine Associate Sound Steward, along with a big fat bonus check, personally presented by a grateful Butterbugs, with Orson himself in attendance.]

41.

And He Hung His Hat
On An Arc Of Righteousness

Four days before principal studio photography was to begin in Hollywood, Butterbugs had a dream. He dreamt he was President of the United States of America.

(Interior. Night. White House, near the East Room, ten minutes to midnight. PRESIDENT (aka: POTUS) stumbles drunkenly along the moodily-lighted corridor, grasping at chairs and even paintings, along the way.)

POTUS: *(under his breath, suppressing the urge to vomit)* Yes, I have served. Served and given of myself. I'm pretty much perfect, but my perfection has been mutilated by my selfless service. So I'm kinda *pissed off.*

(He can suppress the urge no longer, and a hideous stream of vomit sprays out of his mouth, completely soiling him and many adjacent historical items in the vicinity. The official portrait of James K. Polk is irretrievably ruined, and two Ming and three Sèvres vases are shattered. Shocked at the severity of this process, he licks his lips and instinctively reaches for jars of pure grain alcohol and rainwater that sit on the Federalist-style table nearby. After mixing the drink, bartender-style, he downs the flagon, completely puzzled as to why he should do such a thing after this late act of drunken discomfort. The caliber of the drink puts him right back into his deeply drunk state.)

POTUS: A vision strikes me!

(Bright light appears at the end of the hall. An Xmas-card ANGEL appears, like an embryo, or an unpalatable oyster, and makes to speak.)

POTUS: *(interpreting the angel's thought and verbalizing it)* I see you, my infected child. I will follow your instructions. I will create an Arc of Righteousness, as you request. Forgive me, I did not know you were a mute. If I misinterpret thee, then strike me from this earth, like a curse!

(ANGEL exits. POTUS is consumed by quaking and wambling, and vomits super-violently. The ashen color of the discharge issuing from his enraged

333

mouth quickly changes to bright scarlet, compounded by chunks of internal tissue and much later, actual organs.)

(After he literally pukes his guts out, POTUS, in agony, grabs at some lofty curtains, as if to pull himself back up and towards the vanished ANGEL, but the heavy drape comes down in a cascade, and the pelmet follows, burying him in a crimson terrain, in which he suffocates and expires. Lightning flashes, strikes the window, then bursts through the glazing, and incinerates the curtains and the body. Tableaux of SECRET SERVICE AGENTS, PEASANTS and DeMILLE-STYLE EXTRAS looking on in horrah, yet accepting what is obviously providential judgment.)

(Cut to newsreel-style title: 'President Visited by Apostate of Hell. Pays Supreme Price'.*)*

(Cut to B&W scratchy footage of POTUS' burned corpse lying in state on a bed of wilted lettuce, in the tawdry, overgrown capitol rotunda, under a cloven dome. Bit of plaster and fresco drop from Brumidi's 'The Apotheosis of George Washington' 55m. above, killing several of the 'mourners' every few minutes.)

GEORGE WASHINGTON: *(To the corpse below)* You pathetic *failure* of a POTUS! You make me wanna PUKE!!

(Most painful is the fall of the fresco bit with WASHINGTON's mouth (his wooden teeth obscured). It lands directly in the dead POTUS' gaping mouth and crushes his entire skull. A stern rebuke from the Father of the Nation!)

(Schoolchildren with dirty lips file past the remains, and throw dirt clods at what's left of the corpse.)

POTUS: *(VO)* I did so much for them, but I guess they don't like me very much. Can't people see all the stuff I've done? Why can't they be a little... you know, *grateful...?*

(Cut to black.)

Butterbugs woke up, feeling very glad he was not the POTUS.

But what *was* he?

He was about to become, by virtue of the photoplay contract he signed of late, a severe ruler, one with total authority and power. What then, did this acutely disquieting dream signify?

334

In another scene he'd dreamt some time before, involving an actual political figure, the Sec'y of Defense, he discovered that un-admired personage had at least one filament of humanity left in him, symbolized by a sole tear. Thus, a crystalline cyst of hope.

Hope! Which never leaves humankind!

What to do with a dream sequence full of unpleasantness, death and justice – or apparent justice?

(Just to make sure, in the morning he'd call Sharship Mendez-Belumba, FAIA, Architect of the Capitol (AOC), and a darn good friend. Just to make sure 'The Apotheosis of George Washington' was intact and OK.)

Rapid Eye Movement Dreams were never premonitions to him, nor self-fulfilling prophecies, either. They were almost exclusively entertainments, possibly of the symbolist variety, but without dogma or guile.

What then, was he to make of *this* one?

Two days before principal studio photography was to begin, Butterbugs made a key decision. He chose to phase out horseradish, like an old vaudevillian who turns away from his can of backstage beer when the laughs ebb. On the other hand, it was not so much a farewell as it was a thought of pride.

'I don't need it anymore,' he announced to Old Atrocity.

The sage replied, 'Is this a sign of a… lowering of listening, or something?'

'How can you say that?'

'Am I to be your *senex* in the chariot, blabbing about mortality all the time?'

'Nay, my friend. None needed. I am telling you something of confidence.'

'Your confidence, or a secret knowledge?'

'My sureness! This is a big picture. I am up to the task.'

'Then I shall happily turn down any chariot rides ye may offer me!'

'My friend from yore!'

'All the way, and beyond!'

'You understand.'

'Yeah well, it's a probability that you have outgrown your need for the equine radish. But the elevated platforms which now are presented to you each day, which you must ascend, step by step, are well-nigh dizzying.'

'They are.'

'They fuckin' blow me away.'

'A very Old Atrocious way to put it!'

'But I've seen you grow, Butterbugs. Even as the heights rise.'

'I must grow with them. Not in size, but in acumen.'

'Well said, Prince.'

'I thank you, M'lud.'

'Time for a nipperkin of the arcane liqueur of your choice? Perchance from yon venerable skull-cup?'

'Aye! As one high-level understander to another!'

42.

Alfred, Only Alfred

'Can we get Dmitri? The Shostie guy? You know, Shostakovich-type.'
'No way. He's busy revising his 41st symphony. Century 41 Symphony!'
'OK, then. What about Timmy?'
'The other Dmitri? Di-mitri.'
'Of course. Dumbo!'
'Tiomkin's booked up at Bronston. Three pictures this year.'
'Then get me Newman!' Hyman Goth's voice reverberated throughout his office suite. 'NOW!'
Cody was nonplused. 'Paul? Joseph? Emil? Irving? Randy? Lionel?... Bob?'
'Al!'
'Is he a SAG member?'
'Alfred, only Alfred!'
'But he just composed the fanfare for Mega|Goth Pictures' revised logo. Our new audio trademark!'
'You don't understand, peach-ass, I want him to score the picture!'
'Of course you mean 'UWH'?'
'You're catchin' on!'
'Isn't he booked till 20 —?'
'Now you get me Al, my bubbly butt. I want Al, now you get him for me. I don't care how you do it. Here's some spot-cash money!'

Having worked in pictures since 1930, Alfred Newman was pretty seasoned. He had done it *all*, and he was still *doing* it all. But his gaze was not dim, nor had his industry abated. If anything, he had grown more creative, more mature in his style, if such a thing was possible. This was at least the 20th Butterbugs film he was to score, and while it was certainly the biggest, – yes, bigger than 'Nibelungen' (20th-Fox) – it was also the most eagerly-awaited.

This time, he uttered nothing like 'How the hell am I going to write ANOTHER chase scene?!' Instead, viewing the rushes so far, much of the incandescence he saw in Butterbugs' performance onscreen inspired him. Like Ernie Gold with Otto's 'Exodus' (UA, 1960), he got to be intimately involved with the scoring as filming progressed.

He assembled his team of stalwarts, such as Ken Darby, Ed Powell, Fred Steiner, Charlie Henderson, brother Lionel, neph Randy, Varma Skizzill and Dandry

336

Druesrome, and they went to work with a fervor that matched traditional House of Newman productions.

His HQ was not at the studio during this phase, but at his Palisades estate, in bucolic resplendence. Butterbugs often hung there to get away from actors and directors – and especially producers.

'I like them and everything –,' said Butterbugs, the first time he showed up at the coffered door.

'So do I,' replied the musician. 'But let's take a break from the powers that be.'

There were easygoing luaus, chamber music in the afternoon (Brahms quartets were a favorite), and the requisite shots of O'Tarnish, when points of review needed discussing.

These retreats were similar to when the ultrastar wandered off into the art department of a given studio. He could goof around in the back rooms, pick up stuff covered with plaster dust, leaf through old folios of production sketches, and pick the brains of Special Photographic Effects wizards and Set Dressers who stayed late in order to personally work out problems no one but themselves – and maybe their peers – would ever notice. But that was the greatness of the detailing.

Music was one of the preferred goof-arounds that Butterbugs took on these days. He'd always known a significant part of a picture's character was identified through the score, but as he'd spent quiet-time and down-time with those in Music Depts., new dimensions of cinematic power were truly understood, not just observed.

Alfred was as attentive to the written dialogue and the actors' performance as Richard Strauss was to von Hofmannsthal's text, or Wagner with his own words. Tone, setting, and combined mood were always within the sphere of his perfect-pitch coverage of a given film's incomplete physicality. To which he would add his own particular stamp of rounding out the picture's soul. Even if it *had* no soul, he gave it one.

He certainly had his wry moments, of which there were plenty. For what professional in pictures can avoid his/her rights in venting workaday B.S., even in the process of achieving high cinematic art? Alfred took certain delight in burlesquing his own Industry, but never did he mock his passion within that field: music itself, or its dedicated practitioners. If anything, he was their fiercest defender.

'We have a tremendous responsibility,' he told the ultrastar late one session. 'Even if the score's not a conscious element in the film, every audience member's aware of our musicianship. And we'd damn well better be up for the task.'

The day before principal photography in Hollywood would commence, Alfred and Shonnaleen Gubbins were over to Vinejuice for dinner.

'You're sure?' the always-elegant Shonnaleen asked, with all courtesy.

'My lines are known, and I'm not due at the studio until 1:00 in the PM. Confab with DFZ & Co., then a straight pre-makeup still photog session at Hurburt's Lodge.'

'Might I sit in on the confab, Butterbugs?' asked Alfred.

'Absolutely, if you're in the mood.'

'I'm *seeking* mood!' Alfred drew deeply on his cig.

'If you find it there, amongst the Great Ones, then you are truly inspired.'

'You'd probably never believe it, but I can't count the times that Darryl's given me a great idea. I don't play croquet with him, either. They come mostly in the form of telegrams, and now emails.'

'I played him once,' said Butterbugs, smiling wistfully. 'Once. Yes! *Once.*'

'You got beaten?' asked Shonnaleen.

'Nay, I was on the verge of wiping DFZ off the green, unintentionally, and he thought he heard the phone, so he rushed onto the terrace and said he had to get down to the studio right away.'

Alfred coughed.

'Always the competitive one, aren't you? As usual! Futzing with moguls could get you excommunicated.'

'I repeat, it only happened once.'

'Boys,' said Shonnaleen, filling their shot glasses with O'Tarnish's, 'I'll tell you something shocking. Not only am I invited to at least one match a month at Ric-Su-Dar, I am allowed to win. And I *do* win from time to time.'

The musician was blunt.

'What do you threaten the Little Guy with, sitting on him?'

'Actually, dear Alfred, you are most perceptive. That's *exactly* what I threatened to do. Non-verbally, of course. A mere perambulation unto the borders of his personal space did the trick.' She did a sort of hubba-hubba shake of her blubber at key positions, while the other two busted up.

'Scared, boys? Well, you've never seen such existential fear as in the eyes of Old Snaggletooth after one of my advances.'

'I like how you use your clout in this town,' said Alfred. 'Heavily!'

'Literal – instead of implied – *power!*' marveled Butterbugs.

It was a typical mellow late afternoon at the Vinejuicy palazzo. The three went their separate ways for a siesta. Each relished their solitary time at this captivating retreat, with its hill-town ambience, its sweetly independent tenor, and its sparse population. Staff were limited to three: Munna in the kitchen, Nadine as upstairs maid, and Obadiah von Leung as khansammah/chokeydar/groundsman. No team in high-elevation LA was better, and they knew how to be invisible.

Butterbugs did some yoga and ended up in the lotus position for about fifteen minutes, focusing the mind on his craft's essentials: competence, conviction, and style. Each side of the trinity interlocked with the other. Locked into place, without any trace of cynicism or affectation or guile. Memorization, character, creativity... the triumvirate would evolve automatically. The immense script, even though it was still in development, was embedded in his mind. Standout characteristics of the HMD were already in place, to be co-developed with Egaz.

He tested his many voice options, then mixed and matched inflections. He was officially well prepared, and would have a lot to run by his director.

After a while he padded down to the breakfast nook, where he found Shonnaleen and Alfred having a quiet session.

'Too early for dinner,' said the composer.

He'd been discussing some musical sketches, batting about ideas from Shonnaleen.

'No time to get overstuffed.'

Shonnaleen chuckled.

'Lemme do the stuffing, baby. You do the pacing.'

Alfred paced and puffed.

'Are you composing?' Butterbugs asked.

'It's human stuff…,' AN confided.

'We were doing some reviewing,' Shonnaleen said, trying to inform without filling in.

'Life-matters. With musical addenda.'

'We never have it completely *made*, Alfred,' she added.

'I have some more ideas for themes.'

'You can have the Study in the Jaén Wing,' offered Butterbugs. (The suite was inspired by the fine wines of that particular district of Old Spain.)

'Truth to tell, Butterbugs, I can't compose here.'

'There's a piano up there. Bösendorfer, I should think. Of course, it's not *your* piano…'

'Very kind of you, but I just can't compose anywhere but in my chair at home.'

'Like Satyajit Ray! He's creatively dead outside his own pad.'

'That's what he told me as well, and we were in harmony. So to speak.'

'Well then, I certainly won't press.'

'Thank you.'

'I wish I could play.'

'You're not musical?'

'No. Sadly.'

'What about your performance as Adrian Boult?'

'Acting.'

'I see. Yes. Rather good acting. Who coached you?'

'Valery Gergiev.'

'Not bad. Not very English, though.'

'He knows all the styles, all the personalities.'

'A very rarefied community, Butterbugs.'

'I'm just excited to be fraternizing with you on this level; the composition level, that is.'

'Yeah, it's not too common an exchange, except with musicals, but it's definitely OK with me. There are always ideas in my head.'

'Your mind, 'mad with music'? as Tennessee W. used to say?' Shonnaleen re-entered, with a Royal Plush TV dinner, fresh 'n' piping, just out of absent Munna's m-wave.

'No, Big Baby, not mad, but musical. Once you get it rolling, it doesn't have to stop. I dig it, you know.'

'Ever since you were a little kid, Boy Wonder,' winked Shonnaleen.

'Yeah, yeah, don't re-remind me. But you know, it's been a blast.'

'I figured such!' She toyed with the pear-cum-quince dessert before approaching the main Starving Gentleman courses offered within the confines of the jumbo stamped aluminum thali plate.

'Figured what, exactly?' The composer was coy.

'Because, who else could pull off this assignment, but Pappy N?'

'Hear, hear!' crowed Butterbugs.

'Listen, gang, I tinkle the keys on the honky-tonk piannah while the foreplay scene flickers, projected on the bed sheet overhead. That's all. That's all I do. That's all I've ever done.'

'Now you looka here,' said Shonnaleen, who even went so far as to put down her fork. 'What are you looking for, attention? We all know you can make or break a picture. My God, what you did with 'Wilson' (20th-Fox, 1944), 'The Real Glory' (Goldwyn, 1939), and the Mother Teresa biopic – can't remember the title –'

' 'The Long Night Of The Soul' (20th-Fox),' interjected Butterbugs.

'Right! Thanks, Mr. U-star. 'Long Night/Soul'! We all left the picture show on our knees, Al! Half-cuz of your score.'

'When I put on my tie in the morning, it turns into a clerical collar,' Alfred wisecracked.

They laughed with enjoyment, but mutedly.

'Not quite as flashy as TABP's though, honey,' said Shonnaleen.

'Yeah, mine's more sober.'

'And glorious, too,' said Butterbugs. 'I'm so glad it's there.'

'It's pretty nice of all you captured-audience members to say so –'

The composer was obviously genuinely touched.

'Willing captives!' said Butterbugs. 'And there are millions of us.'

'Thanks, thanks,' he replied in a murmur.

'Are you saying that you're a bit down in the mouth about this assignment?' asked Shonnaleen.

Alfred finished his shot of O'Tarn's. 'I guess I could confide in you both regarding that fact – That fact, I guess, is true,' he said.

'Excellent!'

Shonnaleen's outburst came with her mouth full. She really had to gobble some sustenance, which she could easily accomplish between sentences, especially since Munna, back from non-existent absence, discreetly slipped tray dinners in front of the composer and the actor, as well as appending Ms. Gubbins' own TV grub with some really gourmet Vinejuice fare. As a second-string dining experience, the processed food was contrasted with *created* food.

'That's really outstanding, Alfred!' she proclaimed. 'Your sincerity is noted. A true artist you are. Self-doubt, even at this stage! That *proves* you're consummately *up for it.*'

Butterbugs was simultaneously fascinated and comforted. Shonnaleen may have been the biggest gal in the upper echelons of the picture business, but she was also the biggest supporter of artistic achievement in the Industry. Whether it was the dithering first-time extra, or the elder-but-still-evolving professional, such as A. Newman, composer, in this very room at the moment, she was *there* for them.

'Shonna?' said Alfred, almost emotional (which wasn't too much his style), 'I'm glad you're so big. Something's got to be big enough to house that gigantic heart of yours. You're unforgettable, Good One!'

Shonnaleen smiled.

'So's your main theme in 'A Man Called Peter' (20th-Fox, 1955)!'

Butterbugs and Alfred quietly chowed down, as did Shonnaleen, in second-stage mode.

Afterwards, over coffee, brandy and cigars, Butterbugs mused.

'I wonder where it comes from?'

'What, child?' asked Shonnaleen, trimming her Punch Habana-Coolah, though she already knew where this was headed.

'The decisions; what to do; how to score a particular scene… Just, how to *do* it. Don't laugh!'

'Not at all, ' replied Alfred, 'I wonder myself. Often. But I don't question too much. I don't fight it. Just let it roll. And I have guides. Like you, Butterbugs, the actor, up there, on the screen, with the work-print lines running through your close-ups, in cheap B&W rushes (not as common today, it's true). The scenery, whether painterly or stark. Grey slabs stimulate me! Then there's a little thing called the script on my podium, and my team's buttressing, of course… Maybe I'm easily inspired, but when I see this guy,' he gestured to the ultrastar while aiming his words at Shonnaleen, 'Up there, and seeing what he does, it moves me to places I haven't been before. And I've been – *to all those places!*'

'Oh Al, simple, simple. I'm glad it works. So glad. You're lucky. We're lucky. To –' She finished her sentence in wordless enunciation, while pointing toward Butterbugs. 'To have this guy to work *from*'.

'He's a starting point. Central. A hub of departure…'

'…Whence we can continue.'

Alfred still brooded in (temporary) self-doubt.

'I do indeed notice talent on the screen. It gets me through a picture. But Butterbugs? I don't know if I'm… worthy, actually… I really don't…'

Butterbugs was so wordlessly gratified that all he could do was bypass any response and raise his hands and say:

'Can you both join me for a get-together here this weekend? It will be a film composer night. I have the weekend off, so I'd really like to have everyone here. Everyone. I'd be grateful for your presence.'

Party music!

What can one offer one's guests, music-wise, when the guests themselves are composers, each in their own right? Well, pretty much anything will do, because all professional musicians of quality respect each other. They're all perfectly aware that what they do is so esoteric and so respectable, there's nothing for it but to enjoy mutual respect and mutual admiration that inevitably result when such particular birds of a feather gather together.

The Music Department: the most rivalry-lacking division of the Industry. At least that was the case with those who assembled in the musical halls of Vinejuice on the appointed evening. It promised to be *the* unruffled event of the season.

Butterbugs and Shonnaleen were inherently sensitive to the virtues of musical glue. That was why they knocked their heads together and indulged in such a specific clambake with total vim. They knew if they nurtured, good will would result. Without offensive baggage, unlike in many other departments of the picture business.

'Should be a pretty pleasant evening,' said Ms. Gubbins with quiet joy.

'You know, I think Hollywood musicians are pretty much in the same boat,' said Butterbugs as they planned the showdown. Even after principal photography on 'UWH' had rolled (mainly preliminary stills and costume shots), the ultrastar was keen on doing this music gig while he still could.

'It's like camerapersons, and even (most) art directors,' he continued. 'Almost always, mutual respect! It's like, they all have the same burdens to carry, so as to get the job done. There's a trust in competence. Because, if you've got a music department that's pulling off its chores with style, quality, and remarkability, what's not to respect?'

'No shit,' replied Shonnaleen. 'Wish I could say the same about producers, directors – and especially, *agents!*'

'I know everyone's got their workplace politics and all, but...'

'I used to think, in these 'troubled' departments, is it just a contentment with unhappiness, or an unhappy... contentment? Hell no, it's just egos!'

'You should know, Shonna. With all your custodial experience...'

'Music is the language of understanding, baby. That's why we use it in motion pictures.'

The evening was upon them. Vinejuice was jazzed.

'For I am interested in cultivating such positive atmospheres,' said Butterbugs, still on the same train of ponderment, as they were both setting up for the evening.

'How generous, Butterbugs!' Shonnaleen replied, 'Hosting these contributors. They're usually so – overlooked! Isn't that the stupidest thing? Here they'll be amongst us, and available, mostly for compliments. Real humanoids – not just names on the screen. Because, as you say, everybody matters!'

'Just so!'

'Good thing it's only musicians tonight. That being the case, there are over ten teams of film music aficionados and scholars, right outside, in your bower and your backlands, all ready interviewers, anxious to take down sessions, no matter how extended. I call 'em your Music Nerds – fondly!'

'They're gonna record any music-making tonight too, right?'

'You better believe it, child. For free. You and the gang retain any copyrights.'

'Oh, Shonna, you don't know how much this means to me!'

'I *do* know, especially as you embark on the none-too-casual role of HMD, which will dominate your earthly existence for the foreseeable future.'

'True! But it is not within that context that I –'

'Yeah, I know! Cool it, sport! Let's lose our selfness! I've got to get over to...'

'Right, baby, because I have to...'

A touch-screen at the entrance vestibule to Vinejuice, with messages of greeting from absent Saskia (currently in the Makran, doing rewrites) and Justy (in Bangui, in between lining up new puisne judges in the Revised Judicature Realm), welcomed the guests via a gracious ribbon of digital embellishment (quite well-produced by Ms. Gubbins and Ben Barenholtz). Watching it, some of the composers personally thought the background score of stock music to this otherwise thrilling (and sexy) intro a bit tinkly and hokey. But there was a bit of trickery in play. At the end of the vid was a rather lengthy (three minute) fake credit crawl, lain over both women of the house, who remained in the background shot, wearing expectant expressions, as if some bonus awaited. After the silly credits ended, all they said was, in unison, 'Welcome to Vinejuice, Musicians!', before fade out. There wasn't one composer who didn't watch the whole thing to the bitter end – just to hear the music. For a bit of comparative analysis. So here, at the entrance to a party, was a musical issue. Was the average moviegoer likely to ride out the full extent of a composer's carefully-constructed credit-crawl accompaniment, or sit still in wonder at the Exit Music so required by persnickety roadshow production producers?

Every single composer proceeded into the villa with these questions on their minds, so the gambit was successful.

'We gotta *stimulate* 'em!' Shonnaleen had said while she and Butterbugs were kicking around ideas to enhance the party. 'A few *topics* might be in order.'

All the biggies were there. Known, lesser-known, and not-so-known.

Strangely enough, the subject of Exit Music came to the fore.

'My son,' said Timmy Tiomkin to Butterbugs at his earliest opportunity, 'The end of the picture! What are we supposed to do with it? I ask you! I compose for the reason of closure. Completion. I wrap things up, whether Ivan X notices or not. What are we here for, to cut things off like a rural projectionist might do?'

'Have you spent some time in the stix, Timmy?' asked Dave Buttolph. 'Well, I have. A lot. Those guys tend to run the whole thing out. To blank frames.

The best damn presentation I've seen is in the picture show at Anarene, Texas. Completeness! And when the house lights come up, now *that's* closure!'

'Oh, Dave, please don't hate me, but I'm happy for the rurals. They're getting better showmanship than the cities!'

Timmy knew that Dave, to the great unwashed, was basically an unknown name, but that he had influenced untold thousands of audiences' moods at any given evening. Like everyone here tonight.

Tiomkin was born in Ukraine, so to him, a steppe was a steppe, was a steppe (as he said in public many times, in order to prove his qualifications in scoring westerns), so peace was declared.

'Now don't go sayin' nothin' aginst *anyone here!*' announced Ray Heindorf, already pleasantly lubed, and damn sure he wanted a good time tonight. His entreaty became the theme of the evening.

Suddenly Delius' 'Spring Morning' rolled out over the estate-wide stereo system, DJ'd by none other than the distinguished Muster Shade. It had an immediate effect on everyone who was present. Most were overcome with a sweet sadness, or a nostalgia, or an interpretation of some aspect of life that only music, in the key of contemplation, could portray. Some were in tears, as the countryside the piece evoked led to a land of longing, of dreams, of bursting forth into the sunny freedom of expressive sharing. For every composer had their own version of what the tone poem was saying. Each had been called upon to score the same sorts of feelings, in one picture or another. That was how it was done: they all felt their environment and its potential very keenly. Life needed enhancement – it needed scoring.

'Damn!' more than one was thinking, 'Wish *I'd* written that!'

The music was saying, 'Come with me into the tonal realm of another, further, and different perception of the reality which we assume is ours to hold'. It is fleeting, as is music itself, and what comes forth is the sensation of the moment. But what a moment – if it could only be contained! If it could only stand still! But if it did, then there would only be one note, and if it were not the grace note desired, then sorrow would taint the memory. Instead, let the tones roll, let them unfurl, even if the effect is just for an instant, even an instant following an instant, for music flows, as does life, and on and on, in channels we do not necessarily know, for we hear them instead of see...

'...That is why we, on the screen, those in the foremost credits of the photoplays of which we are all part, can only but wonder at the power and effect that you who score us and support us bring. So we rely on you to lift us into transcendent zones. We need you, we need you to help convey our presence to those who watch, for only you possess the means to take us there, and then return us to that place where we can be taken up again, whenever an audience returns! You are the furthest dimension of the Seventh Art! You are the most subjective, and perhaps the most powerful. For, what am *I* when I recite lines? When I emote? True, I can carry a scene without you. I say that in all honesty, but why would I want to, all the time? Why would I not want whatever picture I am in to not be enhanced by your graces?

'We are not, in these talkies, doing opera – though I have done so in the strict sense, and I have to say, specifically, in 'Der Ring' (20th-Fox), Alfred, you saved my ass! And Paul (Smith), in 'Ukanada-Jasta' (Cinemation), you made my role smaller than it was in my mind, but just the right size as far as what it was supposed to be. Great levelers! Do not let my praise over-value you, for such a thing is not possible. If anything, do not let my words or anyone else's, especially producers and studio heads, interrupt what you do. Just keep on keeping on, and we shall not bar your way!'

Butterbugs finished speaking, and as the strains of 'Spring Morning' stepped toward their conclusion, and all wished for a continual tone poem to sustain the mood set by the host, each person, whether they were couple or solo or group, had to steer off into a solitary mode for a time, in which to ponder the significance of music's role in life and love and aspiration, so melded by cinema's additive chemistry.

'We are *part* of it,' Cyril Mockridge said to Franz Waxman.

'And that 'it',' replied Franz, 'is part of the person's mind, part of the audience's mind. We shape it, make it presentable.'

'You better than most!' said Johnny Green.

'No, go on with you!' said Franz. 'I feel that I'm talking from my soul with a given score. That I'm committed to stating what the rest of the picture cannot state. I am only so glad we get opportunities from producers and directors to trust our instincts, if not our melodies or leitmotifs.'

'Wilder loves you, Franz. So do we all,' said Johnny.

Always energetically modest, Franz adjusted his specs and said, 'I'm grateful to the Academy for letting me rejoin.'

'I would have sued them had they not!' declared Bronislau Kaper. 'To resign because Alfred's 'Robe' (20th-Fox, 1953) wasn't even *nominated* is a most noble notion!'

'Besides,' Franz laughed his gentle laugh, 'I had to adapt some of Alfred's 'Robe' themes for 'Demetrius and the Gladiators' (20th-Fox, 1954). I can tell you, they were *worth* adapting!'

'Better than the originals!' Alfred himself sounded off from across the room.

'Too complimentary, Pappy! But I feel that the urge to write a score that could dominate or wreck a given picture is a stigma that has been placed upon us by certain critics. That is, the ones who notice these things. It is an urge I myself have never felt, yet, I strive to explore my assignment as far as I can take it.'

'A reasonable conclusion, Franz.' Bernard Herrmann had just entered, and he'd been listening to Waxman for only a few seconds, but he always hit the ground running, and his fellow composer/conductor was a person he could not possibly repudiate.

'For where lies the expansion of music's expressive desires but in the conduit of the cinema, which can, it seems, go anywhere that music goes.'

'Provided you adhere to the demands laid upon you,' counseled Alfred.

Everyone knew he was academically posing the standard studio line for the sake of clear discussion.

'We all know our business, my colleagues,' said Miklós Rózsa.

'You above all, Maestro,' replied Alfred.

It was a custom (and a pleasure) for this civilized group to compliment each other, often relentlessly. They not only meant it, but it also kept their solidarity tuned up.

Eliot Goldenthal chose the moment.

'Yes, Pappy, we are all part of the same traveling caravan of expansive accompaniment. We're along for the ride, and is that not what it's all about?'

'Indeed. To accompany and assist, but to point out, as well.'

Harold Arlen had to interject, 'And to create memories to be remembered!'

'The constant desires of a tunesmith!' Van Cleave added, with a big smile.

'From our ability to convey the needed support,' said Anne Dudley (just arrived from Londinium, having just scored 'Samson Agonistes' (Pucklechurch Pix), a major challenge), 'there comes a reliance. We are they who can be depended upon. God, how I love what we do! Greetings from Pinewood, all, where nothing is too much trouble!'

Big welcomes were sent in her direction.

On one of her arms, Michael Nyman, fresh from scoring the latest Bond picture, as well as Carlyle's 'The French Revolution' (Rank) and 'Sarter Resartus' (St. Sepulchre Studios), and on the other, John Barry, with two Peter Greenaway productions under his belt. But they were quiet. They wanted to hear.

A Polish contingent slipped in behind them, consisting of Wlodek Pawlik and Wojciech Kilar. Vyacheslav Ovchinnikov was the only Russian who could make it tonight. Quincy Jones signaled that there were still empty chairs in back of him.

'Ours is not to reason why,' said Alfred, in the center of the gathered tribe. 'Ours is but to create within the dramatic framework of what we are given. Otherwise, there's always the concert hall...'

Tucky Pharos, punky girl composer from Cape Verde, who'd done the stunning 'In Ferrero Te Enuxus' (UA) and 'Up On Chinaberry Hill' (Pathé, AA), didn't sit well in Hollywood yet, so she took elder Alfred's safe summary to task.

'How can we limit ourselves to 'the formula'?' she queried.

'An imperative exists in the Industry,' he replied. 'And it happens to be: if you want to score a studio picture, you have to comply. I think you'll find there's considerable freedom within the alleged confinement.'

'What do you mean? How can you sit in the same chair as the assembly line passes by, and you stick in your little components, and call it done??'

She was good and feisty, and promenaded from entry hall all the way out to the terrace and back, broadcasting these noticeable words.

'I mean, *really!!*'

'She sounds like she'd rather do what we do,' whispered Laurie Anderson to Björk, who nodded.

Miklós stepped forward with patience and kindness.

'What Alfred is saying is that, given the assignment, stick with it in spirit, then elaborate in your own way. They will be pleased, believe me.'

Alex North trod into the indirect light.

'That's what Stan Kubrick said about '2001' (MGM, 1968).'

Score rejected in favor of pre-existing music.

'Kubrick is an exception. He changed the whole field, you know,' said Maestro Rózsa.

'Would that I could work for him!' said Tucky.

'Then it will be as a 'Music Supervisor',' said Leonard Rosenman, who knew from (fairly good) experience.

'I don't care,' replied Tucky. 'For it is music, *music*, which writes the scene, makes the grade, does the work, and deserves the whole credit!'

'Now, just a minute,' interjected Butterbugs. 'We are *all* additive elements here. Never mind the many eminents of certain other crafts and arts, who all came to this town on the very same day! Gathered in this one place at this one time. It's probably unprecedented. This gathering is only due to Shonnaleen's and my love of scoring. You can't qualify a joined effort by taking credit because one element is, to you, more prominent than the others. What if directors of photography had been invited tonight? Oh yes, there would be subject-of-discussion-rules laid out at the door! Nevertheless, Tuck, you do bring up a subject that all of you might review. Me? I'm fairly exempt, as I appreciate all the work of everyone here. Thus, there is no rivalry to be accounted for. Yet, there is welcome room for debate, naturally.'

'My dear son! Young fellow! Please don't hate me,' said the inimical Timmy. 'But we are not rivals in the least here. It is *non*-film composers who might think so, but not us! Eh, my friends?'

Sneaking a sentence in before the laughter roared, Miklós said:

'We all know you are above rivalry, Timmy. We cannot possibly compete!'

Indeed, hilarious responses followed, but they all knew that Tiomkin was sincere. He was right. That was why they could all be in the same room together at the same time.

There followed welcome musical interludes on the piano. Bernardo Segall played his End Title from 'Custer of the West' (Cinerama, 1969), Benny Herrmann played the Prelude to Act V of his opera, 'Wuthering Heights' (in pre-production at RKO), Elmer Bernstein soloed with The Wide Open from 'The Commancheros' (20th-Fox, 1961), Dusan Radic performed his Fantasy on Themes from 'The Long Ships' (Columbia, 1964) and 'Genghis Khan' (Columbia, 1965), followed by Jerry Goldsmith playing his Love Theme from 'The Sand Pebbles' (20th-Fox, 1966) in its original piano version, Quincy Jones delivered a wow-medley of themes from 'Mackenna's Gold' (Columbia, 1968), with Timmy, who co-produced the picture, singing 'Old Turkey Buzzard' in Ukrainian, in lieu of an absent

347

José Feliciano. Then Björk sang the Hymn of the Vestal Virgins from Rózsa's 'Quo Vadis' (MGM, 1951), with the composer at the keyboard. But the set was powerfully wrapped up with Maurice Jarre playing his End Title from 'Tai-Pan' (De Laurentiis, 1986).

Other acts followed later, each its own special contribution to a special evening. More were willing to step up, but it was getting on…

Then unexpectedly, Shonnaleen mounted the stage platform (which was thankfully bolstered by solid headers laid flat and tiled over), and the genial group grew silent. The masses calmed, she flourished an LP of the Original Motion Picture Score to Rodgers and Hammerstein's 'Flower Drum Song' (Universal, 1961), and made it clear that it would be the subject of her *testimony*.

'Kats and kittens? Just a moment. You ain't heard nothin' yet! Jolson may have said it before me, but this here blackface is *real*, so you gotta believe me. I know you've heard it *all* because you write the scores that indirectly – or maybe it's directly – make or break the show. Whichever, we non-perf types are eternally grateful. But maybe, with my one bite-sized example, you'll know *how* much. It's nothin', really. Oh hell, why be all humble and bashful about this? That's just a tanker-truck of horseshit. It's *somethin'*, all right. Because I saw it.

'I was still doin' my custodial gig. You all know what I did, for year upon year. Well, I was nowhere and nothin', but I had a few young-y people I knew, mostly white folks, who felt sorry for me and invited me over to their dump so's I could, you know, take a break from my own dump. Am I gettin' too graphic?'

The room warmly responded with approbation, not rejection, as she knew it would. Shonnaleen was beloved.

'And I was there. At their place. A different scene than I was used to. Hip, skinny blonde boys and girls, working in restaurants by day but doing the art-y thing at all other times, or tryin' to. I thought to myself, you whites don't have a monopoly on this sorta thang, but here I am, and I'm your guest, so I guess I'd better take what you offer. It's only good manners. Well, I was surprised, and I guess I was sort of pleased they were all as broke as I was. But not broke in spirit, which I have to tell ya, I was considering taking up, if you know what I mean. But whoa now, this isn't about me. I'm only a witness. And I'm getting on with it.'

There were plain signs from the audience that they were digging her log-in-mono.

'So they plied me with green wine, but I did turn down the cycling witchweed. I realized their status, and I found I could relate. Yeah – me, black, mega-ton, solo, dyke-type, doomed to janitor closets and invisibility. But I mean, how do you lay a life before someone new? But I know, this isn't about me. It's about *us*, cuz I found we all, in this little group, on this obscure night, all appreciated music we didn't know we appreciated.

'Cazzie, the dude in the stocking cap and stubble, wanted music, needed music. Nothin' but a sapphire-needle Xcess ToneSaver turntable. Lemmah, cool Swedish Twiggy girl, who made my eyes twinkle, went over to her durable duffle and filched, finally pulling out some yard sale dime albums she'd fancied because of their covers. I'll never forget 'em. 'Jerry Colonna Entertains – At Your Party...', and – 'Flower Drum Song'. Original Sound Track, baby. That's right, Alfred, *your* album!'

Alfred reacted, but above all, he wanted her to continue without further blandishments.

'Well, my feelings were a bit hurt when the first cut they played on the Colonna album was 'Big Fat Minnie', but I knew it was just chance. What else could go wrong? There were other downbeat incidents that were based on destiny, and not on personal choice or behavior.

'But my point in all this palaver is that, on this particular night, I felt very low and, quite frankly, near the end of my tether. I sat there in a slump, taking up the whole of the daveno and thought, I'm so depressed, I can't even wiggle one ear lobe.'

Shonnaleen's bummer story was heartfelt, but the tone of her narration, peppered by a shake-out of levity, gave the audience cause to suspect some sort of triumph was coming. Also, her story was so entirely lacking in maudlin or self-pitying sympathetic slop, that every film composer there was already scoring her words in their minds.

'And I also thought, the skin on my dimpled ass is gonna graft with this furniture's fabric before I can even muster enough gumption to *end it all* somehow. Hopefully, I'll just do a final fade out.

'It's funny, because my senses were blinking away, one by one. Not cuz of the wine, just natural causes, I guess. Nothing to touch, nothing to see, nothing to smell, nothing to hear...'

Some in the audience were daubing their tear ducts.

'... Until, that Cazzie dude put on the other album. Barely, at first, but it wasn't a few seconds before it came on strong. Symphonic, but showy. A show tune. A show, yeah. Upbeat, movin' on. Main Title and Arrival from, yup, 'Flower Drum Song'. I thought, WTF, what, why?

'My ears were already back, but I guess I opened my eyes and saw, things had changed. Tinker, another guy there, was air-conducting, and pretty well, too, maestros. And then these two blonde babes with bare bellies started doing balletic interpretation of the score. I perked, baby, cuz the eye candy and the swelling, dulcet sounds were restoring my wearily-framed life, jiggling me, and prodding me, and carrying me back to the zest and the best. As the others did their own performance trips, I found I could do mine, too. I mouthed the singers. Shit, you shoulda seen me do Juanita Hall! I'd never heard the score before, but I *felt* it. Know what I mean? It became part of me. I know it's R&H, folks, but Alfred, it was the *way* you brought it alive. Spoke to my heart. Woke me up. Soothed me and comforted me. Gave me something to go home to.

'OK, we were all a little high on a few substances, but it was the music, it was thoroughly the *music* that was guiding us, tellin' us what to do, cuz when you perform, you gotta have guidelines. The score was it for us. These young-oids were gettin' down, rollin' with the music, the dance matched, the conducting worked. Even the wait until the flip side got going had a backstage feel – all was on hold until the music resumed. Man, by the time Jack Soo was doing 'Don't Marry Me', I was groovin' and shakin' with the best of 'em. So were my earlobes. I was *back*.

'This music, on that night – and on this one too – did not 'soothe the savage beast'. Hell no. It did a long shot more than that. It damn well returned the beast to life.'

'Well,' said Alfred quietly, 'it's Dick Rodgers' *score...*'

'Come on, Alfred! Come on. You know what I'm talkin' 'bout. It's what you *do* with it. Besides, Dick sent you the same telegram he'd always send to Russell Bennett: 'You *make* my score!' That right?'

Newman was silent. He of course knew what she was talkin' 'bout, and he was humbled. He was also choked up.

Then, with a conspicuous absence of schmaltz, but with every bit of sincerity she could broadcast, she faced Alfred and said:

''Tis magic, baby. You have it. You wield it. We appreciate it. Thanks, and,' – spreading her massive arms out wide – 'a big tank full of love to you *all!*'

Huge applause, with quite a few misty eyes, and praise for conspicuous attention from this visitor from Hollywood's Olympus, who condescended upon these lowly music-maker-types in their humble shindig. The excitement, chatting, and good cheer in the room were palpable. Shonnaleen was a boffo hit. Bob Newman, film musician agent, was already dickering with her to do a one-woman-and-her-musique show at the Pasadena Playhouse.

And the evening wrapped with everyone giving Alfred best wishes, good luck, and break-a-leg for the 'UWH' score. Before the lights went out, e/telegrams arrived with best regards from DDS and Klimenty Dominchen, among many others. Even Maxie Steiner, who was indisposed with a twisted ankle, sent an email of goodness.

And, as was part of their custom of solidarity, each composer in turn took a magic marker and scrawled out a one-bar fanfare on a short strip of toilet paper, to be hung in sequence as a sort of Tibetan prayer flag in the home of the night's honoree (Alfred), for the duration of the coming score's composition.

43.

Bunker Mentality As Method

At precisely 3:00AM the klieg brutes were ignited and Leon 'Shammie' Shamroy put down his newspaper, bear claws, and coffee-flavored beverage, then climbed into the viewfinder saddle to prepare for one of the most important shots in the picture.

Butterbugs was just emerging from makeup. His stand-in was already in position, as Shammie would get very annoyed if there was no one on the set who was serving as a warm body to light properly. Rance Kemmosch, the stand-in, had already been on the receiving end of one of Shammie's cigar butts, flung at him for reasons of extreme annoyance on the eminent lighting cameraman's part, for similar churlishness on another picture. Today, however, they were both bantering about the mugs in the boxing industry and describing a few they'd particularly like to punch out, given the opportunity.

Egaz D'Varzim stepped onto the set.

Things were plenty tense.

'What would the genius director of 'Plusterbrøarck', 'I Wanna Marry a Chimp Cage Cleaner', 'The Existential Quandary of a Ruthenian Silage Sifter Operator' and dozens of other art house classics, make of the Most Important Picture of Our Times? Half Angolan/Portuguese and half Goan/Portuguese, this brainy auteur's command of English is shockingly limited, but if all sorts of foreign directors could make great pictures just by squinting or making auction signs at actors, he can, too. In point of fact, Sr. D'Varzim has a BigPod full of Berlitzinopolis-style Emergency 'I Wanna Know NOW!' English lessons that run in one ear, simultaneous with his assault on this mammoth production. Our Butterbugs knows all sorts of languages fluently, but will he know Mr. D'Varzim's? Could be interesting!'

– Mitti Mar Mammah in 'Our Industry's Best Minute-To-Minute Blogification'
(A Mega|Goth Stvdios undertaking)

Said the director: 'In what way, ready for shot on set? I want-ta-to have-an-this dry-and-pressed.'

Cody de la Funk, Special Production Assistant to Mr. Goth, was on set and making differences. She took the cravat he handed her.

'Mr. D'Varzim, right over here on the parallel. Mr. Shamroy is ready. Butterbugs will be in place presently.'

To her he almost sounded Belorussian, or something… She was actually beginning to understand him.

D'Varzim: 'Ready! We are all the ready! Tie-up, this, is my favorite. Please-then-be careful with-uh-it. More than.'

'D'Varzim, eminent realizer that he is, is in fact the twelfth director on the picture. Merv LeRoy, Al Shean (who has always wanted to direct), Jon Korkes (ditto), Willy Wyler, Sergei Eickkhrytovich, Debbie Smith, Ingmar Bergman, Randy Ogg, Stevensen 'Steve' Tidd-Tiggs, Ed Ulmer and Lmumba Mbane had all been signed at one time, but it was D'Varzim who got the prize on the strength of his brilliant 'Lemieux of the Ancient Follies' alone.'
– Press Release from Henny Lectrerne, Publicity Dept., Mega|Goth Stvdios

'What the –' thought Butterbugs, as he scanned the inaccuracies, outright lies and balderdash from Publicity and associated blogs. 'Why, 'Lemieux' was ash-canned many moons ago. And there's more to him than just half Angolan/Portuguese and half Goan/Portug…'

That, anyway, was what the Press Kits said. It wasn't clear if the Kit was a Hy Goth production, or just a generic spit-out from Publicity. That is, disappointing hyperbole mixed with a tarragon-like incongruous sub-text of amateur-sounding name-dropping.

P.R. was just another name for 'Propaganda Release' – or snake oil.

Butterbugs noticed the clipboard-wielding Cody, en route to the Assistant Director of the moment. He approached, then danced her around and behind a cyclorama opening, and nostalgia'd her, nice and close up, with a blown kiss, albeit for a specific purpose in the here and now.

'Oh, Butter-boy, you're more charming than ever. It's fun to be whirled and snatched – by you. But I have to –'

'Haven't seen you in too long, Code. Welcome aboard! Hey, I like those new smile lines on your sleek face, luxus. Let's retire to the New Mexican high country. You can show off your tan 'n' taut tummy with one of those knotted tops, on horseback. We'll ride and reminisce. Over the hills and far away.'

'Ultrastar lover! You've got more than what it takes. I remember, child.'

'The nights…'

'The nights… The stars… The stars in our eyes, in the heavens above, and down here on the ground… On my roof… The roof of my palate, too… Ooooh…'

'So I've given you memories. I've done my part. Now, can you lend me a few coppers?'

She became dreamy, flush with sex-shot fondness, and an almost parental caring for this ardent one, who would have done anything for her. At one time. And probably, now again.

'How are the babies?' he asked.

'Well, Butterhunk, I couldn't be more grateful for your foundational help.'

'Glad they're on the right trolley tracks.'

'Oh, yeah.'

'So, what've you got there, an ascot or something? Doesn't seem quite right. Not for this picture, anyway.'

'Oh, it's a cravat that *Mr.* D'Varzim wants pressed for some reason. I'm supposed to be 'please-then-be careful with-uh-it.' He's taking some getting used to, ya know.'

'Brilliant guy, Cody.'

'You sure?'

'OK, since we're past intimates, and we've memorized everything about each other, I'll let you in on a it-goes-no-further-than-our-pressed-together-lips, all right?'

'You can trust me, boy.'

'I know I can, heartthrob. Ya see, that partial-talk Egaz has going is... Well, it's an act. He's about as erudite as it gets. But he wants to go with a cryptic approach to his direction. It's his call, and I think it might be advantageous, especially on so gigantic a production.'

'To keep kind of a 'mystique' at the top?'

'Probably. It's good that everybody believes that's the way he really is. Otherwise he'd get a vat of cynical acid dropped on him. Like it's a gimmick, or something worse.'

'It... *is* a gimmick though, isn't it?'

'Hey Code, I know you're on the wry side of the biz, but easy does 'er.'

'Oh, I will. Especially for your sake, now that I know the 'dreaded knowledge'. Actually, I get a kick out if it.'

'You haven't been snickering behind his back, or anything...?'

She mock-snickered, cute as hell. 'OK, that's my final one!'

The actor smiled and stretched his arms casually. 'I kind of like it. It's rousing me out of my comfort zone.'

'Like you *need* to be kicked out of that nest!'

'Only *you'd* get to do that, Cody. I'm still crazy about you, girl.'

'And I you! Let me know!'

'I serve only you! So anyway, Egaz's secret – totally classified, right? He wouldn't kill me if he found out, but creatively, he'd be devastated. You being near his right arm, you should know it. That's why I don't feel I'm betraying a confidence.'

'I swear it!'

Butterbugs gazed fondly at her noble bust when she crossed it.

'Coming from you, I will revise all observations and opinions regarding Mr. D'Varzim.'

'He is a visionary. We need him.'

'Oh Butterbaby, I believe you. Really.'

They kissed.

'Lots to do,' she said, a bit dully.

'You, uh, seem kind of 'plastic' on this production.'

Cody seemed relieved to hear this. 'I fake it, erstwhile roommate! My babies need a financially solid future. This is a good gig. Fakery is half of studio life. The sun shines only part of the day.'

'Yeah, I know, I know. You're understood.'

'Thanks, ultra. Say, you're lookin' good, even in your High Mad makeup!'

'Well, shot's about to commence. Now looka here...'

'You want Hy-Facts?'

'And even some falsifications.'

'Well, there's plenty of P.R. about this production, as you know. We've had to fabricate, to a certain extent, Butterbugs. We need name recognition. D'Varzim's unknown. Inflating truthiness isn't the worst thing in the world, especially in this biz, old pro. Huh?'

Her collarbones glistened. Her tawny lips were still raised, padded, mindful of rememberéd glories in the sack, and her hair caressed her shoulders, as he himself used to, and she was still bra-less – she of the uppermost measurement's imperviousness to assistance or alteration, and for the most stately of reasons. This, friends, was an exemplary woman, showcased in obvious visual impacts, but possessive of deep integrity, built well below the landscape.

Butterbugs *believed* her. Her credibility was intact. So was her surficial but genuine stun-power. But he was not distracted. Cody was holistic, as always, in her effect. So now, he thought only of the picture at hand. 'UWH' was in a delicate state.

'Let's rev this pageant up, OK?' she continued. 'Otherwise it would just be too unremarkable. There's nothing *wild* (yet) about this picture. Sure, it's a big one, but there's no real hook with the public yet. It's the book that's king. The hook is the book, and we have to create our own. It's assumed that the picture will just be a loyal filmization, respectable and all, (cuz of *you*), but no real...'

'You mean we need a scandal? A tragedy?'

'Look, super-cock, Hy just wants to make this thing work. I'm concerned, as well. There're a lot of producers, but I'm more concerned than they are, it seems. Well, they don't know the half of it. I think you're all just drifting into this one.' Then she added, sing-songly. 'Drifting along...!'

'You don't realize what tremendous pre-production has gone into this thing, Cody. Especially out on location, where your bare shoulders have never sun-bathed. I can tell you that right now.'

Suddenly she got all contrite and 'subservient' (Cody-style: playful first, wry second). He still thought she was hot, but he didn't much care for her all-stops-out loyalty to Hyman Goth, the Dubious-but-Connected-and-Moneyed One.

She knelt down and mock-kissed the zipper of his fly, then quickly rose, touched his nose gently with her pinkie, and said:

'Gotta go. This 'n' that. You know. Everything's intact. What we talked about:

rock solid. You know. Ring me. Let's do an early morning drink in a questionable bar out in the Plains of Id, huh?'

Holy shit, was she *some kind* of fox, or what? Why couldn't *she* be the sole producer of this shindig? What more could an honest actor want?

The cyclo drape caressed her on the way out, in a circular swirl around the flared pillars of her legs, as her shoes fox-trotted back to the freeway of to-and-fro activity, over the curved plywood deck of the immense HMD HQ set.

In the annals of film-within-film films, the present moment was when cameras might dolly in to medium close-ups of those in the cast concerned with carrying the built-up tension implicit within the soundstage in question. Any sensible director would repeat the process regarding all players concerned. In this case, however, it was solely Butterbugs upon whom the next juncture rested, for it was to be his acting 'cred' that would make this little Hollywood clambake worthwhile. His interpretation of the lead role would indicate to all concerned if this under-advantaged-though-huge picture gambit was worthwhile, or if it should be mothballed, out of sheer vanity on the part of those who dreamt of its hatching.

This principal player was definitely used to the predictable load of heavy-duty expectations assigned to his Atlas-wannabe shoulders. For the ruling classes of the studios, courage, fortitude, and determination were all virtues expected of their performers, whatever form they might take.

In all the pictures he'd done so far, Butterbugs had readily adapted to the systems-that-be. Because they really didn't have much to do with his mission of performing as far as the essence of his acting was concerned. Maybe that was because he generally transcended the mechanics of movie-making politics. In actuality though, his working with the system succeeded because he really didn't transcend much of *anything.* He stayed down in the trenches, where films were really made: in front of the camera, on the set, on location. Wherever it was necessary to position himself, in order to get the story told and the picture finished and projected to audiences to interpret. That was the built-in corollary, and it did not abandon him now.

Stimulated by their on-set reunion, Butterbugs and Cody took drinks in front of the Spence Tracy Cabin at the Bev Hills Hotel.

'Just like early times,' he said.

'Olden days!' she smiled.

'Of yore!'

'Only now, look at us,' he smiled back. 'You're practically running Mega|Goth!'

'And you're leading the whole Industry!'

'Towards what, *I don't know...!*' he laughed.

They were joined by Gloria Steinem. She'd just finished a seminar, 'Women Directors Before 1920', across the garden in the Gish Sisters and the Talmadge Sisters Rooms.

'Well by golly,' Butterbugs marveled, 'here we are, the three of us, together again. Just like that time in Knoxville, for 'Lady Delicata' (Klizzington FilmoPix)...'

'My first crack at producing,' said Cody, trying not to smirk.

'That script was a real bastard – er, I mean, *bitch!*' Gloria's tongue was in her cheek.

The picture had been universally acclaimed.

'Back in a flash, you two...,' Cody quipped, rising and trotting off the terrace.

'How's the filming, then?' asked Gloria.

He was momentarily distracted by a sidelong glance at Cody's bouncing hair, super-tight pants and VPL, as she headed toward the luxurious loo.

'For being such a significant male feminist, you sure are slobberingly abstracted by Things Sexual, aren't you? And I'm sure I'm not the first one to tell you that in such stark terms, buster!'

'I *enjoy* it!' he crowed.

'Well,' replied Gloria, 'I suppose that's where your *incandescence* might originate from, hmm?'

Back on set, Butterbugs promptly took his place behind the desk. The shot was being framed and lighted. The gigantic camera required special placement treatment, and special patience was required of the cast.

And then, the gravity of the situation – a distinct, extraneous force – which had nothing to do with his own self-confidence, or experience, or courage, or even talent, sort of... hit him. He looked up at the monumentally complex apparatuses above him. They were filming in the loftiest soundstage in the world: Mega|Goth Studios' Stage 55 – over 400 feet high. 370 feet of stage house space above him was packed with special effects wizardry, enough to make Cirque de Soleil's most sophisticated machinery look like two tin cans and a string. Or maybe two tracks and a whistle.

You see, ever since audiences worldwide categorically rejected digital special effects because they were too 'fakey', the Industry was in constant turmoil: how to hide the digital amidst the real was the Crisis of the Age. Therefore, because of the complete and utter importance of this picture, Hyman Goth himself, aided and abetted by his VP in Charge of Production, Charles Technicolour Clearwater, *insisted* that all effects would be *real* in every application.

Gravity existed. It would be a familiar feature in the weeks and months to come. There was nothing for it now but to live with it, and roll with the tide.

Butterbugs donned his spiral chapeau made of Jimson weed fibers, Upper Middle Eastern Dictator glasses, and patted his Plumpy-pad mustache discreetly, lest the Makeup Marauders notice his fiddling. He was fully prepared for the special Seek 'n' Destroy effects, even down to the lowest basement contingent, to do their tap-dance on him.

(All brands ™ by Allied And Unanimous Dynamix Corporation, a division of Polycarp Davis Systems International.)

Reverie followed preparation for the oncoming scene, due to the a.d.'s advisement of waiting for more of Shammie's lighting plots to come true.

He fell into contemplation over previous pictures of risk he had known.

In one particular film... which one was it? Oh yes, 'For Closure' (Studio+Canal), about the psychological problems of people who want some limb to be amputated in order to be whole. Butterbugs played a psychiatrist in charge of an esoteric clinic for very oddball disorders. He witnessed a co-star having his foot hacked off and then successfully restored – digitally. It was almost as if he were an audience member instead of a participant in the film, for he may have witnessed the event, but he never followed up with any substantial understanding of the whole SFX procedure.

When an actor has been so thunderstruck, he must quickly move on in his career. But the seed of intrigue was certainly planted.

What were the possibilities of such advanced special effects, then? Way past the banal and the predictable? Most likely. Did they really aid a picture that much? Could they make or break a film as surely as a music score could? Were they really that necessary to tell a good tale? What were *really* the possibilities? Supposedly, they were limited to the motion picture screen, but now, in his deep experience in high-level picture shows, perhaps they extended beyond the quasi-designed latitudes of thinly veneered Seventh Art realities. Perhaps they were blurring with *real* realities, more than ever.

Old-fashioned questions, certainly. But for some reason, now that he was embarked on 'UWH', they seemed somehow valid again.

Then there was 'He Sailed... Right Out There...' (Your Basic), in which the star had staked his life in order that a proper and compelling picture show be produced. If he were to sacrifice himself on any cinematic altar, it had better be worth doing.

The script had required him to take a fall. A considerable fall. He cheerfully assented because sincerity in acting was so vital an imperative in fulfilling any given director's or studio boss' wishes or commands. It was all about integrity.

The remarkable plunge into the 'He Sailed...' sphere of the Ancient Ages, which Butterbugs volunteered to do (with ærocopter backpack to be engaged in order to break his fall), was simply a procedure necessary to get the right shot. Each picture had its summum bonum scene, and this was one that really mattered. It went off without a hitch. That was why he did sequences of chance. Because when all was said and done, it was the right thing to do. For the sake of the picture's integrity of character, if nothing else. For his own sense of worth also. Nothing to do with ego. It was merely the required moment of truth needed for all the surrounding effort to be worthwhile. *Meaning* meant so much. Moments of truth bore the meaning out, so that it was cast, molded, burnished

357

and finished. To present, with all honesty, before a public already weighed down with its own cares, woes, and weariness. To be lightened by an insatiable appetite for diversion.

Sincerity then, was one of the seminal reasons why he wanted to do the bunker-buster scene in 'UWH'. It promised to be a complete and exciting success, for the general benefit of the picture.

Recalling his Great Leap sequence back in 'He Sailed...', scored by an adventurous chorus:

'Today I fell 3000 feet. And lived!' he wrote in his diary.

And there was no way he could ever forget that occasion when he unintentionally soared from the belly of the jet in 'If My Pilot Be Khalsa' (UA). Down, out, into the open air, for the longest time. It worked quite well for the picture's veracity, and made for a modest financial success, too.

No further arguments, rumination, or reviews.

Time to be great. Time to grasp and hold. Time to lunge, if necessary. In order for greatness to grow.

44.

He Shall Lead, And
He Shall Teach

Butterbugs' lines of dialogue as High Mad Doctor were, in the sequence before the cameras today, uttered in Imperial Aramaic. Subtitles would appear on the Ultra-Panavision 70 screen, with translations presented in 155 languages in the porta-media versions, with a 460 language translation in the Mega*Nung*-DVD Director's Cut Version, in tinted straw-yellow text, specifically designed by color consultant Henri Jaffa to co-exist with Shammie & Bob's extremely detailed and intimidating cinematography.

And those lines, how he had labored on those lines! The archaic tones gave him the willies, with accompanying creepshow imaginings of ancient Hittites, and Ur, and savage Samarra, all lurking in the back alleys of the faraway past history's downtown. Oh, but he relished these feverish ramblings, and their power plainly inspired his brilliant performance thus far. And so it would be today: his big Talk Back Speech, delivered in the tongue of the ancients! Never was a Doctor so High, so Mad!

The scripting team of Sawlohmunn Rabinowicz Cane, Kerf Cheup, Britney Spears (her first script!), Harry Clork, Ting-Go Lay-O, Sho-Jen Smith, Pramila Jutterjee, Ioweho Kettlesimmer, Chief Standing Cow, Arrah Shencottah, Artie Cheung, John Smith, Johnson Foo, Bertita de la Goth (no relation to Hyman), the distinguished Brit lit lion Sir Fendal Splibbington-Jhares, and of course, Saskia Pingles (here now, and for once!), all sat anxiously in the sound-proof A/C Observer's Booth, provided just for the occasion.

The two 'adaptation sisters', Tulameen and Similkameen Spuzzum-Judgeship (aka: T-meen & S-meen S-J), their work on the script completed, got to sit in a gilded swan-decorated pulpit, unused in this sequence, which made them feel super-special.

Irving and Yosef, deluxe soundstage butlers, wanted everybody to be comfortable, and to have plenty of entertainment beverages on hand, in case anything got *out* of hand. De Bimini Maan was there with his drinks trolley, so everyone relaxed. It was Yosef's long service in Vegas that brought his sort of culture along, and it was a super idea.

Saskia, back from far off Jambutterbugsabad late last night, was so horny for her long-distance three-way member #1, that she burst into his dressing room early that morning, unannounced, ushered the make-uppers out, out, OUT!, and clambered on top of him as he sat, bibbed and napkined, in his barber chair, awaiting further application of his extremely sophisticated and multi-strata'd makeup.

'I've never engaged in intimacy with such a sinister-faced personage!' sang Saskia. 'It doesn't matter a whit, for the face of love has many visages, and on many levels, both lateral and longitudinal!'

Butterbugs enjoyed her logic.

'Good morning. Nice to see you.'

As he was reciting lines today on set, those he knew she'd specifically written in the script, he saw no reason to wax verbal about much of anything at this moment. Only a smile of pleasure passed across his face, and in its current dramatic state, any effort that curled the edges of his mouth could only come across as a satrap's smirk at a concubine's competitive get-ahead gesture.

Saskia happened to like the effect. Preparatory viscosity automatically spread to where it was needed, for she was hot to trot with he for whom she'd created high drama. The words of a leader, whose power would spin out as an aphrodisiac to millions of his female subjects. Not to mention Subject #1, who pulled her knickers until they snapped (even breakaways take a bit of tugging to free), then spun them around his nose, which glistened with spirit gum, in a hazy, heady circle, before tossing them over at his mirror, where they lodged on the topmost Tesla bulb. The imbued fabric rapidly heated up, filling the room with a therapeutic scent of essential oils of musk-cum-patchouli. Pleased with this mood-setter, she wasted no time in fingering her labial system in circular dilation/pucker-mode, for the waiting insertion.

'No nether-region makeup today, eh, dearie?' she hooted, and hopped on top. Her pale bootie pumped up a storm, a hurricane, the eye of which the man playing HMD occupied, and quite contentedly, too. Caught up in the generated energy, with the most prosaic of methods, the film's star found his mind expanding with new ideas and advanced interpretations of the lines he'd already memorized. Filed and valued and ready for creative association with his director, he was silently grateful to his screenwriter-cum-lover for the added inspiration. Perhaps he could wangle her an additional screen credit as Associate Director or Idea Inspirer, or something a little more randy...

Aside from the crazy creativity, it was just plain good to have his beloved Sasky back where she belonged. Oh, but how he marveled at her multiplicity of talents and admired her every detail of refined quality!

Not one carefully-applied detail on the star's face was mussed, but there was something missing. Saskia's mouth, even while her heavily-parted lips breathed, needed cuddling, not just verbiage. To satisfy her kiss quotient, and thwarted by the runny silver spangles on the star's cheeks and lower lip, Saskia was compelled to address it elsewhere on his person.

So now, sated, sitting up in their Observer's box, the excited jabbering amongst the writers soon toned down as the Lights, Camera, Speed commands added up.

Henry King, who was doing Second Unit on this shot, called for 'Action'.

HMD: Mr. President! I greet you with all the cheerfulness that such equivocation (as I feel in my very soul right now) will allow! We greet you with tam-tam and gong – the heritage sounds of my ancient people. Because we are a great people. But you, you are a *New* People!

Butterbugs rose slowly and drew up his robe for a grand gesture. He was feeling super and dandy, and did not mind the heavy Styrofoam wig, the spun-glass-fiber sideburns, the steel wool mustaches, or the pubic hair eyebrows. Behind all the makeup, composed of these humble yet effective materials, the spring fire of his dramatic creation was descending from the heavens. To bring its gift to the masses on the face of this planet. And *he was the one to do it.*

HMD: *(pausing, in Roman senator-style pose and gesture – robes serving toga effect)* So I address not only you and only you, Mr. Presidente *(varied pronunciation intentional),* but also those who call themselves the New People. I care not for labels of inaccuracy. Only mega-truth will suffice. These New People!

Henry: CUT! Print! *(aside, to Cody)* Got it in two takes! This kid's amazing! Best since Greg Peck.
Cody: Thank you, Mr. King. That's high praise indeed, and well placed. Mr. D'Varzim is now here.
Henry: Ready to hand it over. Crew? Take fifteen!

Butterbugs was then attended by several assistant directors, as well as Cody, to get ready for the next shot. He would leave the Throne Room and glide along the loggia to the Grande Balcony, where the body of the Talk Back Speech would be made. 35,006 extras awaited on the plains before the walls of old Bashgong's citadel. This was a bigger setup than the pyramid-building sequence in 'Land of the Pharaohs' (WB) in '55. Bigger than Borodino in 'Voyna i Mir' (Mosfilm, 1968)! And that was saying something.
Egaz took the conn.
'Ac-ca-tions!'

HMD: *(tracking shot, walking along the columned route)* Come, my Deputy Prime Minister Vushgubb! We must prepare! The world is watching, and much of the world is with us. We must not lose them.

VUSHGUBB: I *will*, sir.

Sir Vyvyan Claudeburst, the eminent Shakespearean who played HMD's vazeer, having trod the boards with Sir Henry Irving, with Larry, with Sir John, with Pamela Tiffin, and with Orsonia, stared in wonder and admiration at Butterbugs.

'Never in all my long years,' he thought to himself as the shot was progressing, 'Have I seen a better actor, a more confident player, a more potent teacher! He shall lead us all!'

Then, as they reached the parapet, the very plains roared with jubilation from the gathered populace as their High Mad Doctor, their Leader, Teacher, and Chief Martial Law Administrator placed his hands on the venerable speech pommels attached to the weathered stone, and made to speak.

45.

Butterbugs On The Tribune

Back up behind the terrace, in the loggia lined with drapes, ancient lights, and quietly glowing embers, a space pungent with the aroma of smoldering braziers, with attendant platters of prend-worm sheddings and chicken hawk livers, tankards of roseleaf wine and hogsheads of porter, the whole providing a genuine environment of royal gaiety and real excess that was wholly suitable from which to enact the creative drama of this important photoplay, Butterbugs suddenly found that he was truly carried away by the ecstatic rationale of his powerful role. Propelled by the amplified turbo-generatings of High Mad Doctor, and all he meant, he was now harnessed with the potential of violent fury. Certainly that was what the script called for!

He must consider. He felt like letting loose a huge bellow of rage/force-cum-panic/stress. He knew what the majestic camera movements would reveal on the screen. Would they reveal the turning globe of confrontational energy now operative within him?

He thought of the One Big Shot in DeMille's 'The Ten Commandments' (Paramount, 1956), from the upper reaches of that huge gate to the city of Per-Ramses, with the Children of Israel about to depart for forty fabulous years of wandering in the Wilderness, before crossing over Jordan. That moment – that one C.B.-Loyal Griggs-Elmer Bernstein-charged moment, when galvanization happens on the screen! Such forces were before him and within him now.

This, though, today!

That which enveloped him was bigger, yes. Grander, yes. And more shadowy. Yes, darker in tone and theme. Would he be up to the task of wielding the heavy instruments leading to the necessary galvanization? What would it take for such magic to occur? Here, spread under his watch, was Decadence personified in Imperial terms, and by golly, pride had to enter at *some* time. Was it pride that he finally felt in this spinning entity-ball inside him, back here in the curtained alcove, whilst the camera's railroad was being re-aligned by the second unit's late night crew, during everyone else's break?

In costume, bathed in the dim shimmer of the vulgar sensual influences around him, the graphic introduction of certain irreal ribbons of thought deep within his brainpan dissolved in and out of his picture show consciousness. No Gobbtown hallucination, this. Butterbugs' mind was free of intrinsic persuasion of any kind – neither drugs nor beverage alcohol lay in his cells. (Nor horseradish, either...)

These ribbons of realization were pure and natural, and could be proven valid in any metaphysical courtroom. But this undeniable Truth proclaimed one thing – a possibility. Was it not conceivable, that with all the evidence surrounding him – indeed – *rushing in on him* – that at this strangely marvelous moment – was it not possible that with the mindset he now experienced due to the inculcation of stimuli and identifiable signs at this time – was it not *probable* that he, Butterbugs, was, in actuality, the High Mad Doctor himself?

Really.

The High Mad Doctor?

No mere actor's dilemma of identity, but a positively stunning determination of plausibility. Indeed, he knew who he was through and through, and the fact was, maybe he was something *more* than just an actor.

Just an actor!?

Butterbugs let out such a gasp of amazement that if anyone had been near to him at the time, they would have thought some sort of awful death-rattle would surely ensue.

What if, with this obvious power, despite the cinematic artifice and appliances that now preoccupied him, he could transcend the limitations of role playing, and the limitations of role playing within the repetitive and sluggish apparatus of filmmaking itself, and seize the opportunity of – remaking the world?

Remaking the *what?*

The world.

Yes, the world. The world in which we are all contained.

Did it *need* remaking?

All this time, as an ultrastar, he had seen the world, all right. Lived it, worked with it. Worked in, around, and above it. Below it, too. It had been sweet to him, but was it so with the others, most of the others, who occupied it? Since when was he called upon to analyze any of this? Well, since – Since he had been gifted with the awesome and assumed responsibility for being some kind of phenomenon.

Remaking the world. Which world? His own? That of his Industry? Both the former and the latter were already in play. And going well, as a matter of fact. The Butterbugsization of motion pictures was making sense to all, and progress was proceeding to make it cogent and practical and lasting.

Should he confer with Sonny about this issue? Instantaneously, no. Sonny was a mega-agent, but he was an agent nevertheless. He steered people into roles. He, Butterbugs, had *played* roles, *become* roles, either via the Method or the Brit School, or (dare he acknowledge it –because everybody else did) via his own incandescence...

Didn't matter, he was the Enactor, the Realizer. The Actor who enacts, reacts, and everything in between. That was real, that was felt, lived, acted *out*.

Something higher had been making its presence known for a considerable time now. Something above the ceiling that had been encapsulating his mind-bogglingly successful career.

MGR, Arnie, NTR, Ron Wilson Reagan, and Jayalithia had done it! (Even

Vladimir Putin had been in a talent show...) None of them, though, in so thoroughly Imperial a context as at this moment. Though Martin Begglurr, the mild-mannered insurance agent from Shur, W'scaansin, had gone on to become Emperor-General of Katanga in central Africa, when that troubled province finally broke away from Kinshasa-oriented Congo. (Never mind that his puppet status came to a very bloody end a few months later, when he was assassinated and the province was forcibly returned to its original owners.)

[An interesting and unique example of the reverse of this progression: after being thrown out of government, 'Toawni' Blare became an actor of dubious talent but readily exploitable name value in London's West End, the Old Vic, and the National Theatre, as well as Broadway, where he was even more 'interestingly' received as a novelty. Both critics and audiences accurately pigeonholed him as a 'lightweight' player, appropriately cast in musical comedies and popular entertainments, usually as a bum-goon, or, in British parlance, a goon-clown. Or prat, pillock, tosser, tosspot, wanker, et al. And as everyone knows, after his disgraceful resignation, Richard Nixon was offered a three-month exclusive contract at a prominent Vegas showroom for an engagement that 'involved stand up routines scripted by Norman Panama and I.A.L. Diamond.' The casino took out a full page ad in 'Variety' announcing 'a terrific new show' to be presented by the legendary team who brought you 'Sinatra at the Sands'. The ad's clincher was that 'a new superstar', to headline the show, 'would be revealed when the curtains parted'. The financially-strapped ex-Prez eventually took the offer, but he ended up in a different show altogether. Bebe Rebozo had advised against this particular offer, and bailed him out of debt. Later, he and Bob Abplanalp reorganized and mounted the extremely successful 'Dick Nixon at the Sands' show (later officially retitled 'Richard Nixon at the Sands', as the ex-POTUS was resigned to sounding as presidential as possible, even in post-Oval Office showrooms. His agent, Checkers Milledwhump, fought for all his demands, and won. Certain members of the Rat Pack jokingly called it 'A Dick in the Sands'. In any case, it was a boffo phenomenon that bouffanted receptionists still wish were playing at that beloved venue.]

Pausing, after he had done a complete take in walking the full distance to the tribune and its pommels, so that the speaker could believe, through tactile contact, that he was literally 'steering' his nation in the direction of his choice, Butterbugs felt a rush like he'd never encountered before. It was LSD-worthy, but without Dr. Hofmann's magic bullet.

When called upon to do a second take of the Walk to the Pommels, the ultrastar was almost robotic, so deep in consideration was he. But ne'er betraying his strolling duty to execute the role assigned, he nevertheless dove in, even as the greater part of his conscious mind was taken up by this new and admittedly shallow subject, or even prospect – of power.

The tonnage of the camera, Surtees-run – as Shammie had gone off shift for the day – trundled silently next to him as he strode slowly and ceremoniously toward the balcony of advantage. This take was much deeper in every way, and all on the set could detect some kind of different-brand profundity emanating from Butterbugs. Old Atrocity couldn't put a finger on it, so he watched in spellbound silence as the take transpired, assuming that Butterbugs was onto something big, or else onto something that he didn't think possible.

The wall sconces glared more hauntingly, the richness of the drapes was increasingly palpable, the expressions of the HMD's face were much more defined and even diagrammatic in aiming any audience's attention towards the proper and most edifying aspects of the star's performance. Way down in the trenches was this take ignited, and its efforts fought uphill before moving over the top and onto the battle plain of proof.

In a way, it was sort of guerrilla cinema, beyond Method, in which naked character is revealed by no technique whatsoever, just by presence. Presence, action, interaction with objects, dialogue, interaction with other characters. But mostly presence. Way beyond 'star quality'. Way beyond – whatever.

'Ultrastardom in action,' Old Atrocity thought to himself. He didn't care to tell anyone though, lest he be snickered-at. It sounded so – elementary, so pat, so banal. But he'd figured it out. It, the phenomenon in front of him now, was simply evolutionary.

OA looked over at Egaz, who was following along behind the camera, and, judging from the expression on his face, barely but revealingly illuminated by the reflected fill-lamps and pin-spots that fell on his actor, the director was *getting it*, as well. No squinting, no smiles, no expression of any kind, except steady, resilient connectivity in letting a desired take run its course.

Moments like these were why crew, usually big macho types, or at least those with the pecs to heft a brute from A to B, tended to tiptoe around a set, particularly when they detected that greatness was being enacted in front of the camera. Hell, they'd behave the same way on a Herbert J. Yates production at Republic, because they were professionals first and last. But tonight, those on the crew who were privileged to witness this one shot, as if it were a new criterion from which to judge remarkable acting, based on – very little, really, were transformed within the life they'd always lived.

'Cutta!' announced the director, once the actor had reached the pommels and the camera had dollied into a close-up of his right hand. 'Again, in the please. Star? Grip lacks tights. Not enough. Again, again, the please. How do you say... places? Yowzah! Places!'

Butterbugs was elated. He got to do it *again!* Of course, he could have requested it, but things were in such an exalted state right now, when no dissatisfaction was possible, no verbiage except his director's was needed. His head was full of new ideas to use.

He also found that Egaz's ersatz Butler English was oddly inspirational to him. It was official now. His funky word combos constantly introduced new perspectives and methods in approaching his role.

For example, just this time, when Egaz had said 'Grip lacks tights' – obviously meaning that HMD should seize the pommels more aggressively – Butterbugs mixed in his own little ingredient. What if his hands should act like they're wearing actual tights, chorus girl tights, maybe? No doubt HMD's a real kinky fucker. Plenty to explore there, in occult measures.

'Thank you, Mr. Director...'

Tying into this peculiar but startlingly fertile energy were all the other actors and crew on set. It was like a far new country being discovered. D'Varzim spoke, Butterbugs responded, generating a revised and energetic approach, which in turn was spread to all involved. And, like stage designer (Adolphe) Appia's droplets of oil that remained suspended in the performance space on a stage, allowing for all sorts of compelling lighting and atmospheric effects, the Butterbugsian energy had mighty staying power. In fact, it did not diminish. Not like toxins remaining in fat cells. More like a bulking of muscle tissue. Not binding, but enabling, and awareness-building.

YEAH!!!

Who could possibly identify and explain all this subliminal and subjective activity? Butterbugs knew he couldn't, nor did he try. He simply went with it. Free to open doors in the midst of his acting, opportunities were taken without question. In his wisdom, Egaz went with it as well. If a director cannot spot anything extraordinary on a film set, he or she should be boiled in fatty groundnut acids (for high-temp fry-up and golden coverage). That, however, would never be this particular director's fate, for he embraced the unlabeled and undiscerned creation now transpiring in front of his camera. He also had the good sense to shut up and keep things rolling.

The director was totally aware that the previous take had been simply revolutionary, and he knew nothing else need top it. But he was going for a bit of Wylerian coverage – multiple takes – to see the extent of his star's variation in performance. Hell, the setup was so extensive, so lavish, the conditions so perfect, and the hordes of extras so tempting to exploit! He also looked forward to agonizing over which take to use in the editing process. He was not at all opposed to the idea of perhaps issuing several versions of the finished picture, utilizing varied 'masterpiece' takes to tell the same story. Gargantuan as the picture was, possibilities of a lean agility were opening up, thanks to Butterbugs' sudden new experimentalism.

'What is the performance of great music but the same principle? Existing music – replayed, reinvented, recycled, re-interpreted, re*born*...,' he thought. 'Cinema need not be set in celluloid – BKV Method, or anything else. Capturement, certainly, but freed of one-off editions. *New ideas*, my boy!!'

As the next take progressed, sure enough, intriguing variations virtually erupted in the process. Not overtly, it must be understood, but via gesture, tone, non-verbal conduct, and the implications of these and other nameless forces, combined and organized within the script's preferences. Sequential conclusions were arrived-at with entirely different messages attached, based almost solely on the wholly alternative way Butterbugs grasped the pommel before 'Cut' (or 'Cutta') was called.

(Kinky fucker...)

'Wrap-ups!' the director announced, knowing that any further shooting tonight would be unnecessary, and probably overripe.

'All up! Rest now is the order! Thanka, thanka. Please wrap and extras out. Ever out. All!'

He smiled and bowed.

Within a half hour, the great plain was empty of extras, the crew had secured the equipment, and even Old Atrocity, the Dean of Closure on the Set, was headed home.

Butterbugs though, stayed on.

46.

Stipendium Peccati Mors Est

In an obscure alcove of the loggia set, Butterbugs was approached by a mysterious and gloomy personality.

It was super-late, and with the exception of the utterly non-invasive night security team, the cast and crew had indeed departed for the day. Needless to say, the star had total freedom to do as he wished, and all who were on this picture knew full well that Butterbugs regularly set to purposeful brooding and deep contemplation of his role. They often witnessed him remaining in full costume to properly marinate himself in the galaxy of emotions in play, not to mention the divers factors and possibilities which counterbalanced them, so as to not only intellectualize the role's reality, but to feel it from his very soul. Tonight's manifestations had been a signal example of how this advanced approach was developing.

The actor's voice, in considering a recitation in a monotone delivery, caught the moment and conveyed a few lines from his Tell-Off Speech at the Tribune:

HMD: Star! *(gestures to a specific spot in the heavens above)* Eastern Star – Night-Light of the millions who view you in similar dark: as I gaze up to you now, and have for some time... memorial-time... take *note* of what I bring.

Inflection modulation: work on the second syllables in third words in sentences, to preserve Sawl's cadences, of course. Check.

Cult-of-personality leader as poet: consider Chairman Mao by himself, or, in quasi-symbiotic relationship: QE1 and Ed Spenser, or, leader without benefit of talent: Tsar Nicholas I and Pushkin, Generalissimus Stalin and Pasternak – or even Comrade Lenin and Mayakovsky. Veracity problem? Check.

Cult-of-personality leader as human being *sensitive* to poetry: 'Man From U.N.C.L.E.' (MGM, 1964) villains as sophisticates. Ask Victor Buono for tips. Check.

Over-obviousness of referring to *night itself* during night scene: believable? Confer with Sawl and Britney, who both scripted this sequence. Bring in Jesse Lasky, Jr., soon. Suggest 'opposite-ism' poetics; not contrary, just supposedly inspired in HMD's mad mind. Check.

Click – click – click. Down the newly-generated list. All business first, before any romance in his lonely position might ensue.

Butterbugs, quite used to all sorts of unusual characters who have come out of creation's woodwork that panels the hallways the famous and the noteworthy traverse in life, was neither alarmed nor threatened by he who now appeared. This man loomed, as if straight from an Usher property, clearly in lofty and uncertain standing, in front of the actor's composite role as Leader.

Fortunately, the ultrastar was in contemplative but ready pose at this moment, in picture show production time. It was a lengthy but legitimate identification process in justifying his stasis in expectations, while considering this approacher, in the here and now.

This, this, *Visitor* – (how else to identify him?) – was singular in his bearing. Mrs. Radcliffe might have invented him! Maturin could have scripted his arcane speech! 'Monk' Lewis would surely know his innermost secrets! Fuseli, or perhaps an unskilled but hysterically-determined provincial portraitist in say, New Granada, might have painted his portrait!

Fringe. Suspicious. Silent matinee imagery.

Butterbugs got a better glimpse of him now. His sallow face, half hidden in the chiaroscuro blend cast by the still-burning tapers and the actual moonlight, now shining into the columned gallery.

'Late greetings, onlooker,' was all the actor could think of, as an intro line.

The Visitor was grave and bypassed reciprocal greetings in this case. So he entered right in.

'I have been watching you, and have seen how you have grown in power of late, and not just as a megastar.'

The Visitor uttered this statement in somewhat sepulchral tones. His mien was somber but real. His obvious distance from the mainstream was defined by his usage of 'mega' rather than 'ultra' for star status.

Despite the lack of introduction and his unannounced presence, Butterbugs immediately sensed a certain and soulful credibility about him. Benign even. Helpful, possibly a friend.

'Advisement comes in all forms,' the Visitor said, not as a proclamation, but as a sort of knowledge of sharing.

'Your offering?' said the fully made-up star.

'Your work is only possible via advisement. From writers, from directors, others.'

'True. I do offer my own, upon occasion. It's a collaborative ef –'

The Visitor actually interrupted him.

'I give you this text. It is the unknown truth about the destiny of life on this planet. It will serve to either destroy you or make you more powerful still.'

It was far, far too late in the night for tall and shadowy figures, horror-lighted from a frequently-flaring brazier below, to be making jokes to lone remainders on a film set. However, there was every possibility for a lurking wacko to distract a celebrity with a loony tract, so as to pull out a *kris* and plunge it into his victim's brain stem, for whatever motive might apply.

So Butterbugs took the gamble when he was handed mealy and oft-folded papers and bowed his head to regard the text in the Middle Aged light that was hereabouts.

Any act of violence could now take place, for the reader was instantly captivated, and even peripheral movements would not have been noted. As it went, peace reigned so that comprehension could transpire.

The provenance of the text could not be determined right off, but the gist was this: the rest of the planets in the Sol system are dead because their inhabitants – who had been, unbeknownst to Earthlings, whether in the Ancient Ages or B(efore) C(reation), wholly adapted to their own environments and successful in their entire runs of creating and sustaining places of life and achievement. They had *rejected the call to life*, and so, were consumed. The call to life = the restoration of humanity in light of its degradation and corruption. This did not follow religious guidelines so much as natural, instinctive choices. Thus the validity of the Enlightenment, Rousseau, rationalism, rational humanism, etc.

'What are you, some kind of a *nut?*' the ultrastar inquired, brightly.

Looking up, Butterbugs found he could be playful, even at this hour, in his outrageous makeup, facing this character, and having read this not unreasonable assessment of the planets in the cosmic neighborhood.

'I am informed. And I care.'

Butterbugs was reminded of his title role as Sri Sankara, when he uttered the immortal line, 'I am the seer...' (in the eponymous Grandad Ted release), and as a result, the revision of rational thought therefore commenced in the West.

'You have read and understood?'

'So, there was life on all the other planets?'

'It was so.'

'How did they live there?'

'As we do here. Each planet supported life that was adapted to it. All aspects of these details are generally past human understanding and technique. You will read what happened to all of them in their ways, and what will happen to us, in ours.'

'That is a surety?'

'Not at all. But it is a probability.'

Butterbugs set aside his phial of horseradish, which he was considering resuming, but eschewed its contents, and drew closer to the Visitor.

'Knowledgeable One, why do you come here with these precepts? You are no snake. You bear no apple...'

'And *you* are no Eve...'

Butterbugs hoot-laughed, while the Visitor actually cracked a crooked semi-smile.

'Oh please proceed then! But heck, why the precepts?'

'Because, apparently, you need them. Not in application to your craft, which is unimpeachable, but to the rather half-developed world-views you neither acknowledge nor admonish. The imperative is to latch on and commit to an accredited point of view.'

'I wasn't aware that I was being so… analyzed.'

'How could you think otherwise? You are in the public eye. Thus, you are fully *available* for analysis. Is the extent of your impact upon the world blissfully limited to your conveniently limited view? Or purview?'

'I am not a deep thinker, sir.'

'Well then, that's different. Forgive me, actor. I did not know you were conditional in your understanding of yourself. How could I think you were?'

'In the process of acting, perhaps you take on too much.'

'I, and many numbers of others, look at your pictures and think, here is a mind beyond all others. If not, how could he achieve so much within the Seventh Art's limitations?'

'Quite a question. Perhaps that is best left for they who will follow. They who watch. They who can absorb more than I can. Like you. Those with a bigger picture. Further, on-past we who are *immersed* in said picture. Absorbed in *making* it. Both forest *and* trees surround us when we are in the midst. I am only a component. Do you not know of the collaborative nature of this, the Seventh Art, of which you speak?'

'Oh, Butterbugs, you yourself speak nothing but truth. Not only on the screen, but here, in actual conference, in person, of the moment. I am obscure and unknown of value, but now, right now, I consider myself in the midst of undeserving virtue, to hear you talk to me, and if not that, then to hear you talk at all.'

'Thanks, but I demur from all fan waves.'

'I speak not as a fan, but as a seeker. Of something more than entertainment alone.'

'Film is based on distraction, momentary attention.'

'Oh yes, but we know that for long, the art of the film is based on so much more. Such as stimulating ideas, possibilities. New ideas.'

'Inarguable fact.'

'So that, as truth – truth makes way for other truths.'

'Such as?'

'Your individual statements. Made within your films.'

'Are you a cinephile, then?'

'Not at all. I am, in fact, an advocate of truth, of truths laid aside by a public too pre-occupied with full plates of self-indulgent filler, which is of no purpose when attached to the masses of the day. I do not really know what cinema *is*.'

'You are backing into a pigeonhole, sir.'

'Thank you for the warning. You see? You branch out above our petty limitations. You guide, in the simplest, most valuable ways.'

'I talk to myself often when I talk to others.'

'You are as unsure as any of us. That is why we take you amongst ourselves and value you.'

'Well, that makes sense to my self-conscious soul.'

'It should! For what is self-consciousness but belly-roll gazing?'

'In case some cannot locate their navels?'

'Well, I am thinking of the many.'

'You are well-prepared.'

'I am an intruder.'

'That is true. How did you get in to this level?'

'I am a custodian in this place. I sweep tinsel and broken high-heels. I dust the silent remains of sparks flown from stars.'

'Legitimate! So, can you make a pronouncement, person who's obviously making a janitorial gig support something else entirely?'

'Come away to the East, and awake to your *other role* in moving on, in the direction of the greenish light.'

Color was an item usually left to consultants like Lennie Doss or Henri Jaffa or Morg Padelford, but Butterbugs could well appreciate the point this cameo-ist was making. Why, if even uttered from the most fringe-like of street crawlers, a statement that computed within the range of the universe's meaningful thought deserved at least the most thoughtful bearing-out.

'All right. I will go East. Anywhere east of here. Right?'

'You should. And remember, the reward of sin – is death.'

'Ah! The missionary zeal steals out at last.'

'Not at all, Butterbugs. I am speaking in human-oriented terms. The terms humans themselves made up. It's all they understand. Just as in the dead planets. They, who were there, did not move on. They stuck with what they knew, and that was enough. Thus, they were – *stuck* – and stilled. And they are gone now.'

'Thank you, Visitor. I shall not forget.'

So many setups had to be followed through with exhaustive thoroughness just now. It was mainly because of the thousands upon thousands of cast members who populated the tremendous scenes of 'UWH'. The script's dictatorial backup became such that Butterbugs was exempt from any shooting, both in studio at Mega|Goth and on location, specifically at Jambutterbugsabad, for the blissful range of about two months. For that stretch, he could do anything he wanted with his time.

'Everything but cause it to stand still...'

The first week, he spent in strict retirement in the outer belt of The Lazaretto's properties, combined with distraction-free eves at The Æyrie. He studied the lights of LA, and tried to divine what they spelled at this stage of the game. They served the citizens below, but he knew what they were *capable* of spelling, and that seemed as much a statement of public support as the grosses in 'Variety' would ever spell on their charts.

Then he went to Oxford for the next sequence of the break. Ostensibly, it was to pick up an honorary doctorate that had been granted him. He went through the Sheldonian ritual of having his head bopped by The Auld Don of Dons, Sir Deciduous Barney Uccothwaste, as 'BVTTERBVGSICVS MAXIMVS,

DOCTORVS PHILIOSPICVS CINEMATICALICVS' was duly gifted him, which he accepted with heartiest thanks, before beetling out for a pint at the nearest beer engine.

Actually, all Butterbugs could think about at the moment of bop was, 'Chris Wren designed the house in which this blow occurred... Just like John Eberson designed many of the palaces in which my pictures play. I am as nothing but colored or black and white or sepia'd projected light, whereas, if one seeks the memorials of architects, look around you...'

It was his unconscious way of exerting some degree of artistic competition. Architecture is relatively permanent, whereas cinema is exceedingly fleeting. Why was this 'legacy' issue cropping up in the outfield of his daydream thoughts, in the midst of such achievement?

Perhaps because he had the leisure to do so in this interim time.

Bonk. Doctorate notched at Ancient U. Based on fleeting and flaky flicker formations. Fair enough. Many was the actor honored, based on mere stage perfs, which only the privileged few had ever seen. Consolation was offered on the highest levels. QE2 had already promised him a Special Limited-Edition Full Knighthood. That is, when he had the time to spare to pop down to Windsor, if not Frogmore. There was also Garter-talk in both White Tower courtyard and Etonian playing field.

'When this picture is in the can,' he mulled, I shall come bowed to Queen and castle.' He really felt he owed her one, what with her loyal fandom and support on many a set.

Back in Oxford's fair city, after having his noggin thunked, he repaired, in hurriedly-supplied worn tweed sports jacket, to The Kinked Steeple pub, down Jeremiad Lane, over in Jericho, 'neath St. Barnabas' stolid Osborneian campanile. The somewhat morose clangs from its belfry on leaden-sky days brought comfort to his stressed dramatic sensitivities, and beckoned him to become moderately spiffed with wharfspersons who loaded the skiffs off Fiddler's Island, perhaps bound for Gangetic ports, and likewise with the sextons who rounded up the grave culture of St. Sepulchre's Yard, and those who ran the night-soil expresses, that jangled their bells past the midnight hour, who could quote Cardinal Newman or Isaiah Berlin as well as they could Jona Lewie or Amy MacDonald (e.g. 'Where you gonna sleep tonight...').

'Mind what ya do!' was Carky the Denizen's chief advisement to He Whom He Knew Nothing Of (viz. Butterbugs).

And after that, there was no choice for the brigade of beverage'd scholars but to descend on New College Lane in the sodium glare, a bit past Fulcrumblast Lodge, and scrape age-old grime crystals from the soft stone of the walls, if nothing else but to call a mission past pubbery worthwhile. Because, was the immediate environment of schoolish erection not telling? Here, in silent volumes, were the modified geological evolutions of assembled structures, as they go through the ages...

Never so joyful in recent times, Butterbugs and his mob made their descend on Gown Territory, perchance to make geological analysis of raised product from Albion's B(efore C(reation) scalp.

'Carky the D!' stage-whispered Butterbugs to his boss of the night, 'Behold! Will you just *behold?* See here, how I've dislodged this glob of massy soot. Look what it's revealed! In all frankness and gathered honesty, I can't claim to have actually made a/an historical find, but it looks pretty darn bloody intriguing to me!'

'Get this lad a tankard of Lord Roberts' Final Fuel!' the Denizen charged. 'I must don my monocle and inspect, then approve!'

He did, and flame of bluey butane lighter behind magnifying glass aiding the perusal, he saw, as did Butterbugs before him, the text, engraved in the style of a cheerful Tudor student, out of control, because of a pewteréd pint, proclaiming presence in a moment in time on these hoary – even then – walls. And it read:

'Will Shakesp., Esq., Calling Upon this Foreign Towne, in visit First, none Before, doth Will Scrawl ye Memento, Based on Ye Cunt Conquest, Hereabouts. I Enter 18 Such. *In Acto Anne Sar Sacto.* And Divers Learnings here, for My Say. For I Say, I was Here. I tell You, I was Here.'

(END of Inscription)

The look of the text: John Box could have designed it! Peter Brook might have directed its incision! Ben Kingsley could have made its execution convincing on the screen! Iris Murdoch would've questioned the Bard's crude language! Even the botched Latin looked legit – scripted by John Mortimer!

But the thing was... it was mucking genuine.

'Sure enough! And Bob's your uncle! Who are we to say that the lane between London and Stratford was not pounded by a Bard in heat? And in this variation? And that his steps did not shuffle this way, especially on account of Ye Olde Park Pub, for beer bubbles at the visual terminus of this here walled lane?' gasped Carky. 'Cor! Just *cor!*'

Butterbugs could tell he was on to something, else the Denizen would not have expounded so eloquently.

Besides all this, he lit out alone after the pubbing, generally 'twixt college fabric and flood-plained river, to Isis at dusk, amongst the reeds and weeds and hushed washing of the nervous and undecided solution. The moody skyline of Sarcophagus College's turrets made for a fine Military-Gothic mass to contemplate. The cheery lights from Wuggins Hall sparkled and shone through the darkling eve, and further, rather near that college's chapel, a choral rehearsal, of Vaughn Williams' 'An Oxford Elegy', with even some words discernible from out here. Next the impatient waters, notes drifted yet, touched lightly, as if gypsies from scholardom still sought their quests via revived memories-musicale. The sweet wist filled his mind with recall, or of what might have been, rather than the real implication of such input: that which might yet be.

His thoughts settled upon Saskia, she of the sensual but essentially English realm, when longing for fulfillment through romantic notion is most effectively brought to bear by ladylike nightfall, clothed in wispy garments, barely shielding bodies of a further tint of pale, not at all ghostly, but promising secret sensuality, comfortable with night and shade and moist drives toward contented climaxes.

They rehearsed the musical 'Elegy' all right, in the Perpendicular chapel across the way, but sans narrator, so that Butterbugs could formulate his own lines, accompanied by faint chorus and strings, and it made his eyes moist with portent. In this interval from a role that was becoming, whether he was quite able to acknowledge it then or not, the most demanding of his career thus far, a considerable cargo of sentiment, accompanied by melancholy tendencies, was apparently needing to out. And so, in this time and at this spot, he naturally turned to tender subjects, one of which, perhaps foremost because of her very origins at Wantage, not too far from here, was that *Saskia* came indeed to occupy his mind.

Saskia! Had he, in fact, 'settled' for being without her? She of the equal loves for Justy, as well as the loverly typed-page of her own creations! Was he a mere part of her estates, or did he have preeminence? That is, if he might just request it?

He sought her in places with which she was associated. Along the sapling-lined trails that ran out of sight of any bund, amidst tussock and mud ledge, but avoiding the moribund coypu lairs. Out and along, just here. Along the Oxon Canal he then trod, as the music faded. But another, thinner bell than he'd ever heard in the collegiate zone, dinged out from a wan non-conformist tower, as wood smoke rose from the stack of a funky, long, very long, narrowboat. There, seen through un-shy windows brightly candle-glowing, a small group of hip girls, barefooted and honest, celebrating the new Akyabi boyfriend in their midst. Well now, there's a thing. Sweet, a scene to be wholly left alone, because it is so wonderful.

Saskia might have once been among them, but she was nowhere to be seen this night. If she had been, he would have committed to her solely then and there, on bent knee, and he would have requested that she do the same, fully standing.

If only she had been there and then. Then he could have given it all up, *all up* – Really – What did Saskia care of nights he'd spent in the Burj Khalifa? Now that the tension in his role was acute and the reason nebulous, all commitments were fluid, all futures indeterminate. And if she were indeed willing, they could have lived happily on this placid narrowboat, in search of nothing but that within their immediate vicinity. For what else in life was truly needed?

Ahead was the darkening night. Uncertain paths above the inky river, and no music.

47.

The Further Adventures
Of
Butterbugs In Calcutta...

. . . Will not be recounted at this time. Not now. There's simply too much... Too much to tell! To explain! To recount, to recall. Just too much to say. Oh, way too much...

In the several weeks of hiatus in shooting 'UWH', Butterbugs headed for Bengal. The reason was not entirely known, at least to the anxious public and its media services.

Oxford had been mildly nostalgic, and The Visitor's dead planets resume had set his mind to pondering, but there actually wasn't an encumbrance of motive in his pressing East. No specific agenda, except to connect with well-established ports of call. He deliberately passed right over Jambutterbugsabad, of which he had good views, below on the darkling plain. Brutes and kliegs were ignited, allowing Bob Surtees' lens to do what was needed in capturing non-Butterbugsian night shots – at night, as opposed to day-for-night.

'Butterbugs has certain matters of interest which require his presence in the East' was the official line that rattled-out ultrastar news, and a clamor grew. Raggy media outlets, never very harsh on him, nevertheless thought they'd have a bit of sport. They tried many a dubious tail to pin on him, from excuses to cover up sex-tourist probes in nightie-night Bangkok, to illegal tiger shikar in the Sunderbans, to Buddhist nation-building summits in Vientiane, to gem craving & bantering & smuggling in and out of the Ruby Mines District of upper Burma.

It was all wildly fanciful rubbish, of course. Butterbugs just needed to dissolve into the æther for a spell. He thought nowhere would be more handy right now than the metropolis on the Hooghly, which he had not visited for some time.

'I'd forgotten the heat,' he said to himself, as he settled into his first secret digs in summery Chowringhee Lane, with great satisfaction.

Butterbugs was relieved that the old spelling of 'Calcutta' had been permanently revived and restored. The temporary (and reactionary) Romanization had always reminded him too much of radio station call letters (viz. 'KOLKATA' – e.g. the old KOL-AM in Seattle, Wash., and KATA-AM in Arcata, Calif.; ugh and shivers!). Calcuttans were much more happy about the restoration than even he was. It showed.

Because he was in the midst of an important picture, he was restless but not agitated. Therefore, he tended to change lodgings about every other night. And Calcutta, Star of the East, did not in fact have too many stars in its eyes. Consequently, he as ultrastar could stroll the intrinsically hubbub'd streets in peace.

Actually, in many places of the world, he moved as others did, anonymously. Just another humanoid. Boring, even. Just another set-piece of conventional facial arrangements and other operative body parts.

For an ultrastar though, it was a somewhat oddball feeling to be so 'neutralized'. Nevertheless, his largely unconscious talent as a street-side chameleon was always an asset in such environments. Given his propensity for pulling off roles such as Chairman Mao, that so thrilled persons of Chinese heritage, and Comrade Lenin, that drew respect (and love) from Russians, Tatars, and Slavs as a whole, his 'auto-adaptation' to local looks and ways usually kicked in without conscious activation. No talent or technique, just an inherent asset. Still, doing walkabout in real time required some subjective skills. Perhaps they were distilled from Sonny's magic formula of donning his Old Fitzgerald Bourbon shades, so as to render him into convertible anonymity, when needed. Instant Invisible Man. Butterbugs? He had no gimmick, just an automatic system that happened to grey-down his presence, so that his form seemed to blend with the background of the movements at hand.

Equipped with this apparent luxury, Butterbugs got down to business in making his time in Cal count. His pals for the duration included the legendary Delhi bookseller Faquir Chand (in town for some book-bin shopping in the city's more obscure nooks), Mr. Motwani of Oxford Books, Deepanjan Ghosh (starring in his smash-hit barrister series, season number two, filmed at the High Court, in CinemaScope), Preeti and Samit Roychoudhury of photo and design fame, historian and presenter Anthony Khatchaturian, philanthropist and wit Max Galstaun, Khushwant Singh (not a Calcutta man, but always willing to perch in the Indian Coffee House, Albert Hall, for a yak), a babu gentleman (of great propriety) named Bhudadheb Roy, Sally Hawkins (on holiday), Ypear Yem (the Wisdom Agent, 'from somewhere east of Suez', who was currently enjoying the season in Calcutta), Shamim of Tottie Lane (who always had plentiful lane-life tales), Malik Kubbah the barber (damn, was he ever into cinema!), Harold and Edith Ting (fifth-generation Calcuttans and consummate movie-hounds from Chattah-wattah Gully in Chinatown), Tarasol the Courtesan (a specialty dancer in many a Tollywood mythological, very modest, but with very little reason to be), two assistant production designers on 'UWH', Emmeraud dos Blastos and Dorian dol Drendronden (both based in Calcutta and Baku, and busy setting up the new big Teheran Filma complex, as well as at Bronston in Madrid, and Cinnix in Chimkent), and a somewhat mysterious Bong intellectual who went by the appreciative moniker The Natural Film-Follower.

Oh, how Butterbugs felt at home in this environment, where everything was up, all systems go, and where ancientness could co-exist beside the so-called cutting-edge.

'My life is in rotation,' he told every pal. 'I can come and go, as I will from here on in. You will be with me. All of you. And more!'

That was always a popular sentiment to each and every non-Hollywood cinema worker or fan he'd ever met, anywhere on this here globe.

Whether the gang was all there, or singly, or in any combination, the ultrastar shared many a classic moment in dear old Cal with these intimates, in many a venue. From the Mint Master's House to cubicles in Madge Lane; from the cigar divans near Parsee Church Gullee to the mattress-makers in Cotton St.; from the funky 'n' fashionable paan parlors where Diamond Harbour Road meets Orphangunge Road in old Kidderpore, to the mansions of the Laws, or when simply dreaming on the bunds of Tolly's Nullah, vintage gold was struck during all the addas, the soulful reviews, and even while engaging in a tad bit of carousing. Solo hours also occurred, as there was always some appropriate retreat to be found in this gigantic Star of the East.

In fact, one of his favorite hermitages stood at the very fringes of the Star's metro spread, over in southern Howrah. It was tucked into Rajnarayan Roychowdhury Ghat Road, the very route leading to his secret Seebpore bungalow. This one happened to be the grotty little Shree Jagannath Hotel. There certainly wasn't any reason for secrecy here, as its bolthole was fabulously obscure. He'd selected it for no other reason than he liked the hand-painted signs and ciphers on the frontage, seen while passing by. 'Modest' would be a grandiose term to employ in describing its entrance, which was hardly more expressive than an everyday tea stall's. Yet, beyond the smudgy 'lobby' was a warren of eccentric chambers and musty suites, with enough character and pictorialness to inspire a whole string of Shree Jagannath Hotel photoplays. The clientele were screen-worthy too, mostly humble worker types, with plenty of stories to tell. For Butterbugs, the place was a verifiable delight. A hole-in-the-wall where he could don a dhoti and relax in a naked light-bulbed cubicle and do a few yoga poses. Perchance to take tiffin with chat-friends P.K. and Bipla Murghatagapadhyay in Hawakhana Hall, their curious Victorian mini-mahal nearby, with its rusting cupola and eccentric brickwork. Then, out in the lane for some sanding-down of any rough edges at the Shree Balaji Plywood stall, where everyone was always in good spirits. After that, an evening stroll in the glorious Eden of the Botanical Gardens, with a requisite visit to Bipla's beloved Giant Victoria lily pads, and a check to see how the Great Banyan Tree was doing. (Expanding – ever outwards – as always.) Followed by a cheery game of Carrom with the gang at the R.B.T. Club (est. 1970), just at hand.

What could be better than that?

On this side of the Hooghly, nothing ever came up concerning movies, stardom, or 'UWH'. Butterbugs was merely an agreeable 'gora', passably fluent in Bengali, and amusing to all as 'Mr. Ghee-babu'.

He'd long considered purchasing the Shree Jagannath... as a sort of keepsake. The owner, one C.K. Paul, who lived in Benares, was perfectly willing. However, upon further rumination, the actor ruled out the plan, so as to keep the ambience of the establishment intact. One of his alternative plans, meriting a very high 'C' or 'D' rating (for possible implementation in the event of his retirement), was to settle here in Howrah and apply for employment at the Shree Jagannath as a nightshift desk clerk.

A special dream indeed, to treasure and enjoy in private.

At any rate, he showed up and stayed for a time. Then he'd be gone. But he'd be back.

Over in the city, after studying the old deco-ish Ford dealership sign, newly restored, on Ganesh Chandra Ave., Butterbugs happened to be a bit peckish, so he trotted into the nearby Aventine Restaurant, with its famous Le Corbusier-designed facade. It was dim and Populuxe inside, which perfectly matched his mood. He was pleased with the strangely-undersized lanterns that had been newly installed on the walls of the room, and their tiny-watt bulbs. Taking an acceptable tiffin, he was struck by the fact that four ideal Bengali young women, with perfect cheekbones, were working in various capacities in this establishment. Indeed, they were the proud new owners. But they were unrelated. There was a déjà vu involved somewhere in this realization, but he was happy just to accept it as a characteristic bit of Calcuttan synchronicity, a connection with something or other in his baroque past.

An unimpeachably happy time.

It was a blowsy sort of afternoon. Butterbugs was wandering around the College Square tank, poking his head into some of the curious buildings thereabouts, thinking nothing in particular as he toddled along. That was why he was here. Not to space out, but to walk the ground in groundedness, and with a fleetness of foot. Calcutta was perfect for this purpose. The city and its players, its drama, its sets, its reality, were all far bigger than he could ever be. Within this protective bosom then, did he relish the deceptively lightweight moments of heightened awareness which he could not help but encounter practically everywhere he stepped in this transcendental conch shell of a community.

Arms behind back, clad in a white linen suit, string tie and broad planter's hat, he adjusted his pince-nez and carefully read the text and roster on the memorial to the 49th Bengalee Regiment in the Great War ('To the Glory of God, King & Country'), and let his gaze dance about the cartoonish lines of the Mahabodhi Society's headquarters. What fun to be a sort of architectural tourist, in search of the singular and the pleasurable – and finding them wherever he looked.

These structures! These ceilings! The floors, the shutters, the valences, the cast iron, the stucco, the pillars, the courtyards, the echoes, the coolness, the byways, the alcoves, the nooks, the dark chambers, the sunny loggias, the wistful walks, the contemplative hallways, the historicity, the lived-in heritage, the ghostly memories, the fresh & friendly immediacy, the invitational smiles, the proud restraint, the rough edges, the renegade banyans, the sheer epicness, the welcome intimacy, the inexhaustible greatness...

Back along Lower Chitpore Road, way up above, the huge main dome of the Nakhoda mosque crowned an Arabian Nights skyline, its paint peel actually adding an element of pictorialness, like an abstract mosaic or a globe of an (all-Muslim?) planet, with green oceans and mysterious continents...

Street kids knew him, but not as an ultrastar. They greeted, chatted, and did their street kid things, moved balls with foot or bat, then moved on, as Butterbugs moved on, and all was regular and motion-oriented.

In a courtyard near the Ionic pillars of Vidyasagar's Sanskrit College, he spread out on the grass that was so peculiar to 24-Parganas topography, and thought he might doze for a time.

Someone was attending a smoldering garden-rubbish fire across the way, but otherwise, with only the kik-bird and charlerlollahs providing audio continuum away from the metro din outside the wall, he had his mind to himself. The mild agarbatti effect from the smoke was charming, and for a moment he mused over the notion of trundling on up to Gothpore, to give a big namaste to Fat Chance – er – Moti Charbi Bewkoof Baba, and the gang. Lolling and fantasizing, he soon fell into a dream state. Therein was the notion of a journey to Gothpore taken up and made into a full Technicolor production. His dreams were usually predictably lavish, and this one was particularly fanciful.

Buzz Berkeley could have directed it! James Basevi could have designed it! Laxmikant/Pyarelal could have scored it! Carmen Miranda could have co-starred! Well sure, she could play maharanees, as surely as Maria Ouspenskaya, and with more flash and verve, too!

At any rate, he found himself taking off from Dum Dum. Not in any æroplane, but upon the back of Durga's blaze-orange tiger! They were flying, all right. Really flying, through the air, with no heat-producing hardware or fuel-based propulsion of any kind. Movement with purpose, reasonable, without restrictions or requirements. It was cool, clean, and sweet, and they both took turns hauling the other effortlessly through the air. Below were the great rivers, savannah, dry-jungle and then, uplands.

'I like to fly whenever I can,' said the tiger as they passed over Cherrapunji way below, on this, a rare cloudless day.

'Me too,' replied Butterbugs. 'But never have I done so in this fashion before.'

'Well, neither have I. Really, my good fellow. I'm usually accompanied by my mistress. Durga has all the divine powers. She could fly to the planet Nahchundrahchundrah if she wanted to, packing me and much else, besides.'

'So, if Durga isn't here right now, how are we both able to fly?'

The tiger smiled quizzically.

'You know, that is a reasonably good question, my human child.'

'A question... Do we want to answer it right now? So high?'

'I agree. But perhaps you have similar powers as Durga does. You're providing the power. I'm just along for the ride. I hope you're not going to pretend you don't know that.'

'Now really, my good Tyger, I'm afraid I have to say that that is the case. That – that I didn't know, that is.'

'Well, a fine state of affairs that is! See what you're doing? We're losing altitude. And Gothpore is far off yet.'

The descent! James Newton Howard could have scored it! Astronomers could have known the trajectory! Industrial Light and Magic would have known how to recreate it! (If indeed, they were still in business...)

Down, down, down. Trajectory-wise, not vertically. But the view was tremendously exhilarating, and reminded him of the famous and lengthy boom shot in his own 'Blaze Of The Summer Islands' (Selznick), when the camera travels over and in and about the Tenasserim palm trees during the legendary chase sequence.

It would be a beautiful crash. A beau ideal – the way it should be done on the screen.

Bash! then thrash! then blackout.

Awakening, his chican shirt balled up from his grass wrasselling, he straightened everything out and fancied a bit of Nehruvian coffee as a perk-me-up at the Albert Hall, just nigh.

Shuffling into the echoey, punkah-mixed air of the Main Saloon, Butterbugs spied a familiar face over next the sea-green wall.

Coffee was of course ordered, in double-half doses, and they got down to their adda.

'Let us now consider some film technique,' said Malik Kubbah, barber, from Umbrellawallah Lane near Tiretta Bazar and consummate mad-keen film buff.

'All right, Sir Malik. Which one today?'

'Boom shots!' Kubbah proclaimed, with much pleasure.

'Interesting coincidence...'

'I know, Butterbugs. You have been in some of the best. But tell me, what do you think of their value? I loved the early Indian efforts, especially in 'Lucknow, Delirious Lucknow' (B.T. Rajshahi, 1957), not to mention Delmer Daves' 'Spencer's Mountain' (WB, 1963). Good, sensible use of great rising, to look over the scenes.'

'They are particularly effective in epic films.'

'I'll tell you what I think,' said the barber, sipping from his second cup. 'I of course like boom shots of all kinds. You know why? We in the audience are given a chance at flying. Not in a winged device, but on our own. Our only chance – in our waking hours, that is. We look down, out, and around. It is a gift. In the audience, we receive gifts.'

'I quite like that, barber of mine. That's always been my intention: to give gifts, and to keep on giving. Ah! Another familiar – and very welcome – face! Come, join us, Natural!'

The Natural Film-Follower took his usual place on the ultrastar's left. The two instantly linked their gazes.

'I can tell, Butterbugs,' said The Natural, 'you have had a dream. A most remarkable dream.'

'Was it about boom shots?' asked Malik, just kidding.

'Yes. It was, Butterbugs. Wasn't it?' asked The Natural, somewhat pointedly.

'You know something,' the ultrastar replied, 'I think it actually was. At least I was flying…'

'Achcha – camera on boom,' said Malik. 'Very logical. And natural for a movie star, eh, The Natural?'

'What exactly, was propelling your flight?' the Film-Follower queried.

'Well, it was… I was, quite frankly, I was riding a tiger.'

'Of course you were. Durga's tiger.'

'OK, OK, what 'mythological' was that from, guys?' Malik cajoled.

'No myth. Truth.'

'I think so, The Natural. I think so, Malik' replied Butterbugs, now that he thought about it.

'It was a great effect in 'Sant Gandaneshwar' (Kaisar Talkies, 1956),' said the barber, proud of his encyclopædic recall. 'An early sophistication in special effects here. The tiger was somewhat fakey, though. As well it might be.'

'True enough, Malik Kubbah,' said The Natural. 'But I think Butterbugs was divinely inspired a little while ago.'

'Where's Yem the Wisdom Agent, when we need him?' chuckled Malik. 'You know! To validate the divine stuff.'

'He is out of station,' replied the Film-Follower. 'Besides. Not necessary. Butterbugs, your dream was so simple. You shall be carried aloft in your upcoming role. You shall be taken to heights unimaginable. And Durga will be your guide.'

'And her tiger!' added Malik cheerily.

'Thank you, both, for the extra-sensitive senses! I know these realizations will aid my performance.'

'Yes. Of that, there is no doubt whatsoever.'

'That's why they call him The Natural Film-Follower!' Malik laughed.

The rest of the occasion was jolly, fluffy, and packed with gossip, trivia bits, and Malik-led quizzes. Harold and Edith Ting chanced by, and they all took early dinner at the Chowringhee Hotel. The evening was topped off by a stroll around Armenian Ghat.

'Well, I have to get back to the studio in la LA now,' Butterbugs announced. 'I have a big scene in 'UWH' to do.'

48.

Jonny Requesticus

Today's scene in 'UWH' was a daunting one for cast, as well as crew. A Very Big Deal.

It contained long slabs of important dialogue, and director D'Varzim was in a questionable mood. His progression in English was (supposedly) going poorly. There were many lines of dramatic placement and weight – not necessarily meaning – every actor in the scene was required to deliver. As a result, he was quite (superficially) overwhelmed. Thus, he communicated largely with grunts and hand signals. Refreshingly, but consistently, he seemed to be wringing outstanding performances from his people. Verbiage was light baggage, easily discarded, so he kept things stripped and sleek. Early in the day he'd realized he was onto something. So he moved along.

Great acting was taking place on both sides of the camera.

The crushingly pomp-laden Throne Room set surrounded them now, with its grandly costumed players, vast protocol-obsessed logistics, and the mind-spinningly complex upper mezzanine, housing the High Mad Doctor's chemistry apparatus, hovering heavily above. Everything in the built environment served as a sort of lowering intimidator to all. Most fitting for a despot's HQ.

Old Atrocity had everything rigged perfectly. He approached Butterbugs to notify him of his Final Check, before doing so with Egaz.

'A-OK, there, Lead Player?'

'... Aye...,' Butterbugs replied darkly.

'Nervous?'

'You know it, OA. Gaze around you, as well...'

'Looks like everyone hasn't yet learned to live with anxiety...'

Butterbugs gave the master grip a glare that signified such comments were worming into the realms of distraction, so OA humbly slunk away.

The combined load-factor of script, set, sensitivities, and general anticipation made this sequence one of the tensest ever filmed. Everyone, even Butterbugs, was on edge. Everyone inherently knew that conditions had to be so, otherwise, what the hell was the *point?*

The premise was simple. HMD's power has reached world-domination status. He was propelled there by a wildly supportive world populace. But today, he reveals his true self. Thus, the absolutely critical, pivotal nature of the drama, so urgently awaiting realization.

There were several Grade-A VIPs in the Stranger's Gallery, which Hyman

Goth had specifically set up for publicity purposes. King Chuvkah of Tannu Tuva, QE2 (Her Imperial Majesty was Butterbugs' biggest royal fan; that knight-hood appointment was still hanging though, mainly due to scheduling conflicts), Anjanette Comer, the Maharaja of Patiala, King Juan Carlos of Spain (ret.), sev-eral visiting mehtars (sweepers) and their spouses from Alwar, David Rockefeller, the Incredible Jimmy Smith, Gov. Ross Perot of Nevada, Lindsay Lohan, Bobby Kennedy Jr., The Nawab of Junagadh and his Dewan, Moms Mabley (her scenes were already in the can, so she was kicking back, doing social shit), several offspring of the Nizam, plus a few other corporate elite, relegated to the lower 2x4-braced levels, who were considering investments in Mega|Goth. No matter; QE2 had already trumped them all, even with her divestment of BP and other fossil-ish holdings.

Waycroft Pamiel, who played the groveling courtier Jonny Requesticus, glided forward and adjusted his felt head-case, before addressing the HMD. He'd taken one pill over the recommended anti-sweat specific's dosage, so he appeared especially desiccated and saturnine.

D'Varzim was filming this scene in single long shot, without B-roll. Despite being lensed in Ultra-Panavision 70, one could hardly see Pamiel's mouth move without an opera glass. It was the director's 'upper balcony' effect, operatic to say the least. But his track record in using it was proven: all who had seen any similar rushes from this picture so far sat spellbound through such sequences. It wouldn't be until halfway through this take that the director would command the camera to slowly dolly forward.

'Lae-on! The AC-tion!' D'Varzim announced. Shamroy's crew was ready at the trigger.

JONNY REQUESTICUS: *(smarmy)* Most Dreaded and Horrifically-Gifted Power-Lord! With tears in my eyes, I am down on my knees in order to make the humblest of requests to Your Immensity! I can only grovel so far, or kowtow so low, and now I am in both of those positions in order to approach the sacred Throne upon which you sit, and I cannot hope to be anything more than the very dust upon which your incredible person savagely and rightly treads. So thus, then, do I muchly utter one tiny item for your consideration before you resume your ultra-busy affairs of State – and much else. I am so totally grateful for this minute audience of the barest few seconds with You, and now, because I know your royal atten-tion span is completely correct in its growing impatience with the noth-ingness of my very being, and because I am only interested in engaging in the most crass and perhaps base acts in order to please you and publicly humiliate myself, so I will not be executed simply because I am a severely annoying entity – sort of like the lowliest of mosquitoes which acciden-tally is inhaled into the highborn nostrils of your blessed self, I am no more than a boring gnat, which should justifiably be ground into a few poor granules of powder in order not to cause any impedance whatsoever to your august progress through life! And so, it is with the permanent status of a mere trifling nuisance that I supplicate mine-self to thee with the following, hideously minor and obscure request.

HIGH MAD DOCTOR: *(consummately irritated, all right)* I hear you. It's your call.

JONNY: Most Treasured Hyper-Godlike Chief Martial Law Administrator! Center of Beyond this Universe! I come to you to ask, try to let my people *in!* Your repression has become a *bore!*

HMD: I have warned all who would dare to upset me, that, if anyone crossed me, or crissed me, or spread heckling beyond the ridge and unto the Gates of Zunn, I shall delegate them to the numerous ventilated – or, if their character is dire, to the even more numerous *non*-ventilated spider holes, which it is my pleasure to utilize.

JONNY: At the slightest provocation, your Mega-Lord?

HMD: *(shrieks, in Vegas-style)* Youuuuuu KNOW it!

D'Varzim burst in: 'Cutta! I am must saying, Battarbugs, you must *rage* out this line! Flinging it to at your Jonny with a like dead dart!'
'Should I... roar?... It out?'
'Yessis, like sir, the cleaving and cloven-roar. Now, in from the top side, the ACTION!'
From the top then, did the actors replay the scene, segueing onward:

HMD: *(roars in horrifying style)* Youuuuuuuuu **K N O W** it!!!!

JONNY: *(calmly)* Then, sir, pray, consider. In this, thy home, pray, know, this is also thy heart.

HMD: *(calmly, but with oh-so-fake resignation, as if any of his behavior was anything close to being democratic)* I yield.

JONNY: If thee but a bastard, Protean Symbol of Repulsion, who pretended to this, thy throne, know you not why they who might question – might question, wholly and heartedly, with hard-assed pressing-in, on your very *being*? *Why* they might?

HMD: *(contemptuous)* Your posturing poses the kind of questions I ask myself every day in the strict privacy of my nocturnal repose.

JONNY: Then *ANSWER!* You dirty piece of slime!

(HMD is silent.)

JONNY: So. I let your guilt show. Does Lutrena know? The Lady of your dreary manor?

HMD: My consort does not know. Rascal!

JONNY: Then *why* can you not give me a straight answer, Over-Arching Colonel DeLuxe?

HMD: *(reflective, biding his time, burning with hatred)* Because I did not wish to thrust her into the level field of the heavy cheer of Court Affairs, and my Height prevents me from displaying her honor in front of the likes of, shall we say... dismal courtiers.

JONNY: *(to the* COURT, *gesturing)* I demand that the Lady Lutrena make her appearance.

(The COURT *gasps.)*

JONNY: I demand it, here and *now!*

HMD: I canna turn you down. Send now! *Send* for the Lady Lutrena...!

'A-CUTT! I like the *this* in this! Sham-and-roy! Surtee! Whatevers! Next shot! This way!'

Butterbugs and Pamiel, exhausted by the high-toned drama, took their break over at the box where the royals were. Butterbugs was largely silent, but he was glad, as Moms Mabley was taking up the burden of entertaining those who were there. Butterbugs loved Moms too, but there was something picking at his heart.

'Oh, it's not just the gravity of the lines, Ma'am,' he confided to QE2. 'It's just that, I'm not sure what this is building up to.'

'I know about the burden of State,' said the Queen, with radical understatement. 'And what you are enacting is almost exactly the same, I should think. Except for a rather different standing on such issues as human dignity. But I always keep in mind the psychology of your photoplay. Mr. Rudyard Kipling used to tell me his 'Just So' stories at Windsor when I was a child, but I had no idea what was 'just so' until I took the purple. Mr. Barrie echoed the same thoughts, really. Peter Pan, you see. Larry Olivier told me that, compared to the Tudors 'n' Stuarts, I have it pretty easy, for some of their entire reigns were composed of *annes horribiles...*'

King Chuvkah agreed without equivocation.

'In my case,' the Ruler of Tuva said, 'we've never had it so good. In fact, we've never had much of anything at all. Stalin never would've permitted it. Nikita at least opened up the possibility of an Autonomous Royal Republic when I met him in Ulan Ude that time. But he turned down my invitation to Kyzl. It wasn't until Richard Feynman made it possible for me to return to the davenport, our throne...'

'And you've been terribly popular ever since,' added the Queen brightly.

'I follow your example, Ma'am,' said King to Queen.

'And you, Butterbugs, I fear your role as High Mad Doctor, ruler of billions, is perhaps not as endearing as our excellent Chuvkah of Tuva, hmm?'

'He is the abomination of the planet, Ma'am.'

'And abominations must and shall be exposed for what they are.'

'I'm afraid there are quite a few unpleasantries that will come forth in this picture, much of which is offensive and not very nice, for honorable persons of your sensitivities, Your Majesty. Mr. Cane and his scriptors have included some pretty gross stuff, for which I apologize ahead of time.'

'No need, my dear Butterbugs. For apologies, that is. Oh, Sawl and I have reviewed many of the picture's such qualities, and I have even lent some advisement. You must understand, in my reign, I have had knowledge of more 'unpleasantries' than most have wit to ask. I shall not pollute your ears at such a time when they are needed for concentrated creativity. But in the freer realms of a private chat, I can let you in on some pretty juicy items, especially concerning my predecessors from the Dark Ages. In the meantime, apply all the robustness ye need to expose this germ of power abusage to the peoples of the world, who have need of thee!'

'I endeavor to expose the High and the Mad, as you say, Ma'am.'

'Splendid! Please ensure that you play him to the fullest. Perhaps as an example of, shall we say, *poor leadership.*'

'I am your servant, my lady,' said Butterbugs, bowing.

'Oh, by the bye, Butterbugs, in this moment of fleeting leisure, I shall now dub you Sir Butterbugs of ... Of, what home seat, pray?'

'My humble thanks, Ma'am. Vinejuice, I should think, as 'tis my most cheerful abode.'

Drawing a porta-sword from her duffle bag, QE2 assumed knightage pose and requested the ultrastar do the same.

'Well spoken, sir. I dub thee *Sir Butterbugs of Vinejuice,* Full and Honoured Knight Commander of my British Empire, with all rights and variations therein. Arise now, Sir Knight, and do good in the world!'

Before he rose, Sir Butterbugs (FHKCBE) bowed yet lower, and when he obeyed her command and completely rose, the Queen could see his easy tears.

She herself was choked up. 'Back to work now, Butterbugs of Vinejuice. Much to do yet, and we can share the joy of this occasion another time! Come to me at Balmoral, anon!'

'I *will*, Your Majesty. My grateful *thanks*, Your Majesty!'

The others in the VIP box, seeing the Queen's majesticness, and her new knight's fealty, almost passed out.

Exhilarated by the royal's sage perspective, and his new knighthood, Butterbugs drifted over to the property corner, where Old Atrocity was holding his own kind of court.

For some reason, the Director of Systematic Realization was brandishing a copy of the day's 'Wall Street Journal.'.

Butterbugs desperately needed a diversion. Knighthood was fine, but he was still on set, with much to do. Like the Queen said.

'OA, OA, OA! I've just seen the Queen, and I'm a Sir now, and it's all OK, except for one thing.'

Old Atrocity, never impressed by *anybody*, except perhaps Charlie Clarke, Coleridge-Taylor Perkinson, or Martin Shaw, and still smarting from his earlier 'dismissal' by the ultrastar, answered casually, 'Before your royal-ruler entrance, Sir Exalted One, know this: Her Imperial Majesty in fact took tea with me 'n' the gang. She did impressions of boring and tedious heads of state. Thought we'd bust a gut.'

'Wish I'd been here.'

'You would've had to fan your high hat of goonyness, sport, so many laughs to make us sweat!'

He tossed the newspaper at the star.

Catching it, Butterbugs indeed fanned his beaded brow. Not a bad idea.

'One thing?' Old Atrocity queried.

Sir B. of V. had forgotten it, but he had a substitution.

'OA, why is there a *period* after 'The Wall Street Journal'? In the title. The very title.'

'Why that's easy. Because it's a sentence.'

'The title of the newspaper is a sentence?'

'In the grand old style of properness. A sentence has to be properly concluded.'

Butterbugs happened to notice that, even on the smallest page designations of the 'WSJ', the labeling was the same. It was a consistency he appreciated. Some things had to be consistent, but they were usually matters of repetition, like a business periodical, with its doing of The Numbers. They always added up to the same thing: aspirations of profit. Creation was different. It had to be. It had to vary itself. The sun rose every day, but never in the same manner, nor the same imprint, as if on the repeated page. Repetition was the answer – for some. Not he, though.

'Why the 'WSJ'?'

'Prop, old boy, prop. Date irrelevant.'

'We are men of property, Butterbugs,' quipped Guff Gaff, prop-meister-general.
Butterbugs could only smile and return to his creative cycle, ready to release.

'Hey!' OA called after him, 'Cool about the 'Sir' thang!!'

'Jealous?' Guff Gaff asked.

'Naw. Liz pulled me aside after tea and said she'd try and swing an honorary
garter – or garter belt – or somethin', for me. Me bein' a behind-the-scenes guy
and all.'

'Woo-hoo! Kinky-slinky!'

Then he leaned over and quietly quipped, 'I tell ya Guff, we're just not willing
to accept anxiety any more, are we...?'

'Act-shioné!'

D'Varzim set up his shot to start with a MCU of Lady Lutrena's entrance
through the National Romantic portal in the HMD's Nordic Palazzo – austere
but legendary, chiseled with motifs from the legends he loves, with characters he
aspires to but knows he can never become, part of his active and rapidly growing
resentment against humankind. From Lady L's appearance, in Guinevere-style
costume (form-fitting tunic, defined with 'waist-thigh-pubic lines', anti-chastity
belt, long hair, headband, etc.), the scene unfolded in another extended take, via
a lengthy pullback, the reverse of the previous shot.

(The Lady LUTRENA *enters.)*

It was the sixth rehearsal (others were held the day before), but it was the first
time Butterbugs beheld the actress who played Lutrena in costume, in character,
and under Shamroy's sensual lighting plot.

There she was. She, an actress who would be acting with him in this scene.
She, whom he'd been too fucking self-possessed to properly notice. But here she
was in full force, ready to be unequivocally noticed, in all her splendor.

The birth of love! Her form – Gallen-Kallela could have depicted it! Sibelius
might have been the only one to properly score her appearance! (Newman would
only try!)

Now born, the vision of loveliness grew and instantly matured in Butterbugs'
mind as he beheld her. Not, however, in character – his character. Not as HMD,
who sought her expulsion, if not demise – as in the script, she is a force for good
in the midst of his perverse plots.

No, as *Butterbugs*, ultrastar and star of this picture, did he see her. He beheld
her, and it was insta-love – consummate, serious, a ten-ton gift of brilliant bearing – light to look at, fulfillingly burdensome to feel – a tare he'd long sought
– even if he did not realize it for seeming ages.

She was stunning, she was gracious, she was sexy, she was the subconscious dream of his longing's truth – here – in the transcendent flesh, in front of him – on set, before everyone, as the camera rolled, and as his speech must commence. And that speech was writ with castigation, anger, and character assassination, and he must deliver it within forty-two seconds – long enough for the camera to pull back (in silence), so that he, HMD, must enter on stage left, then gesture in acknowledgement of her presence, and do the same to the Court, so as to begin his lines.

Forty-two lavish seconds, in which to glory in her view, to look, and allow love, deeply pure love, to expand, to enter into his very being, to arrive at last on the high plane of his expectations, his searches, his needs. For his heart so completely *needed* to be stopped so desperately. Love, so long lacking in anything like a full dose, needed to walk right in and seal off any further passage of life. Until it was assured, until it was addressed, until it was for sure, that love was here and here for real.

And that was how an ultrastar fell, even though his HMD character felt rather differently, for Keenah LaVine.

Thus:

(The Lady LUTRENA *enters.)*

HMD: Lady Lee! Lutrena of the Karelian forests and swamp-havens far above Peipus' enstagnated, mozzie-larvæ'd shores! Lady of my bedroom's access, ward of mine own private parts, privy to my dirty bits as well as my naughty bits! You have been duly summoned by he whom I hate – simply hate – and, come to think of it, he who deserves high guile. Why, then, is it instantly appropriate to obey such summons as these, while what I ask of you in my *inner-est* of sanctums goes into coy and snarky eclipse?

*(*HMD *waits for answer; none comes;* LUTRENA *initially in shock.)*

HMD: By your silence then shall you be known to Court. If you rigged this to push for my doom, let it be known now!

LUTRENA: *(finds voice)* Topmost-minded lord of bossiness, and exposer of underthings! My voice has always been primed and my body is constantly aware. Your overpowering mush is depressing, and is no longer tactile to me, nor my uses as your consort. I know that now.

(Camera continues to pull back, revealing astonished courtiers.)

HMD: So. My purty sweet public confection! Tasted by me, but soured due to your impossible haughtiness... Well, what gives you the *right?* What's the fire in your eyes, Mistress of the Conceits? I cared for you! Groomed you! Fostered you! I fed you non-scum; the complete and utter opposite of that which I force upon my subjects! You were everything to me! Now you are lower, perhaps, than a dustbin left open after a fry-up in one of my subjects' most loathsome backyard bug-infested lean-to kitchens, where disease cells rage for revenge and –

JONNY: *(boldly breaks in)* Leader-lord, crazed with mad thoughts, *including jealousy!* How can you unpleasantly evacuate upon this sweetness-girl of love? This merry muffin of the senses? This vision of loveliness? However *can* you? Why must you flaunt your boorish nature so as to inspire hatred in all of us who listen to you at this particular point in time? How –

HMD: *(explodes)* See, Court!? See?! Listen! How he *DARES* to stave my truth with absolute nonsense. He eviscerates my screed! He hurts my contempt for all of you, which I have the high-end birthright to encourage. And how he bitterly insults my Lady Lee with erotic gobbledygook! She, whose soul and still-sweet young bod I own, lock, stock and nipple! Do you know how you shall pay?

JONNY: How do you know I *have* to pay? After the disgrace you have shown us this day?

HMD: Why, *you...!*

JONNY: I fear only one thing, cursèd puke-person! That you will now harm my Lady Lee, as a reprisal for my justified insolence.

HMD: *(aghast)* What did you just say to me – and Court? *Your* Lady Lee?? You cannot *do* that! You cannot *ever* call her that! Only *I* can address her and refer to her as: Lady Lee! That is a private nickname, with sexual associations! Only one who could have – Why, you miserable – Only *I* can call her Lady Lee! Only *I* can own her! Are you saying, by this outrage, that you have had sex with this girl?

LUTRENA: He has! I tell you, he has! And glorious it has been, too. Even within the last hour, love-waste lordy! The thought – the very thought of you and your inherent hideousness, your baggy remnants of something you delude yourself with, the prospect of drawing nigh to your wobbly bits, both dirty and naughty, make my pretty belly wamble with vomitous portent, and the concept of your disgusting attempts to impregnate me, whether via squeeze-bulb or penis-pump'd product (which, despite the fact that any issue from your hulk would have to be limited to nasal mucus, though, to be sure in my own mind, I have even surreptitiously employed a humble coat hanger, soaked in harsh tinctures and preventative potions of all types, as total insurance against any reproductive blunder), fills me not with your semen 'n' sperm (ick!), nor even from your nostril snot – which you tried one time – honestly, he *did*, Court! – but you *do* fill me with the desire to open your neck with my sharp fingernails whilst you sleep, and to expose your tiresome voice box, which gave me such sick and mind-awful commands; to expose it to the air, and then to the nearest drain, to end up in our poor, polluted Sea of Aral, where it might be set upon by the vilest of vermin, while the gap that I opened drains you of putrid life. Yes, I would do these things. I would *murder* you at my first opportunity. Why I have not done so, particularly under more discreet circumstances, I cannot say. Perhaps I was in a constant state of overpowerment from your brutalism. Perhaps it was my fear of your power. I can only blame myself. But none of that adds up to anything worth summing in the analytical sense. Until now, I was not sufficiently bolstered by Jonny's constant pushings and pullings. By my failure of blandishment I expose myself. Only now, at this late, late hour, I might redeem myself... through love!

(JONNY *makes to advance toward her, because of her last statement, but restrains himself when:)*

(LUTRENA *pulls out a long dagger from her damosel sleeve.)*

HMD: *(belly laughs)* Oh, ho! The witch with a knife! How now, Pinwheel? How close I have come to having my sacred balls chipped off, for – nothing!

(COURT *sycophants laugh nervously.)*

JONNY: Leader of lords! May I speak?

HMD: Here comes Jonny!

JONNY: Thank you, Liege of the Highest Arts...

HMD: Why then do you mock-talk me, traitor?

JONNY: To save my Lady Lee – or rather, your Lady Lutrena, from mutual assured destruction, which I share with her. You, sir, are partial to flattery, so I suggest you enjoy it while I offer it.

HMD: *(agreeable)* Proceed.

JONNY: Please don't execute us.

HMD: Guardians of the Height of the Doctorial Throne, seize them!

(GUARDS *grab* JONNY *and* LUTRENA.)

GUARD GOMBO: But Grandeur Controller and Owner, we cannot end the existence of one so comely.

(GOMBO *attempts to feel up* LUTRENA, *now that she is virtually condemned.*)

HMD: No? Then allow *me!*

(HMD *pulls out a concealed Bowie knife and lets it fly, hitting* LUTRENA *square in the neck. Camera dollies in, as fast as possible, but still at a stately pace, for expectations to build, into a CU of* LUTRENA, *who then does her death speech:*)

(*Cue music in final print; arresting arpeggio into sorrowful rendition of 'Lost Love' theme.*)

LUTRENA: See, how I am killed!

(*Camera dollies out enough to show* JONNY, *as he wrests himself from the* GUARDS' *grip and rushes to her side, then camera returns to CU of* LUTRENA; LUTRENA's *vocal cords are exposed, but the area is in deep shock, though still operational, and because of this, she is actually able to talk.*)

LUTRENA: Oh, Jonny! You emboldened me, so. You set me up for this, and now it has killed me. You are as much the author of my untimely expiration as he whom we hated together. Why did we not fly to Kyemtabulask, when I begged you to? I have estates there! We could have *lived!* Instead, your ambitions and your designs kept us *here*, in this seat of my sorrows. You kept telling me, repeating to me, almost haranguing me, that it was possible to eliminate the Doctor, who is so high and mad! Oh, Jonny, how could you have been so – wrong? How could I have been so – loyal? Or some… thing…

JONNY: (*devastated*) Because, dear sweetness, oh! oh!, now in ruins, you were the Ideal: loyal, helpful, sympathetic, obedient, and all because: you – love me!

LUTRENA: Oh, what a failure I am.

JONNY: *(shattered)* Oh Love-Lee! Do you feel much pain?

LUTRENA: Nay, for I am beyond it. I am at the threshold. And Death approaches...

JONNY: *(sullen)* At least that...

LUTRENA: I failed, failed, and all my regrets now carry me away. Away, away to deservéd darkness. I tried to dissuade you. I tried to make you understand – something you are incapable of doing. Oh, Jonny, like most cocksmen, you were possessed by the opiate of world-grasping, whether in my nest, where I tried to trust you, and where I kept giving you chances, or upon these stones, in these rooms of destiny, where world drama should be responsibly carried out, but is usually squandered by power puffs like you and like that abomination just there who captured and claimed me as wifey, and plaything, and disposable property. You are both pure trash, and you do not deserve to be present at my passing. I scorn your deathwatch!
(She begins to fade.)
And now, before me, like a dream, he comes!

JONNY: *(thinking her previous talk might have been a temporary delirium)* My lovebird! Yes, I am here! No, this is not a dream. I am here, love!

(HMD: actually thinking that LUTRENA might be returning, not to JONNY, but to himself, clasps his hands involuntarily and with fervid expectation.)

LUTRENA: *(if she were not such a good person, she would attempt a scoff)* I should have left you some time ago, Jonny. I should have joined my *true* love! Oh, but we would be far away from here. Far away from you. To you he is lowly, but to me there is no better heart that beats with nobility on this or any other earth.

JONNY: *(a stunned whisper)* And who? In *whom* beats such a heart?

LUTRENA: Kuk-Yikky, the stable boy! The mere, sweet, humble, stable – Oh, horrors! I revealed him in my dying weakness! Only because – because I could not wrap-up without the bliss of uttering his name! My one true love... The only love I have ever had. The love at the end... We are so young! Alas... And you, Jonny, have aided my evening-in-common. I die sad – bereft. I can, I can only think of my lost love... And yet! His name!

To carry me out! Kuk-Yikky! Kuk-Yikky! Come, *save me!* Kuk... Kuk... (*dies*).

(*JONNY, grief-stricken but repulsed, withdraws and makes to escape the scene.*)

HMD: You root-pigs! Doing these things to me! You make me retire into a deplorable rage! I hate you! *Hate you!* You hear?

(*HMD outwardly gloats, but, inhuman that he is, he is nevertheless appalled by his deeds this day. Thus, he allows JONNY to speak his piece; camera dollies back to be inclusive.*)

JONNY: (*spitting, chaotic, dazed, but trying to be authoritative*) So, my Absolute and Complete Ruler For Whom It Is Utterly Unnecessary To Have Any Substitute, we are rid of a whore, are we not? A sex-worker vanquished! Eliminated! Before God (you yourself, of course), Court, and Country! Can we not now come together on this matter? Do we not now realize her vaginal guile? Why! She screwed both of us over! Is that not a bond betwixt us now? Can we not work – with you at the awesome summit – to now advance upon the world together, with me as your totally loyal lieutenant – if not corporal – and, free of any annoying love interest, can we not now concentrate our victory urges where they should have been all along: to consolidate our advantageous and strategic muscularity in establishing ourselves as a regional power that nobody will fuck with...? And soon, as a global... power...?

HMD: (*affable*) That is your recommendation?

JONNY: (*thinking that maybe he has an apparently easy chance at redemption*) Yiss! No big deal, huh? Let's do it! I have other good ideas, too. I was just keeping them dormant because we were so distracted for a while by that hooker, but now we can get totally into our conquering. I mean, *your* conquering. It doesn't have to stop *anywhere!*

HMD: (*smiling, mostly with his eyes*) Seize him once again, loyalty guards. This time firmly, no? Grips of drop-forged iron. Enough. Time to wrap this turkey up. I, uh, decree: Execute him in any sicko manner ye all prefer. There is only one mandate: make it slow, and send me the video of it. Pray, do not capture it in the porno style, but, rather, in the mode of pantheon directors, for it will be a video that will live for quite some time in the documentary fashion, for we are making history here, are we not?

(GUARDS, despite thinking HMD *is one twisted muh-fuh, swear complete fealty, and haul dumbfounded* JONNY *off; National Romantic door slams; camera dollies into CU of door, capturing the rebound of the iron ring; then dollies out and in to tight CU of* HMD, *face evolving and transforming as the lens draws nearer, finally settling on a mask concealing an interior crucifixion of agony, coverted by toughness.)*

HMD: *(dismissive)* Oh, and bump off that stable boy in your fashion, whatever the hell his name is; I can't recall it – and do the act without warning, hmm?

'CUTTA!'

Every cast and crew member, and every observer had tears in their eyes. Keenah LaVine's performance laid everyone to waste. And Butterbugs, archest of horrors, got astounding applause and cheers. Pamiel also shared in the audio accolade, which was as passionate as a La Scala swoon over an aria from 'Guglielmo Ratcliff' or 'Parisina'.

Aldobrandino Camposanto, the set designer-cum-decorator, collapsed into the arms of his wife, Assistant Costume Designer Sharna Carsell, and it was a good thing that Associate Art Director Albert Nozaki was there to assist in reviving him.

'I was simply overcome with emotion!' he said once he caught his breath.

'Aldo, are you all right? Come to hospital!' Sharna was understandably anxious.

'Not at all!' the intense Sicilian stood up. 'I am glorying! I have never *felt* such a performance, *of any kind!* My faint was one of the most beautiful experiences I have yet had!'

And he smothered his wife with kisses.

Sharna would approach Porter Parker with the notion that perhaps this was a picture that would require trained nurses to be present at each screening – a twist on the old William Castle gimmick, but with serious intent, this time around.

The set was enhubbub'd with enthusiasm, and everyone was chattering and weeping, hooting with praise, guffawing with amazement, and generally a celebratory kind of 'Can you believe what we just saw here?' mood splashed all over the place. Some sat in awe-stricken silence, unable even to move.

Doing little more than taking a brief Victorian-style bow, Butterbugs found himself shattered within his own private scope of wonder. There was his Lady Lee, and here was the actress who played her, alive, excelling, acting her heart out (and vocal cords) with him, and he, subject to her magic, all of a sudden loved nothing in this world more. Not even acting.

She was the One, and what then could contain his joy, when his consciousness then adjusted its contact points back to solidarity with the here and now? There was thrill and relief from the fact that he didn't *really* kill her after all, for there was a split-second when even a great actor can think, 'What have I done?' while trying to extract himself from a role's hyper– but hyped realities.

Yet, he could only gaze across the set at her, as she was attended to by production assistants, SFX-fixers, and make-uppers. Egaz himself kept his head enough to make sure she was all right. Then he came over to Butterbugs.

There was so much ambient noise about, the director could speak normally.

'Butterbugs! Congratulations, my fine fellow. Bang on target. Dare I praise you, or is your head big enough?'

'I'm simply glad it is still attached, Egaz. But that girl, the LaVine girl – I had no idea.'

'She is great, Butterbugs.'

'Great? Not a potent enough word. Not by a rather long shot. I am, I am taken aback. No idea... No idea at all...'

Egaz, mega-pleased by everything right now, let his star fade off into his reverie.

'Stand-by, please, I'll make the usual inquiries before we knock off.'

Actors can sometimes space out when performances on set become particularly exacting, but directors must be like sharks, always moving ahead and pro-active. Practical, too.

Butterbugs remained where he was, for the awe he felt happily reduced him to an observer. Keenah! She was magnificent, she was lovely, she was covered with blood.

A usual inquiry was made by Leon Shamroy.

'Did we get it?'

The answer given him was... most unusual. The camera did not Cut because the camera did not Roll.

'Paul?? What the fukkkkk??' bellowed Shamroy, his c-gar chomped clean through.

Paul the operator looked straight at his Director of Photography without fear.

'Meter showed we were rolling. Plus, vibration against my thumb, Chief. Motor signified it, as well.'

Key cam grip Leo corroborated.

'All signs show film rolled.'

'Except!' Leon rasped, pointing to the stock window in the magazine (after he'd opened the 300 lb. blimp, which crew usually did after every take). This time, Shammie himself popped the top, due to the obvious importance attached.

'Holy shit. This time we got hit in the Achilles heel,' he said.

'The heel!' gasped Paul.

Shamroy was on the crew's side, and against no one. He could be a tough cookie, but equipment failure only endeared him to his crew, even the mechanic, whom he knew was sincere.

'These fucking old hogs!' Shammie all but kicked the antique U-P 70 camera. 'If Bob were here, I'd take him to... task!'

Bob Surtees knew this system inside and out, but he was currently off to Jambutterbugsabad to do super-important location work with the 3rd unit's director, Yak Canutt. Shammie rang him up, somewhere over the Levant.

'So what gives?'

'I think I know,' replied Bob, always measured, always even-tempered. 'Check the aperture for Bakelite drop-off. If that's Camera #5 – the one I shot half of 'Raintree' with, I'll bet the feed spindle base is degrading.'

'Bob, you're the best!' replied Shamroy.

'I thought *you* were, buddy boy...'

Knowing he was dealing with a competence unrivaled in their Industry, Shamroy simply stood in front of the camera now, with Dirnd Deigh, the mechanic, gazing at its guts (once any previously-exposed or otherwise unexposed stock had been safely isolated).

'Whataya think, Dirnd?'

'Well, I'm not sure. I think it's not all it appears, but –'

Egaz came over.

'No – nothings?' the director inquired.

'How did you know?' asked the cinematographer, genuinely impressed, but apprehensive.

'In. In-stinct,' Egaz replied. 'The word, right? Right word? When – er – the, uh, how do you say, fil-um, when it does not shutter – I know. I seem to know...'

'Then why didn't you call 'Cut'?'

Shamroy of course knew that 'Cutta' meant 'Cut', but he was wary of a civil war on the horizon, if rage chanced to eclipse grief and the sense of loss.

'Valid. Question. Butta – lookette – did you see, uh – the perf – actoriuns – playing. Frames passing – along. Did you viddy? I did. My actors of mine! I was – help. Less.'

What they were having right there was a failure to communicate. Director thought he had a magnificent take. Cinematographer thought he didn't.

Egaz didn't slip out of his Butler English mode, though he came close. He was absolutely blown away by the take. Still. So was everybody else, even the hardasses on set. *Still.* That was why those who had seen it – those who were there – knew that they'd witnessed true greatness in cinematic performance.

Now there was a dreaded knowledge, as yet occult, but known to the few. The take – where was it? There was only one thing to think. And because it was lost forever, it now belonged to the ages, as with every great stage performance. Once the truth was known, the witnesses would surely know that the only way to go was ahead. Either that, or the response would be with fire and sword.

If all were amenable, maybe, just maybe, repetition would be the answer. Chance might smile upon them with something as good, if not better.

It soon became apparent on this intense set that within the immense U-P 70

#5 camera, a bit of 60+ year-old Bakelite, that shielded the frictions of the feed reel from the conductive part of the camera's magazine, had flaked away – from age – and had traveled onto the sacrum of the film chamber, due to a tilt in prepping for the take in question. The offending fragment had become wedged in the old mechanical sprocket advance-chain, which was a non-bind backup device, characteristic of these cameras. In this situation, theoretically, the camera would grind, but the film would not advance. The chances were 250,000,000 to 1, but in this case, the roulette wheel – that is, the one that disseminated the stock to be exposed, which awaited the privilege to pass through the rather large aperture as Butterbugs & Co. enacted their genius before the world – landed not only on the wrong number, but no number at all. And now the world had lost that particular extension of his genius' power.

As Bob had implied, several of the cameras had been used on MGM's 'Raintree County' (1957), for that was the look Egaz wanted for the Throne Room scenes. Thus did he pay the price for the luxus effect he favored so much.

As indeterminate tension grew, Leon took courage and finally ushered Egaz aside.

After discovering the news, the director blinked, raised his chin, and stroked his lengthy locks. Managing to find his voice, he said quietly and clearly, 'Thank you, Mr. Shamroy.'

Then he sought out his star, who was genially accepting compliments from ecstatic cast and crew.

Egaz wisely elected to paper-over his state of shock with bland simplicity.

'Butterbugs? Moment?'

'Thank you, best of all possible casts and crews! Now our director summons me for a private chat. Prepare, all, for a late tiffin of bakes, custarded fruitmeats, and mulgeon-water at my bungalow for dressing, now that our labors in the field are done this day!'

Egaz was hushed, his voice almost a hiss.

'Butterbugs? Friend? Still? Do you and now know. Pray. Again?'

'Eh?'

'Again, all. Again, yes. And yes, again. Pray.'

'All, Egaz?'

'We are as poverty, star! All. Yeses. Sir. Yes. From Lady L's entry. If it please?'

'Why Egaz,' replied Butterbugs robustly, noting that the cast and crew had regrouped in front of them for guidance, thus eliminating their privacy. 'Your English is improving! I hope it is because of Keenah's and Waycroft's performances!'

'What about *yours*, dear boy?' said Pamiel.

'Mine; yes, I suppose.'

'Let's not overdo the modesty at this point, hmm?'

Keenah smiled broadly. Butterbugs laughed.

'The three of us, then!'

Egaz greatly appreciated the assistance...

'Oh, star, yes. No doubts. Places? Oh?'

'Why, certainly!' Butterbugs was ecstatic. He got to do it again!

These were they who were top-flight professionals. The best in the business. There was no shock amongst them, only duty. Their business was capturement of performance, aided by style and artistry. Accomplishments appreciated, but *preciousness* had no place on the sets of the Seventh Art.

Set-side SFX were called in to prep Keenah's features, and a spare prosthetic neck was quickly installed, due to the crack crew's resourcefulness. For her part, young Keenah was a good sport, and her laughter was not particularly of relief, because she knew she had to do the whole sequence again, so she indulged in the luxury of releasing a bit of pent-up steam.

Still did Butterbugs regard her from afar. There was something that instilled and maintained a distance from him to the other. Perhaps it was simply the professionalism of both. He with the heavy lines to pronounce, she with not only heavy lines, but a darned complex set of plumbed-and-wired neck apparatuses, which had to be rebuilt and reinstalled over her existing (and surpassing) fairness.

He was shameless in his staring, but no one seemed to notice, as everyone was on task now. Then, in absorbing her being within the context of the rather demanding situation of Take 2 looming, her significance suddenly expanded. Hidden boxes of dreamt-of expectations were opened, due to this vision of her. Here he was, on the topmost turret of stardom, and there she was, gifted to him by smiling forces far above. He almost felt unworthy.

But no, after many attempts, many losses, many shifts, there was no contest in regarding his lack of fulfillment in matters of the heart. Why should he not claim this opportunity, to at least explore the possibilities? After all, there was the matter of *her* side of things to consider, no?

Oh, but he was just a little bit tired of sensitivity and accommodation. Why couldn't he, this time, be a consumer... a movie star, for pity's sake? Was he not desirable? Could he not command his own choice in mates? Well, he had chosen – or, more fairly, her presence had chosen him by its simple impact. Either way, he would have to make a gesture.

She made one first, however. As she waited patiently, with butterflies in her tummy, for techies to finish her restoration while she remained motionless, her gaze sought distraction in distance. It happened to catch Butterbugs' rapturous stare, and instantly, there was joined light in joined beams of vision. It was incandescent, really. The star noted this with interest. Most remarkably, it birthed a new paradigm: to ingest alternative approaches for Take 2 – not just variations on a theme, or just another old college try, but...

He couldn't help but think a major bonding with Keenah had just occurred.

Assuming that his Take 1 was safely stockpiled within #5's take-up reel, due not only to Egaz's cryptic plea for a retake, but because of his quiet and unexpected revelation over his leading lady in this scene, Butterbugs chose to follow up on some demi-funky revisionist thoughts concerning his plans for Take 2. They would involve taking creative action.

The concept of improvisation was brought to the forefront of his consciousness, and instantly approved by his engines of creation.

Therefore, he would *do a Brando* (who had played Fletcher Christian in front of the same Panatar lenses in MGM's 'Mutiny on the Bounty' of 1962), and let go with some free-form alterations, to be coined on the spot. He grew giddy at the prospect.

He would do it for Keenah first, for Egaz second, for his fellow cast members and crew third (perchance to score some overtime for 'em), for the distinguished guests present fourth, for the picture in general fifth, for Mega|Goth sixth, and for the general public seventh. Or – what was he thinking! For the general public *first*, of course! In any case, what was wrong with a little showing-off to his girlfriend?

Similarly, everyone on the set was communally ecstatic. He'd just connected on a plane – who knew how high – with a fellow thespian who had the added luster of being all-time lovable, and a director who couldn't (or didn't) micro-manage him because he trusted him implicitly. It was 'cadenza time'. Why the hell not?

His amazing power of tone spread to all the cast, crew, and guests present.

Butterbugs knew Sawl and his writers were watching from their own grandstand. But instead of whispering and jotting over rewrites and dissatisfactions, each sat patiently, transfixed. Same for the royals and friends in the other reserved seats. Theirs was total non-verbal attention, not anxious so much as wondrous.

Therefore, he thought that they, as a preview audience, and others in film halls across the world after them, might be pleased at some experimentation, perchance to keep their minds nimble, their expectations humble, and their enjoyment total. Actor and director had some creative building to do on their scaffolds, so to speak, but mostly he was motivated by new energies. He could not possibly repress the shine of his lamp of creation, with its specially-increased lumens, about to be broadcast.

Plus, there was someone *else* worth performing for. Alas, she whom he must, in his dastardly role, dispatch so savagely – on screen, of course. She who would act her heart out for him (really?), and whom he knew he loved.

Yes, *loved*. It was for sure now. So, he would show her how much. He would go the limit for her.

'Ah. It begins,' he thought, after Egaz called for places in the most grateful tones possible for Butler English, which were pretty ingratiating.

'Here goes.'

The camera was now well and turning, with stock active in the aperture, and once again, lights, camera, speed, clapper, and, ACTION.

'All, and all right, ACTIONS!'

(The Lady LUTRENA *enters.)*

HMD: Ladle-y, Ladle-y Lee! Lutrena! Oh yeah! *Lutrena*, of the running desires of my most sumptuous concepts of Nordic standards and purposes, to pant over so-cute babes in ceremonial stride, before me! Well! Aren't I powerful enough to intercede! Do I not have the clout? If I have already achieved possessing you, that means I have *conquered* you. Where you came from, before I sealed you into this high-strung life, your homeland: all full of legendary babes – But! Were you the best? Do you have the stamina that I require – me, of the Plains, down and away from your safe havens of trees to hug 'n' hole up-in, and the wood-smoke of cozy camps in amongst the no-go zone of a people who've known what they are doing for, well, centuries now? Do you, then? Forgive we of the lesser levels, we out here on the overrun marches, where not only the spikéd heels of Mongols trampled us, but those of Huns, White Huns, Galicians, Lichavas, Chermans, and Cossack-stans, aplenty. Forgive my tardiness in evolving into a personality of sophistication. But, you have to admit, I have arrived at that place. How else could I address you with confidence? How then, do you like my authoritarian appearance? Hmm? So then, Lady of my bedroom's assets – ward, not of state, but of mine own right of return – as many times as I want! So... what? That's what I like to acknowledge and show off about, especially in this here power-chamber – You know, that we're gettin' it on, that we're having sex, at my convenience, and thus, if I have such impressive suzerainty over you, I command attention from these here so-called 'Courtiers', who damn well better get with the program and realize that my domination, domicile, and dominion extend to all quarters. Thus, if I can physically rule over you with my sex act, I've surely got the capability of screwing anything that moves, as a deed of warning and coercion. Just in case anybody out there gets the wrong idea. That's the rapist's creed. Ugly force makes us hard. So, baby, you know every centimeter – or decameter! – of me (heh!), and you worship my attributes. I get to flaunt myself all over you, and you must obey. Without any equivocation or the slightest reference to your own past glories. (You were an innocent virgin maid of course, but I allow some fantasizing to have occurred, about a figure less than mine, naturally, who fancied you but couldn't have you.) Oh yeah, and you must certainly conform to any *alternative*, now that we have bonded in locked-in love – if you actually want to use that term. I want to tell everyone here that Lady L. has done some remarkable things as far as responding to my sexual athleticism is concerned. She has served both dirty and naughty. Do you want details, my people? Well, perhaps later. Right now, devotees, behold my sex-toy and consorter, Lady Lutrena! She stands before you! Gaze upon her public lips: full, feminine, and fluppy. Imagine, Court, where they've been, and the exciting

expeditions they've been taken on! Expeditions of privilege and high purpose, I assure you! Well, what next? What's to come? And what *will*...
come? (*directly addressing* LUTRENA). You see, I really can't *stand* the
way you showed up here, today. Want to know why? Don't answer me. No,
no, no. No excuses! I don't want any 'meal' to come out of your formerly
accommodating mouth. You see, you still turn me on. Your octopus lips
down there... You still randy-randy me, though I will keep my robes in
orderly fashion just now. I simply and profoundly revile that guy over
there. That cast plaster of Paris fake! Made of china glass! Plastic cheapie!
Yes, him (*gestures widely to* JONNY). He has revealed to me today that I
have every right, as head of this here State, to regard him as an interloper,
a common opportunist, and a snotty little snit who wants to see my balls
on a platter of, say, Eggs Benedict – for *your* consumption, no doubt. So
that my sacred essence can end up as your excremental statement. I find
that *rawther* revolting, don't you? Even a goddess under my care has to
use ye olde thunder-mug. Huh?? Right??? But I understand the true insult
of such cannibalism. Let me re-state the obvious in highly civilized terms.
The hated human is consumed, *as food*, not because it, or should I say,
he, tastes good, or as a sign of supreme conquest, but as a transformation:
from thinking humanoid to abhorrent stool. By that process, one ends up
as, not fodder for worms, but rather, shit for the sewer pot. Toss a pauper's
cardboard gravestone down the cistern! Well, that's the kind of degradation nobody talks about, eh? Look about you and see the courage of my
Court! Nobody's plugging their ears. Why? Is it because my courtiers are
noble and courageous? Huh? Doesn't really matter. I'm saying things they
long to say! Like, the degradation you and they know to be true. But I'm
talking about it because this is my Court and I can do anything I want!!
(*then, calmer*) Think I'm raving? Hmm? Think I'm, you know... running
on? Think I'm intimidated? Think I'm falling apart? Think I've gone off?
Maybe I want people to think things that ain't necessarily so, hmm? When
one senses intriguers in one's midst, the defenses rise. You, Ladle-y Lee,
may still turn me into a horndog by your very presence, but is it really
wise for us to kiss-off and tell, before Court?

(*HMD* waits for answer; none comes; LUTRENA *initially in shock.*)

HMD: You besmirch me by your inept *silencio*. How else can I interpret cuck-
old strategies, so well laid out in front of me? Isn't it an obvious gambit?
Me – virile Head of State, on the world's roster of the Top Ten Most
Consequential Rulers! Probably up to Top One Most Consequential, by
now. Aren't I eligible for likelihood of Plotting By Mediocre Dumbos
From Within? (That's an official category, y'know, by Vombo Institute
poll takers; asking questions to mobile and landline citizens, the world

over!) You cannot operate in a your-own-little-world vacuum these days, oh, my sexy wife of the slinking buttocks! You just don't have the capacity to put me down in person, do you? Faced with my rather sensible responses, you just can't think of anything, can you? *Silencio* says it all, baby. *Oh! Silencio!* You co-authored a coup, it's obvious. Against *me!* You think I am too preoccupied with thinking with my dick to notice? Eh? How dare you take the intimacy that we shared, that I have on video record, that you swore your bodily– and mentally-oriented perma-troth to me, and now you would conspire against me. Me!, who protected you, who gave you every conceivable toy and property, as well as motorcar and holiday house, plastic accessories currently in fashion, and more jewelry than would choke a vacuum-blowing prostitute!, by which to make you happy in this doofus nation, and by providing you with every opportunity to improve the lot of our pathetic citizens by placing alternatives and new ideas in their collective paths? You did none of these things, except to get your clit off by hooking up with this, this *scarecrow* of a power-plucking traitor! You are the Hurter, I the Hurt-ed. Oh, calumny-causer! Yes, no wonder you can't spitball any eruption from your mouth, that I have genuinely relished! For, do you not remember, I pledged any platform that might please you in bedroom matters that you might desire – no matter how sacrificial or demeaning to me as your lawful husband, be it multiple sex partners, homosexuality, santorum-generation, kinkiness, or even piglet-fondling – as long as it was something that meant something to you! If I wasn't 'good enough', if my dick wasn't 'enough', if you were too discriminate a 'prick lady', all well and good. I could have found you what you needed. And paid for it, too! I have millions, and you wanted minions! You, you, break my underestimated and true-beating heart, glossy gal. I know now what a pain it is to endure rejection. So. Enter. Show up. Blab a little. I'll watch you, as my dick gets hard. You can hear how fucking well-spoken I am, can't you?

LUTRENA: *(finds voice)* Topmost-minded lord of bossiness, and exposer of underthings! My voice has always been primed and my body is constantly aware. Your overpowering mush is depressing, and is no longer tactile to me, nor my uses as your consort. I know that now.

(Camera continues to pull back, revealing astonished courtiers.)

HMD: As I thought. So, I am offended. That's why I wanted this little splatter to occur before Court entire. So that those members interested in fair play could witness for themselves the bummer package to which I have been obliged to respond. Here you are, admitting in public – for we are being broadcast live to all five corners of the nation, and perhaps being podcast beyond the wildest realms of our collective imagination (for radio waves of this exchange could end up on, say, Ceres or somewhere akin, I suppose). And come to think of it, on this occasion do I claim Ceres itself, as a mere start to my Empire Without and Beyond! How many other Leaders and Teachers aspire to such Upthrusts and Impressives today? Well, *I* do! But here on my ground, which I permanently own, a somber wake-up breakfast awaits to be processed. My heart – well, it's healthy enough. My coronaries are clear. But my heart is sick. Grey blood makes my pink tissue turn sepia with grief. I expect a huge and downbeat stroke to lay itself upon me, of such a dolorous nature that it will not be describable in the long train of personal thoughts I carry, on behalf of my people. For remember – you dippy poseurs in your petty power plays carry only your self-inflated thoughts, while I, as Head of an Empery, recognized not only by the United-Now Nations, but by the 'CIA World Factbook' as well, struggle to carry the honor of a Great Country on my back, as well as your hop-on and offensive agendas. So, so. So, put that in your pipe and torch it!!

JONNY: *(boldly breaks in)* Leader-lord, crazed with mad thoughts, *including jealousy!* How can you unpleasantly evacuate upon this sweetness-girl of love? This merry muffin of the senses? This vision of loveliness? However *can* you? Why must you flaunt your boorish nature so as to inspire hatred in all of us who listen to you at this particular point in time? How –

HMD: *(explodes)* See, Court!? See?! Listen! How he poses hypothetical scenarios to divide the truth, from the perceived preferences slathered-on by an elite band of renegades! He (and probably she), stabs my – and your – truth… Through 'n' through, *and through again* – with a selfish blade! He (and probably she), aspires to bending words into a pendant worn by the self-righteous, who are assumed to be so, by the mere fact that they dare to exhibit some form of safe and telling form of iconography that exempts them from scrutiny, especially when they are guilty of indiscretions made void by law! There is a criterion, set by our Laws and our Standards, in which guilty parties experience the practice of a lawful state's Roman-style preference for enactment of civic behavior. Or there is an alternative: to revert to utter savagery in seeing through the courses of justice preferred to most humanoids wishing a full and just life on this here planet at the present time! There is only one truth for peoples like you: you must *pay!*

(Huge cheers for HMD, *from the* COURT.)

The Court, following Butterbugs' lead, was doing their own daring bit of improvisation (e.g. non-scripted cheering). But Egaz did not call 'Cutta!' at this creative insolence. Indeed, from behind the camera he registered silent delight over where this take had gone and where it was going.

JONNY: How do you know I *have* to pay? After the disgrace you have shown us this day?

HMD: Oh, you task me! I let the many witnesses hereabouts judge my testimony. You make me so mad! Why, *you...!*

JONNY: I fear only one thing, curséd puke person! That you will now harm my Lady Lee, as a reprisal for my justified insolence.

HMD: *(aghast)* What did you just say to me – and Court? *Your* Lady Lee?? You cannot *do* that! You cannot *ever, ever, EVER* call her that! Only *I* can address her and refer to her as: Lady Lee! That is a private nickname, with steamy sexual associations! Only one who could have – Why, you miserable – Only *I* can call her Lady Lee! Only *I* can associate myself with her intimate agreements! Yet, you fill my innocent mind with an idea – as a final solution. But never mind that! Are you saying, by this outrage, that you have had sex, and *sexy* sex, with this girl?

LUTRENA: He has! I tell you, he has! And glorious it has been, too. Even within the last hour, love-waste lordy! The thought – the very thought of you and your inherent hideousness, your baggy remnants of something you delude yourself with, the prospect of drawing nigh to your wobbly bits, both dirty and naughty, make my pretty belly wamble with vomitous portent, and the concept of your disgusting attempts to impregnate me, whether via squeeze-bulb or penis-pump'd product (which, despite the fact that any issue from your hulk would have to be limited to nasal mucus, though, to be sure in my own mind, I have even surreptitiously employed a humble coat hanger, soaked in harsh tinctures and preventative potions of all types, as total insurance against any reproductive blunder), fills me not with your semen 'n' sperm (ick!), nor even from your nostril snot – which you tried one time – honestly, he *did*, Court! – but you *do* fill me with the desire to open your neck with my sharp fingernails whilst you sleep, and to expose your tiresome voice box, which gave me such sick and mind-awful commands; to expose it to the air, and then to the nearest drain, to end up in our poor, polluted Sea of Aral, where it might be set upon by the vilest of vermin, while the gap that I opened drains you of putrid life. Yes, I would do these things. I would *murder* you at my first opportunity. Why I have not done so, particularly under more discreet circumstances, I cannot say. Perhaps I was in a constant state of overpowerment from your brutalism.

Perhaps it was my fear of your power. I can only blame myself. But none of that adds up to anything worth summing in the analytical sense. Until now, I was not sufficiently bolstered by Jonny's constant pushings and pullings. By my failure of blandishment I expose myself. Only now, at this late, late hour, I might redeem myself... through love!

(JONNY *makes to advance toward her, because of her last statement, but restrains himself when:*)

(LUTRENA *pulls out a long dagger from her damosel sleeve.*)

HMD: *(appalled by the offense)* Oh, no! My love, in whom I placed complete and unutterable trust – she comes – comes at me, with a *knife!* How should I act? Should I treat her as the traitor she appears? How close I have come to severing these balls, as they certainly be the chief offenders in my perceived offensive behavior, in doing the right thing!

(COURT *sycophants laugh nervously.*)

JONNY: Leader of lords! May I speak?

HMD: Jonny, really, if you can clear up this chilling confusion! Please – help! Pity my new vulnerability!

JONNY: Thank you, Liege of the Highest Arts...

HMD: Oh, how must I respond? Why must I be subject to this onslaught?

JONNY: To save my Lady Lee – or rather, your Lady Lutrena, from mutual assured destruction, which I share with her. You, sir, are partial to flattery, so I suggest you enjoy it while I offer it.

HMD: *(agreeable)* You force me – into compliance, so that my love is protected still...

JONNY: Please don't execute us.

HMD: You give me a way out! You give me a way, to see reason, within the tragic bounds of the tunnel into which you have cornered me! But take note – I have indeed found a way out. As with ty-byamite, with which to blast one's path from the midst of living rock, I do hereby press such a plunger to the roof of its ignition box! So to speak... A crackdown! Not my style, but you place me square in the center of it! I can and will resort to authority. I am the supreme figure here, and you have pressured me into enacting that role. Thus, Guardians of the Height of the Doctorial Throne: seize them with great seizing!

(GUARDS grab JONNY and LUTRENA.)

GUARD GOMBO: But Grandeur Controller and Owner, we cannot end the existence of one so comely.

(GOMBO attempts to feel up LUTRENA, now that she is virtually condemned.)

HMD: Nobody has said that you should end anyone's existence. Is that the expectation of this discourse? Court? Are these not forces that conspire to sow discord instead of cooperative agreements, agreeable to all? (*directly addresses* LUTRENA) Defiance? You retreat? As to go with *him?* How am I to react? Should I not restrain you to cooperate in any subsequent inquiry? I shall protect my rights, even unto radical action! Honor is more important than love! Obeisance matters more than freedom!

(HMD pulls out a concealed Bowie knife and lets it fly, hitting LUTRENA square in the neck. Camera dollies in, as fast as possible, but still at a stately pace, for expectations to build, into a CU of LUTRENA, who then does her death speech:)

(Cue music in final print; arresting arpeggio into sorrowful rendition of 'Lost Love' theme.)

LUTRENA: See, how I am killed!

(Camera dollies out enough to show JONNY, as he wrests himself from the GUARDS' grip and rushes to her side, then camera to CU of LUTRENA; LUTRENA's vocal cords are exposed, but the area is in deep shock though still operational, and because of this, she is actually able to talk.)

LUTRENA: Oh, Jonny! You emboldened me, so. You set me up for this, and now it has killed me. You are as much the author of my untimely expiration as he whom we   hated together. Why did we not fly to Kyemtabulask, when I begged you to? I have estates there! We could have *lived!* Instead, your ambitions and your designs kept us *here,* in this seat of my sorrows. You kept telling me, repeating to me, almost haranguing me, that it was possible to eliminate the Doctor who is so high and mad! Oh, Jonny, how could you have been so – wrong? How could I have been so – loyal? Or some... thing...

JONNY: *(devastated)* Because, dear sweetness, oh! oh!, now in ruins, you were the *Ideal:* loyal, helpful, sympathetic, obedient, and all because: you – love me!

LUTRENA: Oh, what a failure I am.

JONNY: *(shattered)* Oh Love-Lee! Do you feel much pain?

LUTRENA: Nay, for I am beyond it. I am at the threshold. And Death approaches...

JONNY: *(sullen)* At least that...

LUTRENA: I failed, failed, and all my regrets now carry me away. Away, away to deservéd darkness. I tried to dissuade you. I tried to make you understand – something you are incapable of doing. Oh, Jonny, like most cocksmen, you were possessed by the opiate of world-grasping, whether in my nest, where I tried to trust you, and where I kept giving you chances, or upon these stones, in these rooms of destiny, where world drama should be responsibly carried out, but is usually squandered by power puffs like you and like that abomination just there who captured and claimed me as wifey and plaything and disposable property. You are both pure trash, and you do not deserve to be present at my passing. I scorn your deathwatch!

(She begins to fade.)
And now, before me, like a dream, he comes!

JONNY: *(thinking her previous talk might have been a temporary delirium)* My lovebird! Yes, I am here! No, this is not a dream. I am here, love!

(HMD, *actually thinking that* LUTRENA *might be returning not to* JONNY *but to himself, starts making wild gestures and facial expressions, implying regret and horror.)*

LUTRENA: *(if she were not such a good person, she would attempt a scoff)* I should have left you some time ago, Jonny. I should have joined my true love! Oh, but we would be far away from here. Far away from you. To you he is lowly, but to me there is no better heart that beats with nobility on this or any other earth.

410

JONNY: *(a stunned whisper)* And who? In whom beats such a heart?

LUTRENA: Kuk-Yikky, the stable boy! The mere, sweet, humble, stable – Oh, horrors! I revealed him in my dying weakness! Only because – because I could not wrap up without the bliss of uttering his name! My one true love... The only love I have ever had. The love at the end... We are so young! Alas... And you, Jonny, have aided my evening-in-common. I die sad – bereft. I can, I can only think of my lost love... And yet! His name! To carry me out! Kuk-Yikky! Kuk-Yikky! Come, *save me!* Kuk... Kuk... *(dies)*.

(JONNY, grief-stricken but repulsed, withdraws and makes to escape the scene.)

HMD: I am in the dire danger of dissolving into a pile of griefs. Collapsing from overwroughtnesses! Faced with an end to my service to the Nation, and all! Oh, calumny! Oh, grieviousness! *[sic]* Why are ye such a tyrant so as to control my hands? Why? Oh, now *why?*

(HMD outwardly suffers, but, conflicted human that he is, he is nevertheless appalled by his deeds this day – thus, in this extreme circumstance, is the barest shred of his humanity revealed. Thus he allows JONNY to speak his piece; camera dollies back to be inclusive.)

JONNY: *(spitting, chaotic, dazed, but trying to be authoritative)* So, my Absolute and Complete Ruler For Whom It Is Utterly Unnecessary To Have Any Substitute, we are rid of a whore, are we not? A sex-worker vanquished! Eliminated! Before God (you yourself, of course), Court, and Country! Can we not now come together on this matter? Do we not now realize her vaginal guile? Why! She screwed both of us over! Is that not a bond betwixt us now? Can we not work – with you at the awesome summit – to now advance upon the world together, with me as your totally loyal lieutenant – if not corporal – and, free of any annoying love interest, *can we not now* concentrate our victory urges where they should have been all along: to consolidate our advantageous and strategic muscularity in establishing ourselves as a regional power that nobody will fuck with...? And soon, as a global... power...?

HMD: *(overcome with disgust)* You rotten tough! So much for your little affair with my late wife! You make me want to spew moist chunks of bile-heavy pig lard at every one of your vulnerable orifices, you cheap creep. And in turn, you want to butter me up. Look at what I just did: I bumped my wife off for the sake of her and your treachery. Behold, Court, my crime of passion! You saw with your own burning eyes, that he, this... this *man*, in whom I placed both my National Trust and my Inner Sanctum Trust, not to mention all my apples, into his apple-basket, he – he *made* me do it! It was as if he had approached me, pulled the bullish, self-protective blade from my person, and forced my hand to let it fly to its target! *(addresses* JONNY *directly while gesturing to the* COURT*)* My witnesses, Requesticus! *(then, to all)* I realize that I am safely above the law of mine own country. But, with so many witnesses to not only my late wife's faithlessness, but to the fact that this turbo-traitor, her ersatz 'lover', drove her to confess to her crimes, and then drove me to this fit of spontaneous execution, I deem it a certainty that this here Court will see my enactment of justice as quite a reasonable and defensible act after all. *(faces* JONNY*)* That you did these things that I charge you with is beyond question, beyond contest, beyond the need for any further hearing, I tell you! And you still want to partner in my enterprises of power?

JONNY: *(thinking that maybe he has an apparently easy chance at redemption)* Yiss! No big deal, huh? Let's do it! I have other good ideas, too. I was just keeping them dormant because we were so distracted for a while by that hooker, but now we can get totally into our conquering. I mean, *your* conquering. It doesn't have to stop *anywhere!*

HMD: *(in sudden festive mood, smiles mostly with his eyes)* Cheerfully, then, do I command the following mandate, based on my awesome power. High-level guards, grab him, will you? Will you do it? O, *will* you? *(*GUARDS *indeed seize* JONNY, *who is aghast)* Good! Good! Now, Court, consider my position. I have summarily executed one traitor, and you all know why. Now, what to do with the other? If I had to do it over, this turkey would be bone-dead by now, with the girl alive and captured. A preferable situation, I can tell you that right now. But you saw how he tricked me! His methods exponentially increase the heinousness of his crimes. And see how he has no emotion at her passing! Court, particularly some of you ladies out there, fear not! Fear not for your lives, for you do not serve a man who executes gentler sexes offhand. I tell you, he made me do it! And you may point out my own stern and confident manner as I declare my stately but grim business to you all right now. See, no tears border the cockpits of these commanding eyeballs! But inside! Consider. The smoldering, dying fire that is sorrow burns within my shocked breast. Remember, I am a Leader. Great leaders have to steel themselves, even in the midst of personal tragedy, for if they are to carry the burden of State onward, they must place their own cares and affairs way down the list, if not eject them completely. Behold me, then, as a barren and lifeless man in matters of life's joys and pleasures! Understand me to be, though, a tested leader of you and your land, who has become even more hardened – like the burliest of walnut rounds, or the harshest of *montagne* granites, or the keenest of ferromolybdenums, ready to stand impervious to any attempts at carving, chiseling, or drilling into your security. For I lead us through both tragedy and trial, straight on through to VICTORY! Do you hear me? Are you joined with me? *(huge approval from* COURT; *cheering, for some time)* Now, now that you support me totally from here on in, and in all situations, advise me now. Shall we rid ourselves of this man, this, this 'Jonny', who is so repulsive so as to be vile? *(massive approbation from the* COURT*)* I thought so, and I agree. Now then, guards, take him out and END this rotten remainder of what should be holy, but in this case isn't: life itself. End it in him. You may be indiscriminating in your actual methods, only end it within the hour, and document it. All of you will enjoy prosperous rewards for this service. *End* of show trial.

*(*GUARDS, *despite thinking* HMD *is one twisted muh-fuh, swear complete fealty, and haul dumbfounded* JONNY *off; National Romantic door slams; camera dollies into CU of door, capturing the rebound of the iron ring; then dollies out and in to tight CU of* HMD, *face evolving and transforming as the lens draws nearer, finally settling on a mask concealing an interior crucifixion of agony, coverted by toughness.)*

HMD: *(discursive, to the Commanding Guard,* GOMBO, *who tarries a moment)* Oh... and, I don't know, extinguish any other thoughts you might find conspiratorial, as regards your fellow human, you guardian-type personality, you. Isn't this one horror enough? There are, no doubt, many to consider, even all at once. History runs, and runs swiftly, like a cold alpine stream – *(now confiding in* GOMBO*)* none of which we have within our borders. Thus, we are exempt from history. It does not apply to us. The end of history begins here and now. I have transcended it. I am bigger than it is. Way, *much* bigger! By far!!! For, if I were not so, what kind of Leader, in this day and age, would I be? I must carry my country on my back. My shoulders must be stout. If I were to think that I am still chained by history's tyranny, what hope could I offer my people? What would be the point of going on? The late Lady Lutrena and that soon-to-be-late flimp you're about to dispatch are really the founders of a revolution. The revolution of which I speak. They kicked it off. I will commemorate them with a plaque in the candle-flickered anteroom just aft, behind the lowering columns of shadow, so that the people will know of my magnanimity, despite my own personal and selfless losses. I could not have transcended history without their 'sacrifice'. But in actuality, it is me who will perform the sacrifice: by rising to the unexplored heights of power that await. It begins now, my loyalist Guard. Stay loyal, and you will enjoy the lower balconies that adjoin the pinnacle upon which I will stand, as a monument to this heavy task. *(HMD then adopts a false tone of self-criticism, so as to make GOMBO think he is not as conspiring as he is; his guile will out later in the picture)* But, if we are to preserve the 'Rvle of Law' (I do not necessarily condone that tired term, even now, but I state it in ancient Roman characters, for maximum effect), what choice do we have, in risking indiscriminate selection of offenders? Do your worst if you must, but if that worst be put toward experience, and thus, in the force of progress made upon the path upward, toward something like truth and vindication, perhaps force is still to be relied on. How else can I rest easily – if at all? I send you now, Guard of my forces. May my will accompany you on your right-decision mission, though over my heart hangs doubt heavily and with tonnage frightful. Above all, I have deep doubts as to the decisions I have made to keep my ass above water. I should not be admitting these things, but, because of this late afternoon's events, I have been forced to become a man of conscience, and that man is suspended in the funnel of self-inspection. There seems to be only one way out. Downward. Narrowing. And harrowing…

(HMD turns away from GOMBO and the COURT, retreats to the curtains behind his throne and hangs his head; camera, which has followed, rises above him and ascends to the top of the baldacchino, then zeros into a huge CU of HMD's crest: two facing steers' heads, their horns locking, and between them, a naked Eve, holding an apple aloft.)

'…c–CUTTA!'

No one, absolutely no one, could do anything. For a full four-to-five minutes, it was as if everyone was jerked off the power grid, stunned.

Then… there was a bit of shuffling, coughing, low mutterings, as cast and crew were allowed back into life. Within a few more minutes, the whole soundstage was abuzz with chattering and laughing and swooning and howls of amazement and other responses to incredibleness.

There was a whole new energy on the set. No one really knew its perimeters, but they felt themselves in the midst of alternative forces that commanded all the power of dictatorial weather conditions. The collective head turned toward the away-direction of the wind.

The thing was, now Egaz had to concern himself with the course this picture should take. What the hell? HMD as quasi-sympathetic character? The actor as creator. Like Picasso blending paint directly on the canvas rather than on the prosaic palette.

Association and amalgamation of presented elements must be mixed and examined and possibly dried as final expressions after an internal artistic debate.

As a former graphic artist, Egaz could only wave his hands in non-swishy fanning and realize what he'd cracked open here: a painterly evolution by way of an actor's improv's inventive intervention! The revolution of Butterbugs' divinely (?) inspired character development posed unprecedented consideration. No one, not-no-one, not-no-how, had whined for a second about the direction Butterbugs' variations had gone. There were no yakkings of 'He's completely disoriented me' or 'He runs on, doesn't he?' or 'Where the fuck is this leading??' or 'Egotistical actor grandstanding and boring everyone shitless!' None of that tat.

Instead, sheer wonder.

In fact, QE2 herself had touched (!) Egaz's shoulder to get his attention as he was stepping back to assess the scene just tackled. Then she whispered to him – as a confidant. Her Hanoverian face was passive, only because her smile muscles were exhausted.

'Sri D'Varzim!' (her pet name for him, which implied an exchange between close friends, rather than royal chastisement) 'Do you know what you have here? This is a rare opportunity! Quite extraordinary. Some of the language employed is a wee bit... inelegant, but I find the implications most conducive to truths rarely, if ever, spoken.'

'I humbly absorb and agree with your points, Your Majesty. I shall endeavor to see to your wishes.'

She retired from the director's presence. Her carriage awaited, Sandringham-bound. 'This is the artistic highlight of my reign within the confines of Century 21!' she enthused to Sir Cragbast Muldenbloover, her aide.

Then the (ex) King of Spain drew nigh and gently grabbed Egaz by the collar and pulled him close.

'I have not thought of these things before, quasi-Portuguese semi-Iberian! Have you?'

That was all he could say. His eyes glinted like hematite buttons. He was asking for *help*, for Pete's sake. Egaz could interpret the obvious. This monarch, familiar with Almodóvar, cared for all things high quality. This was the shorthand spoken by those lofty enough to not dally on obvious grace notes.

'I know what you mean, Señor! Thank you for your input. I hear you.'

It was a serviceable response, but he, along with the Queen and other royals, seemed to be of one mind: this take was more profound than the first. It had grasped the very picture by the horns – by the balls – by the boobs – and re-directed it – somewhere. But where? Time to confer with Sawl & Team!

Moms then grappled the director.

'Son? Helps us, son! Mebbe you kin make us understands, mebbe we's can makes you understands. Cuz we know. I ain't never seen nothin' so fine...'

She wept for a time, then whipped out her mobile and got TABP on the line, clear over in Jambutterbugsabad, to fill him in.

'Angry Blackie?' she drawled, using her pet name for him. 'We's seen the perfection. And that's alls I gots to say!'

Egaz reached Sawl in the Writers' Cabinet, which remained above the fray. They were all shell-shocked, or so it appeared. John Smith was on the floor. Britney had her hand over her mouth, trying to contain impending emesis. Chief Standing Cow, usually impassive-appearing but always profound, stared straight ahead, past the revelers and into the drape that formed the backdrop to the HMD throne, and uttered:

'He is the Improver.'

And that was *all* he said.

Sawl had his head in his hands.

'Sawlohmunn, baby, I don't know why, but he did a Brando on us. Went his own way, Sawl. I'll get Porter to approach the Producer Team for more bucks to re-stage next week. Schedule won't allow it today or tomorrow. And –'

Thinking that Sawl would either want to slit his own throat right then and there, or else come at him with a hatchet, Egaz froze with terror as the mega-author slowly, oh-so-achingly-slowly, raised his head. He had been bawling, and his hands were soaked.

'I'll impound the film, Sawl. Don't worry. None of this will get out. I'll seal the soundstage until security can be established. Your reputation will remain intact. And impeccable, too.'

It was remarkable how the very exotic Mr. D'Varzim now managed to be sounding very 'Hollywood' in his terms and talk.

'Don't worry Writer Cane. I'll order the Take 2 film to be launched into an acid bath the second I decamp from your – presence… (If I'm still alive…)'

Sawl stood up sharply, grabbed Egaz's collar, much more aggressively than the wussy (ex) King of Spain had done, and glared at him with an Abrahamic intensity that outdid any old Isaac-ish death sentence, and spoke very calmly and very clearly so as not to allow the slightest bit of misinterpretation to crop up in what he was about to say.

'You – do – anything – ANYTHING, you understand? – to adjust – or to harm that take, and… and… I will, I promise you, I – will – find – you – and – then – *kill* – you. End your existence. Give you cause to expire. KILL YOU. That is a promise, all right. And there had *better* have been film that moved inside that camera this time. There just *better* have been! UNDERSTAND?? If not… many – will – *die*.'

Egaz, had never, ever referenced any evidence that Sawl Cane had ever displayed aggressive characteristics within the dual contexts of the crazy bizzes he was involved in, publishing and pictures, but here he was, probably establishing a precedent, and over the picture he, Egaz, the director, was shooting, so the nature of responsibility occurred to him, and super-charged him, and he turned silently, exited the Cabinet, then hooted a holy hellhound howl:

'YYYYYYEEEEEEESSSSSSSSSSS!!!!!!!!!!!!!!!!!!'

Writers mollified in spite of liberties taken! Greatness achieved in this one take! Forward, then! To *GLORY!!!!!!!!*

His intensity declared, the author cleared his throat and called mildly after

Butterbugs, who was drifting around the set in a quiet daze amidst the frenzy, alone, all but ignored, in sickening costume that matched his role-playing, yet as if he had just received Holy Writ from...

'Butterbugs? Could you toddle over here for a moment's supplemental chat?'

'Sawl.' The actor drew near, ready to comfort in light of his liberties taken with the script, or else to acknowledge justified banishment for sins committed. 'I understand your writer's defense of product. I will be its worthy steward yet. You, you must know, that –'

'Yeah. I do know. You see, I can't be happier with what you did in the scene. The whole Team is pumped. Britney's puke is a *good* sign! But I noticed that in the second take, HMD does not ring down the axe on Kuk-Yikky – the supernumerary stable boy. Intentional?'

'Wow. I'm embarrassed. I forgot all about him.'

Butterbugs grew silent and concentrated.

'Sawl, you know, I think that in the scheme of things, might we – you and the team – not consider: Kuk-Yikky *gets away*. In his supreme grief, he forms an underground movement, and perhaps...'

He paused, then resumed.

'He is the element of hope, Sawl. Hope. If the audience notices. If they choose to notice the subtlety, in contrast with HMD's bombast.' Then his voice lowered. 'The lowly stable boy is a symbol – of hope.'

Sawl could not speak at all. He could only think:

'SEQUEL!!'

Butterbugs saw the compassion in the master author's eyes, and knew there was resolve.

As Egaz moved away, Butterbugs called out to him.

'By the bye, Director, I got knighted by the Queen!'

'Finally! Great! I'm not going to be calling you 'Sir', though...!'

Amidst Egaz's elation however, one bit of business.

Indeed, 'Better check the magazine'.

Egaz sought out Old Atrocity, who was still incapable of comment. The director immediately understood and adapted.

'Where's Shamroy and crew, OA? Want to ascertain said take's safety.'

Relieved by his director's appropriate concern, spoken in new fluency, but still a mute witness himself, OA led him to the crew, who'd sensibly retired U-P 70 #5 to the sidelines, while the numerous occupants of the set sort of... partied. Golden moments of tremendous caliber, impossible to ignore, even for seasoned professionals. Cameraman and crew were wiped out, as well.

'Shammie! Found you – plus camera, OK.'

Shamroy's cheroot was a sodden tobacco vine.

'Yeah, well, you could've stuck around, *Varzie*. We were wasted. We got over to the side after the closing CU on high.'

'My desire, and told you to, as it went.'

'Yeah, I guess you're right, King's English-mangler. I mean Queen... We had to adapt.'

'Superb, you were. You pulled off.'

'WE did, Doc. Glad you had the instinct to go with his Brando-tango tangents.'

'Surtees had seen that stuff on the 'Bounty'.'

'Sure as shit. All *I* had to wade through was 'Cleopatra' (20th-Fox, 1963). Oh man, wish he'd been here. But I think we pulled it off.'

'You bet. You did. I'm sure.'

'Yeah.'

'Well, speaking of. Magazine OK?'

'Now *there's* a thing.'

Egaz went blank.

'*Magazine? OK?*'

'That's one thing I wanted to talk to you about, Egaz.'

'Funny, I've never heard you call me that before, but I suppose it's OK.'

'Strange. I've never heard you speak so normally, in QE2's English before, but I suppose it's all right.'

'Screw that shit. Tell me, the footage, the magazine – is everything secured, everything all right? Did we get it? All of it?'

'Well, it's a little bit clumsy...'

'Spare me the personal impressions, Leon! Please, level with me – what's the score? I have to plan my will and the way I'm going to extinguish myself if you've let me down. My last reel's running out. Just think, by midnight, I will no longer be on this planet.'

Shamroy was nonplused.

'I haven't let you *down*.'

'You... haven't?'

'It's more serious than we thought it might be.'

'What??'

'In fact, there's more than we reckoned.'

'More? More *what?*'

'More footage. Way more. One whole take's worth, in fact.'

'You mean – Now wait a minute. You mean we got one and not the other? I knew that. What I'm most keen on knowing, you got the *second* one, right?'

'Of course. Start to finish.'

'Ac-tion to Cutta??'

'Yes, Director.'

'That's a relief. Wow. For a instant there, I thought I'd have to step off the Sepulveda Overpass onto I-5.'

'I wouldn't want you to do that, Director, in the midst of a picture. Especially after I respect the hell out of you, now.'

'Your sentiments are appreciated. But –'

'Hey, what's with the 'accent-banishment'? Or the 'language restoration'? Or, whatever. I thought you barely spoke my language. Yeah, right! I get it now. I *thought* it was kinda hokey. And I didn't even shoot for Curtiz that much...'

'Does it matter? When there's an emergency, communication can break 'up', not 'down'.'

'Oh, I see, you rise to the occasion, huh?'

'Now listen, give me the whole lowdown.'

'Well, the second take is intact. We have it headed for the lab right now.'

'Bravo. And the first?'

'Well...'

'As I thought. Camera malfunction. I *knew* we should have shot this in CinemaScope 55 or Todd-AO!'

'Hold on, auteur! There's another side to this. And it boils down to *me*. Yeah, that's right, little old *me*.'

'Do tell. I've got all night, what with the social whirl hereabouts, and all.'

Shamroy noted the festive, boiling crowd, and figured the director ought to get the full grit first. Before the battery of exec producers – or worse – got it. He tossed his waterlogged 'gar into a nearby dustbin, pulled another out of his breast pocket, and, this time, lit 'er up.

'It's, well, embarrassing. But what the hell. Here's the squawk-down. When I examined the magazine meter for the first take, well I... Well... I *misread* it. Contrary to my sharp-as-shit crew. It was actually captured, all right. Take 1. In full 70mm magnificence. Safe and sound.'

Before he allowed bliss, joy, or full-blown ecstasy to color his reaction, Egaz was immediately sympathetic. Old timer that he was, Shamroy was one of the absolute best in the business, and he needed him to last this one out, for consistency, if nothing else. Bob Surtees was handling other aspects of the picture, and both their work would be seamless if the director's vision was to be adhered to. Besides, he loved Shammie's work, and now that he could talk to him without faking Butler English, he found that he liked the man, as well.

'Solid professional that you are...'

'Yeah, well... OK, so, I was glancing into the magazine window, and I thought, nothing's moved. Stupid fuckin' me. This is Century 21. We're using BMK Method stock now! One twenty-seventh the thickness of conventional Eastmancolor stock! As if I'd just arrived on this planet! Instead of a 20-minute reel in the mag, we got five hours! The whole thing's intact, along with devastating Take 2. Great cinema's within our grasp, Egaz!'

'*He ram!*' whispered the director, glancing to the cosmos above.

'Egaz,' continued Shamroy, in identifiable contrite manner. 'Please, please don't tell on me if you don't think I deserve it, but, shit, did I fuck up?'

Egaz milked the moment, but only because Shammie could be cock of the walk every morning, until now. He truly looked worried, and Egaz didn't want him to blow a gasket.

'Not to worry, best of the cameramen!' the director proclaimed, 'We're in a haven. You captured what I wanted without knowing it. Thank heavens, because, without your – shall we say – 'miscalculation', I would never have gotten that second take, which, as far as I have been able to pick up, has already entered the pantheon of, well, 'greatest scenes ever filmed', has it not? And we *were there!* We caused it to happen! It may change the whole landscape of the picture, but that's the best kind of cinematic generation: new ideas cause new growth. New growth shoots in unexpected directions. We have to be there to put it in the can. I can tell, Director of Photography, Lighting Cameraman, that you're up for it. You are the one to thank first – even before Butterbugs – for the double achievement of the day!'

The old lenser smiled, bit though his second 'gar, and tossed it aside. The big heat was off.

The only speck in the picture was a literal one: the actual Bakelite chip perceived to be such a culprit, loosened by age, duly made its appearance in the first take, for one twenty-fourth of a second, as it raced from bottom to top, and out of the screen.

'Looks like a 16mm print for TV,' Egaz said to the cameraman as they did a euphoric troubleshooting scan of the Take 1 rushes in the screening room.

'Look what it did for the P.R. of this picture!'

Leon was ready to boast, especially in the surety of the event, that DFZ & Co. would balk at the extra expenditure of a second, extended take. But no balking was ever forthcoming. Instead, all lights were green, and they grew brighter and brighter as filming went on.

This whole matter would open up a considerable conversation piece regarding the takes of the great actor and ultrastar, Butterbugs. It was discovered (the very night of the Requesticus sequence filming, as a matter of fact), due to superb record-keeping accessible by common database that, over the span of his august film career so far, over 96% of all Butterbugs' pictures' takes had been preserved under Grade-A conditions at studios far and wide. All who had been involved in each of those pictures knew of the exceptional performances given by the actor in these remarkable but unused takes. Conventional cinema demanded that only one (the best?) take be used in the finished product. However, it was the power of the second take today that caused none other than Porter Parker – who had been peripheral on the set all this time, perhaps because things were percolating in his head – in concert with Egaz's similar concept for 'UWH', to conceive of a certain scheme. Past Butterbugs takes could be assembled into alternative versions of his past films. If his artistry, in all its versions, was to be seen and utilized, could it not expand the very scope of film production, and open it up to more adventurous and inventive development? And could this practice not apply to all films and all participants from this day forward? The value of the material would have to be worthwhile of course, but with Butterbugs leading the way, the bar was already high, and would surely rise with time.

Thus was cinema transcending its limitations. From here it could evolve into the more liberated realm of the theatre. As each night's performance of a given show on stage is different, so could the concept of varied takes carry the viewer toward that more expansive state.

This treasury of Butterbugs takes, in collusion with his co-stars, and their associated variations, made for new horizons in Versioning, on which Porter, joined by Sonny, got to work that very night, to birth and grow Hollywood's next bonanza of product (and box office). Though those who managed the business of filmmaking and its opportunities had intentions paved with gold, no one, not even the most cynical sub-agent, could deny that Butterbugs was only in it for the art. Art was the torch that lighted the way ahead. And an ultrastar held it high.

Thus did Butterbugs continue to re-make his Industry.

It was later found out that *both* the 'Jonny Requesticus' takes had been covered by about 59 different mobile phone cameras, from 59 different angles, operated by persons on the crew and even some members of Court. Thus was the legacy of the picture secure indeed, and additional material for the editing process made profoundly abundant.

And what... *of* Butterbugs?

He'd repaired to the site of his concluding close-up, reprising his arresting pose at the heavy drape, as if to consider its value by returning to the terminus of the sequence. His head was downcast as all on the set continued their revelatory reactions. It was done. He had made it through. But only one thing occupied his mind now. Only one person. She whom he had just 'dispatched' during the photoplay-acting that was his trade.

She: his inspiration to go higher and higher. And he had indeed gone from height to height. Now he had to see her. Had to approach her. Had to understand why he did what he'd just done.

No time for shyness, or modesty, or leaving things lie.

Despite being exposed to a growing tarantella-like atmosphere, the star managed to keep to the outskirts, and chanced to see Keenah LaVine, his leading lady of the scene, moving toward a secondary exit. Slipping away, he followed stealthily, and, by golly, nobody noticed.

It was one of those anonymous passageways to somewhere. Generic limbo. For once, the lighting was not fluorescent overhead, but instead, classic boxing-match hallway lights, with protective cages to keep Billergloss gloves from punching the 250 watt bulbs as a way to blow off the steam of either anticipation – or defeat. Scenes from 'Stan' Kramer's production of Mark Robson's 'Champion' (UA, 1949) were filmed here.

That aside, it was deserted, and Keenah was going on ahead. She, like he, was in another, further world, transported naturally by the dramatic work just done, and under trying circumstances. Perhaps she wished to be left alone. He desired the same, but why couldn't they be alone – together? They could run away... Away, out into the night.

No more thought now, just action. Enough of the schoolboy trepidation. It was just that, he was a tad intimidated – by her acting. She was phenomenal, and this was the first actress of stature – no, the first actress period, who had struck him so.

Now was his time, for he had her to himself. He caught up with her – certainly she heard him from behind. He drew near, but she kept on ahead. A meeting of consequence should always happen under one of those downward-aiming hall lights. It was important, as faces should be clearly and unabashedly seen at the dawn of love.

Sweeping aside as much of his bizarre costume and makeup as he could, he gently took her elbow, and she turned about. Dismantling what little of her stage-bloodied prosthesis and fake neck guts as she was capable of doing on short notice, she gave her 100% undivided attention to him, and with a certain breathlessness. They just looked at each other, unmindful of the world, not only around them, but the corner of it they had just created for the screen.

Just a look. No kisses, no words. The harsh light was enough. Normal skin blemishes rose all about the makeup, and all was well and real. There was enough for them to enfold themselves in the other's gaze, as thoughts, and thoughts limited to mind, served as the only adequate communication of the moment.

But words, to a certain extent, had to be found.

''S go,' said Butterbugs.

'I'm... with you,' replied Keenah. 'Totally.'

So they left.

49.

The Scoring, The Scoring

Alfred Newman was currently absorbed with scoring 'Unholy War Hymn'.
Absorbed was probably not an adequate enough term, because he and his team were up to their furrowed brows in realizing the picture's musical evolution, in artistic tandem with its graphic, verbal and stylistic development on the screen. Never was a dramatic picture more intertwined with all its main creative fibers, so interrelated and interdependent were they. Quite understandably, that was the way all the filmmakers involved wanted it to be.

Because Egaz set such stock in music as a heavy lifter, easily equivalent to cinematography in tone and intent, he applied great attention to the score's progress. Of all the main contributors to this picture's substance, Alfred's was probably the most facile. He could do this stuff in his sleep. But in all the rehearsals that matched the rushes received, there was nothing banal or of 'filler' feel to the music that was emerging.

'Pappy's a veritable factory,' said copyist aide Monnen Mock-Breuwn to Egaz, as if the director were about to announce: 'I'm scrapping all of Alfred's music and replacing it with an adequate score from the Muzak people'.

'But, please, Director D'Varzim, don't think for a second that anything will come out of an assembly line. Trademarks he has. Style he has. But run-of-the-mill or mill-of-the-run, he isn't.'

As if anyone needed convincing.

'Peace!' was all Egaz could say, in reply. 'What all does he need?'

'Peace!' was all Monnen could say, in conclusion.

Ms. Mock-Breuwn made the same declaration to Porter Parker, when he came snooping around one day.

'I would expect nothing else!' replied Porter, who was continuing to evolve into an insightful and not-so-giggly producer, with not a little sophistication under his belt by this time.

P.P.P. was now located at Mega|Goth, next to John Calley's suite, where there were good vibes aplenty. After he failed to entice Butterbugs and Sonny into a three-sided studio-from-scratch venture, which he'd prospectively titled Butterbugs & Buddies Studios (variations: 'Buddies 'n' Butterbugs', 'Buddies of Butterbugs', 'Butterbugs' Buddies, Featuring Porter Pud Parker', etc.), he decided to decamp from his longtime Universal City perch and lease space from Hyman as an independent producer, releasing through Mega|Goth. It was all part of a noble and perhaps inevitable attempt to get the ultrastar actively into the production side of things. Porter's point was, to fully control the creative output of the ultrastar. For custom-tailoring purposes, if nothing else.

The ultrastar was chary to commit. Finally, considering his heavy 'UWH' responsibility, his inner reveries over issues of power and influence, his essentially artistic (and business-wary) sensitivities, his general awe of cinema history high and low, and now a love-of-his-life in front of him, Butterbugs graciously declined. Because he did, Sonny followed suit, as the mega-agent was, somewhat surprisingly, as content as a little old Odense shopkeeper with his current empire. In addition, his occasional dipsy-doodles into independent production, by way of associates and executives, usually involving oddball pictures, sometimes starring his most prominent client, sated any desire to be a production mogul.

Porter hadn't been offended at all. Things were hopping. His new digs, his recent Butterbugs successes, his surpassingly independent role in 'UWH''s production, a profile in 'Rolling Stone', and working with Alfred, the Writers Team, Egaz, and the whole gang, kept him in perpetual jubilation.

Besides, the truly awesome mission of supposedly 'controlling' the ultrastar's creative activities was a ludicrous notion, as probable as opening a Tiki bar on one of Neptune's as yet undiscovered moons.

Even after his vast dream was conclusively consigned to the Kaput Bin, Porter was heard to mutter – in his sleep – 'We really *could* do this thing, gang! Yes! We really *should...!*'

But now, in his waking hours, reason transcended hallucinations. Porter was really shaping up, in more ways than one.

'I'm really very much on top of this production,' he crowed to both press and colleagues alike. And the remarkable thing is, he really *was*.

Alfred had been discreetly present at the Jonny Requesticus Takes, for he had to create a fitting 'Lost Love' theme that would punch the audience right in the – well, *soft*-punch them – in the heart-strings, accomplished with... strings. What better to formulate the right notes than to be present at what turned out to be one of the most remarkable sessions in Hollywood's history.

Consequently, the musician was keen to get together with Butterbugs, one-on-one. So he invited him to his studio getaway off western Mulholland Drive. It was a neat artist's pad, designed by Eric Lloyd Wright, with a closer view of the Pacific than Butterbugs' own The Æyrie. He'd dubbed it, On The Heights.

There, on a balcony protected by classic Wrightian eaves, Alfred had his scrappy 'n' scuffed little Zórymäga baby grand parked. He'd selected it himself, from a little shop around the corner from Liszt's house in Budapest. It had seen composition of scores from 'Captain From Castile' (20th-Fox, 1947) on forward. Some 'UWH' themes, mostly supplemental, poured out of the venerable tuning board, and Butterbugs, sitting there, gazing out to sea, considered the tone poet's contributions, then adjusted his private concept of how the accompanying scenes in question could be acted out. His absorption was total, his comprehension in advanced mode.

Actually, there wasn't much to consider. The fit was right. Quite perfect, in fact. The actor was inspired. Like having an accompanist in the pit as you're improvising on stage. One hand washes the other.

Then, Newman stopped playing.

'Butterbugs,' the pioneer said, clinking the stem of an O'Tarnish's bottle to the rims of two shot glasses, 'Now, what would you think about... this...?'

Not a fortnight later, there arrived at LAX a formidable group of colleagues and students to oversee the proper production of the score. There was Ion Yeetkevich, Potchkeff Zhuvkuvko, Sergei Sprakovnikov, Semyon Bosboltovizitch, Yakov Endellovich Shirityposhnikov and Izok Vaztyzazonovich (*'Those* guys – on the same plane?!' was Newman's first reaction). Plus, Vostyaslavskaya Raslostoslav, Gav Shaposhnikov, Khlur Shiritypopnikoff (the 'three cousins' of the Kiev Conservatory). And none other than Rayakna Bubklevyalenynova, Minda Wainling, Ilya Emmetovich Weelding, Sam Tebb, and Irina Sposspendisspasskayovna.

Alfred was overjoyed, not with just the talent or their cargo, but with the names of his new, and mostly young, friends. Not only were these the top arrangers and soloists and copyists of the Russian and Ukrainian Schools (plus two from Brooklyn), they were all set to be integrated into the studio orchestra for the composer/conductor's recording sessions, as well.

And, most solemnly they bore with them the complete score for Dmitri Shostakovich's latest opus, an expansive symphonic tone poem, to accompany a key sequence in 'UWH'.

DDS couldn't make the trip. Much to his chagrin, as he dearly wanted to see Butterbugs again, and in his Industry town, for a Vinejuice respite had long been pledged. But in lieu of his presence he sent several video chat sessions, consisting not only of greetings & gossip, but also of performance specifics regarding the piece, intended for the musicians at the studio end. All were important documents.

So, Shostakovich was in on 'UWH'. Butterbugs was proud, but only after an evolution of understanding.

It had come about like so...

At that particular conference at Newman's On The Heights, where just the two of them reviewed the essentials of what the score should be, Alfred had dropped a bit of a bombshell.

'Butterbugs, now, what would you think about... this...? I feel that, as much dimension there is in this script and story, it would be dynamic and purposeful to pursue a different avenue of musical accompaniment in *one specific part* of the picture. I've read the sequence over and over again, and I know Egaz wants it intensely scored. Probably something like a fugal cue, I would think. But because that particular sequence stands out so much itself, as, you know, sort of an...

appendage... to the rest of the picture, I thought it might be striking to have it scored by another composer.'

Butterbugs had to admit, he was a bit taken aback. He had not known Alfred long enough to discern if any subtleties were in play, or if a painful subject was about to be approached via indirect methods. He took a gamble.

'You mean... Are you telling me, uh, you're bowing out?'

Alfred almost choked on his nipperkin of O'Tarnish's.

'Oh, my God, man, don't scare me like that! I've gotten into hot water before, on 'Greatest Story' (UA, 1965), which was not my doing, but believe me, I'm *in* all the way on this one, and that *is* my doing. For the duration!'

'I'm relieved, Pappy. But, what's the deal?'

'Well, I thought I'd run it by you first. You're the only one to hear it so far. No, I'm definitely up for the complete score. Or almost complete. You see, I've got a general scheme. Just like always. But in this one part, 'The Build-Up' as Sawl and his gang call it, I have a better concept. The more I've thought about it, the better it sounds. Or, I hope it sounds, literally. As I said, what about having another composer score it? Just 'The Build-Up'. I don't want to alter that sequence – I think it's about forty minutes' worth. I mean, I just don't want to alter, or even wreck, its effect by linking it with my themes. Too predictable. Not necessary. Wouldn't fit.'

'I see what you mean. I never would have thought of it.'

'My age comes in handy, for once.'

'Let's see, 'The Egyptian' (20th-Fox, 1954) comes to mind.'

'Indeed. Benny (Herrmann) and I worked that one out pretty well. We took turns. Alternating cues. But that isn't what I mean in this case. I'm referring to just this one sequence. The forty minutes' worth. That's a concentrated block, I know, but this will be a very long show. Two intermissions, at the very least.'

'Right. So now, I present my next question, one that will embarrass me by its sheer obviousness...'

Taking his cue to interrupt, Alfred announced:

'Easy. Only one choice. Shostakovich.'

Butterbugs smacked the armrest of the daveno.

'Of course! Brilliant! You nailed it, Pappy!'

'You don't think it's pretentious?'

'What, a big name – to outshine you?'

Alfred laughed.

'Yeah, I'd better exercise some humility, eh? But really, if the producers want to look at it as added prestige, fine. They'd do that anyway. I'm looking at it as an æsthetic necessity. I know DDS would really make 'The Build-Up' into something I couldn't. Besides, our scores meshed so well on 'The Aghori' (20th-Fox). That's really what gave me the idea.'

Butterbugs had become such a sponge for knowledge concerning every facet of filmmaking throughout his now considerable experience as a feature player, he could well imagine the effect to which the composer was inferring. And because Shostakovich was both a groundbreaking film composer and concert composer, the linking of both picture show and concert show was irresistible. He loved the idea of such an admixture. He knew Keenah would agree. Oh, and the Producer Team as well, as they had to give the green light.

The two sat back in their opposing chairs for a moment as the mellow afternoon waned. God, was life good. Sippin' liquor with a view, collaborating on a land-mark, with the promise of its height defined by the perfection of *Music's* guidance. Revelation thus resolved, they were allowed a bit of down-time to relax, before the needful source tasked them.

Oh yes, it would task them.

In the meantime, they cooled it.

Sometimes the 'scoring' of the silent times in life itself is just as potent a pro-cess as the more obvious crowding of companion-thought, and its stacking-up, when things in life tend to get intense. Similarly, the decision-making as to where to place music and where to leave it out is one of the most momentous processes in cinematic production, and one of the most transparent. (Or, to put it in musical terms, judging the placement of 'measures lacking substance', like boxcars riding empty, unbeknownst to onlookers.) Truly, knowing where to place music – or silence – in day-to-day existence is a life-skill of high artistic attainment.

Both professionals exercised such skills at this decisive moment. Indeed, si-lence reigned.

Along with the enjoyment of kicking back from the directive notions of a cer-tain picture, that rode roughshod over anything else in their lives at this juncture, the high life on a Hollywood terrace provided a summum bonum option on all projections of influence said picture might have. It was to be assumed that a fin-ished 'UWH' could reach minds and sensitivities that would find the picture's effects at least edifying – if not entertaining – in the gigantic scheme of public reception.

Perfectly relaxed now, and thinking the day's business was done, it was time to talk of absurdities with the Dean of Hollywood film composers.

'You know, Alfred, the other day I saw this goofy guy wearing a propel-ler-topped cap, and...'

But –

'I was wondering, Butterbugs... Well... Would you... Could you, you know, *approach* him?'

Butterbugs instantly remembered that he was, after all, the first to know about the composer's bold idea. But there was no dithering necessary.

Alfred knew of the utter seriousness of his inquiry. He knew DDS would be eager to deliver, and he knew it would be perfect. That hurdle crossed, he could continue with his own composition.

'I shall ask,' was all the ultrastar said in reply.

The Russo-Ukrainian-American team scanned the Shostakovian score. Their fingers were insulated from the white-hot emanations that rose from the fully-or-chestrated pages.

After Sawl & Co. heard the DDS score, immediate script revisions resulted:

Scene: the HMD marshals his military forces.

(Soundtrack: an incredibly powerful score, a similar driving effect as DDS' Symphony #7's 1st movement, but utterly different in content. Duration: 37.7 min. The stylistic contrast is successful and appropriate for this dynamic sequence.)

Now the sequence could be definitively filmed.

As with several of Alfred's cues, Egaz desired to film the scenes in question *based on the music*. It was a great and artistic honor to pivot his photoplay on the creations of these composers, but it was also demonstrative of the admiration and above all, the *trust* that Egaz, Butterbugs, Porter, and, to a more detached extent, the Producer Team, had in Newman and Shostakovich. Collaborative filmmaking at its best: the fact that they would be so integrated into the production.

Sawl Cane himself extolled the influence of music on his initial writing of the work. When he was told who was doing the music, Cane got all dopey, like a little kid.

'Really?? *Really??*' he kept saying. 'You got *both* of them? No! Really?'

Shonnaleen, who had been following the non-shooting aspects of the picture, and who was the one who really got Newman inked in the first place, knew this score would be a crossroads. A crowning confirmation of the style in scoring, which grasped real emotion, as opposed to whatever remained of the ersatz pro-gramming that had ruled the great unwashed motion picture product for the lon-gest time. She and Alfred got a kick out of the notion that this film might be re-garded in such protean terms. They did not especially view themselves as molders of public taste. Yet there was nothing stopping their creativity in doing just that.

Such articulated application of the music's power within the superstructure of the film amplified the meaning of the score's bedrock mission in aiding and abetting the larger collective effect. As far as sophisticated melding of cinematic elements was concerned, this was way past the role of mere mood-settings for a public in need of diversions.

Major recording sessions in big Hollywood sound stages are momentous events. They tend to reduce all who witness them to a state even more minimal than when the widest of screens reflects the latest of rushes, even when a day's shooting has been felt by all to be extraordinary. Because up there, on the unprepared screen, oftentimes the effect isn't quite so magic as the moments in which they occurred. As a result, viewed as a routine daily, they often seem lacking.

Perhaps that's why director, cast and crew do not regularly sit in on such symphonic sessions.

On the other hand, live orchestral music commands the attention of the witness like no other art. Therefore, within the Art of Cinema, where equality is entirely a fluid concept, music can come off, if not as King of Arts, then at least as King of Ingredients.

Music *works* so tidily, so completely, so majestically, in affecting the waking moments of all within its earshot, it risks monopolizing your basic photoplay scene. It has certainly done so on occasion, but usually the score is kept in harness by engineered controls, so that it shall always be subservient. And in the authoritarian world of filmmaking, any rival creative force, however essential, if deemed a threat to other elements that vie for our attention, must be quickly and efficiently kept in its place. And in the case of music, its assigned place is one of yeoman service to the visual and dialogue aspects of the motion picture. This conscious reduction of film music to a sort of second-class status, in both quality of audience interpretation and its standing in the world of 'serious' music, however explainable in its pragmatism, still seems a shallow settlement.

Alfred's talked about these things, numerous times...

Well, in the case of 'UWH', such platitudes were no longer very valid. Surely, its transcendent contributions would raise the respect for pure music within a cinematic context, and perhaps social awareness, as well.

Therefore, it was beholden upon Alfred and Company to prosecute the forbidding task of making-mine-music (as Porter Parker liked to call it) fit 'UWH' in an acceptable manner – like a foxglove placed over a porcupine's mouth. In the pre-scoring stage, the parts of this sprawling film already shot appeared unusually disjointed, incongruous, even unworkable. Could the footage even be scored?

Most of the non-musicians involved with the scoring project were going out of their gourds with puzzlement. As sound engineers, recordists, grips and maintenance crew, they were used to the perpetuity of formulaic assemblages of creation-into-product, cut & dried, pure & simple.

'In all my years in front of a board,' Weenah Ahmad, ace music recordist, declared to her crew, 'I have never seen a more formidable, mind-destroying assignment. Heaven knows where we'll end up...'

She fully expected to see Alfred snap his baton in two and storm out, never to return.

It was clear, though, that, as of yet, the tech side was not able to comprehend the disparate bits and bobs that were showing up for scrutiny. To them, they were ponderous pieces of a cinematic conundrum, falling all about, like squares made of cut felt, scattered in a warm snowstorm. Or something like that. For a team that had to have everything in its assigned place at the perfect time, 'UWH' was an obnoxiously-misplaced prospect. Unholy, even.

But up on the podium, Alfred, the ultimate, consummate, *total pro* in rabbit-pulling – from the deepest of stovepipe hats, *knew what to do*. Because, there was only one thing *to* do. This is what producing a score as the actual picture was being shot was like: an intertwinement of shooting/acting/composing/performing. Parallel worlds joining, birthing, refining, emerging.

After all, these were early days yet. Alfred was mainly getting his musical ideas out in embryonic form first, so as to chart a passage towards refinement, adaptation, and final fit. The tech team need not have been so premature in their thoughts and attitudes. Plainly, the collective stress was a sure indicator of the very mega-ultra-importance of this production.

'Is this… fair?' Alfred asked his orchestra.

'Fair, maestro?' asked concertmaster Felix Slatkin.

'To inflict my sketchbook upon you, incomplete, unsettled, unrefined… ?'

Bows struck strings in conductor-supportive feedback.

'Listen Al,' Slatkin rebounded, 'We're here because… Well, we're not only getting paid, but we're damned excited to be part of this whole trip. Lead on, baby! Right, gang?'

The entire orchestra plucked, tooted, bonged, and hooted.

Up in the booth, the engineers paid close attention.

'Pappy will guide us!' Weenah half-announced/half-prayed.

After an awkward few days, the preliminary-level recordings of these and other surrounding cues-in-progress came off without a hitch. Butterbugs sat in on many of them. He let himself be totally immersed in their full symphonic power, which is what he wanted all along. Even as ultrastar though, he never got invited to attend, except now, with Alfred as his contact. No questions were asked, and he could freely sit in on the varying waves of 'UWH', and be carried away by them.

Transported, he was trolleyed into turbo-powered reveries, via Alfred's 'sketchbooks' and other powerhouse musicales. There he was, surrounded by sonic ideas, inviting him to re-think his role in life, his place in the universe, and whether he had been wrong letting Old Atrocity's nephew Munty run his Querhy-Bike across the Inner Lawns of The Lazaretto, and, failing a sort of Grand Prix finesse in mastering a singular said course, he realized that…

Holy Moly! Look where Alfred's theme 'Along the Embankment', now being recorded, conveyed his thoughts! By itself, the cue, a profound reverie, took every mind that heard it to a different place. But the ultrastar knew that when it would be plugged into its rightful spot in the picture, the notes would perfectly serve the surrounding *gesamtkunstwerk*.

But in these sessions, all who watched or participated in them was pleased and heartened as to what could still be done in this, the Further Era in tonal system composition. Further because it leapt across what had already been done, but with connected ropes of fiber optics to link future with past, and nobody debunked the past any longer, because it was such a gold mine of richness and ideas.

At another session, Alfred gave a brief talk about how studying with Arnold Schönberg had led him to an ability to incorporate all aspects of chamber music into his full-blown symphonic scores.

'In every cinematic tale told by music, lies Brahms' String Quartet #4,' Schönberg had said, meaning that drama only needs a very few notes (or very few words, or colors, or costumes, or sets...) to make itself known. Because, if the drama is intrinsically strong, it needs little more than its tale to justify its presentation.

'But let's put a little 'Gurrelieder' in the mix from time to time, shall we?'

It was Pappy's way of catering to script, scene, player – and studio boss.

'Let us now play for great drama, of all sizes, and for all,' was Alfred's offering at the altar of his podium, before each day's recording session.

Then, when the tech talk took over, there was every reason for all concerned to strive for the maestro's cause. Which was all any film composer needed to produce... you guessed it: great film music.

After scoring 769 pictures since 1930, Alfred was known to say, when confronting a certain type of scene within an assignment, 'How the hell am I going to be able to do *that* again?' But the thing was, he always delivered, with electrifying panache, style, and depth. 'UWH' was shaping up as his best score ever: sweeping, penetrating, a concentration of heavy development in the strings (naturally), highlighting broad themes made contrapuntally intimate and integrated with the soul of the film, crossed with a pathos that was at once epic and heartbreaking. That combination of widely-separated tonal prerequisites made the genius of his scoring all the more emboldened in this watershed picture.

'You know,' said Shanklin Kennell, Music Critic for 'The World's Times In General' on 'Larry King Live' (CNN), 'It is one of the world's marvels, in the light of the challenge of creation, that given the options on talent in the available free market of they who have elected to enhance our everyday existence with products of creative thought, they who are endowed with such talent and vision, it is a marvel that they are actually so *enabled* to realize them, through the production of their entirely natural statements of contributory originality.'

'I take it that you are amazed,' said Larry.

'I am!' replied Shanklin, known for his long-way-around to a point. 'I tell you, I am! I have only been privileged to hear two, and only two, cues from Newman's score-in-the-making, and it clearly demonstrates that Platinum Days are back. Or rather, they are here for the first time. We had our Golden, Silver, Brass and Lead Days, but now, with the Butterbugsization of the Industry, such effects have flowed into all aspects of picture-making. I speak not only of musical aspects, but every associated aspect of the Seventh Art's manifestations.

'So Larry, you should really make an effort to get over to Carnegie Hall tomorrow night. Collodi conducts the New York Phil in those two very cues from Newman's score that so floored me: 'Train to Zlusk' and 'Cheremin, Oh Cheremin!' You too, might be down there with me, groveling with joy!'

'OK then. Now, I can retire!' said Alfred, after he and Butterbugs heard the interview. 'Hell, if I can put Shanklin Kennell on the floor without the involvement of booze, I don't know if this is a world I want to continue working in. No challenges left!'

However, Shanklin – and everyone else who had heard even a small portion of (or having played in) the transcendentally great score – everyone except the composer himself – cheerfully agreed that he had duly earned an end-with-a-bang retirement.

'The hell with *that!*' the composer rasped; there was no finality in his intent, ever. In fact, he'd just signed a long-term contract to return to his old post as Music Director at his alma mater, 20th-Fox.

The score itself? Wagner could not have done it! Not Richard Strauss, Enescu, nor Zemlinsky! Tiomkin praised it, but could find no other composers to thank.

'Alfred only influences himself!' he quipped.

Massed strings. Architectural brass. Themes that would make one weep for weeks. Fifths all over the place in the Rotunda sequence: ostinatos of climbing, then falling. Muscular constructions in key structural spans. Groundwork expertly laid for the DDS 'guest' tone poem. Elegant finishing work afterwards. No entr'acte at either intermission, because new themes are introduced that do major tasks in the following acts. A love theme as haunting as it is tragic – though sweet. An Overture to bring the house down. Exit Music to raise it up again. And a climactic build-up to rival the most formidable Brucknerian or Mahlerian forces. Occasional ruthlessness that outdoes Petterson. Though the tender aspects of the score, of which there are many dimensions, render the picture heartfelt and soulful, to glorious and passionate extents.

It was as if a great trail on a lofty plateau were being followed. A complete awareness of being on an elevated plain. Close to air, sky and sun, with the possibility of ascending higher. There, all round, and at every quarter, exalted landscape and painterly vistas encountered, described and made profound by Alfred's score.

Sustained majesty, delivered in a rarefied atmosphere, not only of elevation, but of epic poeticism and intimate nuance. Music, telling its story by means of a cloud walking at high noon, told through symphonic tonalism. If this were not enough, the arpeggios, key changes, rubato, emphasis on the higher strings, alternating lavishly with extreme low-register in the basses, and inventions and variations, assured that the martial enclosure that accompanied The Trek sequence was inspired by sheer musical talent as much as it was by D'Varzim's direction, not to mention Shamroy's and Surtees' cinematography. And, in this case, last and least, by Butterbugs' essentially supernumerary appearance in a sequence of very long, long, medium, and close CU shots. As a whole, assuredly, epic poetry, of Homeric proportions.

Thundering when it needed to be, and thoughtful, intimate, and even naked, at opportunities not necessarily so obvious.

Bottom line: sheer *art*.

And it was far from finished. Filming was far from finished, too, and both processes seemed to be progressing at the same pace, as they should.

'Pretty damn rare to have such harmony – pun intended – 'twixt simultaneous filming and scoring,' commented Sonny Projector, as he, Mayella (whom he himself was now dating after genial agreements with the newly-Keenah-struck ultrastar), Butterbugs and Keenah sat out on The Æyrie's terrace, while Alfred played themes from his developing score. Ken Darby turned pages and took notes on matters the composer brought up. Ed Powell was already working on orchestrations.

It had been a working lunch, and now Egaz hastened back to the studio, while Alfred, Ed and Ken were packing up, promising to have the first ('of at least two') Intermission cues ready to record, day after tomorrow. Now, for real, the day's music business had been satisfactorily completed.

With personnel successfully departed, Butterbugs was still in the contemplative mood the music had attached to him. (Never mind the musicians' talk amongst themselves; it was the notes themselves that still influenced him now.) Because it was so sweet, he wished to prolong the magic, like a cig at the end of a sex gig adds to the timeframe of bliss, if only for a few minutes.

It would be more than that; an hour and twenty minutes, for that was the running time of the score cues thus amassed, which Butterbugs duly mounted in his Mutuala MP-9 player. It spread its splendor all throughout The Æyrie, via pea-shooter speakers, which were everywhere.

Time to set the mood, to take his girlfriend out into the environment, and take stock as to how background– and foreground-scoring was going to affect his acting, his role, his relationship, and his life.

In the beauty of the aloes, two young people sat in rapt silence.

For a moment, the California sun acted the role of a further clime, where succulents and palms would not live, in the shadow of stone and turret, somewhere cinematic, but from a drama not yet known.

The couple said nothing for a time, because they were being washed over by music of a most personal kind; music that fit them both, if not in this life, then in one they were fashioning for the screen.

'Listen! How it transports us!' observed Keenah. 'I feel enveloped by a legend, by another time and place.'

'I too feel a wonderful distance. A longing.'

Then Butterbugs gazed at her.

'But what I have longed for is *here*, next to me, sharing the same passage. With me.'

She reciprocated.

'I am at your side, never closer.'

They listened raptly, and shared the same dream.

50.

The Poster

Tackling the task of the poster for 'UWH' had begun.

Co-producer Sam Bronston put a whole unit on it. Everyone from Saul & Elaine (Bass) and Paul Rand to Emmerrendrum Parquall and Milt Glaser were signed on. They came (or remained, while dealing over the Net), from very cool graphic studios in sandy Jutland, to the latest hot salons in golden Rome; from Kansas City's finest Graf Ficks Terraces to Singapore's Tock Tock Tick Tock Studios-cum-Agencies of Peony Mansions. Nothing like it had ever been attempted before. It was a big undertaking, *really big*. And in this example, big was best.

At once hologramatical in its dimensions, tactile in access and unabashedly graphic in its design, the poster took on a whole life of its own. It was an entity that grew in stature as the picture itself was filming, and both were duly publicized.

Because of this greater evolution, the designers elected to make the poster an unfolding entertainment as well as a hoarding on many different levels. Like the Cinerama logo, with its string-along band of open book motifs implying more than two dimensions, the 'UWH' poster became a sort of accordion of foldout facets, each promoting the latest development, but as an integral part of the film, as if it were a finished product. Also, plenty of cubic room was necessary for the truly-counted cast of thousands. Butterbugs wanted complete credits for all. None of this 'uncredited' business, as seen in the Internet Movie Database (IMDb) run-downs.

Eventually, more artists than the Absolut campaign were in on the job, and they were invited to interpret 'UWH' in any way they chose. MOMA, Guggenheim, Getty & Sholem/Goldkorn/Schmugwuntz exhibs, and a book set would naturally be issued, but their work would adorn more conventional advertising on a rotating basis.

Dani Karavan, Maciek Piotrowski, 'Plain' Jane and Juan Juab, Dong Kingman, and the inimitable Botero were next into the production design team. There were so many diverse settings in this picture that the more individualistic the contributor, the more purposefully disjointed the look of things became.

'We're jumping from A to B and then to Q before visiting V and back to B,' explained Egaz (few seemed to notice his crisp new English; hell, everybody, it seemed, had had his or her transformational epiphany when present at those Jonny Requesticus takes).

'What's your motive in such disharmony?' queried someone from the press.

434

'*Real life*,' answered Egaz, with feeling.

Within seconds, Egaz's utterance was all over the media. They knew he wasn't talking about the Realife movement in cinema, which strove to be true, but *real life* itself. You know, *really* real. Some were skeptical that it could be accomplished. But most waxed ecstatic over what was to come. Anticipation was already at fever pitch.

However, the makers and players had to distance themselves from the turbo-publicity that was now being laser-guided around the planet. For them it was exacting business as usual. Set designs were incredibly demanding. Exponential details had to be seen to.

When fabrics for the seven-meter-high windows in the Great Big Room at Keem-Gherrun-Drem's palace in Tiflis set were called for, it would have to be fabric that would remain in the background of the largely conversational scenes, probably out of focus, as most of the shots were in CU. Nevertheless, authenticity had to be obeyed, at practically any cost. For a director who believed in the totality of real-life depiction within the framework of manufactured, cinematic-style real life, there was nothing for it but to devote a good chunk of his time to inspecting, then approving (or re-selecting and then re-approving) the million-and-one essentials needed for successful coalescing of the cinematic egg – cracked and popped, on its cooking surface – so it could actually *work* as a motion picture.

So, it was the Hour of the Fabric. And so much more...

Without this attention to detail, the picture would be doomed to mega-failure, or maybe even ultra-failure (that is, commensurate with the lead player's standing; a prospect not yet fully defined at this time).

The legendary team of Tabernacle Smith and Hiawatha Jones were brought in (at great expense) to design the sets and costumes – for the Tiflis scenes only.

'What you're paying us, for less than twenty-five minutes of screen time is, well, exorbitant,' said Tabernacle to Porter.

'But we'll take it!' Hiawatha chimed in.

'If we must, Mary,' Tabernacle mock-smirked.

'Oh yes, we must. *Mary!*'

The two strutted and swanned about, enacting old-fashioned affectations, both audacious and nervous. Probably as a result of the truly exorbitant rewards they were about to receive for this effortless assignment. Plus, they thought they were charming and adorable.

'Isn't your little collar-decoration just *too* festive then, Puddy Porter-Pie?' sneered Tabernacle, waltzing dangerously close to Porter and fingering his conservative, science teacher-style bow tie.

'Oh Tab-Tab, it's not 'Puddy'! Mr. *Pudgy* Porter-*put-upon*-pie is just too shy in the Compliments Department!'

'I just can't believe you're paying us for things we could do whilst taking chapel or grinding through 'Jean Santeuil'!'

'I breeze through Proust, myself,' quipped Tab.

'See what I mean, 'Sis'?'

Porter, even as he practiced his new maturity in dealing with inter-personnel matters, almost passed out at this rambunctious folderol. Instead, he quietly (and wisely) passed out of the soundstage.

Hiawatha was almost squealing with glee, which brought out his classic sibilance, full force. 'Oh Sissy-Sis! Can you just *believe* this gig, Tabby-Catty?'

'Oh Hi-Hi, go on back to Camp Tack-Ee, would you?'

Just then Egaz showed up, and, without a word, fingered the fabric samples the team had brought in.

'I sort of like the coarse-knit chartreuse, aqua and charcoal weave for the drapes,' he said matter-of-factly. 'Can you have them hung by early next week?'

'*Well*-hung it'll be, baby boy. Mmm, next week would be dreamy,' replied Tabernacle, slopping on the peacockery with a snow shovel.

'Very well, Mr. Jones. It should look quite splendid in the general scheme of things. The effect won't be passive at all, even though it's basically background filler.'

'So what's with *you*, Mr. Di-rector?' Hiawatha snarked. 'I thought you only spoke, I don't know, 'Himalayan'... or 'Untouchable'... or something the pigeons dropped off...'

Hi could be blitheringly outspoken, even at the worst of times.

Butterbugs appeared on the scene, but did not impose himself.

'Why, Hi-Hi,' said Tabernacle, feigning indignation at his partner, 'What's gotten into you, *Mary*? Your addressment of our head honcho is... curious, to say the least!'

'But Tabby-puss, I heard this 'rare gem' had a fashionable communication-act going on, and –'

'Hiya helpers!' Butterbugs interjected. 'Let me explain. Our director is a person with a complex ethnic background. I think it's best if you –'

Now Egaz became the interrupting one.

'I don't think we should waste too much behind-the-screen time futzing amongst we Little People for gossip items of 'interest', to distract us from the 'unholy' task at hand. But *hola!* You're the first couple, or the first humanoids, to point out my frankly amazing progress regarding bossing-out directions to my vassals and chattels. Just understand, girls, that I'm a quick learner, and perhaps I know more than you think.'

Even though it was brutally banal, Hiawatha and Tabernacle just *loved* Egaz's response, because they took his point. Which was: this was a very expensive picture, and a very big picture, starring the world's only bona fide ultrastar, and they were getting high pay and perky perks, so shut the fuck up with the faggy bitchin' and the antique 'Mary' shit already, and get on with the hyper-serious tasks of making this production the most kick-ass, incredible, mind-exploding specimen in the history of the Seventh Art.

They paid attention to this notion, which they knew all too well, and were grateful without groveling. Actually, it was a relief for the two *not* to have to indulge in the kind of childish, stereotypical camp-role-playing they felt compelled to play out on other sets, in order to keep delicately disparate factions properly entertained and/or distracted.

Butterbugs regarded the exchange with pleasure and amazement. It was not as if he were at all dim in his interpersonal perceptions, but he didn't quite realize that Egaz was using a veritable Butterbugsian technique of BS-eradication in his directorial communication. That is, the utilization of *plain talk*, a language many in today's modern world thought themselves too cool for, but were actually in desperate need of. It wasn't a question of wit, but it had everything to do with addressing truth via unexpected avenues, such as dramatic licenses. Show people enjoy being entertained, perhaps more than the entertained public.

The two fellows had been Hollywood's longest surviving marriage, as of a month ago. Ross Hunter and Jacques Mapes, the previous record holders, were delighted. Industry people, not just the trashy press, kept track of such things. The comfort zone Hi and Tab occupied had been bloated by this new prestige, thus their swishy swaggerings on the set of this, the biggest picture of their careers. Their professional interactions matched their own private consensual-dom, for when it came to putting set decoration together, they finished each other's sentences, so to speak.

Tabernacle & Hiawatha (as they were referred to, never the insipid 'Smith & Jones', as Hi particularly abhorred the ancient ABC-TV series; 'Duel & Murphy – way too cute!') were a cinematic institution. If they were ever to split up, specialist-seeking filmmakers would be bereft of the most ingenious detail-knowing partnership in film design, and many a scenic dream would be sunk.

However, there was little chance of that, seeing how the two were as relentlessly fond of each other as they were of the high-quality product they kept producing. They had done drapes and home makeovers for everyone from Betty Blythe and Claire de Lorez to William Hung and Daphne 'It's-the-latest-*kick*,-y'know' Zukvuk. That was why Egaz and Porter craved their expertise. They had been everywhere, and their travel adventures were a combination of Evelyn Waugh, Jetlag Travel Guides, Emily Eden, Mrs. Bratchingwood, Ian Wright, Laurel and Hardy, Peter Fleming, and even John Buchan, as far as effects and flavors were concerned. However madcap or risky their adventures, they always made it through, usually with a caravan in tow, groaning with esoteric trinkets, oddball souvenirs, samples of unwanted booty, and downright stunning design discoveries that often set trends when they came into full flower in a film. Too quirky for mainstream rubbish cinema, auteurs in the know snagged them at first opportunity. The boys had eight Oscars to prove their effectiveness. In regard to 'UWH', their regional knowledge was vital to Egaz's dear wish to realize the full expansiveness of Sawl's epic saga.

Tabernacle & Hiawatha were aware of every back-alley boutique in the

Caucasus and every second-string palazzo in the chasms of Kcheffkwek, and they had been to Stalin's birthplace museum in Gori, with its haunting belfry (which the character of the HMD admires as a beau ideal of monument design). Who else could possibly fill this picture's needs?

'You guys are the *most!*' Butterbugs enthused.

'Why thank you, ultra-uptrastar!' replied a simmered-down Hiawatha, as he welcomed a jar of Tibetan chang the ultrastar proffered.

'I'm really not used to being addressed as such,' said Butterbugs.

'Sorry, dear boy, then I'll refer to you as Totally Hot Egg-Hatchling, because it's the *truth.*'

'Ease the cool lingo, Hi,' said Tabernacle, sort of barging in, preferring a thimbleful of Mёkkerbergdorf alcool on the drinks trolley. 'Ultrastars are lofty personalities. They're not to be fiddled with.'

'Well, I was just *trying* to compliment –,' the ultrastar attempted to say.

'You gotta understand, *Butt*erbugs, I'm kind of a 'butt-in-ski'. Tab smiled burlesquely.

'Well you can just butt-*out*-ski!' Hi squawked.

'All *yours*, I suppose??'

'Silly Tab! As if I were trying to hit on him…!'

'Language! Mind what you say, fellah!'

Butterbugs could only watch in wonder, because they next took the gathered piece goods and hung them where Egaz wanted, even though he had ostensibly already made his selection. Then they repeated the action with different bolts, until an alluvial fan of spread-out material transformed the set into a sort of geologic time-span of color and texture. Then they hopped down, ran back to the future camera position and just stood there, facing the director (not the star) in expectation.

Egaz milked the moment, almost to limits bordering on antagonism. Indeed, he already knew what he wanted. But there was judicious reason to disseminate the non-childishness at hand. As a signal to those capable artisans, even if they were down on their luck right now, who possessed the talent to tackle this assignment, so as to understand that, while his set was all productive business, it was not conventionally stress-oriented. In short, he wanted talent to spread itself around, for all to see. For the sake of the picture. Confidence, morale, pride, all the holistic agencies he could think of. He wanted his people to *show* their talent. It was because they were all part of something great, and he had to lead them into greatness, as far as he could. Any typical Hollywoodian shallowness had to be squeezed, excised and flushed. After all, his talent wasn't assembled only because it was getting a certain amount of money to behave in a certain way.

'Uhhhh,' the director groaned. (It was his turn to apply a bit of affectation now.) 'Uhh – Wow! – Wah! – I'm, well, I'm overwhellllllllllmmmmmmmm…ed. But listen, let's just go with Sample #38. OK?'

'Should I be acting, you know, *coy* now –,' Hi began.

'– Or something…?' Tab finished.

'No need, boys. I ask this youngster Butterbugs to do all the acting required. Now that I think of it, I'll be a-talkin' to Leon and Bob. I can open this sequence with a deep focus shot of the whole room. Windows highlighted. The fabric might even show up. A little. Done deal. It's wrapped. That's the one. Gentlemen? See you, next orbit. Ciao!'

Sample #38 was the coarse-knit chartreuse, aqua and charcoal weave. And the director exited the soundstage.

Butterbugs was the only one left. As coincidence would have it, he'd happened to silently pick the same fabric that Egaz had all along. #38. It would look stunning in Surtees' vivid low-light interior. Such was the symbiotic state of mind that bound the makers and the players together in this here picture. Anything else would tank.

'I bend down (but not over) to you, Hi/Tab, in gratitude, for your remedial demonstration, in light of my un-attuned awareness of the possibilities, when it comes to window dressings…!'

After Butterbugs left, the two designers chatted quietly, acting their age.

'#38, Hi. Our favorite. Our director knows what he's doing.'

'And thank your gods, Tab. Thank 'em outright. Tonight!'

That was enough for Hi and Tab. They had won wonder from the ultrastar and approbation from the ultrastar's director. Nothing else could register on their sensitivity meters. They got to work and finished, 48 hours before the deadline.

Perhaps the biggest blast of publicity to hit the 'UWH' production had the least to do with the picture itself.

This being Century 21 and all, Twenty-First Century Scale concepts were now possible. Not just elements of *science* fiction were coming to pass, but ideas formerly associated with *social* fiction were now theoretically achievable, and downright possible. With metaphysical certitude, too. Ever since the Hubble telescope captured universal gas combines in Technicolor for all the world to see, and Tzi Xuci and Sravannah Ramapalayam harnessed once and for all the awesome energy at the center of the Earth, and converted it to steam power to meet humanity's electricity and heat needs for the next 5000 years, no further justification for the advances of science needs mentioning here.

But in the realms of what used to be fiction in the social sense, the stuff that dreams are made of, the consumerist society naturally came to the fore. A vast public, wishing for something *more* than they regularly encountered in this most superficial of day-to-day worlds, were opening up to previously unthought-of realities.

After several decades of particularly fallow fatalism, new possibilities perked up that successfully challenged many of the institutions and beliefs that had run the global show for thousands of years. Gone were the frivolous expectations of those old 'End Times' mentalities, and the oogah-boogah threats of terminal rapturism, the Johnny Revelationists, Sven Ragnarökists, Jyoti Kali-destructionists and Obadiah Apocalypticons that had cleaned up at the bank after fleecing scared citizens for so long. Their gigs faded, withered and dried up, one by one.

And why had these seemingly-organized but actually naturally-occurring phenomena taken place? Because, contrary to the promulgations of certain people, who had nothing else to do but promote the lack of progress in humanity, evolution nevertheless was pressing onward. This, in spite of the fact that most human beings had been led to believe they had complete control over their destiny.

Simply put, the people new on the scene – newly-hatched or newly-aware – had other stuff to do in this newest of worlds, rather than squandering their lives on exhausted notions and practices.

Only one example of this progress in the carbon-based human experience is necessary to cite. Only one example says it all. At first, to those society watchers and academics who pontificated and prognosticated about such things, it came off as preposterous, if not laughable. But the fact was, simplicity, such as that displayed by all the world's great thinkers, both known and unknown, was the framework upon which this next step, this immutable evidence of a transition upward, had its basis and proof.

And that sole example? No one ever really laughed about it, even in the early phases of its recognition. It was because it made so much sense. It stood out so boldly as a mature and sensible truth. It did not require deep analysis or explanation to appeal to the populace of the world. Because its depth was part of the stem that led to the roots of all knowledge and all existence and all connections with our human values, attained through the ages.

And the example was (for it was the only one discernible, so far), and the example *is*: the fact that Butterbugs was an ultrastar. To repeat: Butterbugs was an ultrastar.

Butterbugs *is* an ultrastar.

Butterbugs is *the* ultrastar.

As they say up on the Northwest Frontier of Pakistan, 'khandan nanashad', venerable Persian for 'Don't laugh'. Not that this phrase became the instructional mandate for any jokers who might pass off such a fact as poppycock. But it did actually become a rallying cry for those in search of further horizons regarding the best that life has to give.

The seriousness of the quest established, its validity spread, as did its reasonableness. Thus was the recessional trend in human development braked, placed on a turntable, and guided into a more sensible, less reactive direction. That reality was solely due to Butterbugs' reaching ultrastar status. Because, as a figure who mattered to all, or most, people everywhere, new standards were set as to the value of life itself. And the standards, once they were codified and understood, were followed. Because they were better than what had come before.

Quite frankly, this matter was difficult to articulate, even for scientists and philosophers. So the terms in discussing it were the simplest. It was almost as if scientific method could not apply. Not any more, anyway. One exemplary human figure had evolved, and now, the rest would have to follow – because they *wanted* to follow – and that included all existing perceptions of the world as it was previously known. Truly, then, was a revaluation of all values set into motion.

But wait – to return to the streetside, raw-bone, happenin' groove-thang of those involved with this foundational evolutionary re-grounding, it must be established that the persons who were in from the start had no idea that they were indeed part of something that would change the world. Granted, Butterbugs was a big-time dude, and the 'ultrastar' label had been accepted and tossed about as everyday parlance. But the thing was, life could go on in its cinematically creational course, without the burden of pretentiousness or mind-boggling responsibility. Unlike Messianic or Buddhistic or Prophetic contributors to the world's evolution, an ultrastar is only required to be an ultrastar, and the ultrastar's effects toward those whom he or she shines upon are in turn responsible for the heavy lifting and fundamental changes required for human evolution to plow onward. 'Catalyst' is too light a term to use for this manifestation of evolution, but it might have to do for the present.

Ultrastar as catalyst. Maybe, but the truth was there. Catalysts provide ideas. People pick up on them and implement them. The burden resided with implementers, not originators. Followers thus are leaders.

Load shed unknowingly, Butterbugs belched and farted before returning to his girlfriend's presence. He closed the loo door, as the open window transported his fœtid evacuata vapors into quick dissipation, far aloft from the LA grid, so nicely presented on this magic eve here at The Æyrie, so mild.

Keenah was cool. She was completely untroubled by being left alone for fifteen minutes, or that Butterbugs had a nose hair out of place. She'd been a little spooked by the terrace sans railings that formed the faint line between earth and sky, stretching latitudinally in front of their easy-deck chairs. Now though, with Butterbugs present to steady her, she felt not only at home on this plane, she felt elevated. Not with elevation, but with elation. And love.

'I love you, Butterbugs,' she whispered, her shapely arms joining and pulling his head toward hers in a kiss that would only be regarded as idealistic if it weren't so realistic.

Smooch…! For the longest time.

'Ohhhh, Keenah! I love you, too. I'm aware like I've never been before!'

'We must be equals in every way. I could have said the same thing!'

'Perfect!'

'Yes, perfect!'

Theirs was the exclamation-laden talk of young lovers, newly discovered, newly probing, testing, striving to believe. To believe this was really happening.

In her own version, similar to Butterbugs', Keenah had been a girl on the fringes of self-realization through mate-hood, yet in the thick of things when it came to appearance and potential. She had indeed scored this plum role in 'UWH', not just because of her spectacular and stylish looks, but due to her range, required for acting out the very difficult part of The Lady Lutrena. Though they had already shot the Jonny Requesticus scene of her demise, there was still a whole shitload of scenes yet to be shot in which she and Butterbugs had to expose and amplify their roles, and why things led to his assassination of her in front of Court.

Was their script influencing their real life? They both thought about it, but had not yet shared, which was a blessing. Because, the more each one thought about that angle, the more they thought it ridiculous and embarrassing to even think about. So they didn't. Sensibly, they both decided to love instead. Just love, without reservations.

At this point, they had not yet been naked and bedded together. There was every mutual desire, but not yet the right moment. Keenah had not laid every gent in the county, but she was nevertheless just as experienced as Butterbugs, in her own way. That being, she was not hot to trot until the opportunity presented itself, free of encumbrances. Like equivocation. Like the possibility of regret. Like the fear she would not fill his bill. After all, she was his co-star, but she felt so many notches below him in true human standing that the elongated ovals of her smooth thighs were puckered with pinch-marks, just to make sure she was conscious and not luxury-dreaming.

'This is not a dream!' Butterbugs tongue-whispered in her ear.

'Hey, how did you know – of my self-pinching?'

Her thighs were as yet uncovered, though her tennis-player skirt was darn near the revealing level.

He laughed in miniature, hushed measures.

'Know? How did I know? Oh, Keenah, I did not have to know. I only needed to guess, and, and I was right?'

Her cute bangs were feathered enough to show her dark eyebrows rising in hopes of approval.

'Uh-huh…' was all she could get out.

'Somehow the act of pinching seems inferior to an act of caressing…,' he murmured.

'Oh, lover! Am I not – Do you not – Am I – *good enough?*'

She was serious, he could tell. Self-pinchers usually are.

He drew away from her for a moment.

Her security went into question. Her lips parted. A silent gasp prepared her for the worst. Her eyes were wide. Her knee socks were still all the way up. Her clunker-heels remained on her feet, though up in the air, as she reclined in alert pose in the easy-deck chair. Her nipples became erect under her little shortie top, and her tummy muscles hardened in preparation for the news ahead. Never was a girl's body so in concert with her thoughts.

There she remained in awful suspension for what seemed like full minutes, who knew how many. Here she was, the best she could be, the off-set actress who really was a woman, more interested in being a woman than an actress, here, with the biggest star on Earth, who was plainly a gentleman and one fucking sexy dude, only he was holding back. Back, because of *her*, of course. Or so it appeared.

Whether it is endemic for thoughtful women to hold themselves responsible for every little innuendo of attraction and analysis from the sex partner of their dreams, this woman could not help but indulge, in the full wave of intoxication that came along with being alone with that very partner, Butterbugs.

But that was about to change.

Without further ado, he descended upon her and planted his mouth on her cock-suckingly-full, free-from-filler lips, and she abandoned any further thoughts of qualifications. Now they flew, free of appendages, up into the orbit where sensuous gesture and response were all that mattered, and what's more, where they were all that existed.

Into orals, they both celebrated what they could give to the other, and what the other could offer as tools that pleased the partner. He was gratified by how her lips conformed when they took on his stiff and stand-tall erection: a generous border of flesh to serve as talented border between cheek and dick-head. For her part, appearance was not on the list of requirements, as her face was excitedly taut and aimed at the terrace's roof beams as her lover's lips and tongue, whatever they looked like, sought her longitudinal lips and ventured in, with swiveling, and taste-instrument talent, and lover-licking, mattering a helluva lot more than the obviousness of cock-sucking.

But so what if she were more cerebral than he was in intimate interpretations? They both dug each other so much, they were on an unnamed cosmic dust cloud until dawn, and it was a good thing that it was a Sunday without makeup call, because they lapsed into repose after multiple orgasms, and on the deck of the terrace, without pillow or coverlet.

Some time after 10:00AM, Chun, the androgynous house-attender, probably of Philippine parentage, who ran all things operational at The Æyrie, approached the totally nude couple as they slumbered in disarray, and made to grasp Butterbugs' kneecap, probably the most innocuous part of his body, what with all the detectable film of kissing in most other parts, that covered both their forms like a slug fleet's nocturnal slime trails.

Kneecap rotated, the signal did its job and the owner awoke, albeit groggily.

Frequently had Chun seen Butterbugs' nudity, but never so attractively arranged as on this occasion, with the nearby lady's curved shapes providing stunning accompaniment to the languid male who now stirred.

'Telegram for you, Mr. Butterbugs,' Chun whispered. 'Marked urgent, otherwise I would not have approached you and your guest, until it was your move, of course.'

'That's all right, Chun. Thank you so very much, today.'

'Awake-oriented beverages await when you and your intensely sweet companion are ready.'

Butterbugs regarded Keenah along with Chun.

'Lovely she is, now more than ever. Would you prepare the VistaPanoRama Room's bed? She will go there when I awaken her. Offer her every courtesy, please-and-thanks.'

'I will, sir.' Chun withdrew.

As Butterbugs unfolded the crinkly rice paper, Keenah did indeed awake, then rubbed her eyes and stretched, not minding the hardness of her apparent bed. Her body was young enough and lithe enough to adapt to any topography involving love.

'Long lover!' he marveled, 'Look at you!'

'Am I not *something?*' she purred, coyly. Full confidence was in play, based on memories of a few short hours ago.

'Oooh, what a contraption!' he said in one long exhale.

Rising on one elbow, she gazed at his flaccid penis as he unwrapped the telegram. She intensified her attention until he began to feel a rising of the troops, and so made to adjust and accommodate the change while he read the telegram.

She smiled as she beheld the desired results of her efforts, and prepared to check her moistness for a bit of frolic on these hard but uncompromisingly romantic terrace floorboards.

Instinctively, she gazed about for any spy mechanisms in play. Reassured that the only lens that might capture their sexualities safely resided way up and away on Mt. Wilson, she relaxed into vixenian concentration.

While there was little doubt that Keenah possessed considerable erotic powers, such as making tissue stiffen just by looking at it, there was also another force in play right now: that found in the words that now presented themselves in front of Butterbugs' eyes at this elevation, and at this moment, and in this company.

'Keenah? Listen to this… Better yet, here, you read it. Otherwise you might not believe me.'

Busy with her erotic single-mindedness, she had to break away in order to react to his statement. She thought the interruption might deflate what she had wrought, but no, the reinforcement remained. So she took the paper handed to her and read it.

'It's from Sonny,' he said.

'Son – ny?'

'My agent. Yours, too. Sonny, Projector-type.'

'Yes, big prick – er, I mean, big love. I shall read it now.'

'Yes, read it now. Tell me from your own lips. Because I thought I was still entwined in your long limbs, dreaming.'

'Where you will return, cool-boy.'

'Now? *Right* now?'

'Well, you want me to read this thing, do you not?'

'Read now so that we may resume. There is a comfy bed that awaits!'

'I can take it or leave it, love-mug.'

'You can decide after –'

'OK, I'm on it.'

She rearranged her hair, her lips, her thighs (the pinch marks had mercifully faded), and decided she should get really comfortable and remove her clunker heels. She did, and then settled into reading mode, after being satisfied with her man's manhood in its stability.

Casually did she begin, but after forming the words with her morning-puffy lips, she moved into overdrive in order to project her comprehension of the words in the short telegram.

'Butterbugs?'

He was doing some routine rearranging of his private parts, in anticipation of decamping to the VistaPanoRama Room.

'Yes, love? Find something? Something that isn't a fantasy?'

'Well, funny you should say that. Because, if you read this already, that's what you'd think.'

'That's what I thought.'

'Well, we both know Sonny. You, better than anyone.'

'Me, better than anyone.'

He felt his at-the-ready equipment and looked out and followed her should-be-insured legs up to their panty-less juncture, with its sprig of groomed pubes and one stretch of glisteny labia that pouted out from the casual position she now assumed.

'Me-me-me-me-me! You-you-you-you-you!'

'Butterbugs!'

She sounded odd, almost hysterical.

'Yoe!'

He thought he should respond in kind.

She then proceeded in sustained speech, albeit a bit tremblesome, but generally joyous:

'Butterbugs, do you know, this is what Sonny says. He says, you, 'Butterbugs, ultrastar and strolling player in front of the cinematograph cameras of today's movies, you, are the fist ever, the first single person ever, the first ever recorded, the first of the first, well, you are the first... trillionaire, yes, *trillionaire*, to walk the face of this Earth!' He says, 'All calculations previously have been on the conservative side. All new calculations from multiple sources concur. You are indeed in a new category. Earth's first ultrastar, but also, now, today, Earth's first trillionaire. In dollars, euros, loonies, rupes, pings, and pangs. It is a fact. Congrats, Sonny.' *Also sprach* Sonny, Butterbugs!'

'Well, now there's a thing,' replied the world's first trillionaire. 'Curious! But look, Keenah. Do you think I should trim my pubic hair to match yours?'

Butterbugs and Keenah came together in a huge CU kiss, but in front of no cameras. It was quite a smacker. In it, Butterbugs knew that she wasn't into it for his
money. A trill here, a trill there, but the lip action resonated in hearts, and not
guts. She loved him for his love, and he knew it.

51.

Awake!
The Sun Is Shining Over
The Town! Cast Off Your
Sorrows And Be Glad!

'**W**ill you?'

'Will I what?'

'Awake! The sun is shining over the town! Cast off your sorrows and be *glad!*'

'But my precious, I have cast off everything. All my garments lie at your feet.'

'Still, don't you have other items to discard?'

'Like...'

'I already mentioned them. Your sorrows!'

'But what was that first thing you said again?'

'Awake!'

'I have, dear. Some time ago.'

'Not *that* awake! Your soul, your inner-ness. Do you not know?'

'It still slumbers, I guess.'

'Then will you not cast off the burden of your sorrows?'

'How could I have sorrows, when I am here with you? And you me.'

'And I you!'

'The world shall hear of this joy!'

'And all your sadness and anger and troubles have fallen away?'

'What I carry in my heart – I am not sure it is not secured for the duration of all time. But today, up here, us, in this honesty of body, without modesty from each of us, with only admiration, I nearly feel up to the plane you want me to be!'

'I can change you! Of that I feel capable, as of now! This very micro-second! Happiness! It might yet condescend unto us.'

'I look at your revealed body, then into your eyes, lady, and I cannot now feel the shades which have always drawn me into their uncertainty.'

'Verily then, I have won you with my sweet seduction!'

'Seduction? Why, what? Is *that* what this is, then??'

No director was there to say 'cut', but they did what they knew was in the script.

'Not a bad run-through, Keenah. I like how your dialogue is becoming enveloped around the character's soul.'

'Here is where she shocks him, though. She blows it, actually.'

'Indeed. That's why they want to cut the scene's development right *there*. Lady

447

Lutrena is so in love with HMD. Before things change in her heart, that is. You are getting it, baby!'

'Mr. D'Varzim has taught me much. Almost as much as you.'

'He's a perfect director.'

'Oh, yes.'

'You still call him 'Mr.'?'

'Out of respect...'

'Come down with me. To my level of convenience. Call him Egaz.'

'He won't mind?'

'I'm doing you a favor.'

'All right.'

Butterbugs, sighed, stretched, and tossed his script aside.

'Would you not consider the majesty of this place?'

Here they were, so far above the rest of the world. Not on location, but high in respite, a furlough for love. All their cares had been left far down on the plains of Jambutterbugsabad. Earning their interval, they flew over Hindu Kush's hump and made their way to alpine Zambash, before spending a romantic hideaway night at the hut of Arkshnug, with views down into the defile of Koshtblobb. And in the meadows in the Yintixtc highlands beyond, they tarried 'twixt blossoms and sky, for the season of the intoxicating blooms was upon them. They could not have chosen better.

Ploughpersons' lunches, sour pickle pâté from Pleshtbulb, table-bread from the huge ovens at Shuhttahsh, and the local Kurn wine of fiery blue hue and firm buzz were enough to make them recline upon the flowery bank that afforded a masterful panorama.

Off in the airy distance, the perpetual people's snows of Mt. Communism were a visceral cone of refreshment, and away in the impossible expanse to the western north, surely those were reflections from Lake Balkhash, smiling into the sunny heavens.

'What an exceptional rehearsal!' Keenah gushed.

'And what a place for love to bloom! After all, we are in the middle of it.'

'The picture? Certainly –'

'No, silly-head! I'm not talking about that! Us! Here! Our love's a sea of flowers!'

'Oh, Butterbugs, of course! I've been too immersed in one-track concentration!'

'On me?'

'No, my *part*, because it's my first big – Oh! You! Tricksterby!'

Butterbugs crowed with laughter, which did not even echo because the peaks were too distant, but the peaks probably heard its lusty ring anyway.

Standing up, he took her hands, pulled and swung her around, so that she noticed, rotating past his broadly smiling face, the true grandeur that she'd previously been distracted from.

'Stop, love-player! You're making me dizzy!'

'You see it now?'

'Oh yes, the land is amazing! All of it!'

'And something else?'

He stopped his leading rotation. He then drew her close, close for a kiss, but paused so that she could read his face with the same attention she'd devoted to her dialogue lines.

'You see it now, Keenah? You see what I have?'

'Your... love? Right?'

'You do! You *do* see it!! I am the most fortunate of lovers, for I project my ardor without any words!'

'No lines!' she laughed.

'That's right, but remember, not all of life is scripted.'

'Nor need it be.'

'You love me?' the ultrastar asked, his lips whispering to hers at their closest.

Her turn to be wordless, she kissed him passionately, so as to communicate her answer. In that kiss was enough intent to answer him to the fullest.

Despite the elevation, to which they adapted by way of leisurely progress up the Cart Road, it was considerably heated up here, so sex in the sun was ruled out. Still, they breathed deeply and embrace-walked back to their rarefied lodge, stripped, mounted each other, and really worked up a sweat.

They could carry on no more. Both collapsed out of each other's arms, chuckling and braying, before tumbling down onto the Morris peacock-patterned duvet cover, the terrain of five king-size beds. This great plain rippled slightly from the punkah action above, an indoor zephyr on this hottest of globally-warmed days so far this season.

Due to differing filming skeds, the two stars returned to Hollywood independently. Butterbugs did so via Paramaribo, which is in Suriname.

Just out the door at the Jambutterbugsabad studio, he'd gotten a long-distance request from Edmund Mark Mad, the famous photoplay critic and producer, who was, in point of fact, doing an Associate Producing gig on 'UWH'.

'Butterbugs, could you please do something for me?'

'Well, Edmund Mark, I would be happy to. Shoot.'

'Good! So listen, I'm enjoying an alcohol-enhanced tumbler of Vincent's Punch here at the Ecliptoworks, above the Bev Hills Hotel. Poolside, you know? Hey, wowzah! I think that babe's about to do a topless cannonball off the high-dive over there. Nope. She chickened out! Still topless, though. Yowzah! But let me tell you right now! So looka here, my little brother's chat show is tanking in the ratings. He can be a bit of a bozo-boy, but I'd... I'd like to help him out.'

'Cool.'

'If you could drop off for an afternoon on the old Dutch Guianian shore's chief mart and population center, the kid's doing a remote broadcast, highlighting Surinamese cinema.'

'A worthy cause,' replied the actor, who, as they spoke, punched in a Karachi-to-LAX ticket order, halting in Paramaribo for five hours only.

'I've done several pictures there. The scene is very upcoming and fabulaire.'

'Sweet, baby, sweet. Show up. Yak. Help him out. He's got golden-time global broadcasting mandates. I ramrodded it right through; high up at TeeCzar Sputnik Channels, ya see. He doesn't know I did that for him.'

'And he never *shall* know!'

'You're one of nature's noblemen. The whole world will be watching. This is his big chance. No big deal for you.'

'I am always ready to help a fellow show bizzer.'

'Beautiful. Say, can't wait to (favorably) review 'UWH', baby – 'our' 'UWH'. I've got my hot little feet in both worlds!'

'Oh, neither can I! You're a bridge-builder.'

'Hy Goth let me see some teaser-rushes. It's fucking flame-thrower!'

'Good heavens, that's great to hear.'

'Butterbugs? You, uh, sound kind of, I don't know, kind of – bubbly – or something. I mean, I'm happy you're doing the Paramaribo gig for me and everything, but I don't wanna put you out or anything. It's just that, it's on your way home and everything. But I'll be jimmyriggered if you don't sound – different.'

'That's because... *I'm in love...!*'

ANNOUNCER: [in English, after local announcers make their introductions in Dutch, Hindi, and Taki-Taki] This is DeWitte Benson on the TeeCzar System, a PlanetWide Sputnik-Powered Networks Concern, covering the globe with the glue of sealed communication, encrypted for safety, reaching every and all of you out there on the Earth Planet. Atomic Clock-out-of-Denver time: 9:00PM prime. And now we segue to 'Move All The Way On *With Movies* – And At *Full Blast*', with your host, Davies Mark Mad, film critic for 'The Gold Dragoon' and other mercenary publications, today reporting from the Cupid Movie Auditorium in downtown Paramaribo – Special Spotlight: Surinamese Cinema This Day!

DAVIES MARK MAD: Greetin's 'n' felicitations! I'm glad we're here. Because, folks, we have a lot of local stuff to offer about the obscure cinema of this obscure nation. No offense to those Surinamers who are graciously hosting us This Day, but heck, compared to the guest who suddenly condescended unto us in this audiotoriumite, everything else looks pretty darn dim. For he is a *star*, brightly beamed into our midst, and I just couldn't be more peachy-pleased than to now present the ultra-personality of our time – here – now! In person! All I have to say is: BUTTERBUGS!

BUTTERBUGS: Thank you, thank you. I'm delighted to be back in Paramaribo. My memories are most fond of my picture-making experiences here. Great place. Great people. Great groove-thangs.

DMM: You're most gracious in your homage, movie star. I've never met you before, so I'm kind of nervous.

Bb: Please, don't be. Truly, I'm in pleasure at being here.

DMM: You know, the second you said 'Don't be', I no longer felt nervous at all, and I do not now. I hope it lasts!

Bb: It will. For, why should we be goofed out by blimped-up tensions and wobbly self-flagellating thoughts?

DMM: Butterbugs, you sure know how to comfort! Is that what makes you great?

Bb: I'm not as praiseworthy as a rotting dog I saw in Bangkok once. I'm here to celebrate Surinamese cinema, not to get licked over by shills.

DMM: OK! Well, thanks for dropping in. What do you like best about Surinamese cinema?

Bb: Well, it's a kind of a... Or, rather, the essence of the criteria is... It's, well, it's... *texture*. Yeah, it's texture.

DMM: You're of course referring to the new exiting Eddith Kiser picture, 'Texture' (Elimmany Cranston Pictures Intercontinental), which was filmed here, crewed here, and will premiere here, in this here picture hall, *tomorrow night.*

Bb: In this here picture hall. Right. I'm also struck by the gutsy inventiveness that is emanating from these precincts. The film community is small, but it's resourceful and imaginative. In fact, before I popped in here, I spent a couple hours across Kamta's limpid creek, filming a cameo scene for my friend Airgurn Minnaterio, who's helming 'A Nice, Greasy, Prehistoric Moose-Dog', with many soon-to-be-known Maroon actors and actresses. With Vanessa Redgrave, Due Sutz, Sheila Chi′n, and the fabulous Doutzen Kroes (who just started her own Filmaufnaumoon Institutet Stoomptvaart here). And Renée Adorée's in it, too. Yes, 'Moose-Dog' will be just an incredible picture. Unlike anything you've ever seen anywhere. And I mean *any*thing. Selznick International's releasing it.

DMM: That's remarkable.

Bb: Aye! There's oh-so-much more I could comment on here, if you'd like.

DMM: So, Butterbugs, tell us about your new status as the world's first, well, *you* know what.

Bb: You mean, the world's first fellow to have discovered that he's the luckiest lover in love, and that this is a great place to be, and that I'm glad to be here?

DMM: Well... say, I'm just receiving some information on my EarClear|SendinReceive that, well, there's a *surprise* coming up.

Bb: But I'm already here...

DMM: Something else, because... Uh, yes. You were saying, Butterbugs?

Bb: Oh, just mushy stuff. But you asked!

DMM: Maybe, heh!, we'd better begin again. This is *LIVE* TV! Welcome to my show! It was indeed a surprise that you showed up, and we're all elated. I'd also like to welcome my viewers far and wide across this here globular globe. Tonight we're ampli-casting all over the place. Very fitting, as we have an ultrastar with which to celebrate the occasion... with.

Bb: Big, big thanks. And, ah, yes, I'd just like to pay a tad bit of tribute to your brother, Edmund Mark Mad.

DMM: Why, thank you, Butterbugs. We don't ever speak, but fambly is fambly, I s'pose, as they says down in the incestuous holler.

Bb: Great egg. A super associate producer, too. A dahn good critic. He can do it all! He replaced Randi Chuzzlewit, you know, and a good thing it was, too.

DMM: Who? Who-um did he replace?

Bb: Randi Chuzzlewit.

DMM: Who's that?

Bb: Ah yes, the forgotten one! You plainly don't know. But, realize, he was the most influential cinema critic in the nation and yes, the whole globe, all hemispheres, for a time. The power he exercised cannot be calculated now. He was hated, you know. Universally. Except by me. You see, I never knew him, but I found out, after he had committed one of the messiest suicides ever to be seen in the annals of –

DMM: Folks, I'd like to –

Bb: No, let me finish, Davies Mark. A few words in *defense* of – not in *praise* of… Items like these need saying. The facts are these. He reduced his brainpan's contents to atomized tapioca, all in the name of sacrifice, so that the guard might be changed. I know that now. And so I found out, after he had departed this life-plane in so depressing a manner, that he'd been amenable, even in his final blow-out, to the idea that the old guard, of which he was a member, had to surrender to something new.

DMM: The guard to what? Of what, I mean.

Bb: He had spied out the land ahead. His influence as a critic was ungainly but mighty. He had Hearstian power in the motion picture world. Bigger than that hag Louella Offputting Parsons, but of course, quite different, quite different. I am not understating this. Then, when I came along, he changed. He saw me. He saw the future, so I have been told. I tell you, I don't know how he did it, but he saw something different on the horizon, and he knew he should get out of the way. In one aspect – only one, but a potent one, I was responsible for his demise, though the Industry was grateful for his new non-existence. I feel a bit preten-tious in outlining this bit of cinematic history, but Davies Mark, I tell you, I am a part of it. This Randi dude knew that he could not be part of the new –

DMM: As I understand it, you're displaying a tad bit of uncharacteristic aggres-sive language, Butterbugs, but I suppose it's all right. You're talking n-e-w here. Like, the New People.

Bb: I'm talking n-e-w, but not the New People, for pity's sake. I've always thought that was the stupidest term ever. Yes, I know, I was for a time considered to be a member of, if not the leader of this, this 'New People' mouseshit, but hap-pily, not one soul has breathed a word of it until you just did. To be brutally blunt, I'm wary of anything with 'new' in its permanent identity. Temporarily, in certain cases, such a reference is valid. 'New' is a relative or interim term or state of mind. Sooner or later, things new are rendered more chronologically advanced. Anything that remains 'new' implies a suspicious flakiness. New Road in Kathmandu is no longer worthy of that title. Comparatively it is at least usable, certainly, but who wants to always harbor historical perspectives when dealing with matters of the moment, whether it's infrastructure, or a pop cultural label? Old and new, new and old! Why, I always liked that film title, 'Little Old New York' (Goldwyn-Cosmopolitan, 1923 and 20th-Fox, 1940). Think about it. It teaches us irony. New can be good. Perhaps that's why it's used and kept. It has promise. Like, New College, Oxford – which is positively ancient! Yes, every-thing new turns old. Good new, good new. Let's see. Well, I'm tickled at some results of the kind of n-e-w that I'm talking about. Like, the official name change from 'New York City' to plain 'Gotham' (no 'City' included, Batman fans…!) and 'New York State' to 'Iroquoia'.

DMM: Or, Mohawksylvania?

Bb: You're catchin' *on!* Now, if we can just get them to change 'New Jersey' to 'Hackensack'...

DMM: I daresay, you could, Butterbugs.

Bb: Down with the bad kind of New!

DMM: Your skill as an actor *always* seems new, Butterbugs.

Bb: Why, why, thank you. I always endeavor to play my screen roles in ever-evolving ways. Like a floating ball in the universe that is constantly changing shapes and character.

DMM: A very grand and fitting way for an ultrastar to consider himself.

Bb: Well, I...

DMM: Yes. And now, my audience of mine, I'd like to surprise our guest by bringing out from behind the grand drape, his co-star in the upcoming thundering epic and mega-picture extraordinaire, that NEW personality and NEW – yes, the very BEST kind of NEW – actress, who's starting at the very top, Miss Keenah LaVine! Here she is now, see what you think of her! Would you please give her a bang-up happy-princess' mega-welcome, huh? All right??

Bb: Davies Mark! You stop my heart!

DMM: I hope not! You're gonna need it, as I hear you two are sweet on each other!

Bb: Sweet on each other! Why, you don't know the half of it! Lover-package, it's *you!*

KEENAH LaVINE: Why, hello, Butterbugs. Fancy meeting *you* here! Wanna get lucky?

DMM: Folks, the ever lovely, ever-lovin' Keenah LaVine, who's about as NEW as condensation off a beer tin! And you're new to me, and boy, do you look swell!

KL: Pleased to meet you, Mr. Mad.

DMM: Oh come, come, come, call me Davies Mark! Well, I'm not half as blown away by seeing you as our co-ultrastar here. Look at him! Droolin' an' gigglin' and gollywoggin' you. And I tell ya, folks, I just don't blame him!

Bb: Well! Keenah-keen! I had no idea! Why didn't you wire me or send an alert?

KL: Don't you like surprises?

Bb: I sure do! Especially when they're your super-lovely form and smiley words.

DMM: You two love hounds sit down. Keenah, you've got some explaining to do.

KL: I'd just like to compliment your brother, Edmund Mark Mad.

DMM: Oh. Yeah. So did Butterbugs. If you must, I suppose... Heh!

KL: He's so terrific.

Bb: Sweet girl, how came you to this place?

KL: It was really no big deal, although I did a bit of puddle-jumping. From Kurrachee I flew to Bahawalpur, thence, non-stop to Vladivostok, and thither to the Los Angeles. Then I heard tell that you were shooting a scene down here, so I hopped the freighter and got here about fifteen minutes ago. Not bad, eh?

Bb: Oh, you're never bad, you girly-girl...

DMM: Hello young lovers! That's quite a little tea dance, my young starlet! Now, wait, Butterbugs. This is a family show. No French kissing!

Bb: OK.

DMM: No groping, either! You didn't see that, folks. Uh, Butterbugs, as I said, this is *LIVE* TV.

Bb: Uh, yes...

KL: Mind what we do, Butterbugs.

Bb: Anything. Anything you say, sweets.

DMM: Amazing, that we could all meet-up here.

Bb: You know, that's one of the most exciting parts of this bizzness. Super-charged happenings of all kinds make up my days. And now, since I am currently enjoying the plump fruits of true love on my doorstep and in my bedroom, I am taken to even greater heights of the best that life has to give. Look at her, will you? Camera operator, dolly in to a huge close-up! See her perfections, for all to enjoy. For she is mine, my lover. See, the lips I get to kiss. The lips that whisper all kinds of intimacies into my ears. Notice the shapeliness of features and face. And, cameraman, follow my directions, the first I have ever given, for she inspires me like no other being on Earth. Follow my direction down. Look at her matchless collarbones, which naturally lead the view down to her cleavage. There the slopes rise on either side, climaxing in dual summits of stupendous breastworks, which are, on the surface anyway, the most easily accessible accessories to be appreciated by those of you who are not privy to my bedroom and her boudoir. Are they not elegant and sexy? You can compare them to any number of fine-figured gals the world over, but I feel I have the creamiest of the highest-risen cream. And do you know, she makes me cream my jeans! This – top she has on. Observe! It does not necessarily show off the shape of her torso. But my narration can describe and titillate at the same time. Those lines phase down from her orbs to a flat tummy and recondite navel that might make Raquel Welch ineffectual. Raquel's pretty good, but my Keenah's got plenty of exhibition chutzpah to bottle and put on a shelf for consumption by all those pathetic losers out there. Because, you know, she is just gradually being revealed to a needy public. Men will lust over her, and honor me with their jealousy. Women will feast their eyes on her, and hands-down decide that if they would go lesbo with anyone at all, it would be her, it would be her, it would be her! I love it when she pooches her triangle outward at me as she's on her knees above me in bed, and then –

DMM: Butterbugs, Butterbugs, Butterbugs BUTTERbugs! I can see she's gone to your head! Ultrastars are also actors! Folks, we just might be witnessing a scene from their upcoming picture, coming to you from Mega|Goth Studios, of Sawl Cane's revelatory epic, 'Unholy War Hymn'. Drama it has, in super-high doses!

Bb: Our journey is not yet through. I'm only down to her 19-inch waistline!

DMM: And we'll save the rest for next time.

Bb: I get it. I just wanted the world to be as excited as I am to actually experience an exceptional person. I love to give of myself. I need to share.

DMM: And you have! Oh, how you have!

Bb: And in the morning light, the light of dreams newly faded, when consciousness resumes the mind's night-shift of freedom-oriented thoughts from undiscovered countries, shrouded by the lights of awakened conduct, I see her before me. Whether clothed, or as lovers should see lovers, she crosses and re-crosses the footbridges between wakefulness and dreaming slumber. Proof that she does indeed exist, for my delight. And her coming to and fro is not fleeting, but increasingly reliable, and indeed, part of my daily life. From here on out. Oh! Joy-bringing woman of the gift-giving aspect of humanity! You have presented your offerings to me with such humbleness, with such attractive mien and lines, with your sculptural flesh so willing to be caressed, respected, worshiped, your wondrous descent upon my sorry-ass station is an endowment that has given my life meaning and my art inspiration. You do not distract. You command. And you lead me onward!

DMM: Folks! Butterbugs! Give him a hand. Please do. Great scene!

Bb: Thank you, all. It is the way I feel. It expands with each moment.

KL: Butterbugs, that was sweet.

Bb: All because of you, love!

DMM: Now Keenah, you retain a close friendship with those pesky twin stars, Sugarina and Shastina, who romp through their teen pix like an augur through pink cotton candyfloss, with hyper-sweetened peppermint 'n' soda cake frosting slathered on top. Does that cramp your dating style with an ultrastar? He's in some pretty heavyweight pictures, you know. Like the one you both are doing now.

KL: Davies Mark, whatever are you talking about? Butterbugs is as cheerful and as accepting as one could hope. He thinks Su'ina and Shasts are pretty neat dirndls! Besides, several pictures ago, my Butterbugs starred with them in the wacky confection, 'My Sugary Fry-Up Swill' (Oxidized Onion), which everybody loved! Besides, 'UWH' is peppered with comedy of all kinds, from blud sausage-dark to wispy clouds-lite. Just like humanity itself! I have a goofball levity scene with Jerry Lewis, and kind of a naughty bit of fun with Ron Jeremy and Al Lewis in another scene, to name only two examples. Richard B. Shull is a scream in his cameo part.

DMM: I notice that you're saying 'my' Butterbugs. Can I apply an ear trumpet to the side of my head and detect dim wedding gongs from far up the misty glen?

KL: You're so funny!

DMM: Well, Butterbugs?

Bb: I cannot find an equal to my current rhapsody.

DMM: You were, sir, once involved with the late, legendary Vonda Van Den Dell in those – well, what must have been wondrous days of bohemian joy, before the awesome responsibility of strolling player-ship brought you to the world?

Bb: Pardon the trickle of wistfulness that I now betray when the memory of VVDD is kindled. And to you, my Keenah-keen, know, truly, I did not realize that ye even existed, to walk upon the lucky ground that happily accepted your footfalls. How many truths are hidden from us in the times of our lives!

DMM: You were close to the late star…

Bb: Yes, I loved her.

DMM: I see, Keenah, that you blush. Miss Van Den Dell was so bold, so black, and so monumentally sexy.

KL: She was so beautiful. I've seen all her pictures, and TABP has shown me her personal scrapbooks. I am in awe of her.

Bb: Alas! And such a beautiful person. And you know, at the point at which I knew I loved her, she was taken away from me. Shall I weep? Nay – I spent all my tears in accepting death's finality. And my Keenah is now at my side and in my bed. That is considerable comfort, I can tell you.

DMM: Well, I suppose that if you and Miss Van Den Dell had gotten married, you'd probably be divorced by now.

KL: Why Davies Mark, I think that's inappropriate speculation. I thought you were pro-Butterbugs in your orientation.

DMM: I am!

Bb: It's all right, my dear, Davies Mark, being the popular host he is, is pretty much OK in making such a statement. Not that I agree with him, but he views the Hollywood scene and makes reasonable expostulations. But Davies Mark, maybe you're right. However, the progression of my history has led me to the bright image sitting next to me, and that is all I can attest to.

DMM: Speaking of TABP, will he be performing the ceremony?

KL: You silly fellow! Still pushing!

Bb: I could say more about Surinamese cinema. After Keenah's through, of course.

DMM: Well, that would be great if we had more time, but you're so besotted with love-juice that I feel we should all be paying high-price tickets to see you confess your love for this drop-dead babe here. No mere sex object in her intellectual self, but good God, look at her! And of course our female audience can slaver all they like over you, sir, and your Wordsworthian lyricism.

Bb: Sometimes I'm thinking more in Ovidian terms.

DMM: I'll bet you are! Additionally, I'm told that your plane for home leaves in a mere twenty minutes, Butterbugs. Off you go. On the other hand, Keenah LaVine, you've got about five hours to loiter until your LAX-bound liner takes to the tarmac. Won't you continue to share our survey of local moviemaking with me?

KL: You're so kind, Davies Mark, but I must provide escort service to my Butterbugs to his winged victory home. Then I have to change, which'll take some time in Paramaribo International's powder room, so that when he greets me at Tom Bradley, I am worthy of his affections. What should I choose, hot shorts, high socks, thigh-high clumper boots, abbreviated top? Then again, little black dress with A/C lace is always nice when going from tropical steam to the steamy confines of Butterbugs' bedroom...

Bb: Woooo! Wooo! Wooo!

DMM: Knock it off! I can see by the mutual winking wonders of your facial communication betwixt each other, you'd better be on your way. Butterbugs, can we have a rain check for continuing your guided tour of your wife's – I mean, your future wife's, uh, shall we say, figural geography?

KL: Wife's? Wife's?

Bb: Let's just refer to her as my Idol. Yeah. My Idol's figural geography.

DMM: That would be fine. The terminology is just for the viewers' benefit.

Bb: You *got* it!

DMM: Thank you a lot, both of you. Tah-tah! Folks! Butterbugs and Keenah-la-vine! Now, let's return to the New Important Surinamese Cinema of today. My next guest is Runalda-Bojo van Weenenfoon, and she has just directed a picture for all time. Hear that rumba? Its plot concerns a boho musician who falls for a planter's wife, and...

Home in a hot tub, gently swirling. A Californian redwood-staved white wine afternoon, western view, grillettes on the outdoor kitchen's sizzler, and private moments without Egaz or Sonny or Porter or even Justy or Saskia's ringings, safe in The Lazaretto's outback Cliff May ranch house.

Terrycloth was all over the floor.

'Let me snuggle closer amidst the warm bubbles, girl.'

'Come on through.'

'I loved how you got into the rhythm with Davies Mark on that broadcast. You were great.'

'That was one of the best acting workshops I've ever attended! Your performance was incredible.'

'It was all true, you know.'

'Really?'

'How could you question it?'

'Oh, of course! You were really flying high. Lover, and all.'

'I live to praise you.'

'Oh, go on with you...'

'It's one of life's greatest pleasures.'

'You know, I didn't really mind that you gave that tour of my body on TV like that. (Glad you didn't quite get down to my too-big butt, though...) Do you think that I'm... I don't know, being ... conceited, or something?'

'See these hands, amidst the rushing flood? They could do another tour, with alternate routes, using the known arterials to access the off-road sites, as well as the limited access tracts for those with special permission. They are also ready to concentrate on your all-too-*perfect* butt!'

'Oh, you really *don't* mind, after all!'

'What?'

'Well, I thought you were sort of 'high' or something when you got kind of, you know, intimate, talking about me. I wasn't embarrassed. Really! I was thrilled. I just thought that, maybe you had jet lag and you were...'

'Trying to... show off, maybe?'

She didn't answer.

'Keenah, I know myself well enough to tell you – nay – *pledge* to you, that, well, I don't show off. At all. I don't think I really know how. If I ever got good direction in that department, I could probably pull it off. But it would have to be scripted. When we were on TV, I didn't have a script. No jet lag, either. I felt free, unencumbered by any of the things that drag us down at any one moment. I was reveling in, well, sincerity. I said those things because I love you. Love you. It's simple. And also, you make me erotically charged! As if you didn't know! Based on our, shall we say, private experience, that the public can easily guess at. Quite frankly, I enjoy respect. I don't wish to abuse it. But excitement is excitement, and I know that the public agrees with me if I make a judgment. So, baby, I got, well, I got turned on when you made the scene. I got a... to put it in Augustan poetic terms, a throbbing erection. Even – and it's a real thrill – on *LIVE* TV!'

She laughed at his Davies Mark Mad mimicry.

'If there's one thing that led to my babbling,' he continued, ' – and let's forget about your Best Girl in the World status as far as turn-on appeal is concerned – it was having the opportunity, for once, to talk about someone besides myself when an interviewer comes calling. I was just as jazzed to simply talk about the love of my life as I was to feel it – I mean – her. You. And there you were, there, in Paramaribo, on stage, with me!'

She water-cuddled, trying to lay her head on his shoulder, but found it getting wet, so she opted for a wine-swallow before rearranging herself for display purposes, and stroking his feet in the eddying spa mixture.

'Big movie star!' she teased.

'Star *claimed!*' he replied.

'Scripted?'

'No way! It was writ in the constellations above, æons before we were conceived. Like Gable & Lombard. Well, perhaps that's not the best example...'

Keenah giggled.

'Spence & Kate?'

Keenah sighed.

'Angelina & Brad?'

Keenah shook her head.

'Paul & Joanne?'

Keenah held out her hands.

'Maybe it's just not necessary to equate with any who have gone before us.'

'We're unique?'

'I know so. We are so singular, so exceptional; I'm trying to temper my high-flight instincts with more under-control observations. That way I won't fly too close to the sun.'

'Shall I call you Icarus?'

'Never! Never, partner in flight! We're unclassifiable! No precedents! Only originality. I feel comfortable with that, don't you?'

'Apollo, then!'

'Hey! Enough mythology, already!'

'If it's as good as in this tub, and if it were always like this, that's all I care about. Can you make it happen?'

'It already has.'

'From here on?'

'It is as good as done. I am an ultrastar. You are my mate. That is as sure as anything in this world. Artifice is what we do for a living. *True* artifice. It need not rule what we really want in life. And it *shall* not rule.'

'Oh, but Butterbugs, I wish to be a screen star, in the fullest sense of the term.'

'And you don't think that your role in 'UWH' will not make that happen?'

'Amazement! Yeah! I have to remember that! You're right! When will I feel that this isn't a dream?'

He dropped his legs into the depths of the tub and launched off toward her across the turbid seas. His prepped penis came into a harbor per-se, and the etiquette of coupling did not have to be negotiated.

She thought she might say:

'Sex is *it* with you, isn't it?'

But she knew how he might reply:

'Not at all. It is the additional gift of one's freedom. When love is in play, freedom makes itself fully known. It's when devices and desires are free to roam, without penalty of analysis or judgment, that the truth of what one person feels for another can come to the fore. It's when trust sustains the oncoming event, and love kicks in as scoutmaster and prophet...'

Or some such paraphrase.

He didn't say these things, but her logic, based on his obviousness, accepted the option with reasonable reality. Love? It was easy to spot. Easier to feel. She was sure he felt it.

She herself, wasn't so sure.

She said nothing, but above the bubbly mini-waves, she parted the lips he loved – both sets – and smiled, invitational, of course, and let him advance. That was a woman's intuition.

And she was right.

52.

Allegretto

The rhythms of picture making are: start-stop-stop-start, and variations there-of. The pace can quicken, or it can slacken. The rest is either boredom, or creative glory. Because of this rubato, even professional and seasoned crews can get awfully droll after a while (even Old Atrocity). But, because of the inherent quality of the gig, the bucks & bennies, most usually stick it out career-wise. The general feeling is that, even if one is doomed to clinkers at Monogram or standard 8mm produc-tions (with soundtrack on reel-to-reel tape) at United Pyramid, it's better than driv-ing forklift at some plant, and it's definitely better than Relief. As far as actors are concerned, the established stars have things their way. The makers cater to them, based on their own mandates. Actors on the rise will do anything. They are either neglected as a result, and thus, abused and fallen by the wayside, or else they come to be appreciated, and adopt straight-laced work-ethic approaches. The hard labor might go nowhere, or it levels off, or else it goes up, up, up. And only once has it led to ultrastardom.

Butterbugs, the unlikely ultrastar!

He never acted the part. Perhaps that was why it was not questioned as a stunt or even revoked. Stars come and go, but ultrastars seemed to be fixtures in the firmament, not even subject to the night sky's ever-moving viewpoints of upward locales.

Despite such an exalted standing, for the first time in his life, Butterbugs felt like a day-to-day human being. He had lodging, he had wheels (currently, a '73 NSU Trapezio, just for around town), he had a job – which was also his passion, he had enough money (he guessed), and he had a cool girlfriend. Plus he was an ultrastar, but that was down the list as far as qualifications and necessities were concerned. All things considered, a pretty fortunate day-to-day human being.

So, the main things right now were:

1) Being in love with Keenah
2) Enacting HMD for 'UWH' with the highest fidelity possible

After 'UWH' wrapped, three possibilities and one probability presented them-selves to him:

A) Retire and live in love – *life and love!* – perhaps aboard a longboat on the Oxford Canal

B) Go into politics

C) Continue acting and really dig the ultrastar thing, whatever that was

D) Abandon acting forever and apply at the Shree Jagannath Hotel in Seebpore, Bengal, for the position of nighttime desk clerk, starting out in the Gwuldah Lane annex, in earnest hopes of securing said employment

E) None of the above

Up in The Æyrie, Butterbugs collapsed in the Barcelona chair that faced the Plains of Id. It was white-hot noon out, but he was done filming for the day. The route from Mega|Goth Stvdios had been bone-crushing in the Trapezio. No dampeners had ever been installed – it was a track car – and usually Butterbugs enjoyed feeling the road, but not today.

'A jungle of a shoot!' he announced to Keenah, as she brought him an End-Of-Day punch, with airy steps from the bar.

'Oh, wow…'

'Yup, a buggy, slimy, torrid *jungle* of a shoot today, sweeters. 3:00AM till now…'

'I heard you crawl out at 2:00 to go on down,' she replied.

'It was a descent, all right. You might say, things aren't going particularly well.'

'You mean, with the picture?'

'Most definitely.'

'I'm not on call till next Thursday. Wish it wasn't so.'

Keenah wanted to act and keep acting! All the time!

'Yeah, baby-baby. Thing is, you should be glad you're not down there. Tension rules. Things are amiss. Old Atrocity says a distant planet has gotten out of alignment somehow. Nothing else to explain it. My lines were OK… You know the scene? It's rather violent. Not that we're shooting in chron order, but Egaz seems to be tackling all of the pressure-building sequences right now. Anyway, in the dawn light of the back lot, I'm pushing the Womm of Kuertrell around. You know, that ruler guy of the rival satrapy. I'm supposed to pop him in the neck. The camera crane's hydraulics blew out. We all couldn't believe it. Shot ruined; scrapped. Yoh and Melbo, the mechanics, got completely covered in hydro fluid. I handed them tools. Shamroy was pissed, but he got his coveralls on! Then Waycroft started arguing with Chutney Brassington over cricket scores. Really. It took three assistant directors/high-level production associates, the three Millah brothers in fact, Skookumchuck, Squillchuck, and Humptulips together to quell the riot they made. Couldn't believe that, either. Probably happened because of all the pent-up angst. Easily explainable. And yet… a tone of 'amiss' is in the camp. I've never seen this much difficulty in a day's shooting before. Everybody knew my presence wasn't helping, I'm sure. They say I always bring magic. Not this day. So I came home.'

'What does this mean – for the picture, B-bugs?'

'Well, there's some jeopardy to deal with. The producers went into a brown study and didn't come out, at least as long as I was there. I could go back down, I suppose…'

'Oh, no, honey. You've got to relax.'

'You talked me into it. Beverage refill, my dear?'

'Of course.'

'Boy, I've never seen Egaz so steamed.'

'Really? Is he all right?'

'Oh, I think so. Well… It's just that, because the private planet that only Old Atrocity knows of is so mucked up, the travails of this production are snowballing and I'm not sure the people involved can bear the tremendous weight. I *know* that *I'm* stressed. To be sure. And a thought strikes me, so uncharacteristic, I scarcely dare give it utterance. It just occurred to me: that's not my style. I'm not sure how to interact with this new, on-the-very-edge quality on set. I'm used to working on harmonious and successful pictures. What has happened, I wonder?'

'Dear fellow! It's not your fault.'

Despite the tedium of which he told, Butterbugs did rather fancy this end-of-the-day sharing with a mate. Even with Justy and Sasky, he'd never quite had it on this intimate a level before. So cheered, he rattled on.

'Quite frankly, I don't see how it could be. But things have changed. From the days of undiluted glory on the set, when scenes rolled off as easily as rain off a shellacked hog, there's now a certain detectable 'backing-up' of some kind. The emphasis is on what we *can't* do, as opposed to what we *can*. Roadblocks! Problems with intellectual approaches to the logistics and the means of interpretation. Quite frankly, it's on the director's part to realize the script's challenges. That's how things have evolved. I don't know how to articulate it more fully – yet. Bob Altman said that directing is basically problem solving. I don't know if Egaz is a problem solver or… a problem creator.'

'Of a sudden, I feel uncertain.'

'Sorry, my kettle. I didn't mean to flood your day with unwanted drama.'

'I don't know quite what to expect.'

'Do not be troubled.'

She prepped a selection of offerings from the drinks trolley that was hard by the settee, plainly glad to have some occupation for her hands, while she weighed this dynamically different angle of reportage from her ultrastar lover.

Satisfactorily exhausted by not only the tone at the studio, but with the long hours of required shooting, Butterbugs lay back on his special chair and got as comfortable as he could.

'Keenah?'

'Hmm?'

She was completely absorbed at the trolley.

'Are you – shall we say, content – with your involvement on this picture?'

She paused in her futzing.

'Sort of. I mean, I wish I had more scenes.'

There was a brief interlude of clinking glasses, stirring and swirling, and other piquant sounds.

'Keenah? There's something I want to ask you.'

'Hmm...'

'Is that OK? I mean, if I ask you something? Just that, nothing more.'

'All right.'

'Are you – well, would you be interested in, well, retirement?'

'As in – re*tire*ment? You, retiring? Me?'

'I've been thinking.'

'Are we not in our youth? You – two winters older than me. I'm not a kid, but neither am I ready for the nursing hall.'

There was a moment of silence, in which humorous opportunities were not taken up on either side.

'I was just pondering the matter.'

'What've you got to *ponder?*'

'Just a progressive change, is all.'

'But – re*tire*ment?'

'It's just that... maybe it's time to... decamp.'

'From LA?'

'Oh, I don't know...'

'Then, from... picture shows?'

'Perhaps. Maybe I've done my thing out here.'

'Oh. But I thought that...'

'Yes?'

'That, uh, well, this is my first big picture. I thought...'

'It's my biggest, too.'

'But, it's my *first*...'

'We have so much already.'

'But honey, I want a career! On the screen! I thought that... That this would be my entrance, with much more to come!'

'Why... yes. Of *course* you did.'

'I don't want to stop here, baby! Not with such a step *up*. It's only the beginning!'

'I see. Yes, I understand.'

'All the striving, the hoping, the fearing. I came from less than nothing, honey, and here I am, way up here, with you. Sure, there are problems, but I'm just starting out. I came from nowhere. Now I'm *some*where.'

'I know what you mean...'

'And... everything came together so fast, and with so much uplift. I walked on air, scarcely believing it. And when you held me, and when we actually were... you know, in front of the camera... together, and you got me to stand on my feet, and when I stood, you approved, and after you approved, you loved. And here I am, with pathways cleared, walking in pure sunshine and freedom, with wishes being granted and heads held high! I treasure all of these things, and I don't want them to go away! No, I don't. Not at all!'

Genuinely moved, Butterbugs regarded her with new insight and respect. He felt he had to explain this perceived fork in the road.

'I just thought that, in case things *go off*, there might be another life, another way in which to live within the times of our lives.'

'You mean, you expected me to – ?'

'My love, my love… !'

Neither spoke for a few moments. She left the trolley and approached him with full impact: her super-high heels imposingly resounding on the hardwood floor, her long legs fully exposed up to the mini's horizontal triangle at mid-thigh, held, further up, by the world's largest Stefan Bhreng belt buckle, her activated persona projecting, now that a challenge was in the air. It wasn't as if he were distracted by the lower half of the tour he loved to take, it was just that, for the first time in his high life, he was engaging on a truly mature level, that of committed partners, plotting their course for the future, and the debates therein. Perhaps distractions were purposeful, but because the combined years of both participants were less than sixty, youthful summaries were to be expected, amidst the attempted wisdom and its attached responsibilities.

'Butterbugs? I have to ask you something.'

'Anything, my dear.'

Then he thought:

'My God, does she look cool!'

'Well, you've been with a lot of women. Many…'

She was non-accusatory.

'That is a truth I wouldn't dream of altering. Not for any reason, let alone with you. Yes, I have, I humbly admit.'

'It's not a bad thing. I've always been impressed. And, I know why. But, you haven't seemed to remain with anyone on a… you know… sustained…'

Butterbugs suddenly looked morose.

Keenah drew close to him and massaged his dome.

'Oh, B-bugs, I'm sorry. I didn't mean to pin you to the wall.'

'No, it's OK. You were right in doing so. It's just that…' And as the emotions gathered, he almost started bawling. '…No one… struck me… as, someone to… *love* – You know, really to *love*, before you came my way. I suppose I appear callous with such a track record. Or too superficial. Or else that I'm, I don't know, a closet gay case… (Which is the first stop for speculators, I suppose…) Or something. Some… *rumor* flitting about, for P.R.'s sake!'

He scoff-laughed through his near-tears, fully knowing the truth, but feeling relieved at listing the possibilities of misinterpretation.

She laughed.

'No, Butterbugs, I think the latter one's off the list. Remember when they branded Sinatra 'gay' in Australia?'

He smiled.

'Or Ellen, as straight?'

'Come closer, roommate.'

They snuzzle-kissed and enjoyed early-afternoon intimacy.

He gathered himself. He may have done some heavyweight HMD scenes today, but who the fuck cared right now? This was real life.

He massaged her thighs with comforting pleasure. So smooth. She liked it. He loved when she wore this couture stuff around the house, but without the finishing fuss of either makeup or hose or accessories. Her hair looked like she'd just gotten up, a sexy style all its own. Fuck, she was so... Well, she always looked terrific, and so did her soul.

True relaxation was achieved.

'So Keenah, are you bored?'

'Bored. It's just that, there's so much waiting. Waiting everywhere. All the time. I'm impatient!'

'That makes complete sense. I don't blame you for a second. Pictures entail a lot of waiting around. But you know, it's not time that needs to be devoted to pensiveness or...'

He drifted off when he saw she was distracted.

'I think,' Butterbugs resumed, getting up and drawing the wispy white curtains across the LA view so as to confine their dialogue to the room at hand, 'that our perfect director is in turmoil. He is at the root of the current dilemma in production right now.'

'Oh?'

'He's staying at The Nookery today, on Boulevard d'El Fontaine de la Los Angelinos dos Temple Expiatori de la Sagrada Familia.'

He paused, with as much pregnant portent as Elia Kazan ever endowed him, the exactitude of the director's current address raising a red flag of obviousness, before continuing.

'*Go* to him, Keenah. See if you can't level him off on my behalf. He is a reasonable fellow, and brilliant. But his artistry has clouded his skills of commanding a major production. Perhaps it was too much to expect that a person of his lack of experience could manage such a gargantuan picture. I don't know who he can relate to right now. He and I are somewhat fatigued in our collaboration. The Writers Team is alienated, and the producers are disgruntled at overruns. Bronston's trembling from bad memories, but at heart he's fine with it. On the other hand, DFZ's thinking he maybe wants to scuttle. Can you imagine? They shouldn't be surprised, with all their experience, but they are. Porter's actually lost thirty-five pounds in trying to keep them from blowing out. Or bowing out. I don't know if this is a crisis or not. All I know is that Egaz isn't taking it well, obviously. He doesn't confide in me anymore. That's certainly a bad sign. You see why I'm considering alternatives?

'Yes, *go* to him. It's a brilliant idea, if I do say so. Access him on any level you can. And to modify your impact, ask something for yourself. See if you can wangle – I mean, *manage* to get – more scenes. I know he's shelved some of Lady Lutrena's best ones. Someone needs to fight for them. Like, The Lady Lutrena herself. Sawl has written a whole sub-plot concerning your character and the farmer-peasants who stage a march. It's rather superb. But Egaz, in his error, has sidelined the sequence. With a little – persuasion – he could easily shoot it in a week's time, while we retool the main unit, so to speak.'

'Sounds like *you* should take over, Butterbugs!'

'Not a chance. I'm only an observer, and maybe a bit of a critic. You have no items in the left luggage that the rest of us burden him with right now. Go to him! Besides, you are fresh right now, and I am tuckered. And you are impatient, dear girl. Take the Facel Vega. It rides smooth as the first milkin'.'

She looked at him with a responsible air of restraint, just short of doubt.

'Oh, *go* to him, Keen!'

'All right. I will. I had no idea things had reached this critical a mass.'

'Well, you haven't been on set for over a week. It's as if some tipping point was passed. Subjective stress has surfaced in diverse ways.'

'Are we all in danger, Butterbugs?'

He hesitated. He'd had no intention of indulging in these subjects just now, as his early release today was a promise to have frolic-time with his lover, but that lover was engaging him, resulting in a non-sexy shoptalk spillover. He had no choice but to be entirely transparent and reasonable.

'No, we are not, per se. Not personally, though the cast of thousands could very well be inconvenienced. But the *picture*... Well, yes, I'll be brutally frank. I think it's very much in danger. And Egaz – Egaz, is, perhaps out on a limb. I'm not sure how far out, though.'

'But, but, why?'

'Why? *Whie?* A behavior that I can only ascribe to stress has turned him into a creature of fear and equivocation. I wasn't going to say 'fear and loathing' because he hasn't been that demonstrative. Besides, Dr. Hunter S. Thompson warned me never to use that term so casually, so I won't. Suffice it to say, long-limbed lover, he is a contained person, but I know him well, and all his innuendos speak of a rising tide of overwhelming tension. If he has, say, panic attacks, they are strictly private. Regardless, he is not himself. I have tried to cover for him, but even my ultrastar status cannot prevent a meltdown, if a multi-crore picture is derailed by its commander's going all wobbly.'

'Oh, oh! Suddenly I feel so despairing!' said his beautiful co-star. 'Would that we were all sprites with angelic powers, so that sparkle-dust or some efficacious substance could be cast out into the air above the needy one, so that its matter could settle into the pores of both head and hands, and the troubled person would be freed of his yoke. Then he could emerge, refreshed for the heavy tasks ahead. Alas! If it were *only* but so!'

Butterbugs gazed at this remarkable girl, who was not merely someone whom he loved, but just at this moment, with her face turned toward the æther of her recited wishes, she took on a sort of transcendental quality, possibly proof that she indeed possessed some of the extraordinary talent she desired to wield.

'Go to him, Keenah. Oh, *go to him!* See if you can save him. Oh Keenah, please! In pure pragmatic terms, if nothing else, he is essential at this juncture. Too much of the picture has been shot for a replacement to come in. But high up, closer to where money lives, it's possible. Besides, that's the last thing all of us want! How could we, ever! We love him, and he loves us. But a cloud has come to settle over the land. Go to him now, and return when you deem the task completed to your satisfaction. You will know.'

She turned and drew into a CU with him.

'Butterbugs, my Butterbugs! You are so *good!* For that alone you deserve your singular status in the world.'

'No more words between us now, dear thing. Time to go. To *him!* Plenty of opportunity for our love to flow without valve or meter. Right now we have a picture to save. Do your wondrous best, and convey my love, felicitations, and respect to our perfect and beloved director.'

'I will, perfect and beloved fellow, and thank you for the opportunity.' She gave him a smacker that smashed the formality, and as she receded toward the exit, he called out,

'I love the way you move, Keen-neen-ah!'

Then she giggled.

'*What* was that address again? Of The Nookery?'

'Ah! 1349986 Boulevard d'El Fontaine de la Los Angelinos dos Temple Expiatori de la Sagrada Familia – Mansion #2. Can't miss it!'

She turned and gave a fluff-wave, then dissolved into light evanescence, as befitted her sprightly nature and mission.

He hopped up and opened the curtains, then positioned his chair so as to scan the plains below, which he did without benefit of magnification.

'Keee-nah! Keee-nah!' he breathed, and officially kicked back into glorious neutrality.

For a few moments he actually felt like a producer, what with the political assistance he had just rendered his director and all. Plus, relying on his girlfriend to be an agent of change in this task was a genuine power-play worthy of exec producers, or even studio heads. He thought of Hyman Goth in his supreme dictatorial position, meting out destiny to all who performed under his suzerainty, and the security he must feel as a result.

'Hy Goth, Emperor of Hollywood! For life!' he mused.

No one could quibble over the paternalistic power of Hyman Goth, but at this moment, it would take someone of his stature to approach Butterbugs, sitting back in his working-class mode of exhaustion after the day's work, and declare, 'Butterbugs, you have *trillions* now. Why don't you simply *buy* 'Unholy War Hymn' and make it your own? Save it on your own terms, above the storm & strife of

Industrial pettiness! And while you're at it, why don't you just buy the rest of Hollywood, and save us from ourselves…!'

But the ultrastar didn't have any such person on his doorstep right now, and besides, he didn't think like that. He just wasn't that kind of guy. He was the kind of guy who saw a friend in trouble, and sent help.

Yes, he had sent his most treasured person on Earth over to parlay and heal the wounded soul now on trial. It was mid-afternoon. She would be back by quittin' time at 5:00 or so, for certain.

It was no longer mere rumor that 'UWH' was in crisis. Circumstances had turned on a dime, into the realms of misfires, bad luck, questionable juju factors, and an absence of grace under pressure.

'Have I caused these things?' he asked himself.

'I was fourteen minutes late one morn, when my Trapezio wouldn't start without pushing it. I told Egaz that his curly locks were particularly oily one day. He didn't take it as an insult, because I've commented previously that I think the coconut oil application gives his hair a refreshing appearance. No, couldn't be those things…'

He checked to see if anything was on color television, and nothing was, so he repaired to the terrace with a Penguin of 'Bouvard et Pecuchet', the one with all his margin notes, but he couldn't exactly concentrate, regardless of the hilarity.

Perhaps there were issues in the current 'UWH' fluxus that had been kept even from him. The sort of money and/or logistic matters that filmmakers suspect artistic types won't understand.

'Oh, but I *do* understand,' he stage-whispered. 'And I've always known what the principal angle is. Everybody's got an angle. Including me. That's not a cynical point of view. It just *is*. But then, why am I so accepting?'

He happened to look up at that moment and behold an urn of Bellenkhand/ Choo Brand horseradish. A yellowish scum rimmed the opening and a couple of youth-flies pizzed dismally around its orbit.

'I'm sick of that flavor…' He sounded like a spoiled child. 'In more ways than one. Besides, I just don't need it anymore.'

It had been a few days since he had 'dosed-up'. Coincidental to the malaise at the studio?

Sip-sip-sip. Keenah knew all the right tricks of the vermouth in constructing her martinis. Just a bit of tipsiness encapsulated his brain at this midday hour. It was fun. Liberating, too. For so long Butterbugs had devoted his waking nanoseconds to the craft of the drama, and this, the first impasse of sorts, had been cause to set him down in another room entirely. No wonder he was pondering such matters as a potential non-strolling player life – whatever that could mean.

Was this then, the real Butterbugs – he who was now likkered up and all de-horseradished, who sent his prize girlfriend out on a fixit mission? Well, it was a Butterbugs in love, and love's a catalyst stronger than a mountain of quartz.

Along about 3:00, the afternoon atmosphere was thickening and worsening. Such conditions allowed for more compelling light-plays to experimentally frolic over the madness on the grid below. The super limited-access telephony instrument rang.

'Yoe.'

'Butterbugs?'

'Sah-nee?'

It was indeed Sonny – Projector-type – but the star was a little disadvantaged by lyrical snooziness, and all things were daydreamlike and matinee-tinted, and not a little liqueur-syrup'd.

'Awake!'

'Sonny?'

'It is.'

'What, ho?'

'Home?'

'That's... I think, why I answered the super limited-access phone.'

'Early to home, then?'

'I'm awake Sonny, trust me. What's shakin'?'

'Well, I'll tell you. I take it you're sitting down.'

'I'm prone, in fact.'

'Mr. Drunk-so-early-in-the-morning?'

'Why you – I'm nothing of the sort. And anyway, it's approaching late afternoon. What time zone are you in?'

'I just left the cultural hearth of my homeland.'

'Super! I was just down Suriname-way a short time ago and –'

'Yeah, I saw you on Davies Mark's worldly-broadcast show. Made a fucking sap-filled pinwheel out of yourself, did you not?'

'Guess that's what happens when you're in love. But say, Sonny, you don't exactly sound yourself. So, how's Bolivia?'

'I just told you. I left it, lover-boy.'

'Oh, oh, oh, oh, oh.'

'I'm holed up, I tell you. And you'd better not tell anybody else, that's for bloody-ben sure.'

'I swear it.'

'Upon the book.'

'Sonny, I'm not near any Holy Scriptures at this charted moment. There's a copy of the 'UWH' script over in the bedroom...'

'On a telephone book then, ya jackass! On *any* book!'

'OK. I swear it. I used the Peeper's Corner Phone Pamphlet that was a prop in 'Harold Of The Country' (Mega|Goth). Remember?'

'You crude oaf!'

'You are surely stressed, Sonny.'

'I surely am, Answer-Man!'

'Thus, your sarcasm.'

'And my meanness.'

'That, too. So, you are in an aircraft after having vacated the high Bolivian plateau?'

'No, you flimp. I'm across the border. I'm… in… well, Paraguay.'

'A place of habitation, or in the wastes of the Chaco?'

'Well, if you must know…'

'Yes? Sonny, I might *have* to know, depending on what you fancy telling me.'

'I guess so.'

'I'm glad your stress is lessening as we chat, Sonny. And your sarcasm has practically vanished.'

'I'm huddling in a tin chair set upon gravel, in front of a beat-up card table, with a tiny demitasse of *mate*, spiked with palm alcohol, at a tawdry cantina-cum-cerveza hall. A crooked kettle of firewater steams over a smoldering corn-sheaf fire.'

'You mean the tavern has gravel flooring?'

'Sí. I mean, yeah. It used to be an abattoir.'

'Why ever are you having *mate* in a demitasse instead of a calabash?'

'It's because I'm Hollywoodized and don't give a damn about local customs right at this particular moment.'

'And where –'

'All right. I'll reveal the locale. Keenah isn't there with you, is she?'

'Negative. I sent her over to Egaz.'

'Oh, great! That's *all* we need, now!'

'I don't follow you, Sonny.'

'Skip it. I'm in General Eugenio A. Garay.'

'Ah yes, I know it well.'

'I figured.'

'You must be at the El Tinko Cantina y Taverna y Cerveza Palacio! One of my *favorites*.'

'Uh-huh.'

'What is it that you wanted to tell me, Sonny?'

'My agency, Butterbugs. It's – my agency. Associates & Ultra-Creators Agency for Management – or Sonny's Trip – whatever the fuck you wanna call it these days, is in gothic horrorshow trouble. Penny's in jail. His habeas corpus was revoked. We're in deep dark doo-doo in River City.'

'How could A&U-CAM be sunk?? How could they imprison your son? Why was Penny arrested? Drug world?'

'I should say NOT. He was at table in office when the Feds arrived. I was already fleeing country. We were lighting out until this thing blows over. Or up. He was supposed to follow, anon. His single-allowed phone call was to ME, Butterbugs! Doesn't that just make you weep? And I didn't say that A&U-CAM was sunk. Cooked, maybe.'

'Sonny, steady. Steady, Sonny. You've got to tell me what this all means. What it *means*.'

473

'Since I'm in a safe place, and since the encryption on our communicators will last for an hour after I utter these lines, I will tell you my innermost thoughts. The NSA shall not have us!'

'What about Justy?'

'Justina's too damn busy with her 'Central African Empire' to even acknowledge my tears.'

'Go ahead.'

'From my Inner Sanctum do I now pour forth to thee.'

The ultrastar saw no reason to continue bantering, but his breath was bated.

'Butterbugs, do you know a fellow named DeVault Lurgan?'

'Why, why yes. He's that guy from the All-American Institute of Responsible Famous People.'

'The very one. He's a pus-licking, fangless, sex-neuter, dirty snake-tit.'

'I thought he was a fairly pleasant personality, who –'

'He's been infiltrating my stable – sorry, my agency, and futzing with my studs – I mean, my clients.'

'Despite the terminology, I know what you're saying, Sonny.'

'Yeah, well… I ran into this Lurgan fucker at Stav Quintrum 'n' Bob Evans' place. Big cocktail/pool party. You missed that one. It was great, except for the fact that Lurgan was casing me out. When I called him on it, he branded me as – get this – *anal retentive!* Just because I was getting into detailed questioning about the shit he was pulling. So I said, right in his rotting face, 'If *I'm* anal retentive, I guess that makes you *rectal retentive*. You know, *further in*, back with the residual shit.' All he could come back with was, 'Where'd they get this guy?' So I shot him down with, 'Probably *not* the same place where they got *you*, which was under a 55-gallon drum of greasy weasel 'n' ferret vomit, combined with slime scraped from dead whales washed up on Bikini atoll after the nuke blast.' He just slanked away, while Stav, Bob, Babs Rilplay and I yukked up a storm. That FUCKER!! I *hate* him! You should, too!'

'Slank.'

'What??'

'Slank. Slank away, not slanked.'

'Fuck-shit! *Whatever!!?*'

'You really *are* stressed, friend.'

'Yeah, well, it's pretty damn shocking to have a subversive in your midst.'

'DeVault Lurgan? I don't think DeVault's ever attempted to futz with me.'

'He's a slim customer, pal. Has he been to your studio bungalow?'

'Why yes. Several times.'

'Then you're perhaps cooked as well. HOLY SHIT!!! HE GOT MY BIGGEST CLIENT!'

'Easy, Sonny. Shrieking wears down your mobile battery faster. I'm not sure about BattPaque purchase or recharge in the El Tinko Cantina y Taverna y Cerveza Palacio, or for that matter, in beautiful downtown General Eugenio A. Garay, *or region*, for that matter.'

'No worries. I have my MegaBattPaque.'

'Then go ahead and shriek.'

'Lurgan is a hidden agent for both the HETSA and TMG. Have you any idea what that means?'

'So, he's a Homeland Enforcement Total Security Agency guy, AND a Tarpit Mercenary Groups actuary? Are you sure?'

'Never more so. The evidence is staggering.'

'Why, that miserable liar!'

'You're in the danger loop too, my son.'

'Uh…'

'Those bungalow visits? Did he spend any time alone there?'

'Why yes. I'd be coming off set. He'd be there with a welcoming beverage in his hand and ready for a cheerful chat on how to be responsibly famous. Hy Goth wanted him to genially circulate at the studio.'

'He'd be there right now with a rope in his hand, ready to string you up, if you went down there at this minute.'

'But Paris, Lindsay, Beyoncé, Taylor, Rihanna, and even Britney recommended him.'

'That makes six more sweet innocents in the loop! I swear, the tide is rising!'

'How could he have been that kind of a person, and just *whie?*'

'No doubt he rifled through all your secrets in the bungalow, photographed them, and air-wired them to both his central controls.'

'Secrets? What secrets?'

'To DeVault Lurgan and the dual monoliths he represents, ye are one subversive puppy, Butterbugs.'

'And you?'

'I am my agency. A&U-CAM represents you. They came after me first.'

'Came? For what?'

'Butterbugs, can you wing off to Jambutterbugsabad at the earliest?'

'I can be at Bronston's private airstrip in about forty-two minutes.'

'The second we hang up, which will be when I finish this sentence, LEAVE.'

Sonny hung up.

In about fifty minutes, the ultrastar was buckling up in Sam's VroomStar Meridian-To-Meridian jet, which taxied and took off across the Pacific without further ado.

Thank heavens that Judah Fitz-Judah, Sonny's on-the-road associate, who virtually lived out of an attaché case, was a fellow passenger. Before even a handshake, Judah handed him a thick packet.

'Welcome aboard, Butterbugs.'

Now the handshake.

'Sonny appreciates your loyal trust. You might've thought that you were being kidnapped if he hadn't contacted you first. That's why he had to cross over into Paraguay, where his phone coverage kicked in.'

'Otherwise?'

'Otherwise I would have had to compel you to come with me, though I would not have been able to provide you with an adequate explanation until we would be in the air. You would have protested.'

Butterbugs presumed, correctly, that Sonny's associate was packing heat.

'And what if I do protest now? How do I know we're going to Jambutterbugsabad? What is this, pre-production for a Matt Helm picture?'

'I don't believe Mr. Dean Martin has been contracted to do any more of that series. We are indeed headed to Jambutterbugsabad. And because you aren't *actively* protesting now, I conclude that you won't start, unless there is something that is not to your satisfaction on this flight. Would you care for refreshments?'

'As long as you don't slip me a mickey...'

'That's very funny, Butterbugs. I'll bring a trolley. I suggest that you turn to the packet I have handed you, for some instructional reading as to the situation at hand. You will note that the seal has not been broken on it, and that Mr. Projector's thumbprint, which you surely recognize, is plainly impressed in the wax.'

Sure enough, he recognized his agent's thumb in the red concave image.

'I am uninformed as to any further data in this matter,' Judah continued. 'But Mr. Projector has assured me that you will brief me, as per the enclosed instructions.'

Butterbugs was not particularly dazed by this sequence of events. It reminded him of the comfortable roles he had played in several spy pictures, which ranged from comedic to harrowing.

But this was real. And, apparently, serious.

There, in the warm LED rays of the every-seat-a-first-class-seat's reading lamps, standing out against the rest of the empty exec cabin in which he sat, with the soothe of a carrot, celery and Old Man Cuisine Hot Sauce cocktail, Butterbugs abandoned the picture show imaginings of the greater situation in which he now found himself, and instead, dove into the role of 'traveling businessman with a lot of material to cover before the banal conference at the exotic location that awaited him'.

Sonny's thumb-seal yielded but reluctantly to his earnest scrapings, and for a time he contemplated ringing up the tall, blonde, miniskirted Aussie hostess ('G'day! I'm Joby. I'll be serving all your needs on this trip; welcome aboard!'), who could probably provide a Juggosch breaker hammer if needed, but he managed to pry it open with the plastic stir stick that accompanied his pleasure-beverage. What he found within threatened to twist his canines and make his hair hurt.

Here, gathered by Sonny's operatives on many levels, was an array of exhibits that proved the urgency of the somewhat dubious call from the agitated individual down in General Eugenio A. Garay in Paraguay. With growing obviousness, these preliminaries were a legitimate warning, but positively understated as far as the associated implications were concerned.

Document after document, photo after photo, testimony after testimony, each offered proof beyond a shadow of a doubt that certain elements in the Con Murn Administration (that is, the President of the United States of America) had very specific reasons to target he, Butterbugs, and all those associated with his enterprises and his pictures. The reasons why remained to be exhibited. His life in general was profiled in digest form, both public and private, in cheap, typed, mimeographed form. There was something about a 'Person Extraordinary', and mention of an 'Enemy of the People', but they couldn't possibly be references to *him*.

Then, sensibly placed at the rear of the collection, as if the viewer would surely weary of the voluminous presentation of tiny example after tiny example, of how the subject of this file's character must and shall be *assassinated*, an identifiable Conclusion appeared, in photocopy form, on cerise paper.

(The eminently discreet Judah, by his skill and instinct, was actually able to refrain from reading any of the text during the assembly of this packet. He would remain so, until green-lighted to peruse the material for legal purposes by Sonny – or Butterbugs.)

'Person Extraordinary' and 'Enemy of the People' stood out on the page. There they were again. Those very terms painted a stark portrait of the éminence grise, therein:

A Non-Conclusive

Conclusion

*(as the **Person** Concerning these here **Points**
continues to operate, uninterrupted)*

For The

Times
To Date

Some reasons listed for this particular treatment (see Exhibit #4456 for recommendations and partial solutions) are these:

Preamble: This is a testament to a threat that must be seen to, as soon as possible.

1. Because he raises consciousness among the masses

1a. Because he has proven himself to be a **Person Extraordinary**, whom the world willingly brands an 'ultrastar', a term we as a group refuse to recognize as legitimate

1b. Because all signs show that he, as **Person Extraordinary**, in ways in no way conducive to our interests, merits the only label that may be applied to him, as a result of the grouped offenses contained in this list and in countless other files: an **Enemy of the People**

1c. Because the preceding charge is a very solemn charge, it is made because the charge is irrefutably true

(**1d. – 1m.** deleted)

1n. Because the term **Enemy of the People** has been coined by us as a group and used here for the first time ever, the phrase shall have to be copyrighted, if not patented

2. Because he instills hopeful and troubling aspirations into the peoples of the world that might confound them and fill them with false and restless, and *dangerous*, desires

2a. Because he dizzies the peoples of the world up

3. Because he is undeniably attractive to most peoples of the world

4. Because he is not particularly identified with causes or concerns in concert with the present US administration or their associates

5. Because he is an oddball, and we do not know how to deal with oddballs

5a. Because he cavorts and associates with other oddballs, some more odd and dangerous than he is, including freaks, weirdos, lesbians, uppity negroes, artist-types, homosexuals, the gays, strange minorities, and geographers

5b. Because he is an oddball, and we do not know how to deal with oddballs in ways harmonious with causes or concerns in concert with the present US administration or their associates

6. Because he has mightily-charged sex appeal to women, who look up to him

7. Because his influence on people transcends race, creed, or policy

7a. Because he is particularly adept in influencing people of great attractiveness and power in the entertainment industry; this is especially troubling in that attractive persons command respect amongst the people, who look up to them and aspire to their status and influence

7b. Because, while he generally appears in pretty good pictures, if not artistically outstanding, that is all the more reason to point out this **Enemy's** rivalistic and envy-inducing characteristics, for they cause anguish to sensitive minds

7c. Because, by exhibiting remarkable excellence in all he does, he makes others feel like worthless failures

8. Because he is currently involved in a very big way with a motion picture that can only be labeled as subversive

8a. Because there might be evidence that he is in collusion with an **Enemy of the People** in another undisclosed country

8b. Because of his attributes of influence and importance, as well as his celebrity, he could use all those things as a cover to engage in covert activities of the most maddening kind

(**8c. – 8q.** deleted)

8r. Because we do not like subversive threats

(**8s. – 8dd.** deleted)

9. Because he stands to be able to marshal great masses of the populace, if he so chooses

10. Because it is the universal conclusion by all agencies, operatives, consultants and participants in the interests of the Murn Administration and its Associated Partners, that he must be apprehended in his progress of influence immediately, and without delay; prejudice of even the extreme kind may be employed in the enactment of this mission

11. Because said 'mission', briefly alluded to and outlined in Point #**10**, is duly recognized as legitimate; similarly, it is duly made official by all participants in this concerned study, none of whom will be mentioned here, for security, legal, and religious reasons

Conclusion: BECAUSE of the preceding eleven points and their codicils, and many others besides, it must be ascertained without a doubt that Butterbugs and his people pose a major threat to the interests of most of the enterprises of the world; therefore, it is recommended that he be stopped

Postamble: This is a testament to a threat that must be seen to, as soon as possible.

(signed)

(Over 800 signatures of parties interested in the *Elimination of Butterbugs as a Threat to the Progression of Purposeful Interests of the World, Inc.* a.k.a. 'EBTP-PIW, Inc.'; additional sheets attached.)

N.B. Additional signatures or 'x'-marks available upon request, pending security clearance and security rating results of requestor(s).

'Why,' thought Butterbugs, 'I've never seen such absolute nonsense. Questionably drafted, terribly written, amateurly assumed. Plus, they haven't even read Ibsen!'

He didn't tear-up or choke-up. Didn't even bother. He knew he was innocent. But he also knew that, in the eyes of the signatory parties, he was guiltier than shit.

Each point was initialed by high-up officials in the Murn Administration, or by Dark Side players whose names were not known to the public. 'C.M.' appeared most often, along with 'M.R.' in second place.

'Who the fuck are they?' scoffed Butterbugs. It didn't yet occur to him that such initials indicated the POTUS himself, and way down the order of precedence, his Assoc. Sec'y of Defense…

As he scanned the material, Butterbugs held his jaw from dropping, and tried to pay attention to the level of his beverage, so that when Joby the hostess came back, he would be able to answer her caring inquests coherently instead of the drooly *gah-gah goo-goo, blaaap!* response these documents tempted him to make.

In the background of his mind was a sort of cycloramic pride in causing this sort of consternation with people he didn't admire, but the deep trouble in all the implications therein was nothing to take casually. So, he was largely aghast, more than anything else.

'You know,' said Judah coolly, noting that Butterbugs had taken a break from the packet's zapping effects. 'I'll bet Sonny restrained himself as far as his commenting on some of those issues. He has interests in several of these listed parties' concerns. But I would fault him not. I council patience. I know that Sonny would place his heart on a stake, to present to you, as proof of his loyalty, if it were the only gesture he was allowed, before expiring. As legal council, I believe him! You must understand, that as a businessman in a very big business indeed, Sonny has ethical choices he must make. But I am confident he will not only make the right choice, you will see him as a new man, a man reborn, with all the awareness of one who focuses on the things that matter in life – and little else.'

'An intriguing assessment, Judah Fitz-Judah. I'm sure you're right. I would rather have Sonny come clean than to remain in the hinterland of uncertain discernment. I hope my famous last words do *not* consist of: 'I completely trust him, yet!' I want such words to last, but I do not want them to be famous, naturally.'

'Of course. Being a player in pictures, you are used to all sorts of scenarios. I imagine your imagination is constantly heightened to accommodate all the scripted possible plots that pertain to your ultra capabilities. I must say, Butterbugs, I am in awe of you. This, from a member of A&U-CAM, who does not at all deal with people face-to-face, but instead relies on principles and practices to steer policy and persons in their proper direction. All from the luxury bastion of my telefoon, tapboard, mouse-cage and cyclopæan monitor. Well, I guess I don't know... I...'

Such was a man used to splendid isolation from his perceived humanism. Butterbugs beheld him amidst the turbulence from a thermal updraft launched from Spukka Island in the eastern North Pacific, below.

The plane pitched, and because Judah was no more a globe-trotter than he was a people person, it was all the more remarkable that his footing was altered so that he was rendered diagonally off his feet, from the aisle into the avenue of Butterbugs' spacious long-range comfort zone.

Conventions were shaken loose, especially after the turbulence died down and retired into the more characteristic Pacifist long haul's welcome dullness.

Judah came to rest amidst Butterbugs' outstretched legs.

Like the Mobile Director Chair option available on 1967 Imperial motor cars, each row on this BronstonAir craft was, with the shift of a lever, capable of swiveling round to face the row behind, lest diplomats of both statecraft or artcraft chanced to engage in council on these voyages. Too bad then, that Judah, obviously in need of hobnobbing in order to compare notes of loneliness with someone else, instead chose to remain in the landed position that turbulence wrought, and as the seconds ran out in which to laughingly apologize and realign oneself, he remained in actual bodily contact with the sole ultrastar on (or aloft, from) the planet at this moment in time.

By his gaze at Judah did Butterbugs allow the agent to forget his post and behave as a normal human being.

And because he'd never had such a chance on a business trip before, all pretensions of professionalism suddenly fled.

'I... I need to kiss someone...,' Judah said, his teeth clenched.

'In the circumstances, in these limited surroundings, I guess then, let it be me,' said Butterbugs, his empathy reaching pragmatic proportions.

They were hours and hours away from being even 25,000 feet over Siem Reap, where numerous creatures of service were handily located, but they weren't stopping there, as this craft had the capacity to sail halfway round the world without refueling (thus the 0 to 180 degrees Meridian-to-Meridian ploy).

In the world of entertainment, the full spectrum of life's preferenced variations comes into play, as a matter of course. Butterbugs was no stranger to these wavelengths. In many of his roles he'd played kinksters and pervs and philanderers and queers, be they ever so noble or disgusting or sympathetic. Yet, his personal choices for his own love life tended to be conventional, though with many successive partners, as his Keenah so recently pointed out.

Here though, was the passion of Judah, a plain indicator of a stressed-out, repressed-out individual, who merely needed some living lips to press, though what it would lead to was uncertain. Like everything else in his world right now, Keenah and thoughts of her lovin' form went right out of his head. Nothing mattered but the moment, because, when one is in a plane heading west, after having decamped out of an emergency, with the future holding little but anticipatory apprehension, despite the fact that one of them was an ultrastar, all sorts of permissiveness might be considered. If, for no other reason, than to savor the moment, Omar Khayyam-style, and the only way to do it was with what was at hand.

'You may kiss me now,' the star almost said, reflecting lines he'd spoken as the gay King Pukus of the Durrazzo Crusaders, in Martin Ransohoff's production of 'The Brave, The Bold and the Beautiful' (RKO), directed by George Stevens. In that part he'd 'had relations' with Sean Connery (as Richard), Bob Redford (as Emperor Alexis), Matt Dillon (as Sir Jean d'Azy), Omar Sharif (as Saladin) and McParken Janeway (as Peter the Hermit), and it had been no big deal. Acting is acting, when reality has to be constructed on a movie set. Aside from any etiquette applicable to the situation, there was also the need – Butterbugs' own need – for a bit of distraction, given the drastic changes in this one very long, very weird day. What better than sex?

So, despite the temptation to bring logic to this progression by verbalizing its legitimacy, Butterbugs said nothing, and when Judah saw that the star's lips were plainly invitational, he made his move.

Like a hunky lead, the agent gave in to his current desires and glided into contact area with the green-lighted guy reclining on the first-class chair. It was a kiss that was manly but judicious, heartwarming rather than lust-filled, a simple statement of honesty that fit with the moment. Everything was on the level. No sub-currents.

Now Judah was quite a handsome fellow, but Butterbugs, truth to tell, wasn't, for lack of a better term, very inspired by his bodily presence. Homophobic he was not, not even when he was faced with this prospect in private. Closeness is closeness, but it has to be right. Orgasms were special to him, as he was a romantic. The ladies were his thing, from start to finish, and he had nothing to prove. After all, in the past 24 hours, he had seen one of the hottest women in Hollywood without her clothes on, and he had touched her, too. It wasn't as if mere closeness to a generic body, regardless of gender, got him going. For Judah's tastes he could not speak, but he had an idea that might just tip the scales in a direction he, Butterbugs, might feel rather more comfortable with.

Judah, debonair exec that he was, always used to dealing with showbiz VIPs, turned out to be mannered enough to open his eyes after the kiss of generosity, and he saw the ultrastar's face closer than any CU he'd ever seen on the silver screen. Instead of being intimidated, he felt as if Butterbugs was just a normal guy, the type of fellow that, well, he'd like to be with. Because, right now, the revelation had been exposed, and the verdict was in…

However, because this was such a shake-up flight for he and his agent-at-hand, the thing that Butterbugs now enacted made him relax and feel the beauty of young bodies in concert.

The alleged 'Enemy of the People' pressed the call button on his special chair, and in about one and a half shakes of a lamb-i-kin's tail, Joby the Aussie, premiere hostess, was on the aisle. She saw the two guys together and didn't bat an eyelash. Though she privately and very professionally reveled in the remarkableness of the world's sole ultrastar and a dreamy agent both in sensual poses. This remarkableness got her own moist and tender responses up and running – with potential for coffee, tea or me extracurriculars, *but only if requested*. After all, strict conventions regarding her duties provided for her to engage such requests *if she herself consented to them*. That's what she loved about the premium life of jet-serving out of Dubai, on whatever private craft she hopped on: everybody wins. Producer Sam Bronston, her usual charge on this craft, was a genuine family man of preferred restraint. Nevertheless, this was the high-level domain of adults with needs, where mutuality could interact with mutability, with pleasing results for all.

Joby was hip to whatever applied on a given flight. Renderings of an intimate nature were gratis; tips not accepted. No call girls these. They made their own decisions. Tonight it was Butterbugs and associate. How top-flight was that? She was a little surprised that the ultrastar was gay, but any pull into judgmentalism was nonexistent past that. For all she knew, they could be rehearsing a scene or something, and she required no explanation. Besides, any reportage of it would never go past her magnificent frontage. Her short Oz-blondie hair was done up in one of those period shag cuts that nicely capped her verticality with perfectly reasonable gorgeousness, making her a vicereine as much as a care-giver on a private jet. Such top-notch flight attendants drew inevitable comparisons to your basic cheekboney supermodel, but it wasn't just the required proficiency in a minimum of five flight-path languages, or the expected masters degree in linguistics, or political science, or history, or art that made them qualified for this rarefied level of jetting hereabouts. There was also something *alternative* about them, a higher-honed intellect, a look of transcendence, that fit well with their lofty locations during a working day. Not to mention the bearing of distinction they invariably carried with them. On the whole, a compelling and undeniably attractive combination to have for a person you want on your side.

'Joby?'

'Yes, Butterbugs. What can I help you with?'

'Would you care to join us?'

The palm that had spread before the Roman masses in 'At Last, Hail!' (Bronston) and currently employed in the world's most wondrous production ('UWH'), gently gestured to this six-foot-three hostess-with-the-mostest. She smiled the smile of an efficient and canny specialist to all sorts of VIP needs.

Joby then strutted towards them up the wide aisle, her working girl's heels enabling a rather haughty high-step, as an announcement of her intentions. Drawing nigh to Judah, who was now reclining in the chair across the aisle from Butterbugs, she raised her miniskirt, which was joined with her tony top, and twirled about for examination. Providentially, she was pantyless, causing Butterbugs to marvel, 'Boy, they think of everything!'

Butterbugs discreetly eyed his companion across the way so that Joby could follow the innuendo, which had to remain wordless. She saw the signal and instantly knew the score: friend of ultrastar needs a warm encounter on a lonely flight.

After all, when a guy makes a pass at another guy, it can often mean that he's agog at the hostess at hand, but he's too shy to show her, so he 'asks' a buddy to do it for him. Butterbugs was only too happy (if that was indeed the case) to help out.

Joby then bent over Judah, her D-cleavage highing into view, her butt cleavage making itself known to Butterbugs, here as an afterthought. Since gentlemen usually react to the non-orificial simplicity of breasts as the first front in sizing up a lady, Joby's instincts were wholly appropriate and hopefully pleasing to her second-foremost passenger's desires. In the midst of her show, she was getting a bit choked up. Bringing pleasure to others was a heartfelt passion that, when she saw admittedly obvious signs of its happening, she wanted to melt all over the observer. For to bond with someone rather than cause strife was one of her dearest standards in life. How lucky, she thought of herself right now, that she could share her rather spectacular endowments with appreciators who sought sincere connectivity. She detected nothing but that one objective right now, so her earnestness was embodied in a really stunning display of admirable female physicality. She always felt empowered, but never manipulative. This was how she projected her love of humanism.

Slight but confident smile on her lips, she worked her hands along Judah's well-haired chest, across his stomach, and then indulged in some grope choreography. She made both wrinklings and smoothings over and around his trousered crotch, but after she'd done her job of assessment, with sensual add-ons like knowing eyes, brushing her bangs off her forehead, heavy breathing (easily heard due to the aircraft's state-of-the-art cabin's quietude), and some bodily twirling and organic exhibition, she concluded that she wasn't the center of the known universe for Judah Fitz-Judah at this time. Girl views, girl tastes, and girl scents were not his thang.

No worries; she put two and 2 together and knew what then to do. Full-but-non-Botoxed lips came together and pressed against Judah's, offering naught but non-French friendliness, which she felt as perfectly cordial and appreciated, but not conducive to further progress in any predictable campaign. His flaccidity was explainable and helpful to her.

Therefore, with all the style of a supreme Monna Vanna, Joby, by a few low-key signals of approving facial expression and polite acknowledgment to Judah, turned on the balls of her feet and zeroed in on the actor. A little showy wiggle's worth drew obvious response from the region of the ultra's private parts, and pieces flew into place with all the alacrity of a fly-apart puzzle, reborn through understanding.

Autobahn-smooth the flight was, and whisper-quiet, exquisitely perfect for Joby's sage course of action. Therefore, having pantsed the ultrastar where he reclined, by way of an ever-so-slight domineering of a woman who knows what she wants, Butterbugs lay exposed to this private club with as much willingness as a man was wont to show.

Sure enough, the stage now set, Judah rose to the occasion now that circumstances were congenial to his just-stepping-out-of-the-closet expedition. He spied Butterbugs' offering and had no choice but to face his own honesty. Thus informed, Joby did her expert utmost to keep Butterbugs' equipment exposed enough for the attorney/agent to get high over its exhibition, while at the same time performing stellar action on the VIP of this voyage, making sure every aspect of excitement was extracted from his diversion-needy physique.

Stealing sidelong glances whilst sucking Butterbugs' dick, Joby, with her boyish hair and demi-butch expression, saw the almost-writhing of Judah as a sure sign that he was on his way to fulfillment, without any embarrassment of not being true to himself, or putting Butterbugs in an unwanted position.

She thought, 'I can well imagine the warming of a hooker's heart-cockles, what with giving this much satisfaction to others, by every means, emanating from my sexy talents.'

Where was it written that a girl serving these lucky ducks in a private flight couldn't derive deep pleasure from a bit of extra service if that service be delivered within honorable and mutually-beneficial conditions? The closest she had come before this was with some aged but randy-wishing CEO asking, 'May I just kiss you on the cheek and pat your bottom? Then I will cease and desist.' Why, that had been cause to almost question her value as a human being. How she had wanted to give him much more than that, whether as a tribute to his late wife, or as a salute to his fleeting love of feminine things, that so enhanced an otherwise cruel world. But now, here, being freely-drilled by the ultrastar beneath her, Joby had attained a certain grace in the esoteric atmosphere in which she worked. The purity of æsthetics was where the truest of cultures could not only be born, but thrive.

On top of Butterbugs, first one way, and then the other, without missing his beat, Joby rode the actor, her skirt rising higher and higher, until for a few moments it was like a Magritte image of a face masked without explanation, until pop! the garment was ejected by her long arms, and all could then see her startling beauty revealed as the realizer of these men's potentials. No tattoos or piercings, either. Just pure outback tangibles in action.

'Bravo to the growing-up culture of Broken Hill!' Butterbugs hooted, whether she was actually from there or not. (She was, in fact, from Woollygollygoongah.)

His choices made early on in observing who really mattered in this exchange, Judah was the first to splooge into the sick-bag he'd sensibly employed. Meanwhile, across the way, Butterbugs built his climax on the pyramid of cares and metaphorical baggage, collected since the onset of this flight, so that the tantric head of bursting climax, spreading itself from his groin up to the lantern of his dome, was enough to heal him of recent hurt. In fact, it successfully created enough scab tissue to withstand any picking, likely in any ordeal to come, at least for a while. Surely this was the case.

For her own part, Joby thought Butterbugs' fuck was divine. She came quietly, in a quintet of earthquakes, en route to his own impending but compact mælström, and it was good that the aircraft was as straight-arrow as it was, as the three sensualists brought forth enough turbulence to require instrument-only navigation as a way out of a vortex.

Meanwhile, as Butterbugs and Joby (and Judah) were getting it on 33,000 feet over the Pacific, Keenah and Egaz, coming into a very similar and universally-desired congress of intimacy, realized they were absolutely and unquestionably in love with each other, and the dam having burst, consummated that fact with a cathartic love-make that sealed their new bond.

When Butterbugs landed at the private Jambutterbugsabad airstrip, he gave Keenah a ring on his mobile.

53.

Alarm,
Or,
The Tocsin

'**M**y love! My life! My very dearest notion in all this world! It's me, Butterbugs! Lovely girl! Keenah, my blessed! Are you well? Are you safe? Do you miss me? Are you in love??'

'Butterbugs?'

The connection was silvery-clear.

'Oh, love of my life, how very good it is to hear your vox! Are you OK?'

A meditative light glowed off the grandiose cliffs that always reduced the mammoth sets and cranes and walls of the studios of Jambutterbugsabad to a sort of – nothing – especially this time of day. If a camera pulled back from an extreme CU of Butterbugs, while he was on the phone to his lady-love, it would not be long before his form would be swallowed up in the confluent perspectives, as they blended their pixels to unite in the much greater context of nature's palisades, which kept the Makran protected from humankind. He sat on a low wall, separating the outskirts of the studio from the maze of nullahs and scars that filled the waste ground before the yawning heights. He was so absorbed by the object of his conversation that his gaze only went as far as the powdery earth, directly at his feet.

'OK? Why, yes,' Keenah replied.

'Beloved! This is monumental! You don't know how good that makes me feel! Oh, joy! Now I can be *joyful* again!'

If his words in a given sentence ended in an upswing, the cliffs caught the echo, but only for a second or three.

'I'll come right over. I didn't hear from you, so, I –'

'*I'll say* you should come right over!'

He wanted to laugh, but he paused for effect instead.

'But guess where I am!'

His little-kid jubilation was not exactly contagious.

'The Æyrie?' Keenah said quietly.

'Nope!'

'The Lazaretto?'

'No, ma'am!'

'Vinejuice?'

'Nay!'

'The Bungalow?'

'No way! Keep guessing!'

'A soundstage?'

Some weariness of tone was setting in.

'Nah!'

'I'm running out…' But then she brightened, partially because Egaz kissed her earlobe. 'How about… Paramaribo?'

'Close! OK, I'm at Jambutterbugsabad! Just landed!'

'Whoa! I mean, wow! What for? What's up? I thought that you…'

'Can't really explain it all now, baby-Keen. Gotta make it short, due to tracing. My unit's NSA-proof, but you never know!'

'Tracing? Why the caution?'

'Just wanted to see if you're OK. Just get over here as fast as you can. Too much to describe, but I think you're in the clear. But get your cute ass going, huh lover? Please be quiet about it. Don't tell nobody. Not Porter, or the Sams. Or Egaz. Nobody. Just fly Bronston. They'll know.'

'I'll – come. (In due course…?)'

'Love you, love you, love you. See you soon! Soon, soon, soon!'

'Love you – too –'

Click-off.

'UWH' was in suspension of production. The Producers' Group had called a halt to filming. Porter Pud Parker had the high honor of making the announcement on behalf of the higher-ups. The communique happened to be released about three hours before Butterbugs' plane landed. All aspects of the picture went into the aspic-can, so to speak. Even the janitors who covered the fourteen soundstages of the Mega|Goth lot in Hollywood that were packed with all things 'UWH', and the sweepers at Jambutterbugsabad, which was wholly devoted to the picture, were flat off the job. The hangar doors were actually locked by little strips of metal with Saturn-like coupling balls (usually used to seal boxcars), making these halls of cinematic creativity off limits to all.

The freeze was the talk of the nation, the international media, and the blogospheres. No, there was hardly a person on the globe who *didn't* know that something had gone horribly wrong with 'Unholy War Hymn'. Plus, they knew it before its star did.

For his part, studio head Hyman Goth had convinced – nay, ordered – The Producers' Group to kibosh activity then and there. He had rashly decided to take the stonewalling route. He was sequestered, garrisoned, and ready for a siege if necessary, in the central office blockhouse of his Goth Hall.

'Who does he think he is?' muttered one of The Producers, in an anonymous phone conversation to another one of The Producers, 'Jack-Fucking-Warner?'

'No,' the other The Producers member replied, 'Jack's only Tinker-Toy. Hy's Architect of the Known Universe.'

The Group were essentially opposed to the shutdown (there was plenty of Second Unit work to do) but Hy was the real estate baron who had their goods on his land... And, he was also God.

It was left to Porter to manage the aftershocks. He lost more poundage in the process, rendering him lean, hungry, and bedraggled. Not to mention, scared. Big, big, big expectations were in play with exhibitors, the press, and, yes, merchandisers (which always irked the acceptably-high-minded Butterbugs). How dare the supply side flake out on the consumer side?

All-important placements of the players began to fall into order.

As far as the media could tell:

– Hy, of course, was in his den. 'Hy Mad Doctor' was first coined by *Rags* at 'Variety'. A typical headline: 'The Hy M.D. Is In', 'Doctor Hy: Mighty Mad', 'Hy Mad Cuz Off Meds?' etc. Needless to say, he was not granting interviews. (The 'meds' banter was sheer coincidence. No one in the media had any idea one of the Industry's chief moguls was a martinet druggie, and thanks to the ever-loyal Stuart Curtain, Hy was definitely *on* his drugs, uninterrupted.)

– Porter, along with many an associate, and the core Producers Group, were all positioned in Hollywood. DFZ was on call in Palm Springs, on and off his croquet lawn.

– Associate Producer Arimanes Jugbash shuttled between London, Trieste, Luanda and Moscow, working on PR as if nothing were amiss. His diplomatic charm kept everyone calm and mature.

– Assistant Producer León Alastray was working his Mexican magic in the salons of Paris, and having considerable success in engaging the local intelligentsia with the breaking news of the 'UWH' controversy. Sartre was pissed off. National industrial action was contemplated as a protest to this cessation of the progress in cinematic art. The international solidarity spread.

– The Writers' Team were scattered in a selection of romantic retreats.

– Saskia was in the Shetlands somewhere.

– Sawl was in Canaan to see his mom.

– Britney was in Palestine with dinner friends.

– Others were hither and yon, from Corfoo to Asmara, but it really didn't matter, as the script was solid now, and scenes in the can vastly outnumbered scenes that awaited realization.

– Countless cast members awaited notification as to which way this thing was headed. For the present, it was nowhere. Many a livelihood depended on it. The Screen Extras Guild was ready to go to court. Barristers in six countries were prepping cases. Word was spreading amongst the masses of extras that Butterbugs would come through with a specific programme of Hard Luck Grants and Loans, but there was absolutely no evidence of this. The sentiment was probably correct, however. As an ultrastar who was also a trillionaire, Butterbugs might even find himself besieged by an expectant mob, perchance at the gates of The Lazaretto...? (That is, if he were even in the hemisphere...)

– Robert Surtees and Leon Shamroy were cool and professional; their lives were not particularly held up in light of these production problems. Either one could be at either studio in about a day. They certainly had their thoughts and opinions, but were simply standing by. After all, Bob had weathered 'Mutiny on the Bounty' (MGM, 1962) and Leon had survived 'Cleopatra' (20th-Fox, 1963). This was as nothing, at least for the present. Happily, all the UP-70 cameras were secured by Panavision and held at an undisclosed location, personally guaranteed by Panavision head Bob Gottschalk himself.

– Old Atrocity was holding steady in Jambutterbugsabad, along with 60% of the production crew.

– Egaz was in LA, at his rented quarters, and in eclipse right now. He wasn't even mentioned in any media explorations into the story. Apparently, editors and reporters approached it from the business angle instead of a work of creative cinema. Typical.

– By the very, very few who knew of his whereabouts at the dawn of this crisis, Sonny was presumed still in the border country of the Chaco (sans publicity of any kind). Either that, or, as several rumors insisted, he had slit his throat.

– Keenah was in transit. Probably five persons, if that, knew this fact.

– Butterbugs was rumored to be out of the USA. Speculation was the only option. The rest was silence.

The whole situation was like a general strike. An entire planet, ground to a halt. Conditions were duly reported in frenzied journalistic-cum-media fashion.

Porter was stressed, but with his new non-blubbery frame, he was coming to the fore. He even avoided a 'Vanity Fair' reporter (Tips Klarelow, no less) who wanted to do a follow-up to his legendary original profile in the mag. Porter eschewed on the premise that he was too busy right now, which was absolutely true. Faced with critical mass if the actual created property wasn't protected from extortion or confiscation for whatever reason, he wisely put a private armed guard around the Footage House at the bottom of the Selznick lot, where the cans of the complete exposed stock (so far) were stored. No one else seemed to think of doing anything like that. The cans had been spirited out of their vulnerable racks at Mega|Goth by revolutionary brigades, whose devotion to Butterbugs and the picture verged on the felonious. Their fleet of three old Divco milk trucks, used as studio rubbish haulers, caused no notice from gate guards. If any of them had cared to follow the tiresome flow of the usual discards to recycle oblivion though, the dull aluminum glint of stock cans could be seen inside the vans.

Despite interested parties presuming that Hy had corralled the priceless takes at Mega|Goth for use as a possible bargaining chip, the studio chief's overview was laughably myopic. Thinking he'd thought of everything, the physicality of the film itself hadn't even occurred to him. His crack pipes were all accounted for, though.

The secretly-sympathetic Selznick location was perfect as a covert depository, safer than a cave in Switzerland.

After all, if things went dreadfully wrong…

Much of the world away, Assoc. Sec'y of Defense Montague Realms hung up his phone. His higher-up had just made his own announcement: that this first phase of Realms' scheme had been brought to fruition.

'Beautiful,' he mused as he sat back with hole-riddled socks on desk. No one was down under there, blow-jobbing though (as if anyone ever *had* been), so he fantasized about that particular 'if-only' for a few minutes. He farted, then inhaled deeply. Good shit. Because he was a *hot* shit, all right.

Now the second phase could be implemented. The cloak could be eased open a little, but the dagger was still firmly grasped. Realms' can-do agent had excelled. Time to give him a chitty-(but *not* shitty)-chat.

'Toodles 909? This is Entablature ZtX-4007. Codeword: Prowlercat.'

Pause. Click. Whirr.

'It's OK now, DeVault, I enjoy the status of hack-free telephone conversations once our code-names and codewords have been muttered. My exclusive OnGuardForPeace mechanism engages. I know, I never told you that before. You hadn't proven yourself yet. Now you have. Talk freely! ProwlerCat? Why, she's that mini-cute actress that's *probably* sucked Butterbugs' dick. Wouldn't mind taking *her* home.'

Realms thought of DeVault Lurgan, Agent, as a friend. Sometimes you can be boss and buddy at the same time. Sometimes you can't. Notwithstanding this, he generally felt that anybody he sent out on a mission where they could get killed was a pal. In the absence of cash incentives or promises of afterlife goodies, 'When a feller needs a friend' could be manufactured to order. He licked his fingers and groomed his thin mustache, then picked at his chronic ear fungus.

'At any rate, you heard? Course ya did. We're *winning*. Do you *hear?* A big-titted but totally disgusting and subversive movie is about to be relegated to – *I* don't know – how's 'Nowhere-Under-Obscurity-Is-More-Forgotten'? Heh-heh! You *like* that? Yeah, I think it's pretty good, if I do say so *myself.* It's fun to be a *ba-dass* against a – goody-goody – isn't it? That goody-goody guy. Now looka here. Time for the physical bits. Yeah. But you have to do one more *play.* Your plane leaves for Karachi in less than three hours. We know for certain that Butterbugs is in Jambutterbugsabad. Yeah, that's *actually* what they call it! Can't help fuming. Conceited little prick… But I suppose it'll have to do until I can make up something to call it that's more cutting… How about J-Bugs-Is-*Bad?* Ha-hah! *Huhh??* Anyway, that's perfectly fine with us that he's there. You will meet with him, *in person.* I *know* you're a known entity now. That's the *idea.* This thing *is* planned, you know. You will *clear the air* with him. A cordial but *frank* discussion. You're on his *side*, as it were. You still are *there* for him, and *magnanimous*, even after all the hurt he's brought upon you. Play it up. Do a mind-*fuck*, specialist. Make it personal, very *personal*. Make it like he's really *hurt* you; he's really *hurting* you now. These actors don't get smarter the more lines they recite, y'know. Now look sharp, and pay attention as to *how* the air shall clear. Here's the deal...'

Meanwhile, though, in his mega-fortified HQ in Arkbash, in the roguish country of Khwhy, Chief Martial Law Administrator Ool-Akzad Nazah proceeded with his plans of jacking up his nation's commodity prices to unprecedented and craggy heights. This was sure to drive the Murn Administration totally loco. Unaware of 'UWH''s hiatus, the leader was downright looking forward to the picture. All was vanity. He assumed it would be a biopic of the most flattering kind.

At the present moment in Arkbash, a special arena-sized cinema was being built to accommodate the forthcoming picture (acquired by piracy, if sanctions were in play) for 24-hour showings. Reconditioned Sovscope hardware had turned up and was being positioned. Master architect Lev Rudnev, of Moscow State University fame, had produced some really dandy designs that were now being realized to the fullest. Giganticism was not an issue, *it was an imperative*. The buzz was that it was going to be an outrageously wonderful place to see a picture show. A destination venue. Mega|Goth's eastern hemisphere distrib, Tooth-Of-Time International Pictures, stood ready to shepherd the film throughout the region, and a series of Khwhy-based offices was inaugurated, with great state-fed pomp. All that was needed was a finished picture. Everything else was nearly in place, from the daily rehearsals of an invocatory cantata composed by the esteemed Bwoshkov Vtyannutvuvv, down to installed doorknobs which sported a 'Bb' (Butterbugs) logo, in Roman, Cyrillic, and Spratatash (e.g. Khwhyresiumnnik) scripts, ingeniously intertwined.

Mists of quick time whooshed by as the earthen globe rotated-cum-revolved.

DeVault Lurgan, aka: Agent Toodles 909, having cleared Karachi Airport, made his way incognito through the Indo-Gothic brick'd-arched galleries of the Empress Market and was met, according to plan, by a mysterious figure near the tinkling Osborne Fountain.

Contact: male, c. 37–62 in age, of medium height, in a native-style and non-hooded Indus Valley garment, with Sindhi cap, of indeterminate race (though not South Asian), but passing adequately. Dull appearance, attracting no attention whatsoever. Effective participant.

Toodles 909: c. 49–81 in age, of less than medium height, with stoopéd shoulders, comes off as plainly-displayed American, in Dokkers ersatz-khakis, a Burkmart bush jacket, Land's Endless other stuff, with a stupid turned-down sailor's cap (Jippy's Wharf Brand) as head covering.

A dead giveaway, but Karachi is a busy place. Even though the everyday masses astutely notice the kit of the man on the street, and note the credibility therein, they nevertheless have work to do – things to deliver, and business to accomplish. As a rule, no tourists here, so little reason for locals to analyze tinker-toy intriguers at the public market. If any do happen to show, they're just too predictable, and just too inconsequential...

Granted, this easily-disposed anonymity was a strength to anyone purporting to infiltrate themselves within the bazaar culture of old Kurrachee (as Toodles 909 thought it was still spelt). But any seasoned onlooker, of whom there were many 'on duty' around there, had already pigeonholed these two as mere bozos on parade. If they made any trouble, there were already scores of bored but ready personnel to kick into action when the innuendoes got suspicious. But this was Sind – anciently civilized. No need to be impulsive.

In any case, a meeting was at hand; a joining of like beliefs and goals.

The fine old Empress was the busiest place in town, but absolutely no one cared when these two forgettable figures linked and apparently made some sort of social connection. The Sindhi-hatted one patted the capped ferringhee-type on the back – with his left hand. This naturally defied any local etiquette, though there were drunks and drugoids who were of course below the norm of bazaar society. They themselves would probably be liable to make such blunders, but these two looked like they weren't even nerdish philatelists, or resembling anyone near to such semi-interesting characters. Spies? Nah! Merely space-filling humans of little consequence. At least these bazaar-denizen observers had high æsthetic standards – for the most part.

After faking some 'window' shopping in the stalls that featured copper pots & pans, then along to the paraffin lanterns and LPG cookery hobs – and doing it very poorly – the two evacuated the premises, but did so *together*.

Bad show.

Nevertheless, no one bothered to pay attention as they climbed into their little Bolan van in a side street and clumsily skedaddled. Beyond the casual idlers' keeping of tabs near the Empress' way-out exit arch in the rear (a non-embellished yet significant Victorian relic), the two then went into the automotive-only arterials, bound for Karachi's further reaches. Thickly then, through all the goths and the suburbs, and unto the colonies they wended, thinking they'd lost any followers. Actually, there were none to lose.

They spent two days in a Drigh Road barracks, a permissible pit-stop.

'Near here, very near,' said their ostensibly-friendly host, who would only go by 'Alam', 'T.E. Lawrence once lodged, in his incarnation as T.E. Shaw, airman. We preserve his historic digs. Surely you will be interested.'

'Who's that?' inquired Toodles 909 dully. 'A friend of yours, or something?'

'Surely you will know of Lord Napier then? 'Peccavi' as the ideal code message for the Britishers conquering Sind?'

'What?'

To the relief of everyone thereabouts, the two secret agents then made their way out of the mega-city, supposedly bound for far-off Jambutterbugsabad in the west.

However, their route was unnecessarily circuitous and inane. Since Drigh

Road, they had the huge advantage of one of those Toymotor 4x4 comfort rigs. But instead of adhering to the sensible mandate already writ in spiral-bound standard-issue road guides, based on the definitive and classic 'Topee and Turban' itinerary, they buffooned their way onward by blunderingly heading up to Sukkur, *to the northeast*. Once there, they thought the Lansdowne Bridge over the mighty Indus was a big fish-trap. Then, after a bit of consideration, they assumed it was a full-blown motorway.

'To the west we must head, I would guess,' one of them declared. 'But wait a minute. We must cross this stream at all cost!'

They proceeded towards it with great difficulty and got up to grade, which was plainly railed. Then they barely avoided a train. Facing it head-on, the locomotive wisely braked upon encountering the dipshit-piloted foreign rig. Stepping out onto the middle of the epic span, the engineer himself advised them as to their proper route, once a safe halt was accomplished.

An idler emerged from the Military-Gothic southern gatehouse of the bridge and observed the encounter. He happened to be an unemployed geography teacher, and entered into conversation with the foreigners, hoping to avert an international incident. With impeccable English (which the visitors thought everyone spoke in this land) the teacher patiently explained that he knew the greater region well, and was very good at problem-solving. Armed with Mr. Hughes' Gazetteers of Sindh and Baluchistan from the 1870s, he proclaimed that he had never been lost, *and never would be*. After learning of their dilemma, he agreed to guide the boys onward to Jambutterbugsabad, providing terms were favorable.

The ploy used by the wildly-dislocated pair was disturbingly preposterous: to hunt the rare and endangered Kelatian klorn-hen at close range. At least they got the Kelat locale correct. Further 'intelligence' was not so mighty. Klorn-hens had been extinct in the subcontinent for over two years now, a well-known fact. Klorn-hen kurma was a long-lost delicacy, mourned over by millions.

But the geographer only acceded once he'd been paid a lot of money, which came easily enough from the goofball couple. Even if these 'silly ones' were up to some naughtiness, for one who was almost at the end of his rope after dreaming himself into deep depression, this crazy opportunity was nothing less than the biggest of lucky breaks – inshallah.

In brief, their progress was scenic enough, and through highly historic territory, but because they were on a mission and had no intrinsic interest whatsoever in the harshly austere but fascinating region at large, theirs was an agonizing, *stupid-stupid* progress. Plus, the terms agreed by the unemployed geography teacher engaged him only as an 'advisory sub-companion'; with the proviso that 'Asiatick natives shall be treated with indifference, if deemed preferable' – as instructed by the 'Secret Manual of the Secret Agents', the 'jokey' title of their CIA manual, handwritten on a piece of notepad and cello-taped over the title page, meant to deceive.

The two spies then tried to show off their hubris by attempting to 'guide' their guide through Jacobabad, but only succeeded in getting hopelessly lost on the rocky road to Bibkot. Just outside Dera Khuzzah Khan, one of them fell asleep at the wheel and hit a beef-calf, killing it instantly. In India proper, they'd be in deep doo-doo, but thanks to the diplomacy of he who was treated with such indifference, the justifiably-enraged cowherd was paid off with a rather handsome sum of one thousand euros (US dollars not accepted).

Still bent on their superiority trip, the two insisted on going on a wild goose chase clear up the Bolan Pass towards Sibi and Bostan, before facing the dead-end drop-off at the Chappar Rift.

'I shoor wish they hadn't removed that bridge. We'd *be* there by now...' was all one of them could say.

'No. No, you wouldn't...,' their disempowered but well-paid guide silently replied.

'Oh, but how I pine for the fleshpots of Quettah!' one of them howled, with unintentional comic effect.

The guide rolled his eyes, mainly because neither of them even knew what Quettah *was*, let alone the fact that there *were* no fleshpots in that ultra-conservative and nearby town. No, such words were from 'The Ballad of a Subaltern's Failed Desires', by Greaseberry Groams, the 'Cheap Kipling'. A musical rendition of the ditty had played on the radio earlier, while one of them fiddled with the search button.

So they had to sullenly retrace their steps, all the way back to Jacobabad – the hottest place in Sind – before finally cooperating with their more-than-competent 'advisory sub-companion'.

While the Americanskis slumbered from burnout in the back seat, the 'Asiatick' slipped behind the wheel and easily found the correct route, all the way down through Kuzzulbash, Khuzdar, Khazzaddah, and Khazadzabad. Then to Bela, and beyond. It was a very arduous process, based on the dimbulb-ishness of certain guest drivers in this part of the world.

And it came to pass that, seven days later, the unemployed geography teacher, Ablam Yoonus, fed up with the folk he'd successfully brought down onto the Makran bench, wherein Jambutterbugsabad lay – as any self-respecting and cinematically-aware South Asian could have done, decamped from the now beat-to-shit Toymotor rig, and happily placed himself in Chance's gallery, for to hitchhike back to his native riverain residence. However, due to the contract agreed upon, he was amazingly 17,073 euros richer (US dollars not accepted). He could now embark upon the educational effort of his dreams, and within sight of his beloved Lansdowne Bridge, too. Upon such 'dirty money' was a worthy institution built, and from those two ancient gazetteer volumes – which had never let their users down – a great regional library grew.

'I am only following an inspiration that stems from the efforts of *Butterbugs*,' Prof. Yoonus declared at the school's inauguration ceremony, to great acclaim. 'For Butterbugs would *do* something like build a learning resource in a place like this. So I shall do it in his name. And like the appeal of Butterbugs himself, I do hereby open these doors, these books, these ideas – to all humanity!' Hundreds cheered.

The chosen name for his institution? The Butterbugs Bahadur Madrassah for Poetic, Cinematic and Land Studies. Hundreds enrolled.

Discovering the ultrastar was indeed in-country, Professor-cum-Chancellor Yoonus excitedly prepared a request for the ultrastar to appear at his creation's formal dedication, in person, at his convenience, perchance between interior and exterior shooting schedules on his latest picture.

So, at length, the dark-side workers came unto the place of their assignment.

DeVault was now at the out-of-alignment control of their rig. (His disdain for the handle 'Toodles' no longer burdened him, for they were beyond the range of Assoc. Sec'y Realms' cell phone jurisdiction.) He randomly pulled off the road at a highly significant viewpoint. Way over there was the great studio complex, standing nobly before the marching mass of up-cliffs. Over to the left, the faint line of the Arabian Sea appeared in its mid-day haze.

By all accounts, quite a magnificent scene, worthy of a David Lean-directed Kodacolor snap, perhaps designed by John Box, in preparation for a major Maurice Jarre-scored desert picture. ('Shaw of Sind', maybe?)

But any artful composition of the prospect was lost on the two tin-eyed, physically-bushed motorists. DeVault switched off the ignition. The CD of Durdle Duddles' 'Live From Branson!' album died a dusty death as a result.

'Companion!' DeVault declared, while the waver of 'Is This Finger Pointin' In The Right Direction?' – as if from a wrinkling filament of 8-track tape – faded into the antique noontide ambience, which hadn't substantially changed since Alexander the Great's day.

'I need to know, as this song has reminded me, that… what… What then, what exactly *is* your name, be it real, or encrypted? *You* know, your *real* name, like. As we approach our theatre of operations, which I guess this Podunk stretch ahead of us leads to, I think it would be pretty likable for me to have that all that stuff, you know, like, your name – you know? – in my safekeeping, as our journey comes on in.'

Naturally, the turkey at the wheel didn't know he was in fact burlesquing what was a very serious proposition: prosecuting the mission at hand with the most severe prejudice now known in this here universe.

But they were *players!* Consider their ordeal! Bone-jarred for so long, brain-jittered, judgment-tangled, after progressing in second gear mostly, with the engine over-revving to an alarming extent, the tachometer busted from wear-out, the front end calf-damaged, the catalytic converter so white-hot it could just as well set the rocks below aflame, their native reserves had been unwisely jangled, tweaked, and retarded more than they already were. Under the hood, the Japanese engine, fed up with the abuse, was ready to throw a rod right out of its block from sheer spite, even though it was actually stout enough to proceed to either Pole, if needed.

They had stared ahead in stentorian silence – until now, when the 'humane' American formerly known as Toodles desired a kumbaya advantage.

His companion was highly austere. So much so, DeVault was, somewhat understandably, chary to 'connect' with his colleague, at least on 'rapping' terms. So, after his questioning, he could only stare at his profile, which was aimed dead-ahead through the cracked and spattered windscreen, as sure as a pointing dog's.

DeVault, who for purposes of furthering his profession, had toyed with pursuing a homosexual lifestyle in the great tradition of Britty super-agents associated with setting the East ablaze (like Burgess and Blunt in days gone by), wisely chose to admire his companion in the artistic, sort of portrait-sense, instead of just groping over there somewhere as a tension-easer, on the off-chance that his companion had the same built-up devices and desires as himself.

Good thing he chose restraint, as the admirable but remote one in the opposite seat revealed himself to be a dedicatee to the mission at hand. Of the *a*sexual kind.

'I will tell you,' the passenger said in generically-foreign English, as he quit his characteristic gaze ahead and adjusted his nighttime-PeneTrayVision-capable eyeballs on the needy pilot of his delivery vehicle.

DeVault was worshipful. Yet he wanted to splatter attentions in admirable blots, with 'Yeah? Tell me! Now? Tell me! Tell me!!!!!' But his training kicked in and he became totally professional as a listener.

'My name? Which one? Which from the list? Should I say? Should I pick just one? The most appropriate? To you, a high-up success-nik in the banks of US intelligence-suckers, I can say, I respect you. Really! I know of your deeds and of your brown-nosing the people who matter.'

DeVault was nonplused, but he could not deny he was impressed by this fellow's scope of understanding. Spooks of all ages were artists of the amorphous.

'I see things,' the passenger continued, his eyes suddenly closed. 'And I contain myself. For, what am I *for*? To serve the larger purpose, don't you think?'

'Larger? What's larger than... me? I mean, you know, *you*?'

'I see. You're only in it for yourself.'

'Isn't everybody?'

The companion opened his eyes and frosted DeVault with them.

'There is a larger purpose.'

DeVault, amazed, held steady. The exhaustion of the road had given way to skewed intellectual debate, a mindset that was key to his profession as a spy, yet subject to shipwreck if charts were lost at sea.

'You're not one of those sacrificial lambs, then?'

'I do not detect a standing altar in my work.'

'To die?'

'Why would I want to do that?' reasoned the companion. 'To return to the nothingness from which I sprang – for no reason?'

'Well… I wouldn't want to, you know, *die* for this gig, or anything…'

'No doubt. I see you much clearer now, even though my gaze has previously been riveted on the road ahead.'

'The road…?'

'Ahead. I know what I have to do. *Do you?*'

'It's dusty here, and scary. I don't like it here.' He'd wanted to add, 'Take me away from this horrid place! Take me to where we can be safe, and happy and…' But he controlled himself. He was silent. It was a question he didn't want to answer.

'Roads are of the mind. I do not take them literally.'

DeVault liked the height of his road trip buddy's reasoning. That's why he felt comfortable using terms like a wuss-meister's 'scary'.

'Please tell me your name before I ask you my next question.'

He was going for broke, but hoped he didn't reveal it.

'We are talking too much. If your talk takes on a personal characteristic, it must mean you sense disaster. And failure. I do not think that way. I cannot. I do not even know how. But I know you are from the lush safety of the District of Columbia's luxurious suburbs. You have too much to lose, even though you are probably already a loser. Isn't that what they call people who can't do much but the lowly thing that they do in fact do?'

DeVault thought for a second, and then was tempted to say that he personally knew the Assoc. Sec'y of Defense of the United States of America – a sure sign that he *wasn't* a loser. Because, hell, most of his high school classmates were upstanding farmers in Iowa, or they were busy doing some other *truly* loser-oriented occupation. But he continued to censor himself, because he knew his companion spoke the truth, and there was no reason to heap obviousness or any humiliation on the already resolved issue that cornered him right now.

'I, uh…'

DeVault was smart enough, though, not to dissect the words coming at him at this juncture.

Surprisingly, the companion opened up. 'Because, I know… you can sense my mission. And I think you are in love with me.'

A blast! Vroooom-hah! Even asexual spies get horny when the talk turns seductive! For his own part, DeVault deliriously, punchily, gave in.

'Yes! I am! I tell you, you have been mine own rig companion for these many days, and I, fairly driven out of my mind, knowing that we are here, out on this deity-forsaken landstrip, and I know we are in danger, but I think, can't we experience pleasure before we are sacrificed? Isn't that permissible? I mean, *really?* Sometimes I think, it's as if I'm in prison! In solitary! A fella has tenderness needs! I have felt this every time I meet potential death in the face. It has spurred my selfishness. It has been my perpetrator of showcase-hope, otherwise I should have slain myself years ago.'

'I cannot relate at all to your superficial desires. I am on my track. Take us on in.'

'You destroy me, rightful one. I will take you on in. But one thing remains. Please, I beg of you, without loving prejudice, for I am cured of the carnal distraction of one so dedicated as ye be. Forsaking all other desires, pray, what be your name – so that I can die with it on my lips, if called? In these remote missions, we serve not country, but each other.'

'I now admire your renewed dedication to our mission. And your understanding of severing the connection between our covertness and the loyalties that commission it. Thus, the two of us have passed beyond mere annoying personality hassles. So. When you die, you may utter 'U.X. Vunn' as your farewell verbiage to this wasteful and pathetic plane.'

'You are – oh my – you are... *the* U.X. Vunn?'

'It is sufficient that I tell you I am.'

'You mean, you aren't? How can I...'

'If I tell you I am, that means you are on such a lofty plane of security that you are privy to such name-bandying, which is not, I have to emphasize, due to persons *not* worthy of its rewards. Why else would I recite my treasured name to you?'

'Oh! Oh! May I debark from this vehicle and bow on down?'

'No! That is the penalty of me telling you my truth! Fie! Fie upon you!'

'Oh, please don't kill me!'

'I won't, because I need one bit of additional information from you.'

'But U.X., no longer burdened with my trepidation in addressing you in the style of: 'as-yet nameless VIP passenger', I nevertheless need, even at this place of godless desolation, to empty the bladder that so primitively expands due to my survival tactics in such a drastic environment!'

'Well go, then! Take your pissoir! What the fuck – as you people are wont to say...'

'And I promise not to diddle with my John Thomas in memory of you, and, uh, oh, that, as I, urr, exit this vehicle, I will be gone *some time*, but only long enough to perform the nervous loser-activity that I am forced into, because...'

He finally had the sense to shut up, mainly because the need to go was becoming poundingly pressing. It was all he could do to perform the several-stage process of unstrapping himself, igniting the auto-door unlocks, grasping the hi-impact plastic release lever that liberated him from the saloon, and making sure that his deerskin boots reached the Makranian ground in unison. Because, for all the world, he was rendered unto watery pudding just knowing that U.X. Vunn was his project partner, and how *ever* was he going to pull off this mission to U.X.'s standards of excellence?

OK, one step at a time. Evacuate first, damage control next. Boy, did *he* feel like an idiot.

That was the problem with the spy service today: all these imbecilic baby boomers who thought they'd be stars after growing up. That it would just, you know, *happen*, and everything... It wasn't even a case of entitlement. It was just a law of physics. Wasn't it? Faced with the prospects of reality, one couldn't be much of anything but a FUBB (Fucked Up Baby Boomer). An ongoing destiny, until death.

Oh, gawd…

Usually canny in most ways, as befitting a proper, if not perfect, spy, DeVault was nevertheless pretty sloppy in his piss site. His act proceeded fittingly enough at the back of the vehicle, but in full juxtaposition with the passenger-side rear-view mirror. And the passenger within *noticed* all right, even though Objects In Mirror Are Closer Than They Appear.

His dribble moistening the terrible flats in a few spotty spaces for a few seconds, the spy basically known as Toodles 909, disadvantaged by his humanization through ordeal, returned with humbleness, mainly because his passenger hadn't done anything bodily since they left Dera Khezzi Khan, or wherever the hell it was – which was horribly out of direct route to their goal, for what, three days?

'Sorry –,' DeVault expostulated, once back in the driver's seat.

'No problem.'

Could it be that the super-spy's sudden softening was the result of absence making the heart grow fonder? Or did he approve of the private parts now revealed?

'Oh, thank you, spy; I mean, U.X.! Pardon, I am flustered.'

'I see. I hear you.'

'You do? And so, can we now proceed with what you asked? Maybe?'

'I shall give it without further equivocation, if you so desire!'

'I do. You have to, if it please you, repeat the thing which you… wanted.'

'My patience is running.'

'Sorry! So now, name your one thing. Surely it couldn't be anything of consequence, so near the end are we.'

'EVERYTHING is of consequence in this mission,' U.X. said gravely.

'Yeah, of course! Now, name thy desire.'

'I'm sure you wish I would give in to something sexual –'

'Oh, no, wondrous one. I am cured. Shoot!'

'You must tell me the name of Butterbugs' chambers.'

'At Jambutterbugsabad cantonment?'

'Yeah.'

'All right then.'

'A simple bit of information.'

'For goal purposes?'

'Mmm.'

'But U.X., there's just a remaining trifle. I mean, there are those at Agency who, once they find out that I met you, and I'm telling you right now, they *will* find out, one way or another, even though we be on our last detail, they will ask, in all innocence and sincerity, just what *race* you assign yourself to. Pray, please consider, it is not that they're racist, it's just that they crave to know the heritage of our finest agents, so that we may promote diversity amongst our minorities – I mean – our fellow agents. Oh U.X., why *won't* you tell me of the non-white heritages from whence you originated?'

For a second, U.X. was tempted to say:

'You kinked-up fuck! How did I ever get burdened with you as a team member? You already made one mindless request, *and I granted it*, even though I was not required to do so. And now, *you make another one* without even answering my simple question, which, by the way, pertains to our mission, whilst your gossipy jabber does not!'

But he restrained himself.

Instead, despite the seriousness of the assigned task at hand, U.X. nevertheless listened to his admirer's queries. And due to a sprig of vanity that was chanced to grow after this grueling tour, the super-agent relaxed somewhat. It was most unlike him, but perhaps it had to do with something, despite his training, he had not perceived on any subjective level. Something unspoken, though it be on the surface. And it had to do with *Butterbugs.*

He waxed reflective. Poetic, even. As if he sensed the cinematics of the moment.

'My heritage! My background, is it? I can say, with my characteristic reticence regarding my profession, that I am one who straddles two opposing hemispheres as far as my parentage is concerned. For when the sun is low and – *HEY!* Wait a minute! I am on a fucking *mission* here, and no force can stop me, you insidious and faggy-agenda'd fuckface!'

U.X. immediately went into prejudice gear, grabbed his kit bag, and debarked from the vehicle. Just before he slammed the door, he ejected the StartGo card from its press-in port beneath the glove box, rendering the Toymotor helpless as a baby runt kitten. It was going nowhere.

Neither was DeVault, who was a fairly effective agent in dainty surroundings, but in places like cis-Jambutterbugsabad, he was as a stale and stalled packet of pale meat, tossed in a moat before the goal presumptive.

U.X., on the other hand, easily pressed into progressive action. And as the day proceeded into dusk, he covered the deceptive ground on into Jambutterbugsabad with nary a wisp of rising dust to identify his trail. Binocularization could not even produce any sign of his presence. He was that good.

Sullen morn found DeVault Lurgan arriving in Quaid-i-Azam Gunge on a farmer's hay wain, for the man had sprung-to after the shock of revulsion at his haughty agent-mate's spurning of his sincerely-offered love. Therefore, after spending devastation in darkness, the pre-dawn sputter of a peasant's transport into town brought him back to the value of service to his country. Which is what he was here for anyway – or service to his boss, one Realms, his ostensible 'friend'. So he hopped to and got himself up unto Jinnah Bazar, which hummed before the mighty Saracenic gates of the studio.

As luck would have it, great shipments of straw-toned light were splayed across the collective blockade of highland surfaces behind the studio complex, providing a moderne-contemporary illumination to all activities down here, in the comparative 'orchestra pit' of human-scale activity.

Back on his two deer-skinned feet as an agent once again, Lurgan quickly reconnoitered. He clearly remembered that he hadn't given U.X. the piece of info he most required. The very reason that he, Toodles 909, existed at all. That is, the name of Butterbugs' local address. He hadn't imparted it. He wondered if doing so would have made a difference. Rivalry between agencies was rife in his business, but rivalry between allies closer-in was even more intense. All the Smiley novels and Cold War pictures didn't come close to making it real. You had to live it to believe it. And even then, orientation toward deception proved to be an exception to perception.

Actually, DeVault *did in fact* know the precise location of Butterbugs' digs within this vast industrial estate-cum-encampment. It was part of the treasured knowledge he himself had successfully extracted from Butterbugs in person. He'd scored it simply, successfully, and solo, in the star's studio bungalow in Hollywood, no less. What did people think he was hanging out there *for*, anyway? To worship some egomaniac tap-dancer? Time he got his self-worth back. Forget about Mr. SmartyPanties U.X. Vunn! Time to celebrate the magic of his own considerable standing as being On His All-American Majesty Montague Realms' Secret Service!

'Toodle-oo, UXV! Blow it out your ass! Hyuck-yuk-uk!' snarled Toodles 909 out loud. He'd even changed his own private codename for U.X., downgrading 'TigerPenis' to 'MosquitoBladder', and it felt good.

He proceeded to sneak around the bazaar, so as to prove to himself that he was a superstar secret agent after all. Besides, he was scared of a chance encounter with MosquitoBladder. Hopefully, his rival hadn't detected his rather careless but cathartic taunt. Like the good observant agent he was, Lurgan had spotted a shotgun mike in U.X.'s armaments kit.

'They'll make a movie of this, someday!' he enthused, 'And when they do, I shall sit as consultant, and I will tell them of all my sacrifices and my selfless glory in doing so! And there will be those who will bend down in awe and thank the old gods that people such as I exist! And there will be children full of terror-imbued wonder, arrayed at my feet! And there will be those ladies who, as single failures in the arts of both love and marriage, will know of my story and think: 'Why was I not able to be with he who gave so much service to his country, and, down the line, service to me as a lonely gal waiting for his type to rescue me?!' And the aged and the infirm will cling to their nursing hall pillows at night and wilt with gratitude that fighters such as me exist at these, the Outer Lines of Freedom! And the babies of the field, they will giggle and gurgle in their buckets of parental care, and yes, even *they* will know in their tiny hearts that it is those such as me who are, in their painstaking efforts, out here on guard for peace, which starts on the battle-plains before mine enemies! And who but the town criers and the wayfarers, and those without franchise, who waste my tax dollars in idling and waiting, perchance even *they* will come to the realization that it is my selflessness that keeps them liberated! Who but they! For when the sun is low and...'

Wah-de-doo-dah...

In this new but classic conurbation, way out here in these wilds, in this 'Talkienagar' as it were, there was indeed to be found the classic subcontinental combine of City and Cantonment, the former being the dwellings of the inhabitants who labored at the studio, and the latter being the studio itself and its appurtenances. So the delineation was well-defined and easy to navigate. But the ultrastar's current tented quarters, characteristically austere, were positioned out toward the edge of the concern.

Across a barren ground on the western edge of the cantonment was an old idgah, little-known and lesser-used. The whitewashed wall that backed its eminence was an ornamented yet organic uprise of minar-lings, scallops and flourishes. From the confines of his dooryard nearby, the ultrastar loved to scan this skyline late in the day, especially when contemplating the significance of his work.

Unto this very idgah then, came DeVault, just as the blanching light on the palisades above came on down, brighter and brighter, though the depths were yet in blue gloom. The spy stole over to the recess of the mihrab, lest he be seen, even on this Id-less forenoon. Stealth was reborn in him, and he well knew it would have to remain engaged, right up to his encounter with Butterbugs – which was his goal. If his rival spy did not know the tent's location, then surely he, with the advantage of the moment, would be able to clinch this mission by being clever enough to remain in its vanguard.

From the weathered wall he scanned the near neighborhood and quickly located what must be the actor's enclosed shamiana.

'Aha! There stands 2, Mulgie Lane! Where an ultrastar breathes in station! I am close to my glory! Fuck U.X. and his gay deception! That stupid MosquitoBladder! I'm in this for *me*, and *me* only. Realms may pay me, but when all's said and done, I'll go public and rake in book & movie deals that'll make Michael Jackson look like a Quaker! The whole world shall tremble, because of *me!* Hell, mosquitoes probably don't even *have* bladders! And now, for my approach...'

Insensitive spy that he was, DeVault proceeded, fully shoed, across the paved assembly deck of the idgah, in plain sight. Infidel! Who the hell would care? Then he casually strolled on over to the player's quarters.

Shut-down was everything around there, with only a stillness that later-on heat of the day would melt into place. Or else, if the swooper-nest wind blew, rag doors and canvas coverings would be fastened and shutters closed, rendering everything in the afternoon a grave-quiet qabristan, lacking life, but with certain interior brooding quite alive.

502

Formal gateway there was none, but as DeVault approached the dwelling, he could see that the only colors on the somber façade were thin bands of fluorescent greens and yellows, encrustations of efflorescence-beads from the Hoochee peoples within the Shookreeut tribe, up past Gonzar Mountain. That was where the Agony in the Wastes sequences had been filmed with much difficulty, though with great feeling, a few short weeks ago. These decorations were gifts from the native chiefs as signs of exaltation and protection. Butterbugs had been hailed a poet-saint in their regard, on account of his caring and thoughtful treatment of their race, and his giving many of them gigs in this picture, as valued extras.

'I pray that their qualities not catch the notice of my competitor…,' whispered the spy to himself. For half a second, he thought of pulling the arts and crafts down, lest their singularity attract U.X. in, before he'd had his time.

How strange this scene was, the lonely and weathered tent-lodge, like a dollop of limestone rudely scraped and molded to stand, more like a mausoleum than a tent. As if readied for outsiders, washed onto this further shore, without the will to move on, coming here, to make an end. To grow into the earth. To die. Indeed, a place for those who could do no more in life but blend in with surroundings many times larger than they.

As a result of the harsh environment, real peace was all around here, the sort of peace that comes from things long ago decided, and from a great distance away. Here was an edge to the experience of life, the signs of which were less apparent than a boneyard, were it not for arcane knowledge of varied activities hereabouts, of late. Such as, the filming of a great film.

So the spy drew nigh to the flap that served as a door, and as convenience would have it, a post of holey pearter-wood served as a knock-plate, from which vibrations would set off a dim gong within. Tapping it, a narm-cricket was dislodged, and its ratcheting sound as it fled into the gurm-mounds was almost as loud as the rap on the plate itself.

How long then, should he respect the interval that followed? It went on, and on, and on. Finally, when the first ray of sun, diffused by airborne particulate matter, shone through The Crack of Moolyab on the cliffs far above and landed on seven of the strips of Hoochee hospitality beads, the structure became as an energized and vibrant nerve center. Or something even more extraordinary.

Einstein might have defined it! Lynch could have communicated it onto the screen! Something metaphysical, not even necessarily real, made the phenomenon highly debatable as to its actual existence. But as seasoned Jambutterbugsibadis had learned from their life out here, all sorts of displays of things once thought irrational or improbable might occur in the span of a single day. Or, in nights of torchy limits, the back country might be bathed in electric blue or subtle yellow, with pure and broadest noon most likely to allow light-play of the strangest and most beautiful kinds, in the hot silver sun. Maybe it was because of the water, which trickled out of the quirmatite caves and into the deep cuttings of profound and silent stone, and there made its wait before serving the communal thirsts of the new filmic community. A ferment of gathered minerals, aided by distillated hours of the day, forming a perfectly unique and living elixir of cinematic effect as normal life... Or it could be nothing organic at all, only the notions of a desert province newly accessed, little understood, but appreciated without benefit of portfolio.

But as the effect of the sun dulled and became scattered, the building at 2, Mulgie Lane returned to its lifeless state, where it remained.

Until the dullest of stirrings was detectable from within.

Anxiously, the door flap seemed to be unfastened inside. Question marks of dust were launched at each anchor point, until the whole drape of exhausted canvas was furled up and aside, as a face known by all the world emerged out of the brown murkiness and spake in a tone not so familiar:

'She comes?? She's here?? If it be so, I'm *saved!*...'

'Butterbugs, Butterbugs, Butterbugs, *BUTTERbugs!* No *one* 'she' is here. Only me. And I come in peace.'

'You! *You?*'

'I, DeVault Lurgan.'

'I know who you are. Deceiver!'

'Why call me – Oh, but never mind. The speed of darts flung in the world now travel in nanocruiser style...'

'I am of a revised mind regarding you, DeV. Lurgan.'

'In whose estimation, friend?'

'People I trust. You – you are a dirty piece of slime.'

'Please! Peace, kindred soul! Would you hear me out? *Might* you? Then, if it be your choice to relegate me to you list of hates, I can bear my fate in due course. Pray, can you spare the bare time to venture into my tale?'

DeVault was becoming quite anxious about being spotted by unscrupulous rivals, even out here.

On pins and needles, anticipating the arrival of another, loftier person, Butterbugs agreed to take in the one he had been warned of, if only to pass the desolate moments which were readily perceived as centuries.

'In, then! Enter, but under a sort of protest.'

'I hear you, great actor! I will protect you as much as you wish yourself protected.'

'Remember, untrustworthy one, I have the power to arrest any untoward efforts you might enact within this here chamber which lies ahead. Only remember that!'

'Agreed, strolling player, agreed!'

They shuffled into the shadowy interior of the yurt-ish structure. A lone window of translucent muslin was the sole light source, and it caught a thin wedge of the wan chasm-shine from up cliffside a ways. The disarray and lumpishness of indeterminate stuff in the room reflected a depressed and brooding personality.

'Strange!' thought DeVault as he judged the layout tawdry. 'How shutting down a picture can quickly dissipate these movie people's dissolute lifestyles, so used to excess and babying are they...'

The self-righteous ethics of James Jesus Angleton were always at his side, to guide him through the appalling things in life a spy sees. And does.

Unbeknownst to him, though, this was not the star's official shamiana. That spacious and luxurious headquarters was clear on the other side of the cantonment, and it was, at this very moment, being scrutinized from a judicious and camouflaged distance by none other than U.X. Vunn.

Butterbugs knew strategic discretion better than any spook. A life in pictures took place in *front* of people, not behind the scenes. He'd applied evasive action in order to achieve solitude by bunking at this moribund address, used earlier in the picture by Old Atrocity's C-team grips, long departed to the confines of Stateside now.

How remarkable that it was mere coincidence the star had given this particular address to Lurgan when back in Hollywood. Crisis or no crisis, Butterbugs always had to hedge his bets when giving out personal location information.

'Protection? Why, you are no guard-type...,' Butterbugs uncharacteristically thought out loud, uncharacteristically fingering both a scimitar and a blunderbuss of the antique kind.

'I rely on craft more than weapons of mass destruction, capable one,' said DeVault, raising his arms, ready for frisking. He knew that the actor, skilled particularly in pictures exhibiting ferocity enacted on the plains of a Tartarstan or thereabouts, could hack both his legs off at a whack, then inject a whole bell-load of mini-canister into the pith of his pitiful torso, before rendering his skull flat with the carbon-coated door gong that still swung in the twilit belfry near the door. So he simmered his commentary down, and would now solely rely on guile, a tool he never mentioned, as his prime preservation mechanism from now on.

'But I am your guest,' he said easily. 'Do with me as you will.'

He knew that Butterbugs was well aware they were in the region (here and in the great Afghan tracts to the north) where maximum courtesy is always by practice extended to guests. Be they your most mortal of enemies, guests nevertheless deserve at least a morning's head start before deadly pursuit ensues. The rest of the world often considers this part of Asia to be a savage cauldron of ruthlessness, but how civilized is *that?* So, DeVault stood some chance at carrying out his mission, in search of a time-buying parley. Even a seminar of deception might yet come off.

Butterbugs put down the forceful toys and resumed the weary mien he'd had here for some time now. He was weakened by both his cares and his unbearable suspension of being. He didn't understand anything any more. He didn't know anything about time, either.

'When will she come!' he let escape.

'Oh, my friend, you must be so lonely here!'

'I only desire *her.*'

'Of course, of course. Of *course* you do! You could not possibly feel for any other. Her... Yes. Might I venture – Is this the one known as Keenah...?'

'Oh, how did *you* know? How *would* you know?'

'Because you two have worked so hard together on this picture, friend.'

'We have, you know. The world doesn't know *how* hard. But now the world has changed. *My* world has become changed. I know not what is right-side-up. I admit it! I *must* admit it! An actor has to be naked with himself. I have been, in my strict privacy here, trying to sort it out.'

'Let me help, Butterbugs.'

'You??'

'Tell me, son, how came you to hate me so?'

'I believe that I trusted you.'

'As well you might, as I reciprocated. My record shows it. I swear!'

'Even deadly snakes can appear benign.'

'I have been all about reason with you. Everything I *do* in your name is reasonable! As a famous person, I brought you help in the form of guidance through your celebrity. I brought wisdom to our little chats.'

'At my pleasure.'

'Of course. But I gave of my time.'

'And I became your doormat.'

'Let's leave off that unhappy subject just now. I would like to help with your current miasma.'

'Where, oh, *where* is my girl?'

'Perhaps she will be here on the next gharry…!'

'Could she?'

'Most probably.'

'I will dare to hope!'

'Do. Indeed, do. Hope is a hopeful sign!'

DeVault glanced out the primitive window and almost started.

'Say, that looks like –'

Butterbugs gasped anxiously.

'Naw, I guess it was just a dustman's cleanup cranchee, now vanished over an undulation.'

Butterbugs, totally taken in by the fictitious observation, remained in situ and sighed.

DeVault took in the whole room with a good-natured gesture.

'Your quarters – those of a bohemian artiste! A retreat from the boils and the tears of the sets and the fans, I'll wager.'

Such a drippy attempt to make light of things in order to win the actor back! Butterbugs was merely stationary on a rumpled ottoman and allowed his face to evolve into Stanley Cortez-style chiaroscuro.

'I guess that wasn't very funny.'

Butterbugs had absolutely no reply.

A few extremely awkward moments passed. The actor had no choice but to wax impatient.

'So??'

'Butterbugs, now… I'm afraid I have to bring up the solemn subject of my visit.'

'Oh?? Well, what the hell are you *doing* here, anyway? I suppose you want to continue your sick 'Responsible Celebrities' come-to-Jesus talks, or something.'

'That's not a very nice thing to say, Butterbugs.'

'Yeah, well…'

DeVault calmly resumed his statement, by way of explanation.

'The subject as to the Why of my being here will settle all things. Not only will it make us friends and partners again, it will set you upon a new path toward recovery and light, *and* your lady.'

Butterbugs was listening, even though he thought it creepy and weird.

'And the thing is, we can all be winners. However, there's a little intermission here. I wish popcorn, lollipops, cotton candy and cupcakes might be served! Even here! You know? But not in this dump, eh? Heh-heh. Well anyway, there's now a sad prologue to the upcoming features of my treatment of this storyline, though…'

DeVault thought he'd inject a bit of cinema-exhibitor lingo into his spiel, in order to make his client feel more at home. But the dreadful look the star gave him, which was especially atmospheric in this scene, was so deadening in a film noir sort of way, he immediately abandoned this tack and returned to the gooey but plain talk of his successful days as a responsible celebrity councilor back in Butterbugs' studio bungalow.

'It's, uh, *sad* because… Well because – Er, Butterbugs, do you mind if I sit down – somewhere…? Like… somewhere?'

Not at all thrilled about any of this, Butterbugs gave the most minimal gesture possible as an indicator that some sort of seating arrangement was actually feasible. That is, if his guest chose to place a slivery piece of board between a smudged crate of worn-out Chapman crane gears, cotter pins and bearings, and a tub of unused Enfield rifle grease from the Property Dept. This from an ultrastar famed for his trademark hand gestures of presentation, in scenes both grand and intimate, contained within some of the greatest pictures ever made.

Once he got into this project, the guest, much to his distaste, encountered all sorts of grody and infuriating details of futziness, but he persisted in rigging up a barely serviceable plank-davenport that was extremely brutal on his internal piles, but the stakes in this mission were, he reminded himself, extremely high, and his performance in it had the potential of outdoing that of Philby, Maclean, and all those guys. (Was that a good comparison to make?)

'So, I know we are surrounded by sadness right now, OK? But I have to emphasize that it's better to agree we've got a really sad situation here than to try and deny it. Then, that makes fixing it all the harder, OK? I mean, all the easier…'

Butterbugs cast a look in his direction that implied, 'Would you get to the fucking point?' but the ultrastar just didn't feel like wasting good vulgarisms on this tiresome visitor. Besides, this intruder had better fucking explain himself, and pronto. The selection of weapons was still within the aspect ratio of his vision.

Now was DeVault in need of plucked courage, for he sensed a growing hostility in Butterbugs. He had to go on with his angle. He had to project confidence. The chances of him botching this thing loomed as a very great possibility. It could all fall apart in seconds. Therefore, he'd have to go for 'Shock and Lying', as they tended to say in Langley.

'OK. Here's the deal. Your agent has been giving you falsehoods. Yes, falsehoods! Of the most bald and stark kind! He's plotting against you, Butterbugs. You know that, now don't you, now? He wants to take advantage of you. Well, not just that – he wants to *take you down*. Don't you see?'

Now that DeVault was getting toward specifics, Butterbugs stopped thinking about Keenah for a moment.

'*What?*'

He paused.

'*Whie?*' he asked in a stunned whisper.

'I suppose you've heard from him? From somewhere… South of the border, shall we say? Excuse me, somewhere in Latin America?'

Butterbugs was grimly impressed.

'Maybe.'

'Oh, we *know* he's probably in the vicinity of old Bolivia. He has startings there, you see. Not many people in his Industry know that, but *we* do.'

'You talk of him as if he's a – criminal, or something.'

'Butterbugs, when I tell you, you might think of him as that, as well. But you be the judge.'

'Well, you just tell me now, Lurgan.'

'We also know things about you too, Butterbugs. But please, let me immediately say that our intelligence is meant to protect you, and with benevolence! We agents are working for peace and safety, you know. Peace, with honor!'

'At least you're admitting that you're one of the most reprehensible manifestations of a poor career choice on earth: a spy! You rat on people for a living. The only kind of 'agent' I know is Sonny Projector. You are… *rubbish.*'

DeVault held the tiller steadily. Without missing a beat, he serenely resumed, knowing that the bombshells waiting would erase any anger this overpaid ventriloquist act could ever serve up.

'We happen to know that your earnings in pictures have placed you in the very front rank of the globe's most endowed individuals. I believe the term 'trillionaire' is generously jockeyed about. To be blunt: your 'agent', Sonny Projector (if that really *is* his name…), has taken steps to deprive you not only of your wealth and linked resources, but he is well advanced in a plan to engineer a situation wherein your career is rendered kaput… *finished.* In a word, your agent has betrayed you.'

'You *fucker.*'

'Poor fellow! Poor little orphan lamb-y! I'm afraid your agent's judgement is against you.'

In past pictures, this would be a cue for the actor to rise and cry foul, to sweep over to his weapon of choice and to commence dueling with this villain, or to force a confession of his lies before chaining and imprisonment, or to strike his head bloody-well off. Big damn head.

Instead, he winced and continued to listen weakly. Anger to be re-directed?

'You know, Butterbugs, we really don't have much time for me to give you every last detail. There will have to be some trust going on here. Trust between us. Don't you think it's about time we arrived at such a station? Hmm?'

'Go on.' Butterbugs' voice was filled with pure hatred.

'Well, it gets a bit unpleasant for you now. Sonny has committed felonies of embezzlement and robbery, money laundering, conspiracy, uncleanness, absconding, fleeing the country, and even gunrunning. His agency, it seems, was involved in all sorts of nasty activities. It has been shut down, the building taped off, and evidence and assets seized. All this has been happening while you have sat here in hermitage. Do you realize that? Projector's son has been arrested and is now in jail, with bail, originally set at US$10 millions, now denied.'

'You *LIAR!*'

'Hardly, entertainer! Look on my NewsPacket contained within my Wristie. The documentation is all there. A media meltdown. There are no lies to contest.'

'Surely, with a little explanation...'

'Oh, grow up! It's *that* severe. Drugs are also involved. Can you imagine anybody going to Bolivia and drugs *not* being involved? There is plenty of evidence to show that he is an addict.'

'Unpleasant for *Sonny*, you mean.'

'Heavens, I can't say anything sympathetic about Sonny Projector! The thing is, he left considerable evidence and documentation that you, Butterbugs, are in collusion with him, and that any conviction based on this evidence would put you in prison – probably Leavenworth – for a very long time indeed. As an actor, you would be entirely discredited and invalidated. Depending on the extent of the case, all your pictures, and every aspect of them even, and especially the negatives, as well as all prints, could be destroyed. It would be demanded by all those thou hast offended. The terminal result would be as if you *never existed*. You are heavily, and I'm sorry to say, fearfully implicated in Projector's case. I don't see how you can successfully fight it. Of course, you may want to confer with a lawyer or something. Please, Butterbugs, do not collapse in shock and depression! I said I am here to *help* you. I will now cheerfully offer you a way out.'

'What's next, suicide?'

'Why –'

'After all, if I'm going to non-exist, I might as well do it myself.'

'Ha ha. Yes, I can see why you'd joke that way. (Strolling player, and all!) But look, there's a significant thing going on here. Notice that Projector left the country, and we know the general vicinity of his hiding. Then, notice that you, too, left the US, upon the advice of Projector. We know (quite obviously, right?) of your very location – in front of me now! – Isn't that *special?* Sometimes extradition laws can be overruled. South America has often done so. Perhaps this 'Stan' in which we now sit, might, as well. You don't know. No guarantees. But the big deal is that both you and Sonny Projector lammed on out of your native soils. The coincidence is damning. In the palazzos of jurisprudence and in the cinema halls, the television lobbies, the cigar divans, and the countless homes, and for all I know, the peep-show booths, both juries and the great world-public will cry out at your treachery. You have betrayed the public trust. I'm afraid the judgment is against you.'

'You stupid shit-ass! You're wrong about Sonny. So wrong! He would strip nude for me, just to show he had nothing to hide. Will no one now come forth and ask him to strip? He will! I tell you, he *will!*'

'I can understand your emotional rejection of my tale,' replied DeVault with noticeable condescension. He now took significant pleasure in reducing Butterbugs to a tantrum-throwing brat. The more epithets, the better. Happily, he felt his MinnieTaper6000 recorder humming along next his breast. The mike that passed as a hearing aid was capturing their dialogue with Neumann-like quality.

'Sonny's strip-tease huh?' Lurgan continued. 'That's a good one! But you see, you just don't have the time to research this whole thing, buddy-boy. You are obliged to trust in me. The international clock is running.'

'No, you're wrong about his native soil,' Butterbugs said sullenly. 'It's Bolivia, not the US. He didn't desert his native place. He went *back* to it, ShitLips.'

'Funny! Funny. Droll… But yes, I don't blame you for rooting out some levity in this appalling dilemma. You have been left alone. Alone! Think of it! Where are your fans now? What are you and your resources now, here in this hideous place? You wouldn't want to bring the Lady Keenah here for a tryst, would you?'

'No… I… Keenah!… Keenah…?'

'That's what I thought, gentle friend. Now consider – I have a scheme.'

Butterbugs didn't know whether to feel he was being hornswoggled, or if things were closing in, due to the heretofore unknown mischief of others. Truths were dangerously elusive right now. But it was true: he was isolated, for the strangest of reasons. Where *was* everybody? Things had gone dreadfully amiss – he guessed. Everybody had vanished. That Judah Fitz-Judah guy, whom he'd let kiss him (!). Now what the hell happened to him? No further contact with Sonny had been possible. Out of his phone coverage again, or just sick of General Eugenio A. Garay? He'd tried to find where Penny was incarcerated. No luck. A&U-CAM was entirely shut down – phone avenues sealed off, and he daren't call the studio, lest Sonny be correct, and now, lest DeVault be correct about Sonny being incorrect. Justy was at a UN conference in Svalbard. Saskia never took her phone with her when she went to the Shetlands; on Ochterlony Island, there wasn't even a telephone kiosk anyway. Egaz was surely sealed off, presumably at The Nookery, on

Boulevard d'El Fontaine de la Los Angelinos dos Temple Expiatori de la Sagrada Familia – but maybe not. He didn't even want to think for a second what kind of danger his Keenah might be in, just now. These were the only (former) securities he had to go on. So now, apparently, DeVault Lurgan was his only asset, his sole comforter, his single ticket out of this, this – pickle – or whatever the hell it was. With him, then, he would have to throw his lot, at least until he found out more tangible facts. Right now he was dependent on a sort of *trust*, even though it be with an agent of espionage, whose only portfolio was verbiage that could not be corroborated.

Plus, this, this, *agent* was one of the most disgusting fuckers Butterbugs had ever encountered.

'Shoot,' was all the lone ultrastar could say.

'Good! *Good!* Now, what I'd like to do is this: you will maintain your privacy at this here hovel for the day. Yes, the long hours of a full day. You may brood, but please, do not use your mobile. Global-wide YurkaCover Spot technology can trace your calls in a matter of seconds now. You must remain in neutral undercover – I mean – in hiding, until the next phase is revealed unto us. It's only for the course of this day's light, I should think. No big deal.'

Butterbugs was beginning to wholly believe the spy's trip. It was making too much sense, maddeningly annoying though it was. This DeVault just *knew* so much, and the pieces were fitting together – he guessed.

'And then?'

'Consider!' said DeVault. 'This unscripted but sure-shot scenario. We have learned of your thoughts concerning a potential retirement from the screen – Please, Butterbugs, hear me out. Do not balk at the covert data I have acquired. You must accept the long range of intelligence's means in learning truths, for it is truth that can save us all. Now then, research has shown that, not too long ago, you considered repairing to a contemplative retreat called, um, I believe it's called *Goth*pore? Something like that?'

At this name, Butterbugs perked a tad.

'Why... yes.'

'Good. *Good!* I'm glad our inquiries were truthful. We *always* prefer truth! Well, therein lies a terrific opportunity for you and yours, Butterbugs.'

The ultrastar discreetly clasped his hands, which were hidden in the darkness below his face.

'Tell, please.'

'Certainly! It's rather an attractive scheme, because it includes spiritual options. So. Your circumstances being what they are, I and certain associates who are assisting you already – though you know it not – are ready to ensure that you have safe passage to ground that is *sanctuary*.

'Oh! *Sanctuary?*'

'Yoe! Also, too, there is another element here which you should know about. It will either be cause for you to rise in your stirrups and smite the offending force, if that be your choice, or else to heed sage advice and take a less fateful avenue. Either way, it's up to you, my fine fellow! It's *your call*.'

The cheerful rise of tone in which the last sentence was uttered made Butter-bugs ram a thumbnail into his index finger. What did he do to deserve this National Public Radio-like treatment?

'Go. On...' was all the ultrastar could get out.

DeVault's verbosity, delivered by the lousy actor in him, outing itself perhaps because of a sour grape mash he'd distilled for the great Butterbugs to steep in, threatened to loosen the compelling grip his earlier reasoning had made on the star. Once again, a mere glance from the artiste to the yakker made the yakker dump the flowery prologues before every explanation and cut to the chase.

'Yes! Well, the thing is, Butterbugs, the FBI have it out for you, too. Also, too. Plus... That's a really *big* plus... That's right. Certain parties of a conservative nature have been spreading lies (well, I should *hope to shout* they're lies!) about you being in partnership with the tyrant Ool-Akzad Nazah's interests. You know, so as to squeeze the American people out of their rightful favorable deals with that roguish nation. After all, you are playing a role in that 'An Un-holy War's Hymnal' thing, that, as wags have it, is a thinly disguised portrayal of that troublesome and tiresome personage and Epic Renegade in question. You know, the Nazah fellow. Don't take it from me! But there are considerable congressional forces who are aggressively pursuing this supposed connection. They don't need facts, only noise. Now, I'm not saying I agree with them. No, no, no! But the reports coming over the media have been, well, somewhat convincing. So that's another thing.'

(His misquoting 'UWH''s title was intentional, but such a stupid thing to do – it wasn't even funny in a sardonic way; it was just stupid, and reeked of the sourest of not-so-tender-vined grapes.)

Though he surprised Butterbugs by declaring, 'They don't need facts, only noise', DeVault could have used phrases like, 'It looks like you're being framed' or 'There is no hard evidence to suggest...', but he left off. Instead, he noted Butterbugs' droopier stance and his wearying posture, which he deemed promising to his cause. Besides, *lying* was the most obvious tool in his kit bag. Guile, which was fancier, too.

'But now, Butterbugs, a plan of hope! A surefire possibility of renewal. Hark ye, hear ye! Your new life will proceed as follows. But first, I have to ask you a question. Are you up for it?'

The star was encountering shell-shock territory like no filming of even 'On Volga's Ensanguined Shore' (Mosfilm) could instill.

'The question itself, or what the question *implies?*' he managed to ask.

'Well gosh-golly, it seems you've been in some thoughtful, even psychological, dramas!'

Butterbugs looked at him with an expression of utter 'You have *no idea* whatsoever'.

At then the spook grew dead serious.

'Now listen, fella. We're talking about *both* the question itself *and* what it implies!'

'I am – I am – I, I, am up…'

'All right then, stout-hearted one, my question: if you and those you hold dear had the option of stealing away to a place of happiness, peace, and sanctuary, pray, where would it be? Oh yes, it has to exist on this planet, and it has to be, you know, real. Not some movie thingie…'

Then, the look on the face of Butterbugs: Werfel could have described it! Bernini could have captured it in marble! Mahler might have symphonized a portrait, out of its passion!

'I can tell you – I can state, without the least bit of equivocation to interfere, that that place on this eventful sphere, wherein I and my people might dwell, would be none other than that place *well away* from the madding crowd. Far up the valley, toward glory. Away, oh! *away* from the world at large. Sequestered in peace of mind, hand and bowl, guiding staff, and selfless worth! That terminus of questing and longing and dreaming! That final destination of this finite existence, at least. The honest and dear settlement, wherein dedicatees to truth and the interior life have made something of themselves in this less-than-satisfactory world. Where there is perfection of understanding and a release from our superficial distractions. Where the air is more rarefied, but closer to truths. Where there is, nearby, a bulwark of rising ground, which leads not to a higher elevation only, but to a higher plane of consciousness. Where, yes, truth and the mind meet, perhaps for the first time… That place, that place I have helped *build*, have helped *remain*, have helped *launch* into the unknowable future: GOTHPORE!'

'Praise! Praise, now, to and for your choice!'

'Yes, *Gothpore!*'

Butterbugs was struck with a sense of coming home…

'I knew it. I *sensed* it…,' whispered the spy, supportively.

DeVault was genuinely moved by Butterbugs' delivery, though his heartfelt conviction actually caused a boil of hatred to grow in his heart. For what *right* does a man have in feeling so sure about his desires, and what *gives* him the right to be so damn egotistical in proclaiming them?

After his mental applause for the star's dramatic performance, admittedly admirable in itself, quickly abated, an inflamed contempt for his confidence in happiness now took pride of place. Not only was the spy suddenly elated in proceeding with his mission's task, he was totally resolved in regarding Butterbugs as a force to be eliminated. For how could such a wonder be tolerated in an imperfect world? No, the world must *stay* far from perfect. And he, Agent Lurgan, would be absolutely central to the perpetuation of evolution's stasis. If he had been a believer in any sort of religion, he would have felt positively *Satanically* endorsed and empowered at this point. But no need for the validation of mumbo-jumbo. He was well on his way to a success so total as to spread its plunder before his master Realms, like a cape of drebb-flowers, funereal in their feeling,

513

but solemnly triumphant in their intent. Beyond that lay Empire, of which he would certainly be an intimate part. Intimacy! Why was it associated with sex at all? Real intimacy meant power over others, and the power to choose how to use it, and upon whom. What else *was* there?

'Your choice,' DeVault continued, picking up his serene persona after the heady reverie set off by the word *Gothpore*, 'is an inspired one. It is a place none of us but you can aspire to, for you are its soul. Also, Arunachal Pradesh does not subscribe to any conventional extradition treaties. Attaining Gothpore, you'll have it made! Just think! At Gothpore you will be able to retire into private interior life! Perfect, baby!'

'Perfect...?'

'Why, you'll have Keenah at your side and in your bed, or cot, or floor – Heh, heh! Whatever!'

'Keenah! My love! What can she be doing? Here we are, plotting her and my future together, and I cannot even share it with her! Oh, irony! Heartless commentator on all mismatched events! But, I have to be strong and patient, do I not? We've done some big scenes together, she and I, you know? Both off and on the screen...'

'Lovely!' DeVault's jealous hatred for women was kindled. Steady though, pardner.

'She can come with?'

'Oh yeah, most – I mean *most* assuredly, Butterbugs. That's what all of this is about! Happiness, perfect happiness. Isn't it?'

'I am comforted.'

'Good. *Good!* Next, a sequence that is right out of one of your pictures, Butterbugs. Your line of escape – er, departure. Let's toss around some ideas. It's just like something out of one of your big adventure pictures. Like your 'Cities in Flight' (Universal*), n'est pas?* You know, departure to somewhere *better*. Want to hear about it?'

'Yeah.'

Apparently, Butterbugs was going to have to wade through this ongoing Children's Story Time in order to get the lowdown on his wimpy ditching of all that he was, based on hearsay and all.

'Just get a load of this, Mister! It's all *set up*. We – me and my helper – plus you, and Keenah, that is (of course!), get to take off on modest conveyances through the wilds of this here 'Stan' and over its roads, which are more like our American *off*-roads, if you know what I mean. Anyway, we'll all get to depart on whatever means of transport we can cobble up. So as to, you know, be secretive, and head for the good old Kurr Valley, an easy coasting downhill to the coast, and into Gwadar town, a place of total picturesqueness and charm. Some time may be allowed to wander about the native bazaars, if scheduling permits. Souvenirs are encouraged, but only if light in weight. Miss Keenah will like that, don't you think? After a bit of refreshment at the Alexanderus Drinks-cum-Kebub Bar, we take a hired car out into the molten wilderness of S'shirr and stop off at the H.M. the Jam's Meteorological Station, Up-the-Country from Gwadar, at Pundit Point, where you will take ship aboard a special weather balloon. It shall be equipped with wicker stateroom, perfectly adequate for the rollicking sail-away which awaits, guided by a special British (and Dickie Branson-trained) balloonatic, who will take you and your Lady Love on up the mega-spine of the Roof of the World, and down into Gothpore Vale at the end of the third day. All of this do I pledge to you, upon my honor, as your assistant, subservient, and helper.'

The prospect of escape from this miserable post, and via a really quite reasonable route, appealed greatly to the brooding ultrastar, despite the sick-making presentation made by this stranger-creep who knew so much, and was, thus, chained to his testicles, as it were.

'And now, Butterbugs, I must announce that, well, certain conditions must be enacted in light of you getting what you want. In return for this glorious sanctuary, you must drop your participation in the 'Hymn' picture, and indeed, you must renounce it utterly, so that you will be entirely purged of its associations of burden and of guilt.'

He didn't define what 'guilt' might mean in this instance, but he'd made his point, and to great effect. And then he clinched it.

'The final and permanent bottom-line in all this is that you cannot reverse any of it. Once you have committed, your cinema career is concluded. For *ever*.'

Butterbugs was hunched. 'Concluded' and 'For *ever*' were baleful enough words, but he just plain didn't much care for the term 'Lady Love'. Bastard! What the hell did he know about the wonders of Keenah? But, but, what could he *do?* Clouds there were on the horizon, but when they cleared, and they *must* clear, they *would* clear... Gothpore, only Gothpore...!

'Do these things, Butterbugs, and you shall have the pleasantest and most fulfilled next stage of your life in happy Gothpore. This I pledge. Come now, I have some papers for you to sign...'

At last, Butterbugs broke down. The petcocks were twirled in the corners of his eyes, releasing the saline fluid of angst and grief and sorrow and longing that had built up. It was a condensation of lonesome love for Keenah, combined with the realization, despite the glory of his cinema career, that the edifice containing it was capable of collapse, implosion even, and the true import of such a possibility simply made him weep. To have come to *this!* It wasn't as if he had been aloof all this time... He remembered the Fall of the House of Isaac Davis with a vividness that could only be filed away by his dedication to his craft. But now, his *love* was involved! It was just that the trust he had lived from day to day seemed lasting and contagious. It was surely built for the ages, and perhaps, all by itself, it could be regarded as a significant step in human evolution.

But maybe not.

'Haven't heard from Sonny,' he sniffed. 'Haven't heard from anybody! I'm really worried. Have I really been abandoned, so?'

The grand processional way – was it closed now?

Both questions, one consciously asked, the other below the surface, were rhetorical. He'd already concluded that yes, he had been abandoned. This served to answer many an inquiry. Maybe he had indeed been abandoned by everybody, including his love. He could only guess. These things can happen in this world. He thought it was so. But still, he didn't want to admit it to this, this *flimp*, who just sat there on that appalling plank, with the fecal-hunting smile/leer on his greasy face, waiting, waiting to get what he wanted.

Indeed, what was DeVault's stake in this gig? Money? Real estate? Stock options? Oh, he forgot: government agents serve their country before anything else.

'Notice, though, Butterbugs, that *I* am here. Here you are, an ultrastar, and everyone has left off of you! But *I* have not abandoned you, like some! Well now! You are a subversive, Butterbugs. You – have to *go*. It's that simple. You will retire from both professional and public life. I say 'life', but there is also another choice.'

'You'd... bump me off?' The ultrastar almost... whimpered!

'I have nothing whatsoever to do with such sick prospects. But there are others who do. Their nameless identities are writ in deepest obscurity, yet highest ferocity, and first-quality efficiency.'

If this was a scare tactic, it worked.

'I get your drip. I've been *had*. I'm screwed. Cooked. Fucked.'

'No! No! Not at all! Why do you think I'm here, famed actor? Will you not consider the noble concept of vindication when it comes to your regard of my poor self? I cannot hope for redemption, or even partial forgiveness. But if you might grant me a tad bit of consideration, that I seek to aid you now in compensation for your fears, you might, at the very least, consider me an *agent* – of the travel variety! How's that, you ask? Very well! Can you not conceive that the plan I have outlined will *actually work?* This is not a movie script we're talking about. This is the real world, and it is free from script conventions, and thus, limitless in its possibilities. The good of the world is as limitless as the bad; I think more so.'

Startled by the spy's halfway intelligent statements, Butterbugs brightened, ever so subtly.

'You, you think? Can there ever be a tomorrow for me – and my love?'

'I've been telling you...'

'Then, let us enact your scheme. I consent! I tell you, I give my consent. Purged of our temporal ills, my beloved and I will be able to retire into private interior life. I'd rather live in love away from the world than to resign it without resolve. Oh, DeVault, lead me! Take my trust and let me move my life and love up into the great mansions of the mountains, to find a fulfillment I have never known, though I know it exists!'

'So, Butterbugs, you would steal away to Gothpore, then?'

'I... would.'

'Perfect!'

That word came out in disgustingly cheery decibels, but Butterbugs didn't have the stuff to analyze it any more. Right now, he was out of gas, and his head descended slowly, and in this wilderness of anti-comfort, his neck found the rim of the Enfield rifle grease tub to rest on. And the man actually slept for a time.

Outside, the disc of sun was well-washing all over the muted settlement. Silver it became. Then, as inevitable apogee approached, white, all dusty white.

Time ran. DeVault, with all kinds of arrangements to make, let the star slumber for only fifteen minutes, as a courtesy and trust-builder. What better for the star to see upon his awakening than a steady soul on the lookout, guarding without complaint, like the hamadryads of old, who sheltered Akbar the Great in the desert, as well as a million gods, godlings and chosen chelas before him.

Rising in the gloom, his numb ass suddenly shot through with ancient ache, DeVault stood there and regarded he who was both hero and inspiration to billions, sleeping innocent sleep. Yonder, the blade of the scimitar, a most realistic prop, glinted dully.

'If I were to wield it now,' Lurgan thought, 'I should be more of a hero than any actor ever could. I should start with his private parts, for they have caused so much grief in the world. Then I should remove his liver, to ensure that it is devoured by gross-kites and other vulture-y flyers. Then I should render his body in half, so that it could never be whole again. I would do these things, and go forward into glory!'

He actually approached the weapon, and attempted to pick it up, hilt-side. But his clammy fingers were no warrior's tools. He clumsily let it fall with a thuddy clang.

Butterbugs slept yet.

'Oh, it's so heavy...,' he whined.

Butterbugs slept yet.

Then he considered the other life-destroyer at hand, the formidable blunderbuss, stacked against the canvas wall. Dainty fellow that he was, he didn't even bother to inspect it any closer.

'Looks too complicated!' he complained.

Butterbugs slept, even yet.

'Should I go through with the plan, or kill him now? I could always brain him with that icky gear-cog thing. Or that board, I suppose...' The insipidness of his reasoning surprised even the super secret agent himself.

But no. Not today. He leaned over and reached out his hand to gently touch the star's shoulder. This was the climax of the reverie he had been playing since Butterbugs had lapsed into sleep. Intersecting thoughts of power, influence, logistics and glory met in his mind as the shoulder was gripped, in all friendly helpfulness, and he knew that now, simple enactment of the program's features was all that remained in this mission. The tough John Le Carré part was completed. Now the Alistair MacLean bits could proceed.

'Gentle actor,' murmured the spy, turning on the schmaltz, 'Did you sleep with dreams of merry flight and dreams of deserved bliss? With Keeny, perhaps? Hmm?'

Butterbugs, awakened now, looked up at him with a 'Don't ever, EVER touch my body again; that is the province of my 'Lady Love' as you so disgustingly put it' expression.

DeVault then realized his charge might be a little difficult to deal with.

'I'd forgotten the heat,' he said, as if he were waiting for tires to be put on his RV in a Tucson Big Meats Wheel 'n' Hub outlet.

'Shut up.'

Butterbugs sounded as if he were hung over. It was not a restful nap.

'Tonight we go. Until then, lay low!'

Stupidly, DeVault had kept on with the insufferable cheer that Butterbugs obviously hated.

'Just – shut up,' the big star muttered.

'I promise I will, but I have to brief you first. I really must. There are a few minimal matters to discuss.'

'Oh, well, all right then.'

'You aren't having second thoughts, are you?' he smiled.

'Well, I think I do.'

'Just remember, future hilltop philosopher, your girlfriend has yet to connect with us. A lot can happen to her, especially if she doesn't link in a timely fashion.'

The threat worked: Butterbugs *became* 100% on board. They shook hands on it. The hatred each felt for the other was communicated through their sweaty palms. But right now they needed each other completely, though for utterly different reasons. All-business could now be the ruling tone.

'Now listen,' DeVault said, as if he was going after 'The Guns of Navarone' (Columbia, 1962), but had to deal with group dysfunction to get the job done, 'You've got to keep down here until darkness covers these bitter rocks. I'm out to link with my associate, and to acquire our getaway vehicles, etc. It's boring stuff really, but heck, if you go out of this dumpy haven, the recognition thing will make our efforts blown. In conclusion, I wonder, Butterbugs, if you might not surrender your mobile to me for the duration.'

'You sleaze! Don't trust me, eh?'

'I would rather you loathe me personally than to let the potential weakness, ignited by your understandable passions, cause you to attempt ringing-up your loved ones. You would be traced in quick-time, and this hovel would be surrounded by S.W.A.T. teams of unknown origin, with even *more* unknown agendas to enact. As an agent, and yes, as a '*fucking spy*', I have to warn you about these things, and demand your cooperation, now that we have shaken on the deal.'

Butterbugs almost laughed.

'You said that 'f-word'!'

DeVault almost did, too.

'And I said it for the first time!' lied the spy. 'And I hope the last. Forgive me.

Please? Oh, *will you?* Nevertheless, you comprehend the emphasis its usage carries.'

'OK, Filthy-Mouth,' said Butterbugs mockingly, remembering his character Crownie's role in 'The Mugs Of The Alleys Behind Broome Street' (Goldwyn). 'I'll bide my time and await your imperious orders.'

He handed over his mobile, but with a protest toss, into the DeVault's fumbling hands.

'It's only because we are very close, Butterbugs, to making this thing work. Very close. This is not a drill! Please, let's not – (get ready) – *fuck* this thing up! I save such words only for emergencies.'

No near-laughter now. Butterbugs was won over by the spy's perceived sincerity. He would put his life on hold until DeVault returned. Unsaid promise to himself.

'Affirmative,' said the ultrastar. Then, as DeVault made to go, 'Who is this 'associate', then?'

'Oh, he's a very nice guy. Very resourceful. He can pull a Kwunthuthian Crowing Hare out of a hat when everybody else uses the same pink-eyed bunny you saw every week on 'The Hollywood Palace' (ABC). You'll like him. Peace now, and dream of the heights of Gothpore! Oh, and Keeny!'

'The heights of... yes...,' breathed Butterbugs, as the spy enfolded himself in the canvas front door, and was gone. 'And it's Keen-*ah!*'

'That fuck-fucking pig-shitting egotistical piss-hissing spoiled shit-fucking ass-smooching playboy'd shit-lipped fucking *assmouth!*' muttered DeVault as he attempted evasive action in retreating from the safe-yurt into the noonday sun. 'I just hope that bizarre-fucking-*prejudice* is what Realms has in mind for that vomit-box of a shitty fucking-fucking-fucking human 'actor'-turd!'

(He'd always aspired to join Army Airborne for its freedom of speech, but never made the grade.)

Speaking of fecal matters, he suddenly felt a cramp in his gut and was forced to succumb to severe 'rice-water' runs. He did his hideous business next the low wall of a Raj Era cemetery, populated by forgotten Sappers and Miners. Here in the white-hot block of mid-daytime, their leaning regimental markers of cast iron and fatigued marble, set amongst the dead narl-stags, came off as nothing more than a few harsh, charcoal sketches.

'What a place to expire...!'

At least he did not befoul consecrated ground.

In his hot flushing agony, he cast his eyes, bleared by greasy tears, round the neighborhood. Here, on the slope that ran away from the newness of Jambutterbugsabad, with scrub and powdery soil, broken-down simply by the sun's rays, rather than the more elemental techniques of erosion, there was little indication that anything had ever changed past 1890 or so. Yonder, the ruins of an old garrison church and vicarage, as if imported from the prettiest little vale in the Cotswolds, looked like a heap of melted bouillon cubes.

[Actually, the spy had stumbled onto an exterior set complex, designed for the future production of Kipling's 'The Strange Ride of Morrowbie Jukes' (P.K. Kharve Talkies), scheduled to go into production after 'UWH' wrapped. Butterbugs had only recently signed the contract to star, under David Lean's direction. The atmospheric weathering of the set was coming along very nicely.]

The idgah, which DeVault had frequented just before his Butterbugs conference, stood blindingly in the near distance, heat waves rising from its white-washed deck and walls like vibrating solution in a sonic denture bath.

Indeed, it was hydration he really needed right now. His thin lips were cracking so quickly, he could almost *hear* the process. But returning to 2, Mulgie Lane for a tin cup dip into that probably-polluted goat-blimp full of 'water' – no doubt from the bottom of the tube-well out near the graveyard – did not occur as an option to him.

With his soiled monocular magnifier, he searched in vain for a vending machine or a Sparklurtt's dispenser in the shadows of the idgah's wall. He did, however, spy a sight that was not so surprising as it was lucky. It was *the* U.X. Vunn, doing his classic undercover maneuvers, feeling his way all along the wall, in direct sunlight, but trying to blend in. Methods practiced had led him close to where Butterbugs was. Not bad. He'd get a gold star. But he, DeVault, was ahead of the other's game. Way ahead.

Nevertheless, he would surely become vulture grub in about half an hour if he didn't get electrolyte replenishment. He'd already shat out his entire water reserves, the stupid nut.

No doubt U.X. would be annoyed to be found out while still in high stalk mode, but he had to get this bad-boy project rolling his way, before dying trying.

As a signal, Lurgan produced a little blowpipe from his polyester leisure suit jacket (which he mistakenly thought would be effective regional wear), and popped in a FethrTrakr cartridge. Then he bit off the tallow-coated seal to activate the micro-switch, and a bit of patooey later, a swift and steady dart left a trail of sage-green smoke, making its way to where the noonday spook might get its message. The dart then combusted into a telltale husk, like a Piccolo Peat, soft-landing as a harmless splotch on U.X.'s left shoulder.

Before the smoke-trail dispersed, U.X. gazed down its route, and saw, at its launch point, a spy's old fashioned hailing: gesticulating hands spelling out, 'Hi! I'm your associate! Let's get together (Yeah, yeah, yeah)!' boldly articulated in All-American Signpost Lingo.

In his reply, U.X. signed:

'OK! Happy to see you, matey! Come on in, why doncha!'

Even though no local person or beast in their right mind would have been out and about this hour, the spies behaved as if they were at Checkpoint Charlie, circa 1965. Every precaution was taken. U.X. oozed over onto the other side of the idgah wall, where it was only slightly cooler, while DeVault covered his entire person with the fried dust from the Makran's floor, in an attempt at camouflage. The result was something like an ash-smeared Hindoo sadhoo, none of whom had been seen in this zone since early August, 1947. The effect lapsed about halfway along his predictable zigzag to the idgah anyway, leaving him with every wrinkle filled with a sharply-defining line, and the general dirtiness of a drunken foon.

Absolutely no one saw them because absolutely no one was around to care.

And so, up under the ten centimeters of shade the idgah's wall provided, the two made their reunion. There was plenty of bickering, but they essentially agreed to combine forces in order to follow the mission's guidelines, which DeVault reviewed for U.X.'s benefit, once again.

'I will not argue with you more, Lurgan. Because your preliminaries fit with my upgraded instructions.'

'*What* upgrade?'

'While you were doing my job of handling our 'client', I was in receipt of revised instructions regarding carrying out our mission.'

'Pshaw!'

'I've never been more serious about anything in my life.'

A new frankness was stealing into U.X.'s relationship with his ostensible partner. Privately, he was overjoyed to see him. He regarded DeVault with – he couldn't help it – a new feeling. Something was distracting him, so he stuck to his guns of agency protocol in elucidating this development.

'So, *wow* me,' said Lurgan, confident of his mastery of mission.

'Wow?'

'Yeah. So serious, huh? OK then. You've got to prove there's an upgrade. Otherwise you're just a lying sac of buggery-santorum.'

U.X. actually felt sort of tingly.

'It's from Realms himself.'

'Bullshit. Nobody but *me* gets it from Realms (or sticks it in him, either).'

'I'm going easy on you, Lurgan, because we need each other right now. That I freely admit. And I grant you your progress with that fancy-schmancy Butterbugs over in there. But right now I've got the winning hand. You had your mobile turned off the whole time, and –'

'What the hell was I supposed to do, blow cover by having an intimate with Entablature (additional code not included), right in front of our prime client??'

'– And so Realms got a hold of me. Me! He's *pissed off*, by the way.'

'At me?'

'Uh-huh.'

'Get on with it. What's the beef?'

'Can't say. Yet.'

'Full of pork, eh?'

'You're not very funny, Lurgan. You never have been. Besides, I don't *like* jokes.'

But privately, he sort of liked the *sound* of the last one...

'So *you* get to crack the jokes, huh, 'You-Ecks'? What's this secret 'Realms' BS, but a joke?'

'No joke.'

'No jokie, Vunnie?'

'You don't own me, 'Lurgie'. *You never did.*'

'Un-*real!*'

'It's real, Lurgan, and *I'm* real.'

'Well then, I don't believe you. *You* never heard from Realms! You're just jealous of my achievements. You thought you'd mop the floor with me, way out here, didn't you? Well you looka here, bub, I'm running this show, as if Realms hisself was here.'

He felt all quivery and wambly and weak inside.

'You're really a dumber fuck than any of us thought, including Realms,' snapped U.X. 'He's frying-mad at you. That's one of the reasons he's upped the ante.'

'What do you mean by *that?*'

More than his volcanic bowel uprising, DeVault was genuinely ill at ease just by the words 'Realms' and 'pissed off' and 'you' (meaning he, Lurgan), appearing in the same spoken paragraph.

'I *mean* that we've got revised orders. It's all being jacked up.'

'Jacked up, or *off?* Just prove it, you mouse-ear! I can't stand this game!'

For a second, U.X. thought of bedrooms, riding crops, handcuffs...

'Well then, *OK.* Let's settle this then. Here's the word that'll prove I got the *in* from *on top.* Uh – I mean *the* top.'

U.X. mouthed the word 'Pantywaste' and watched DeVault's own mouth drop. 'Holy, *holier* shit.'

What clinched it for DeVault was the startling fact that U.X.'s precise mouthing actually delineated the difference between the more conventional (but non-applicable) spelling of 'pantywaist' from the unconventional (but here applicable, and more secure) 'pantywaste'. Good spy methods in action!

'Can we, um, *proceed* now?' U.X. stood triumphant.

'Yeah. Yes. Yes! Certainly! Can you elaborate yet?'

'Not yet.' He paused. 'I like how quickly you came around.'

'Well this is just too big. No more fucking around. It's big-time now, Vunn. You're at the top. With me. In all seriousness.'

'I know Realms is a bigwig and all, but what's the bigger deal?'

'Since you were good enough to let me into this, I'll tell you. It'll make the orders upgrade you're privy to take on a whole new sheen. Codeword you gave only means one thing: the ball's coming down from WH.'

'WH? Who that, William (Henry) Harrison?'

'Right address, wrong era.'

'Duh, address?'

'You may be just a hardware guy, but if you can load an Uzi, you can figure out my banter.'

'Address...'

'1600, Pennsy.'

'From the top?'

'That's what the codeword means, baby. And that par-tick-you-larr *spelling* of it, too. Which you nailed quite nicely, by the way.'

U.X. half-smiled, the first time he'd done so on this trip.

Renewed seriousness as to their professions instantly kicked into their chuckleheaded personalities. What other kind of human being would be suckered into such a mission?

Instinctively, they became more efficient. And there was a side effect. They actually softened toward each other. No more 'Spy vs. Spy'.

Now that they were the most important agents of the hour, a camaraderie surfaced and provided a bonding. DeVault utilized it as a deck-clearing. As of now, he didn't have to get fouled up in agent-to-agent bitching, or distracted by some screwy infatuation. Unburdened, he got back to being a Spy of Some Specific Talent.

For U.X. the change brought with it a rather more unconventional manifestation. He developed an erection. One that just wouldn't go away. He wasn't sure what made him hard, whether it was the excitement of their now totally-testosterone-loaded mission, or whether it had something to do with the other guy carrying it out with him; a sort of 'togetherness'. Regardless, it was one of those things that was rather hard to ignore. And because of the tightness of their revised schedule – and the tightness in his already-tight bellysuit – it was a condition that would just have to be addressed *and treated* – but later on.

As a result of the upgraded orders, U.X. told DeVault he had some private prepping to do, which could be done after their immediate duties were successfully completed. He wasn't exactly specific. With great shame, he realized he hadn't packed any protective cupping in his kit bag. But as of right now, much needed to be done. Relatively immediately.

'So??' Lurgan tremblingly asked, straining to hold his distressed lower sphincter shut.

'Revision time,' U.X. said quietly, holding his own special urgency in abeyance.

The projected shade upon DeVault's reddened face increased just a bit, just as he nearly fainted from the heat radiating from the idgah's wall.

'We need to combine knowledges, U.X. Now.'

'Right. My testing shows it's OK to do so verbally out here.'

'Super.'

'You go first,' said U.X. In his excitement, he almost added, 'How do you like it?', but he remained wholly professional.

'We need to get the bikes.'

'Check.'

'Well, Chet –'

'I said *check*.'

'Oh, oh, oh. I thought you were referring to the Chestre Alun Aurthur Alternative Plan.'

'What's *that* all about?'

'Oh, it was back in Springbok Cloven Hoof, in the Métis lands, when we had that stupid Commie to deal with, who ripped off the Presidential name and – hey! That has *nothing to do* with today, dumbo!'

'OK, back to just 'check', then.'

U.X. kind of liked it when Lurgan called him 'dumbo'. He futzed with his leggings, and coordinated his armaments, both organic and synthetic.

'Did you contact the Branson dude at H.M. the Jam's Meteorological Station at Pundit Point, so as to get the balloon prep going, so that –?'

'That stop will no longer be necessary,' U.X. interrupted.

'No longer... Oh.'

'Nope.'

'The bikes? Still on?'

'Yeah.'

'Then let's scare some up. May I suggest the studio runaround bikes?'

'You may,' said U.X. gravely. 'There's a postern, with three leaning against the back wall. Circa four hundred meters, that way.'

'OK, but we'll need one more. Four, total.'

'No we won't.'

'We won't... Oh.'

'Won't.'

'Three bikes only. *Revision*, remember?'

'Yeah, OK... *Three*, then.'

'Three, total.'

'Down the Kurr Valley to Gwadar? Still?' asked Lurgan, hopefully.

'Basically.'

'I see. Well, let's proceed.'

'After you, WH.'

'Funny. Funny! Droll... But U.X., one more thing. Might I have a swig from your PortaJug WaterGlass?'

'Can't it wait? I want to get those bikes.'

'True, we have a mission, which comes first...'

Then U.X. spotted something ugly, way over by the cemeterial wall.

'What the hell's that splatter over there? Looks like new shit. Somebody on our ass?'

Speaking of panty waste, Lurgan hadn't the heart to tell U.X. of his wimpy defecation-storm. Nor could he impart that the First†Dress panties he'd been trying out were at the bottom of it all. Gawd, was it difficult being a conflicted spook, or what?

'Oh, probably just a mirage... Let's get cracking... A lot to do. No more distractions, dopey, OK?'

Fortunately, any communicative airflow was lifeless and static just now.
U.X. rather liked 'dopey' better than 'dumbo'…

Meanwhile, in the cooker-yurt, Butterbugs was down on the floor, in order to absorb what little cool the earth hereabouts was yet prepared to give. Sometimes it seemed as if air had been removed from the world, as the need for it apparently could not be met by mere inhaling.

After a time, the anvil of the sun was moved on to a different location. The majestic cliffs, having absorbed an incredible register of solar radiation, efficiently dispersed it upwards. Then a light but effective breeze from the vicinity of Gwadar, down on the coast, considerably eased the oven-like conditions.

The stalled ultrastar stood and moved around. Wisely wetting his whistle, he guzzled about a liter from the plumpy goatskin reservoir that had been so forbiddingly regarded by DeVault Lurgan. It was always full of bell-clear water, via a spring that seeped from the living, giving, rocks above the flying cliffs. Its drops were so sweet, so pure, and more bacteria-free than the supercooled foundation currents under the Southern Ocean. Hydrated, the ultrastar recharged somewhat.

Eager for the least bit of input from the outside world, he couldn't get much info from the muslin window that faced massive rock. Then he lazy-walked over to the front door flap and worked its chinks so that a series of jagged strips allowed for head-slanting views of the dooryard without.

Deadly dull it was, though its classic Makranian characteristics brought comfort to the actor. Indeed, he loved this land. All through his career he'd striven to publicize, then aid, many an obscure cause or region in the world, and this meant there were plenty of unsung efforts in places only he knew.

He cast a glance over at the lurid but strangely romantic burial ground, with its cracked sarcophagi and other baked monuments. As of now, even he did not know it was a set for his next picture, so convincing was its character.

Death! And all that came with it! And being buried *here*, of all places! Such an exquisite terror! He made a mental note to have just that wish entered into his will.

'If I could cast my magic wand in any direction that caught my fancy,' he mused, 'I would restore anything of deemed and worthwhile value, bringing stability to the peoples therein, and causing peace to spread over the world. All achieved with this simple formula. If I can get through this tight situation, that is what I would like to do.'

Whether this noble notion was to be his destiny or not didn't really matter at the present moment. It was a sign of life, and a sign of moving past a troubling obsession with only Keenah. His sweetheart was right up there, but there were other matters and other persons within his sphere of influence to be considered and cared about. Annoying though he was (Lurgan that is), Butterbugs nevertheless had to admit he was the very man who'd busted him out of his neurotic and limited state.

In Jambutterbugsabad itself, he had created a community of liveliness and accomplishment. How appalling that a production shutdown, from an unknown source and for unknown reasons, way, way over in Hollywood, could reduce everything here to a slab of inaction and retrograde steps. Talk about unsung – no one would ever know the labors made by the many, mostly locals, who made this Studiostan a reality. In 1950s Oscar speeches, hotshot winners called them 'The Little People'. But to Butterbugs, they were bigger than he was.

'Why do greater powers always suppress the smallest threats?' he wondered aloud.

It was characteristic of the ultrastar to truly consider others before himself, no matter how shocking and offensive that stupid 'Report' he'd read on the plane out here was. Greater powers usually sought to oppress threats – the smaller the better. The smaller the easier. Now, he himself was apparently their target. But within his perspective, never mind that. There was a picture in jeopardy, and it affected many thousands.

Just then, he beheld a sign of somewhat animated life without. As chance would have it, the person whose life it was reminded him there were actually persons of worth who still walked this earth.

It was Yusuf Malik Khan, the alcalde of Jambutterbugsabad, great friend of Butterbugs and carrier of his cinematic dream here, who'd had, until now, astounding success in making both their concepts come true.

Peering from his pathetic retreat, he was tempted to call out, if only to say:

'O great Khan, come unto this door, and let us consider the fallacies of the world at large, for they become as candy to children, and when *consumed* by children, they grow and become accepted, so as to appear the norm of the world. But so do they prevent transcendent and advanced knowledge to lift humankind up into its next stage, which is waiting – and worried sick about the delay...'

He'd wanted to speak out, but –

'Truly, I can talk to him in such terms,' whispered the star, noting the Khan's deeply contemplative progression, with hands behind his back. The sherwani he wore on this heated day was the very same as when he greeted film folk entering his new Industry town. The very invitational quality of his being unfailingly projected good will and best wishes.

However, as the Khan bent his steps along Mulgie Lane, his eyes did not travel with any features along the way, as was his custom. Instead, they kept to the guiding ruts in the roadway, as if they were rails. A dictated route, pushing cooperative eyeballs or whatever vehicular traffic chanced to travel this by-lane, out into the virgin Makran. To face whatever nature might give there. Or take away.

Could that be where he was bound? To never return...?

Not one to be swept away by such environmental power, though, the Khan was plainly troubled and plainly in search of solitude. No doubt in order to sort out an understanding, if not a settlement. In fact, he was brooding over a statement that required delivery to both public and staff, regarding 'UHW''s fate, the studio's, and perhaps his own.

Butterbugs looked after him, and yearned for just a few moments of conference, as he was sure they both could find a solution to this critical problem that
had everyone so stymied. Surely it was not so complicated as to wreck the destinies of the many distinguished and sincere collaborators in this vast mix of
international cinematic art! How *could* it be?

"UWH' is not in itself worthy of jinxing Jambutterbugsabad, nor ruining any
associated lives!' the studio mogul proclaimed out loud. Only the dust heard him.

He then proceeded toward Sunset Rise, as it was called, and paused, as if he
could use a companion to share his thoughts concerning these troubled times. If
only he had known of his ultrastar's location, his longing, and the direness of his
helpless standing!

The ultrastar himself continued to view his Khan through the chink, and then
called out – but the cords in his throat would not vibrate. An innate sense of ethics overrode his will, keeping his physical self in thrall to the absurd-appearing
pledge of silence to DeVault. Was this really the judgment he should heed?

Now was his current state of mind so very like the pre-success days of his life,
when everything was one big introspection festival, in which this-and-that were
debated ad nauseam, and precious little resulted from all the self-indulgence.

Then, the great and very sane Khan went on over the Rise and turned into Moolkah
Lane, which headed back to motion picture civilization. Often a stroll did not necessarily produce tangible results to the questions of life, but it was always good to get up
and move around.

It was as if they were under the walls of a long-deserted Rajasthani fort. Prick-
le-weeds, rock dust and a lack of snakes were the sole extent of life and non-life
out here. The two spies had no need to be concerned about observation. Much of
the studio's working population had decamped to the delights of Gwadar, Karachi, Bombay, and even Dubai for the duration, or else they were well off enough
elsewhere in the not-unpleasant cantonment hereabouts.

The studio itself was of course secured, but not every bicycle had its own Kon-
Ippton grade lockup.

Everything the two spooks really needed for this (upgraded) mission stood in
front of them now. With tires plump enough to go, they almost cheerfully worked
out an agreement by which they would take turns handling the transport of the
third bike, taking the long way around to 2, Mulgie Lane. DeVault, who had a
considerable spare tire round his middle, nevertheless managed to pedal his own
rig while steering the spare with one hand grabbing the middle of its handlebar.

Through nullah and dale, past many a silent shamiana on Muldah Road, which
progressively shrank and became unmetaled, the selection of dwellings grew
more sparse as they progressed, decreasing in rent value the closer to the wastes
of Sunset Rise they got.

Things went like clockwork.

But past Mundah Gully, as he prepared to hand over Butterbugs' bike to U.X.

for the final leg, DeVault felt something – *crack* – inside him. Not a tear, not a rupture, but a crack. True, he was pretty dried out, but what had happened to his usual no-physical-problems-while-a-mission-was-in-play reliability? Even his turned-down sailor's cap seemed too large for his head now. Apparently, he was desiccating. His stupid clothes sagged. At least they weren't falling off. But this, this – crack – did not bode well at all.

No comment, though. What the hell would U.X. say at a time like this? What was he himself supposed to say:

'Hey Mr. Vunn, wait up while I reset me pipes inside. Shouldn't take but a jiffy'...?

Stoicism was *the* sign of a perfect spy.

DeVault's boss should be so lucky as to have known of such perfection.

Montague Realms sat at his DeeCee desk, all alone in the office suite. Past 6:00PM at the end of the week.

'Why did I turn out to look so *much* like Michael O'Dwyer?' he asked himself, gazing into his floss-speckled vanity mirror that faced him on his desk throughout the livelong day.

'*Sir* Michael O'Dwyer, that is.'

Then he picked at some dried lunch munch that had coagulated on the scrub-brush edge of his mustache, and started to play around with his private parts.

Phone rang just as he was getting going. The voice at the other end did not cause him to cease his jagging though. It was the White House calling, V.P. Division. More than any potential choice of sex slaves, Realms subscribed to Henry 'Young-Executive-Glasses' Kissinger's love-mandate: 'Power Is The Ultimate Aphrodisiac'.

'Charm Bracelet CK-001?'

The Assoc. Sec'y of Defense had the leeway to assign impressive code-names for his own identity, like 'Entablature', but only for his subordinates' referral. As far as his connection with his own superiors, they had the right to assign their own names, in turn, to persons who occupied the tiers below them, even though they be high in themselves. Such names were often of a slightly or even significantly demeaning nature, lest any ambitious hack in a plum but subservient post get up-pity and attempt to storm the gates of the tower of power above them.

'*Good* Late Afternoon, U.D. Just plain *good*.'

Realms was pretty excited. This was the frikkin' V.P. he was yakking with. Skill-fully balancing the phone's controls to synthesize his voice so as not to reveal any orgasmic possibilities, he pantsed himself to have full access to his unremarkable pee-pee. Stale sweat from his butt-crack quickly stained-cum-soiled the Idaho Wolf Grey broadcloth of his exec chair as his pulse quickened, but he was too preoccupied to care.

'Pardon the pause. I'm being discreet. Security time-lag, just making *sure* the jamming's on.'

'Naturally it's on, Charm Bracelet,' said the technically unidentified high-ranking White House official at the other end of the line, not without an obvious trace of smug condescension in his voice.

'If I'm talking freely, it's because I *can*.'

By the way, 'U.D.' obviously stood for 'Undisclosed Location', which was code-name enough for persons at or near the top of today's pagoda of power.

'Why, why *naturally*, U.D.'

'No need to rattle on today, Jerk-Off. Just essentials now.'

It wasn't that U.D. was putting down 'Charm Bracelet' by this particular epithet. The self-diddling was a given. Besides, everybody did it, and everybody knew it, because exercising power throughout the livelong day was such a foxy turn-on. Sex workers might be able to relate, but the understanding was not reciprocal.

'I *await*, U.D. I stuck around *because* I was anticipating your call.'

'Yeah, right. Loyalism comes out of the barrel of a gun, huh?'

'That's *funny*, U.D.'

'Shut up and listen. The subject of the current mission. OK? He's to be taken out. Code C-alliss-26. Got it?'

Realms was managing to almost get hard on account of the sexiness that was being batted around. He always thought he was something that he wasn't, and that mindset extended to limp-dick-thinks-it's-a-stud-dick. No amount of Peter North viewing ever did any good, but today there were a few faint touches of solidarity, perhaps over the prospects of a commendation, for what he was about to say.

'U.*D.!* You're not gonna *believe* this, but I anticipated your very wishes. I took the *initiative*. At this very *moment* GreasePuff-69 and StoolMule-5 are, as I want to *totally emphasize*, at this *moment*, out onsite.'

(Hell, why not make up some agent code-names to impress U.D. with?; and well-placed repetition of terms made higher-ups *remember* you...).

'Go on, Bracelet...'

'They are, U.D., and – hold onto your *family jewels* – prosecuting your *very desires*. He will be removed, ere sun-up. You can '*World Bank*' on it. Heh-heh.'

U.D. didn't buy into the smarm-marketing. All he said before hanging up was, 'I want him *executed*.'

He didn't even need to add:

'I'll hold you *responsible!*'

The three Rollfastest bicycles now parked at 2, Mulgie Lane had served many years at the Selznick lot in Culver City. They'd recently been airlifted to this busy and needy studio. Tonight they would have to roll fastest indeed, as the vital mission at hand – to perhaps save the free world – was going to be heavily reliant on them.

They were big-barred hauler types, with oversized parcel & packet baskets welded to the front forks. Single-speed only, coaster brakes, no handlebar tassels. Proportionately, they had as much metal on their chassis as a 1961 Chrysler New Yorker.

'Perfect for their purpose,' U.X. mumbled.

Now came time for U.X. to become bicycle repairman and ready the rigs. Having moved all three into a shadowy but convenient lean-to behind the shack-yurt, every advantage for easy garage work could now be enacted. His old kit bag provided for every bolt-on plug-and-play item's installation, all nice and pukka, without fuss or debate. That was what perfect spies *did*, for God's sake.

There was plenty of time to kill before sundown, after which they'd set out on their gloaming's ride.

'I shall repair to the interior to keep an eye on our charge, and to school him with my charms,' said DeVault. 'I assume you will be occupied *some time* in prepping our vehicles? I think we can be leisurely at this point. So as to shipshape everything. To see to every last infinitesimal detail! All is darn well.'

A perfect spy never dishes out orders. He *implies* them.

'Yoe,' replied U.X., who silently rejoiced at the prospect of an interval.

Who was the more perfect?

DeVault smiled and turned, then winced, holding his torso, but hiding the fact. It was as if there were parts missing inside him… or something.

'Why Butterbugs,' he stirringly announced amidst confusing pain as he flapped back into the yurty shamiana, 'How good, how *very* good to see you again! How sweet it is! Now, let's have a bit of a pow-wow about what we're going to do. Tonight's itinerary is shaping up nicely.'

The afternoon heat had implied a certain celestial anger from above, but because all was now so silent about, any potential emotions were held in suspension.

The open front of the lean-to out back had a widescreen view of the old Raj cemetery just yonder. Hotter than a stovelid, the cast iron obelisks and markers endured their trial with more resignation than the fortitude shown by the gnarly remains of trees that stood slightly taller. Kudos to the art director and the set dressers!

U.X., who sat on the ground next the cycles, gazed out. Because he had the leisure of a lengthy pause, he found the scene posed a confrontational incongruity he had never seen before. Here, in hot Near Further Asia, were Victorian-Gothic architectures and designs. By their very nature, they should be darkly-lighted and drippy to the touch, not whisked with dust and able to fry up a steak if such meat be slapped down upon any of their exposed surfaces. By their very presence, they asked him baldly, 'Is the world not a bizarre place?'

The question startled him. Used to 'A-fuse-is-a-fuse' and 'A-plastic-explosive-is-a-plastic-explosive' and other common platitudes, his workmanlike mind could not compute the imported styles of the Queen-Empress' Empire, as mute and as telling as Ozymandias' stark declaration of time's burial. Because, he was a dumbo. A dopey dumbo, too. Movies were not for him. Neither was an imagination.

'How horrible, horrible, horrible to lie in such a fearsome territory as this! Bones in kilns below, baked and re-baked, doomed and forgotten! And those who would stand with mourning tears on the bitter earth above – themselves would *die!!*'

In spite of his specialized skills in life, he was perhaps a poetic dumbo.

'Better to have never existed at all. Better to have never loved at all...'

He caught himself.

Yes, he was a dumbo. Hopelessly dopey. Surely he could sneak around and wire things, and wreak havoc without ever getting caught, but he had no sense of truth, nor beauty, nor understanding of what makes souls tick.

Until now. It came to him in a rushing cloud: not an understanding per se, but recognition that something out there had to be acknowledged. Or was it within him? Something about himself.

Several challenging issues had been visited upon him during the span of this mission so far, especially upon halting on the plain before Jambutterbugsabad. They did not concern the mission itself, the entire work of which he could perform while handcuffed during a somnambulistic promenade. No, these issues were contained within a subjective layer that had been identified by his fellow spy. That bit about –

The words, those words that DeVault had spewn, so long ago it seemed. But those words – he could not expunge them from his mind. Those words: '...*and I know we are in danger, but I think, can't we experience pleasure before we are sacrificed? Isn't that permissible? I mean, really? Sometimes I think, it's as if I'm in prison! In solitary! A fella has tenderness needs! I have felt this every time I meet potential death in the face. It has spurred my selfishness. It has been my perpetrator of showcase-hope, otherwise I should have slain myself years ago.*'

What did the words mean? He knew. He now knew. They made him hate himself. He was a homosexual. Why, he hadn't screwed a chick since that hæmophiliac hooker out in Sarawak's jungly tracts, what, seven years ago? That fact alone must surely prove it.

'I've been so busy...' was always his rejoinder.

So, this DeVault guy, by yakking about his own needs, had inadvertently busted him – U.X. – out of the closet of his mind.

By that dumb-ass and drooly entreaty in their SUV before moving on in to their objective, Lurgan had popped his gay cherry, in effect.

Fucker! Cocksucker!

Status of mission: fucked-up, as of now.

He had to rescue it. And at all costs. So what if he was a latent, self-loathing queer! There were resources he could draw upon to realign strengths. He was used to that: doing it solo, out *there* somewhere.

He admired former senator Lerrie Kreg, whose homosexual denials had propelled him to great heights, first as US Ambassador to the UN, then Peacemaker-General At Large, which included a crusade to bring carpeting and full-length privacy screens to lavatories for the masses, and finally, to the Vatican as a Cardinal, having converted to Papal Dogmatization, purely out of heaven-sent conviction. Such was a man who'd turned his life around through the proud accomplishment of deeds, in spite of what others thought of him.

Right now, U.X. wanted to do something like that. To make grand gestures. And the grander they were, the more his cure would be assured. But could he erase the troubling distractions that now dominated his consciousness? He wanted to, but how he wanted to get it on with that – oh God, he couldn't help himself, no he couldn't – with that, that hideous DeVault dude...! (Because DeVault really *was* hideous.) He wanted to supplicate himself before him. He wanted to be peed upon, trampled if need be, in order for him to be worthy to kiss both his idol's dirty bits and his naughty bits. And his feet. How else could he make himself whole again? He would have to dive down into the very depths of the crucible in order to emerge, purified.

What the hell – was that how he would have to make himself *whole* again? By what method, exactly? Why, by a suitably grand gesture, not a humiliating one! The dilemma was, his dick was telling him to do the latter, while his ego plumped for the former.

OK then, what would the grand gesture be? Why, to carry out the mission, of course. An ultrastar was involved. The mission had expanded in scale and import, certainly more than he knew, though his was not to reason why.

But U.X. sensed, if he was to do just that, and to follow his duty, sure enough, that bitchy DeVault – well, he'd hog all the credit, making him, the great Vunn, into a little poncing Po-Beep, all alone, with only his Liza Minnelli cassettes to comfort him while he continued to crank out those tacky pink doilies to sell at that virginal Gramma Atticus's AnnTeeky Attic in Langley, the back alley door of which he was wont to hang out by on melancholy afternoons, sipping sicky-sweet Bublchams and pouting the moments away.

That nasty DeVault! Claiming all the glory! And making Vunn be a bottom and a kneeler! Why should he have to put up with that? He would be nobody's bumboy.

Indeed, he being the mechanic of the mission, *what the fuck??*

He didn't have to be told there was a quick fix to this shitty situation. Respect was within the grasp of his hot little hands.

Screw this brooding over an old graveyard! He knew how to finally be a *man*, and get cured in the process. If thy eye offend ye, pluck it out, ya yo-yo! Ya jackass!

There was a bicycle to fix up. More than one, in fact.

'*I-I-I-I'm* nobody's bum-boy...!' he off-key whisper-sang. Repeatedly. Obsessively.

'So you see, Butterbugs, I've told you the other half of the story now: Sonny ratted on you to the authorities, who now want your head, as you are considered a ringleader in illegal international activities, which are cloaked behind your standing as an ultrastar. Talk about fabrication! You have obviously been abused, framed, slandered and extorted. And, truth to tell, you have been *had*. But you should sensibly avoid the long years in jail (now that habeas corpus has been permanently suspended in cases like this), and by the time you would prove yourself in court, your young manhood would be spent, your virtue would have been violated on a truly dehumanizing scale, and your legacy would have been reduced to a few bootleg prints of probably no more than a handful or so of your great films, rendering you an impossibly failed personage and a victim of the most heinous kinds of calumny. And, if 'tis prison life that occupies the years between, unpleasantness becomes multiplied.'

'So I should flee, I suppose? Run away?'

'Yes! Flee! It is the only sensible thing. But let us not use words like 'flee' or 'run away'. Or even 'crap out'. Why! Can we not think of this effort rather as a product of a *transitional motivation?* Should we think of it as a step backward, or a great leap forward? Why should we limit our concepts of the new life to come, in the context of mere words and phrases? You *do* want bliss with Keeney, do you not?'

'Keen-ah!'

'Whatever. I mean, yes, sorry, Keen-ah. *Bliss* with her! Think! Don't you just *so* want it? Free, easy, and with epic marvelousness, all in the ageless heights above fabled Gothpore?'

'I do! I tell you, I do! But where is her call? Why does she shun me? Can't you tell me?'

Butterbugs was sounding desperate again. It was just that this whole ordeal had gone on for so long now.

'You will see my wisdom, Butterbugs, once we come unto the balloonatic departure stage, way over on the Pundit Point. And surely you will see Miss Keenah waiting for us there, for I think she is in transit to that very spot, as we speak.'

'You think?'

'My covert sources are powerful, ultrastar/actor! I should know more as we are in transit, cuz my TransItSpeakIsStar HomeIn system can be employed once we are on the move.'

'Then let us be gone from this unhappy place!'

'Good! *Good!* We will duly leave, though not yet awhile, as the orange-and-sandstone-tinted sunset has not melted into blue dusk yet. Hail, though, the high heat's departure for the day!'

'Ready when you are, D.L.'

This, from an actor who many times had said a similar line to C.B. DeMille in huge productions this pismire spy couldn't even guess at. But this was no time to bathe in past *coups de cinéma*. There was nothing for it now but to effect a practical escape from the forces of collapse that so threatened from nearly all sides.

Thereafter, the shack-yurt was bathed in anxiousness, impatience, and anticipation – inside and out.

'I see that your modest haversack stands ready to be grabbed. You will find ample room for it in your vehicle's luggage area,' counseled DeVault.

'Great! But I don't see any motorcar or transport van outside.'

'And you never will! Our adventure is going to be something more exciting. In fact, fancy a bit of Jules Verne?'

'A submarine? A space ship?'

'No, silly! Bee-cee-clets!'

'What are you, some kind of *nut?*'

'Remember, I said we would depart in conveyances *to be determined.*'

'You said no such thing.'

'So, you cannot negotiate a bicycle?'

'You flimp! I've been in pictures demanding far more than that! You have *no idea!*'

'Then you should be at peace regarding the means I have procured in order to save your ass from a fate worse than doom, Mr. Movie-Cool!'

Butterbugs did not quibble with the spy's rather well-placed put-down of his churlish and elitist attitude. After all, this was one whale-assed emergency. History might be written tonight. Shut up and get on with it.

Dusk fell, as it does in the subcontinent, like a blue chenille grand drape at the neighborhood Loew's State after the matinee comes to a close, with the evening's show to come.

It was *certainly* to come.

Despite the fact that 2, Mulgie Lane was decorated with those remarkable talismans from the Hoochee tribe, Butterbugs left that place without looking back, for it had been a citadel of pain and anxiety these long hours. Though he was heading off into parts unknown, they that awaited offered more of a sense of liberation and safety than any old defunct studio could provide. Besides, he was a wanted man. Prison was a great setting for the drama of a ripping good flick, but he had no desire to do a decade or two of Method preparation for some minor incarceration picture.

'Let's GO!' he sounded off.

They went out to the lean-to, where the prepped vehicles awaited. Butterbugs didn't warm to the sullen and silent U.X. at all, and as no verbal exchange passed between them, the ultrastar dealt wholly with DeVault all through this exodus. There were no introductions. A perfect spy can't be boss and buddy.

Departure was in the air. A sense of resignation, farewell. Goodbye, possibly to the routine of Apollo's chariot-ride across the known sky. Au revoir to the process of elimination based on nature's call. Adios to the hassle over what to have for breakfast. Auf Wiedersehen to the prospect of 'What are we going to worry about today?'. In contrast, the blissful simplicity of a millennium or two in Gothpore seemed better than heaven itself.

Amidst his own thoughts as to where he was headed, a waiting tremor of new beginnings was promised. A gamble, to be sure, but the house was safe to bet on.

'Behold, Butterbugs, our stable of conveyances. Humble, but effective. And healthy, too! You are a hearty type, as the rest of us are, so perhaps we can '*tour de France*' on out of here, in style.'

After this stupid attempt at cheerleading his charge into this nitwitty project, DeVault dodged out of sight round the stable and doubled over in order to curtail the waves of pain that seemed to shred his thorax, but the attempt was limited in its efficacy. Still, he was able to swivel about and smile in the direction of Butterbugs' searching visage.

'I was just going to hawk and spit a bit before we shoved off,' he lied. 'The mund-dust in this land enrageth mine own mucus.'

'But DeVault, you said there was plenty of room for my modest haversack in the hauling basket on this here bicycle,' observed Butterbugs, when he encountered a large canvas packet in his bike's basket.

'So I did, trouper! But wait, pass along your scant cargo to my associate's bin. We are, you know, as a caravan, with goods aplenty, but they may be spread amongst our wheeled 'camels' as space allows. Provisions, notions, rations for the ambitious journey ahead! For we are of the same cause, and make for the same destination, which promises freedom and renouncement of this sorry world, in order to make way for a better life, a simpler life: a life of love and glory!'

So inspired was Butterbugs by the upbeat speech of the spy – he was reminded of the dramatic pitches of master auteur Wieriold-Tim Macanda – that he grabbed his pack and tossed it in U.X.'s wire tray without further thought. His mind was only on Keenah, and Gothpore, and sweetened freedom. Motion pictures, misfired dreams, traitorous persons, and the unhappy life – adieu! He'd been *so right* in asking Keenah about retirement. Now, certainly, she would see his point and love would wisely pilot her to his side, whether behind a wicker railing, hailing snowy Bundarpunch and glacier-clad Monkey's Rump, or deep in dharmsalian bliss, on a bathing ghat stair at dawn!

And U.X. was increasingly sullen in his interaction with the others. The jolt of the conceited actor's pack onto his bike, which he straddled, was like an assault and battery to his sensitized body. He was as a Hardyesque rook-boy, unspeaking, but unyielding as well. No help was he. It was all on DeVault's shoulders to get this carrousel rotating.

Not filled with slush-pile scripts, or decoded film stock, or Baby Jane doll props, or portraits of Jennie, or any such familiar cargo, the bikes were mounted and directed out from the lean-to garage with little ceremony.

Three men on three bikes.

Yet, DeVault rose to the occasion.

The sun's afterglow vista managed to lessen the impact of the crushingly powerful Teezah Mountain's brow into a hard-to-distinguish line between reality and dream-state. The spy noted this phenomenon, as well as that of their passing from one world to the next. With one still deer-skinned foot on an upper pedal and t'other firmly splayed on dusty ground, he fancied that making such an observation was a good rationale for decamping from somewhere so politically and ethnically important as Jambutterbugsabad.

'We came to this location in good faith! But now, we hie unto the road that leads from it, for our time has expired in this place. There is nothing left for us here! If I had a faith above, I would ask that we be given a safe trip. But, my heart being too wise, I expect nothing less than the luck of the moment, for experience in life has taught me to indulge the lowest common denominator in all things, and to consider disaster as imminent, if I cannot have total success in my undertakings. So, let us hope this night's ride will bring us unto the resolve of closure, because if things don't work out, I shan't be able to contemplate a future without the freedom to choose. To choose my own poison, if need be. I have long lived within the pale of acceptability like a good little boy, but lately, I feel a need to break out into the springtime of universal selection, for the liberal tub-thunk is preferable to me over Neocon Stalinist order. So I will lead them. But oh, Ahura Mazda, it is a weary way amongst the Yasts, but I will do better than my best to struggle. Leaders who lead down the path always land right, and I desire a comfortable flat in posh-side Damascus, where I, from this spot, will bend my steps in foremost hope, though I have exceptional beings to place along the way before I sleep!'

'Hurrah, DeV! You have given me hope! You have given me a reason to go onward, because right now, things are looking pretty black, and only my Keenah's love or something better – if there *is* such a thing – can sustain me in the long night to come. Lead on, oh Plotter, Navigator, and Deliverer!'

Butterbugs, strolling player of both classics and further-light dramas that he was, fell into line with the immediate simp that took up his cause, as of now.

And that was how three men on bikes traveled out of that mainstay settlement and into the wilderness, in search of a freedom to live that was not so accessible as was once thought.

DeVault was in the lead, trusting on the remaining glow from the ceiling of the world above to guide him, followed by Butterbugs in virtual tow, while U.X. lagged behind, unnoticed and unaccounted for, though his mind was on sexual matters associated with the vanguard.

So they went on down into the Kurr Valley.

Deep were the countless defiles, lost in the purply dusk, impossible to fathom. The swore-birds headed home for the eve, their 'rairrah-rairrah' howls emboldened the desolation of their passage, for they knew that hardly any animated atom made its life in this country, so bereft of common vermin and their poachers were they, not to mention the solution to all: water itself.

There were no exterior lamp designations on their vehicles. They were dependent on the ambient half-light emanating from the long line of cliffs that accompanied them at a distance to the north. It was as if the white-hot sun had shot its radiation into those palisades, which in turn had no choice but to emit a muted illumination, if only because of saturation, so that any creepy-crawly thing on the floor of the slope below might benefit from this strange endowment.

Sometimes the rutted road, subjected to the harsh caprices of seasonal wash-outs from the heights, threatened to derail the riders, and in the dimness, many other hazards were possible. Steadiness at the handlebars saved them all individually, either from bashed knees or scraped teeth. Steadfastness was also guaranteed by the sturdy welded structure of the bicycles themselves. How many gorilla suits or rumpled draperies had they hauled, or how many extras, late to a shoot, had hitched rides around the Selznick lot? Plus, the flabbiness of the balloon tires, which rendered the bikes somewhat hard to pedal, in these conditions worked as an asset, as their flexibility conformed to the ravages of the Earth's crust hereabouts.

There was no talking. Each rider was wholly preoccupied with simple negotiation of the route, which, contrary to DeVault's assurances, neither of the spies had ever traversed before, relying solely on verbal and vague instructions received back in Langley. Perfect spies relied on native intuition, which, once spy skills were polished, was always correct. It was all up in the noggin. DeVault absolutely knew they were going in the right direction. They would not get lost.

Though the general progression was downhill, the pedal pumping was a considerable grind. There was no opportunity to coast, no straightaways, and no smoothness at all.

Butterbugs had been depleted from the recent stress of uncertainty and upheaval, but his essentials were hale and capable of long-range stamina. He'd also draped his goatwater-bag over the center tank bar, from which he swigged regularly.

U.X. was in excellent physical condition, which his persistent erection proved.

DeVault was overweight, severely dehydrated, and actually doing quite poorly. But he didn't let on. If gauges had been hooked up to his vitals and meters read, any technician would be dreadfully mortified that all of them were well into redline territory. Tumultuous inside, but serenely neutral on the outside, except for sporadic grimaces safely hidden by twilight, made his face an amorphous Carpeaux-like mask, seen by Butterbugs at regular intervals as he glanced around to make sure the others were following. Many things were horribly wrong, but he kept going.

For Butterbugs, it was good to be moving. Each rotation of his pedals was bringing him closer to a new and previously inconceivable existence in a location he would not have been able to fathom, had it been pointed out on a globe, while a directionless youth in Carstairs.

Considering the drasticness of his current events, he thought, 'I could be worse off. I might have been in jail by now, gazing at a dreary linoleum floor, or rubbed out by untrustworthy agents whom I might have given myself to, in all naïveté. Here I am, en route to a better kingdom, which is what I want, really. For me and Keenah. Perhaps there might be a time when I can come back to the world at large, but this is something I have to do for myself and my love now.'

And so it hit him, but touched him gently, as if a kiss from an invisible but helpful nymph, that these people were indeed helping him after all, and at great peril to themselves. He was as a child, having grown up, who realizes, but not too late, that the sacrifices made by his parents were for his own good.

Churning onward, he thought, now that they were on the road, maybe they could take a break, and the opportunity to say a modest thank-you to these stalwarts was in order, especially in light of his earlier snottiness to the indefatigable DeVault.

He tried to call out for the leader to pull over for a time, but in this instance, his cords did not activate because they were starkly coated with a dust-imbued and very viscous mucus, totally devoid of necessary wetness. Apparently, DeV wasn't the only one so affected. If nothing else, 'twas time for a guzzle, and for the goat-bag to be passed around.

Managing a clear course amongst the rocks and rubble, Butterbugs fished in the pockets of his bush jacket and found a blessed item: a small bluelight torch. With it he took a chance, pressed the thumb-button, and its beam came to illuminate the face of DeVault, who had just turned about to discern his followers' presence. As chance would have it, an expression of turbo-pain was projected from the spy's visage, and it shocked Butterbugs with a power that was naturally cinematic in its punch, but in a horrorshow way.

Like much of the route so far, the rocky track sloped up to a drop-off they had been skirting for some kilometers now. There was ample room to pause. So, responding to the plain signal from his charge, DeVault chose to do it at a vantage point, as if there was a scenic view out there somewhere. True, the hills might be riddled with agents manning green-lamp night viewers, but he once again obeyed his intuition, which *knew* there were no such watchers out there in the dark. And he was 100% correct. Standing here on the steep grade of this lonely road, they were obscure enough to be casual. Why, seen from afar, Butterbugs' torch might be easily mistaken for the Shayne-fly's nightglow rotor-strobe. There were in fact some of those very insects out, but they were well away from their party, which was good, as their defensive pus-bites caused considerable lesion eruption on the surfaces of unaware prey.

As the spy Lurgan, straddle-walking his bike, drew closer to him, Butterbugs saw by the mute-light that an easygoing and confident look was on his face. Perhaps he had misinterpreted the 24th-of-a-second frame of view that had characterized the image of immense suffering that the spy seemed to betray. Therefore, the ultrastar-on-the-run gathered the goat-bag and, careful to rest his bike's rear axle against an eccentric boulder of aggregate sedimentation, approached his guide with Gunga Din-type sensitivity.

Taking a couple of frugal sips of water, just enough to loosen up the old cords, he smacked the cap back on and held out the jolly reservoir.

'Fellow human, take refreshment! Our progress, arduous as it is, requires it. I share my valuable resource with good cheer.'

For his own part, DeVault was taken aback by the sudden charitable ambience demonstrated by his difficult mission's object, but his entire senior canal was so enraged with thirst and its associated demands, he went straight to the promulgated goatskin, felt its cool sweaty suppleness, popped the cork and drank deeply.

For his own part, U.X. stayed on the fringes, not even trying to assimilate or intrude on the Lurganism in play between spy and his subject. His pounding dongwood was hounding him relentlessly for satisfaction. But the austere side of his nature still tried to ignore it, as if it was a cold turkey craving to simply combat by sheer stubbornness. He refused all entreaties of Butterbugsian help by the coldest of looks, which penetrated the gloom with marvelous intensity.

DeVault glugged yet more. He wasn't keeping track of how much was left in the goatskin, as his terrible thirst had made him into the most selfish of creatures.

To better deal with the awkward gullet grunts, Butterbugs tried to make narration.

'You know, this overlook here: we cannot discern it, but we know it is there. We do not know its dimensions, but somehow, we know they are considerable. I recall a moment on the set when we were filming 'Marius the Epicurean' (20th-Fox), and Joe Mankiewicz asked me, 'Butterbugs, when you stand in front of that Roman crowd, do you really see anything at all?'

"Faces, Mank,' I replied.

"In your mind, not the character's mind.'

"No. I see a void.'

"Good boy. Empty vessel, occupied by a shadow.'

"The guest I host.'

"Exactly.'

'Well, he was ascertaining my priorities as far as my character's reality was concerned. We perceive nothing until we resolve our own identities inside. Here I gaze at the void, which is without, but my real void has been within. I think I finally know myself now.'

As DeVault listened in the midst of his self-irrigation, he recalled that he had indeed seen 'Marius' and he had worshiped that picture as a perfect and all-embracing work of art. It wasn't exactly Butterbugs' difficult-to-define charismatic effect on audiences that had captured his person via this one picture, it was the film as a whole. The message brought forth by one's interior meditations in the midst of sensual extravaganzas, which provide aid in determining the correct path one should choose in life, was only one collective notion that elevated him, for a time at least, above the fray of mundane life. Yes, for a time. Wholly because of 'Marius', he had wanted to actually quit the spy industry and do something magnificent instead of something subversive. But enough time had passed, and he was away from picture-going, off on all those assignments, and the brief gift of idealism had morphed into the temptation of opportunism.

Gravity carried the water down, down.

It suddenly occurred to him that here, standing nearby, was the star of that seminal film, and now, here, more than ever, he felt the same magic as had emanated from his 'Marius' revelations. So it was *Butterbugs*, after all, who had made it an exceptional experience. Exceptional enough to instantly want to scuttle this mission, break all ties with his boss and associates, and *truly* help Butterbugs escape from his emergency.

More swallowing accompanied radically revised plotting. Settled. He would have to take U.X. out. Soon. Well, immediately. That would be phase one. Obviously a mission-dedicated opponent, U.X. wouldn't exactly take on his sudden creative admiration for the actual person they had been ordered to 'process'. He could rig U.X.'s exit without Butterbugs' knowledge, under the premise of an accident. His carbon fiber Pinfire shooter could make an asymmetric matrix of 246 boreholes into U.X.'s skull, simulating contact with, say, a falling rock. Projectiles could be fired even in the opposite direction from the target, with pre-programmed heat-guided course determination, tapped out on the matchbook-sized control board. He was pretty sure U.X. wasn't armed or even aware of such a device, though no doubt he had his own kit of weapons of mass esoterica. He'd have to act fast.

Guck-guck-guck. Gulp. Dook-dook-dook. Gulp. Well, that should have replenished his fluid depletion. Almost emptied the supply! Indeed, that should do it. Now he could get back to his robust leadership role. Now, where was that Pinfire...?

Amazed at his own Dolokhovian capacity, though not on a St. Petersburg windowsill guzzling brandy, DeVault tossed the nearly limp skin at Butterbugs with comrade-like goodwill, and said, after a throat-clear:

'Thanks, mate. Did the trick.'

'I'd just like to say, DeVault, that, uh, I'm sorry for all the rubbish I said and acted back there. I'm a slow learner, and sometimes I cannot see my real self. Sometimes I cannot see to the bottom, which is what we all must do if we are to recognize when others are trying to help us.'

Genuinely moved by the ultrastar's contrition, the spy suppressed a disturbingly large water-belch, then gurgled a little before he was able to speak.

'Why Butterbugs... most kind of you. I knew you never meant me any ill. But listen, I too am a candidate for apologies. I too have changed, instantaneously, for you have given me the water of life. *New* life. So now, if I may confide in you a little, I –'

His speech, which quickly became lowered in volume after '*New* life', accompanied by a bit of body language that indicated a desire to distance himself from the other spy that lurked way back there in the shadows somewhere, was cut short.

A pulmonary rattle, sounding jello-y and over-saturated with liquidity, shook DeVault's frame in a sequence of spasms that went way beyond a mild bit of choking.

The etiology associated with Lurgan's sudden presentation was this: neglect of internal systems based on H_2O intake caused distribution and drainage routes to desiccate and become brittle, while endocrinological functions were obliged to come to a standstill. Blood pipes reached critical mass in pliability capability. Compounding these pre-existing conditions was the inundation of locally-produced H_2O that, because of its volume and not necessarily its composition, over-taxed said weakened systems in every sense of the word. The effect was similar to releasing a deposit of molten lead by way of an open valve into a network of conduit composed of isinglass (e.g. muscovite mica), or possibly even paper products, such as tar-imbued Orangeburg drain-tile, but of the 50+ years old variety, with resulting flakiness and leakiness that leads to complete breakdown. The flood of cooled fluid, in lieu of a preferred I-V of 30% saline restoration solution, administered while patient is inert, indeed reduced many internal passages to the consistency of dissolving gelatin, and thus, a continued saturation, spurred by the tongue's taste bud pleasure at experiencing long-denied sweet-water, ensured without debate that immediate and terminal trauma would result from this voluntary and overwhelming infusion of H_2O that, in cases like these, guarantees shut-down-death, due, if nothing else, to blown-out kidneys, if not epic collapse of distributary systems, as alluded to above.

For DeVault, there was no time to writhe as a result of his guzzling. Surpassingly awful internal collapse was now upon him, and he instantly suspected U.X., even though U.X. had absolutely no part in this bodily meltdown.

He was startlingly noisy, though unarticulated in his reaction, which echoed amongst the nullahs and chasms that were nearby. He behaved like a tubercular dinosaur in the throes of expiration. After the water-oriented channels within him had blown, the blood pipes, so dependent on support from beverages, both high and low, began to crack, pop and go POW! His body's new mandate: to wrap this turkey up as all life support systems were being denied their right to work.

Curiously, on the surface, as witnessed by Butterbugs, there was no sign that DeVault was unraveling inside, though at close quarters in the nightland, his eyes were wild and his mouth started to take on clown-like contortions. In general, his face exhibited Zero Mostel expressions of considerable quality, due to their theatricality. Nevertheless, the lighting for viewing this performance was patently lousy. So Butterbugs had only a sloppy mezzotint sketch to operate from.

'DeVault! Are you *infirm?*'

Lurgan, all this time managing to stand with his bike between his legs, started to tip over. Butterbugs, himself straddling his bike, attempted to disembark and draw near to his comrade in crisis.

DeVault was devolving into shock, but his spy's eyes caught a glimpse of a glowing sapphire diode attached to a box in his handlebar basket, newly revealed by the bike's listing, displacing some oilskins designed for balloon flight, which had been lain over all.

Thoughts were still being transmitted with lightning speed within the realms of DeVault's non-flooded brain, regardless of his 'Titanic'-like sinking.

'I have a bomb on board,' he correctly inferred, *'And it is armed.'*

Butterbugs rushed over to right the bike, which he did, in order that DeVault could proceed on their mission in peace. Far too late for that, the spy was quick to utilize the capability he still had. Once righted, he super-pushed Butterbugs away from his bodily presence, and declared:

'I love you, Butterbugs, with the peace of all nations.'

And he floored it as far as his pedals were concerned, peeling out in the pulverized dust of old Makran, so that he headed off into the indeterminate foreground, the slope of which became almost vertical after a distance of about three meters.

Yet did Butterbugs follow, in hopes of arresting his newfound ally's forward-bloc push, perchance by grabbing the rear fender's edges, taking care not to get his fingers sliced off. But then, realizing that DeVault's bike had in fact no rear fender, and facing the fact that he had done all he could do and advanced as far as he dared, the ultrastar stood in place, just centimeters from an edge of consequence, while his guide's bicycle plunged down into the undefined shaft, into the basement of the world.

There was no cinematically-convenient intermission, in which speculative thoughts might coalesce about what could happen next. No courtesy was extended, except for the fact that DeVault had just saved Butterbugs' life by a timely evacuation of site, for the clock hardly ticked at all before the downward scene exploded in plastic flames, lighting the age-old cliffs with terror-reflections, while the falling central ball of fire raged and spun and quickly evolved into sensuous globes of matte-black smoke, too easily lost in the aggressive darkness that had settled over the heavens.

Rooted in his horror at the slashing pageant before him, and blazing with a light that sure enough showed the depth of the defile before him, which was probably about three hundred meters or so, Butterbugs nevertheless stood tall. And how acute was his observation, even as a responsive spray of atomized DeVault guts plastered itself onto the actor's frontage as a result of blowback enabled by the chimney-like circuit of the rocks that provided the blowup's setting.

Brain, bone, and blood, all a bit roasty, were mingled on his person. The slight BBQ bouquet instantaneously recalled Lamb Slurp Days each summer back in old Carstairs, when whole broadtables were set up in Dizman Park and the public was invited to a Generalized Chuck Wagon Grub-down, with hominy-on-the-cob, gray-veal chops, or rosy sheep shanks, lentil-colored sprats, and sap-green melon spheres, sponsored by Babby's Bib 'n' Rib. It was the one event in his childhood years he really looked forward to. And it took an event like DeVault's fiery splatterment to awaken such a nuance from his faraway past history. Would that he were there, in Dizman Park right now, chowing down to beat the band, with nary a tethered care to his name!

But then – this here BLAM!

Would that he could reassemble his scattered guide again, starting with the material on his trousers and shirt, so as to restore a new friend to his rightful status. Grief, which was instant, manifested itself in one long and sustained howl from

Butterbugs, which matched the rising bunches of coal-specked smoke that rose into the un-receiving skies.

DeVault Lurgan, on the verge of a breakthrough, was no more!

A perfect spy at last: dead because of his flaws.

'It was an *accident!*' Butterbugs hissed, taking immediate responsibility as a first response.

Then, as he swiveled in his disbelief, he caught sight of U.X. emerging out of the extremities of the campfire-lighted scene. He was heading straight for him, in plainly warlike mode.

No movie shoot this, though the flaming defile on one side and an approaching creep with a noteworthy bulge in his pants on the other did remind him of a picture or two, though he couldn't quite recall the titles and corresponding studios just now.

An uppercut to his dropped jaw convinced Butterbugs that he was dealing with an enemy. He struck back, popping U.X. square in the nose, and drawing blood in torrents.

Already decorated with expanded tissue, Butterbugs added to U.X.'s pulpy gore by head-bashing him in the belly, after which the two rumbled and struggled and dirty-fought in the sandy soil, without words and while enacting mankind's most primitive instincts: survival at all cost.

As he was getting up from a big Butterbugsian blast to his neck, U.X. succeeded in finding on his own person a little Velcro-attached thingy, and, as the ultrastar of the world zeroed in on him to wreak holy havoc, the spy made his stumpy fingers dance over the thingy's super-mini keyboard, and then, once 'enter' had been tapped, the lamp-endowed edge of it came alight in the common fashion that any geeky device of today possesses. An everyday amber glow, as banal as a shaver's recharge transformer diode, here lent a plebeian tone to the high-level hostilities between these two elevated warriors.

If U.X. thought at this moment that he was in the center of a video game – as one of its main stars – well then, fine. Any game player has intentions of winning, as do its stars. Pizza-stained fingers on the joyful controls, he or she (but probably he) knows that the luxury of detachment is a built-in right within the player's abilities. To retire unscathed from the platform of battle is one of life's basic guarantees. Nevertheless, when one is in real straits and still thinks in video game terms, that person will probably not succeed with any sort of triumph. Fiction and non-fiction need a respectable no-man's land in between them. But, with so many young people weaned on gut-building-ass-loading-thigh-packing-finger-pudging video games, the skill of split-second decision making, as DeVault had so nobly and recently practiced, becomes prosaic in the gaming context. Thus, one can fantasize about making tough decisions instantly, but one need not enact any policy that is not fun, not ego-reducing, or pro-losing. The higher the points, the more dead are counted, the more time can be spent lolling in the winner's circle. That's the name of the game.

The thing was, U.X., who had rigged DeVault's bike with a holy-fucking-fart-ing-whacked-out-dangerous BOMB, had not counted on the fact that the far-lean-ing of the bike itself would activate the bomb's arming, due to some sort of pres-sure-sensitive inner switch option, the default being: option *chosen*. Sensible bomb-planters, all too aware of this well-known bit of unnecessary and annoying software, always opt to un-check that very option box during setup. Like a nurse who should read a prescription thrice before dispensing its dosage to a needy patient, the sensible bomb-planter will thrice-check all options, so that everything can naturally proceed in hunky-dory fashion. However, if a bomb-planter happens to be preoccupied with sexual titillation whilst undergoing advanced arousal of the male organ, compounded by the combative effects of an ultrastar bent on mayhem, such methodical practices, like seeing to any and all basic details that ensure a safely-delivered impact, might possibly be... passed over – though *not intentionally*.

So, in the greater scheme of things, U.X. was not particularly judicious in bodi-ly attacking his next subject for demolition: Butterbugs. The ultrastar himself. Certain things hadn't quite been seen to yet.

In the occult regions of spy vs. spy, a dead spy is either noble – or inept.

Because, when Butterbugs, in their close-range struggle, happened to knee-kick U.X. in the crotch – truly, an unwitting move on Butterbugs' part (he'd just wanted to get a better footing from which to power his next honest punch) – the blow from the opponent's knee on U.X.'s stubby but chisel-hard erection simul-taneously triggered the usually-fearsome spy's unperceived shut-down button, as it were. Too much 'ouch' to keep up his campaign. Then, escorted by a siren of screaming pain, the spy took a dive in search of escape. Interestingly, he happened to land on Butterbugs' bicycle, harmlessly parked-and-propped-against-an-eccen-tric-boulder-of-aggregate-sedimentation. His impact tipped it over entirely.

Everything afterwards was merely academic. Bike upset. Explosive device, rotated from original plumb-line position.

Like its successful mate, this device was programed with the very same pres-sure-sensitive inner switch option setting, the default being: option *chosen*. In addition, within this popular software program – beloved by superpowers and terrifying militaristic insurgents alike, there was *another* option box, this one left unchecked. Again, experienced bombers gave great consideration to this item, as each explosive assignment required its review, to be reviewed *thrice*, remember?

It was the Five-Second Delay option.

Often referred to as the 'Courtesy-Pause', allowing five eternal seconds for those in the know to clear well away from the impending disaster, or else five fleeting seconds for the suicidist or nihilist to utter either a dedicated prayer or a supercharged 'Fuck you!' In any case, true professionals almost always *checked* this box, as their preferred implementation presupposed they would not only be well away from the impact, but free to decide whether praying or cursing was appropriate for the act itself.

And in one of those maddening examples of software funkiness, authored by some witty troll too super-sized and sugared-out to care, the selection of its option was the reverse of the previous all-important delivery choice. That is, the Five-Second Delay would be deactivated by *selecting* the box with a finger-poked checkmark. Left unchecked, she rolls. Alas, once again, when programming these dual jewels, U.X. was sufficiently distracted so as to skate over the finer details.

Therefore, the canvas-boxed bike bomb, tipped on its side and relieved of its restraint, now allowed for a courtesy-pause to be enjoyed by U.X., in which he had ample time to contemplate the gravity of his custom-tailored deeds, and what the outcome would surely be, before –

'Oh, fudge!'

He'd meant to say 'fuck', but there was only one second left, not enough time for a proper, he-man shout-out. Here, at the very end, his true, dainty self was finally expressed.

– BLAM!! – *again!!*

These were really nasty-nasty box-busters. A heady cocktail of MowLawn white phosphorus, Kritchurd Puerile Brand NitroGlobs, and fuming TanJel-lUm-8, the bomb performed perfectly, dissolving in a ghastly explosion of bike frame-melting firepower, which, due to the rocky mass behind it, enabled the expanded mash of U.X.'s remains to be shot right onto Butterbugs' already-seasoned frontage.

Thus, two spies, significantly kept apart in life, were now chemically immingled in death. A tacky apotheosis (or apocalypse, rather), but there it was, the destiny of spying, blossomed into full (fiery) flower.

The U.X.-based blots on the ultrastar were far weightier and closer-range in their impact (and thus, less roasty), than DeVault's rather more conventional taste-type product, so they oozed off the ultrastar in a foody slide before he was able to step back and assess the situation. DeVault's remains, in effect sensing an escape plan, demurely followed suit.

[The latest kick in the gourmand's world was 'flash cookery', utilizing dangerous and sexy means to fry meats practically instantly. Here, in the Kurr Valley, were two variations, both with fatal results. Consumption not recommended; trace elements of starn-flesk and other hypertoxic substances that make up the miracle of the new plastic explosives are absolutely imbued in any and all material rendered fissile or fissile-contacted. If taken as a 'flash cookery' tutorial, this example would be for chemical-reaction demonstration only.]

U.X. Vunn, then, in search of final solutions, would not be missed.

'Good. *Good!*' was all Butterbugs could think of to say.

A failure of a spy: dead because of his own efficiency. Correction: for 'efficiency' read 'titillation'.

Indeed, aside from some insipid bruising from U.X.'s silly assaults, the body of Butterbugs was intact and unharmed. And, astoundingly, his mind was processing its input with the same methodology it encountered on any movie set. Compared with 'Scenes From The Late Parthian Empire' (MGM), this shit was *nothing*.

Resourceful as ever, he quickly went over to the remaining Rollfastest, U.X.'s own, and inspected it to make sure no waiting bomb was on board. Then he hopped on and headed back to Jambutterbugsabad without any further memorializing or attendant thoughts.

'Too bad about that DeVault guy. He had a tough time, there at the end. We were just getting to really know each other. I didn't like that other fella, though…'

After about five kilometers of difficult up-slope pedaling, in which the tires sunk further into the sandust of ruts already made, he was met by a corps of mounted constabulary. They were Bund tribe members all, who had detected the firepower out in the Kurr and had come to investigate. Their garrison was located near the mud volcano zone, just this side of Gwadar, and they rode these tracts with Kit Carsonian expertise. Their bearing was proud and they bore lanterns and pitch-torches, which gave a legendary air to their horseback finery. Not ones to trifle with, though.

Butterbugs' words were in Baluch to the officers of the earnest patrol, and readily accepted as the lingua franca of the moment. They knew who he was at once. Each was an enthusiastic fan of his pictures, and all were supporters of his efforts at Jambutterbugsabad, which overrode any possibility of arrest or even questioning about the Kurr incident, in which they rightly presumed he had taken part. In any event, they were on his side, 1000%. They would convey the star back to his proper shamiana in total security and secrecy, each offering to take turns to have him in saddle. However, the chief pointed out that the studio property of the bicycle should be returned as well, so all the junior officers volunteered to offer up each's steed for the actor's use, so that one could ride the actor's bicycle back. Lots were drawn, a lucky fellow dismounted, the exchange of transport was made, and Butterbugs, his garments still caked with the dried horror of exploded human pulp and krig-soil, which impressed the corps to no end, spurred his mount behind the gallant leadership of the chief, and on into Jambutterbugsabad town.

With the star back in station, the elite members of the corps did not leave until they were satisfied he was bathed, re-clothed in a local khuss smock down to his heels, pleated at the waist, with loose drawers and a long cotton scarf, so as to sit in peace, surrounded by flickering lamps, a beaker of comfort-chai, and other luxuries of stability that were well and truly built into his domicile here.

These noble and caring chaps would have to be content that Butterbugs thanked them with his eyes, for he uttered no words to them, and would not, if pressed. So, alerting the absolute minimal number of the star's serving staff, lest his security be compromised, the authorities retired to their beat, full of wondrous chatting regarding the world figure they had just facilitated. When the foreign authorities came calling, they would know what to say: the name of Butterbugs wouldn't even be mentioned. Each was sworn to a secrecy of noble intent.

After all that, he just sat. Butterbugs sat and sat, in the midst of his shamiana's suspended state. Kane Hall, his abode – named in honor of Sawl Cane, but here Baluchized – was isolated, splendid, but suddenly deeply melancholy.

Post-Traumatic Stress.

'I survived, but so what? What now?' he asked himself, as an inertia deepened around him. There was no sense of triumph, or 'winning', or prevailing over any-one. If anything, there was a great feeling of loss, as DeVault was a sympathetic persona, tragically snatched away as soon as his true nature was known. No, life was brutal, and it had just gotten worse. People were dead, and he'd tasted their fat and their sinews. Gross, and ultra-downbeat. Everything was hitting him, as he sat in quiet comfort.

What, then, was the incentive for going on? Really, now? The obviousness of the cumulative items flipped through his mind like a newsreel review: the con-stabulary would support him to the hilt, but he didn't want to get anyone into trou-ble, though they would probably remain behind the background. DeVault Lurgan, his controversial guide, his evolving mission having failed due to betrayal, was gone from the world. And what of Keenah? Keenah! Keenah the Lost! Probably a no-show. He loved her, but… If she couldn't communicate with him, she was either dead by now or gone over to the enemy. What the hell else was he to think? If it was the former, he could join her. He really could follow her, couldn't he? Du-tifully, lovingly. Yet, if it was the latter, how could he live with that? Such a thing would be unthinkable. Her voice, the last time he'd heard it, somehow lacked… conviction. Then there was all the mess with Sonny and his crimes, plus the blank-out of the studio and the abandonment of any and all whom he held most dear –

Where were those who mattered?

Well, in Butterbugs' current state, the concept of 'incentive' was a quaint no-tion at best. Any witch doctor would have immediately prescribed uptake inhib-itor injections, a fast track toward the flatness that lies between the Arctic and the Antarctic of the soul, with advice not to 'buy into' anything negative. What, though, does one do when one has been splattered with yin and yang personalities, and in the literal sense? Just walk (or pedal) away, with blithe acceptance?

Well, both voodoo physician with prick-worthy doll and Johns Hopkins loy-alist to Big Phat Pharma would no doubt agree on the next step: psychosurgery. 'Clinical trials now show there's a lot to be said for both prefrontal and trans-or-bital lobotomies, now that we understand them better…'

Uh-huh.

Maybe he was being too extreme and 'actorly' in his own blank response. No, there were damn good reasons that he was shorted-out.

Yes, he was indeed shorted-out. *Hell* yes. Career explosion, fugitive isolation, a mission gone wrong, terrible violence, fate in the balance. That was all. And what about the horseradish issue? Hellfire – damn *straight* that he was practically drooling from event-impact!

So then, what to do about it? Human life as a problem-causing experience; human cinema as a problem-solving enterprise. There was some sort of connection there, but he was too depressed to track it down. He presumed that was now the remaining task. Thus, something had to be done. He'd better get to work rather than remaining a human pincushion for anything that might now transpire. Sharp objects must be avoided, whether voodoo needle or trans-orbital icepick.

Butterbugs was now a wise person. His experience in pictures, and dealing with people on all levels of the Industry and in public life, his talent as a creative artiste, his canny sense of right action and right thought, and his preference for fun, were all part of his assembled personality of achievement and conduct. All these elements, and so much more, were intact, present and accounted for, here in this shamiana.

That being the case, there was every reason to shut down this here show, here and now. The whole shootin' match. Done. Good enough. End on a high note. Wrap 'er up.

So thoroughly had he been imbued with the dramatic skein of life, that a good deal of showbiz common sense had sneaked into his world outlook. When a show was no longer good any more, call 'Cut!'. That's what the director did at the end of every take, good, bad, or indifferent. And at the end of every one of his pictures 'The End' was written. 'Fin', 'Fine' 'Finis' – and 'Das Ende', too. Not to mention hundreds of other languages and calligraphies. Reels always ran out of film when running through a projector, and they *really* run out when the picture is over. *All* over. The arc light is switched off, and the houselights come up. Life could be like that, or even more often, life *should* be like that. For the sake of good taste, if nothing else.

Same thing in the thiertre. Final curtain, rung down.

'That's where the term 'curtains' comes from, ya know…,' he muttered, a little bit of Butterbugsian naiveté still glimmering amongst the dying embers.

So then, there was an awful lot of gathering thought, that maybe, at this stage of the show, the curtain should indeed be rung down, the film should stop rolling, and the thought should stop occurring.

Just, *end* it. All.

In the immortal words of Howard Cosell, 'It's ovah! It's *all ovah!!*'

Yup, the argument was convincing. The very grand and very fine mess surrounding him now was unprecedented and without comprehensive analysis. But its power and scope were irrefutable. Meaning, it was probably impossible to resolve.

Granted, this was only Butterbugs' overview, and, given his state of mind, it coalesced at hardly the best time. That is, while alone and in neutral. Yet all the points entertained were inarguable, and if their truth was ever proven, liable to malfunction. Why not make a clean break and shut 'er down, as the decent thing to do?

Quietly, sanely, Butterbugs got up and went over to a tall cabinet wherein his prop arms of the most realistic kind were kept. Not the most receptive person to guns as a way of life, despite heavy cajoling from his good pal Chuck Heston, the ultrastar had nevertheless mastered the technique of blunderbuss culture. It was required for the role of High Mad Doctor, who is a fanatic about that sort of thing, a certifiable gun-wacko, based on self-loathing due to an inadequate penis. There had been several sequences involving the blunderbuss, including drunken snipe shooting, purple partridge blasting, and a merry romp in search of crippled peasants, ripe for potshots. Butterbugs had been properly appalled at these provocative parts of the script, but he'd agreed to perform them, if only to show the true nature of the psychotic Chief Martial Law Administrator/Generalissimus.

Right now, a genuine, fully-functional prop might handily serve to clean up one mess made by making another, albeit on a much smaller scale, and with a competent staff to mop it up.

It was a Keeffey BellShot Speciale, from the 1910s, platinum-plated, with a generous supply of original shot, still in the Wanaganthah packets – a collector's wet dream. Schooled in the tind, parth and gellum procedures of blunderbussery, Butterbugs prepped the wide-shot firearm with cool (Travis) Bickle-esque finesse.

One would never know that a few hours ago he'd been confronted with burning human flesh, both good and bad, so steady were his fingers and methodical his accomplishment. In essence an Alvin York, Butterbugs the pacifist acted now as Butterbugs the sharpshooter. A guy has to be pretty sharp to get a blunderbuss properly beaded on its target, lest incompetence shine through, exposing humiliation and worthlessness in the process. Besides, the main incentive for the High Mad Doctor's special proficiency in firearm operation is to prevent anyone from ever, *ever* suspecting him of having a woefully disappointing penis. Gun studs are *always* master cocksmen. Aren't they…?

Schooled in all aspects of the Keeffey, he even knew how to activate the Self-Eliminating Standard, as recommended for troops and/or hunters in tight spots, so they could go to their Gawd like soldiers if there was no way out. It was a simple mini-tripod setup, with pull-cord, back-spring for trigger, with yardarm for cord hookup, and a cheap edition New Testament paperback provided in the kit (which would probably go for thousands on eBay). In just a few minutes it could be all arranged and ready to go.

But hell, still, what now? Was this *it?* Was it really *time?*

Probably… yes. Yes it was.

At any rate, that was the coin-toss.

The verdict?

So, as if taking direction from a John Sturges or a Zwaynah Kerratay, Butterbugs, in acting mode, duly set up the Keeffey in that very self-elimination configuration, complete with cord extension and digital video interlock controls, if it was wished that the event be taped, with delayed broadcast options in the satellite upload menu.

The shot went down the bullhorn like iron peppercorns into a mule-grinder, and all the other flintlock and guncotton stuff was worked out to perfection. The dry-lubricated pull cord was run through the accessory guide pole circles, which ran their course like miniature telephone poles on a model train set. The firearm itself was successfully anchored from pull cord rip by its basing in the Ground-Slow cast iron weight group, promising minimal kickback, making the arrangement about as pukka as it could get. Result: TAL – Total Assured Lethalness™, guaranteed by the Keeffey people: 'An American Tradition Since 1813™'.

He sat down in front of the silent horn, as if it were a Techniscope camera. If he were a musician though, he probably would have been comfortable with the trumpet aspect of the view, despite it being sans a Satch. At any rate, the curve of the platinum bell had the same reflectivity as a camera's bug-eye lens. The lens had the greater depth, as if deep things swam beneath its glassy surface, whereas the blunderbuss' opaque smoothness promised nothing past its metallic end in itself. Both were a conduit to an audience of sorts. One would be live, and the other would be live – but posthumous it its authorship, and far more sensational than even a hit movie.

True Crime always commanded a huge fan base, as did True Tragedy. The latter had also spawned a massive industry, as Naomi Klein's Shock Doctrine had so fully demonstrated, time after time. (Oh, but if Naomi herself were here, now, it would be a day worth saving… But never mind…)

There was naturally a series of interconnected parallels mixed in with all such factors, but the true actor wasn't really thinking along those lines just now.

Because, at the moment, there was no audience to play *to*. None of that mattered, or was even contemplated. The actor was acting in real life, and there were no rewards looming, either in dollars or in kudos.

All was set for imminent departure. The cord end dangled in his loose fingers, poised as if about to grasp a demitasse. Nothing urgent, but the blowhard power waited, dawdled, taunted. But it was all so boring. Like waiting for a bus.

There was a notepad over there, with pen, but nothing had been written. Butterbugs felt lazy. An executioner's song had yet to be heard.

Review drill, then. The cord would be pulled. His head, and perhaps much of his upper trunk, would be reduced to a variation on the theme of roasted guts that had been sprayed on him earlier. It would complete a trilogy, though riddled with the Revolutionary War huntsman's bane of crunchy shot-waste in the killed prey, instead of high-tech annihilation fallout.

Killed prey. Self-killed… prey? His own prey? Killed? For what reason, exactly?

Now the real tedium could set in. Reviewing the whole thing again – Hadn't he already done that? Why not say, 'Goodnight, disappointed prince', and end things on a romantic artiste's upswing? Gals in nighties would be weeping into their pillows every night for months.

Gals in nighties, is it...?

The gals, girls, ladies, women, females of the earth! Were they not still in their places? Did they not still love him, adore him, want him? What *about* all that stuff, anyway? True, that 'stuff' was all fairly intact. Whoever said it wasn't? But now his mind had become changed – But changed by *others*, right? What had he, Butterbugs, actually done to get caught up in this apparently intractable web, the only cure for which was – death?

Oh *really*, now?

But that's what desperation does to you. It corners you, it rubs out options, possibilities. Then it rubs *in* all the reasoning, the perfectly obvious and incontest-able rationale for proceeding. All the dreaming and aspiring, romanticizing and learning. All the hoping and planning, all up the spout. The only thing left is the doing – the committing of the act. When one is in a corner, one either rots into entropy, or else one takes action.

POW!

Just at that instant, he almost did it. He almost pulled the string. The POW! had gone off in his mind, though. Only in his mind.

Then an overwhelming wave washed over him. Not the drowning kind, but a wave of motivation, of wavelengths really – power movements from far off the bandwidths of light and sound. From way out there, not as far as thought can reach, but from somewhere yonder or out back, came non-verbal instructions.

He dropped the trigger-cord and got up. He knew exactly where his *other* mo-bile was – not the atomized one surrendered to the late Lurgan. It still lay on the austere bedside table next to a dimly flickering star-lamp, where he'd inadvertent-ly left it before decamping to 2, Mulgie Lane. He powered it up. The 'low battery' icon was flashing. More instructions came. He went over to a small wardrobe of the Jacobabad kind and found a spare battery without any difficulty. The mo-bile perked into action and awaited his command. Thumb-work got him into the less than well-known files of his phonebook. He never memorized numbers, only lines. Where was the number? What was the name attached? Where was he going with this? No continuing instructions came through.

Blankly, he kept punching his thumb on the minute, padded key. All sorts of names in the Industry faded in and out in rapid succession, like the credit roll of the greatest picture ever made. They were all there. But he selected none of them. Then he came to the end, the last name in the lengthy group. Often, at the end of a credit sequence, lavish care is lent to special messages, for if the viewer has stayed down to this point, esoteric names or personal messages may be shared, as if in a specialized community.

He saw one of these esoteric names, and it was as if a lofty chime went off somewhere remote, but nevertheless, quite noticeably. He selected the name and hit 'dial'. No further instructions were now needed.

A pause, as the anticipation of waiting for electronic transmissions of consequence to do their nearly instantaneous work tend to make sweat beads appear on foreheads, and adrenalin effects always heighten the tension with flush and flutter.

'Heatherette?' he whispered.

'Yes? A voice – that I know. Your voice — Butterbugs? You are Butterbugs. Your voice! It is transformed somehow. But still, I know it.'

She was Heatherette, oh blessed socks! She had answered, when no one else could. She was as Susannah, but there were no elders about. Private as always, and free of clothes. *But she had answered.*

'It is the midnight hour where I am.'

She was calm.

'Therefore, you must be on the marches of Baluchistan.'

'You... follow my progression... even now.'

Slowly, slowly he got his words out.

'I do. All the nations of the world do as well, though the trail has become vague of late. None know why. You sound... dim. Not the connection, but your conviction.'

Naturally, she wanted to say, 'Is there anything wrong?' but restrained herself in case over-obviousness might cause consternation. Her intuition told her something was plainly wrong, but there was no open approach to it, yet.

'By... the most minimal of signals... do you know me.'

He seemed to be feeling his way along a wall in the dark; toward a drop-off.

'I am without guile.'

'I know. I know.'

He was warming to her voice; it was real, it was inviting. Was it entirely sympathetic, though? Regardless, this was really happening. It was a time for the most naked of honesties.

'Your call is indeed a surprise.'

'That's why I call you now. Heatherette? I am at an edge. Not like the last time you found me in such a state, but here the edge is figurative, not literal.'

Holding the phone gingerly, he slowly sat back down, facing the horn of death.

'I see. You describe it. That means you are in earnest. You are objective and of clear mind...?'

She regretted 'clear mind'. It sounded too like Last Will and Testament. She would have to repair.

'I am,' he answered, without emotion. 'Clarity can enter now, because all endings must be done with a clean conscience.'

'Endings, then.'

Taking note of every word, she was struck by his use of 'clean' instead of 'clear'.

'Endings?'

'What sort of endings, Butterbugs? Clean, clear ones?'

'Like in a film, maybe. But no! No! This is *life*, not a *film!* I don't know what to do. I don't know where to guide myself. No one is here. No one around.'

'I am here, right here.'

'Yes. Yes, you are. Heatherette, I, I have been near real death tonight. Twice. Should it be thrice? I don't know what I am moving toward.'

'Tell me, Butterbugs, what is your exact situation? Right now.'

'I have an instrument of guaranteed destruction aimed at my face as I speak. It is activated, and awaits my command.'

'Butterbugs! Don't!' she wanted to say, but didn't. She could make no further gaffes. The tyranny of distance that ruled between Yniguez Terrace and Kane Hall was nothing but a modifier. Instead, she remained silent. It was an agonizing gamble, but she did it. The silence grew unbearably long. If any loud noise from his end should punctuate it, she would hang up and seek her own way to the waters of oblivion.

This was such a childlike moment. Everything was suspended on delicate strands of hope, mingled with anxiety. During the span of this deep interval, hope hung in the balance.

Then, it had a chance.

'Heatherette?'

She was humbled that her name was what she heard instead of an explosion. He wasn't playing from any script.

'I am here, Butterbugs.'

Rock-solid were her words.

'It's strange, but playing to a phone is much more difficult than to a live audience, or a film crew.'

She dared to install a bit of a breathy laugh.

'It is *playing*, then?'

The gamble was allowing for a certain development: he sounded more human, familiar, even.

'Oh, Heatherette, I'm afraid not. I'm all apart.'

'My friend. I am here. Your circumstances? Please tell.' Her tones imparting 'Please tell' were like a Chinese bridge: low at each end, high in the middle. They conveyed great and powerful meaning to the man at gun's gate.

'Where I find myself now – I never thought I would ever be left with *nothing but where I am* at this moment.'

It then came to Heatherette, that the subjectivity of *vibrations* in the life experience could actually be a real, coherent thing. She had, in her current state of contemplative nudity, in fact just been thinking of the ultrastar – the whole sweep of his being, and she had had a terrible feeling of loss, though none of this had been palpable to her. Yet, at that moment, he had called, and she knew she must pick it up. For it just *had* to be Butterbugs calling. No premonition stuff, no self-fulfilling prophesy or gimmicky synchronicity. Just straight, direct, vibrational connecting, almost Vedic in its foundational solidity. Now she knew. She was moved and humbled in the most profound of ways.

There were plenty of silent pauses, in which one's opinion of the other might shift tenfold, so that plenty of distance might add up between one mind and the other. Any points they made, because they were so adjacent to one another through this connection, were required to be differentiated and individualized, whether via an obvious spreading of facts, or a controversial knife-blow of opinion.

'Why don't you try one thing, Butterbugs.'

'And that is?'

'Remembering. Rear up the gathered back-file. Think of all you have said and done in your considerable range of motion picture experiences. What is the harm in looking back in this instance?'

'I have never done so before. Never *truly* done so…'

'Life of the moment is a precious gift, but what about a perspective of directions?'

'Can it be that I have never paused to reflect so?'

'It doesn't really matter too much. You have certainly desired affirmation as to your standing in the world?'

'Not if it reveals conceit in any way.'

'Perhaps that juvenile point of view had merit at one point, but now, what is its value?'

'I don't know, Heatherette. I think it's an immature thing, certainly. Based on – well, I'm not an intellectual. I act under direction, realizing scripts and associated ideas.'

'An intellectual process.'

'Please, no…'

Determined to treat him right, Heatherette wasn't sure, even at this juncture, how delicate he was. So, she would avoid praise or the argument for it. She could well imagine that he had rather a heavy load of such things all the time, being the world's sole ultrastar and all. Was *that* what had driven him to this point? Time to latch on to more obvious factors.

'Butterbugs, where is Keenah?'

'Oh, I don't know. She never came. I am bereft. If she no longer lives, why should I?'

'I would think that you'd want to know for sure, before you did… I don't believe you have ever played Romeo, have you?'

'Why, why no.' He almost allowed himself to laugh.

'You might, still…?'

A vague chuckle.

'Too old!'

Keep it flexible and moving.

'Your verve for acting – where is that?'

'Tipped upon the ash heap!'

'Not your preference, surely.'

'No! No! That's right. Not because of me. I feel so powerless, despite what everybody says of my station. And pointless. Even the President hates me!'

Heatherette was incredulous.

'What? Of Mega|Goth?'

'Of the United States. You know, of America.'

'Oh.'

She decided not to pursue that one. She genuinely doubted he was delusional, but how dramatic! Cinematic! Automatic!

'That's quite a range. You feel cornered, then?'

'Well. I... guess so...'

Somehow the urgency she felt was going flat. Vibes can fade.

'I'm still here, Butterbugs.'

'I know. I'm... I'm grateful.'

She was afraid to ask, 'What should *I* do?' because she knew she was already doing it. Being there. Nevertheless, what else could she really do? An 'intervention' or something? Did she have the leverage, the skill?

'What are you doing now?'

Her question had a casual ring to it, as did his reply.

'I'm sitting here, thinking: I have a horrible firearm pointed at me. Can you believe it??'

'No, Butterbugs. Quite frankly, I can't.'

'I'm not fibbing, Heatherette.'

There was the faintest trace of haughtiness in his voice, much to Heatherette's pleasure.

'I mean, I believe that that's certainly the case, but what's unbelievable is that you have gotten to that point. The point where you are.'

'Well, I've been trying to describe why I'm *to* that point.'

Even though he hadn't described very much at all, she of course wanted to remain supportive.

'And I think it's completely understandable.'

'You do?'

'It's perfectly reasonable. You're a reasonable person. You are not outrageous or emotionally out of control. No matter what you might think. You are in your current situation because you have been driven to it.'

'Driven. I think so, too... But... To... you know... *suicide?*'

His first use of the word.

'That's the premise. An unrefreshing one, granted.'

'Unrefreshing? Why? It's an answer, isn't it? Suicide!'

'Certainly. It's the getting there that's, well, rather shocking. Violent. Unpleasant. It's supposed to be.'

She didn't say 'selfish'. Did The Samaritans use that term so early in a case?

'Supposed to be, what?'

'Protection from dangerous things is essential to the life force.'

'Oh yes, I agree. I want mine back!'

'Your protection?'

'Yes! Yes! I want it back! You have it, why can't I?'

'We all must strive to preserve it!'

'"We all!' What does that matter? This is me! I'm the one! I need out! I need what cannot be given!'

Obviously, things were falling apart. She had to think of something. She had to jump ahead. Another gamble, but a jolt had to occur.

'Butterbugs, when you do it, what will happen? Describe it. I'm not there, but you could at least let me know, while you're still alive, what the act is going to be like. Besides, when you pull the trigger (if you don't wuss-out and hang up, first), I'll be listening for the right moment. I'll be the last one you talk with, and what am I going to tell the Press, and indeed, the world? We're actors, you and me. Rehearsal now. Rehearse with me. Paint the picture with reds and purples and Karel Appel colors. What's the pitch of the Theremin score? What are the famous last words to be uttered? Glom it on. Slop it on. I want emoting, not boring depression. This is a big scene – don't fuck it up!!'

He didn't hang up. Instead, he went to work.

He assessed the blunderbuss, checked its cord and the entire setup, which was intact and ready to go. He stared into the black-hole center of the flared horn and took the sequence apart frame by frame...

'...And then – OK, the cord jerks, setting the whole ball, or balls, lots of 'em, rolling. Seen straight on, a flash of orange light; I don't think it'd be white light; not hot enough. But it's pretty dang high-temp. Big crack of flint-snap and hammer-smack on soundtrack, just before the blowout. From POV, switch to CU and MCU, as needed. Profile of blunderbuss horn, muted lighting, to increase menacing look, then face, receiving shot, in real time. Then, repeated, in 125-and-up-to-1657 fps slo-mo. Every detail shown in un-compromised graphicness. The nose hairs collapsing, the pores giving in, the punctures starting, the facial expression that betrays momentary disappointment that the deed was actually done, just before the brain-shield caves and cerebellum activity has a limited time of response, before shutdown. Does this make *sense* to you? And indeed, the mind still has considerable time to reason, reflect and review, not only on this one instant, but a whole life, as well. Plus, what's to come. What's to come? And, uh, what *will* come...

'What comes is more devastation and surrender. Expansion gas from each bit of shot projects itself just ahead of the advancing pellets, so as to make an explosive and rancid environment on the tissue surfaces before they are rendered ensanguined and newly pulpy, as the dangerous objects *advance*, inexorably *advance*. Bone fibers, eye pieces – blasted-out rods and cones – mucus chunks caught in transit amidst the cashed-in sinus galleries, all are dislodged and thrown clear of the composite *ex*-head 'n' shoulders, which the huge CU of the, what, well, certainly widescreen coverage of this event, yields us.

'If possible, a dolly-in during this slo-mo is essential, or certainly desirable, as the shot, as it advances further into the interior of the blown-up person's remains, needs to scrutinize all the diverse destruction from as close a quarters as possible, and indeed, as the camera dollies, it follows the horn's baleful projectiles, all the way in. ALL THE WAY IN, I tell you.

'Soon we arrive at the ruins of a brainstem and its spinal cage, the way having been cleared with the utmost blitzkrieg-like efficiency. It is a dolorous sight, like an old Spanish castle, clinging to a parapet of conquest that countless and anonymous cannon fodder gave their lives to *not conquer*. Shaggy hacked-off end of said brainstem, so newly denuded, flops around a bit before expiring, its system of reflexes loyal to the end.

'Never mind covering the blown-apart masses of skull and brainpan that are the first to be sacrificed in such a campaign. The scatterment is too extensive and impossible to cover without a second unit, or perhaps even a third, and even a camera network on the lines of both 'Ben-Hur''s (MGM, 1925, 1959) chariot race sequences would probably not be sufficient. The spectacle of blood and brains will rival anything in the 'Tale of Guzman's Family' in 'Melmoth The Wanderer' (20th-Fox), in which, incidentally, I starred.

'There is the tongue, still protruding from its bloody pedestal, trying to click against a palette in order to articulate what the hell has happened, down to the edifice in which it was once part, but now, stripped of its rights, it can only faux-lick and paw the reddish atmosphere around it, operating for a few seconds on dying reserve power. And given the chance, certainly having something wry to say about how this thing turned out. But all words being denied, the done deal has hit home in the most appalling ways ever.

'So then, once we've dollied in, we've got a lot of overhead angles to tackle, as the lateral punch of the action has revealed a WWI-style landscape of ghastly-grim features. But instead of a range of Belgian grey, Verdun charcoal, and Somme taupe, and possibly lifeless lavender and muted blacks, we have color spread all over, akin to that, you know, coincidentally Low Countries artist (as requested), Appel, for the mélange of tissue, fluid, and – I say, Heatherette, I didn't forget Karel Appel in this scenario, because, that's a good examp – Heatherette? Are you there? Respond!'

Butterbugs cut off the storyboard talk. Instead of gasps or crying at the other end, he heard obnoxious vomiting sounds. Really awful, drippy, pukey, emetic drooling and spitting, with associated trauma-cum-self-disgust grunts and moans. It went on for some moments. Then a distressed voice moaned, amidst the inevitable follow-up of enzyme-spitting and evacuation:

'Butterbugs!' Heatherette squawked, 'I threw up all over my bubs and thighs! And all over! In fact, I am sitting in a pool of my own spit-up! Oh, heavens! What a horrible mess! Look what you did! Alas, you cannot see it, but oh, woe! A fine brunch of hollandaise, pan-fried prunes and duck crème! From the fount of my troubled mouth, the discharge churned within my soft but wambling belly, all sprayed and splattered in disgusting stages! Oh! Oh! This will take hours to clean! How *could* you! What *made* you! Have you no pity? No caring? Why must you be so selfish? So self-absorbed and naughty! You mush-head! How could you *do* a thing like that??'

Assuredly then, Heatherette's sterling acting ability was paraded over the phone with panache. But like the medium of radio, in the case of conventional telephony, everything beyond sound must be left to the imagination. Art's honor system inevitably requires trust.

Reaching over for a kerchief to daub the genuine dribble that resulted from her Grade A fakery, she returned her wide and plump lips to their usual sensual status, and added a few gauche grunts and throat clearings to validate her heavy-cheer recovery.

'Oh, Butterbugs,' she added with mufflement, not to imply that another wave of upchuck was on the way, but to impose a notion in her listener's mind that perhaps his little situation had placed an innocent in some jeopardy, and thus, he might emerge from his own inertia to think about *someone else's* ordeal. 'Oh, how *could* you be so…'

Her voice trailed off into a weakening, highly disturbing trickle…

'Heatherette! Are you OK? Oh! Wait! Don't die! Please! How could you slip away like that! You cannot! You… ! Oh, no! Hurry! Live! Live! I *will* you to live! *LIVE*, DAMMIT!!!!'

His last utterance had an effect similar to Sensurround in the reverberation that came screaming across the phone.

From Heatherette there was silence.

'Heatherette! Do you hear me? Can I yet reach you??'

From far at the other end of the line, in old Hollywood, a bit of gurgling could be heard. Not quite a death-rattle… Followed by a hawking, then a spitting, then a cascade of coughing. Finally, a human voice, like the first cry of a newborn babe, made its way all the distance over to Kane Hall at Jambutterbugsabad:

'Oh, Butterbugs! Your intervention… has… saved me! I was about to choke, really choke, as my epiglottis was stalled. But your voice jump-started its involuntary action, and I was able to swallow the remnants of sour stomach and breathe pure uninterrupted air again, despite the horrendous fumes from my scattered kaka. You have saved me! I knew it was dynamically providential that you called me from afar, because by that act you have saved my very life. I bow down in grateful and happy acknowledgement for your selfless heroism! Thank you! Thank you! THANK YOU!'

'You are saved? You are well? Oh glory! Glory to you! Returned to life! To life! Life and its glorious, adventurous sureties! Welcome back, girl, a hearty welcome back!'

'You too, Butterbugs. You too!'

After they hung up, both in restored fettle, Heatherette gave a big sexy smile, something Butterbugs had never seen. She naturally reflected on the phone conversation just concluded. Somewhere in there was a testament to her superior acting capabilities. She realized though, that she didn't possess Butterbugs' mobile's number. Her clunky 1949-vintage phone possessed no digital guts. Any follow-up would not be possible. Then she started bawling.

It was now, as part of Butterbugs' duty to the world, that if he was to well and truly return to said world, some form of contrition must take place. He knew what to do. Shed tears. Not for himself, or even for those he loved, or for the whole world itself, but for what might have transpired. He was very sorry, and it wouldn't happen again. The blunderbuss set-up was dismantled and its junk went back to proper storage quarters, without any further needful thought of what its capabilities were. Reverted to prop-dom, whence it came.

So he wept.

While the actor wept without any attempt to shield his feelings from the world, the sound of those feelings did not go unnoticed. Though Butterbugs reckoned that aside from blessed Heatherette, all caring persons were gone from the world, the fact remained there were many whose concern had been thwarted by confused means, so that distance was created, and obfuscation as well, which led to misinterpretation and manipulation in general. It had been someone's master plan somewhere to isolate the actor, and in that isolation, to erode and eliminate such a thing as the world's only ultrastar. The mission had nearly succeeded. But because it didn't, space and time now allowed for a rebound of sorts. The ultrastar was in quarters. Word was getting out. The studio started to come alive again. Courage had returned to the world, and in its footsteps trod persons who lived in relative normalcy, and they were once again in evidence.

Old Atrocity had been beside himself. Confined to the soundstages during this tense hiatus of information blackout, he'd worked wonders in rigging sets and effecting cinematic wonders in SFX and associated requirements, while filming awaited. He had accomplished much. But now he was restless and anxious and in need of some sort of resolve. Was this a production that would proceed? If not, *why* not? What the holy hell was going *on*, anyway?

Taking notice of the movement of humans in the chasms between the soundstages, and catching the air of machinery moving again without even asking anyone, the Director of Systematic Realization hustled his bib overall'd bustle over to Kane Hall, to see for himself.

Reaching the ultrastar's neighborhood, the thoroughfare nearby reminded him of the Warner Bros. lot during the night shoots of 'The Music Man' (WB, 1962), when all the extras were knowing their way to and fro, while assistant directors out of sight kept them organized and occupied. Tonight, there was the same kind of busy energy, undefined as of yet, but things were happening, seemingly without overview or control. Etiquette was in play however; this was not anarchy. It was as if high filming were underway once more.

Pausing at the dual pilasters that flanked the public entrance to the star's Kane

Hall abode, Old Atrocity heard the weeping. It was as if the sound was old as the ages. The burden of so many years was heard in its soul-wrenching dirge. Yet, there was an element of weightlessness to it, as if a purge after whatever needed dirging.

The veteran film worker knew it immediately, that his ultrastar was within, restored after some terrible ordeal of which he did not know. But credit in all ways was given that something of an ordeal had transpired. Such were the vibes that passed about this community.

Still, OA paused under the gas jet that subtly flared in the center of an iron hoop that arched between the pilasters, the flame thick and viscous, like flammable yogurt. As 'twas getting very late, the other forms in the lane dwindled until OA was left alone in the jittery shadows at the gate. Still, he heard the weeping. It was time to know it.

He approached the shamiana's flap door and knew he had rights to proceed on in, but he hesitated.

'Just because I am facile in my work and am knowing of the ultrastar's qualities,' he thought, 'Doesn't mean that I am necessarily privy to any emotional meltdown he may be enduring at this time. But, oh hell, just think about it, bub! I've done everything for this star but change the plastic non-frayers at the tips of his shoelaces! I *know* him, and he is family. If I do not connect now, I lose him, and I would deserve banishment, as my total humiliation would require me to take up, in all honest earnest. *I'm going in.*'

He did go in.

The scene: Joe Biroc could have lensed it! Surely Perry Ferguson's interior designs set it all up! The chamber was headachy-hot, and spot-lighted by the isolated flicker flames. A very indoor image, but like Charles Foster Kane's Xanadu seen from afar, and at night. This particular Kane Hall was intimate with the sound of sorrow, and its occupant sat in the featured middle, with head in hands.

Knowing another humanoid was near, the weeping lessened. Butterbugs looked up. OA's face was concealed in shadow, but his trademark bib was plainly noir-noticeable.

Butterbugs said nothing and did nothing but stretch his hydrated palms outward. OA advanced out of his lighting plot and grasped the actor's hands fulsomely.

'Butterbugs, friend of the world, you reach out!'

It was the kind of declaration OA had seen many an actor attempt on the sets he cared for, but no one had ever said a non-scripted line with such heartfelt integrity. Actors have their lines, but OA had his *soul* to speak from.

'Old, Old Atrocity! You've come! I scarcely can imagine who is here and who isn't. Am I alive, or beyond the ridge? Your presence is treasured, but can I be sure?'

With the grip of his profession, OA pulled the star up from his sitting and as the invisible creative team would want it, both faces, raised into position, benefited from impeccably placed happenstance illumination, as they steadily came to address one another.

'Butterbugs! You live yet! We had heard – We had heard that you – that you might have...!'

He was referring, of course, to the Kurr Valley debacle, as the u'star's late crisis in Kane Hall was, as yet, an inner sanctum secret.

He couldn't finish. Seizing the burden of empathy, the craggy grip took on the other's tears until his eyes welled into giant raindrops. Personal pride required him to withdraw momentarily to daub and to regroup. Raw emotions were best left to performers. He, on the other hand, wasn't afraid to cry, but he knew Butterbugs wanted sturdy affirmation, not creaky-weepy. He approached again, grasped Butterbugs' shoulders, and patted them in soldierly style before standing back a little.

'There's a good old man! So glad to see you intact and here and *yourself.*'

'Thank you, OA. Sufferin' bleedin' Chickamauga, eh?'

'Music to my ears, survivor! Are you then, well enough?'

'Enough, yes. I am *changed*, but as one who is emerging. It is good to see you, and it is good to be here, at this time, right now.'

'You are the one I know, all right. I can truly relax and rejoice now.'

'Wonderful, friend. Yes, please, would you take wine?'

'A jar of beer, perhaps?'

'Absolutely. Over in the almirah. Cooled, I think. You just *take*. Try...'

'No beats are missing in the noble pulse of the Butterbugsian life force! But what a holy hellhole horrorshow you went through! I've only heard the basics, man.'

Talk was helpful. Ventilation was possible, whereas just before OA's appearance, a dangerous pressure was a-building. Now it was rendered neutral by the sense of normal human interaction.

Busting open a tin of Jabe's 'Old Ferringhee' Sukkur-Bukkur Style Ale (Brewed Under Supervision of Bob Sandeman's Favourites), Butterbugs kicked back and dove into the OA gab, finding it fine balsam for his rapidly recovering self. As if they were on a Burt Kennedy set, the two pros kicked back and yakked about what had happened of late, with all the ease of Mark Twain meets Rudyard Kipling, with Perry Como, Terri Garr, Sessue Hayakawa, Myrna Loy and Oscar Peterson as guests. It was a beautiful overlook of the current events, with just the right nip and tuck at just the right moments, thus securing Butterbugs' grounding in the black loam of sanity and familiarity, where he belonged.

Several tins later, OA felt really good. About Butterbugs. That established, he was content to be a pilaster in the overarching and protective mechanism that could now be re-employed, after the ultrastar's obscure odyssey had sufficiently reached into the portends of society's future. It was that big a deal. So now he made room to watch.

Some time-bends of serenity then passed, and they were so appreciated that OA and Butterbugs became downright lazy in their 'responsible' assessment of their eventful panoply. Rather, they might appear callous and detached, but instead were practical and forgiving toward themselves.

Then the flap of the tent was swept aside. Into the flickery chamber, its dim corners causing the central figures to be accentuated even in the low light, a force now entered, and with it, tone change. It did not bring more illumination, except perhaps of the soul.

It was TABP.

'What the fuck are you doin' here, Atrocity??'

'TABP! Thank sufferin' bleedin' Chickamauga that you're here!'

'Oh, man, you saved the day. I just had a feelin' that I should get my ass over here.'

Having looked intensely at Butterbugs, and seeing that he breathed yet, and that a few disjointed components of the firearm kit yet remained on the floor, un-flashed powder still intact, he broke down into sobs.

'Dear fellow...,' whispered Butterbugs. 'Dear, dear fellow.'

Gesturing with considerable emotion to the ultrastar, TABP nevertheless aimed his statement at Old Atrocity.

'We almost *lost* him, man!'

OA could only nod his head, as the known fear of that very possibility was writ large on his expression.

'The gravity of that fact is something none of us even bothered to ever con-template,' muttered The Angry Black Priest, taking his principled disgust for all concerned – which included the whole world – onto his broad shoulders.

'You speak for all of us,' OA said with great somberness.

'All of us encounter close calls in life, but when we hear of our dearest friends and their emergencies, and we fall back on the excuse of 'Who knew?' there is nothing for it but to self-consume our own loathing of our conducts, and to mourn how low on the scale of moral responsibility we've come.'

Butterbugs knew that TABP's sermonette was for the right reasons, but he saw no cause for self-flagellation. All he cared about was the presence of these fine people.

'TABP! TABP! Be not so troubled!'

'So, Butterbugs, grant me a fuckin' solemn pledge to make to you, OK? I pledge that you will never, ever be allowed to again sink into anything like the bottom level you had to suffer on down-to. Know what I mean? It will *not be possible* for you to do that again, friend of mine. The ever lovin' The Angry Black Priest will not tolerate it. You can and will rely on me, and I will always be there. Remember now, so long ago, before your ascendancy, when we sat on that sunset slope, checkin' out the future? What has happened here tonight was not in that plan. It was an aberration. It cannot and will not happen again. You are saved, and you remain safe. With me. Know that. Believe it, now and always.'

Butterbugs, gazing at TABP, could not speak, but his eyes filled near to over-flowing, and that was enough. Even his very ears conveyed the same powerful acknowledgment of blessedness. The imperative was obvious: he did indeed grant TABP's fuckin' solemn pledge – with all his heart.

The wrapper/priest's throat tightened and it took a couple of tries, as he looked over at OA, before he could get out:

'I've been granted, man! I've been *granted...!*'

Returning to his deep regard of Butterbugs' eyes, TABP could not help but indulge in a bit of interior meditation that bespoke several possibly misogynistic points of view. Whatever the interpretive label, he had to review the plain fact that in his state of crisis, Butterbugs had not received any help from the women in his life. Not that that was their specific responsibility, but it was a reflection on the re-ality that Butterbugs was one who gave of himself without conditions, and oddly, those women who had aided him and supported him and enjoyed the benefits of a Butterbugsian relationship, no matter how deep or sensual or loving, none were here on the front lines with their man at his crossroads of life and death. Was such a phenomenon possible, though? Thus, he could not judge them harshly. All were responsible and engaged and busy human beings. Just Justy's accomplishments in a single day were enough to justify her responsibilities away from her Butterbugs, but her Butterbugs had made it entirely possible for her to *be* in such a position of leverage today. No, there was no need to consider all the ultrastar's women to be selfish and self-absorbed creatures interested only in taking, taking, taking from the resource known as Butterbugs – for their own needs and agendas. He simply thought it was sad that none of them, apparently, were able to channel their usual-ly remarkable gifts of intuition toward the critical-mass vibes that surely had been emanating from the most remarkable man in their lives, albeit half a globe away. He was sad that no transcendent rendezvous had come to pass. Of say, all of them showing up here, at precisely the right moment, in order to save the one who had done the most for them. To save him, from himself or from those who wished him harm. It was a blessing of cosmic shakti which he most desired, because he'd always thought the eternal feminine was the ultimate savior of the universe.

However, he obviously did not know that such an occurrence had indeed come to pass. Heatherette's intervention, utterly indirect that it was, was meritorious of being cosmic in every sense of the word. Had TABP been able to consider its existence and its import, he would have regarded it as an effort of the highest and most beautiful order possible in this whole sinking world.

This perception of failure in regard to the women in the ultrastar's life was, he fully knew, a mere and cheap-ass excuse for avoiding a more bitter truth: that the *men* in Butterbugs' life were the chief culprits in allowing a crisis to have a chance of occurring in the first place. Therefore, it was wholly appropriate that he, a man of both spirit and talent, assume the role of responsibility for this near-tragedy. It would be the only way he could be able to cope with the awful thoughts of what might have happened, and how they would all have had to face the consequences.

'Where is my spiritual integrity now?' he silently asked himself.

The answer – was immediate. Just there, in front of him. There it was, in the ultrastar who so soulfully regarded him with such gratitude. Just there, the message already delivered. From that moment forward, TABP was renewed, and his own private crisis passed. His innate intuition was now allowed to be liberated, and it provided for possibilities such as Heatherette's right-moment role. The facts need not be known so much as the wonder of unseen potential.

The two embraced in a bond so wordlessly effective, there was nothing more needing saying or doing. Only a musical resolve from the likes of a Franz Waxman could seal the encounter without the slightest trace of cloyingness or any other awkward tool of Hollywoodian technique, employed in order to convey the audience into the next scene.

After TABP left, Old Atrocity and Butterbugs looked at each other with re-moistened eyes.

'Whatever your ordeal is, Butterbugs, you are not without friends.'

'I cannot articulate the caliber of the meaning of TABP's visit, nor your own. With friends like you two, slaying myself would have been like murdering family, for the three of us would die at once, a triumvirate deed of total worthlessness.'

'You know it! But, wait… Butterbugs, uh, *slaying* yourself?'

True, there were bits of blunderbussian self-kill appliances around, but still, it was Kurr Valley all outsiders would know.

'Yes, well,' Butterbugs hastened to protect all outsiders from unnecessary worry. 'You know, placing myself carelessly in harm's way, and all. Whether it's near explosions, or other things that go BAM! or POW! in the night!'

'Aye,' murmured OA. 'Ye see reason now.'

'I do,' answered the ultrastar almost inaudibly. 'I tell you, I do. I think we might be on the verge of a great truth, OA.'

After they had been refreshed by some pumpkin-flavored chai, served by loyal khansammah Kuzzah Randi, who'd been worried sick about his charge but now quietly rejoiced with other support staff, Butterbugs and Old Atrocity were able to verbalize their thoughts within more normal states of mind.

'Have you ever noticed, Old Atrocity, how life imitates cinema?'

'I was following no such script,' OA replied. 'You players and your type are required to be scripted in your actions. That's why so many actors are fuck-ups.'

'I know,' Butterbugs smiled. 'But instinct is often script, mostly, is it not?'

'If one is conditioned enough, I suppose.'

'Well, it's not for me to work out.'

'Yass indeed. You're trying to rationalize your emergency behavior. You came so *close*, man.'

'Closer than I can handle.'

'You can handle it. Consider it scripted.'

'That's what I was trying to say.'

'I see your point now. Otherwise, the reality would be too crushing.'

'I am, however, not crushed.'

'Triumph, then. You sure?'

'Never so.'

A knock at the tent door was heard.

'Come,' said the star.

Skookumchuck Millah, high-level production associate-cum-assistant director on this production, and a talented director in his own right, entered.

'Butterbugs, someone to see you. Someone special, I think.'

'Suffern' bleedin' Chickamauga...'

'Special... !' wondered Butterbugs. 'I am already in the company of *special*...'

The tent flap swept aside, causing the lantern flames to waver, so that she who was now illuminated in the doorway seemed an evanescence created by an old-fashioned dissolve, made within a camera itself.

She was Keenah.

She stood in the doorway until the waver ceased, and then, fully in frame, she advanced. She wore a plain cloth coat, but after the flap of the tent returned to privacy position, she chucked it aside, revealing a scanty black bikini underneath.

Without a word, she approached Butterbugs, knelt down in front of him, and put both her hands on his knees.

'I have come,' she said quietly. 'I have heard. You are here, still here, and I am overpowered with relief. I am comforted. I came as you asked me to.'

Their faces were close, and they regarded each other with new honesty.

'Butterbugs, beyond my joy at seeing you alive, I will now tell of myself. Rapidly-here, and quickly-now. The pure and simple things. *I am with Egaz now.* We have found that we love each other. We are committed to each other. We will go on together. To you I apologize in the most profound way I can think of. I am sorry, but I must be honest, as my abiding love for you requires it, and its power frees me of a troubled mind. I can only hope it frees yours, as well.'

The suspension of this lightning-bolt instant kept her from shedding tears, whether of happiness or shame.

Butterbugs, without hesitation or comment, moved closer and kissed her lightly on the lips. Sealed with a blessing. A glorious chapter closed. He treasured the beauty of the moment, and was mysteriously but pleasingly satisfied with the new news. Delighted, even.

Again, music was the only adequate resolve for an encounter like this. Alfred could have written it! Or Suk! Certainly Dmitri!

Lacking such a cinematic luxury, everyone relaxed.

'Dear girl,' said Butterbugs, ''Tis lovely that you are. 'Tis sexy that you look! What could be better in life?'

He could now ogle a bit at the bikini wear.

'You like it? I got it at Belsum's. $395!'

They all laughed. Ice cannot last for long in Baluchistan.

'Makes you look like you literally rushed out the door,' wagged OA.

'Well,' she giggled, 'I came with a full kit. I didn't dream of a tease, no matter what I would have to do to win my baby over.'

'Appeasement?' OA tossed in.

'No sir. You see, nothing in the world was more important than for me to know that my Butterbugs would be OK in this matter, in spite of what direction the cookie might crumble.'

'You felt that way, my dear?' asked Butterbugs, his voice revealing well-placed emotions. 'You really did?'

She looked at him with as much sincerity as it is possible to assign to one's interaction with one's own kind.

'Kind sir and honorable lover, I was always endeavoring to meet your standards of quality, in every way. Perhaps I betrayed them by my ambition.'

'You could never be a traitor, Keenah. You are too real and too rare by half.'

Still on her knees, Keenah bowed her head and lowered it still further into the folds of her beachy thighs.

'On the long flight over here, Butterbugs, I wished... I wished... I could *die* for you. I would happily take your bullet. I still would!'

He gratefully fondled her cute hair as its bob'd tresses came into his hands' range.

'Dear girl! You will never, ever have to do such a thing. We are at total peace. You have found the one whom you really sought, and I, even though I thought I did, am still on the quest, which, you know, I really quite relish after all.'

'You mean you don't want me anymore?'

She sounded serious of course, because she in fact was, despite her reassigned love.

Deciding not to make a sitcom joke out of it, Butterbugs drew her up so that her kiss-target nose was level with his, and well within the frame of a CinemaScope-grade profile close-up of them both.

'Keenah-teenah! Oh, Keenah! You are securely ensconced in the uppermost galleries of my everlasting hall of fame!' He looked over at OA. 'You see? My 'Great Truth'! Keenah to Egaz, and I to my role. Thus do Keenah and I join in a new way: to follow Egaz. She for his love, I for his art.'

'Oh, Butterbugs!' Keenah burst out, with tears of joy. 'You lovely, lovely, caring fellow! Oh, how could I be so lucky?'

'I feel the same way, dear girl. Nothing but lucky. What more could we want?'

'Indeed, indeed!'

'And indeed!' echoed OA. He had previously thought Keenah might be a trifle shallow for the ultrastar, and that he deserved someone with more dimension. Now he was almost brought to tears again tonight, by the sweet and deep sincerity she had shown to all.

'OK, where *is* Egaz, anyway?' asked Butterbugs, with genuine good nature.

'He's probably... at home...!' offered OA, with a bit of a teary twinkle.

Keenah stayed sincere.

'Why, in his chambers back in old Hollywood, awaiting your counsel. He is on terrible pins and needles. And he has not found alleviation of any kind. He genuinely suffers, Butterbugs.'

Without hesitation, Butterbugs grabbed his mobile, dialed the director, got him, and delivered the most movingly beautiful explanation of a situation that Keenah and OA had ever witnessed. He rang off, and his magnificent smile told the others that the exchange had gone well indeed.

There followed lots of hugging and kissing, for all three were bathing in the wonders of relief and repair.

Then Keenah laughed specifically.

'You know, Buttery-dear, I *still* can't remember that whole silly address where my Egaz dwells!'

'Truth to tell, babe, neither can I. Something about 'Los Family of the Expiatory Whatchamacallit', or something even worse!'

Everyone indulged in a lot of free-form laughter, jollity, and relieved-as-all-getout merriment.

'I have to tell you, Keenah,' said Butterbugs at last, 'I'm really happy for you. Egaz and I are close. We understand each other. Always have. There's no one else I'd rather see you with.'

'Oh, amazing fellow, I'm so grateful for your understanding. *And* your love.'

'It's all intact, too. Except now we two can proceed with our (love) lives. You with Egaz at your side.'

'Egaz! Egaz!'

'He's a great and talented fella!'

'Oh, *isn't he?* Isn't he awesome?'

'You will be perfect together. I totally *mean* that, Keenah.'

'And you, boy?'

'Me? I'm experiencing new things. New ideas. New love, though I don't exactly know what it is. Or where. Or, I guess, why!'

Even now, Butterbugs did not really comprehend Heatherette's recent role in the scheme of things.

'You will find it soon, no doubt, sweet king!'

'For the first time, I know that I will.'

'So now, big one, what wilt thou do? What is thy heart's best desire?'

'To *act* again.'

'Oh, baby, yes indeed, I think that's a good plan. Stroll your play, act your role, finish this picture.'

'Let's do it together.'

The two then silently and dreamily regarded each other with the delight of a nouveau sweetness and light, unencumbered by anything having to do with the past.

'Well,' sighed OA, 'It's getting on...'

The two still-lovers smiled knowingly and appreciatively at close range. Keen-ah dropped her top and then let her hands stroke the slabs of Butterbugs' inner thighs.

OA, appreciative almost to the point of getting choked up yet again, at the trust displayed by the youthful-but-wise actress with the poetically-perfect breasts, turned on the balls of his feet and flipped the flap of the tent door, making the flames shake, and things in the shamiana dissolved into a whole new sequence of young love.

Without burden of either marriage vows amongst all those involved, or the expectations of greatness in the minds of the two now falling all over themselves with hot lust, there was no reason not to freely love each other in a revised way: to simply clear-the-decks, clean-the-slate, spread–'em, prep it, and pumpa-pumpa them pistons 'n' cylinders like nobody's business. There was nothing like a no-frills but still fancy-free fuck to level life back to where it was sane and sensible again.

Never was intimate bliss so baggage-free or so wisely-used!

Goodness had returned to the world.

They were cured, all right.

After a boiled-egg breakfast, another curative act was accomplished. Butter-bugs got into telephonic contact with Judah Fitz-Judah, who was tracked down in Tehran, attempting damage control of A&U-CAM and 'UWH', from the haven of Nadeer Studios. Judah in turn managed to get Sonny in on a three-way conference call from General Eugenio A. Garay, Paraguay.

'Let's clear all this up, you two,' said back-in-the-saddle Butterbugs.

'Why, Butterbugs!'

'Why yes, super-agent. It's me. Things have changed.'

'For the better?'

'Uh-huh. Better believe it. Now, define your status.'

'Well, I'm pretty ashamed of myself, Butterbugs.'

'Not for the first time, Sonny.'

'Boy, we go way back with that history, don't we?'

'Uh-huh. Better believe it. Now, explain yourself, sir.'

'He's been briefed a little,' offered Judah helpfully.

'But I wish to hear it in his own digitally-transferred words. J F-J.'

'You will!' said Sonny, eager to please now. 'Some polluted atmosphere has cleared. In fact, I can see the sun again. And my own son, too! Yeah, Penny's out of the jug. Seems there was a bit of a misunderstanding.'

'Yeah?' said Butterbugs, as Sonny paused clumsily.

'Uh, it's a tad awkward.'

'Good heavens, Sonny, you're a super-agent and you feel *awkward?* I should say!'

'Thing is, old rubbish, our #3 guy here is involved.'

'Judah? *Fitz*-Judah?'

'As a matter of fact… yes,' said Judah.

'But let me tell it, fellas,' said Sonny. 'I don't think you know, Butterbugs, that Penny's gay. He's *gay*, Butterbugs.'

'Yeah? So?'

'Well, I told him to go head-on into it, if it was real. It *was* real, so he went head-on. I'm not being funny here. I'd rather have the kid go for quality than flop-pability, so I encouraged him. I said, you can be gay in my agency, but you have to keep 'em separate, huh? He said fine.'

'Could you condense a bit, Sonny? In acting we have to be concise. In management, you *should* be concise, but often aren't.'

'I'm not as conservative as I sound, ya know.'

'I know, Sonny. Again, conciseness, maybe?'

'Awright, kid, message punched in. But this is all important in the big pic sense. So anyway, Penny's going along and you know what? He got himself a relationship. It turned steady, and I approved of the other guy. In fact, he works for me. They *both* work for me.'

'So you had Pennefold thrown in jail?'

'For a second I wanted to, but then I saw who he was getting into bed with: my right hand man on my third set of arms. The third party in this here conference call, in point of fact.'

'Judah?' Butterbugs heard a muezzin sounding off from way behind Judah's corner of the phone space.

'It's true, Butterbugs. Crazily true. But we're committed. Mr. Projector can explain it better than I can.'

'*I'll* say I can! I've been in many a funky situation, but nothing like this partic-ular one. But don't think I'm mad about it.'

'Mad-angry, or mad-keen?'

'Cut the Brit crap, Mumpkin Boy! (Just kidding!) Angry-mad, man! Can't you tell?'

'You don't sound mad at all, Sonny. In fact, you sound sort of… proud.'

'Yeah, well, whatever. So anyway, it's late in the day and after hours, see? Penny's in station and Judah joins him. They have assured me that work comes first, and it goddam *better!* And here they were, in our favorite conference zone Butterbugs, where we've brokered many a deal, and they're, you know, goin' at it there. Hell, I've had a few liaisons there myself, of the opposite sex always, don't ya know! Right, Judah?'

'That is correct, Dad. I mean, Sonny. Mr. Projector.'

'Yeah, I suppose you can call me Dad, my probably soon-to-be-son-in-law…'

'Thanks, Dad.'

'Don't mention it.'

'Your family is growing, Sonny,' smiled Butterbugs.

'But let me tell you…'

'Right. Where does *jail* come in?'

'I'm almost there, actor-sahib. So, my kids are gettin' their rocks off, and our security rent-a-fuzz happens to come in, ostensibly to check because all the lights were on. (You don't make out in the dark, Judah?) So this cop, he's a cocky bastard. He knows of my lofty standing, but he nevertheless does the unthinkable. He mocks me and my family. He comes in and finds the two having consensual sex. And despite it being none of his shittin' business, he starts haranguing, mocking, laughing, and finally, *preaching* at the two, as if they're in chapel school or something. Can you believe that? He ends up drilling a Deuteronomy dart at their collective ass, and spits and barks his way into a tizzy. I'm sure he's a self-loathing closet fag himself – of the most toxic kind. Isn't that right, Judah?'

'You speak the truth. It's just… that, it's painful – to go over it again, and… in front of others…'

'Yeah, well, Butterbugs is a cornerstone to me, son. The *foundation*. He has to know everything.'

'Of course, S…onny. I didn't mean to imply… You've been most gracious to Penny and me, Dad. Most understanding.'

Judah was beginning to feel far more comfortable calling him Dad.

'Sonny, I get the picture. No need to drag Judah –'

Butterbugs could well now understand the equivocation and sexual tension Judah had undergone during that memorable flight they shared (…with Joby the flight attendant…). So much had been unresolved in the world he was leaving behind in LA! Similar to Butterbugs' own, actually. They could all bond over like issues. He made a mental note to give Joby a call, to see how she was doing.

'We're almost there, my movie star. I want you to get the whole story.'

'OK!'

'So Penny gets a bellyful pretty fast. Justifiable rage set in. And yeah, this is where pride in my boy comes home to me. Penny calls for peace and for the cop to move on, but the preaching takes on a maniacal tone. Right, Judah?'

'He was getting quite out of control, Butterbugs. And he was armed.'

'With a pea shooter.'

'Possibly a pee-pee shooter.'

It was Judah's first attempt at levity. He was healing.

'That's funny, Judah. Hey, were you dudes buck naked?'

'Not at all, Dad. It was all very civil and un-sensational.'

'Yeah, well, you're in SHOWBIZ. If you've got it, *flaunt* it, baby!'

Butterbugs laughed as Sonny continued:

'And Penny, he doesn't waste any more time. He pops the cop – hard, really hard – in the schnoz, and that didn't go over big, at all. Cop started bawling, then calls his support in nasally tones. They show up and slap assault and battery on my son! Can you believe that?? They haul his non-virginal ass downtown, and it was only my good name that kept him from being dumped in with the freakazoids.'

'Shameful, Sonny. Simply shameful.'

'OK, so while he's in stir, gossipword gets out that big Sonny's son's been busted.'

'In what way, Sonny?'

'What would they say? For drugoid activities? Sorry if this offends, Judah.'

'Why, not at all...,' said the man in Tehran.

'Naw, Penny's clean as the first milkin'. Naw, rather, mine enemies seized the opportunity to fabricate a tale told by idiots to bring forth *my own* downfall, so's they can carve up my empire. Gotta be on guard for peace. Simply said, they spread foulness about Penny being an embezzler at the top levels, and taking orders from me, with the goal of cleaning out the coffers of other people's monies. Pretty lame, huh? And they came down hard on Penny cuz I happened to be conveniently out of the country. As if we're making off with the swag, to start a new plantation life in a sympathetic South American 'democracy' just like the Bushoids did! Pretty preposterous, if you ask me. Never mind that my voyage down here was to see my aging grandam in Potosi, who would've been heartbroken if I hadn't been there in person to celebrate her 111th.'

'Give her my best wishes,' said Butterbugs.

'Will do. She's writing her memoirs, due out in three months. I took out an option on it. Hey, can you play my grandam, ultrastar? Think about it! Helluva saga.'

'When I have time,' Butterbugs replied in all seriousness, star-to-agent.

'Well, that's the extent of my little scrapings 'n' scraps. 'Tain't nothing compared with your little bicycle-bombed-for-two ride, B-bugs.'

'Yeah.'

'But officially, it's eight bells and all's well at A&U-CAM. Sonny's Trip is *back!*'

'So Judah, you'll proceed with Pennefold as your significant other?' asked Butterbugs.

'I'd like to. Very much.'

Sonny had to interject:

'Well! My son Penny, folks! That rascal! It'll take some fixin', but we should be able to beat the rap.'

'But he doesn't face doing time or anything.'

'No. Not at all.'

'Does Justy know?'

'She does not know. But she will! He'll need her clout, as well as ours.'

'He shall have it,' said Butterbugs, ready to exercise his power in all ways, even now.

'He'll be punished for freaking all of us out this way,' said Sonny, who chuckled, '...But not very much. I love my kids. We got family values up the ying-yang, heh!'

'Resolved: A&U-CAM is now salvaged.'

'Check!' Sonny sounded off.

'Check, too!' Judah sounded just as jubilant.

'Your agency is *saved!*' added Butterbugs. 'But I have to tell you, another threatens. Another sort of agency. There still remains this troubling onslaught from some forms of government. And, in a more shadowy vale, some from *non*-government, as well. Lest we forget. The work of HETSA and TMG goes beyond the mere efforts of Lurgan and Vunn, I should think. The slander, the allegations, the nonsense, not to mention the suffering therein. Will it ever be said of us: THESE ARE THEY WHICH CAME OUT OF GREAT TRIBULATION...? Why, they call me an **Enemy of the People**.'

'Oh, that's right,' said Sonny, somewhat crestfallen.

'DeVault Lurgan – was everything he said a lie?' asked the ultrastar.

Judah spake:

'We will have to confer further as to the details, Butterbugs, but my facts show me that not one iota of the material against you and Sonny (and all other associates) is factual or based on reality. You are the socio/political force 'They' fear most. We just wanted you to be aware of your standing in the presidential eye. Sort of like Sidney Poitier and Paul Newman, on Nixon's shit list.'

'Well then,' Butterbugs thought of the poor, late exploded fellow wistfully, 'I blame DeVault's ruses, as well as his fate itself, on his employers. I believe that near the end, his paradigms changed, though. I have no evidence other than a hunch, but I think he was going to help me escape to Gothpore, all the way. Really. Otherwise he would not have been sacrificed for his change of plan.'

'They meant to take you out, then?' asked Judah quietly.

'I think so. At least the other agent intended on it. He tried to blow me up and it all went wrong.'

'I'm not going to make any smartass comment at this juncture, Butterbugs.'

'I appreciate that, Sonny.'

'My research shows that the other agent, U.X. Vunn, was a member of the mega-elite Buckmeister Gang, who worked in the upper-level, super-secret, black-budget realms of the agency,' said Judah. 'I assume he perished out of his own miscalculations.'

'Yes, I suppose he did. But why were *both* bikes rigged to go off?'

'Hedging his bets, old boy,' answered Sonny. 'You know how freaky those spy dudes are. Remember your 'Gary The Bubbah, Superspy!' (United Pyramid) role, and its 'Secret Sam' sequel, 'Pins And Cardboard' (United Pyramid)? Totally hilarious!'

'Well, I guess so,' answered the actor, fondly remembering the spoofishness. 'And by the bye, I'm not political. I may be socio, but I am not a political force. And who are 'They', anyway?'

Judah, who thought it not quite best that they dissect all this right now – and over the phone, simply said, 'You are a force, Butterbugs, whatever you choose, or not choose, as a label.'

Some trans-oceanic pause-filler-type throat-clearing and shuffling followed, while the ultrastar put it together that indeed, all this should not be dissected right now – and over the phone.

'I guess we're each in good positions,' said Butterbugs. 'To fight it. And, we all happen to be out of the U.S. at this moment. I hear tell Egaz is in transit, as are other vital personnel, including Porter, and we have all we need right here in Jambutterbugsabad. I'm sorry to say we lost two studio bicycles, though. My pay will be docked accordingly.'

'Far out, Commander!' hooted Sonny. 'I'll be on my way over, as well.'

'And I, too!' said Judah. 'I will bring all the relevant files for our composite case.'

'Judah's all the legal team we need, Butterbugs.'

'So, we will be a united front to face the challenge,' said the star, with relief.

'It'll be one helluva reunion, gentlemen!' crowed the agent.

With the arrival of Porter Parker at Jambutterbugsabad, production on 'UWH' resumed after the space of one day.

Less than a week passed before needful personnel were gathered and the cameras rolled again. It was a testament to the mightiness of The Producer Team as far as responsible action was concerned. Hy Goth may have still been sequestered in studio in Hollywood, but here in Jambutterbugsabad, who the hell cared?

'We've got a picture to finish,' DFZ declared. 'Nothing else in this universe matters.'

'Except one thing,' replied Butterbugs, without the slightest trace of timidness while facing the sunglassed, mustachioed, cigar-punctuated visage of the great Zanuck himself.

'What's that? Go ahead, tell me before I say 'no'.'

'I have to make a quick trip over to Sukkur, to help open an educational institution that a new friend has founded. For some strange reason, he actually wants to name it after me…'

'Oh, the Butterbugs Bahadur Madrassah for Poetic, Cinematic and Land Studies?'

'Why, why yes, DFZ. You know about it…'

'Course I do, kid. We all know. You're the lynchpin we all serve and protect. Now get your ass over to the Indus, pronto.'

'I've always wanted to see the Lansdowne Bridge, too!'

'You've got two days, buster.'

'Two days! Why, thank you Mr. Zanuck! You won't regret it!'

And the ultrastar departed the mogul.

'Regret!' DFZ snorted. 'It's him we all have to thank! For everything! All the time!!'

The Madrassah dedication was a huge success. Conferred with a doctorate under the ægis of the BBMPCLS (Sukkur), Butterbugs immediately founded a new discipline, Motion Picture Production Based In The Landforms Between The Potwar Plateau And The Gwadar Hammer –with Masters and PhD options. In addition, he pledged to be the course's first guest lecturer, after 'UWH' wrapped. DFZ signed on as well, followed by practically everybody who was anybody at Jambutterbugsabad.

So the grand machinery moved forward again. And thank your gods for that. In all the caring and sharing, all the investigation and the explanation, all the attention had been concentrated on Butterbugs' close call with the spies. It was deemed his sole near-death experience. It was known that a prop blunderbuss was in Butterbugs' quarters, but no one knew it almost shattered the ultrastar's head into seventy thousand-and-one bloody shards. No one knew how close he came. No one knew how he was saved. No one knew who did the saving.

No one knew it was Heatherette.

54.

You FINK!

The return to production made a monumental statement of strength and determination, heard round the world: revolutionaries in rebellion were making a renegade film of much value and high art.

And it was true!

Only a fraction of the real story had percolated to the media's circus, but the effect was one of heroism in the face of an adversarial unknown.

Whatever reason for the shutdown, thought the public, a massive benefit of the doubt should come out in Butterbugs' favor. He and his team were lauded to the skies. Anticipation and interest in the picture were reaching new heights, and there was a new hope in many lands that large entities, thought to be insurmountably powerful, might well be superseded, given the proper leadership (in this case, Butterbugs) and the proper goal (in this case, Butterbugs' newest production).

Even though it was not an MGM release, when filming was taken up again, it did so with a mighty roar. Right out of the gate, the three great battle-plain locations were opened up and all three sequences were filmed in magnificent succession.

There was not one actor or actress, extra or extress, camp follower or quartermaster who did not, after the first day's shooting, say to one another:

'It's good, oh so very good, to be back!' or 'We are part of something truly great!' or 'Butterbugs is involved. That is all that matters.'

Everybody worked.

Even amidst the raging warfare being staged in the background, significant dialogue-driven scenes were interwoven, and, additionally, a drawing room-style banter of witticisms was required to take place, involving the detached and haughty set of sissywimps who designed the film's war(s), and their stunningly awful bossing-about with the seasoned, but sadder, wiser, and obedient military folk.

One particularly strident scene involved a grandee (masterfully played by Frank Thring) dressing down a capable but harried field marshal (masterfully played by Nigel Stock) in front of hundreds at a grand ball. Butterbugs was not in this particular scene, but he hung out, just to watch. He could not help but make correlations between himself and his film on one side, and the Murn Administration, and all their 'Non-Conclusive Conclusions' regarding his subversive role in the world, on the other.

In the next scene, the grandee's bratty daughter confronts the field marshal's wife (nicely played by Julie Cox and Shirley Temple Black, respectively) with the news, sneeringly-delivered, that her husband, the field marshal, has committed suicide as a result of his shame, though he was virtuous in his actions.

Again, Butterbugs made a correlation of sorts.

Here in the Makran they all had their freedoms. Back home, control smacked of Neo-Fascism. The ultrastar couldn't quite banish this dispiriting thought while witnessing the glories of instantly important, instantly classic, filmmaking in the making.

And there was Egaz, returned in fine form, directing with unprecedented confidence and brilliance. He was everywhere at once, missing no subtlety, but strongly reigning in the larger waves of cinematism, in order to retain the picture's overarching integrity. He fearlessly stood his ground, right in the thick of the hottest part of the battle, as well as on the terraces of the Detached Ones' stage of observation, where fops traded many a bon mot with their sycophants, while silently disapproving generals looked on in helpless horror.

Everyone knew Egaz's inspiration came directly from Sergei Bondarchuk, who aside from his important role as Diplomat Zokannavoz, would get screen credit as Strategic Consultant. The maestro himself even did a bit of assistant directing in the charge of the hussars over Chab Hill. Pappy Ford had done similar service a few hours earlier, in the Disaster at Straffc Creek, much to the thrill of Egaz.

All thought Bondarchuk and Ford were inspired choices for inspiration. This was not Borodino, but many of that very sequence's ideas were in play here, including color schemes, Empire costuming, and the dramatically perfect compositions based on battle paintings and eyewitnesses of yore (even though there was no yore involved in the time span of 'UWH', except for the refined æsthetic choices in the director's choice of coverage).

This 'war-oriented' act of the greater picture happened to be shot in sequence, as the plot evolved in a startling, even nihilistic way, with several of the generals taking matters into their own hands by falling upon the sissywimps with fire and sword. Removing them for ever from the decisive role of dictating policy, they then engage in the Dolorous Pause, in which, on this bright forenoon, the newly-empowered commanders take time off to read their Clausewitz and Tolstoy, and even a viewing of 'Stalingrad' (Senator Film, 1993), so as to turn the tide of the battle and move it on to their victory. In directing this powerful scene, Egaz improvised on the spot, and he depended on Butterbugs, who was at his elbow, for perspectives and suggestions.

In a way, Butterbugs had saved 'UWH' by transferring the powerful love of Keenah from himself to the director, who now found the strength and inventiveness to carry on, doing what must be done, and doing it with unqualified genius. Besides, Egaz could also tap into Keenah-love directly, which had its own high-potency benefits.

The helper-star was also quite tickled to see another familiar face out here, production-managing to beat the band. It was Borah, the sweet girl he'd maybe-fancied way back there in time, up near Mt. Palomar, when they'd been decent nobodies pondering the lights of LA far below, and not quite sure how they should go about distilling its significances. She'd leveled with him then by confessing her engagement, and now he was gratified to know her husband Glairy, a prominent coin collector, and her two neat duckling-like kids, Tinky and Derry, who were doing production assistant gigs on the set and doing them well. In fact, Glairy had been invaluable in securing impossible-to-find coin props for the immense Plundering of the Foundational Vaults sequence.

Pabbi Khan and Muhammad Goonah, the Location Managers, would surely attain poet-saint status because of their devotion and expertise in the production. Every day, Egaz and Butterbugs uttered some variation of the following sentiment to them: 'What you are doing for this picture is beyond words, or praise, or even measure', but the two Bahadurs took in others' wonderment with polite and professional aplomb, and simply continued to enact their heroic and beatific creative service in making 'UWH' a reality.

'*Inshallah*, we shall complete the task,' was their humble reply.

And through every scene, there was Starla the Script-Girl, as stamina-possessing, and doing it with as much noble bearing as the most bear-like dress extra, totin' a Brown Bess. Starla did it all, and without flaw or complaint. More than most who were associated with this production, on Starla's shoulders was 'UWH' carried, with a sprightliness, and with style.

Over in the all-important second unit, there was Script-Girl Bibsey! One of the best in the biz, Bibsey and Butterbugs went way back – to his first strollings in front of a camera, in fact.

Such as these were just a few of the solidarity-proving filmmakers who were giving their all for this show. And thank goodness that none of them knew, or ever would know, about Butterbugs and a certain blunderbuss, lest all their hopes and efforts be in vain.

'These are they which are my *family*,' thought Butterbugs, not without a plainly ecstatic emotional twinge. Everything he beheld and felt now had an added enhancement, for he was *glad to be alive*.

Additionally, all the battle filming came off without a hitch. Not even a single band-aid was needed, either. Bondarchuk, always a hater of trip-wires, though forced to use them in 'War and Peace' (Continental, 1968), was proud to report that all his horses used in the charge sequence were buoyant and hearty.

That night, the whole company toasted guest directors Ford and Bondarchuk, and all was well in Jambutterbugsabad.

Even though he still sported his eye-patch despite successful eyeball surgery, Jack Ford, the Dean of Directors, still made his rounds with patch flipped down, just to spook the ladies and impress those who might question that, despite stereoscopic vision capabilities prevalent in the masses, motion pictures still came out of one 'orifice', so to speak.

Bondarchuk had no better argument. To him, the cinema, in the individual's POV, was for him, the destiny of (a) man.

In the present picture, placed in the next-to-last act, after the ultimate intermission (which, after final editing, would probably be the *third*), the title card for this sequence would read: 'The War Of Civilization's Survival'.

Which civilization, it didn't say.

Meanwhile, way in back of the tremendous outpouring of support for the inspiring filmmakers, one sat apart, away from the joyous resumption, brooding in his lair. It was he who had tried to stop it, but he had been overridden, despite approbation from much higher up. Higher than any paltry entertainment edifice's highest point, that was for sure.

He was Hyman Goth, controller of Mega|Goth Stvdios, Lord and Mythic King-Emperor over both facility and its productions, seen by millions, and worth billions. He was not quite up to Butterbugs' trillions, but by gum, he would get there somehow, clawing over human flesh all the way, if necessary.

Hyman Goth, at the top of the Seventh Art's premiere chateau, was nevertheless nothing but a six-cent crack cocaine addict. Besides himself, only one other person on the globe knew this. And right now, that one person was on his way into the studio, having Special Ongoing Security Clearance in the midst of the big lockup that had gone on for some time now.

Stuart Tibbs-Curtain was that man. For the longest era, the erstwhile Lawyer to the Stars and Their Creators, the onetime Irv Thalberg of Legalia, had been kept in thrall to the great Goth, sacrificing his once plummy career and his chance to forge his own Sonny-like empire – though on the legal counsel plane – only to be lassoed by Hy's sadistic ego and reduced to a stressed-out runner for some cheapie crackoholic's daily, if not hourly, needs.

As a mogul in abeyance to his own needle-clawed chimp on his back, willfully taken on because he enjoyed its perverse company, and, by the way, because of the fact that he was probably the most powerful dude in Hollywood, Hy was an infinitely happy man. He wanted it all, and by golly, he *had* it all, many times over. Every day Hy got ripped, and having a ripping time in the process, not only deluded himself by his standing as probably the most powerful dude in Hollywood, he was indeed facile enough to manage his actual status. So that *yes*, he was *indeed* the most powerful dude in Hollywood. If ever awards were to be given out for Most Capable Enactor of Power Whilst Under the Constant Influence of Crack Cocaine, Hy Goth would have to open a Louvre-sized display cabinet of trophies.

Impregnable. All-powerful. Higher than shit, but in control. He was a testament to the drug actually *working*. If word ever got out about his usage, he would no doubt enjoy prestige as an inspiration to addicts of all kinds everywhere. And to aspiring addicts, waiting in the wings, to fly. The fact was stark: crack addicts *can* be successful. Wildly successful.

He ran the studio with a hand made of crush-proof granite. Firmly, but capably. Some would even grudgingly admit, brilliantly. Nevertheless, his petulant decision to enact the current lockout/shutdown of the studio was a patently insane gesture, if not brain-dead. Beaucoup bucks were being pizzled down the drain of lost momentum and opportunities. Perhaps the substance was getting to the old boy, after all.

While he was high, Hy's chief emotion could not be called joy. Nevertheless, he was having a damn good time. That was the only way to put it. On the other hand, his partner in this activity, Stu T-C, had never ever ingested the fire-drug. As the runner from supplier to demander, he only had sealed packets on his person, and none of their effects had ever sopped through for him to understand what the big deal was.

His life as a blackmail-threat victim consisted largely of driving the same old route, to/from one of the more sleazy districts of east LA, which shall not be named, and to/from the bland and lightly industrialized quarter where the behemoth stand of Mega|Goth Stvdios was. Concrete streets, taupe-y-beige walls, and high voltage telephone poles were the stuff of his waking hours, with glances into his rearview mirror about every twenty seconds or so, lest LAPD got hip to his erranding.

A life that was impossibly dreary to imagine, and drearily impossible to change.

He was still a steel-trap legal mind, but a real doofus as far as being taken advantage-of was concerned. It had always been his plan to do that to others, not to have it done to him. There was a perception problem in there, somewhere. The stunning reality though, was that he was an indentured slave. He had to live with this somber and humiliating fact every day. He'd lost practically everything he'd built up in the brief, meteoric years of his rise, by involuntarily participating in this 'programme'. Gone were his mistresses, all the Goon Cars (those DKWs, NSUs, and many other such toys he'd once prized, long ago hocked), swimming pools, vacation pads, stereo equipment, kids, patio furnitures, homes, and even his wife, pretty Clairol. He now drove a shameful Ford Maverick that didn't even have an air cleaner on it, so the constant sucking noise of the carburetor made mockery of what he'd become. The radio actually worked, but the cone of its speaker had largely crumbled away, causing the Spanish dialogue station it was stuck on to sound exactly like a buzzy, heckling insect, always on the wing, refusing to be brushed outside. The smoggy atmospheric pressure on the boulevards was terrible. Monoxide monotony, no-mind freakazoids as pedestrians, and low-rider drivers with rapidograph-thin mustaches and single-tear tattoos. Nobody smiled.

He existed in a sponge-bath walkup located somewhere within a laughably worthless 1970s apartment block, behind Slurry Way. A hopeless motel sort of thing. It directly faced the San Piño-Los Coldrés-Alcalde Rapid-Freeway. Exhaust pipes spoke their minds only a few meters away, and the noise was never something one could ever get used to. The nails holding the plywood that lined the treads of the entrance stairs were coming up. No hammers seemed to exist in this region, nor hammer-like rocks. Everything had already been stolen. Domicile-wise, not much to relate. A front door that had been picked and kicked numberless times, now left unlocked because everyone knew there was nothing of value inside, occupied or unoccupied. Burlap curtains spray-painted avocado-green to (unsuccessfully) hide the coke dust. Stale bile-blue shag carpeting, totally unspeakable. A plastic Jippa desk lamp with garbage-spill on its cracked shade, doing service as the living room's prime lighthouse – on the floor. Black & white TV, naturally. A few stations via antenna. Spoiled cottage cheese in the fridge. Bloated dust kittens. Devastating light from half burnt-out ceiling lamps. Humus-like buildups in the plumbing. Needle dumps. Condom-flings. Chew-wrappers with rejected content. Old urreen bouquet everywhere, from derelicts committing nuisance. The sourness of the daylight, the menace of nightfall. Cheap crime, drugged minds, decline, depression and dinginess everywhere. Nothing rated of much value or quality there. How could there be? Why *should* there be?

A shattered person's 'home'. A crash-pad awaiting the bulldozer. However, its owners reasoned, it *wasn't even worth bulldozing.* Even after a demolition, sowing the ground with salt would be wholly inadequate to purge the land of its perversity.

Stuart had this one lousy, low-paying job. (Yes, Hy doled out a few coppers, so technically he was an indentured servant – one micro-step up from slave rank.) But otherwise, he didn't have shit. Proof of the latter was that his in-situ toilet had been busted for the longest time, so he invariably performed his toilette on an existential concrete slab at the rear, his modesty ensured by all the shrouded, newspapered, and foiled-covered windows along the range (veiling drug-oid festivities within), with bucket, faucet, and crap-bin.

At least he wasn't in deep-jail for the mega-illegal activities he was committing each day, though the anxiety of that threat accompanied his every step. It was as much a critter on his back as the rather more fun simian that Hy freely welcomed into his Bigger-Than-Master-of-the-Universe life.

'I really got *burned*,' was Stu's endlessly repeated chorus.

For his own part, Hy was much smarter, and he always had all the cards to play. He never – even when he was mellowing after a crazy but boss inhalation – offered to share any of his goods. He never wanted Stu to get high, either in his company or at all. It was one of many things he insisted on, under threat to rat on Stu's naughty deals in the past, the gist of which they had both essentially forgotten – Hy because of his sturdy but Swiss-cheesing brain, and Stu because of his erosive burnout.

'A sharing user is a worthless guppy,' was the proverb Hy'd invented, in order to defend his selfish but protectionist policy in that regard. Besides, he didn't need a pipe-buddy. Couriers supplied services, not companionship. Why get the mailman fucked up?

So, this over-a-barrel ex-lawyer-now-drug-runner was a rather unhappy fellow. In fact, with each successive trip 'crost-town to ferry his out-of-control cargo to the Encyclopædia Britannica of Hollywood Studios (Hy's phrase, illustrative of his creativity whilst high), deep resentment expanded in Stu's heart, and picked at it with a battle axe.

Today, the rage was especially thick. Having gained access to the world's highest-security studio in the midst of its current Emergency, as usual (his privilege in this respect was the sole point of pride in his joke of a life), a sense of laconic approach suddenly came over him.

Here he was, in the ghost town of Mega|Goth, its peripheries manned by Tarpit Mercenary Group elites, and the borders were secure, but the whole massive core of the plant was devoid of humans. So he had the place to himself. Almost. Packs of wild puppies and prides of dumpling kittens padded about the canyons between the soundstages, where everyone from Spence Tracy to Charlize Theron had once trod, for this was the *pied en Terre* of feral things now, and tough luck to any timid soul who tried to take it from them.

'GO, *BABIES!*' cheered Stu, as he saw both felines and canines united in making their stand against corporate control of this, their squatting-rights homeland. He brought dumpster-culled soup bones and fish heads for the canine/feline gangs, who engaged in prehistoric gobbling and grinding. Knowing his reliability, they left him be as he bent his troubled steps to Hy's citadel.

Toward Hy's citadel rather, not necessarily *to*. In the general direction, not specifically to it, for its own sake.

The day was getting on. The Pyongyang-style mercury vapor lamps (Hy's covert purchase from the Dearest Leader saved him c. $75,015 per month in expenditure) were igniting, turning the warm SoCal tones of the great slab-sided buildings into Antarctic-freezy sastrugi-like corridors. Hy wanted the night shift workers to be repelled by the exterior lighting, so they would remain inside and work through their break time, as an escape from the punishing illumination just outside...

But because Stu felt particularly sick at heart over what his life had become, for this reason, on this eve, for the first time, he deliberately tarried en route to Goth Hall, which loomed in the distance. Its Forbidding Deco imminence could always be seen from any soundstage lane's prospect, but he successfully resisted its toxic magnetism, so he dejectedly aimed for the forge shops and their godowns, just to be contrarian.

He milled around the Slop Yard as the sun fully set. Distant quit-whistles were heard at non-showbiz factories in the region. Melancholy images of a once-thriving concern hit him as yet another example of the existentialism of his life: stacks of used lumber; trashed plastic disco lamps from a Gary Crosby picture; a pile of used coats from a Joan Staley vehicle; case after case of castors that needed the paint from their single-time usage chipped off so they could be used again to transport a Buzz Berkeley set smoothly to the sidelines. Maybe, maybe not.

But, did everyone look at such things in this moribund way? Definitely not! Memories of the Hollywood high life came flooding back as he strolled amongst the overflowing grease drums and bins of reject *cast* items – not the cast of a picture, but those cast as prop items, often from lost wax.

'The life I used to live!' he mourned, scanning the grunt-end of the studio's butt-job dangers. The hanging hooks ready to pull over collapsing Atlantean fora, the chains to move pagan temple gods, the busted candy glass from all the bad guys plowing through saloon windows, all those sharp and rusty screws pulled up from the canvas-lined tank for the sea battle of the miniatures, in the remake of the studio's own 'Admiral Ushakov'… (starring, incidentally, Butterbugs…)

'I was so much higher than these, the grease-industries of lower life! If I'd stayed in Bloodhusband, Arkansas, ten-to-one I'd be a board-bender or a mastic-stretcher, as a career. My hands would be raw with lime-spread, or else my lungs would be rife for Shend's Disease, but at least I'd be settled into a life that *meant* something. Here I am, scratching around the greatest studio in Hollywood, and I'm a zombie before my time. I am less than the shadow being projected on that wall, yonder. If I had a X-ray of my person right now, it would come out as an opaque sheet of glass…'

Empty, empty, empty. Nothing left to even piss away.

Never having been in the back parts of a back lot, or even on set during a shoot, and despite being in the picture biz, but without contribs to the creative side, it was because Stu had no interest whatsoever in the Industry. There was no romance. No aspect of it interested him. All he had ever cared about was soaking as much as he could out of this callow bunch of clients (and he'd fit right in as far as callowness was concerned). So as to rise to the top of it. He hadn't known who Irv Thalberg really was – that complimentary epithet was from producer Sam Engel, on account of the young advocate's whiz-kid performance at top levels. Stu duly adopted the phrase with pleasure, to appeal to the non-goy members of the Industry he strove to tap. He wanted to fit in, but only to his advantage.

At heart, all he *really* cared about were his 'Goon Cars', those wacky esoteric specimens of postwar German attempts to have success with the 'people's car' concept on a sub-sub-compact scale. Any Messerschmidt was a pet to him, with instant housebroken status granted. Each Janus deserved a temple for worship. Every Heinkel Kabine was welcome in his living room. And Crosleys, though American, were always invited to frolic in the fold.

These were the daydreams that allowed Stuart to keep placing one foot in front of the other, day after day. Otherwise, surely the man would have died of solitude.

He of course had relished the sex-laden dolce vita of Bev Hills & Such, but his secret goal had been a rather gentle and even altruistic one, in its own way. Once the power of his (former) position had allowed for tons of income, the possibilities began to really open up. The dream of acquiring every Goon Car in existence materialized in his mind, and then, the 'Stuart Tibbs-Curtain Museum of Goon Cars' idea was born. He had dynamic designs drawn up by Albert Kahn, Ohzus Kwigk-wup and Eric Lloyd Wright, and plans had gone ahead to purchase the dying town of Keezus, Nevada, which was on the road to Vegas. There he could found his Museum, attach an associated Institute and Librarium, where in-depth studies might take place. The whole would form an idealistic combine (he even thought of the concept as a *commune)* in which to gather all the remaining designers and parts and ephemera, and present the whole caboodle as a way of life, a destination, a whole culture as lived by the surrounding town, and an all-important societal contribution, with he, Stu, at its benevolent center.

Oh, but there was a master plan that overarched all. There was only one thing left to do. Build a Goon Car of his own. The Tibbsmobile, naturally. (After very serious consideration, he'd vetoed 'Tibbs-Curtainmobile', but planned on models bearing 'CurtainCoupe' and 'StuartSedan' badges, and even envisioned a 'Kürtin-wagen' line for export to sympathetic German markets, maybe even with factories in Chemnitz, Cottbus und Coburg!) Based on his projected billions, to be extract-ed from the trivialities of showbiz, the factory in Keezus would crank out fleets of brilliant bubble cars, ready to drive across the world, and maybe even to the Moon – and, why not Mars, too?

What a dream! And it was way bigger than these here flickers on a shadow-re-flecting screen! Not to mention coked-up creeps in control.

So sad, so pathetic, that all of this was no longer possible. None of it. And Kee-zus had been sold for the sum of $1.95 to the Lingre/Roast Futuremost Coy., who had planned to site their Final Repository for All Toxicity from the Known World just there. (At least that company soon went bust, but Stuart couldn't even come up with the revised $600.00 asking price for the wretched, trashed-out remains of a once pleasantly-degraded Nevadan village...)

'Oh, tragedy!' he would often moan, fist held at the sky. 'Where is your *rea-son?*'

It was just so stupid that he, the supposedly-canny lawyer, had fallen in with such bad company. Which, incidentally, he never suspected he'd find at the top of Hollywood's control apparatus. Naively, he'd thought that a sort of virtue would predominate amongst those who had not had to hardscrabble their way to the top, like he did. He expected enlightened despots to be throwing all the switches and levers. Eagles, even. But even eagles prey on little bunnies and innocent cow pla-centas.

In spite of this discovery and adaptation, he'd achieved his own sense of sum-miting by age twenty-five, and at that age, one relies on one's invincibility to be permanent.

Now, as a wreck, a mere shell, a stripped chassis, rods thrown from the crank-shaft before their time, he stood in shattered 'n' shorted-out simplicity, staring straight ahead. He'd ended up in the motor shops, where studio vehicles were repaired, and where those soon to go before the cameras were either customized or dolled-up. The place was as cluttered and greasy as any chop shop or walk-in city of car fixits the world over. In or outside the Industry, all were similar, for the universal truths of vehicular physics always command their environment instead of conforming to it.

'Oh, fate!' he would add to his moaning mantra, 'By what legal precedent do you hound me, without even a plea-bargain?'

Straight ahead, positioned in the canopy-covered garage, in line with his stare, was a goofy little car hulk, up on blocks, wheel-less, beaten and bashed, as if burped-up from a deep, oily orifice containing a mockingly-personified demolition derby. It was certainly an oddball, and because of those characteristics, which were identifiable instantly, Stu was jump-started into primitive thought.

'That form. Those lines. That delineation…'

He needed further proof from the exhibit.

'Why…'

He drew closer.

'I used to *own* that car…,' he thought blankly, defeatedly.

Then, a realistic rage hit him.

'Hey!! That's my *car!!*'

He rushed over to the rig, the baby remains of a '58 Goggomobil, and got even more peeved. Scrawled on the windscreen, in chartreuse felt-marker, was: 'FUNNY CAR FOR THE CROSBY PICTURE. SMASH AND SCRAP AFTER SHOOT.'

'What's so *funny* about it?!' Stu growled.

Then he got all choked up as he closely examined the car.

'What have they *done* to you, sweetheart?' he mourned as he saw the thrashed interior, the holes poked through the engine block (with what had obviously been a huge iron chunker-pole), and the obscenities scratched into the remaining window glass.

He laid hands on the rear deck of the wreck and probably uttered some sort of blessing or prayer to the not-so-powerful – apparently – Teutonic gods of the mini-wheels, so devout was he as to the soulful worth of these poor abused orphans.

'Wer taten dies – und *warum?*'

He didn't even understand German, but somehow, the poor Goggomobil *speiche* to him. Then he himself said it, in translation:

'How could this have happened? Who was responsible?'

Re-gaining steady breathing after the emotional eulogy-cum-keening, he searched above the workbenches and near the doors for an employee roster or schedule. Then he saw it: one such reference clipboard hung under a 'water balloon'-type fire extinguisher grenade, attached to the wall. Significantly, the names for each shift were highlighted by magnified bars of light, shining right through the grenade from a nearby incandescent night-light, with perfect spotlight effect.

They were names of anonymous worker-bees who, Stu realized, couldn't possibly be responsible for what comes and goes in and out of this shop, let alone what each transformation should be. They only did their work by following orders.

Responsibility for atrocities usually gets hung on the low echelons of a power structure, though the obviousness of its real authorship – higher up or at the very top, usually shines like the Wisdom Angel beacon that sits atop the apex of the LA City Hall.

Abu Ghraib, Guantanamo, Birkenau, Charkax Camp, Bergen-Belsen and other horrific scandals were not successfully resolved until public hue & cry set the truth free.

At that very second, even an individual so crushed by soul-robbing and other disheartening life experiences, such as Stuart Tibbs-Curtain, still had the stuff to recognize when he was faced with a considerable coming-to-grips. It smote him, as if his big toe had just been smashed by a complete bound set of the California Penal Code. Responsibility! Now! His blood began to boil. Well, come on – Who ran this here popsicle stand, anyways? Who, who, who?? Who was the cosmic and overruling deity-on-Earth who reigned in absolute terms over these barns, like some Kublai-Pasha-cum-Turbo-Leviathan? Why, he who now surely brooded in waiting rage at this moment – He who was Simultaneous Creator and Wrecker of Persons and Careers, Determinator of Destinies for the Masses, the Goth of Goths, the Hyman of Hymans: Hyman Goth, was doubtless *he!*

Resolved: Hy was he. He was Hy.

It didn't take any more argument for the prosecution to form its case. For today, he took the unconventional pathway. Leaving advocacy to the successful ones, Tibbs as Lawyer reverted to textbook ethics and instinctual morals. There would be no rest. In lieu of a proper trial and sentencing, independent carrying-out of *guilty status* could now proceed. Incumbent on the obscure precedent of Goobah vs. the State of California, 1931, allowance was made for an isolated party in Death Valley to enact a self-determined sentence in the absence of authority – rather like the Law of the High Seas.

Well, if there wasn't an entire match-up – no matter. Comparative precedence could follow in review. Right now, it was imperative that action be taken in this, a case that cried out for responsible pro-action. For the egregious abuse of these innocent automobile remains – and perhaps others as well, justice *must* ensue. Forgiveness was not possible, but justice, as determined by the beau ideal of Law, was the next best thing. That was how those who fancied themselves Christians could rationalize capital punishment.

A faint drumbeat of righteousness began to be heard in his head. Max Steiner could have scored it! Leo Forbstein could have conducted it! Chords of hope! Chords of *justice!*

In jurisprudence, rendered improvisational due to conditions of isolation, a judge-penitent can write decisions. While he, Stuart, was certainly a penitent, this outrage had qualified him to be a judge, as well.

Settled, out of court!

Couple things remained: 1) Sentencing. 2) Carrying out sentence.

How – to *do it?*

Of a sudden, the whiz-kid legal machinery returned to action. Method presented itself with exhilarating obviousness. His bone-weary stare had been inadvertently aimed at one of the auto-restorers' most basic starting-point images: What is the condition of the battery, if there *is* a battery? It's ten-to-one that a long-ago expired battery will have its connectors coated with, in varying degrees, oxidized battery acid.

And here, on this squirt of a Goggomobil's six-volt, positive-ground battery, its mini-mass covered with frippertree needles and its three cell caps gashed or missing, great cauliflowerian deposits of whitish essence were gathered. As if from the merry nozzle of a wedding cake frosting bag. Or was it old clotted cream that had stood out so long at Miss Haversham's wedding reception?

He clearly saw where this was going. *Would Hy?*

Analysis followed. Samples gathered. Nearly as white as cornstarch. Or laundry detergent powder. Or dishwasher detergent powder. Or – anthrax. Or cocaine. White was always the most lethal of colors – or lack of color.

Stu flipped on a fluorescent workbench tube and set his bag of coke – which was in transit, and not at all his property, except by possession on his person (and which was, by the way, overdue at its destination), and examined it.

Good shit, as always. If there was one thing that Stu had become, it was a competent runner, the breed of which must learn what good shit is and what bad shit is, because bad shit could cost one one's life – or worse.

Then he got a stainless steel vessel from nearby, grabbed an average screwdriver, and went back over to the car's battery. He chipped off virtually all the oxidation, leaving the posts and contacts looking unremarkably normal.

He found a bit of gasket-pack cardboard, bent it into a tray, then opened the Burkmart PlastaSac™ of coke and poured a generous amount out. Next door, in the stainless basin, his flat blade screwdriver dug into the snow-covered volcano of acid. Retaining a sample on the expository tool, he aligned it with the cupcake of coke hard by, comparing the two for value and consistency.

'Not quite the right color. Too… snowy.'

So he proceeded to grind the mound of acid compound in its newly-native vessel, using an awl handle as a pestle. Expecting off-gassing from the substance to wilt his tear-worn eyelashes, he'd sensibly donned eye protection. But the acidic fumes, which usually have a corrosively 'fresh' sort of scent, weren't particularly pungent. Too old? He hoped not. The car and its battery had plainly sat through the ages, until they were discovered as star material. Sometimes the older the acid oxidation, the more virulent its effects, despite deceptive somnolence, such as low fume output.

As luck would have it though, the collective grease on the awl handle had darkened the tone of the nicely-ground powder, so that it not only made a pleasing match of complexion, but the consistency of the texture was absolutely perfect.

Pride having returned due to his craft, Stu did an effortless mix/addition of the acid into the coke, bulking it up quite a bit – sure to greatly thrill its owner, and the product was ready for consumption.

One thing was wonderful about the trade in which he worked, whereby to live: no finicky Burkey Belser-designed 'Drug Facts' or 'Nutrition Facts' naggings, or warning labels of any kind. Product-ready! It was the triumph of the honor system in action.

Trust now, trust for all.

'How fitting,' thought Stuart, 'Fitting, and fulfilling too, that justice can be meted out directly via a controlled entity that has been so rightly wronged! And not because Cole Porter sang its anti-praises. Resolved: cocaine can kill, but if we want our cars to start, our Priuses to pose as no-carbon footprinters, and our sex toys to out-perform weakened flesh, battery acid must and shall be one of the most vital parts of our daily lives. Indeed, it should enjoy the honorific: the Acid of Life! Oh, but how huge is the family of white powders! Life, death, they do it *all!* Bones are the ultimate in remains, so their white, powdery meal might make the ultimate statement of, well, *revenge.* But – in the legal sense, of course!'

Stu's stream of corollary thought bubbled along, like a puttering, lovable, old Fuldamobil Attica 200. Right at this moment, he dared to feel elated. And with elation, came confidence.

'Boy, it's getting late,' he ejaculated amidst his thought, after glancing at his Wyler watch, one of the few things remaining from his old glory days. (But with no connection to director William.)

'Better get on over and get the goods delivered! Bet he's hopping mad…!'

Before departing for Goth Hall, Stu went back over to the hulk, and with an emergency-orange marker he'd found, under the 'SMASH AND SCRAP AFTER SHOOT' statement, he added, 'HOLD OFF SMASHING. CAR TO BE FULLY <u>RESTORED</u> – ON MY NICKEL'.

He then vigorously X-ed out the SMASH words and skillfully forged Hy's signature under the notice, which would make the shop workers tremble.

Lightly kissing the troubled, crumpled roof, he whispered some sweet somethings.

'Not to worry, baby. Daddy Stu's on his way to rescue you. Hang in there, Little Wonder! Wiedersehen!'

After judicious disposal of the implements he'd used, and eradicating all signs of his activities by plunging them into the resident Hot Tank, Stu packed up and returned to the sastrugi-of-the-mind alleys, bound to his mission and its new addition, and glad to have a purpose in the universe again.

Once again, in his mind Stuart ran over the West's Key System™ procedure in ascertaining the permissibleness of the action he was about to prosecute. It would not, could not be classified as self-defense, or even justifiable manslaughter (even though both were personally appealing to him). His case, if ever he were taken to task by Authority, could be proven by way of a path that was clear to him, as enactor, but no doubt utterly befuddling to any others.

It was: a drumhead court option, wherein the 'Opinion of Judge Metempsychosis Q. Burlburrah of 1844', in Boiler County, Missourrah, containing a judgment brought down concerning renegade Yankee soldiers, who lit out from the Fifth Seminole War, and who were causing havoc on farms in said county by keeping the farmers and their families hostage, so as to reap illegal tribute from them by waylaying octroi deliveries, until the group was summarily picked-off by repressed vigil farmers. This, only after much trial and suffering under the threat of said renegade lawbreakers. Judge Burlburrah's wise verdict of Allowed Capital Execution by Interested Parties was a resolution that remained ironclad in precedence.

Resolved: in the (not yet enacted) case of Stuart Charlie Tibbs-Curtain vs. Hyman Hubmunnum Goth, any decision would be: Allowed Capital Execution by Interested Party. Perfectly normal. Perfectly legal. Indentured servitude just this side of slavery, especially in the distribution of a crop best controlled by certain lords of the trade in other hemispheres, *shall not stand.*

As if striding the streets of Dostoyevsky's St. Petersburg in bleak midwinter, Stu now aimed for the administration building with a steadiness and a purposefulness he had not known before – at least not within his recent recollection. In the glory days, he would zero in on any studio head who was all set to make a hassle of themselves, then sum him or her up in an opening statement or two, before moving in for the kill, so to speak. Now it was time to remove the 'so to speak' from the equation.

Since its beginnings, the cinema has fitted its low-tech silence with musical accompaniment, in keeping with the dramatic traditions of opera and thiertre. Certain filmic sequences demand scoring, others should be but aren't, while some definitely do not. The same applies to real life, upon which the cinema is usually based.

Often in film, the wedding between a series of images and its companion score is complementary, harmonious, and one serves the other to make a whole. The projected image is king, of course, as image without score is still cinema, but score without image is only... music. Combined, as Alfred has maintained many times, music is always the handmaiden, and never the... maiden. And if the composer is especially talented and reliable, chances are, a compelling and total cinematic experience will result.

Consider then, the steps now taken by Stuart Tibbs-Curtain, as he made his way through the soundstage canyons of Mega|Goth. Except for the echoey footfalls, all was silent. Even the wild things had gone back to their dens, due to the lateness of the hour.

The silence beyond his slightly gravelly shoe-scrapes continued to fill the soundscapes before Goth Hall. Then, with the way wide open to the vast Deco entrance, the scene suddenly cried out for music, to help fill the anxiously looming voids. Indeed, it needed embellishment, as the generated tension grew into a high anticipation that *something was going to happen.*

It is poor practice in filmmaking when effective music has been re-used in another picture altogether. Certainly this is not the composer's choice; more likely the effects of a cheap studio in search of cut corners.

But this was real life all right, enacted in A. Edward Sutherland Plaza, before the great Hall. Undoubtedly, the growing anxiety of the moment needed enhancement. That is, if its portent and import were going to come off as credible and explainable.

As the lawyer ascended the expansive set of stairs toward the Grande-Entrée, this was what needed to play: Dimitri Tiomkin's cue in 'Duel in the Sun' (Selznick, 1946), in which Herbert Marshall, portraying the wronged Scott Chavez, makes his approach to the townhouse wherein his extravagant but slutty wife (Tilly Losch) has taken up with a no-good gambler (Sidney Blackmer), and, pistol in hand, prepares to dispatch the both of them. Tiomkin's buildup of rising chord progressions becomes as an inexorable march toward some kind of awful moment of truth, though it be under a starry Technicolor sky, with warmly-comforting adobe all around.

The gunshot climax of Dimitri's perfect score cannot play now, though. (In the picture, Chavez is hung for his crime of passion...)

Stu did not pack such heat, only fizzies for the nose and throat.

Once the doors of Goth Hall were opened and the courier entered – no more music. Any director – or composer – would want it so. Breathing and heartbeats perhaps, but no score could now guide the man onward. He was on his own, and under his own counsel. So no help, no embellishment, no enhancements.

A great administration building – without life! The corridors icily lacked even the slightest operative presence, human or otherwise. But on a higher story, a life form was indeed very much in operation.

If there were possible signs of Technicolor outside the building and even in its passages, in one specific space, which was very large and even mysterious, all was cast in monochrome tones. A sort of low-contrast black-and-white, that could serve in a cheaper film noir, without the charm of any chilling romance, not to say a cinematographer's art.

Compelling details there were, though. Moody lighting showed off Deco fountain-style wall sconces and brass ash receivers, built into the wainscoting. Sullen etchings, some particularly and bizarrely erotic, perhaps by Rops, were tastefully arranged between unlighted candelabras. If the heavy filters of obfuscation were removed from the lenses of observation one needed to take this space in, all would be mahogany veneering, brown velvet, and gunmetal.

These style choices were significant, because in his past guise of being *the* Goth in Mega|Goth, Hyman Goth had several offices of a far more average and style-less ambience, including a stripped-down writer's rat-cage of a cubicle, used when he was virtually masquerading as an administrative nobody, in order to cower a bit during the corporate merge. He also spied on who was with him and who wasn't (the latter were all vanished from the scene, and not because of the shutdown of late).

In actuality, this muted suite wasn't Hy's office per se, but his inner sanctum getaway, a black hole in the midst of the studio's series of VIP HQs. Bennamin Spandahau was just down the hall, as were Nurnfeld Gold, Nelwyn Kluknik, Jasp Groonman, Jeighmes & Morry Krutzel Pieces-of-Stone, Wainling Cavága, Hosea Densman, Schmuel Lataga, and the venerable Jack Cummings. Plenty of other bigwigs too: execs, exec producers, producers, and associates. But not tonight.

Except for State Entries, the front door to Hy's sanctum was always barred. But there was a further entrance in a faintly-lighted alcove, lurking behind theatrical exit drapes, by which certain privileged persons might access the suite. For if the buzzer combination was correct, with final approval only possible by Hy's personal flipping of a knife-blade switch from his desk-side control board, powered by waiting servo-motor, 'The Servants' Entrance', as everybody called it, would open sesame.

No buzzing yet, this night.

On said desk, an ultra-dim SightLight was turned on. The hands of a mogul shone like etch-a-sketch gloves, covered with purply earthworm veins and those horrid age and liver spots. They hunted around the empty-framed blotter, which was so void of form that one could take a dive into its brown study and never return. Sepia-stained fingers picking and smoothing, hunting and pecking, to remove the last atom of white particulate matter that might remain on its surface, owned by a conspicuously obsessive and compulsively-minded man. But that wasn't the motive here.

Higher up, where little dark light ever reflected, pursed lips greedily accepted what little the fingertips brought to them, and the twilit nostrils yet further up were not neglected, either.

Rage could be extracted from the air of this office with a pitchfork, where it would add up on the floor like a big bull's monthly manure heap. Interwoven with the waste was frustration, its fibers linking rage upon rage like a spider's web might, holding it hostage in powerless suspension.

'Where the fuck is my shipment????' were words that had been bounced off these walls scores of times tonight, and with very little variation. Rage instigated the statement, and frustration brought on the unimaginative repetition.

Yet, he was not quite at Code Red. For the umpteenth time he would successfully simmer himself down and seek out something to provide not only distraction, but reassurance and reprieve.

'Fuck the cracking; I'd settle for just an old-fashioned doing-a-line right now. *Five* lines!'

Next to his pipe, mirror, and lucky dollar bill paraphernalia (for the present, the man both smoked 'n' snorted), Hy Goth's constant desk companion was that charter of purpose that had taken over his life even more than crack cocaine ever had. That particular mandate of heaven explained everything as far as his immediate course of action was concerned. This, and much more 'instructional' information besides, had molded his mogul mind into that of Follower rather than Molder, as morbid-fear and self-loathing, stack-loaded with generic loathing of most things past the confines of the self, had transformed him from Leader into Lackey, based on contempt and trembling. Plus, the promise of hollow optimism, with 'lunge' options (that is, get all you can *now*, in spite of everyone else), all guaranteed by the Con Murn Administration and their associate feeder elements. These temptations had turned his head toward that imperious power group, and he'd signed on, with his very own soul-blood. There had indeed been a soul-sale somewhere around here, but it was lost in contractual gobbledygook that even a Stuart Tibbs-Curtain might find difficult to sort out.

Stuart Tibbs-Curtain... not a name that brought reassurance right now.

Hy thought, as the head of Mega|Goth, 'Am I not *in* on such gain, and do I not stand to benefit from supporting every and all aspects of Murn's reach-out goals and dreams, no matter what all the faggy liberal opposition might propose?' So now, to comfort his anguished and impatient soul, Hyman settled down for a sustained timetable of about a minute, in order to re-read and savor the comfort-text of the following retread document:

A Non-Conclusive

𝕮onclusion

(as the **Person** *Concerning these here* **Points***
continues to operate, uninterrupted)*

For The

𝕿imes
To Date

Some reasons listed for this particular treatment (see Exhibit #4456 for recommendations and partial solutions) are these:

Preamble: This is a testament to a threat that must be seen to, as soon as possible.

1. Because he raises consciousness among the masses

1a. Because he has proven himself to be a **Person Extraordinary**, whom the world willingly brands an 'ultrastar', a term we as a group refuse to recognize as legitimate

1b. Because all signs show that he, as **Person Extraordinary**, in ways in no way conducive to our interests, merits the only label that may be applied to him, as a result of the grouped offenses contained in this list and in countless other files: an **Enemy of the People**

1c. Because the preceding charge is a very solemn charge, it is made because the charge is irrefutably true

(**1d. – 1m**. deleted)

1n. Because the term **Enemy of the People** has been coined by us as a group and used here for the first time ever, the phrase shall have to be copyrighted, if not patented

2. Because he instills hopeful and troubling aspirations into the peoples of the world that might confound them and fill them with false and restless, and *dangerous* desires

2a. Because he dizzies the peoples of the world up

3. Because he is undeniably attractive to most peoples of the world

4. Because he is not particularly identified with causes or concerns in concert with the present US administration or their associates

5. Because he is an oddball, and we do not know how to deal with oddballs

5a. Because he cavorts and associates with other oddballs, some more odd and dangerous than he is, including freaks, weirdos, lesbians, uppity negroes, artist-types, homosexuals, the gays, strange minorities, and geographers

5b. Because he is an oddball, and we do not know how to deal with oddballs in ways harmonious with causes or concerns in concert with the present US administration or their associates

6. Because he has mightily-charged sex appeal to women, who look up to him

7. Because his influence on people transcends race, creed, or policy

7a. Because he is particularly adept in influencing people of great attractiveness and power in the entertainment industry; this is especially troubling in that attractive persons command respect amongst the people, who look up to them and aspire to their status and influence

7b. Because, while he generally appears in pretty good pictures, if not artistically outstanding, that is all the more reason to point out this **Enemy's** rivalistic and envy-inducing characteristics, for they cause anguish to sensitive minds

7c. Because, by exhibiting remarkable excellence in all he does, he makes others feel like worthless failures

8. Because he is currently involved in a very big way with a motion picture that can only be labeled as subversive

8a. Because there might be evidence that he is in collusion with an **Enemy of the People** in another undisclosed country

8b. Because of his attributes of influence and importance, as well as his celebrity, he could use all those things as a cover to engage in covert activities of the most maddening kind

(**8c. – 8q.** deleted)

8r. Because we do not like subversive threats

(**8s. – 8dd.** deleted)

9. Because he stands to be able to marshal great masses of the populace, if he so chooses

10. Because it is the universal conclusion by all agencies, operatives, consultants and participants in the interests of the Murn Administration and its Associated Partners, that he must be apprehended in his progress of influence immediately, and without delay; prejudice of even the extreme kind may be employed in the enactment of this mission

11. Because said 'mission', briefly alluded to and outlined in Point #**10**, is duly recognized as legitimate; similarly, it is duly made official by all participants in this concerned study, none of whom will be mentioned here, for security, legal, and religious reasons

Conclusion: BECAUSE of the preceding eleven points and their codicils, and many others besides, it must be ascertained without a doubt that Butterbugs and his people pose a major threat to the interests of most of the enterprises of the world; therefore, it is recommended that he be stopped

Postamble: This is a testament to a threat that must be seen to, as soon as possible.

(signed)

(Over 800 signatures of parties interested in the *Elimination of Butterbugs as a Threat to the Progression of Purposeful Interests of the World, Inc.* a.k.a. 'EBTP-PIW, Inc.'; additional sheets attached)

N.B. Additional signatures or 'x'-marks available upon request, pending security clearance and security rating results of requestor(s).

Oh, but what sterling sayings! That, combined with sensible and intelligent assessment of a warning tract, was a package pretty much on par with that Bill of Rights, wasn't it?

'For it is Butterbugs, Butterbugs! *BUTTERBUGS* who wants to destroy my way of life! He uses terror as an intimidator! He hates my freedoms! He wants me dead! He is a thug, and a coward! That's what this thing *says*, anyway. Will you just look at it! It's all there. I must contribute to any cause that brings him to justice. I must hasten to add my signature to this sacred document!'

In lieu of having done it when it was drafted and when it mattered, he grabbed an almost-dry quill pen and scratched out his name on the photocopied parchment.

'There! My John Hancock makes me independent at last!'

Never mind that it was actually a signature on a Declaration of Dependence.

It was not only a testament to the persuasive efforts of the Murn Administration, but to the absolute shallowness of the mogul himself, that he would seek to eradicate he who had brought so many bucks to his studio enterprise. But no, of course not. Going Murnside promised to be so much bigger than the Butterbugs Follies could ever hope to be. And the promise of a President had a lot more gravitas than some strolling player's flaky shadows on a wall. Diversifying into heavy armaments, trade-line mastering, and nation-adjustment was where the truly grand action was! Movies were for mediocre Meghans and masturbating Melvins.

He used to *love* the movies though. They were in his blood. But blood can go all watery and slimy when the pump is no longer primed with passion. Plus, it was the lateness of his daily delivery that was shoving him into such anti-rationale. Wasn't it?

'But I am worried, lest I do not make it through this trial. The trial of tonight! Oh, where is Stu? Where could that man be? Sweet Judas, there have to be a few speckles around here *somewhere!*'

For the fiftieth time he ran his fingers all around his blotter and his desk at large, snorting what few dust mites remained, and fancying there was a micro-high in there somewhere, as a result.

'Hey – haven't tried the *floor!* I'm *saved!*'

The floor had only floor-like qualities to it.

Then the 'Where the fuck is my shipment????' resumed again.

And like film noir is wont to do, by introducing dramatic touches at just the right (or, script-wise, the wrong) time in the tale, just then a cascade of buzz-tones was heard through speaker cloth that looked like a 1950s science teacher's sport jacket. The heralding of a tardy but welcome appearance, not of human form, but plastic bag-ette.

Like he'd done countless times before, Hy charged down the gloomy corridor to the Servant's Entrance, swung wide the door, grabbed the goods, let the panel slam in the face of the deliverer, and rushed back to his launching-pad blotter for prep, letting that Stu person fumble with the door, comport himself, and then hang out by the wastebasket, like a lowly punkah-wallah, looking embarrassed and humiliated, while waiting for a flimsy bit of freshly-laundered cashola – never cheques, and never *ever* money orders – to be tossed in his direction.

Back at his world headquarters desk, absolutely no sound or interruption were possible as Hy dressed his coke zone, cleaned off his mirror yet again, and got ready for a humungous and simultaneous snort/smoke of the product in order to make up for inexcusably-lost time.

Silence got busted-up all of a sudden.

'I was *just* about to press the 'send' button, shit-fuck!!!' raged the studio head in big pre-inhale-tones. 'You know how close you came??'

He held up a wobbly index finger for maximum effect.

Never mind that no 'send' button was at hand. Never mind that nothing awaited to be sent. Never mind that no computer was even in this office. Never mind there was no early-warning worldwide network of backups and auto-sends, to be triggered if someone didn't manually deactivate it daily. Never mind there was nothing inside an email message that didn't even exist. Never mind there was no substance for blackmail, whatsoever. Never mind that only hollow words had ever defined it, threatened it, and that the words themselves were lies. Never mind there had ever been any of these threat-mechanisms in play.

Never.

But never mind. Why, it had all been bullshit. Every last syllable had been composed of the finest high-class waste products from the most audacious and thundering male bovine in Hollywood, and by the BS' very power, lesser mortals were controlled and made to do the most contemptible, degraded, objectionable *things*. All within the highest humiliation standards known on Earth.

Stu, still compelled to be a believer, just stood there.

'Suppose I don't care anymore,' he finally said.

'You care. If I'm still controlling the world in my state-of-*high* at my age, while you're busy licking my gag-inducing asshole, I figure you care a lot at yours.'

Somehow, the ancient institutionalized intimidation and fear just weren't the same any longer. For the first time in, he didn't know how long, Stu felt totally confident with his course of action. *Judiciously* confident. There were no thoughts of a last minute reversal, even though he'd retained the sizable amount of 'clean' coke that had been displaced by the Goggomobil's droppings. Just in case he had to make a peace offering, or something.

Even though Hy wasn't high yet, he now acted like it. A wee bit of softening and conspicuous mellowness projected from his waspish facade. A comfort in the theatricality of his home-base sanctum was kicking in. Perhaps it was because the studio head could dodge in and out of the noir shadows that made up his vast retreat, intercepted by rays of unexplainable key-lighting and artistic touches. And sweet drugness was dead ahead.

He was in the picture business, for crying out loud, and he had Industry professionals at his beck and call to rig up the best effects, even for his private use. (One of Old Atrocity's first electrical gigs as a freelancer – way back when – had been to wire this very Gothic space...)

If one is around sets and lights and special effects and glass shots, even as an executive, sooner or later, they're going to say, 'Hey, I'd like some of that.' The old Orson Welles quote that a film studio was 'the biggest electric train set any boy ever had' rubbed off even on the Hy Goths of the world.

No fancier of train sets, Hy could nevertheless twist dials and adjust rheostats in this, his private party cave, right under Hollywood's collective nose-in-the-air. His own nose was happy to vacuum all the snowy flakes it could stand, and the hairs within were about to look like flocked Christmas greens.

A proverb crossed the mogul's mind as he shifted his accessibility to his guest by adjusting his own lighting-coverage, so that master lenser Ernie Haller might just as well have been in the room:

'Ahem! It's all about sex. Sex, which creates, though it also destroys... What could be plainer?'

Silence.

Then he shifted, and spat out another maxim:

'Families are as much about hate as they are about... love.'

More silence.

Then Hy tried another pose, which was weird, because he'd always hated the 'actor' thing and all its catering to weaknesses, and how its rigmarole made the strong into fairies.

'Don't speak ill of the dead... or the soon-to-be-dead.'

Now this last utterance struck a chord with Stu. He moved away from the wastebasket.

'Wha –,' began Stu, before being preempted.

'Well, you old fink, then,' Hy rasped, simmering a bit.

Once Stu stood in front of the desk, his shadowy form was immediately erad-icated by the mogul, who flipped on the specially-aimed GrillerFollowSpot, flooding the lawyer with hot, interrogatory light. Hy felt back in control, where he permanently belonged.

'Well sir, you can use your... stuff, now,' Stu said quietly, amazed that Hy hadn't torn into the bag at first grab. Of course, it was just cussedness that fueled him, even more than drugs.

'Shut up! What do you think I am, *desperate?* I can go at my own pace, any time I want. And I will right now. I'm in no hurry. This powder may be magical, but it doesn't *own* me, you know. But you were *late*, pal. What?? Huh?? Fucking with me like that! You've never pulled anything like that before...'

'You've – you've got it now. Sorry I was late. Car problems.'

'Oh? Busted down, droopy-drawers?'

'Yes, sir.'

He wasn't referring to his Maverick.

'Got 'er going again, loser?'

'With some help, barely.'

Skilled at remaining totally operative as he did his drugs, Hy prep'd his dosage while continuing the conference.

'So, what the hell does this mean – that you'll be pulling this 'breakdown' guff on me every day now?'

'Car's all broken and vulnerable.'

'Yeah, I'll bet. Get it *fixed.*'

'Needs a full restoration.'

Hy was going to deliver some snotty zinger, but he really needed to be practical here. There wasn't any precedence to Stu having one over on him, he'd been so bowed, so cowed and so cooperative while he, Hy, had successfully chipped his chump ex-lawyer's life away. Stu was the perfect defeatist, the ideal blackmail victim-evolved-into-slave. And he was needed. What better setup could he have?

Almost a sort of sympathetic softening slopped over the studio's führer as he regarded the loyal runner.

'Well,' he said in a beefed-up grudging tone, 'I'll see if I can't be of – uh, I don't know, some... *assistance*, I guess.'

He leaned back, pulled out his billfold and tossed three hundreds onto the desk before Stu.

'Get yourself some better wheels, Chuckles. Before it's 'Curtains', heh-heh. And remember, it's on *my* nickel.'

'Thank you, sir.'

Stu took the spot cash money meekly, but with a dustbowl farmer's gratefulness. Inside, he was elated. Those C-notes would probably cover about half the cost of one of the Goggomobil's taillight lens replacements, with maybe a bezel included, depending on the seller. He'd try the Aussies first. They *did* taillights. They had everything.

'Me gonna do smoke first,' said Hy, in an awful First Nation parody voice. 'Peace pipe? No way, bozo-boy! How!'

Stu might very well have witnessed the owner of the film studio's first attempt at 'acting'.

'Well, Mr. Goth, I'll leave you to it, then.'

'Wait!, lazy-ass. I've been thinking. Seems I've been a bit pinchy about my attitude towards you, huh?'

'That's OK. I've got to go now. Long march home.'

'Relax and siddown. *Now.*'

Stu, if he had been fully returned to his normal state of logic, would have known that there was nothing legally binding about obeying Hy's *every* demand, and even if not, he would have been well-advised to exit via the Servant's Entrance, without further equivocation.

But he sat down in an over-stuffer, still within the rays of the GrillerFollow-Spot.

'Stu! Cool it! You're among friend. Heh! 'Friend'. Get it? *One* friend. The only one you got. And I is it! Ha ha ha ha ha!'

Stu looked increasingly uptight.

As he continued to futz with his substance to abuse, practicing a little foppish snuff sniff here and there to ease into the coming blast of high-ishness, Hy actually waxed genial.

'You know, Tibbs-Curtain, there's a whole lot of things I've been wrong about about you. I've been awfully darn selfish, no? I know you agree with me. I can see your hungry face as I feast on my twinkle-snow. I bet I know what you want: some dummy dust! I can see the envy in your eyes, the jealousy contained in your minimal comments. And I see how your nose twitches. Its mucus lining panting to feel the glorious creep-up of high-flying fun! And you've been frikkin' impeccable in not lifting any o' my snowstorm... Oh, yeah! Snow! It won't be long before... Snow...! You know, I sometimes dream about snow. Warm snow. Snowflakes, drifting down into our Southland yards. And it stays till spring, cuz you know, it's *warm*. It's not the cold stuff. I dream about it... Hello, why, hello you snow...! You know? Like a welcoming blanket of – But! But yoe, you, uh, never jittered with my stuff, cuz, well, I'm gonna let ya in. Yup. Know what? I weigh it ever-time you exit my dandy presence. Only reason I've *not* got the scales out right now is that yer still here. See how conscien –! Conschushen –! You know, the con-shuss thing – I am??'

Hy burst into a self-congratulating laugh.

'*And* hungry! Hungry for my bounty. Huh? Well, brat-boy, you're in luck. Sometimes the charity weevil bores into my butt and up to my brain, and then? Well, I've just gotta do somethin' goody-goody *good* alluva sudden. Yeah, I got you figured. You're one deprived dude, I can tell you that right now. *So join me!*'

Indeed, it was probably a wise strategy to get Stu hooked at this point. Better control – better security. Though there were risks... Hell, if this busted-down hotshot flamed out, there were plenty of kids he could replace him with. 'Cept, what if they turned on him? Risks, all right... Best to stick with Stu. Stick with the names you know. Well, Stu would have to learn how to drive while he's really fucked up, and then there's the problem of...

Hy gestured to the blotter in front of him, which was now rather nicely dressed with two sets of two lines. His lucky dollar was next to one, and a very classy Dutch gold 'nosepijp' (technically for guests) next t'other.

Stu, rooted in true horror, characteristically said nothing.

'Stu, baby! Consider it part of the job! No charge whatsoever! My nickels! Really! Enjoy! I know, you're probably worried about that paltry three hundred I just gave you. Hell, boy, that was just a warm-up!'

Hy was getting out plenty of verbal butter. He couldn't afford to lose this guy, as the best and most talented, not to mention the most trouble-free, courier ever. Butter, honey, free coke – anything but badmouthing and slave/master treatment! He'd seen the error in his ways. He'd now dump the tyrant image and adopt his usual schmooze frontage. After all, that was how he'd cracked the great Who's The Biggest-Cocked Mogul in Fucking Tinseltown? conundrum. He was a winner who'd keep on winning.

'OK, buddy-boy. Get thine ass over here. Lean in and snort 'er up. On me! My nickel bag! Heh-heh! Oh, and keep that there golden snort bauble. My treat! Gold does wonders for the high. This old pro prefers his trusty dollar, though! Hell, I may need it when I'm out on the street, ha-ha! Come on, step right up now, don't be shy. If you're a virg– I mean, a greenhorn, y'won't get no ridicule from me! I'll talk ya through it, if yudd'd like.'

'Oh, Mr. Goth, I'm, uh, not really in the mood now.'

'Course ya are! Listen, baby, things'll change for the better. I admit, I've been ever so slightly harsh with ya. No longer! No need! You've proven your loyalty! Why, I see a great future for you here at Goth – er, I mean, Mega|Goth! (Never *can* get used to that pesky merger!)'

'Really, Mr. Goth?'

'Why, soytenly! And call me Hy! Play yer cards right, you'll be a producer one day.'

'When?'

'Why, well, OK, *now*, if you choose. Can do, if it please ya!'

'Oh, may I?'

'Sure! Want a picture? I'll even cut you in on the gross.'

'How about, 'Unholy War Hymn'?'

Hy was impressed. Impressed at what a dumbo Stu was. Here was a picture that was frozen out of the Hollywood plant, but still, someone actually wanted in!

Totally stupid, or what? Little did Stu know that 'UWH' was about to be 86'd once and for all, Jambutterbugsy unit, or no. Well, no harm in funnin' the kid a little. He'd have the shit shocked out of him when he realized he'd signed onto a worthless enterprise. But hey, might as well let him down easy and give him a fuzzy Irving Mushmash picture or something. For his training wheels. Hell, a great way to learn the biz.

He figured that having a junior producer to boss around, and who was also a crackhead, might be sort of a fun hobby.

'Well, you talked me into it, kid. You'll be signed in as an Assistant Producer, reporting to Pud Parker, who's a wombat, I know, but if he gives you any shit, tie into me at first milkin'. Let's see, I've got a whole stack of contracts for 'UWH' written up, right here. Not too many partners yet, but they will come. You'll be in on the ground floor. Plus, you'll get screen credit in the opening titles after the Overture. Hell, I'll cut you in for 10%.'

'Most kind of you, Hy. I mean, Mr. Goth.'

'No, no! Hy! You *promised!*'

'Hy!'

'Hey, what's the money *fer*, anyway?'

'Where do I sign?' asked Stu, still in a sad voice, but he'd scanned the contract and it was legit.

'Right there, Pluto-Boy! Now here. Here's your copy. We'll have it notarized at first light.'

'Well, Hy, uh, allow me!'

Stu was indeed a notary, and still, to this very moment, he carried his stamp in his pocket. He'd fingered it whenever he needed tactile encouragement via remembrance, just to get through the day.

Hy was more impressed than threatened. As the clamp made a relief of legal-ness on the contracts, he himself signed.

'So now that the biz of the day is successfully concluded, we can party!'

Stu returned to his apprehension.

'I, uh…'

'Step right up now! Say! 'Produced by Stuart Tibbs-Curtain'! How does *that* sound? Huh??'

'You know, Hy, I uh, I thought you said you were gonna – going to – smoke first?'

'I did. Pretty sharp, kid! Yeah, I did! So, you wanna smoke 'em first, huh?'

'You show me. I'm not really – you know. Well, I'm actually a *virgin*. I admit it. But, you know, in *that* department, only!'

'Very good! Very good! Heh-heh. Well now, first time can be good and it can be bad, ya know…'

Stu was struck by the banality of this pronouncement.

'Thing is, you're a lucky duck. You happen to be in the company of one who prefers smoke to snort. Not to gross you out or anything. Smoking's so much more civilized. So much more stylish. OK then, if you wanna be my Assistant Producer, it starts right here.'

Pride now took its place foremost in Hy's mind. Not only had he hornswoggled his slave in a lesson of obedience, now he would show off his prowess as a role model. What a perfect combination!

From a superbly-crafted mini-cabinet in the dark recesses of the western plateau of his great-plains desk, which he unlocked with a platinum-coated key, Hy brought out a fancy and jumbo-sized crack-cum-coke pipe, held it in presentation mode with a wink, then chirped:

'Got this muthah in the depths of old Tangiers' Casbah! You like romance? You're lookin' at it. Now, observe!'

The man at the top of motion picture showbiz indulged in a bit of shtick as he ceremoniously filled the bowl with white powder, so as to make a huge impression on the novice, even though it wasn't the best technique employed by the professional puffer. But Hy felt like he had *family* right here, so he chucked the old paranoia right away.

A bit of suspicious fume-clouding rose into the air as he primed the pipe with powder.

'Hmm! A trifle acrid!'

He paused in his process.

'Just part of the adventure!'

He looked up.

'You know, Stu, you have to watch these things. The, uh, 'cut' factor and all.'

Stu's back began to feel a waterfall of insta-sweat pour down all the channels and recesses.

'But hell, when you've got a feeling that you've got the best, and you actually *do*, why hell, let 'er roll!'

And he resumed his merry task.

'OK, now watch. Here we go. ACTION! – as dey say in da movies! Heh!'

Lighter to pipe, inhale a-go-go.

As Hy was puffing, an almost indeterminate stream of what looked like *steam* seemed to emanate from his aft nostril, rather like the waiting blow-by on a Saturn rocket, as seen ad nauseam before Apollo blast-offs.

All entreaties to share in the spoils evaporated. Hy was in his cubicle, and there was no entering.

'You know, Curtain-Tibbs, I might wanna do this round first. On my own. To, to, check 'er out. Know what I mean… On my… On my…Own…'

He grew kind of quiet. He belched. Then, as if to change tack again, as far as handling Stu, he belch-coughed and straightened himself up so as to make an announcement.

'I've – you'll be glad to know, all but killed this 'Unholy War Hymn' abomination. I've saved the public, I've saved the studio, and I've saved the world from its scourge. And Stu, I've saved your sorry ass, as well. I await the world's gratitude. I know I already have yours, as always.'

'But, filming proceeds in Jambutterbugsabad as we speak. Besides, I just signed a contract…'

'Not worth the bubble-jet grease that landed on it.'

'I'll see you burn!'

'Don't get so uppity, errand boy! What the hell do *you* know about my things?'

'Well, I know that you're a cokehead – crackhead – whatever.'

'Why, you – !'

Hy was easily licked. His tongue flicked over his fingers and then he let them scrub his gums for the forty-seventh time since Stu's ship came in this evening.

'Aw hell, I'll show *you*, you rat-livered whore's nit!'

Then the head of the studio tossed his obviously inadequate pipe aside and lunged toward the greater high, inhaling both remaining lines on the runway of his desk, one per nostril, in a flyover that was genuinely stunning to behold.

'And besides, you're a, a, a *chicken*head!' was all Hy could add, after he'd straightened and faced his courier. Once the transcendental drugs would hit though, his wit 'n' wisdom would return, and he'd *really* give Stu a proper tongue-broasting.

In another instant though, Hy blew up.

'Holy! Holy! *HOLY… FUCKING… SHIT!!!!* My mouth's a – a – river of lava!!! My throat – oh lordy! It's being stripped open! And oh! The brain! The brain! Its pan is full of fry-gravy! My brain is br-br– r-r-roasting – like a pig heart! I tell you!! It's got holes in it! Junk is leaking out! AAAAAAAAAARRRRGGGHHHH!!!!! Help me! Somebody – *HELP MEEEEEEEE!!!!!*'

One eyebrow on Stu's forehead rose. He had no idea this would be the reaction to the 'acrid' cocaine, or that it could even take this long. Things promised to be interesting from this point, and to know where they would end up.

'Oh! Rigorous awful! The ripping pain is – is – oh, globby! I be choking with fire-mucus! Doctor Wheck! Where??? What happened? AAAAuuuhhhhh!!!!! Oh, ukkkkkkkkk!!!'

The screaming was terrible and fearsome. So was the mogul's attempt at extinguishing the fire. He tried to gain access to his sinuses and throat by attempting to open them up with his fingernails, so as to let the offending crème flow out into harmless air. He tore at the inner burning flesh, but only punched holes, so that blood, not the poisoned ichor, fountained out. Quivering and hooting, he sought and found a letter opener and commenced jabbing it at the problem area. This succeeded in accessing the fiery vaults, and there was indeed some outflow of the angry toxin, but once it actually reached the air, it immediately coagulated and formed a tough and scabby seal, ensuring that the deposits within could freely continue corroding and melting and doing their natural chemical conduct, as they had a right to do, without further interruption. The pain of his self-inflicted violence was as nothing compared with the reactive fury behind the fastness of his cranial fortress.

Positioned so near by, and already shaken by the invasion, it was his brain's turn now to fully come under the influence of the terrorizing consumption. Hurting steamy vents had been opened under the cerebellum, and the poison was advancing without shame.

This was an emergency!

As his vision began to swim with vile liquidity and *noir*-outs, Hy made one last bid to quell the acidic riot that had been visited upon him.

'Blabbariah!' he shrieked. 'Ow! Ow!!!'

In a somber corner armoire were various arms and armor of a historic nature, trophies from the filming of 'Holy Water Sprinkler War On The Volga Plains', a Butterbugs picture in Technicolor, produced in creative association with Hyman Goth (though released through Bronston).

'Oh no – OW! Shuh-shubbah! Oh, narbah! Quck! LABBBAHHH!!!'

With hands insanely fluctuating but sensibly guided, Hy made it to the door of the case, flung it open, and grasped one of the very objects that had given that great war picture its name. This 'holy water sprinkler', straight from the dungeons of the mediæval Wartburg, was indeed a baleful thing of leaden klusp-metal, anxiety-inducing to behold, and heavy as a clutch assembly from a '63 Isetta. Assuredly used by some Alaric-like wreaker of barbarian chaos in the endless land wars of the Dark Ages, its action-end possessed a spiky ball, wherein unholy blood would be spread in place of water. With such a wry title attached to such a terrible, swift weapon, its effectiveness dare not be questioned at this late hour.

Grabbing the tool, it would at first not give, as the secure StealrPrufe mounts were doing their job. But they did not reckon on the searing pandemonium within their owner's head at the moment, and in its own sick way, enough super-human strength was, for a split second, allowed to be distributed to Hy hands, so as to wrest the healing instrument with urgency, so as to utilize it in this vital procedure.

Its weight actually steadied his hands. He went over in back of his desk, stood up straight, and stared dead ahead at Stu, knowing then and there, with a clarity that dawned even in the midst of the current catastrophe within his head, of his courier's traitorous deed, his sabotage, his complete and utter betrayal, and the outrageous knowledge, with attendant horror, that he, Hyman Goth, had been *had* by a lowly slave!

Stu just stood there, fully expecting to have to dodge this blood-sprinkler, flung by his tormentor with final but deadly vengefulness. Because, without any word transfer, Stu knew full well that Hy knew who had done this to him.

And the mogul wobbled as he stood there, limply croaking, 'You FINK!'

repeatedly, as the fizzing, sinking, devouring action hugely advanced in eating away his brain.

Then Hy did the needful. He would have loved to have punched Stu's skull down first, but because his own needed first aid first, he'd get that out of the way before finishing Tibbs off. After all, first-things-first was how a studio should be run, so as to beat any rivals at their own game.

On with it!

He bashed the weapon square onto his own pate, so as to fly-swat the problem once and for all. The trouble was, the sutures of his cranium, acting as meandering distributaries for the now liquefied acid, had weakened the skull's superstructure so that the spiky sphere's heavy contact and invasion of the brain-house was akin to a ladle smacking into a chocolate-coated bombe by a disgruntled pastry cook.

Thus and so did his crown collapse utterly under the onslaught, every bit caving in to the point where the spikéd ball might even be considered the globular limit of Hy's skull, though the image of it was not nearly so bizarre as that of an etching on the wall, that now caught a few drops of Hy's sprayed blood. It was indeed by Rops of course, in which a skeleton with fleshy woman's breasts stands next to a grotesque bust on a pedestal, its skull-face composed entirely of Rosicrucian thorns. And the face is smiling.

His body hissing and seeping, the remains of Hyman Goth collapsed in on themselves, ending up as a dud on the floor, while icky things continued to do their shutdown act of finishing off what was left of the host.

'Revenge and vindication!' Stu declared, looking past Hy's no longer-twitching corpse, and into the future.

'We now advance! Our task of avenging the wrongéd one has been wondrously completed, and I have been vindicated by my persistence of suffering and honesty. My thanks be to my beloved Goggomobil for bringing me back from the zombied dead! Now, it is my turn to return the blessing. Get ready, oh my Goggo, ye shall *roll again!*'

Grasping the 'UWH' contract in one hand, and the keys to the saved Goon Car he'd kyped from the shop, he strode out of the office majestically, using the front door for the first time.

No one was around. No security cameras were on. His hands had been gloved, and Hy hadn't even noticed.

Resolved: he had never stopped being a skilled lawyer.

55.

The Wise-Apple

'Variety' headline: 'HY GOTH'S WRAP SHOCKS PIX INTO STYX'.

In the center nozzle, the second h'line: 'Could 'UWH' Sink In Underworld River?'

Naturally, the Industry was shaken to its foundations.

There were plenty of incidents involving public reaction.

Several theatre chains had already booked the epic, and they had rights to show trailers long before even the Roadshow release. Since several progressively-re-vealing previews had already been shown, the public's appetite was not only whetted, it was positively panting for fulfillment. As more and more glimpses were had by viewers, demand was becoming intense.

Riots broke out at hundreds of cinemas worldwide, as newsreels, shown just af-ter the trailers, announced that 'UWH' might be sunk for good. In Cleveland's Ex-tremadura theatre, after both enticing trailer and damning newsreel were shown, bold young firebrands charged the projection booth and unplugged the Simplexes as a protest. The blank Spanish-style wall behind the wrought iron chandelier defined all the dead space between audience expectation and the empty screen. The public had nothing to look forward to, and justifiable rage would surely erupt wherever pictures were shown. There were arrests, but all were released without charge.

In Pressburg, Slovakia, projectionists in all the metropolis' cinemas were taken hostage and their livelihood, if not their lives, was reluctantly threat-ened. That is, until the UN intervened, informing the masses that 'UWH''s interruption was due (as far as they knew) to one man alone, now deceased: Hyman Goth. There was no call to hold anyone else responsible. All protests were plainly not the preference of the frustrated peoples of the world, who only wanted their Butterbugs picture, as they had been promised.

This scenario was repeated in scores of cities throughout the world. As a result of intervention from the UN, the Vatican, Sai Baba, and Jan Egelund, a shaky peace was secured, for the time being.

And in Reepsville, that hallowed starting point for the new expectations in pic-ture shows, children gathered under the Spanish-moss trees to weep, as old folk choruses sang the saddest of Stephen Foster's tunes in the background.

It was as if the public had lost their way, so impacted by deprivation were they.

Black baseball-capped and generic beef-ball guys with predictable shades and

Uzis lined the walls of Mega|Goth Stvdios. Eclipse still reigned, though securi-ty-cleared players in the upper echelons of the studio's operation had been al-lowed in. Action had to be taken by the few, but in this case, there were *very* few. In Hy's very Inner Sanctum (in its post-janitorian, post-splattered era), they convened in crisis-council conformation.

In some ways, it was a mottled group. Those who were there were up for the challenge. They had no fear, because all had been before some kind of firing line during their careers, and with the 'UWH' crisis, none had anything to lose, for they cared implicitly about the picture, and their love for Butterbugs was un-bounded.

'If only the Mob *had* been involved,' mourned Chas. T.C. (e.g. Charles Techni-colour Clearwater, High-Up Exec at Mega|Goth Stvdios). 'That would have been a lot simpler than drug-dealer pinwheels.'

[This is perhaps an appropriate place in which to cite a germane bit of trivia, ably chronicled in 'Speppy's Industrial Alternative Facts, Fake News, and Possible Truths' by Carbel Speppy and Kreince Yunnah (Wum: The Jingus-Vox Concerns). 'The Technicolor people attempted to sue Mr. Cheam Prail Clearwater and Mrs. Baby Cambio Clearwater for daring to assign their registered trademark brand name to their newborn child, successfully spotted by loyalists after it appeared as an announcement (in tiny print) way in back, on page 36, of the Vomero, NJ 'Daily Blab-Whistle' (3:00AM Limited Edition). A red flag indeed: a grievous copyright infringement, even if only as a middle embellishment, though rarely seen. The case attracted huge media attention, especially in the Industry. Nevertheless, Judge Gradtag Guzzard immediately threw it out of court when he happened to notice that the actual spelling of the middle name on said birth certificate was rendered in poetic form (n.b. BritSpell), instead of the assumed registered trademark version. In point of fact, the attentive typesetter at the 'Blab-Whistle' had indeed 'corrected' the spelling to the more familiar designation (viz. AmeriSpell), perhaps assuming that said newborn might be a member of the extended Kalmus family. Ironically, this affair was unspooling just as the Technicolor Motion Picture Company was aban-doning its famed three-strip technology for more modern methods, so the general public interpreted the suit as a ballyhoo stunt, and flocked to Technicolored films as never before. For his own part, as a budding Industry exec-producer in the making, Charles Technicolour Clearwater proudly proclaimed his full nomenclature at every opportunity.']

'I assume there was percolation upward,' Sonny replied. The agent had just arrived breathless from LAX.

'Not up to any recognizable source. From what we've been able to find out, Hy used lean-to, back-alley meth-lab-in-the-potting-shed suppliers, the most difficult to trace.'

Chas, by universal decision of the Board, and upon urging and advisement, had taken control of the studio. There was much jubilation in circles in the know, because he was the man most of his colleagues had plumped for all along to run the Mega|Goth show. The only one who'd barred him from presidential powers had been Bleak King Hyman himself. And despite the opportunity, no one on this planet formed any bogus theory that Chas had done Hy in so as to secure the throne, although they *could* have. But that was ridiculous. Chas had persisted out of duty, never ambition. Besides, the LAPD investigation was complete. There had been no arrests whatsoever. None were pending.

Up in this office suite, there was some speculation, but no theorizing.

'I've never seen such an extreme reaction to drug usage,' said a redhead in the room. 'But I can't say I'm surprised. Hy's decisions of late were uncharacteristically radical.'

The front door, now the exclusive access point to the Inner Sanctum, blew open.

'And looky here!' announced Porter Parker, just entering.

The headline blared off the five-star final broadsheet of 'The Daily Porridge':

CASE CLOSED: HYMAN GOTH'S BLOW-OUT RULED SUICIDE JUDGE MACABY DECREES SELF-DEATH BY MISADVENTURE ONLY FOUL PLAY WAS MOGUL'S OWN

'Well now,' said Hazel Snyder, the redhead in question, 'That wraps 'er up, then. Now we can get on with it.'

'Thank heavens!' said Chas. 'The public can be appeased, from this day forward!'

'That should quash any conspiracy theories,' offered Whimpei Groyle (the guy who'd once shot Butterbugs in the arm because of a situational misunderstanding; he had now risen to Consultant-General within the Butterbugs organizations).

Chas was circumspect.

'The stress of having to close the studio… God knows why he did such a thing, and on the verge of the biggest hit we've ever imagined. His reasoning had fled outright. Right? But he loved those old weapons. They were very dear to his heart. I suppose we'll donate them to The Hyman Goth Memorial Collection of Mediæval Weapons Used In His Pictures, which will be housed at the Getty.'

'That's touching, Chas,' said Sonny, sympathetically.

Sympathetically?

'We all hated him, you know,' said Chas.

'Amen. About as bad as Isaac (Davis),' said Hazel. 'Now we can get on with it.'

'As bad as Isaac?' asked Porter. 'Are you sure? Well, a tyrant is a tyrant is a tyrant.'

'Well eulogized, sir,' said Sonny.

'Oriana and the Borzois get everything. Surprisingly.'

Chas, like Hazel, was ready to move on. They'd done more than enough respectful commenting on one who didn't deserve it in the least.

'I love Gabby and Prissy,' said Hazel. 'I'm happy for them. Now we can get on with it.'

'By that, Hazel, I take it that you want to open the studio again.'

'Today, if possible, Chas. Like, in a half hour, say?'

'That's a tall order. Hy fucked up so many things. It could take weeks.'

'I'll help you, Chas,' she said quietly.

'You mean it? On top of your 'UWH' chores?'

Hazel took a drag on her Virginia Slim and shook her curly red hair.

'Absolutely, baby. I'll HQ right here.'

'But what about the daily needs of Hazel Snyder Presents?'

'Chas, dearie, we dames can multi-task better than you dudes.'

'You're on, Haze!'

'Delighted. One more condition: I want Tibbs-Curtain on board. He knew Hy intimately and no doubt he's got insights galore as far as running this place. One of Hy's last official acts was to sign him up. Some kind of sweet contract, too! One of the best things he ever did.'

'Agreed, Haze. A-OK. Stu's in, and Haze, I can't tell you how tickled I am that you're gonna be on-site.'

'Now Chas, if you'll allow me, I'd like to get on with it.'

'By all means.'

With Chas' approving gesture, Hazel repaired to her new commanding position behind Hy's old desk, which had basically been fire-hosed, decontaminated, and detoxed, but was worth saving because it had once graced the offices of Norman Bel Geddes. And, seeing no further impingement, she took control of the 'UWH' unit at Mega|Goth.

'Purrby, you'll be my Exec Sec. Up for it?'

Purrby Burrburr, erstwhile porno star of the most respected caliber, who'd been scooped up by Chas when he heard of her script-girl talents on the sets of grind-em pix, and after they'd dated for a responsible period he brought her to the studio as his Secretary At Large. She gazed at Chas as if to ask, 'Oh, *may* I?' So Chas, giving the most encouraging wink he was capable of, pleasingly acquiesced.

'Oh! Oh, YES, Ms. Snyder!'

'Goody-good-good. Ready?'

'Yesss!'

'Purrby, first, a laundry list:

'– Fire all the Tarpit homeboys. They're outa here within the hour. No exceptions. It's 1:10 now. One creep in charge here was enough. Bust their contracts. All to hell. Stu will handle the trench warfare involved, based on Hy's illegal hiring practice in this particular case. We're getting our studio back. Now.

'– Reinstate our usual security team.

'– Re-key all locks.

'– Production of 'UWH' (and ALL other productions, both in-play and sked-ded) resumes: to-*day.*

'– Everybody works. Notify. By day's end, please.

'– Protect and preserve all the puppies, kittens and other small furry animals now on site; set up a nursery and adoption center.

'– That's it for studio-wide mandates; now:

'– Whimpei: can you form a consensus as to some of the occult reasons why Hy shut down production, i.e. possible subversive interests, covert mismanagement, creepshow bullshit, anything at all; you have carte blanche; I want worldwide input. This picture, occupying the media for so long in its perpetual state of filming and preparation, should not be considered a *horror vacui* for the Industry. We've got a lot of corrective work to research before we speak it.'

'You got it!' declared Whimpei, more than ready to get going.

'– Porter: line up your associates and channel the following: nuts and bolts pro-duction items. You know what I need. Also: a full rundown on start-up priorities; by sunset tomorrow, I want to issue an expertly-produced explanatory trailer to all the-atres worldwide, announcing a return to FULL production; highest urgency in this one – life and limb may be at stake! Beef up the drama angle of our struggle. Here on the lot: because all post-production is done here, we go full-blast now. Music's been waiting; Alfred will record over at Selznick and 20th. And yes, please get the Producers Team up to date. The grand old stalwarts need to stay right in the thick of things; we must formally thank them for their support. It didn't waver, ya know.'

'Check, Chief! Comin' up!' crowed Porter excitedly.

'– And Sonny: latest, latest, latest on Butterbugs?'

'Yup, Haze,' said Sonny. 'Just saw him yesterday. In Jambutterbugsabad. I'm not even jet-lagged. He's ready, I tell you. We're ready. Because Butterbugs kick-started the whole thing, and did it over there, independently, the momentum has been preserved. And get this: all the battle scenes are in the can!'

'Super, all. Magnificent. This is more like it. Now we'll pick up the heavy lift-ing here at this end. Because that's what we *do*, without question, and with highest of high quality!'

Everyone in the room cheered and applauded. At least four wild studio animals were spoken for in the process.

'Got all of that, Purrby?'

'Every bit,' returned the secretary.

'Oh, and Purrby, can you give Radan a call over at Art and have this room re-done, all in sage green?'

'Yes, Ms. Snyder!'

'Call me Haze. Love ya! OK team, let's *go!*'

After they all left, Hazel leaned back in her new VP in Charge of Production chair and blew Chas a kiss through her bright scarlet lipstick.

'I want that squid-mouthed puppy and that blue-plate special kitty that live on the steps outside. Perfect mascots!' she announced.

'I knew we shouldn't have divorced!' he smiled broadly.

'Which time?' she smiled coyly.

'Yeah, we've had a crazy ride, huh?'

'I like the way things are now. You're my best bud, Chas. Purrby's adorable. You're a lucky kluck.'

'She'll slave for ya.'

'Yeah, I could use a little girl-on-girl action. Mind?'

'Not at all. She's been asking me. Really!'

'Well, don't worry, I'll keep duty and passion separate.'

'In thee I trust.'

'You cool guy. Thanks for the gig, Techie.'

'Don't mention it. You haven't called me that in ages.'

'Haven't felt so copacetic with you in that long.'

'A good feeling, no?'

'Indeed, sir.'

'Sky's the limit now.'

'We got us one big-titted studio here, Techie-love.'

'You're not so bad yourself, Rhode Island red. About a 36-C, I'd reckon. No push-ups needed. You're in some kinda great shape! And you haven't called me *that* in even more ages!'

'The old smoothie!'

'You're still hot, Haze!'

'And you're still my country gentleman.'

'I bow, and am at your complete disposal, ma'am.'

'Every courtesy granted!'

'You're my production veep!'

'And you're my studio head. I'll serve ya, lover.'

'You saved our collective ass, Haze.'

'Thanks, but it wasn't me, Chas. There's a guy way out there somewhere called Butterbugs. He made it all possible.'

'Right, babe. The world will never forget.'

These were they which came out of great tribulation. These were they which saved the great and mighty creation that was 'Unholy War Hymn'.

There was but one more sequence to shoot: the grande climax.

56.

In Fustian Chemistry

Look sharp!

For those in Empire's drivers' seats (as there were many), it was a time of troubles, for there had been several setbacks of consequence that threatened to throw otherwise on-track agendas out of gear.

One such driver, Montague Realms, having aspired to keep his place within Empire, and by so doing, surpass it, got himself down to the familiar local theatre, the Audion picture show in Yougah, VA. Seeking a little explanation from Butterbugs concerning his much-publicized role in 'UWH', he duly saw a trailer for the still-shooting but soon-to-be-released mega-epic.

Who the hell should be more powerful in this nation, anyway, Pentagon lever-throwers (and civilian ones, to boot!) or amateur-hour skit performers, gallivantin' around in flickering silliness? And really now, it wasn't a question of who *should* be, but who *was*. Way beyond this prosaic point though, this Pentagonian civilian was seriously ANGRY.

The Assoc. Sec'y of Defense was in luck.

[Actually the title was now 'Assist.' – he was demoted after the Lurgan/Vunn disaster, but that humiliation shall not be designated here, until all official nomenclature (e.g. calling cards, nameplates, websites, matchbook covers, etc.) are fully and appropriately altered.]

It was a special half-hour Advance-Advance Preview Peep™ of 'UWH''s progress, and the house was predictably full. What he saw in the ultrastar's performance, one whole sequence, that of the Gathering of the Councilors for the High Mad Doctor's Planning and Accomplishment Programme, was so tantalizingly presented it hit his sensibilities like a doom-laden mushroom cloud. Aside from Butterbugs' acting knocking him out of his still toeless socks, the underlying message the scene conveyed was one of uncanny familiarity. For his part, he saw the future, the future he himself had built with hoodoo methods within the very government he served, and it suddenly hit him how full of holes it was, as if all his failures to construct the perfect fascist storm were now displayed very handsomely before him.

More exposed than if a viral photo was flying up to the cloud right now, revealing him, posed in full-diaper kinkiness, tap-dancing to Chunky Urine's 'I Wanna Win, And I *DID* Win, So Neaner, Neaner, Neaner!' at top volume.

How could such a thing be possible? There it was, up on the sheening screen, in dramatic form perhaps, but he was aware enough to recognize allegory, if not a thinly disguised personal attack, which is what he settled on, as an interpretation of choice. Because it would, in due course, seal his fate.

Realities were smacking him in the face. His scheme, to boldly wrest control of the US government from others, this coming Sunday during church, might have been dunderheaded in its megalomaniacal naïveté, but it was in place, and about to be set into irreversible gear.

Butterbugs, this hated Butterbugs, whom he'd failed to 'get', was now flinging panic in his lap! If any leaks or cracks in his plan came about, any and all investigations would lead to *him* at his P'gon HQ penthouse. He was working with traitors, as he himself in fact was, but traitors betray fellow traitors, too, and that is what he knew was about to happen. The austere but inspiring independence of the intelligent individual that had so struck him in 'I, Doughboy' (Kemmendine) so long ago, had now morphed into the obvious ultra-tragedy in this upcoming 'Unholy War Hymn'. He now had a terrible and unhappy realization: by sheer co-incidence, anyone of authority seeing this picture, by its plot development alone, would instantly have knowledge of his (Realms') covert plan to take over the US government. He would be unmasked. It was a certainty. The rage he at once felt against everyone responsible for this perverted picture, and especially Butterbugs, was positively prehistoric in its blocky force.

Butterbugs' acting odyssey had always carried the ultrastar from strength to strength, but for Realms and his kind, drama on the screen could not reasonably be coupled with the consistency of any sort of constitution, let alone the highest law of the land.

Gradually, rage was giving way to problem-solving. As Assoc. Sec'y, he could *still* halt the picture's release. He would take them *all* out, one way or another. He'd have to get more fuckin' ugly than he already was. Why, he was poised to become Advanced Severe Leader of the New American Combine! (That's what he'd named his fascist dream-horror.) What was this ribbon of celluloid, but a pesky tapeworm of poncing faggy drama queens, putting on makeup and airs?

Well now, *that* was his best put-down, yet.

Strengthened by his own anger, he knew he could nip this thing in the bud.

'That fucker must be *stopped*,' the Assoc. Sec'y muttered.

Some moppet in the seat ahead, mouthing a squeaky-deaky wad of Rubbery Poodle Gums, heard him curse Butterbugs, despite the roller-coaster modulations of the epic trailer's soundtrack, and turned around.

Seeing Realms' mug in reflected light, all grotesque and sinister with plotted-power lust, made him yelp. Out popped the glob of Poodle Gum, and it pasted itself like a dart on the chinnie-chin-chin of the recalcitrant Realms.

'You stupid *kid!!*' he wailed in his nasally manner, and stood up fast, grabbing the sticky sweet and flinging it back at its owner, but not hitting anything but the floor. He was on fire inside, but tonight he looked like a chilled piglet, with a sheen of greasy sweat, packed into a tight suit and trousers that probably concealed vast plates of venereal warts, so awkward-moving was he. The most important thing this kid had to know was that he was dealing with a really disgusting person, and to not let him touch him in any way.

Others in the audience nearby, not realizing the gravity of Realms' interior flamethrower miasma, merely shushed him, as if to avoid a spitball fight or something. Indeed, there were lots of kids in the audience, good as gold, as they were just as hot for 'UWH' as anyone else. But apparently it was an adult who was misbehaving. Stupid, stupid adult.

Wishing he had a death-bolt to aim at the kid, the high-ranking governmental official nevertheless grudgingly settled back into his seat.

Then, as the next trailer commenced (for an intriguing new Perry Flask and ProwlerCat picture), he felt the rage return with even greater command. The idea, the very *idea* that Butterbugs was still alive after his world-class attempt to remove him from the planet for all time was not a truth that could be tolerated any longer. That he had commissioned the execution himself, even before the VP (and higher) crowd ordered it – well, that effort was *his* baby. But alas, the mission's total failure was the same child: miserably retarded, then D.O.A. And he didn't even know about Butterbugs' much more real brush with death, nor of she who really brought him back.

In any case, the truth was unforgiving in all its terrible unfairness.

'Butterbugs *hijacked* my career!!! For that alone he shall *really* die *this* time!!!!'

The rage was much more urgent now, and an awful flush made him gasp for air. Nearly blinded by this turbo-anger, he got up, bungled his way out of the seating zone, pissing off many a patron, and felt his way all along the curving wall before managing to leave the house, down at the stage right exit, while accompanied the whole time by the trailer's samplings from the brand new (and catchy) Rodgers & Hammerstein score for the Flask/Prowler picture.

After flailing through the curtains, he paused in the ghastly red exit light of the stairs, just before the alley, and felt the pure horror of Butterbugs' power. The power that had emanated so relentlessly from the screen seared into his rotten soul. Blood was all he saw, but he wasn't sure if it was Butterbugs', or his own.

Panic-gripped, he charged up the steps, pushed the latch bar down, and found himself in the most turgid of alleys, a place so obscure and vile that it was unbelievable that his seat of power in the Pentagon, where his haughty satrapy had led to his bid for Empire, was only a few lonely miles away. What a place to come apart!

And that is what he proceeded to do. Because, what exactly *else* was he going to do? What action could he possibly take?

He saw, on the slimy brick wall, a splinter of old wood that used to house a button box for an Iron Fireman coal augur. He ran over to it and pulled it from the ancient mortar, a bent rusty nail coming with it. It was such a ghastly image to him, he almost shrieked with both fear and elation.

'By this humble tool will I *kill* Butterbugs *once and for all!*' he gurgled. 'I will set out *now* to do the job! The job that *others* could not even *start!!*'

Debilitated by his delicate state, he only stumbled around in circles, dropped the lethal weapon, and on another orbit, stepped on it hard. The curl of the nail made a new hole in his left sock and dug deep under his big toenail.

Physical pain merged with mental pain, the union of which was so frightful, it showed no sign of being verbalized, either with a shriek or (in)coherent words. It had virtually silenced him, increasing the negative pressures multifold. His looniness now unleashed, he sought relief in any form. There, on a horror-lit ledge below a bricked-up window, he saw two bottles. Unbeknownst to him, one was half-filled with urine (the receptacle of a conscientious street person, who happened to be an ex-CEO of certain refinement), while the other was half-empty of country liquor (which had rendered the ex-CEO drunktank-able, and whither he was hauled).

The Assoc. Sec'y was not particularly discriminating at this juncture, so he downed both in quick succession. He was kind of thirsty.

For a person who fully deserved to be tried, found guilty, and duly executed for the loftiest of treasons, what happened next was sheer mercy for him to have to endure, albeit brashly delivered, perhaps ordered by some celestial court, whose jurisdiction covered regions beyond the earthly coil, which waited impatiently for this case to enter its docket.

As a result of this grisly concoction, the Assoc. Sec'y's bodily systems were thrown into toxic shock, which activated Conclusive Cardiac Boiling Striasis, 9th-stage. It was like a bunker-buster bomb to his heart, which blew out after a half hour of convulsions, and his body, vibrating as if zapped by two electrically-charged earthworm harvester rods, ended up in an un-grated cistern that received the picture show's daily detritus of popcorn old maids, chund-nuts, soda syrup dribbles, and mopped vomit remains, often peppered with Ju-Jubes and other soft and chewy candies (e.g. Rubbery Poodle Gums) that so often cause distress for young and excited Jerry Lewis matinee viewers.

Thus, Butterbugs' performance in this particular picture preview justly claimed its most needful victim. The public had long forgotten Randi Chuzzlewit, but Chuzzlewit's self-demise was essentially a service to the Industry, while the Assoc. Sec'y's end was a service to humanity. For thus was one of the world's most dangerous persons removed from the scene of power: discreetly, and even naturally. When his rat-gobbled remains were found in an unspeakable sump of the capital's rejectimata, his death was ruled, by Justice Beepus (who had personally been repelled by Realms' very being, though it never affected his judgeship), as 'Death due to heart attackage, based on autopsy findings, robot-performed'.

In his Pentagonal office, which was duly fire-hosed of his nastiness, the only valedictory response made by the Assoc. Sec'y's underlings concerning the death of their boss was nothing more profound than: 'Boy, I'm glad it wasn't *me!*'

Still, after his judgment, a hoary proverb from 'The Yanagariat' momentarily flashed across the mind of noble Beepus: *Hatred is always hardest on the Hater, who makes it harder yet for the Hated to endure...*

Without its master planner, Realms' traitorous scheme collapsed in on itself.

Thus was the nation spared.

Another case closed.

But there were other – deeper even – threats.

Not very much clock-cycling within the scheme of things passed before there came a dolorous stroke. That is, dolorous for those who received it. Most others in the American land saw some value in its occurrence, while some who weren't so sure at first came unto elation when they fully understood what it all meant. Never in world history was a fulcrum for change better used.

It should be understood though, that Showbiz, Hollywood-style, is decidedly different in both nature and evolution than is characteristic of Showbiz, DC-style. Both are highly performance-oriented, but if one be firmly rooted in fiction, while the other purports to treat non-fiction, one might be deemed more honest because it is fictional without pretension, while the other, which purports to be honest, is all too often guilty of trickery. In the former, convolutions are possible; in the latter, they are probable.

Showbiz, DC-style, which captures the nation on such a trivial yet all-encompassing scale, usually stands a good chance of dizzying up a public's mind. Presented via silly old nonfiction media, those elements of the populace who actually pay attention assume that reality is being properly dealt with behind DC's white marbling, rather than the clearly fictional mandate further behind the scenes. Over on the Hollywood side of things, with dramatic wisdom in play, attention-payers have always been able to see through such snake-oil-spraying. If reality-based non-fiction occupies a state of trust higher than fiction, it is only in the minds of the devoted, as all others with access to any positions of decision-making will opt for using it for their own agendas, rather than aiming at the objectives of truth in the non-fictional sense – and beauty in the fictional sense.

Oh, but weak and weary it renders one, weighing and valuing these issues. And the monitoring of such trends burns minds out.

Alas, dissection, adieu!

To hell with all such rubbish. It is *power* that rules and *power* that is sought – in order that it be kept. As Machiavelli said, 'What the hell else *is* there in life?'

The next phase, involving other – deeper even – threats, happened like this:

In Las Vegas, at the Joe E. Lewis Commons, that spectacular stretch of the Strip donated by the casino grandees for the people's enjoyment of great pageants and durbars of all kinds, there had gathered an assembly of almost the *entire* Con Murn Administration.

Gunboat Vanttool buses of butch appearance and sickeningly cool distractive graphics had ferried each concerned party in from many different directions and at slightly different times. Neatly joined, they were all here in order to rally those who cared into enthusiastic gift-giving mode. For if the upcoming election was to be not only won, but uninterruptedly lorded over by the condominium now in power in this country, gestures had to be made before the power could grow. The all-wise strategists had divined that the freebooting culture of Vegas would be the perfect re-launching pad for the renascent desires of the party to which they belonged. Confidence had no dearth amongst these people. Used to such a winning streak as the last term's contest had brought, they adopted a steady strut, walking through constituencies as if they were mere Burkmarts or Vonses. One had only to appear in the proper department, make a few laff-lines, then appeal to the ditzy standards of those who bothered to show up, then retire to the bus and count the gold just acquired. Your basic traveling clip-joint. This pattern had gone on to such an extent within this Administration, its practitioners were virtually apathetic if they were regarded as such.

Any lengthy régime ancien becomes susceptible to erosion after a while, even though it is within the United States' system of quadrennial review. If the regime possesses a 'sort of ego' though, the kind to which all bow down, there are few worries that percolate upward to the policy-makers and gearshift-throwers. The insular effects of kowtowable power weaken as much as they protect. Such was the case on the Strip today. Personnel in the Murn caravan were almost yawning. Of course, money in the desert can do that to one.

Here was the setup: Murn & Co. were here for photo-ops in front of cripples and other disadvantaged persons, in order to flaunt a benevolence that did not necessarily exist in their program, except in a couple of State of the Union sentences. Obligated to make such scenes every once in a while though, the power team deigned to show up for a benefit or two. Vegas was always a money-spinner. So, what was the harm in patting the pathetic on their collective head, before turning to the really big dealings amongst Clark County's higher echelons, later on?

Plus, after business, plenty of FUN awaited, forbidden-style. Sex workers of all makes slapped on the depilatories and prepped their private parts. For the flab-bos who preferred food porno, the crab legs and multi-creams were all stocked up. Pretty much every self-respecting hotel/casino in town now had at least 15% of their toilet facilities fitted out with mega-wide porcelain steering wheels and gatherment-bowls – under 'ADA-Approved' auspices, naturally, which always pleased the corrupt contractor crowd. Casks of trumpet-beer and puncheons of bergin were tapped for the boozers, and the boutiques were straightened-up and dumbed down into more comfortable kitschy realms for the jewelry hags.

Look sharp! The guv-ment was coming to town!

The pennant-flown plaza was arranged so that devotees could approach the raised altar housing the Chosen Ones, via one central avenue of slowly-moving darshan-ites. Consultants had been brought in, representing the Bin Laden Group's Haj-All™ family of products. They expertly handled first-quality pilgrimages for high-class folks, so their advisement on how to handle cult-of-personality attractions was especially treasured. It was they who suggested this central mass approach to the Desirable Ones, as it was always a crowd-pleaser. (Tramplings in Mecca were downright unfashionable to mention.)

Security was never a problem, as threat-scanners and DRIN-optics operated well with the sluggardly crowds.

So the Designers set up a great review field, wherein the people could behold those that ruled them, to wonder at the actuality of their reality, which was larger than life. Indeed, when Leadership showed itself in the flesh, and, by doing so, proved its existence, it also established its requisite staying power as *permanent-seeming*. Today's mission – to establish staying power as *permanent-really*.

The Folk always tended to soften their grumblings after seeing leadership in person, no matter its character. One only had to behold the wonder of Dmitri Mochalski's 1949 masterpiece mural, 'They've Seen Stalin' (or 'After The Demonstration'), to see how even little kids are transformed by the magical powers of their leaders.

Many an enthusiast showed up and went through the security protocol in order to qualify as marvelers, and the place soon filled to capacity.

Astoundingly, they were all there: the President, his VP, all his secretaries (save one, just in case), and most of the Supreme Court (save Justice Beepus, who didn't fit in at all; he brooded in chambers, á la 'What the hell happened to mine own country?'), as well as notable senators and other Congresspeoplement.

It was an all-star cast because the Murn Administration felt it had to 'Hit 'em hard, hit 'em low, and when they get up, hit 'em again', as Yodeler of the House Cheech Malan had been harping, over and over again. Because, underneath the bravado and the overtly projected confidences, there was a thick layer of neurotic depression pressing down on the stage managers. The worries incumbent on the promotional team in maintaining the Administration's hegemony were almost as extensive as the bemused smugness spread by the top leaders on show.

All audience members were encouraged, once they got through security, to pay obeisance in the most explicit ways possible, so as to catch the attention of the numerous cameras and media capturements that packaged the event for worldwide consumption. This sort of intimidation was easy to inflict, as the carefully-selected audience consisted of persons so physically– and mentally-diminished that they would do anything for a free snack, a commemorative keychain, and a bit of cameo-ing on *LIVE* TV. Verily, they rated as extras in a cheapie production's crowd scene. Without a union, so to speak, but with an 'important' job to do. And others were indeed watching, all over the globe, to see, if nothing else, how the peoples of the US were so lovingly devoted to those now ensconced in DeeCee's power perches.

Persons of advanced disability (PADs) were especially catered to, for the hell if the Murn Administration was going to be caught going soft on the nation's ADA millions, as losing their vote meant relying on the goofballs of the religious extremes, whom they accommodated in words, but held in high contempt in private, as they very well might do. Trend-watchers such as the omnipresent Fish Darnley, Tappa den Teighp, and Joey 'Jeremiah' Wigplap had all counseled the Murns: 'America's disabled population is increasing exponentially. Hook, line, sinker 'em, then *reel 'em in*, before someone else does'. (Fish Darnley was especially proud of originating this analogy, based on St. Peter of course, to simultaneously appeal to the Rigorous Riligeous Rites, obviously.)

President Con Murn wanted to parade the cripples in order to show how perfectly capable they were, and therefore, any and all programs for them could now be scrapped. His speechwriter, Pemp Bapplastre, was already penning lines to be read momentarily, after this parade of human waste had gone by. He'd copied Jerry Wald's technique of penciling ideas while his hand was in his sport jacket's pocket, but instead of terrific movie concepts, Bapplastre's scrawlings were usually sneaky thoughts on how to screw over the public.

'Our diversity in cripples shows how they thrive. They're in the traditions of 'Don't Tread On Me' and 'Leave Me Alone To My Rugged Individualing'. So let's just let 'em be dignified and free from coddling. Wouldn't YOU want that for YOUR crippled or soon-to-be-crippled family member?'

...and much more bullshit like that.

Down's Syndrome people, cripples of all stripes, oldsters who fancied their scooters because they had the enthusiasm but hadn't the stamina (nor their driver's licenses anymore), and some really hardcore cases in motorized gurneys and boy-in-a-bubble portable ecoworlds were given bypass privileges onto the dais where the Olympians were. Of course, they were thoroughly scrutinized first.

The rally was really a good PR move, because every damn reporter on the scene was profiling this generous and humanitarian 'access to leadership'. Plus, it gained even more admiration by exceeding ADA requirements by half. With such heavy media coverage, the upshot would lead the nation into thinking that the Murns truly cared about the disabled. If the Administration could just get 65% of your average George W. Americans to say, 'Boy, if that cripple was *me*, shaking the POTUS' hand (despite my hand being laced with leprosy or Ebola or sarcoma), just the fact that he's touchin' me makes me wanna do anything he asks...' then they'd have the USA safely secured in their bag, *in perpetuity*.

It was a wildly brilliant strategy, and one that promised to wildly succeed.

In that very lineup, on this cloudless and freshie day, with a crutched friar before him and a three-year-old in an automated wheeled device behind him, none other than Marshall Vogg was positioned. *The* Marshall Vogg, the quadruple amputee from his long-lost existence in the Russel Arms apartment scene, who'd made such a sudden and surreal impact on Butterbugs during his ordeal there.

Now, today, Marshall had managed to steer and gear his ol' reliable battery-powered bathchair along, albeit with the only stumpy tool he had: what was left of his right arm, which wasn't much, though it was more than his other selection of limbs.

Marshall – the guy whose flat Butterbugs had crashed when he was so needy in spirit and so vacant of mind. So long ago.

Marshall – he was here on a mission, because, as a veteran and a (severely) disabled one at that, he had an interest in what this Administration planned to do with types such as he.

He had taken a long time to reach Vegas from LA. Because, hell, he had aimed this very bathchair thither, along the Barstow route, on a journey that would rate with Cherry-Garrard's as one of the world's worst. No journalist had championed this heroic effort. No journalist even knew of it, nor VA officials, either. It was accomplished deep within the obscurity that enveloped the rest of the cripple's twilit existence. However, after adventures beyond the scope of most people's imagination, Marshall had actually arrived in Clark County's metropolis, in plenty of time for today's gathering. About a year ahead of time, in point of fact.

So, he'd hung at Caesar's and made a tiny but tidy fortune laboriously pumping slugs into the slots. There were nights when he'd motored to the bus stop with an open plastic barrel full of silver dollars, but people were generally so repulsed by his appearance that he progressed without fear of robbery, and his coin-heap had grown gigantic. One beverage waitress, who covered the lesser slots, made a point of being especially kind to him, but she was soon fired on account of 'customer favoritism'. Mercifully, Marshall never learned of her subsequent suicide.

The days passed and he bided his time. One slot after the other.

The day came, and he was ready.

Predictably, Marshall looked poorly, as there was no way he could present himself as someone who could actually compete in looking normal for the political people. What remained of his hair was long and lank. He had all sorts of skin problems. Sad eyes, red-rimmed. Snot gobs clung to the wild strands of his nose hairs, and the presentation of his body below chin level was nothing short of disturbing. As in: an introduction to all sorts of thoughts for the observer to perversely ponder. Such as, how does he manage to do this, and how does he manage to do that...

Indeed, what was it *like* to be Marshall Vogg? Tod Browning might have responded, via film! Lon Chaney could have attempted a portrayal! Or cast members from 'El Topo' (ABKCO, 1970)! Regardless, all would invariably look away...

But that was how Marshall was, and he had been this way for some time now. That did not mean, however, that he had totally accepted his condition. There were questions still to be asked, and yes, scores to be settled. Because he had gotten fucked-up in service to his country, and nobody had cared, so far.

For years he had heard all the bullshit explanations for the firefights and gas-leaks that had deprived him of his limbs, and how they'd been so important for the transmission of liberty and democracy throughout the world. The genericness of the explanations (especially regarding the specific disaster in which he was altered, somewhere in Mesopotamia) had worn thin. Because that was all they – those in power – kept repeating, out of convenience. You know the line: that such sacrifices are necessary to keep the theoretical peace. This, despite the fact that there was no peace at all. Only protracted low-level warfare, for the benefit of the few, at the cost of the many, both local and imported. Thus, the not-so-beloved Military-Industrial-Congressional Complex (as highlighted by Ike), doing what it does best, and business was darn good. Better than ever.

So, there were just a few things that had never been resolved for Marshall in his debilitated state. He'd hoped, in this session with the Administration, here in Vegas today, to address a few of his concerns to the people who had access to the power to do something about his and others' concerns. After all, it wasn't only himself that he cared about...

He figured, if they could just see him in all his sincerity, all his reality, a point might be made. No tokenism, no fakery. On the other hand, he'd made points before, and always, the response was the same: 'You should get some help.' True, but 'help' was very selective about who it actually helped, and how. The complications had been soul-destroying. Right now, for Marshall, the company line was down to this: 'Hey, you signed up, and you were in the wrong place at the wrong time. Sorry.' Authority had determined that no entity was responsible for his condition, except one: Marshall himself. So he'd just have to 'make do'.

He'd bided his time. One slot after the other.

But today, he'd have to try another approach.

That was why Marshall was at the rally today. That was why he was in the lineup. It was still worth making an effort to make his point. And he was going to make it in front of the Commanders themselves, and the Commander-in-Chief *him*self.

At last, some justice seemed possible.

However, as the occasion progressed, it was soon apparent that the Administration present had no intention whatsoever of doing anything but appearing for appearance's sake. An appearance of smiles and glad-handing and ineffectual claptrap, that added up to nothing. Why, the devoted who'd waited so long in the lineup were not even allowed to deliver testimonials lauding those whom they regarded as their champions! Neither a single word, nor a concise paragraph. Not even boot-licking or blowjobbing. Nothing.

Plainly, they were requested to 'Move along, and keeping moving. There's a good cripple...'

Seeing this in the company ahead of him, Marshall let his laboriously-typed speech, which he'd held between his few teeth up to now, drop down onto the matted surface of the bathchair's footrests, which his stumps of course never reached.

It was time to engage in his Plan 'B'. For there *was* a 'B', all ready to engage.

Well, that was what he expected, really. That was why he was more prepared in

'B' than 'A'. He'd already feathered his thorny bed of expectations, so as to gird himself for the actual encounter.

'B' it would be.

Comforted that his limited existence might now be granted some sense of purpose, so that his upcoming 'appointment' might be accommodated and realized, Marshall smiled for the first time in years. Assuredly, he was on the threshold, and hoped beyond hope that his sole involvement in seeking resolve regarding so many of the issues of today might be achieved. It was almost like a gift of charity, this sole notion, this one hope. Was it possible? He could truly be himself now, the real man, rather than just a shattered image. A man of great depth and courage, which was all he ever could be, and was more than enough to make his point. Whether that alone would be sufficient to ensure its success had yet to be proven.

In the meantime, an obstacle course had yet to be negotiated.

As a vet, and a very bunged-up one at that, Marshall enjoyed a mini-bit of backstage privilege. His cards and his papers were shown. How nice that the guard didn't say, 'Could you take 'em out of that plastic envelope?' No, he was all legit. Preliminary security sent him on his grasping way, with his bathchair proceeding at just-engaged speed, which really ate up battery time.

It ate up other things too, like bodily-function time. The wait was so long, the assistance so minimal, that embarrassing breakdowns were sure to happen. They did. Marshall's waste retention system, tenuous at the best of moments, was compromised to say the least, due to the lengthy queuing to reach the Selected Ones.

So, now that he could truly be himself, his thoughts ran. They ran at top speed, on strong legs and with pumping arms, free. Free at last.

If it was one thing Marshall had evolved into, it was a thinker. Stephen Hawking he wasn't, but, in a way, maybe he was even more advanced. It was because, unlike the great Hawking, Marshall had done his thing alone. And his thinking. Every last thing had been sorted through, strained after, suffered through, all by his lonesome. So while the far more publicized thinker had access to every technical aid, and the love of millions, Marshall's long and winding road led to bungalows without Bills and wildness without honey pies. Plus, he was so very much more capable when it came to facilities. After all, his appendages had been radically altered is all; not his entire physical being.

At any rate, Marshall had thoroughly researched the players in today's game. He'd tapped a lot of politically-savvy website clicks at his local Milldnumb branch library. And because the public was so repulsed by him, he could hog the terminal in the Reference Dept. all day. He even had a 12-hour piss bucket capacity, so all he did was learn, learn, learn. Hell, his sicko 'mates' at the Russel Arms thought he was out gambling or begging all day, but there he was, improving and edifying himself. Purpose-wise, he wasn't quite sure about it all. But all he knew was that he'd found purpose, and there was nothing else to do but to go forward…

Forward to…

He was so brilliantly organized in his mental sensibilities and critical responses, that if he had had Hawking-like access and tech assist with online and social media, a rather erudite and pithy pamphlet might have emerged from his sardonically-accurate assessments. They were of course formulated on the spot, immediately upon witnessing, which transpired so rapidly that no conventional chronicling could ever ensue.

Nevertheless, as if any document of record could indeed have resulted, here is what it might have resembled:

Marshall's Non-Written Mental Notes On A Gang Of Many Who Run One Of The World's Most Noteworthy Nations

Preface

Well, here I am, on the scene. Here in Vegas. It's a big deal. I'm right up near the people who run my country. Here are some of my observations, in the order encountered. And the weird thing is, I'm really physically close to them, and despite my fucked-up body, I can see and hear them pretty good. So it shouldn't be too surprising that I notice a lot of physical stuff, and how people come off, even based on superficial first impressions. I use cuss words a lot, throughout.

They're all so hard to believe, these 'top leaders', as they call them on the official websites. And for an Administration which is blatantly racist and bigoted, the selection is breathtakingly diverse – in the weirdest of ways. Just wait! And please believe me, I take no great pleasure in outlining these – these *fiends*. I'm an always-sick man, and these entities make me feel sicker.

I have to ask questions like: Is this a parody? A satire? A burlesque?

Here's what I found firsthand, to back up what I already know, what *America* already knows, but hasn't done anything about...

Keep in mind folks, these people are *criminals*. Their offenses are document-ed. It's just that they're so well protected, they've become invincible. Latter-day Rome was a bubble gum 'n' creampuff party for 'Ding Dong School' (NBC, 1952–56) graduates, in comparison.

Only one thing to do: read this and shriek. *THEN GET ORGANIZED.*

Cabinet Positions

0. VPOTUS Fendal Kraypstane. What the fuck kind of name is *that?* He's just like I thought he'd be. A Vice-President who can run stuff without doing all the 'president' shit. He's too fuckin' ugly anyway. Yeah, he's the Great American Psy-chopath who hates himself first, so there's only one thing to do: hate everybody else and make it look like it's for a good reason. Sorry, but I'm prejudiced. I hate this fucker. I wish there was something I could really *do* to help everyday people be relieved of him. Un-frikkin'-speakable.

0a. I just have to mention his wife, Lally, whom I've heard all about. There she stands, the whole cow, right next to him, feeling him up. Can you believe it? Hell, if I had my hands, I'd push 'em *both* onto a flaming rubbish heap.

1. Sec'y of State Hope Cripe is actually pretty harmless. But she's always so mealy-mouthed and simp-brained, there isn't one half a cell of originality in her being, virtuous *or* devious. She's conventionally attractive and happily married, which helps on the diplomatic front, but Murn Inc. keep her in the dark on everything of importance, and she loyally follows all orders, probably fearing for her and her family's lives. I have to admit, I find her quite admirable in the looks department, and she's eschewed the conventional 'dressing for success'. There she is, in a Gaultier bustier-cum-halter top, a gauzy boho flounce-skirt, Nancy Worden junk-jewelry, and blonde hair-twirls down to her trim derriere. But sorry, looks just can't make up for deeds. She's essentially contemptible for her participation with these psycho freaks. I brand her 'Hope*less*.'

2. Treasury: Bean Block-Bisteard. He's such a tiresome cliché. Corporate, Wall St., whatever. He's done it all, mainly through armaments. He looks like some guy who'd be driving an obnoxious Gurrywander motorcycle – with training wheels, no less. Cuz he's really a wimp. Dainty motherfucker can't even handle looking at any of us disableds. Glad we make him vomit. He's a sin-kisser and a dissolute rake-humper. Total pervert. Buys used mattresses then jacks off on them while wearing budget pantyhose.

3. Defense: Rhadamanthus Smith. *This* shit-lipped ass-sucker has done everything contemptible in the book. And it's not even *my* book. How the hell else would he get to be Head War-Cheerleader for our very own POTUS? Hatred isn't a strong enough word for how I feel about this soul-destroyer and children-crippler.

4. Attorney-General Dippie Bluppo is a head-injury rubber-stamper who has nothing to do all day but agree to what the Murnists lurking above may require. Plus, he is a drunkard of the most base incarnation. While drunk, he's a perfectly sweet guy, but at other times, his rage is incalculable. 'Rage gets things *done*,' the VPOTUS is known to say in trusted circles. And he goes on: 'Rage keeps a man alive. *My* kind of rage, of course. *I* believe in justice first. Love really doesn't come into it. Bluppo agrees.'

5. Perhaps the most shameful is Sec'y of the Interior Yohn Smith, who, as everyone knows perfectly well, is a convicted sex offender, whose specialty is young boys and girls, specifically from ages nine and three quarters, to twelve and seven eighths. That's how fucked up this psycho is. However, the Murn Administration has always maintained that he may be one batshit-crazy individual, but he's a pret-

ty decent Sec'y of the Interior. Mainly because he got General-Standard Grain and Chaff that terrific deal on back-door access to the Cambie Goodfellow Permanent Relief From Human Infiltration Tract in the Missouri Coteau, and that was good enough for the Murn Cartel.

6. Agriculture: Vent Spylz (non-present Government-Preserver). He's kind of an OK guy, and not 'in' on any of the others' shitty acts.

7. Sec'y of Commerce Fabian Lavandar Squeeqwux is an especially curious case. An African-American ex-Burgerball player from Arkansas who's more conservative than anyone else in this extremely conservative Cabinet. He has so much contempt for his race that he coats every inch of his body with PailMor Créme twice a day, so as to de-emphasize his blue-black complexion. The results are insultingly obscene, with his whole being having the æsthetic effect of a person masked in places of orificial access, then pressure-washed with a kerosene-based solvent, before spray-painting from a vat of children's spit-up/kaka from overindulgence of butterbrickle milk shakes. The effect is one to illicit an 'oh...*ick!*' response from any onlooker. Yet this fellow's (blurred) signature is on every legal tender note in the American money system. He looks more genuinely sick-making than even I do.

8. Candy Bootmeatt, Labor. Looks more frightening than me! Face is a virtual zit-board, hands a landscape of blackheads and suppurating whiteheads, more used to masturbating flaccid hopelessness than sorting taters or toting frozen fresh-pack boxes. Some laborer! In my high school days I was hauling 75 lb. fish-pack boxes at Jale's Freezery & Fishage Jetties, and it built me into quite a fella. I had me three girlfriends at once, folks. Although you'd never believe to see me now... This candy-assed National Laborer has a sicko wife named Yurma, with eyes that look like bags of blood. I'm not makin' *any* of this shit up, you know.

9. Babbs Klawdatsch is Health & Human Services Sec'y, with enough outrageous irony to render her impossibly incapable of empathic – let alone sympathetic – service to the public. She is a vape-freak, mainlines muffreine (a nicotine distillate), and spreads cold lard on her sugarslab pancakes, just to give health nuts the finger. She is rumored to have taken a contract out on her husband Fiep, so as not to submit to his sexual advances, as she is even more terrified of children than she is hateful of them. The fact that Fiep evaded her contract and ended up marrying the glamorous actress Feather Saltchurch (after a judicious and respectful period following her affair with Butterbugs was concluded) makes her even *more* twisted with sociopathic abnormalities.

10. Jennysuckle Hawfpijp, Sec'y of Housing & Urban Development, whose parentage stems from the obscure Dutch enclave of Spoorio in Western Sahara. Had

never seen a community with a larger population than twenty or so until her six-
ty-seventh year. She's largely confined to her Digberry Ave. housekeeping studio
apartment, as a shut-in. Strange to see her here. She looks like she doesn't even
know what day it is, or who the President is… Poor thing. Or should I say, *Lucky*
thing. She hates 'the poors', as she calls them.

11. Transpo Sec'y Plasta Keip-Vastoway's body is so bulemiactically distorted that
her abdominal aorta plainly shows through her skin-tight yoga top, which showcases
her baboon-nipples to an almost prurient extent. Then she's got a dirndl outfit below
that, which showcases nothing. Plus, she is so profoundly bucktoothed, her upper
chompers protrude from her rubbermouth at an almost horizontal angle. It is true that
I admire girlish torsos that have more straight lines than soft curves, but this bundle
of 2x4s – with compositional roofing tacked on – (cuz that's exactly what she looks
like!), is positively libido-crushing. Her slutty posings amongst her cabinet companions plainly betray a horniness that does not care to settle for any male escort offerings
that surely await in her suite of privilege. Anyone with any sense would be hopping
transport AWAY from her boudoir, as fast as possible.

12. Sec'y of Energy, Barllt Cobamuck. Without a doubt, the most violent of
Murn's cronies. He likes sawn-off shotguns, Flitcher knives, and rape. He's
enough to bring credibility to Phrenology. Droolin', pawin', pantin', disgraceful
bastard. I wish I could warn all the sex workers in Vegas to avoid him tonight. Or
better yet, to set him up for a sting operation. Oughta have his balls arrested and
sent to Death Row. Along with the rest of him.

13. Sec'y of Ed, Cobb-Cotter Secksmarque. You know, this dude is *probably* the
most bizarre of 'em all. No, *the* most bizarre. I think he's an Annamese who got
some French time, then opened the FryMelt Chicken Silo in Chantilly, right next
to the Pentagon, when he met some guys, who got him the Ed gig. He has a brush
haircut, wears big Allen Sherman glasses, beige skin, thin black tie, white short-
sleeved shirt, black frock coat, and fishing gaiters. He sports a button that says,
'Hey! Who Made Off With My Rod 'n' Reel?? HUH??' He just stands there,
saying nothing. Hell, I don't know if he even knows how to spell, let alone talk.

14. Then there's my very own ostensible Carer and Steward himself, Ho-Wo
Dean-General, Vets' Affairs In-Charger, who presides over a Department soon
to be axed from the American scene. That's the Murn Administration's plan, I
tell you what. Not even a military man (or even a man at all, but possibly an
amorphous hermaphrodite), the person overseeing millions of vets' affairs is a
paper-pusher of the most odious character and mien. His/her ectomorphic embodiment, mercifully draped with macramé hangings today, seems no more than
some sub-animated pile of grey art-dough, excremental clay of a lesser kind, and
supremely malleable by powers higher. A flabby-lipped mouth-breather, childish-

ly nose-picked, fartingly-stalled – right where the POTUS & Co. want him/her.

15. Sec'y of Homeland Security Bentram Risticalifrum is a sadistic SOB who wants nothing more than to hurt the world's people – on a huge and unprecedented scale. Even Con Murn thinks he overdoes things a bit, but privately thinks him advantageous in the high labors of empire-building that lie ahead. 'He'll be my badass in the many wars to come,' the POTUS was known to whisper winkingly to the VPOTUS, in moments of merriment. I always insert the 'In' prefix before 'Security' when referring to Sec'y Risticalifrum's still-infantile department.

16. Postmaster General Greggus LoPlampoMus possesses an outthrust gut that is so herniated a steam-powered wheelbarrow probably couldn't budge it. There he sits on his special ironbar-reinforced blob-platform, working on his fifth Big Breakfast, specially ordered from The Trop, clear down the Strip. I doubt if he could even hand-deliver a cyber-dimensioned e-mail, let alone 55 lb. packets of explode-o-gel ordnance that I myself had been hefting that day of my... accident. Of course, he's not even a fuckin' Cabinet-level schruzz, but Murn installs him here because he thinks the public needs a grotesque icon to fear.

(Other Top Leaders are present, not worth noting.)

Non-Cabinet Positions

Yodeler of the House: Cheech Malan. You know, ever since they officially changed 'Speaker' to 'Yodeler', so as to keep Congress 'light' and 'just plain folks', the cheapness has become unacceptable. There's just no other way to explain it. The Yodeler doesn't even have to be able to yodel, either. A far as Cheech Malan is concerned, he's a huge believer in apartheid, and just because he sold used cars for Cal Worthington and Ralph Williams – and was fired by both – that doesn't mean he can wield a gavel in today's House. Then again, maybe it *does* mean he can... It's *that bad*...

(Other Congressionals are present, scarcely worth noting.)

Chair, Joint Cheaphs: Daylon Geppuchchiatta. I think he's actually a general, of 'Nam experience, though I don't know how honorable. He's the most shady, shadowy, and mysterious of the Murn crowd. Can hardly find anything *on* him. I think he was heavily into the Dirt Wars in Rinlinplaster, Orange Free State. Really bad, raunchy shit. He was undoubtedly involved with the Maj. Bepminster scandal as well, but I can't prove it – yet. Bigamist, too.

(Other Militaries are present, totally not worth noting.)

CIA Arranger: Marp Clantrums. Probably the most perverse individual in the USA. How could the head of CIA *not* be? Was personal friends with the guy in Enumclaw, WA who wanted a horse to fuck him, but his senior canal couldn't handle it. Clantrums read the eulogy at his black mass funeral. Short, cocky bastard, too.

Nat'l Security Targeter: Queirum-Eulellus Jakenail. A repellant snake-like person, notorious for being a cheapskate. Yet in his vanity, he wangled federal funds to build his own mansion, on his own private property, an exact replica of the White House, but seven times larger. The entire basement is given over to dungeon culture. Passionately interested in the movies, his contribution to the cinema is to facilitate the production of snuff films, shot in his basement. He usually gets Executive Producer credit, too.

(Other Securities and Agents mixed all around, impossible to note.)

Beilan Sprakcode, Fed Chair. He's a real loser. And guess what, he's a cripple. In a bathchair. Lifeless legs, but arms of devious power. He hates democracy more than your basic shithead CEO. Does everything he can to spread hate 'n' discontent. Takes out his impotence on poor folk. Hell, I could take out *everything* on him, if I wanted to, and I'd have the better excuse. I hear tell that old Alan Greenjeans, confined to the crazy house now, calls him up twice a day and yells, 'Beilan? You seen my plastic dinosaurs?' And this fucker puts in more time and attention soothing that old despot, and lying to him that he's *found* the dinosaurs, and he'll be right over to deliver 'em. Fuckin' A, he should be fixing the economy, not giving the Devil a blowjob.

(Other Financials are up there with the biggies, too sickening to note.)

Supreme Courters

0. Pricemore Terry Fieastakins is an entirely different kind of Chief Justice. He collects fingernail clippings he finds on public transportation while incognito (usually a comedy mustache and tinted pince-nez). His personal hygiene is simply nonexistent. The general feeling is that anyone in his courtroom can't wait to get out, the conditions of environmental degradation are so objectionable. However, Chief of Justices Fieastakins has won award after award for efficient justice-giving, even though an astounding 72% of his cases have been overturned, and he's had an alarmingly high rate of defendants who've been summarily executed, yet found to be innocent upon DNA test run-throughs, later on. What a pig-shitter. Call him, 'Chiefly Justice', I cheerily quip. But hardly for *all* – if any…

1. Associate Justice-ette Mellory Peastisz is another piece of work. She was born in a court's backroom in an unspecified west Texas courthouse, the result of a corrupt judge's unholy union with a Salvadoran sex slave, kept in the basement. Therefore, Mellory thought it was her birthright to dictate terms from the bench. So did others, who elevated her by every sleazy method to the top court hall of the nation. She is a complete and utter fake, knowing nothing about Law, or jurisprudential reasoning. Incredibly, she is totally illiterate – *still!* – and functions wholly from a well-planted earphone (as if she's supposedly ear-challenged – another fraud), which receives every last instruction to recite in her less-than-illustrious record of botched decisions, (ghost) writings, and flubbed posings. She also has no teeth.

2. Associate Justice Justus Pestus Cleumichael is a study in hideousness. He bitches about everything. Bitch, bitch, bitch! Nobody has ever heard anything like it. Married nine times, he always self-divorces himself just for the fun of it. He also regularly urinates in the many plant holders that he insists on having in his court, despite prohibiting regulations. 'Well then,' he said when challenged, 'looks like I'll just have to prohibit the prohibiting regulations!' What an asshole.

(3–8. Other jurisprudencers are present, absolutely not worth noting, except to say that those who can still stand are clapping their hands and discoing to the connivings of Con and the gang, but they scarcely merit my dry and sober evaluations.)

9. Associate Justice Roarald Tennunian Beepus (non-present Court-Saver). His record is upright and solid. I'm glad he's back in DC and not intermixing with these felons and boobs.

President

00. Conelrad 'Con' Padpompom Murn is the current President, and I'll bet you anything he plans to take over the government and become President For Life. Oh yeah, he does. Bob Jones degree in Indeterminate Studies. 'Distinguished' grad work at Drumpf University (Secaucus campus).

00a. Belle 'Belley' Murn (née Jelleigh). First Lady, but not much else. Married to Con Murn, anyone would be in the deepest of the shadows that resulted. So she drank. Still does. Big time. Betty Ford was a name no longer known in the White House. Belley also has the quality of character that is basically nonexistent. Plain beyond hope, inaccessible, forgettable, childless, talentless, she is the perfect foil for her husband's bisexual peccadilloes, and the perfect audience for Lally Kraypstane's endless blabbing. No sympathy-sink though, Belley privately hates everyone and everything she comes into contact with, especially all those cancer kids she has to smile at, 'every other minute', as she puts it.

Conclusion

Previously, I asked the following questions: Is this a parody? A satire? A burlesque?

I can answer them now, each with the same answer:

No.

I wish people could know what I've thought here. Or read it, hear it, *understand* it. But know this, world: I deplore violence. Not just because of what it did to me, but everything about it in principle. Violence is a failure. War is a failure. *I* am a failure. Thus, my decision to…

Here I am. This is remarkable. A life of misfortune, fulfilled at last. But you know, seeing this shit today, I'm so happy now – that this is the life I've lived. I'd do it all over again. I couldn't have wished for more.

They're all here.

Vive Valeque!

[END of Marshall's observations.]

'These are they,' Marshall starkly yet sagely observed, 'who occur when fascism reaches its true operational capabilities.'

In his limited huntings and peckings, as proven by his trenchant 'Non-Written Mental Notes', he'd thoroughly researched these top leaders and their hangers-on, and that gave him all the confidence he needed to serve the nation on this occasion. In light of such disturbingly aberrant company, he was actually glad to be a severely limited and disadvantaged person. For if those with their full facilities, where scratching their balls or plucking their eyebrows were unconscious acts of great capability and ease, nevertheless chose to pervert and exploit humanity rather than raise it up and improve it – hopefully on an unprecedentedly egalitarian level – then it was a world he did not necessarily wish to…

'Hey, you! Look sharp! You're approaching the leader of a free world!' a sour voice hollered to no one in particular.

'Yeah, HIS world,' thought Marshall bitterly.

Since his own personal disaster, he had always hoped his bitterness would prove such a caustic secretion from what glands remained that it would corrode his systems as surely as the bottom of a water heater rusts-out from hard times that result from hard water. All he hoped for was the peace of nothingness. But no, deprived of even that, he lived on, writhing in the self-produced acidic generations his body, mind and soul would never release him from. It was as if he lay in a tray of his own bilious discharges, as if he actually needed reminding of bitterness' purpose in the human experience.

'Get with it! Spit-polish them shoes, and do it NOW, troops!' the sour-dude bellowed, without even noticing that Marshall had neither feet, nor shoes worth polishing, nor shoes at all.

'Wait till yore Cummandr-in-Cheaph flunks yer sorry-ass inspection!'

'I'll bet that overweight, head-shaved, aviator-mirror-sunglasses-wearing bastard usually never gets away from his desk job typewriter the whole time; that is, while he isn't sex-slaving, either for some sergeant's wife, or some sergeant himself...,' Marshall mused, as he observed the ersatz 'Marine' traffic cop who attempted to keep this battalion moving. In his own active duty days, he'd seen plenty of such types enjoy sex servitude, while his buddies slew themselves from guilt, depression, or trauma, one by one.

'No, I never did it as *they* did it,' Marshall self-reviewed. 'Mainly cuz no fingers to press a trigger, nor palms to hold enough pills...'

Actually, this was no time to retrospect about past choices and consequences. The national leadership was yonder, and maybe, just maybe, Marshall's very presence, insignificant and damaged though it was, would make a difference.

'Could my country's fate be this dire?' Marshall asked himself as a lump grew in his parched throat. 'Oh yes. It could. And it is. That is why I am here this day. That is why I am in this lineup. That is what my studies have shown, and what I have overheard just now. The reason I am here. For my moment. Of truth? That I do not know... Besides, why should *I* be the one to answer such a question...?'

Holy shit, then! How he had contempt for these poseurs! Why them and not him? Well, that was already settled. No argument now. In fact, a certain serenity had floated over his daily ordeal. Just think: the nightmare was about to end. Amidst the distraction of making sure the inexorable progression went ahead, there were also ancillary thoughts as to the finiteness of the moment, and about how he wouldn't have to go through daily life as an appalling four-strong amputee any longer, and that it would all end as it should've when his first big bang had hit, although Providence had other ideas.

Providence! *Was* there a Providence?

Actually, this was no time to forecast about future choices and consequences. The national leadership was yonder, and maybe, just maybe, Marshall's very presence, insignificant and damaged though it was, would make a difference.

Now, he himself, Marshall, had other ideas. He was taking command, and being responsible in his actions. Here he was, poised to do what most people only dreamt about. All those poor, disadvantaged ones who went to their daily jobs and bitched about stuff, yet hadn't the stuff to change reality, even though they were far better-placed to do so than he, a member of the *truly* disadvantaged and disenfranchised. Oh well, this was his solemn and bitter role in life, and now, at this stage, and up *on* it, he was either going to enact his destiny – at least the one he most wanted – or else he was going to fail and fade into a thousand filaments of forgotten fibers, on his way through the cracks below.

He had already made the choice, because he foresaw failure in every other possibility. Therefore, resolve was set in concrete, and it was setting-up fast. He was happy about the future of the country, the country he had served. Oh yes, the VA certainly would have assisted, after a fashion, in his presence here this day. They would have straightened his crookedly-mounted medals and seen to his comfort. But that wasn't Marshall's point to be made. Unlike those Administrators way up there, his was no mere appearance, left for others to interpret without knowing his story. Any such agency could acquit themselves by doing what they were created to do, by doing only the minimal. Marshall didn't want such support right now, for his attention was anchored on the Policy Makers, not the Caretakers (who could only act after the Policy Makers' deeds). Anyone could sit back and claim benefits. Marshall's solo mission was to concentrate on sources. Only there could the truth he sought be found.

Alas, he had indeed messed himself, and the consequences were pretty dire. Because there were no trained helper-persons along the way at this juncture, cases such as Marshall – and he wasn't the only one – were simply ushered along, lest unpleasantness linger, even amongst those who mindlessly assisted in the über-cause. Any enfouled cripples could be hosed down later, probably in a gravel parking lot.

A roll of paper towels, the disableds' best friend, was made available in case he needed them. It was placed on the mat next to his fallen speech by a peon-ette named Hi! I'm Becky, who wore a stars & stripes miniskirt, had thick thighs, and winced at Marshall's plop-leak, then mockingly held her nose, so that her fellow 'helpers' could snicker playfully from their hang-outs near the far sexier Tarpit security dudes.

'Oll jist tuck it on down there, darlin', so thit nob'dy sees what a nasty li'l ol' mess yer in…,' she giggled. 'Ewww-weee! Looks like yer mommy fergot ta pack them dy-purrs!'

'Fuck! What a cow!' thought Marshall, and quite merrily, too. 'I'd hate to see *her* nude!'

He was especially cheered when he noticed that the paper towels, so conscientiously-tucked, nevertheless slipped off his rig, the entire roll newly slimed with his soft-stool gravy, as a gift.

Even when it came to the vaunted Secret Service, they looked at him askance. Here was this mutilated guy with his bulky and very dated electric bathchair, all soiled and icky, grandfathered in by his admitted veteran's prerogative. And what the hell, the dais was ventilated enough, and the sentiment lay with the vets. Simple assignment: move 'em on through and keep 'em rolling. The SS were doing their duty just by being here and using the 'Think Method' on all these harmless cripples. Besides, after this little tea dance, all eligible agents could dine later at the CircusCircus's buffet (for free), and chow and chew over the day's labors amongst themselves. Meanwhile, the Nation's VIPs would HQ at the Heavenly, Vegas' newest and most elite hotel/casino. ('Heaven's Our Theme, And Sky's The Limit's Our Meme!')

So Marshall moved on through, and kept moving, at baby-crawl speed. The miniature American flag on his poorly-mounted baseball cap tried to flutter, but seemed more suited to a froufrou cocktail glass.

Empty glass. Soiled. On a rubbish heap.

Diane Arbus moments!

His own shit certainly disgusted him, and its public appearance really was unplanned, to say the least. Yet, it was opportune. The Secret Service had indeed noted and processed his tainted craft. They'd run their (surgical gloved) hands over it, and yes, the run-out of the owner's bowels had been duly noted. But it was the demeanor of the driver, the poor fellow who'd been disadvantaged by his disability, that softened the heart of the guardians to the upper fields of Elysium, just ahead. Besides, a Hispanic cleanup crew waited on the further side, to see to such casualties. No fire hoses, but they *were* sited on a gravel lot... The imperative was to just get these cripples through the VIP bottleneck, then do mop-up afterwards.

Coupla 'consultant' types, very privately contracted to Murn, versed in the 'new' PR, considered him.

'Hey Brandendenen, cover this guy, aiming at a sympathy slot. Can't even hold his crapper, either out of fetishistic devotion to the Führer, or because of inherent breakdown. I say we let him proceed.'

'No problem there, Gatekeeper. He'll make a good poster child, but not with the shit scattered hither and yon. Nevertheless, it *is* a badge of sorts. Last I heard, everybody has to take a dump sometime. If the public see it, Con might lay on hands. He needs more 'Bernadette' moments, let me tell you that right now. The Healer! I like that. Let him on through. Sympathy's got a big boner in anticipation. Inform all of them up the line, via earbone phone.'

'Oh, OK. The more pathetic the better, I suppose. Holy shit, that guy don't have nothin'! Can you imagine being him and having to take a crap? Well, Hell's belles, I guess he just did, dint he? So *that's* how he does it. Wonder how he takes a piss? I mean, really! What the hell. Let's move him on in.'

'Secure?'

'Shit's more secure than anything.'

'OK, roll him on through and we'll take the consequences. I'm sure the committee will thank us in the end. If we'd missed the photo op, we'd be fried, ya know.'

'Right this way.'

Though Marshall's battery had only a matter of minutes left in its weary loyalty, it nevertheless conveyed him on up the ramp that led to the holy moments with the Essential Ones. The annoying whine of his way out-of-date conveyance added to the tension of those who noticed it, as all security personnel are wont to do. But the urgency of making this whole show work included all possibilities of participants, just to keep it going, even though this parade involved some fairly forbidding entities, such as Marshall's 'float', as it were.

All right, enough exposition as to Marshall's attaining the sublime level of show-off and approach, but was he really going to do what it took to portray his honesty in front of the world?

He glided toward the people in power, and he heard them speak. Professionals all, they spoke in a sort of casual patois that was their own. Nothing memorable, but all was geniality and even good-timey.

Then, as the atmosphere became more rarefied as the ramp leveled off, Marshall slowed to a stop before the *Very*VIP stretch. He bore his humiliation with overt serenity, as he always did, and remembered to hold his head high, though up here, no one was really looking. It was one of those unexplainable phenomena, wherein a person or thing can be in plain sight and hearing, but its existence is inextricably denied. Probably because some sort of aura hovered around him that warned of his utter repulsiveness, so as to keep the sensitivities of others protected and at a distance. It was true, nobody noticed him.

Except one.

'Goodness, sakes, we can't have *that*,' said Lally, the wife of the Vice-President of the United States of America. She being a bit of a hands-on Western gal, who still bragged about shoveling her own horse's manure whenever she visited the ranch at Nashua, Montana, now took up an oriental rug (loaned by Dimple's Bollywood Hotel & Casino) and she herself draped it about Marshall's bathchair so that all foulness was concealed. Characteristically, she didn't even notice the actual passenger of the bathchair, but only her handiwork, which was successful. Many a camera snapped and whirred at the photo op, which ceased the moment Lally withdrew, brushing her hands off and leering at her people, as if to imply, 'Can I cook, or what?'

Lally, with a horse-gal's ass so wide Super Technirama 70 wouldn't be able to take it all in, was in her glory. Here she was in *Vegas*, with the imperial power structure nigh, posing next to her husband, whom she controlled, who in turn controlled the nation. Never was there a more perfect life than to be Lally Schippurkee Kraypstane, Mistress of the Known World.

She nudged the First Lady, Belle 'Belley' Murn, with another tall tumbler-drink.

'Last night, when Lane 'n' me was whoopin' it up in the Rope 'Em Bar, when I commenced to hear 'tee hee! tee hee!', I *knew* there was a fight a-brewin'! Peoples from the intellectuals an' from the internets always say to me, 'Yer a bunch of hicks 'n' such, runnin' this here greatest country *ever*. What gives *you* the *right?*' Well Belley, you know th'only thing I say? I sez to those jackasses 'n' yoyos, 'Pardner, *we're* the real 'Muricans aroun' here. *Yer* jes' the misfires 'n' slugs sittin' aroun' spittin' bitter. *We're* the leaders 'n' doers cuz we're the winners. 'N I got a

Peston 45'er packin' on my horsey hip to defend my Second *Freakin'-A* Right fer bein' so!' That's all I say. Works ever time.'

'Yoo tellum, schisthter!' Belley slur-replied, shitfaced on Gurgle-Gal Basic Ginnies (provided by Miss Texina's Hotel 'n' Casino Fer Real, Tough, Chicks).

'Guzzle-pourer? Round up 'nother one for the Firstest of Our Ladies, huh?'

As the servant poured another spruceberry wine, Lally rolled over to her vice-presidential mate and looked back down her nose at the nearly falling-down drunk who was the nation's frontline dame.

'Sassy Lal! Whatever have you done, *now?*'

'Belley's all oiled 'n' ready fer her top-bunk bed – already,' Lally smiled to her hubby.

'Yeah, *big time*,' he smirk-answered.

'Derlin', you think she ever might... you know... *talk?* This here Vegas moon-shine makes her loonier than a drunken Comanche.'

'I hear ya, Big-Beautiful-Butt. But hey! Mindreader! Cuz later tonite, we've arranged a little floor show, after which she will 'expire from too much laughter'. In the faggy Rip Taylor Suite, too!'

'You is a genius, Bighorn. I won't miss that bitch. Does the Con Man have summun lined up?'

'Shit, I dunno. Summun's *always* lined up. He's into 'black trans' right now. Can you dig a 'First Ladyboy'?'

'Sounds like a spice-up to a borin' party, babe!'

'As long as it ain't Muzzlummns 'er Jieuws in the pilot seat! An' our Leader 'n' Teacher's got 'er sewn so that'll never happen anyway.'

'Merely genius, Derlin'.'

'Hey, wanna hear one a my own rare jokes? OK. This ugly Jieuwish dude goes up to this Muzzlummn fee-male covered with a black rag, and he sez ta her, 'Hey baby, wanna come be Jieuwish with me?' An' she sez, 'Sure! We're both Sem-mettics. How could we be 'anti' to each other?' Huh? And they say I don't have a sense of humor!'

'Fuck me now, Big Chunk. Here and now. Fuck me any way you want. Even in the ways I hate, but I love the way you think of 'em. Fuck me – in front of the Nation!'

'You mean, in front of these here li'l ol' cripples?'

'Them too. I wanna make 'em jealous!'

'They already are, More-Than-Full-Figured-Gal!'

'Come-own, come-own, come-own! Kiss my belt buckle – if'n yieu kin *find* it!'

'Back to work, Sex-Trap Fishbait. We gotta see this drive, all the way thru the cattle chute first. No time even fer brandin'. 'Sides, don' wannem ta overhear our, you know, *plans*...'

'Oh hell, Derlin', they're all got busted eardrums from all your shocks 'n' awes 'n' such.'

'Well, it takes a real *man* to defend this country. And the real *men* are the ones who conceive of the strategies, then give the orders. Those who *do* the orders are mere servants. There's good 'uns 'n' bad 'uns. No need to make 'em into *heroes* or anything.'

'Like, looka over yonder, at thet baby-sized freak on the rug I tossed aroun' 'im. Probly shoulda just burryed him with it. Put 'im outa his misery.'

Her husband's response was purely vice-presidential: 'Fuck! Hope *he* passes by faster 'n' a snot leak!'

'Shit, *he* couldn't do nothin' with my boobs. Guess they're safe. Maybe, 'stea-da that rug, I could bury him in my butt crack, then turn on the gas. Yeeeee-*haw!!* Watch this!'

The wife of the Vice-President of the United States of America mega-sashayed over to Marshall's conveyance.

'Hey li'l bundle of 'whatever', you could prob'ly use some lovin', huh? You know, without havin' to *pay* fer it? What you think of *these* curves, huh?'

She turned about and wiggled her industrial posterior.

Abashed at being so solicited, Marshall figured he'd better answer Mrs. V-P in a manner akin to her own casual, folksy style of speaking. So he cleared his throat and said the last thing he'd said to his fiancé when she visited him in the hospital after his horror, right as she turned to leave the room, and unbeknownst to him, left for the last time:

'You know something? You've got a *great ass!*'

He said it because it was true then, but not so true now.

Lally just *knew* that's what he'd say. What else *could* he say?

'Yiss ah *do*. Oh, but pity you, poor thang. Guess you cain't caress it, or do much more than kiss it, raht? Sorry hon. But them 'lips' a yours jes' don' seem up to muh *standards*, ya know? Might *chafe* the goods. But maybe I'll let ya, some day! Bah-bah!'

And she cute-walked away, assuming he'd be imploding from sperm-retention stress by now.

'Oh lady,' Marshall thought, looking askance, and then, heroically up into the skies, 'you know your patheticness not. And how you celebrate heartlessness!'

Only a gentleman would substitute 'heartlessness' for 'sadism' *in his own mental dialogue*. Yet, he allowed himself some levity: 'My God! What would *Goliath* do with such a thing...?'

There, as the setting sun was turning the great sky behind him rosy, and a far-up streak of cirrus seemed a faint pastel sketch of a laurel-leaf crown above his head – (also unnoticed, as it could only be discerned from one obtuse angle) – was Marshall, with the rug causing his bathchair to look like an oriental throne, and the delicacy of nature painting his features in soft and forgiving light in the seconds before he entered the harsh xeeron lamp zone. The much-altered veteran sat in a kind of magnificence, evanescent perhaps, but demi-divine.

He knew now that his whole life had been leading up to this one seminal moment, and he felt, for the first time, that it had all been worth it. Every atom of his remaining body and soul had come forward and were present in their unanimity, and he was at peace. There was still a performance to give, however, and he was up for it.

The white light of the lamps kicked in and the idyll vanished. Over-amplified blare-music turned the procession into a tacky frug, right out of a Burkmart Budget-Givers commercial. The taste and the tone of the Murn Administration was fully engaged. Even a cheap likker dive in North Las Vegas had more class in comparison. Character, too.

Closer, closer.

Then, despite all his intellectual analysis and insight, a protective amnesiac was instantly generated, and it descended over Marshall's brain. For the sake of the mission, analysis was no longer needed. Resolution *was*. Consequently, all of a sudden, he didn't know who most of these people were. Several in black robes were standing and clapping, like they were at a disco. Others were not remarkable in any way, at least to look at. He did know they held power, though. If he hadn't had his epiphany a few minutes before, surely he'd be highly intimidated right about now.

There was one he did recognize though, up ahead. President Con Murn, busy yakking, glad-handing, smiling and buddy-buddying on an almost frenzied plane. Marshall suspected he might be on drugs. As someone who wasn't a druggie but had every right to be, the vet's powers of perception were bell-clear, and all his interpretations rang true.

Then, another traffic director took over and impatiently whisked his hand into a fluttery beckoning motion, like a driver giving instructions to another motorist because they themselves don't know the rules of the road, but act on impulse only. It took a minute or so to figure out that this hired prig was ordering the motorized devotee to pull over and get his due from the Prez. As if it were a fucking favor or something. However, such conditional benevolence was the sort of casual aspect that had won over so many folk who thought themselves unworthy, but because of this down-home good-guy president, who'd said 'Well *hi* there,' instead of, 'What is this, Fatima? Lourdes? I never seen so many cripples in my life!', most were sold into slavish admiration of him, quite probably for life.

In the wonder of the moment, President Murn asked the cripple just ahead, 'How're ya doin' today, anyway?' and 'Got enough Attends? How about Depends, then? If not, I wanna know about it!' etc.

'Most kind of you, Con!' called out Sec'y of the Treasury, Bean Block-Bisteard, in particularly mocking tones. 'Save some for me!'

So many who were here today thought Murn was their savior, but only because of his rather limp talk, and maybe due to his rather icky presence. It certainly wasn't because of his agenda-driven deeds. So here he was, obviously exploiting the weak and disadvantaged, who were letting him do it, as if they'd be 'getting something' for their obeisance. A lie, mostly.

In the scheme of things, there was little doubt that Marshall was a challenging bit of imagery for the average person to encounter. He just didn't fit in to the average spectrum of human experience, as displayed in the daily media-flood. Even dirt-babies bawling in war zones were more acceptable, provided the war zone was remote enough. At any rate, it wasn't just the vet's tragic reduction in overall mass. Like a pariah dog infested with too many infections, parasites and tumors to list, he had several other conditions that rendered him sickly and damaged, from facial pock-marks to alternating patches of greasiness and dryness on his public frontage, and on and on. But when Marshall himself drew nigh to the Commander-in-Chief, he, Marshall, was the one who almost got sick to his mutilated stomach.

Portrayed in the media as a tanned, rested, and relaxed pardner, seen in these close quarters, Con Murn looked rather tawdry indeed. Cameras certainly had the technology to capture such truth, but only if the go-ahead was given by arbiters, which it universally wasn't. Only flattering depictions merited approval, naturally. But this was in-person stuff right now. The President, the very leader he'd served when his catastrophe occurred, stood very near to Marshall now. His face was an explosion of capillaries, giving him the 'red-man' look so common to Anglos who fancy themselves as saddle-leather characters – supposedly seasoned, appealing, healthy, confident, capable, and *sexy* – yet their blotchy self-delusion invariably comes off as troublingly hollow, especially if posing next to true persons of color in the world. However, 'tawdry' was the color of the power structure now in play within the most powerful nation on Earth.

In any event, Marshall was struck by the lax attention to detail that had been lavished on this evening's top-drawer celebrants. The President was a *mug*. Crusts of tinted pancake makeup, appearing like a combination of friction-spun smegma and dried vaginal lube from a failed congress of another kind, had been patted onto the slab-sides of his visage, in order to cover up the red menace – those alkie-fueled facial blowouts and gin-blossoms. Except that this foundation was peeling off like incognito plaster from Vincent Price's horror-face in André de Toth's 3-D masterpiece, 'House of Wax' (WB, 1953).

Surely the man and his handlers were drunk, drugged, and didn't give a damn. Didn't his handlers and the broadcast media *notice* this stuff, though?

He glanced around. The Sec'y of Labor's face was still a virtual zit-board. The eyes of the Sec'y of State's wife Yurma were indeed bags of blood. Nat'l Security Targeter Queirum Jakenail's whole ambience was reminiscent of the Ghost of Christmas Yet-to-Come. Justice Justus Pestus Cleumichael looked like a BDSM-Meister. And of course, Ms. Smarty-Pants Lally – Mrs. V.P. herself – was a Montana cow gal gone horribly, horribly wrong.

Protected by his mild amnesiac, Marshall was discovering the horror at the top all over again.

'What the fuck…? Are *these* the people running mine own land??'

Marshall's mental line of questioning was perfectly reasonable. He should know. Everything he did was based on his appearance. Mediocre minds might blithely say that Marshall Vogg, his appearance noted, might very well fit into the grotesquerie of this ruling gang. If considered on such a superficial plane, yes, assuredly, there were some connective stylistic possibilities. Past that, no one could perceive the beauty of Marshall's unpretentious right-mindedness, the very motivator for his presence among these cheaps and shills.

Still, for a commoner to see rulers close up, the overt grotesquerie came as an obscene shock. However, being a driver of a pathetic, outdated tub, he wasn't aware of such technology as InstaDidge/EnhansaFix and SubstiTootaSound software, built into each camera, that automatically applied pre-approved appearance-script templates to the President's form as he showed up on screens across the world. Another cool feature was that the program automatically altered the mouth-workings of the leaders, so they could not be lip-read. And if they were within mike range, voice-sampled tripe-lines, such as 'We're going to engage in fiscal responsibility, just like the American people want', and 'It's good that the American people trust themselves, and because they elected us, we have to earn their trust!', and other goofy sayings, were automatically substituted. That's why no one was giving a shit what they said, or what they looked like in front of the millions watching. Every revision happened instantly, too, like the names say. The finished product was a virtual animated film.

Of course, such curative magic would not apply to any of the Marshalls who appeared on camera today, as their digital profiles would have had to be created, then loaded into the software, and preferences made.

As for the in-person and largely unpleasant flesh Murn was seeing today, they weren't worth dolling himself up for, anyway. This was just a bozo gig to whack off before partying in the Heavenly's Musical Meatsticks Elite Club on the 34th Floor...

And there were other reasons...

Marshall's verdict: the dais members had naively but willingly come under the influence of that old Vegas Welcome curse: 'If you got the dough, the liquor will flow'. It seemed that the DeeCee entourage, used to everything going their way, chose as a group to view Vegas culture as less than human, and to condescend unto it and, thus, to abuse the opportunity. Therefore, the goal was to *party*, ostensibly like adults, while coming off as Spring Break retards who are in way over their heads.

'Now why,' thought Marshall, 'would they let this guy come off like that?'

Because, dear Marshall, when a feller has his beady eyes on the Dictator For Life office in a nation that has sacrificed its Democracy for Empire, such details *don't matter*, particularly out here in the West, and particularly in Vegas, where people-watching proves that Americans, as well as others of their ilk, from practically every nation in the world, are about the ugliest polyglot of human clay on the face of the planet. So why *bother*?

'Does that mean I fit in – at last?' queried the disabled vet. Indeed, a kind of honest nobility descended on him, rendering him truly superior, though he active-ly pitied those he beheld. This reversal of his usual life experience was genuinely graceful, and brought with it a lofty beauty and a relaxing peace.

Lots of Blue Hawaiian-poured glasses, like glowing Sterno-pads, littered the landscape of the Chosen Ones (provided by Wayne Newton Hotels International Concerns), which had resulted in a pretty wasted constituency by this point in the early evening's pageant.

Thus, the practicing power structure of the USA was, at this moment, carefree in its pottedness, right here in Sin City. It was as simple and as sad as that.

His bathchair hesitantly whining onward, the vet eased up just short of the assigned stopping point and came to a dead stop.

Battery. Dead. Stopped.

Oh, great! Fucking *perfect*. No, fucking *fucked*.

The fussy traffic director was fuming. Yet, he could do nothing but hope for the best. Grips and Secret Service, ready to pitch in with other comrades, to wheel this carpeted nightmare out into the desert somewhere, as Sammy Davis Jr. was threatened with that time, stood by to push, if necessary.

Instead, a wondrous thing happened. President Murn, who had every intention of seeking his third term after his plan of constitutional hijacking passed through the underbelly cloaca of Congress (as it was assured of doing), allowing him to be Ruler In Perpetuity (though that wasn't the sneaky language employed), made the supreme effort to appeal to the masses by accommodating them, no matter how un-rinsed. Besides, he was just spiffed enough from free drinks to get a little *fawnky*.

And just then, a mandate descended from heaven this night (or some ersatz version of it). It provided for the sitting President to descend among his approach-ers and take several steps *out of his way*, in order to draw up to Marshall's stalled vehicle. And, as all the media cameras and even the satellite coverage in the lower realms of said heaven above adjusted their cameras to the lesser-lit area – a tad bit short of the proper position of center stage – the Man-in-Charge himself came up to one, single, sad soul, over whom he was Chieftain and Protector. Citizen Marshall, fucked-up vet and gnarled personage, the type by which Murn would ascend to total cynical power over these united states.

President Murn said aside, to his aide, Pompetto Pumpkins:

'Well Pompky, don't he look like a freakin' penguin! Tennessee Tuxedo! 'Cept he ain't wearin' the blacks 'n' whites. Got flippers though, real flippers. He'll be real impressed when I *touch* him. Makin 'contact' *does* 'er. Hope he can press a vote machine button! Pumper, or Wandy, you got them Wipe-Oops ready?'

Another aide, White House lawyer Kairman Kumptian Kweston, had been promised a Supreme Court seat before the year was out ('We'll dump that ol' Bali Hai Injun nigger – or wooden nickel injun – or whatever the hell he is, 'Un'-Jus-tice Beepus, 'fore he can make it to the shitter' was the Prez's promise). He set down his Giant Gin and took a good look at Marshall.

'Say, isn't that the kid who told you to fuck off when you were good enough to award him his Purple-prose Heart, number of year ago?'

'Oh yeah? No! Yeah? You mean you memorize these fuck-ups, Kwest? I've seen so many body parts, still livin'! Hell, the VA oughta take a part here and a part there and slap together a real man – one who'd still be able to get it up.'

'I remember his demon-glare, Con. He still got it.'

'Well, when a feller's been blown apart that far, guess even he's got a right to be pissed off. 'Course, he's just mad at hisself. If he's mad at me, well then, he's mad at 'Murica. That's what these stupid-ass types do: sign up, get all fucked up and then soak us with the bill for the rest of their stupid lives. Fuckin' *A*, he's got a glare. That's what the powerless do when they see the powered! Haw!'

The carpet's weave, somewhat suppressing the fecal bouquet, hadn't reached the POTUS yet. Then that very man stepped forward and addressed Marshall in the most poli-plastic of politicians' ways.

'Well now *howdy,* Vet! Way over here, are ya? Don't be shy. It's just that, holy crudhoppers, you got a lot to be shy about, don't ya – I mean… Well gosh dern it, you served my country, all right. Right? Bet you're proud. Lemme shake that – uh – busted flipper – er, I mean, *hand* a-yer'n. That's right! Lemme give ya a *hand.* Thanks fer yer service, li'l guy!'

There was a noticeable smirk in his last sentence, which made mockery of any potential sentiment in the words. This was probably a result of excrement-discovery on the person whom he approached. But being the pro he was, President Murn kept his wits about him. It was a point of pride. His elitist opinion of himself skyrocketed, as it always did when privilege met the pavement upon which it was implanted.

'Holy shit but I've got some raunchy motherfuckers in my domain, don't I?' Con thought. 'Ain't I just the nice guy to grin 'n' bear it? Too bad fer him, but what the fuck's that got to do with me? But, hey, easy to rule, easy to rule…'

In his years of power he had learned not to say naughty words in public out loud. So successful was this discipline, there were those under his rule who thought him truly godly.

Boy, but were such words handy for use in private, though.

'Dang, but that untreated shit stink-stank!' – Like most of his subjects, truth to tell.

Yes, Con Murn was that most perfect of clichés: power, whether gifted or earned, had corrupted him totally. What else was new?

Here they were, president and peasant, connecting.

Marshall, humanly equating his response on the most level of playing fields, couldn't help but let his new honesty rule the day in his chance at expression. While he shook the POTUS' hand, he made a sarcastic reply. It wasn't what he'd planned, but because of his dubious first impressions, combined with his new status as over-viewer, stacked on top of the overheard 'Wipe-Oops' talk, it just tumbled out of his mouth, in free fall.

'A *hand!* Giving me a *hand!* Well, isn't that super? My president delivers, don't ya know! By the way, uh, might you have a penis for me, as well? Mine's missing, but they wouldn't let me in here naked to show you, so you'll have to take my word for it. Balls shot off, too. I'm trimmed up all around.'

Was the president listening? *Truly* listening?

Still somewhat respectful, Marshall made a follow-up effort for the learning-disabled.

'OK, what's my point?'

The President continued to shake and smile, making sure the flashbulbs got every good angle, though the realization that he was touching something loathsome and post-amputated struck him more than the ex-soldier's words. To an observant person, Marshall's increasingly pressured facial expression might suggest an ushering toward some sort of climax. The whole scene was a multi-media package that a Blue Hawaiianed Prez might consider a threat. That is, if he were capable of recognizing one right now.

'No?' Marshall continued after receiving zero response, and exercising what little muscular crimp he could muster to keep his President physically engaged.

'Hey, what the fuck –,' said Con, realizing there was something forbiddingly funkadelic going on here.

'Notwithstanding,' continued Marshall, still barely hooked to him while the Secret Service closed in, 'It's too late in the world for *hands* and other *implements*. Far too late. An *end* now, an *end to all*, you sissyhawk 'warriors'! So – so, what's my *point?* I'll tell you! To *teach!*'

He let go of President Murn, and the Service halted their invasion, then tried to look cool. Because this weird cripple was confronting the President, and everyone around him was a giant in comparison, the earbone instructions from Langley were: back off, as bullying a vet, no matter how hideous or disaffected, was a no-no the media would pounce on, given the chance, given their control.

So all forces indeed backed off and let the Prez stand tall over this pathetic, puke-making freak, whose presence could be easily edited out of tonight's hullabaloo soon enough. (You *still* not heard of InstaDidge/EnhansaFix & SubstiTootaSound yet, or what??) In addition, online and analog means in the print media were, even at this point, fixable in a breeze. Besides, media-borne memory had a life of about 4.2 seconds. Simply moving Marshall along would be the best solution to this uncomfortable glitch. If any of his 'material' made it through to broadcast time, he would be forgotten by viewers in about 5.1 to 9.9 seconds (source: C-Gympra Sono-Sets Pollwich, plc), and they could readily go to a commercial for Borry's Berry 'n' Beer-Toasted Eggplant Wedges, if necessary.

So, on principles more practical than ethical, everyone let Marshall *be*.

On past the stage lights, the sky was a pleasing deep navy blue. Nothing beat the desert heavens off-hours, and that included the approach to night. Butterbugs, reclining in his long-ago Vegas wasteland-chair, while in eclipse, while lost in the dirt, had learned much from the night sky. And now, with power-play-people on the scene, they might learn from it as well. At least it was a possibility. For the sky is the ultimate witness, and witnesses stimulate the conscience, as to the consciousness of decisions and actions.

Then, an intermezzo of compelling peace descended unto Marshall, as he maintained his position of poised attentiveness to destiny. Signaled by a heavenly chorus, time was suspended for as long as it took for him to absorb the grace that was offered.

There, right in front of him and amidst his sub, semi, and real-time consciousnesses, was a scene in which he was blessedly the focal point. It was right out of 'The Robe' (20th-Fox, 1953). And it was stately, edifying, and euphoric. There he was, Marshall, walking along. *Walking*, with a beautiful lady on his arm. Yes, *arm*. She was Jean Simmons, no less. Lovely Jean. And the two were slowly going forward, forward to –

Wait a minute, a discordant voice intervened. Caligula! (as played by Jay Robinson), shrieking at them, something about going into a *better kingdom*. Maybe they were, and maybe they weren't, but as an intact man, walking tall, with Jean Simmons, and Alfred Newman's Hallelujah voices assisting, Marshall couldn't imagine a better exit strategy – the ultimate escape from tragedy.

Then Jean stood aside, Jay ceased his harangue, and Alfred suspended the orchestra and chorus in mid phrase –

Even though there wasn't enough power left in the bathchair's battery to move its sludgy wheels forward, there was just enough reserve to make the chair's withery horn beep for a second or two, once its button was pressed by Marshall's prime flipper.

Somewhat moisturized by Presidential oils, the flipper tip just about slipped off the button's convex surface. But with more determination to give life force to his efforts than he'd ever done since before his debilitation, the vet brilliantly nailed his mission. The button was pressed, the battery delivered its power, and the horn buzzed, just after he declared, 'To teach!'

And then —

BAM.

Or rather, **BAM.**

…Marshall hand-packed that high-plasticity explosive play-dough into the motor housing of his bathchair… For weeks, patting in a bit here, and another deposit there, all with his one good flipper… the one that would eventually determine *the* American destiny of the epoch.

An image out of Kaz's 'Underworld' comic strip, which sometimes features a digit-less character called Petit Mort...

...And Marshall looked into the sunset sky, and there he was...

...Walking, joyfully, with Jean Simmons, Caligula receding, music resuming, rising, glorying, free at last, walking, towards –

A rather *huge* **BAM.**

Just one, which was enough.

Diced, smashed, pulverized... Meatloaf, strawberry jam, cranberry catsup, ground hamburger, mashed taters... Tatters, shards, specks, flakes, black *snow*-flakes – of scorched clothes and flesh.

A President and all the other VIPs, scattered into shattered molecules... That was the *big* news.

Along with a soldier – of agony, not fortune – his second and last big **BAM...** That was *bigger* news.

All were no more.

Extremely sophisticated explosives.

It was a pretty big deal. Everybody on the dais was wiped out. Some (sniff) were actually innocent, but not many.

The dusky sky was clear, the palms were tall. The sun was honest as it left for the day. Whatever happened on planet Earth, there were plenty of nature's witnesses.

As the cloud of blow-up smoke rose into the heavens over the meadows, old-timer Vegasians were reminded of the last big atmospheric atomic blast out Air Force Base Nellis way, with its mushroom cloud rising above the gambling hall neons of Fremont St.

Both signaled ends of eras.

The Executive Branch of the United States needed replacing. Congressional leadership, too, plus some leading military, financial, and other figures. And there were significant vacancies on the Supreme Court's benches.

None who perished were outstanding human beings.

Except one.

Marshall left an End Note, addressed to Senator O'Wayne Kebbah (D-NV) punched out on a Moultin/Dichter Derlip keyboard with a pencil in his mouth, explaining that Butterbugs – the actor, strolling player, and ultrastar – was an inspiration to him, and that he once had a dream in which Butterbugs himself bodily lifted him up, when he was in distress:

'I was like a tiny baby, all helpless and undeveloped, but with the mind of one who was consumed by his own loss. I'd run into trouble. What, I ask you, would *you* do? Then, out of my un-expectations, a strong and pure set of hands grasped me, firmly, but with direction. They raised me and repositioned me, and set me straight. Who *were* these hands? Who were they attached to? I later dreamt they were those of the actor Butterbugs. If there was one who on this Earth could successfully straighten me, it was he. Who better to dream of as my guide? I used to use some of my allowed pennies to attend matinees of Butterbugs' pictures over at the Carbox cinema, three blocks away. Sometimes the charge in my electric bathchair would fail and the neighborhood kids who didn't run from me anymore would push me along, knowing what I was trying to do, and they'd join me for the matinee. I'd be their mascot and they'd get into the Butterbugs thing as much as I did. I, to get through the day, they, to look ahead to their lives. It was beautiful, really. If you ever get all your limbs blown off, you should be so lucky!

'I sat there in the dark, in wonder, and thanked that person up there on the screen for showing me that I could be allowed to still think of myself as a person. You know, a *person*, instead of a fucking *thing*. Nobody told him to do that, and nobody told me nothing. This was between Butterbugs and me.'

And then,

'All the world's a tragedy for me, but by my last deed, perhaps I have lessened others' own tragedies, and other, future tragedies. I have to tell you, I pondered at great length about this mission. Now that it has been executed, I confess that I humbly let myself be taken out by my own purposeful – and peaceful – actions. Please understand what I have taken on. For those of you who seek revenge for my act, I do not wish to sound absurd when I say that perhaps I have already endured my punishment. However, blowing the fuck out of the US's rotten rule is no act of correcting any punishment I myself have considered unjust. The corrupt rulers whom I take with me were not worth remaining in power. After the dust clears, all America will agree with me. You will know what they have done with your treasure, your lives, and your souls. And now a sad part. To any innocents who may have been slaughtered in my deed, I am truly and permanently sorry, and contrite as it is possible to be. If I am yet to be punished for it, I can tell you, I am already pre-seasoned for it. To those who believe me, no forgiveness is necessary. To those who do not, no forgiveness is possible. Know, though, that my conviction is based on experience, while, to those I take with me, their conviction is based on notion. I cannot say I am correct in my actions, but I cannot say I am wrong, either. You, the public, be the judge. So I am going on alone. If I fail in this attempt, others may join me in accomplishing it whole.'

(signed by mark)
Sgt. Marshall Tiptop Vogg
Rigger 1st class, Special Forces

If it was a dream, if mated with possibilities in the world of the waking, it was the kind of dream in which all things might come to fruition. In that one hour in Vegas, the inspiration was in the subconscious while the doing was in the conscious. Marshall Vogg achieved both, unlike most of the occupants of this Earth, who are grounded in either one or the other of these worlds.

The vast majority of the nation (and the world at large), sided with the viewpoint involving experience and suffering, rather than notion and nothing. Thus, the Union was preserved.

For Butterbugs himself, there was especially no need of forgiveness for Marshall's deed. There was nothing even to discuss. Thus his vacuousness when the media came to him for perspective. It was all transcendent simplicity, where there was beauty of the highest order.

'I am mourning for Marshall Vogg – serviceman. His destiny was noble. He is a new hero for all.'

And he meant it. The media knew it, full well. There they left off.

Uncannily like Marshall, his memory stirred by the epic End Note, Butterbugs had his own dreamlike recollection of some sort of personal encounter with the late hero. Also like Marshall, back when they had actual but brief contact at the Russel Arms, Butterbugs himself had the mind of one who was consumed by his loss (for him, of identity, instead of appendages). He'd certainly run into his own kind of trouble in that encounter. That image – of the screaming Marshall on the floor – nightmarish, not dreamy. But now, after this world-steadying event, it became a miraculous vision. Even if he did not understand its mystery, he simply regarded it as a gift.

In death, Marshall Vogg merited instant status, right up there with JFK, Martin Luther King, Jr., Bobby Kennedy, GXT, Jere Tentmouth, Malcolm X, Mrs. Kraulerton, and Abe Lincoln. It didn't take too much to figure out.

But he was not so much a martyr as he was a deliverer. That would be his shining legacy. Plans were already laid down for a National Memorial, on the spot where it occurred. A Campus Tragicus Dignitas – the National Field of Tragic Honor. In its center would stand an ingenious and humble dual-portrait of the man: powerful human-scale statues of a 'Marshall pre-catastrophe, standing tall, and a Marshall post-catastrophe, pre-glory, finger [*sic*] poised on the decisive horn button'. The Memorial's theme would be, Marshall as Deliverer, and the Relief from the Corrupt Ones. Marshall and the Two Unknown Innocents were commemorated by cenotaphs. The names of the Corrupt Ones were nowhere. It would be a place of pilgrimage, especially for the mighty of the world – to reset their perspectives.

Almost by the hour, huge reports of the late Administration's corruption, illegal dealings, vote-rigging, international dirty dealing on a completely dispiriting scale, and creepy activities that made the nation's collective corpuscles freeze up were released by the freighterful to the public. The dam had burst and true freedom of information returned to the land.

645

Apologies were made, restitutions were awarded, critics were vindicated, former supporters were disgusted then indignant at being duped, the media reported the stories responsibly, and the healing began almost immediately. There were still boils under bandages, but lancing always led to truth.

Most shocking to the masses of the world, though, was all the evidence that Murn & Co. had declared all-out war on Butterbugs, his allies, and his goodly effects, and that they had planned to eliminate them so as to secure their grip on the jugular vein of the nation. The final straw was the release of the infamous 'Non-Conclusive Conclusions' declaration, a paper that was almost too much for the world to accept. All the signatories of that document, if they weren't already dead or executed privately, were arrested, held without bail, and set on the fast track to trials by jury in Washington DC, The Hague, and Ulan Bator.

Butterbugs was so admired and so respected, so treasured, so loved, that hordes of people from all places and all walks of life pleaded with him to understand that they would have gladly been taken out in his place, if only they had known the ugly background truth! Now that they *did* know, they also hung their heads for having been so successfully taken advantage of. Indeed, it was a humbling sort of comeuppance for a modern world in which trust was placed with insufficient scrutiny or insight, in the name of convenience, though it was actually mostly apathy. No longer.

They would never, ever forget.

The government transitioned peacefully, and with vigor. Sec'y of Agriculture Vent Spylz was the one who had stayed home. An innocuous man, Murn-selected due to his place-holding and non-controversial nature, he would serve as Interim Office-Minder for the Presidency of the United States of America. There was no opposition to the appointment.

Eventually, the wonderful and beloved Justice Beepus of the Supreme Court, who had so ably served as Technical Advisor to Butterbugs in his role as Chief Justice Taney, was declared President. ('The Roger B. Taney Show, With Special Guest, Dred Scott' (UA).) Reversing the route blazed by Wm. H. Taft, he was a hesitant Cincinnatus at first, but so genuinely called upon to serve that he left his plow on the Bench and rose to the executive office with great effect.

'A massive step in the right direction,' breathed Butterbugs to anxious Justy and thrilled Saskia in a conference call. 'And proof that hope shall never leave humanity.'

The Murn Administration was so reviled by they, the people, that no days of mourning were declared by a relieved Congress. All the funerals were strictly private, and any protocol and etiquette that provided for respectful treatment of those horrible people was summarily junked in this instance. Thus ended the first, and hopefully last, bonafide mafia presidency of a troubled nation.

All through the time of the Murns, Butterbugs had done his cinema thing, independently, nationally, internationally, but with few expectations that the world's political leaders would save the world from itself. After being so hurt by his reading of the Murn Concern's 'Non-Conclusive Conclusions', probably the most significant subjective factor in his near nosedive in front of that blunderbuss, his thirst for just reform had come to the fore. Mobilized by his current film role in 'Unholy War Hymn' as a power-politician and warrior-administrator, the conjoining realities of power and its upshots had never meant as much as they did now. Art could threaten politics all right, but it was invariably politics that brought its own house down. So, rising up from all this event and experience was the realization that he, Butterbugs, as a screen artiste, was indubitably a player of signal consequence in the world. As usual, he was duly humbled, but there was more to it this time: he accepted the responsibility therein. If Marshall could sacrifice his life, however damaged, to prove a point of liberation and edification, Butterbugs could desist from the tiresome trap of modesty's soft denial, and properly account for his influence on the world. It was a matter of maturity. Truly, he had arrived at a fuller embodiment of what an ultrastar really was... and should be.

Without any persuasion or preparation, Butterbugs made the following pronouncement:

'The US! A nation where unbelievable things truly happen! Therein lies our decline. Formerly, it was t'other way round. In these, our days, realism has trumped the dreaming aspirations of the idealists. Thank heavens we do not have to *lead* anymore. For they, the mafia controllers, were leading us into an oily river to nowhere, the waters of which drown rather than sustain. Indeed, they were Sadak's Waters of Oblivion, distilled by Marshall Vogg, and finally drunk by our former rulers of corruption. Onward now, oh country! Return, return with me to the greatness of wisdom, earned through our review of knowledge thought lost. A knowledge that helps us evolve upwards, as we were meant to do, by dint of our virtues rather than our power. With this exciting prospect, we are carried forward by each and every one of ourselves, rather than an authoritarian regime of deception and repression!'

In its complete form, it was a somewhat curious tract (Butterbugs utilized analogies praising the pleasures of gumball-chewing, the cosmology of Sri Aurobindo, and the return of the Forward Look in automotive design as incentives to benevolent excellence), but the expanded broadside edition, which appeared at every newsstand, tabac and webstop on the planet, was consumed with a nouveau and robust awareness. This worldwide relish allowed for a peoples' awakening, to be one with realistic aspiration in revaluing existing values in the life experience.

There was talk that President Beepus would approach the ultrastar with propositions of officialdom, but nothing, at least for the present, transpired. It was all big movie-story stuff, but the ultrastar's plate was already full of both collagen and gristle.

The new President and his family were an instant hit. Plus, they were sterling evidence that America had fully accepted the fact that yes, it was the world's most diverse nation and society, *and it was OK to admit that fact*. Roarald Tennunian Beepus was the country's first Associate Supreme Court Justice – and president – of First Nation (aka Native American) heritage. A member of the Yakama tribe, he'd studied under Justice Wm. O. Douglas, traveled with him, and clerked for him. His beauteous Montagnard-Malawian wife Kellah was a Goethe scholar and culinary artiste, whose chief cause was the restoration of critical thinking. Their four adopted kids were: 1) Ahmad, originally from Nizamabad (Deccan), now a brilliant techie nerd; 2) Lo-hei-Mlama, the White House's first fulltime (and openly declared) transgendered/queer resident, of Tibeto-Uighur parentage, now an up-and-coming painter; 3) Mabel Lake, a færie-like girl so white they could've named the entire race after her, newly-graduated from Goth-Jayne University with a PhD in Museum Curation – at age nineteen; and 4) Chad Gringurry, a nice young kid of (American) Samoan heritage, with a great future ahead of him.

Taking Butterbugs' shooting schedule as a gracious demurral of public service (for the duration of 'UWH', anyway), the new POTUS cast around for a suitable VP. His first (and successful) choice was Washington State's governor-general, Ms. Kshama Sawant. Together they melded the priorities of the nation into an *incandescent* reality: an ascendance to equality, reason, and right action, in their truest forms. VP Sawant would undoubtedly be taking up residence in the White House upon the conclusion of Pres. Beepus' first (and only) administration, as the presidential term of office had just been unanimously amended to a single five-year timespan.

Further offices were filled swiftly, and with universal approval. The beloved philosopher Mahomet Quaruzz went to State, Yobus C'chunga brought sanity to Treasury, Betty Lomax restored lawful Law as Attorney General, Rev. Dayla Barrison Chisterston conscientiously guided Defense, Bernie Sanders inaugurated the new Peace Dept., Rev. Wm Barber at the new Human Justice Dept., Dad Wambox healed the land of Interior, Hlako Wuorbornio at Commerce, Maxine Waters got Labor working again, Elon Musk at Transpo, the Venerable John Lewis at Education, Dr. Vungus Volcanoe at Health & Human, Pei Ping Nohamazaki at VA, Dr. Harry Edwards at HUD, Vent Spylz was warmly invited to stay on at Ag, Naomi Klein capably took on Energy, and on down the line.

Perhaps the most pleasant surprise was that Michelle Obama had been so delighted to accept the invitation to fill the high office of Chief Justice of the Supreme Court.

'A New Excitement As America Reforms' (this in 'The Universal Gazette') was about as complicated as headlines needed to be right now.

The appeal of these long-held hopes led to genuine conviction on a universal scale. In the simplest of terms, the collective populace of stewards, money-ists, and citizens had literally *come to their senses*. Thus, the massive edifice of a newly checked and balanced government was transformed. It was a fact: at last America was prudently headed for the destiny that had awaited all along: *democratic socialism*. That is, *Social Democracy*. The 's' word had been vindicated, and the 'd' word was finally understood. Not *just* because of Butterbugs, but as a result of his indirect facilitations, certainly.

Out of violence was this freedom born, but beyond such trauma lay the wisdom of a genuine Pax Americana. There it was, for all to see and honor, to be taken up and enacted – in toto this time – and for the *first* time.

If Marshall had been the igniter, then it was Butterbugs who was the spirit that fueled the lamp. Its glow rapidly grew into a great and benevolent light. Stronger and stronger, until it enlightened all – even those who'd fiercely opposed any such possibility – usually out of spite and selfishness, of course.

As manifestations of this transformation progressed, one imperative of human evolution could finally be proven to all: that such a process could actually be a conscious choice, rather than the foregone conclusion that humanity would always be locked into its doom-laden tendencies. In the months and years to come, the proof would spread across the entire planet.

Never was a world more ready to receive a picture like 'Unholy War Hymn'! An ultra-powerful cautionary epic, dramatizing a world where *all warnings* are shunned or suppressed. But after absorbing it, viewers everywhere would be able to breathe easy. Because the story of 'UWH' wasn't how things would come to pass. After all, it would be 'only a movie', but also an object lesson in dodging a very big bullet. Most importantly, it was destined to be one of the noblest and most resounding demonstrations of global awakening to right action yet to occur in the human experience. Never would the power of cinema be so effective in changing Earthlings for the better.

These were all things that were in progress, but they were things that would *be*.

Old Atrocity, hearing the epochal news of these thrilling changes, climbed to the roof of the biggest soundstage in Jambutterbugsabad, raised his hands to the heavens and, his voice resounding even unto the frowning cliffs above, bellowed:

'A new dawn! A new day! We *live again!!*'

57.

Have You Seen A Girl Called Prairie Browne?

So, the wave of clustered crises had conveyed Butterbugs into a mælström. But then, in one of those inexplicable tangents produced by the imperfect laws of physics, the trajectory caused by the latest radical jaggedness of the Hyman Goth demise and the wholesale removal of Murnism happened to carry the ultrastar off to the side, into a lagoon of sorts, if not palm-lined, then at least dream-like in its placidity. Perhaps it was the calm before the aneurysm, the sidetrack before the head-on death-embrace, but there was palpable quietude, and the High Mad Doctor was able to turn aside his costumed mind, his role-wracked body... Because the surrounding waters were now still and lamp-lit, even if they were just a concept.

For Butterbugs, even now positioned amidst the flare-ups on the battlefields of opinion and passion, there was still 'UWH' to finish. The marvel that he silently maintained, of the panoply of super-remarkable aspects in this, his life, was properly filed. But he needed some neutral time in which to level the balance of his private life with the public gargantua that always loomed.

The flurry of returned production had brought with it elation and purposeful recognition of triumph on a huge scale, but the person at the center of the grouped spotlights fancied a bit of retreat, while the machinery and apparatuses were being set up for the sequences that would wrap 'UWH''s shooting sked.

Therefore, he repaired to a notable and particularly obscure place for contemplation: at The End of the Camino Real Hotel. It was one of those old time hostelries of the type that used to pepper the LA of the teens and twenties of the 20th century. It had large, rambling verandahs, runway halls with acceptably creaky floors, a slight sanatorium feel, but with overstuffed furnitures, esoteric but sophisticated foodstuffs, a deep amber glow of soft lamps after hours, plus a sleepy clientele, which always meant for a mellow ambience.

With a jar of afternoon wine, darker than blood mixed with rubies mortared and pestled into the same cave-compatible glass, one could sit in the Bamber Porch out back and muse not only on oil-cured olives, lemon wedges bordered with salt crystals, black prune-pomade tarts, and regular-chicken-in-the-dust-leaves (a specialty of the house), but one could also fancy that a foxy Mae Murray or Anna May Wong or Blanche Sweet or a manly and confident Wally Reid might stroll in, the bunch of them to settle down to a glorious gossip about the latest Ince crisis or an eagerly-beaverly-awaited Frances Marion or June Mathis script, while the sideways-sun covered them all in gold – a sure indicator that not only was life good, but pure proof of their worthiness, revealed by that true-minted color, shown off with Olympian surety.

A place for golden players of a golden age.

In the here and now though, the interlude was tinted with the same gold, but the tone was one that brought with it matters of gravity rather than pleasure. For there was much to think about. Still, the moment gave pleasure because of the environs, and that was why Butterbugs came here.

Here he might be spotted in the solitary afternoon idyll beneath the vine tunnels, hands clasped to his forehead, not with 'Now is my soul troubled' intent, but as a posture allowing for a reasoned and high-level discursive session of the internal kind, in order to weigh, debate, and justify the reviews of his current events.

'Consider,' whispered Butterbugs to himself, 'The psychology of our photoplay. I am the Leader. I am also – as Sri Sankara said, as I played him: I am also – *the seer*. But what do I see ahead now? The terms 'tribulation', 'equivocation', and 'trial' circle about my mind, but what are their values? How will I deal with them?'

He placed other intellectual problems, such as 'Whither 'UWH'?', 'Whither my country?' and 'Whither my course, now?' on the platter near the olives, so to speak, in order to rate their worth in the balance. His fingers picked the oil-cured items, instead of the abstract lack of promise that came with his ideas of worry and doubt. Then he continued to ponder as he slowly let the savory olive-mash melt into his afternoon.

He took a turn around the verandah. It was a quiet time, impossibly lyrical hereabouts, and a few nooks were populated. Tucked into a love-seat cubby, framed by grape matrices, an elderly couple were ensconced. He was a dead ringer for Cyril Delavanti, and she resembled Maylie Rigstoff. But they were neither. Probably just got off the train from Biggler's Corners, Iowa.

'Hello there, folks,' greeted Butterbugs.

'Hello,' said one. 'Hello,' said the other.

They struck Butterbugs as *the* perfect through-the-years couple. Cozied next to each other, as close as they could get without indecency, both hands clasped both hands.

'By golly, you two are so sweet! You just don't want to let go of each other!' the ultrastar marveled. 'Do you?'

'If we let go,' began he.

'We'll *strangle* each other,' finished she.

Back to the olive tray. The afternoon continued to mellow, the wine glowed, and wryness was replaced by the piquancy of cornichon goodness.

The verandah floor creaked. Not as noticeably as when some hefty long-timer tromped that long stretch, but Butterbugs could tell full well that someone was a-comin'. One of those dreamin' California-type girls, though not necessarily from the Golden State, came by, trim and baggage-free. 'Penthouse'-worthy, really – oh, shit, not to pigeon-hole her, but by golly, those pages are where she could've emerged from, as in the '70s, with honesty showering in all directions from her confident form... It wasn't a matter of discernment on the retiring actor's part, as he wasn't even alive at such a time. But some persons, by their very nature, exude an era by which they might be identified, however unjustified. Which, if they are exceptional, might simultaneously include the broader era of *timelessness*...

She even had a headband on, and a choker, too. And a wispy tie-dye scarf, chosen not because she wanted to *be* somebody, but because she liked it. In any case, she was beautiful and her attractiveness had a netting quality to it: catch her or she is gone.

Butterbugs of course could not ignore her oncoming figure. He'd seen many a blessed practitioner of the eye-candy-maker's art, but here, obviously without pretensions, a remarkable female took a place of respect in doing what she chose to be doing in this place and at this time. Highlighted by the Camino's strategic light, she was particularly vertical in her bearing, but not a string bean and not a cat-walker. My, how quickly such escapist activities as pedestrian observation swept aside the more pressing insistences of one's self-made tedium!

The thing was, all things taken in, there was no reason *not* to talk with her. She a neat girl, he a single (and yes, lonely) guy. Throughout his picture show career, there was scarcely a come-on line that did not work for Butterbugs. Not that he was a cad or anything. It was just that, in this timeless place, and within its beauties, the instantly-recognizable significance of the opportunity seemed to him more advantageous to her than it was for him, to 'pull' anything that might work against her. So he made an outgoing gesture, but only after assessing her choices made, just now.

She slowed and then tarried momentarily, regarding the hors/condiments selection that was near to Butterbugs' nook.

'Life is good, here in the afternoon.'

Not the most fetching pickup line; more appropriate for a wistful middle-ager, nostalgic for something to believe in, be it ever so minimal.

'Oh! Is it afternoon? It *is?*'

'Did you just get up, Miss?'

'I did, yes.'

'Comfortable here?'

'Ever so much, thank you.'

'I like it too, whenever I stay here.'

'This is the first time for me. My parents wanted me to stay at a respectable inn once I came to the place where pictures are made.'

'Then, you have just arrived?'

'Mhm. But I should be reticent here, without introductions.'

'Yes you should. I can tell you that right now.'

He was prepared to withdraw, but she remained, glancing down at one of her sandals that needed adjusting, but choosing not to do so, lest it be a premature move. Feeling comfortable enough with the holding pattern, she nevertheless re-aligned some bangles on her left wrist, which made an appealing clinking sound.

'Are you a native, Mister?'

Butterbugs took up the offer.

'In body, but not wholly in mind.'

'Whuh...?'

'Rather, uh, yes. Yes, but I'm, you know, on a sort of holiday from my usual place of residence.'

'That sounds nice. Sort of like a day out, or something.'

'I think that's a good way to put it, yes.'

'For me, I guess I'm trying for a *lifetime* out, not just a day.'

'That's a very balanced way of looking at things.'

He was trying not to sound parochial.

'You think so, Mister? You think so?'

'Oh yes. There's nothing better than an even-handed way of approaching new ideas.'

'That's good! I'll do that!'

He sensed she was open to sensations and opinions.

'It will serve you in your quest. Perhaps better than it has in my own.'

'Yeah, my... quest... I guess I *do* have one...'

She sounded almost wistful.

'Everybody's got one, whether they know it or not, I should think.'

'That's what life *is*...?'

She couldn't help but make an intended statement sound like a question.

'It's a good idea to look at big things in the simplest of ways.'

Now she looked at him as if he were someone to truly pay attention towards.

'Some advice, from you...'

'Oh, I'm reminding myself, really.' He was quick to claim his statement for himself. 'Thinking out loud. Thanks for helping.'

She looked over at the foodie bits again. The verandah floor creaked far down the way, as someone quit the light for the shadows of the hotel's interior.

They had the whole place to themselves.

'Who *are* you?' she then asked, in all reasonable innocence.

'Only a resident of this here hotel,' he blithely fibbed, but with just as much sincerity, only so as not to shock her. His hands, thrust out in carefree anonymity comforted her.

'Me, too.'

She seemed OK that no names were contained in the introductions, which her receding reticence required.

'I'm here for some time *off*, not just a day out.'

'Well, as for me, I am here to try out for picture shows,' she said without further discussion of Butterbugs' being. No reason not to make an announcement to this handsome fellow.

'I would like to be a strolling player of the screen.'

They both paused; Butterbugs to politely raise his eyebrows and take up a crunch-muffin wafer, and she to modestly flounce her long dark hair. Not to flog the 'Penthouse' similarities, but she was one of those Cherokee/Irish/Swedish cocktails so dear to Pet-dom. Here, she was the real thing. And with her dazzling 36–22.5–36 form, standing 5'11" in the sidelong sun against the mellow shadows bordering the area just behind Butterbugs, the motion picture screen would definitely be the preferred showcase for her great potential. Image-wise, at any rate.

'Are you *sure* about that?' the ultrastar said at length, genuinely concerned for her.

'Well, I guess so. I think it would be sort of fun.'

'Do you? Is that your only reason?'

'I think it is. I want to try out different things. I'm sort of in a hurry, 'n' stuff. After high school, I looked in the mirror, and I thought, you're similar to what you see in the movies. You have the same things. To use. *For* use.'

She plainly wanted to belong.

'Makes sense. And what if it doesn't work out?'

'Oh, I have a degree in art history, and I have a job waiting for me at Sprackington/Nillinuningham in London, any time I want it. Friends of my parents, but I don't mind. I *like* them.'

Butterbugs was impressed, and instantly reassured. Now here was a sensible girl. He knew the people at the gallery in question and thought them unimpeachable.

'Are *you* in pictures?' she asked him.

'I know some in the Industry,' said the world's only ultrastar.

By this, he was not at all dallying with her, but he found that he indeed fancied her. There was nothing much to figure out in that respect. Nevertheless, he proceeded with care. As usual, his reasoning was pure, but it could always be misinterpreted. Still, the more he chatted with her, the more he thought she would not be prone to misinterpretation. In fact, he had a growing feeling about her. Was she worth knowing? Could she have the potential to be… the *one* that…

Non-conclusive conclusions.

Her body language was sensible, dignified, practical.

'So you *know* about this town? Places to get a good hot meal? Where I can shop for books?'

'Oh yes. All that and more. I know a bit, I should think.'

She liked the rapport. Not jokey, but easy. She was sick of that 'everybody's a comedian' crap she got from here to breakfast. Plus, she liked the ambience that surrounded him. It was the first attractive moment she'd had in LA. Time for identities.

'What's your name, Mister? I'm Greenah!'

'How do you do, Greenah. I'm Butterbugs.'

What the hell. Perhaps she would think he was a wannabe and pass him by right then and there, and the problem of desire would be settled by her swift and decisive judgment: to flush this bozo instantly.

'I've never heard that name on a man before, but I suppose it's all right.'

'Never on a man?'

'Well, I've never heard that name on *anybody* before.'

'You haven't?'

'Is is common, then?'

'In today's parlance, I think it… might be.'

'Well, not in mine!'

'Then you have come from some remote district?'

Greenah was completely matter-of-fact: 'Kansas City, Kansas!'

'Well, that's a pretty busy enough place.'

'Yes sir. It is.'

'But the name Butterbugs is unknown to you?'

'I should say it is… Butterbugs. Sorry!'

'Well then, do you go to picture shows?'

'Not yet, but I suppose I will. I want to act in them, and all.'

'Yes, you may want to prepare yourself.'

'For fun?'

'Oh yes, certainly. There's nothing *more* fun. Being in the middle of it, the communing, the creating, the essence of it – when it's right *there* and you're part of it. It's hard to explain. You have to feel, and you have to calculate, too. It's not just a wish.'

'A wish! I wish I could be in a picture show!'

'It's a lot of work, too. A different kind of work.'

'I want to *do* that kind of work!'

'Playing roles.'

'Yes, yes, yes! Being someone else and seeing what happens!'

'What would you choose, if you could? Who, that is.'

'Shakespeare's Cleopatra. She has the spunk, but appreciates the tragedy she's heading toward.'

'Aha! You're a book girl.'

'I'd rather you didn't classify me, Mister.'

'Of course, of course, how unthoughtful of me. I apologize. Say, would you care to sit and have a merrill-leaf drink and some olives, or something?'

'Well, I had thought that I'm gonna get me a tin of Royal Crowned Cola and go *think*.'

'You could, but I myself was thinking, I could give you some tips on approaching the acting thing.'

'The *thing*. Ah yes, the *thing!*'

'Care to?'

'Tips from you?'

'Well, I know about some of that stuff.'

'You never really said…'

'I do now. Yes, I know about acting. I think I do.'

She reckoned he was one of those guys who did those workshops she'd heard about. He sounded pretty good. He spoke well, and he seemed pretty smart.

'Don't mind if I do, Mister. Butterkwugs, was it? Butterworks?'

Though she was funny, he knew she wasn't trying to be. Nor cute.

'Uh, Butterbugs.'

'I knew it had 'butter' in it somewhere!'

'It's there. May I scoop some oily olives in a finger bowl for your pleasure?'

Greenah sat her dreamin' rear down in the flowery poofy pillow of the williwaw chair next to his, the late sun casting its good-time glaze onto her tawniness and darkish-but-honeycomb hair. Guccione might have snapped her in soft focus! Jeff Dunas could have emulated him! Crazy Horse could have spun out a 75-second song of memories over her! Dylan could have *married* her!

Greenah's lips took on the sheen of the olive oil, and the merrill-leaf liqueur made her eyes close.

'Wooooh!' she sighed, stretching her arms skyward, 'Those are *great!*'

'Here, try some St. Faune d'la Zœranne fromage.'

'What's that, Butterbugs?'

'It's a cheese from a legendary castle. I visited it, once.'

'Oh, that's fantastic! I didn't know this place had that stuff. I'm used to…'

It was such a quick transition she made. The exoticism of the snacks, the punch of the sippings, and the languidness of the locale brought her to a place of real connection: very close to Butterbugs' face in order to whisper her renewed impressions of the moment to him. She really liked his vibes, those he'd sent her, on account of being in such an intimate proximity.

Kremel-drizzled peach studs, glisten-dough trapezoids, and above all, the fromage and the Jubba olives, elevated her to 'Friends 4-ever' bliss, so enjoyable did she find this verandah-stop on this long afternoon.

Tipsification led her into home-style cuddling, and soon they were sitting next each other on the old wicker love-seat (as close as the elderly Strangulations), arms wrapped from body to body, with piquant cornichon juice mingling with the dolmades drippings, which ran down their faces as they kissed.

'Whieeee-ooooh' sighed Greenah.

That grape-leaf essence, it came off her chin and landed onto her slanting chest. She wordlessly pooched it out to him, and his tongue served as caretaker, for it followed the stream down, all the way down, past the collarbone gateway, through the cleavage pass, down the path opened by the parted blouse, in and around the shallow pool of the swirly belly button, with its centerpiece of effortlessly-tanned firmness, and south to a walled-off domain.

As their oral gratification sequence, fueled by food, drink, and unabashed touching where it mattered, went from self-conscious questioning to a commitment to quality and a desirable agenda to be met, Greenah suddenly blurted out:

'This stuff... oh man, it gets me horny. It *must!* So horny. Come on, take it down further. Here, I'll add to it.'

She let loose some of the dolmades fluid she'd been slurping, a neat stream from her mouth, so that it gathered on the sleek roll that barely gathered between her navel and her crotch, and its flow continued gravitationally, so she had to hustle to let down her jeans-cum-panties combine, that Butterbugs' tongue might keep up with the consensual rill, which gave her linear thrills that were headed in the right direction.

Gosh, she was baring herself in a sense, but in another way, it was all for art, because the premise was sensual absorbency, not seduction or guile. Swept away by the delights of consumables, she led the list of requests, and Butterbugs followed.

Just then, the verandah floorboards creaked again, this time with more purpose, as there came along two grandees in the Industry, senior member Bob Evans and young power-buck Sebastian Transept, who was poised to have a bumper year of hits, what with his securing of the Darley Dickell series and all, based at Oxidized Onion Studios. Besides that, he was classified, by Industry insiders and those who could absorb such palaver from the consumer side, as being the hottest dude in either-side-of-the-camera pictures – hottest after Butterbugs, of course.

The two producers, well-versed in the etiquette of a company-town's needs, didn't even interrupt their rap on their Industry's trends of the moment (which invariably concerned things Butterbugsian), while at the same time observing the casual encounter taking place in this verandah's best nook. Some dude was eating out some fantasy chick. So what? Cool, in fact.

'How nice though,' each one of them thought, independently and subconsciously, 'That we live in an environment where such things can freely take place.'

Everybody here loved free love.

They both would defend such freedoms to the death, as would Butterbugs.

Butterbugs, for his part, having nothing against either Bob or Sebby, nevertheless wished to remain anonymous just now, so he didn't look up, either to Greenah's superstructure before him, or toward the other two on promenade. Instead, he firmly plopped his face into the always-reliable triangle of ultimate devotion, all of it in favor of when a man loves a woman, in order to stem the flow of the sensual rivulet that was turning this girl so 'on', naturally.

However, Greenah, in the midst of her ecstatic food 'n' semi-sex experience, happened to catch a glimpse of Sebastian Transept's profile as it passed. The shades, the sideburns, the golden chains and things, the white belt and white shoes, all said something to her: this is a picture person. Somebody who's in the biz. This is a person to approach. This man will lead her to fun, to movies, to showing her stuff.

Without further indulgence in her sensual pleasures, Greenah stood up, passed over Butterbugs' head, a few drops landing on his noble pate from her intimate archway, then she amalgamated her minimal kit back into presentation mode, zipped up the fly, and got her sandal-carried little ass going down those verandah planks, after Sebby and Bob, for to make her first real contact in Hollywood with someone who *mattered.*

Butterbugs, down on his knees in the retreating light, gathered himself against the fabric of the overstuffed chair and felt the thin trickle of unresolved Greenah seepage moving toward the static climax of his chin. He squeegeed its flow with his index finger and installed it in his mouth as an agreeable coalescence of the pleasant encounter now interrupted.

'Mmmm,' he mumbled. 'Nice.'

Nice, but a marked emptiness remained as a legacy of – what was her name again? She was lovely, to be sure, but truly empty. She was an e.g. of the *new* new people hitting town. Book-smart perhaps, but street-smart? Who knew? These, the brave new people coming into the Industry, that's what they were: empty. Even less tied to precedence than he himself was. Yet, he was strangely envious. They had the sort of emptiness that was 'free'. Detached. And vacuous, without self-consciousness. You read a couple of Shakespeares, then you *say* you did. That was enough.

Come to think of it, passing up and over him in search of opportunity, Greenah had shown her apparently true self. Hippie chick she was not. Impeccably shaved, in fact. Come to think of it, Sebastian Transept maintained an Adult wing of his Sebastian Transept Presents outfit, which was a good little earner. Their team was famous for always having fun. Young girl in a hurry, but knowing where she was going.

Silly, silly Butterbugs!

He sampled a bit more of the gobblers' options from the trays.

'Funny, these things don't strike me as aphrodisiac in their nature…'

Always learning, this ultrastar.

He walked certain streets, at night, and thus, under cover. Of course, night on the LA backstreets was far from dark. The great bowl of always-accessible ambient light in the city was nearly as omnipresent as the Big Gaming Rotunda's luminescence at the MGM Grand in Vegas; that kind of soft reference-like glow that never quite leaves you in the dark. On the other hand, such an atmosphere was almost as if someone were always watching over you, for their own voyeuristic purposes.

Lately, in this interregnum of both a nation's rebuilding and a production's final preparation, Butterbugs had to decide whether to wholly return to his progressive life after much devotion to such a specific ideal of escapism – that is, the dreamy Pepper/Prairie bliss – that had been his standard for the longest time. It was certainly not the aspirational Shangri-La of Gothpore that he contemplated right now. Nothing so concrete. Rather, it was retrospection on the not-quite-obsessive but admittedly remote prospect of 'la vie idéale' that Pepper Carlson occupied. And Pepper's Puck-ette, that sweet Prairie Browne, who started the whole thing, who'd led him thither. *She really, truly DID!* And if… And perhaps, dear Prairie – dear, dear Prairie Browne – might yet lead him back, all the way back… to she, whom he really, truly loved. Love in its most poetic and fulfilling form! Not the worst thing on which the ultrastar's searching attentions might be concentrated. There was no one to hate in this instance, no one to blame for his frustration, disappointment, sadness. Not even himself.

If only he could attain some sort of contact with those girls, and climb aboard their world, complete with its epistemological sanity. If he could, he certainly would, leaving 'UWH' incomplete, for an unfinished world to wonder after. Now that so much else had been accomplished in his life, the old pursuit of happiness remained in doubt, like an ungainly child abandoned at a sock hop.

Sadly pathetic, he tromped all around the flat sidewalks, bordered with dead grass, from somewhere deep in the past. Marshall would have known them. Yes he would. And would he also know where Pepper and Prairie were?

'I've been looking *all over* for them…'

Marshall, with his knowhow in matters both elusive and impossible, might answer:

'Sorry, but they were probably just *maya*, as is most of life.'

There he was, out there in the dark somewhere, whispering:

'Have you seen a girl called Prairie Browne…?'

It was a question he asked himself over and over again as he stole away, all the way up, in fact, to the old home town – in secret. It was a question he would keep asking, even if he were to become a poor wayfarer, lost to the world, derelict, even unrecognizable, and broken. With endless steps, surely towards entropy, he might be seen in obscure lanes or on barren tracks, feebly inquiring of anyone or anything at all that lived, from bunched speargrass to martinet townsman:

'H-have you…? S-seen? A-a-a *girl?* A g-girl – ? Called… *Prairie B-Browne…?*'

And any animal, vegetable, or even mineral might peer after him, shaking their heads, reflecting grimly on this pitiful and hopeless mission. And his inevitable doom in its assured failure.

Carstairs! Lonely remnants of something or other… Something once vital, viable, and visionary. Something patently, even peculiarly, American. An optimism in the wilderness, gone wrong somehow. Like the Nation itself under the previous administration, the streets and bricks he once knew were teetering on the edge of oblivion. The Nation was though, on its way to amendment, to preservation. The same could not be said of Carstairs.

On account of the ultrastar having spoken of his origins to neither press nor producer, nor even in any intimate relations, there was no special guise taken

659

up by the town as having witnessed the nativity and provided the setting for the world's most honored picture player's unknown years. It had indeed fostered him, but no one really knew. Here he was now, in his years of achievement, virtually sneaking around the place he may once have called home, but had never really believed in.

With certainty then, did he know he wouldn't be finding anyone called Prairie Browne hereabouts, nor would he ever locate she who was called Pepper.

At midnight, under a Fred Remington sky of blue stars, while standing in the abandoned Ludge plant's evening shade, gazing at the towers and mansions of the municipal core, he officially and finally gave up his quest.

'The girls are gone...,' he murmured. 'Gone from this land. Gone from this universe. And gone from *me*...'

It was a strange resolve, but a closure nevertheless.

Somehow he knew there was no one in these precincts who might know him in his present guise. Surely though, any inhabitant of Carstairs would be aware of his big screen personas, like anyone anywhere. But as to the man himself – nothing to say, nothing to even guess at.

Somehow he knew that the trickle of blood, the bits of dust, and the fragile framework of bone that had once been Old Dad were no more. Long ago no more. As forgotten as a red ant's decision to go around the rock ahead, instead of over it. Old Dad was a *nothing*. Is that, then, what he was becoming now, as part of a family tradition? The acreage he once lived on was no doubt more dissolute than the somber structures in the town's barely-breathing center. It probably didn't even exist on this planet any longer.

Notwithstanding this, he refrained from uttering his most reliable self-identifier: *I am a stranger here*. Because, he wasn't, really.

There, over there: the Goth Theatre. That was where his life really began!

Stealthily, he made his way across the vast waste ground that spread towards the grand old house's flying buttresses. He drew nigh and sought refuge in the arched gallery beneath, noting the great tower's ecclesiastical profile as the three-quarter moon rose behind it. Feeling his way all along the polychrome wall, he arrived at a set of side exit doors, and, all of a sudden, the bare spark of an impossibly distant memory was kindled in his recollective mind.

It was *here*, at the very beginning of his true life, when he was playing a top-hatted-and-caned New Year's Baby, that those who'd minded him carried him out from the venue of his premiere. He could not recall who such people actually were, but he remembered that half the theatre's elevation extended well below ground level, so that if a person was exiting at this particular point, they would have had to ascend far up the main balcony in order to arrive at the Earth's surface once again.

As a performing tot full of wonder, fresh from his first Stage Left exit, such a fulsome impression had made a huge impact on him. Its lastingly profound effect was undoubtedly the actual inaugurator of his intrinsic sense of drama. *The* Drama. The very force that would propel him inexorably but gloriously to the place where he stood today.

At the top of all possible stardoms.

Was *that* where he was now? At this obscure, erstwhile house of entertainments, hunched in secret, with trembling hands, ready to try to part the double doors to nowhere?

Incongruity did not occur to him just then, only a stasis of mind, unaffected by drama or any of its notions.

Chained! Closed! Dark now!

However, the once-confident panels of the portal gave somewhat, and the clank of linked hardware inside told of a very long closure, but did not echo into the dead air therein. In the gap he was allowed to squint through, there was just enough half-light to detect row upon row of still-intact balcony seating, marching down, down, down. A dim well, a vast cistern below, full of rising damp, and, with it, an odor of things moribund, motionless, morbid. Yet, way over there somewhere, a lone bulb in the last illuminated exit sign gave dimension to the mysterious space, and he recoiled with fear, lest he be sucked into what was once a realm where fantasy reigned, but now a nameless abyss.

Never was 'There is nothing here for me' a more potent maxim in the self-reflection of an ultrastar. Better to return to his present self, hollow though it was, than this dead end of failed findings. There was little to question in the matter, as the way back into any former self was blocked by bricks, chains, closed doors, and darkness.

'There is nothing here for me,' he said in a stunned whisper. 'There is nothing here *of* me.'

Butterbugs was still a dreamer. Then he woke up.

58.

The Remnants of Dignity

The most glittering, the most spectacular, the most-attended gala, probably in Hollywood's history, was now about to take place.

The Occasion: Victory – Signaling *Pax Bvtterbvgsicvs*
The Venue: The Lazaretto
The Host: Butterbugs
The Presenter-Generale: Shonnaleen Gubbins
The Line Producer: Tuan Jim
The Time: 7:00PM till whenever
The Guests: Everybody who is anybody in classless Hollywood, on divers planes
The Only Ground Rule: C.lean Y.our O.wn V.omit

Needless to say, all the creative and productive might in the film metropolis was available to make this *the* star occasion of the epoch. Not that the occasion's purpose was intended as such. But that was what it *must* be. A nation's liberation was something to be joyous about, and the cinema burg's version of its celebration would naturally outdo any attempts elsewhere in quality, color, style, and, if considered all by itself, its cast.

Contrary to cinematic buzz, the festivities were not at all a wrap party for 'UWH' (the whole cast and crew of which, were of course invited, however). How *could* it be, anyway? Firstly, the filming itself was not yet wrapped. Secondly, Butterbugs was very specific about a separation of film and state. This was a national celebration – localized, but honorific.

Those being the basic guidelines, the host was immediately petitioned by two people who were very close to him. Hazel Snyder and Charles Technicolour Clearwater showed up at The Little Grass Shack in the upper levels of the estate, where Butterbugs was currently camped out, studying the drill for the final sequence of 'UWH', coming up soon.

The teamed decision-makers were still not wholly committed to where it would be filmed, whether in Jambutterbugsabad, or out at Lasky Mesa, in the absurdly close-by wastes of the Santa Monicas. This was not a dilemma based on poor planning, and its development had nothing whatsoever to do with the late Hyman Goth. It did, however, have something to do with the late Montague Realms. In a grand gesture unique in the annals of moviemaking, exact duplicates of the colossal grande climax sets (e.g. the HMD's monstrous citadel) had been success-fully commissioned and built in *both* locations. The cost of this bit of insurance matched the size of the constructions themselves, obviously. But, due to a gener-ous infusion of funds toward this end from an intensely popular public subscrip-tion, spearheaded by newly-inaugurated President Roarald Tennunian Beepus as a token of national gratitude, the option was thus realized. However, the lion's share came from a single source. And it was a dramatic one: massive amounts of gold and silver, illegally acquired and hoarded by the traitor Realms, to serve as his war chest to fund his post-coup regime (had it come to pass), were discovered 'neath the subbest of P'gon basements.

The treasure's status immediately fell under the Confiscated Gold (+ Silver, Tantalum, Yttrium & Several Other Fast-Elements) Amassed For Purposes of In-surgency and/or Coups (Bloodless or Violent) Against the US Government Act of 1900, which provided that such confiscations, once cleared of restitution costs, must be allocated to: 1) Charitable concerns, such as orphanages, fishermen's widows, etc.; and 2) Cultural pursuits that edify the People, such as the Cinema of Enhancements, etc. (The 'Cinema of Enhancements' clause was added in 1911, just as film was taking off...)

Unanimously, 'UWH' fit right in.

So the new sets rose out at the Mesa, providing a sort of 'famine relief project' for the Industry's second string of artisans and hammer-slammers, recently tossed out of work. This was due to several Sebastian Transept Presents projects that had gone tits up (though they were not, it might be noted, any in his Adultia wing, some of which would feature his new sensation: one Greenah de la Lonndaire).

The proximity of the Lasky Mesa location to the Mega|Goth home base really turned the heads of most of the production team in the right direction. Especially ol' Porter Parker, whose huge weight loss was mostly due to the 26-hour one-way commutes to/from Jambutterbugsabad.

[Although the real reason for his astonishing weight-dump was that he had formed quite a bond with Joby, the cool Aussie flight attendant, who was working the route regularly on the Bronston planes. As their relationship intensified, Porter found it a tremendous opportunity to trim up, so that the previously unappealing producer was now dating one the foxiest and smartest young women to be found in any community, let alone movies or jet-setting.]

Butterbugs was passionately devoted to Jambutterbugsabad, but he had to ad-mit, the sheer practicality of a local grande climax was an attractive notion.

The set construction being a situation that was well in hand, it was thus not the reason why Haze and Chas now bent their steps to the L.G. Shack, where the host was in station, decked out in Lucknowi chican comfort-clothes.

'Hey, you two! Come on in. I was just brewing a pot of ketterick-pendaboll tea. Would you care to join me?'

'Delighted, Butterbugs!' said Chas cheerfully.

'Most kind of you, Bb!'

Haze had the same sound to her voice.

Cups poured, butts on pillows, reclines accomplished, Butterbugs knew the visit was social only.

'You wouldn't believe how the Industry has responded in prepping for this Victory shindig,' said the actor. 'I haven't had to lift a finger. Everything's coming together under Tuan Jim, who's exec producing. Shonnaleen was here a little while ago. All I have to do is show up.'

'The grounds are stunning,' said Haze.

'It's going to be perfect,' added Chas. 'I especially like all the different lanterns.'

'Good stuff, all the way round.'

'Yeah.'

'Indeed.'

Butterbugs considered the pregnant pause that now descended.

'You two have twinkles in your eyes, you know,' he said. 'They're easily detectable.'

'You tell him, Hazey. Straight up.'

'All right, Techie. Straight up it is. Butterbugs, we're *betrothed!*'

'Again? I mean, that's terrific news, you two! For keeps this time?'

'Oh, I think so, Butterbugs,' said Chas. 'You see, there's an added element this go-around.'

'We added it up,' Haze joked.

'We're not only betrothed, we're expecting, too!'

'No way! Really? I think that's just super! Really?'

'I think it'll work out nicely. Haze is 55, and I'm all of 60. I know, it's crazy, but our other kids, from – get this – *four* marriages besides the two of our own, will do team-parenting for the kid when our time runs out. They're more excited than we are. It's all set up!'

'You two! An elegant solution to love's outcome! I'm thrilled! Baby's OK, ancient Haze?'

'Blissfully normal! Calm sea and prosperous voyage forecast!' she smiled broadly. 'I'm in fantastic shape.'

'Agreed, agreed!' Chas planted one somewhere in her trademark low-cut top.

'Now, what can I do for you that's special?' asked the ultrastar. 'Cuz *special* it's gotta be!'

'Well, sir,' said Chas, 'We'd love it if we could be hitched sometime during your sure to be swingin' party – As a footnote, mind you, not in any way a centerpiece. No showboating, no way.'

'We don't even want it announced beforehand,' added Haze. 'No warning. None. Hollywood's favorite Marryin' Sam, Pastor of the Peace: Abner Artoch Hale, will already be there, of course. It would be a high privilege, if you're amenable.'

'Otherwise we have to do a Belvis wedding in Vegas,' said Chas, in all seriousness. 'Don't really have *time* for that…'

Butterbugs waxed enthusiastic, and his own eyes adopted the same twinkle.

'My super-producers! Well, I guess I'll just have to nab P.o.P. Hale at the right
moment,' he said with instant agreement. 'After all the national respectful stuff is
concluded, we'll have it done on The Terrace, where all can see and participate!
How's that for a playing-plane?'

'Oh, that's what we were hoping for, my fabulous fellow,' said Haze.

'Thanks, turbo-friend!' said Chas. 'Oh, and there's something in this for you
too, Butterbugs. We'd like to name the baby in your honor. Middle name status
OK? You know, works for either sex!'

Butterbugs did a mock-tension pause before quietly saying, 'You have my permission…' after which they all exploded into laughter, with kisses, hugs, and all
that stuff.

Seven PM on the night-of-nights! Vintage balm in the liberated southern Californian air. Gentle layers of eve that even the Mediterranean cannot emulate.
Mild and mellow temperateness to allow the skimpiest of dresses and the whitest
of suits. Everybody got to wear what they wanted though, and while the spectrum
of togs was wide, the accent was on pizzazz, from pixyish to plantational. This
was *Hollywood:* dress-ups expected, but tonight, not from the likes of Western
Costume.

The glow of soft lamps! Rich aromatherapy offerings! Gawker artist exhibi-
tions throughout the grounds! A sort of candy-land was laid out, democratized, in
keeping with the Peoples' Triumph way back in DC. (A mighty national celebration was in progress on the Mall, attended by millions, sure to come off without a
hitch, produced by the inimitable Urnan Tarquesquieu, Jay-Z, and Robert Emmett
Dolan.)

Here in LA, the festivities commenced right on time.

Because all who knew The Lazaretto tended to love it, and all who would know
it for the first time tonight would also fall in love, the spell of enchantment was
so effortlessly universal, it suddenly seemed like the most *healed* place in the
nation. Its effect was downright catching, and for all the right reasons. Internation-
ally-broadcast coverage of the night's events certainly had a peacemaking quality
to it, for the benevolence its scenes conveyed was the type to inspire rather than
deride. No 'Hollywood-Types' labeling applied. It was a feeling very akin to the
ultrastar's films themselves, and no wonder: Butterbugs' throwing open his doors
to the world had predictably wondrous results.

If peacemakers are blessed, that's what everyone happened to become during
this night's gathering. Of the lucky invitees, whether high or low in the Industry, many were engaged in perfectly normal work-related feudings or fussings.
Most took their beefs home with them, in the great tradition of modern work life.
Conventional wisdom might dictate that if facing an adversary in a looser party

environment, some might be tempted to stoop to fightin' behavior as an egotistical or vengeful gesture, with the excuse of 'proving something'. Always a potential. But as the gala unfolded, everyone forgot all cause for grievance or fault or annoyance, and got on famously with whomever was at hand.

That was what Peace was all about. Not being bugged, bothered, or bewildered by other people. Maybe – just maybe – the effect would be a lasting one.

It began right here, tonight.

And who was on hand? Well, *everybody* in the Hollywood picture scene. Music, legit, auditorium, exhibition, online, art, and TV too, but mostly picture folk. Ages raging from prams to hospital beds. Mostly persons in between. Too many names to even start mentioning, and while official documenters of the event were swamped with work in covering it from start to finish, there was a remarkable lightness and lack of *duty* (except for enjoyment) to the party, even though this was, in the scheme of things, an important festival. And the fact that everybody got along so well, without pretensions or conflicts, wasn't just a matter of best behavior. It was true civilized evolution in action. Nothing else quite like it had ever taken place.

In warm turquoise light they mingled and chatted, nibbled and sipped, giggled and gurgled, greeted and rendezvoused, laughed and exclaimed, hugged and kissed, petted and foreplayed.

The Annals of Victory Night were extensive and distinguished. At 9:00PM, Shonnaleen assembled the hundreds of celebrants on the huge Oval before The Terrace, where speeches and testimonials were given, honoring the nexus of what this occasion was meant to signify, specifically within the larger-than-Hollywood sphere. She declared that an aura of remembrance should be maintained, though cheerfully in concert with the whoop-whoop-whoop of hardcore celebration.

The great Gubbins played it for solemnity, as the bottom line and the theme of the evening was one of gratefulness to a nation for waking up, standing up, and remaining standing. True, it was a somewhat rude – and crude – stirring of public consciousness perhaps (Marshall's demolition of the Murn Administration, that is), but no one questioned its Great Purpose any longer. Conversely, in a wholly cinematic context, blowing up things to solve plot problems in a given movie were now viewed with some dubiousness by many filmmakers here this night. But what explosions accomplished in real life was another matter entirely for debate... It would always be argued whether removal of an entire corrupt edifice was the most effective way to manage bad behavior in a civilized way. But sometimes a mere tea party is just too subtle a gesture for the peoples of Century 21. Gestures of a more dramatic kind are how we deal with things now.

'In a summation that brings us up to this night's cherished occasion,' Shonnaleen proclaimed, 'It must be stated, with the clearest comprehension, that revolutions often entail violence. Ours of late was indeed a grisly demonstration. Yet, given the intractability of our plight as a nation under tyranny, a harsh exit from it, unto enlightenment, was apparently needful. There is no doubt whatsoever though, that upon this Earth, our *Second* Revolution, just concluded, closes the book, for *ever*, on Change Through Violence!'

Gigantic applause and high cheering erupted after those epic words.

There followed a fireworks display of great inventiveness, the equipment of which had just arrived from Butterbugs' favorite 'By Appointment' fireworks shops in old Canton. And rigged up amongst the cypresses was a frame that supported a quite spectacular 3-D firework portrait of Marshall Vogg, whom Shonnaleen had eulogized as the real hero of the occasion. And while his recognizable visage sparkled and glowed over this gathering of goodness, toasts were made, not a few tears were shed, and more than one picture deal was signed, down in the crowds somewhere, for a Marshall biopic.

The official duties of the evening having been obliged, Butterbugs was quick to keep the crowd roped-in before they dispersed into advanced partyizations.

'My friends and neighbors!' he announced, with both hands raised high, having climbed up on one of the urn-lined pediments of The Terrace's semi-circular edifice, 'How *now?*'

Hearing the ultrastar's voice aimed at them, and seeing his Joshua-like figure, up on the romantic heights, all were galvanized. Just like in picture shows across the globe, wherever a Butterbugs picture played, whether at this moment, or any time in the future.

'You came tonight, and I thank you. Humbly and with the most felt of hearts! You venerate the hero of our times, and I thank you, especially, for that. He thanks you, too. I met him once, you know, though I was wholly unaware. And I lifted him up... But he lifts us far higher, and to a grander plateau. Remember, always remember, the moment when the world changed. You saw its nadir. Now we ascend to its apogee – and *beyond!*'

Great cheers.

'Tonight we commemorate. Tonight we celebrate. You come, you promenade, you enjoy. Which, I might add, you shall do at this place until it is your pleasure *not to!* But before you vanish into The Lazaretto's æther, where many fine pleasures await your discoveries, please consider, another jim-dandy task awaits to be enacted.'

The partiers were hooked. They weighed on his every word, with high anticipation and respect.

'Speaking of a distinguished *Jim*, please, cinematic citizens, a dandy round of applause for my Production Manager, Chief Khansammah and Sommelier, the unique, and very ubiquitous Tuan Jim! Never was any Victory Hullaballoo better served!'

Praiseworthy applause, as tumultuous as any tonight, surrounded the Tuan on all sides.

'Oh, and *one more* thing. It has been entertained before me, that in fact, since tributes have been duly made and never-to-be-forgotten memories are now ensconced where they should be within our progressive consciences, the idea of another kind of solemnity, a sweeter kind, should be given a chance, as long as all you fine peoples are here to witness it. After all, for legal purposes, it *needs* witnesses. At least two.'

The audience wasn't quite sure...

Then, the actor burst out:

'Are you *with me??*'

A vociferous 'You betcha!' and countless other affirmations resounded from all who were there, as they thought, 'We don't even have to *think* about how to answer *that* question!'

'Thereupon! I should like to invite you all, right at this moment, at this location, on this very night, to a most deluxe kind of ritual. Right here, right now! It is a ceremony I think ye all will take into your hearts and treasure. For at this very time and this very place, in front of everybody, and indeed, to further honor our Marshall Vogg, I present our beloved Pastor of the Peace, who has married everyone from Jimi Krinki and Elessa Drundaraboundn to Angie Dickinson and Joey Bishop! Would you please welcome, ladies and gentlemen, the Rev-err-rund Abner *Hale!*'

Tremendous applause and cheers greeted the celebrity hitcher, famous for his hip-length platinum hair. Last week, while a guest on 'The Zurk Clamson Show' (VXTc), Rev. Hale revealed that he was 105 years old. Asked what his current condition was, he'd replied that it could be described simply by referring to his last name. '*And*, hearty!' he cracked.

Tonight he wore a long white frock coat, grandad pants, and trademark collar, which he personally starched himself. Holding an epic circuit rider hat and brandishing his 'All-Purpose Technical Texts of Marriage' pamphlet, Padre Hale reminded Butterbugs of a southern-fried Finlay Currie – or else C. Aubrey Smith in a fright wig.

'Because,' Butterbugs rode the crest of the approval-wave generated by his fine onlookers below, 'We are about the witness the union of two of our *favorites*. Get ready to wish them the best (yet again, but for the rest of time, *now*). For they deserve it as the best of any group does. May I proudly present: Hazel Snyder and Charles Technicolour Clearwater, who are about to be joined in high-toned and total wedlock! For the ages!'

Most cheered, some swooned, and all rejoiced at the mating of these two top-flight cinematic eagles, who were universally admired by the entire Industry and its associated communities.

The ceremony was positively thrilling, with Butterbugs as best man, Purrby Burrburr as bridesmaid, but no others were in train. With the procedure stripped-down and all-business, the couple kissed after only three and a half minutes.

The obviousness of the outcome, combined with his stepping aside to allow for the newly-reweds to bathe in the limelight, did not require Butterbugs to do any follow-up presentation talk. So, retreating back into the shadow of a grotesque statuary, he felt as if he had not only given away a couple, but that a piece of his longing had been lost in the transaction.

Damn moods!

'What about me?' he thought, perhaps importunely, as this was supposed to be a time of great luster.

Well, what *about* him? A parade, it seemed, was passing him by. If in fact he thought about such things, he might well become quite surly. All about him were happy people, almost all of them coupled – and happy – largely because of him. And here he was, a single fellow, generally *un*happy, because of them.

Did anyone not notice? Did anyone not care?

It was an equation he did not desire, and its effects over him were even more unwanted. But he couldn't help himself. He was bummed and felt left out. Way out. On such a night!

Then, emerging from the brush of the sonnah-kroo acreage that butted onto the Oval, like two teens who'd just discovered each other's attributes, Saskia and Justy came out onto the stage of The Terrace, holding hands.

'Butterbugs,' called out Saskia, while virtually addressing the whole crowd at the same time, 'Justy's *just proposed* to me – *formally*, this time! I'd just like to say, on behawf of both of us, we'd like to tie the knot in quick succession after Haze and Chas, if we may! That is, while Parson Hale is still available. Oh, Butterbugs, *might* we? Wilt thou give us thy blessing, lover of ours?'

Justy went over to Butterbugs, who had come forth from the grotesque's shadow, and took him in her arms. Her voice was hushed.

'Dearest lover, it is our most intense wish. After we three have been through so much, one must grab on to any reliability that will carry us into the future. We love you, but since tripartite unions are not yet legal in this here state, I'm starting by setting the foundation with Saskia, my sacred girl.'

Both she and Saskia, who drew in to join, then shed copious tears, for they knew their desire could only make Butterbugs an outsider, no matter how close they pressed to him.

'Sure. Why not?' he said.

The great actor was… sort of… casual. And the tone in which he said it was… flat.

But no one noticed. The thrilled couple were in bliss, cheers went up with hats and bouquets, and the merry-making rose into a kind of tarantella.

No one heard, either, when Butterbugs muttered, 'The hell if *I'm* going to be the one who objects at their moment of forever holding peace…!'

From flatness to downright sourness. His face became a prune of disassociation. Even the great man, Butterbugs, that paragon of selflessness, was jealous as a trashy 'National Suspector' headline's intent right now. He just wanted to… spit.

But hell, it was *he* who had neglected them both, and had gone wandering, right? Quite some time ago, in fact. It wasn't just because of all their busy careers. He'd let them go and he knew it. The least he could do now was shut up and respect their fidelity to each other.

And he did. He shut up and went back over to them, kissed them, and held them tightly. The three bawled with bitter-but-mostly-sweet joy. They all cared so much, and they were so enriched by each other, that the tiresome premise of what anyone was going to 'get' out of a given situation (here, as applied to Butterbugs, the acquisition was 'loss') then and there melted away, like spilled gum-apple juice licked up by a dog. Which was what Hugo, The Lazaretto's star hound, was doing right now. With his baloney-tongue, he delivered his love and fidelity directly to Butterbugs' right hand, as surely as the left one cupped Saskia's shapely bottom.

While Hugo's tail wagged briskly, tousled face devotedly looking up with marbly eyes, the ultrastar and his gals realized what was happening and burst into a great infectious laughter, then welcomed the sweet and excited pup into the center of their loving huddle. As the star of the hit Butterbugs family picture, 'Hugo, Dog of Peace' (20th-Fox) and its sequels, in which a dog ascends to the US presidency, this canine was true to his character, and all hearts grew warm from the wisdom of his gesture.

Right on cue, the youthful and equally lovable Hudson, Hugo's student, protégé, and snuffling associate, all leonine and rangy, romped into the action like a big toy, making a showy splash. Himself a budding actor now that his beard was in, Hud's swashbuckling elegance was a perfect compliment to his co-dog-star's noble and Byronic character.

The two great Griffs then went into vaudeville mode, tearing up the boards with hilarious goofiness and operatic hound-sound, before shooting off, stage left-right-left, with sheer joy, certain to sign many a claw-tograph for many a faithful and obedient fan this festal night.

'And another thing!' a voice suddenly sounded off, 'I – or we, would like to toss our hats into the marriage ring, too!'

Why, it was none other than Porter Parker, in a big white suit of colonial cut, who then commanded the jolly crowd's attention.

'Now I ask you, lai-tees and gempmun, what better time than *this here present* to join the marrying kinds around here and do it up, fit and proper? Butterbugs, my friend, my star, I humbly ask you, before all these here witnesses, might we – my bespoken and myself, that is, might we line up behind those two lovely ladies in order to plight – or pledge – our troth? Sorry to put you on the spot, *HMD*, but we're so in love!'

The crowd was mirthful, with cries of 'Wedding march, wedding parade!'

One anonymous voice even cried, 'Follow von Stroheim's lead!'

And who might have snagged this perpetual bachelor? Sure enough, Joby the high-flying flight attendant, who emerged from behind a rusticated pilaster, held out her arms, and advanced toward Porter in ultra-high heels, mini-mini, old-fashioned hostess blouse, neck scarf, and cute pillbox hat, to generous applause and whoops.

Conductors Joe Lilley and Walt Scharf were each handling the musical chores for the evening, while Parlor McKenna, Randy Newman, Neil Young, Sinatra,

Bob Dylan, Fred Kaz, Les McCann, Tracey Chapman, Amy Macdonald, Mobuda Kinchendh, Joan Armatrading, Esa-Pekka Salonen, Professor Supertime, Drave Christianson, José Carreras, Placido Domingo (both solo), Suzanne Vega, Kaycee Chambers, Tze Qung, King Pig, Iggy Popp, George Clinton and Parliament, José Greco, Nora Jones, Charles Ching, Sheryl Crow, Richard, Linda, and Teddy Thompson, and a whole bunch of others were ready to serenade, in due course. The only rule was: one song per artist. Sinatra got away with three, Dylan with two. Conductors Joe and Walt, partying but professional, with their one-hand-washes-the-other bands that flanked The Terrace's stage, got their inevitable 'Lohengrin' asses into gear and pleasantly scored the unfolding surprise saga. They did a cool 'one band talks to another' back-and-forth rendition of the Wagner classic, followed by all sorts of inventive variations, minted on the spot. It was fortuitous that they put this much effort into what was becoming a show, because there was more to come.

'Yes!!!' Butterbugs honked in reply. 'Why of course! You *know* it!'

Emboldened and normalized by the love of his Justy and Saskia, he rose to the occasion without any more churlish equivocation – and with relish.

'I see no reason why a triple ceremony is not called for, do you?'

Butterbugs gave one of his fine hand gestures toward the throng. One would think that they of the cinema had seen every variation of dramatic posture known to humankind, and some in multiple takes, but somehow, whenever Butterbugs struck a pose, it was with Picassian originality, with Tolstoyan credibility, and Wagnerian tonality.

'No! No! Not at all! Bring on the brides! Bring on the grooms!' sang the crowd.

'But wait!' sounded off a voice usually soft-spoken but now stoked with confident jubilation. 'Could we not make it *four?!*'

Coming forward from the safety abaft a vine-clad obelisk, was Judah Fitz-Judah, hand-leading his partner, Pennefold 'Penny' Projector. Given the impromptu occasion, an interesting role-reversal occurred between the two. Penny, usually the more outgoing, was a bit chary about seizing this unprecedented opportunity, while for Judah, it was the opportunity of a lifetime. Maybe because Penny's very mom was on the ceremony list ahead of him. Justy smiled and winked at him, which bolstered the young Pennefold instantly.

'Come on through, you two, *too!!*' Butterbugs happily shouted out.

Though a yarmulke and wineglasses were still where Judah'd left them on the obelisk's pedestal, they would not be needed in the here and now. Since Pastor of the Peace Hale's programme was firmly secular, there was no conflict in the civility of his union-making power. He could officiate at a Yummunelkia tribe's mass wedding on Island X, if called. All creeds, castes and persuasions were welcome.

'Now that you mention it, how could you leave *us* out?'

Well, well, well, like son like father (and like mother).

Sonny Projector!

Amidst his own crisis of both family and worth, Sonny had tried to retrace his steps into something meaningfully long-lasting. It couldn't happen via the demands of his wildly successful agency. Which, despite the glitch with his soon-to-be-married son, was restored to new-heights ascendancy. It had to happen through humbleness and willingness to concede: to the reality that he was an idiot when it came to understanding human needs through human interaction. In other words, an intimate partner was desperately required to keep his train on the tracks. Sonny's experience with so-called train troubles could no longer be ascribed to anyone in the White House. Rather, because of his own impulsive nature, and because that train had been coasting so long on sheer luck, there was bound to be a more thorough derailment ahead. That is, unless an intimate partner was located and secured. Silly, but true. He'd had a succession of serious affairs with premium women (including Butterbugs' erstwhile g.f., Mayella – who herself was somewhere in the crowd tonight), but nothing had felt right. An evolution toward something lasting was evident, though. Perhaps it was simple mathematics, applied even to these privileged few.

So he'd put in the effort. He had changed. Not conformed, but adjusted. Then he saw her. She was in a restaurant alone, and they'd clicked, allowing for head to roll over heels. They were both ready, and so it had to be let loose.

'Our union must and shall be preserved,' was Sonny's proposal line.

The she in question was the enchanting Sydney Desh, whom Sonny had pursued on and off for years. Well now: Syd Desh! He was finally mature enough for her Sino-Winnebago charms. One look at her was to love her. That's why she eschewed a screen career, of which she had a brief fling, in which flakes of all kinds coated her with unconscionable demands, so magnetic and transporting was she. Then came the long times of building her own thoroughfare through this jungle of a business. Finally, after she was secure in heading filmdom's top casting agency, she considered herself free to wed. For to be wed was to write off a gap that came to be prominent once other goals in life could be claimed as won. The groom was nothing if not willing. Sonny was essentially opposed to marriage, but if he could get the love of his life into his life, he was ready to line up, right after his son, if needed, for the same treatment. Oh, and after his ex was properly fitted-out, too.

'And, folks, tonight will be our *first time* in bed!' Sonny hooted. 'Really!! Give us a shivaree, huh?!'

He was actually quite accurate in this flimsy-sounding statement, as their dating had been conducted along the lines of Syd's great-granny's 1890s northern W'scaansin etiquette.

They joined the queue, with mass approval from both a floored Butterbugs and a grateful filmic community, who knew that Sonny's agency was going to be one helluva lot more pleasant to deal with now, and that Syd's Gurnelf Castings would be, as well. Pots, pans and wooden spoons were gathered by the faithful.

Speaking of Mayella, whom the ultrastar hadn't seen since Heck was a pup, she simply approached him and casually said, 'Oh hi, Butterbugs.'

'Oh, hoyy...,' he answered politely.

'You remember Conductor Ukaiji, I presume?'

'Why, why *yes*. Of course!'

Conductor Ukaiji stood strongly behind Mayella (who, true to her presentational innocence, wore practically nothing this night).

'You conducted us safely during the emergency at Burj Khalifa in Dubai!' remarked Butterbugs. '*Welcome*, sir! How do you like being in unit production on 'UWH'?'

'Just super-fine, Butterbugs. I'm swiftly moving into production management. Thanks to you, sir.'

'Oh, and Butterbugs?' added Mayella, sort of antsy to get away, 'The Conductor and I are getting married. Tonight. We'll be joining in on the business of the evening. Thanks.'

As they moved away, Mayella was heard to say, 'OK, good. We'll get the civil ceremony over with tonight. I'll give a call to a Qadi in Gaza I know, to cover my Palestinian side, and I just *know* Rabbi Mendelowicz will do the wine-glass trip for us later. We might have to petition Pope Frauncis to do the Cath'lic thing – in Wrocław, of course. You're not already Catholic or anything, are you…? And are we gonna do a Kenyan wedding too, or something…? Is that what you want? Might as well…'

Conductor Ukaiji looked back with a 'That's Mayella for you' look.

'We're totally in love!' he called out.

Butterbugs smiled weakly and shook his head.

Then, along came Yakov and Katya, doing art direction finishes on the Lasky site, just in from Moscow.

'If you please, super ultrastar, we are ready to join,' said Yakov in his Rasputian elocution, through his Old Believers beard. There was Katya, as pellucid and inviting as ever, entreating Butterbugs with her eyes to either marry her here on the spot, or do what she really wanted: to validate getting hooked to Yakov, which is what she'd wanted since day one, and was the very reason why she had seduced him (Butterbugs) at all, in order to draw her closer to Yakov, who, unfortunately at the time when they were all together in Moscow, was going through a voyeuristic phase, but now that he had burst through it, he was a more heroic lover than ever, and keen to marry her at first opportunity, now joined with her in seeking Butterbugs' blessing in their much-anticipated coming-together.

'You friends from Mother Russia!' Butterbugs announced, 'I cannot imagine two people who were more meant for each other! Saltyakov-Schredin might have scripted your progression! Tarkovsky should have filmed it! Ovchinnikov could best score it! I know that all I can do is provide approbation, as its inevitability is pre-ordained, to say the least. And all I can add is that, Yakov, you're getting one terrific girl!!'

Then came forth, and not wholly within an element of surprise, two persons with whom the ultrastar had been particularly intimate: Egaz and Keenah!

'We apply, too, Butterbugs! For the Parson's unification qualities! In auspices such as these, we have reached surpassingly beautiful realms,' said Egaz.

'You lover!' blurted Keenah, still mad about Butterbugs. 'So much love in this proximity!!'

'Here they come,' announced Butterbugs. 'More close ones, more creators from within the center of what we're trying to *do* here tonight. Given these two, we're succeeding. I welcome them into the waiting line. They should be as one, because quite frankly, I know what it's like to be *as-one* with both of them. Egaz has been the anchor of our prized 'Unholy War Hymn', and Keenah has shared her total goodness with selfless charity. You will be blown away – very far away – by her performance up on that big ol' screen. She gives great head, too! Welcome them! Welcome them *now*, in their prelude to togetherness, for it is a unified bastion from which to leverage not only our Industry, but the world in general. Because, just think how Egaz is going to have to handle said world after our little photoplay is complete. I do not envy him, as the onus of competitiveness will be upon him. I tell you, with these two people, do not hassle them, for they are both front-runners in conveying our Industry's latest capabilities, and what it can do into the future. Know that I love them and will stand behind them, in all circumstances!'

The two great figures bowed to Butterbugs' wishes and moved into the queue with a near genuflection, on account of their good fortune, which was not at all taken for granted.

Next, as long as the awareness was up in front of the party's feature offerings, a seasoned couple made their way carefully along, and without asking the ultrastar for validation. No need, for it was Pappy Ford (recently widowed) who made his way thither, with not a good deal of rightful entitlement, and without any verbal permission or entrustment. Yet, there was his usual element of charm and even gentility, primarily aimed at she who kept his company on their way to the altar.

'May I please have another cigar?' was all he said to Butterbugs, as Vera Miles joined him there for the rest of the journey to spousal completion.

To the awe-struck crowd, Butterbugs simply recited their names, as they needed no further introduction or explanation. With show people, mere presence accounted for everything.

The ones made bold by this evening's special matrimonial feature continued to come forward.

'And then there's... ProwlerCat!' marveled Butterbugs.

There was the kittenish superstar, come up to make her vows with none other than B.K. Vendacardamom, genius of the BKV Method, the film stock that was traveling through many a camera at this party – and through every camera of consequence worldwide – to capture it in techniques mixing realism with artisticness, in the most compelling ways.

'I have never seen a finer combination of minds molded to both art and science,' Butterbugs extolled. 'She who knows compassion and how to apply it, and he who knows not only *of* it, but how to *capture* it. Two like and complementary minds, and their bodies will be as one tonight. Please salute them!'

674

Great cheers went up, comparable to any that had come so far this evening.

If Butterbugs had been a more intrinsically wry character, he might have spun off into Mel Brooks-like dialogue by now, what with the gameshow-like aspect to the proceedings and all, which threatened to turn things into parody-ville, despite the distinguished lineup. But the emcee/host kept his wits about him and played it appreciatively and supportively, despite private thoughts that actually bordered on jealousy and envy. This was a *gig* though, and he was the most professional of pros.

There followed a slight lull, in which the revelers noticed that staff were setting up dozens of champagne access-points all throughout The Terrace's campus. (Eustæché et Quœune, too. *Very* expensive champagne.)

'Any more?' was all the trouper asked the audience.

'YEAH!'

Shonnaleen Gubbins, power-wielder extraordinaire (just rated #1 in 'Vanity Fair's Most Powerful in Hollywood list), and presenter-generale tonight, strode boldly into the center stage lighting plot.

'You all know me by first name,' she declared. 'And tonight, I'm getting *married!*'

Shonnaleen-sized cheers erupted.

'And for the first time, too!' she continued. 'Some of you might know who it is. And if you don't, you will, cuz we're teaming up in the biz, as well. All my life, I wanted a cohesive family and work-unit. All the same thing. That's what me and my mate both want. So get used to us, and *work* with us. Everybody benefits. Everybody *wins*. And now, to present…'

Shonnaleen reached around in back of herself and, emerging from the mighty curtain of the power-wielder's form, was…

'Purrby Burrburr!!'

Hazel Snyder's exec secretary-at-large – no longer.

'Well I'll be dahned…,' Butterbugs mumbled airily. He had previously thought, that in order not to make his mateless evening a total loss, he himself had planned to ask sexy Purrby to share a flute of the bubbly with him. Turned out she'd been doing so – and was now – with the multi-gifted, full-of-surprises Shonnaleen, whose upper arm, he noticed, was thicker than Ms. Burrburr's waist. So what! Granted, the great Gubbins had her own magnificent sexuality. Sure, she and the ultrastar had gotten it on a few times, and fun was had by all. Back then, she'd just wanted to feel a man again, but that was enough, and afterwards they'd toddled their merry ways. Was Purrby sleeping her way to the top, then?

As he gazed at their faces though, he saw how profoundly happy they obviously were. Rising from hopeless janitoria to the topmost flight-plans of Hollywoodland had been nothing less than a triumph for Shonnaleen, but she had found those stratospheric reaches to be most lonely as far as affairs of the heart were concerned. For her part, Purrby, emerging from her porno past, had intended, upon the suggestion of friends, to indeed approach Butterbugs, perchance to go out for a soda or something, sometime. Recently however, she and Hazel, after a long day at the office, happened to run into Shonnaleen at Bob's Keg 'n' Cork, who joined them for cocktails. Haze knew the two were really clicking, so she feigned a phone call, allowing the two to – fall in love. It wasn't long before each knew what she wanted: the other.

If Butterbugs saw before him a mountainous black sumo wrestlerette holding the hand of a slightly past-date ex-porno princess whose boobs and buns weren't quite as elevated as even a year ago, it might be the perfect oddball game-show postcard image. But all he saw were two mutually loving people who had found themselves in each other. Poignant. Sweet. Well-deserved. End of unnecessary analysis.

The ultrastar choked up, but he was able to get out, 'Ladies and Gentlemen, may I present Shonnaleen and Purrby – together at last!'

Everyone was just as touched. There were as many 'Awww's as there were applauders.

The next couple did not wait for an invitation. Perry Flask, who had indeed been acting with Butterbugs from the start, ascended and requested that here, in front of everyone, he'd like to renew his marriage vows with his beloved wife Darcie, whom the whole film community knew was worth vow-renewal after vow-renewal.

'Oh, *may* we, Butterbugs?' asked Perry. 'It would mean so much to dear Darcie, and the babes!'

'Yes! Yes! By all means!!' cried the audience to the popular star. 'In front of us all!! *Please*, Butterbugs?'

'I add my vote, dear boy!' said Butterbugs. Then, to the crowd, 'Behold! Two long-marrieds, wishing to renew, prolong, and eternalize their bond!'

Muse Darcie, in flowing powder-blue gown, her lack of affectation always preceding her, went over to Butterbugs and kissed him on the cheek.

'You have been our beacon,' she whispered. 'Without you, this moment could not have arrived.'

He thanked her with his eyes and kissed her back. Her loveliness was not calculable. It only required simple witnessing. He planted his hands round her waist. The tips of his fingers still met, just like they always did. He sighed, but without a Vitaphone of nuance, so she never knew.

The audience gave one collective lump-in-the-throat swallow.

'Oh, picture-show people!' Butterbugs stated, 'You have magnetized our magic this night! Love streams through the very air that we inhale, as surely as love flows through our veins, with a priority over blood! Look above! See! See! how passion streaks through the firmament! Love is the good feeling, the essential settlement upon which we base our lives. Consider these heroic ones tonight, following in the inspiration of late Marshall Vogg. Why? Because they are all and each seizing the moment of projectile action, from which their lives, and the creative output therein shall always affect us. It moves them ahead into purposeful achievement. As I have saluted them all along, I am prepared to do so again, but only after we allow *one more couple*, if one is so in-waiting, to declare their marital desires in front of all of us tonight. For there are limits that even vaudeville dictates, as there are only so many act cards to place on a Stage Left tripod, before even the most appreciative audience stands up, and would to home. Believe me, this is *no occasion* for The Hook!'

Huge audience laughter.

'And now, if that particular couple fancies it, they may step here-up, and proclaim themselves, so that good and patient Pastor Hale may be about his business. One more, please. Only one more.'

There was a milling, but no specific coming-forward of an interested party.

'I might add,' added Butterbugs, 'Our good Hale has agreed to supplemental marriage chores by appointment, as always, in which all the panoply of tonight's ceremonial significance might apply to couples joined in *later* union, as if on the same evening's magical roster. I stand on that principle right now, you see. In that case, no further couple steps up?'

An unsettled noise came from the masses, as a current of urgency spread through them. Then, up the steps to the presentation module of The Terrace did the next and final couple tread, and just in time, too.

The only thing that Butterbugs could do as a result of this couple's appearance was to engage both members in the deepest hugs of the evening. Words were completely inadequate. The ultrastar had been floored many times tonight, but with this ultimate male and female, he was not only surprised – he thought: 'In a just and cool world, these two who now come forward *absolutely and positively* should have gotten together all along, in order that the world be made a saner place. And besides, they are just so fucking transcendent/wonderful, that all the woes in the world, if they were followed-up by these two, would no longer be woes. They would be wonders.'

That was what he thought.

'Butterbugs, from the super-surprised look on your face all through this show, I can tell, you had no idea so much fucking was going on while you were out to lunch!'

TABP was serious, but he and Butterbugs still howled with laughter as this shit came down, like peach blossoms, raining from heaven. Butterbugs vividly remembered what TABP had done in building his confidence that time at the Roxy, and now he felt he was repaying the debt.

'I thought ye were set on that country-girl, Keremeos, high priest that you are.'

'Butterbugs, history is populated by players, man. Some don't stay past the intermissions. You gotta check out who's left in the second balcony lobby.'

'Usually the last place people look...,' the ultrastar host replied, thoughtfully. There were no second balcony lobbies anywhere at The Lazaretto.

''S right, you unholy warrior hymnist!'

TABP had on a spectacular chartreuse clerical collar, but in spite of its conspicuousness, he added, 'I can't marry *myself*, can I? Nor all those dudes & dudettes in any Hale overflow! Hell, I'm on holiday!'

TABP they all knew and loved, but who was she who now joined him, up on high? Whomever she was, she earned the wow and the flutter of everybody who looked up in awe.

Oh now, well, what-the-hell: there was that trademark black tank top, the tight jeans, lace-up boots, and stuff like that. Oh gosh, but she looked great. Better than ever, really. The perfect match for The Angry Black Priest.

Cody de la Funk. No mere left-over choice. No consolation she, only a central goal, thought unattainable by all. And so she was, except for the right guy. Someone always to love. For nostalgia's glowing sake, if for no other reason. Always in service to the Industry. No single person more than she deserved her new position: V.P. in Charge of Production at Mega|Goth. A title that meant she was running one of the world's largest studios, not only in cinema history, but in cinematic reality. The biggest of times. All that effort and sacrifice she'd spent, assisting that sickening psycho Hyman Goth! A certain kind of quasi-revenge had resulted, though. A brief week before, the trades made it public that Hy had willed her his entire interest in the studio.

'WHY, THAT SWEET OLD GOAT!' chirped 'Variety' at the news.

Chas and Haze could not have been more tickled. The studio was ironclad now, and everything was firmly in place to kick off a new, Golden-er Age, with a bigger splash than had ever been seen: Mega|Goth Stvdios presents the Producer Team/Porter Parker production of BUTTERBUGS in an Egaz D'Varzim film of Sawlohmunn Rabinowicz Cane's 'Unholy War Hymn'!
!

'He never laid a thumb on me, Butterbugs. Not the whole time,' she'd confided in him after Hy's wrap. He knew she'd spoken the truth. Hy had embraced erectile non-function in exchange for cracked bliss – which was fine with her.

At any rate, filmdom's smartest (and sexiest) mogul gazed at her former lover before embarking on what would be an exceptional life with TABP. She approached Butterbugs, and before the whole assembly, said more with her eyes than seven pages of dialogue possibly could, to which he needn't reply. They both knew they had had their time together, and now, at least for her, things were going to be better than they had *ever* been. Still in plain view, she kissed him in consummate movie star style: fully, dramatically, but with total honesty, while catering to the coverage camera's big close-up. Then she stepped aside slightly, hands in pockets, and drawn-in a tad, as if she felt just a little bit pretentious in proclaiming her love and obvious relationship with the actor in such a way, despite the completely supportive audience.

Then TABP came over and placed both his strong hands on the actor's shoulders. For a moment or two, it was as if TABP and Butterbugs were on that remote but sunny slope so long ago, where they had solidified their rapport. Way back, when TABP had referenced his former wife and her reaction to the black star's nature. By non-verbal communication, in the form of a penetrating look, Butterbugs asked TABP if this might not be the same kind of deal. In a similar response, TABP replied, 'No; absolutely not, brother; an impossibility.' Butterbugs understood. He knew TABP was correct. There was no way that Cody would not be perfect in every way. Not because she tried to be, but because she was hard-wired that way. TABP's same-level fuse-block was a natural hook-up.

But inside, Butterbugs was experiencing a sort of... cheapening, as the evening wore on. He thought to himself, 'I could've had Cody for all time if I'd wanted. If I'd been smart enough.'

She was another one who'd gotten away. Because of his own failings. Bitch! But how could he not still love her?

Then TABP did something really cool and heartwarming. He pulled out a flasket of Œyuoénaire liqueur, and first offered it to Butterbugs, before downing a nipperkin of his own.

'To Vonda, eh, fellow-chosen one? To Vondakins, now and forever, huh?'

'Huh!' Butterbugs agreed, with a tear to prove his bonding. Another one, who got away...

'Yoe. The triumph of time's progression. It all adds up, but all we have is the coin of the past, the slick of the moment, and the promise of the dawn. Well, let's do-do-do it, baby. We all got rocks to burn, huh?'

'We all...'

Except Butterbugs.

With this preeminent emotion, there was nothing to stop him from being the most touched by this last couple.

'So much coming together on this day!'

'*You* brought it about, man.'

TABP gave a clap on his shoulder before stepping back with his bride-to-be, so that Butterbugs could utter:

'Here and now! All right, then. No more. Not yet awhile, anyway. No way! Therefore, let the knot-tying commence! O Pastor Hale? Is your assembly line in order, I ask you?'

The hale and hearty uniter signaled his readiness, and the ceremonies began. Each was as brief as the Haze/Chas union, so no couple was upstaged. And in Pastor Abner 'Grab-Her' Hale's ingenious style, he gave each a different homily (in the secular sense, of course), touching on the great themes of sex, food, love, travel, and filmmaking.

No one chickened out. These weren't mere larks, and none of the participants were particularly swilled or dummied with any kind of dust. Their commitments were plainly measured against the contemplation of their already-existing desires, while seizing the moment of opportunity with a euphoria that was not vacuous in the least.

Over there, standing in the wings, stage-crewing the event, was Old Atrocity. Butterbugs hastened over discreetly, so as not to detract from the ceremonies now in play.

'OA! What about *you?* You mean *you* aren't going to surprise me?'

'Naw, got a picture to wrap. The Jambutterbugsabad set is all finished and se-cured. Now we gotta do the same out at Lasky Mesa. Too damn busy to sign up for the ball-and-chain programme, buddy-boy. But lemme tell ya something right now. It could happen one of these days, maybe sooner than you think. Remember Tarlah, that girl electrician? She and I are, well, we're, uh, dating – and it's so fine! Looky over there, she's crewing on stage left. Ain't she a cutie?'

Crushed, Butterbugs looked over, and he had to admit, 'Yup, she's cute all right. She's a cutie... She's Chief Elec at 20th now, isn't she?'

'Thanks to you, man.'

'I thought her name was Perrill.'

'That's her *last* name. We're on a *first* name basis now, if you know what I mean.'

Yeah, yeah, Butterbugs knew what he meant.

'Er, see you later, OA.'

Then, out on the stage, Pastor Hale donned his wide-brimmed hat and pleaded for order.

'At this point in the providential space-time continuum,' he declared, 'All done – the nuptials so ordered. I'm a tad tuckered. I did my best, with a humble padre's recitation, for to make mates' lives whole.'

The crowd, suitably amazed by the whole climax-to-climax spectacle, toned down, anticipating a fit & proper wrap-up speech before a resumption of partying.

'You know, marriage is an institution we can take or leave, enter or re-en-ter, or forsake at will. No matter what 'others' may say or think. You may find it remarkable, but I myself have never taken its vows. Never considered it. In-deed, never *believed* it. Until tonight. Tonight, I looked upon all of you here. No assembly line, despite the inevitable comparison. Then I looked around for Butterbugs. Couldn't find him anywhere. Still can't. But all through my vow-rec-itation and pronouncements, beyond the loving couples under my supervision and destiny-direction, I *thought* of Butterbugs. Guess that's all I needed to do. And when I thought of him and his deeds, his generosity, and his wisdom, never have these aging eyeballs witnessed such an inspiration! So it is *Butterbugs* who has infused special significance within these ancient bones ye see before you. So that now, this minute, in this phlegmatic ooze of blood, a new passion flows, with new ideas, and new beliefs! Thereupon, I, single-gentleman-committed, this past century-and-five, now take this occasion – to be wrung by the neck – *just like a chicken* – to hold on, for one more act, to be committed, if it may, for my benefit. Tonight I seek, as so many others have sought, a helpmeet and partner, who shall share the royal path of life with me. You see, I guess I've waited for the right mo-ment, 'cause everything's falling into place. And I have now decided to actually conform and agree to the principles of marriage! I have! *Oh, yeah, I have!*'

The crowd was dazzled.

'I'll be brief. These past seventy-five years, I have been a loyal lover to one whom I've waited for. Waited for, because she was not available till now. O, loyalty! As a young salesman of bibles, texts of Nietzsche, Voltaire, Rousseau and Irwin Sperber, whose field covered Biloxi to Buenos Aires, I was tramping through the jungles of interior Haiti one year, with a bag o' books already succumbing to damp and worm. Well, there she was, the love of my life, Muu-Uu-Alli, just standing there! Though her family was dead-against our love, we loved from afar. I dwelt in that land thirty-five years, but was eventually compelled to come to Hollywood town, so as to become the matrimonial master of the stars and their kin. Who of you knew I was simultaneously pining for my love, back in the lush security of our love-land? Well, now that the ages have passed, her immediate family has been consumed, and we are free to marry! So here she is, you children of film, just standing there – *Hello, young lover!* – waiting for us to get on with it. And to *get it on!* We have been patient, but now we're hot to trot! Though she is a mere ninety, to me she's as fresh today as when I first cast eyes upon her, a barefoot girl from the voodoo wilds of that wonderéd isle! She is my beloved, and tomorrow we shall take ship for that Hispaniola shore, for to found our own church, which shall be, as a sort of further, loftier marriage, a combo betwixt my Lord Teacher church, and her St. Ju-Ju temple, and we're gonna make hot, mad *religion* together!!'

The crowd erupted in super-wild enthusiasm.

'But wait, my children! Wait a while! You all, those who are hitched & those not-ready-yet! I make this appeal: is there not one of you out there, who might tie the knot 'tween myself and my Muu-Uu-Alli? Can't do it myself, you know! We'd *so* love to marry in the midst of the magic of this night! Will no one now do for me what I have done for so many? Come! Tie us up! Take up the burden!'

From way in the back, past the great camphor urns and triobelisks lining the Oval, someone called out, 'TABP!'

Others joined in.

'TABP!'

'TABP!'

'Yes, TABP!'

'Why *not*, TABP?'

Soon the entreaties increased, gathered, and joined in a crowd-wide chant.

'TABP! TABP! Yes, TABP! Why *not*, TABP?'

And in no time at all, the man TABP himself joyfully departed Cody (for the moment), and emerged from the mists now spreading from the newly flowing and carnival-colored fountains, and spread his arms wide.

'Fellow man of a different cloth, here am I, as fully capacitated to perform unions as ye! Here and now, *do* I take the burden from your historic, not-hunched-at-all shoulders, and turn it around for your favor! Hell *yes* I'll marry y'all! Oh, hey! Come to me, sister Muu-Uu-Alli! I dig your voodoo charms! Blessy girl, you are. Dig this duffer preacher with yo' magic dolls & push-pins 'n' stuff! Too cool, you two! Lemme make ya whole! At last!!'

Quick-changing from his already-festive chartreuse dress-collar to his special dolphin-blue neon-lined clerical identification neckwear, he switched it on, and in its cool glow leafed through the 'Technical Texts of Marriage' until he located the Vaudou section. Then he folded over the pages until he found the entry for Mel's Churchings (Pastor Hale's well-known denomination), then recited an ingenious blending of the Creole vows with the Melistic ceremonials.

'Good, blessed TABP,' stage-whispered the venerated, beaming padre at the moment of climax, 'I've waited three-quarters of a century for this moment! Kindly pronounce over us now, will you?'

And TABP *pronounced.*

So these were wed – and epic were the commitments and epic was the occasion. The bells in the Campanile rang out their congratulations, and Pastor Hale and his new Mrs. tucked into much-deserved swelled-meat sandwiches, with jars of beer, before joining in the jig session at the estate's little thiertre, up-country.

But as the evening waltzed on, while every sort of celebratory blandishment was in play, a change came over he in whose spirit the success of the whole party lay. It was as if, after the last bride's bouquet had landed in the forest of glovéd and star-dusted arms, a shutter came down on Butterbugs' open door to generosity of feeling.

Minglement followed, as the party really got into social mode. No more requirements or shows, except to celebrate, respect, enjoy, and get a little plowed. Or not. Butterbugs enthusiastically supported the production of non-*alcool* Grape Glurk at his tiny vineyard within the terroirs of Blaye, Bordeaux region, and there was plenty of Vincent's Punch to offer those who were teetotal.

Everything was under control and running swimmingly. Catering Chief: Muaz-José Khirigh (the onetime beverage procurer, of Isaac Davis Affair fame), who was accomplishing Five-Star foodstuff offerings. There he was, moving amongst all the grub venuettes, his wife and five kids assisting.

Tuan Jim was doing a terrific job as producer. The only thing Butterbugs *didn't* like about his work was that, after tonight, some studio head would surely be offering him a gig as a picture producer that he couldn't refuse. Heaven knew, he deserved one. Oh, another thing that bugged him about Tuan Jim: his hot & heavy girlfriend, the formidable Lady Fashionettah was snogging him every opportunity she got.

'Something for everyone...,' Butterbugs mumbled, as he drifted through the crowd. He knew everyone, of course, but his somewhat saturnine mood brought with it a sort of invisibility. The world's sole ultrastar moved through his own party scarcely noticed.

Then he saw a girl who nearly knocked him over. Talk about a (pleasant) stab from the past! She was that lone flute player of the hills, she whom he'd encountered in the clear air of the uplands before his other sort of ascent – to where he was today. She, the musician, practicing her instrument out in the solitary wilds.

She was here, this night! And what a girl – intact in her alternativism – That is, no make up, no boot-up, and no get-up, with real-girl substance and neat glasses frames; a bit more jiggliness in her figure, but there was that same foamy pudding-delight of hair, that same genuineness that made him want to surround her with a frenzy of digital picture-taking, if only to capture the naturalness of her extraordinariness. And after the photo-session, a lifetime of fun and love.

'This is amazing,' he overheard her say to one of the band's musicians. 'This wedding theme! In a coincidence which matches up well with tonight's melody, wouldn't you know, I was actually *married* for the first time just yesterday, up there on the alm, where I usually do my practicing! Yes, I really was! Can you imagine? And now, we have all these happy newlyweds in the neighborhood! Why, just yesterday I was playing Grieg's 'Wedding Day at Troldhaugen' as an exercise, but at my own ceremonials! We laughed, we cried. And earlier today, just before we were ready to leave for our honeymoon, Krimnos and I wandered over here to see what all the fuss was about... Tuan Jim said it was OK to come on in, as the host's magnanimity is as reliable as winter frost at midnight. What a neighborly fellow! Now we've decided to honeymoon right here! It's so magical. I wonder, though, if I have enough nerve to introduce myself to Butterbugs. I've loved all his pictures from the start, and I have to confess, I always have worshipped the ground he walks on, which is, well, right here, next door to me! Can you imagine? He has touched these stones, these drinking fountain handles, these cypress needles! Oh, how I had wanted him to touch – me! Oops, I've gone and done it. Too many champagne bubbles! I've spilled my desires of the heart. But really, I'm one of millions, aren't I? Or, I *was*, rather. Such a thought is really quite inappropriate now. So I, a mere flute-playing idiot, dare not have shared my deep desire to serve him and to be his playmate or pet! Oh, but that's just dream-talk now. I'd love to introduce Krimnos, the love of my life, to him. He'll give me the nerve I need! Oh, there's Krimmy now, just over there...'

And then the strangely unperceived Butterbugs saw the disgusting outcome: this lovely and sensitive girl led some Greek with a mustache through the crowd and on into his own oblivion.

'*Krimmy*, I suppose,' he thought, mockingly. 'Looks like a 'kriminal', all right...' ??

He couldn't bear the fact that he'd missed out in attuning to such a person, and a neighbor, at that. There she went, his solitary one, a soloist, but solo no more...

Missed opportunities, missed everywhere. In spite of his own C.Y.O.V. law, it was enough to make him want to induce puking, and then to *chew on it*.

Surly-cues danced around his mind. Was every fucking person hereabouts blissfully coupled, or what? Was that the qualifier at the entrance gate or something? He felt like reaming Tuan Jim a new orifice, and in some location more unpleasant than an asshole.

'Why is this happening??' his thought raged. 'Because! You're lonely! LONELY!' was his wail, that no one heard. '*That's* fekkin' why!'

Even long-denied Pastor Abner Hale was this night completed in joined love!

'It can happen, but I canna wait three quarters of a century! Hell, if he'd pulled a charwoman wearing crumpled foil out of his hat, I'd've married her...!' was the gist of his self-centered mourning, just now.

For a moment, he almost ascended to the roof of the little Greco-Roman Temple of Fame that stood on the Arcadian hillock that overlooked the huge The Terrace scene, backed by a Böcklin-like stand of cypresses. Standing atop its authoritative cornice, he would make an eyetooth-curling Cry From The Heart's Soul, a thunder-cum-lightning bolt all here would never forget, which would send them scuttling for cover from a wrath not even Adam nor Eve could escape from. For was he not the High Mad Doctor, omnipotent beyond even *his* own reckoning?

But too many lovers were gamboling in the folly's circular-columned openness, and he lost heart. Lost! Along with everything else, it seemed.

What now, was it all about?

He headed up to The Lazaretto's Far Grounds. Far more shadows than discernible light surrounded him, but everywhere there were revelers out there in the dark, knowing full well what they were doing, and doing it with joy.

The sickening round of questioning continued to heckle him. But indeed: what was it all about? Indeed, everyone who was anyone was here. But what was achieved? Was it just a distraction from the inevitability of what, death? Was it that mundane? Or was it just a tacit subconscious diversion from his failure to achieve the elusive ideal of Pepper Carlson and Prairie Browne? Oh, *why* hadn't he stayed at that remote Lodge in that other dimension, or whatever it was, while it was accessible? Why did he not climb into that chopper to send the others away, and then return to his true love?

'I swear on the smallest stone of that Temple of Fame, which possesses more veracity and integrity than any of my pictures, that I was *there*. I *saw* Prairie Browne! I *touched* Pepper Carlson! Yes, I kissed her, and the kiss was so real – so real I can feel her soft lips at this very moment. So real, I can recall the scent of her skin beneath her falling hair! I tell you, I could testify in a court of law as to these things! Oh, *why* was I allowed to experience their wonder, if it was only going to be revoked? How cruel is fate? How brain-dead was my decision to conditionally leave that site, even though it be in a dream state? Why is perfection not allowed down here on the ground? Why is there the brutal trade-off – that I can achieve success in shadowy picture shows, but I am denied the joys of tangible love? *Why?*'

He knew the horrible answer, the dreaded knowledge, the awful truth: the triumph of his ego had led him to this defeat in victory.

Again, he longed for Marshall's exemption from further earthly punishment.

'Oh Marshall! I am one with you! More, than I ever could have thought! Your longing, my longing. How could they be so very different?'

Butterbugs had hoped for a kind of grandeur to result tonight. Instead, it was just a party. And a wedding reception, to boot. Plus, a honeymoon for some. He was of course happy for his studio execs and colleagues, but there was a wistful reality that bespoke exclusivity – as in, 'Things work out great for some people, but as for *me...*'

Butterbugs wouldn't dignify an emotion such as Envy to take pride of place, but he couldn't help it... As the newlyweds and their party reveled, he himself would have to evaporate into the æther this night. It was just too poignant, and ultimately painful. In addition, his anger was rendering him sullen and stupid.

The nagging issue of personal fulfillment overrode all the smiling faces and pretty bodies and successful careers now on his property. He had achieved so much, but here, at the top of stardom, he seemed an empty cipher. All challenges had been conquered, 'cept one. Now he was rendered clueless, as puzzled as he was disappointed, and, admittedly, as angry as he was puzzled.

Observing The Terrace from the midnight shade of an upper grove, Butterbugs gazed down at the framework that held the firework portrait of Marshall. A few plugs still flared dully, while most were burnt-out sockets, where non-eternal flames once proclaimed their tribute. His envy was just as applicable to the dead as it was to those who were livin' it up all about him. Again, he envied the dead hero just then.

Not quite ready to fall 100% in love with easy death, he settled amidst the rime-cones and jacaranda-waste next to an eroding balustrade and reviewed the might-have-beens of this night, even though it was so early.

Why had things gone so wrong for him?

Had they really gone so wrong?

Yes. They had.

Otherwise, why the uncharacteristic negativity that so clamped him now?

Why, even Purrby, one of the delightful dedicatees, along with t'others, to 'UWH''s assured, unqualified success, and whom, he assumed, had gotten tips from Haze on how to hit on Butterbugs tonight – Why had she other plans? Why had she suddenly become bold enough to reveal her true self? Why had she made it clear that she was sweet on Shonnaleen Gubbins, above all others? And why tonight? Tomorrow night, fine, but tonight, when he was so weak – why? In considering her as an impressive and honorable personality (with a really cool look and demeanor, by the way) the ultrastar thought he might've dated Purrby so they could check each other out. One night was sufficient for things to succeed or fail.

Fail...

But then the nobility of altruism, in the name of others' joy, a role he had played in many a picture's scenes of decision, now was allowed access to the scope of his self-pity. That was certainly the case in the immediacy of the moment anyway, for he admired both Shonnaleen and Purrby in the purest sense, and that admiration transcended any po' boy's self-absorbed expectations of 'I-want-this/I-want-that'. Brakes on, a wall with a plain sign stood ahead: SACRIFICE *AS SENSIBILITY*, IS YOURS.

His 'Stella Dallas' (Goldwyn/UA, 1925 & 1937) moment! Sweetly sad, and scored by Alfred, no less...

Oh, but he was glad that Purrby had zeroed in on Ms. Shonna. That gal had gone through so many mutations, from dead-ender to selfless power broker. It was as if the trail thither could only be littered with happily-shed pounds of blubber. She so deserved to have a really neat girl like Purrby, flying her way within a happy and golden route of possibilities.

There were so many deserving people about. There were so many...

Then, in his stalled hermitage of huddling amidst the underbrush of his estate's nether reaches, he glanced at a particularly crumbled spindle in the adjacent balustrade lineup. Now reflected with gay light from the festivities below, there was revealed a line of forn-crawlers that spiraled up the belly of the poor old spindle in question. It was a tough climb, and in the process many a crawler, who did so much good to the earth organically, even with their phenomenal hooks and grabbers, fell to the ground and were shattered. Yet, there were just as many who, having attained a good grip in the weathered cast stone, paused in their inexorable upward passage to think of another of their own kind, and extend a helping tendril down to one about to fail. And thus did the tribe of crawlers preserve itself by this charity, and the passage up the spindle was attained by not all, but most.

It was a moment of learning, in which the chain of *we humans*, as observed by those aware enough to realize it, that we are bound by duty to pull each other up on our way toward glory. For was it not in the interest of every climber, to be fulfilled in life by helping his or her fellow climber experience the same exhilaration when reaching the top of an arduous life's course?

Because of that fact, and his review of it, Butterbugs now elected to bow out, and into the darkness of the underbrush. Behind and away from all the vivacious and engaged persons that graced his estate this eve, and at an hour just before midnight. It would be an avenue of escape of course, but there was nothing for it but to retire into non-existence on this particular plane, so that the players associated with him could get on with their lives, unencumbered by the ponderous entity popularly labeled an 'ultrastar'.

But ultrastars, even though they may be a new phylum, needed their basics, too. He didn't quite escape without some slippage in this respect.

A shaft of horizontal light from a frisky couple's Davy lamp shone in newly-discovered Venusian directions. It chanced to hit upon Butterbugs' great profile as he was moving toward the nearest accessible postern.

'For sarrtin! Butterbugs of the Ultrastars! Here in these wilds! There he is!' exclaimed big-time producer Nesk MacFahrquahrsonton (releasing thru UA, Paramount, Your Basic, and Universal-International), who caught an image that any professional cinematimagician would catch, if for no other reason than to make some coin from.

'Why sir, come and join us in our encampment, for to guzzle cheer in the name of those who have gone before us! Also, do you think you could get me in to see Porter Parker? I've got a super new idea about a vehicle for this chick I know called Brero Bonavalleyvista! In fact, she's right here, and she's a dandy ornament to pin on your shirtsleeve. Heck, you can taste her honey if ya want, and –'

It wouldn't have been so bad to endure this standard-issue entreaty from such blitzed barnacles as this Nesk & Co.'s pathetic beggings, had not Butterbugs stolen a glance straight past those pinwheels who now addressed him, and seen, in the popular avenue behind Nesk, his flute-girl heroine crunching the gravel determinably, with her Krimmy in tow, no doubt in search of he, Butterbugs himself, in order to say 'Hi'. All so he could be melted-down in the process of meeting this wonderful girl, face-to-sweet-face again, and hearing about her settlement for Fourth Best, in light of what *could've* transpired betwixt them.

Well, hell, there was NO WAY he was going to undergo *that*. The only option was violence.

Therefore, in his very first act of non-screen aggression as applied to another human being (in a non-self-defense application), Butterbugs lit out with a right uppercut to distinguished producer MacFahrquahrsonton's jaw. But half-sensing the error of his ways, he deliberately put on the brakes as his fist entered the balding but virile producer's jowls, thus sparing him from certain bone displacement and indeterminate brain trauma. As it was, he would get off with a boastful bruise, by which he could relate 'How me and the world's only ultrastar got into this fist-fight over my gal – and I won', or equivalent.

Bruise inflicted on this particular member of the elite producer class, and nothing more, flute-girl and Krimmy passed on by, still in search of an impossible ideal. The same as Butterbugs himself had attempted, and having found it, and finding it spoken for, abandoned.

Producer Nesk massaged his trophy batterment, and looked to his protégé Brero, who was indeed worth noticing, for some baby-powder comfort.

'Hell, they ought to rename him *Bitter*bugs…,' he whined. 'He has achieved all, so why is he acting like this? So cowardly! So estranged!'

Indeed, why?

'Will greatness sustain him, or will it overcome him?' wondered the glamorous mega-star-turned-producer Scheherazade Wong, who looked after Butterbugs as he fully faded into the gloaming, whilst sipping her polished martini in which the reflection of The Lazaretto became drinkable (e.g. the cover of the February 1963 'Playboy')…

Looking in the direction of the departed single male, Nesk spat:

'That stupid shit-ass! What's *with* that guy, anyway!?'

It was the first time (outside of the late Murn Administration, that is) that discouraging words were aimed at the world's sole –and very solo – ultrastar.

'Decline is the only option, when one is at an apex,' Ms. Wong added. '*Unless one can ascend to the stars.*'

Butterbugs kept moving forward, into certain darkness. He thought momentarily of the old horseradish tonic that'd kept him so even-keeled for so long.

'I could never take it again,' he brooded, 'As I am beyond redemption now.'

At this juncture, his self-criticism did not have the capacity to brand such a thought consummately melodramatic. Disillusionment was what he was leaving, in the midst of his heading for – somewhere else. *Anywhere* else.

'Steal away!' he advised himself. Yet again.

To where? His imagination had fled before him. To somewhere familiar, then. Somewhere like…

Somewhere like…

…The alley behind Yniguez Terrace.

He hopped onto an old black Raleigh three-speed, and pedaled off into the night.

Victory achieved.

Now, the secondary theme of the party entered into its own: the Pax Butterbugsicus – the ultrastar's peace. And even though he himself had broken it, it nevertheless started tonight, with or without him.

59.

The Night Before

An absent wind had commenced, which broadcast the passelberry fronds and blapper-pods that lay along the smooth pavement. A great amount of similar tree rubbish was swept under a parked car, like the nocturnal waves of an underground ocean.

The car was a lumbering hulk, long lain-up here. Its lengthy skyline of swooping metal was rusticated with rot-leaf particles and bird-splat, and the sallow glow-light from the moving cloud cover above brought out its topography in almost lunar relief.

An aged DeSoto station wagon! One of those truly old-time rigs! Butterbugs approached. Despite torn-off license plates and a bit of disinterested vandalism, he knew it was his own. The vehicle that had brought him to fame and fortune! Still here! A wreck – forgotten within the very cityscape that had brought him to such heights. Such was the apathy in this backwater, a nether pole in a city of extremities.

Like a sailor returning to a port he thought home, only to find the grave of his loyal hound as the sole remnant of his former life, the ultrastar embraced this inanimate wheeled object as the only tangible route to some sort of comfort, and folded his arms around one of the tail-fins, as best he could. The tears he shed fell upon the plastic backup-light lens, dull with dust. The clouds far above the tree canopy scudded, and the full moon shone through a ragged and temporary hole. The round reflective dome of the lens, unexpectedly lubricated, caught it and radiated back up at him. Through his misty vision, what did it look like? The footlights – in the form of dying-battery flashlights, held by Chester Stradley – and Digger, and... Ernesto! And remember poor old Esteban the Cerveziac...? Dead now, for sure. Dead and gone...

The nights of the Tailgate Performances! They were *here!* This was the place!

The birth of The Drama... Or at least *a kind* of drama...

More steadily now, he faced the back of the wagon, then reached through the shattered rear window opening and released the chrome slab of the tailgate latch. It still swung down easily, its rubber buffer strips resting with fond familiarity on the bumper below.

Wendcroft sandals stepping up onto ragged black shreds of carpeting, Butterbugs returned to the launching pad of his career. The shock absorbers still allowed him to play the springboard act, ready for a swan dive off into fame and achievement. But only after a worthy performance. Well then, what better than Usynus' Homecoming Speech from Sir Tex Wong's 'Wambian Philpot'?

689

USYNUS: *(stoically)* I return! To a land of quiet. Though fountains still tinkle in my palace of yore, no voice other than that of she who is *nature*, is to be heard. All are dead now, and I return, to know only that. Why it was me who was to survive, the world might soon tell. Will it? Oh, *will* it?

Butterbugs' performance was mute. He mouthed the lines only, for fear of attracting a new crowd, perchance to emerge from the tremulous undergrowth. They might not have the same sense of understanding as his former alley pals, all of whom were now certainly extinguished from the scene. But, as he performed this pantomime in the shadowy moonlight, his elocution and expression were superb, bringing light, as it were, to this place of uncertain darkness. Yet, the longer he tarried, the more he actually felt at home here. His tactile contact with the old car triggered a nostalgia of times that may have been tough, but they were purposeful. Focused, even.

If only there were someone down there in the audience who would seal these welling feelings... perhaps with a kiss.

The monologue complete, he bowed to ghostly applause. Then, standing straighter than he ever had, made to bounce up into his famous dive. But where were they – those former railway workers and longshoreman and truck farmers and grips, still stout after decades of country-likker usage – to catch him? He bent his knees to break the flight, and the DeSoto grew inanimate once more. Silently he stepped down and shut the gate with a hushed click.

The performance over, dismalness returned.

It was then that he thought of the words of U Po Wine, film critic of the 'Weekly Bundle-'Em', who once said of the character Butterbugs played in 'In Inebrious Centrifuge' (Oddball):

'He remembers too much of too little value'. And, 'Propaganda is always selective in how it chooses to present reality.'

The dead tree matter rustled and dropped in the intermittent breeze.

There was a feeling of unrest to the scene. Not necessarily a nervousness, but the atmosphere of an impending show, a performance of some kind, whatever it happened to entail, was palpable. Something perhaps related to stage fright, but nothing so specific. It was a feeling not entirely familiar to him. For these long times now, he had gone about the process of picture making in such a free, easy, and vigorous manner. There had been no anxiety or stage fright or anticipation to color his mind in the somber tones of damaging introspection or self-destructive tendencies. In other words, his creative thought and its appurtenances had been refreshingly lacking in internal conflict. That was what his Incandescent Realism had brought about, and that was what had sustained him for so long.

There was intermittent moonlight tonight, but nothing shone from within the ultrastar below.

[Oh, but it is late, so very late in the picture, when everyone's butts are sore and the longing for resolve is on each viewer's desire list.

But wait awhile. Here are stationed scenes of vital assessment and judgment, perhaps a bit on the quiet side, but definitely noteworthy, amidst the pressing insistence of attention-getting last-act expectations.

Those critics who bitch about 'Third Act requirements' when assessing a given motion picture – well, what the hell is up with *that?* Don't they know about a tragedy's classic five-act structure? Whoever sent them this textbook of 'have-to' balderdash, as far as film structure? What audiences generally require in going to the movies has always been moronically simple.

Entertainment, entertainment, entertainment!

Though they were and are a dying breed, film critics still attempt to inflict timid readers with their reviews. Readers who, when in audience-mode, are usually quite comfortable with being couched in the lower regions of a common denominator. Even with the rise of Butterbugsian cinema, which inarguably created a permanently higher standard in film, basic audience needs remained simplistic, even primitive.

The dude with non-Butterbugsian cinema in mind, after seeing a worthwhile picture as an aid in an umpteenth try at scoring a flesh-union with the female receptacle of the moment, manages to snazz himself a date with the age-old desire-goal. And any girls' night out isn't necessarily going to be devoted to Butterbugsian ethics, no matter how sexy a guy he was in 'Wulfnoth of Cartobia' (Magna).

As far as film criticism itself is concerned, who might be the intellectual pointer-dog? What direction to follow? It sure as hell wasn't André Bazin or his ilk. And Randi Chuzzlewit was never very analytical, only mean. Incredibly though, a feeling was growing in film study circles that it was Randi C. who actually *discovered* Butterbugs. Sometimes people pay for their discoveries with their lives!

But now, that particular discovery, Butterbugs that is, took pause in this unchanged alley of his past.]

Having left behind an evening's festivities that started out as a tribute to both a nation's restoration and a nation's hero's sacrifice, and then morphed into a fucking wedding march, with which he had no association whatsoever, the ultrastar now became fully disconnected, distanced, – maybe even disenfranchised.

He nevertheless had the objectivity to ask himself, purely in stale, academic terms:

'If you yourself had a mate of the marrying kind tonight, would you have been in the lineup before Pastor Hale's vowing mechanism?'

'Yes, certainly!' he responded. 'But that wasn't the case. That wasn't the way it was. So I'm sour and pissed off.'

He didn't have to justify his attitude to himself anymore. The reason why was irrefutable. So, he was correct in his attitude. But so what? What was the sum total of his righteousness?

Well, *not much.*

He looked about, absently. There was his station wagon, neglected, but largely intact, and before it, his dooryard, so to speak. He was in its familiar quadrangle.

Looking around, then hanging around.

Looking for something of value, he guessed.

It was as if he were again entering the House of Hur. Not late in the first part of the MGM picture (1959 version), just before the intermission. Not like the time after he'd recoiled from that miserable 'Music Hallelujah' janitorial job. But in this instance, the applicable parallel was a plugging-in, late, very late in Willy Wyler's same picture, when a purging rain has brought miracles. But none appear to Judah Ben-H. He pauses at the mezuzah at the front door of sadness, and while emotions pour out, he nevertheless meticulously places a broken part of the mini-shrine's assembly back where it should be, before proceeding into the neglected estate. An embryonic sign of hope amidst despair.

A signal, perhaps, of miraculous things to come, still unperceived.

After all, the last time this sort of cinematic comparison occurred with Butter-bugs at this site, he was on the verge of his first screen role.

Dim lattices in his mind hung down at too sharp a decline for him to pick up on any synchronicity that might bring with it a sense of emergence. Instead, he let his palms do the walking across the oxidized paint of the wagon's hood, pointlessly arriving, near the jet-like hood ornament, at a fine prospect of the great Bupp Mansion. There it was, past the overgrown border wall, a scene in itself most satisfying, for the rich detail it provided. But to one in Butterbugs' current state, why would such things matter?

However, there he was, witnessing, if not wholly seeing, the spread before him. It was the same view he'd had, that first glance out of this very car's window. Right here. Eons ago, if time measured in heart-and-mind spans be summed. Into this strangely placid, even lyrical backwater he'd ended up, after his odd odyssey in succumbing to some of the more esoteric of the universe's magnetic currents.

After all he had experienced, after all he had emoted, here he was, neutralized into the negative funnel of the mind's upper-tier analysis, perhaps sliding down the spout, heading for lower-level fluid build-up, without any anchor and certainly without any tiller. Unfulfilled, unredeemed, and now, uncaring, he was blazing new trails to the very limits of ultrastardom: over-the-top, under-the-rock, no-where-in-between… For, if not he, then whom?

The fantastical skyline of the mansion worked as a kind of space-maintainer in his mind. Even though he had tackled extremely sophisticated roles, enacted on sets and in locations far more exotic than this gifted but humble alley, But-terbugs was at this moment unmindful of any such achievement. Why didn't he feel smarter, wiser, and more transcendent than most humans right now? Was it because motion pictures really weren't an art of much substance, after all? All that 'Seventh Art' bullshit? And those who played in them, were they, truth to tell, not really worth the shadows they were lighted on? Was that it?

And what about –

Enough! Enough! Enough of this torturous innards-gazing! What he wanted was a deep and lasting relationship! That's all! Why all the precipitative squabbledeblather to clutter up what should have been an imperfect but irrefutably triumphant time for him? All this picking and tweezing and needling and brooding and syrupy violin-playing to accompany the profession of self-pity that had taken over his very being!

Because! Because! Because, in the midst of his heightened success – admit it! – an emptiness! A misery, in spite – that was the key phrase here: *in spite* of all things achieved... The glaring emptiness had become undeniable. And well, he could look forward only to it becoming unbearable.

The clouds above, as dreary as an occluded eve in Northumbria, rolled along in X-ray hues that were no more hopeful of miracles than X-ray results, waiting interminably to be read by a specialist who was never appearing.

Late, so very late, for miracles. Judah Ben-Hur eventually found his, or rather, they were endowed upon him. No such alignment for this actor though, who stood in the bordered dark, having come up against a stone wall.

Gone was the bickering, the internal clash, the firefight over what he thought he deserved but did not have. Now that the central gap in his soul had been identified, and grips had come to be obvious, all expectations within the man wholly died.

'There's nothing in that black bag for me...'

Air, moving aloft of the plains of Los Angeles, then elected to act as feather duster, relegating all cloud masses unto the Riverside side of things, there to be dispelled. No replacements were coming from the waters of the Pacific.

So, lo, like a heat-shield rising within a film projector's aperture housing, so that the arc light's rays might shine through both film and lens, now was the full moon able to project its full candlepower on this city of the vaunted Seventh Art.

Nature always out-performs the creative products of humanity, but every once in a while (not as rare as a blue moon, though), natural effects seem to emulate those of a talented art director or production designer. Whether 'tis evidence of 'intelligent design', according to Ussher's system, no person in the Industry cared to say. Any film person who witnesses such phenomena is either flattered at the imitation, or immediately sets to work with sketchpad, pencil, brush and gouache, or with a Gæpetto's ElectroVortex/DigiHelp software packet, to capture the visual idea for a prospective motion picture.

At this instant, in this night, and from Butterbugs' particular standpoint at the wall, such a phenomenon was about to unfold.

Observe: the cloud-line moved, exposing the perfect lunar disc at its bottom on up, with the effect, as seen from Earth's surface, of a rising thiertre curtain, rather than any heat-shield. And through this opening escaped a fulsome illumination that acted like a spotlight's beam. At least that was how it appeared to blank-minded Butterbugs, who just stood there, mindless as a camera's mechanism, recording what was before it.

Whether projector light or spotlight, no actual lens was set in its path to provide magnification, so there was no transposition determining the celestial direction of the moonlight's movement. No special effects were utilized. Thus, the lower aspects of the mansion were highlighted first, and as the effect spread upward, the bulwark became a mighty silhouette. Proceeding further, certain features of the house, coming under the oblique glow, now stood out in clearly defined detail. A weird but intriguing selection of lines, shaped and surfaced, became apparent. The curve of a lofty window arch. A pilaster's vertical rise from podium footing to upper cornice. A bas-relief tracery of strictly decorative purpose, to fill an otherwise blank expanse of wall. Also, a running balustrade on a lower rooftop terrace, previously invisible, now lap-dissolved into the developing frame. Warm-white light painted itself onto the ornate lines of the flowery architecture, which here stood out from the austere bulk behind. It was a beautiful example of nature enhancing human creation.

Then the curtain's rise revealed an end to the inanimate exclusivity of the scene. It happened to be another sort of human creation, a different kind of beauty: a woman, standing up there in the most frozen of poses, who was becoming delineated by the same warm whiteness that held her surroundings, and now she herself, in nascent suspension.

A vision to startle, and also to arrest. Startling in its loveliness. Arresting in its familiarity.

She was Heatherette, upright, completely still, nude, facing the darkling west. It was she all right, naturally au naturale, but strangely… without life. The waviness of her hair and the waviness of her body were all exquisitely drawn with quietly theatrical dimension, in thin but sensuous lines, but the voluptuousness almost seemed to merge with its adjacent railing, as a pediment's statue might. Indeed, a statuesque figure, but one plainly living, instead of inert marble.

Now did she stand in the moon's full radiance, plainly and honestly revealed.

The roaring silence of a tableau of transfixion.

All of a sudden, whirlwinds occurred in the mind of the watcher. They were signs of life, spawned by the revelation of what he saw.

What then, did he see? It was a stupid question, because in it was contained the stupidity of he who now was relevated. Later rather than never. In fact, at last. He held out his hands to receive the gift. For he was being given something here, something almost unfathomable, only it *was* to be fathomed – easily and simply.

Because it was love.

Of course! Why – why, of course! She was Heatherette. *It* was Heatherette. It had been all along. Heatherette was *it*. It was *she*. His chosen one, the one who was the one from the start. Submerged reality, repressed, kept in the background, whatever. Here it was, presented to him without cinematic technique, in terms concrete instead of manufactured. How perfectly wonderful.

He loved her, he loved her, he loved her. He loved her! Understand?

He understood. As if graven in stone before him, he had only to gaze in her direction to know all she had done for him. Each time she had done so, he had known it, and he had registered it. Really, he had. But because of his ambition and his ego and his distraction, plain and banal self-absorbency had always trumped her goodness, and his owed response to it. Something between them, something that was exceptional, something unlabeled, had been there right in front of him, all along, all along. Only now did he really notice. And on its label was to be read the simplest and most universal of truths to be found in the universe.

'Gubbah-gubbah!' he thought, baby talk being the first impulse in his stupidity. Now that it and its behavior were called on the carpet, stupidity vaporized.

It had been a gift, then. It really was! Whatever cosmic majesty had led him here, he dropped to his knees in order to thank it. As there had never been anything like a script that had led him to this spot at this time, he could only ascribe it to vast controlling powers, whether divine or instinctual. Whatever the case, he rated them benevolent and beneficent.

But he did not hate himself. Not now – nor would he. There was no room for hate of any kind. Only love, for he knew *her* love provided for all things. Her love was up there, down here, and all around; abiding, patient, forgiving, and almost, it seemed, not of this earth.

No tears, no regrets, no nothing – except, yes: love. Her love. Their love. It was mending him, and quickly.

'Oh! Oh!!'

His mental vocabulary capabilities were rapidly maturing.

'Oh, but gosh!'

Yes – yes – yes! Heatherette! All along!

How magnificent the realization! How saving! How restorative!

'A fool there was!'

His mind, wind-whipped with clearing currents, progressed at exponential speed.

'A fool no longer!'

Love in the moonlight. Love up on that terrace. Love in the night. Love in his heart. Love in *her* heart. Love omnipresent.

He lived again!

No doubts crept into his revelations, because part of their endowment was to banish all possibility of them. As in, 'What if she does not return my love?' or 'Could she ever forgive me for my mindless negligence?' No doubts existed, because they were impossible. Past some superficial equivocations, there was never any doubt in Heatherette's mind, so why should there be in his?

Neo-neuroses, adieu!

Connectivity was of the utmost importance now. Only to let her know! Only to seek her love, from her – in person! Only to proclaim *his*, face to face!

Kindness in the night, delivered by the moon. It was his move now, his message now, upon the heels of the moonlight. His message. To deliver it…

Though her face up there was in shadow, perhaps in contemplation of the effects of the moon rather than of its bright face, there was no mistaking her identity.

The effulgence of her hair, the smooth contours of her torso, here seen mostly in the form of her back, down to balustrade level, could only be Heatherette's, and no one else's. In her own house, no less.

He could not speak outright yet – Could not verbalize anything – yet. The scene's impact, too strong, too wonderful, still enclosed his usually formidable powers of speech. Fair enough, and so as not to startle her, as a voice from down-here, out-back, might be an assault on such a sensitive soul, he would make his approach with convention, while his voice had a chance to return, en route. Then all would be in order to declare his heart's truth. Respect for his new love began right now. Consequently, he would gladly embrace the gallant lover's pathway to a glory deserved, but a glory still to be earned.

'Oh, but by golly, but I'm in love!' he thought as he got busy.

This was bigger than any picture, any role, any dream he had ever had. And because it was, he secured his joy with a care to see it through. That utter care that he was famous on film sets for: that nothing, absolutely nothing would he allow to get in the way of a successful enactment of an important scene. He was not only back on track as far as his talents were concerned, he was BACK, period.

Sullenness, sourness, saturninity, adieu! For all time!

This infusion of love was also curative. In its intersection with his body and soul, certain chemistries commenced, permanently altering him for the better, in which flaws, such as the need for compounds like his longtime horseradish elixir, were rendered null and void. Also deleted was all that busy-busy quagmiry intro-spective inertia, blasted, as with ionic zappers, from his very psyche.

Transformed, empowered, and just plain in love, he went forward. Pure prag-matism now. Only to tell her! Only to let her know!

Then, she moved. No apparition, no statue, Heatherette. At the height of the moon's art reflected on all things eligible, she chose to retire into the dark man-sion, where no lamp burned.

To the great front door, then, would he make his way. It was a door he had not frequented for these many moons. Did he still know the way? Epiphany or no, he nevertheless had to navigate through a challenging physical environment. The estate was so much more neglected than he'd remembered, and the obstacles were many, the first of which was the wall and the fence.

Recollections returned with full recall, along with the sensibility of love's in-centives. Stepping cautiously through dead weeds and alley rubbish, the longitu-dinal slabs of moonlight, which appeared a deep blue back here under the trees, led him to the postern, with its vacant lanterns atop guarding pilasters, choked with pea-paste vines.

How derelict! How undeserving to the Occupant within! How arcane a passage toward love awaiting! Yet he was thrilled, not just because of said love, but be-cause of the dearness of every detail, no matter how decayed or gothic, for they were all part and parcel to the love of his life, and because, at the center of this estate of decline was her romantic freshness and sexy splendor. True, these qualities he'd duly noted in the past, but never had he thought they might be applied to *him*.

Ducking down to avoid the old chain that kept the crooked cast iron bars of the gate somewhat joined, their footings anchored in hardened soil, Butterbugs had to then pry his way through, thus entering Heatherette's property on his hands and knees, which was rather appropriate.

Strangely, no alley person, no delinquent kid or stray animal would appear to have done what he just did. There were no discarded syringes or condoms cast about, nor any nuisance committed, nor any litter to speak of. Apparently this back yard's appearance and portent were forbidding enough to keep any element out, bad or good. Until now that is – in the latter category, for sure.

Erosive powers, even within an urban context, can be just as steady and as ruthless as the bald domain of say, southern Wyoming's barrier-free subjection to the elements. If anything, man-made environments are the most susceptible to decline, whether they are hell-for-stout or jerrybuilt. Cessation of maintenance soon reveals how long any ruin-to-be will last before complete vanishment upon the face of the land takes place. There are much harsher environments in the world than the coast of California, but all things lying out in the open in Los Angeles will fry, rot, desiccate, or collapse ere long.

Well, Heatherette's mansion was indeed a blockhouse for the ages, but its surroundings, dependent as any hereabouts on a grounds-person's care, had fully descended into the most picturesque but pronounced scruff and tawd. Here, seen not for the first time, but now, even in this lovely-izing moonlight, all things in thrall to the mansion were eroded in advanced states.

The sundial in the stroll-garden was knocked over due to a crumbled base. Sideways, it read high noon. Shrubberies were mere sticks. Pleasure-walks were hard to trace, and low walls were almost one with the surrounding country, as vegetative waste and dropped branches filled the spaces of their lees. No vandalism by any hands but nature's. Because there was so much of it, and because every detail was now linked to his devotion to Heatherette, Butterbugs defended this state of things as a sign of her desire for the wistful, the dramatic, and the nostalgic, perhaps as a memorial to her illustrious forebears. All in all, the grounds had a dreamlike quality that only heightened the experience of going toward bliss.

Rounding the main dwelling, he could see something new: a great wall, of the drabbest character, had been erected across the formerly open frontage of the huge lot. Yniguez Terrace was nowhere to be seen. Here was a barrier on which the moon did not shine.

The front verandah was easily accessed, but significant signs of what could only be called aggravated neglect were there. Old newspapers, breeze-blown remnants of blossoms, a screen door barely operable on its dislodged hinges, a caved-in tread on the main steps...

Was the place closed, and maybe sealed, due to litigation... or death? Did Heatherette even live here any more? Was the nude on the terrace... an illusion?

An illusion of his desire? He had seen and touched and even kissed illusions before...

No, he would have none of this questioning, none of this probing speculation. He saw what he saw under the most brilliant of moon's lightings. She was there. He saw her. She was within. He would proceed.

Once past the wreckage of the screen door, the comparative order of the verandah was welcome indeed. Even though filtered by the large expanses of begrimed bug screen, moonlight made the arcade consummately romantic, with its venerable old unpopulated settees and ottomans, while the front door was, quite frankly, a bit baleful in its looming statement of guardianship.

Standing before the blackened varnishment, the ultrastar felt his heart leap. A forward leap – to glory, because he knew where it led: to his long-misplaced love. She would be surprised, assuredly, but great things would follow. Why, surely she had felt his presence down there in the alley. Surely she was on her way down, without even the faintest touch of a door clang. Surely the power of their love involved tractor beams and other such non-mechanical links?

Now for the conventional moment, within this oddball milieu. The moment of moments. He had no flowers, no present, no trinket, no nothing, to offer. Except the biggest load of love that was possible for one man to house on his person, or tote on his back, as that love overflowed his person and into anything that could carry it. Light as air too, high air. He had no speech prepared, and indeed, he did not know if his voice actually worked yet, but he wasn't worried, as he knew the power of love would see to all things needful and all things loving.

His finger found the oxidized Bakelite button, which it pressed, expecting ancient solenoids to loyally cause the Usherian chime. Its sound would issue from away up there somewhere, a welcome punctuation to his feeling of growing uncertainty. Despite the presence of love's active embers in his entire body, Butterbugs found the remoteness of the moment somewhat disheartening.

Not to worry. After several more attempts, he resorted to knocking, first in friendly knuckly singles, arranged in syncopation after a time, then with double-knocks, as the taxman might use, followed by blows meted out by his hammering fist. The blows of a lover sensing something perhaps amiss, but still trusting that the size of the pile and its romantic degradation precluded conventional approaches, at this time.

No worry warts sprouted on his sore hands. Nor was he affected by any soreness. Instead, ideas bloomed in his brain. There was a short cut to his love. He'd taken it that first time – the first time he'd seen her and talked to her. He had been a housebreaker, and she wasn't even mad at him. Instead, she'd welcomed him in. How many people in this world, loving or not, would have done such a thing? And there he'd been, bumpkined-out, too much a dumbshit to pick up on her invitational subtleties. Aw, so what. What mattered was the moment and the future. Time to set things right. He knew just what to do.

Quitting the facade of the palazzo, he trotted round back and gained the old

Silent Era Party Plain of flag and slate that made up one of the best and most unknown surfaces for socializing to be found in the film capital. Tonight a wasteland of indeterminate hummock and ruin, Butterbugs made straight for the batted wall at the extreme end, wherein was contained the plant and rustic services for the great house. Here, intact, was that very window through which he had crept in order to enter the confines now hoped-for. What had formerly been an easy swing-in window was now locked fast. Very fast.

'Damn!' he thought, 'I'm *really* in love, and I have to take the *long* way around!'

There were many other windows he could try. Too many. Then, it occurred to him to seek out the elevated terrace upon which *she* had appeared lately, and perhaps obtain another view of her returned peerlessness.

Back across the Party Plain, until the base of the other wing was reached. Backing into the ragged grounds to assess the top lines, nothing but balustrade, even more artfully moon-bathed than before, was all the scenery to be had. He scanned the actual structure of the wing, undoubtedly a later addition, and there were no climbable notches or gutter pipes or ivy growths. Only barren framing with minimal style exhibition, reflective of the main mansion, but without its stylistic assets.

No Romeo-romantic opportunity presented itself then, which was actually fine with him, as that play was one of earth's greatest tragedies. Heavenly to act in (as he had several times by now, at Grauman's Metropolitan, with the punky-cool Eevy Sprarestnopp as Juliet), but 'twould be hellish to *live* – he presumed. No interest in compelling but wasteful tragedies, just now.

Back to the rudiments of the known basement window, by which a passage to the upper galleries was assured. That pane of glass was probably the original, but it had to go. Besides, what if Heatherette had stumbled or something, all alone, way up there on an upper floor? A lover's concerns now overrode any obedience of civic propriety.

It wasn't hard to locate some bludgeonable something there on the Plain, with which to first attempt a tapping, to discreetly dissolve the pane of prevention from his path. But the old glass was tough and unyielding.

Cut the crap, pilgrim! Bust that bad boy now and get yo' ass through it without any more timidity-based *scheisse!*

Tool flung full-force, original glass flew everywhere downward. Shatter-noise was curiously shrouded by the thick air down under. The coast lay clear.

To think of it: just his luck, passing through the empty casement, the opportunity presented itself to catch his sincere neck on a bit of unattended glass shard, sharp enough to diggeth into his full-flowing jugular, which emptied at an excited-enough rate, more suitable for erections than nervous lover-searchings, but nevertheless ardent in full-capacity blood-movement. There was a drain down there somewhere to accommodate the mortifying volume of blood that might leak out of one's closed system, and it could easily happen here.

No, in fact, that wasn't what happened at all. Just an anxious lover, used to acting in imaginative picture shows, letting his mind run a bit. Reel it in, Sport! He did. Safe passage was now assured, away from the glass-bust.

He thought that love was supposed to sail him through these kinds of reasonable scenarios. Love could do a lot, definitely, but a man still had to be responsible for his actions. Thus, the value of love: use, but don't abuse.

He stood up on the floor of the basement, listening carefully for any household response to his willful vandalism. There was none. Nothing.

Not even any signs of life from that old hoary boiler that knew him when. No longer used at all, its system's seals were failing, and there were drip-drip-drops from back in the corner somewhere. Indeed, there was still a working drain in the floor.

Memory strung memory together, and in this murky catacomb the actor was reminded of many a script's demands that he take up an Ariadnean thread in order to navigate his way through some labyrinthine action sequence. Only, because of his new imperative, he thought not a bit about such director-dependent scenarios. This was him alone, without any production support, and he was liberated at last. His free will, now driven by love's mission, provided more confidence than the best of writers or directors.

Crockery-housing suites, chambers with earthenware storage jugs, hallways hosting empty picture frames, bunker after bunker containing countless film cans, cellars of wine puncheons and champagne bottles awaiting rotation, closets filled with draperies and pelmets, stacks of books that rose above intact basement windows with thin slices of moonlight sneaking in, a room he couldn't access through half-ajar elevator-style doors because it was jammed with smashed junk of all kinds, and finally, nearby, the staircase leading to the halls of the main floor.

That's right, he remembered what a chateau this was, a place instantly captivating. But when he was first here, as a young man in a hurry, it seemed much too much an end in itself. Perhaps that was contributory to his glossing-over the wonder that was Heatherette. Perhaps, perhaps. The manse and its girl were too closely associated with each other. Quite a call for a greenhorn dipper into the showbiz vat-full of easy conclusions to make! Now, however, all that stood here, all that surrounded him, became instantly sacred, as it housed his beloved. No further justification was called for.

Nothing structural was faulty (despite the Big One in '33), but there was a lot of cosmetic decline within these impressive precincts. The Great and Grand Hall looked positively balletic in this light, with the moonbeams streaming in the two-story windows. But there was plenty of peeling plaster up in the internal domes, and wallpaper was drooping everywhere. If one was patient enough, the slight sound of paint giving up its grip on the coving way up there somewhere might even be detected...

Butterbugs hoped no beams or chandeliers dropped on him, but if they did, it would be worth it, because there was huge love cuddling him from all around, providing protection, and he knew from whom it emanated.

Where might she be?

His voice stubbornly remained in mothballs, so there was no question of calling out into the echoey voids, and no way to ascertain her whereabouts except by sighting alone.

He discovered there were two grand staircases, one leading to the upper salons and the other to the numerous apartments and boudoirs. Judging from the open plan, in which each staircase tried to outdo the other in sheer showmanship (for this was a show people's manor), the one by which Butterbugs had initially ascended behind Heatherette's swaying hips that first time, was still the one to choose. Her residential chambers had to be up there somewhere. At least he knew what floor to aim for.

He mouthed the words, 'Lover, lover, Heatherette, lover of mine!' to test if he was still tongue-tied. Yes, yes he was. If worse came to worse, he could always make ghost sounds like foot stomping or door slamming, or breaking something ceramic, though he earnestly hoped it wouldn't come to that.

Would there be paint and brushes available soon, to pen his love on the great walls, if nothing else?

The problem with his previous visits here was that he had always been so utterly preoccupied with other matters that he'd relegated both manse and girl to peripheral consideration. A really asinine thing to do, given all the detail-y integrity he applied to his acting craft.

So he was flawed in a few ways! Whatever!

Right now he was on the threshold of starting his life anew, and helping someone else do the same. After all, it was now undeniable that Heatherette had placed her whole existence on hold, because of him. Everything about this place communicated that fact. If it was an unconscious act on his part, what better than to take her in his arms, apologize from the bottom of his feet, and to now go ahead, enjoined, in any direction they decided on.

Because the mansion was so spacious inside, with ingenious angles to exploit whatever moonlight was accessible, the walls seemed to give off their own special light, or at least enough so as not to need a torch or klieg-light for his searching. But no, whatever light there happened to be at his service now had to be love-generated, as well.

The first landing gave off to the Damask Loggia. The second to the Sleeping Porch. The third might just access the terrace itself. It did not; only broom closets and packet-lockers. On to the fourth, via a narrowed and more plainly residential flight. He was drawing nigh to the very ceiling of the Great and Grand Hall, and the sense of height and conception of the nocturnal space were dizzying. One in such love had to keep his head about him.

An upper lobby, frozen in Great War ambience, and devoid of moonlit tone painting, nevertheless led to double doors. Past that point was – Heatherette's Sky Space. Out on its otherworldly surface, he looked slowly around. It was as if no kind of urban concentration lay beyond this elevated platform. And because the

LA heavens were so trouble-free tonight, all observations upward were dominated by the light source that had set his love in motion. With such a lack of restrictions, no wonder she promenaded here, sans vêtements.

Indeed, she had walked here! A short time ago, too. Vainly did he seek any signs of her presence, his moonlight pantomime in searching the whole terrace, eccentric though it was, had a poeticism that proved his immersion in love's motivations was total.

Magic, pure magic was possible on this plane, but he must press on. Her footsteps could not be too far ahead of him. One more level upward, inside, as he had thoroughly scanned the fascination of the mansion's roofline. Quite frankly, the territory on up from here did not seem too conducive for a naked girl's explorations, no matter how sporting or skilled in mountaineering she might be.

Ascending yet another flight, this one particularly long, he left behind the enormous void downward and entered the attic structure, which was nevertheless dressed as an active part of the household. In fact, he now accessed a most wondrous zone: a vast space, which might well house an entire corps de ballet, or a mural painter, or a full tennis court – or five or six silent film sets. Instead, it accommodated a series of lengthy tables laid out in orderly fashion, piled with masses of materials that were indeterminate in their nature, despite the generous though subtle illumination. For high above all these arrangements, huge skylights let in Earth's satellite's reflected light, all shutters and gauzes having been drawn to every perimeter.

His gasp was without audio expression, for the place brought delight as much as mystery and intrigue. Oh, why couldn't he simply call out, 'Heatherette! I'm here! Will you have me: Butterbugs . . ?'

But still he couldn't. If he were on set, a throat specialist would be glaring at his tonsils in about six minutes. Six minutes of production time lost.

Time to get serious in finding her, as this was the terminal level on which such a search could ever be resolved.

Lest she steal down the stairs in case she thought him a threatening phantom, he closed the exit door and leaned an iron pry-bar against its shadowy section, so that at least a noise would result if she opened it.

With the carbon-lamp pipes above, curtain rails to divide the expanse into sections, the several dressing room mirrors on the walls, and even a production manager's blackboard with '12/03/27' chalked in as its dateline, there was plenty of evidence to suggest that indeed, this was where small-scale motion picture scenes were shot, undoubtedly in Hollywood's infancy and youth. There were offices and anterooms and storage parlors, and relics of old-time filmmaking were cluttered everywhere. With no time or inclination to assess or appreciate this fabulous clutter, a certain sense of anxiousness now grew from one footstep to another.

There was a lot of ground to cover up here, but he was closing in on all the possibilities. Despite his ecstasy of self-realization and the absence of doubt as to its validity, what was going on in this rarefied zone? Was this another Pepper/

Prairie/Carlson/Browne – *'hallucination'?* Oh no, he'd gone and thought of *them*. He'd created a distraction of rivalry… So what! They and their world had been pre-empted. Now he had someone *real* to love. At least he *thought* she was real… And around here… Somewhere…

He got to a point of pre-franticness now. He searched behind doors, in wicker hampers, and in fireproof film lockers, as if this was some Easter pageant egg-hunt, with its participants pulling gag stunts or even practical jokes.

There was sweat on his brow. This feeling of wonder couldn't be digressing into melodrama, could it? Was he, yet again, to be the loser, the pathetic survivor, washed up on the sterile beach of the Isle of Incompleteness, a shipwrecked sailor, alive, but without hope? These thoughts were not based on doubt, the doubt of his love. Rather, they were rooted in simply being scared. Scared of what he might find – or not find.

He covered the fringes of the great studio room yet again, quickening his pace, rifling the matte-black drapes, which looked to him like stygian columns of deepest oblivion. Plowing into one particularly thick hanging, he whirled around and got lost in their velvety but lightless expanse.

Staunch enough not to succumb to panic, he nevertheless knew he must escape from this enveloping prison in the next few seconds or –

Then he did something he was never known to do. To call up an experience from the childhood he never, ever, thought about. He stopped thrashing, dropped to his knees, and rooted into the realm of the bottom hems of the heavy curtains. Just like he'd done at the Goth Theatre in Carstairs as a two year-old New Year's baby, who'd had the chutzpah to crawl under the Grand Drape after it had come down, in search of one more tin horn toot, one more whoop, one more cheer from the audience out there in the house.

So, with his new act, 'Root Pigs In Love', the ultrastar had returned to his – roots, as it were. It worked. He cleared the dusty black barrier. On the floor, on all fours, he found himself staring straight ahead. At a naked girl.

A statue? A glass painting? A hologram? No, no, no. Impossible. He'd seen this view before, in this very house, going up stairs and such, albeit with some filmy but revealing garment as civil adornment. For in the here and now, she faced the opposite direction. Hair, back, bottom, right there, moonlit-pale, ethereal, but warm. She seemed… had to be… verifyingly living and breathing womanhood. Besides, he heard her belch – ! – the discomfort of the gas and its passage upwards caused her body to respond with the shifting subtleties that anyone anywhere might show. She was real, to be sure. He had found her at last!

She was Heatherette.

There she was, in a yet-further studio, similarly sky-lit. It was easily entered, through the dark box of a small vestibule, which he stealthily crawled toward. Simple enough, but he was terrified of scaring her, as she was facing away from him.

A soft call-out would have been appropriate to alert her, but heartbreakingly, the vocal vibrations would still not come. The will was there, and even the words (e.g. 'Heatherette! It is your lover, Butterbugs! Be not afraid – I come in peace and love…!' etc.), but the ability mulishly remained stalled.

So be it. If he was to be mute from now on, it was enough that he had found her at last. It was enough that he beheld her in such a mysterious but artistic pose, so that he could well take in her perfection of feminine beauty. This from a man who had seen, felt, and touched many of the best that cinema's world of exceptional beings had to offer. Not only was there the connoisseur's appreciation for her æsthetics, there was also the erotic pull of hyper-normal lust that tended to result from such an exhibition.

Actually, she wasn't quite totally nude. She had on a pair of really wild high-heeled black leather boots, calf-length, undeniably created for purposes of arous-al, both for the wearer and whomever might be the watcher.

She was indeed an exhibitionist! How could she *not* know he was here? Hadn't she heard his shufflings and rootings and crawlings? Were women not superior to men in sensing their surroundings and their effects on those whom they knew to be voyeurs?

Then, a gesture that suggested a decision on her part to perhaps enter into the language of the dance. One of her high heels rose gracefully and then moved backwards in a carefully calculated step, followed by the other one, duplicating the act. So there she was, backing up in slow motion, without looking around.

Was she indeed putting on a show, here in the comfort zone of her own do-main? If she was, he had no intention of spoiling such creative expression. She undoubtedly knew where she was going, and in such an unexpected and captivat-ing way. So, he continued to view her peepingly through the black framework of the intervening room.

And what exactly *was* in said room of brief but profound shadow?

An empty elevator shaft.

60.

It's Getting On Now

Heatherette spake.

And, because the studio she faced for her statement had very sophisticated acoustics (which was curious, as it was intended for silent picture shows), each of her carefully-delivered syllables was bell-clear and expressed with unique emotion and technique, which indicated original talent.

'On this perfect night, I see perfection all around me. It is here, even within the words I'm trying to form into some sort of farewell. Fare… well…! In the details of existence, nothing can be left out. In the large scheme, invention is constant and evolves in perpetuity, regardless of our impatient recognitions. I have to begin with the sky then, and looking down, the world can try to make sense of itself. *I* can make sense of it. I think I do, even at this off-moment, when I have to regard it from the edge of the room, and maybe even from further out. Out in un-surveyed domains.'

She stood still now, in verbal hiatus. Enjoying the view, Butterbugs assumed she'd resume her backing-up, so as to pass from her room into his, via her special-delivery choreography. He'd be there with an introductory kiss, when she was safely harbored in his waiting arms.

However, she kept her brakes on and remained perfectly poised in sleek but rigid station. No wonder French curves influenced the baroque movement! She had them, but it took a voyeur's daring for her admirer to access them. If he'd not been her lover, his current practice of sneakiness would have been unthinkable, except as part of a writer/director's auteur vision, in order to make a cinematic point. His new dedication, his new self-realization, his new *self* was thus allowed entrée to her inner sanctum.

Rigid beauty, just there. There was no way not to appreciate it. As far as the ultrastar's tastes were concerned though, and if he could have his way with them just now, she could at least relax one leg and let her hips and shoulders slant into classic sensual pose. But at the dawn of love, you can't have everything quite yet. Plus, upon discovery, his covert position on the floor had the potential for controversy. With such an odd but compelling setup, he still hadn't a Plan 'B' as such. That is, if his Plan 'A' of automatic reception and perfect union went awry.

She then resumed her soliloquy, as if each pane of glazing in both windows and skylights of her surrounding studio was a person. Her absolute focus of concentration was a high achievement of acting's art. If this actually *was* an act.

'One thing is certain. I'm not afraid. I never have been. If I were, I dare not be

705

so sure-footed. Without fear, risk is as nothing. Without risks, life is as nothing. And without life... love... is as nothing. So I have become... as nothing...

'Without love? Not me. I have it. I have love in reserve, love all about me, love in play at any one time. Why then, my melancholy resignation? Is that what this is? Oh, it's just that, well, how can I fit into a world in which I really have no place? What do you do when you're alone in the universe, and you know it, and you're at peace with knowing it, but because you're at peace with such knowledge, you're still not resolved? What do you do? A conundrum inside a frustration! I long for a conclusion of some kind...

'Is this, then, my escape from what might've been? If I were in love – which I *am* – but were I in *active* love with a giving recipient, would I feel this notion to bow out? Of course not, Questioner!'

Hearing this, Butterbugs immediately became choked up, which made his vocal cords all the more helpless.

'I think each thing in the universe itself has a kind of perfection. Yes, I see it all around. But as I find myself an occupant within it, I cannot deny my own emptiness. I wonder, can I be part of it, *become* part of it, by vanishing into the æther? I do not desire extinguishment. On the contrary, only by a joining, a transition, a transcendence can I be... whole? Is *that* it? I want to be around for the grand show, not excluded from it. And possessive of a new, enlightened state of mind, not this human reliance on limitations and barriers. But if I were a child of the cosmos, I think I would be happy. Because, I wouldn't just be witnessing love, or even feeling love, I would *be* love!'

While her poignancy was in itself heartbreaking, Butterbugs as lover felt a simultaneous exhilaration. Heatherette was giving one of the finest and most genuine performances from the soul he had ever beheld. Enough to reduce him to a wasted puddle on the floor. Heartbreak duly noted, but founts of elation joined in the mix, and came to predominate in his superior sense of marvelment. Keenly did he feel his love actively interweaving with Heatherette the person, in which her life and character became graspable, dimensional, and understood by him.

In a way, he was glad his own voice was stilled. Love was already present, but the opportunities of unspokenness allowed for other powers of intuition, empathy, and insight to evolve naturally, without some cinematic interpretation, or some wiseapple-minded scenario to develop as distractions. He was the perfect naïf: he had nothing figured out. And from that point he became the perfect student: knowledge becomes wisdom, wisdom becomes conviction. And from that point he could become the perfect lover: sincere, constant, and true.

Here was her gift to him, an intimate introduction without pretension or any embellishment of attachments. Soul as bare as body, Heatherette was unconsciously offering herself up for the most personal of scrutinizings, ready to be judged and expecting to be found wanting.

While he was so affected by her monologue, his eyes, now wholly used to the darker framework around her exquisite and patient model's pose (stiff, but elegant) cast their gaze down at the square of mystery that made up the foreshortened floor of this conspicuous border between he and his lovéd one.

Suddenly, there was something about that floor he didn't like – A quality that awakened distant memories, close-up fears. Indeed, he detected an enclave of fear within his new fearless self. It now made itself known in terms not to be ignored.

He didn't have to pull himself to the edge to instantly know what the darkness contained. Here, at this portal, were similar doors he had seen down in the basement, and for a second he was impressed at the apparent freight-elevator configuration of this residential lift, as it opened on both sides, and in a uniform, series application, such as those in department stores. Then he became particularly impressed with the impending horror that threatened Heatherette, which was seemingly one of her own choosing.

Computation next. Conspicuous wreckage at the bottom of the elevator shaft in basement; Heatherette's statement, however beautiful and lonely, of alienation; signs of her giving-up evident everywhere in the house and its greater estate. The sum total: holy shit – she was backing into a deadly voyage downward!!

Speaking of the old Goth Theatre in Carstairs, it had an elevator shaft in its center stage that had carried a medium-sized Wurlitzer up and down for decades. But once the organ was dismantled and sold off to a church, the lift had a role in all sorts of big plans for Vegas-type extravaganzas, in which dancers and crooners might enter/exit at opportune moments. However, after one attempt at a revue took place on those uncertain boards, in which the singer Enelldah Whambo accidentally fell into the open space, broke her back and spent a few feeble months in a bathchair before expiring, the Goth's organ lift was pronounced jinxed. It sat idle until it was utilized by unknowing others who got it going for the New Year's celebration of '83, so that a dancer could rise onto the stage, do a 'taps' farewell to the Old, and then referee the entrance of a hobbling Father Time from stage left. And the crawling New Year's Baby (Butterbugs) from stage right.

Right now, here in Heatherette's attic, did he in fact remember the gaping hole left on that New Year's Eve, when the dancer, her job having been completed by joining the old man and the tot of the moment, retreated back into the earth. When his baby eyes saw the square of solid stage that dropped away and left a cube of uncertain emptiness, the fear of something being taken away from him made quite a mark on the future ultrastar. It all made sense now. Here, even in the gloom, that square space before him had the same quality of void the old organ shaft had possessed. A void that led to nowhere.

'Oh my God,' he thought, 'I think I understand this…!'

She stood before the shaft's opening, surely a step into another dimension, way above a fractured elevator car and its snapped cable, six stories down in the basement, complicated with banged-up furniture, busted glass, and other items conducive to human termination – if encountered from any sort of height.

Yet, she was being drawn into it. What should be holding her back? Judging from her extolling of fare–wells, nothing. There she stood, before the indiscernible abysm. What grimly glaring treble-brandished scourge awaited down below? Assuredly, one that needed no further description.

Thus did he see Heatherette through the double-sided doors of the old lift shaft.

Then it became official: she continued backing into it, INTO IT, with her shapely bottom, the folds of which undulated back and forth, slowly, slowly, leading the way.

Super-shocked, Butterbugs was frozen, as if zapped from unconscionable 220-volt fondling.

She had three steps to go.

Flash – forward: she, into the void. He, to save her, as some kind of expiation because of his delay in comprehending her value in his life, bald evidence of an essential and irreversible flaw in his character. What would follow? An *attempting* of something, at least. The vividness of an undesirable downward plunge everyone can imagine. Who doesn't dream of some fall, however long or short, in which dread, disaster, fear and failure are not intermixed as a deadly cocktail? We feel it in our guts, and mercifully, we wake up. Not this time. Not enough chance to even watch the floors go by. She, fully capable of screaming, but does not. He, can't do anything verbally. So they descend. Then they hit a bunch of terrible and sinister objects that make any landing much worse than if it had been a plain stone or concrete slab at the bottom. And yet worse, they are not killed by their fall, but are so horribly broken up that ——

'NO!!!!!!' Butterbugs screamed internally. 'That *cannot* and *will not* be!!!!!!'

Two steps remained. One and one half, actually, as the last half of the second step, taken on the fifth story, going down, would be without foundation until purchase was found on the minus-first story.

'Heather — ette…!' he whispered out loud, with all his might. But a whisper – not even one fit for the stage – was all he could manage.

One half step remained. She stopped. One stiletto heel was actually over the ledge.

His voice rose an octave.

'Heatherette! I love you! Now! *Now do I love you!*'

The only sign of either surprise or acknowledgment she gave upon hearing these words was, her fingers sprang out at right angles from her sides. Plus, her feathery tresses waved slightly in their cove at the small of her back. And, at hearing *'Now do I love you!'* all her wobbly bits became firm.

These were signs of attentiveness, not startlement or fear. But the rhythm of her tightly controlled movements had been interrupted. She started to waver, to lose balance. She was going to fall into the abysm after all.

From his all-four position, Butterbugs launched himself into a mighty long-jump, not thinking of targets or world records, only missions. To save her, or to go down together. It was a split-second decision totally worth making.

Was she about to die for him?

Would he die for her?

Was the moon *round* tonight?

He was in flight. So was she. His velocity exceeded hers. Instinctively, she used her superior feminine sensitivities to feel the potential of his oncoming impact. Surpassingly supple, and like a classic model, yet lithe as a ballerina, she turned on her one remaining fifth-floor stiletto just in time to avoid the onrushing battering ram of Butterbugs' shoulder, which would have broken all her ribs, or perhaps caused even worse injury if she'd been in its way, despite all her high-quality padding. And because she was now narrowly off to the side of this juggernaut's passage, she was not necessarily free of its influence.

Fortunately in this world, there are manifestations of the movement of spheres and similar phenomena, which cause actions like slipstreaming and sail and wind power. All such terms might now have been applied to Heatherette's consequent change in course. Because, swept along by prevailing gales, they provided for her neat body's solid, even graceful, and *safe* touchdown, on a floor she'd never really left: the Fifth.

It was a pirouette landing, ably executed with a skater's double-axel finish. In those sexy boots, too.

Butterbugs was a different matter. But it is not to say this guy was a klutz because of some impulsive and non-supervised stunt-work. Why, Yak or Joe or Tap Canutt might've done it in the same style, or directed its success! For it was indeed successful.

He landed on each of the fours he'd started out on, and aside from a mere rollover and a bit of over-compensation in trying to look reasonably cool as he was getting up, the ultrastar stood there, nearly breathless in pure moonlight, trying to discern if his girl was over there in the dark somewhere.

She was, also breathing excitedly, now facing him for the first time tonight. Certainly proud enough of her nakedness not to feel prudish at a landmark moment such as this, she nevertheless decided on prudence, not prudery, and trotted over to a nearby settee, still in the shadows, and donned a barely chaste little nightie thing that, because it was lemon yellow, gave the middle of her bod a coolly phosphorescent look, so that Butterbugs could now really believe in her actual presence. Besides, there was no evidence that any crash – bang – shriek from far below had occurred.

Here was a tableau worthy of any master of painting or cinema. Yet, none who had come before these two could have designed such a beautiful love scene. No one else could have even conceived it! Here was an exceptional couple, one known by the world, and the other not, come together at last, before it would have been too late!

But here they were now, slowly circling, each alternating between light and dark, getting closer, knowing that such a spiral was bound to join. Before it did, each stopped and regarded the other, both in full lunar essence.

Well, what else could they do? Engage in banal greetings? Or express themselves in a wordless pas de deux, so as to put off the inevitable?

Whatever the case, despite the bit of excitement just past, there was nothing but joy all around. Delight, too. What better than to draw closer, to join, without resisting the magnetic naturalness at all. To come into contact with each other, to touch, hands first, then closer, close enough, almost, to kiss.

Heatherette saw nobility of character and structure of strength before her. Butterbugs saw peerlessness of spirit and loveliness of form. Plus, the very sheer, very skimpy lemony nightie only enhanced her appeal. The unusual color scheme certainly differed from her characteristic amethyst and sapphire preferences. However, it did not in fact change her personality. But it did alter his attention from holistic to specific. Her body became a citric blur to him, while his prime focus was her face, and then it zoomed in on her eyes.

The grey of her eyes suddenly grew – incandescent. No other word for it. The exact and same sort Butterbugs possessed, manifested via his remarkable acting. There was a melding now taking place, of like souls and their cosmic kinship. Only those who had never or would never experience such wondrous exchanges would dare call them trite or sensational – or unlikely. For it was happening, as sure as the moon shone down on them.

And then, indeed, they kissed. Finally. For the first time.

All things previous were not only in the past, all things previous had been mere prelude to this one meeting of lips, with eyes closed but bodies open, mouths in consummation, providing their own sort of overture to higher communion, a union that had to happen, and having happened, was the preservation of all things *now*.

Then came the bliss of relief, a pure and saving grace, flowing from one to the other, one to the other.

Their kiss went on, to a yet greater expansion of love's permeation, love's sustenance and love's rest. Indeed, now they could cast off their incompleteness and rely upon the trust they had in each other. No further figuring or defining or explanation was needed, except to say it over and over again: 'I love you', and 'At last! At last!' and 'Now!' and other expressions of surprise, liberation and pleasure. Because, it was all so fitting, and besides, it wouldn't mean so much right now if the possibility of actually missing the very chance of it hadn't been so closely avoided.

Let now the device of a filmic lap-dissolve come into play, to render any opening words between the two unnecessary. Why relegate 'I love you' to cliché status? Why look for a hand to guide us through what is better left to the imagination? For who cannot put themselves in the place of either of the young lovers in the moonlight studio?

Also, a dissolve in time ensures some privacy, for how does one very public person present his most private self to one very private person who has just shown some very public tendencies? Actors must always operate both lever and fulcrum by which to keep the two opposites in harmony. But right now, with each at their own lever's end, they had attained a level ideal, a ramrod-straight road, as much a belt of communication as it was a metaphor for sexual congress, for which they were both hungry. All these things, all the things that involve coming into a close proximity of life and love were now within their joined efforts.

Let them have this time in private, so as to experience the ecstasy of their defining moment, all to themselves.

In due course, the moon was moving westward.

Heatherette: 'I knew it the first moment I saw you. Those long days ago. You knew it, too.'

Butterbugs: 'You say what *I* was going to say! Oh, Heatherette, I *did* know it, but I was in a Forest of Error! So callow, so unboiled, such a dimbulb – I couldn't see the truth for the life of me. And now, *you* are the life of me!'

'Isn't it cool that we both feel exactly the same way?'

'I couldn't agree more. Such a feeling I've never, ever had.'

'You've played some roles…'

'Scenes where I had to act it, yes, but it was instinctual acting, certainly not method! You, you've given me the method. Shown me.'

'Like Marlon before us.'

'Yeah. Maybe we out-Brandoed Brando this time.'

'If anyone could, you could!'

'My co-actress. You never let on.'

'We have much to *really* talk about, you know.'

'I can't wait to plunge in, girl.'

'Me neither! So, let's!'

'OK. Questions, any questions?'

'Butterbugsy, tell me, how came you to chance your approach to this lonely hall and to jump my way on such a close-call night?'

'It's a bitter tale, dear one. That is, before this nocturnal discovery of ours. I will respond in full as soon as I collect the thoughts in proper sequence in the osier of my retrospection.'

'Dear boy!'

'It was a rough evening, to say the least. Pretty eventful. Bottom line was, I was out in the cold and holey-headed deranged about it. I cannot at this time know why I made passage to your alley. I can only praise the planets and beyond for guiding my withered mind's direction. In any case, I came to the place I formerly knew, and there was my old car-cum-domicile. You *can* go home again, but at your peril. At least that's the easy thing to say. Out of the very depths of peril's threat sprang a kind of magic. This homecoming proved to be my self-actualization, because I saw you, *you!*'

'From that old romantic land-barge?'

'Well, after I'd moved on from its fossilized vestiges…'

'Funny thing, those vestiges. Because that car originally brought you to me.

Somehow, I suppose quite wistfully, I more than hoped it might bring you *back* to me.'

'Oh, it has, dear girl! It really *has!*'

'Assuredly! Though abandoned – temporarily, as it turns out! – I protected it, and turned away every attempt by heartless others who made to haul it off. Finally the city gave up... and, I have to tell you, coincidentally, so did I. That's why it slid into the degrade in which you see it now. I wanted to have it moved into my garage, but with the long gap between seeing you, and zero expectations of ever seeing you again looming always, I lost heart. My only consolation was that, if you ever chanced upon it again, it would be a land-mark to you, perhaps from which to navigate your progression from nowhere to somewhere. If I think about it, I suppose I was inspired by Judah Ben-Hur's homecoming to his ruined palace.'

'Sweet soon-to-be sex-princess! That's the picture I thought of, too! Subcon-sciously, that is...'

'Both versions?'

'No, for me it was the '59 release.'

'As some of my family members were involved in the '25 version, that's my choice.'

'Well done, film-girl. I praise your loss of heart. Irony sometimes serves they who are usually its victims! If the DeSoto had not been there, I would have had no compass in my foundering lifeboat.'

'Nobleman! You are a wonder-hero. My hero! My only one! My very own!'

'Matched by you, lovely-ass! Er, excuse me, 'derrière' sounds better. Say, shall we have the old hulk preserved after all? It's really quite intact. If my fan clubs only knew about it, they'd flip!' He chuckled. 'We could donate it.'

'As good as done, my super-love. Or, ultra-love, I should say!'

'Now, my unknown-fantasy-come-true, I have one for you: You didn't really want to – throw yourself down... in... that... there...? You know...?'

As his question mark formed, he was in fact thinking not of his saving her a while ago, but of her saving appearance on his terrace at The Æyrie. This, rather more than her *second* saving (and sick-making) gesture, via the phone, while he was in Jambutterbugsabad.

She smiled, and then answered with all sincerity:

'Not at all. Never. A subconscious desire to fly, is all – Only I was awake. But to fly away – not to dusty death, but somewhere wholly grander. Perhaps death is only a stop along the way... But suicide is not at all my style. But if I was going to go, perhaps I felt drawn by my forebears.'

'What do you mean, sweet and saved treasure?'

'I can tell you now, similarly-saved one. When I was not yet three years of age, both my parents, who were obscure but brilliant experimental filmmakers – (in-deed, they used my great grandfather's old silent studio just here, to make their cinematic works) – well, they plummeted to their doom when the cable holding the car in this very lift shaft snapped. There was talk that rivals may have filed the cable, but private investigations revealed nothing, and the whole affair has been under hush-up right to the present day. Were they murdered? I cannot say. I have done a screenplay on the subject though. Perhaps it will kindle an interest in re-opening the case. All the evidence is still here – down there – virtually intact.

'They were true artistes in film. In all its elements. Their entire œuvre, unseen as yet by the world, remains intact in the basement (and not one frame of it is nitrate stock), just steps away from where they parted this life.'

'I'm so sorry, dear girl.'

'Thanks, Perseus. I suppose my life has rotated round that tragedy to a level I had not previously known. Until tonight, when you have freed me forever from it.'

'I'm delighted I could provide you with that humble service.'

'Yes indeed! Now I can face the world with good cheer!'

'Together!'

'You and me, baby-baby!'

'Gubbah-Gubbah!'

'You speak my language, boy!'

'Our close calls…'

'Yes, yes,' she replied. 'Sometimes we are compelled into avenues of thought which we were never meant for. But because of the actions of others, they appear to make sense.'

'*My* actions?'

'I think it all comes down to my own actions, not those of others.'

'But, would you have *done it?*'

'Would you, the two times I encountered you in similar situations?'

'You know,' Butterbugs said, relaxing over the preposterousness of his question, 'We have quite a bit in common, you and me.'

They rested.

As their stories came out, their admiration for each other grew. This was just the beginning, too. The night was getting on, but it was still young because there was new life within it. Mutual commitments were born.

Butterbugs looked through the awful elevator doors and to whence he'd come.

'How do we get back over – jump? I can take you on my back.'

'Come with me,' she giggled. 'Right this way!' and led her new and rightful boy back to the main studio by means of a not-so-obvious bypass. It was directly adjacent to the elevator shaft, but concealed by soundproof curtains and easily missed because of the dangerous attention-hog of the stuck-open doom-doors. In a mere jiffy they were safely on the other side, the most mundane accomplishment of the night.

'Had I known of this occult but easy bypass, I would have…'

The ludicrousness of his words made them both cackle. Still, he needed closure.

'Tell me, Prefectioness of Perfection, why do you keep that threatening breach un-shuttered?'

'I guess as a sort of memorial. But from this night they shall be closed for ever, as the curse has run its course, and a new era has entered this place. I never paid much attention to minding the gap, probably because I grew up with it and the novelty wasn't there. But now that we have both felt the suction of its hazards, it must and shall be sealed.'

As a person of independent practicality, Heatherette muscled two big plywood sheets into the lift door gap on both sides, pounded in some retaining nails, bent them into place, tossed the hammer to the ground, brushed off her hands, and arranged her nightie back into presentable configuration for her very welcome but still untested gentleman caller (even though said caller liked the workpersonlike configuration that said nightie had gotten into, due to her hard work).

'I have never seen a more lovely person doing heavy physical labor,' said Butterbugs, truly bedazzled.

'Oh, go on with you. Not that physical, not that heavy. But thanks for letting me do it my own way, and remaining in the wings.'

'My turbo-pleasure, infinitely-capable one!'

Then, safely on the main side of this attic-studio concern, she took his hand and led him to the labyrinthine table arrangements that occupied the space where Olive Thomas once acted and Efrem Zimbalist once fiddled.

'Now, dear guy, let me show you some of my things. The moonglow is totally romantic, but if you'll allow me to interrupt it for a few minutes...'

She went over to an archaic but mint-condition rheostat mechanism, cranked it, and lo, a lighting plot of great invention and warmth rose into existence and made the contents of the vast space well defined and exuding of intrigue.

As the house lights came up, Butterbugs now beheld the full extent of what had been somber shadow and shape before. Tables were laid out in linear fashion, end to end. Some were only two or three in length, while others doubled, tripled, quadrupled back upon themselves, like labyrinthine trains of thought. They groaned under the weight of texts, manuscripts, research materials, books, and, more specifically, typed print-outs, copious notebooks, sketches, models, along with keyboards, paper-blocks, watercolor tubes, brushes, DobianColor pencils, and rapidographs, amongst other art and writing paraphernalia.

'My projects for the cinema...'

She held out her hand in a gesture that was purely Butterbugsian in its grandeur.

'All – by you? Your doing?'

She was then wordless, most likely out of modesty, now that she had revealed her crafts, and maybe with second thoughts. But she was in love. All must be exposed.

As he browsed the collections, he could see they were very much her doing. Each had a kind of energy that rose from it in different strengths and tones. No mere displays or relics, each project was alive with activity, and brilliance was all around.

In the midst of her studio, Heatherette guided him through astonishing lay-outs, storyboards, script deposits, set models, costume designs and all manner of pre-production essentials for a huge array of original productions she had been nurturing, month after month, year after year. Pictures written, designed and di-rected by she, Heatherette, starring Butterbugs – as well as herself. This was the life of her mind, the product of her hands, all here, all ready to go, but dependent of one thing, one man: Butterbugs – who regarded her work now, and in-person!

'When you'd said you'd done a screenplay, I, well –'

'You thought I was jesting?'

'No, no, certainly not. A little metaphorically-intentioned, perhaps.'

'My script about my parents' elevator tragedy –'

'A heady story?'

'Well, maybe you'd be interested in perhaps appearing in its filmization?'

'Baby, I'd be interested in appearing in your launderette hamper, if you asked me. I'm totally thrilled at the prospect!'

'The launderette one, or the film one?'

'Both! Hell, my dear, I had no idea! None whatsoever! Only you never let on. I knew your ancestors were picture pioneers, and you suggested 'The Ag-hori' (20th-Fox) to me and all, (which you never received screen credit for – but I tell you, you will!) But I hadn't the faintest inkling you might be an auteur, and an actress to boot! Heather-eather-ette-r! Why! Where've you been?? Away here in storage – that's where! Busy, sure enough, but in deepest obscurity! You should've hogtied me the last time I was here, hooked me up to a block and tackle in that there elevator shaft, and hauled me up here, then forced me to gaze at this fantastic repository of greatness! You'd be living the life of total cinematic im-mersion by now!'

'Again, not my style, Sir Butterbugs. To hogtie and haul and force, that is.'

'And definitely not while wearing that outfit.'

He winked. She blushed.

'You mean, you're interested?'

'Interested?'

He went over to a natty set of script shelves, her thirty-six photoplays so far, carefully arranged in alphabetical order, according to title. Then, second copies, arranged according to subject, genre, etc.

'Now looka here,' he continued, randomly opening the first one he selected, to the third act of 'Pinebane of Shickleshack', silently reading the lines, then grab-bing another, 'Sureenum Magnum', silently reading some second act dialogue, then from yet another, 'The Chimneys of Tiebulbus' reading to himself again, this time moving past the sampling and into true engrossment for a couple minutes, before slamming the script down (for effect, not harming one sweetly-scented page).

'I can dive into your work at any stage, at any place, and in the first sentence I read, I know there is something profound, something great that surrounds it. That's my test, and I just did it. Thrice! You have to understand, one knows these things without too much rigmarole attached. I am pro enough now, dear girl, to spot talent and to recognize its quality, and to instantly know such a talent needs to be placed before the public instead of being hoarded away from view! We who have talent are all publicists in a sense, but some of us need to be publicized by others of our kind. Like you. Like me. This is the nature of our Industry, and I am always happy to break its staid rules if I can be of assistance. I know these things not (just) because I love you, but because I myself am what you should and shall be: surrounded by the completeness of a creative cinematic life. I do not need to reinvent my own wheel to prove the point. What I need to do in this case is not to help you invent or reinvent your own self, but to facilitate your cinematic realities. You are plainly, even painfully, *ready*. I want to do it. My lover needs me! It is my desire. Nay, it is my *duty!*'

She almost swooned. At his words, at their meaning, and at his performance. Never was love's bounty so giving or so keep-on giving!

'Oh, Butterbugs, I wish I could sing a rapturous aria to you, just now!'

'These scripts! This art! These concepts! Your aria, lover!'

They all but leapt into each other's arms, happy to get lost in the nuzzling and the touching and the exciting boom-boom-boom of ideas, prospects, and bodily urges.

Like a Carmen in playful joy, she then pushed him away and coyed toward a teapoy, which itself strained to hold up a jewel-like array of decanters and thimbles.

'Refreshments in light of amazements.'

'Don't mind if I do. If *we* do!'

Now had he the precious leisure at last to simply look upon her as she did beverage presentation. He thought not only of her grace, and her tangibility that was breathtakingly earthbound, despite the filmy briefness of her intimate apparel, but also, he discerned her obvious genius as a filmmaker. Unmade films do not disqualify any filmmaker from her or his rightful role as a conceptualizer, a visualizer, or even a storyteller. Making films is not necessarily defined by filming, developing, editing and release. Ideas, scripts and pre-planning qualify just as much. Bean-counters expect product, while artists expect processes. Though Heatherette would now get her chance for cinematic fruition, she was obviously not lacking for artistic achievement.

For her part, while she clinked crystal upon crystal as colored fluids flowed from one to the other, she could feel her man's recognition of this other side of her true self. She felt his appreciation, his pleasure at the discoveries, and his awe in her candidly exhibited talents, hidden till now. After all, she had long known of his own genius, and her belief in him had never wavered.

Also, she relished his admiring gaze, so effortlessly felt, and so excitingly welcome. After all, she had beheld him in countless scenes and guises, admiringly, from the vantage point of a seat in the audience. It was his turn now, to absorb who she herself was. She loved giving him the pleasure of doing so.

Indeed, she keenly felt his look as it flowed over her, and when she approached him with the nipperkins of Ghoabshuh Savours, her Athena eyes interlocked with his, and she knew of all the right action and right experience that could now take place with this one, sole ultrastar, her truant but treasured find.

Indeed, the rightness of everything made up the bulwark of their love. Right, and natural, and so very timely.

Sip, sip, they sipped the turquoise fire-oil, relaxing on her beat-up Empire work settee.

'Gosh, Heatherette, one thing still troubles me. Your monologue, delivered just before I saved you. Your being lost in the universe and all. Should I be concerned?'

'Oh you dear sweet heart! I'm glad you liked it.'

'I liked it. Loved it! But what *about* it?'

'It's called thinking out loud. I may use it in my latest Butterbugs-specific screenplay. Your thoughts?'

'You mean, it was just improv?'

He sounded almost naïve.

'Well, *now* it is. Now that you saved me from my foolishness.'

'You were about to sacrifice yourself for a script?'

'Apparently! Though not really. I don't want you to confuse the destructive spark with the creative spark. I guess I just needed saving – and you were the man for the job!'

'Lucky me!'

'Lucky us!'

'Now we can move forward!'

'To glory!'

They toasted each other.

'Now,' Butterbugs waxed professionally cinematic for the first time since the 'UWH' hiatus was resumed, 'What ideas, what fabulous ideas have you? In addition to those tables'-worth over there, that is.'

'First I have to ask, are there any cherished projects you'd like to do that so far ye have been denied?'

'I have a dear desire to be in the ultimate filmization of the 'Darbidiah' saga.'

'Superior! Coincidentally, I myself have recently completed a six-part treatment of that very saga, for realization as a major motion picture series.'

'Perfect!'

Ever since Butterbugs had encountered amazement at Dmitri Shostakovich's preemptive composition based on a vital property that was imminent, he thought preparatory treatments of possible pictures perfectly normal. Being in love with the preparer made things even more perfect.

'Now it is perfect, as of this instant of your agreement! We can collaborate with Kevlurr Kaarson and associate on the final screenplay. Could Hazel bankroll it?'

'She will! I tell you, she will. Upon my recommendation.'

'Oh, Butterbugseth!'

'My goodness, Heatherette, you seem so *with it* – as if you've been an Industry heavy player for the longest time.'

'I've been waiting for my chance, and you have set me free. The prospect of being your partner in every way is the most sacred thing I can think of!'

Their Ghoabshuh Savours-flavored kisses were really quite fine.

Then she told him more about many but not all of the projects she had created in her self-exile here.

He applauded.

'So, let's review a bit of background, Butterbugs, to see if we want to consummate our newfound relationship.'

'An excellent idea, princess.'

'So we can say we did it.'

'Or didn't do it.'

'Consummation?'

'The whole shootin' match,' he said with a satisfying exhale.

'To cover everything.'

'So no one can blame us.'

'No one is at fault, I shouldn't think. But my years of detachment added up to a true isolation. Errors of judgment… result. As if abusing some kind of substance that prevents the expansion of the human mind.'

'You were always there,' he said. 'All the time. Right along. In my heart, and I, I somehow knew it, yet I didn't act upon it. What would have been my… motivation? The actor's raison d'être. Acting! What I *do*. Still, I didn't know how. Didn't know how…'

'As if *I* did. So much for my own skills.'

'I came to you a broken man, I think.'

'Why? Because of that Pepper Carlson?'

'You know of my loss, my emptiness, then?'

He was not defensive, only the recall of a melancholy memory reminded him that he and Heatherette were people with histories, and if they had a problem in reviewing them, this new thing would never work. So they reviewed, proving that the thing would indeed work.

So he added, 'That was a major part of it. But I was in love with an idea, not an actual person. That idea has been utterly and irreversibly superseded by you, yourself, and your love.'

'I'm pleasured to hear it, sweets. I knew that when the media plastered all that publicity about your search for Pepper and Prairie, you were perhaps in search of an elusive ideal. Not an idea, but an ideal. Your love for her in spirit… For her spirit, yes. I can well understand that. I know how you loved her, won her, wanted to be with her. I know of the empty space of... Of unknown dimensions, that existed in your heart, though it did not occur to you.'

'I'm glad you use the past tense, lovey. 'That exist*ed*' – That's right, *used* to exist. It does no longer.'

'I believe you, Butterbugs.'

'Upon my very soul!'

'Good!'

'And I think I have found her.'

'You mean...That Pepper girl...?'

'Naw!!'

'OK...'

'No! Right here, in this room. Tonight! And I have kissed her. Tonight! I am *home!*

'Better!'

'She – you, have been the one I've always sought. The only one. The only *possible* one! You must understand, that knowledge was not fully understood, until – until – Tonight!'

'Best!'

She knew of his search for the lost ones, true, via the yakking media, but most of her knowledge was accurate intuition. Even she, the believer in færies and limitless combinations of nats, munchkins, winkies and hobbits, privately doubted if his Peppering on the Prairie had ever really existed. The fantasies of strolling players! She comforted him on this issue, but then waxed surprisingly blunt: if he had had his way, and indeed, was able to retreat into Pepper's world...

'...The Earth would have been thus deprived of the profound gifts you have brought to billions. You have not sacrificed, Butterbugs, so much as you gifted all of us. You are a bearer, not a taker. You were meant to provide, not consume. You taught us not to live by selfishness alone.'

He shed a few tears of liberation, at last, from the fantasy and its sad reality. And she, feeling free of her own nightmare within the crashed elevator car in the basement, joined him in making each other's necks wet with saline solutions.

They both figured they were a bit potted from the liqueur, which they immediately dubbed The Bawling Tincture.

The moon ran west, so she dimmed-out the conciseness of her working studio and they went back to the mysterioso wall-washes of selenite light and its reflected effects. For their moon was retreating now, its squares slowly traveling up the walls, as the night got on.

Their gambol on the settee was supremely soothing. So much so that Butterbugs dropped off into a deep-breathing slumber.

A slumber that allowed for a dream sequence. Not formally scripted, but ultra-high production values. Probably widescreen. Maybe even 3-D. Color by DeLuxe. Production Design: Perry Ferguson and Hans Peters. Music by Dimitri Tiomkin. Directed by (unknown – signed by Alan Smithee). No studio designation, nor main titles, nor end titles. Box office potential uncertain.

Fade in.

The night before Butterbugs' big scene, an affecting visit to Heatherette's abode. Tiomkin scoring: a soulful chorus in the distant background, implying wistful nostalgia and longing. In the twilit mansion, intimations of mortality, truth, glory, and the poignancy of Heatherette (now like a delicate pre-Raphaelite or Arthurian princess). Butterbugs is *still* not committed to her in his heart – till he leaves the verandah's edge and resolves to propose to her after his restoration following the big scene.

Atmosphere builds.

The night before – the very night before – yes, the night before Butterbugs' big climactic scene is to be staged, the great man himself manages to steal away from his incomplete life. Where-o, where-o does he direct his DeSotomobile? For some reason, he searches for anchors into the past. It is a balmy but moody evening, with the given searchlights, way in the distance, perchance a premiere of one of his pictures, off in Glendale or somewhere. Where then, should he spend his 'last' night on Earth? Boulevard upon boulevard decide for him. It is to the wistful world of Yniguez Terrace. Despite the length of time that has passed since he was last on this side of the alley, everything appears the same. But there is a degree of sleaziness that he can't deny. Several of the grand old piles have been razed, one is virtually collapsing, and the brown lawns and broken roof tiles on front terraces bespeak a woefulness rather than a wistfulness. In 'Citizen Kane' (RKO, 1941) there is a pronounced sentiment of rot amidst plenty, and in this scene is found the same sense of dubious accomplishment. Yet, in the operative path he now takes, there is a synchronization with the inevitable decay, once such a peak has been achieved. How else would it have been possible for the world of 'Sunset Boulevard' (Paramount, 1950) to have existed only a few short decades after the heyday that created it? It is an aspect of Hollywood to which he is inexplicably drawn.

So, what is he doing here? He would pay – pay a visit – a very deep visit, to Heatherette. She is there, as she always is. Loyal, in a sense, without any sort of commitment. As is her custom, she appears in a hastily donned royal purple bathrobe, at the dusky doorway, all surrounded with terracotta tiles in an absent-minded Byzantine configuration, which Butterbugs has never noticed before.

'There is *a lot* I never noticed before,' he says breathily to her. 'Including how lovely your kissable lips are. If only I had known!'

He plows gracefully into a locked kiss that can only be described as truant in its sadder but wiser electronic impulse.

Gracefully as well, Heatherette draws him inside, and still engaged in the ca-noodle, waves her bare foot in an untried but unexpectedly skilled manœuvre of closing the great Nouveau door in one gesture. Then she goes almost limp.

'I thought you fainted…,' Butterbugs utters in the gloom.

'Butterbugs – you're here! Such a – *re*-introduction! I cannot –'

'Don't speak, Heatherette. I hardly can, myself…'

And then there is the necessity of great romantic music's providing shelter to the scene, by defining its background limits. Tiomkin's cue now: a further-out 'legendary' sound, almost mediæval, to accommodate the lady's distinguished standing.

'Oh, Butterbugs…!'

'Heatherette! If *only* I had –'

'Don't say it… Yet… If I could only hope for the færie-land of my distant dreams!'

'We live in it already, if we care to look.'

'You know of it, then?'

'I have tasted it. And I have even been there. But not with you.'

'Can you take me?'

'I can and I will. After I do what must be done.'

She cannot help but become plaintive.

'What? *What* must be done?'

'I'm going to do the scene. The final scene.'

'So, the rumors are true.'

'It is not yet in the press, Heatherette.'

'I know. Remember, I have sources.'

Butterbugs eases up.

'Of course you do. Thank heavens for that. You I can trust.'

'And I you. Although I must question the wisdom of your decision. Oh, Butterbugs, I cannot lose you!'

'Nor I you. But you shall not. It is only for a week or so.'

'Or forever!'

'Nothing will be lost. Only gains will be made.'

'How can you gain when the risk is so high?'

He laughs, almost stridently.

'You don't understand. It's all under control.'

He lets her loose and makes towards a decanter of indeterminate liqueur in the adjacent alcove, 'neath a votive lamp of distinctive Turkish origin.

'How could such a situation have come about?' she asks, not yet feeling abandoned.

'Well, I'll tell you. It's all built into the power structure of the Industry.'

Not wanting to discomfit him by his somewhat naïve (despite his magnificent standing) presentation of power politics & policies in Hollywood, Heatherette chooses to be patient, oh so patient, even though it is getting late in the day as far as her agenda in the matter, and she aches now for resolve.

'Yes, Butterbugs, I should think that would be the case.'

'So now there's this thing about making the biggest impact possible.'

'Oh, Butterbugs, drop this unhappy situation and come to me!'

'I would be happy to.'

'So you mean you'll do it? Come to me? Now?'

'In a bare week's time, my love!'

He draws nigh to her and cups her posterior in his large hands.

She trembles with melting expectation.

'Come upstairs…'

'In one week's time, beloved.'

'Not now? The heavens are still shielded from stark day; night is for new lovers – Like us?'

Tiomkin cue: more intensity of passion.

'I came tonight just to let you know.'

'Let me know, what – Just a statement, just a promise? After the long time I have waited?'

'I must *prepare*…'

'For a mere scene, or for a lifetime of love?'

'My makeup call, it comes, in a mere hour!'

'Surely they can use someone else. Your stand-in. I will tell them myself, so as to spare you the embarrassment. I'll say you have an indisposition, anything.'

'That would be against my practices, loved-of-mine.'

'I have to *protect* you, I have to shield you from…'

'My anxious one, I understand –'

'No, I don't think you do. Not at all!'

'How can I make you understand…?'

Tiomkin cue: a development of urgent longing; e.g. the jail scene, just before Scott Chavez's hanging, in 'Duel in the Sun' (Selznick, 1946).

'If I can't have you this night, well, I guess… No, I *know*. I can't have you at… at… all…'

'Why? Why not? Why the extreme conditions, my love?'

'Because I cannot bear those very conditions. If you – if you *never return*.'

'Why of course I will. Other actresses, other babes, other admirers, they mean nothing to me now. You'll see!'

'That's not what I was thinking.'

'So, you trust me?'

'Oh, glorious one! Of course I trust you! With my very life, my very being! But I don't know if I trust *others* with it.'

'You are safely here, Heatherette! I'll see to that.'

'No, I mean, trusting others – with *your* own very –'

'Oh, that! I'm a professional, lassie! So is everyone I work with. We're a merrie band of fearless filmsters!'

He laughs, hoping it will infect her, but it doesn't. She stares at him directly, soberly, and pushes him away slowly.

Tiomkin cue: somber tones.

'No, I can see you will not bend.' The tone of her voice grows flat. 'Therefore, please leave.'

'But Heathery-bank, I love you!'

'I love you too, but I cannot *lose* you.'

She gently but purposefully pushes him until he is out the front door. She releases her touch of his shoulders with great regret, but with resolve. She can look upon him no more. Her eyes travel down to the ground and her face vanishes into the dark as she closes the great door.

He is out on the verandah now, looking mournfully at the fast-closed barrier.

Dissolve to Butterbugs out in front of the house in the troubled night. He raises his arms in despair.

'Heatherette, Heatherette! I cannot, cannot lose you! I cannot lose you...'

He lowers his arms sadly, turns about, hangs his head, and exits the scene.

Tiomkin cue: a tragic climax (mixture of minor and major keys).

Fade-out.

For her part, Heatherette did not doze, despite the urge, but rather, let Butterbugs do so as her first act of consideration for his domestic welfare. It was an enriching moment, to have someone else to minutely care for, and she reckoned she'd be quite good at it. Besides, the opportunity was there to simply gaze at him, in the cherished still of the hour, as her lover. Focused on his fascia, she mused fondly on the love to come, whether in his arms, or he inside her.

Time ran, though not much. About twelve minutes.

All Heatherette did was shift her ankle just a bit, and the ultrastar awoke with a start.

'I cannot, cannot lose you!' he blurted out, then opened his eyes and sat up.

'Dear boy! An appendix to your dream?'

'What? You're here? I'm here? But –'

She sensed, quite correctly, that he'd had an anxious time of it, so she wisely and hastily brewed up a samovar of Sarve-tea to restore them both, and to take advantage of its slight but effective amnesiac qualities, which worked very well to erase one's troubling dreams upon awakening.

'It was about... loss...,' Butterbugs said.

Heatherette's only reply was to serve his cup of Sarve.

With the tea they indeed perked and reveled in the excitement of being up all night together. Butterbugs mentioned nothing more about his dream, because he had forgotten that he had one, and on such a night, Heatherette had no desire to hear about its perceived drama. She was fully aware of the classic Actor's Muddle, when a Player of the Drama, no matter how even-tempered or stellar, gets a bit 'mixed up' over what is dramatically *real*, and what is really *dramatic*.

But there he was, fully Butterbugsian once more, relishing the moment, without having to be pinched.

'I like your slumber parties,' he said, smacking his lips in order to catch the buzzy herbal vibes the Sarve-strips – of the horehound variety – would deliver, to best advantage.

'It's about time you stayed for the duration of such events.'

'I'd forgotten their charm. I'd forgotten a lot of things.'

She drew close, and with her tongue frolicking with his, shared in the pleasant high the flower-pot-raised tea-strips brought, until all of them were dissolved between the two.

For a time they appraised each other's relaxed bodies, another step toward passage to bed, and neither found the other wanting in any respect. Heatherette was somewhat familiar with the lay of Butterbugs' land, what with many a bared screen scene, all the way up to explicit (but never, ever gratuitous) statements of cinematic sensuousness. But at this moment, she couldn't have been more pleased with the transition from widescreen portraiture to casual slump on a raggy day bed. A real man, wholly suitable, all three dimensions in front of her now.

For his part, Butterbugs' appraisal of his new girl was very simple – primitive, even: sheer admiration.

Filmmakers may film their works out of sequence, but their conceptualization tends to be linear. Not just because of the basic roll-of-film format, but because of our storytelling tradition. Strings are followed, whether in chronological fashion, or via flashback or jump cut. All sorts of innovations in varying the progression exist, but nevertheless, film is all about fade-in and fade-out. Another wheel that doesn't necessarily need to be reinvented, only added-to.

For their own part, cinema actors usually think in terms of scenes, and not necessarily of the whole in which they are comprised. So Heatherette, polymath of the Seventh Art, utilized her gesamtkunstwerk capabilities, which she now employed, and without guile, on her dear one, as he was in need of some direction regarding one issue in particular.

'My beloved!' she began, as it was conducive to his reverie.

'My – dear – Hurrette –!'

'You're as dear to me as I am to you, not so?'

'So!'

'So,' she continued, 'since, in a way, things loom large, especially on the quickly-coming morrow – though later on in the day, I was wondering about an issue of business that lies slightly beyond our newfound and rightful bliss.'

'A matter of motion picture affairs.'

'Check!'

'Shoot!'

'What we must do. Now, *that* is the question.'

'Aye,' he agreed, gazing at the loveliest lover he had ever encountered, or was ever liable to.

'Well, dear boy, what about the climax to the impending agreement? It is what so largely loometh. Will you, then… finish it?'

'You mean, of course, dear love-mate, 'Unholy War Hymn'? (Notice that I do not recite that picture's title in the hip acronym-only manner.)'

'It is of that which I ask.'

'Aye, there's the rub. You know of it then, and all its demands.'

'It is as if I've been on the Producers Team from the start.'

'And you should be! And you will!'

'In any case, sweetheart, what about it?'

'My remaining scene-sequence! I am required by contractual law to fulfill it. But, you know what? I don't want to! I want to move on to other things. *Your* things. I do believe I will chuck the 'UWH' finals.'

'Will you? Oh, *will you?*'

'The great question of our times.'

'Whatever may be the case, B-love, the question must be asked, for to-morrow, the multitudes will ask it, again and again.'

'Perfectly correct, my sacredness.'

'So, we of the joined bliss must still deal with the on-the-ground realities.'

'And I am perfectly happy to do so.'

'Good! *Good!* Now, what say you, cinema-summiter?'

'It is the last hurdle between my existing obligations and our unified dreams for the world! That being the case, I guess I believe in honor after all, and *above* all. That's why, dear skin, I would have sacrificed myself to save even one discarded superficial flight off your swooping breasts – swooping toward my cheered face!'

They were both a little baked by the mild high of their herbal infusion.

'Ye loving and grounded beast! Yes! Talk to me of these things in bed, but only after we lay to rest the urgencies of the moment, so that we can get on with our true love's truth! Having been close to snuffing it this night, I need to know your intensions, lest I think regressive thoughts regarding your picture show obligations.'

'I know. I agree wholly. For, how can we begin our new lives if residual draggings remain, by which to keep us anchored to dreariness past?'

'Sweet guy, don't get too hung up on the properness of the bullshit. Let's purge and come clean!'

'Oh, yes! Lover, you! You see how I am liberated by your purity? Teach me! Lead me on!'

'Just so…'

'Yes, thank you. All right. I think I see your point. Fulfill all obligations outstanding so that we may proceed into your love's patient creations. I agree!'

'So then, you will comply?'

'With 'Unholy''s remaining tract?'

'Yes. To my mind, we need closure.'

'That's what I don't like about it. It is the last remaining hurdle between the past and the future.'

'The two, so closely intertwined.'

'I have to say, Heatherette, I don't want to finish it. That's my first instinct. I want to start on *our* pix – tonight!'

'I too desire the same, devoted boy! But you know, you are bound. We cannot start by having the Industry, to which we wish to contribute, as a hostile entity.

Besides, your friends must be my friends. I cannot be regarded as your spoiler. We shall all be making pictures together. I have so many plans – and you do too, now. Finish what has been so grandly started, and we shall go forward together – to our own kind of glory. No pretensions, just happiness, in all its forms.'

'Oh Heatherette, is that what you want?'

'Our glory, yes!'

'And to *get* there, I must fulfill my agreement and finish the picture… I suppose I must…'

'Just so, lovey. It's just a short hop, really. Can you hop?'

She stood up and did just that, backwards, in a parody of her near-catastrophe.

He burst out laughing and followed suit in a sort of bumbling choreography, also aimed backwards.

Then they swept toward each other to a full embrace, with lots more kissing.

'My new and true lover,' she whispered breathily in his ear. 'Now comes time for us to share what we really are.'

'What we really need,' he replied.

'I've waited so long. So very, very long. Unto weariness.'

'And I, too. I never knew *how* long!'

'I'm no longer weary.'

'And I'm not exactly snoozlechugging! I kind of want to fiddle with that flimsy thing you've got on.'

'The crotch of which grows soaked.'

'If you would be so kind…'

'Come now, to a place you've never been. I think you will find it suits you.'

Oh, but how they exchanged so many secrets and longings and fulfillings on the considerable walk to the paradise garden of her fabulous bedroom.

They passed in front of one of those theatrical dressing room mirrors, but despite their miracle of joining, there was no cinemagic that lighted their forms. Perhaps if they'd entered its frame a bit earlier, a cogent image of their grouped effect would have appeared, but the moon was heading on out. Choice moments of great night lighting were passing. In spite of these conditions, their silhouettes were attractive enough, and absolutely perfect for any upcoming film noir scenarios – several of which were already committed to paper in Heatherette's feathery hand.

Butterbugs paused for a moment, examining her elegant profile. Every curve, every wave, every flourish was pleasing, edifying, inspiring. All he needed really, to erect a temple around.

Heatherette, needful of something *more* just now, leaned forward and flipped a wall switch. All the surrounding showbiz bulbs came to life, revealing the couple as they really were: Hollywood's best-looking people.

'Why Heatherette – you're – you're beautiful!'

It was something he already knew, but how many times can one say it?

'You've gotten plenty of screen exposure, lover,' she replied. 'I suppose you already know how I feel about *your* appearance.'

She kissed him on the cheek.

They were the perfection of the matches. The screen would love them. So would the world.

'I think we're ready for audiences, don't you?'

'Ready when you are, Bb.'

He gazed at the light bulbs, some of which were the old Edison variety.

'Why Heatherette, I'm glad you use electricity when it's most effective!'

'It's good for a few things,' she answered coyly. 'Such as running light through a projector, and for seeing who we really are. Now let's explore how we really *feel*.'

He ran his hand lightly up her side, and she shuddered, then moaned.

'I'll lead the way,' she whispered, leading the way.

There was a hilarious outburst from both of them when he opened the exit door to the stairs downward. The great pry-bar he'd set against it, as a security guarantee, crashed to the floor, scaring the piss out of them. The mirth of the situation told them to quickly howl.

'Well, I believe you would've heard me if I tried to escape,' she laughed.

'Had you tried!'

'Of course, with two other exit stairways, plus a fire escape to choose from, it might've been an entertainment to humor you by, testing your little system, here!'

How tickled he was to find out that she had such a playful trait within her. How tired he'd become of the reverence shown him by most everyone else in the universe. Here was someone he could not only worship, but laugh with as well.

Now was their urgency to become physical, reaching its randy/fancy/grabby/ panting-over-panties, and mutual-stripping stage.

'Right here?' Butterbugs asked, gesturing to a bit of cape-like drapery on the gymnasium-type hardwood floor, made available via curtains hung lower than they might.

'Well, that's a sexy enough spot, but I have more comforts to offer. If we can hold out, it'd be worth it.'

'Lead on, baby. I can steel myself. No problem. Remember, I've done nude sex with Lacplesis, ProwlerCat, Keenah, Feather, Jes, Nic, Liz, Kim, Scarlett and many another in front of the camera's gateway to the masses. I'm a 'pro', doncha know!'

'So... I think you'll 'do'! And you will do so with me – in front of *my* camera and *my* crew, ere long. Wait till you read the scenes I've written us!'

'Well, if you want to, I suppose...'

She laughed, 'I think we'll act them out in private, first! Come on! The virgin lands await.'

In the long trek to her private chambers, they were able to freely exchange some of their lighter thoughts.

'So, when you saw me standing there –'

'In your naked majesty!'

'Which is all yours now, Bubsey-lover! But there I was, and you heard me and my, well, gassy hello, eh? Good thing I had that sheen-pepper stew, earlier!'

'Was it tasty?'

She smiled with the fullness of a rapidly growing confidence of love.

'Yup!'

Pepper, schlepper. No subsequent reference to Pepper Carlson from him, and she knew he hadn't even thought of her. That entity was dissolved into the æther from which it had come, and it wasn't because of any old Sarve-tea infusion, either. Thus, no further references were possible. Time for them to get physical and prove their bodily mass' worth, as a joined unit.

'I am doing nothing but rejoicing, sweetie!' she announced.

'Yeah, yeah, yeah, cool one!'

Her bedroom suite was a magnificence. He had snogged starlets behind pedestal'd busts in Versailles, pinched bottoms in the Forbidden City, stroked long legs at Bald Hills, made raga-love in Bikaner Palace, tested bitch-goddesses at Chatsworth, and even copped a few feel-ups in the US Capitol. But this chamber, Heatherette's seat of solo power, was to him, the summit. Everything about it was perfect, and as he led his wide eyes around, all he saw, even though it be shrouded in late-late night substance and shadow, met with his amazed approval. A few strategically-placed jar-votives happily prevented appearances from becoming *too* modest. Like a lush set out of the Silent Era, with a comforting bohemian heart inserted, the bedroom was heady in itself, and ready for love. With appropriateness then, he silently thanked the stars that reigned at his nativity for allowing him to *even be alive* (and sensual), so as to be present in such an environment.

'Thanks be to stars and all powers therein,' he murmured.

'Did I hear you speak of star power?' Heatherette called out, as she puffed both pillow and duvet to make her lover acclimatized to her nest.

He was acclimatized, all right, and ready for romance in its most fetter-free freedom.

'Of stars, I sing, and associated heights of all kinds!' he replied. 'I feel like we're up there. We've joined them.'

'We're climbing together! Oh, I know, I feel the ascendancy as well. I can just look at you, across this crowded room, and feel it. Now, will you come over as I strip?'

No words, just an approach. He to her bed, and she to him, drawing nigh. The little yellow wisp of a thing became like butterfly wings on the floor. As she slipped out of her boots with lyrical talent, he was able to spy the contours of smooth thighs, the plump generosity of lips, the sumptuous hair just above, the triumph of gently full breasts, and the reappearance of her belly button as she stood up straight.

Confident that her strip was a success, she rotated so as to show the complete, unedited version of her calves, the well-formed smoothness of her butt, the musical lines of her back, and the tress-decorated sureness of her shoulders.

For his part, Butterbugs shed his unremarkable party duds, and stood facing her in Apollonian pose.

They dove into bed.

It may have been coming on to the hour when cocks crew, representing the closing of one day to allow for the next, but there was no shortage of passionate crowing now on its way, signaling the two lovers' unification.

They were naked, and they were in bed, and they were enfriskened.

He sniffed her body, doglike, and the results made his saliva viscous and plentiful.

'Horny boy and girl,' she whispered. 'Oh yes, yes to everything!'

'We have waited so long, you and I.'

'Though we knew it not.'

'Now we know. No waiting, ever again.'

'Will you fuck me now, expected-one?'

'With all the oncoming messages before the season's wind!'

'In from the wilds, to flow over me. Around me. In me.'

'The spreading of the seeds.'

'For me? A seed for me?'

'With the many, all for you, as you desire.'

'Oh yes. All you have. Come, come in me, without limits.'

'Feel me, hard for you.'

'You've got a nice cock.'

'Yours now. Let me lose myself in you for a time.'

'Come down, love. I will receive you. Soak into my sexy body. All the way.'

He did indeed, and at length, the product from his balls equaled the invitational passacaglia of her pleasure-moans. And his resulting motility thrust her into ecstasy, so that her body was transformed into its next, higher phase.

He bellowed, she cried, he grunted like a warthog, she panted like an antelope. His shrieks were such that it was a good thing a considerable mansion was at hand to contain them. She held not her ears. To her, the place rang with song, like it hadn't in years, and like it never had at all.

Then, in an interlude before she approached her first climax, his own hearing was exquisitely tuned to her progress, which he engineered with finesse. Rapture-breathing, surefooted selecting, then a quivering, shivering *landing* of the nexus right on the sexus! Past the stratospheric zing of her zest, she found her bearings again, and applied a gorgeous sophistry to her kegels, while her hot talk was lower than the dirt. Pure, primal pumping was his reply.

Their overlapped visiting along the glorious rainbow of their fuck-suck-slurp-workout was nothing less than a grand tour through the other's most private treasure galleries, both astonishingly varied. Her Symbolist visage, with its abstract expressionist intellect, and his neoclassic figurativeness, entailing impressionistic depictions – together at last.

A perfect melding of arts, sciences, and majestically-compatible fucking.

729

To be *in* on this communion was to behold harmonious friction between two naturals, previously deprived of such moments. With a beautiful certitude, they made their encounter into something truly celestial. But it also had foundations – a congress that linked heaven and earth. An event, a trust, a sharing, and a fabulous flesh-fest, sprung from the ground and into the empyrean. Some might call it tantric, others might say it's magic. Whatever its label, they were without naked vanity. Only naked *will* mattered. Two lovers had achieved the best that life can offer, realized through their sincerity, their mutual appreciation, and their shared truths.

With this maximized experience of hyper-drive sex, in which all bodily systems joyfully signed on to high-performance mode – after the perfectly-timed double-climax – came a sort of pastoral bliss, a new standard for our times, in which ego is transcended by the sheer marvel of existence, and where the limitations of comparison or etiquette or even self-awareness have vanished. Like the scattering of birds before a calm that has been misinterpreted as a wind. For true peace must be tested before it is allowed to rule.

After their session of fantastically fun and furiously passionate lovemaking, all in the pale light-and-dark of Heatherette's boudoir, they repaired to the Damask Loggia for a nipperkin of crystalline amethyst beverage. Their looks at each other were direct and full of soul.

'Butterbugs – your vitality, your virility! Oh, gosh! Better than your acting!'

She was playful, one of her natural tendencies, long kept suppressed by solitariness, now radically altered at being accessed by the foremost personality in Cinema.

'You make me that way, Hot-erette! *So* hot! My goodness! Your lavishness is a splendor that needs no description!'

If their words came out somewhat purple, their passion inside glowed red with lovers' lust.

He planted a sloppy kiss on her exclusive neck, sending a tremor of shivers throughout her still-galvanized body. The semi-baboonishness of men was new to her, but she was not repulsed nor priggish. Sometimes fully mature persons, long single, respond to others in ways contrary to their settlements in life. But for Heatherette, she couldn't wait to abandon old ways. This was *him*, in all his layers, and each one was a component of her newfound life in love.

It was funny and touching how Butterbugs was reduced to this sort of simplicity when he was around her. Almost an innocence. After all he had done in the world! And what he would yet do…

And then a nightjar somewhere without reminded them how late, how very late, it was.

'Heatherette!' he uttered, as if of a sudden, he had one lonely hour to live, 'I, I, uh…'

Here was Butterbugs, the reciter of orations, of soliloquies, of lines always remembered and memorized, coming up short, as time itself was short.

'Speak, my daily baby.'

'This – *this* is what I've really wanted all along,' he said, gently slapping her fine and quite lusty rump, as a representation of her whole being.

'And, I tell you, it's what you deserve,' she replied, pleased beyond measure at his prowess and his endowments, not to mention his tasteful appreciation.

'And you deserve me saying so,' he said. 'Plus... *you* get to have what *I* give.'

'Which is rather more than my heart's desire ever was, I can assure you! Very much more!'

There was so much to admire and appreciate in each other's pulchritude. And they did so, for they were picture people, unafraid and unhesitant to show and interpret the power of the image as a vessel of meaning and anchorment.

'You are the love of my life,' he told her directly. 'Because it's true.'

'And you're mine. Here is truth. Truth all along.'

'Now, to complete a picture.'

'And upon its completion, our lives begin!'

Wordless but melodic dawn was breaking all around. The moon, still visible as a white melon over the Pacific, was rolling out of power. In the aurora of another day were all the ideals, aspirations and actions of an upward-seeking human instinct, long dormant, now activated anew. And they, who personified these elements, lay together, related in body, mind and soul.

So, they had gotten it on, at last. Finally, theirs was a love that was already *built* to last.

And because of this, he, Butterbugs, had been redeemed.

Through love.

61.

Exegi Monumentum Ære Perennius

Exegi monumentum ære perennius
Regalique situ pyramidum altius,
Quod non imber edax non aquilo impotens
Possit diruere aut innumerabilis
Annorum series et fuga temporum.
Non omnis moriar multaque pars mei...

I have reared a monument more lasting than brass (or bronze)
And more lofty than the royal memorial of the pyramids –
A monument which no devouring rain,
No violent northern blast can overthrow,
Or the innumerable succession of years or the flight of ages.
I shall not wholly die, and a great part of me shall escape death...

– Horace, Odes, Book III:30 [tr. F. Brittain]

The First Day

Their early morning leave-taking was ecstatic, he to his obligation, and she to her sequence of progressive waiting. Here, by this newel post at the bottom of the stairs, where they had first met, they parted – he for the East, and she for her studio.

The two lovers, extremely mature individuals that they were, cheerfully agreed to link after the span of one week. That was indeed the contractual time it would take to wrap 'UWH', and truth to tell, both felt sufficiently injected with the high-octane juice, generated throughout the previous night's lengthy glory, to provide them with the kind of sustenance they needed while apart. With full mutual accord that the old saw, 'Absence makes the heart grow fonder' was true enough for their purposes, they reasoned that this picture, being the rather important production it was, should be seen to its conclusion without any distractions whatsoever. That was the undeniable mandate. But they were doing this course of action, each for the other, because they loved each other as much as they did. It was as sincere as that. What higher calling was there?

732

'In this legendary week, should we speak by the telephone?'

'You know, babe, I don't rightly know,' answered Butterbugs, warming to the glee of their affairs. 'Good question!'

'For to have a bit of... shall we say, phone sex?'

'Well, my dear girl, if you keep chirping so, I'll get all excited, and I'll have to take you right here, in your door-gong's alcove! It *is* curtained and private, though.'

'No distractions allowed!' she barked while winking. 'No phone calls. Your character must remain intact. Your performance must be High, Mad, and *Doctoral.*'

'Yes, dear,' he mock-timided.

Then she took his hands and placed them on her breasts. There was now a touch of the earth-mom Erda to her voice. Out of sheer admiration, he wanted to drop to his knees and be worthy enough to touch his tongue on her pussy lips, but he held his ground as a role-realizer, simply enriched by her explicit advisement.

'Feel them well, Butterbugs. Engrave their contours and plushiness into the most prominent parts of your memory, though please ensure they aren't in the middle of any roads of memorized dialogue! Rather, choose the Memory of Witness rather than of Performance. Do this, and you will be sustained for the full week – after which, ye shall possess them – that which ye hold – from that date, on out.'

'I cannot imagine a better parting gift.'

A tear escaped from his sensation-inspired ducts, which expressed so much of his mind's rightful emotions, just now.

Thus, after the tenderest of temporary-farewell kisses, and plenty of sweet somethings whispered to each other, their outstretched hands lingered together for as long as they dared, before reluctantly letting go. Kisses were blown until there was no more air, and then, the great door of dreaming-minutes and waking-hours now settled the matter of their separation – by closing.

Heatherette being Heatherette, this did not mean she was biting nails next to a crank-up phone. Rather, she directly repaired to her topside studio, springing up every step on each flight, and threw herself wholly into her work, the latest of which, inspired by the previous night's rapture, she herewith commenced: 'Where Stars Are Constructed: A Tale of Earthly Hollywood, Not of the Heavens'.

He set out. Hoofing it over to Drum Blvd, he hailed a taxi, and marveled that it was a 1948 Brazeler Toccata fastback, a bit ramshackle but still husky, its pilot being a reverent B-bugs fan, from Tegucigalpa. Realizing the status of his fare, Jozé the driver requested that Butterbugs autograph his chest with a fluorescent highlighter, and that he would later have it permanently tattooed. That accomplished under the shadow of morning high-palms, with the assistance of a blurry old dome light, the big impending actor was duly dropped at the curbside entrance to the Selznick Studio, which was the nearest starting-point for his return to the world of 'UWH'.

Butterbugs was penniless at the moment, but he signed a chit which the cabbie joyfully waived. The trillionaire ultrastar offered to purchase him a new cab if only he would care to donate his remarkable rig to the Brazeler Society, of which he was a patron. The cabbie was flattered but fiercely protective of his wheels, promising to keep them rotating for as long as he lived. And a chit from an actor so beloved?

'No, mega-Señor.'

The tattoo-to-be was enough for Jozé. He was a fulfilled man, who would have a fine story to tell.

After the Brazeler's throaty resonation died away, the ultrastar turned to face one of the most familiar of all cinematic icons: Selznick's knurled sign before the Mount Vernon façade. Every time he'd encountered it, including right now, he swore he could almost hear Alfred's gamelan-ish chimes.

At that moment, in a coincidence worthy of any event that might be classi-fied as 'post-Discovery-of-the-True-Heatherette', while he stood there, alone in the Washington Blvd morn, the front screen door opened and out came Perrison Voog-Ug, one of the Industry's most meticulous producers, who had been Butter-bugs' champion in such lapidarian masterpieces as Pater's 'Marius the Epicurean' and the exquisite 'Gaston de Latour' (both 20th-Fox).

'I say there! Is that Butterbugs yonder? *My* Butterbugs? I say, *salve! Salve!*, I say! My stars, but fancy if I'm not vaunt-courier for an anxious giganto-produc-tion, the fringes of which I have been attempting to haunt!'

'Voogie!' quoth Butterbugs, overjoyed to see, first-off today, someone so sensi-tive in his æsthetic and ethical understandings, as these qualities applied not only to motion pictures, but to human hearts. He may have been an old auntie to some, but to Butterbugs he was the antithesis of Hollywood's all-too-common pushi-grab-bi-bossiness.

'Marius de Latour!' Voogie's favorite gag name for his star, although 'Gaston de Epicurious' came in a close second.

'Salve to you! And an 'ave', and perhaps most importantly, Hail! At last!'

'Will you join me for a mayonnaise brunch, my dear fellow?'

'I would be tickled, Voogie. Where?'

'Just nigh, at Parkle's.'

Everyone who was anyone at Selznick avoided that eatery – just across the street – like the plague, because it wasn't hip enough. But Voogie, who was close friends with both Pierre Franey and Madhur Jaffrey, had made it his best-kept secret, where foodies might squirm in bliss before, during, and after each session of 'Parklefaction', as the Voog-Ug himself put it. It was the quintessence of an occult gourmet outlet, intentionally kept arcane – Or was it *elite?*

Ensconced safely in a dim booth, one of those avocado-tinted living room lamps of vaguely Spañada-ValuMart design helped keep them incommunicado, especially from the heavy-lidded types taking refuge here from the healthy sun outside.

'Can you believe it, dear rag, I missed your adorable hullabaloo last eve. Crabby the Maltese was sicky-poo. What could I do, do, do in such a deep?'

'Well, funny you should say so, Voogie. I missed it too, after a fashion.'

'Don't tell me, plebeian, but let me look at you for a second.'

The stale green light was perfectly adequate for an old queen to read a star's face.

'Why Butterbugs, World's Only Yultrastar and warden of our Earth's most envied schlong, I think I detect a young supporting player *in love*. Who is she? Please, please, please. I'll never tell a fellow cretin in this room. Or across the street, either.'

'Can I trust you?'

'You are talking to a man who wants to produce you in a screen version of Walter P.'s 'Portraits in Miniature', bizarre as the prospect may be. Some day I will. But in the meantime, I am the proud possessor of that dream. If I can maintain an erect construction over such a desire these long years, you can certainly trust me with your most sacred name – of your beloved flame, that is.'

'She is – Heatherette…'

Voogie gasped with pleasure, then slapped his hand over his mouth, lest the few others, under neighboring rusty-red, harvest-gold, and beer-can-blue lamps might read his enslavered lips. Then the tears came on.

'Oh, Butterbugs! That's so wonderful! You mean, the one and only Heatherette of Lumière-Pathé fame? The recluse? The Great Cryptogramette of Yniguez Terrace?'

Butterbugs was suddenly tremulous.

'You… you know of her?'

'There's only *one* Heatherette! Oh, but don't be alarmed. We, that is, those of us in the know, have done all we can to protect that wonderful girl. You are a new arrival to this arcane but sacred trust! Our covert mission: to protect her from any harm or alteration. She has no idea how much! I'm proud to say there are many unsung aunts and uncles, cousins and second cousins, who have kept tabs on her through this, our era, in order to sustain her amidst the ordeal of her legacy. And I'm also proud to say that she knows of none of our efforts. This is a girl who can hold her head high, because she has carried on in style and grace and dignity. And with this news, we are all, and I can instantly speak for all the others, humbled and well-nigh delighted. There is no one in this universe more deserving than you, child, to have the award of Heatherette. Oh, and vice-versa.'

'That's remarkable, Voogie. I am gratified beyond belief. She has earned my awe in more ways than one. How chivalrous of all of you.'

'It can be a cold world out there, dear boy. Some of us just rub our hands together once in a while for one who needs it. Not that sweet H-ette is a Little Match Girl, or anything.'

'You will be pleased that she has not been idle. She has created such a body of work, our Industry will be endowed with surpassing product for the foreseeable future. She is a cinematic artiste par excellence.'

'Oh, *really?* I knew the girl we're talking about is one of the smartest in this galaxy, but I confess, I knew not where her true talents lay. Delightfully superior! Oh, Butterbugs, that makes me doubly glad you two are in love!'

Now it was Butterbugs' turn to shed silent greenish tears.

'She will be coming into her own very soon.'

'May I ask a positively vulturish question?'

'Feed, old scavenger.'

'Might there be possibilities of we three clunking our heads together for a bit of dickering?'

'Assuredly! I think some of her scripts are tailor-made for your producing style. They're all very advanced in their development. She even has production designs executed. I'm sure she'll agree that you're *in.*'

'My grateful thanks, Epicurious!'

'In fact, there's one of her scripts in particular that I can go over with you right now. It'd be a brilliant holiday season picture, in which –'

'Tut, tut, tut, old egg. Lest ye forget, this here conspiracy brunch is a mere last station of the cross before your duties come due – in about an hour, thank me very much.'

Butterbugs sighed.

'I know what you're driving at.'

'Mmm.'

'I was going to give myself up at Selznick, until you waylaid me.'

'That's because you still have a grace period. At 12:00 noon they are going to send out an APB, Hollywood-wide. It's nice to be wanted on the set so badly, isn't it?'

'Yeah, well…'

Then Butterbugs simply thought of Heatherette, and their agreement over what the coming week would hold. His face became radiant, even in this odd light, and he was infused with fresh and vigorous resolve.

'Yes! Why, yes! To finish what I started! Resolve, resolve now!'

His recognizable voice caught the attention of one particularly reptilian personage under the sallow light in several booths down. A yucky tongue darted in and out of a gash-like mouth. No autograph-seeker he, but someone with an interest in this particular ultrastar.

'Very noble and law-abiding of you, my dear Marius,' said Voogie. 'It's a mere mammoth climax sequence that awaiteth, that's all.'

'It'll be fun! I'm rather revitalized about the prospects. Quite frankly, Heatherette taught me how to do just that. She taught me not to live by sex alone!'

'That sagacious girl! I'll have you lucky ducks over after all the hooprah's dribbled away. Holy Crayolas, look at the time!'

They gobbled the rest of their mayo-plastered pancakes and got their asses across the street and into the administration building. Sonny and Porter were in the Ince Suite, pacing and frowning.

'See you later, Voogie. We'll confer, anon.'

'I'll wait in quiet and loyal euphoria, dear boy.'

'Hey, newlyweds!' crowed Butterbugs, seeing his two associates' palpable angst. 'Honeymoons delayed until after 'UWH' wraps?'

'Why you miserable – Hey! It's the *kid!* We thought you dead! Delayed? You *know it*, pal!' responded Sonny, incredulous at the fact their lead was showing up at exactly four minutes to noon, the very cell-phone by which to sound the general alarm in his very hand – and pre-dialed, too.

'All of us are on hold for the duration,' added Porter, who was vastly relieved more than he was incredulous. With Butterbugs, every undertaking always took on a slightly miraculous tone. He'd learned to trust miracles, like a true believer should.

'Say, what was *with* you last night?' asked Sonny in his more-needling-than-angry mode. 'We haven't even bedded our new wives on account of you, you know. I got one hour of sleep last night. Or this morning. Or... whatever.'

'I got a half hour,' Porter piped. '*Maybe.*'

'Well, I got about fifteen minutes!' said Butterbugs, cheerfully. He didn't mention that he'd managed to fit in an actual bedding of someone special, regardless.

'C'mon, baby,' said Sonny. 'Let's over to Mega|Goth. Haze and some of the Team are there. It's decision time.'

They hopped into Sonny's rare '65 Red Flag limo, which reminded Butterbugs of his giddy time as Chairman Shing's guest at Thousand Candle Hall in old Hangchow, back in 'The East Is Red' (August 1st) days.

'So what was with the shitty attitude last night, Butterbugs? How could you flake out at such a wedding feast?'

'It wasn't designed as a wedding, Sonny,' said Porter, more content with now being happily married than in making a point. 'A guy named Marshall was sort of involved, too.'

'So what! It was a coming-together. It was full of wonders. Old grumpypuss here must've been jealous, or something.'

Butterbugs laughed.

'Well, I'll tell you. I *was* rather pissed off, actually.'

'You? Why? Just jealous, I suppose.'

'You nailed it, Sonny. I was pissed off *at* my jealousy.'

Porter was better at reading into the presumably perfect ultrastar's psyche.

'You probably felt pretty left out, didn't you?'

Butterbugs looked over at Porter gratefully.

'Then why so chipper today?' asked Sonny.

It occurred to the agent that the twin pillars of Saskia and Justy no longer stood on Butterbugsian ground, and that his actor might be kind of sad about that.

'Oh, I'm very much better, that's why.'

'Came to your senses as a mature adult?'

'That's a good way of putting it, Sonny. I had quite a remarkable late evening and wee hours of the morning.'

737

'That sounds intriguing, Butterbugs,' said Porter.

'And we want to hear all about it,' said Sonny, as they pulled up in front of the Selig and Luetta Goth Building.

[Hyman's parents were pretty good eggs; the Goth name as it applied to the studio and all associations had been officially converted to commemorate *them*, rather than their beastly son.]

'Is it because you're happy for all of us?' asked Porter.

'Sure!'

'Guys, can we do the personal stuff later? I wanna join you in gabbing onto that subject, cuz I'm pretty happy as well, but we've got a thousand tons of 'UWH' balanced over our heads right now. Let's get it all in the can and up on the editor's shelf, OK? Hey, looky up there – another newlywed who can join our club. Butterbugs, you can be an honorary member!'

There, in the middle of her window, situated in the exact center of the building's Deco symmetry, looking out at them, was Hazel Snyder. She waved, obviously ecstatic with relief.

Emerging from the Red Flag, Butterbugs waved back and bellowed, 'Hi-ya HAZE!!'

'Man, he *is* happy!' said Sonny to Porter.

Sonny didn't really mean to come off as a prick right now. In actuality, he was supremely pleased, even content. But the stress of piled-on current events was making him impatient for their resolve, largely so he could settle in and see what life with his very own lover, the totally cool Syd, would bring. He knew it would be worth the wait, because he knew even more that 'UWH' was the picture of the age, and it would make history, and he was part of it, so yer damn *right* he'd delay the honeymoon! As a result, he simmered somewhat.

And thus, some of these who were wed were gathered in the headquarters of a critical picture that screamed completion, and loudly enough to put some of Hollywood's most powerful people into eclipse – as far as their private relationships were concerned.

Before they got started, every person present, with the exception of the ultrastar, was hitched as of last night, and each of them couldn't help but be drawn to that specific exception, that exceptional person whom they required to wrap this turkey up. For on his face and from his being emanated an extraordinary ambience that made them skip a beat and smile. In short, they were picking up some sort of uncommon vibe from bachelor Butterbugs.

'Why Butterbugs,' said Haze, 'On behalf of all of us, our heartfelt thanks for hosting, facilitating, and *believing* in our rather impromptu life-changing moments on your stage of truth and love last night!'

Saskia, Porter, Sonny, Chas, Judah, Egaz, Cody, Purrby, and TABP – they all applauded, and from the very depths of their beings.

Butterbugs beamed, making personalized eye contact with every one of them.

'It was super! And I will never forget all the magic moments. It was a remarkable time. Something we can take throughout our lives! *We were all there!* You are each so severely special to me! And I made it happen! I am only so glad. Hurrah for each and every one of you, and also, to spouses and couples not present here today, at this signal moment! And what's more, as Nicolai Rostov would say – Hurrah – For the whole world!'

More applause erupted and was sustained by this blue ribbon group of showbiz top fliers.

But Haze was nothing if not anti-neglectful.

'You, wonder-boy, are officially thanked and kowtowed-to for your outstanding generosity of treasure and spirit, and we can only hope you yourself will some day share in our joy, perchance to not only copulate (!) but to couple with the mate of your dreams, as we did last night at your entertainments. You have our undying support and best wishes.'

Butterbugs would have been overjoyed to blab about his very wonderful own future contribution to what Haze was speaking of, but keeping in mind Voogie's purposeful and protective imperative regarding his not-yet-prepped-for-the-world's-stage heartthrob, he thought it best to exercise restraint.

Oh, he would have loved to parade his proud tidings in front of these fine friends, but Heatherette was too much a treasure to experiment in how impetuosity might impact her. No, best to reveal all to these wedded ones (and the world) when the time was right. Such as: after the last frames of 'UWH' had added up on the exposed take-up reels in Leon's and Bob's cameras.

In the meantime:

'Oh, hey gang, it was my distinct and unique pleasure to be the one on whose estates your lives were transformed into gem-like examples of transfigured hope! May you all bathe, lounge and frolic in all the glory your new lifestyle brings with it!'

Sonny and Porter, having earlier heard a more frank explanation from the star himself, chose to let the matter lie. Besides, they couldn't wait to get down to the business at hand, which fortunately, Hazel now did.

One thing about Mega|Goth Stvdios, the access to the administration building was really rather casual. This was because some in the Industry were interested in making the corporate frontage to the world of the studios invitational rather than sequestered. Such a mindset was subject to debate, but the upshot in this case was that persons approaching the Goth Building might do so directly off the street, rather than having to attain a domain behind security barriers. This was not to say the Goth Building lacked security. It did indeed have it in spades. The thing was, anyone with a pea-shooter could potentially at least *touch* the walls behind which some of the most powerful and influential persons in pictures today passed their waking/working hours.

And it was with that humble instrument, a plastic tube included in a SugarTex

Croonchies box in fact, of sea-green variety, that came to aim at Haze Snyder's longitudinally-placed window, and after a lizardy inhalement, fœtid but sufficiently-forced air was generated in order to send a little putty-like ball of sticky something or other up to that elite third story, so as to glom onto the A/C-engineered glazing, with no more impact than sparrow's poo carried by a zephyr, to ultimately *pah!* onto any old windowpane in its way.

This particular spitball had landed where it was intended, and it immediately transmitted waves invisibly from its waste-appearing insignificance with certain authority and purpose.

'We'll come to order now,' Haze announced. 'Everyone knows why we're convening in this manner. So, let me get your input, individually, please.'

'You know, peoples, I'm really plumping for using the Lasky site,' said Chas. 'Because, you never know about international situations. They can come under certain risk factors.'

'In what respect, Charlie?' asked Cody, Mega|Goth's bran-new V.P. in Charge of Production.

'Well you know, riots, spring uprisings, wars 'n' stuff…'

'You're referring to that botched and fucked-up attempt to atomize our own B-bugs by that kinked-out anti-vaudeville act, Lurgan & Vunn, no?' asked TABP.

'Why yes, TABP,' answered Chas. 'Exactly.'

'OK, but that action translates to anywhere on this here globe.'

'Agreed, TABP,' said Haze. 'But let's get a consensus first, followed by debate, if necessary. TABP?'

'Chas is cool, but I can't get behind his reasoning. On t'other hand, sometimes convenience trumps everything else. This has been a particularly demanding production. My life's been on hold because of it, which is tolerable, but since we're in the homeroom now, my wrap tells me to wind this muthah up. Let's go the short route instead of the long way around. Let's do the Jesse Lasky thang.'

'I like the Jesse acknowledgment, TABP. One of our Industry's great pioneers. I'll tell Jess Jr. He'll be gratified. Chas, we've basically heard from you.'

'And you will again. I'm with TABP, for the same reasons, and more.'

'We can just imagine *what* more, dear. Let's continue. Purrby?'

'I'm all for Lasky Mesa, too,' the high-level secretary-cum-advisor replied. 'I was out there three days ago, and I have seen the polished quality of the work. Rather spectacular, really. Plus, it's easy to get to. Talk to the vets who've shot scenes out there in the illustrious past. I did, and they're all sanguine about such a location. I vote for Lasky.'

'Well spoken in the brevity department. Judah?'

'I can't speak highly enough of Jambutterbugsabad. My time there has opened my eyes to the *reason* of the world. Considering legalistic and logistic concerns regarding the tedious details of my end of things, I would nevertheless suggest Lasky Mesa. Local limitations, but local freedoms, as well. Regulations are already in place, union relations, etc. Nothing to negotiate, nothing to doctor. Plus, along with the simplicity, a gesture of respect for the benefactors who made this duplicate possible. I would add that the Jambutterbugsabad set has been and will continue to be used extensively for fill-in shots, and back up, ably handled by our capable Ridgey Callow, 3rd unit director par excellence.'

Hazel was methodical in her around-the-room fairness. Order was not according to importance, but it was proceeding in a sort of increasing-volume fashion.

'Many thanks, J.F-J. Cody, what does the Studio think?'

No one knew the management of Mega|Goth better than its rightful heir and operator, Cody the Exceptional.

'Mega|Goth is totally favorable to both options,' she said. 'We are in the absolutely luxurious position of being able to go either way. I wish we had Dera Ismael Potwar Khan or our Yusuf Malik here right now to state the Jambutterbugsabad case, although it really isn't necessary. Their sterling work stands on its own, and we all know it. So, the other side is economical, not artistic. My bottom-feeding lentil-counters a mere one story below us tell me that actual filming at the Lasky site will save the budget approximately ten millions. Because we, the Studio, aren't strictly producing the picture except in a partnership arrangement. With no less than 346 partners in toto, Mega|Goth does not have any budgetary problem, as we are flush with funds. And funds from some very attractive sources, I might add, as all MurnCorp influences have been happily purged.'

'Excellent,' replied Haze. 'That being the case, I still have to corner you. What is your personal preference?'

'Lasky Mesa, quite frankly. Personal note: my nearly-grown kids are at the Kloomagawn School out at Kunky Creek. I can see them in the evenings. Oh – and along with my husband of c. 18 hours, I should think.'

She winked at TABP, who winked back, even though his shades veiled the fact. But she knew. To her, his clerical collar was blinking rapidly.

Cody added, 'Please understand, that's my selfish side speaking. Personal matters are irrelevant. I will gladly abstain if that's a problem.'

'Me too, if conflict of interest starts adding up,' offered TABP.

'I don't think any of us want to slice this too finely,' said Haze. 'OK, Saskia?'

As the representative scriptor in the room, Saskia had a firm hand on the Writers' Team's tiller. As an intimate of Butterbugs and a past sharer of his household, she had to divorce herself from any temptations to associate with his private life on ethical principles. Being a writer, her imagination could successfully evade any such complications.

'Dear friends, I've considered all the emotions in play as we review our strategy's possibilities. My love knows no bounds any more. I love all of us too much to be selfish at this juncture. (Sorry Codykins!) I also love this picture, which all of us have given our souls' right arms for. If I can paraphrase the poet Merrill-O, I have given of my vagina, which flows, flows, and flows with good will. I want the flow to continue, but I do not wish to deplete it. I am a child of Internationalia, but in this instance, as the duplicate set at Lasky meets our script's needs, why not head across a valley rather than several oceans?'

'Our grateful thanks, Saskia. Porter?'

'For my part, I am ready to go fly with my new wife to the planet Prapp, if needed. (A terrific idea for a picture!) Or I can do the trans-Pacific run any time. I've got about 36 return trips under my tighter, trimmer belt. I love the Jambutterbugsabad setup, but I could easily be persuaded to 'go native' in this instance. Why? Because we have the same thing here. The same thing. For a producer, that's one helluva singular situation. Plus, let's be practical: we have two more UP-70 cameras on this side of the puddle. I can go either way, but I think I'd go with Lasky, as my lazy, not-so-fat-as-it-used-to-be ass sort of likes the idea, for its own sake.'

'Well Sonny, like Porter's belly, the lineup's firming. What say you?'

'Lasky. I know the territory.'

'Simple, simple,' replied Haze.

There was then the matter of the picture's director and his sensitivities to consider. He was supposed to be the last word in location approval, what with lighting, ambience, and artistic vision. And so he was.

'Egaz, what does the director himself feel?'

'Both sides, of course. I am more adaptable now than I have ever been. That is because I know we have a great picture here, almost all of it in the can. We have not saved the best for last, though. There is no 'best' in this picture. It is *all* 'best'. Nevertheless, we are unconventional. Selznick filmed the burning of Atlanta at the dawn of 'Gone With The Wind' (1939), but in the coming week of the here and now, we shall truly film the climactic last scenes. We are prepared. If I had to flip a 1-pice coin though, my first instinct, I guess, would be to hope it landed on the Lasky side. I'm keen on getting my cameras rolling within a day.'

'I hope you have such a coin on you, old boy, as we might have need of it,' semi-joshed Chas.

'Egaz, what's Old Atrocity got to say about this issue?' asked Haze.

'He's of course keen on the Jambutterbugsabad site, as he put the most care into it, and he feels very comfortable there. However, knowing his standards, I think he has every intention of producing a duplicate here. Well, he and his team *have*. I believe I can say that with confidence. They deserve a hand.'

Everyone joined in stormy applause.

'I don't think we'll need any coin-toss,' murmured Sonny to Porter.

'Well-stated, director D'Varzim. We're most fortunate to have such a perfectionist team. They will be grandly rewarded. So now, Butterbugs, your turn, please.'

'I'd like to do it in Jambutterbugsabad.'

'We might need said coin, just,' murmured Porter to Sonny.

'And, why would you like to follow that course?'

Haze was gentle. She loved her new position here at Mega|Goth, and even throve on the pressure, but she saw no reason whatsoever to abandon her trademark sweet sincerity.

'Well, we've had a remarkably fruitful run at Jambutterbugsabad. I can hardly express the depth of my experiences there. All of you are so intensely involved, so I don't really need to. You already know. Besides, time is on the short side, isn't it? One week? But uh, you should know that I confess to a firm loyalty as well, a loyalty to those there. Which is basically everybody, who've all bent over so far backwards that surely they must be yogis of the highest order. There's a good feel there. It's so *right*.'

Everyone in the room agreed. There was much simultaneous yakking on the subject.

Haze called for order, smiling broadly.

'Well, team, I think we'll all be catching the afternoon flight to our great facility at Jambutterbugsabad. At least five LearJets can be booked. So, I'll leave off, as we've got our preppings to see to. I'm claiming my usual port window seat, with Campari 'twixt Rangoon and Karachi.'

'And I'm claiming my usual Joby!' said Porter, in good cheer. 'Better to see her at work, and try to steal a kiss, than not at all!'

As the breakup hootenanny got going, Butterbugs set himself to pondering. The office door to the non-Inner Sanctum world was opened and people were about to go through it.

'*However*...,' Butterbugs ejaculated.

Everyone froze.

'And on the other hand...'

Everyone came back.

'I was just thinking...'

'Yes, Butterbugs?' said Haze, drawing very close to him. 'Your word means the world to us. We may all be newlyweds, but with this picture, we're all loyalists, first and foremost. To you.'

'That's what I was thinking about. You know, Jambutterbugsabad is a tad bit of a winged-victory effort across this here globe, isn't it? But gracious me, we're all pretty immune from jet lag now, aren't we? Nevertheless... Ye are indeed newlyweds, and my heart melts in the light of that knowledge. Why ever, if we possess an OA-approved duplicate here at Lasky Mesa, should all of you be away from your newly betrothed mates at such a time? Really, *at such a time?*'

'Dear Butterbugs!' said Cody, 'We've basically waited our whole careers for something like 'UWH' to come about. Never has the road been so clear to fulfilling that dream.'

'In concert with that, Cody, is the fact that you've all been waiting for the perfect mate your whole lives. I know that is a fact. Now that you all have them, why squander the promise of joy? If I were in your position, I would champion matters of the heart even over our artistic endeavors. Besides, we have our duplicate set of HMD's great citadel right near here. I have awakened! Do not worry about

Jambutterbugsabad! The set there can be adapted for any use. I think we all know they will go from strength to strength from here on out.'

'This may be the biggest fuckin' photoplay the world's ever seen, ultrastarred-one,' said TABP. 'But we're merely followers.'

'Such respect humbles me to no end,' replied the ultrastarred-one.

'Das fine enough baby, but what you gonna *do* with that *respect?*'

'Well TABP, I…'

'Butterbugs, are you sure?' asked Porter, privately elated.

'I don't see any reason not to be, Pud. And I can read you like a script. You'd *love* to do it at Lasky, right? Am I right? Hell, if I were linked to Joby, like you are, I wouldn't want her to be stewardess-izing right now, even if it's on our own group flight. I'd rather be in the sack with her, safe at home every night! This way, you can be.'

Porter blushed.

Butterbugs thought of himself, as well. His Weeklong Pact with Heatherette would indeed be honored, but there was no escaping the fact that knowing she was a few dozen-ish miles away rather than 20,000 leagues brought comfort to his heart. Maybe that one thing was the reason he gave away his Jambutterbugsian loyalties to the universe unknown.

There was laughter, some cheers, and not a few tears, over Butterbugs' supreme consideration and generosity.

'Boy, I thought he was soured out,' Sonny whispered to Porter. 'What happened, did he get Ticed or something?'

Porter shrugged happily.

'So yes. Lasky Mesa. Yes, yes, yes. That's my vote,' said Butterbugs, with some finality.

'Team?' asked Haze, 'Does this make *sense* to you? Are we in accord?'

'Yowzah!' was the general outcry. 'Strength-upon-strength to Butterbugs! Glory all the way! HMD *rules* at *all* 'UWH' locations!!'

They were as children rendered grateful by their dad's magnanimity. So the matter was settled.

Instead of a 23+-hour flight, these who were so recently hitched had about a 75-minute motorcar ride to look forward to. And sex every night in wedded bliss. Thanks to Butterbugs.

From the rise on Kullugfrarrmund Road, before it descends into the Lasky Mesa lands, there was a pull-off-and-lay-by where any motorist might seek opastus-style information on the new arresting sight that dominated the great vale. It was an architectural structure of great power, intricate, with almost phantasmagorical decoration, yet austere in its essentially conical rise into the sky. It had a strange quality of disturbance, not just because of its size, but because it seemed to communicate something of a remote, even ancient, dreadfulness. A finer setting for a tyrant's triumph did not exist. Without a doubt, it was the most splendidly terrifying construction ever made for a motion picture: the High Mad Doctor's Citadel of Gyugganthropristixc!

The ultrastar had set out from the studio a little while after the meeting's conclusion, alone, and after everyone else had gone on ahead. His request for solitude in approaching the location was immediately honored, having declined the company of Sonny and even TABP.

'That's cool, man,' TABP had said. 'There's the *respect* you so characteristically talked about. It calls for reverence. Just you and the object. Dig it deep.'

'I dig!' Butterbugs replied. '*Oh*-so deep, TABP!'

Hazel made one of the studio's plush prestige rigs, a '57 Dodge D-500 yellow-and-black convertible, completely at his disposal. Feeling a déjà vu that presented itself as a montage, consisting of his old DeSoto, Heatherette's alley, the 'D' in the pushbutton block, as well as the omnipresent Heatherette herself, he got the hell outa Dodge, as it were, and headed for the mesa country, to see the climactic set for the first time – for himself.

There he paused, on the rise, in the pull-off-and-lay-by, on this, his first trip out here. Butterbugs was absolutely struck with this imposing erection, rising to over five hundred feet in height.

'It is reminiscent of Boris Iofan's Palace of the Soviets!' he said in a stunned and epic whisper.

He aimed his binoculars all over the structure and was astonished at its adventurous constructional believability. A pukka three-dimensional set, to be sure. The perverse decor, whether a blatantly pornographic gargoyle or ill-conceived modeling of the most subjective kind, perfectly reflected the high, mad taste of the Doctor/Dictator.

'My character is one freakazoid sum'bitch!' he muttered with satisfaction, utilizing one of OA's numerous epithets for the HMD he had yet to finish off.

Imbued with unstoppable Heatherette-erings on every level of body and mind, he felt true artistic exhilaration, which was compatible with his role, the film in general, and his new personal life.

'I can *act* here! Truly act! It is like having the newly formed Earth to have as my stage! Heatherette was right – there's no end to what the human spirit can do when it is planted in air, so that it can fly! Yet, I feel the earth at my feet, upon which to stroll my play. And down there is the stage for my greatest role yet. It awaits me, and I am ready for it. Ready – a state in which I have always lived, to be sure. But until last night, I was only *ready* to be *ready*. Now I have attained something more advanced, and I know what it is. I am complete in my readiness. Love has led me here, and within its overarching sphere of wonders will I prove myself to she who recalled me to life once more!'

He raised both hands high into the air, clenched his fists as if to say, yet again, 'I am ready', then opened his hands as far as they could go, as if to say, 'Thank you! And now – to begin!'

Then he reclined in the yellow weeds, on his side, elbow holding palm holding head, as if lying next to she whom he had invoked, and after an imagined discourse, he enjoyed a light repast of kaxx-pudding and a sachet of wafer-waters. There was ample reason to partake in this pastoral interval before the great task began.

Up on a bluff of dead grass, a lone figure stood against the sky. A silent sentinel of uncertain duty. A tube of lenses allowed for ascertaining the identity of the convertible driver down below, who continued to scan the prospect of the vale at his apparent leisure.

Seen through the glass, judgments were made, analysis formed, speculation reduced. For all intents and purposes, every indication was that an ultrastar would shoot here, in this locale, and not on the other side of the world.

'Oh, translucent day!' declared Butterbugs, noting with pleasure the subtleties of the afternoon light on the baleful but awesome set. 'Come! Let me be part of you!'

He whirled around, as if to sample all 360 degrees of the land and the very air that housed this remarkable citadel.

His peripheral eye, in its busy rotation over these lands, then snagged on the upland figure, who made no attempt to alter his stance, but appeared a living entity, affecting Butterbugs with a sort of romantic pictoriality.

Why, Butterbugs himself had played such brooding Byronic-appearing roles in past pictures, so there was a sort of instant kinship with this one, who stood up so starkly amidst the land. Like the monstrous structure across the vale, the lone form seemed to possess a like sense of identity and isolation.

So it was with the same sort of admiration for the set that Butterbugs regarded the lonely one up yonder. He gazed at him as long as he dared before reaching out into a sort of linkage effort. He cupped his hands together.

'Wayfarer! Care you to take up the opportunity and ride with me as I progress further into the vale? Surely you require passage the same way, at least. I offer you plain transport, and in the open air!'

His call was indeed heard. The figure stood still on up the slope, its wide-brimmed hat keeping everything underneath in moody shadow. Both hat and head beneath shook in slow abnegation of the kind offer.

'All the best to you then, free wanderer of the hills! Find joy! Though your sole companions are the doughty clouds as they pass in fluffy bunches in this fresh blue sky, that is enough to give you comfort and cheer along your route, is it not? Well then, happy wilt thou be in such simple safety of need! Farewell, wayfarer! Fare-thee-well!'

The figure gave an ever-so-slight bow of his hat in acknowledgment, denoting at least a cordiality often found amongst those who haunted such wilds, though they do not necessarily desire human company for any number of reasons, whether exploratory, through brooding, or via melancholy.

From this hour forward, Butterbugs was truly unencumbered in approaching the waiting magnificence, created for the furtherance of the cinematic arts. Incredibly, a vast palace set, linked to the citadel by a wide processional way, also became viewable once a large brow of a hill was cleared. Granted, the scale of everything was titanic, but the whole scheme looked fully integrated into the land itself, as if 'twas born here of organic purpose, an ancient imperium, rather than a false front for a mere picture show. So decidedly different from the plainly-procured siting and utility of the other version, away at Jambutterbugsabad Studios! A pleasant realization, really. Mainly because everything before him was basically within his beloved's neighborhood, so to speak.

'I chose well,' he thought.

He motored at parade speed along the grandest progression of the route, as it wound and descended along the gentler inclines and down into the straw-yellow vale, so as to savor the views of the mighty pile built for him and his use, for his art, and for the world.

In a merry yet gravitas Richard Straussian heldentenor then, perhaps in reminiscence of his role in 'Friedenstag' (Oceanus), he sang into the sky above, as he drove on down:

> 'In a world which is a feast
> If we care to look, if we care to feed,
> There lives *love*, embedded in all things!
> If we look, if we try,
> There will be all manner of choice in these before us.
> And Master Trouble, seeing our consternation,
> Comes to dizzy us up in our silly dilemma.
> For we cannot, in our entertainment,
> Recognize the opportunities of love,
> That lie amongst the more dazzling distractions
> At such a table.
> We know, however,
> That love is what we *should* aspire to,
> What we *shall* aspire to,
> What we *must* aspire to!
> But, where is it?
> Will we question, will we care,
> When Trouble guides us, chooses for us,
> While we are content with the matters of surface,
> And the wiles of distraction?
> Past them, that is where the glory lies
> Even though we be told otherwise.
> Seek beyond the obvious, then.
> For then there is love, love, *love*,
> In the guise of the higher ideal,
> Which we might not perceive at first,

But if we can tear ourselves away,
Even for what passes as a jiffy…
Then we will stand *so good* a chance
To see her in her helping ways,
In her caring ways,
In her ways so subtle and tender and right
There, waiting, waiting for us to say,
Waiting for us to ask,
For she must be mute to test our sincerity,
Our will to discern, our choice to change,
There, somewhere out there, if we try,
If we attempt, if we dare!

(Orchestral intermezzo, here hummed.)

At last! Long last!
There! I see her! Up above the current of lower life!
She is there, smiling at me!
Reaching out her hand, her lovely willingness shared!
Thence I will go, because all I need do
Is aim myself there, straight there,
Where she will take me up, to join her,
To remain, the two of us,
In joy, in bliss, in peace!
Peace of love, love… of peace!'

It was a rapture that flowed from his very soul as he progressed around curved hills and through dill and dale, until – until – the road idyll's dissolving.

Down at the flats that now rolled away in front of him, he arrived at a strip of service facilities that catered to the location. There was the usual Tuttle's Trading Post, the Li'l Burkmartetta, the Porta-Den and Porta-Doc shoppes, and then the impromptu bungalows and yurtopolises for staff and extras, now filling up with personnel, all due to a staggeringly complex yet efficient logistical crew. All because Butterbugs had said 'Lasky Mesa' instead of 'Jambutterbugsabad', earlier today!

Indeed, the cruise-y idyll *must* end. Here were a thousand distractions, in matter-of-fact stases, to divert him from his needed meditation of the HMD's peri-climactic and climactic head-trip. Hell, he'd better get this D-500 steered to his quarters chop-chop if he were to pull off this little pantomime for the mud pie-purchasing public.

Not that he really felt that way. Cynicism was not possible within the concentrating brain of Butterbugs, the world's sole ultrastar. Focus to duty was kicking in, brought on by the ambience of a great production on location, and there the dreamer/lover gave way to the actor/fulfiller.

He discreetly glided the majestic spaceboat next to a group of grips, gathered at a pop shoppe that served this quadrant of the great and revving cantonment.

'Who can say...,' he almost said to them, '...where might the quarters be, wherein alleged player Butterbugs must lodge?'

'Butterbugs! Butterbugs!' said fine-grips Dougie Pejsa and Juan 'Hoowan the Pawn' Gonzaalez, in unison, 'You come to us! Fodder for our stories to the young ones, when dandling them on our knees! Gracias for your attentions!'

'In a playa of practicality, hombres', yakked the actor, somewhat amused to be treated with Our Fellow of the Wastelands respect, 'I need a place to rest my weary you-know-what.'

'In that case, leading caballero,' they both said in turns, 'Follow this lane to its obscure end, then hang a right, and you will enter Calle Rarefied, as we name it in the Anglo tongue. You, our Butterbugs, are to bunk in Kelat Lodge, so that you will feel the affinity with your *other* studio of late, which we respect, but are glad you chose us as your super-qualified crew. After all, we are pretty laid-back when the camera does not roll. But when it does, we are hardass slaves to the daily rushes, for they matter more than we do!'

'Muchas gracias, team associates!' enthused Butterbugs. 'If it were up to me, all of you would have seats in my highest heaven, on account of your service and your trust.'

'And you in ours!' the two sounded off.

'An attractive deal!'

'Everyone's attractive here!' Dougie cried.

'Hola!' Butterbugs added, 'I hear tell that Sanchez the Scaffolding Expert is supplying support for our sets, all through this shoot.'

'Por supuesto! Of course! He is! I tell you, he is, Señor. He is around some-where, everywhere!'

'Give him greetings, por favor. Hope to see him!'

'Anything is possible at Lasky Mesa, Señor!'

'Excelente!'

'Vaya con dios,' said Hoowan the Pawn, while the convertible drove off.

The ultrastar regarded his assistance in Sanchez's becoming the premier scaf-folding and frameworks agent in Hollywood as one of his greatest personal-help achievements, all from putting in a good word for him, here and there.

Butterbugs managed to get through a sand trap when he turned into Calle Rar-efied, as he had to push the 'D' and 'R' buttons back and forth in quick succession to get the lavish and very heavy babe rocking. Having made it through, he was indeed pleased at how similar to the Makran conditions the general setup was, hereabouts. Richard Day, Colasanti & Moore, Hal Pereira, Jack Martin Smith, Leelah Bomeko, Boris Levin, Perry Ferguson, John DeCuir, Lyle Wheeler, John Box, Wilfred Shingleton, Mark-Lee Kirk, Ed Carrere, and of course Malcolm Bert (just to mention the biggies) had busted butt in not only designing and realiz-ing two mammoth climax set complexes at opposite ends of the earth, they'd also laid out the Lasky Mesa cantonment in similar style and tone.

He rolled into the dooryard in front of a yurtish hogan that was indeed reminiscent of Kane Hall, his favorite residence in Jambutterbugsabad. It had been specially fitted and kitted within the last hour, by Old Atrocity himself.

The detailing was impeccable. Even the outdoor potted plants, a trademark of subcontinental landscaping etiquette, here appeared, lining the walk from driveway to front door. A trivial item perhaps, but in a tradition of quality, provided by the world's finest cinema greenspersons, just to help the actor feel at home. Everything in this location cantonment told of speed, organization, and integrity.

Butterbugs had a lump in his throat.

Having parked the luxus-cruiser in its specially prepped bay, he 'came home' to the homey hogan that would be his HQ for the next week. Inside, under its cornstalkish beams, was the same singular blend of austerity and pleasure that made for a non-neurotic but sensitive cinema artiste's inspiration-conducive environment.

To a hard-ass producer, pampering a star was usually a good investment if the star was rising or reliable on an ongoing basis. But in the case of Butterbugs, no producer had ever had the need to primp him, as it were. No artifice came with this ultrastar – only a real connection with a real sense of life. Great minds in the world, in search of detailed and credible analysis of the Butterbugs phenomenon, invariably returned to platitudinous, even banal, conclusions that were usually their starting points, involving words like 'real' and 'reality' and the always resorted-to 'incandescent'. This was most often the case because, probably all this stuff was… true. Therefore, critics, journalists, bloggists, academics, and other inquiring minds simply let Butterbugs and his phenomenon *be*, because he just *was*, and what he *was* was some body, some thing, that was probably indescribable. Even people with sensory deprivations, whatever they were, knew of his transcendence, which went well beyond the ancient Greek tradition of labeling every atom in the universe. There was a Greek god or goddess for everything. Was there one for Butterbugs – or was he one himself? No one quite knew.

His solitude was not disturbed for the rest of the evening, which he spent in study, meditation, and reflection.

So endeth the events and the progress of the First Day.

The Second Day

The trumpet-dawn of the following day was in keeping with the scripted needs of the climax sequence's first scenes.

'Awake, Butterbugs!' called the soft voice of Terra Tar Tingles, the production assistant assigned to his affairs for the day. She opened the drapes of the small eastern window so that a shaft of pale blue could penetrate the gloom.

On a flight out to Bangkok for location work on 'Supplayashurncorn of Channalostachuppaya' (Goldwyn), Butterbugs had spotted this lovely erstwhile flight attendant, all in purply-orchidy silk, and after a discourse concerning the drama of the ancients in Thailand, he sensibly hired her on the spot. Consequently, she had served on each of his pictures since. Mornings like these were totally familiar to her, as the two had spent some weeks as lovers on location. She had recently married Bongo Enumba, the rising actor from Lomé, who was playing a courtier in the Palace scenes.

'Your High Madness!' she cooed. 'Your esteemed presence is required at court after makeup call is complete!'

Butterbugs smiled before opening his eyes.

'I gotta get up, I gotta get up, I gotta get up in the morrrr-ning!'

'You Irving, you! Berliner!'

'I look forward to our day together, Terra,' he said as he dressed, whistling Irving's tune.

She was tempted to ogle him, but being on the job and in her own love, she modestly returned to the window.

'If you squint a li'l, li'l squirter, the citadel, seen here in silhouette, is not wholly unlike Wat Arun.'

'The Temple of the Dawn!' yawned Butterbugs. 'Where we climbed that time and had chai on the busted crockery.'

'Phrasemaker! So witty you are!' she chortled, while stretching her rail-thin body and touching her mound for effect. 'You were very fine that day, and particularly at that elevation, prong-master. And at fiery noon, no less.'

'Oh, those days! Such a time.'

'You think we should have married?' she asked wistfully.

'Had we, you would have missed your Bongo.'

'You're right. Sorry Butterbugs, you're second-best.'

Outside, two bicycles, late of Jambutterbugsabad, awaited. Not at all like the turgid Vunn & Lurgan types, these were the latest Chibbabulbs, all in carbon fiber, 32-speeds, weighing one pound each. It took Butterbugs a little practice to adjust to his conveyance's non-weight factor, but once they reached Makeup at Vidor Plaza, he would have no other get-out-and-about, in-costume or out.

All the old team were there, and much high jollity ensued.

'A House of Westmore on every continent!' the ultrastar crooned.

751

Instead of finding staff & crew at the end of their endurance because of this super-demanding production's long-longer-longest run, the star instead found everyone refreshed, enthusiastic and even effervescent. And this translated to everyone he encountered on the entire location shoot. Such was the effect of a Heatheretted Butterbugs. Such was her effusive power, and his transmission of it.

In full costume and makeup, Terra led his way as they biked over to the Palace set, not surprisingly, immense in its own right. From its upper steps was a fine view of the stunning Citadel. Butterbugs could see painters and plasterers far up the shaft, adding final touches, as instructed by Mal Bert and Dickie Day at their telescopes, via wireless talkers.

The first scene today would be exterior, on the Palace's side steps, expected to be in the can before lunch. As the script's requirements for the entire week were to be filmed entirely in sequence, via an ingeniously planned scheme, Egaz, cast, and crew would be free to experiment with and even improvise around this final act's drama. The precedent, of course, had been the seminal 'Jonny Requesticus' scene, and there had been plenty of inventive, expansive, and mind-blowing scenes since. For the next week then, there would plainly be an unavoidable but hopefully inspiring sense of increasing intensity to all things, as they went along. This sustained movement toward the undoubted majesty of the final fadeout was absolutely interwoven with the communal elation that everyone felt, due to Butterbugs' presence. That was why everyone on this picture right now considered themselves The Chosen.

Butterbugs was in classic form. Every bit of his dialogue was intriguingly delivered, and because the usual number of takes numbered about seven, he brought forth seven variations on a theme, each intrinsically valuable, and each sure to give both Egaz and his editors cause for lively seminars of choice and preference.

They called them '7V7A', aka 'The Seven V's for the Seventh A'. Script-As-Shot breakdown was as follows, e.g.: Scene 372A: 7V7A/1; 7V7A/2… 7V7A/7. If takes exceeded seven, count would continue in bonus mode, e.g.: 8V7A, 9V7A, etc. Traditionalists might balk, but in a picture where each variation had the highest of values, this system, forged by Bibsey the Script-Girl, would be key in the heavy decision-making during the editing process, which was already in full spate, headed up by team leader Margaret Booth. Right now, the general feeling was that the film would be released in multiple versions, perhaps as many as…
seven.

The ultrastar's distinguished co-stars reveled in every aspect of the art-making and they were stimulated in ways that could not be pinned down to any definition.

Today's scene's argument: HMD, just returned from victory in the wars, points out the near completion of his citadel, gleaming in the noontide sun. It is a symbol, not only of his massive, conclusive victories, but of his dominance in the world for centuries to come. Two scene-stealing soliloquies are highlights, alternating with speeches from timid sycophants and a rather more bold architect. The latter feels he can assert himself for his own benefit, because of his great achievement across the valley. HMD wants to enter its fastness now, but the architect compels HMD to take an oath not to enter until the final worker has left and the key is presented to him on a special Rexene pillow. HMD agrees. Break for lunch.

The afternoon was filled with utility shots, B-roll long shots, reactions, and retakes. Terra then conducted him back to Makeup to be made *down*, and they kicked back for a while.

By the time evening came round and the best light was gone for the day – on this day of exteriors – Butterbugs, spurred by Terra, decided to take in some of the dailies. This was not standard Butterbugsian practice, as he thought their influence could interrupt his core of concentration. But with Heatheretterization fully integrated into his systems, the ultrastar thought it might be a kick to lay into the b&w work-print a tad.

Egaz & Co. were delighted. No other cast members were present, so it was just the commander and crew, artistes all, ready to react.

After an hour of viewing the full run of the morning shoot's results, things quickly devolved into wordless silence on the part of such a distinguished audience.

'Egaz…' began Bob Surtees.

The veteran of vast experience and achievement, who'd been doing alternate coverage from separate but equal angles, as was now the standard approach on this too-important-to-do-otherwise picture, faced with the mighty teamwork up there on the screen, struggled for expression.

'Eeg-az. This is really… *good…!*'

Bob *never* made such statements. That is, before a given picture was properly wrapped.

'Yeah,' was all comparable vet Shamroy could get out.

Massive, enormous praise from two crustbucket geniuses.

[Shamroy and Surtees would get equal credit onscreen. But, at Egaz's insistence, he would follow the fashion of an interesting precedent. In the billing of 'The Towering Inferno' (20th/WB, 1974), Steve McQueen's name reads first, but Paul Newman's is placed slightly higher, off to the right. A diagonally-elegant solution. Thus, Shamroy first, Surtees second – but higher up. Equality, conforming to the physics of graphic design and aspect ratio, in action. Shamroy: 'You wanna go first, Bob?' Surtees: 'First is lower. Second is higher. I'll go second…']

With the cameras grinding again after the late hiatus, it came as a grouped astonishment that they could be coming up with such exceptional footage, completely uniform in style and dazzling in content.

Egaz, who maintained the best overview, kept his thoughts to himself.

'If I do say so,' he thought, 'The whole picture has been absolutely consistent.'

And who better than the auteur to know that he had something special on his hands?

It took Butterbugs and Terra about a half hour to finally find speech capability after they left the Garmes Viewing Hall. They had been invited to stay for the rest of the rushes (sign language was the only means of communication that anyone was able to employ at that moment), but the star and his p.a. thanked them with a grateful wave and returned to their bicycles.

They pedaled to one of the fluorescent-illuminated tea hovels that lined Rosson Road and had an anti-perker cup, a lullaby mix of lotos and wavel-root. Pretty harmless, but a fair ensurer of solid sleep.

'You know, Terra,' said Butterbugs at length, finding a bit of prosthetic mollusk hair still in one eyebrow, 'I never realized how the power of film can be found at any stage in the process, and in any corner.'

'Really?' she replied, assuming his statement was a bit of over-the-top Butterbugsian modesty. 'Are you sure? We, the public, want a bit of pride in our ultrastar, not just self-effacement-ization.'

'That's not exactly what I meant, princess. On some shoots, I might think, if I went to the dailies or hung out in the editing booth (with Margaret, Dorothy, Qingha and Hal), I don't know, I guess I thought it might be like hanging out with the fiddlers as Rome burns.'

'You thought you might jinx things?'

'Yeah! That's what I was trying to say!'

'So, it wasn't just out of modesty?'

'Oh no, I was always desirous of being *in* on stuff. And I have been a bit, but not on any great level. Music, quite a bit...'

'You thought your presence might wreck things somehow. In these other aspects of picture show making too? Past acting?'

'Mmmm... My insecurity?'

'You?? Insecure?? Maybe a little timid on this issue, but hardly insecure!'

'I guess I've always saved my security for being on set in front of the camera. You know, while it rolls.'

'Precisely what you *should* do, actor of mine.'

'So what's the big deal?'

'Yeah. What's the big deal?'

'I just feel so, I don't know, more 'opened up', I guess. No more thoughts of jinxing, no more selective security or conditional confidence. Just open truth.'

'Open truth, Butterbugs! What a glorious concept! What a gem, a gem for all of us to share.'

'And take it with you!' the ultrastar sung-sang.

Back in the quietude of Calle Rarefied, the two could detect night crews putting the ever-continuing finishing touches on the towering set and its consequences. The location was nearly as busy with graveyard shift as it was during the day.

The two did a little sibling-ian smooching.

'Look!' said Butterbugs, 'There's the moon rising! The moon of my Heathe-' He chopped himself off.

Terra didn't need a thing more tonight. Butterbugs could say such things if he wanted to. She smiled in the dark though, because she knew he had someone special on his mind. As a matter of fact, so did she. Her Bongo awaited.

'Nighty-night Tinglesome.'

'Nighty-night, Magic Lantern Boy!' and Terra rode off into the night.

So endeth the events and the progress of the Second Day.

The Third Day

A little brass horn sounded from the center of Butterbugs' dooryard. Not one of those kazooey things of tin, but a throaty song from the Roof of the World. A fine tooting then, on behalf of a most becoming entrance. For a day destined to *up* the pitch of this location's role as the 'non plus ultra' of contemporary filmmaking.

So much was at stake. Yet, the huge community hereabouts was of one mind: to push this sequence into a transcendental realm of cinema, the dimensions of which none of them knew, except to press forward *toward* it. When a script exists as a vision's blueprint, talent and means have the elevated responsibility to deliver the highest-level of interpretation humanly possible, which was the Producer Team's principal task, of course.

Dinzorra of Mundgod was behind the brass horn. Her lips were perfect to encompass the mouthpiece, so as to enact the ideal tone. From her Tibetan forebears, though they had been relocated to the Indian town of her name, she learned the classics of both text and tuzzle-horn, with which to keep her heritage alive while she did her production assistant gig on this big Butterbugs picture.

'Hi, sleeping beauty,' she said with a matter-of-fact all-American but resonant voice, to the lazybones on his Napoleon-style cot.

'Is that my Princess Charmingling?' he replied, feigning aristocratic levee.

'You know we can't commingle any more, Butterybuggsi,' she answered. 'All our chang has been drunk. Now open those boiled eggs of yours!'

It was Hollywood fact that this rare kid was head-over-heels in love with her husband, aged but hearty Merv LeRoy, but that particular vet dir/prod/exec got off on her circulation as a production assistant amongst the best that studio pictures had to give, which left him office time and project preparation.

''Tis me, Dzongkung, Sky-Witch of the Ridges, come to prod you like a zebu, in order that you belly up to High Mad Doctor's trough of servitude. Now rise, central Asian cowboy!'

She loved such funning, and so did Butterbugs, because they'd shared both life and love one super-y summer month whilst filming 'Zeebah McMrairtylochs' (Oddball) in the canyons of the upper Salween. Merv had directed, but their bloom of love did not sprout until the pic, in which D. served as assistant director, reached its editing phase, in beautiful downtown Burbank.

'So you're my mistress today?'

Dinzorra did her big smile.

'Oh yes, yes, and again, yes. You get me. I get you. Crazy!'

'Dress me, my operator. You know how.'

'The delight is mine, Jiggles.'

'Mind Merv when dealing with the naughty bits.'

'Always.'

'How is the wizard? Give him my best.'

'Nothing else will do.'

'I hold him above few others.'

'And we you.'

'My dear girl!'

'You sweet-ass!'

'How are the babies?'

'I dwell in pride. We're holidaying in Mundgod this year, to show them the southern heritage.'

'Might I link whilst you are all there?'

'It's our tradition. Nothing else will do.'

'Well, that leaves just the minor task of today.'

'Which I heralded in appropriate style.'

'Indeed, helpful one. But only a few dreeps! Well, oh, well… Let's go to it.'

'Now, here's Egaz's revised script. He wants you to emote a certain kind of distance, like you have recalled a childhood memory of longing, of sweetness, of windy days in spring, when the land lies uncomplicated and full of potential, but without portfolio, nor its maintenance. All open, upward truth.'

'That's good. I understand. I can link. I can provide a portfolio on call.'

'Egaz was hoping so. Knowing so.'

'For sure. There have been a few glimpses before, of HMD's repressed humanity.'

'If we can *call* it humanity.'

'Good point. Let's just say, 'humanity characteristics'. His self-torture could not ever be contained.'

'So he must spread it across the world.'

'Which he has done, my child.'

'With super-success.'

'So now, at his triumph, Egaz wants me to introduce a new angle on his more contemplative style. I get it. In the manner of his previous monologues of conscience, so to speak?'

'No, not like his meditation after the slaughter at Gelgarn Field, or on the Cornish moor before the Battle of Halsetown. This is more expansive.'

'I should say. His ego and its justification must be big enough to fill his new citadel.'

'A phallic thang.'

'To prove to the world that he does not have erectile dysfunction.'

'If you can pull it off.'

'I believe I can. HMD has wrestled with me this whole time, yet I am completely dominant over him. He does what I say. What Egaz says.'

'I should hope so! If not, we're all up cracked creek. How'd you like *him* to rule the world?'

'Well, we're just coming out of a near miss at something like that.'

'That Murn guy?'

'Our first overtly tyrannical president.'

'Not something you Americans can be proud of.'

'Not at all, and it was left to an American *outsider* to remove him and all he represented.'

'Now *that's* something Americans can be proud of!'

'You got it, Zorra-Din!'

'We're OK for time. Lines ready, Butterbugs?'

'Let's go over the sacred texts.'

They had roughly twenty minutes or so in which to do it, and they alternated sides and signatories, thus loosening up the script's dependence on metaphysical certitude, even at this late date.

Some of the really big scenes today: HMD's procession into his palace, which stood to feature the highest number of cast and extras, next to the grand finale. However, this was a much more complicated setup, with elephants, a fleet of wild but tamed bull moose, a battalion of midgets (the most little people assembled for a picture since the Munchkins descended on Culver City), a phalanx of topless, one-breasted Amazons, and...

Some of the many, many tributaries to HMD's new planetary hierarchy, in which the world is now coming under his one central authority. This is a victory celebration. His enemies were many, but they are vanquished. Thus, there is no reason to show magnanimity. Losers are not invited. This is HMD's peacock moment, to show off his conquest, as if it were something good.

'Are you pumped about the menagerie to come?' asked Dinzorra.

'You just *know* it!' Butterbugs enthused.

'I love how you approach these demanding tasks with such incredible relish.'

'Why Zorramund,' Butterbugs was almost taken aback, but in a totally joyful way, 'Now you looka here. When I think of what we're doing in this place, and how it adds up, not just as a picture show for folks to see, but as a life ponderment, a life... force, really, I can and must take on the canvas, in *full*. Everything about it is appealing, and this conversation is a very great part of it. I am not shaken by lack of confidence. Not even when I review the world's watching of us and what we will ultimately offer. I am not rattled by any onerous duty, even though all our labors have been Herculean.

Instead, I am as a greeter at a docent convention, or a doughboy reaching the picket fence of his own rental shack after years at the wars, or as a dimpled button-molder whose assembled products in front of him give his life added meaning! I'm telling you, this is rare and rarefied stuff! How privileged are we, right now, to be, at the start of *this day*, sequestered in its sacredness, to ready ourselves for good-gravy-greatness! Thus our happy carrying-on, eh? Moments like these are enshrined within all the universe's great creations, and just think, for us, it is not just one moment, but many, sustained into an epoch really, and not just a random one. We have made it *last*. Yes! a lasting spark! I tell you, it pumps me, knowing this. So now – Why! I am pumped about everything! Everything, do you hear?'

'I can hardly contain my excitement!'

'Me, neither!'

'Are you sharing this with someone special, Butterbugs?'

'Well I know *you* are!'

'I know I am. But I asked about *you*.'

'You have cornered me. But listen, I'm glad you did. I'll reveal my joy, but only a little.'

'So as not to… jinx it, eh?'

'Oh, you kittenish thing! I'll just tell *you*, on your honor that you won't tell anyone, not even Mervyn.'

'On the honor of our past intimacy, of course I won't tell!'

'Until after we wrap this here picture.'

'That's easy! I swear it.'

'Then I can only say, I am, yes, I am sharing this with someone special. Ultra-special, I think.'

'Oh, adorable news! Is she in station?'

'No, girl. We're linking after the final fade-out. I've too big a beam to raise in the meantime.'

'Then let's over to set, via Makeup, shall we? Our two-wheeled gizmos await. I share your joy, actor.'

She was actually quite solemn, as she did a Potala-witness' bow toward him, her horizontal color-band smock revealing its fuller assets at such a tipped angle.

'Then take out your tuzzle! Lead us with its otherworldly sound – here, in this world, today! Yoe! Forsooth, as Ruskin said: To-Day! To-Day! To-*Day!*'

All the way to Makeup and then all the way to the set, Dinzorra triumphantly tuzzled through their passage, while clearing the path ahead through the thronged participants in 'UWH''s high honors. Many cheered. Most applauded. All looked on in wonder.

Reaching the High Mad Platform of Speeches and Doctoral Reviews that was set up to overlook the progression, Butterbugs bent over to Dinzorra and said:

'They warm me up! Look! Way back there! Plasterers on the war-elephant frieze are taking notice! The people of the streets! The everyday passers-by!

Those who do their thing, all the livelong day! They are here! They care! Caring – for what we are doing!'

'Butterbugs! You are different! More elevated; raised up by both material and the energy of the moment! And also by your ultra-special one, I'm sure!'

'You're the preciousness of the day, dear girl.'

Then came Egaz to the scene, and set it up. Blocking was obeyed and gospel-script followed, with the free association of an actor's interpretation attached.

They commenced working on these heated, legendarily-couched heights, above the organized masses. The members of which, now fully installed as extras, were in position for shots that depended on the ultrastar to deliver his lines in a mode of performance that should carry all their accumulated weight. As breathlessly as a baby-delivering stork. Yet, with all the subversive and perverse purpose of a (behe)moth-eaten Lord and Coercer, over a world that had become drastically and draconically changed.

High-level set up now in play, high-tension wires connected.

'All right, *ACTION!*' commanded Egaz the Dynamic.

HMD: All you assembled things of mine! Take note! I command your awarenesses. *(*THE MASSES *take immediate notice.)* You gather here at my minimal whim, and I want you to know, my performance way up here is to be appreciated! I come from triumphs of vast war and prize-taking that you, as street-routiners and boredom-inhabitors cannot possibly comprehend! Do you know that – well – if I tried to explain the plain truth about war culture to you, you would all pollute this brilliant square with your nerve-released effluvia, and you would *still* not intellectually absorb all the juice and junk therein! So, here I statue-stand, tall in isolated understanding and ceaseless service! You must adapt to the reality: that I know so many more things than you do. Thus do I condescend unto you in the role of Leader and Teacher. You must and shall accept this truth. If you choose trust as your avenue of acceptance, we will get along in ways more beautiful than any sort of Garden of Eden-type thingy. If you choose any of the other options beside the far more desirable trust route, there are going to be some problems. Ones of your own making. So! Let's get accustomed to the total-trust-all-the-time ideal, huh? You know, I like that term! So let's adopt it. Trust In Me *Rules!* That being the case, you must strike obeisance to me! Endlessly! From this pernt, forward! I have given of my very celestial being for you people, and you hardly know why. Why do I do it, then? Why? Because I love the world that I now own and control! Put yourself in my place, why don't you? I ask you, especially you thinkers out there, what would you do if you had won the world for all your right reasons and you had to tell that world as to *why?* I challenge any of you stalwarts out there, *way* out there: how would you come to terms with this incalculable issue? Well, I can say, these are the matters your ruler struggles with in order to see your lives through to their daily success. That is why I stand up and in front of you now and draw this aspect of my selfless service to your regular lives. It is a sacrifice, let me tell you! I dodged both firebomb and canister to fight for my rights, and, having won, transfer their benefits to your choice roads. On the battle-plain of Khunschwashkrelmn, I dodged a spear aimed at me, so that it pierced the breast of my most fabulous general, just behind. He was a great guy, and a really super general, who did everything I asked, even though he always spoke his mind. He may have died for *me*, but I did it for *you!* Understand? But, look what I did! I did that for *you!* Understand *now?* That's why it's so important that you see my side of things. I have given of myself for you, now it's your turn. Nothing else than complete trust *in* me, and total agreement *with* me shall do. Have you any idea what I go through, even now, having survived your wars, which I so selflessly started and won for you? Won, so you can continue your little lives, whatever they are! Or, or, have you really any notion of how much I suffer for you? Can you not reward me?

(GRUSHPYUNRAG, a streetsman, [as played by George Clooney] has the courage to emerge from the throng and raises his hand in complete and utter obeisance.)

GRUSHPYUNRAG: *(deeply respectful)* Oh golly, Sacrificer! Had we known! Would we be worthy! Now, in lieu of this pathetic crowd, do I offer my ox-like hulk to you, to be presented and then positioned under any conveyance you might offer – to be crushed in order to serve your high purpose: to You, as one who has given two billion times more than I could ever possibly offer. But if I offer it, perhaps many, many others will offer themselves similarly – to prove our fealty to you without any conditions whatsoever! Will you have me? Oh, *will you?*

HMD: *(pleased but haughty)* I am well nigh pleasured by you pleading, insignificant other! Indeed, Garrison Rigs of the High One? Hear me now! Rake your high-tonned, groaning chassis over this fellow, if only to show the front row (at least) of the thousands here gathered, that what I demand is indeed to be attended-to, and most importantly, in my own severe fashion.

(Chariots rage over the prostrate but totally silent GRUSHPYUNRAG, and though it takes some doing, due to the devotee's toughness and gristle, they duly mutilate him unto death; THE MASSES gasp, but mostly with impressed surprise, and relieved that someone besides themselves stepped up.)

HMD: You see? I mean to have you damn well fall into where you *should* be. There are many, many meaningless additions to the pavement such as this minor but noble one who just gave of himself to educate all of you as to my importance and power. And I welcome your giving of your ultimate selves. Yeah, I really do! But right now, let's not get in the way of the Parade of the Vassals that, at this dawn to The Age of Me, is prepped to stream in front of us like so many boxcars of tribute. For they represent my COMPLETE, UTTER, TOTAL, ABSOLUTE, FINAL, FINAL, FINAL – and above all, LASTING *victory* over all you peoples of the world, and for ALL TIME.

'CUT!' announced Egaz, with obvious delight.

'I've never heard his voice so clear, or with so much purpose!' soundman Alan Splet said to audio ministers Murray Spivack, Doug Shearer, and Sash Fisher. 'It has entered into a higher plane.'

'Do you have it?' asked Egaz.

'Most assuredly, director!' answered the sound designer.

'That's all I care about in the world today,' he replied, hastening on to the next setup.

Egaz, in a moment while the grips moved the immense cameras to the next shot's plot, came up to Dinzorra.

'He sinks his teeth into the tissue of mattering,' he said.

'Indeed,' replied the important production assistant. 'His engagement in this heinous character's persona is total. Yet, I think he has reached a level of detachment that is almost divine. Or at least in the perspective of Nirvana. He is plainly inhabiting a very lofty parallel. He knows how to project but not lose the essential mastery of life's connection with consciousness.'

'And thus, to super-consciousness,' said the director.

'I think so, Mister. He *gets* it. He makes it so that we too, can *get it.*'

'Oh, my cherished wish. Can you believe this? Excuse me, I've got to give Keenah a call. I'm so happy.'

'Good idea! I'm calling Mervyn right now!'

All were up there on that heat-blasted plane till 7:00 in the PM, when the light was failing, though superb late, late, late-in-the-day shots were to be had. And they were *indeed* had, caught by a Nirvana-deserving crew.

'You know,' Butterbugs said as he and D. of Mundgod relaxed at the Ladyl-e-Lee-Lee Honey Tea Nook in Jennifer Jones Court, 'I think I was able to show a real validity out there – somehow – today. You know?'

'Oh, Butterbugs, I don't know if I can actually talk about this. So far above my head! So advanced! So many levels! I feel almost a fool.'

'Wait!' the ultrastar was needle-sharp in his rebuke. 'You can't say that! I cannot abide someone so beyond the atmosphere saying they are left behind! You are in the vanguard. There are indeed so many levels, but we are all on the same one. Now don't elevate me to unreasonable incorruption! I cannot bear it!'

'Right, erstwhile lover. The power of your performance swept me away, is all.'

'In the right direction?'

These were people who did not know what flattery *was*. They only conversed in the most objective and honest ways, from the heart, and from the brain. And no one was trying to be funny.

'Most assuredly! Nothing but good came of it. You should be able to handle that.'

'You're right. I'll simmer. I'll reflect. And I'll think of her, the special one, the one I can speak of no more until these few days have passed. And they are passing surpassingly quickly.'

'I can well respect your distance from her, for the duration. Still, I am aghast with admiration. *Still*, you need to think of your role.'

'I thank you, girl. You're absolutely correct. Come now, step highly as I waddle-pedal home. Then you to your chambers – without my body or my thoughts. This tenure is as a monastery to me, and it will sustain me. Austerity in the name of the role, in the name of the picture. Now let's up and out, so we can 'night-night in right action, all the way.'

'I will not speak more tonight,' D. of Mundgod replied. 'You did it, for all.'

So endeth the events and the progress of the Third Day.

The Fourth Day

'**I** am not attached, and you know I am not attached, so I awaken you with an intimacy that I think you will appreciate. For I am Juba Xudr, late of the greatly-placed Somali marches. I am a river girl, born on it, so I *became* it, and here, as I present myself to you, I run my current in your general direction.'

It was Juba Xudr all right, the production assistant-aspiring producer-actress/model-cum-social activist, who now was rewarded with Butterbugs-assisting duty on this next great day at the Lasky Mesa shoot.

'Please, Butterbugs, speak to me! I know it is cruel dawn – before dawn really, when goblin and goofball are both still out, but when warm-toned and warm-spreading arms reach out to you and pull you toward one-of-a-kind moistness, ready to play, ready to bond, and ready to get you over to Makeup by 6:51AM.'

It was Juba, attempting to muscle in on one she'd been eyeing, only because he had been kind to her on several previous occasions, and only because she felt sorry for him because he didn't have a steady girlfriend, and he seemed so open to the possibility of having someone he could pal around with. Juba being quite pal-able and eligible, as Butterbugs was himself, what the hell – she got this p.a. opportunity, so the least she could do was to offer herself up, first out the gate, so that all options would be on the table.

'Juba?' the ultrastar stirred. 'Juba, here? Ready to face my bed-breath and my tousled moptop, and my general disarray?'

'It is indeed Juba,' she replied. 'And I am without prejudice or hang-up of any kind. You know why? Your faculties outweigh any distractions that might occur in the sphere of our time together. So, I just think, wow, Butterbugs, let's get together in your way of ways!'

'Er, roll a couple of bummers and –'

Butterbugs didn't really register who this p.a. exactly *was*, as he was just emerging from a dream-sleep in which he had lived through riding on the front of a polished locomotive with several others, going at about 110 mph, and realizing it wasn't as hazardous as he'd thought, and that one of his companions in this ride was this gorgeous Somali girl who now stroked his dream-greasy cheek with her long graceful fingers, and that he liked those strokes and that he wanted her to lay herself down next to him so that he could begin this next big day with a fulfillment of his horny dog's imperative in a better-quickie-than-none-ie, and that if she was willing, he'd certainly engage in...

She was Heatherette – in his mind, and she didn't wear a halo, but he'd keep his own counsel, thank you very much, without any scripted rhetoric or conduct mechanisms to dutifully follow.

No, she was Heatherette, and only Heatherette. No Juba or any other, no matter how dazzling, could enter in right now.

So he yawned and gave Juba a peck on the cheek.

'Your wake-up call, Butterbugs!' she announced, with full sincerity, despite the fact that she was nude.

'Gosh, what personalized service,' he replied, all sleepy and groggy and un-comfortable. Then he loafed for a while, semi-dozing, trying to recapture the valid parts of his dream, so that they could perhaps be utilized in his waking hours' powers.

Mildly frustrated, she resorted to tried-and-true earthenware techniques and first passed her underarms over his face. Then, when that didn't get a rise, her superbly hirsute crotch made its pass-over.

Ding! His erectile response was practically instant, so she positioned her lean form right over his campanile and made to plug it into her outlet, by which she would propose her person and personality, by which to make a reasonable claim to his attentions. After all, she was approaching him with the best will in the world. Based on what others had said, the ultrastar at least needed an escort, a compan-ion, as even ultrastars no doubt cottoned to a soft set of chests to hold, and a warm bod to curve around.

Just because Butterbugs' fingertips came into close contact with her air-brush-smooth breasts did not mean he instinctively grabbed on. The air between the two different sets of flesh indeed crackled with responsive volts, but the fingers were connected to a mind recently transformed, so there was conflict that resulted from the nearness of such attractive impact.

Here was this Nut, this sky-goddess, her body curved over in an arch of heaven above his receptive pharaonic form, ready to lower her span for the sake of a goodwill goodmorn. But he sensed his departure from the old ways as tangible, so he turned on his side, even as she descended onto the vacated flat of the bed. And to prove her sincerity, the sheet was indented and moistened by both her mound and her pursed lips.

'Juba, Juba, so willing to rouse me! Your beauty has already done that, and your closeness. I thank you.'

Indeed, she had performed an essential service. Girl Friday for the day. For starters, the ultrastar had been awakened.

'You don't remember me, do you?' asked Juba, as she handed him a tomato-filled bearclaw for breakfast.

He regarded her striking and imperial looks.

'Quite frankly... no. But I should! 'Tis a soothingly beauteous view that you are.'

'Well, thank you, you matchingly handsome fellow!'

Juba was beloved for her tell-it-like-it-is-baby! manner.

'Juba – Juba, weren't you in... 'The Expedition to Punt', and its sequel, 'Unksunnommah' (both WB)?'

'Good memory! I was the Æthiopian Representative in 'Punt', after which I chucked acting and gripped for the sequel. Besides, Somalis don't make credible Abyssinians... Now I'm a production assistant!'

'Next stop: producer!'

'How did you know?'

'It just came to me. Now then Juba, we've been properly re-introduced. I'm not so certain that you should have abandoned acting. You have the talent and the looks. Those I cannot deny.'

'Can I be in 'UWH'?'

'Well by golly, I don't see why not. I'll fix it with Cherramona in casting. Is a crowd & court scene OK, tomorrow? That's about all we have left.'

'That would be dandy! I hope that'll give me enough time to prepare. Thank you, Butterbugs!'

'You can have some lines, too. Egaz likes this flexibility. You're already SAG, so this may revive your acting career.'

'Or else I could have both! That and... producing...'

'And why not? It'll be fun.'

'Wow, my head's spinning. But we'd better attend to the business at hand.'

'We'd certainly better!'

'Do you require more grub?'

'Not right now.'

'Then let's bike off to Makeup for a cameo, followed by some grandeur shots. No dialogue this morn.'

'Good! I must save my voice for later, and my soul for what is to come.'

She sort of snuggled up next him as a 'Let's break a leg' gesture, and he was amenable, not just because showbiz was touchy-feelie, but because he was really attracted to this impressive girl in all non-lust-laden ways. Well, the door to carnality could easily have been thrown open, but when one is in true love, the urgency of another who happens to brush up against one is not so dominating as much as it is flattering. So mere admiration is the outcome, not orgasm. Besides, she showed she really cared about him, and that was nice in the midst of his joyous but semi-lonely sprint to the finish, to make way for all-new things. Also, it was how a really good p.a. *should* be, pure and simple.

Butterbugs loved cycling through this city of cinematic undertakings. It really was a city, so healthy, so absorbing, so giving of its all-encompassing love. Everyone loved what they were doing, and the dedication of each was plainly displayed.

He thought, as he followed Juba on his bike to the places of shooting, and observing the perfect-fit harmony in all he saw and heard and felt, '*This* is how the world can be. This is how the world *will* be. Never mind that we are making a picture about a tyrant, and how he was created a tyrant by the powers of the world. Here is an ideal achieved, not by forcing it, but by simply allowing it to happen.'

If there was one flaw that Butterbugs visited upon himself, it was his genuine inability to admit that the reason for such harmony, ideals and perfect fits was the fact that he, Butterbugs, was their facilitator, their inspiration, their reason for being at all. But maybe this lack of consciousness as to the how and why was the secret of its success.

Some of the setups this morning were basically a job of work. Those fill-ins, mendings, resolves, and matters of utility that would make the raw footage of the past couple days more coherent and polished in the final outcome.

'Filling the cup, mug, jug, or hogshead' the actor called it.

After some of this feather-dusting, which would have been tedious had Butterbugs not spread easy cheer all about him, there was a generous hunk of time until the string of necessary setups was due. It was late morning, and the location rhythm was in its full swinging and ringing. Juba and Butterbugs had a full three hours though, so they goofed around.

He was in 'lite' makeup and costume right now, so he was pretty mobile.

'Let's explore!' said Juba.

'Er, hokay!'

They looked around, taking in the hordes of laborers swarming about the giant sets, and the legions of extras rehearsing their complex operations, the only way it was possible: by a Hawks-like pan of 360 degrees, each handling a 180°-half, and they both came to a meridian that dominated absolutely everything hereabouts – predictably.

'Your Citadel!' proclaimed Juba.

'It certainly *is!*' Butterbugs was equally bemused and flabbergasted.

Here, in the stark sun of broadest day, much closer-up, it was like beholding the thing for the first time. Instantly, he was filled with ideas he could use in his portrayal, depending on how many takes he could get out of Egaz for the upcoming 'Regard!' scenes.

They made their way thither amidst the swirling and many-layered activity, where dress extras engaged in a massive choreography that would form only a part of the HMD's deviant celebrations. Five groups of five hundred extras, each one a skilled dancer, were being shepherded by such eminent choreographers as Hermes Pan, Twyla Tharp, Bob Alton, Jack Card, and one eminent director, Julie Taymor, all under the supervisory vision of Buzz Berkeley, who was phoning in directions, broadcast through stacks of Vox of the Drive-In Thiertre speakers (ingeniously integrated with rostral columns, pavement gratings, and flaming tripod plinths), from his office in Hollywood, no less. Buzz was so stimulated, he didn't even need his oxygen tank any more.

The mega-dance's eventual coalescence would form one of the picture's largest master shots, captured from a camera parallel way up there somewhere.

Further along, they dodged any number of set decorators, groundspersons, greenspersons, and carpenters who were furiously dressing the sets so that a great motion picture could be born from their efforts.

'Looks like it's gonna be a great show!' said Butterbugs excitedly, ogling the dancers without reservation.

'Lots of sick twists, licentiousness, and raunchy strip-teases, too. As befitting your good, high and mad self, of course!' added Juba.

Such was the total professionalism of cast, crew, and extras alike, that they took no notice whatsoever of Juba or Butterbugs. All were equal here. All had equally important tasks to perform.

Coming into the shade of the mighty high-rise, they were able to pause for a few seconds and look up. While the mass was in itself startling, the detailing was even more so. Wild, culturally-indeterminate decor was plastered all over the lower masses of this vanity-pile, from which the sleeker main shaft sprang. Nothing quite like it had ever been seen before. It emulated no sci-fi or fantasy sets in pictures past, and it certainly had no grounding in any of the world's heritages. All Butterbugs could think of for the moment was that it was some violently-fevered fungus, of world-shaking proportions. Utterly dangerous. Completely diabolical. Totally perfect.

Up on its depraved heights, 5th-unit cameras were already being manned on all levels and galleries, capturing its magnificence for all sorts of shots, whether needed or not, as some unit directors particularly creative in their ambitions. Plainly, the footage they would submit was multi-functional, if not historical.

'I think all aspects of these sets are being well-nigh utilized,' said the star to his p.a. as they neared a side entrance.

She replied by planting a smacker on his cobalt-ish cheek, out of pure thrill.

The side entryway was still under construction. To get to the main entrance, they would have to trek way, way around, as it was the only other interior access. Too far for their limitations.

'You had no idea it was this Brobdingnagian, did you?' she chuckled.

'Not at all, girl! Not at all! It renders us into needless seedlings!'

So it was with an even more heightened sense of awe, and not a little trepidation, that Juba led Butterbugs into the Citadel set, via a gangway of 2x4-framing that was, as chance would have it, about to be pulled up by justifiably impatient grips.

The 5th-unit was all ready for an essential cover shot of this particular angle on the set's exterior. They duly noted the weirdly-costumed creep crossing the flimsy bridge as, indeed, the principal star of this picture. Hardly a usable shot, however. The creep and his bridge had to be cleared, NOW. Even though the one worth billions was totally cool, he needn't be treated like royalty or anything. Nevertheless, they waited with all the good-natured tolerance for on-camera talent any professional crew was wont to give. In fact, as the two VIPs made their gangway dance, unit director Kevin Corcoran and his grips golf-clapped and tastefully hooted their approval.

'Make haste, Butterbugs!' Juba called out.

Their pace made the boards wobble and crack.

As he put his trim-boot down on the right-footed plank, it split and gave way, causing the HMD to tumble into the dry moat below, about five feet down.

Juba, having successfully reached the fiberboard-and-stucco curtain wall, spun about in fright.

'Oh, great follower! Are you OK? Are you infirm? Oh! Bash my soul for being so careless!'

'I'm all right! I'm *all right!*' the ultrastar gaily announced from down there somewhere. 'Perfectly fine! Perfectly normal!'

'It was an accident!' she declared to the instantly-gathered grips, her arms outstretched helplessly. 'It was... an... *accident...!*'

The grips poured down into the moat and skillfully swarmed about the star, who was confidently standing and brushing himself off.

'Not even the wind knocked out!' he laughed. 'Except the bit that 'broke', heh!'

'You are one sturdy, totally corrupt leader!' joked unit director Corcoran.

'Thanks for reminding me, Moochie! That'll sustain me in the heavy work ahead!'

Then did they all laugh heartily.

'I say, gang, be good enough to hoist me up to yon portal, where my lovely guide awaits. It's high-high time she showed me my very own citadel, or whatever it's called.'

Barrison Thek, the Key of the grips, then procured two fashionable hardhats and handed them to the visitors.

'Here, star, for thy domes. Rules 'n' regs, fiercely enforced! You and your striking p.a. are indeed welcome and under our watch, but for fucking A's sake, have care, will you? We've got everything in there up to pukka grade, all the way to the top, with many a warner-sign. But the average tourist must also exercise un-instructed common survival sense, lest high stakes (such as yourself) be put up against unacceptable odds. Especially in the Producer Team's view, if you know what I mean.'

The star's eyes sparkled, but not quite as much as the grip's.

'I know what you mean Thek-Sahib.'

(Barrison, whose grandsire hailed from The Gambia, had served on many a tough location with Butterbugs & Co.)

'I'm green-lightin' ya then. I'll inform Production Management. Mind what ya do!'

'No Barrison, please don't notify Production. They wouldn't know what to do with it. Because... I mean... You know, whether they should send the cops after us or not. Everybody's just too billy-be-wigged *busy* right now for such truant churlishness. Pray, let us sneak up with teen glee, for to seek total awe. Like the two tots in the tower, from Meindert DeJong's 'The Wheel on the School', which Porter wants to film after 'UWH', perchance with this very set – after Dutch-iz-ing, of course. So *please* don't tell on us! Best left on the quiet side.'

The Key Grip got all tender and wistful and soft-hearted, as he happened to be a huge DeJong fan. Simply hearing the news that one of his most cherished books was to star his friend and idol rendered him helpless in watchdogging the set, not to mention his idol's welfare.

'Man-oh-man! I hear ya. Notwithstanding that, I implore, mind what ya do, OK?'

Butterbugs, his memories still pretty fresh from the big construction industry picture, 'Hell For Stout' (20th-Fox), in which he had acrobatted his way through-out a stupefying matrix of intimidating and utterly dangerous sets, did not at all look down his nose at Barrison's warning (an attitude he was incapable of inflict-ing on other living beings, anyway), but instead merely answered:

'We *will*, sir!'

'Hope to grip for you on 'Wheel', Butterbugs!'

'Oh, you will, Barrison. I tell you, you *will!*'

Just inside, away from prying eyes, they scanned the vast Grande Lobby, naked in its framing, but ready for decorative cladding, if needed. It was a full-blown soundstage.

Steadied in their new headgear, Juba's top priority was contrition. Such an emo-tion also couldn't help but enhance her now undeniable turbo-crush on her charge. Her self-appointed duties well and truly included responsibility for his very life!

'So sorry am I, Butterbugs. I wouldn't be offended in the least if you rejected my service flat out. And, quitting these precincts, after you make your way to Location HQ, you should have me written up and sacked from this august assign-ment of a lifetime!'

Butterbugs looked at her with immeasurable kindness, and saw the true apprehension in her stunning eyes.

'Is that what you want me to do?'

'Oh, no, no, no! Sir Bb, not at all, all, all! All I want is for you to accept my overwhelming apologies and my Mariana-Trench-deep regret for my stupid and potentially dangerous actions –'

'Juba? Aren't you laying it on a bit thick? Well, aren't you?'

'It isn't thick *enough!*'

'That trench I toppled into – of my own accord – was hardly Mariana-grade…!'

'My regret, sir! My *regret* is even deeper than that!'

'OK, OK…'

'I'm almost finished! But now – now that all danger has passed and my apology has been made, I want more than ever to continue our enthralling expedition into this mind-blowing set, just here!'

Her confidence and get-on-with-it personality was obviously successful in rebuilding her persona, erasing any equivocation he might have had about her being a capable producer.

'Then let us proceed, for all apologies *for all time* are accepted. All dangers in the world are a thing of the past. And my own explanation, that I was a clunky oaf back there, which had not a whit to do with you, which now I present as conclusive evidence, make me rev up and say, indeed, let's get a move-on before we have to be back on set. I must say, this is absolutely as profound a construction as I've ever trod upon.'

The surroundings alone were enough to realign their minds into a mode of discovery. Because both of them thought inside, 'I have to ask myself, *all this*, for a picture show, of which I am a part? Yes. *All this*. For I am a *part of* it!'

Ramps and utility runs were everywhere. They moved past the Grande Lobby. The whole was exposed studs and nail boxes lying about. Unlike the Palace set, the Citadel was entirely an exterior display, though it could be readied for any application at a moment's notice. No scenes would be shot in these interiors, save for the Upper Penumbra Chamber, topside, where the HMD would make his triumph complete.

'You know,' said Juba, 'In the Horn (of Africa) from where I ultimately originate, there are several aged Gothic chapels by the sea. A legacy of our colonial past, which I accept as part of our recent heritage. But I have probed them and prowled through them, and in every case, I was always seeking the highest possible point accessible for the casual explorer to reach. Attaining the uppermost height usually allowed me to see beyond the fringes of my horizon, and that elevation is what really gave me the push to make it to these North American shores. All that aside, dear Butterbugs, it is the ascent, the rising up, that brings us to truth, for we must be elevated – or self-elevate – in order to command our location in the universe, even if it is out on this particular location.'

Butterbugs listened carefully and thought, 'She may be a kid, but I am more than endowed with hope via such a person'.

Now he himself was laying it on a bit thick, but it was a truthful pleasure to do so.

'I must say, Juba, you are my interlocutor, for I had to be introduced to the setting of my super-climax scene by someone, somewhere. What a wonderful way to do it, here and now. With you.'

'Oh, Butterbugs! That's so romantic – I mean, well, Egaz and any of the producers are too busy, so why not me? I can even show you the blocking tape on the floor. I've studied the script and I know all about it.'

'Shall we ascend – by foot? I need the circulatory and respiratory exercise.'

'Perfect!' she replied.

The lift was just at hand. For the sake of cinema audiences near the end of what would surely be a very, very long picture, it would enable the HMD's hastened ascent. It was highlighted externally, so that the camera could follow his signal progression to the apex. Keen on beating any assistant director to the punch, she showed him what he must do to navigate the lift, and the timings involved therein.

'Stairs, just here, my film's star!'

So began the alpine-seeming climb. It was indeed a solid back-upon-itself staircase, a zigzag of unerring plumbness, carpentered with the greatest sincerity. And so it rose, flight upon flight, height upon height, without relief, with no Eiffel Tower's first level, no Elevadora Santa Justa (de Lisboa) escape route, no fireman's pole to slipslide down and out. No, this wasn't any pansy-assed party-booze-cruise through isles of interest. This was a mucking out-on-a-limb set for a gutsy actor to fucking act his socks off within and upon. A husk of utility. A helpful and supportive shell, from which to hatch a brilliant performance.

The passage to the upper lofts and galleries was now clear. Nothing remained to stand in the way of making their quick tour a sprint, given the mechanism of the inclined plane they followed being so simple and so responsive. They got up very high in a very short amount of time.

From a vantage point, over halfway up, composed of a trustworthy floor inserted for utility purposes, the two tots found an opening in its middle, which they inched toward.

This access to the empyrean below allowed for several future function possibilities, in the event the structure should be preserved beyond its cinematic usage. A carillon installation, maybe. Perhaps its destiny would be as a for-its-own-sake monument, something for onlookers simply to wonder at, as did Butterbugs during his grand descent into this very valley. A curious feature for the detached visitor, rather than for any intrinsic purpose, such as a bell tower or a shot tower or semaphore station or lookout for any invaders from the Pacific, which from here appeared as a very distant line of silver to the west. Indeed, the entire core of the Citadel, basically hollow, was as tough as a Cape Wrath lighthouse, with all its overbuilt pendentives and wish-bone-lash, hurricane-proof-linking, interacting with Sumurum-brace systems. All this opened up to them, with vertigo-inducing detail.

One role it would never fulfill: as a memorial for any recently-dead POTUS.

Even though he actually found this drop-off scarier than Pulpit Rock when filming Wagner's 'Ring', Butterbugs couldn't resist a little childishness and grabbed a nearby discarded Ken's Ale bottle, then let it drop through the opening. It was hardly a feat of hubris or post-juvenile delinquency. Rather, a simplistic act of one who thought he was in virtually derelict precincts, despite their being brand new.

'You know,' he said, after the distant poof-bust was heard far below, followed by a sturdy silence, which meant that his stunt was met with approbation by any crew member down there, if there actually *was* any crew member down there, assuredly hard-hatted, 'I've been in close proximity to a number of significant situations of verticality of late, some of which would send you around the corner. And, I have to tell you Juba, I'm rather... you know... *comfortable* being on the edge... and stuff...'

He was not quite admitting to the testicle-grabbing effects this particular verticality was having on him just then. Perhaps it was his latest rescue-bound across Heatherette's black hole that enabled a bit of the Insufferable Showoff to bounce around his adolescent frame of mind right now.

Juba could only approach the void at hand by crouching down and crawling on all fours, then halting, just so she could peek over, chin on the edge's molding, butt in the air.

'Can't say... that... I feel the same...,' she mumbled. Her stomach didn't go wonky, but she had the good sense to remain low, while the guy...

For his own part, Butterbugs felt some sweet nostalgia for his new love's elevator shaft, and had a thought.

'I think, my dear p.a., that I could easily leap across this here opening. Why, I've had greater chasms to cross!'

Juba, her cinematic recall always ready at the offing, which in this case referenced the Dare of the Cossacks in 'Taras Bulba' (UA, 1962), lowered her rear to the deck and cleared her throat.

'Uh, Butterbugs, – ultrastar – star of this rather important picture, which incidentally, *isn't quite completed yet* – uh, I rather think that, uh, that isn't the *best* idea, just about now. *You know?*'

Then, in a voice that could only be assigned to the cinematic creation of the High Mad Doctor, Butterbugs burst out:

'Are you, then, my keeper?'

Juba, seeing Butterbugs' power in both sound and gesture, as well as physically lying immediately next to the possibility of perdition itself, nearly swooned.

'No one can contain you!' she managed to get out. Then, with more authority and confidence, 'See now, the time runs! We must either proceed aloft or to the ground – and not in the fastest way possible.'

'Well, it was just a fancy, I guess.'

The puff of performance passed, the role retreated, and the actor remained. He thought of his character's more acceptable attributes: boisterous, pressured speech, a Gordonesque approach, a raging bullock...

'I'm so used to taking direction on account of my pictures, Juba Xudr. I'm not quite as used to being my own director in my life, especially between shots. Like now, if you know what I mean. There's a twain that has to be met there – somewhere. Pardon, dear girl. Sometimes I need an authority, and not just on the set.'

Juba rolled on her side, then thought better of it and returned to her previous position, where she flipped up the back panel of her black mini so that her bright scarlet panties were revealed.

'If I can help...,' she said, daring to be openly seductive at last.

It wasn't as if Butterbugs was dim or even distracted by the surroundings, or even by the nearness of gravity's revenge. He was, without the burdensome reputation of being a letch, certainly accustomed to making surgingly important love to the women in his life under all sorts of conditions – many of them exhilarating. Some were threatening, and many involved a pressure of some kind. However, right now he was somewhat oblivious to this rather spectacular young p.a.'s overtures. Simply because, the all-encompassing block of Heatherette-love was protecting him from all external influences, good, bad and everything in between. If it made him invincible from fear, fairly impervious to acrophobia, and strong in the face of scarlet panties over bubble-butt components, then he might consider himself a man transformed by the power of love.

Still, he was no isolationist. Juba had endeared herself more than ever to him. He perked from his risky reverie and gave a friendly pat to her pretty buns, then offered her a big hand up.

'Rise up and further ascend with me! We are past the point of return! There is plenty of time for grounding, later.'

Back on her high heels again, she gazed straight across into her hero's eyes, with a dreamy notion that she was definitely making progress in her mission of becoming his steady g.f.

'Oh, *Butter*bugs...!'

'We'd better go on up,' he smiled.

'All right,' she answered, as if they were about to make their first appearance in the Rainbow Room as a couple.

Now, in the manner of upper, less-traveled routes in high-rises worldwide, the staircase grew narrower. The scent of new lumber was more concentrated and there were a greater number of un-pounded nails to be wary of. After all, more swiftness of erection had been applied to this upthrust than the Great Hall of the People in Beijing, with no evidence of jerry-building, either.

Up, up, up, and *more* up, above the valley below – How much higher?

There were plenty of openings from which to get a true sense of their ascent, and every once in a while access to some gallery or balcony came their

772

way, but they hadn't the time to follow every intriguing and invitational pathway.

Out of the corner of his eye, Butterbugs thought he saw a large buzzard or kite-like bird, reminiscent of types he had come into close but unintentional contact with, when roaming through ramparts in Jodhpur once. It appeared to perch on one of the ledges outside, but it must've flown off or shifted when it saw them. Probably spooked by his costume and makeup.

The Upper Penumbra Room was their goal, where they would be rewarded panoramically, for sure, and perhaps with some chocolate milk and cookies.

Juba led for a time and Butterbugs, as a pleasant distraction, noted how shiny his p.a.'s thighs, exposed torso, and arms were getting. Such an athletic performer! She was able to reach around, yoga-style, and adjust her sport-bra strap, then give her hair a straighten as its strands gathered the moisture around her shoulder blades, all without missing one high-heeled step.

And she, ahead of him, knew he was giving her the once-twice-thrice-over while his own athletic engine, which perfectly matched hers, kept him right under – or behind – her stilettos. She had been up and down here lately, seeing to certain production needs, but had never attained the summit. Therefore, she earnestly hoped there was a comfortable bed up on top somewhere. She also wondered if there was an observation deck. If so, she could drag the bed – or even an old mattress pad out there, and they would make glorious love, with nothing between them and the sun's approving face.

In their trek, Butterbugs noticed there were no light fixtures all along the way.

'Boy, I wouldn't want to be going up here at night,' he commented, a bit breathily by now.

'Just think, though,' replied Juba, 'This is merely a code-fulfilling fire escape. You'll be riding in luxury in the lift, over there.'

Their constant companion in this journey was the exposed cage-work of the elevator shaft, itself a brick shithouse of an engineering affair (by Obadiah & Otis, of course).

'Anyway, there are plenty of batt-opp torches at top, and also, at these Reference Stations along the way. See? There's one. Nice little kits. You don't have to break the glass or anything. These details were all part of my p.a. duties, sir! I myself directed the work be done, all for my super ultrastar!'

'Well, that's pretty good! There's a demi-military quality to this whole undertaking, Juba. Every filming location always has it, but this one, especially.'

'Yeah, we're Soldiers of Fun, huh?'

'I'm so glad that I got the tour from you – So in-the-know is Juba the Special!'

She stopped her climb and turned about. His face was at aureole-level, and he knew it, as it was pretty... obvious.

Here, in this airy belfry, was a perfect place to fall in love. Shybirds flitted past the glazeless windows; the light on the star's face came in laterally. Even in his makeup of hideousness, he was *her* hideousness. She would claim it. Just think, here was the world's ultrastar, stopped in mid-flight because she herself stopped! Here he was, near enough to turn her on where it mattered most to her. Lanterns on her dual domes went pop-up/pop-up simultaneously. Priming was progressing.

She glanced upward for a few seconds to viddy just how much further it was to bedded bliss. Not far at all. Right up there were beams supporting the ultimate chamber, beams husky enough to support two wedding bells: his and hers.

Then she looked down. It was something she'd prudently never done during her duties way up here. But now she did, just for a bit of sport, to see how far they'd come to their reward. There was her smiling, paused lover, and beyond him, the astoundingly complex superstructure of her damsel-tower's interior, in all its giddy struts and supports.

She went a bit maroon and wobbled a little. It was genuine, not feigned, and Butterbugs could tell. Then, she faltered. There were no railings up here, as only adults were admissible this far, and only those who knew of the standards which Barrison the Key Grip had noted. No kids allowed, no matter how sneaky – or horny.

If she would then totter, she stood a good chance of plunging into this hundreds of feet-deep well, into space that, to her mind, should be occupied solely by the nuptial bell rope of her dreams.

She did indeed totter, and through it was no choice of hers at this particular instant, she nevertheless soon felt Butterbugs' hands on her body. It was a sensation of explosive magic. If their fate was for both of them to then travel over the edge, that was all well and good, for a liebestod with her man was worth every glory in life she had wit to think. And besides, such a loving exit from a world worth renouncing would be *the* most romantic moment in cinematic history! A true tragedy, but one all the world would tearfully enjoy!

'You fainted,' was the next thing she heard.

They had come to rest on a landing just a few steps down. Fortunately, safe in a haven next the outside wall. But her elegant head was just a few inches away from fearsome sinker-nail sharpies that held a vulgar ornamental swag onto the exterior of the tower. Her temple would have been punctured with great gusto. That aside, no bruises, no busted limbs, just a bit of sawdust on a little black mini and some displaced cobalt-tinted facial makeup on an actor, who, just as prone as his girl companion, was looking down at her closed eyes from an extremely close angle.

'My dear p.a.! I do believe we will take the lift on down, don't you think, Juba? Juba! Speak to me, please?'

He made sure their hardhats were where they should be, as per rules & regs.

'I… what?'

'Oh Juba! Now it is my turn to wax apologetic, larger than the full moon! How could I let you come up here this way, and so fetchingly, as I did not consider your delicacy, which must be protected and preserved so much more than I thought! I hate myself for this brush with doom! My flaw in this respect glares at me, as I gaze hopefully on your great glowing beauty. Surely your trust in me has been completely blown! Please, *please* forgive! I can't ask you ever to forget, only to forgive!'

She opened her eyes, then closed them, and parted her generous lips.

Thus, this then, was the moment, the time when he would warm to her, when their mouths would meet, which they did, and the time when –

He kissed her passionately, fully, in francophone combinations, with preludian intent – perhaps as a superior form of apology, but most likely as a mere surrender to sheer sensuality. Then he grew hard and was ready to spring it.

'Not quite here, lover,' she pillow-whispered. 'Not quite yet a moment. For what if we were to let our passions out in full force and roll into yon abyss?'

She had a point. Butterbugs, wordless and as if possessed, which he was, by her complete set of brilliant attractions, straightened all the way, gave her another big hand up, and, without losing any of their ignited hots, brushed themselves off and trotted briskly up the remaining flights. Past the wedding bell level, Butterbugs made goo-goo eyes over her trimly-placed assets of all kinds. He could hardly be blamed, especially after his semi-bumbling heroism.

The top. The Uppermost Penumbra Room. No exposed rafters here. Drywall installed yesterday. Walls painted last night, in very un-HMD saffron tones. Minimal decor – to emphasize the last CUs of the HMD at his zenith. No observation deck, per se. 2.76:1 aspect ratio windows all round. Superviews. Stunning, simply stunning.

Next: a flat place to lie, over there, a futon for crew-persons' break times. Good enough. Who cared? Young people in a hurry, a hot, hot hurry, with pulsating sex-exchange flurries to address: now, Now, NOW!

Hard hats ditched, clothes and costume ready to be shed, but there simply wasn't time. Some scraps of fabric would have to remain on. Because, though stripping is a very sexy act for both parties, right now, still in the lunch hour, automat impatience was peaking and there was sexier business to attend.

Juba almost literally dove onto the futon, flipped about and readied to de-drawer herself, while the dick of Butterbugs was delayed in making its entrance, simply because the ultrastar was mired – yes mired, in the maddening impracticality of extracting himself from the complications of the superb Walter Plunkett/Ann Roth costume, which happened to be one of this picture's more simplistic sets of HMD duds.

They actually gasped at the sight of each other, randy push-pulls in full spate, the kind of plush and perfect hotdog sex they show in the movies. But things were so real right now, that picture people wouldn't even be talented enough to invent a reasonable facsimile to stage for multi-take recreation in front of any camera.

The real thing, in its essential, blasting-caps-of-lust purity.

Then the two sex-kegs let out another kind of gasp, for there came a verbal influx from unexpected quarters that split their congress into a house officially divided – before it even had a chance to unite.

'Looks like your starring ass has seen some sense by coming up here, boh. 'Bout time!'

Hell's belles and likker cabinets, it was Old Atrocity! Just returned from a daring finishing-touch visit to the cupola's finial, which was now fine, dandy, and ready for photography. He beheld Butterbugs from behind the barrier of a half-height soft wall, so that only the star's head and upper torso gave the great Grip a portrait of a contemplating man in profile, looking diagonally down – a solo actor coming to terms with his weighty assignment ahead.

Down on the mat and still unseen, Juba knew what to do: enact the same trip that had worked so well in order to get through the Ogaden intact that time. She feigned infirmity. Sweated-up, slightly but fashionably disheveled, as befitting a showbiz context, this canny girl played her scene with aplomb.

'Oh, Glory-Gary!' OA ejaculated when he drew closer and saw whom Butterbugs was looking at so anxiously.

The actor's anxiousness was so pronounced, he didn't even become startled by this alarming interjection of OA-ishness. That old voice was so familiar and so comfy. And so famous for sounding off at the most remarkable times – none of them ever inopportune. Besides, there was no flagrante of the delicto variety to impugn, only a scene of incomplete possibilities. Thus, it was quite suited to a film-in-the-making's sensibilities.

Butterbugs kept staring at this splayed girl, who was almost in a Jane Russell pose, as in Howard Hughes' 'The Outlaw' (UA, c.1943), sans straw of course, but knowing the trustworthy veteran would approach with appropriate wisdom. As a consequence, HMD's wood became wet paper pulp in about four seconds, as if on command. So there was no telltale evidence to be found in the region of his rather tightly-drawn midsection.

But this was Old Atrocity here, the hippest dude on international filmdom's tech side. Hey, he'd not only be cool to let in, he'd dig the staging of such a tryst. No set had ever provided a more spectacular venue for gettin' it on at penthouse altitude.

Notwithstanding OA's reliable confidant/workmate's status though, Butterbugs and Juba both, without the need for any communication past a zeroed-in eye-link, elected to play the innocents. There was just too much on the communal plate of 'UWH''s Lasky Mesa location right now. Besides, both participants were a little embarrassed, she for botching her romantic interlude, and he for, well… falling *towards* temptation, for lack of a better term.

Butterbugs found some words.

'Old A – my, uh, dear fellow. Yes. My p.a. here, know her?'

'Juba X., I presume,' said the old pro. 'Girl-about-set. Is she OK?'

'An exercise in over-exertion, I should think.'

'You OK, Miss?'

'I'm… all right, Mr. Atrocity…'

'What the – Did y'all come up the peasant route or something?'

'We staired it, OA.'

'Shagbags! Let's get her some water or equivalent beverage.'

The Grip of Grips grabbed a flask of stone-water from the mini-bar just nigh and approached the significantly-quiet super-girl. As it happened, part of his crust-bucketness as a signature of his surface character was the fact that, in earlier days, he had done many a thumbful of snuff as a gentleman's diversion from the interminable tedium of soundstage filming, as is the Hollywood studio way. Therefore, his sense of smell was so diminished, he had no detection whatsoever of the positively smog-like eminence of sexually-aroused scents, distributed due to Butterbugs' influence over this quite splendidly-draped-and-poised production assistant.

'If you please, Miss… Just here… That's it… Slowly, slowly… We're gonna get ya rehydrated… Everything's gonna be OK… That's it… You're doin' fine… You can *do* this…'

So, the old letch of quality gave her liquid refreshment with much propriety, as they were in a Josiah Blimphurst Sunny-Baptist film, starring the always-virtuous Prenny Prinkles. A truly touching sight, and it betrayed OA's natural preponderance for helping little fuzzy attractive critters in need. Not to mention stately, stunning ladies of wit and elegance – in distress.

Butterbugs felt he'd just dodged a hail of bullets. One with OA concerning Juba, one with Juba's mishap, one with his preposterous prance near a death-shaft, one with avoiding authority, one with stumbling into a moat, and another with 'UWH' in general. And probably a flying bomb with the media, regarding any or all of these zanyisms. But most importantly, a projectile, fired point blank at his face, now remained, about a millimeter from his nose. An over-obvious reminder for an idiot, of the sacred recollection of his very own Heatherette, whose sustaining über-presence now returned to him. He was vastly relieved. Oh, but he would tell her about the episode, by all means, in detail, if she wished. Would Heatherette take it in with hospitality? She would. Oh yes, he *knew* she would, and without question. That's what their relationship was all about: a relationship without questions.

'There,' OA reported back to still-primed Butterbugs, 'I've refueled her. She'll be all right in a minute.'

OA paused next to the star, arms akimbo, regarding Juba like a problem solved, without really regarding the looks of the problem himself. Or herself.

'Well look, pal,' he addressed Butterbugs directly now. 'C'mon! Lemme shew ya some stuff.'

'So you think…'

'Yah, she's fine.'

Juba made eye contact with Butterbugs, signaling complete stability in her own dodging of uneven projectiles.

'We're going out on the ledge now, pallie-wallie,' said OA, virtually pulling Butterbugs away from his Juba-view. 'You can handle it. Whole route is lined with foot-grip tape.'

And indeed, it was true. Butterbugs felt like he was attached to four-wheel drive interlocked rails, as the tape on the ledge anchored walkers with almost magnetic security. They were about as exposed and out on the roof as was possible. There was every opportunity for breath to be taken away, even unto asphyxiation, so sweeping were the views. So dangerous to all gravitationally-bound life – so seemed this environment. But that darn tape kept such fears in check, so the thrill of it all was the exclusive emotion felt by both seasoned pros.

This monumental distraction also made Butterbugs realize the implications of the awkwardness with Juba, so that he successfully defused himself without having to do any acting. This was a key point in his quickly improvised quasi-deception, as few knew his acting style better than OA, who sensibly believed the situation as it appeared on the surface. Once they reached an inspection point that was safely railinged, allowing for a mind-churning vista almost 551 feet to the valley floor, OA drew close to the star and discreetly mentioned something of finger-snapping freshness.

'You know, a thought just occurred to me. Probably somethin' you haven't even thought of. You might just consider dating that there Somali prize, who lies a-recharging back in the Upper Penumbra Room! You know? She's a honey. A gem, doncha know! And I bet she'd be sweet on the idea!'

'*Sweet* on it?'

'Why sure...'

Never had Butterbugs seen OA so – he didn't know – naïve, or goofy, or fallen off the turnip trolley, or something. Proof that the old guy had an innate goodness about him, a benefit of the doubt, even after all these illustrious years in an often wry and cynical biz. Or maybe it was because he was dating that Chief Electrician he'd mentioned the other night. Electricians had a way of softening grips of the hardest core.

There was no wind way up here, and the masses below were ant-ized, but Butterbugs was fully sobered now, and he took a deep and judicious-appearing breath.

'I shall ponder the matter, OA. An intriguing possibility, to be sure.'

'Ponder?! What've you got to *ponder?* She looks like a million dollars! Acts like a million, too. Or two. An architectural build that just... won't... quit...'

'True! Too true! But in the meantime, my dear Genius of Operations, we've got a picture to finish.'

'That's the chorus I hear every hour, so it seems. But of course, you're bang-on. Lemme show you the lowdown, way up high.'

'You think she's OK?'

'It's only been a few minutes, B-bugs. She said she was better before we came out here. Guess you're *pondering* my bright idea after all, huh?'

Meanwhile, back on the futon, Juba slumped a bit, drooped a bit, then took a deep breath, put herself together a bit more and smiled broadly. Even with broadcast pheromones and a generously-lubricated essence, she could take a rain check on things hot & heavy. After all, she now knew he fancied her, and that sooner rather than later she would have his consent, thus mutualizing the inevitable. The water she drank was good, the sky without was blue, and all was welly-welly-well with the world.

Now involved with the facts and figures OA fed him like rich beer at this top o' the world pause, Butterbugs absolutely marveled at the structural detailing surrounding them as he looked down from this dizzying height. Heroic-sized cartouches and grotesques served as horror vacui filler, while the general surface upon which they were attached was embellished with the finest sgraffito and embossments, even in quarters never to be seen by the most prying of lenses.

Butterbugs gestured to these details, both immense and intimate.

'Was it all really necessary, or is this the worst kind of budgeting overkill?'

Privately, he was charged with a ticklesome faith in humanity – that persons of power would make such choices in selecting artistic enhancements as the preferred route to take when cladding buildings, even if they were for a mere picture show. Who better to lead the way to civilization's restoration than showbiz people of quality and taste?

Back at the futon, Juba was 'getting better' yet. All day she had been moving toward this heightened encounter, this protracted moment, and all day she had been subjectively preoccupied by Butterbugs on an imagined level. Why the hell *shouldn't* she place her emphasis on him, the most eligible bachelor in the known universe? Thus was based her horny but unimpeachable sincerity.

'As I said, OA, necessity or flight of fancy? Because, I *like* such flights.'

'Then you'll like this: if you must know, Bronston led the way in pushing for completeness, my Lord Highly-Mad. And you know why? He's right. New BKV Method stock, developed just before principal photo on 'UWH' rolled, is arrestingly hi-res, especially via Ultra-Panavision. You won't believe your jeepers-peepers when you see non-work-print, best-quality presentation. You know, when you see it in final theatrical. It even picks up flyspecks, pal. Every boil, every tear. Near and far. Gregg Toland was right those many years ago. Deep focus was the future, and with BKV, we're seeing what Toland's *mind* saw! The gang at MunnLabs is really going all out. Henri (Jaffa) and Morgan (Padelford) were just here, raving about the big screen bits they've seen back at the studio. Makes me wanna take an all-nighter and spend it in the projection room, but I've too much shakin' right here.'

'That being the case, dig it, and don't scrimp on the details!'

'You *know* it, baby.'

They started to head back, noting how steeply-raked the mansards were.

'Hey Butterbugs, I just have to say, this is the most high-tanked *gas* of a picture I've ever worked on! Can you *believe* it? It's going to be the absolute and ultimate in motion picture experiences. Of that I'm sure. I'm a total believer! Oh, I know what you'll say. What happened to my 'droll' demeanor? I had doubts at first, but now I know. I *know!*'

'You've been in on every element. Far more that I've been.'

'Yeah, and I don't have time to get into all the sympathetic slop of thanky-kind-lys or credit where credit is due, or anything…'

'We'll save that for the Wrap Party, OA. Plus, on that occasion, just a few days hence, I'll have a… *surprise*… for everyone at the party.'

'Well, well, well now…!'

OA grimaced knowingly and winked, nudging his hand toward where they knew Juba to be.

'Huh? Hmm?'

'Something like that – only I've discovered that –'

All of a sudden, a Buzz-Rang All-Encompassment Serial Informational Public Broadcast Bulletin pierced the air, filling the entire location with an audio announcement of great import. Art Gilmore's voice of authority was heard absolutely everywhere.

'This is Production Central from the Kiosk on the Mall, near the Actual Director's Chair. Request: will Butterbugs please report to the Advanced Viewing Loggia of the Palace set, within three quarters of an hour, so that long shot proceedings, needed for Scene 3701-D, may come to fruition? Apologies for this emergency interruption. Thank you…'

'Art's going to do the voiceovers for all 'UWH''s trailers,' said OA. 'That was firmed up today. Norman Rose is in, too.'

'Jiminy Crickets! – gotta go!'

'It's the lift for you,' said OA. 'I'll bring 'er up.'

'Yowzah, my friend, and leave us not forget my treasured p.a.'

'Oh, most assuredly, Butterbugs. I know. Wrap Party surprise and all…'

Butterbugs let it ride. How could he have the energy to explain all the right Heatherettian perimeters to everyone, regardless of their history with him?

Therefore, it was written that Butterbugs should approach Juba and say:

'I must head down to the needful. Will you come?'

OA stood behind him.

'Yes, Mr. Butterbugs. I am well now. Well enough. Thanks be to all!'

'I meant to ask…'

He approached her and gave her yet another big hand. He grasped her long, narrow fingers, and just for a second wondered how they might have felt around his balls, but –

Old Atrocity rode down with them in the VistaVue lift and proved to be a virtual chaperone, which for Butterbugs was good, though for Juba it was so-so. Had it been just the two of them, she would've proposed a quickie, for there was certainly time enough for two hopped-up candidates to pull it off. The lift traveled at one preset speed: pretty darn slow. Such was the calculation, to make the greatest effect in the grande finale shot, which still awaited its formal rehearsal.

However, the passengers were able to actually put themselves in the director's chair for a while, as if they were riding a camera crane on down. OA was reminded of J. Lee Thompson's 'Kings of the Sun' (UA, 1963) as far as logistical

crane-work integration was concerned. For all three professionals, the scene below was truly compelling in all its film-in-the-making manifestations, which were
quite simply as epic as the artistic product itself. The mind of every person down
there – many thousands at any one time – knew exactly what to do, not with ant-
like devotion, but with very human independence and critical thinking. And the
communal mind had only one priority… (that universally-known refrain will not
be needlessly repeated here…)

Because the call to service was a Listed Grade I Request, premium transport
was needed. A Wolseley Westminster Extended Wheelbase saloon awaited, with
Chief Driver Wilsey Pictoorblaup at the foot-feed, and au pair Nixie Bill-Bullen
riding shotgun. Like so many others this day, both had loyally served the ultrastar
on countless location shoots and backlot trolleyings, always in the best of rigs,
from oddball to godball.

Star and p.a. hopped into the back seat, positioned their lap robes, and prepared
to get lectured, a particular specialty of Wilsey & Co.

'Wow, Butterbugs, cuttin'' 'er close to the vine, aren't we today? Like that time you
almost missed the train out of Moldavia, me roddin' to get you to the station, cuz you
were lollygaggin' at the beer hall with all the little missies! Holy kasumbah!'

'Wilsey's right!' Nixie sounded off.

'Course I'm right. Close calls are fine, but on a picture like this…? I mean, *my
God!*'

'Wilsey's right!' added Nixie.

'Course I'm right. And that time in Yakutsk, when I had to get you to that private lunch date with Putin, and you were still dithering on which salt and which
bread to bring! Jeepers cramps!'

'Wilsey's right!' reinforced Nixie.

'Course I'm right. And that damn Ruta Nacional 81 in the Argentine, where I
had to yak at you for seven hours straight, all the way to the end of the road, cuz
you *wanted me to*, so's you wouldn't drift off 'n' fergit yer lines! Damn if *that*
wasn't a jimmy dickens of a night! Judas Priestus!'

'Wilsey's right!' Nixie chimed.

'Course I'm right. And that time up in northern BC, in the Dodge Charger R/T,
when you had me pick up them hippie hitchhikers, and they tried to share their
wax paper-wrapped fried chicken with us! Hell*fire!*'

'Wilsey's right!' confirmed Nixie.

'Course I'm right. And that –'

'Chide me not today, Wilsey. We've enough time. But I know you're right.'

'Course I'm right…'

Then, once they reached the straightaway to the Advanced Viewing Loggia of
the Palace set, the distinguished babe was put into overdrive, and they sped across
the plain with a rooster-tail of dust that rose higher than the Citadel just quitted.

And when they alighted at the huge plaza before the Palace, production could
now officially proceed.

'Grateful thanks, Wilsey-cum-Nixie! And you're *both* right, as usual. And when you're right, you're *right!*'

'*Course* we're right!' concluded Nixie.

Juba and Butterbugs ascended the wide, wide steps.

'Our star is back amongst us, crew and associates!' announced Egaz, with appropriate decorum. He was enjoying this final countdown as much as any, perhaps more than every. His inventiveness was so in-play and his confidence in creation via the conduit of the cinema had sustained him in his deliverance of masterful and inspired results.

Even though the Citadel was plainly there across the valley, no one could have guessed the vast heights from which Butterbugs and his assistant had just arrived. But that wasn't the point. It was supremely important that the script and its story be enacted upon these specially prepared environments, all just at hand. Thus were such matters as personal desires and wishful gestures reduced in the gargantuan perspectives of this picture's mechanics.

'Welcome back, boy!' the director called out. 'I was beginning to think that you had eloped!'

Jests were still fresh from the other night at The Lazaretto.

'I say, Egaz, I have a young lady here, my p.a. of the day, Juba, who needs to be in this scene. Can you accommodate her? She is SAG-current. Any assigned dialogue attached would be appreciated.'

Egaz was all about nimbleness, inventiveness, adaptability and experimentation – all simultaneously – even as he captained this Jupiter-sized production. In fact, he had become even more flexible in the crucible of its testing, and had achieved a capability of thinking in virtual parallel universes regarding the construction of this filmic monument. Some people in this world can actually do such things. Most can't. He was one who not only could, he got better at it with each succeeding hour. Plus, he was having a ball. It was plain to see, and his facility, combined with Butterbugs' incandescent effects, made for a sort of elevated state of consciousness out here at Lasky Mesa.

'An accommodation? Why, of course, Butterbugs. I think we might be able to line something up. I'm doing some improv inserts today. Well, way past improv, actually. Juba? Welcome! Let's see. Sawl & Co. submitted a new scene only this morn. A monologue that I see as very important. Well, it's vital, really. Vital for dimension reflected by HMD's victory interpretations. I like this scene. I only just scanned it. Haven't read every word of it. Don't need to. I know it already. Yes. It's going in. Oh, this is fantastic! Your timing on the scene is inspired. I was *just wondering* who might act it, as every single player in the valley is locked into their assigned roles. I was having to face the possibility of airlifting 87-year-old T'zukkah Muantmuorentsy – who would be perfect – in from West Texas, but she's so frail, the journey might kill her...! And it would cause an extra day's shooting (if she survived!). A-heh! But Juba! Juba, Juba, yes, let's see. All right. *You*, Juba, will be Yimvinctrah, the Indoctinaire Liaison! Settled. Børnie? Con-

tract, please & thanks – short form. Juba? You are she who stands as chief hyp-
ocrite in league with HMD, spreading his BS so as to gain support amongst the
bewildered classes. However, I think Sawl deemed it wise to use her as a rotating
weather vane in revealing HMD's true self before the masses. I think so, anyway.
So, as you utter the lines, they will be the first time any of us have heard them. We
will act upon them, because we will *have* to. We will be compelled, naturally, but
it will be a willing conformation. I dare to take up this uncertainty because Sawl
has proposed it at this late date, and I trust Sawl implicitly, as I trust Butterbugs.
And I trust his trust in you, Juba. Therefore, I trust you equally, as well. It's a
small, but key, role. OK? Can you take it up?'

'Oh, y-y-yes, Mr. D'Varzim! Might I memorize s-script?'

'Naturally. Keenah's my script-girl today.'

'*Hi*, beloved Keenah!' said Butterbugs.

'Hi, my maestro!' she answered, then handed the necessary text to Juba. 'Egaz?
I'll brief her on stage directions and stuff. She'll be ready to shine in just a few
jiffies!'

Script clutched to her breasts, Juba staggered, albeit gracefully, over to the
ultrastar, who began quick-scanning his own lines. She drew close to his ear for
privacy.

'O-h-h, n-n-n-noble B-b-butterbugs!' she hiss-pered, practically hiccuping, 'I
thought – I thought you said – such a role would be possible on the morrow – n-n-
not right *n-n-NOW!*'

'By golly!' he exclaimed out loud, 'I guess I forgot! No big deal! We'll all help
ya through!'

'But – but – but – Really?? W-w-will you?'

'No more worries in this universe, Juba! We'll help you with that stammer too.
If it's a problem! (But I think it's only temporary.) *Later!*'

Keenah then hustled her off to Costuming. It was with a purgative sigh of
relief that he now looked after the wonderful backside of Juba, fast receding.
He couldn't help but note, wistfully, a bit of annotation regarding the two who
were now arm-in-arm: Keenah, whom he'd fully accessed, and Juba, whom he
could've.

In fact, the two gals hit it off instantly, and would serve each other in their
newly-engaged tasks.

'Heatherette?' he murmured to himself, 'Why didn't I just bring you along for
the week? *You* could've taken the role of Yimvinctrah…!'

But then he resumed his line-study.

The activity on set was tremendous. Camera and track placement, crew com-
munications, makeup touch-uppers, smoke-effect techs, mike-boom trials, light
focusing, blocking adjustments, a.d.s barking, extras milling, testing, testing, 1-2-
3… Places, everyone. Action imminent…

With no time for further Heatherette or Juba musings, he allowed a tad for
beloved Keenah.

'From star-girl to script-girl, in one easy – backward – step…! Apparently…' After all he'd done to promote Keenah's acting career, he wondered about the propriety of this latest discovery. Then he remembered: she was married up now. To the director.

All Keenah's scenes had been in the can for some time, so she relished her script-girlishness with her husband at the helm, but only on an informal basis, so as not to nudge rightful others out, like Bibsey, who was mega-busy elsewhere on this sequence. In fact, it was Bibsey who'd requested the helping hand. This was a very *moral* production as far as consideration of its makers was concerned. Nobody got left behind, or out. Quite frankly, there was morality everywhere. Nobody was saying things like: 'I deserve that (role/duty/position) just as much as that ignorant little *jerk!*'

Egaz approached.

'I'm glad you brought forth Juba, Butterbugs. Very opportune. I saw her in 'Punt' (WB) and was turned on.'

'So am – I mean, so was – Yes, that's swell.'

'Mmm, what a contraption!'

'She's not just a sex-thing ya know, Egaz.'

'No? I, I mean, I know. Yes, I know, Butterbugs. You may not believe me, but on a Jambutter flight recently, Juba and I sat across the aisle from each other. I was sort of thinking of Keenah a lot. Juba was reading a book. So I asked her about it. Incredibly, for the next six hours we discussed Schopenhauer. Kant. David Strauss. And, Nietzsche, natch. She's really interested in revaluing all values.'

'Oh. Well, I didn't know *that*. That's good…'

'Yes it is. Very good.'

'Say Egaz, I just wanted to quickly say something.'

'Ja, mein Herr?'

'I just wanted to say, I'm… I'm really *glad* that you and Keenah are, you know, together. And please, don't say that you wouldn't be together if it wasn't for me…'

'OK! Thanks, B-bugs. We're glad too. And yes, grateful. Now… Here's Juba's lines. Take a look, but don't tell me! You two have some fun with the thing. My crew and I are made of Plasticine. We'll adapt!'

'OK' was all Butterbugs said, after he glanced at the new script.

'Now, all, *places*. Everybody report to their coordinates, now, please.' Then, to Butterbugs, 'And by that time, our new cameo will be ready, and her lines must be spoken with golden intent, as they are a sendoff into the future of this picture's message to the world.'

Egaz really *lived* the Epic Life.

'This sequence comes into play, sir, as it should,' said Butterbugs, who was beset upon by touch-up wizards and primpers, some of whom were puzzled by the displacements down in the crotch zone, but who gingerly restored correctness where it was needed, and with maximum discretion.

The assemblage of filmmakers and their charges then did what they were placed in this world to do: to stage a complex and transcendent scene before a series of cameras, so as to record them for public consumption and consideration.

In this particular master shot, which would be captured as the day grew long and the memories of the masses turned to the way the world was *before* the High Mad Doctor's new era, a procession of slaves passes by the tribune, all lighted in the reddest of sunsets.

The sunset was right on cue, too.

There stands the HMD, with the stoniest of faces, listening without emotion to 'The Song of the Outgoing Ones', and 'The Plea For Farewells On Into The West' (both composed and now conducted on the spot by Alfred Newman, sung by the Hall Johnson Choir, Jester Hairston, conductor; with the essential Ken Darby, vocal coordinator), which, in its very first bars, broke the hearts of anyone and everyone who heard it (including Butterbugs the Man – though not Butterbugs the Actor).

[Between shots, Butterbugs gave Alfred a jingle across the way. Asked how things were going, the Maestro replied: 'Fine and sugar-dandy, Sir Knight. We've got our own special terrace over here. Hardwood floor, too. A helluva lot better than that on-location golf course me and my band had to play on, accompanying Jolson and Langdon *live* in, 'Hallelujah, I'm A Bum' (UA, 1933). The grass was wet, no even ground, and the 7th hole sand-trap almost swallowed us up.']

So the great sad and soulful hymn accompanied the somber procession as it passed into the sunset, and there were many in the court who looked after them with tears inside, for they knew those who departed into exile and bondage were the last righteous ones, who now faced certain death in the distant mines of the HMD's mineral strategies, in order to keep the world within his sway.

The music built up, and built higher, and built highest, and it maintained its power all the way, so as to contrast with the shallow iron tyranny of the new world's regime. Not for a second was the significance of both sound and image to be squandered on mere sensation. For, at this late point in a very long picture, there were still sections of the heart to melt with unprecedented emotion. In this case, via musical breaker-bars. Hearts would indeed bust up, and for the greatest of dramatic reasons, as there was a pukka climax that now impended.

But here, in processional arrangement, cameras rolled, big-time.

In her preset place in the foreground of the shot, Juba's heart fell from her soul. Acting gears engaged. In her filmy robes, she slowly came up the pantheonic steps, and, in an expansive gesture toward her mourned-over ones, she framed the crisis around not only her own private thoughts, but of those who now marched against their will, away, and toward nothingness.

(Camera, on crane, has YIMVINCTRAH *[as played by Juba Xudr] in MLS, in a diagonal composition, due to the short-rise Palace steps. During her speech, moderately-slow crane-dolly in further, achieving big CU of her by the end of her speech. Take will continue via a crane sweep over to* HMD, *for his response, in MCU.)*

YIMVINCTRAH: *(over music themes, continuing, as a counterpoint to her speech)* I see multitudes moving away, away from this place of building-up, away from things assembled, and into the scattered realms of unhappy life broken apart by unconventionality and undesirability. I pray that you hear me, Leader, for this is my prestige effort, to be placed before your omniscient face. Oh, but is this a lost opportunity? Am I its only witness? There go those who might have served you, if only the lash had been replaced by the olive branch! Do any of you know how savory-sweet such a switch is, on one's quietened being? Taking a respite from the burden of such severity, the soul rests and re-evaluates its role in this, a safe shell, from which there is a chance to make a statement of – I dare not say on these steps, except to mold certain words in an order that can be disassembled, if necessary – and probably at my peril. So: in my humble but expert opinion, I DO NOT THINK IT WISE TO DEPORT THOSE WHO WOULD OTHERWISE SERVE THE CENTRAL CAUSE, IF THE CENTRAL CAUSE WAS SOMETHING THEY COULD RELATE TO, SOMETHING THEY COULD BELIEVE IN. *SOMETHING OF VALUE.* Oh, High *Mad* Doctor! You, who stand up there and are my permanent idol, hear me please! Those without, who have overpowering love, and those who lately depart – they have so much love in their beings for you! Love is really a factor here. For it is the basis of devotion. The devotion of family values, the devotion of one lover to another, the devotion of political loyalties, the devotion of citizen to leader, the devotion of subject to all-powerful and powerfully benevolent and just and wise and wonderful ones – just *one* – such as you. You! YOU! Love expands if it is given a quarter of a chance. From there, it attaches to the flimsiest of parallels. Will you not support my dream with a symphonic and choral matrix? *(gestures toward the departing ones)* Ah! Listen to them! You tolerate it! So! You do! And it does not aid me! Listen to their poignancy! Their pleas, amidst the resignation! Can't you hear it? Is your heart not approached by those of humbleness, those who have humility? They are not merely conquered, they are really expectant of great things from your goodself! They will respect you with highest respect, if given that quarter chance! Even a 64th of a chance! Indeed, the most insignificant of chances... The chance of a lost cause being reversed. So you let them sing their song-cycle of departure and passing-on, and their leave-taking. The sad beauty of an abschied! You make your point. Yet, *their* point is stronger than *your* point! Do you hear? They sing from their souls, and so I ask, with deep respect, Leader of My Life, do you really hear them? Can you imagine? It is not difficult for persons with hearts to witness these poor rejects and their advance into their oblivion? Would that I could go their way, if only to hear of the events which might pass between the bulwark of your High Mad everyday life, and so as to delve into a deeper descent into documentarianism as such reason and intelligence might illuminate... For beyond the You-set limits of impossible mind, can we not venture in ways above even the topmost finials of citadels (which I have lately visited), where lie imaginings beyond even your ten-thousand-year timeframes, that come to be frayed in the endless winds of human-oblivious elemental forces? Remember, you are mortal, Leader! That is a happy thing. Indeed, a happy thing for this world! That's what this is all about, isn't it? You are as mortal as those you send to their certain deaths. That is why you send them out wholesale and with their sad presentation. You think that by letting them have their sorrow so displayed, it will serve your cold concrete promise of ego-based control! Instead, who has not been moved by their hymns? By the dignity of their music alone, you should be vanquished, for you are not worth one eighth of the waste products lately shrove off by these banished/condemned ones. I would indeed treasure their cast away shit in comparison with your ersatz and psychodramatic life-grasp. Listen to them! Don't you know how to be affected? No? You stand there in sullen priggishness, devoid of feeling or talent. You are a machine, efficient perhaps, but deadly-dull in your reflection of life. A greasy gear turning here, a punch-down die, cast there. So what! You have arrived at an unprecedented point of the human experience. Nothing could be more vapid and boring. What do we have to look forward to? Ten thousand years of your tedium – grim, selfish, sniveling, mind-numbing. Of course, you will take pleasure in that. Your revenge. You send persons to their unwarranted deaths because you hate yourself. How can I tell? Because you plainly hate yourself more than you hate anyone else. You are not trained to hate anyone more than yourself. You simply don't know how to do it. Did you know that? How could you! You are hardly eligible for excuses, though. You are beyond any. And because your survival instinct cannot allow *self*-destruction (sadly), you must enact it on countless others. You will preserve yourself all right, but the whole world must pay the price. It is an immutable truth that –

HMD: *(growing impatient, and now, fed up)* Enough.

YIMVINCTRAH: *(noting his displeasure)* So! Your petulant pants have tightened around your insipid scrotum? Tired of my rant? Go ahead, blowhard, spew your indigestible lint! Give it the full force of your mediocrity, the genius of your dumbshittedness, the action of your skuzzy –

(HMD *raises his Slammszchupp mace into the lurid sky. It is a signal for the* MUVUPPIAN GUARD *to close in on* YIMVINCTRAH, *who nevertheless stands firm. The camera follows all this action in the same fluid take.)*

YIMVINCTRAH: *(not resisting her restrainers, but maintaining her impressive stance)* You, are the fucking most murderous bastard of all time. Not just our own time, either. Something to be proud of. Something to get you destroyed, which, I should think, is not according to your plan. That's my curse upon you. You'll have to live with it, for a time perhaps, and then you'll have to die with it. You will find out. I'm not going to be around to see it. But that's fine with me. Profoundly ugly things disgust me. I will be seeing to the needs of my people, instead of gawping at some bone-bunioned and profoundly excremental fuckface like you...

(HMD, *having heard beautiful* YIMVINCTRAH *bare her soul on this subject, and because he cannot function with women, whom he might love – (or fancy, as his capability to love is not at all a given) – and because female influences upon his absolute reign are a mortal threat to him, decides to eject all in front of all, and with all's approval. This, as a cheap-ass, up-front display of his all-power: fully and 24/7-erect GripPower, in Masses'-Proof ™ undeniability. The point here, in his character's role, is to establish a reticence in any power relinquishment or alteration. Therefore, the weaker elements of his edifice must take up the strongman's burden.)*

HMD: *(truly enraged, but with impressive power through restraint)* Then go! Then you just go, and get out! GET OUT! Go with all those dirty dirge-wailers with whom you sloppily sympathize, and play your own gross-out fugue! You shall not only join them, you shall be in their dust-clogged rear, and in shackles, for by your bogus revealment, you have signed your license over to those un-people who you are so in love with! You are now one of them, my onetime sex-slave! You are now an UN-PERSON. You want to know what a curse is like? I'll show you and it'll be rammed down your rotting throat, that vomits forth such unspeakability! Go, un-person that you are, and begin your entropy! Go and decompose in obscurity! A curse is only a statement, and I let you have your say. *(to THE MASSES:)* Didn't I, subjects? Did you not witness my charm and magnanimity in indulging her hogwash? (THE MASSES *offer their approbation; then, addressing* YIMVINCTRAH *directly:)* So, you 'curse' me, do you? Hah!

Hah-hah-hah! Empty, empty non-words from an un-person! Take note now, 'Unny', as I not only curse *you*, but I enact my own curse sent. I stand behind my words, unlike your little yak-wobblings. When I fling out a curse I back it up, because I have the power and also the integrity to do so! Unlike your little mewlings and pukings. *(rambling on, because her curse has genuinely freaked him out)* You know, I don't mind saying this in public, but because you were so sexy to my tastes, I had *plans* for you! You could have sat at my right, and in between sessions of licking my pecker – a duty most of the world would give their right souls for, I might add – you have elected, by your traitorous sentiments, to leave off to failure, while championing a brief sustenance within a fading belief that what you did was right. How pathetic! *(almost effeminate)* It's just... pathetic! See how charitable I am? I use words like 'pathetic' to describe you, even at this point, even after you have hurt my feelings so with your calumny – and in front of all my friends, too! Your attempt to slime me has failed totally, and everyone here has seen you do it. Some might question why I allowed you to rattle on so, but it is a signal example of my fairness and my balancedness. None can contest my sincerity! Thus, they've seen the totality of your failure. That alone is why I look so good to my peoples. And I *always* look good, baby! They regale me with PRAISE, NOW DON'T THEY???

(The crowd cheers in huge waves of sound, drowning out the song of the departing ones. The MUVUPPIAN GUARDS *slaveringly strip* YIMVINCTRAH *of all her clothes, and though she stands nude, it is not with humility. In fact, it increases her nobility and her resolve. They drape her in rough lime-coated burlap and hustle her down to the floor of the plaza, where the grim single file of exiles shuffles. The* MUVUPPIAN GUARDS *take perverse pleasure from watching* YIMVINCTRAH *suffer from the effects of her torturous costume on her skin, until she can join them, last in line. As they slowly withdraw from the scene, the music draws down as well. Sequence intercut with varying POVs, including from high on the Apex Parallel.)*

(Cut to huge CU of YIMVINCTRAH, *who is no longer able to speak, but her full lips part, as if...)*

(Cut to matching CU of HMD.*)*

HMD: *(quietly, not revealed publicly)* I loved you, Yimvinctrah! *(a lengthy pause, in which his expression reveals conflict, but only on a selfish basis, as pity or regret are both impossible for him to feel; then, with a sort of evil satisfaction:)* But now you must die.

(Geo. Stevens-type dissolve into stationary GS of YIMVINCTRAH *being taken down to the humiliating position of rearmost exile. Sndtrk: intense orchestral interlude of Newman's 'Departure' theme, infinitely tragic and sad; chorus resumes when progression continues anon.)*

(Stevens half-dissolve into new CU of HMD, *with the setting sun making his face florid, while the sorrowful scene of her departure prep remains in the dissolve's other half.)*

HMD: *(almost jauntily)* There she goes! Off to her destiny of dust... and, and... digging her own grave. That's what we make sub-humans like *her* do! That is what must be done! Because... because, they are so polluted. Therefore, my proclamation will be law. For I am the greatest Chief Martial Law Administrator ever! We shouldn't have to touch anything having to do with them – these un-people. So, does anyone here feel sorry for her? *(sounds of 'no, no')* She did it to herself. All of you saw her do it! I tried to stop her! Does anyone wish to go with her and help her with stuff? *(no sounds at all)* I like the sound of that no-sound! It says it all. *(his voice almost wavers; then, with pumped-up enthusiasm:)* Therefore, I say to you, will you, my Loyalites, will you not come in and party in my Rather Generous Space For The Masses, while I and my select few do the same on my upper level, so that I can watch and see which ones of you are *truly* loyal to me? If you are, great rewards await, and along with them, a few great treasures, and more!

(HMD's expression betrays a true sense of loss, but without its comprehension. His slide into silence implies a sort of inner devastation. For a second he almost reverses his act, but pardoning her would reveal his weakness. Oh, why did she do this to him? Why did she speak the truth? So, he lets her go, he lets it all go, and in this beautifully-composed state of sustained dual-image dissolve, he shows all this, through his visage alone.)

(Stevens dissolve, fully into MLS of YIMVINCTRAH, *in her burlap robe, shackled by those who once knew her as a princess, heading away from the camera, and into an almost lyrical cow-dust time, with its golden motes caught by the setting sun. Cut to big CU of* YIMVINCTRAH, *dollying with her, at her slow gait. Spangles gather on her hair and tunic, a sort of benediction of unknown but beatific significance, which is entirely lost on* HMD. *She has an ecstatic expression, implying liberation. While he is a tragic figure, he is not poetic in the least, and* YIMVINCTRAH's *departure is tragically poetic. Cut to medley of associated shots to cover the scene in general. The chorus resumes for a time, then music reverts to*

orchestral variation, which fades as the company heads out for the long trek into the toxic wilderness of Gnulb.)

(Fade-out.)

'Oh, now CUT! Cut, my friends! Was that not fine? I think so! I cannot help but think so! Oh, my Community, are we not all en*riched?*'

And then the director whispered to himself, 'A masterpiece of performances; I know it is. I shall send a gold bug to Sawl and all, and diamonds to Juba, and a star-like mantelpiece to Butterbugs, as tokens of my appreciation of their adaptability and reasonableness, not to mention their creation/invention. Great speeches! Juba – instant success of genius! The inculcation-thought of Butterbugs *worked* on her! No second take possible! Plus, I just love to be surprised. I cannot believe the unadulterated luck we are having. This is what creative bliss is like. I am living it.'

Then, onward, to a pipsqueak of a scene in comparison. It was the 'Light Supper of the Fabled' Sequence:

(HMD, attempting some sort of show-offy gentility after his act of very public banishment, so as not to let his unbridled savagery hog the lime-light, hosts a late feeding of lem-chow for a small circle of VIPs and elite intimates. It is a high-dress occasion though, and the leader is duded up in fanciness, his appearance dominated by a huge satin bow tie, à la Randi Chuzzlewit, of disturbing dark blue hue, and the ladies are all crinoline and cleavage and pearls. KAMMAH, one of HMD's favorites of late, [here played by Doutzen Kroes] *sits across the circular table from HMD, and gazes at her lover with seductive and knowing expressions.)*

This scene, shot by both Shamroy and Surtees, was specially lighted by the great Arthur Miller, who was joyfully brought in for a cinematographic cameo. He cast it in dark tones of turquoise and brown, set amongst profounder shadows. Lyle Wheeler, Mark-Lee Kirk, and Gaultier designed and dressed the set with ob-noxious French curves of cold old gold chromium, heavy draperies spilling onto the floor, and a cartoonish but predictably baleful sort of octopus thing lurking on the ceiling, done up in spangly plaster. The general effect was luridly dreamlike, though not nightmarish.

(THE DINERS at table engage in chatter, with no perceivable dialogue emerging. HMD catches sight of KAMMAH's sexy overtures, done via playing with her food and the best kind of solicitous looks. He responds with somewhat receptive awareness. An exchange of CUs between them

follows, each one successively closer. KAMMAH's *expressions now border on the frankly lewd.)*

(Then, in MS, KAMMAH, in key-lighted glow, with flanking DINERS in turquoise shadow, makes her next move most obvious: with her right index and middle fingers, she reaches under the table, negotiates the mass of her full and billowy 1840s-style dress, and pulls at her delicate bikini lingerie until it snaps in two – a moment that makes her jaw drop with horny excitement – and, with her face continuing to narrate the process in wordless manner, she then gathers a generous sampling of natural vaginal lubrication – currently in high production – and then her fingers gracefully emerge from that mysterious realm with the product intact. As camera dollies in slightly over the table, KAMMAH stylishly advertises her prize with balletic hand gestures, the moistness glinting like jewelry in the cold warmth of the mood light. CU of HMD, definitely paying attention, whilst the perverse small talk continues round the table.)

DINER #1 *(in shadows; with interest)* [as played by Richard Pasco] Now, what's that bouquet? Some hors d'œuvres that escaped my hot little frisky clutches? Huh? *(no one replies).*

(KAMMAH then rises and sashays around to HMD's side. Her now split-crotch panties, having dropped, trophy-like, onto the void-like floor, merit their own cool key-light, while her form, still bathed with an illumination that effortlessly travels with her, as if it emanates from within, passes by the insignificant DINERS, who remain in shadow.)

(KAMMAH then draws close to HMD's right, and bends down, as if to give a kiss. However, she does not. Instead, she elegantly sweeps her right-hand fingers around, still loaded with the fresh and private lube, and playfully smears them on HMD's problematic but ruling upper lip, then places them in her own mouth and sucks.)

KAMMAH: Hmm! Good! *(she gives a soft bedroom-giggle, and makes to return to her place setting).*

HMD: WAIT! *(considers her for a few seconds, then, quieter)* – 'Dear one'. You have just dared to *touch* your Leader and Teacher in the flesh, and without his permission. Do you know what that means?

(The table goes utterly silent.)

KAMMAH: But, my porno-lord – You cut me to the quick! I had no intention of –

HMD: *(angry, but contained)* You dared! Now I command!

KAMMAH: *(entreatingly)* I am your body-slave!

HMD: Yes, well, I have been without issue of edicts on your behalf, but now you have gone too far. *(twitches and wrinkles his nose, implying annoyance and discomfort, if not battery, while actually and deeply inhaling the ambrosia of her perfume box).*

KAMMAH: But you usually let me – nay, *command* me – to go *much further* with –

HMD: Silence! Shall we...?

(To fully establish and embolden the new officialness of his consummately misogynistic policies, lest another uppity Yimvinctrah personality raise her beautiful but tempting head, HMD now embarks on his harsh declaration. He is proud of the craftiness and good sense of such emergency preparedness.)

HMD: I now ejaculate this edict. If I can't have obedient courtiers, then, by Wally, I will *e-dict* them! Hear! Take this wenchy whore out onto the Platform and away, away from my discomfort, and *destroy* her! Oh, I weary of 'mates'. They are so careless and dumb! They disabuse their positions of hyper-privilege! I say this now! And now, again! What a hassle they are! I've changed, people! I'm going to get into loving *myself* much more from now on. Oh, YEAH! If I want a dalliance, I'll let you know! We do things *my way*, see? *(to the CAWLTRONIAN GUARDS, just at hand)* Take her. Destroy her. Now leave me to my pudding in peace!

KAMMAH: *(scared and shocked, but strong)* But, honey-pile, you always used to *love* that! *(makes a wiping gesture across her own upper lip).*

HMD: *(to himself)* She is right... She had a gift! *(inhales fully and exhales almost wistfully)* But now she, too, must die... I must prove myself to my people... I *must*. Her destiny. My duty.

The following sequence was already in the can:

(CAWLTRONIAN GUARDS hustle KAMMAH indelicately out of the chamber. One of them slips on the shiny and slick panties, and makes a fool out of himself, though HMD does not notice. Music cue is 'Stealing Away'. Clearly sympathetic with KAMMAH, the CAWLTRONIAN GUARDS have no intention of performing her execution. An unsuspecting substitute will be found. In the gloom of the exiting corridor, some of them make grabby and improper advances to her, but CAWLTRONIAN CHIEF PAZAH censors them and safely delivers her by torchlight to the quarters of VUZZAPC, the Sub-Vizier-cum-Dewan in Charge of General Payroll [played here by Vincent Price] *who has championed CAWLTRONIAN CHIEF PAZAH in the past. KAMMAH is relieved and delighted, and the trio do a 3-way before making their prudent and successful escape.)*

(Cut to fuller CU of HMD.*)*

HMD: *(still to himself)* **By my wholly effective demonstrations of tight control over the comings and goings of lifes and deaths under my permanent watch, thus do I show my proof to my peoples of the world. Let 'em know my sexings, my habits, my tastes, then! All the better to weld fear into their hearts and stanch their intentions before they are even embryonic!** *(inhales in a big cocaine-like snort, then wolfs down a huge chunk of dry-pudding)* **Hmm! Good!!** *(gives an arid and narcissistic chuckle).*

'Oh, yes – that's a CUT! Indeed! It's special!' Egaz enthused. 'And super-big thanks to our Arthur, for his Artistry. Arthur, you are blessèd! A big hand for him now, and for all his crew! Lyle, Mark-Lee, Jean-Paulie, take a bow! Doutzen, darling, aren't we all glad you get to escape? (Oh, *what's that bouquet?*) Hah, and heh!'

Everyone cheered in total agreement. Doutzen K. gave Egaz a big smooch. Even Butterbugs applauded, as he was still stuck as HMD for a time.

It was past eleven in the PM.

Porter Parker himself picked up Butterbugs and Juba in the Dodge convertible and headed for Calle Rarefied. Almost immediately, the two actors zonked-out in the back.

Porter was kind of *hopped-up* about something, and it wasn't newlywed-dom in this instance. He was all swirly and grinning, with cheeks like baked apples, twirling and shining.

'You know, Butterbugs, I'm *so* glad we're all very much on top of this production. I know *I* am!'

Butterbugs was adrift and almost proto-snoring, his and Juba's heads taking turns wobbling over the 'V' emblem that emblazoned the rear speaker grille between them.

'And now, after all we've been through, you 'n' me, I think I've finally developed big enough balls to give you the bird's eye lowdown on a little – no, pretty darn big – private secret I've toted about my now-sleek person, for so long. Listen up, OK?'

No response from out back.

'Great! Finally got them ears of yours! You're not in on this, Juba, but that's fine. You were absolutely terrific on the set today, by the way. Glad you have such a photographic memory for those pages 'n' pages of dialogue! Your perf seals this thing as a classic! So dig my praise lovely one, while B-bugs and I commune. Cuz this is a historical thing. Nothing to do with 'Unholy', but everything to do with me. Oh, and uh, you too, Butterbugs. Ya see, it's like this. One time, before we even knew each other, we were on the same set. Really! But let me tell you. It was that big 20th-Fox re-film scene, you know, that Darryl commanded. The logo deal, that your mug – er, heh-heh, visage – still graces! We rubbed shoulders in the big ol' mob scene, and I heard you say they should just *rotate* that monster set piece so it could be photographed without the big re-schedule nightmare. Well, you know me! All right now, don't bust my shoes or anything. Don't get mad before I finish, OK? I know you know where this is going, and all. Well, I cribbed yer idea about the rotation thing. Hell, *I* didn't know it could do that, but I figured you were a grip or something, and knew what the hell you were talking about. Producers like me gotta take *chances*, ya know. (Or crap-shoots!) I mean, for crying Pete Parker's sake Butterbugs, *you* weren't gonna trot up there like I did and tell 'em what to do! Were ya? So anyway, they liked my – er, *your* idea, and word got to Darryl, who knighted me then and there, and I was off and running. Rest is history! So thanks, big guy. Thanks for the break. I really mean it. That's it. That's the whole thing. This has really been bugging me, Bb, and now I'm tickled that my jig is up! Hope you're not mad at me, and that you never *will* be, ever again!'

Still, after such earthshaking truths, there was non-event reaction from the back seat. Just a few crude sleep-snorts, drowned out by the rig's dual resonator rumble. Porter figured he'd blown 'em into ecstasy by his triumphant becoming-clean.

'You showed us what we're made of today, so that's what gave courage to, you know, let you in on my little – no, *big*... secret...'

Porter thus concluded his remarks, to both, hoping they could now all have a good day's-end review, as a wrap-up. However, none was forthcoming. He glanced in the handy, dash-mounted mirror. Their babe-sleep in back told him he'd achieved total success with his come-to-Jesus integrity.

'From confessor to *protector!*' he mused, stumbling upon a new role: that of Father Hen to the world's most valuable player in pictures – and his probable lover and possible future wife(?).

'Am I a lucky duckling, or what?'

He hummed merrily, then broke into an Irish tenor-ish warble, pinching the old Jare Panklooby tune:

'On account of all our *love* for him
Our boff for him, our goff for him
Our helmets and mobcaps *doff* to him
Our liberty-belling playing *off* of him…!

Wellllllllll… then…
You just… gotta… *love*… him!
Cuz he's rarefied and always standing TALLLL
Dooby-pubba-bubba-prango-jibbston-DAAAALL
Cuz we're bonafide to come at his beck and CRAWL!
To never swerve
To stay in the curve
In order to serve
…buh-bub-bub-buh-buh *buh*…
Poosh!' [high-hat imitation, this]
That greatest nice-guy-actor *of them ALLLLLLL!!!!'*

On that last, particularly cracked note, the two passengers snapped awake, almost simultaneously. Porter, cheerily piloting the huge convertible into the residentia zone now, fell silent as well, glorying in his self-induced relief, his sincere words back in the dust somewhere never having traveled through the ear canals they were meant for.

He, the great nice-guy-actor, brooding and handsome, makeup-free, woken, yet somewhat pensive, as if he almost took to heart his harsh banishment of a beautiful girl called Yimvinctrah (the mildest of his character's deeds of the day) whose body was next to him right now. In reality, hardly banished at all. In addition, he was drained, his energy having been sucked out by the virtuous one's going into exile, and the sexy one's unexpected and covert escape to happiness.

She, Juba of the here and now, awakened, post-costume, returned to her neat little getup, her head back, gazing out at the brightening stars above. She herself was pleasantly exhausted, all her force having been withdrawn by facing the tyrant up on the podium.

So, after Porter smilingly dropped them off and parked the rig, and saw they were in the front door, he, the line producer on this massive production, having revealed his secret (if only to himself), modestly took off on foot and walked through the dust and darkness two miles to his own wife, who ecstatically awaited in their humble hogan.

'I did it, babe!' he announced to Joby. 'I'm glad you talked me into it! Now I'm free as a bubble, and ready for love!'

Butterbugs and his p.a.-cum-supporting actress both entered his Kelat Hall quarters in a sort of magical haze. Having achieved high art without pretension in their own ways, they could bathe in the afterglow, without concern for its identification or dimensions. Such a condition was part of the rarefied delights that allowed those fortunate enough to cross over into that quasi-state that defies chart-ing or documentation. This was the land that Butterbugs dwelt in much of the time, and it was the reason that, as a person, he might be circumscribed, in the opinion of others, as having his head in the clouds... For lack of a better term.

Then they got a second wind and kicked back with a couple of fashionable bread-dough/orchid drinks.

'Juba, you were nothing short of superlative today. I have never heard a soul at work as much. You will be what the audience *remembers* in this whole important sequence.'

'You are too generous, my lord.'

'Your character is the surprise. I don't want to indulge a comparative perspec-tive, but we did, after all, share this scene, and, and... wow! Because, my charac-ter is predictable. HMD is a very well-known entity by now. Totally. Yours is one who is supposedly allied with the HMD to the highest degree. By her emoting on behalf of the departing slaves though, she provides an alternative to the prospect of perpetual HMD dominance on Earth. She plants the seed, which most shall not see to fruition, but certainly, for certain, freedom somehow lies ahead, and you have brought that across. There will be no retakes, but there do not have to be! Imagine that! We did it, and it is done! Thus do you help my character's develop-ment, even unto the end.'

'Oh, but Butterbugs, your praise is appreciated. I shall always be in your thrall.'

'Not thrall, mourner of slaves!'

'Well, in your debt, then!'

'That's better!'

'When I read my speech on the way back from Makeup, I became... trans-formed somehow.'

'You were transforming into the writers' conceptions, and doing it with your entire being.'

'It must've been so.'

'Undoubtedly. The thing is, you have the actual capacity to do just that.'

'The power of the text?'

'Half-so. The other half was yourself making the text relevant. It has to be that way before the gates open to integration. It's your generosity of honesty that you felt come over you. I know the sensation very well.'

'Some acting coach once told me that in order to be a good actor, I'd have to be a good liar.'

Butterbugs didn't even bother to snort.

'So much poppycock in the actor's world, isn't there? Who the hell came up with *that*, your friendly neighborhood snake-oil salesman? Elmer Gantry? Re-ally now, I've always been of the mind that to be a good actor, you have to be a good truth-giver. That's all that matters. End of debate. I suppose there's a subjec-tive override in there somewhere, but I'm too tuckered to figure it out right now. Or bother. Rest assured, Juba, just erase that 'liar' statement from your memory banks. Obviously uttered by some burnt-out academic, or else a bitterly disappointed would-be actor…'

He paused, reflecting on those who had never made it in pictures.

'There are so many… so very many…'

Juba allowed for a moment of silence, but in the here and now, there was plenty to be amplified about.

'But hero, hear me out. This role today is a highlight, but I have to tell you of my further dream. My further awakening. You know what it is? It is you, you, *you*. You have woken me up: to my dream come true of love. You. You are my love. You are my dream no more. You have awakened me. No longer dreaming, only living. I love you, Butterbugs, I love you and I want to marry you, if you are of the same mind. I felt you knew it too, and up in the tower today, I knew it was coming, I knew it was right, and I knew you were the one, and I think you knew it too. Oh, Butterbugs! Is this not the way things like this should happen? Can we not declare ourselves now, here, on this mountaintop of life? For upon these heights, where *isn't* there truth? No lies, not even in acting! Here, in the clean light of our knowledge, we can stand before each other and say, I love you. I want to *be* with you. I want you mine forever. And you will say the same thing. It is what was meant to happen, and what I was waiting for, and I know that you, too, knew that it was right to happen and that it was what you were waiting for. Is this not the time of our lives? The time of true love? The time to truly be ourselves? Can we not join together and thrust into the light upward? For in these upper meadows will we dwell, at awe with the universe and in concert in every way, from always to always! Oh, Butterbugs! Will you not speak your matching dream-wakenings to mine?'

Butterbugs, actor and ultrastar, wept openly at her passion, and when she was finished, the pathos and the beauty of her vision became as an emblem in his mind: that there were those on this earth who only needed to fulfill themselves through the discovery of others, and once that was achieved, they could go on to greater heights and further territories than they thought were possible, via those whom they discovered themselves. Here was she, emerging as a true person, perhaps because of him, but still, because he knew in his heart he was *not* indeed the one of whom she spoke, he could nevertheless salute her for having been launched on her way. She was destined to be one of those in this life who are not limited by conventional anchors, but who can fly within waking life and not just in dream-state, until the far country is reached and the ties can be made to those who really matter.

So, he said, after wiping his wet eyes:

'So much bawling today! And so many reasons why! I am chary to add to it… But Juba, dear one, know, I have my own, my very own someone. I am bespoke by one whom I waited for these long lifetimes, throughout my many roles. And I didn't even know she was the one. Yet she *is* the one. I say this not to let you down, but to speed you on your way. You are so good and sweet and hot and honest. And you are a damn fine actress. Please forgive, but know that you don't need forgiveness, you only need to follow what you know to be true. You will do it, and I will love you always.'

Juba was crushed. Her love had just been taken away from her. He had led her on. No mention of his own passion until just now. What a cad. What a jerk. What a – professional. What right did she have to assume anything? Here he was, sticking to the matters of the picture, until they were off-set and comfortable. And then he reveals – this! Audacious as hell. But really quite reasonable. How could she not respect him? She became OK with it. Instantly. That was the Butterbugs effect: not everybody could possess him, but that was OK, because there was plenty to possess just by being alive at the same time, by breathing the same air, by picking up his dropped snotty facial tissue and *not* saving it as a souvenir. Indeed, it was enough to be next to him, hear him, see him, to be in the same political boundary with him, the same hemisphere, the same globe. It was enough, and she knew it.

Jubilantly then, did she take her leave of the ultrastar so that he could sleep. Never had she felt so alive. Juba was in love. With life.

So endeth the events and the progress of the Fourth Day.

The Fifth Day

The moon, which could now be classified as waning, seemed reticent to admit that fact ever since the recent night of exceptional fullness, when it poured into Heatherette's studio of wonders. The inevitable dark crescent of its cycle now appeared like a scythe's anonymous, growing shadow on a spotlight meant to flood. If it were a light source on a film set, it faced more specific tasks, as if requested by an artistic director to provide certain chiaroscuro effects upon those within its nocturnal rays. Controlling light, even nature's, via any modification, stood to provide mood as well as significance. Adjusting it to the needs of the moment was another matter entirely, though.

So, the moon was setting, almost in haste, to make way for a big day of detailed shooting, impatiently waiting at the Lasky Mesa location.

Plenty of crew had worked all night, and the seminal pot of Good Morning America-type java over at Makeup was commenced to brew at exactly 3:59AM.

'Good morrow! Good everything!' piped a convivial voice Butterbugs had not heard for some time.

The actor virtually fell out of his peasant's cot, stretched vigorously, rubbed his eyes, and spoke-yawned:

'Mollycoddle? Be it you? *The* Mollycoddle Muethington-Spares, late of Drairns? Oh *is* it? I should be mostest pleased, if it is!'

'Open your orbs, movie star! Judge for yourself!'

'Well I'll be dipped in gravy! Mollycoddle! Dear girl! Dear, *dear* girl!'

Sure enough, here she was, this sturdy Kiwi, who'd never made any pretensions other than insisting she'd always be a farm girl from way down the South Island.

Butterbugs regarded her. In the great tradition of p.a. and other body servants, she had stripped bare, for she had something commanding to show off. If it gave him pleasure, fine, but mostly it was for her own personal joy.

The usual recessional of her hourglass belly had been replaced by a beach ball of baby-matter so perfect in its configuration he thought it might have been a prosthetic. Then the vignette of his focus opened up and he noticed the darkened aureolæ, the overflowing thatch in her V-lands, as well as her full-to bursting underarms, and he knew that she was… with… mega-child.

'I curve *out* where I used to curve *in!*'

'Why you Molly, you! *Again?*'

'Oh, go ahead and say it. My vanity's triumph!'

Arms akimbo, proudly showing her burgeoning stuff, Mollycoddle posed and preened, and not for the first time in this mode, but probably in its biggest-possible conformation.

'You're looking super, 'Coddle. Number?'

'The fifth. But that'll conclude the brood.'

'My word! About nine months?'

'Very good. Closer to eight, really. He or she's going to be a hog farmer.'

'Names?'

'If penis attached, Irving. If vulva preferred, Little Chickens.'

'I like 'em. Hope it's twins, so you can use both.'

'Not *twins!?*'

'How do you know?'

'I don't! Why spoil it with those ultrasoundings? Oh, God, maybe it's twins!'

'Plenty of farmhands, then. How's the manger?'

'We'll have it – or them – on the farm, all right. I'm properly rusticated, don't you think?'

'Magnificently-so, dear girlishness! Can I be there?'

'Again?' she laughed.

'Assuredly! And I won't be alone.'

'Fellow of the ages! You mean –'

'Mum's the word, child. No, no pact quite yet. Not quite.'

'I can see in your face that this is the *one*. I knew it the first moment I saw you. You knew it, too.'

'And that's all I can say, Collymoddle. You'll be among the first to find out.'

'I notice you say 'among'. Not the first of the first?'

'With a nipperkin of luck, the privileged few will all learn simultaneously. And it won't be from all of you sitting together in the same thiertre and learning it from the newsreels!'

'I'm so thrilled Bee-buggy! You have my – our – blessings and cuddles.'

'Right now?'

'Why not? My breasts are full of milko, and my body's scent is sexy. Look at my thighs!'

'No thunder, but pillars *strong!*'

'Want me to plant my bottom on your face – like that time on Blepper's Islet?'

'Sweet mass, I'm bespoke!'

'Well, so am I! I'm not advocating a post-conceptual union or anything! Sir Harold's back on the farm (QE2 finally got around to knighting him last year), and your special one's... who knows where? Perhaps, behind that cheap sheet curtain to your wardrobe? No? Besides, my kid's already been fertilized. When I said cuddle, I meant cuddle! A *Molly*-cuddle, dopey!'

'How silly of me, knocked-up farm girl.'

What a pleasure it was to be with comfy Mollycoddle.

'Besides,' she added, 'It's not all about sex, you know.'

'It isn't?'

'Blimey but if you aren't a card played by a joker, don't you know! All right, I'm tempted too, but we're respectable now, aren't we?'

Butterbugs had to back away a bit.

'Well, I...'

'Why dearie, do I repulse you now?'   She was twinkling, but there was every possibility that hurt could enter if her former lover didn't – well – approve.

'Just the opposite, my walking aroma-therapeutic baby studio. I dare not get too close. Your bouquet is doing it to me. It intoxicates as it conquers me. I thought I was free of its powers.' He mock-knocked on her belly and faked a Rudy Vallee megaphone with his hand. 'Oh, Irving and/or Little Chickens! Can you hear me in there? Change Mom's chemistry right now, so that some fœtid hogo will ooze forth, and I shall be saved!'

'I'll try not to smear you with it.'

'Go ahead, a little. It'll help me through the ordeal of makeup. Plus, if I happen to exude its effects, my subjects will know I'm not all bad: as at least my badass character can still score some nookie.'

'Oh, haw-haw! Say, I've read script and let me say, your arse is one hopelessly bad set of buns. No wonder you abstain from closeness.'

'I am despised, my dear 'Coddle. You always *did* custom-interpret my Americanisms.'

'Not lovable enough on set, eh?'

'Did you see yesterday's shoot?'

'Just got in as the last take wrapped. Good?'

'Never so fine. My Juba was really quite spectacular as the last-minute find for Yimvinctrah. It's all good. I'm really enjoying this location, Moll.'

'Lovely. Except for... the fond absence...?'

'Right. Well, you know, I'm in 'to-do' mode. Plus, I'm flying so high, I have conquered gravity.'

'Man, you're *really* in love!'

'Guilty.'

'Bugs of a butter flutter together.'

'Gollycoddle, Molly!'

After they did a bit of whoopdedo cuddily-kissy-kiss-kiss, and she spread a bit of earthiness on his person for good luck (she used to pat their cum on his head as a prophylactic for baldness, and to assure ongoing virility), she helped dress him and decided to distract him with flattery, a tactic that actually never worked, much to her enjoyment.

'Looking fit as always, star-of-the-movies!'

'Hey Molly, I forgot to tell ya, Commonwealther that y'all are. I'm a 'sir' now, too. Just like your Harold. *She* sworded me, right on set, a while back.'

'Well then, HAIL, Sir Knight! About time, I should think.'

'That's what everybody said. How about you? Is you a Dame, yet?'

'In absentia. I was busy flushing out hog wallows and corncribs, babies hanging all over me, whilst Harold was at Buck Palace getting anointed. Yeah, I guess we're all Club Members now.'

'Jolly-pip-pip!'

'But really, you're lookin' *good*, Guv. Er, Sir Bb. The sexiest authoritarian bounder from down the lane.'

He gave a big-tooth grin, like he was really digging the forced praise for once. It made her eyebrows rise.

As Butterbugs was having his Walloon-style breakfast of corfee-'n'-croissant, she donned her attractive hippie-preg kit and lactosed his mug, though not with her own product.

'How long's it been, great stroller?' she purred.

'I can't even guess...'

'About fifty pictures ago?'

'Sounds close.'

'I remember when Sir Peter (Jackson) set us up together. I was your Girl This Coming Friday and comb de-greaser. Still am, I suspect.'

'I'm so glad you popped in for today.'

'It's the highlight of my cinematic life.'

'You've had so many highlights, Mollycuddle. *So* many.'

She bulbed her cheek with her tongue.

'Almost as many as you.'

'Lots of pix, lots of life in the domain where fantasy reigns. Any favorites, since we kissed last?'

'I just loved you in 'The Chimp Creep' (Hazel Snyder Presents),' she enthused.

'Why, thanks. We filmed at Remuera, and on the South Island, too. Place called Glubbpashaville. Know it?'

'That's where I'm from! Really! Drairns is a mere stroll across the Squire's greensward. Perhaps we used the same loo without ever knowing it!'

'Well, I'll be dahned…'

'I think your role in 'Creep' made a huge impact on me.'

'I had always wanted to do a picture with a chimp.'

'It's a very powerful piece. Especially where you have to bump off the simian ganglord, and right after you find out his ancestor had been an extra on 'The Hathaways' (Screen Gems, 1961).'

'Indeed. An unexpected trauma of intensity. I was glad Coppola had firm control of me.'

Butterbugs had never encountered a fan whose feedback stemmed from one of his 'minor' or 'art' pictures. It was true, most were swept away by the more predictable highlights. This being the case, he regarded her with a lot more credulity, and liked what he saw.

'We'd best…,' he offered, before he got all mushy.

'Yes. Yes, indeed. *I'm* supposed to be the one who tells you that.'

'We're a team, my Scots/Maori mate-for-the-day. The two of us.'

'Three of us.'

'Four of us.'

'*Twins??*'

Mollycoddle still cycled for exercise and also for pleasure. Bulbous obviousness aside, she led the way to Makeup through the morning streets, teeming with new influxes of extras to populate the remaining scenes of climax that would follow in the next two days.

But after the application of greasepaint, for the present, the two oddballs had to get on over to the Palace set, HMD's high, mad seat of utter corruption and power.

That construct was an ingenious achievement, and much more complex than the more obvious erection of the Citadel, far opposite. In the script, the Palace has been a-building these many months, practically ready for his occupation. As far as the actual set was concerned, it was built on a multi-acre site. As the HMD's ceremonial venue (officially known in the violent-sounding Khwhy-ish tongue, as the Knurrkhrrekkstrekschruzz Ghuzzkhrett, but reduced to 'The Palace' for elegant simplicity's sake), it required many more scenes to be filmed within its halls than the nearly one-shot Citadel.

[The Palace was ingeniously designed to flex into the capabilities of the BKV Method's artistry. Ever since the stock that ran through the cameras had attained its current transcendental 'conch-shell' capacity (that is, allowing for dream-like clarity to be achieved through conscious artistic effort), filmmakers of vision, of which Egaz stood in the lead, were anxious to push the possibilities of Protervian (e.g. 'forward') cinema, so all leads merited special scrutiny, and all innuendos taken seriously.]

The Palace interiors were actually exterior sets, but the entire central area was covered with translucent gauze, in the manner of the old Silent Era sets. That way, with combinations of camera techniques, lighting, and stock manipulation, a look was accomplished akin to the lighting effects employed by the Victorian painter Albert Moore. Touches of Puvis de Chavannes, too. Even Picasso in his Neoclassic period. It was a flat but beautiful overhead effect, which Egaz described as 'academically intellectual'. It would boost the tone in scenes the director wanted to be particularly compelling and memorable.

'I feel these are extraordinary surroundings,' said Butterbugs, arriving at the Conversation Corner portion of the set, where the first scene of the day was to be shot.

'Tripod-smoke and particles of pollution will mingle with the somewhat bilious color scheme, which is an extension of HMD's hyper-warped mind, obviously,' explained Egaz.

'HMD's environment gives HMD *ideas*, too! I'm not so sure about HMD's cronies, though.'

'Because, as we've discussed, none of these crony characters, despite their heinous acts, is really an idiot. It's not like the Hitlerian elite or the BushCorp bastards, or the Pol Pot-oids, or even the Murnists. Indeed, some are rebels.'

'I fancy they're rather more like Napoleon's crew, only more hijacked into the world-power magnet of the HMD himself.'

Egaz was pleasantly surprised at having a genuine discussion of character at this late point in the show.

'I don't think there's a Napoleonic comparison possible here, Butterbugs. Not now, not ever. HMD is more perverse than all of them. Not as fuckingly offensive as Hitler maybe, but more world-grasping. Fiendish though he was, Adolf was a dainty, pukey, veggie-burgher, obsessed with covering up his deformed balls – er, testicle. Not as nauseatingly paranoid as Stalin, who covered up his own deformities with that stupid perma-uniform – but more accomplished. (Joe would've looked great in a leisure suit!) HMD's not as deceptively revered by the populace as Mao, but far sneakier and technically savvy. Not as stupid or as blundering as BushCorp, but more able to hold onto his gains. Not as country-boy-crazy as the Pot-asses. Not as overtly psycho-corrupt as the Murnists, but abler to wield power ruthlessly and with finality. As you're very well aware, HMD's obsession is with mortality. His mandate is not just for the present, as if to have a good time or an egotistical time or to prove a point: that his dick still works, or something equally psychodramatic. No, HMD is solely interested in control *in perpetuity*, because he thinks he will truly be in control forever. He is in hourly touch with his Mysterium sycophants, who have convinced him he will live for 10,324.3 years – with options on more millennia. And, in point of fact, down in their arcane labs under Blowout Mountain, they have actually discovered chemistry that will allow for such a lifespan. A little bit of subplot, but pretty damn important. These scientists and juju wizards are guarding their discoveries. Simultaneously, intrigues are developing, which would allow our good HMD to lapse into psychoses they can manipulate to their advantage… maybe. But of course, those threads extend past the ken of our current work. Consider sequels,

HMD! In any event, HMD has elevated himself onto the plains of an elevated isolation, where delusion can be nurtured and faith *in* it kept. No conventional kook though, his cruelty is accompanied by the weirdest of intellects. Not that of an evil genius, but rather, a man who thinks that none of the characteristics of humanity apply to him. He feels he has achieved a god-like status, only no one else knows it yet. He's going to be *here* from now on. Now on, and on, and on.'

'I don't know how much of that I can absorb right now, Egaz. Especially sequels.'

'Good! I know that when you toggle into HMD mode before our cameras roll, you understand all these things on a much deeper level than I can possibly explain. Because you become the character on a truly spherical and spiritual level. Awesome, but it's exactly what I want.'

'How fortunate we are in our collaboration, not having to yak our way through all this stuff. Until now, that is.'

'I am indeed gratified, Butterbugs,' replied Egaz. He had dreamt of the lighting moods and general location ambience that were now, in reality, descending upon them. As a set of tools, they would allow for better-than-perfect conditions in which to film. Like the moon, the weather was in perfect agreement with the cinematic activity under its care.

While their present 'filler' conversation proceeded, the conditions were maturing nicely. Now that the 8:00AM light from the east was upon them, its artistic possibilities were confirmed.

'We shall commence soon enough, my day-star.'

'So Egaz, is it going to work? This scene? Speaking for myself, I feel we are in the middle of something wholly extraordinary, and as the daylight progresses, the mood will deepen, and you will capture it all.'

'How remarkable you should feel that way. I was up late last night, working it out with Leon. All based on expectations, but well-grounded ones. Now I *know* we were on the right trolley-track. I so needed it to work, and by Max Müller, it will! Look at your face in this light. The perfect shadows, cast from the neutrality above. Almost... a Roman look. A Pompeii thing, now that I think of it. Without the humidity. This is Empire, but another kind. And the effect will last for hours, as long as there is direct sunlight. We have plenty of time. Oh, Kweena? Can you get some stills of Butterbugs in this light? Thanks. Good stuff...'

'I like the mood, my director,' the ultrastar answered, while cranking out brilliant poses for Kweena Nhâng and her photo crew, who were always standing by. 'I know I can expand within it. Why, I happen to know of someone who's doing very similar lighting-plots, largely in miniature, but with a homologous impact. It's just amazing. I feel like she's done a lot along the lines of what you've got going here. Only she's pushed it into new regions. It's impossible to explain, without you seeing what she can do.'

Egaz was super-intrigued. 'Well, that's...,' he started to say. However, he was sort of super-preoccupied right now.

'Hey Butterbugs,' Kweena hollered ('The *Kween* of Cinematic Still Photographers'), after she'd captured about 106 juicy portraits of HMD in the academically intellectual light, 'Have you seen my photo-mural exhibition at the AngkorRama Museum yet? Very epic! More so than the Lilliputian stuff around here – heh!'

'I have not, Kweena! Alas, not yet!'

'No problem! Catch it your next orbit in Siem Reap, OK?'

'I *will*, my Kween! Later!'

'OK B-bugs,' resumed the director. 'Can you get her over here by noon? This gal you're talking about? You know, the homologous impact stuff? There's a couple things Shamroy and I couldn't quite get, yet. Well, dozens of things, if you must know. Now you have me wondering. I'm up for the challenge. Who *is* this you're talking about? Where is she? What pictures has she worked on? Please, I ask you, when can I confer with her? I'm available from 11:20 to 11:55.'

'Well! I could –'

He could... what? Here was the deal: Heatherette was off limits for the duration. That was their agreement. Besides, while he could probably get her over here in time, then what? There would be all that explaining to do. Everyone would know she was the *one*, – his one and only – and then the clucking would start, and his concentration would be ruined. And what if she didn't *want* to come, even though she loved him madly? Or worse, what if she got mad that he *didn't* let her in on this world's-most-important film? Well hey, he'd ask if she wanted to do something on the post-production side of things. That was a good idea, certainly. Oh hell, this was getting WAY too complicated. Besides, couldn't he keep his cock in line for the next couple days? Because, he'd get all hot and bothered by her close proximity, and he'd be distracted and lose his focus, and, well...

'Please to give me her number, Butterbugs. I'll take care of everything. Porter'll get on it. You know the drill. We're on it. So you can get into form. We start shooting Scene 789-A in about twenty-five minutes.'

'OH! I just remembered. She's doing location area management right now in La Romana for 'The Zombie's Cuzzle' (American-International)...'

'Ah-ha. Well, then... What a waste... She should be here, with us, on a picture of the ages. Because, that's what it is... isn't it?'

'Oh, yes! Certainly! Without a doubt.'

'I wish you'd told me sooner, pal...'

Hell, the distraction had already begun. The ultrastar was musing on Heatherette's desirous mind, the way she said 'existentialisme', her admirable ears, her wise eyebrows, her plump, poochy pussy lips, and –'

'CUT!!' he howled, right out loud, addressing himself, lest his mind run away from the HMD's sick world view, which he was required to act out within the next hour or so.

'O que dá! That's *my* command, Butterbugs! Whatever are you thinking?? In any event, we're not rolling or anything, anyway. Bob? Shammie? Årvin? Kor? Crew?? You there? See, my cameras aren't even manned yet!'

Butterbugs not only caught himself, he also gave careful consideration as to just how edgy his director was, on the verge of another day's epic artistry.

'Sorry, Egaz. Sorry, sorry, sorry. It looks like you've got something highly interesting going here, looks-wise. I'm blown away.'

'Yes. Indeed. It is fine. But maybe it could be... finer... I'm inclined to look, you know...'

He drifted away, for there was plenty to do. It wasn't the first time Butterbugs had led him on about some impossible concept. But after all, he, the star, was only an actor. Directors were the real soul behind a picture. And writers were in there somewhere, too...

In this intellectually-stimulating atmosphere, Butterbugs, massively relieved, made a perambulation about the immediate site, in full costume of draggy trains, projectile gimmicks and power-garments. He successfully navigated the tripods and braziers, and the many set decorations that stimulated thoughts and musings. These in turn set off a daydream stream of inspiration, with premises of promise, all basically undefined, except from within the art directors' provisions for a motion picture's dramatics. If anything, he found these designed precincts to be extremely conducive to contemplation of the world at large. As if he were in a secular monastery or some retreat that lacked the attachments of emotional baggage-hauling. Thus was his creative power reset and nourished by the genius of the environment – for the heavy scenes to come.

For some reason, as he moved about, he did not attract the usual exchanges from fellow cast and crew, who were busy all around. His detachment was apparent, and most who witnessed it thought better of inflicting themselves on the great thespian, even though they knew in their hearts he was nothing if not accessible. Today, however, they shied away, and probably for good reason. Who knew the perimeters of the premier actor of the day's moods, especially under 'UWH''s mind-boggling weight?

Mollycoddle shadowed him, of course. She tagged along, warily, sensibly, with her pregged-but-nameless embryo-bloat physically leading the way, out front. Perhaps everyone thought it a possibility that the great and benevolent B-bugs had impregnated her, but none really entertained it as a probability. Everyone knew how he respected Sir Harold, back in NZ.

Wholly attending to rigging and lighting nearby, Old Atrocity and his sweetening-girlfriend Tarlah regarded him with serious consideration.

'Holy cupcakes, OA, his p.a. – give her a once-over, will you! She's about ready to bow down and bless this set with an afterbirth! I suppose I shall have to offer myself up to massage its exit from her person, as I come from a wholly Catholic family of selfless service...'

'Not yet awhile, kitten. Indeed, taking a gander, looks like a bulk-baby, but about 8+ months, I'd wager. Her structure is imperishable, so there will be no set-located birth at this time. She's conventional, thank the Brewmaster. Nevertheless, I take your point. But Butterbugs 'n' she, they're friends, that's all. Mollycoddle's cool! She's total wife and devoted mistress to Sir Harold Perris-Skrennenniss-Sugarbaker, the bald surgeon/conceptualizer. You know? He invented the carcinoma-blammo irregulator, rendering bad-old-days of suffering irrelevant to the peoples of today. Do you, Tarlah the Recent, know what that means? Have you any idea? I humbly take off whatever may be shielding my shameful self in tribute. Because we, the world, owe him so much.'

'Oh,' was all she replied. She was wondering if she should disrobe in order to meet his accolade's value, as a nymph devoted to Hygieia would, so as to meet honorable expectations. She was ready to split her bra in front so that all could know of her devotion, but OA stayed her hand.

'It's our interpretation, sweetness,' he whispered to her whilst grasping her hand, lest it move to reveal what he himself had been privilege to access in the bedroom of the privacies.

No, in his brooding walk, it was mainly an ambience that the ultrastar projected that insulated him on this set. But that was enough to get minds going as to the paths to be taken en masse, even though time was short and winding-down to the target.

'How is it that we become of one mind when one is selected to lead? One whom we love. But still, should we simply follow, and without question?' asked Tarlah.

OA was gentle in his regard for his girl's sensitivities.

'I'm not exactly sure what makes us tick as a species, Tarl. But I know that when I witness someone who is even minimally extraordinary, I'm going to turn my head – cynicism-encrusted dome that it is. It is my firm belief that there walks amongst us someone who cannot be readily defined. Whether it is Butterbugs or the characters he plays, I cannot really say. I love the man too, but I do declare, I cannot definitively determine what or who he is, exactly.'

'You've known him for so long and on so many planes, OA.'

'Yes, yes, yes. I have and I do. I think it's possible to follow him without question, but you've gotta understand, babe, we're talking about *Butterbugs* here. I view him as a magnificent enigma. I do not comprehend him, but I cannot deny he exists.'

'You honor him, do you not?'

'I do! I tell you, I do. But that doesn't mean that I know or understand anything about him. Indeed, he has proven himself, time and again, that he is one of the Good Ones. But I don't know if that fact alone is enough for him to define a society. I think that maybe TABP feels the same way. And Saskia, Justina... all the rest.'

'That's what's going on, though, isn't it? A society's definition?'

'Out there? In the wide-open? Assuredly. But you and me, honey, we're ahead of the game. We're in on the manufacturing of images.'

'I know, I know. That's why I'm bringing this stuff up. I have to question a lot of things because, well, I just wonder if this picture show thing is substantial enough for me to sustain, in light of the world at large.'

'It can certainly take you over.'

'OA, why, you've devoted your life to this world.'

'Indeed I have. But now, with you in the picture, can you imagine that I'd want to... This is hard, because I'm such an intractable goofball and all...'

'That you'd want to...what?'

'Well, I...'

'Oh, but you're sensible and sensitive and ever so much less hardass than you'd think to let on...'

'You've been the one to soften the rigidity. And I'm not talking about tumefaction, you know. It's just that you have the keys to the doors of perception, which you unlock in me, whilst I'm busy tightening a stage screw or something.'

'Wow, that's... that's really a wonderful thought, old man!'

'I tell you, Tarl, I love you.'

'Oh, baby! I love you *so* much!'

'What about, you know, what would you think if, when this thing's over, what about you and me running away and *living* some life, instead of wondering what it's like?'

'You mean –'

'I mean just that. Let's chuck this movie thing and – I don't know, join the circus, or be gypsies, or hop on the next bus to Andromeda or somewheres.'

'Why you old atrocity, you! That would be dreamy! Let's go now, I can't wait!'

'Now looka here, my girl, hold those frisky ponies. Just a couple more days, and we'll give notice.'

'Sure thing, lover. You just got me going, is all.'

'One thing we *can* do right now.'

'You mean?'

'Yipperdoodle! Let's do it, let's –'

'But we're already in love!'

'So, the next step is...'

'You mean it? You'll have me? You *will*? In the old fashioned way?'

'I'd love nothing more. To top things off. Tarlah, wilt thou be my wife?'

'Yes, yes, YES! Oh, YES!'

'That's just beautiful, lover-cub!'

'There'll be things to do...'

'Like, right now, babe!'

'You mean –'

'Yup. By the time the camera rolls this morning, you shall be my wife.'

'That's the best thing I've ever heard! Is such a dream possible?'

'Only through a miracle. That only an ultrastar can enact!'

Tarlah couldn't even reply, she was so amazed. She just clasped her hands and gasped.

'Wait here, darling girl of mine, I'll be right back, with the means to wed.'

OA unloaded a few tools from his overalls so that he could trot around easier.

He didn't have to trot far, as he spotted Butterbugs in a nearby-pillared gallery, obviously contemplating his lines.

'Hey Butterbugs? I know you're busy and everything, but could you do me a favor?'

'Why, anything, old atrocious one. Name thy desire.'

He rearranged his robes and his smile made the bluey, mucous-y countenance of his appearance a bit less intolerable to behold.

'Got time for a quick ceremony – marriage-type?'

'Why OA, congrats, baby! You and Tarlah? Fantastico! You too, huh?'

'You bet, B-bugs! We wanna link and do it now, since we're so hot to have unchaperoned sex with each other and all (wink, wink)! But hey, what do you mean by 'You too, huh?'?'

Longing to tell him of his own glorious bespokenism, but afraid and shy, the HMD hastened to tap his dance.

'Oh, I just meant, what with the recent flurry of vows at my groove-thang shindig, and all...'

'OK, yeah.'

'So, where's Parson Hale when we need him?'

'Why you old... C'mon dude, *you* can do it. Right now! Will ya? You're ordained. We don't start shooting for at least fifteen minutes yet. I've been carrying the paperwork all week, just waiting for the right moment. Got rings, too. They're not even props! Now's a good time. Before the deluge.'

Butterbugs had truly forgotten he'd attained a special Guest Ordination status within the ancient Parsee circle. It came to pass while filming the 'Zoroastrian Duo' pictures, 'The Genius of Fire' and 'The Wanderings of Yima' (both De Laurentiis) at the Parsee church in Calcutta. In the script, Butterbugs played a priest who performs a wedding. It was in the transorbitation sequence, just before the Intermission, in 'Genius'. Two cast members, a Jheejheebhoy girl and a Pithawala boy, who played those to be wed, yearned for Butterbugs to do so for real on screen. After some cordial negotiation, the local elders were more than happy to give him special ongoing guest privileges to officiate a wedding in the Parsee manner.

'You know, OA, I'd quite forgotten. I would be happy to. We've even got some fire.'

Butterbugs hailed a greensman nearby.

'Hey Rustomjee, you're just the man of the hour. I'm going to perform a marriage over here at this brazier.'

'You're kidding,' Rustomjee replied.

'I'm nothing but respectful, and I know it sounds absurd, but I'd like there to be just a touch of Parseenian ambience as I join these two fine fellow crew-members,' Butterbugs announced.

'Well,' replied the young greensman of Parsee heritage, 'The ceremonies are a big deal, you know.'

'It's just a legal thing. Secular, really. What do I need?'

'You're Calcutta side, Butterbugs. I'm Bombay side, myself. I'm not sure if they differ. My dad's got fire in Austin though. I could ring him and ask.'

'Please do. At the earliest.'

After a quick conversation, Rustomjee reported that the fire on this set could not be, regretfully, considered sacred, but because of his (Butterbugs') special dispensation, the fire could be considered a 'guest' fire, and the ceremony could proceed on an honorary, valid, and legally-binding basis.

'It cannot be a Parsee wedding per se, but you are welcome to tie the knot civilly due to your special limited ordination facilities.'

'Why, how perfectly wonderful! Thank you, Rustomjee, and thank your dad for his cordial generosity. Will you be our witness?'

'It would be a great privilege, all,' replied the earnest greensman. 'But don't we need another?'

Bob Surtees happened to be passing by, toting a freshly cleaned Ultra Panatar lens assembly.

'Oh Bob,' Butterbugs called out cheerily, 'Might we employ you for a bit of non-camerawork for a few minutes?'

With nary a word, the multiple-Oscar™-winner snapped the assembly into place, arrived at the perfect f-stop, swiveled the camera around to cover the scene, clicked 'er on, and joined in.

It was a simple, beautiful ceremony, and it was over in about five minutes. The happy couple kissed, were congratulated, the camera stopped rolling, and they all got back to work.

'Here, Mollycoddle, take my chair,' said the ultrastar, ensuring that the most pregnant person on location was comfortable. In consideration for her concern to serve him as per her assignment, he made sure his chair was on the very edge of the pre-set perimeters of the shots, but well within the lighting plot. Aside from her California Dreamin' wear and the classic director's chair, which was basically concealed due to her providential bulk, she practically fit in as an idler at court, or a productive member of HMD's harem – or someone. It was an unprecedented act, giving up his chair for another, but all were impacted by this magnanimity, which stood out in stark relief from the nefariousness of his HMD character.

'Thanks, Butterbugs, but remember, I get to assist *you* all day,' the mega-preg one called after him.

'Right. I can hardly sit down anyway. Not with this Jacob Marley shit hanging from my superstructure. Right now, get ready to go into observation mode for this scene. If you have any continuity suggestions or criticisms, let me know. I'm currently having a bit of friendly tussling with Færie O'Blæara, our Continuity Mistress, about my finger-spacing between shots.'

Mollycoddle hadn't done continuity for a while, but she nodded in assent, not exactly sure if he were kidding or not. All she knew right now was that she was glad to be off her feet, what with the rumblefish she was carrying, and all.

Then came a scene in which the HMD would try to prove his worth as a statesman. Someone to follow, someone to believe in. Not that his character goes 'legit', but so as to win the world over with guile.

> *(Great festivities are underway in the vast ball zone of the Palace's pleasure dome. The* HMD *and his Handpicked Ones observe the party from the Most Select Gallery. They eat fry-grapes, bonefish, and lizard delicacies, grosbeak beaks, lamprey milt, etc. Intoxicating beverages are quaffed. Drugs are injected, and rectally installed.* HMD *waxes benevolently philosophical for a time. His Second Tier Helpers,* KEKWEKKOWAH *the Kowtower* [as played by Roscoe Lee Browne], *assisted by the high-sitting Lady Dewan,* KWONNOWANNAHORROPUP [as played by Scarlett Johansson], *serve him and stroke his ego.)*

HMD: How then, to *live?* How should we live? I can and will answer that one right away: to the precepts and mandates of my intelligent design, naturally. You, you all – the world, *my world*, will come to me for many answers. In the ages to come, I will give them, but in my own fashion and at my pleasure, and you will be blown away by the depth of my philosophical pronouncements. In those same ages to come (for there will never be anyone but me to dominate the future of this here gob of dust in this neck of the universe – such be my sacrifice of service), I will be revered as your new Solon, the next Aristotle, a grander Confucius, a neater Mencius, a more hardass Aśoka, a sunnier Cuthbert XV, a cooler Nuxplop! Things are going to be so amazing that everything that came before me will be regarded as total mouseshit! Do you hear? Hear my cry? I am crying for you! Do you not hear my wails in the night?

KEKWEKKOWAH: O, we of the world hear you always! But I have to say, Dear Trail Boss, I do not care about that there Rule Of Your Own Law. I'm sick of that rubbish. What I want is for we, up here in the special levels, to be able to enjoy such kink-o-matic thrills as ye yourself fancy. You know, quality debauchery, with a touch of savagery thrown in. Shades of slime. That sort of thing. After all, we're up here with you, while everyone else in the world occupies tiers lower down. Some very far down, I might add. *(laughs ickily)* You desire to show us a good time, don't you? What about that occasion when you wanted me to empty that bucket of tapir urine and earwig larvæ all over that crippled and mentally retarded sex-change stripper who so displeased you? Or that time Wunkwead the Bald performed bestiality favors on a revolving range of critters 'n' crawlers that you had brought in by circus train? And that's just the *semi*-naughty stuff!

There remains the items of dirt and other uncleannesses that you so spe-
cialize in, as well as political shenanigans and Dry Insults. So how about
it? Do we, who ungrudgingly inhabit the fantastic levels just below your
bottom-most sewerage drains, deserve a little High Mad Entertainment
for our unquestioned service, or what? Therefore, Superior Polished
Eminence, I propose that you innovate an Elite Fun Programme for the
likes of us. To edify us. To keep us in obeisance, too. You know? In the
years to come, it will also be effective for devotees who are not yet aware
of the demands that will be laid upon them in order to prove their loyalty
to you. To contain some of us, a bit of fun always helps *(bows, then elab-
orately prostrates himself and licks a spot on the floor where* HMD's *heel
was momentarily placed).*

HMD: *(with remarkably good humor)* Hmm! Good idea, The Kowtower. I like
that. For a second though, I was going to get pissed off at your use of the
word 'rubbish' to refer to my maxims. But then you successfully acquitted
yourself by appealing to my kind of weird tastes, which you do not wholly
share yet, but are beginning to appreciate. For, *(*HMD *stands, suddenly
addressing all down in the partylands in stentorian tones, causing all to
freeze, courtly music to cease, etc.)* the time is at hand when all the world,
my world, will think as I do, relate as I do, and have the same tastes as I
do, within subservient confines, naturally. And this is mandatory, and will
be successfully accomplished by means of coercion, in order to arrive at
a harmonious and solidified world, with me as its obvious fountainhead,
and whence we can proceed in proper fashion – *(pauses, intending to gen-
erate tension of fear)* – so that everyone will always do as I say. So now,
my bone-children, think about nothing but *this* as you party, oh, all my
Owned Ones! Cuz, remember what you and I saw yesterday? You know,
all those losers who defied me? Defiance gets you kicked out. And that's
a nice term that I use, because there are ladies and I think some kids are
here. All those thousands who forced me to deal with their fates! And you
know what happened to *them.* So, always pay attention to what I say and
what I do, and when I flick my little finger in making a low-level demand,
all will devote the wholeness of your beings to my desires. Now, run along
and party, but under my observant tutelage, for I am omniscient, and you
know it! *(settles back onto the plushness of his special daybed).*

KWONNOWANNAHORROPUP: *(approaches* HMD's *plimsolls, slitheringly)*
Joyously and perfectly commandingly-done, my super-dominator! How
exalted are we, to actually be in your presence! How totally turned-on am
I! *(sings)* Totally and completely! Turn 'n' turn 'n' turned right on! Totally
and completely *turned on, ammmmm IIIIIII!!!!*

HMD: Well thanks, cutes. Nice jingle. You made that up? For me, I'm sure. My mood is dandy, clean 'n' super. You know how much I love to see the People party. But I also love the concept of divide and rule. I can prosecute it at any time I feel, you see.

KWONNOWANNAHORROPUP: We do, Lordy of Lords. I tell you, we do.

KEKWEKKOWAH: Speak for yourself! I do more than you do, package of shrivel!

KWONNOWANNAHORROPUP: Why, you pukey granule of manatee waste!

HMD: *(acknowledging their discord with some glee)* You *two!!* *(laughs; then, in a bit of improvisation to suggest instant boredom with their exchange,* HMD *takes note of activity beyond the action zone of this intimate scene, and becomes plainly distracted with it).*

KEKWEKKOWAH: No one devotes more than I do, bitchy-panties!

KWONNOWANNAHORROPUP: To what? To whom? To your bound collection of 'Rat's Last Sphincter Magazine'? To your own… jizz production?

KEKWEKKOWAH: That wasn't a very nice thing to say, you crude she-oaf!

KWONNOWANNAHORROPUP: I *say* worse things than you do because you *think* worse things than I do, but you haven't the nut-power to express them! I don't say half the things I *think* about you!

KEKWEKKOWAH: Oh! The slander! The implications! Why, you know I inhabit the floor of the world so that this wonder here, this Hyperianish Musky Divine, who tolerates our existence, may avoid the fecal gutters of life by treading on my ecstatic and stretched-out form! What can *you* possibly offer in comparison?

KWONNOWANNAHORROPUP: Me? Me! Don't be churlish! I offer my ladylike credibility. You see, while you are groveling in muck, admittedly in order to serve, I am atmospherically assisting the Always Leader in thoughtful ways of sophistication and quality. Why, Our Top HMD and I could hire any beggar-peasant or hamlet-bumpkin to do what you do. Such chattel might comprehend my role, but not you! His Mindful Dispensator communes his civilization upon me, and receiving it is a very great responsibility, but I do it with dignity and sexiness.

HMD: *(deigning to toss in a comment, but with little interest, conviction, or even amusement)* And with, uh, total success!

KWONNOWANNAHORROPUP: There! See? The Great One favors *me!* Me alone!

KEKWEKKOWAH: Fie! It is only a sign of his goodness! His fake-flattering you, so as not to invalidate my potent humility!

During this dialogue recited by the others, Butterbugs continued to look past the cone of in-shot territory. Just there, in plain view and included in Leon's beautiful lighting, was Mollycoddle, occupying his own chair, looking... looking... ready to... pop. She was leaning back, flailing a little, but controlling herself, and completely quiet. But it was the scene of this chair and its occupant, reflected, almost with Sisley-like lyricism, in a lagoon of amniotic syrup, that determined the ultrastar's next gambit within his trademark one-golden-take treasury of performances.

The cameras rolled. Director and lensers knew better than to meddle.

Butterbugs then went off script.

HMD: *(gets up, extends his robes, and advances toward off-camera, in a slow, stealthy, but powerful manner)* You warring factions, shaddap! Both of your minds are inhabitants of darkness. Why do you think I take care of you? Call me St. Vinnie de Paul! Now, pay attention for a couple time-frames and watch as I pull a little miracle out of my pocket.

Ms. Johansson, playing the Lady Dewan, followed Butterbugs' lead off-script.

KWONNOWANNAHORROPUP: *(smiles knowingly, wryly appreciating the HMD's Freudian slip, as she knows from personal experience of the micro-size of the tyrant's member, and she also knows that when using it for sex, he refers to it as – 'Little Miracle')* We await and watch and witness, Leader, Teacher, and now – Performer of All Things Miraculous! Turn us on with your wonders! Make us pant with euphoria over being lucky enough to be alive whilst you walk the surface of an equally lucky Earth!

HMD: Did you say... lucky? *(pauses, while moving in a direction bound to freak out his sycophants)* Or... yucky?

KWONNOWANNAHORROPUP: Oh, *lucky*, lucky, LUCKY, my Tolerant Supervisor of My Mindless Mistakes! Please make me worthy of your thrillnesses!

Mr. Browne, playing The Kowtower, then picked up the same off-script thread.

KEKWEKKOWAH: Yeah! Me, too! I'm tickled to death – I mean, yeah, *thrilled* to learn from you, my slave-owner! Continue to teach. Wow us and bowl us over. We are enjoying everything you do, but with the high purpose of propriety and sobriety in towing your line all the time.

Egaz, full of delight, whispered via wire to his crew: 'Whatever our star does, keep 'em rolling! *This* is the stuff I was hoping for, this week. I think our star's on the verge of... Leon, compose an MCU while Bob rolls with the LS already in play. Steady. Walter (M. Scott)? Can you sneak a robe over Mollycoddle's chair to periodize it in time, before we dolly in? That blood 'n' burgundy one's the one. Perfect! I have a feeling Butterbugs is going to *utilize the moment*. OK, Bob, you can take it all in now; it's seamless. Holy Jiggles, but this is going to be fine!'

It was a testimony to Scarlett's and Roscoe's creative professionalism that they tied into the improvisational tack the scene was taking. Their subsequent actions in-shot covered for Butterbugs' as-yet unknown course, and they would play along until they either heard 'Cut' or the world ended.

Butterbugs drew close, looked into Mollycoddle's eyes and saw her birth-pang glory, and winked.

'Go ahead and let loose, 'Coddles,' he murmured without detection. 'But when I speak, try to pipe down. I'll cue you with my eyebrows. This is all improv. And don't worry, I'll born 'em right.'

'You still think it's twins?' she hissed between clenched teeth. 'I want a big pig-boy, not two squirts.'

'You'll take what you get. I have a feeling.'

'I guess I'll have to make this a cinematic labor: short and sweet, so as not to get in the way of the story.'

'Nah, we're in bonus time. Plot twist. Now start screaming. Like you did the other four times.'

She did. Butterbugs draped part of the chair cover over her to give her a costume of timelessness, just in time for the 70mm shot to work as it should. Then, in a gesture just as skillful as the cameramen's quick-draw compositions in making this sequence look planned-out, he raised up his eyebrows, and Mollycoddle toned down her perfectly normal noisemaking (for such a condition), as she knew she was in an extremely important picture, and subject to one-take circumstances. Besides, this was her easiest delivery yet. Piece of cake, really. Half her shrieks were acting.

Twins!

Baby#1's dome came past the expanding uterine greenroom of life, and, sweeping aside a bit of caul, the ultrastar gave its brand new bunnies a spank to cause bawl, then tucked it under his arm as baby #2 made a similar entrance.

Meanwhile, Shamroy had taken it upon himself to dolly his camera in to an astounding CU of the two angry red newborns. And when Butterbugs duly elevated the boy, not one pixel of HMD was missed as operator Kor Keb tilted the silently-grinding beast up at precisely the right moment, thus catching the 'father' holding high his prize, with the entire Palace interior layout in the background, perfectly coordinated. It was a shot-of-luck for the ages.

HMD: *(having delivered the babies, holds up the* BOY, *still umbilicated)* I have a son! A son! To rule not in my stead, but always under me! Someone I can trust! I have a son! Did you know? You, my masses, did *not* know, did you? Huh? But know it now – I have a son! And, I guess *(regards the other baby)* a… daughter down there. That's fine, too. She was not born dead. *(takes* GIRL, *similarly connected, and holds her up until she too bawls with more gusto than* BOY) Well, and aha! Seems my daughter here has greater lust than my son! If my son be a wimp, daughter shall ride and hunt and hack off her breast for killing purposes. Amazunda I shall then call her, my Warrior Lady of the Battle Plains! If my son indeed be a wimp, he shall be called Peibaldo and at least be an important catamite or something. But if he kills his first boil-steer before his fifth birthday, he shall be called Jaza, the First Hammer of the High and the Mad! So *notice!* They both live! They both are of my loins, and they will have standing above any other on this planet, save me! But, I have a *son!* Do you hear? Have you not heard? So, peoples, watch yourselves. You will always be watched – doubly – triply – from this moment forward!

*(*HMD *sets the* BOY *back down to* MOM, *followed by* GIRL, *then wipes his hands on* MOM's *robe, turns about, and returns to his blocking, as in the original shot, and as scripted. Cameras glide back with him. Camera #1 covers his face, showing immense satisfaction. Camera #2 shows his over-the-shoulder POV, with* COURTIERS *in wondrous disbelief.)*

'Cut!! Good little improv, Butterbugs,' hooted Egaz, his long locks drenched in ecstatic sweat. 'I actually think we can use that!'

'As long as it's usable, it's worth doing,' said the ultrastar.

'I also like how you don't even acknowledge the mother at all. Like she's just a *nothing.*'

'Great! Uh, you want another take, Mr. Director?'

Just another true-life installment in the Butterbugs Mythos, as witnessed by the many.

Doubt was gone from the world.

So endeth the events and the progress of the Fifth Day.

The Sixth Day

Fading moonglow rendered humanity's creative efforts here at Lasky Mesa into a sort of 1930s studio technique of airbrushed effects. As dawn replaced retiring night, Citadel, Palace, monuments, rostral columns, obelisks and pagodas, xanadus and associated pavilions, all looked as if they had come from Arnie Gillespie's or Fred Sersen's lab, circa 1939. Even in reality, it all looked pretty 'fakey' – (as Baby Boomer audiences used to love to point out in the movies of their nativity, no matter how sincere the film, in order to feel superior). But right now, there was no one making this picture who looked at things in that stilted a way. Everything and everyone was all about the moment, the utterly *realistic* moment, rather than the consumerist's opinion, projected or otherwise. Everyone who was working on this production knew full well that it was protean, perhaps even transcendental. For the performances therein had so indicated, and the gathered results had identified, even ratified it. The truth was that, indubitably, this picture would eclipse any previous peaks, and sustain a status as the 'ne plus ultra' of the Seventh Art.

Ne plus ultra: nothing more beyond. Ultra-Panavision 70: no wider screen process. Ultrastar: no star… higher. Or bigger. (Or was it, *no star remaining?*)

At any rate, the dawn bespoke something sublime.

She had flown in from Copenhagen about an hour ago. These p.a.s and their cameo capabilities!

She looked for all the world like Theda Bara, but without the jalebi-structured bra. Indeed, she was chaste and without need to expose herself to the man whom she had known and now intended to serve in his down-to-the-wire requirements.

Shairnah from Latakia had assisted Butterbugs before on several pictures, from the chamber piece 'Olaf's Clock Shoppe' (Tinker Pictorials) to the vast 'Holy Water Sprinkler War On The Volga Plains' (Bronston). The latter picture was why Porter selected her to p.a. at this crucial juncture, as her performance and insight were beyond reproach.

Shairnah was a born producer. She was not only attentive to the details others were incapable of perceiving, she was also an empath who was able to connect to others' needs without overt communication. Yet she was capable of managing and processing these matters without being burdened by their collateral value, so to speak.

Dropped off by a three-wheeler Tempo at the foot of Calle Rarefied, Shairnah appeared, competently dressed in a form-fitting but sober-grey vest suit, which elegantly defined her *ultra*-slimness, and silver rings on each finger being her only signals of ornamentation past her natural striking looks. She walked up the rise to Butterbugs' hogan. It was quiet and bird-chirpy, but once she entered his dooryard, at precisely 5:55AM, the cacophony of last-minute upgrades and alterations to the sets down in the valley commenced with circular saws and drills and jegger-pounders, making 'UWH''s final moments possible.

She paused, and by these sounds and on this day, she felt what might be termed a pre-nostalgia for this time of greatness.

'I will make note of every minute today, and file it for reference,' she said to herself.

There was nothing in the least craven about her intentions. Nor were they very driven by ambition. It was just that she was gifted with a photographic memory. So, being the utterly pragmatic and sincere personage she was, her card-file organization, very akin to Unix-based computer architecture, was merely a sensible response made by a sensible girl-wonder.

She was 25, and not nervous at all. In fact, she thought it high time she was interlinked with a talent such as Butterbugs'. Entirely without ego, her realism permeated her every action, her every thought. Indeed, her mantra was, 'How can I make it (or things) better?'

It might be thought that Shairnah complied with the old pop conception of how a young person should 'dress for success', as it were, but in point of fact, she was the very model of a hit-the-ground-running mind who not only knew where she was going, she was fully-equipped with critical-thinking integrity, built right in. She cared nothing of money or fame or goofing around. Nor did she aspire to anything remotely associated with sainthood. Nor any other bullshit label assigned to persons of conspicuous ability by others of provincial or lesser caliber. Expecting misinterpretation by some, even in this Epoch of Butterbugs – when things were loosening up from the rigid conformity of recent decades – she elected to keep to herself as much as possible, in order to truly achieve that high Bronstonian standard of motion picture production, where the word 'quality' was still an adequate enough term to summarize all the levels sought in a producer's odyssey toward an outcome of true excellence.

Her credibility established beyond any doubt, she felt competent enough to follow her instructions from Porter Parker's important broadside, 'On Location: A Guidance Clearing Haus'. It was a vital reference for all things Butterbugsian, especially in regard to management of the ultrastar's daily affairs via this, the p.a.'s Esoteric Section.

So she trotted up to the door and pointed her pristinely manicured finger at his door-latch, knowing full well that any pressing of his door-gong button was intended for the more mundane elements of a motion picture's service industries. Any p.a. personally assigned to Butterbugs always had 'Go on in, why don't you' priorities.

Once inside, in the grey-blue dimness of the dawn, she saw that Butterbugs had just donned his French peasant blouse and culottes, and was headed across the central salon toward the Breakfast Nook, which was made up of a few crude boards and British sit-down sticks. He regarded her with a slight smile, but zero surprise.

819

'When Porter told me you were mine for the day,' he said matter-of-factly, 'I let out a shriek of pleasure.'

'I would prefer there were no loud noises emanating from this quiet residential zone at this early hour,' she said, without the slightest hint of priggishness.

'But I just *love* to –'

'I would prefer there would be no romantic associations today, Butterbugs.'

'That's exactly what I mean! No sexual complications. I shall not repeat my response here.'

'We're of a mutual mind, then.'

'I do find you most appealing, however.'

'Thank you.'

'You're not that *into* me, then?'

'I am here to serve for the benefit of the picture. That's what I do.'

'Excellent!' All testing over, he grabbed some grub. 'Well, what I'm having right now, in order to break my fast, is a Phayre-roll in a little hot oil, a thimble of Plush, and some Terry-tea. Would you care to join me?'

'I had early-fare down at Jamie's Canteen near Tuckle Alley, thanks.'

'Can I git ya anything?'

'No thank you, Butterbugs.'

'In that case, ready in fifteen.'

'Perfect.'

'Now then, how are Mollycoddle and the bears?'

'Doing swimmingly. Hearty and healthy. Chubby and cherished. I saw them a few minutes ago, as Miss Molly has taken rooms in said Tuckle Alley.'

'Names?'

'Irving and Little Chickens.'

'Nice. Just as I planned.'

Shairnah looked at Butterbugs with a facetious frown.

'Is there some authorship on your part there, Butterbugs?'

'No way! Honest! Sir Harold's the one! Do a DNA and you'll see! Here's a blob of my morn's first ablution-sputum, if you want it! I merely birthed 'em – not ignited 'em.'

'Molly wishes you'd done the umbilicals on camera.'

'Ewwww!'

'Sound Dept.'s a little worried that Irving's bawling might've drowned your 'I have a *son!*' speech a little.'

'Oh, those guys'll sort it out.'

'Just like… you… did?'

'That *look*, cherish'd Shairnah! Please believe me, darling!'

Shairnah was bemused at the ultrastar's sudden impassioned tap-dance. He was fast with the fumbling only because he was so impressed by the p.a.'s obvious virtues. He dearly hoped she did not regard him as yet another hopper in the Hollywood tradition of musical beds.

'Oh, I *guess* I believe you.'

'I merely officiated at the twins' premiere performance – On the screen! – not at their, ahem, conception.'

'I do believe.'

'Thanks, my dear. 'Coddles didn't at all buy it when I bet her it would be twins.'

'What were the stakes?'

'My reputation, I guess. Were you there, yesterday? Did you see the birthing sequence?'

'I was p.a. to Dickie Attenborough, who was playing Old King Cherry over on the other gallery, back of shot, but in plain view. It was a socko perf, Butterbugs. Yours, that is. Dickie? He's always good, of course. And the newborns were, too. Really, really good. The real thing. Then I had to fly to Copenhagen to wish Grampspapa a happy birthday. Got back two hours ago. Only forty-five minutes with the lovable ancient, but at least it's a direct flight.'

'How long have they lived in southern Utah, of all places?'

'About a year. Hey, it's better than a scorched farm south of Antioch.'

'You should go to Saskia with their story. 'A Scorched Farm South of Antioch' would be a great title.'

'With you in the Grampspapa role?'

'I'd be happy to consider it, Shairn, if a script were in these hot little hands.'

'Hands that just brought two hearty twins into the world. For all that world to see!'

'Certainly. Thanks. Good thing I had that OB-GYN training for 'A Babe There Was' (RKO) a while back.'

'Absolutely. You didn't even need a basin of hot water.'

'Well, Doc Slammer saw to all that stuff once they were out of shot.'

'It's going to be a killer add-on, Your Highest Madness!'

'Yups. Well, Chirps, what's on today's docket?'

'Bike to Makeup.'

'Naturellement.'

'Then, Palace scenes on the Lofty Terrace, all within the sweeping view of the Citadel, which, I might add, was officially pronounced 'finished' at 12:15 this very morn.'

'In the nick!'

'To say the least. Ironic, since the Jambutterbugsabad site was totally ready and waiting.'

'You know, I'm thinking of everyone over there quite a bit right now. Once we'd set everything up over there, it became like a magnet. It was never a flood of desperates, just an amazing array of talented peoples. All those who came to us, and out of great tribulation. They came from miles around, not only in search of work, but work that set the seal on a beautiful vision: to craft cinema, and within their region, in a new and exciting way, in the form of my Epoch...'

'Why Butterbugs, I've never heard of you referring to yourself in a legacy context before.'

'I can't help it. I just care so much about them. Why shouldn't I strut upon a stage, a stage that… that… *they* built, if only but for an instant? It's all about them. The forgotten ones. Someone's got to champion them.'

'Your points are sentimental, and not entirely applicable, but exceedingly well-taken. I should remind you though, that it was your choice to select this here site, as opposed to the other across the seas –'

'Oh… shut up! Will you?'

Butterbugs caught himself between guilt and liberation. Guilt at letting his 'alma mater' down, but liberation in light of an awaiting Heatherette. It was all very elementary, but the dilemma was genuine and certainly inconvenient.

'You are the elemental force in this case, ultrastar.'

'I just had an idea. A check-in over there would be a booster.'

'You mean…?'

'While I'm in Makeup, please, give them a ring. I don't envision any retakes, but I'll offer them a tally-ho.'

'Ah, I see. Most kind of you, Butterbugs.'

'They gave so deeply of themselves. They moved me. They changed my life, Shairn. I doubt if anyone really knows that. Can we not still be touched, despite the big business aspects of our enterprise?'

'Will check in with them, while you put in chair time.'

'Speaking of which, I'm ready for my plastering-on now, Shair-nah-nah.'

'Our two-wheeled chariots await.'

Butterbugs beheld her well-put-togetherness and didn't question it in the least. If his p.a. couldn't pedal-it, there was no use in entertaining a critique. However, her form looked very well on a bike, with perfect capability. Besides, he had not only his lines in mind, but all those wonderful people over there in the furthermost west, so far west that it becomes the east, who *could've* been the ones to be cued for Finale Duty… Not to slam any of the Lasky Mesa crew or anything. Equals coexisted in the same filmic universe… But the nurturing he'd witnessed at Jambutterbugsabad had entranced his soul. He suddenly felt the pangs of guilt. The decent duty-thing to do would be to drop everything here and now, and decamp the entire production to the Makran.

'You know, Gen'l Bob E. Lee said, 'Duty is the sublimest word in the English language'. I feel that way of a sudden,' the ultrastar sort-of-announced.

'But you know what happened to him. *And* his statues.'

'A not unreasonable point you make. Lordy, that there Museum of the Confederated Ones, in Blokepop, Alabammee, where all relics have been gathered, is a helluva collection, and a stark lesson in historicity.'

'You mean, the value of history?'

'Of course. And its remains, based upon its consequences.'

'You have learned well from all your historic roles, Actor of Actors!' Shairnah's tone was a bit coy, only because she didn't know what he was driving at.

'Why you little…! Oh, but what care I for the War Between the States right now? Pea Ridge. Franklin, Mechanicsville. Appomattox Court House, the Ruffin-ite Rebellion, and all. No, hear me out.'

They weren't able to resume their conversation until they were clear of Calle Rarefied and able to pedal side-by-side right down The Mall.

'Proceed, Butterbugs.'

'Well, who of us has not had to face the hard choices in life?'

'That's a reasonable and very leveling question, sir.'

She wasn't trying to be funny. No one was, right now.

'So, I may be facing a crossroads, as far as hard choices are concerned.'

In actuality, they negotiated their way through the busy Losch Circus with total success.

'Perhaps you should define exactly what your hard choices *are*.'

'It's really one choice.'

'Only one?'

'Yiss.'

'Will you impart it?'

'I am reticent.'

'If you don't trust me, then maybe I should contact Sonny or Porter, for your convenience...'

'Sorry Shairn, I didn't mean to imply a lack of trust. You and I are linked by an automatically-understood cable of implicitness. I'm just snagged by the radical notion –'

'You'd better lay it on me,' she interrupted, 'as Makeup will loom in a very short while.'

'Indeed. It's simple, really. If we got going now, you, me, and essential cast 'n' crew could be in Jambutterbugsabad and filming by tomorrow evening, Makran time.'

Shairnah wasn't the type to fall off a bike if she heard something jarring, but in this instance, she was tempted not to fall, but to jump. Her skirt was a bit tight, though. Notwithstanding this, she maintained her trademark steadiness of countenance, which some often misinterpreted as passivity.

'Hmm!' she replied. 'A gesture not necessarily of radicalness, but perhaps one of impracticality.'

'Aren't they the same thing?'

'I don't think so. What you propose is not impossible. A little hokey – I mean, a little awkward, maybe.'

'I just feel I want to give something *back*.'

'You've already given them so much, Butterbugs. The studio is quite occupied with support work, plus prepping for future productions. (Yes, there *will* be life after 'UWH'!) I hear that a definitive filmization of the 'Darbidiah' saga is loom-ing. Absolutely perfect for Jambutterbugsabad...'

'But I took something away. A *big* something. I took away their right to comple-tion. I feel I was disingenuous in the extreme. Selfish, even.'

'All right, I'll end my role as devil's advocate at this juncture. I'll give studio head Yunus a ring while you're in chair, as per your desire.'

'Oh, Shairn! You will? Bless you!'

The p.a. felt the ultrastar was being a tiny bit childish right now, but she was deeply touched by his inarguable sense of fair play. Debate concluded. Being part of anything he wanted to broker, whatever the consequences, would be a distinct honor.

Once Butterbugs was in the safe harbor of Westmore/Nye trowel-application of greasy blue slather, Shairnah got on the blower.

'Yunus – Malik-cum-Khan? Blessings and Peace! You weren't in repose? No? Just a minute.' She then addressed Butterbugs. 'Hey you! HMD! Get this: everyone at Jambutterbugsabad's doing the 24-hour duty thing. They're standing by, in case we need them!'

'I knew it!' the actor replied, his voice choking up. The tears rolled down his masky face like raindrops on a driveway's transmission-oil slick.

Shairnah listened intently to Yunus' rundown, and did not respond until he had finished.

'I see,' she finally said. 'Hold the line. I'll tell Butterbugs.'

Butterbugs strained to receive Shairnah's report while he underwent the unpleasant but utterly vital process of Makeup's installation of bloater tendrils in his armpits and on his forearms, so that icky hangings of troubling and unsanitary appearance would protrude from his toga-robed sleeves.

'Butterbugs, now listen. There is a very great thing going on. At Jambutterbugsabad, as per the Producer Team's wishes in lieu of your vast busyness, they are absolutely on top of a very awesome process. That is, they are filming mirror scenes.'

'Mirror scenes! Oh, oh, oh, oh, oh, JOY!'

'Yes, it's true! In constant contact with our crew, mirror crews half a world away are pulling off what we ourselves are accomplishing here, shot for shot, using the stand-ins of the ages, just in case we are somehow lacking in anything at all that might come out during the editing process!'

When everyone in Makeup heard this astounding news, they could not help but freeze to a halt in their activities, regardless of their obvious urgency.

'Let me – let me talk to the hero!' Butterbugs pleaded.

She held the phone near his ear, made wondrously putrid and objectionable by the makeuppers' arts.

'Greetings, Great Khan!' he said, his enunciation made juicy and sibilant and excruciating by the prosthetic cracked-and-rotting teeth attachments in his mouth, meant to fuck up his speech into the authoritarian and tyrannical patterns that were his character's own, and which were intensifying in these going-toward-climax scenes.

Seeing her star's passion and sincerity, Shairnah remained stoic, while inside, she melted.

'Oh, yes, my Khan!' he lisped/spewed/masticated/munched out. 'Your loyalness of feeling and action is *everything* to me! I hear of your wise proactive efforts, and can well imagine the effectiveness of your carrying it all out. Yes, I know we have a beautiful team! It's everybody! Same here at the Lasky's Mesa. And thus, I must compliment everyone here. But I'm talking about all of us – *all* – together!

'But Yunus-Khan, can you not remember? All we have talked about over this long shoot! So much! And now, we are near the resolve. Closure is nigh. Therefore, I was humbly... mubbl... wondering, yet, uh, in the very grandest of terms, what would you think ifffff... faaa... faa... splupp... pluppl... splurr-plep-plupp... pluppl... PLUPPLUH! P-pluh, pluh, pllhuhlluhllpl...'

Unfortunately, a particularly voluminous cyst of salivary sputum (certainly packed with DNA), caused by an Egaz-ordered injection of a Camzokevulkulumn-23 compound into his buttocks, designed to cause his oral lube-coating to go a bit wild (so as to make his verbal performance more sickening in today's scenes), had gotten lodged on the green fang that was attached to his right-upper wisdom tooth, and he had to beg off the conversation until the slippery offender could be captured by the techies at hand.

It took some doing. For a few minutes, unbeknownst to anyone present, Butterbugs' life was seriously endangered, as a spit-cyst of this composition, if it adheres to enamel, causes its giant molecules to expand exponentially, thus extinguishing the life of the victim in a shockingly brief time by way of a diphtheria-like disaster. By chance, makeup wizard Chance Westmore had selected a more raunchy-looking green fang of Perro-plastic instead of the less-offensive enamel-made one. Still, it was only a matter of a few minutes before the plastic would be engulfed and the enamel encountered.

'Khruszplipp! Ploorplapp! Pluppa-sluppa blah-blubp...!' Butterbugs tried to say, before he was constrained by Chance and his assistants, who, surgeon-style, got scalpel and drill to extract the dirty piece of slime.

Shairnah, full of understanding, and privately marveling over the fact that the two of them had just been discussing sputum earlier, returned the phone to her ear and by her sympathetic facial signals, promised Butterbugs she would be the interlocutor between he and Yunus overseas. Thus, the star relaxed while his mouth was flooded with ViscousDestroyer tinctures and purees. Suckers and graspers now entered, and by their means, the ultrastar was saved.

'Yunus-Khan? It's me, Shairnah again. Blessings, peace. Yes. Butterbugs, who is momentarily indisposed, proposes the following: he is prepared to shut down the entire production at this, the Lasky Mesa end and resume it at Jambutterbugsabad, no doubt in time for tea, tomorrow evening. Will you take up the challenge? You will? I shall tell him. Wait. Butterbugs? Listen to the pronouncements of our Yunus. All would be ready to serve on your authority, and at the time and place you require.'

Chance & Co. were in the process of irrigating the star's oral cavity with silicon/pumice cleanser, which was a dry liquid, really. He who played HMD couldn't quite speak yet, but he heard, and he was tickled.

'He will call you back, Yunus, with the mandate of his choice. Salaams to you and yours.'

Restored to at least a rasp-level, the star was able to croak, 'Thanks Chance and team! You preserved my life, and the life of the picture, too! You're the *most!*'

The team gave him a thumbs-up in return.

The blubbery cyst removed and relocated to a special high-rise Petri dish, the Makeup team withdrew in order to let the made-up one recover and contemplate in repose.

Then, in need of serious counsel, Shairnah drew the heavy soundproof drape about the chair in which he sat, and their privacy was secured.

'Butterbugs,' Shairnah said, drawing up close to his glossy mouth, 'Are you infirm?'

'I rebound, Shair. My grateful thanks. A player must be steeled for the challenges of a role, and not just the role alone, but all the preparation for it. The struggle continueth, always.'

'Good! You live yet!'

'I do. Shaken a bit, but stirred.'

'That being the case, there is time enough to ruminate over the effects of your proposal before it is enacted. You still wish it enacted?'

'Why, why heck, Shai... Yeah. *Shit*-yeah.'

'Very well.'

'You're not smiling.'

'Butterbugs, before you decide for sure, is there someone you might want to call, in case you possibly have a dinner appointment or something – You know – that you'd have to cancel, on account of your being out of station?'

She had no idea if there actually *was* anyone coming to dinner, but she had to stall for a little time, in order to prep her own explanation to the powers that be (specifically, the august but theoretically forbidding Producer Team) as to the ultrastar's radical – indeed *radical* – (and awkward, not to mention slightly expensive) change of plan.

'No Shairn, I don't think so –'

Then he caught himself. Caught, on the helpful domes of remembrance that tended to protrude from a girl's body. She was Heatherette, of course. If he embarked into the Makran, she would have to know. Therefore, he would break his own commandment and inform her, out of courtesy, if nothing else.

Shairnah handed over the phone, not knowing any number to dial, and retired from that fabric cone of ultrastarred seclusion, scarcely knowing if she had done what was required or if she had caused new nightmares of conscience to come to the fore.

Alone now, Butterbugs regarded the phone as if it were a bull before Sevilla's formerly ensanguined but freshly purged sand, in the Plaza de la Maestranza...

'I dial,' he mused, punching out the long-classified numbers, 'In shadows of my own making...'

It rang in those dreary but suddenly dulcet tones of the American telephone clicker panel's selection.

'Are you... Heatherette?' the ultrastar inquired timidly upon the answerer's generic 'Hello?'

After all, he had so recently dealt with her exclusively on the high plains of instant love. Such a girl can make a boy shy when there's day-to-day stuff to do, like saying he won't be home for dinner.

'Butterybugs! Butter of my bugs! Ballyhoobugs! That, too! It is you, it is you, it is you! I *knew* you would call! I – just – *knew!*'

'Indeed, love of my stokéd coal-fire! My intrinsic motivator! I am in Makeup and sit, before on-set.'

'To business then, based upon your position and the obviousness of your needful brevity.'

'Indeed. Well, uh, I am still in harness.'

'The most expected thing in the world! Of course! Do you need counsel? I am happy to oblige. In any event, I am happy, no matter what. Past the remnants, sex awaits, always ready, always aware, always 'Et in Arcadia ego.''

'I rejoice. But Heatherette, as per our no-bullshit relationship and our needs that are already inter-strung betwixt us, let me be frank.'

'It is the only means, Butterbugs.'

'Tell me what you think of me. For my part, I wish to, even at this late, oh-so-very-late crossroads, convey the current trip from this child's vantage point.'

'Just spit it out, lover.'

'OK. Sensing that I've hornswoggled Jambutterbugsabad as I have, by my callous disregard for all things separate from Butterbugsian affairs – apparently, some sort of amelioration must transpire, and not merely as a discussion point. Thus, in this, my rightest of minds, related to you from a mere across-town platform, I feel a need to make it up to them by moving the entire production within their ken.'

'Super! I think that a worthy goal.'

'Fan-summer-tastic!'

'All right, that's done. So, when can we do the season in the Makran?'

'Why, why... tonight.'

'I was anticipating such a reply. That's fine, but let us consider the real concept behind the sentiments.'

'I choose to listen, without condition.'

'That is wise, for let us ponder a basic thought.'

'*Ponder??*'

'It is *very* basic.'

'You're going to bring up money, aren't you? Oh, I don't care about the money – I shall pay, and out of my own coin-purse.'

'Money? No. Not money. That does not compute into this soulful equation. Rather, it is a question of honor.'

'Honor?'

'I rather think so.'

'I am honorable, Heatherette.'

'Think past the obvious, Butterbugs. Not your honor. Theirs.'

'Those who serve in Jambutterbugsabad?'

'You're catching on.'

'Their honor?'

'So, you don't think your rash and emotional gesture in taking the last day's shoot over to them in Jambutterbugsabad is anything remotely like... condescension?'

'I hadn't really thought that...'

'Perhaps not. Perhaps you were wholly thinking of... yourself?'

In a way, Heatherette couldn't quite believe what she herself was saying. Never before had she been so outspoken, never had she risked words that might be misinterpreted as wanton critiques, never had she attempted to exercise her will – or the gentle implications of its potential – so that it was flexed in front of others so. But because love was out of the bag and had sunk its possessive (golden) claws into both of them at either end of this phone conversation, liberation was at hand: she of her former constraints, and he of his current burdens. She must facilitate, and he must act. They had very little time to do so.

'And that...'

'Thinking of yourself, maybe?' She kept him on track. 'Forsaking all others?'

'Myself...,' replied Butterbugs, after ruminating on her bold question, which he took up with honest cheer.

'Beloved,' she interjected, 'I am thinking of they over there who might receive your imperial request. What are you, a god-emperor, or something?'

'My character is.'

'Well, that explains everything.'

'Yes... That... I have adopted similar characteristics... Perhaps?'

'It certainly sounds like it.'

'Heatherette! You sound so ordinary!'

'I'm sorry. Any particular reason why?'

'Yes! Many! I think it is wonderful! I'm not casting aspersions! You speak sense, and sense I need, let me tell you that, right now.'

'Because, well, I was imagining, aren't you being overly condescending to the peoples of Jambutterbugsabad?'

'I think that yes, I quite possibly could be,' he replied with a new quietude.

'And that they would always reply with politeness and agreement, to whatever you told them, out of principle?'

'I think that yes, I most definitely am.'

'Condescending?'

'Yes. Condescending.'

'But not on purpose, surely.'

'I hope not, but I have underestimated the potential for it. Say! Let me play back the conversation, for your consideration.'

Butterbugs then tapped out the replay commands with his metallic-greasy finger, and Heatherette considered.

'I have to tell you, love-speaker, the tone I heard in Yunus' voice when I heard his reaction to your proposal... Well, there was high anxiety in its timbre.'

'I imagine that I brought much mega-stress upon his decent head.'

'Yes, you can imagine.'

'Now I feel like a kluck. But I want to help them without appearing condescending or patronizing. Can you not sympathize with my desires?'

'Well of course I can. But sentiment must be crafted into caring instead of remaining as shallow show.'

'I follow you! Readily! But how can I...'

Then Heatherette's voice grew more solemn.

'I can tell you this, Butterbugs. You, who are my life-via-my-love (and vice-versa): I envision a whole long sequence of pictures, to be shot at Jambutterbugsabad, and nowhere else. Why, they will make what has come before look like... like meatloaf! In short, in this briefest of meantimes, finish thy picture at the nearest facility, and then we can be free to ponder and to enact and to produce our *own* cycle of Seventh-Artistic offerings, and do it the way we want and where we want. I am planning all of this and much more, and keenly await your involvement. Surely you know this! What do you think has sustained me in this long week's walk, so far? Why, in your own dealings, you have said picture to gambol in. Me? I have dreamtime potentials, and I have bucked-up enough to now handle the roughly 36-hour hiatus in my life which looms, until I can suck you back into my arms' orbit, by gentle and outrageously-sexy reimplementation of our plans: as Filmmakers-DeLuxe in a world awaiting our concoctions.'

'Oh, unrivaled love of my ages! I never conceived reality at this juncture in the ways you could – and *can!* Pray look upon me as your chela, and indeed, as a chela in need of guidance. *Ongoing* guidance!'

'Nice and flattering language, love of all time, but you speak the truth. Yes, you must simmer and perform art before grand strategies are tackled. In that sense, your aspirations overreached.'

'How good of you to be there, in your Jadoo [Wonder] House, before I plummeted to my foolish doom!'

'Crisis averted, Butterbugs!'

'Oh, aye, aye, lover-tone!'

'Do you want me to pop over under cover of darkness tonight, so as to top off the comfort factor?'

'In a more perfect world, more would be possible. We dare not, pomfret, if only because the time-gulf between us has been so drastically reduced.'

'I know. Oh, how I know! But I just wanted to let you in on the option, in case ye be privately wobbly.'

'Thanks, sweets. Thing is, you're entirely and totally *in* already on my privacy, and what do you hear?'

'I hear a fellow strong and sturdy and steady and steadfast, and at the top of his game, without any doubt whatsoever.'

'Beautiful dreamer! Your dreams walk through the day as examples to follow, by which they glow with reality and clarity and love!'

'Your concentration is intact, dear one. Now you can finish your role in the upper echelons of the human creative experience.'

'You have placed me there.'

'And by your climbing, you have made it fully executable. Strength to you, dear boy, and we shall kiss in the full flower of our love, in several hours' time!'

'Several hours! How much is several?'

'More than a few.'

'I am content. For the duration of those hours, however many.'

'For the duration. They will pass and we will duly join in ongoing unitedness.'

'Love and love and love again to you, my main figure. And when we join after the short time in front of us now, there shall be so great a wonder, we shall surely become the true One of our dreams! Out of two, One!'

'Good night, sweet ultrastar!'

'In the soon-ness we shall both light the sky with our love!'

And they both then clicked off at the same time, lest the protraction of the farewell statements become unbearable, though such would certainly eat up some separation time, though not nearly enough.

Resolved: a picture would be completed as planned, because of the love a man felt for a woman.

Shairnah, outside the column of draped privacy, determined that the conversation was concluded when she saw the HMD's chainmail-clad foot appear in a slight and arched chink of light near the front entrance flap. Waiting no more, she drew aside the curtain and discreetly slipped within.

Here, in this cylinder of white light, she saw the ultrastar had indeed stood, fully cured. But he stood motionless and with eyes closed. Nevertheless, knowing his p.a. was in such close proximity after a time, he held out the phone, to return it.

His eyes opened, and the two looked at each other in huge close-up.

It was their one erotic moment, and one to remember on both sides of the mere air that separated them.

The moment experienced, it quickly passed.

Shairnah, with sober duty on her mind, then ceremoniously drew aside and away the deadening curtain and Butterbugs stood revealed in all his restoration.

'I am returned!' stated the ultrastar, who advanced from the near-fateful chair and beat his breast comically to prove his soundness, which was bona fide. It was a distraction, naturally, from the inner agony he'd suffered over his now-decided crossroads.

Unspeakably happy at Butterbugs' return from unperceived danger, all of Makeup resumed their glorious work, all united in their total commitment to this picture's storied values.

Shairnah drew back in.

'Butterbugs, to proceed.'

'I'm afraid,' Butterbugs announced, 'That I have to make a statement to them, then. To all of them. Over there.' He gestured grandly toward the far, furthest west. 'I'll make it short, as the camera will be waiting.'

Shairnah handed him the phone once again.

'Ultrastar,' she informed him, after tapping out the Jambutterbugsabad Complete and Utter Access Code, 'Your voice will now be broadcast to every corner, every lane, every soundstage, every film storage vault, and every yurt of the vast studio complex of Jambutterbugsabad.'

He took the speaking device.

'Beloveds of our Jambutterbugsabad! These are the *days*, aren't they? Know, each one who breathes in your precincts, that this is me, Butterbugs. I dearly and delightedly hope I approach you with not too heavy a cheer. Know of my high and permanent regard for each and every one of you. Know that all your names shall adorn the credit sequence of 'UWH', and that you shall have seats at its premiere, and at any venue in which it plays throughout the world that you desire. Know that I canna make it over to film with you just now. Know that it was one of my heart's most valuable and super-cherished desires to *do* so! Know that I beg your forgiveness, and know that when we are all together again at the very first opportunity – which will be *soon* – (it will! I tell you, it will!) – I shall cheerfully confide in you all as to the great Reasons Why I could not select your fine facilities as the chosen site of this last, home-stretch sequence. So, in farewell for the present moment, I can only leave you with this newly-minted gem of wisdom, while at the same time pleading for your understanding. In addition, I baldly apologize that I am unable to utilize your combined facility at what is plainly the most opportune moment in this picture. However, I happen to know you are all well occupied and confident in your contributions. So, I apologize for my condescension over you. The ownership of all the collateral results is all mine. My mistake, and my miscomputation, in respect for all of your capabilities and anticipations, and my comeuppance is entirely in order. Hoping against hope, I hope you will find it in your collective heart – to *forgive*. And now, here is the gem I humbly offer as a gift: in a more perfect world, more things would be possible.'

He then repeated the message in Urdu, and again in Baluch, and finally, in slightly abbreviated Dari and Farsi versions.

As a postscript, he added:

'And I now whoop all of you on, to keep your lenses focused, your cables plugged in, and your pulleys greased, as I expect we shall be shooting the vast majority of footage of a beautiful new show, the epic saga, 'Darbidiah' at your beloved studio. Nothing has been inked, but I tell you, I will strive to make it happen! News – to *sustain you* through this difficult time of letdown…'

It was a postscript meant as a rally, but in all frankness, it was sort of a whimper.

Hanging up, he then hung his head in shame, and shed tears, pretty much like Mollycoddle's twin babies were doing just then, across town. Except, those babies were merely keen on supper, while for his part, Butterbugs had let his people down. Somehow, he would have to make it up to them. For the present, he had forgotten Heatherette's sensible suggestion to engage Jambutterbugsabad for future productions of all kinds.

In order to forget this wrenching chapter, he would have to immerse himself in work. In that sense, he was fortunate, as Egaz, cast and crew, were patiently, even *reverently*, awaiting his arrival.

And they pedaled along.

'Let us finish a picture – one remaining step at a time!' he managed to say to Shairnah. It was supposed to be a sort of battle cry in the generic sense, but it came out as a pathetic sniffle.

'It's all right, Butterbugs. They all understood. I think you're taking it much harder than any of them.'

'As well I might! How would *you* like to botch a face-saving attempt? Who do you think was supposed to lead them along the Seventh Art's risky ridge route, to lofty achievement? Not me! Oh no, not me! That august role is best left to others far more capable than my strolling player-self. But I was supposed to be there at trail's beginning, to encourage, to give hope, and to point the lantern toward the way ahead!'

'Oh, but you have! By this choice, you have taught them to stand on their own.'

'To stand… proudly?'

'Their pride was palpable, Butterbugs. As you were lecturing them with your passions, I was viewing InstaViddy of them at the other end, and the effect was staggeringly galvanizing! You achieved a very great victory in what you did. I swear it.'

'Oh, Shairnah – if I could just believe…'

'Dry your tears now, Butterbugs. Your close-up is at hand.'

They rounded a massive pillar and stood facing the cast, crew, and extras, which ran into the thousands. The ultrastar looked confusedly at Shairnah.

After a whole minute of petrifying silence, the entire company burst into applause.

Egaz came forward from behind one of the cameras.

'Well done, Butterbugs! Well done! We all heard your entreaty to our mates at Jambutterbugsabad, and the solidarity, of your own making, has raised us all – *all* – to new levels of understanding, partnership, and camaraderie!' Then he turned to the rest. 'Hurrah now, hurrah for Butterbugs!'

The roar of the masses added up to one huge approval, in the form of advanced jubilation in which all hearts present were warmed. Simulcasting to and from Jambutterbugsabad doubled the effect.

'And thus,' the director resumed, as the volume of the cheers lessened, 'Will you take up the player's burden? Will you grace us with your presence in this here Scene X-597-c? *Will you?'*

His overrun cup refilled and vigorously bubbling with potent vapor, the ultrastar cleared the liverdumpling from his throat and cried:

'Here I am! For you! All of you! From this very spot on Lasky's mesa, to the cliffs which gaze down upon that further lot, near Alex of Macedon's shore! Dare we resume? We dare! Show me the way – or take me with you!'

Again the massive company cheered and applauded, so glad and excited were they. And when a signal bell was judiciously sounded in the Palace's Dorian-moded carillon, all the celebrants prepared to get back to work, with smiles on their faces.

'None too soon!' whispered Porter to Egaz and their star. 'DFZ and the Prod Team are keen on resumption. Very. Keen.'

'And they shall have it!' said Butterbugs, knowing that Porter's genteel terminology dolled-up cruder synonyms.

'Places!' Egaz commanded.

Fabia Drake and Dorothy Dandridge, who played Xnekseldrier the Scribe and Vurra the Herald, respectively, recited their lines after Egaz's go-ahead signal:

'All right, ACTION!'

XNEKSELDRIER: [as played by Fabia Drake] *(gesturing broadly)* Oh, but greatness! It exists! He comes!

VURRA: [as played by Dorothy Dandridge] He does! *(to the crowds)* Peoples? He comes!

(A symphonic fanfare in troubling tones, to illustrate HMD*'s perverse but triumphant personality.)*

HMD: *(emerging from behind a bevy of topless houris)* I announce myself! I actually do! Because, who amongst you would have the very stuff of the universe to pull such an assignment off? Who amongst you has the primal guts to make announcements meaningful – especially those that emanate from a being of uppermost occupation – a being such as – me? Well I can tell you right now: none of you! *(The* CROWDS *show their huge approval with bellow and pipe and drum)* I thought so! Ye love me, don't you? Why, you'd better! *(laughs heartily, then attends to the business at hand)* Lord-Boy, approach! *(*LORD-BOY [as played by Emmanuel Lewis] *cometh to* HMD*'s presence, and grovels)* Lord-Boy, there was a time when I wanted to have sex with you, but now my mind is changed, for you shall be the first.

LORD-BOY: *(nonplused)* The first? What the – I thought you'd had many dozens such as me...

HMD: *(in reasonable tones, to his* SURE-FIRE GUARDIANS, *indicating* LORD-BOY*)* Take this up to the highest pinnacle of yon Citadel and let it see if it can fly all the way down. Make sure at least two of you escort it on this mission, to ensure that it makes it all the way down. *All the way,* do you hear?

SURE-FIRE GUARDIANS: Yoe!

HMD: *(to* LORD-BOY*)* I need a sacrifice, not an uncommon want.

LORD-BOY: I go with total and unrestricted joy, Highest of Mad Doctors! I have to tell you, I was terrified you would *not* choose me to inaugurate your high and extremely phallic symbol of your potent power! I'm really *pumped!*

HMD: *(to his* SURE-FIRE GUARDIANS, *noting* LORD-BOY's *pleasure, and so, wishing to spoil it for him)* My Sure-Fires, as you descend – at least two of you who accompany that thing – dent in its skull with thy cludgeons, so that its fake joy shall be extinguished before its supposed fulfillment at bottom. Hah! Ha-ha-hah!

SURE-FIRE GUARDIANS: Yoe!

*(*LORD-BOY, *stunned beyond belief, and wordless, is led away; as the scene unfolds, we will see in various shots and, in the background, the execution of* LORD-BOY *by several of the* SURE-FIRE GUARDIANS, *who have volunteered to go down with him, while the drama and dialogue continues in the foreground;* HMD *duly makes note of the aftermath.)*

HMD: Court? Surely you know I am about to enter my stronghold. Very soon now. And every one of you is asking, 'Will I be allowed to follow?' Hear me, O golden goons! *(then, to* 2ND TERTIARY VIZIER CCYKLVX:*)* What do *you* think, CX, The Overrated One?

The great Larry Gates, who was playing 2nd Tertiary Vizier Ccyklvx in his usual brilliant style, was nevertheless a bit burdened by his costume, which included a rather bizarre but stunning Saturn-like headdress (with certain attendant moons arranged in Calderian æstheticism about his head), and even though his robes had motor-assist transport mechanisms, he felt a bit faint.

'Gang, could we maybe break –' was all he had time to say, with cameras still rolling, before he started to pitch forward.

The script called for him to answer with:

CCYKLVX: I exclusively follow you, True One. I can only hope you'll have me, my Truth Regulator. If not, there is only one course to follow...

Sawl Cane & Co.'s screenplay then required him to pull a Slape-knife out of his robes, so as to slit his own throat, as he suspects that, because he has been singled out, he hasn't a chance of being saved (never mind that all the Court will be 'graciously' allowed to enter the Citadel, albeit well behind HMD, as HMD is just 'kidding around' right now, as an amusement). HMD, spotting the Slape-knife, and thinking that Ccyklvx is intending to assassinate him, seizes a spear from a nearby Carrier and lets it fly, hitting the 2nd Tertiary Vizier square in the gut.

That, anyway, was what the script commanded. But there was a possibility Butterbugs' improvisational ignition could instantly choose another pathway to drama, if it was absolutely necessary.

All was in place for this carefully rehearsed scene. SFX were on point and ready for their cue, in which the radio-controlled projectile would make its flight and end up safely in the globe of BluBlubbah TipStop SupraSalve, specially formulated by the special effects industry to provide plenty of protective flab, concealed under Larry's voluminous chasuble. The compound's coolest characteristic was, once pierced, the BluBlubbah immediately set up, braking any penetrator in about .567th of a second.

Unfortunately, things went horribly wrong.

The cameras remained rolling, but the players went off script, due to unforeseen circumstances.

Larry faltered, and was only able to make the 'Gang' utterance instead of his lines. As misfortune would have it, he was positioned – very dramatically – on a ledge at the edge of the Great Marble Flats, upon which the lion's share of today's scenes at Court were being enacted. In front of him was a ceremonial cistern, perhaps four meters deep, and one-quarter hectare in breadth. Just below the edge was a narrow gallery of smoldering basins, full of incense and bakery-jar remnants, which caused a decadent but painterly Chinese-screen of azure, silver, and greenish smoke to rise contemplatively, somewhat obscuring the hazards of the site.

Egaz, seeing his supporting player totter, was ready to sound red alert to save this national treasure of Thespia. But Larry's stamina was sustained long enough for the director to adapt the scene accordingly, based on the marvel of improv, on the part of talented actors. It worked before – it could work again.

Many an advantageous twist and turn can be used to a picture's advantage, even down to the wire. Misfortunes can often be spun into gold. The director figured he could even find a use for the line, 'Gang, could we maybe break', as a lead-in to, well, a breakdown of some kind.

But that was as far as he might take the ploy just then, as Butterbugs himself took action faster than anyone else could. Happily, the provisions of UP-70 kept all angles covered.

Butterbugs, in high mad character, saw Larry falter, and, within seconds, had a plan: Ccyklvx, made haughty by HMD's challenge, instead of intending to slay himself, now attempts to assassinate his ruler with the Slape-knife just drawn. To thwart CX and show off his prowess to the Court, HMD shall make a great leap forward, across the gulf of the cistern's corner, in order to attack and destroy his would-be attacker and destroyer.

This Butterbugs now did. He made an astounding Baryshnikovian thrust, in full costume (obviously), over the void's right angle, just as Larry, his standing finally spent, fell forward, toward one of the fuming basins, just below. The ultrastar's gymnastic talent, so recently exercised in his saving of Heatherette, was so fortunate that after a flight which would undoubtedly look stunning on the screen, his feet landed on the ledge next to the dangerous basin, just in time to gain purchase enough to gently break Larry's fall, and usher him slightly upward and backward onto the Great Marble Flats once more, so they both careered – none too swiftly, thanks to Butterbugs' inherent flight engineering – into an adjacent and very expansive wig rack, a legitimate prop that displayed the vanity of the courtiers, who were wont to change wigs regularly and without notice, as required by the script.

The scene still played, seamlessly. Larry had the wind knocked out of him, but that was all. In fact, because he was prone amidst the carnival-colored hairpieces of great extravagance, he fully recovered his faculties and rose, metaphorically at least, to the improvisational occasion quite magnificently. As Bob's camera came in for a MCU, Larry and Butterbugs continued playing the scene.

> (HMD, *having tackled* CCYKLVX [as played by Larry Gates], *feels the Slape-knife between them, wrests it from the shaken 2nd Tertiary Vizier, and with overblown and show-offy gestures, plunges it into* CCYKLVX's *lumpy midriff, then steps back to the very edge of the cistern's opening – also a show-off gesture – and stands proudly, to examine and appreciate his deed.)*

CCYKLVX: *(mortified but bitter, then with force, though dying)* Well now. *(an ironic snort-laugh, then angry)* You creep of a Lord! Why, you – ! But hold... I will not add coarse language to my final report to Your Baboon's Rump of a 'Highness'! No, I will not pleasure you even now, for I am killed. And by your murdering me, I leave with my corpse a toxicity which, *(winces)* or that, *(winces)* will seep like acid-mist into your visceral hump, where it cannot escape, and where all manner of hideous symptoms and effects shall bear themselves out on your person. Not instantly, but with deep time. All these things, which I cannot possibly name now, as ye have robbed me of the years it would take to relate them, will strike you like a merciless karmic review, except without the luxury of innocence through rebirth. No, you shall have the knowledge of your crimes and grossest of misdemeanors. For you are the trickster, the dirt merchant, the searingly pissy pustule of dissolution and anger in which all of humanity's faults have gathered to a boil – *in* a boil or wen, of toxic pop, to be popped, so as to poison our failed world. Oh, but let me rave! Let me roil! Let my rant be heard down the hundred ages of the soul's mortality! So, you inane creep, you puncturing stabber, you sick-making jelly-bone of unsavoriness! And, and… you LIAR! I cannot hate you enough, even in my dwindling moments. I cannot stand the fact that your horrific mug fills my fading vision's aspect ratio as I wrap 'er up on this doom-laden globe! Therefore, I shall raise mine eyes unto the cloud-streaked heavens, where the dying embers of the sun tint all in a reassuring rainbow of farewell colors, so as to make my crossing into the Underworld at least a memorable one, so when Pluto hassles me about being your sycophant, I can at least remember that your throttle-reign over me ended with a tonal enhancement. For me, I care nothing. Nothing at all! For this poor world, under your unspeakable and wretched tutelage, I can only say, this planet we call Earth – not your sullen 'Urth' – even at its lowest ebb, was at least a place where potential was possible. And, as your sub-vizier, I thought I could make a difference in the long run. I dreamt that… somehow… I could, in my weak but determined ways, have you eliminated by whatever means it took, even via violence, which I have always spoken out against, though I stupidly witnessed many of your egregious acts in a state in which we courtiers are enacting, even now, a neutered muteness. So, I have failed in my dream. Oh, but I am speaking my piece, and you are inane enough to let me! Yet, maybe you will not now hack my head off, for I am about to give you credit. You're right, H.igh-on-drugs, M.ad-der than a brainless hare, D.octor of a hundred-and-one morbid degrees of lust and pig-behavior! (There, your name is spelled out complete, and for the first time.) You're right in that I was certainly hatching a plot to take you out. I would have proceeded with it, even at my peril. Alas, a peril that has now punctured my belly, and at the worst possible time. But I leave you with this one thought of horror: I depart, but, *who else* is plotting against you? Who else will not just pull their Slape-knife from their tunics of silent protestation, but perhaps bump you off with Judge-missiles and Prindon-dust? Maybe it will even happen ungrandly, when you are performing some vile personal act of unspeakable uncleanness, and someone will wrap you up with justified techniques of which I cannot even conceive. Nor would I wish to! I would not ever slumber again if I were you! But, oh, how I wish I could be there, when – oh, oh, oh, now it comes! Now! It actually does! I have lived to see it! Death be my guide, my conductor! *(Even though he desires to take her hand, he dares not invoke his wife, comely young* STERRATOPPA *[played here by Marvel Mirkry], who is just nearby, so as not to associate her with his transgressions, despite her longing responses, her knowing of the repression and now this tragic resolve, that catch and hold his heartstrings; then he rallies)* Look! Look, as the late colors stream in the heavens above! The colors of freedom! Far above, but so near! They are free – Like I am now – free! Just think! I am… fre…! *(rolls off the wig-comfort onto the Flats; dies)*

STERRATOPPA: *(wife to* CCYKLVX, *nearby; cam moves nearer to her in short series of closening shots; weepingly whisper-sings* [dubbed by Laura Gibson] *her sad lullaby)* Hush a bye, don't you cry, go to sleep little baby, when you wake, you shall have… *(finishes song, in two-verse version).*

(She mourns her lost love. A montage of close-ups, combined with Newman's variations on the song, designed to emotionally wipe the audience out. When the song ends, everyone's heart is broken. Except one.)

Subjectively, this insightful and moving improv set a new and profound factor into HMD's character. Butterbugs, so pleased with Larry's perfect invention that he was almost distracted, picked up on it with boundless understanding.

HMD: *(to* CCYKLVX, *unmindful of* STERRATOPPA's *pæan to the tragic loss of her mentor and husband)* Oh, shut up! Get out! Get out, you old misery! Clear him off my deck, people who wait upon me! I say this now, so *do* it now, otherwise many shall die. I'll let the grave people inhale that fœtid acid-mist he was talking about. Me? I shall *de*hale his time on earth and its apostasy, and notice now, how I turn about, how I face my people, how I inhale, and how I shout: This is MY world! See how I hold it!

(HMD raises his arms in a mighty gesture before THE MASSES.*)*

HMD: There! You see? I have saved the nation once more! This rotten trash, who lay awaiting with gangland actions, wanted to 'break' me! Did you hear? In case you didn't, I'll repeat it for you. He said, 'Gang, could we maybe break –' But he didn't finish, because he knew I heard him, and he was about to say, 'Could we maybe break the High Mad Doctor?'! Instant treason! Punishable by death! And you saw me carry out the sentence, which was based on his aggressive act of weapon-drawing!! Oh, my justice is thus demonstrated to the Masses without dilution or delay! If this false and dirty garbage-hulk had broken me, he would have destroyed *you!* See how I have saved your collective ass? See the Slape-knife he carried upon his person, by which to carve my solar plexus into a knurled doorknob? Here! *(tosses the bloody Slape-knife at two* CLEAN-UP KNAVES, *who approach in terror)* Cast this hideous death-tool into the Intercontinental Boiler, where all things opposed to me are consumed! Witnesses! Observe! Once again, a Leader saves his Nation! Only *I* can do it! I am the Only Leader of you people! *(pauses after impacting the* COURT *with these words, then adds, in weak and mealy-mouthed tones:)* Remember, everything this guy said was a lie *(this goes over like a wet dud-balloon).*

Still off script, but rolling, with Egaz gesturing his cameras, their expert manipulation capturing the new ground as if it were after a hundred run-throughs, Butterbugs as HMD lowered his arms as the first camera (Surtees) dollied over to where Larry lay at the edge of the terrace, while the second (Shamroy) pulled back for a crane-rise.

The shots were very grand and valuable beyond words, the drama progressing without words themselves, as the tension remained and grew. Egaz's desire at the moment was to have stalwart courtiers raise up the dead man's body and exit down into the cistern via stairs in the background, while the HMD watches from his terrace, brooding. Such was his quasi-mystical communication with cast and crew that his directions were realized via a few gestures, a bit of pantomiming, and an exercising of a further, less explainable melding of receptive minds.

In order to get the shot of the corpse's removal, essentially from above, which would make a striking composition, Bob's camera was required to swing out over the parapet of the terrace, above the gloomy cistern, four meters below. In order to progress, the camera would have to rise to a level that transcended the smoky curtain, so that the efforts of the servants carrying their expired cargo would be lavishly and artistically revealed as the smoke faded with the achieved height. It was a shot the operator and director of photography would have to take as it came, for they alone would know how to pull it off.

Only Bob's camera could take on the challenge, as Leon's was on the wrong side of the barrier. So, the progression commenced, with glowingly magical results. There, behind a diaphanous barrier of columnar smoke, back-lighted nicely by the natural sundown, the servants went about their task with an impulsive ritualism, Larry playing dead nicely, and the camera capturing it all, with increasing closeness.

However, there was a line of liveried extras standing along the parapet to provide population to the scene, and some of them were potentially in conflict with the approaching crane's neck.

Chuck Heston, who was playing Bhuhureluckcx the Cross-Eyed Seer-in-Residence, let out a baleful warn-call of considerable electrification from his perch on a bridge that spanned the cistern. This stalled others who were positioned along the parapet from a startlement of the crane's movement, which was partially obscured by the smoke, the contact of which could have launched them into the fire-pits of perdition. It was a cry that probably saved many a player from flame-branding, and besides, it sounded appropriate on the soundtrack, as if someone in the HMD's elite guard was letting out a warlike but supportive whoop.

The barrier and extras thus cleared, the camera crane, controlled by grips at the anchor end, following the director's devices and desires, continued to rise in a forward mode.

'Swing out, swing out *more*,' Egaz whispered to the grip crew, one of who happened to be Old Atrocity.

'She can take only so much,' the veteran hissed.

'Tell me when it's dangerous, OA.'

'It was dangerous two meters back!'

'I need the shot. Look, they're getting the perfect angle now.'

OA said nothing but hopped on the anchor end for ballast. Egaz took his place at the push handle, and they inched along.

The front wheels of the crane neared the ledge's edge, while the camera itself was almost over land, so to speak, with the long neck serving as a bridge across the cistern. None dared consider the perimeters of catastrophe if this entire apparatus were to go over and down, as the holiness of the shot, which, for countless reasons, would be impossible to retake, was not to be impeded upon.

Bleobaris Vosstkoff, Bob Surtees' operator this day, put his life on the line in getting the shot. The mechanism was already overextended, as Bob was riding it right beside Vosstkoff, and this unexpected demand of coverage had turned the crane's route onto an uncharted tack, for which counterweights had not been calculated, so everything was extended way beyond its capacity.

This was unacceptably and obscenely out-of-order practice of course, but due to Butterbugs' bold and wonderful improvisation, director and crew could only follow along, helplessly but creatively. The risk was clearly producing outstanding results, both artistically and dramatically.

'We have to be ready for anything,' Egaz had warned his crew before the ultrastar's arrival that morning. 'Butterbugs is in a sort of exalted form, and we must not stand in his way. I feel this on a transcendental level. And really, who of you could ever question the value of his inventions? Silent? Yes, me too. So, we will be adaptive and we will do it right, whatever course he leads us on. This is Butterbugs' picture. The rest of us are merely custodians of his creation. If anyone wants out, now's the time to scuttle, and no one need feel dishonor.'

Egaz's heads-up speech had gone over particularly well, even with the sometimes critical safety inspection team from the state and fed agencies. As a result, all stood firm in their duties.

'Art shall not be regulated!' Mil Mal, the safety team captain, declared. 'Whatever he does, we must inspect, then inevitably approve,' he'd confidently told Egaz.

So now, with the obviousness of the increasing risk apparent to all concerned, even then, there would be no call to 'Cut!' No one would have the gall – nor the bald audacity. Nor the courage.

The giant matte box on the camera, free of the hypnotic smoke, now captured the corpse's rise to the servant's shoulders, to be borne out in Siegfried style, but without honors.

In continuous 70mm shots, the hardware, because of its mass, tends to move in stately time segments; not that screen results are stodgy, but a certain allowance of physics is required when considering Ultra-Panavision's movement through the universe.

Within that context then, the threat now settling upon the over-reaching crane advanced in a sort of slow motion. Butterbugs himself, in character, was able to look about (and not solely after the victim HMD had just murdered), as if to check out the Court's reactions. He noticed the pronounced listing of the great apparatus, and once again was compelled to think fast.

As a vampiric statement of Empire, Butterbugs as HMD then struck an electrifying pose: hands stretched skyward, feet in wide stance, face in ghastly humor, a long shriek of absolute victory coming from his mouth.

But the crane had reached its tipping point – literally. The front tire had passed over the ledge, and the other five, usually straddling the ground with Richter-proof stability, now seemed poised to surrender their authority. All who now rode the crane, OA, Bob, and operator Bleobaris, were in high jeopardy, and Egaz & Co. were losing their grip. The rolling shot was still safely proceeding, as the camera's fluid head absorbed most of the crane's unwanted vibrations and movements, but even that threshold was about to be compromised. A teetering commenced.

For a second, all who were crewing expected a 'Day of the Locust' (Paramount, 1975) moment, when a collapse of something massive on a film set precipitates an inexorable doom, and all anyone can do is look on with powerlessness.

But once again, it was Butterbugs who saved the day.

Within the confines of his shriek, almost as if he had a dog's multiple sets of vocal cords, the actor was able to convey the following disguised message:

'Bob! Get off!'

That was all he said. But it saved the day.

Jarred by this strange new warning amidst the audio gobbledygook, Bob had been so wrapped up in getting the shot, he was riding the crane, even unto his and the others' apparent peril. From his vantage point, Butterbugs had calculated it was the extra rider's presence that was dictating the collision course in play. So, now that the camera and bucket seats had barely cleared the abyss, his unconventional but canny advisement for Bob to abandon ship was opportune, down to the second. Message received, the old guy was still agile enough to accomplish the feat, and jumped the half meter just before it would have become at least four, and so the crane was returned to balance, and the grips regained control.

Once Bob had disembarked and crawled to safety, the crane, lightened and braked by the grips and Egaz, was no longer in danger of clanking into its death-pit. However, in the most unexpected event yet, it shot up about two meters, a barber-chair movement so shocking and sudden, surely the shot was ruined.

On the contrary, the splendidly solid fluidity (an oxymoron only in print) of the 70mm film stock and its gimbal-like adaptability to change provided for a gripping effect, the least of which was a pullback in composition, by which not only the departing corpse progression was kept in frame, but now Butterbugs' menacing figure and its accursed pose was in-shot, just to the right. Pure art, achieved by way of an unplanned but striking jerk, back and up. The results were beautifully composed and dramatically purposeful. Bleobaris calmed any fears that Egaz and crew might have had by sneaking a thumbs-up sign, while continuing to roll.

(This effect, the 'Butterbugs Thrust-Up-and-Back' (e.g. BTUB) as it was dubbed, would be emulated by filmmakers, with mixed success, for generations to come.)

Still the cameras rolled on, rock-steady, rocking on. Still the scene played. Elation reigned en route.

Sash, who was doing sound, breathed a sigh of relief, not only for a disaster averted, but because the 'Bob! Get off!' interjection would be covered up by Alfred's scoring, though he retained the track in a VEFFNIKEFF file, in case Egaz might figure a use for it somehow. On the other hand, the more Sash ran the dialogue, the less he heard consonants and vowels within the same track of Butterbugs' shriek. Truly, it was a 'Paul is dead' moment.

Both cameras then rose (in safe fashion), to get two pristine overviews of HMD in his gorgeously operatic farewell/fuck-you gesture toward his old nemesis, with that very nemesis being hauled off to obscurity. Shots of nothing less than Shakespearean impact. It was a blessed moment.

'ccccttt,' Egaz choked, then shouted, 'CUT! The CUT. CUT. CUT!' Then, mindful of his civilized duty as a leader of a great enterprise: 'Now – safety check! All stations secured! First Aid – do the essentials! Now! Set, mobilize for any damage! Do your duties of helping!'

Other than for the benefit of his own conscience, Egaz really had no reason to give any commands at all, for the crackness of everyone was in instant play and already enacted. OA hopped off the anchor and secured his crew within an instant. Set-wide, it took only about thirty seconds before it was ascertained without a doubt: 'No casualties or equipment damage; engage in emotional impact scrutiny to those involved.'

Nobody was outraged at anyone for the close call. Instead, a feeling of wonder, of deliverance, descended over the whole company.

'Larry!' Butterbugs called out, 'Larry! You're OK? Crew made it, but you... you!'

He rushed over to where Gates had been lain, on a Roman debauchery-style couch.

'Larry! Speak to me, trouper beyond compare!'

'I am restored,' said the veteran actor in his steady and calm 'Twilight Zone' (CBS) voice. He had been comfortably quasi-napping and mentally reviewing his perf. 'If it were not for your easy heroism, I should feel the deepest of fools for causing this brush with catastrophe, but you level and settle and simmer any such controversy entire, and, by your powers, I am, as I have announced, *restored*. For that and much more, I thank you, Butterbugs!'

Doc Slammer, who was just at hand, nodded his approval.

'Thanks, Doc. As long as you're safe and well, Larry. The remainder is naturalness, not extraordinariness. Except for your performance, that is – under this unexpected duress.'

'Mine? Yours! Oh, yours! My speech was in my character's heart. It, or he, was the author, not me. Facilitated by you!'

'Same here! I tell you Larry, *same here!*'

'Then we both had that most rare of thespian experiences: mutual discovery through un-expectation, and the transpirations therein!'

'Joy to you, actor. Rest where you are, while I see to the matters of the set, and to the follow-up welfare of others who have suffered.'

'I will, Butterbugs, ultra-ultra-star! Care for them, as they so care for you!'

Larry gazed after him like he was the exact opposite of the character his costume represented.

'Youuuuu *dirty dog!*' he mock growled.

'My favorite kind of compliment, Larry!' the ultrastar chirped.

His heart melted with emotion as he gazed around, seeing everyone in cast and crew seeing to everyone else. There was nothing he need do but celebrate the wonder.

He then lavished praise upon Egaz, the crane crew, OA, and then Bob, all of whom were OK, and especially upon Bleobaris, whom, *Sir* Butterbugs insisted, should get a knightship for his superb work. He gave QE2 a quick call to set it up.

Once again, legendary was the scene so captured this day, a take that could not be retaken. Once again, the 'Seven Versions of the Seventh Art' approach was being challenged.

The impact of Butterbugs' rescue of the camera team, which was not only vital to the interests of the picture's completion, but was an act of high humanitarianism, made in order to save one of the Industry's most beloved lenser teams – out of decency if nothing else, was completely electrifying to the whole company on set, and the world of cinema as a whole.

'It was a moment of wonder as much as shock,' stated Egaz, who took up the heavy gauntlet of the production's conscience, supported by Porter. 'And because some of you may be experiencing rather more of the latter at this moment, I'm granting a suspension of further shooting for the rest of the day, and of the week, if needed, on Porter's and my accountability.'

'But Egaz,' said Bob, plainly shaken despite his sterling stoutheartedness,

'We'll become grievously behind sked if we did a suspension, and that would push us past tomorrow's ultimo finale deadline. Quite frankly, I'm hearty enough to continue. Doc Slammer's just checked me out, and I'm as spry as a cricket. Besides, Shammie would mock me for my cowardice.'

Bob glanced in the direction of the other master cameraman with a jaundiced eye.

'I'd rather you be mocked than have some trauma surface, due to my negligence,' the director replied.

'I must say,' offered Porter, 'If Shammie's going to get ratty, he can do it to me in person.'

Shamroy himself was within earshot.

'I make no judgments, folks. Bob & Co. just had a near-death.' Leon lit a long-nine cigar. 'Far be it from me to analyze, much less get sport from it. I'm just happier 'n shit that he's still a rival and not a martyr I'd have to pray to for inspiration. It's your call, in-charge boys.'

Impressed with this A.S.C. solidarity, and his director's and line producer's high considerations, Butterbugs nevertheless now spoke his mind – and not just from within a context of self-interest.

'Gentlemen,' he began, after waiting for a lull of indecision to settle like a huge wad of wet pink fiberglass insulation over a rainy construction site, 'I am surrounded by persons of honorable principles. Hard workers all, and for the same cause, too. Well past the concerns of Industrial filmmaking, I must say, I witness – regularly – the highest standards of ethical behavior on this picture, which at any time could easily digress into a miasma of civil, artistic, or egocentric conflict. Incredibly – but in actuality, and not surprisingly – I have yet to encounter any sort of discord or the slightest inconsideration on this here set, throughout this here picture. And with such exemplary ethical and humanistic standards in play, I have come to expect nothing else but mega-quality conduct from here on in. And because the 'in' in question is a matter of mere hours, I'm wondering if I cannot speak in terms that would not be wholly foreign to the big time Producer Team above us all, and other hardass agencies involved. May I speak?'

'Why yes, of course, Butterbugs,' said Porter.

'Indubitably,' agreed Egaz.

'Well then,' the ultrastar continued, 'I think we should continue the filming uninterrupted. Why? Because, despite this mishap, there were no casualties of any kind. Larry is cheerful, Bob himself is willing, and I, even with my involvement in the incident, however minor, make it known that I have absolutely no equivocation about pressing on… To *forget* the near-miss trauma, if nothing else. For who among us cannot say our beloved and vital activity of making pictures does not cancel out any possible trends and tendencies toward feeble-mindedness, unhappiness, and worry? So, as time's a wastin', I vote we get a move-on into our next scene.'

Who then, would step forward and challenge Butterbugs? Who could possibly? Not producer, nor director, not even those in the avenue of possible trauma brought on by the near-death so recently dodged. No one on set.

One did, though. None other than Shairnah stepped forward into Leon and Bob's beautiful lighting plot.

'Butterbugs,' she addressed him directly, 'I cannot call you heartless, but I cannot call you entirely sensitive, either. Or even sensible. Rather, how came you to such demands of product over cares for the human factors within the usually calculating procedure of commercial film factory output? If no other will speak it, then I, Shairnah, must call your hypocrisy. For you would sacrifice others for your own gloriousness. So many people are so unhappy in this world. It seems as if those who have reason to be the happiest are the least entitled to spread hate and discontent to those who are already overburdened with it.'

'Shairnah of Latakia!' Sonny Projector burst in. He had just arrived on set and knew nothing of this debate.

'I'm calling his bullshit,' replied the now-feisty p.a., without requiring any further commentary from some agent.

'As well she might,' interjected Butterbugs. 'For she is correct.'

'What a thing to say!' Sonny stormed, somewhat sanctimoniously. 'After all you've done, Butterbugs! Your tiny-time p.a.!' He then faced Shairnah straight on. 'What do *you* know of sacrifice? It's because of Butterbugs that we are at Lasky Mesa at all. Did you even know that? I doubt you could ever conceive of such a comprehension! Why, if it hadn't been for our star's goodness and generosity, we would have had to decamp to Jambutterbugsabad en masse! Did you even *know* that?'

'Peace, Sonny. Peace!' Butterbugs intervened. 'Let me inform you with purpose, in front of all. You've just got to know it all. Yes, 'tis true: my selection of this here location. But that's only a third of it. Twice did I desire to yank production here and move it, if only for a day, to my beloved Jambutterbugsabad. Most thoroughly then do I plead guilty to such a notion. But know, it was through the wisdom of Shairnah of Latakia that I reversed my determination to see through such an impetuous scheme!'

To those few on Earth who might know of the truth – that in fact such counsel emanated from Heatherette and not specifically on Shairnah's behalf – the effects of Butterbugs' generosity might have gone unappreciated by those who had no idea of such things. For if Shairnah chose to put Butterbugs on the spot in front of everyone, thus giving him the option to speak in actual terms regarding his location preference, and if he chose to protect the identity of whomever it was whom he phoned while in the privacy of that curtained chair in Makeup, well then, that was his own business. By such benchmarks would his reputation be added to or subtracted from, if ever the truth be known. With his actions of admission though, the p.a.'s regard for him only increased multifold. She knew everyone concerned was perfectly all right with the immediate continuation of filming, but to see him protect someone who was obviously very special to him – perhaps topping all others, by assigning an act of nobility that she, Shairnah, did not in fact commit, instead of to his anonymous champion, who obviously had done so, was an unadulterated example of his magnanimity, the depth of which one could only guess.

She was also mature enough to let pass the notion that it was she, Shairnah, who did indeed introduce the concept of condescension in connection with Butterbugs' harebrained scheme, and by it, so moved him to consult his someone special, his 'dinner appointment', whom intuition told her was a real and secret source of guidance for him. No need to take any accurate credit when enough *in*accurate credit was already presented, so as to settle the matter.

'Might I suggest then,' Shairnah declared to the entire company, and with impressive brio, 'let us proceed upon our pre-determined course. That is, shall we not continue to roll the cameras in the here and now?'

It was most appropriate that she, a 'mere' production assistant, should pose the option as a question. The answer came quickly and democratically. The company applauded and cheered her without reservation, and not just because she was honoring Butterbugs' wishes. By her audacity she had acquired new respect, and not by design.

'A future producer of repute is Shairnah of Latakia,' OA whispered to his wife. Tarlah nodded in awe.

'In that case,' Egaz announced with high pride, 'we shall shoot Scene EF-514 after lunch, viz. in the space of, let us say, fifty minutes. N'est pas?'

'We *will*, director!' the company replied, almost in unison.

Following a cardboard-box lunch, there were scenes filmed that contained some of Butterbugs' finest acting to date, if not ever, as well as similar work from his co-stars, who were many. It was as if, in that brief and essentially groundless confrontation of the morning, some small cloud had passed in front of the sun's enlightening rays, and with its passing, a liberation of sorts had occurred.

As a result, nothing now stood in the way of Butterbugs' full efforts in applying the brilliance of his art to the remains of the picture. Not that anything had been denied previously. But now, after the near-death-by-camera earlier, the dental boil this morning, the shenanigans up in the Citadel tower with Juba, and heavy guilt over shooting locations, as well as other traffics and alarums, whose authorship could only be ascribed to him, his was a deep desire to make peace with his conscience. To be followed by a will-to-power, entailing completion, closure, and achievement necessary to conclude this major chapter of his life and career.

Butterbugs could now make his move to solidify his intentions.

'I intend forthwith,' he thought to himself as he completed yet another of his vile character's soliloquies with the effortless genius as was his strength and style, 'to move into Heatherette's cinematic world. And to do it with even more dedication than I formerly thought, regardless of being at the dawn of the new and permanent euphoria of our mega-love. Not that I decry pictures of the type in which I currently serve… Quite the contrary!… But, after the advanced accomplishments made within its realms, I am allowing myself to *evolve*. And with this evolution,

I shall be transformed – willingly – into something I can only hope will be more purposeful to the world and its inhabitants, whom I love so fully and soundly.'

Such a manifesto seemed daring to him, even at this juncture, but he knew it was what he had always wanted, even from back in the early days, before his ascendancy.

Those early days! He in fact never thought of them much, so how could he have known of this secret desire? Such were the unfoldings of life, and the goodnesses therein.

The final scene of the day came, as the others organically had, at sunset.

(As HMD *attends to trivial selfishness, such as nose-hair grooming and dead skin picking, performed in front of everyone,* LORD-BOY's *execution is clearly seen in the distant background. As ordered, his attendants duly cheat him of full glory on the way down. His head is splattered in the air, before all three end up as mere spots in the waste before the Citadel.* HMD *happens to look over into the sunset just in time to see the essential act.)*

HMD: *(noting the aftermath of* LORD-BOY's *successful execution, as an aside)* Well, at least my new pad has been consecrated by the elimination of that stupid *kid.*

QISUMYTIMUX THE ATTENDER: [as played by Harry Wilson] See how his blood makes your soul shine!

(A remarkable and eerie glow emanates from the Citadel, and it grows with intensity; music score builds to a powerful crescendo.)

HMD: *(casually, in huge CU)* Yeah.

(Fade out.)

'Cut! Cut! And I mean: Cut!' whooped Egaz, swimmingly pleased at the whole one-of-a-kind sequence the day had brought.

OA, regarding Butterbugs in his fade-out posture, almost felt like lying down on his stomach and measuring himself in order to advance along, in the manner of the sadhoos of Gaya District, as an act of devotion to this non-god, but seemingly godlike person. But instead, he relied on his usual sensibilities and merely raised both his palms as transmitters, to broadcast whatever waves he was capable of – waves of honor – toward his ultrastar, over there in the outrageous costume.

'And yes: cut!' yelled Egaz yet again, out of pure happiness, after this last scene of the day. He was ecstatic because all had gone much better than he possibly could have wished. Rather!

'Superior, Butterbugs. You leave us in a sunset of excitement, perfectly lining us up with a future of *cinematica gloria*. I can't imagine how we're going to top this picture in future, but we will! I tell you, we will!'

'And we shall all drink toasts in Pluto's underworld tavern, for the next millennium, if need be.'

'Or in Shiva's foamy nectar mahal,' said Egaz.

'Even better! Up Gangotri way, I should think.'

'Indeed, hip ultrastar.'

'Memories of Gothpore... Oh, Gothpore! How things must *be* there!'

'Nostalgia is the guide of we filmmakers. We're always trying to recapture some innuendo, some notion, some subconscious revelation, from our childhoods, maybe even from material we dreamt as children. From the womb, even? Thoughts of the world as we think we know it for the first time. Would not the best pictures in the world be the actual encapturement of those golden nuances? I tell you, that will be my cinematic mission from now on. We will realize at least *some* of them in the cinematic lives we have left to us, on this superficial but really quite enjoyable planet.'

The need for making manifestoes was spreading, apparently.

'In any case,' the director continued, returning to the moment, 'you have perfectly lined us up for the demands of the morrow, in which we shall see the climax of all we have striven for. Can I buy you an entertaining beverage or some such, whether in the halls of beer or the coves of liquor-thimbles, which cover the night-needs of this location city?'

'Oh, no thanks, Egaz, as much as I'd like. This week has been a sort of monastic exercise for me. Good for the concentration, and all.'

'I cannot argue with you there, my boy. You are transparently and transcendentally incandescent, you know.'

They both burst into laughter in a big way, at the pretentious balderdash-terms others bandied about so gleefully.

'You and Keenah have a night out, why don't you? Oh, and have real fun for once. If for no other reason, just to say you both did so while the picture is actually in production, rather than... you know... after it is all over.'

Egaz suddenly teared up.

'Butterbugs! After it is all over! It is *nearly* all over!'

'Why Egaz! Comfort be yours! There will be weeks and weeks of editing and post-production yet. Your tray will remain full for some time.'

'I know, I know, but the verve of the shooting, the vim of the rigor! The lusty camaraderie we've had! Gone... A set sun...'

'There will be voice-over and dubbing work yet. Scoring! Publicity! Exhibition! Glory!'

'Yes? Why yes. There will! We will still have sessions to do!'

'Of course, Egaz. And you will be happy, as the footage will be in the can, and the excitement of the crafting of the footage will be yours.'

'And yours, as well.'

'Of course. And do not forsake the beauty of those scoring sessions which await.'

'You're right! Alfred wants you there.'

'Wouldn't miss 'em for anything. One of life's highest privileges!'

'Many high-points yet, hmm?'

'And the roadshow release planning, and the credits sequence, and the presentation design – we're intrinsic to it, Egaz.'

'You're right! 'Tis really midway that we are!'

'Glory be!'

'You know, Butterbugs, that first time I saw you, in the surreal vale of a fluorescent conduit – a nowhere – you, you were *somewhere*, though I could not get a bearing on it, even with my additional powers of perception.'

'Some things do not need to be perceived.'

They hugged in true friendship.

'Have a super repose then, Butterbugs.' Egaz daubed his eyes and smiled brightly. 'And Shairnah?'

She was at Butterbugs' side now.

'What you have done for us today I cannot really put into perspective as of yet, except to offer you profound thanks.'

'I'm not sure what I *did* exactly, Mr. Director.'

'You straightened us out. You pointed to the very fact that we were a bit too preoccupied with our great selves and our great project to remember the world still revolves around a sun – and not one of our fabrication. Good luck, dear girl, and thanks for thy service.'

After a cup-dinner at the Boiler Rack in humble Coy Lane with the launderette crew from Costumes And Their Baggage, Butterbugs and Shairnah wandered wordlessly home.

As they stood before the entrance of Calle Rarefied, they passed the pilasters and looked back on the huge Citadel set across the valley's expanse. Work lights were illuminated way at the top and other light escaped from the lancets in the shaft of the tower. A lightweight sea mist had stolen in from the Pacific yonder, which made the rays project out into the mysterious night sky. The vision was no small reason they should experience a mutual shiver, although the sea mist had brought with it a slight chill factor.

'Come in for a moment,' said the ultrastar quietly as they reached the door of his residence.

'A remarkable opportunity to thank you, then.'

'I have more thanks for you than you could possibly have for me, though I shall attempt to even out the possibilities.'

'Yes, I shall tarry… and I formally thank you now.'

'Thanks for the thanks.'

'A memorable day, Butterbugs. A memorable time.'

'More than most.'

'It cannot be properly described.'

'Not by the longest of shots. I can only hope the picture will be worth all our efforts.'

'It will, Butterbugs. I know it to be true.'

He beamed.

'I have no doubt of it either, super-girl. I've known it all along.'

'Yes of course, how could you not? You are its very body, mind and soul.'

'Monitor your praise, Shairnah! Save it for after the completion of this feature picture, and include yourself in it, if you please. Your name shall be proclaimed on the big screen. In proper placement, naturally.'

'I will quell my gushings, then. We're talking too much about it, aren't we – as if it's all in the can.'

'Assuredly, but the condition is an understandable one. I always get a tad impatient toward the end of shooting.'

'Yet, will you miss it? This production, I mean?'

'Deeply, I should think. You know, I was reticent at first. I thought it beyond my means; past my capabilities to even conceive of a plan of approach. But then I read Sawl's novel, and the truth of it hit me like a baseball bat made of mercury, splattering all round. The truth was self-apparent. I only had to look at it and react. Egaz's insights have been vital, for I have hung my very life on them. The writing team – what an expansive communal mind they are! Always inventing, improving, energizing! And all the 'little' people along the way! That's certainly movie making for you, isn't it? It has been a demanding shoot, and in many ways a difficult one, mainly for my too-deeply-felt sensitivities. But I have been refreshed as well, as many have kept my mud-puddle at bay, while one has even shown me the bridge across it! Yes, I am refreshed, and in ways I could never have imagined.'

'I'm happy for you, Butterbugs. No one deserves it more.'

'And you, Shairnah, what's next?'

'Well, I always thought I would make a good servant-girl. Or, I could always work in my father's rope and twine factory back in old Damascus. What's left of it, anyway…'

'Would you like to continue in the Industry?'

'Oh yes, I would. But I could never imagine the opportunity would come up. There are so many who want so much, and there is no room for all.'

'Always a problem in the picture world.'

'Even in this Epoch of Butterbugs!'

She had a look of longing on her sweet face, so caring and feeling.

Butterbugs tossed his keys on the kabuki table.

'Would you excuse me for a moment?' he said. 'I have to make a phone call.

You can have a cream-punch from the icebox, or else you could watch 'Michael Kohlhaas' (Columbia, 1969) on the color television if you want, whilst you wait.'

'Will it be long? Big day tomorrow, Butterbugs.'

'Oh, I think not so long.'

'Fine. Then I shall wait and simply contemplate the dusk, and all after it.'

'Fitting! So much in it is worth pondering, my fine p.a.'

He retired behind a curtained alcove and dialed a number with quiet pleasure.

'Porter? Butterbugs at this end of the line. Yea, I know there is much to do on the morrow. I have a request. Please designate Shairnah as a full-blown producer and assign her to the latest picture under your control, either at Klizzington, Your Basic, MGM, or even at Oxidized Onion. I also happen to know you have several projects cooking at Oddball. Porter, I tell you, she is ready, though she may know it not. I cannot contemplate letting her slip away due to my negligence. She will be perfect. Thus, I myself will also utilize her in the very near future, perhaps in my Esoteric Section endeavors. Yes. That is all. Thank you Porter. Until I see you then, anon.'

Returning to the main salon, Butterbugs paused as he saw Shairnah sitting in her quiet mood, purple-grey twilight supporting her all round, as she gazed out the little window into the gathering night.

For the briefest of seconds, Butterbugs questioned as to whether he had done the right thing.

'No, I did her right,' he thought. 'We want her. Our Industry needs more of her. Yes, we want her.'

Gently did he clear his throat (which actually needed doing, as he was emotionally touched by her silently beautiful pose), causing her to turn about without startlement.

'I want to thank you, Shairnah, most sincerely, for calling my bullshit when and where it mattered most: in front of everyone today.'

'You're most welcome, Butterbugs. I'm glad I didn't disappoint you.'

'Disappointment did not exist this day in the hearts of any of us. Perhaps it has even been banished from the world.'

'*Would* that ever be a possibility? *Could* it ever be?'

'I believe it has already happened. Hark! I hear a tapping at the back door.'

He entered the soft gloom of the back passage and felt for a match, then ignited the wick of a lotus-shaped grease lamp in its wall sconce.

Tuan Jim, in for the day to butle for Butterbugs and tidy up, entered the chamber and approached Shairnah with a handwritten note on a plastic tray.

'For you, Missy-Baba.'

'Thank you, Tuan Jim.'

'What's the deal?' asked Butterbugs, pouring some cola-sharbat and other cup-fillers, before tucking into his treasured pan-fried grape seeds.

'Why, it's from Porter Parker,' she answered.

'Oh, oh! Read it then, lass. Without further prefacing.'

'Here, in hand-written characters, is his message to me. It is a wonder! He – he – wishes me – to… Now wait… To, to *join his team of New Producers*, with my first assignment: to produce the DeLuxe-color screen version of the smash Broadway musical, Weightn and Orbul's 'A Jar of Beer', starring none other than Lord Peter Ustinov, Kerry Washington, Olivia Newton-John, Henry Jones, I.S. Johar, Celine Dion, Ronald Pickup, Glicka Feng, and Eva Green! Oh, Butterbugs, a dream come true!'

'Shujah! How perfectly beautiful!' said Tuan Jim.

'Shairnah! That's just super!' added the ultrastar.

She rushed over and kissed him on his still gucky-blue cheek.

'You superior person, you! You didn't have anything to do with this, oh did you?'

'Shairnah, you proved yourself to Porter Parker today beyond a shadow of a doubt. You did it yourself.'

'What a gift, a climax!'

'The first of many. Congrats, my dear p.a. The only thing I'm sorry about is that thou shalt p.a. for me no more.'

Their mutual laughter was joyous and needed no further words. Only a departing kiss was all that ensued, to cap the day.

Solo in the night, Butterbugs collapsed into his cot and tumbled into slumber in less than ten seconds. He was happy, deliriously happy: for what he had done for others, and for what was to come.

'Good night, my Heatherette! I'll be home soon, oh-so-soon now.'

So endeth the events and the progress of the Sixth Day.

The Seventh Day

Hushed was this particular early morn. More so than any other on this location. Therefore, as the front door of Butterbugs' residence was opened, it was imperative to she who entered to be as stealthy as possible, lest the petals of a delicate kloorah-blossom wrinkle and cease projection of their rarefied (most fitting for this calle) bouquet-set for any olfactory reception.

A Polynesian/Latina girl came into his quarters, fully knowing what she was doing, even though she did not know he who dwelt within.

Bearing this simple gift, she looked about for he who would need her.

There was a stirring. Yonder, a cot in the gloom. Its occupant shifted under the Vinalon coverlet. She knew it was *he*. She approached, as if with license. Pulling in quite close, she saw his face and eyes closed. It was indeed he. Her brown hand caressed his bluey cheek.

At her touch, he opened one eye, then the other. Viscosity clouded his vision for a moment, then he swirled his eyeballs and saw her. She was there, in big CU. He let her speak.

Another day, another p.a.

'I am Vu'unaatatoa Zulloh,' she said, in pleasantly Tahitian-Venezuelan-accented English.

'Butter... bugs is – is my name.'

Her beauty and her demeanor suddenly made him shy.

'Butter. Bugs.'

'No, no, Butterbugs.'

'No-No Butterbugs.'

'Yes, yes. That's right.'

'One and only.'

'That's what they tell me.'

She was new, so very new to the Industry, but the buzz from Sonny was that she was very, very good. In fact, he had great plans for her as a p.a.'s p.a. He had a very good instinct for these things. She had just shown up only the day before, and now, her sincerity was undoubted by her offering of a kloorah-leaf to Butterbugs as he awakened. He was very moved and instantly thought her special. She was.

She had the cheekbones, but she also had what was obviously a fiercely competent intellect and a natural canniness for all levels of the cinema. After fifteen minutes with her, he thought, 'I've never seen someone with as much punch, as much instinct, and as much raw talent for the very rightness of what she is doing here at this location.'

He was already formulating plans for her within the context of Heatherette's upcoming feature productions.

Fascinated with this heretofore-unencountered combination of two lively cultures, Butterbugs insisted they get to know each other a bit before any production assistance proceeded.

'Call me Veezee,' she said.

'I will.' Butterbugs was suddenly perky. 'You better believe I will! Veezee, tell me of yourself.'

'We need to get going. You are the star. Big day. The biggest.'

'Aye, for sure. But take a moment and indulge my cinematic need for a prelude after the Main Title.'

She smiled, with pearlescent effect. That was just how she herself felt about things! Life was a movie, but it had to be designed, and with conciseness. What was wrong with that? She instantly felt comfortable with the ultrastar.

'I was born in a little grass shack on the lonely shore of the island of Terratator-rakahannahpa'pattee in the remote but idyllic Kummakutungah Group, fourteen days' dugout paddling SSW of Papeete. My father was a wayfarer from far-off Maracaibo. One desolate day, he encountered my mother on the beach and detected a sort of aura around her. He approached her, and they rubbed noses, then kissed without words. And it came to pass that she took his hand and led him to her shack, which was hard by. There, in an anteroom, was a small kit of oils, a few brushes, a bit of turpentine and buggle-mix, a rickety easel, and an empty canvas. An artist's survival kit! A scene was set. She let her muumuu drop to the ground, and he painted a wonderful full-length reclining portrait of her, then and there.'

'A modern Gauguin for our times!'

'Not exactly. Papa became Official Artist to the Chief of the Kummakutungahs, a post he retains to this day. He's painted many a portrait, including Walfrido Seza of Anzoátegui.'

'Really? I did a biopic of that great figure!'

'That I know, fellow. But Papa's the *most!* My true hero. My mom, Merratatoa, is his manager. Many of her family served in the Betty Grable picture 'Song of the Islands' (20th-Fox, 1942). A William LeBaron production.'

'That's terrific!'

'My parents didn't say their first words to each other for a whole week. And at some time therein, I was conceived.'

'Veezee! How delightful!'

'It is. They are thrilled that I am finally in pictures.'

'Finally? You mean it's been a very long time in coming?'

She *was* rather young…

'I might have some other gigs for you,' he said, rather carelessly, but it was very early morning. 'I have some interesting things coming up, if you're interested.'

'But you haven't even seen me in action yet.'

She wasn't trying to be fetching, but she was. Nevertheless, that wasn't Butterbugs' motivation in his reply.

'Oh, but you see, I have an instinct about these things. Just stay tuned-in and give me your all.'

'It starts right now: I think we had better be getting our asses in gear, Butterbugs.'

'My stars! You're right!'

'I have a pennyfarthing, and your usual wheels await. You will be taking the convertible?'

'First strike against you, my dear. Not at all. I enjoy the style of the grand finned space-boat, but I shall pedal with you, on my clattery old Chibbabulb.'

'Actually, I was over-compensating. I had a feeling you would bike it, but I wanted to be most thorough when it most matters: right at the start.'

'Veezee, I knew my instincts were in the right direction. You knew it, too. We shall get along.'

She nodded, and they set off. Her pennyfarthing was of junior size, so the heavily-costumed star was not at all concerned for her dexterity, which was considerable.

'I enjoy the cycling,' said Butterbugs, as they cruised down Bickford Boulevard toward Makeup on Vidor Plaza.

'It seems that anything is possible at Lasky Mesa,' Veezee commented, marveling at the general environment as the Catalina mists, never very thick, decorated both mesa and Citadel in the developing sky.

They clattered along.

'Such good progress, Butterbugs!'

'Darn tootin'! But hola – draw aside for a sec...'

'But *set* awaits!'

The ultrastar caught sight of someone he'd wanted to check-in with all this past week.

'Sanchez – El grande! El cid of mine!'

'Señor de Butterbugs! Buenos dias!'

Sanchez the scaffolder was supervising a load of framing used for the Petit Abattoir set. His enthused family was watching, perched atop hay bales on his personal Studebaker flatbed pickup.

'How is the chief of Scaff and Hold (aka Scaff y Asimiento)?'

'Never, ever better, mang. And this is a production made of love, Señor B!'

'You guys have been fantástico!'

Then he noticed Señora Sanchez and their four youngest kids, Wilfredo, Oswalda, Coromodo, and Princesse.

'Howdydo, gang! Ho-la-la-la!'

Everyone cheered, giggled and celebrated.

'And how is the chief of stars, Butterbugs?' Sanchez hastened over, and with his big mitts on, gave the ultrastar, still on his bike, a big bearhug, taking care to not disturb the raunchy moss-like hangings and critter-nests that adorned his costume of craziness.

In return, the chief of stars clapped Sanchez on the back, leaving a great grey-blue handprint of HMD greasepaint on his genuine, official 'UWH' Crew jacket.

'Oooops...!'

'No problem, Señor B! Souvenir that is unique, eh? Heh-heh!'

'Big scene today, Sanchez. One of the biggest. We've put a lot *in*, haven't we?'

'Si Señor. Love! It's all good. Because of you.'

'And *you*, remember. How's the family? And where's... Chita...?'

'We are enjoying the season here. The smallies are jazzed! And our Chita-quita? Next month, she will happily marry Caballero Manwell Vanóñez!'

'Governor of Durango State?! You mean it?'

Sanchez beamed proudly. 'Si-si-si!'

'Well, I'll be dahned. Enhorabuena!! We shall fiesta!'

Bursting with joyful emotion, tears coming, Sanchez could only crow, 'Mi propio pequeño insecto de la mantequilla!'

Without further words of jollity, Butterbugs dismounted and approached the flatbed, making goony sounds and gestures, as if he were in a Hallowe'en costume. The kids squealed with ultra-powered fun.

'Mis cuatro burbujas! Hey-hey! Here, niños of mine! Souvenirs!'

He winked at Sanchez.

Peeling off some gooey shingles and intricate tangles from his complicated garments, he presented a unique bit to each one. Wilfredo, Oswalda, Coromodo, and Princesse were so blown away, they didn't know whether to laugh, whoop, or cry, so they did all three.

The star bowed to Señora Sanchez, up on the hay, then kissed her hand, leaving a conspicuously yucky bit of makeup on it.

'Encantado, El ultrastar!' she responded, with decorum. 'But – what about your makeup?'

'I have an amazing touchup crew, Costamana! Not to worry!'

'Then I shall treasure your 'offering'. Because I will not be returning it to you, Butterbugs estimado! Next week, come to our usual fiesta. We will set a place for you!'

'Muchas gracias, Señora! It's a date! And a perfect time to plan our Chita's *mega*-fiesta!'

Then he stepped back, did an epic turnaround, mounted his bike, gave a big wave, and he and his p.a. went on down the line.

'Vaya con dios, Señor Butterbugs,' whispered Sanchez, more than a little choked up. 'El grande!'

They pedaled along, in the midst of street activity every bit as crowded and intense as one of Nagpur's most average thoroughfares.

Veezee looked over at the ultrastar, who had a faint smile on his lips, and a couple of tears on his cheek.

'That was wonderful, Butterbugs. Really sweet!'

'*They* are the sweet ones, my dear Veezee…!'

'Cute kids. Happy family.'

'I call Wilfredo, Oswalda, Coromodo, and Princesse My Four Bubbles. They've done so much to brighten their parents' declining years. A quadra-powered blessing!'

'Oh, they couldn't have kids… till now?'

'No no. Four daughters! The three oldest are grown and have complete families and successful lives. In fact, they all became neurologists and have practices at the same clinic – their very own – in Memphis, believe it or not.'

'Hey, aren't they the… the famous 'Brain Sisters', who basically came up with the Parkinson's/Alzheimer's/ALS cure??'

'One and the same, my Veezee. One and the same. Or, *three*, I should say…'

'And one more… daughter…?' The p.a. was careful, lest the fourth was no more – or worse.

'Yowzah! Just got the scoop! Chita – little Chita shall soon be wed – to none other than the Gobernador of Durango! Manwell, a fine fellow withal, is a pen-pal of mine!'

'My best wishes! But, what about the Four Bubbles?'

'Merrily adopted from an orphanage of which I know, but shall not name. Down Guatemala City way…'

To the rookie p.a., it was perfectly obvious this bizarrely-costumed ul-trastar-cum-philanthropist, puffing along next to her at this very moment, had facilitated in making such wonders realities.

Veezee leaked a few tears of her own, of heart-warmed gladness.

Further along, several crowds of extras were being managed and assigned av-enues of duty, in line with the complex filmings of the day ahead. There were showgirls for the HMD's SleazBall Follies, touts to hang around selling souls, and toughs to see the sales through. The Scruffians were a punked-out girl gang, utilized by HMD for roughing-up timids and hesitants, to help keep his Rule of Horror in play.

Their baleful column extended across the street, preventing the two bikers from proceeding effortlessly along their way, so they drew up and halted.

'Bunch of tough chicks!'

'HMD-types!' Veezee smiled.

Upon seeing the HMD himself drawing nigh, the Scruffians completely went out of character and mobbed Butterbugs with fan-ism, girl-ism, and enthused-ism. He autographed everything from driver's licenses to bared buns. He cajoled and selfie-posed, gamboled and tarried, roar-laughed and snazzed with these punk-puffed, tough-muffed babes from gangland. That is, until Veezee took her foot off the pedal, put it clear down, and sent out appropriate commands.

'Blessed peacocks! Pay big attention now! Time to get back into configuration! Back into character! An *actor* must report to Makeup anon, lest we all get arrested and ejected from the greatest picture ever produced! Plenty of time later, plenty of time at the Wrap Party, for your idol-worship, and your prostrations before pow-er! Back now! Back in line, ladies of the scruff! Let us pass! Thank you for your attention. Thank you for your cooperation.'

Orders like these helped to facilitate the Scruffians' return to their roles. Con-sequently, there was grumbling and hissing, spitting and cursing. Yet they were thrilled beyond measure. The crowd milled, shooting love-glances and kissies at the star, then slowly broke up.

One Scruffian, however, remained in the background, and even in the company of the ultrastar-cum-HMD, she averted her gaze from his. Because of this very motion though, Butterbugs took particular notice of her.

A Familiarity Lantern was suddenly ignited in the whizzing mind of an actor on the verge of his most demanding scene ever.

It was she! Treasured Shawna Lee! She, whom he'd courted, admired, and cooed over, well before he'd ever had the nerve to even approach the LA conurba-tion, practically for the first time. Back then, Shawna, with her very fine bearing, her looks, and her good-as-gold standards, had helped *give* him such nerve, and for that, the ultrastar felt he owed her something, if only a few minutes of retro-spective comparisons and news items.

'I say, Shawna? Shawna *Lee*, is it? *The* Shawna Lee of my past? Me, from the forgettable North, you, in the lands East of LA, but Vegas-bound? *Could* it be you?'

His memory, virtually blank when reviewing such a time, was here re-developed, because of the verity of this face, this personage, who was indeed the Shawna he meant. There was no substitution. Plus, the impact of her physicality galvanized his rather prosaic and focused sensitivities, so scattered in their duties, and conventional in their intent.

Indeed, seen even from a clunky bicycle, through the flux of jittering and yammering Scruffians, the woman who hesitatingly kept to the fringe was arresting in every way. He had no choice but to immediately make assessments. In contemporary/cool impacts, she reminded him of Cody, but in a way, she rivaled Cody, with many of Cody's attractions inherent, but here transformed by the demands of Scruffian designations.

But how changed was she! And here today, in such a place, where pictures are made, a far ways past his last glowing memories of her. They appeared with ding-ding-ding logic: that sweety-shag haircut, tawny body, lithe and flexible limbs, and the go-to-the-action energy she'd broadcast, while he was still a pointless, dream-obsessed turbo-nebbish. Here she was, in his movie studio, no less! Still stunning, even in a costume consisting of a raggy little shortie top, revealing the same trim, flat tummy he'd known and admired, but had never gotten to stroke. Waist on-down in tight, distressed jeans, with cliched tears and rips. Bare feet, just like all the other Scruffians. Couple of glue-on tats, one of a wolf's head with a cartoon muzzle. Her hair was a bleach-blonde crewcut, spiked and pomaded, with a big prosthetic scar on her forehead! Quite a dramatic touch!

She was instantly endearing.

'Shawna?'

At last, Shawna gave in and approached Butterbugs.

'Well, hello. Butter… bugs… Yes. It's me. Hi. A long time… True! I knew you when! And I've admired you since, from afar, oh so far!'

'And I have admired *you*, though from nowhere, as… as, I've, I've… Well, we went different routes, didn't we? But here we are, well-met – again.'

'And you are the *star*. The star of stars, really.'

'How *are* you, Shawna. Shawna Lee, isn't it?'

'Uh-huh!'

'How *are* you, Shawna Lee?'

'*So* glad to be here. I couldn't have imagined…'

'Wow! Delighted and amazed. We are, both of us, eh? Somewhere, planets concerning us have been properly aligned! I wonder, how *are* you? Could you update me, please? Oh, but…Just now, as I'm kinda busy, could I get the, you know, sorta 'Reader's Digest Condensed Version', as they used to say?'

She was plainly embarrassed on a generic level, but in the snare of his focus, became perfectly and willingly frank.

'With all my heart, Butterbugs! So: that sunny day, I left you for Vegas. Then I *stripped* in Vegas. Then, *trouble* in Vegas. I thought I was no good, so I linked with losers, louts and lunks, and lowered my thoughts yet further. I hung with a wretch who went loco and... did *damage* on me, after which I went into strict hermitage back East, and thought I'd never emerge again. Oh... Much more, much more...'

She made to cover the scar, as if to mop her brow.

'Oh, girl! But wait, what are you hiding?'

'I guess... you caught me... trying to hide behind... or in front of... oh, hell...!'

'You mean... that scar's for *real?*'

'It's not makeup, Butterbugs.'

'Not for the...part...?'

'Afraid not...'

'But you're one of HMD's Scruffians... My – *my* Scruffians... My very own!'

'And this scar is really why I *got* the part. It looked just right.'

'Isn't that just the *bunk!* But when *I* knew you... admired you...'

'I was 'awarded' it, later. That was the, uh, *damage*. Done by one of my loser 'friends'. He just went crazy one night and – Oh, Butterbugs, it's an unhappy story –'

'Why that miserable – When I get my hands on *him*, why, I'll –'

'Stay those hands, caring one! He no longer walks the earth, nor does he create scars any more.'

'Surely you might not think of... protecting him... from my wrath?'

'Oh, not at *all*, sir! For another, unspeakable crime, far past me, he served time, and is no more, an object of pure hatred, ending with his head down a... Leavenworth loo... Oh, so ugly...!'

'Scar... or no scar, you are beautiful, dear one!'

'Oh, *Butter*bugs!'

'Time for *restoration*. Let me think...'

Amidst the backlot's ceaseless activities of equipment transport, personnel migration, and general urgency, all of which swirled around them, Veezee reached out and put her hand gently on the actor's gesticulating arm.

'The Makeup team, the director, the scene – all await!'

'Yeah, yeah, swell, yeah...'

Shawna too knew their time was short, yet she was so entranced by the ultrastar's power, instead of passing out, she was happily compelled, and drawn further along. By his very presence, a birth-cry of hope sounded off deep inside her.

'My minor self should not have been swept into your passage, this morn. It was really wondrous to see you, but now I must be off, myself. Would that I had never interrupted your great task...'

'But, I'll be jigger-swimmied! What a saga! We shoulda stuck together!'

'But we *didn't*, and it wasn't your deal.'

'Nay, but somehow I *feel* it. Perhaps because... Still, we shoulda faced the future together!'

'No, no, no. If we had, we wouldn't be here, facing it today!'

'Well hell – got a picture to finish – Say, let me – lemme help.'

'The likes of *me?*'

'*Especially* the likes of you! We go way back. Now, we go forward...'

'Forward to...?'

'To good times, good deals, and fun projects of all kinds.'

'You're sure a sweet guy.'

'I was sure sweet on you, Shawna Lee...'

'Sweet on me? You *were?*'

'Honeyed Girl of the Lyrical Fields – Before Film!'

She gazed up at him with passionate admiration, then cast her head down.

'But I'm such a loser. Just trash! Trash, trash, trash...!'

Butterbugs reached out his hand, and with one finger not yet soiled with HMD grease, he raised her chin.

'Look up, Shawna Lee. And not just at me. Raise your chin now, *and* your spirits!'

Never had her tears been so deep, so grateful, so soulful.

'At least I can die happy now!'

The humanitarian regarded her with great affection and respect.

'Dear girl, you shall now be happy, and *not have to die* for it!'

'Your words are so comforting!'

'Their meaning is the most heartfelt thing I can offer!'

'Kind sir! Kind, kind sir!'

'But hey, my brain is in a perfect storm! I've a whole slew of solutions for you. Listen! Don't worry a jot. This is how things will be.'

'*Really...?*'

Her expression was all about hope and its possibilities now.

'Say, Shawna, you're not making a... career out of... mere extra work, are you?'

'Oh, no sir!'

'I know your... your... *scar* qualified you for a supernumerary role as a Scruffian in today's mob scene, and I'm delighted to have you aboard, but how came you to be known by Extra Casting's all-powerful gatekeeping?'

'Well, it's kind of a long –'

'Brevity, sweet S! Please?'

'Brev – brief – OK, er, well, after I came back West, I had to – Well, a couple weeks ago, I had a gig at a place on Figueroa, a real dump, but I had to –'

'Was it – *Edie's Place?*'

'Yeah! It sure was. Why, is that a big deal? Was it...'

'A part of my heritage, is all...'

Butterbugs reflected on how, so long ago, his strange visit there had led him to knowing Sanchez, and further along, to –

'As a strip club, it's pretty –'

'You mean, Edie's is a strippery now?'

'Oh yeah. It's also a dump. With Virg Klumbuls on the Lowrey organ. Sha-Boom, cocktail piano, the old songs, all that stuff...'

'But I still –'

'Anyway, dear guy, I was doing my strip there, and not very well, I'm afraid.'

'I'm sorry that you've had to... Unless you *want* to... I mean, ecdysis is an admirable profession in the better venues, but... But how came you to *this* place, here, at Lasky Mesa? To be in this picture, at its very climax?'

'Well, the last hour of my act, which seemed to go on *for ever*, because, you know how, when it's getting late, and –'

'Brevity, child, in the face of moviemaking, here!'

'Yeah, yeah. OK! Well, there was sort of moviemaking *there*, too. Sort of. Anyway, after my act, I got propositioned by this stout guy who was, I think, playing with himself in his pockets, and –'

Butterbugs prepared himself for unsavory tidings.

'Total sleaze?'

'Well, I *guess*, but he said he was doing 'research' for a picture. Said it was going to be a remake of some striptease movie, or something... Anyway, it wasn't a come-on or anything. In fact, instead of a grabby pass at me to go into the back room, or the back alley, he handed me a card. And you know what? It was an actual *pass* – to get on as an extra in this very film, here, today! I guess he felt sorry for me.'

'Glory be! Thank your gods he did! Did he give his name?'

'Well he just said his name was 'Jerry', and that he'd produced that first 'Strip-per' film, and now he wanted to do a remake. I guess all *I* cared about was a gig that didn't involve me dropping my kit to garters only. I actually believed him, and boy, he was right and true, and here I am. So I guess he was a good guy.'

'Shawna Lee, you don't know *how* good. That was the one and only Jerry Wald, mega-producer, not only of the original 'The Stripper' (20th-Fox, 1963), but of many fine and important pictures, unto this day!'

'Gosh!'

'He's one of the greats.'

'Well, I must've pleased him, because he gave me that pass, and it worked, and all...'

The ultrastar glanced down at Shawna's show-stopping body, and wondered why Wald hadn't signed her – as the *lead* – then and there.

'Indeed! Well whadaya know! Cool! By the way, he wasn't, ahem, 'playing with himself' in his pocket. That was Jerry working one of his wonders. He was *taking notes* in his inimitable way, as if no one would notice. Former newspaper guy. He can actually write like that!'

'Oh!! *Interesting!*'

'Well, Shawna Lee!'

'I have to say, I'm pretty tired of doing the strip act, Butterbugs. I'm good and everything, but... There was a time when I thought of having breast reduction surgery, but no, I like 'em just fine now, whatever I do.'

'Oh, so do *I*, Shawnee – I mean –'

'But this play-acting, it looks fun, and…'

'It's tough to make a living as an extra, though.'

Veezee was just about to bike over to Makeup and bring the team back *here* to do their touchups…

Butterbugs looked Shawna over, then made a polite request.

'Could you just do a quick twirl around, please?'

She did. He was finishing Jerry's job.

'Listen Shawnee – I like callin' ya Shawnee…'

'Oh, I like ya to, too!'

'You do? Well, listen, time is mega-short, but here're some ideas to kick around. You weren't doing the strip show *all* this time, were you?'

'Oh no, not at all. Back East, I worked in a bead store. I'm bead-oriented! And other stuff. I make jewelry, too. See?'

She showed off a rather spectacular necklace of blotchy and horrifically-appealing little skulls, suspended down the slopes from her elegant collarbones.

'I made it myself. In about two hours, just on an outside hunch that I might get on as a Scruffian extra! Not only the scar helped, but this necklace. The sub-director says he'll put me right in front of the camera, too!'

'Fantastic! Reminds me of the Durga Pujo in Calcutta! Er – no-no, her Kali incarnation, rather!'

'Oh, how incredible! Will you take me there?'

'Some day! It's really cool, Shawnee. Your necklace too. That thing's *spooky!*'

'Heh-heh! Just a tiny sample of what I've got. It'll help me act like a 'bad girl'!'

'Which I know is not your natural condition,' he winked.

'Oh, no sir! It isn't at all! I've always tried to – It's been so *hard* – !'

'Sweet Shawnee, I know, I was just funnin' a bit. Now's your chance to act for the camera, like I do. Put your costume, your necklace, and your intentions to work for you. But remember, it's gotta come from inside, too. The *act*, that is. Believe, and keep believing. The assistant director, as we call them, will tell you where to stand and when to move, but *you've* gotta supply the character. Just like me.'

'Thanks so much! I'll remember everything you said. I think I can do it pretty good!'

'I *know* you can, Honeyed Girl!'

'I'm *so* looking forward to this!'

'OK. Gotta think fast, for, you know, down the road a ways. Think fast! For starters, let's get you into a bead shop groove-thang, OK? How about a shingle that says, 'Shawnee's Buttery Beads 'n' Bugs' – or something *worse!* Huh?'

'Oh, sir, you take my breath away!'

'You'll need it, babe! OK, I purchased some frontage awhile ago, pressured by associates, I don't know why… But now I do. For your store! It's the Blürger & Börgerbeer Block, along the best part of Melrose, not at all boutique-y, but in need of sincerity. You can rig your shop just there. The way you want it. You just wait, folks I know'll be in line to help you set 'er up! Next: lodging. You can stay at any number of casuals at my very own The Lazaretto. Or, and/or, in addition, there's a modest but pleasant flat that recently came available in an apartment block I own in Valentino Place, right near Paramount. That would put you in close proximity to your future shop on the mellowest stretch of old Melrose! How does that stuff sound? How about it?'

Shawna could only answer with her gorgeous, welling eyes.

'Super, girl! Say! So, you do jewelry and beads and stuff, huh? Know it well?'

'Oh, I do! Quite nicely, too!'

'Then you shall be in charge of jewelry and other adornments in all my subsequent pictures, some of which promise to be very small-scale and quite close-up. Can ya do 'er?'

'For you, anything, dear sir!'

'OK, guess I'd better be off. Wonderful to see you again, Shawna! So good to link! Lucky us! I've many dandy people for you to meet, plus one very special one.'

'*You* are a special one, Butterbugs! *So* special!'

'Pleasure, pure pleasure.'

'And thanks again! Now and always. You don't know *how much!*'

'Very well. My p.a., Veezee here, will see to each and every detail. Veezee, meet Shawna Lee. Shawna Lee, meet Veezee. Veezee'll get everything set up. This is going to be *fun!*'

Veezee presented her chip-enhanced ContactCard to a grateful Shawna Lee. The novice p.a., so newly carried along in the high midstream of big-time starry acts, genuinely marveled at the ultrastar's awareness and attendance to all his non-picture affairs and their divers details. Shawna Lee wasn't the only deliriously-lucky one hanging around the ultrastar right now!

'Oh, say, Butterbugs, can I get you a cup-coffee, or a maple bar, or – just *anything?* Anything at all! There's some good breakfast items over at the extra's check-in!'

'No need just now, Shawnee, because…'

'Because – *we've got a picture to finish*, eh?'

'Dear, dear, heart-of-gold girl, you took the words *right outa my mouth!* Be seeing you!'

He coordinated his pedals below.

Veezee regarded him with more than a bit of mixed concern. Past the admiration, she was afraid she might be held accountable for the dawdling of the world's sole ultrastar. Yet! It was all so magnificent, and *worth it!*

'Makeup, Butterbugs! To Makeup – now!' she whined, low enough so he almost couldn't hear. '*Please??*'

'Yeah, yeah. Jes' sec…'

'Shawnee? Oh, Shawna Lee-Eeee…!'

She turned around, hands clasped.

'Oh, yes??'

'Hey Shawnee? Neglected to ask. Partner? Lover? Mate? Any kids?'

'Nope! Only me. And you know, as things that be, I'm happy that it *is* just me!'

'Pure poetics of independence, girl!'

The hubbub did not let up about them. He finally got his pedals arranged, but did not pump. Instead he turned about again and called out.

'Shawna Lee? One more thang. Mind if I call Jerry – Jerry Wald – and set it up so you can audition for his 'Stripper' remake?'

'Oh, *yes*, Mr. Wonderful! I'd like to at least *try!*'

'Perfect. And I happen to know that all strippers are just plain born actresses. I'll coach you. In fact, I'll make Jerry an offer he can't refuse. If he gives you the *lead*, I'd be happy to do a cameo in the picture, or whatever the hell he wants. How's that? Game?'

'Never more so, Mr. Spectacular!'

'Super! OK, *now:* be seeing you!'

'Love you!' Shawna called back in a clear and newly-reinforced voice.

'Veezee? Set all that up, if it please you.'

'Will do, Mr. Butterbugs. With greatest pleasure.'

Then the star spun about, yet again.

'Oh, Shawnee?'

She rotated freshly, yet again.

'Yes, star of mine?'

'Be sure to be a good Scruffian!'

And the star and his p.a. cycled off, at last.

Shawna gazed after him in bliss, kissed the card, and lightly touched her scar, which had brought her such good luck this day.

They pedaled on, Makeup-bound. Now it was Veezee's turn to have a faint smile on her lips, and more than a couple of tears on her cheeks. She fully expected wedding bells to eventually chime above both stripper and star, together at last...

'Oh Butterbugs! That was really so very marvelous! So touching, heartwarming, poignant! I so admire your gesture!'

'Thanx, thanx, and thanx once more. Erp, I almost fergot agin! Veezee, contact my own Dr. Cantrell. He's got access to a whole lineup of today's most talented surgeons of the 'plaustic' variety.'

'Why certainly. But I thought I heard Ms. Shawna Lee say that she... She preferred *not* to have reduction of her... bosoms...'

'You heard correctly, my p.a.! Rather, I was considering the facial scar that fucking psycho 'gifted' her with. I would imagine she might want to be rid of it, at last. That is, if she's finished with it. No more Scruffian gigs after this, I shouldn't think. No need for it to further her fortunes. Indeed, it's time to do the 'face-saving' deed, don't you agree? Right away – and paid for. Please see to it, in its entirety, Veezee.'

'I'm so embarrassed, Butterbugs!'

'But – but, *whie?*'

'These intimate matters, of personal feeling, and personal body. I'm not used…'

'Young p.a., we are in *showbiz!* Bodily measurements must be declared! Pimples must be popped! Hernias must be patched! Drug intake must be known! Anything that affects the *show* must be dealt with, in *biz*-like manner, with the utmost professional finesse and detachment. In ways of knowledge and honesty, the participants of showbiz shall be protected, enhanced, and strengthened. We're all in this together!'

'Humbly do I appreciate your helpful wisdom, Butterbugs. I look forward to the fruition of every one of my assignments!'

'Love it, baby!'

'Ms. Shawna is so promising. So grateful, too. For your help.'

'Good thing we ran into her just now. I just *love* to do things like that. She's a great gal! Good memories. Them's was good times…'

Somehow, Veezee had the feeling that what the world needed was a Butterbugs to run it, not just some High Mad Doctor, mucking things up in some old picture show…

Those Catalina mists, never very thick, soon retreated and a turbo-clear sky gradually revealed itself, precisely like the preceding six days. It was a location manager's dream. Indeed, unit production manager C.O. Erickson was becoming downright complacent, what with a winning streak of weather, presented on a platter.

'It's a gift, Doc,' said Old Atrocity on their way up to set.

'Nothing is a gift, OA,' the super-seasoned vet replied. 'It's all gravy; we just have to keep dipping our bread in, while it's hot.'

'Doc of Philosophy!'

'That's why they hired me. Say, what's this guff I hear about you chuggin' on out of the biz once this shoot's wrapped?'

'Where did you hear that, Doc?'

'Well, now that you're married up and all…'

'But where did you hear… Oh hell, doesn't matter. I love Tarlah, and she loves me.'

'No debate, baby. We just – I don't know, I detect a feeling of farewell around the set. From more than one quarter.'

'Well, we should be wrapping today, and all.'

'OA, I've been making pictures with you for thirty-five years. There's a different scent about the camp.'

'I hope it's not foul.'

'Nope. Just different. Like a suitcase dragged out and opened, waiting to be packed for a trip. But it's with a different travel agent, somehow.'

'Interesting way to put it, Doc. Well, thing is, you're sort of right.'

'Sort of?'

'Yesh. I'll level with ya. Yeah, we're takin' off. Points unknown, so far. We want some *life*, non-manufactured, you know?'

'I know. I could make some kind of announcement myself.'

'Doc! You? You've got splicing glue in your veins.'

'Well, you always take a shower with your nail gun! Thing is, them veins is hardening.'

'Fergit the nail gun! Now I've got Tarlah to bathe with! Retirement?'

'Maybe. I guess I just want some reassurance.'

'Doc, you turn in your card when it feels right. You and Thetta have a good life with what you do. Me and Tarlah? Hell, that's a new one for me. If it warn't for her, I'd be grippin' an' grinnin' till they make the hit pic of the Apocalypse, *after* it happens.'

'That's what love does, boy!' smiled Doc.

'And for once, I'm payin' attention. We're headed out right after the Wrap Party... While the gittin's good!'

Today – this exceptional day! What a day to film a great big fat climax sequence of an epic! Everything necessary was in place: a fantastic script, a setting of indescribable magnificence, a cast and crew of unrivaled talent and ability, and a virgin day in which to contain it all.

'You's *late,* Butterbugs!' Belt Nye, Ben's other master makeupper son, semi-chided.

'Too true, Belt! But behold, I do indeed come more prepped than ye might think!'

On such a morning, today's makeup requirements were perhaps the easiest Butterbugs needed to undergo on this picture. There was so much built-up foundational substance on his exposed parts (as he had only sponge-bathed all week, so as to maximize the patina effect of his sickening-looking complexion), that it was just a matter of freshening up what was already there – which was something akin to a Böcklin sea creature's greasy cobalt mug.

Veezee gazed at him with wide-eyed self-confidence, dark eyebrows slanting slightly upwards. He was of course captivated by her beauty, a nice distraction while all the primping was going on. He returned her look of engaged concentration. Then he grinned, but her expression did not change.

'You were right, Butterbugs,' Belt sang off-key. 'A couple of trowel-slaps here and a few filler-packings there; a spray-job of fat-mix over your shawl, that's how we prep you for a badass day – as the horrible leader of *all!*'

The whole shop exploded in laughter and applause.

'Very good, very good, Beltie!' the ultrastar chirped. 'I'll tell Arlen & Harburg to fit you into the next remake of 'Oz' (MGM, 1939)!'

Finally, as his makeup session was winding up, Veezee eased her expression and addressed him at close quarters:

'My purpose here is to serve. But while on set, I might be able to contribute in other ways. I might make a comment here and there, about tone, about values, about intent. You have taken on quite a bit of façade enhancement, and that is what your role calls for, but I find it curious that you're using makeup at all.'

'Curious?'

'Yes. Because, when I look at your face, in your eyes, I cannot even discern any makeup on your personage. The same with your performance, though I have yet to witness you performing in the flesh. When you talk, I only receive coherent abstractions, perfectly assembled.'

'You are beautiful.'

'So are you. I sing a hymn to your intellectual beauty in my heart.'

'Thank you. I will compose one for you sometime soon.'

'Will you kiss me now?'

'I will. Draw close, please.'

They touched lips, not erotically, but with a loveliness that was plainly mutual in its admiration.

'There. You've done it,' he whispered, with genuine respect.

'Now we can work together, and without distraction.'

'That's a good way to look at it. Though now, you have cobalt lipstick. It is not unattractive.'

As the peoples of Makeup did final prep to his skins, then primped all over his costume after removing his protective smock, Veezee got down to other aspects of business.

'I hope you don't ruin this production,' she said, 'by your conception of it.'

'My... Please, continue.'

There was no question that hers was a great mind, and perfect for the Seventh Art.

'I have never heard the word 'ego' used in conjunction with you, Butterbugs. Tell me, so that I can serve you better, do you have one?'

He was taken aback. Some actors, hearing this sort of talk, might feel threatened or even upstaged, that some punk kid with metallic lipstick would have the temerity to take such a chutzpah-laden gamble, but Butterbugs was entranced, if not impressed. Also, relieved. He knew the other's instincts about him to be correct.

'Another one to add to this sincere and promising p.a. lineup of the past several days,' he thought. 'To carry on.'

Their thin, thin, 16mm tires reached the set of the morning: the Substantial Grade, a gigantic sloped plain of fuchsia marble, the launching pad to the processional way to the Citadel of Gyugganthropristixc, across the valley.

'I think it's just brilliant,' Veezee chimed in. 'The *rake* on this set! Utterly dynamic! And just the fact that they're filming these last bits in sequence. It's all so relentless. It will positively *yank* the required performance out of you.'

'A completely reasonable perspective,' replied Butterbugs.

He was really finding her to be in possession of a darned intriguing mind. What he wasn't sure of though, was if he were falling in love. Lightly, lightly in love.

The countdown to Heatherette's lips continued.

For her part, after seeing the ultrastar's humanitarian, philanthropic, enterprising, and thespian philosophies in action, and very close up, she felt her own intellectual contributions might well be appreciated by this most consummate of actors.

What she was *sure* of though, was that she had fallen in love. Heavily, heavily in love. With his mind.

Up on the Grade, that was where some splendid scenes would be shot. Leon, who was principal photog in these scenes, was finishing his tone settings, which were priceless in their quality. Bob, in excellent fettle, nevertheless chair-directed his operator, the noble Sir Bleobaris, on second camera today.

'What do you need?' asked Veezee, her upraised chin a mere cat's whisker away from the star's breast.

He wanted to say, 'I need Heatherette, so as to keep your wonders at bay', but he knew how intact his love for his lover was, so he saw no reason not to indulge in and enjoy her attentions.

Looking down into her face, he actually felt... old. Or, older. Older than she, by a long shot, though in real life, not HMD terms, it was not so. But there he was, in this huge and flagrant costume, like a sculpture on the frontage of Gaudi's Sagrada Familia, a monolith climbed by a pixie. A pixie with incredible cheekbones.

'Yes, well, how about a hot-water punch?'

'I can do more than simply get you beverages, Butterbugs.'

Egaz approached.

'I'll let you know, Veezee. Oh, and I need my script. Please and thanks.'

'He wants to see his lines as they are written, so he can methodically change them,' the director laughed.

'You are there in spirit, actor,' said the mere p.a., sounding directorial, 'and as long as you keep to a relatively synonymous path, your talent will carry you through. I'll be back with the Cane & Team script – oh, and a 'hot-water punch' – in a moment, hmm?'

She breezed off, and the two old(er) farts turned their heads after her.

'These are the production assistants of our times, Egaz. They know no fear, and exude more confidence than a plankton telling a blue whale to blow it out his hole.'

'What's with *that* p.a.? That's what she is, isn't she?'

'I'm quickly getting used to her style.'

They were both amused, magnetized by her long swaying hair, as they tailed her tail.

Hazel Snyder casually walked up.

'That's V.Z. Or Veeeeezeeeee. How do you like her?'

'Well Haze, she takes my breath away… a tad,' replied Butterbugs.

'Thought she would,' she said knowingly. 'One to watch.'

'I like her. Yes, I'm watching her, all right.'

'She's not dating anyone, Butterbugs.'

'I think she likes you,' added Egaz. '*Really* likes you.'

'Thanks, guy & gal. I like her, too. And she's a better p.a. than you might suppose. She *thinks*. In, how shall I put it – uh, shall we say, purposely obtuse ways.'

'Most appropriate for your tastes, which appear to be going through a refinery.' They chuckled.

Egaz went over to confer with Leon.

'Say Haze, how's the baby?'

'Just fine, OB-GYN. When the time comes, you're the man.'

'I kind of enjoy birthing. Have you seen Mollycoddle's twins?'

'You mean, in real life and not on the screen (in the rushes)? Uh-huh. Looking bouncy. Your talents are all over them. Quite an improv, old boy.'

'I tell you, I had no idea.'

'Everyone on the Producer Team was spitting joy droplets over it. They won't tell you though, until the Wrap Party. Bronston and DFZ, especially.'

'Glad they liked it. I liked it, too.'

'Now you looka here, High Mad. Here we are, on Climax Day, and we're bantering so!'

'I've learned that, on these big ones, Haze, to tread as if it's a matinee musicale or a goofball's holiday. That way, when the dual premieres at the Roxy and the Metropolitan roll, we'll be sufficiently exalted by the occasion itself, which comes on top of this incredible shoot.'

Hazel regarded him with deep admiration.

'It's strange, Butterbugs. I've never heard you open up like that before.'

'As well you might. Those are essentially Veezee's words, spoken to me on the way over here. Glad I am, that she's right at my side this day! Glad *you* will be, when she's producing for you.'

'She will?'

'Aye. Hers are the qualities we need in tomorrow's producers, if we are to reduce schlock to a minimum.'

'Sounds good. But she is very… seductive… in other ways.'

'In what respect, Haze?'

'She's rawther… impetuous…'

'Hazel, are you intimidated?'

'A little. I'll have to keep an eye on Chas.'

'Well, with me as your deliverer and Chas as a stay-at-home dad, you'll have little to worry about. Besides, I may deliver you twins – my specialty.'

'Oh, fearless one!' She suddenly hugged him closely, despite the goo of sparkle-juice dribbled on his robes to represent his character's high, mad spit-ups. 'Your towering strength rivals that of the penile campanile yonder! You are our torch! Hold me, Butterbugs. Closer.' Then, she whispered, 'You feel the life in my belly? I do, every moment. You feel it? Each one of these location days, six so far, it has grown, exponentially, I think! The dreams of a pregnant girl? Oh, Butterbugs, I confess, I tell you... I wish it was by *your* seed. This child in waiting! Yes, I do! I had to tell you. I love Chas no less, but what a magnificent hope it would be, to bear your inheritor for you! I can run a great studio – for you, but I can also receive your legacy between my legs and make it into someone worthy of you and your achievement. Oh, dear one, I know you have always lusted after me, and even though I am your, well, 'senior', I yet possess wild and unbelievable lovemaking powers. Though my current state of mother-to-be is sacred, after you see my babe's dome take center stage in my red-haired pussy, will you grant me the most singular honor of being your vehicle to immortality?'

'I love you, Haze. See, a scene awaits.'

She looked about and saw the whole company in readiness mode, and Veezee was closing in with the actor's annotated script 'n' drink.

'I yield. The business at hand.'

Just then, out on the Substantial Grade, a battalion of HMD's Scruffians traipsed by, on their way to scenic placement. There was Shawna Lee, right in front, primed for Ultra-Panavisionary capture, in all her punky, skull-hung, stripper-strutting glory. She gave a big wave.

'Yoo-hoo! Shawna! Shawna Lee-Lee-Lee!' Butterbugs sang out. 'Go get 'em, Scruffian-chick! Hold me hostage, and never let me go!!'

They exchanged blown kisses, two or three times.

'Who the hell's *that?*' Hazel asked no one and everyone. 'Who's this 'Lee-Lee-Lee'??'

No one answered.

'Almost there, Haze. I think we're winning.'

While Shawna receded and Veezee approached, Hazel drew especially close and spake as sensuously as she dared.

'I take my leave, but I am with you. You are my center, my focus. Not only are you up there on the giant screen, you are here, in my heart, where you have always been, and where you shall return.'

'Dear Haze! I think Egaz is about to call 'Places'. What a goofball's holiday, no?'

She could say no more, but gave him a truly soulful look that bespoke her undoubted sincerity.

'Best damn girl studio head in the universe,' was all he thought while looking after her redheaded withdrawal, which she enhanced with her loaded hips, white skirt, and black VPL.

'Yes indeed, nothing wrong with *that*'.

He would consider what she'd said, but rather later. Haze was cool and sexy, but there was a lot to do yet, and a lot of Heathery-ettery love-feasting to look forward to, from this day forward.

Verily was an ultrastar's legacy worth consideration. Others no doubt wanted 'in'. No time to consider them now – or maybe ever.

Doggone showbiz!

'Alvez mit dem temptations!'

Veezee placed the worn volume into Butterbugs' hands: Volume XII, 'Finale', and hot water tray on a porta-teapoy.

'What did Snyder want?'

'Why Veezee, there's determination in your voice.'

'We could get behind, dangerously behind, if we don't keep to sked, you know. I'm just trying for expediency.'

'And you shall have it. Find my current page.'

'It's already flagged, see?'

'Ah, good. Let me study awhile.'

'Very well, but I want cameras to roll within fifteen minutes.'

'I will fulfill your wishes, Miss. And secondly, the director's.'

She wasn't sure of his humor until he winked at her. She scoff-laughed and went to liaison with Egaz.

'Your name is Veezee?' asked Egaz.

'For short, yes. Have you anything to communicate to the star?'

'I'd like him to explore more of a lightness of being today. Here he is, having shed so many enemies; HMD is virtually sitting pretty. The world has been conquered, and now there is a seat of power – real power – to take. Symbology must come to the fore. Butterbugs will know, however, that his murder of Ccyklvx has changed HMD somehow. Down deep, a linchpin has gone missing. Though the act inspired fear and obedience in others, in him, way inside, a motivational torch has been extinguished – up his ass, if he knows what I mean.'

'He is transformed, but in a direction undesirable,' said Veezee.

'Yes, that's right. I'm sure Butterbugs knows it.'

'You think he really does?'

'Now listen girl, we know what we're doing here.'

'And so do I. Remember, I just walked into this scene. I have no history in this production. Therefore, I am as a viewing audience member. That is my perspective.'

'All right, that makes sense. Give me your ideas. Be brief, as we roll in ten minutes.'

'I thought you might. Butterbugs has already been sufficiently alerted.'

'Good. Now impart.'

'Well, I think HMD should retain his utter dedication to his nightmarish intentions. However, if he can let some of his inner blowout leak out, as he supposedly moves toward his highest of triumphs, that would perhaps give the audience some semblance of hope at the end.'

'Hope? How do you know that's what we *want?*'

'Granted, hope is a tricky thing.'

'There's the matter of the script as it is – even with Butterbugs' freedoms with it…'

'Let me tell you something, Egaz. You and the others around here… You may be a little too detached. For, if it ends on a totally successful note for the most awful of all world dictators, how can audiences face their future? It will be *that* powerful, and you know it.'

'Shall we betray Sawl Cane so?'

'No betrayal, this. We shall not alter a thing. It is up to Butterbugs to convey this unscripted occult notion, by way of his genius. He must employ the means. We can only suggest.'

'I follow you. I think he can do it, if we set the tone. He responds very well to indirect suggestion, though he be grounded more than the very earth we stand on. Let me approach him now, as the company pants for seeking resolution on this great day.'

Veezee let him pass, and the director approached the star.

'Butterbugs, I –' was all he was able to say before the ultrastar spake.

'Egaz! You know, I have a concept. It just came to me, based on the dialogues I have had with that new p.a.'

'Veezee?'

'Ahem, yes. Veezee. It occurs to me that, uh, I should convey HMD's trueness by cracking his falseness, but without words.'

'You're onto the same thing we were just –'

'And then, and then…' Butterbugs trailed off.

Egaz knew he was working it out. Thus was the higher path of communication open between they who went way beyond trust. The director withdrew, knowing he'd made his point.

Over at Butterbugs' chair, Veezee knew it, too. She had been tied-in. She knew their hearts. Now the cameras could roll.

'All right, ACTIONNNN!'

(HMD's *High-Toned Financier,* NAHGUARRANEX [as played by Robert Middleton] *blithely strolls in for a bit of biz-talk before the Massive Symbolic Gesture of the Citadel's consecration/entry. The two talk privately in a marble gazebo of elaborate design with stunning carved screens, behind which super-activity continues, all around them. Despite the attractive look of the gazebo, it is executed in pelican-puke pink marble, and is most sick-making.)*

NAHGUARRANEX: *(makes himself comfortable)* Well, biggie-boy, I can see by your early morning soiree you have aggrandizement in mind.

HMD: What gives you the right to talk to me like that?

NAHGUARRANEX: Right? Do I... need one, exactly? Oh, yes, I guess for a show in public, I should engage in all that icky, squishy, swishy robe-strutting you adore so much. The posing and the preening and the primping and the picking and the mincing...

HMD: Funny, hearing such a critique from a dude with *your* tastes.

NAHGUARRANEX: Let me tell you something, Goalie. *(these two were on the same football team in their youth; HMD's nickname was Goalie – as he never made any goals, or prevented any from being made, the whole time, and NAHGUARRANEX'S nickname became No.1, as he was always a team captain's last choice; rejection on the playing field was the biggest incentive for each to excel in the arts of vengeful evil, in which both have had hyper-success: HMD as warrior/conqueror/ruler, and NAHGUARRANEX as master of the known corporate universe)* I dally with persons of quality who are just at the discovery point of who they might become in the world. I help myself because I can. If I *don't* happen to help them in the process, I certainly change them. But come, come, come now, we're only talking about a mere hobby of mine. Your own perversions are absolutely heroic in comparison, and I acknowledge my respect for you on that account.

*(*NAHGUARRANEX *realizes it probably isn't such a good idea to be too cocky with* HMD *in sexual matters, so as to piss him off further. On the other hand, in affairs of hard business, he has an agenda this morning: he carries an iron, so to speak, to strike while hot.)*

HMD: That's better. Oaf.

NAHGUARRANEX: Oaf! Yeah... After such an argument, let me make more peace. Let it be in the form of a secret dram. Have a flask of baked animal juice. *(hands him a Spirk-glass)* It is a fine bone-tea from furthest Lake Ktjxczim.

HMD: *(considers its properties)* I *do* fancy products from that region.

NAHGUARRANEX: Ah, splendid. Here.

HMD: *(takes the flask)* My taster, first.

NAHGUARRANEX: Naturally.

HMD: *(after successful tasting by a pale, trembling, skinny girl waif)* [as played by Cara Delevinge] Mumph! That's the flavor of my new enterprise.

NAHGUARRANEX: It certainly *can* be, if you wish it. You remember the deal we made in the mass marketing of this fine item, certainly.

HMD: Deal?

NAHGUARRANEX: Surely, my High Minded Madness, you recall our scheme to peddle all the Ktjxczim zone's treasures, as a no-brain front to our mega-munitions managements, so as to exploit the super-region's possibilities to the fullest, no?

HMD: I will not talk about such sleaze on the day of my momentous Includement Ceremony.

NAHGUARRANEX: Sleaze? Listen, buddy-boy, this here deal, as you very, very well know, is one of the foundations to your post-kick-ass world. This is how lasting empires are built – not by some damn 'vibrator tower'! A-heh!

HMD: You take that back, right now!

NAHGUARRANEX: What?

HMD: What you said about my Citadel!

NAHGUARRANEX: No. I won't. You go ahead and make the world sit on it. I don't give a fig. I just want my deals.

HMD: *(seriously does not like NAHGUARRANEX'S points, but he cannot deny them)* So, No. 1, what do you want of me?

NAHGUARRANEX: That's better. That's the sort of attitude you should have displayed when you first saw my prideful face this clear morn! Yes, that's better. *(reclines on a bolster and glances through the discreet screen at the incredible activity without, including preparations for the Ceremony of Entrance, to be held later on, in the early evening)*

(In the background, HMD's crowd-agents, such as the SCRUFFIANS, hassle citizens, heckle them with crude behavior, and generally serve HMD's goal to keep the crowd anxious about his forthcoming spectacle; intercut with CU shots of noteworthy SCRUFFIANS and their activities.)

NAHGUARRANEX: You've done well, Goalie, very well, with your warfare and your violence… Made entirely possible by my dark industries, I might add. So, before you sequester yourself in that life-proof dildo over there, I want other deals, signed in blood, if necessary. You see, old Goalie, we've come such a long way, and I want to go further. Much, much further. Doesn't really matter if you're along or not. As you mean to consolidate your power now that the wars are concluded, so, by brains, do I. But I can't understand you! Here I am, the perfect complement to your ruler trip, and you reject my overtures, or else you are tremendously suspicious of them. Now I ask you, what kind of way is that to act? You handle the politics and war, and I'll handle the market. I can't stand the stuff you have to do, and you'd never, ever want to take up my activities. What the hell could be better? One hand washes t'other. Separate, but equal – and united, too. Well, you can rule out front. I will grant you that. I'll kiss your knuckles in public, but you'll flush my commode in private. You'll do things my way, see?

HMD: You are one sick snake. And a stupid one, too. I have firepower about one millisecond from your nose.

NAHGUARRANEX: You know, of course, that I could have tapped a tincture of prissitt-acid into that there enjoyable beverage of yours. No tint, no bouquet, no way to detect it.

HMD: *(casts the flask to the ground)* You dirty dog!

NAHGUARRANEX: My humor annoys you, victorious one?

HMD: I am so utterly victorious that it makes all your puffed-up enterprises look like lamb-worm secretions.

(Intimations of their youthful football failures have been shown in several flashback sequences, earlier in Act III of the picture.)

NAHGUARRANEX: Admittedly, yes. Or, no doubt! I mean, perhaps, Goalie, and maybe. I guess you are too delicate right now to traverse my old locker room joking-around. But do not forget that heavy guns are what you hold a possession with. Only the heaviest of guns. Any possession. You just exercised that right with your threat to my person. It has always been so. Will always *be* so, especially under your tutelage and other august auspices.

HMD: You are a flatterer.

NAHGUARRANEX: I am, and you need it.

HMD: Don't fuck with me, No. 1.

NAHGUARRANEX: I won't! Honest! I just want this next sequence of deals firmed up.

HMD: Proceed, No. 1 Sycophant.

NAHGUARRANEX: *(gives a social laugh)* Let's not squander this elevated moment in this classy location, all in the sick pink of your soul. Leave us not fumble with boutique-y items like wabbit beer. As a mere preliminary, I want guarantees on the Polar Armament Claddings series of contracts, and I want exclusive, open-ended controls. We will arm and armor both North and South to your pre-set specifications, but if I cannot prevail the way I wish to in profiting in the No. 1 position – heh-heh – 'No. 1' and all – !, I will be compelled to derail other schemes that you probably are interested in *(massive understatement)*.

HMD: Like?

NAHGUARRANEX: Now, I'm just a trifle disappointed in you, Mad Doc. If you really trusted me, why would you have to ask? Hmm?

HMD: Don't all your CEOs – the smart ones – ask such things? To protect themselves, if nothing else.

NAHGUARRANEX: Very good, very good. Spoken like a true and successful World-Grasper. I know you didn't get where we are by unraveling Granny's knitting. But I'm telling you now, I want every fist-fucking military-industrial-complex contract that you, as Global Controller, will engage in, from here on out. Under*stand?* Not just a one-shot deal, but *all* of 'em, *all* the time, *all* the way, and without question. Does this make sense to you?

HMD: *(pacific)* Immaculate sense, No. 1.

NAHGUARRANEX: Huh? That was too easy. We should *argue*, Goalie!

HMD: You said it yourself: you don't understand me. Here you are, the perfect compliment to me. You're right about that. I need someone like you, probably now more than ever. I need you to run this biz stuff, while I glory on, in my heavy role as Chief Martial Law Administrator and Sole

Responsibility Person for the Planet Urth. (HMD *has officially changed the spelling of 'Earth' to 'Urth', to reflect his taste in things crude and perverse.*) A dual role you, as you're counting all your chips, can scarcely comprehend. Yes, you have my permission. Ransack my world at will. Nothing matters but my power over the people, and if you help hold it, fine and dandy. You're working for me, and don't you forget it, see? Let us sign the papers without further equivocation. See here, in this Crixite vial, blood I have given the nation. The fruits of my veins. We can dip our quills in it and lay out our signatures, which will define the universe for ages to come. Are you with me?

NAHGUARRANEX: *(pleased beyond hope)* Give us thine purply artery-ichor, so that we may sign our lives away – *to each other.*

(Camera dollies in for CU of the fateful signing.)

'Cut!' commanded Egaz, but without comment, except to say, 'Once again, please, from top of scene', and Take #2 ran its course with another display of competency in fine acting on everyone's part. There were certainly variations on a theme, but not many on Butterbugs' part.

In both takes, Shawna shone as the most prominent of the Scruffians.

'Break for tiffin,' the director announced. 'Next scene in 65 minutes, please.'

No conferences ensued and all went their ways.

Butterbugs and Veezee got on their wheels and sought out the further lights of lunch at Lasky. There was a curious and crooked lane, Basevi Gully, that led up to a knoll with a view, known as Scandal Point – where director King Vidor had stormed off the set of 'Duel in the Sun' (Selznick, 1946) on account of David O's non-memo meddlings, and his attempt to helm a few scenes at this very location in Vidor's absence.

Truxton's Pop Shoppe was a humble little establishment up there, and, quite puffed from their pedal-pumping, Veezee suggested – nay, ordered – a stop, so as to partake.

'Why, how thoughtful!' the ultrastar ejaculated.

He was so preoccupied with non-'UWH' thoughts right now, he might have simply gone on cycling to the end of the line, and then headed overland from there, to points unknown on the edges of suburban sprawl.

'You need me rather more than you thought you would,' muttered Veezee, under her breath.

'Not many 'Looky-Lues' today – as Porter is wont to say…,' observed the ultrastar, spying out the Eason and Rennahan Lay-bys up on the straw-grass heights, where groups of touristas gathered with their binocs, fizz-juice, and jellycorn concessions, in order to spy out the on-location land.

'Looky – *whats…?*'

'I guess it's not well-known that we're doing the big wrap shots today.'

'We are not a tourist destination,' quipped Veezee, and then told Butterbugs to pay attention to the menu. 'Besides, Publicity's been chary to reveal all our secrets publicly. A dahn good idea, if you ask me.'

Butterbugs felt a bit sorry for the bakery-capped concessionaires up there in the heat, doling out plate-creme, barrel-peas, knuckledrops and calf-bars to bawling no-neck monsters, blimpy shutterbugs, and other unwashed 'Looky-Lues'.

'Oh, they're all right, those curious ones,' he mused. 'They have their rights...'

'They also have hard coin at the box office,' Veezee added, with a wry Venezuelan-Tahitian twist. The hard-boiling of her 'movie' personality was bubbling along nicely.

They managed to get set up nicely at an outdoor table, with a remarkable view of the vast Location, though that wasn't what occupied them within this valuable time segment.

Veezee happened to have a P(ress) H(ere) D(ummy) camera, and she got some shots of the menu-studying actor she thought were significant, if not historical. He didn't take notice of her at all, as she photographed him from many angles, ranging from a series of evocative and sensitively composed CUs to a wide angle shot of him at table, facing the busy panorama that formed the background.

She may have projected an attitude of all-business canniness on her surface, but inside there was almost a giddiness at being a part of this monumentally exciting production, in this place, and with this person, who chanced to be the sole ultrastar on 'Urth'. Nevertheless those feelings were confined only to the immediate media her camera's shutter exposed. At table, she got right to the essential points.

'I'm not a critic, Butterbugs, but in the scene in the Gazebo with Bob (Middleton), lately finished, I noticed that, um, your creativity was limited to character development within the existing script. I had wanted to call out, 'Butterbugs, you're not projecting!' But I was hamstrung in my wishes. There were moments when you seemed like a block of wood. Or a – a *wall*. No expansions, hardly any variations... I'm puzzled.'

'Perhaps you should be, given your justifiable expectations. We actors have to be constantly aware of audience interpretation – well past what the director wants. I don't wish to minimize the realizer, but once that funnel – his wants – has been cleared, the actor must project the role through its divers possibilities, choose the right one, and finalize it. In the scene you refer to, I was in fact battling distractions, so I played it safe in both takes.'

'Do you want to re-take them?'

'Not at all. I think I was more than adequate in them.'

'Adequate, yes. I would agree. Your craft must be effortless for you.'

'Not when I have distractions.'

'How can you possibly be having distractions? At such a time!' Then she mellowed. 'Maybe you're experiencing some of the true mega-stress this turbo-powered day's demands might solicit? *Tell* me, Butterbugs! I will be kind in my analysis. *Tell* me, ultrastar. I can help.'

Butterbugs well appreciated her benevolence.

Truxton's JFK-style-special-of-the-day chowder-sticks and MLK's favorite soul-gravy arrived, along with Kester & Idbash soda (surprised they could get it here), some duck-lips crisps, plus a combo of dog-milk and bill-milk. They tucked in.

'I may be an ultrastar, my dear Veezee, but I am still happily chained to everything human that you or anybody else on this planet are allowed to act out. Every day! Actors of any caliber deal with distractions on an almost frame-by-frame level, sometimes. Today's were... Well, I hope I've ushered them out of the way now.'

'I think if you impart them, they might relieve you of their imposing presence.'

'I embrace your theory, Veezee. Gawrsch, this gumball-oil is good on the broasted treasures from the sea, is it not?'

'Your appearance in front of me now is bizarre and disgusting, as per your character's persona, but your goodness in all things shines through, Butterbugs.'

'I think I could fall in love with you, Veezee. Easily, over lunch here.'

'That would be a wondrous and natural thing,' replied Veezee, straining to remain professional.

'Wondrous! Natural! Those are the best things in life!'

Veezee proceeded somewhat cautiously.

'So Butterbugs, is that the... nature... of, um, your... distractions on set...?'

'On... set...'

Even now he was falling prey to them, those distractions. Loyalty and love were two separate things to him. He figured, best to take his p.a. up on her cathartic proposition. He snapped to.

'Yes, distracted I was and am. You are correct: that I should get them off my chests. Not that they are burdens of the soul, but they are probably hindrances to my artistic declarations on film. Yes, yes they are. Well, *one* distracting thing I'm thinking of, at this juncture, is a pretty big deal to me. In which, the whole bottleneck of this picture, my career, and my very life, is about to be cleared. I cannot but regard it that way, as circumstances have shown.'

'You are sounding scripted right now, Butterbugs.'

'So I am! Yes, yes. I am. I always admit everything! And why not? It's all part of an actor's credibility. We are actors, but we are not *liars*. Sounding scripted: admitting it. Honesty is my only policy. My conditioning as a strolling player. But you must know that scripted-ness is also inherent in me. It is part of what I am. A structured means to a productive output. And as of now, I've made quite a few pictures. Rather a lot, actually. Yet, yes, let me go off script, as it were. And I *do* know how to do that, when the situation demands it.'

'It does so now. Please desist in prefacing.'

'One more thing, my dear. You have to understand, a person in my position cannot, as they go on, reveal too much of their inner self in front of the public. One tends to retreat to an Inner Sanctum, lest the thought that travels through the spread-open French doors to the public's collective mind becomes too indistinguishable from that which actually exists. Me, I have to employ Dutch doors as an alternative. Upper one, perfectly glad to be open. Lower one, definitely relieved to be closed!'

'I'm not sure I understand what you just said. It was obscure. But I understand all the other stuff, Butterbugs. Now, what about those distractions?'

He let the obscure remain obscure. Behind the lower Dutch door.

'I guess I can bat them about a bit more easily now. It helps, yakking with you on this intimate scale – especially with such an epic overlook as we have before us! I am so guarded, you know. One must protect what one thinks is worthy of a private residence within one's Inner Sanctum.'

'Butterbugs, I'm becoming impatient. Look at the clock tower yonder! Half our time is expired.'

'Of course and affirmative. I am a wee bit nervous in telling you, lest the jinxie come to pester me.'

'I didn't know you had all these hang-ups. I won't tell another carbon-based life form of your confession – ever!'

'Good. *Good.* I shall tell you because you are in my Potentia-Love category. I hope you don't take that the wrong way.'

'No, no, certainly not. I am humbled. There is a saying in the Îles de la Société, and I translate, 'It is always good to have an alternate route to Bora Bora – and back'. Now, the distractions, please. I need to know, in case I have to rescue you on set.'

'But I don't know…,' he drifted.

She readied her hammer and nails, to pin him down.

'Your distraction, is it the girl?'

Veezee was referring to Shawna Lee.

Butterbugs thought she was *probably* referring to Shawna, because that was the only 'girl' she was aware of. It could also have been Hazel – or Heatherette – or… Veezee herself…

'Yes, of course you have to know, don't you?'

It suddenly occurred to him that this p.a. was not only lovely and smart, but extremely perceptive and resourceful. He adored the idea of knowing there was someone on set who could and would rescue him. All this time making pictures, and now he had what he'd always wanted in filmmaking. Besides, what he had to tell her was, well, sort of… nothing.

'We are finished with our repast now, Butterbugs. So you can tell me without gobbling or crunching or quaffing or slurping, or any *further* interruption.'

By anyone's measure, Veezee looked and acted absolutely scrumptious while uttering this rather ludicrous line of command. Her dark eyes flashed, she batted her hair around, and her cheekbones stood supremely out. So determined, so serious, so cute, but impossible to trivialize.

Now that he had a lifeguard, Butterbugs relaxed completely and opened, not his Dutch door, top or bottom, but a more invitational set of French doors.

'In my mind, here is my mission, which I must manage: on the morrow, well after the present joined tasks are fulfilled, and before the vaunted Wrap Party, I will showcase the new Special Person in my life. Before the hog-sparrow's first peep at dawn, I will ring her (to whom I referred in the previous sentence), for she is of high standing with me. Unprecedented, in fact.'

Veezee heard this elevated talk, and found nothing unusual about it. She was relieved to hear that Butterbugs obviously had a sweetheart. That Shawna chick was OK – a little bizarre, kind of damaged, but not at all hokey. This let her off the guilt hook. Now she could pursue that extensively hot guy on the Ninth Cyclorama Erection and Maintenance Crew, who'd smiled at her when she'd caught a glance of him way out in her peripheral vision, when they were biking from Makeup early this morning.

'And you know what?' Butterbugs continued, 'Because our pre-arranged 'separation pact' dissolves at 6:00AM on the morrow, I'm going to surprise my Special One-and-Only by hiring her as a worthy successor to you, Veezee, as you are my girl for the Seventh Day, for the Seventh Art. She will be my 'p.a.' for the Eighth Day! She will thus get screen credit. That being the case, I will be compelled to shun my bicycle tomorrow, and I will commandeer that majestic convertible that bore me to this here location, for I have a journey unto the gates of the city to make, and even as far within them as Yniguez Terrace. I cannot tell you the address further. She will be waiting for me. By 8 o'clock high, I will have her back here, to present to the world, as the highlight of the all-day Wrap Party!'

He paused.

'So you see, V.Z., I *do* have my alternate route to Bora Bora – and back, all set up.'

He ran the whole sequence, in fine cinematic flash-forward style, through his mind's eye. There was Heatherette, whose presence eclipsed anyone else's, at the party, as if arrived from heaven. To grace herself on all those who had labored so nobly on this picture. All those who now sought a celestial figure to focus on, as a sign their efforts were worthwhile, and that they were blessed by an otherworldly entity of note.

Oh, these were the moments he longed for! When his chosen mate would share the role of ultrastardom, and they could go on together in high achievement and increasing bliss. So superbly executed in the best filmic techniques, who *wouldn't* be distracted by such a dazzling show? Everything in the present was as tinsellated-trifle compared with the glorious and long-anticipated things to come.

The Neo-Gothic clock tower nearby, which was modeled on Henry Astley Darbishire's spectacular Columbia Market in London, and specially constructed to supply pre-existing architectural fabric to HMD's audacious giganticism – as shown in the picture's long shots – officially struck the hour. Way across the vale, perfectly positioned as a match in the widescreen frame, stood another tower of much magnificence, this one a copy of Thomas Edward Collcutt's Imperial Institute in Albertopolis. Clockless, its star feature was a complete Deagan carillon, which confirmed the advancement of the hour in appropriately solemn tones.

[To round out the vast Periphery Set, which formed a distant background to HMD's central edifices, the Production Design team, headed by the infinitely-resourceful Richard Welsted Day, included life-sized replicas of Alfred Brumwell Thomas's Belfast City Hall, Edward William Mountford's Old Bailey, George Gilbert Scott's St. Pancras Station clock tower, George Edmund Street's Law Courts, Halsey Ralph Ricardo's Oxford Town Hall, Alfred Waterhouse's Eaton Hall clock tower, William Burges's Cardiff Castle towers, Cuthbert Brodrick's Leeds Town Hall, William Young's Glasgow City Chambers tower, etc. The addition of Sir Charles Barry and Augustus Welby Northmore Pugin's Palace of Westminster Clock Tower (Elizabeth Tower) was vetoed by the team after Old Atrocity mentioned that it might remind too many audience members of London and/or Calcutta and/or Dubai, occasioning a most unwelcome distraction from the drama's intensities.]

Therefore, if they were to be good little cinema bees, they only had two handfuls of minutes to get back on set.

'Time's closed,' said Veezee in biz mode. 'Next scene's up.'

She was thrilled with Butterbugs' thrill-dom.

'And now,' the ultrastar said quietly, placing his serviette in his dessert basket's remains of oil-limped chang-fries, 'We shall proceed to the very end of all things.'

As they walked to their cycles, Veezee remarked, 'This production has extended over a very long time period, I believe. Like, in glacial, or even geologic time.'

'That's why I speak in such terms,' he answered, 'And not solely in jest.'

'Yet, I detect a joyous morale. The sign of a good production.'

'Why do you think that is?' Butterbugs was in all earnestness and sincerity.

'Many reasons,' she replied, up for the challenge. 'But all of them clearly distill to one essence: you.'

'*I* am the reason?'

'You are the catalyst. The reason. It rescues the rest of us. If you were not part of this, it would all be absurd. You are the catalyzer. You are the *seer*.'

A revelation – not a lightning strike, but a quiet – intimate even – climax of sorts, throve in their minds. Interior, Inner Sanctum-ed. Nice in its presentation, and wonderful in its message.

He'd made a mental note, all this past week, that each p.a. assigned to him had basically sounded the same notes. Similar personalities, in a position of proving themselves in a job where one had to hustle, be subservient, but simultaneously bossy, and always there. An apprenticeship for life skills, preferably applied to its cinematic side. Also always present was the imperative of *rising* somehow. Towards producership. Or motherhood. Or some heart's desire – whether via talent, ambition, or… love. Plus, the closeness of personal involvement invariably spiced things up.

But what set Vu'unaatatoa Zulloh apart was the penultimate part of her utterance. Not the catalyzer part, but the bit about absurdity. Oh, and the notion of rescue. In two key words, she had summed up his existence as a strolling player upon the screen: a validation, and also, a vulnerability.

Finally, he especially appreciated her ultimate statement: that he was the *seer*. Yes, he was. He could see Heatherette, all right. Not Shawna, not Hazel, not... Veezee...

Everything was Heatherette.

With this new strength and clarity, he was ready for the home stretch now. Invigorated, reinvented, and most importantly, inspired.

'It is almost as if Heatherette spake through the vehicle of Veezee,' he thought, as the crooked lanes gave way to the broad thoroughfares and plazas that led to the Substantial Grade, where his super-heated finale scenes could now take place, free of diversions.

'Heatherette has been trying to tell me the same things for the longest time, and only now do I realize what she was talking about. What I am doing *is* purposeful, but I am one in need of others, like all of humanity.'

To Butterbugs, never the smug know-it-all, these simple thoughts were as a kind of enlightenment, a go-ahead signal to realign definitions of his place in the universe.

A Mahlerian brass fanfare, practice-performed by Alfred's full orchestra off to the side, on their special elevated hardwood-floored terrace, unconsciously heralded Butterbugs' return for his next scene.

He trotted up to say hi to the Maestro, who was at his podium.

'Strength to you, Alfred, and your stalwarts, all!'

Composer/conductor and his band gave the ultrastar a noble and loving salute, in the form of an impromptu Newmanesque flourish, ending with an arpeggio higher than HMD's Citadel.

'It's your score, Sir Butterbugs!' Alfred enthused. 'I wrote it for you. We play it for you. You're the *best!*'

It would be time for easy tears later. Right now, a grand Butterbugsian wave, and off to the cameras.

Everyone wanted to toss an anchor out in order to slow down time. Now that the climax was nigh, a collective longing seemed to flourish on set. A desire for these hours, these minutes, these seconds, to linger more than their time-value allowed. If only so that the greatness, the sweetness, and even the tension, encountered along the course they had set upon, could be savored. Or at the very least, *examined* more.

It is not often that they who are in the midst of a historical sequence of consequence are allowed much scrutiny of the action arena they occupy. The obligation of the moment dictates duty, not appreciation. And within that duty, no great freedoms lie. Even cast and crew, when witnessing great performances by their peers, shall not become distracted *by* those great performances. Cinematic brigade work is serious business, but does not preclude that many experiences therein shall not be golden. In fact, most of cinema workers' treasuries are privately kept. Many are they in pictures who never go to the picture show at all, for they prefer to keep their memories confined to *production* rather than *product*. Product is for audiences out in public. Production is for the privileged few.

Never, all throughout this lengthy shoot, had anyone ever uttered the old saw, 'Who do you have to fuck to get *off* this picture?' No one. Not even in jest. Indeed, there were those, particularly amongst the extras, who received cellphone calls from persons of both sexes – though mostly female – who might declare, even in these hours that dwindled before wrap-up, 'I would be happy to make my body available for cheerfully consensual sex-play, provided that single act secures me some kind of pleasant and remarkable involvement within the wonder that is 'Unholy War Hymn'. Thank you.' (phonering, zuckerlink, twit-tag, and selfie attached, natch).

But alas, the job ahead trumped any reflection at this point. However, non-fiction crews were ceaselessly covering the whole circus, from dawn to dusk and after, and had amassed a body of footage that eclipsed that of 'UWH' itself. An extensive series of documentaries, shorts, series, and features, created and hosted by every docu luminary (and some dimbulbs) in the biz, were now in the making. Theirs would be as much a legacy, it seemed, as the original novel, its script, and the picture show it created. Such was the holistic magnitude of a film as contribution to civilization, not just what its grosses are in the first weekend.

Deanman Xecugnipip, probably the most distinguished of these documentarians, perhaps said it best in his personal introduction to 'When Something Unholy Becomes Something More' (WongoTV), his twelve-part series on the film's making: 'Do you know what an ultrastar actually *does?* Do you know how an ultrastar actually *does it?* Come with me now, for you shall see so great a saga, and such monumental efforts, that you will surely review and revise any thoughts you may have had on whether life itself has meaning or not. They are efforts made not only by an ultrastar, but by all those *other* stars – 'ultra' in themselves – who do ultrastarry things. And they are doing them, not only for our viewing *pleasure*, but for our viewing *purpose...*'

For there had never been one trace of cynicism or sarcasm or snarkiness or scorn displayed by anyone in or associated with this picture, *concerning* this picture during the whole of its shooting. Respect and positivism prevailed on a genuinely wholesome level. No one had even attempted sitcom humor in reducing it to just a money-spinner or a crowd-fooler, or even as a sacred cow. Cynicism was blissfully absent, but so were pretensions of high-mindedness. No, never had such a clear-conscience production existed. There was no front office-requested-or forced reverence, such as with DeMille's 'King of Kings' (Pathé, 1927). There had been no ego, no puffery, no divide-and-rule on any plane. No gossip even, though a fun endeavor sometimes; the 'UWH' company got their jollies through simple dedication to the film itself, and this seemed to work for every-one. That was why, at the beginning of this last afternoon of shooting, the long-ing for the prolonged moment came to be.

The moment passed when Butterbugs, followed by Veezee, stepped up onto the Substantial Grade after a few mostly unnecessary primps from Makeup. (Some road grit and touslement from their lunch hour journey was OK'd, to make HMD look more scoundrel-like, even at the height of his glory.)

Egaz greeted him as if the two hadn't seen each other for months. The director was very demonstrative and accommodating, though Butterbugs was his usual low-key self.

'They're trying to butter him into a stellar performance, hoping for profitable improvs...,' Veezee mused. This thought was the first bit of cynicism to creep into the entire production.

In fact, she was both right and wrong in this speculation. About 20% right and 80% wrong. To be sure, Egaz sought to cater to his lead actor's sensitivities, but mostly it was out of joy and respect, so that cordiality overflowed freely, for what momentous times these were! This was an aware company, aware that they were part of something great and lasting, and now it was fleeting, so very fleeting.

In addition, from the pure perspective of filmic craft, Egaz had thought over the earlier Gazebo scene, and Butterbugs' comparatively tame performance within. The basic ingeniousness of it had struck him: Butterbugs' rubato effect, which was in downplay during that particular scene, would intensify the rhythm of the final sequence, when assembled.

'My God,' he marveled to himself, regarding the actor as he moved onto his blocking marks. 'The man sees *past* what the world sees. He is already 'there', though we do not know where 'there' is. But we know it is somewhere remark-able, unprecedented, more enlightened. Surely he shall lead us to that desirable locale. Could my film – our film – be *the way?*'

'All right, my able bodies, places!' the director called out. It was as if he had started roll call for the last boat out of Atlantis, the lost continent, for every member of cast and crew was with him, 100%.

'In this scene, my people, there will be a confrontation betwixt HMD and his perceived adversary, NAHGUARRANEX. It is rather intense. So get ready, please.'

It was most unusual for Egaz to address the company in explanatory terms, and with terms like 'my people'. He thought all deserved to have an avenue of appreciation opened to them, to elucidate, particularly for those who did not have script access, where the perimeters under which a great performance is motivated are based.

'All right? ACTION.'

(Emerging from the low-down opening to his noontime nest of perfidy – a steamy little porta-pleasure dome on a purpose-built and plum-tinted

granite podium near the top of the Substantial Grade – HMD *stands after a debauched crawl-out and wipes his hands on a* COURTIER's *robes. Before wiping, his palms were full of some unspeakable bodily discharge, the same foamy viscosity that has formed a pool, as it dribbles over the sill of the nest's doorway. CU of said doorway, showing indeterminate but troubled movement of anonymously naked body bits in the shadowy interior. Sexual activity has certainly taken place, probably involving S&M molestation and possibly even mutilation, though the discharge is not bloody. Adjacent* COURTIERS *make note of unhygienic scents, but suppress their reactions.)*

*(*HMD *stretches and puffs and makes it known that, after a virile frolic, he is ready for a session of statecraft once more. He strolls up to a stout* COURTIER, *slaps him or her with a discharge-sheened hand and grabs a flabby durp-fowl leg that the* COURTIER *has been gobbling. He sniffs it grossly and grimaces. Then he flings it across the Grade, making a greasy streak, before it hits a* KNAVE [as played by Anthony 'The Mooch' Scaramucci], *who attempts to clean the mess up.)*

HMD: *(with very nasal haughtiness)* That meat had Pott's disease! *(then, shriek-laughs)* I was just kidding!

*(*THE COURT *explodes in coercive merriment.)*

HMD: *(to* THE COURT*)* You like-a my naughty skits? Huh?

*(*THE COURT *cheers and applauds.)*

HMD: Well, I thought you droops could use some chucklesomes. I was laughing all through my noontide leg-overs. Didn't you hear me? Huh?

THE COURT: Yes! Yes, O Wonder-Leader!

HMD: Didn't I inspire you?

THE COURT: Yes! Yes, O Wonder-Leader! The only *real* Leader of Wonders!

HMD: Well, great. Whenever you're down in the mouth, think of my antics! But remember, grim pressuring will be brought to bear on anyone who over-does it or thinks he's/she's funnier.

THE COURT: You, you only, are funniest!

HMD: *And* the most talented!

THE COURT: You, you only, are the most talented!

HMD: *And* the brightest!

THE COURT: You, you only, are the brightest!

HMD: *And* the sexiest!

THE COURT: You, you only, are the sexiest!

HMD: That's enough. Now, bring me a barrel of carnival squeezings and bring me my Mandates of Court, which I shall proceed on, as Your Statesman.

(A puncheon is brought forward with dispatch, taste-tested by a burly TIBETAN [as played by Tenzin Gyatso (the Dalai Lama)], in chains. It passes the test, and HMD himself places a sucker-valve in the corner of his mouth, so as to suck-sip and get high, at his pleasure.)

(CHAMBERLAINs bring the trolley with his human-skin-bound Mandates of Court, along with a cheap popular paperback edition for hand-holding and threat-gesture use, which MORPRESSUECX, the Chief Chamberlain [as played by Sir Chips Trolleypinch], hands over, with kerchief protection, to HMD after crawling to him.)

MORPRESSUECX: Mandates now, Higher Than Highest, from the heaven of your creation.

HMD: *(takes the item, strips the kerchief off, hawks into it, then flings it at MORPRESSUECX, the gob in the kerchief sticking to the Chief Chamberlain's forehead)* Leave us.

(Without having the nerve to attend to this humiliating blight, MORPRESSUECX humbly retires after being cur-kicked by HMD.)

HMD: NOW! Bring me the head of —

Butterbugs had gone off script. The hair on the company's collective neck was raised. It was because the shooting schedule had been determined down to the three-minute count, and there were quite a few script pages to cover yet. Daylight itself would dictate when the final sequence had to be filmed. Earlier, Egaz and Butterbugs had made a solemn pact not to do a 'John Ford' this day (e.g. tear out a bunch of pages from the script, so as to be ostensibly 'on schedule'). When he heard of the deal, Ford himself, inspecting the show from his chair up in VIP Seating, had quipped to his new wife, Vera, 'They bettah not. If so, ah'll escort 'em to the horsewhipping pahlah myself! Besides, the whole ploy was horseshit anyway...'

'Cut' was not a word to be heard in all the universe at this moment.

HMD: I mean...

Then he went back on script. Hairs on necks deflated. SFX would not have to be 911'ed to procure a fresh human-head prop at zero-hour notice, after all.

HMD: Bring me the current form, human or otherwise... *(meant as a joke – many laugh)*... of my High-Toned Financier, Nahguarranex, who jes' happens to be – drum roll please – *(the* MAJOR-DOMO OF THE HIGH MAD BAND [as played by Phil Harris] *hustles to get a drummer to rattle out a roll, and a goofy puttering erupts).* Now cut that damned noise out, drummah! I was just kidding! *(drum instantly silenced)* Can't you tell? Is everyone here that *stupid?* Now where was – oh yes, the Money Wiz, my closest and dearie-est associate-type person. Oh, and uh, snap it up.

*(*NAHGUARRANEX *enters, escorted by* PRÆTORIAN-ISH GUARDS, *but non-aggressively; indeed,* NAHGUARRANEX *regards it as a badge of his office, and a super opportunity to act pompous in front of* THE COURT.*)*

NAHGUARRANEX: *(casually)* Oh, hi-hi, High Mad! Hi! How fares the rat race?

HMD: *(sneeringly comic)* The rats are winning – as Paul Lynde used to say.

*(*THE COURT *laughs heartily.)*

Old Atrocity was at Egaz's elbow.
'Was that line in the script??' he whispered.
'It was indeed,' replied the director. 'One of Britney's lines.'
'Sufferin', bleedin' Chickamauga...'

NAHGUARRANEX: Nice li'l ol' private garden party and seminar, mein Herr. Or should I call you 'Goalie'?

HMD: Nice is it, Nugg *(a derogatory and wholly disrespectful moniker).* But even though you have shown up, it is still possible that it can remain nice.

NAHGUARRANEX: You're a riot, baby.

HMD: The funniest you ever heard?

NAHGUARRANEX: Hell no! Not by a long shot. Slightly amusing, though.

HMD: Attitude and opinion noted. *(pause then, for a nearly excruciating time; HMD makes a wide array of facial expressions, as if trying them out; CUs within LSs)* I think that, um… *(facial expression)*… You see… *(facial expression)*… I think that… *(facial expression)*…it's about time… *(facial expression)*… that you were more respectful toward the world's prime law-giver… *(facial expression)*… and enforcer… *(facial expression)*.

NAHGUARRANEX: *(genial)* Well maybe so, but where's the moolah gonna come from? *(then serious)* Money purchases respect, pal, and right now, you're doing deficit spending.

(Some COURTIERS titter mildly – but mistakenly – when they see HMD's souring expression; they cease.)

HMD: Fancy yourself as a pretty big deal, don't you?

NAHGUARRANEX: I can't wait for this stupid vaudeville matinee and bozo Ceremony (the term's not worth capitalizing, but I do it here and now, just to please you!) to both pass into the toxic waste cylinders of history, so's that I can really get *my* schemes going, Law-Boy.

HMD: You classify yourself as Owner-Fellow of the Populace's Own Currency Fundamentals? Huh?

NAHGUARRANEX: I am their Furthest-Up Handler.

HMD: *(making sure THE COURT and, now, all THE MASSES can hear)* So what would you think if I clued The Masses in on your control factors regarding *their* monies? *(indicates THE MASSES)*

NAHGUARRANEX: *(angry, but realizes he could be over a barrel, so, in low tones)* Why you miserable…

And then… And then, Butterbugs went *completely* off script. And he didn't just go off script, he *flew* off script. Bob M. as Nahguarranex not only kept up, he was having the acting experience of his life.

HMD: *(flaunting, strutting, mindful of his advantage in public, his next utterance is a surpassingly awful ancient curse, in the Kshullituz tongue)* Worpay skoozah plimliacco shor shummah vkux!!

NAHGUARRANEX: Ohhhhh! Your foulness now stands revealed!

HMD: You *KNOW* it! Now, in the moment, there's a time to rise in my stirrups on behalf of the peoples of my planet –

NAHGUARRANEX: *(dares to interrupt) Your* planet? You incredible pig! Root-pig! Pilfering the world's gruntings, like you forged 'em yourself!

HMD: *(addresses* THE MASSES*)* How does a root-pig root? Why must he do so? For his own satisfaction? His own greed? Nay! I tell you in the strongest terms possible, my Own Ones, NAY! This rotting piece of human meat? *(indicates* NAHGUARRANEX*)* Why, even a root-pig wouldn't stain his snout with the corporeal decay emanating from his unspeakable recesses. For he is the beau ideal of selfish greed – words not powerful enough to describe his excesses! I'd like to interrupt this purposeful screed to point out the following: notice, my bone-children, how I have made the easy transition from pleasant and fun-loving entertainer to parable-teller and exposer of this Lucre-Oriented Corrupticus. Notice my diversity, and how it applies to fair play. Some of you out there may think I'm kind of a creep when it comes to meting out justice. And yes, I can be – you know – *firm*, but anyone who has not personally experienced my justice can rest easy because I haven't aimed it at you. So don't worry about the justice stuff I tend to do. Just support me without question as I mete it out, and you'll be fine. I won't bug you, because you haven't pissed me off. Isn't that a rather elegant solution to your anxieties? You know, I say this to all my world: just go along with me and you'll be dandy. Cross me, and I'll do other things. I will molest you or possibly destroy you. So support me without question, always, and thou will rise with me to new, unattended heights. And I'm not talking about that bran-new gorgeous Citadel over there. (Only *I* get to go to the top of *that*), but feel free to use it as a met-aphor for your hopes 'n' dreams. Make me your inspiration, and thou can feed at my charitable trough.

NAHGUARRANEX: *(hissing in low volume)* You traitor. You liar and traitor, here and now. *(addresses* THE MASSES*)* You mean, you actually *believe* this, this mega-criminal?

HMD: Back to this Corrupticus here *(gestures with reasonable graciousness to* NAHGUARRANEX), whom we all trusted with all our dough. You and me, fellow Urth-Occupants! He was supposed to make us and bake us bread with the raw, innocent and honest ingredients we cheerfully turned over to him, but what does he give us in return? Pure slop! Can you *live* with that?

ONE OF THE MASSES [as played by Edward Petherbridge] *(stepping boldly forward)* How *can* we, Lord Over All Protectors? Save us, and *keep* saving us! That is our fulsome entreaty!

(Great chorus of objection from THE MASSES, *along with passionate agreement with* ONE OF THE MASSES' *plea.)*

HMD: You see, Corrupticus? Hear *them*, not me. Hear their whines? Understand their desires? Know their verdict? It's becoming quite clear, isn't it? You ground-oaf! Pure silage-creator! I hate you. My people can't stand you. Your arrogance is an embarrassment. Because we believed in you. And you do *this* to us!

NAHGUARRANEX: May I speak?

HMD: I suppose you want to acquit yourself in the face of absolutely impossible odds.

NAHGUARRANEX: Oh, but may I, Leader and Teacher?

HMD: That's better. Yes, you may speak, but I reserve the right, on behalf of all my Dear Ones here and across the universe, to stop you, censor you, to cane you, and to protect my Dears from your objectionably horrific corrupting powers, which certainly caught *me* by surprise. And as for my Ones, I can't imagine the trauma you've caused them. They hear me now, and you also. Some may never get over it. Can you conceive of the lives you've aggressively ruined? Do you know of the little babies out there whose ears and minds have been irreversibly bashed and puzzled-up by your chippings and your further nefariousness? Before me I see the sullen face of a stubbornovitch who defies me! A face I totally gave credence to, a face I confided in, even with secrets of my intimate life. That's why I warn my Dear Ones about you, and that you may utter some things they know in their hearts to be lies, because how could they be true – how could their Permanent Grovel-Guardian On High, their Doctor Who Gets Mad At The World's Injustices for them, do things that become lies from the mouths of scheming traitors? Nay, they, all of them, *they* know me as you couldn't possibly know me. Not in a bazillion years. Their faith in me is *total*, and I will never let them down. Right, me Dear Ones?

(Gigantic approval from THE MASSES.*)*

Egaz was staring like a bozo-boy in sheer god-wonderful awe. Butterbugs of the Blessed Improvs! Everything he'd wanted in this scene, this *film*, his players were giving to him. His expectations were so vastly surpassed, no measurement was possible. The crew was entirely hip too, and tackled the actors' high flying with unparalleled aplomb.

HMD: Do you see, you pathetic, remaining mess of a 'person'? They follow only me. Know that, and obey, lest ye place yourself at Their mercy! *(then, in lower tones, to* NAHGUARRANEX *personally, in magnificent CU)* Mob mercy! Can you imagine anything more just, more powerful, or more reasonable? All those sours out there can beat in more brains than I have wont to note! *(returns to public address mode)* Time now for your speakings. Beware! The Song of the Populace is a cantata of highest warning to they who might evolve as threats. We don't like threats here, we don't cotton to them, or they who would aspire to threaten. So, your yakkings, which I and my Dear Ones now generously allow you to spew forth, *better be good.*

NAHGUARRANEX: *(bursting with hatred, that one more corrupt and awful than he is is using his mandate of power to spoil his own public life, and is rapidly getting away with it; yet, he remains cool, so as to outsmart this ruler flimp at first opportunity; he knows he will not be allowed to say much of anything, though)* What then, *exactly,* Treasured Care-Minister and Instigator of the Genuflections, am I accused of?

HMD: *(somewhat nonplused, but enraged, though completely playing to* THE MASSES*)* What *exactly??* Exactitude is what you require? You hear that, The People? He wants a report in triplicate, I suppose! He can't rely on what we've said – what you, my Dear Ones, and what I have said, *exactly,* this afternoon – alone as reason for his treachery! He doesn't believe in me, and us; in my goodness, nor in my caring for you. Oh, he *calls* me all the proper titles and addressings – (in that he speaks his sole, bare truth) – but with the cheap and lying tongue of a sneaky and sickening holo-me-tabolous pupa. He's icky, and we know it, don't we, gang?

(Crowd-pleasing response from a pleased crowd.)

NAHGUARRANEX: *(taking advantage of a chance to get a word in, as* HMD *turns and turns again, pandering to the crowd)* I'm just going to barge in on you, you calumny-spurting sphincter! Oh, how I hate you! Fiercest fire-hatred! It's mine! And all who are here, and those beyond the Pale you have fashioned by your boorishness, should join me in my barbed feelings. I tell you, I'm going to hold the floor. Yes, we call each other names here. Mine are truthful – yours are not. True, I am a bum-goon and a cash-pimp. I go for the lettuce leaves in life, and that's all I could ever want. I hate love, and have only contempt for fellow peoples, including *you*. In fact, you're the most banal of my contemptibles, due to your mediocre madness. If you were a genius in that department, hell, I'd happily give you a homosexual blowjob. But you'd have to *earn* it. Instead, you are verily *beneath* contempt. *(he then attempts a vaudevillian aside)* Besides, I hear tell that I'd need some sort of GPS search-device to even locate that thing of yours. Some of the gals I've successfully bedded – and you've *attempted* to bed – say that they never *could* find it on your putrid, maggoty person. Heh-heh! Well, now. *(pauses, then finds he can indeed continue, as* HMD *makes no outcry)* No bones can be made from those kind of statements, huh, Loser-Leader? I have succeeded beyond your wildness dreams, and you are thus scalded with jealousy. Plus, I am much more handsome. Yours is an ugly mug and a mucus-puke-inducing body under those fœtid robes. You and your big, cowardly cover-up! I'd joyfully compare members with you in public at any hour, and the day is not too late, today! And your soul is uglier yet. All the built-up disastrous bulk of which I speak really *bugs* you, doesn't it? So I announce to the world: your vanity has gotten you into quite a pickle, no?

Here was now enacted an improv through Bob's own enlightened talent that fit perfectly with Butterbugs' expanding and expansive concept of the scene. So now, without pause, he resumed it, having received the bounty from his co-player's helping hand.

HMD: *(laughing maniacally)* You see, Peoples of Mine Urth? I done *told* you what he would do, and he did it with all the freedom that my love and nurturing brings with it. You plainly witness how he heaves projectiles at me, how his arm winds up as if to chuck a boulder, but what comes across the blameless space between us? Mere dirt clods! And they don't even reach me! Nothing more than gnatspecks of angry spit-up, that not even my Knaves or my Gravel-Prisoners should have to sweep up! Bitterest of joke-lives, Corrupticus, you are audacious, I grant you that, and therein lies perhaps the most admirable side of cowardice, but only because the scale of your crimes and naughtiness has become too invasive to contain.

NAHGUARRANEX: You still can't handle my inquiry. You still haven't itemized my alleged crimes. I know the truth: this is a show trial, you ridiculous foonman. You stupid *nut!*'

HMD: Well, did you evah?! It's a breeze to pass at least a preliminary judgment on you, you mass of shavings from crud-lumps! Just for that, you don't get to enter my Citadel. Not even well behind me. Not ever. Ever! Do you hear?

NAHGUARRANEX: I once dreamt that you were a sort of god. Even though I reject all forms of divinity. I at least thought that perhaps you could invent your own godhead, and that you would be patron to my interests. That you would bring goodness to our blightful world. That you would have the power to cure even sorry fucks like me. I waited, and waited and waited. No cure ever emanated from you, so I, in my helpless way, proceeded freely on my reprehensible pathway, not only with your approbation, but accompanied by you at my side, and on an equal basis. I want everyone on 'your' Earth – not 'Urth' – to know these and many other things, from this moment forward. The disappointment I feel in you is too monumental to even begin to summarize.

HMD: Shut up instantly, you old jar of excrement, you! Hear how I protect the People! People? What do we *do* with things like this clotted devil-sputum? *(to* NAHGUARRANEX*)* I'm sick of you. Fed up, too. So sick. If I and my Ones were to trust you and your corrupt business dealings, why, we'd really get burned! And more than we already are. Ponderment of these and other threats has produced some resolve. I see what I have to do now. And I'm sure you, as you regard me with that most wicked of expressions, know exactly – *(mockingly)* 'exactly' – what I have to do. That's what you want, isn't it? Exactitude? You drippy packet of condom-waste! Already super-burdened with the duties of State and Protection, I must now add Pecuniary to my imperviously strong shoulders. I short you out of your status, Corrupticus. *(addresses* THE MASSES*:)* Note, my Urth Peoples, this, this *thing* here can only, from this instant forward, be referred to as Corrupticus. Anyone who defies me on this will have their head struck off. *(then, to himself, while scrutinizing* NAHGUARRANEX/CORRUPTICUS*)* Which isn't at all a bad idea. No, not a bad idea at all.

CORRUPTICUS: See, Masses, how he robs me right in front of you! Even my sacred name of glisteny entitlement! See how he shamelessly appropriates the empires I myself have built up, and which he merely has shares in, but hogs all the turnings from! See how –

HMD: *Cease* your fire, horror! Cease, or succumb!

CORRUPTICUS: I won't! I won't! I won't let you do it! You Crime King! You –

HMD: My warning is severe.

CORRUPTICUS: I expect you to gaol me for life, but first I shall tell all.

HMD: Your warning has been posted, asp!

CORRUPTICUS: You know your law – or should. I know it better than you. Notwithstanding, you wrote it yourself: 'Enemies of the State shall be gripped and preserved in my strongholds for the duration of their lives, lest the sentiment for their otherwise expired selves corrupts My People with hogwash'. *(holds out his wrists)* Boldly and lawfully now, enchain me, so that I will live in your dungeon, so that I can pen my full knowledge on parchment for an appalled public to read! 'Tis by your own law that I surrender myself.

(Tense silence as HMD *struts about, while* CORRUPTICUS *remains frozen in his stance. MLS to wide master shots. Silence, waiting; unbearable.)*

HMD: You... surrender yourself, do you? *(*CORRUPTICUS *nods)* Morpressuecx? What does my Mandate say in this regard?

MORPRESSUECX: *(quasi-groveling; gob still on his forehead)* What regard, My Weighty Authority?

HMD: *(with firecracker anger)* How dare – Wait, my crackpot Chamberlain. You mean you are unfamiliar with this codex?

MORPRESSUECX: *(whispers to* HMD, *as this is classified information, after humbly but courageously approaching the Ear of Stern State)* Not wholly familiar, My Only Lead Torchbearer. It is because the clause is an obscure one due to disuse, My Serene Denoter and Delineator. All thine enemies were crushed into infernal guts-dust by fire and sword, My One True Dominator. As a result, you currently have no enemies or other classifiable adversaries, although... *(slowly looks over at* CORRUPTICUS, *still standing fast)* My Super-Governor, you stand today victorious in all ways. Thus your Ceremonials (which should proceed, if arrangements are to turn out successfully, My Total Authoritarian Guider). But, but, to conclude my answer to your completely justified inquiry, you have no one to whom engaolment would ensue, due to your Mandate in this respect, My Sole Discriminating Warlord. Your prisons have thus been rendered wistful places, on account of their emptiness, My Turbo-Aware Master. Currently they are godowns for your new arms and armaments, with plenty more on the way, as I understand, My Solemn and Ultimate Fountainhead.

HMD: *(actually appreciative of this update, but chooses outward boorishness as a show of strength)* Get away from me, you sick and pretty much disgusting old jackass! I knew my Mandate was in complete effect, and, with such brilliant guidelines, I shall rule with steadiness and exponentially-expanding wisdom.

(Ever the paranoid, HMD *senses impatience for a pronouncement of High and Mad Doctoral Jurisprudence emanating from the huge crowd of both* COURT *and* THE MASSES, *so he figures he'd better wrap this show trial up, pronto.* CORRUPTICUS, *fully expecting the letter of the law to be enacted, especially in front of the gathered subjects, knows he can be sprung from any of* HMD's *gaols by employing his considerable influence, so he remains calm and confident.)*

CORRUPTICUS: Do you now desire to sentence me, Sacred Man of All 'Urth'? *(utters last word sneeringly)*

HMD: Yeah. As a matter of fact, I do. I'm done with this thing. I want to move on to my Glorium. I've got schedules to keep, Time's Waste. *(visibly pleased with himself at his impromptu but mediocre coinage)*

CORRUPTICUS: Let me then step out of your way, while under your perpetual and infinite care, to the nearest or furthest stronghold, in which to pass out what is left of my failed life, so that I might not clutter up the avenue to your, uh, 'Englorifications'. It is an avenue as broad as the rings of Saturn, but my presence would be as a Great Red Spot on your parade. So, now, if you'll dispatch me thither, I will thankest thou with great thanks. OK, 'Goalie'?

HMD: *(gives* CORRUPTICUS *a look of pure hatred)* I stand here, trying not to loathe you, but I can't. I have to communicate what the Peoples feel, and do you *know* what they feel? They hate enemies of mine own state. Therefore, I let them determine what will be their pleasure. I now sentence you. *(a distant drum successfully rolls)* You just wait. My sentence will be fair and just and really very good. I want to be the best for my People. I therefore brand you an Imperialist Merchant. This thing, this one to be labeled Corrupticus, he doth and hath caused Offense to our kind of world! Heed! Heed!! *(*THE MASSES *cheer enthusiastically;* HMD *acknowledges them)* Hail, My Many Ones, prepare for justice delivered! *(then, to* CORRUPTICUS*)* You hear that? The word of the groups! They call to me, from their councils and their plazas, from their mountain fastnesses and from their scullery boats! My Peoples have need of me, and as they need, they talk to me. They do so now. What do they tell me, by their yelling, their noisingnesses? Nothing but support! Therefore, anything I say goes, and why should I care if only a single voice, like yours, rises in dissent? Maybe they didn't hear *you*, cuz they only have ears for me. They didn't hear that you essentially agree with me. You know, you *want* to be sentenced, you *want* to be engaoled – for life, no less. So I have to act on their behalf. Who else would do it, for they are as inexperienced children. *(more intimately, and close up to* CORRUPTICUS*)* Because, we have quite a bit of *contempt* for those stupid kids, don't we? You and me. Think of how far we've come together. All the way from losing game after game on those dreary playing fields, all the way up to fatherhood of a worldwide nation. That's a fair piece, Sunny Jim. Thing is, we gotta do things my way, see? There is no way there could be room for anyone else at the top. Not any more. Not now. Not ever. You knew I was going to say all this didn't you? You knew it would be a safe bet that you could be hauled off to one of my defunct prisons, didn't you? My prisons! With their abandoned systems and their cannonball-sized escape holes, perfect for a speedy frigate to come alongside and whisk you off to Rebellion Land! A safe plateau, from which to plot and organize and raise a secret band, so as to return in some future century, and raise high-cited *REBELLION* 'gainst your only opposer. This, in order to– to– *hurt* me, or something. That, mule-shit, will never transpire! You see, Corrupticus – Number #1-type – I am *some kind* of 'on' to you. You had no idea, right? *(plainly impatient now)* Well, enough blabbing. That'll just prolong your gloating. You need some shortening… 'No. 1'…

(HMD pulls out his fearsome gark-blade from under his tunic/robe and starts swinging. He hacks off CORRUPTICUS' *hands, then his forearms, then his elbows, and then his nose. He howls with laughter as* CORRUPTICUS *shrieks, then* HMD *braces himself, stands in wide stance, and would strike off his enemy's head with one blow, but the blade thuds into the neck and stays there.* HMD *croaks a response, then cries out, as he tries to loosen the blade. Then he commences hacking the neck, which turns out to be as solid and gristle-bound and stubborn to the blows as a dense asparagus stalk against a dinner knife. Cords and strings of tissue are exposed, as* HMD *continues to hack away with growing hysteria. For his part,* CORRUPTICUS *stands there and takes it, though he emits ungodly howls and gasps, in total horror, but he somehow remains standing, which has* HMD *completely wigged-out. The hacking, hacking, hacking goes on, with little progress, making* HMD *look like the insane degenerate he is. He's bawling now, like a spoiled child, but with an off-color tinge – very disturbing and very revealing. Others in the* COURT

attempt action, but they are either rendered helpless by his presumed threats, or else they wait to see him burn. Blood is everywhere, and it keeps on spurting in all directions. These black-red sprays form a sort of lattice across the screen, speaking of the poetics of such violence, but only in a detached, visual way. This liquid texture that so fills the screen only certifies to the viewer that HMD *is beyond all classifiable madness. He is moving past the orbits of human existence into sheer psychopompos; from simple rage into hyper-articulated multi-tasked power-abuses, the perimeters of which can only worsen and widen. Hack, hack, hack: all who witness are rooted in disbelief.)*

*(*HMD *continues to hack and shriek and weep, believing in his hatred, but wondering about the significance of its latest manifestation. Exhausted, he slows, then stops. Shockingly,* CORRUPTICUS/NAHGUARRANEX *remains standing, his head half severed, eyeballs rolling, nose blown-out, trying to speak of his horror.* HMD *resumes the terrible cutting, which becomes a chop-chopping now, but makes little headway, so he drops the blade and desperately tries to push* NAHGUARRANEX *over, groaning and whining the whole time. He barely succeeds, but it is no victory. He even attempts to urinate on the mutilated remains, but nothing will come forth. Besides, he can't even find his penis. Crying selfishly,* HMD *slowly goes down on his knees, enraged at this horrendous backfire. He grabs the blade and starts hacking at the Grade's granite flooring, a striking image, perfect for fade out. Clear coverage, with wide profile shots.)*

'CUT!' bellowed Egaz, but only once. Butterbugs' own cutting, which continued after the cameras stopped rolling, seemed to render any further 'Cut!' utterances redundant.

The director rushed over to the bloody mess and made sure Bob was still breathing, just in case the SFX had failed and he had indeed been sacrificed for the benefit of the scene. A team of attorneys naturally stood by to bulldog insurance companies in the event of any accidental catastrophes. He breathed yet, so Egaz could resume his own respiration.

Deep in a Method-y funk of advanced-level acting, Butterbugs was still in character, continuing to attempt devastation of the super-polished flooring, as a sort of voodoo doll concept, his own mug reflected in the impervious stone, perhaps a substitution for the remains of Nahguarranex's defiant head, a suppression denied him, creating a sort of self-devastation for the high, mad character. Such were the exceptional cinematic psychological inventions of the ultrastar.

'Butterbugs!' Egaz clasped his actor's shoulder.

The actor acting suddenly ceased the blows on his mirror image (handily captured by Leon's camera, which now descended in the background), and faced the director with wild eyes.

Egaz automatically went into mysterium mode, a sort of samadhi, in which pure serenity and bliss were communicated just by vision-power traveling from his dark eyes to Butterbugs' in-character face. It was like a caress, for the wildness went out of Butterbugs like a thrown switch, and his gark-blade fell to the ground.

'It is passed,' said Egaz. 'We have it, and it is special. Indescribably special.'

Butterbugs became his total self.

'We do? Good. You want another take, Egaz?'

'Not really necessary,' Egaz remained measured and samadhi-sustained. 'Unless you think you'd like another one.'

Oblivious to the synthetic blood-spatter everywhere, not the least on his face, Butterbugs pondered a few moments, then said, 'I wonder if I was too hasty in scuttling that marvelous monologue that Sawl & Co. had slaved over. Well, I guess not, as it's getting on, now.'

'It's your call, Butterbugs.'

'My bits – and Bob's – were passable?'

'Passable, yes.'

Here was the highest trust an actor can place in a director. If said actor is basically modest and understated, he can talk in those terms, even after a stunning performance. And, if they have a close working relationship, such talk will be taken seriously and not in a comic context. Butterbugs' usage of the term 'passable' was made in somewhat lighthearted measures, but Egaz knew it to be genuine. So he accepted it as nothing to fuss over, in order to soothe a personality who may have said one thing but really meant another. None of that tat existed between them. All would have hustled to beat the band if the ultrastar wanted another go, but because the director didn't, and because Butterbugs was given the courtesy of the option, artistic sensibility was given a chance to rule on the matter, not budgetary limitations, or studio demands, or dissatisfaction of any kind. No, the take was done, and it was perfect.

'I don't think we need another one, do you Egaz? I mean, *really*.'

'I agree. Sometimes one is enough.'

'You have it?'

'I do, and I will fade out while you're still hacking away. Point made, thrust-filled exit from non-conclusive sequence. It's a real blowout. Powerful! Moving! A knock-out!'

'You think it was just a bunch of traded insults? Just a big… argument??'

'Butterbugs, this drama is being enacted on a world-stage. The whole of HMD's world is watching, on the edge of their seats. Even if you two were having garden-party-time on such a stage, the court, the masses, the world – and our audience, would feel the same. Aside from that, we are illustrating what people in high power *do:* insulting each other, plotting against one another, and destroying each other, all while neglecting/exploiting/fucking-over the masses. The masses can just go fuck themselves – which they inevitably do – gifting the luxury and leisure to those in high corrupt power to continue doing what they do. As Gibbon wisely said,

'Corruption: the most infallible symptom of constitutional liberty'. (I think we'll put that quote at the end of the Forward, just after the Main Title, don't you think?) It's all a simple equation, but it continues to work – every time. The tide is rising. Something *huge* must give. And it will! Yes, good fellow, this is indeed a political picture, but it is so much else, besides. Insults, arguments, violence, these are the ingredients of our message, our accelerated statements on corruption, leadership gone bad, lessons to be learned. No, I am at peace with the war in this film. It is necessary to show, and we are showing it, Butterbugs. *Actor.*'

'I feel nothing but love,' replied Butterbugs, actor.

So there it was, in the can: another fine Butterbugs improvisation. The Cane & Co. script had called, in great detail, for HMD to specifically imprison Nahguarranex by way of a sensational six-minute-long monologue on HMD's part, which added up to a show trial in which Nahguarranex was declared guilty and sentenced to life at hard labor on October Revolution Island. Butterbugs' rather radical alternative boldly scuttled the monologue, saved three minutes, and Egaz asked for no retakes, proof positive that those who mattered were properly wowed.

Ahead of schedule without 'doing a John Ford'.

And final approval came from Sawl Cane and his Writer's Group, himself and itself, not at all surprisingly, who'd seen the whole thing from the Observatorium behind the Palace set, and all gave their rowdiest endorsements.

Even the fringe-level violence was endorsed, as it rounded out the HMD's character quite nicely.

And there was Butterbugs, immediately after the 'Cut!' became final, down there on the ground, making sure his co-actor Bob Middleton was all right and secure, though his prosthetic head flopped off his shoulder, still death-rattling and disbelieving its partner in crime had split his brilliant mind in two. The freshly-sliced pipes of the faux-circulatory network were still dribbling little surges of plastic blud [*an Old Atrocity-coined term for the synthetic prop blood utilized in this picture, soon to actually be registered as a trademark by the CinemaSanguine Corporation, the manufacturer, with OA's blessing*] and synthetic pus from the below-stage reservoir into which Bob remained plugged. Surely its 370 decaliters must have been close to empty by now. Bob himself was indeed fine, ecstatic in fact, and he was blown away by the scene's power. Production assistants and SFX folk were in the process of busily de-specializing him. He could not stop raving with enthusiasm, for all to hear.

'I had no idea whatsoever though, Butterbugs, that you would chop all that stuff and my head off. You bloody well *clipped* me, man! Good thing I had the clown-nose on. Head's not quite off though, I guess. Good thing my neck was tough as tightly-wound cable! Guess I'll need a new noggin and a coupla hooks!'

'Good thing your improv reflexes clicked in when they did. I've never seen a ducking/replacement transaction so quickly or skillfully done for a decapitation sequence.'

'I had no problem. I ducked into costume on the outside chance that I knew what you were up to, and my 'stand-in' took the punishment in my name. I am no longer 'The Man With Two Heads'. You worried in vain, my best-acting friend.'

'Actually, I had complete faith in your talents, Bob. I knew our last day on location wouldn't be spoiled by my accidental slaying of you. Once again, great job, thespian of exceptional creativity and resourcefulness!'

'Man, I totally dug how you made HMD turn a merry sentencing into a soul-shattering meltdown!'

'Your hands OK?'

'Yoe. As chipper 'n' grabby as a teen nerd on his first date with a buxom cheer-leader! Me arms got tired from the hold-out though, so I engaged the prosthetics.'

'I could tell they were the fake ones. That's why I decided to take 'em off.'

'Reminds me of 'Sholay' (Sippy, 1975),' Bob added.

'Totally. But without the nobility!'

Bob started to sing 'Mehbooba Mehbooba', and Butterbugs joined in the wob-bly wail.

They continued to congratulate each other.

Old Atrocity, having overheard, ambled forward and had his say. Actors could get a little *too* into themselves, sometimes.

'Good thing… that, you know… *our* effects were forward-thinking to all possi-bilities, and that Bob's neck-gristle gave you a hard time, B-bugs! Made of tensile fiber from the body-bulb of the Pruxnoxian whistlepig-gnawing spider! Boy, that HMD bastard sure made an ass out of himself!'

'That above all!' Butterbugs declared. 'Memorable commendations to the SFX teams involved! Miendr! Taiga! Wiglaf! Debbie! Helferich! Gang, you were tre-mendous! I thank you. Bob thanks you. Nahguarranex's dead head thanks you. Or should I still call him Corrupticus?'

'By his valor – too late displayed! – his title was restored!'

'Bravo! Now, let's dine to our success!'

Indeed, a banquet awaited. All were invited, all were fêted.

Veezee, full of recharged belief in the absolute genius of the system – Butter-bugs' system of dramatic expansion, as she chose to classify it – had to remind herself not to clasp her hands in full-blown fan pose when she now rejoined him. Her professional substance intact, her sense of appreciation for the ultrastar as an actor *first* and a star *second* was a revelation. It was as if she'd hopped onto a sky-rocket. Audiences, she knew, would do the same. So she had to mentally hustle to retrieve her somewhat hard edge of purpose, lest her effectiveness as a rising p.a. suffer and be eclipsed by her own distractions of worship.

'Butterbugs? Right this way. A table has been prepared in your honor.'

'Ah, Veezee. There you are. My grateful thanks. Yes, I'm coming. Makeup? Begone!' he jested in HMD-mode to the primpers. 'Plenny-a-time fer *that!*'

The elevated members of the Producer Team were throwing this Pre-Wrap Din-ner ostensibly for Butterbugs, but the ultrastar wanted to make it clear that it was to celebrate the entire 'UWH' company, complete with vidlink (and joined catering) with the busy and time-zone-bucking Jambutterbugsabad Division.

Butterbugs, in his swollen and now blud-creamed garments, could not help but walk with a ceremonial gait, with Veezee on his arm and the famished crew behind him. They all followed Bob M., who was being wheeled along in a bathchair. This was due to no infirmity, but because he wanted to chow down with everyone before the four-hour sequence of removing his costume, which rendered him restricted in his movements, could commence under specialized supervision.

'You're still leaking blud, Bob!' Butterbugs called out playfully.

'Then I hope I make it to table in time for a life-giving refill! Hopefully, they got tankards of Corpuscle Brew #5!!'

Everyone exuded good will and gratitude. Noting the outstanding bearing of the whole company – all at once, and exhibited so universally – Veezee had to comment.

'My goodness Butterbugs, you are portraying a *mega*-mega-tyrant, while in real life, we find ourselves in a sort of Utopia, a world at peace and full of hope – A genuine renaissance of resumed civilization, culture and mindset.'

'I feel it too, Veez. I'm so glad to be part of it.'

'Could it be that... I don't know... that *that's* how things'll go from now on?'

'You used the word 'hope', sugar-kitten. I can think of no word which is better, except 'hope achieved'.'

Veezee realized that not only was Butterbugs part of it, he was *responsible* for it. But she had no desire to embark on any sycophantic tack as his p.a. Instead, she underplayed the courtesies.

'Your performance in the scene was very good,' she said with a straight face.

'Good enough?'

To him, a serious inquiry. At her slightest suggestion, he would press for a retake if she'd detected some shortcoming on his part. He readied himself for the possibility.

After all, his p.a. had earlier proclaimed herself (to Egaz) in the following terms:

'Remember, I just walked into this scene. I have no history in this production. Therefore, I am as a viewing audience member. That is my perspective.'

Therefore, despite the fact that, as of this very moment, Veezee did indeed have considerable history with this production, the high value of her audience perspective climbed higher than ever.

She wisely kept her strategy simplistic.

'Yes. Good enough.'

And they promenaded onward, in great pomp.

The banquet, which was solely a grub-trough, without entertainments or other appendages that required a running time of over an hour (because there was the little trifle of an ultimo finale to be filmed yet tonight), took place within the immense Feastus Courtus set that occupied a major open-air portion of the HMD's

Palace complex. The enlightened art directors, headed by John DeCuir and Lyle Wheeler, had modeled it after John Martin's 1821 Belshazzar scenery, but with their own touches of expansion, color, and alterations. Grandiose it certainly was, but because the script dictated that it was operated under a debauched totalitarian/ fascist regime, certain angles, adornments and design fundamentals had to come across as suitably debased and decadent. Flabby columns, disturbing vents, profane statuary, stench-hung vomitoria, nerve-wracking hues, and clashing resolutions in architectural vocabulary were just a few of the tools employed to make this palace of perversity effective. It was a startlingly original work, with all parody avoided.

Ever since the mammoth Food Fight sequence (filmed the day before Butterbugs' arrival on location and involving him only in subsequent medium and close shots, heaving buckets of yesterday's soup onto out-of-frame but hapless courtiers), the set had undergone a massive cleanup for this one occasion. So it was a really big deal. The tone of the environment was one to induce emesis all right, but it was the only space large enough, and a hungry cast and crew, undiscriminating at present, wanted tray and grub, and they wanted them *now*.

The VIPs arrived at the portal to the feedery, with its bizarre tendril-hung arch scallops, just in time to see the linkboys busily lighting the crazily-lensed lamps. A team of assistant directors stood by to conduct the star and his escort to their table by relay, which happened to be in one of the more unpopular sectors of the great plain. Regardless, Butterbugs was tickled to be there, and once his place was achieved, he immediately dug into the mound of blump-paste and Tatar oil that served as a love-generating appetizer.

None of the Producer Team were present. Not a one. This was intentional, as none wished to snitch the slightest part of Butterbugs' rapport with the masses of the company, lest complaints erupt concerning any sort of ruling class. These were issues the ultrastar planned to tackle face-on after the HMD makeup and costume came off for good. For it was his long-cherished dream to see a truly classless/casteless Hollywood.

It was definitely under classless circumstances that the ultrastar now sat with his p.a. at table in the enormous and unappetizing Feastus Courtus arena, way out there, on the plain somewhere. The tin chairs were creaky and cramped, the folding tables distressingly borax in appearance, dressed in worn, uninteresting Formica. The paper 'n' plastic dinnerware was dreary and leaky. However, the company, all of them, had never been so happy or jolly. Not only was it old home week, it was a signal chance to chill a bit before the filming of the ultimo finale, which in itself wasn't exactly a dreaded entity. But with the dying day dictating terms of lighting, and the dependent timing therein, all the essence required for suitable filming made for considerable justification of group nervousness.

'Where the hell are Leon and Bob S.?' asked Butterbugs, scanning the diners hither and yon, while wolfing down chibb-toast smothered in many a packet's worth of grain-sauce (the banquet's second taste-treated appetizer).

Veezee was discreet.

'Well, Butterbugs, they are most busy doing setup for the ultimo finale. It is a rather demanding set to light and plot. And there's only one chance to do it.'

'Yeah, well...'

Suddenly the ultrastar caught sight of his good little badass troupe of Scruffians, marching in for their tough little repast, which was waiting over on a special scruffed-up terrace. To his delight, none other than Shawna Lee herself was in their vanguard, obviously their leader, the most competent and scruffiest of their number. Their eyes met, and traction ensued. She waited for the ultrastar to make the first gesture, as she expected to lead the brigade on over to their containment sector, sans ado.

Butterbugs had different ideas. Instead of a quick-wave and carrier-kiss, he went for the big dramatic flourish. Practically upsetting his table, he plowed through the rows of surrounding diners and approached the girl gang. Having grandly arrived in the middle of the clearing before them, he prostrated himself, all the way down on the shiny linoleum, with its stale veal-chop-grey marble look.

'*Butter*bugs!' Shawna exclaimed, amidst the revved-up Scruffians.

'Jes' doin' my normal, reg'ler, hourly kowtow to thee, honeyed girl of the west, my ever lovin' Shawnee!'

The Scruffians gasped. Others began to gather around the spectacle.

Rather than assuming the classic Scruffian attitude of what-the-fuck-do-*you*-want confrontation, Shawna stood before him like a demure Aphrodite, awaiting Parisian judgment. Indeed, she was prepared to strip for him then and there, should he wish to exercise his Zeus-given rights. But no, as HMD, the actor stayed in character enough to simply drool-up a puddle on the polished floor. Notwithstanding the dribble from his flat position, his actor's voice then projected with godlike validity.

'Hail, Shawna! Chieftainess of My Very Own Scruffians! How goes your acting gig, dearie?'

'You were right, Butterbugs! There's no limit to what the human spirit can achieve!'

'Good show! Thank you for your service! I shall very much look forward to seeing your beauteous, starry form in full-scale widescreen splendor in the final print. Just as I'd hoped!'

'I will *always* be thanking you, my champion!'

Still prone, the ultrastar craned his neck upward, and bellowed, 'Here she is, media, cast, and crew! My new discovery! Miss Shawna Lee! Take a look! Get to know her! You're gonna *love her!*'

Amplified by the on-board microphone he wore for such moments, Butterbugs was sure the masses in the vicinity had gotten his message. Approaching his dead-looking mass, Shawna had just enough time to bow down, finger her way through the Medusa-like tangle of wig-rubbish and indeterminate discharge, until she found his (scarless) brow, then kissed it in the corresponding region to her own unique badge.

'Hey there! Here they be, Shawna. You'll know what to say! Dig it!'

'Bless you!' was *all* she needed to say.

In less than a minute, the formerly down-on-her-luck stripper-with-a-heart-of-gold straightened herself, assumed a genuinely epic pose, and prepared to morph into a star.

Dozens of reporters, photogs, documentarians, image specialists, and Sonny representatives gathered intensely but politely around her, ready to do their thang, and with an ultrastar's personal approval, no less! Never had they seen the birth pangs of a star emerge in such a classy, cheerful, and welcoming manner.

Descriptive terms like 'intriguing', 'uniquely-branded', 'courageous', 'alternative', and 'totally cool' were already being bandied about.

To ensure all these people knew for certain that Butterbugs himself was proudly associated with this ingenue, he repositioned himself on his knees and announced, 'HEEEERE's Shawna! I go *way back* with her. Further than most, if not all! Here she is now, see what you think of her! She's got a gig to finish tonight, but after that, she's available for birthday parties, telephone kiosk dedications, farmer's markets...' He then winked in her direction. 'And WHATEVER *SHE HERSELF* WANTS TO DO!'

As a result, no one asked of her, 'Who the hell is *that??*'

She bowed with utter professionalism.

'See. You. Latah, Shawna!'

If anyone there was inclined to think that Shawna was his Special One, so be it. No big deal. There was room for everyone, in every thought combination. He'd give a revised standard version of his standing soon enough, as the Heatherette Countdown continued, apace.

For her own part, Veezee was certainly convinced this stripper-into-star was indeed The One. Past that, she'd made copious mental notes amidst her fascination of witnessing, firsthand, a bona fide act of star-creation, pulled off in one stroke, by the star of stars!

Meanwhile, she prepared to assist the hideous, living miasma that was HMD, by getting him back on his feet again. Because of his little charitable stunt, his outrageous costume had made quite a substantial mess on the floor, which standby crews could cure in a trice.

'Sorry floor staff!'

The star bowed low to them.

'Just for laughs, you might find some blucky 'souvenirs' down in that mix, but souvenirs they be! Don't sell 'em all in one place!'

Over in her spotlight, Shawna was really making a hit. However, since she was still on the job, and time was crimping to secure a bit of banquet, the media mavens let her go with courtesy, and resumed coverage of the surrounding day's yet unfinished tasks and events.

'Heh-heh' Butterbugs chortled to himself, 'She's on her way – at last!' Then an idea struck him. 'Vee and Zee? C'mere a sec. Closer. Quieter. Veezee, remembah that I asked you to contact Dr. Cantrell about some scar eradication for our Shawna over there?'

'Of course. It's on my 'to do' list for tomorrow morn. Like everything else Shawna-oriented.'

'Super. But hold off on Cantrell awhile, until we review. Our Shawna just might wanna keep that thing – maybe as a good luck charm or a trademark, or somethin'. It's her call.'

As Veezee was helping HMD get his kit back together, they overheard one reporter ask another:

'Say Mulge, you think it was *Butterbugs* who laid that scar upon her?'

'Why that miserable –,' Veezee hissed, 'He should be banned from these Elysian regions, if he'd going to spread lies and –'

'Stay, Veez, stay!' counseled Butterbugs calmly. 'We're in *showbiz*, remembah? These things happen! Besides, we have nothing to worry about. Truth is easy, and Shawna knows her truths. Because, she has Sonny, me, and *you* to protect her, doesn't she?'

'*Still* – that kind of stuff makes me so goll-darned *mad!*'

'Grub now! Grub for all!'

Standing tall once more, ultrastar-as-HMD resumed his role as Actual Producer of this intimate little late-tray / bib-and-chow extravaganza.

'Oh, *boy!?*' Butterbugs called out to a waiter. 'Get some of this yum-grub together in kits and bongo-cups and make sure our valiant camera crew is supplied with nourishment! Chop-chop! Jaldi! Jaldi!'

It was a barked order. Always mindful of the travails of any given wait person's life of servitude, the u-star abandoned all manners, as the urgency of the situation weighed upon him in this respect. (Never mind that the legions of production staffers had already seen to this and myriad other tasks; it was the sentiment of a super-nice guy that mattered just then.)

'I *will*, sir,' answered the waiter, Zurchur by name, son of St. Zeppelin ConGraf von Zmunchluppy, an eminent member of the picture's editing team, currently swamped back at studio with daily footages to process.

The ultrastar was peckish. Without attending to much socializing until his creepy face had been at least partially fed, he charged into a basket of Cuttdorff serve-rolls (his *favorites*), sprayed rolled-bolled peim-jam on a few and gobbled them quick. Then, having slurped all his pressure-soup of winebone-clobberfish crinklings, he tucked into the main course of plain boiler-steak cradled in deepfat-fried artichoke and hemmelin leaves, with steamed mustards and grape poppings. Churchvine and frostbulb plantings posed as toasted veggies, paul-corns and brightlip sauces as salad substitute, with a dip-cup of jave-gravy. Plus, reap-chutney, lamprey-milt, tilled bonefish scraps, and blammo-pea syrups on the side. And just a dab of horseradish...

'Yumbo! Yumbo!' he crowed.

Everyone else in his quadrant felt the same way, so there wasn't much conversation quite yet.

Then came plate-fry, Waterbeard's discs, smashed pupa flakes, and engenderald clippings, all sharp-cooked to perfection. HMD cuisine had some pretty stunning charms.

'Oh, oh!' Butterbugs called to no one in particular. 'Is there none among you who will send out for cold beer?'

Lord Peter Ustinov, over at a neighboring table, as if connected by wireless communication, snagged a waiter and inquired, 'May I have a jar of *bieh?*'

Butterbugs heard, turned about as far as his fibrous costume – with its criss-cross grating plates – allowed, and chuckled.

'Bravo, Peterkins. You've got guts – and good taste, too!'

'I daresay, *your* guts are the ones most needed at this hour, dear boy!'

The veteran costumer was playing the oppressed man-about-Court, Pate Plimb Plummox, who'd had many fine lines of debate earlier in the picture, and was in the ultimo finale largely as ornamentation. His character now served as a trophy of HMD's Heckle Campaign, after having suffered much humiliation from him during the Wars sequence. He is treated with Versailles-like observation, control, and condescension.

Then came tankards of quaff, the suds of which barely gave Butterbugs a buzz. He also called for piñon likker, and consumed several nipperkins and thimblefuls of Chadd-serum.

Fortified by this and other food and drink, bottle and beer, he raucously picked his teeth and made sure the ejections gathered on his cluttered costume.

''Tis quite properly *mad* you indeed look,' said Mettie Lampshade, super-sized seamstress in Costuming, who was installed across from him.

'Why thank you, Metts. You people have done so much to make me good and properly mad, and I add my own poor bits, as an actor's pallid contribution.'

'Indeed, you have arrived at a brazen and awful appearance, my modest one!' said Carmen Trasch, the only one remotely producer-ish present at this fest (he was production manager on this sequence), who lolled at the end of Butterbugs' table.

'Will I scare little kids, you think?'

'Gadzooks, your very first lines will serve to teach kids everywhere valuable lessons,' said Hope Summers, who was playing Lord Peter's henpecking wife, Shurmah.

'Lessons on how *not* to run a planet,' said Veezee.

'Indeed, my children,' said Butterbugs. 'The morality of Sawl Cane's epic tale is our chief endowment to the nations of the world. And our deep duty to the imperatives therein manifest themselves in the undertakings of our production. Dost thou, my fellow workers, think we might have *success* with this thing?'

Lord Peter stood up and addressed every last diner.

'Our chief player... That is, he who is High Mad Doctor on the wide screen, has, in case you all were not in his sphere of hearing just now, a question for us to ponder, and I shall repeat it in his stead, as he is currently enjoying the viands and bubbly brew so graciously provided by our all-powerful gods and goddesses of the clinking money box. He said, and I paraphrase, shall we have success with our picture, this 'UWH', this unholiest of war hymns?'

Lord Peter knew what would happen. Since a food fight had already been staged and filmed here, he knew that repetition, no matter how fun, was an unlikelihood. Nevertheless, he sort of ducked down in case the tumult of adulation became rather intense.

As a matter of fact, it wasn't so much adulation (intended for the grouped effort of the production, not specifically Butterbugs) as it was a statement of solidarity. What resulted was no cheering or anthem-like demonstration of picture-show patriotism. No, it was something out of a prison picture, as everyone at the venue started banging their plastic tableware against their cheap zinc beakers, and the whole twelve tones of the polyphony that rose became joined and rhythmic. And haunting: here was the great company, not quite entire, rapping out their reply on this spooky set, the torch and lamplight coming into their own within the scary arches and back-loggias, as the day inexorably waned toward the ultimo.

Truly, a tremendous memory forged and welded into every mind present.

Then the noise stopped almost all at once, and the repast resumed.

Bob Middleton was wheeled to his place at the other end of Butterbugs' table, way down there somewhere.

'Where *were* you, Bob? We must've lost you en route. Platter's getting cold.'

'Well, I had to *go*, High Mad Doc,' replied the esteemed vet, still in high costume, complete.

'Whizz?'

'Yupp. SFX had to see me through. All girls, too!'

Veezee frowned.

'I hope they weren't obliged to do any additional services,' she said in all seriousness, expecting the worst.

Bob responded with the same gravitas as hers.

'In point of fact, those ladies had the perfect slimness of hand to – you know – gain access, through that blasted trap door, as it were. They were most kind, and were perfectly proper, I might add.'

No one attempted cheesy sex or evacuata jokes. Despite his gruff appearance, Bob was a happily married gentleman.

Veezee felt foolish. Not everyone behaved in a sitcom manner, especially here amongst the professionals working on the world's most important motion picture.

'They should have hooked you up to a porta-tank, Bob. Plenty of room in that bell-person robe,' offered Butterbugs.

'If your improv hadn't been so damn *lengthy*, I would've made it through. And I've got a trucker's bladder, you know.'

'Poor Bob, abandoned Bob, Bob of the dead-twin head…,' Butterbugs quipped, almost in ditty-song.

Another more lyrical personage nearby took up the challenge the ultrastar had laid down: to serenade the disadvantaged and dependent Bob 'Nahguarranex' M.

Sir Parabola Manewayster of Droxwater Chapel in Humberside (who played a Courtier) considered himself a troubadour of sorts, so he waxed poetic.

'I feel a recitation, Bobe,' said he, facing the estimable Middleton. 'I think a rigmarole by Skulgeon Skulgeoniumite might be apropos:

> Tea-boil Bobby's nose,
> Par-boil Bobby's ears,
> Char-boil Bobby's eyes,
> In greasy mutton fries.

There! You have now been processed, and await consumption.'

'Oh, Pabbi, I don't feel quite 'done' yet, though I'm cooked!'

'Your role, my stoutness, was a phenomenon. I can't wait to see it in velveteen Panavision! I'm jealous as hell, but the feeling I feel is heavenly, so it must be a virtue. Where is he who brought all that dramatic magnificence inside of you out to play? Oh, Butterbugs! Perk and respond!'

TABP, basically a producer, but of special value, sneaked in for a few minutes, and plumped a pulter-cooked basement-meat leg down in front of the ultrastar, who set to chawing into it with savage gusto.

'Jes' wanted you to have some of my home-bibbed gristle on this fine occasion, man. When this is all over, gonna teach Cody the secret Vonda Sauce. Bet she memorizes it as good as you did! Well, gotta get back on set. Grind on that bone awhile. But not *too* long. And guess what: when this is all over, we're going on holiday. You, me, and Code. And your selected guest, a-course. Maybe this Shawna? She cool. Start planning, start thinkin' where we should go. Cuz we're gonna *go*. Say, somebody's hassling you, Butterbugs.'

'Thank ya kindly, TABP. Home cookin's da best, baby. Yours included. OK, if Cody passes the test in memorizing Vonda's recipe, I'll voluntarily erase it from my mind, as I've never imparted it to another living soul!' Even Heatherette would never know it. 'And *yes*, I'll plan, I'll think, and yes, for my selection, maybe that Shawna. But maybe *another…*'

TABP was gone.

'Yeah, apparently, I am being paged by Pabbi! Hey Pabbi!! What gives?'

'A message concerning Bobe's welfare!' Sir Parabola yelled.

'Oh no,' replied the ultrastar, regarding his second-tier dinner, fearing an interruption. 'A delayed reaction to my hacking him apart? Could we be faced with a funeral, of a sudden? *And??*'

'He's *done*,' the poet/actor/Sir replied.

'Oh hell…' thought the possibly-accidental killer. 'Bob's had some kind of blowout…'

'And fully cooked, to boot!' Bob himself sounded off, when he finally got a chance to talk, meat-strings visible to the public when he opened his mouth wide. 'And such happiness I've never known!'

'Why you old…,' Butterbugs began, but noting his co-star's joy, he couldn't even think of a comic comeback, so he simply asked a serving girl to go over and dish out an extra helping of smashed spudadoes to the vet actor. He was *so* happy, in spite of being encapsulated in a bluddy nappy of corkscrew plumbing and pizo-motor bossiness, that he knew his performance in this last act would most likely steal said scene from the ultrastar, which actually gave the ultrastar the deepest kind of pleasure, short of drowning.

Sonny supped just across the way, and passed a platter of broiled cupcakes down the line. But he was more hungry for pussy than he was conventional sweets. It was only a matter of a few seconds before he disappeared under the groaning board and pulled into the safe harbor of his wife, sexy Syd Desh's chair, where he literally chewed through her panties to reach his port. Her upper body being in the public eye, Syd's conduct, in carrying on a conversation with Chuck Heston and Arnie Schwarzenegger about antique firearms, can be imagined.

Oh, but this was a steam-releaser of a banquet! Not quite through the hoop, those who toiled on this picture nevertheless bathed in end-tunnel light, as if all were said and done. And for many, like Bob, in fact, it was. Over half the banqueters in the great Feastus Courtus could call this picture successfully wrapped, in their estimation. Job done, soon they'd face the bittersweet combo of relief and 'Now, what? A gig over at Monogram?'

But for the other percentage, there was still a steep mountain to climb as the sun set, and a summit to take as the sky yielded to lights artificially inseminated.

Then, without warning, came the voice of Producer Porter Pud Parker over the public address system.

'This is your little old Principal Line Producer speaking, OK? Hello everybody, and I'm glad you could come to this little get-together for a few friends. What, about two or three thousand? Heh! We'll have the stats later. Super-praise for our cookery staff, huh? Right-o! Send 'em a postcard of thanks! At any rate, as the dinner hour is about to expire, I entreat those who are about to go ahead with tonight's shoot to ready themselves, as girding is nigh. Please debark in seven minutes' time. In the meantime, I want you to… enjoy your cupcakes and…'

Then he got all sappy and everything.

'I just have to say – and I want to – I really do want to say it, that this whole experience – this picture – has been, for me, a transcendental experience of such magnitude that I can scarcely dare rise to the duel of giving it utterance!' (sniff)

The company listened in rapt attention, even suspending mastication and swallowing procedures.

'And all you wonderful people out there in the Valley, the expanse of Lasky's legendary mesa spread wide... and,' (choke) 'our friends and neighbors out in old Jambutterbugsabad! Oh, the things that have been gifted upon us! Oh, the wonders we have seen, and more importantly, those we have made! By our own hearts and hands! This may be the epic of the ages, but for me, it has been the picture of a lifetime most blessed. We shall not see its kind again... The last of the wine! Or, or, *will* we? You know,' (brightening) 'as I think about it, maybe this is a dawn of a *nouveau* new era – when penguins will fly into the strato-sphere, and all diseased ones will find comfort in a bit a waiting until they are cured, in routine assembly-line fashion, and – wait a moment, that's perhaps a scenario of the next Butterbugs picture in situ... But, uh, back on my track, let's see, just a beginning – of a time when new pictures, with a new, and I mean a *new*, perhaps never-thought-of before, sense of mentality will emerge. I can just imagine that, somewhere there's a someone, who's maybe shut away from our productive world, who has new ideas and new items to offer. Can you imagine? Some high-echelon artiste, in a loft or a garret, waiting to be discovered! May-be? Just waiting to emerge! In fact, I feel this inevitability in my heart. My soul, too! And there is one reason why I feel so sure. And *he* is starring in this, our picture. Yes, Butterbugs is the reason, the raison d'être for our future. He is the leader, not as HMD of course...' (laughs a little) 'but someone to show us the way ahead. As if he hasn't already! But I sense something's coming, and from obtuse angles. I just *do*. Anyway, sorry, folks, to run on like this and partially rob you of your brief respite here and all. I'm glad it's only my voice you can hear in the present, because I'm an emotional mess (but I'll rebound in a few minutes to fulfill my line-producing duties – trust me!). I don't know, I guess I just wanted to add, in the few remaining seconds of my broadcast, that I'm so excited about the future – not only for – and I'll break my own law and enunci-ate it fully: not only for 'Unholy War Hymn', (Mega|Goth) but for our cinematic Industry in general. Butterbugs is heading in new and exhilarating directions. To paraphrase Al Jolson, you ain't seen nothin' yet! So, thank you all. And just get set for a Wrap Party tomorrow to end all wrap parties. Lots of special stuff planned, plus a few surprises. And now, people, a notice: active cast and crew for ultimo finale, report to stations in seven minutes sharp (I will take personal responsibility for the work time I've hogged from you in our accrual system, cuz of bending your ears for these here irreplaceable minutes. It's sure been worth it, though!) In closing, I address you, Butterbugs directly: give your gift to this last sequence like you've never done it before. Meaning, stress invention! Be an innovator! And cool it, regarding conventions! You see, I'm a selfish and greedy fellow. I want everything you can give in this finale. Because, it is a sort of launching pad into the world of tomorrow. You are going there, and we all want to – nay – *need* to go with you. Take us! Do not leave us behind! If only you will remember us, poor company though we may be, but we shall serve you without complaint, and with every courtesy. Strength upon strength to you, strollingest of players! Go now and do what you were *fated to do!*'

Porter's voice, which was steady until he went silent with his passion at the end, left the company in revelatory stillness after the last echo died away.

What could anyone say after that? Part of the harmony inherent in this production was due to the fact that all present were in general agreement – and, most importantly, they were in accord on one main thing: that all were in the company of someone who was beyond-exceptional: the lead player in their picture.

There was hardly a clink of poly-china or a crumple of cardboard doggie bags.

It was Butterbugs himself who broke this silence of continental proportions.

'Veez, can you get me some washrags and burp-cloths for my next scene? I think I'm short on all of 'em. HMD is kind of gross, you know?'

Immediately, the whole scene returned to the jollity of a splendid banquet – abbreviated perhaps, but full of golden moments nevertheless.

Without ceremony of any kind, Butterbugs rose from table, stuffed a few more tea-prune porridge wheels and Bittnurr Bakes into his maw, so as to conclude pudding, wiped his shiny blue lips with his bib, then splattered some mouseberry liqueur (the dinner's cordial) on the front of his bluddy robes for more effect, and made to go.

'Egaz loves the costume filth and its attendant vermin and bouquets,' he said to his dining intimates, 'Though Makeup and Fittings want to have me arrested for property damage.'

All those in close vicinity were delightfully casual.

'Have a good one, Butterbugs,' said Barn Buppa, property master assistant (under Walter M. Scott), 'Gimme a call later in the week.'

'Gotcha,' the ultrastar replied, gathering his weighty shawl of glass fiber.

'Don't stay out too late!' added Munn Troute, talking with his mouth full of cinnamon broccoli. The famous broadcaster would be giving the Possum Evening News from Location Central Control over at Butterfly McQueen Hall in a few minutes.

'What time's curfew?' inquired Butterbugs.

'Your discretion,' replied Munn. 'Reasonable and prudent.'

'In you we trust,' said Lata Mangeshkar, who was voicing in the Chorus.

Tuan Jim, who was of course Caterer General for this one, happened by.

'Hi, Tuan Jim! Hi!'

'Oh, hello, Butterbugs.'

'Great grubbsy, tonight!'

'Well, that's something to reasonably thanky-kindly for. I think we might have pulled it off. The party will continue for those at leisure, for some time.'

'And with my hearty endorsements! They can follow the fun on the VidBoards, which the grippers are setting up right now, for the pleasure of the manys.'

It was true – all non-participants in the U.F. could follow the scene's shooting out on the Grade, without having to leave table or their special chairs.

Tuan Jim then remembered something, and conferred privately with Butterbugs.

'Will you require The Lazaretto to be prepped for your presence later on, to-morrow night?'

'Well, we have the Wrap Party, which starts at 9:00AM, so as to run the whole day, and beyond, even to the outer limits, if needed...'

'I know that. I'm catering, for Pete's sake.'

'Of course, of course. Oh, Tuan Jim, don't worry about The Lazaretto. Not to-morrow. The day after, though – Could you possibly start prepping, particularly the grounds, for something *really* special?'

Tuan Jim was all business, as he should be, and more than a bit harried right now, even with an ultrastar in tow. However, he dutifully took out pen and pad, noting the requests, in all their glory.

'What is the occasion?'

'Well, I can't really tell you as of yet, but ye will be among, as they say, the first to know. Sorry for the inconvenience.'

'Truth to tell, I've got a fairly target-achieved bull's eye region as of now. Lots of missing shind-nelfs, but that's not the point. Plate-upon-plate is full to over-flowing, just like this unholy affair.'

'Sanctify it, then! With gravy and love!'

'If only I had the time and the means!'

'I'll make it up to you. You will get screen credit for all you do, of course.'

Tuan Jim beamed.

'Why, I am most touched, Butterbugs. You didn't have to do that.'

'For one so vital? Of course I did.'

They made to part.

'Oh, Butterbugs?'

'Yessims?'

'I'm sorry to have to tell you this, although I understand that others might be too timid to do so, but since I am your khansammah, I must.'

'Proceed, please.'

'Butterbugs, you have fearsome upchuck and other unpleasaunce on your robes.'

'Thank you so much for bringing that to my attention, Tuan Jim. I've been so distracted – occupied – you know.'

'I know.'

'I'll see to it. Not to worry. Something you don't have to take on.'

'Thank you, Butterbugs.'

'Thank *you!*'

'Oh, hi, Lady!' the ultrastar greeted Lady Fashionettah as she pulled on Tuan Jim's sleeve. And he left them as they were making out quite randily, dangerously close to a big bombe of rose-apple/cut-meat pink-gelatin.

Though their passage to the banquet had been a ceremony in itself, the return to set was absolutely routine. Butterbugs accompanied by Veezee moved as com-moners along the busy thoroughfare, where everyone had a job to do and no time or opportunity to either yak or make marvelous.

They came to the Grade. It was entirely transformed. While most had been stuffing themselves with delicious grease, a tireless team of selfless grips and electrics, under OA's masterful supervision, had trundled in a segmented series of decks forming an Incline Drive, the thoroughfare leading to the Citadel across the great expanse that lay in between.

'Superb!' murmured Butterbugs as he and Veezee surveyed the ready scene. 'Thus is my way to glory provided.' Hastily, he munched a dozen Tarson's Blips ('The Actor's Bodyservant'™) for voice mellowing, and hawked up the purifying lavings.

'And there stands the way to our climax in this picture,' the astounded p.a. added. 'See, Butterbugs, how your people have come through for you.'

'I will never forget it, and I am moved more than I can say.'

'My beloved cast and crew!' Egaz announced broadly. 'Places?'

Everybody was there. The entire Producers Team, all the Writers Team, every damn backer and investor and contributor, everybody who'd had anything whatsoever to do (and some not to do) with this picture, its book, its funding, its management, and its cast, whether they were in the finale or not. They were all there, as well they might be. With such an expansive location, there were plenty of Visitor Galleries, VIP and otherwise, the Observatorium, lookout nooks, and even bleachers on the sidelines. It was indeed a scene with a cast of thousands, as it had to be. No half-measures; all stops were out. The sun was setting, and the sky was exquisitely colored, and was getting better with every minute. 3rd and 4th units were capturing sunset, skies, ambient tones, and reflected light on set facades. The results were going to be absolutely stunning.

First, a brief expository scene.

Egaz's voice was strong, possessing every degree of maturity and professionalness that this picture had brought to him.

'All right, ACTION!'

(The Assembling of the COURTIERS, *with* THE MASSES *in observance. Processional march, with highest pomp, in characteristic HMD style.)*

While the preliminaries to the scene played out front, Veezee escorted Butterbugs to his preset position behind set.

'Well, this is it,' she said plainly.

'I want to thank you, girl. Deeply. You have been a prize p.a.'

Suddenly she went all mushy.

'Oh, dear man! You sweet one! I care for you so much!'

Appreciative of her passion, but mindful of its timing, he put an index finger to her lips in 'Hush, child' code, and winked.

She knew and understood. There was a scene to do. She went back on the job. But there was one more thing to do.

'Butterbugs, may I kiss you? For sustenance!'

He smiled, as he knew it was for love.

'Why, of course you may. With more to come, later!'

Costume and makeup did not conspire to create any barrier to the loving gesture that followed. His makeup was so burnished into his lips that no trace of it
remained on hers. If there had been more time, she would have gone down on her
knees to respectfully service him then and there, as she could feel his erection,
even through the hideous hangings he was compelled to wear. Though he was a
sort of prisoner to this aspect of his craft, her sexy passion was not to disrespect
the lovings he was about to give to another. To the love of his life, whom Veezee
was, by the way, dying to know in full. It was just a part of a job she felt she owed
him.

'Rise now, Veez. Go, with all my love, and watch from your rightful place next
the director's chair. It's going to be a great show.'

'I will go, as you ask. But remember, if you need rescuing, you know where I
am, ever vigilant!'

He watched her retire with the tenderest of smiles. Few, in his estimation, managed their derrieres with such effortless and automatic style as she. Few, so very
few... Let's see, there was Vondy, and Justy, and Sasky, and Cody, and... Well, no
time for a complete rundown... But – oh yes, Veezee just now... And... And...
HEATHERETTE!

That's right – Heatherette! *His* Heatherette! His *very own!*

Just like a jump-cut, Old Atrocity then appeared out of nowhere, to aid
Butterbugs' entrance on cue, from the prescribed mark behind a pillar.

No matter how blissful the reveries, in this biz, they always dissolved at the
instant of services needed.

'Why, *Old Atrocity it is,* then!' The ultrastar's voice was mellowed by his late
meditation. 'Your presence, OA, is my good luck charm. Now I can continue with
the resolve.'

'I didn't know you relied on charms, nutball.'

'I'm just starting, because it's a new world from here on in. All is ready?'

'Affirmative, High Mad Doctor! Most hated! Are you ready for the disgrace?'

Butterbugs was almost all the way into his character, but 2% was in reserve to
answer OA with a pro-to-pro comment.

'HMD's victory, you mean.'

'Yeah. And the world's disgrace.'

'It's certainly the largest-scale scene I've been in, but is it the best?'

OA was without words to assemble for this curious question.

'My coffers are full,' added the star. 'But with what?'

OA sensed a few jitters, so he aimed to calm them with the comforts of sex.

'I hope you've got what I've got. A feeling of a woman's love, is all you really
need for living...'

'That isn't what I was referring to, but I have that now, OA! I do! You will see,
and you will meet her. She's on my threshold. From this day forward!'

'You mean it? You're not being scripted, here?'

'No script, no manufactures. Just pure, sweet scenes of perfectly-matched love.'

'I'm just so glad, starry varmint. You two wanna run away with us? Tarlah and me?'

'Maybe! Oh, *maybe*, OA! We all will talk and we all will push and pull. Is it not the *best?*'

'It is, bub. Finally. Finally, and now. But you'd better be on point. Next scene: imminent. All thought on hold. Acting needed.'

'Yowzah, loyal supporter! With more reason and heart than a thousand elephants. You were there. All the way. Nothing could be more unforgettable!'

OA gave him a soulful look.

'Give it yer fanciest tap-dance then, strolling player!'

'Luck to me, or a broken leg?'

'Maybe both, you goon. You remarkable, lovable, exceptional, transformational mishmash! Go on. Go on, now! To your glory! You'll do it by the simplest of actions, and get there by the quickest means. Don't you know what you do for us… all of us?'

'I act in picture shows, OA. Just that. Nothing else. Nothing more.'

'I bless you, hero. Keep on keeping on. And now, FORWARD TO GLORY!'

Butterbugs went out on set, as Egaz sent his cue for entrance.

'There he goes… goes… goes… He's *going*… Sufferin' bleedin' Chickamauga…,' the wizard-grip whispered in stunned respect.

(HMD grandly enters the showiest prospect of the Grade, which is all set up with an open-air proscenium, so as to serve as a picture frame for a real-life presentation of a particular scene (the High Mad Presentation of the Citadel), in landscape proportions (specifically, 2.76:1), but curtained off yet. The setting sun is behind it, and the great disc glows through the curtain's fabrics, which fills many in the Court with some sense of foreboding. But there is an edge to the moment, which also spells excitement; and, to the more ambitious persons at hand, the promise of opportunity.)

(HMD knows this to be an occasion of epic significance, so he rises to the occasion.)

HMD: Look! Look! Draw back the drape –

(The camera slowly dollies back as the wide terrace is revealed, by laborers drawing the heavy burgundy curtains aside, à la the title sequence in 'The Robe' (20th-Fox, 1953). Footlights on the curtains dim, and the pale blue light of – desolate – day fills the scene.)

(A gasp erupts from the great crowd of COURTIERS.*)*

HMD: Regard! Regard yon pile that I of my own power have raised! Elder structure, protean-grade! Connected to the ancient foundation and arc of planets, and just as strong! *(shouts)* Approach! I have, under the ægis of all my
talents and sway, erected a monument more lasting than brass! A monument for *all time!*

*(*HUONZUX, *architect* [as played by Richard Burton]*, draws in, so as to
assert his importance.)*

HUONZUX: Power-Generator of the Suns! Your Citadel is finished. I have seen
to it: from the first rock excavated while the dream germinated in my
mind, to the last light switch bezel in the 46th Floor Janata closet – I was
there, I instructed, I enabled and I guided. Is it not a splendid work? Have
we not brought you to supra-glory? Can you not bestow your thanks upon
the deeds of myself and countless devotees, a huge number of whom have
sacrificed their lives so that you may spend your leisure on the heights,
in which to dwell in rare and full-blown fabulousness? Here I am, agent
for all of us who have accomplished and executed and suffered, so that
you may cruise in most magic bliss. We await your homage, as the turkey
thanks his executioner, so that his elegance may grace table for his eaters
to preen at. Here it is, what we have done: your very own Citadel! It
awaits your spark of life, to legitimize it into the world's greatest build-
ing-cum-controlling schemes.

HMD: I am well pleased, architect. *(notes* HUONZUX's *aspirations of pride
and he enjoys a sinister pause; then, with devilish pranksterism, and a
sincere determination to be more efficient in his missions of dispatch-
ing tiresome enemies)* Now, Guards, sew his eyelids shut, so that he shall
not stray to others' halls on account of flattery. After a few minutes of
horror, then take him out into the Tainted Zone, well away from anything
remotely created by him, and wholly crush the instinct of life out of him
by mine own block-grinding mechanisms. His work is done. So is his time
in my care. I have other, grander, more ingenious architects in mind. For I
am their Chief and Guider. We will produce structures that will instantly
make this present Citadel seem kind of, I don't know, revoltingly silly, I
suppose. Thus, I cannot tolerate this plodder further, nor put up with any
coy commissions he might accept away from my total control. Better and
more talented practitioners of his art await, so as to make yon Citadel
appear a mere gopher hole. For his work out there is only a teensy way-
post in my progression to ultra-ness. Now snap to!

(PRÆTORIAN-ISH GUARDS lead out the stunned architect, who is mute with shock.)

HMD: *(to himself, as all others are bowed to the floor)* So now. So now, so now, so now, so now! All to myself! My unstoppable, winning self-same self! I feel the victory of the world's long saga, waiting for this moment. And I have delivered it. My gift to this planet. Was there anyone more somber in victory? More mature? More godly? *(then, addressing the assembly)* Who can now contest my right to world-context super-hegemony? Who, who, who? I ask! No one can answer. All shall be as wordless as that architect nut. A fool he was! No one, NO ONE can refute my truth!

(A musical intermezzo, while the assembly prepares for the processional.)

HMD: And when I enter that stronghold, this Urth enters an entirely revised ultra-epoch! It will be a time of my own, on mine own globe, in which mine own and no one else's own Will shall be in all things. *(he faces his COURT, in large CU)* Courtiers and cooperators! Notice how I trust you. If you trust me, you will rise with me, albeit at a distance I am satisfied and comfy with. Watch me now, as I take strenuous command of the center of the universe, which I personally own, and from which I will dictate terms to my world from this instant forward. For I have *won*, haven't I! All my battles and wars and strifes were for this one moment. But from this moment, my universal rule commences, so all the struggles were for that purpose, as well. Watch me well as I take what is mine. The entire world will be watching of course, for it will be darshan's proof that I live, and *will* live, to command and control. Those who have tried to stop me are no more, and never again shall there be any challengers to my rightful office. Everything that I have won I fought for, and when one fights for oneself in this world, and one wins, one has been right all along. And I am right. So it is my right to *take* the world, because I fought for it, and won. *(he then moves away from CU and toward the great entrance in which the vast Citadel is framed, with the pile lighted in the most dramatic ways possible, now that the sunset has become particularly intense; HMD regards it for a moment, as we hear a tremendous and gruesome crash sound off camera, indicating the loyal architect HUONZUX'S execution. Death-scream.)* Free am I now, to have it all to my rightful self! The Self! For, look at what this Self has achieved! Most who are born without poverty think they are so special; that they are automatically going to be stars in life, or some such, as if it is a birthright! I piss on your 'entitlement'! I? Me? I have worked and earned and struggled and fought. Nothing was placed in my hands for its own sake. I had to take, for none would give. So I took, and now I own. So now, yes – yea, and fucking-verily! I am the rightful one! The Rightful Self! I earned it. Now I shall take it! Who else can say such a thing? Whoever could? I am first! *(pause, while he readies himself; then, addressing the* COURT *and beyond them,* THE MASSES)* See, see, see me now, taking possession of the very epoch. An epoch open-ended, stretching way, way, far, far into the future, a vessel to be filled – with my dreams, and more importantly, my intent. Watch now, how I do it. *(prepares for his grand-most gesture)* My command to you is to follow. And at a respectful distance, as befitting one so noble and accomplished. You will not deny me the independent superiority of my ownership of the world. No one ever will. Now watch, AS I ENTER MY STRONGHOLD!

(Camera then dolly-follows HMD *in his long and very grand progression along the Incline Drive, now dubbed Ceremonialistic Way, unto the fastness of his Citadel of Gyugganthropristixc; it is one long take to the end, in which the camera, after dollying after* HMD *at a distance that still allows for him to be prominent in the frame, then eases off and rises on a very high boom to get the final master shot of the picture... The score is magnificent and transformational, and communicates aspects of the story that images and dialogue cannot possibly convey; familiar leitmotifs from earlier in the picture evolve into a new and final World's Pyrrhic Triumph theme.)*

And the script went ahead with:

(The camera continues to rise slowly until it reaches the Apex Parallel at 300 ft., where it is secured without interruption, capturing the master shot, with 2nd to 7th units covering from divers angles. HMD's *figure grows remote, and as it nears the Citadel's front gate, the assembly enters the bottom of the frame, following, as ordered. Sndtrk: a high-reaching symphonic cantata (with sparing chorus), full of portent. By the time* HMD *reaches the gate, the sunset has faded, and he has officially attained the Citadel, which is indicated by the fading-in of hundreds of vertical spotlights, some which rotate and adjust, moodily exposing the structure's exterior. Now inside,* HMD's *ascent within is shown by a special guide-glow, emitting from the exposed lift. We see it rise all the way to the Upper Penumbra Chamber, over 500 ft. above the floor of the valley, balefully-lit in reds and maroons, the combination of which intensifies considerably once it is clear that* HMD *has arrived, and, most importantly, is installed at his Central Control. His technology of dominance cannot be enacted until he is virtually sitting at his Vast Master Control Board, whence he will run the world his way for unknown time blocks ahead.)*

(Cut to MS of HMD *in control at the apex, with a grandiose view of the Palace and the assembly slowly advancing from it. Grasping his Shabgar scepter in devastating victory, with its sharp spike as its most prominent feature, he raises it up in total and permanent conquest.)*

HMD: *(with steely resolve)* Triumph. Victory. Control. Mine. Now, and in perpetuity!

(Dissolve to master shot from Apex Parallel, with HMD *plainly highlighted – due to finest-resolution BKV Method stock, via Ultra-Panavision 70 – holding till score reaches its climax. Final fade-out.)*

THE END

That was what the screenplay said. That was what was written. That was what was required. That was how the story should be told, and how this particular story should end, with the victorious tyrant-god-emperor entering the fastness of his headquarters. And in the manner of 'So let it be written, so let it be done', that was what the filmmakers and the cast strove to do.

And there was Butterbugs, in the Upper Penumbra Chamber, holding his pose as the script and director had asked him to do, the remote-controlled #37 UP-70 camera rolling, its special Ektoplasmically-Transported BKV images captured and instantly beamed to the lab in Culver City, where they were instantly printed out on 70mm stock, so as to prevent the lofty æyrie's set from being weighed down more than was allowed within the safely-tested live-weight limit, rated for Butterbugs, costume, camera, lighting, and needful props, *only.*

'I don't even want to say Cut!' Egaz's voice came over the remote speaker. 'Perfection exists! Perfection itself! Perfection, perfection! Do you hear? All of you? PERFECTION!!!!!! I will keep rolling, because the view is so fine. But you may rest from your labors now, ultrastar!'

Butterbugs lowered his arms and carefully placed the scepter on the floor of the set. He drew a deep breath and gave a sigh of the ages.

'It is wrapped. I am now free. Free for LOVE…!'

Then, an action came to be that no script or even any conscious thought within the constructive art of filmmaking might conceive.

It began as a flash of light, not the kind generated by klieg-lights or brutes or SuperTroopers or VastMansBeams. It was an immense *flare-up*, that illuminated the entire valley without, along with the still-advancing extras that streamed from the Palace, the Palace set itself, and the fully-extended camera boom and the Apex Parallel, far up and away.

Butterbugs knew that the Producer Team, Porter, Egaz, Hazel, TABP, and Sonny had planned for some sort of celebratory pyrotechnic display upon the picture's completion, so this must be it, he surmised. He noticed the remote camera was still whirring.

A millisecond after the flare, came an explosive boom. It drowned out Egaz's voice coming over the remote:

'Butterbugs, we're still rolling #37 UP-70. I'd like a MCU of you regarding your control center. Paul's zooming in now. You're still in frame. Good. I'll talk you through. Then, I'd like CU reaction, and then we'll – Oh, holy jade-priest hell!!!! Whatever is – Oh, *zhond-duscht kaym pronnstch!* Ohh — NO!!!!!!!! NO!!!!!!!!!!!!! NO!!!!!!!!!!!!!'

Old Atrocity grabbed the mike as he stared at the Citadel, which was bloody well exploding.

'BUTTERBUGS!!! Get out! If all downward passages are invalidated, evacuate via the Upthrust Parachute Harness, at any of their eight stations! There are four in the Upper Chamber alone! Butterbugs! Can you hear me??'

All scanned the skies for any such upthrust – in vain – so far. But so far, the tower was surrounded by flames, which, fanned by solicited winds from the floor of the vale, spiraled around the structure with a horrific grandeur that was not to be believed. The approaching extras fled in holy terror as the superstructure threatened to collapse.

The terrible impact of the catastrophe was increased by a thunderhead forming far above the agitated moil of rising smoke and ash, which soon caused bolts of lightning to strike out amidst the friction of disaster, wreaking their own kind of tremendous damage all around.

A twisting of superstructure, a shedding of painfully-applied decor, a yielding to forces more violent, more perverse, than the degraded audacity of a high and mad egomaniac's vanity scheme, mortally-threatened by mere fire and wind, their anger kindled by sudden invitation into action, now took control of an entity so carefully, hopefully, and lovingly wrought.

And this vision was all the more striking, as the waning full moon now rose quickly, as if, full of awful anxiety, it had to cast its benevolent eye over what it preferred to see: romance in its glow, instead of signs of war below.

So endeth the events
and the progress of the
Seventh Day.

62.

Bombastes Furioso

Præludium

Some day, the truth would out. Some day there would appear The Explanation, for the benefit of audiences everywhere.

That day could only come after the world's heartbeat resumed, and its respiration returned, after its brain stopped spinning. Shock, disbelief, horror, grief, tears, wailing, loss: that was the terrible mixture the world found to be present in its collective mind. So much giving for so long, and now, so much taken away.

Then, it was time for The Explanation.

Even the most grandiose of meltdowns might have, in its primæval germ, an element of the most squalid kind. The most epic tragedy of the epoch was thus reduced to the most wretched atom of venality.

It was revealed in a telling bit of evidence, the form of which was an anonymous calling card, on VapourPapour, delivered to Hazel Snyder, who had taken to her sickbed at Mega|Goth Stvdios directly after the ultimo finale annihilation. It was delivered by an anonymous dog working for PuppyMail, that respected firm whose motto, 'Only Delivery, With No Trace', brought such heavy cheer with it now. And the message read:

'Done because of Conelrad Murn, Martyred Hero, Heroic Martyr'.

Just that, nothing more. No mention was made of Murn's onetime status as President of the United States. Therefore, authorities were quick to assume this dolorous stroke was an act of loyalty to Murn's still very extant mafia-cum-cult forces. Clearly, it originated from beyond any known extreme element who 'legitimately' still honored the late ruler and his crew, e.g. nameless agents, in league with esoteric sections in creative association with all things Murn, who did the unspeakable deed.

For it was true, only too true.

However, those agents who pulled it off did so under the most foundational error it is possible to conceive. As agents of revenge, their mission was born under a perverted star of mass misguidance and brain-dead reactions.

Without any debate whatsoever, these austere and hateful persons concluded that it was:

'BUTTERBUGS – and *only* Butterbugs – who was responsible for Marshall Vogg's prosecution of the assassination of Conelrad Padpompom Murn, President of the United States of the Americas, in Las Vegas, Nevada, on that… *terrible day*, along with members of his Cabinet, Family, Constituency, Top Leaders, Business Associates, Officers, Officials, Courtists, Beloveds, Corporatists, Distinguished Guests and Friends, and Other Innocents Associated with Murn Trusts, 'n' Charities, 'n' Good Concerns'.

[So read the nomenclature plastered on the MurnCorp's floating website. No mention whatsoever of the hundreds of staff and volunteers, hired for the occasion, and having nothing to do with MurnCorp, who endured Marshall's solo-executed explosion. Though the actual number of 'innocent' deaths was two, Butterbugs had created a trust for these victims' families, and had been a leader in mourning them. He also ensured that their memory should be fully understood, as a profound separation from anything intrinsically Murnish. Butterbugs himself commissioned and paid for a companion monument, built in the Lutyens-esque manner, styled 'To The Disassociated Fallen', that was raised on another part of the Campus Tragicus Dignitas – the Field of Tragic Honor. In the years to come, after more of MurnCorp's horrible deeds were known, the monument would also honor 'Those Many Hundreds, If Not Thousands – Indeed, An Unknown Number – Who Suffered And Perished Under The Tyrannical Policies And Covert Deeds Of Conelrad Padpompom Murn, His Cartel, Corporation, and Henchmen'. Capped with: *'NVNC PRO TVNC'* ('NOW FOR THEN').]

This dreaded knowledge could only but add to the mountainous grief that came with the realization that Butterbugs *was no more*. If there existed the possibility that the world would now choose a pathway that led to Butterbugs As Victim, it was nevertheless not taken up by all the peoples. Instead, they wisely elected to regard Butterbugs for what he gave to humanity, rather than how he was taken from them.

There were those who, in after times, deduced that any Butterbugsian saga would have had to end this way, no matter what. He was just too *good*. So, in the great traditions of sub-humanity, he just *had to go*.

But for the predominant masses, no, that wasn't their choice of view at all. Not by a long shot.

'He was a gift,' a crippled child in a tiny village in central D.R. Congo was heard to say. 'That is all I need.' And thus, there was no consolation for the loss. But this child did not die of a broken heart, although she had good reason to. Because, that night at the La Vieux Globe Oculaire cinema-tent, they showed a Butterbugs picture, 'A Nice, Greasy, Prehistoric Moose-Dog' (Selznick), and this child was so touched by the picture and its characters, both canine and Butterbugsian, that she was renewed. 'He is still gifting. And that is *more* than I need,' she stated in her valedictorian speech, when graduating magna cum laude at the TABP Académie du Médecine, in Dakar.

And for anyone who did not understand the beauty of this simplicity, all they need do was to look up in the sky for his presence, and his legacy, and its meaning, to be felt. Not as a godhead so much as a natural reminder.

But more about that, after The Explanation is fleshed out fully. It is based on primary sources that cannot yet be named. They are entirely reliable though, and therefore, said Explanation may be regarded as conclusive. A law of nature, as it were. A particularly heavy-going one.

If only this had been a plot confined to an opera! Or a *film* of an opera! Verdi, or Berlioz, or Wagner, or even Charpentier could have scored it! Mascagni, certainly. Boito, D'Annunzio, or Hugo von Hofmannsthal might have written the libretto!

Sadly, in the stark, fluorescent light of a quack's illegal clinic, the mechanics of the deed are reminiscent of the cheapest of dime-box novels, in which the crudest of tales are contained. There wasn't much to it, really. An insipid little tale of revenge, or something like it.

And Now, The Explanation

Since it had been determined by MurnCorp (the handiest appellation for the united individuals whose mission this was), and on the most reactionary of presumptions, that it was Butterbugs – *and only Butterbugs* – who virtually authored the destruction of their hard-won edifice of power, he would, as high penalty, have to be taken out.

There were those in this shadowy organization canny enough to know that based on the tidal waves of publicity causing a daily charybdis in the media waves, filming a major and extremely dynamic motion picture presented all kinds of opportunities for things to go wrong, and that inevitable casualties might result from such wrongness.

Since the interested media had been awash in 'UWH' coverage from the start, the schemers had only to demurely choose which dangerous site they wanted an 'accident' to come about – and when. They considered motorcar tire blowouts, snipped brake tubes, electrical short-outs, and shaving mishaps. Or even more prosaic disasters, like a fire at Butterbugs' trailer, or in his dressing-closet, or yurt, or hogan, or anywhere he slumbered. Or a knife accident on the set (since HMD was doing so much killing). But they were frustrated by the fact that such small-scale acts would be so completely traceable to their dooryard.

In the urgency of their studies, they accelerated speculation and arrived at careful assumptions. If Butterbugs and his partners – like that Sonny Projector guy, among other gentlemen and players – had been able to get that miserable (and obviously suicidal) Marshall Vogg to carry out their requested act, even in the face of presidential security, then in order to properly respond, in order to give a fair fight, they'd have to match an already below-the-belt act with one further on down the belt-line. Way down. From a position of strength.

Hiring a suicide bomber was a trick as old as the hills. Marshall had been so obvious!

Being about ninety-nine times smarter, MurnCorp couldn't possibly have very much trouble bumping off some – *movie star*, now could they?

Indeed, their euphoria knew no bounds when they found out 'UWH''s climax would take place in and around a huge tower the ultrastar himself would be occupying, *solo*.

There it all was, fully mapped-out on the nationally-adored 'Derrold 'n' Mindy Magstaff Breakfast-Television Show' (XBS N-wirx). In one of its co-host's 'Fave On-Locations' segments, there was Porter Pud Parker, innocently walking Derrold through the Citadel's Upper Penumbra Chamber itself, gleefully and meticulously describing what the star of the picture would be doing, all by his lonesome, way up here.

'That totally independent-minded Butterbugs is goin' it alone,' Porter grinningly explained, 'in order to conform to the strict safety standards, of course! But, more importantly, to fulfill an artistic and dramatic sense of *perfection* in this super-finale of a sequence. Isn't that something? Isn't that *wild?*'

That was all MurnCorp needed to know.

After all, the studio's PR staff had worked TwentyFourSeven, bragging about all these and other details. Their constant drumming had worked the public into such a state that, indeed, the world was panting with bated breath in anticipation. 'Eagerly awaiting' is far too wimpy a phrase to describe the hunger and thirst that waiting – always waiting – endlessly waiting, for 'UWH' brought forth.

Speaking of Butterbugs and his alleged 'co-conspirators', in MurnCorp's view, bagging the ultrastar was the prize that truly mattered. Even if they weren't in on the plot, the others could wait, but they would be made to pay, though probably not so spectacularly. Besides, for all the 'innocents' who died in Vegas, matching innocents would have to be found.

The plan quickly came together. It was surprisingly competent, even exquisite. Several arcane and austere explosive specialists, completely current in the properties of the New Plastics, were themselves so obsessed with revenge, they beat down secret MurnCorp doors in hopes of sacrificing themselves in this mission. Hate was their motivation, not heaven. To be relieved of the terrible burden of being a deranged suicide bomber, they demonstrated as much enthusiasm as that devoted Lord-Boy kid had in wishing to die for HMD – if not more. These were they who, as aspiring murder/suicide players, were never going to do the world a favor by committing the suicide part first.

Many auditioned for the role before one was chosen. For it had to be only one. As a counterpoint to Marshall Vogg, if nothing else. Fair and square. That wasn't the reason a team effort was eschewed, though.

No, one and only one could pull it off best, especially when it was ascertained that the Citadel set, complex though it was, was just an empty vessel. Essentially for exterior show only, there was no shortage of places to hide, and perfect for rigging up some wiring inside. Under these unrestricted conditions, multiple systems and even multiple backup systems could be planted, then installed in virtual privacy, and even luxury.

But the schemers were faced with an agonizing dilemma. It was a fact that the most damnable detail was one based on a crapshoot, with 50/50 odds. That is, an utterly unique quandary presented itself. This major motion picture had, because of unlimited bankrolling (though not from banks), the insanely lavish ability to construct not *one* entire climactic series of sets, but *two*. As everyone knew, one fully independent, film-ready complex, entirely completed and totally prepped, was at Jambutterbugsabad in Makran, while another had been commissioned and successfully built a little later at Lasky Mesa.

Q: Which one, then, to wire up?

A: Both, of course.

No debate needed.

The problem was, after the fiasco of the late Lurgan & Vunn's spastic antics in faux-spy work over in the Makran gummed up MunnCorp's aspirations in that theatre of operations, there was just too much damage done to infiltrate the area for a potential assault. Besides, the tight control established and maintained by the tip-top triumvirate of Potwar, Yusuf, and Old Atrocity (aided and abetted by the ruling Jam himself) would've made any influxes impossible. No, the Jambutterbugsabad site was secure and intact, and it remained so. Option closed. Mission, most likely, scrubbed.

Then, evil stars shone down.

The Lasky Mesa site was no joke, nor was it any mere backup site. The revitalized Mega|Goth Stvdio busted ass in making it the best it could be: a helluva clone, surpassing its Makran mate in factors of convenience, approachability, and tap-water safety. But because of the hasty environment in which it was born and the fruition of assembly, certain aspects of casualness came into play, so that the entire location remained considerably vulnerable and subject to accessible, even easy, futzing.

The argument might be made that even if the climax had been filmed at Jambutterbugsabad, the plotters would simply have chosen a later time and place to enact their deed. Butterbugs was marked in any case. Without a doubt, they would have pulled it off some way or other. Except for the fact that every last one of them – the schemers and all their associates – were busted (and would have been in any event), two days *after* the actual catastrophe of the Citadel's destruction. This, the biggest internal mass-arrest in the US government's history, was due to investigative efforts on the part of President Beepus, already in play, from some months before.

Two days!

So, it was the gamble of Lasky Mesa where the unlucky number came up. On the outside chance that Butterbugs would select the California site the MurnCorp duly put all its chips.

The world knows of the humanity that influenced the ultrastar's decision to commit to Lasky, and much emotion has been spent on the significance of that tragic choice...

But, to continue with the bare Explanation of the saga's inexorable progression...

Oh, there were signs, but who knew? What, is an artist supposed to notice aberrations, and instead of interpreting them expressively, police them with authority?

Butterbugs saw a wide-hatted figure in the landscape as he motored out on location. Then, a 'buzzard' high up in the Citadel. He'd even noted some sullen nobody who nevertheless was paying inordinate attention to him in a place like Parkle's restaurant, before reporting for duty at Lasky Mesa.

Indeed, there were signs to notice, signals to pay attention towards. But when one is flying high on love and art, one makes special allowance for all the possibilities in the world. A sort of *benefit of the doubt* quickly reigns. Because when one is high on love and art, the world is doubtless a transportational banquet, to be sampled with good will and honest intentions. It is a place where innocence is a gift of expression, rather than a sexual barrier, or a fool's nameplate. Thus, a sense of civilized place is to be assumed. In other words, wonder has free play to present itself, and the artist can merely select what is to be sampled. The factor of innocence is manifested by the exclusion of the possibilities of untoward behavior, and any awareness that it could possibly cloud a world of wonders is thereby disempowered.

Thus was the innocence of Butterbugs institutionalized. But after so many pictures, made within this positive and nurturing framework, really, why *shouldn't* an ultrastar think that love was universal and that evil was gone from the world?

Perfect, then, for an agent of that very evil to go about a business that pretended to tragic dolor and fatal mischief.

An operative who was profoundly professional and effective, unlike the secret agent bozo-patrol that bumbled through the Makran before, was elected. This particular person would have fit well into the deepest of impossible missions, because he had the stuff of seriousness and self-sacrifice for his cause. He was also seventy-two years old, and had terminal softening of the brain, which was an added incentive to 'service', sealing his Murn-devotion and Butterbugs-contempt. Remarkably, his condition did not affect his work, his energy, nor his effectiveness, though there was an unknown timeframe before it actually would. It could be hours, or possibly weeks. In any case, his own curtains were closing in. Why not bow out with turbo-boomed bombasticism?

After a bit of expert espionage on his own part, when he learned that Butterbugs had indeed chosen Lasky Mesa as his location of choice, via a little bug-splatter on the window of Hazel Snyder's studio office, which opened up the whole sound world of the decisive conference therein, the bile-green light of 'go' started strobing in his mind. How touching that Butterbugs was so accommodating to his horny colleagues, who were just embarking on goody-goody marriages which, as show biz people, couldn't possibly last the month out.

No matter. Next stop: scan the region from the hills overlooking the Mesa's valley. After that: get a job.

After a little genial cajoling at the Hiring Shack, he scored a 'temporary non-permanent' gig as a doorsman and sill-checker. Passing as 'Pop', the easygoing, folksy, mainstream backstage handyman and jury-rigger, willing to do those non-union little-jobs no IATSE pro bothers with, he set up at the side entrance to the Citadel, and quickly became an institution of affability and convenience. And as the interior work on the Citadel all but ceased, and the exterior was being finished by sky-boys and cranesmen and painter-jiggers who were way too busy to police or protect what they had wrought, it became a common trust that Pop would see to all that stuff. And because the Citadel was at the center of the location lot, yet isolated from to-and-from activity, security elements around the peripheries were also content with the harmony of all operations. Things ran smoothly. Threats were deemed non-existent. As Butterbugs was beloved by everyone; no one was his enemy.

Apparently.

In this environment, Pop had virtual carte blanche to rig his systems, and at his leisure, too. He was certainly well-liked, but remained low key and virtually had a license to keep to himself. Somewhat carelessly, he still had the dialogue of that fateful meeting in Hazel Snyder's office on his PeeperPlayer, with which he amused himself via ear buds, during the long hours he had to lie low. He silently rejoiced and knew that his preliminary work, made before the craps-die had yet to be rolled, would not be in vain.

'Pop' had the complete freedom to come and go in the studio's little old 1939-vintage White Horse hauler, and there were many errands to a variety of hardware, electrical and farm supply depots in the region. He also took advantage of contacts with more shadowy suppliers of such items as the New Plastics. He would do his rigging at night, having convinced the happy division location manager (who shall not be named) that if he, Pop, bunked on site, as his needs were simple and his devotion to Butterbugs and the picture in general was total, his guard duty job would be all the more efficacious.

Once again, it should be made clear that the attitudes of trust and responsibility, not to mention a cheeriness and sincerity, capped by an automatic civility, were all hallmarks of a Butterbugs picture, especially in light of the new post-Hyman Goth (and post-Murn) epoch that had liberated the entire production. Thus, the freedom for misbehavior's inception, regardless of the surrounding climate of unlikelihood.

It is not necessary to document Pop's progress in his arranging the Citadel for complete destruction. It had all the dreariness of wiring, say, a Butler building for irrigation pipe storage in Gupper, South Dakota. If asked what he was doing exactly (it only really happened once), Pop simply responded with, 'Doing a bit of safety wiring for when Butterbugs is on set.' It worked. No further questions. Indeed, he installed a helpful series of guide lights on the Emergency Get Down stairs, so he wasn't even lying.

The multi-talents of Pop therefore ensured success in all his undertakings, as everyone now knows, and in the years to come would be the fodder for CSI work, as well as the public's deconstruction, speculation, and conspiracy theories. (Which would be creepily creative. More on that subject below.)

As the mysterious 'buzzard' figure on one of the upper exterior galleries that Butterbugs thought he saw when he and Juba ascended the Citadel, and the one who shadowed from Parkle's in Culver City to Hazel's office window at Mega|Goth, who then stood there above the pull-off-and-lay-by, en route to the location itself, and ultimately to its Citadel, this agent, who can never be properly named or even identified, successfully eluded notice or investigation all the way through, while prepping the premises and evading all, so as to see the suicide mission to its proper conclusion.

(If Pop had thought for one second he would ever be caught, he would have unreservedly flung himself from the nearest parapet or even the topmost turret, as surely as HMD's Lord-Boy.)

Because he became a veritable Quasimodo of the Citadel, Pop also made it his home. He even snoozed on the futon where Juba and Butterbugs nearly convened that time in the Uppermost Penumbra Room. The toxins of his infernal sweat were already there, in the fabric, for his rigging the place, to blow up in the most thorough manner possible, had been the hardest task any solo-performing death artiste could ever do. What's more, he pulled it off.

Ironically – for irony is no mere literary tool, as it positively dominates the world of cinema, due to its remorseless drama possibilities and its infinite capacity for plot twists – to Pop's great credit, his rather ingenious design was arranged so that only Butterbugs – and himself – were affected. Thus, as enormous as the destruction was, there were no other casualties. No other human was even very close, as the extras were en route to the entrance, and being a long way off yet, they were successfully evacuated once the purpose-driven demolition was in progress. Inanimate losses there certainly were, the most prominent being the awful-but-stupendous tower itself, not to mention the great Ultra-Panavision 70 camera #37, which was posthumously awarded a citation for bravery by its patriarch, Robt. Gottschalk himself.

In the spectacle of horror, trauma and loss, the fact that Pop had gone missing went, amazingly, unnoticed.

There were many who thought the whole business of Butterbugs being the sole occupant of the Citadel set for the final shots in the picture wholly preposterous. What the hell was a highest-value star doing up in such a contraption, all-alone, with only robotic camera coverage at the topside location, and with no other standby assistance?

Even Old Atrocity could not argue the issue, though. The facility in the Upper Penumbra Room was so perfected in its automation, and the master grip's presence was so required on the Grade, no one even considered the intelligence of the ultrastar's procedures aloft as lacking in any way, shape or form.

Well, in this day and age of you-can't-fool-me criticism, critics just don't *get* the need for thinking out artistic drama and what it takes to achieve it. That is, they don't really understand much beyond the explainable, and thus they are limited and dull.

In such a picture as 'UWH', everything is heightened, super-larger than life. The same goes for the intent of its effect.

However, the solo act in the Upper Penumbra Room was wholly Butterbugs' idea. Publicly, the reason for his lonesome self at the top was that the structure could not support a full crew and equipment at such a height, without doubly expanding the structure from top to bottom, and doubling its expenditure at the same time. That was basically true, but still, the Room was rated for at least five persons and two cameras, which would have been more than adequate for superior production values.

No, the solo act was Butterbugs' *preference*. Unconventional in the extreme, it was nevertheless the only bit of ballyhoo he had ever formulated or contributed to a film with which he was associated. He posited that the public would be properly awed if they knew of the logistics of his lone progression up into a tower that was spookily empty. Just like the script specified it should be, thus stressing the monomaniacal insanity of the High Mad Doctor. Perhaps it was also an effort to give those who had strived at the Lasky Mesa site more appreciation for the signal job they had done, and to show off their achievement a bit. Maybe it was to demonstrate that the most stringent safety standards were in practice. Perhaps it was even to showcase the robotic options of filming, if a crew were to be at risk. But above all, it was loyalty to the script and its writers. No Butterbugsian improvisation was to be entertained at this point, no matter how transcendent. All opportunities for creative improvisation had passed.

Really, all that mattered to him was that Heatherette was waiting, and he didn't want to be late.

Up in the Room, mechanical workings now had to be obeyed, without question or argument. And because of that insistence of physics, Butterbugs would not cheat his writers out of their climax, nor was he of a mind to. It was the proposition of a selfless actor, but it made sense to all, and that was why the unchaperoned route was implemented. In addition, he thought it would heighten the Realife effects for the audience upon viewing, as a sort of reward after an unimaginably long but compelling picture.

He was correct in all these matters, of course, but within a context very much different from that in which they were conceived.

Even at the risk of plunging into morbidity and vulgarity, it is perhaps appropriate to mention aspects of the folk legend culture the catastrophe spawned.

Conspiracy theories, however much annoyance they cause, are nevertheless stubborn salmonberry seeds in the molars of those who purport to classify and understand the world via scientific method. But because conspiracy theories are often rooted in the same turves of cultivated, fertile soil whence dramatic arts spring, many such theories are often labeled: 'It sounds like a movie (plot)', on or around their final resting place. So be it, but theory also poses possibility, and in the world of drama, the impossible, possible, probable, and the positively practicable all coexist in varying measures.

But there is this: the cracking of pots is sure to continue, and the size of the vessels shall surely grow.

Thus the following short selection of popular Butterbugs Bump-Off Theories, packed with what-ifs in the present tense. All such theories have their degree of truth, so they are perhaps worthy of perusal. If they fall short of objectivity, they at least provide a sense of survey, and serve to broaden the perimeters of The Explanation.

Here is a sampling of what several philosophers, speculators, spectators, tricksters, quacksalvers, beguilers, bullshitters, and other thesauric figures who line the fringes of Butterbugsian Studies think:

– OK, ready? Here goes. The lust for power pushed Butterbugs to go through with a planned bombing of the Citadel, and through the miracle of digital restoration, Butterbugs would return in a transcendent and messianic light of a 'resurrection', from which he would seize power on a generic world-level. Through a Judas-like leak, the White House discovered this by bugging Heatherette's house, and a conspiracy was born to prevent Butterbugs from reaching his goal, thus his demise. (Klorry Kilindell's Source For All Things Unsaid)

– The White House conspiracy fails. Butterbugs is indeed restored and proceeds with his plan. Due to fanatical followings worldwide, he does indeed achieve, not High Mad Doctorhood, but High Enlightened Patrium, and the world actually evolves to a higher plane. This real/fictional alternative scenario is actually taken seriously and entertained on the Full DVD kit of the Director's Ultimate and Final Forever Cut of 'UWH'. But none of this can happen, because they killed him. (Mega|Goth Stvdios Public Relations & Purposeful Publicity Dept.)

– There was a school of thought who determined that, after Butterbugs' horrendous experience with the Isaac Davis building, which was inverted underground, the disaster of the Citadel, which thrust almost equally, but *above* ground, formed a 'yang and yin' prophetic package of astrological validity. The triumph of survival in the earlier 'yang' event now gave way to the non-survival of the 'yin' event. Book-ended by the verticality of these two circumstantial and seminal occurrences, the destiny of the ultrastar was evidence that his fate was determined even before the creation of the stars. Thus, the universe's right to create *new* stars. (A Compendium of Sympathetic Spiritual Thinkers, on ComSymSpirThin.bs)

– The remains of Butterbugs are indeed splattered and scattered, but Old Atrocity, strolling through the smoking remains in somber devastation, chances upon the remains of Butterbugs' unmistakably blue lips and scrapes them up. Butterbugsian slime, but pure. For DNA use. He *knows* some people. Clone time!... (unknown sources)

– Even if, as some purport, Butterbugs has indeed expired (which he most certainly hasn't; he is most likely lounging with King Arthur, JFK, Benazir, and Marilyn in Avalon), he changed the world forever. And in the after years, when the adolescence of the world has come out of the wages of tribulation and adjusted to the benefits of maturity, they will observe that there are many, and indeed, most of the world, who call him their pioneer. (Oxford, Cambridge, Bologna, Univ. of Calcutta, Beijing Univ., the Sorbonne, Harvard, Jack Pelbo's Colleges, MIT, Princeton, Harold's Learnings, and 14,006 other institutions of higher learning worldwide, in a United Consensus Communique Regarding Some Butterbugsian Significances, on several well-known websites)

– There's just so much bullshit about this Butterbugs stuff. I think it was all those producer guys who blew him up because they wanted 'Unholy War Hymn' to be a bigger hit than it would've been otherwise. Blowing up stuff makes a good movie end. (Pelman Doorspilf, A Blog For Me And Mine)

– I tink he got rubbed out cuzza da Budderbugses musslin' in on dat Prezadenchul creeps turf (Tony Blorretti, in 'Tony's TeaTime For Da Boys In Da Mob', on Joizynetting.mil)

– We don't even have to acknowledge that Butterbugs is no more; *something* went upstairs, though. Above everything. (Granny Mbambo, aged 116, President, Concerned Olders of the Tuerkistan Settlement Home, Bizzpuerk, Ungava)

Truth, or illusion? Few know the difference in this case. But maybe some do.

And now we come to the sum-total point of The Explanation.

No matter what anybody thinks or believes, Butterbugs' demise was engineered by Murn interests solely for *blowback* purposes. In the fast-lane of the world's most serious power players, hardball-flinging is fast, furious and merciless. Intended targets are often missed. Mere revenge usually stops at evening a score, but with blowback, damage is usually ongoing, indiscriminate, and (to use the hip-happen' term), collateral. The cross-fire is often more dangerous than the target.

Despite their top echelon's population of morons, psychotics and perverts, the Murn Concern also had its own versions of the Dulles Brothers, the J. Ed Hoovers, the Pulbur Vankratchers, and other insidious types, who were the real brains behind the sleaze. Regardless of Butterbugs and his Effect, they were up to all sorts of shit, worldwide. MurnCorp had determined, via knee-jerk responses, that it was Butterbugs, Sonny, and their effects, who were behind the President's knock-off in Vegas. But unlike frontman Oswald in the JFK case, Marshall Vogg had *truly* acted alone, and for his own reasons. This fact is corroborated by tons of irrefutable proof, which verifies, time and again, Marshall's complete independence, and indeed, his shunning of outside influences.

Marshall's much-publicized End Note, in which Butterbugs is mentioned as a life-affirming inspiration (though *not* a guide for any violent pathway), never should have been released. That is, until Murn elements had been arrested and tried – which they were, with dispatch.

Marshall had sent his Note to Senator O'Wayne Kebbah (D-NV) because he trusted him as a fellow disabled vet – Kebbah had lost both ears and most fingers and toes in the disastrous Murn-led invasion of Nambia – and was a vociferous opponent of Murnism ever after. Incredibly, responsibility for the Note's release to the media was the sole responsibility of Sen. Kebbah's Main Letter Opener, Paury Quoon Plapp-Plaupp, a disgruntled person who hated life – and those who lived it. Though Marshall had specifically addressed his Note to Kebbah alone, the senator never set eyes upon it, until the headlines screamed its existence. Later, the truth emerged that when Plapp-Plaupp opened Marshall's sent packet, not one but two separate letters were within. One was the End Note itself, while the other was a private message to Sen. Kebbah, requesting his Note should repose in the senator's personal safe for not less than five years. Though the Note was typewritten, the private message was penned by Marshall himself, with a crayon gripped by his toothless gums.

Not caring one whit about Butterbugs, Marshall, or even the Murn Cartel, Plapp-Plaupp did happen to harbor deep contempt for his boss, Sen. Kebbah. Though he did not fully understand the significance of Marshall's Note, he nevertheless considered any personal letter directed at Kebbah should be exposed as controversial, on the outside chance it would lead to the removal from office of the senator he so hated. His entire reasoning for 'going to the newspapers' was the Note's simple existence, not its explosive contents! The origin of Plapp-Plaupp's contempt was mindlessly simple. One day, Sen. Kebbah 'got mad' at his Main (and only) Letter Opener for allowing mail to pile up, causing delays to his staff for answering. That was it. That was all it took for Plapp-Plaupp to desire extreme revenge. On his own volition, he discarded the private message (later found and presented as conclusive evidence), and forwarded the Note to 'The Kemp Terker

Neo-Conservative Radio Show'.

Plapp-Plaupp granted a brief phone interview, which aired on the Terker show. He was stupid enough to admit everything. When queried as to why he hadn't included Marshall's private message with the Note, the Letter Opener explained it was 'unreadable' because it was 'written by a cripple'. It was in fact perfectly legible and coherent. He also stated that 'company policy' dictated that all hand-written (and mouthwritten) letters should be discarded, as they are considered 'terrorist acts'. This and other statements by Plapp-Plaupp were outright prevarications.

With the authorities closing in for questioning, Plapp-Plaupp escaped to Kneemipe, Keewatin, where he was murdered by hooligans, after he insulted them.

Thus, based on Marshall's End Note, so witlessly exposed to the public by a vengeful nobody, the MurnCorp plotters placed responsibility for Murn's removal squarely at Butterbugs' feet.

'Never, never forgive' was their barren motto. 'No questions. No answers. Just *plow back* at thems that wronged you.'

That, at any rate, was the goal. And it was a goal achieved.

That Butterbugs' end was due to such a banal reflex as irrelevant, broad-based revenge – and poorly-researched revenge at that – shows the appalling dangers of any decision-making that wills blowback as a viable option. An option that will, in any application, cause far more problems than solutions.

In this case though, the blowback *blew back* at the blowers, and in a rare case of blowback solving problems, problems were indeed solved.

Butterbugs was not a martyr. Nor was he a redeemer, or any cosmic burden-carrier of debts payable by death. He was a victim of a crime, however, an innocent slaughtered, and that alone gave him the *demeanor* of a martyr, a redeemer, and a cosmic hero.

Across the globe, another motion picture set remained intact, ready for filming. It represented heartbreak, unjust action, and things undone. Because, over in Jambutterbugsabad, the beautiful mega-set of the Citadel and its satellites stood safe, quiet, and waiting for their master.

END of The Explanation.

The Eighth Day

Back to the aurora at the start of that Eighth Day. When the world changed forever, and everyone alive of Earth would remember where they were.

And Heatherette, knowing nothing of collapses or fires or possible astronomical alterations, knowing nothing but the fact that the new day was rising up over her world, went out onto her terrace to address the dawn. All hopes were boundless and forthcoming. The sky was bright, all stars retired for the night. But no, there were luminous elements still up there. Like those seen on a jetliner's landing gear, say. Yet, they were stationary, and remained so. Then, as the morning awoke further, past expected arrivals and anticipated kisses, light-points in the sky persisted, perhaps like those on the wall of a mere swimming pool, though not marine at all.

Daystars then, punk rivals to the sun.

Sol still lit the world up, all across Earth's surface. From vast structures in the uppermost perches of the entitled, to the burrows of the humble. The sun inspired and led everyone who chose to look, unto an upward path. Yet it also shone upon they who once aspired to those very lights but now were lower than the dust. High or low, all were covered. Even solo persons on terraced plains.

But now, as of today, Sol had company.

Standing as witness, naked to both the flats below and the sky above, Heatherette raised her arms all the way and saluted these celestial lamps, whatever their provenance. An inviting benevolence, instantly attractive and infinitely comforting, seemed the domain of their eminence. What was more, she felt some sort of connection, of understanding, of creation, with that which now shone down on her.

Then she lowered her hands to her breasts, and held them in giving pose. And when she ran her palms down to her smooth belly and held them there, she knew, fully, that as a woman with a footing in the here and now, she was not alone. Neither here on Earth, nor in the heavens above.

63.

A Constellation Is Born

Majestically, symphonically, Miltonically, the ascending column of light rose inexorably to the heavens. Despite its epic proportions and implication, it was not an entity that projected fear or toxicity or bellicosity. It was a phenomenon, sprung from catastrophe, yet wholly divorced from it. If it was beyond the ken of humans, no matter.

Indeed it existed, obviously an imponderable form, but remarkably without any perceivable forbiddingness, whether as inspirations of Vedic impendency or threatenings of Calvinist severity. Grandly and expeditiously did it travel upward, lighting the ionosphere with spectra never before imagined.

Bursting through this last barrier of the home planet, the column, now seen in posterior perspective, freely transformed itself into a luminous polygon with fluctuating corona. It grew even more tremendous in power, and hurtled ever forward, akin to a comet in principle, but, in actuality, like nothing so prosaic.

What the world then saw could only extend into the realm of non-sensual discernment, for this thing was becoming not only an image in the heavens, but an unutterable truth.

Physicists and astronomers would go down on record in explaining the occurrence, which the entire world had now witnessed. A trophic collection of linked/distressed atoms and sub-atomic particles, displaced by the larger-than-expected collapse of the 'Unholy War Hymn' (Mega|Goth) set, duly assembled in series, as a result of conflicting effluvia and atmospheric counterforce made volatile under conditions attributable to global warming/global upheaval. Thus prepared, the assemblage then caused a pyrogassic transfer progression. This process, possessing some forms of probable part-anti-matter, naturally responds conversely to gravity, and by the inviolate necessity of neo-Charnockian laws of hyper-driven super-atomic material movement tends to be ejected from carbon-based environments by the volumetric compositional ratio of intergalactic membrane flow. Or, in more colloquial terms, the detectable patterns of a subtle æther of space, responding to an intrusion. The latter force has no mercy regarding management of such foreign entities, and is thus obliged to impel them at great speed through universal (non-planetary body) space. Two other significant factors contribute to the collective phenomenon. Within the same quadrant of the target area, that is, the picture plane of the activity, as seen from any given non-aberrant point on the Earth's terrasphere or hydrosphere, regardless of atmospheric perspective (night or day, high noon excepted), an Octagonally-Intramatrixed Ultra Nova had, it was recently discovered, taken place in the Exexis 17 System out past the FP-723 galaxies, over fourteen Local Group full-length time-bars ago. And, it was calculated, this impressive celestial display was just becoming visible to the naked eye of infinitely inconsequential Earth. Combined with this phenomenon, never before witnessed, was a Prismatic Dustpin Explosion Overlay of staggering proportions, coincidentally evolving within the same line of sight as the ultra-nova community. And taking into account the properties of Bent Space, conventional alignment of image-projective subtle mass caused holographic-type optics to transpire, which, as chance would have it, in effect, 'joined-the-dots' of the ultra-nova clusters, by providing simultaneously painterly/sculptural shading and modeling, to create, in the heavens above – it had to be admitted – an unmistakable and wondrous portrait of –

Butterbugs

Butterbugs. The actor. The strolling player. The ultrastar. The star. Or rather, stars.

Butyrum Cimex!
Ultra Astrum Ultimo.

At least it certainly looked like him.

Exsilium Umbra.
Fiat Lux.

In the communal, beholding *mind* of all who observed, there was music to score the event; none so fitting as the long finale of Shostakovich's Symphony #7, where the notes climb to a level of majesty and exaltation equal to that of the stars. Right at the ne plus ultra of the Seventh Art.

And when this multidimensional and all-colorful constellation had indeed been humbly certified by all cosmic scientists on the globe, there were still those of the behavioral and psychic studies remaining to declare the phenomenon was one of mass hypnotism, or that all beings on Earth had been brought under some central persuasion's power by electro-chemical means. Or, in all its bathos, one theoretician speculated it was the work of a particularly aggressive moving picture studio's publicity department.

Some mass power of suggestion at work?

Indeed, the lighting of Los Angeles is under the control of humans, and it is humanly possible to write one's name on such a slate. The stuff of outstanding memories! How many though, looking up from Earth, remember the name of Butterbugs from that time? Do they now complete the sequence, in which that name, articulated in the lights of one of the world's great cities, was only a preliminary title card, a subtitle of prescience, for the awesome image now in the world's sky above?

[As an aside, it is necessary to interrupt this utterly epic and essentially solemn moment to reveal that, at the safely-distant long-shot parallel from which the collapse of the HMD pagoda was being lensed, director D'Varzim, watching the entire spectacle from one of the best seats in the house, and now reduced to speaking his erstwhile broken Butler English out of sheer shock, anxiously questioned his cameramen as to the coverage of the holocaust before them. And he was struggling, *struggling* with the reversion to the stumbling patois with which he commenced the picture, after he and the whole crew experienced the event in stunned silence, until the obvious conclusion of the 86-minute sequence:

'Shammie! Bobby! Totally – shot! Getting the shot! Totaled? Getting it??'
Leon Shamroy and Robert Surtees, both A.S.C., made it baldly official, in turn:
'Yup. Whole damn thing. Twin coverage.'
'Full magazines. In the can. We were prepared. Helluva shot.'
Each camera's operator sent secondary affirmation, as well.
'Tremendously ending for my picture! Any re-takes – later. Excited to see said rushes!!'
Shamroy had the final word:
'That last bit – That wasn't in the script, was it…?'

One of the cinema's most extraordinary resolutions then: with this last sequence in the can, 'Unholy War Hymn' (Mega|Goth) was well and truly wrapped. A very grand and inarguably ultimo finale had been all that remained needful. Butterbugs had loyally fulfilled it.
'This… *completes* my film… And… And… it… *completes*… Butterbugs…! *Our… dear… Butter…bugs…!*'
Such words could only be uttered in the midst of high drama, and higher-yet trauma. But, for a practitioner of action, spoken with a well-honed instinct for pragmatic dedication to the mission at hand.
In an instant, the voltage of reality dialed itself upwards with crushing intensity. The bringers of loss stepped forward to overwhelm, with heavy cheer.

At some time-post soon enough, with all that had been lost duly mourned and assessed, what had been saved came into universal focus: a great motion picture, a triumph complete… and most poignantly, *authentic.*

An undertaking of consequence can still be finished by those in a state of shock.
Verily, there was a picture to finish. Now it was so.]
Remarkably, not one functionary or representative or member of any theological, philosophical or ideological belief (or non-belief) on the planet had any

negative response, misinterpretation, or misjudgment of what this new set of stars in the firmament meant: that now, here, in this time and place, the whole world, and perhaps all that lay beyond, was moving towards something higher, more extraordinary, past the sphere in which all thought now existing was contained. Past its limitations, and past its freedoms.

Meaning had returned to the universe.

The essence of incandescence.

There the lights burned, from everlasting to everlasting.

And a new truth remained. Represented by a new constellation in the sky – the best and the brightest – and the closest – forming an extraordinary image, that could only be taken to mean one thing: proof, known in every living being's heart, that the gates to the higher planes of existence were at last opening up.

We, who inhabit all the world, had only but to begin our ascent. A leader had already shown the way.

F i n

CURTAIN

End of Apotheosis

Next: Beyond *Fin*

Coming Attractions
IV. Beyond *Fin*

Butterbugs is now history. He has come, made his mark, and gone, leaving an even bigger mark in his wake. In retrospect, Butterbugs as actor, ultrastar, and humanitarian, deserves further examination.

The epic certainly continues here – beyond 'The End' (*'fin'*, as the French say) – not only within a bonus chapter that details the ultrastar's most outrageous cinematic gamble, but in a Filmography, where each of his 1001 films is listed, charting his forward path to glory – and beyond.

In *TEMPERING, EXPOSITION* and *APOTHEOSIS,* the saga of Butterbugs was tackled through a lens coated with elements of satire, epicness and noir. These three checks and balances in this larger-than-life saga serve as a kind of modifier, otherwise the lamp of illumination would burn with too lurid a flame. Satire protects us from cults of personality, noir reminds us of the validity of melodrama, and epics tell of grand achievements above the usual human experience. Mixed together, up to this point, *FORWARD TO GLORY* stabs at the world of contemporary media, of show business, and of hero worship, in a time when clarity is needed to make sense of it all. *BEYOND* FIN continues in that spirit, then backs off into more objective territory, as if to cool the jets of high-flying legend-making, and embrace the comforts of documentary fact-finding.

As Butterbugs receives more scrutiny in this welcome encore, so too do those in his circle, who were with him in many of his compelling moments on Earth: Saskia Pingles – lover and writer, who pens his most powerful lines; Zeenah Cazire – teen director of his most awesomely difficult role; Old Atrocity – loyal realizer of filmdom's most complicated logistics; Yoby – the apprentice, who has the guts to put an ultrastar on the spot, and for all the right reasons; Climb Girl – who dares to storm the dizzying heights that intimidate even an ultrastar; and Heatherette – the miraculous protector, who waits patiently for her dream to come true. Plus – the thousands of fellow actors, creators and technicians who helped make Butterbugs what he *really* became: a force for good in a world that not only needed it, but heeded it.

All things can be withstood, because of his going forward, *FORWARD TO...*

The *FORWARD TO GLORY* Quartet

I. Tempering – the Actor's struggles
II. Exposition – the Actor's rise
III. Apotheosis – the Actor's climax
Your next stop:
IV. Beyond *Fin* – the Actor's legend

A Bit Of Bio: Brian Paul Bach

Brian Paul Bach has been a worker in the theatre, an academic library, and the music business. He is a student of film and its lore, an occasional dramatic performer and voice impressionist, an appreciator of theatre architecture and operation, and an architectural writer. He is a lifelong artist, photographer, traveler and filmmaker, a casual blogster, assertive political cartoonist, media-watcher, a socializer via media, and writes a regular 'Calcutta Chronicles' column for 'Kolkata On Wheels' magazine. Golden ages of film production, automotive design, and world architecture are of especial interest, as are his dogs, music, history, environment, society and culture, as well as most things concerning the Indian subcontinent.

As a youth he embraced teenage filmmaking, worked in fringe show business in Seattle, and later probed the filmic corners of Hollywood, London and India. From these pursuits he has adopted cinematic thinking as a built-in facet of everyday life. As a young person he ran his own neighborhood theatre, for which he produced acts and short movies. He has been immersed in performance arts and associated activities all his life. Writing has also been a constant, fiction and nonfiction.

Accompanying these efforts has been an ever-present production of drawings, paintings photographs, videos and designs that have added up to a very personal statement of style and expression.

Bach's other published works, illustrated with his photos, drawings, and maps, include: THE GRAND TRUNK ROAD FROM THE FRONT SEAT, in two editions, 1993 and 2000 – the Author's travels from Calcutta to the Afghan frontier; and CALCUTTA'S EDIFICE: THE BUILDINGS OF A GREAT CITY, 2006 – a major examination of the architecture and culture of the Bengali metropolis. The book was presented to two successive Chief Ministers of West Bengal state, at the 2006 and 2012 Calcutta Book Fairs, the latter attended by the Author. Bach has long observed his own generation's behavior, its choices and its outlooks, resulting in BUSTED BOOM: THE BUMMER OF BEING A BOOMER.

He lives in Washington State with his wife Sandra, an accomplished ceramicist and chef, independent cat Condell, and faithful/glorious hound Hudson.

www.ingramcontent.com/pod-product-compliance
Lightning Source LLC
Chambersburg PA
CBHW060207030726
47499CB00004B/944